THE PILGRIMAGE OF THE LYFE OF THE MANHODE

VOLUME I

EARLY ENGLISH TEXT SOCIETY

No. 288

1985

Guillaume de Deguileville

THE PILGRIMAGE OF THE LYFE OF THE MANHODE

Translated anonymously into prose from
The First Recension
of
Guillaume de Deguileville's Poem
Le Pèlerinage de la vie humaine

VOL. I

INTRODUCTION AND TEXT
EDITED BY
AVRIL HENRY

Published for
THE EARLY ENGLISH TEXT SOCIETY
by the
OXFORD UNIVERSITY PRESS
LONDON NEW YORK TORONTO
1985

Oxford University Press, Walton Street, Oxford OX2 6DP

Oxford New York Toronto
Delhi Bombay Calcutta Madras Karachi
Kuala Lumpur Singapore Hong Kong Tokyo
Nairobi Dar es Salaam Cape Town
Melbourne Auckland

and associated companies in
Beirut Berlin Ibadan Nicosia

Published in the United States by
Oxford University Press, New York

British Library Cataloguing in Publication Data

Guillaume, de Deguileville
[Le pèlerinage de la vie humaine.
Middle English]. þe pilgrimage of þe lyfe
of þe manhode.—(Original series/
Early English Text Society; 291)
I. Title   II. Henry, Avril   III. þe pilgrimage
of þe lyfe of þe manhode
IV. Series
841'.1   PQ1483.G3A6
ISBN 0 19 722290 0

Printed in Great Britain
at the University Printing House, Oxford
by David Stanford
Printer to the University

CONTENTS
VOLUME I

VOLUME II

LIST OF PLATES

(between xcvi and page 1 of text)

ABBREVIATIONS

Excluded here are references which are obviously to items in the Bibliography, such as 'Trilhe, I, xxx'; sigils of the six Middle English manuscripts collated for this edition (see Stemma); sigils of the French manuscripts cited by Stürzinger; common abbreviations and those used only in the critical apparatus, such as '*add.can.*' (listed on pp. xciii–xciv), since though these do appear in the Introduction (where they are not italicised) they are lengthy to explain. Grammatical abbreviations such as 'poss. pron.' are italic in the Glossary, roman elsewhere: in the list below these appear with the roman form in brackets, thus: '*poss. pron.* (poss. pron.)'.

a(a)	article(s) [in an Aquinas reference]
Abb.	Abbildung
acc. (acc.)	accusative
adj. (adj.)	adjective
adv. (adv.)	adverb
anon.	anonymous
âme	Deguileville, *Le Pèlerinage de l'âme*
Apoc.	Apocalypse (The Book of Revelation, in AV)
AV	The Authorised Version of the Holy Bible
Bibl.	Bibliothèque
BL	British Library
BM	British Museum
Cant.	Canticle of Canticles (Song of Songs in AV)
Cat.	Catalogue
CE	*The Catholic Encyclopedia*
Chron.	Chronicles
compar. (compar.)	comparative
conj. (conj.)	conjunction
Cor.	Corinthians
CSEL	*Corpus Scriptorum Ecclesiasticorum Latinorum*
DA	*Dissertation Abstracts International*
Dan.	Daniel
dat. (dat.)	dative
dem. (dem.)	demonstrative
Dept.	Department
Deut.	Deuteronomy

Diss.	Dissertation
DNB	*Dictionary of National Biography*
Eccles.	Ecclesiastes
Ecclus.	Ecclesiasticus
EETS	Early English Text Society
Ep.	*Epigrams*
Eph.	Ephesians
ES	Extra Series
Etymol.	*Etymologiarum Libri XX*
Exod.	Exodus
Ezech.	Ezechiel
F	Stürzinger's *Le Pèlerinage de la Vie Humaine*
Facs.	Facsimile
fem. (fem.)	feminine
f(f).	folio(s) [before a number]
ff.	following [after a number]
FQ	*The Faerie Queene*
fut. (fut.)	future
Gall.	Gallicism
gen. (gen.)	genitive
Gen.	Genesis
Heb.	Hebrews
IE	Indo-European
imp. (imp.)	imperative
indic. (indic.)	indicative
inf. (inf.)	infinitive
interj. (interj.)	interjection
interrog. (interrog.)	interrogative
intr. (intr.)	intransitive
Is.	Isaias
JB	*Jerusalem Bible*
JEGP	*Journal of English and Germanic Philology*
Jer.	Jeremias
Jhésucrist	Deguileville, *Le Pèlerinage de Jhésucrist*
JWCI	*Journal of the Warburg and Courtauld Institutes*
Lam.	Lamentations
Lat.	Latin
Levit.	Leviticus
Machab.	Machabees
masc. (masc.)	masculine
Matt.	Matthew
ME	Middle English

MED	*Middle English Dictionary*
Metaph.	*Metaphysics*
MLA	Modern Language Association of America
MLN	*Modern Language Notes*
MLR	*Modern Language Review*
n.	noun [in Glossary only]
n	see Explanatory Note at this line [after a line reference in the Glossary]
N & Q	*Notes and Queries*
NCE	*New Catholic Encyclopedia*
n.d.	no date
neg. (neg.)	negative
nom. (nom.)	nominative
n.pag.	no pagination
NS	New Series
NT	New Testament
num. (num.)	numeral
Num.	Numbers
ODCC	Cross and Livingstone, *Oxford Dictionary of the Christian Church*
OE	Old English
OED	*Oxford English Dictionary*
OF	Old French
OS	Old Series
OT	Old Testament
Paralip.	Paralipomenon
pass. (pass.)	passive
pa. t. (pa. t.)	past tense
PBA	*Proceedings of the British Academy*
pers. (pers.)	person
PG	Migne, *Patrologia ... Series Graeca*
phr. (phr.)	phrase
PL	Migne, *Patrologia ... Series Latina*
pl. (pl.)	plural
PMLA	*Publications of the Modern Language Association of America*
pop.	popular (non-classical Latin)
poss. (poss.)	possessive
pp. (pp.)	past participle
pres. (pres.)	present
prep. (prep.)	preposition
pron. (pron.)	pronoun

Prov.	Proverbs
Ps.	Psalms
q(q).	question(s) [in an Aquinas reference]
RDK	*Reallexikon zur deutschen Kunst-Geschichte*
refl. (refl.)	reflexive
rel. (rel.)	relative
rpt.	reprint
RES	*Review of English Studies*
Rev.	Revised
Rom.	Romans
s.	(*saeculo*) in the century [immediately preceding a lower-case roman date-number, e.g. s.xiv]
sb.	(substantive) noun
sig.	signature [if used of the *Biblia Pauperum* blockbook, identifying the pages distinguished by letters of the alphabet in two series: a–v and .a.–.v.]
sg. (sg.)	singular
Soul	Guillaume de Deguileville, *The Pilgrimage of the Sowle: Westminstre, William Caxton 1483*
ST	Aquinas, *Summa Theologica*
subj. (subj.)	subjunctive
subs. (subs.)	substantival
superl. (superl.)	superlative
Supp.	Supplement
Tim.	Timothy
Tob.	Tobias
tr. (tr.)	transitive
TRHS	*Transactions of the Royal Historical Society*
u.v.	ultra-violet light
v. (v.)	verb
var.	variant
vbl. n. (vbl. n.)	verbal noun
Vie[1], *Vie*[2]	Guillaume de Deguileville, *Le Pèlerinage de la Vie Humaine*, First and Second Recensions
Wis.	Wisdom
Zach.	Zacharias.

PREFACE

The List of Contents shows that the Explanatory Notes to the text, and the Bibliography, will appear in Volume II of this edition. It is hoped that the inconvenience caused by this delay will to some extent be offset by the resulting ease with which the reader will be able to consult text and notes at the same time—an important consideration when so little has been written about the *Pilgrimage* or its French source.

The need for a critical edition of the anonymous Middle English prose translation of the First Recension of Guillaume de Deguileville's poem *Le Pèlerinage de la Vie Humaine* was outlined by Rosemond Tuve in her chapter on Deguileville. Rosemary Woolf gave me the vital initial encouragement to produce a critical edition of Book 1 of *þe Pilgrimage of þe Lyfe of þe Manhode* for my doctoral thesis (Oxford 1976). My greatest debt is however to Professor E. J. Dobson, who for so long patiently supervised my subsequent work on Book 1. Any errors in the completed work are wholly my responsibility, and are due to my failure to meet the standard he set.

I am particularly grateful to the following for permission to reproduce pages from manuscripts of the *Pilgrimage* in their care: The Syndics of Cambridge University Library; Glasgow University Library; The Master and Fellows of St John's College, Cambridge; The State Library of Victoria, Melbourne; the Bodleian Library, Oxford. Sion College's manuscript is not included here only because a reproduction page of it in John Shirley's well-known hand is already accessible, in Furnivall's unpaginated *Autotypes*, four plates from the end.

In addition to these, I should like to thank many other libraries to which I owe gratitude for the skill and courtesy which is the hallmark of Librarians and their staff: London's British Library, and Sion College Library; The State Library of Victoria in Melbourne, and at Cambridge, the Libraries of Trinity and Magdalene Colleges. All these supplied microfilm and gave every assistance during subsequent consultation of the manuscripts themselves. The courtesy of Mr T. A. Kealy, then Principal Librarian of the State Library of Victoria, and the willing cooperation of the Cambridge University Library, made possible consultation of the Melbourne manuscript in Cambridge during 1971. Towards the cost of insuring the manuscript while on deposit Oxford University generously gave a grant of fifty pounds, and the Charles Henry Foyle Trust a loan of fifty pounds, in the days when this represented a sizable sum.

The computer units of two Universities have given invaluable assistance in providing a concordance, which offered very much more than a mere wordlist from which to extract a Glossary. The University of Cambridge Literary and Linguistic Computing Centre did most of the work for Book 1. Similar facilities have been provided from 1970 by the University of Exeter Computer Unit, who processed the text of Books 2–4, and finally the whole text, Jim Baker, Migs Reynolds and Ivan Dixon appearing to enjoy the problems I made for them.

Special thanks are due to those who have assisted with the preparation of the book itself. Guidance on the preparation of the edition has been willingly given by Dr P. O. Gradon and Professor J. A. Burrow of the Early English Text Society. For the last few years I have been fortunate in the help of Mr W. J. Osborne, who has shared with me his learning and his time. My late father's steady understanding and support over many years of anti-social editorial activity were just as valuable as all these.

SUMMARY OF ÞE PILGRIMAGE OF ÞE LYFE OF ÞE MANHODE

For a study of Book 1's elaborate structure, and the overall design with special reference to Books 2–4, see my two articles in *Neuphilogische Mitteilungen*, 87 i, ii (1986). Briefly, its complexity and meaning derive from three formal devices. First is the sequence of sacraments. These are indicated in the summary by being between * and *. Second is the manner in which two sacraments, Holy Orders and the Eucharist, are 'interrupted' in various relevant ways. The sections making up such interrupted sacraments are numbered; for example, Holy Orders is in three separated parts (at 509, 530, 785), being interrupted twice by parts of the sacrament to which Orders are so closely related: the Eucharist (in a Mass of Ordination). The Eucharist spans 525–2708. Its separated parts are numbered not simply in order, but in a manner intended to clarify the fact that some of these separated sections are themselves interrupted. For example, *EUCHARIST 4* is the Communion of the congregation, but in two parts: 4a (merely a move towards the action) and 4b (the action), separated by 5. Sections of the Eucharist, totalling eight, have italicised titles. The third device is the use of two extended images: Tau (in the Baptism sequence beginning 260), and Pax (during the Eucharist, at 1341).

BOOK 1

The monk collects his audience to hear his dream. In a vision of the New Jerusalem which is his goal in the next world he sees that access to it is difficult, but that some find special ways in. He dreams his birth, and in the Church is shown the main equipment for his life-journey. First and most important is GRACE herself, then the means to Grace, the SEVEN SACRAMENTS. Into accounts of these are inserted the duties of the clergy, who administer the sacraments. The dreamer is offered ARMOUR OF VIRTUES, the STAFF OF HOPE and SATCHEL OF FAITH, and sets out, assisted by MEMORY: though he will not practise the Virtues, he can recall them.

The Dreamer introduces his dream (induced by reading the *Romance of the Rose*) as he slept in his monastery at Chaalit. He saw:

THE NEW JERUSALEM in its glory, an angel with flaming sword guarding the main entrance, by which Christ and the martyrs entered. Members of some religious orders, and other people, now by-pass the angel, flying or climbing over the walls, or stripping to enter by a narrow gate.

The Dreamer longs to make a pilgrimage to the city, but realises that he is not equipped to do so, lacking the staff and satchel of a pilgrim. At once he is born, and instantly GRACE DIEU appears, explaining that only with her help may anyone enter the city. She shows him:

THE CHURCH hanging in mid-air, fronted by water he must cross to enter it. Grace Dieu summons a priest, and the Dreamer receives the first of the Seven Sacraments (the first three of which are linked by the use of Holy Oils):

BAPTISM by the priest admits him to the Church, in the centre of which is the Rood—a Tau Cross, the sign used also by a bishop in the rite of Confirmation, given to the Dreamer next.

CONFIRMATION. The bishop then gives the three Holy Oils to the priest who baptised the Dreamer, explaining their uses in Baptism, Confirmation and the next sacrament described (not received by the Dreamer):

EXTREME UNCTION (Last Rites). We move to other uses of oils:

(a) The bishop explains their use, by bishops only, in Coronation, Consecration of bishops, Ordination of priests, Dedication of altars.

(b) REASON arrives to extend the discussion of Oils, and insert an account of further EPISCOPAL (and PAPAL) DUTIES: the Oil of Mercy as it should be applied by a bishop, whose horns and labels (of the Mitre), and rod (Episcopal Staff) mean Justice and Mercy.

(c) The priest puts away the Holy Oils given him at 289.

MATRIMONY is solemnised by the priest, who turns back to   436
the bishop still listening to Reason; the bishop then administers:

FIRST TONSURE (the shaving of monks' heads). Reason ad-   452
dresses the monks on moderation and rationality, and explains the
meaning of Tonsure. We move logically to the next full sacrament:

HOLY ORDERS 1 (the first six of the seven Orders): 'insignia'   509
and duties of Porter, Exorcist, Lector, Acolyte, Subdeacon,
Deacon.

THE EUCHARIST 1 The altar is prepared: cloths laid, bread   525
set out. The mixing of water and wine may signify either preparation for Mass, or arrival at the OFFERTORY, at which the
Sacrifice itself begins. Either way, the celebrant does not proceed
to the Consecration, having unfinished business:

HOLY ORDERS 2 (the seventh Order): Ordination of priests   530
(part 1): the power to judge and absolve is given: the Sword and
Keys signifying some DUTIES OF PRIESTS. The Dreamer receives only the sheathed sword and bound-up keys appropriate to
the layman.

THE EUCHARIST 2 Consecration of the Host.   776

HOLY ORDERS 3 Ordination of priests (part 2): the power to   785
consecrate the host is given.

THE EUCHARIST 3 Communion of new priests (?) and offic-   788
iating clergy.

Consecration (Transubstantiation) is discussed. It baffles Reason,   793
who departs. Nature, affronted by it, argues with Grace.

THE EUCHARIST 4a Communion of the congregation: the   1083
celebrant merely moves as if to distribute the Host, but first there
is an account of the next sacrament (and the state appropriate to
souls about to Communicate):

PENANCE (PENITENCE & CHARITY appear together).   1087

PENITENCE (? as guardian of the Sanctuary whence Communion is distributed) explains that she cleanses and prepares the soul for its guest.

CHARITY explains the significance of the Host, and that souls receiving it should be in charity. She reads:

THE PILGRIM dons, and immediately doffs, the armour. MEM-   2453
ORY appears to carry the virtues which he can remember but not
practise.

THE EUCHARIST 6b The Pilgrim (after Communicating?)   2705
puts bread in his Satchel, and sets out on his journey.

*Books 2 and 3 form a unit in which the pilgrim learns something of
his own mental, physical and spiritual nature but is nevertheless at-
tacked by THE SEVEN DEADLY SINS (Sloth, Pride, Envy,
Anger, Avarice, Gluttony and Lust) before whom he is almost helpless,
not wearing the equipment supplied in Book 1. He survives by the
Grace of God.*

BOOK 2

*The Pilgrim, puzzled by his inability to bear the armour of virtue,
learns to know himself better in mind, body, and soul, but still falls
victim to the first four deadly sins.*

The Pilgrim worries about his inability to practise virtue.

NATURAL UNDERSTANDING (*Rude Entendement*) at once   2771
objects to the very practice of Faith (the Satchel) and Hope (the
Staff), preferring his rough staff Obstinacy which Grace, through
Reason, orders him to abandon. Foolishly, he tries to use logic to
prove Reason unreliable, but is defeated by her ability to distinguish between name and object. He then fails to show that
Scripture forbids Faith and Hope: Reason distinguishes the
changed circumstances that mean a change in rules. He remains
imperceptive and inflexible. The Pilgrim passes by him, fearfully.

The Pilgrim goes on worrying, seeking Reason's help.   3080

THE UNDISCIPLINED BODY is revealed as the cause of his   3094
weakness. Reason distinguishes between the Pilgrim and his body:
a duality which divides his will. She explains the subtle relationship between body and soul, and man's potential as the image
of God. Momentarily, she separates the Pilgrim's body and soul
so that he feels the true power of his spirit. Reason agrees to

accompany him, though often obscured by the physical world from which Penance may give freedom.

THE TWO PATHS. IDLENESS and OCCUPATION appear, separated by the thorns of Penance. Though knowing himself betrayed by his plausible body, the Pilgrim rejects honest but humble employment, accepting Idleness's spurious argument (a parody of Reason's 'distinctions') that the body alone, not the Pilgrim himself, will pay the penalty for following her.

GRACE warns the Pilgrim to cross to the other path through the thorns, because they grow thicker further on. While he is still looking for a gap in the hedge, he falls victim to the first Sin:

SLOTH snares his feet. She is wife of the Devil, mother of Idleness, armed with the *axe* of Life-Weariness (Depression) and *ropes* of Negligence, Lethargy and the Desperation (Suicide) which destroyed Judas. The Pilgrim's suicide is averted by prayer, enabling him to retain Hope: but Sloth continues to prevent his passing through the hedge. The result is the arrival of the oldest sin:

PRIDE riding on FLATTERY, self-obsessed. Bred by Lucifer, she caused his Fall, then Man's. Bloated and disdainful, she is responsible for war and extravagance. Her *unicorn-horn* is Cruelty, opening wounds for other weapons; she carries the *bellows* of Vanity and a *horn* of Boasting which announces her; *spurs* of Disobedience and Rebellion drive her backwards; Obstinacy, her *staff*, was carried by Natural Understanding; she is winged as if with virtues; her *mantle* of Hypocrisy is white wool outside but foxfurred within. She does not attack yet.

FLATTERY her mount holds up to her a *mirror*, Repeating and Agreeing With What Is Said (like Echo), to mollify the Unicorn-Pride's cruelty. She is logically followed by her daughter.

ENVY has two riders. Other people are her obsession. This shrivelled figure has, instead of eyes, *spears*, the antithesis of receptivity: Anger at Others' Joy, and Pleasure in Others' Pain.

TREACHERY, mounted in front, has a *mask*, a *dagger*, and a *box of ointment* unctuously applied to her victims.

DETRACTION has, instead of a tongue, a kebab for her mother's meal: a spear thrust through the ears of all those whose good name she has stolen; in her mouth (with which she destroys people) is a *bloody bone* barbed with a spike as if it were bait.

From behind they attack the Pilgrim's (newly perceived) horse, whose four hooves are the qualities necessary in one who 'bears witness': good name, legitimacy, sanity and free status. PRIDE now joins in. The Pilgrim still retains his Hope, but another Sin approaches while he is down:

ANGER (called Touch-me-Not) is hedgehog-like with hatred; she carries two *flints* to kindle the fire in which to forge the *saw* (Hatred) for severing relationships (including her own with God). It was made on the *anvil* of Spite with the *hammer* of Chiding, and ironically toothed by the action of Justice's file Correction (which Anger will not tolerate). She causes uproar and discord, even in the microcosm of man himself. She hopes to hand over to the Pilgrim the *scythe* Murder, making him a murderer and then executing him.   4711

MEMORY begs the Pilgrim, overcome by the four most 'intellectual' sins, to put on his armour of Virtues. He is too idle (and yet too busy) even to try, but he does get up with the help of Hope.   4807

BOOK 3

The Pilgrim now descends into a deep valley, signifying that he is about to succumb to the last three, most crude and materialistic, sins. They bear a logical relationship in their addiction to wordly 'goods': the fruits of Avarice facilitate Gluttony, which leads to Lust. When he is subjected to all seven sins, and has lost even Hope, he is regretful (not quite remorseful: lamentation is not repentance). As a result of this minimal movement to virtue he is simply given Hope, and taught the 'A.B.C. to the Virgin', after which cry of repentance and supplication he is led to bathe briefly in Penitence, and is again supposed to make a choice of direction.

AVARICE is in tatters, and yet appropriately cluttered. Spider-like, she has eight arms—or *six arms*, and *two stumps* of her 'giving' hands. The six profitable arms are Rapine, Theft, Usury (holding a *file* and *scales*), False Beggary (holding a *dish* and *bag*), Simony   4853 (an S-shaped *hook*), and one for corrupting Justice, with five names (including Conflict, Trickery), which moves unpleasantly between her *diseased tongue* (Perjury) and a *sore* on her hip (Lying), lamed in flight from Truth and Equity. There is an idol on her head, and a hump (of possessions) on her back.

GLUTTONY AND LECHERY are interdependent, and attack together.

GLUTTONY is disgusting, showing many traits of Lechery. Long-nosed and staring, she is an animated stomach, thrusting food through the funnel of her throat into the bag of her belly and leaving a dung-trail as she goes. She resembles Pride, for in her cups she is unicornish in rage; she also resembles Envy, because like Detraction she ruins reputations, with her drunken gossip and foul language.

LECHERY is hooded, masked make-up and riding a pig (Unnatural Desires). Her instruments, too horrible to show, are Violation, Rape, Incest, Adultery, Fornication and a sixth too horrible to name. She leads the last attack:

THE SEVEN SINS rob the Pilgrim of Hope (but not Faith). He laments the loss of penitence, chivalry, the sacraments and heaven, at which Grace hands him back his Hope, and teaches him:

THE A.B.C. TO THE VIRGIN (Chaucer's translation).

THE ROCK OF PENITENCE is revealed to the Pilgrim by Grace, in answer to his appeal to the Virgin. A great eye in it weeps tears into a basin below. The Pilgrim bathes in it, but climbs out before quite healed. His new journey is at once hindered.

BOOK 4

BOOK 4 is in two contrasting halves: life in the turmoil of the world and the calm of the cloister. Attempting to skirt the treacherous SEA OF THE WORLD in which the DEVIL nets those not trapped by shoals, whirlpools and other natural hazards of ordinary life, the Pilgrim successfully resists challenge to his Faith from intellectual HERESY. Irresponsible pleasure-loving YOUTH carries him above the Sea until TRIBULATION strikes him down. Back where he

*started, GRACE shows him the SHIP OF RELIGION. Entering a
monastery on it he watches the orderly MONASTIC VIRTUES.
Submitting to OBEDIENCE he is at once overcome by INFIRM-
ITY, SENILITY and DEATH. The terrified monk wakes.*

THE SEA OF THE WORLD confronts the Pilgrim; afraid to   6136
cross it, he is at first prevented from skirting it by the DEVIL.
For the first time, the Pilgrim's Faith is challenged:

HERESY, running backwards with a *faggot*, denies the truth of   6187
Scripture. The Pilgrim's resistance earns him the support of
GRACE, who explains the Sea and those who, choosing or forced
to swim in it, are weed-tangled, or blindfolded. The traps of the
Devil (which the Pilgrim now passes) are described.

YOUTH now lifts the Pilgrim for a while over the sea's dangers—   6343
the sandbank of Individual Will, the whirlpool of Worldly Occupation, the rocks of Adversity, the equally dangerous quicksand
of Prosperity, the singing siren of Pleasure—until (Grace simply
forgotten) he is distantly addressed by

TRIBULATION, who is comfortable on the sea. As Heaven's   6442
Gold smith she bears the *hammer* of Persecution, *tongs* of Distress
and *apron* of Shame, made of her victims' skin. With different
commissions from each, she serves God and the Devil (depending
on her effect). She strikes the Pilgrim into the sea, where Hope
supports him until Tribulation beats him to shore and GRACE.

GRACE sends Tribulation away, promising the Pilgrim a short   6647
cut (equivalent to the hedge of Penance which he never braved) to
New Jerusalem.

THE SHIP OF RELIGION (Monastic Life) is at hand, its ribs   6700
bound with osiers of Observances, some so broken that the ship is
weakened. However, its function is to bind up again the
disintegrating souls of men. The mast is Christ, the wind the
Spirit; Cluny and Citeaux are on it, both available to the Pilgrim.
The Porter of the one he chooses is The Fear of God, who strikes
the Pilgrim with a blow equivalent to the pains of Penance.

THE MONASTIC VIRTUES are harmoniously at work inside,   6802 some wearing the Pilgrim's rejected armour, and each with a place or direction.

Outside the enclosed monastery/convent:

CHARITY (who held the Testament of Peace) is hosteller.

Inside Cloister and Church are, in or near the dormitory:

VOLUNTARY POVERTY singing, wearing only the *Gambeson*,

CHASTITY is making the beds, and wearing the *Gloves*;

moving to the Chapter House:

OBEDIENCE, Prioress under Grace, bearing *cords*, with

DISCIPLINE, a *file* (Correction of Evil) in her teeth, and wearing the *Shield*;

moving to the Cloister:

LESSON (STUDY) with a *document*, followed by the *Dove of Spirit*, the *food of Holy Writ* carried in parchment;

moving to the Refectory:

ABSTINENCE wearing the Gorger;

in the Chapel:

PRAYER with a heaven piercing *awl* (Fervent Continuation) and a *box* of prayers for the dead, who feed the living;

WORSHIP, an entertainer with a *musical horn*.

OBEDIENCE is accepted by the Pilgrim.   69

INFIRMITY comes to him. She has a *bed* on her head, and   70
wrestles with HEALTH, sometimes losing because of MEDI-
CINE; though she drinks blood and eats flesh, she is essentially
friendly, recalling Penitence.

OLD AGE brings him *crutches*; she and Infirmity beat him to his
bed.

MERCY suckles him with milk compared to Christ's blood (the   71
sacraments) which Charity turned to the milk of kindness. She
pulls his bed to the Infirmary.

DEATH approaches; Grace comforts the Pilgrim, promising him   72
Resurrection. He is at the gate he saw at the start of his dream,

and must promise Penitence payment of outstanding debts in Pur-
gatory (the subject of *The Pilgrimage of the Soul*). Death scythes
the Pilgrim.

The terrified Dreamer wakes to Matins in Chaalit, and explains   7271
the aim of his writing.

GUILLAUME DE DEGUILEVILLE, EDITIONS AND CRITICISM

The little we know about Guillermus de Deguilevilla[1] is inferred from his work. The evidence is listed in Faral, *Histoire*, which also offers the most complete descriptive analysis of Guillaume's work. Evidence of this kind which may be relied upon is distinguished from the rest by being 'signalled': it is in acrostics, or presented as direct address to the reader, or gives actual dates or periods, otherwise absent.[2] The meagre facts to be gleaned in this way are as follows. Deguileville was born in 1295, the son of Thomas of Deguileville. He entered Chaalis in about 1316,[3] at the age of twenty-one, spending the rest of his life there. He wrote eleven Latin poems[4] and an allegorical poem 'Roman de la fleur de lis',[5] all undated. The first recension of *Le Pèlerinage de la vie humaine* (*Vie*[1], the source of our text) was written in 1330-1, the second recension (*Vie*[2]) in 1355, *Le Pèlerinage de l'âme* between 1355 and 1358, the latter being the approximate date of *Le Pèlerinage de Jhesucrist*,[6] written when the poet was over sixty.

It is important to distinguish between this evidence and that mistakenly based on identification of the Pilgrim with the poet. Faral, while questioning the assumption that, like his Pilgrim, Guillaume must have been robust and given to youthful indiscretion (as if one needed proof of that), himself says that it is clear from the poem that 'il avait pourtant reçu une partie des ordres et . . . il etait, à tout les moins, moine de choeur'.[7] In fact, the Dreamer-pilgrim does not seem to receive even the First Tonsure, which he witnesses (*Vie*[1] 831, 452 in our text), let alone the least of the Minor Orders, though at 6992 he submits to some kind of monastic discipline. Surprisingly little attention has been paid to the French text. For example, no study has yet been made of the influence on it (remarked but not explained by Faral) of the noted theologian Jacques Therines.[8]

---

[1] The name written in acrostics in two of the Latin poems, in *Vie*[2] (unedited, see Faral, *Histoire*, p. 45); *l'âme* 1593-784, 10751-981 (see Stürzinger's note); *Jhesucrist* 3579-966.

[2] It is found in *Vie*[1] 397-9, 5775-82, 5965 (in our text, at 210, 3127, 3226); *Vie*[2] Prologue, and in lines (having no equivalent in our text) which follow what in *Vie*[1] is 13023 (Faral, *Histoire*, p. 44); *l'âme* 9376, 9773-4, 11144-5.

[3] See Explanatory Note 18 in Vol. II.

[4] Faral, *Histoire*, p. 77.

[5] Edited by Piaget, *Romania*.

[6] All three *Pèlerinages* (*Vie*[1], not *Vie*[2]) are edited by Stürzinger.

[7] Faral, *Histoire*, p. 8.

[8] Faral, *Histoire*, pp. 6-7; see Explanatory Note 18 in Vol. II.

Indeed, very little work of any kind has been done on Deguileville's three major poems *per se*. This reflects the marked difference between late medieval taste and our own, for it is clear that they were highly popular in the medieval period. Rosemond Tuve lists the evidence which shows how Deguileville's contemporaries and successors valued the work.[9] More that fifty French manuscripts of the *Vie*[1] alone were available to Stürzinger. In the fifteenth century it was translated into German, Dutch and Spanish.[10] In addition to the various early French printed versions[11] parts of *Vie*[1] and *Ame* were dramatised.[12]

Most so-called criticism of the *Vie* has been simply descriptive. This is understandable in assessments as early as that of De Visch (1649) or Goujet (1745), who deals only with the longer *Vie*[2].[13] Hill's *The Ancient Poem of Guillaume de Guileville . . . Compared with the Pilgrim's Progress* (1858) is not even based on *Vie*[2] but on Lydgate's free version of it.[14] None of these writers was interested in the poem's literary qualities. Even after 1893, when Stürzinger's edition of *Vie*[1] was published, Piaget (1896) deplored the great length of the work and declared himself content to look at some of the manuscript pictures.[15] Gröber (1902) provides the usual formal account of the poems, as does Hultman (1902) in his attempt to trace further sources (Galpin in 1910 did the same for *l'âme*). Gaston Paris (1907) simply observes that dream-allegory moral poems 'a reçu un développment prolixe au xive siècle dans *Le Pèlerinage de l'homme*'.[16] Langlois, "Pèlerinages" (1928), limits his treatment to paraphrase of the first two poems; Delacotte (1932) limits his to partial paraphrase of all three, spiced with quotation.

Lofthouse (1935) attempts evaluation, but she is the victim of her manuscript, a curious amalgam of *Vie*[1] and *Vie*[2], elements from the latter

[9] Tuve, pp. 146-8.

[10] For an account of the three fifteenth-century German versions see Langosch, pp. 897-900: the Berleburger version is edited by Bömer, and the Cologne by Meijboom (both under Deguileville in the Bibliography). Middle Dutch versions ("Pelgrimagie van der menscheliker creaturen") are in Berlin, Staatsbibliothek der Stiftung preussicher Kulturbesitz, MS. germ.fol.624, and The Hague, Koninklijke Bibliotheek, MS. 76.E.6 (Deschamps, nos. 78, 79 and Pl. 62). See Deguileville, *Dat boeck* for the Dutch printed version, and for the Spanish, *El peregrino de la vida humana* (Toulouse: Henricus Mayer, 1490). Miss Tuve doubted the existence of the latter: I have been unable to consult it, but there is a copy in Seville, and there are four in the U.S.A. (*Incunabula*, p. 284; Dulcet, p. 470).

[11] Discussed fully by Faral, "Études". Manuscripts and editions are also discussed by Lofthouse, pp. 178-81 and Tuve, p. 147.

[12] See G. Cohen, *Mystères*, and *Nativités*, pp. 263-302; Langlois, *Pèlerinages*, p. 207.

[13] Lofthouse, pp. 180-1 has shown that in *Vie*[2] Guillaume added 4000 French and 1100 Latin lines..

[14] If it is Lydgate's: see Pearsall, p. 79, also Walls (1977), and Green.

[15] Piaget (1896), p. 207.

[16] Paris, p. 154.

being least acceptable to her: 'Deguileville does little but parade his knowledge. He brings together in the most extraordinary way, discussions on the vices of the world, astrology, etymology, the doctrines of the Church, the works of Ovid and Saint Augustine'[17] (so, of course, does Chaucer). The negative approach to Deguileville's methods is evident in Wharey's reference to the 'crude conceptions . . . far removed from the wonderfully life-like personifications of Bunyan' (1904, p. 66). It is evident even in Dominica Legge's *Anglo-Norman in the Cloisters*:[18] he 'wrote allegory in quantity though hardly of quality' and is 'intolerably dull'. Surprisingly, the same attitude is evident in Graham's dissertation 'Allegory in Mediaeval French Literature' (1955): the passage on Penitence (*Vie*[1] 2023–382, 1095–1298 in our text) is condemned as 'very poor allegory, for the ridiculous broom and other accessories make it impossible to visualise Penitence as a real person' and 'the argument between Aristotle and Sapience . . . has nothing to do with the pilgrim's journey'.[19] One can only assume that, in someone obviously well-read in French allegories (for example those by Rutebuef, Raoul de Houdenc, Baudouin de Condé, and Jean de Condé) which show still less characterisation and an equally medieval delight in combining debate and didactic narrative, this is an echo of what had by then become an unthinking critical commonplace. Even Faral (1962) damned *Vie*[1] with faint praise: 'une oeuvre touffue, d'une invention mal disciplinée, mais qui, malgré beaucoup de superfluités et d'incohérences, répond à une intention plus fermement conçue que ne laisse d'abord paraître la forêt broussailleuse de ses treize mille et quelque vers'.[20]

Not until 1966, and Rosemond Tuve's clear-sighted refusal to allow previous opinion and present taste to obscure her view of the allegory, was the critical attention it deserved given to this 'most striking and well-shaped of mediaeval treatments of the subject', which when compared with the *Pilgrim's Progress* is 'more truly figurative, more subtle and closer to the ancient ways of pursuing enigmatic truths'.[21] It is one purpose of this edition to clarify the shape and subtlety of *þe Pilgrimage of þe Lyfe of þe Manhode*. Perhaps the French source itself will receive more sympathetic attention in years to come: though our poet is outside his brief, M. R. Jung (1971) says of religious allegory in the mid-fourteenth century 'le seul grand auteur sera le moine de Châlis, Guillaume de Digulleville'.[22]

[17] Lofthouse, p 175.
[18] Dr Legge's book is invaluable, *inter alia*, in its list of English Cistercian monasteries containing French manuscripts.
[19] Graham, pp. 296–7.
[20] Faral, *Histoire*, p. 12.
[21] Tuve, p. 145.
[22] Jung, p. 292.

English Editions

Until 1869, the only 'edition' of *þe Pilgrimage of þe Lyfe of þe Manhode* apart from Lydgate's was a modernisation by Miss Cust, based on Lydgate's translation of *Vie*². Addressing 'uneducated boys [sic] and young children' she bade her readers 'go forth to meet the same ruthless foes as the Pilgrim, girded with the same spiritual arrows'. She took fastidious Protestant pride in omitting anything in Lydgate which smacked of Catholicism in general and 'Mariolatry' in particular.²³ Not surprisingly, this left little of the original at all—not even the charming 'A.B.C. to the Virgin' (familiar to the liberal-minded reader in Chaucer's translation) and certainly very little of Book 1, which deals with sacraments.

W. A. Wright's 1869 edition of the Middle English *Vie*¹ is unfortunately less well known than Lydgate's version of *Vie*². Perhaps this is because though easier as a text it is more difficult as an edition: based on manuscript C but with only slight reference to four of the other five manuscripts (he had examined O partially, and seen only 'a specimen' of G, the main witness), it reproduces most of C's errors. His edition is not only unemended but also unpunctuated, and has only a brief glossary and notes.

Perhaps because of the difficulty (and rarity) of the Wright edition, sympathetic criticism of the Middle English prose translation is hardly to be found outside the exceptional work of Rosemond Tuve, who used both the French and Wright's edition. S. Brook's unpublished dissertation on Middle English Religious Allegory (1955) refers only to the Lydgate, where, apparently, the 'motif of pilgrimage lacks the real imaginative force needed to control the rambling, overgrown allegory', which is a 'medley of topics' presenting 'thinly-imagined incidents' where the 'shaping plan of the allegory is lost in a vast mass of didacticism'.²⁴ Matthews (1962) is one of the very few to comment on the Middle English prose version, in his account of the excerpt from Wright which he presents: 'despite its close relation to the moral handbooks and its tendency to load the story with too heavy a burden of exegesis, the work remains reasonably entertaining by virtue of its autobiographical mode [sic] and a narrative of marvellous adventures . . .'. It is no *Pilgrim's Progress*, but that it is far from being so tedious as critics commonly say may be judged from the present specimen'.²⁵ Unfortunately it may not, since the beauties of the *Pilgrimage* are largely invisible in excerpt, especially when that excerpt is not only a modernisation but a corruption of Wright's already corrupt text.

I have already disposed of the idea that much autobiographical material is to be found in Guillaume's work. Neither is pilgrimage *per se* the

²³ Cust, p. vii. I cannot trace *Pilgrim's Progresses during More than Three Centuries, from Guillaume de Guileville, A.D. 1330, to John Bunyan, A.D. 1687* announced as 'In the Press' in a publisher's advertisement inserted in the front of Cust, *The Booke of the Pylgremage of the Sowle*.

²⁴ Brook, p. 124.

²⁵ Matthews (1962), pp. 243-4.

'shaping plan' of the work, which is also ill-described as a series of 'marvellous adventures'. Its artistry is considerable. The structure manifesting it is, as the quantity of previously adverse criticism might suggest, not obvious. It is correspondingly hard to describe. The unusually long summary on pp. xv–xxv is intended to make its remarkable coherence and subtlety as clear as possible. For a study of the large design of the whole, and of the elaborate and hitherto unnoticed structure of Book 1, see Henry, the two articles already mentioned (p. xv).

DESCRIPTION OF THE MANUSCRIPTS

References which follow each manuscript's location and number are to catalogue descriptions, all of which (excepting those for M and S) are brief and if correct incorporated below. Folio-measurements given in old catalogues are often approximately 5 mm. too large, the skin of the manuscripts having shrunk. Extant descriptions of M and S are long: my accounts of them are supplementary or corrective. I follow the conventions adopted in Ker, *Medieval Manuscripts in British Libraries*, except that I include captions to illuminations in M and O, which are not in the critical apparatus.

Often, particularly in matters of provenance, more problems are defined than solved. In the matter of scripts I have not even attempted to define the problem, so varied are the elements in these fifteenth-century hands. Provided instead are actual-size photographs of samples from near line 1670 in all the manuscripts except Shirley's (S), for which a facsimile reference is supplied. All the manuscripts except J show extensive annotations in various hands. Those relating to the text appear in the critical apparatus but without any distinction between the various annotators, all of whom are subsumed under superscript 3, except for the rubricator, indicated by superscript 2. Folio references to some of the more important annotating hands are given here since locating them from the critical apparatus is laborious. Jottings not related to the text are listed only here.

Except for C and M, the manuscripts contain only *þe Pilgrimage of þe Lyfe of þe Manhode*. The colophon common to CGMO (incomplete in M, and missing with the end of S) which begins *HEere endeth þe romaunce of þe monk of þe | pilgrimage of þe lyfe of þe manhode* and ends *Preyeth for þilke þat maade it. þat hath maad it. and wrot it. Amen.*, is in a sense part of the text, originating in French manuscripts of Stürzinger's A^7-type. It is mentioned if in red or a distinguishing script. Chaucer's 'A.B.C.' is not itemised.

No attempt is made to describe the language of the manuscripts. The high incidence of northern forms in JMO has often been noted, but some occur also in CGS, even G presenting a mixture, and the stemma does not facilitate identification of the translator's dialect. Linguists may find the G-correctors of interest, since they so laboriously alter spellings.

C. CAMBRIDGE UNIVERSITY LIBRARY: MS. Ff.5.30 [Catalogue of the Manuscripts Preserved in the Library of the University of Cambridge, II, p. 492, No. 1320; V, p. 596]. s.xv[1].

1. ff. 5–140[v] *þe Pilgrimage of þe Lyfe of þe Manhode*; Books 2, 3 and 4 begin on ff. 54[v], 93[v], 118[r] respectively.

2. ff. 141[r]–164[v] *Heere biginneth þe xii. chapitres of Richard heremite of hampool* red (anon. translation of *Emendatio Vitae*; see Allen, p. 241). Colophon f. 164[v] red. ff. iv + 160 + iv, numbered 1–168 throughout in the modern foliation cited in the text. 244 × 160 mm. Written space 175 × 108 mm. 31 lines. Collation: iv (i, ii, iv paper replacements) + 1[8]–20[8] + iv (ii, iv paper replacements); some wormholes in the surviving old flyleaves have no counterparts in the adjacent quire. Signatures: a–r A–C first leaf in each quire marked 1 in modern pencil and each fifth leaf (which also marks iii (f. 3[r]) presumably as the beginning of the second half of a quire of four); but older signatures (sometimes cropped) mark quires c–r as b–q, and B as b, numbering the first four leaves in each quire i–iiij. Catchwords: in the scribe's hand, on each eighth verso except f. 140[v] (the end of the *Pilgrimage*) and f. 164[v]. Initials: Five 7-line illuminated in blue, red, white, orange, gold extended into borders; 2-, 3-, 7-line blue capitals ornamented red. Binding: Stoakley, Cambridge, 6.5.1918. Secundo folio (f. 6) *feedere of briddes.*

Provenance: From the library of John Moore Bishop of Ely, d.1714. Cambridge University Library holds many of his manuscript documents.[26] I have not found his hand anywhere in MS. Ff.5.30—not even on f. 3[r] *in . . . bye* [?] *Johnes bysshop* where there is also *Thomas hows* twice in a s.xv hand. F. 3[v] has *Liber Johannis Malet*; f. 68[r] has *Wille Crane* [?] *did me* in a space in the text, and in the same s.xv hand is f.79[v] *Inmybe* [*In my be-*]; f. 80[v] *In my begynnynge*; f. 81[r] *I In me by gynde god me spede*; f. 84[v] *I*; ff. 111[r], 112[r] *Wyll*; ff. 140[v] *W . . . m . . .*, and scribbles on twelve other folios. F. 165[v] has the beginning of a conveyance: *Omnibus christi fidelibus ad quos hoc scriptum Indentatum peruenerit Ego Williamus Dalyng Junior dedi conssesse* [?] *& hac carta mea confirmaui Willielmo P. de M. in comitatu deuoniensi armigero etc omne meum messuageum et terram meam in manibus de anton gefferd habendum et tenendum omne et singulum.* Several notes reveal no names: f. 3[r] has *. . . omnia est terra qua admir . . . est nomina tua*; f. 3[v] *A le bone estoire bone guerdon* in a s.xvi italic hand; f. 164[v] *Thys bill {mad} the xxiiij• {of} Januarye* in another s.xvi italic hand at the foot of the page; f. 165[r], in another script: *This bill made the xxiiij of Januarij | In the first and Secound yere of | phylyppe and marye by the grace of god kynge and quene of Englond* (with *he that wyll* and *he that* scribbled nearby); above that in a different hand *Estimastis me ducere In falsum gaudium* and *He that hevyn wyll wyne whyath his | Nebors he mist be gyn | O lady So louly off cheyr hellpe vs all | Bothe fayr and Neyr*

---

[26] Accounts (Dd.14.26[8]); Catalogue of quartos in his Library (Oo.7.49); Letters (Add.2.no.192; Add.51.nos.204–5; Add.4251.nos.977–8).

followed by *Sant Christophorus* [?]. *He that in yought no vertue will vse* | *In age all honor will hym refuyse* is visible at the top of f. 167[r] under ultra-violet light.[27] (On MS. Hunter 400 f. (vii)[v] this couplet is followed by ~~sic dixit seser~~.) Also on f. 167[r], in another hand, is *He that in yought no vertu will vse* | *In age all honor will hem refuyse*, minor scribbles, then the nonsensical *fuit homo allabernum necuit patrem* | *et non peccavit p*/*Miles virgo lupus divictus phebula phebus* | *offert ceperat nesciat et optat*.

In the margins of the text, crosses made with a fine pen mark passages on ff. 91[v], 98[v], 109[v] (two), 143[v], 145[r], 160[v] (two), 164[v]. A 7-like mark appears in the margin in Book 1 on ff. 6[r], 7[r], 9[v], 12[r], 15[v], 17[r], 21[v], 25[v] (two), 27[r], 28[r], 30[r], 31[v], 32[v], 33[r], 34[v], 36[r], 38[r], 39[v], 40[v], 41[r], 44[r], 48[r], 50[v], 51[v], 53[r] and in sixty places in Books 2–4. Conceivably these were made when a scribe using C as an exemplum finished each stint. Perhaps the same hand is responsible for the grotesque on f. 64[v].

Notes and corrections directly associated with the text occur in at least three hands. The scribe himself provides glosses (especially to pronouns) and occasional inserts, for example f. 14[v]/13, 27 have *pilgrime* written over *me* and *I*. Similar additions are on ff. 15[r], 16[r], 17[r], 19[r], 22[v], 23[r], 23[v], 27[r], 30[v], 32[v], 40[r], 43[v], 46[r], 46[v], 47[r], 49[r] in Book 1, and thirty-one places in Books 2–4. Another group of glosses and corrections is in a small, neat corrector's hand, whose work was commonly erased once the original scribe had implemented correction in the text. The erasures, let alone the original marginalia, are scarcely visible without ultra-violet light, but some words are unerased, for example on ff. 24[v], 35[v], 114[v], 149ᵃ 150[v]. Examples of corrections made by the scribe in accordance with marginalia now erased are on ff. 21[r], 23[r], 27[r]. F. 103[r]/2, 3, 7 are particularly interesting: the first gloss is in the corrector's hand, the last two in the main scribe's. On f. 27[r] the rubricator cancelled three words where the scribe anticipated copy.

Transcription is dealt with under Editorial Method, pp. lxxxix–xcii.

G. GLASGOW UNIVERSITY LIBRARY: MS. HUNTER 239

[Young and Aitken, pp. 190–1].

The catalogue wrongly identifies it as 'Gallopez' French prose version translated'.[28] Workman, and Locock, refer to it by pressmark Q.2.25. Mr. M. B. Parkes kindly dated the hand to s.xv[1]. Books 2, 3 and 4 begin on ff. 37[r], 66[v], 85[r] respectively. Colophon: f. 102[r] in Textura-based script not that used by the scribe. Ff. v 104 iii. 293 × 207 mm., cropped. Written space 200 × 135 mm. 34–6 lines. Collation: impossible with accuracy, so tight is the binding; probably v (i paper 'Pro Patria', ii, iii showing countermark not in Heawood, Churchill or Shorter, iii conjugate with leaf stuck to board under marbled end-paper, i stuck to marbled paper

---

[27] Brown and Robbins, and Robbins and Cutler 1151; Whiting Y29; see also *RES*, NS 20 (1969), 48.

[28] Faral, *Études*, pp. 90–3, 101; Tuve, pp. 148, 216.

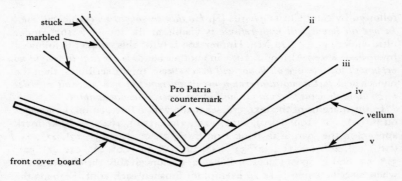

conjugate with marbled end-paper) 1^8–13^8 iii (paper 'Pro Patria', iii stuck to marbled paper which is conjugate with end-paper); wormholes in iv, v, 1–11 suggest missing leaves probably blank between v and i.

Ff. 1–102 numbered in modern pencil. Quire signatures (mostly cropped away) at the bottom left corner of first recto of each quire, scribe's hand: f. 49^r the first now unconcealed by binding. The first four leaves of each quire signed, not by the scribe: the first visible signature f. 35 *diij* (where one would expect *eiij*, which is not used, *f* appearing on ff. 43-4). Catch-words. Decoration: one 6-line and 1-, 2-, and 3-line blue capitals ornamented red. Some ascenders at the top of first quire elongated and ornamented. Binding: s.xviii, rebacked 1936 MacLehose, Glasgow. Secundo folio: *non were his*.

Provenance: The sale at which Hunter purchased the manuscript might be identified from catalogues dated from 1755 (before which Glasgow University Library's records do not show him purchasing any manu-scripts) to 1793, when he died. Mr N. Ker's searches of the library's annotated catalogues of sales at which Hunter is known to have bought proved negative, as have searches of its other catalogues made by Dr Nigel Thorp. Dr Munby found no relevant information in his own catalogue collection.[29]

[29] I am much indebted to all three scholars for allowing me to use their work or for their direct assistance.

Various signatures or initials appear in the manuscript. *Sum liber Antonij Bircham teste Roberto Bowyer* in a s.xvii hand once visible to Young and Aitken at the top of f. 1ʳ is now only partially visible under ultra-violet light. F. 104ᵛ shows various s.xvi hands: *Johanes Hill*; beneath that, verses, the first in an 'italic' humanist-influenced hand, signed *JB* (not *HB*): *Optima quaeque fere manibus rapiuntur avaris | Implentur numeris deteriora suis: | Qui satur est pleno laudat ieiunia ventre | Et quem nulla premit sitis est sitientibus asper. | Os homini sublime dedit coelum*que *videre | Jussit et erectos ad sydera tollere vultus* (the last two lines Ovid, *Metam.*, I, 85-6).

Transcription. There are two main reasons why G, though nearest to the archetype, was not used as the base manuscript for this edition. First is the comparative unfamiliarity of its forms as against C: for example f. 1ʳ/19, 27, 28 *slepptte* for *slepte*, *Gladdschype* for *gladshipe*, *schorttleche* for *shortliche*, and f. 1ᵛ/12, 14, 20 *a bayscht* for *abashed*, *money* for *many*, *cleerkys* for *clerkes*. Another reason for not using it is its common ambiguity in abbreviation, especially in the use of the superior horizontal. For example, ff. 1ʳ/10 and 6ʳ/29 *wōman*, is probably for *womman*, in full at f. 31ʳ/1-2; but G often uses a long vowel, so f. 7ᵛ/34 *wōman* may be for *wooman*, and f. 17ʳ/32 *womān* may be for *womane*. Perhaps the strokes are otiose, as they may be in the common *cōmē* (though *coomen* appears at ff. 1ᵛ/17-18, *becoomen* at 19ᵛ/16). There are similar difficulties with *begān*, *Cherubyn̄*, *comūn*, *doūn*, *dronken*, *gaȳnēpayn*, *koorouned*, *m̄an*, *mēn*, *sertēy n*, *sīgne*, *soūndede*, *sou'eȳgn*, and many others, as well as the stroke over *pp*. In most cases (except the last) I expand where expansion is reasonable, in order to warn the reader of ambiguity; but G's inconsistent spelling (in contrast to C's relative consistency) makes certainty impossible. The same is true of expansion in words which may or may not end in *-ents, -ants*: G habitually uses the forms without *t* (f. 6ᵛ/25 *argumens*, for example). F. 4ᵛ/9 *ōygnemēs* is probably for *oyngements*, since *oygnement* occurs in full at f. 4ᵛ/15, but what about f. 24ᵛ/6 *couenāus*, or *Jugemēs*, *seruāus*?

Ambiguities are also caused sometimes by an indeterminate loop on *t*, *k* and *d*, and a superior sign which may be *a, n, an, ra*. The loop certainly means *-er* at ff. 3ʳ/24, 36ᵛ/28 *aft'ward*. At ff. 1ʳ/9, 2ʳ/11, 3ʳ/2, 13, 18 *folk'* may be for *folkes* which appears in full at f. 1ᵛ/20 (but *folk* at f. 2ʳ/19). At f. 2ᵛ/5 *lord'* may be for *lorde* but cannot be plural. One is unsure how to expand *whñe* (f. 5ᵛ/2 *whañ*, f. 24ʳ/2 *whanne*), or *thñ* (f. 32ʳ/13 *thane*, f. 16ᵛ/17ʳ *thanne*). The use of ȝ with the functions of *y*, *gh*, *-s* is retained.

Marginalia. As in C, the correctors are important. Not only does their work (G³) point to the existence of manuscript *Y*, but at least two (probably more) are contemporary with the main scribe. Indeed, if the early α-branch manuscripts were, as I suggest, checked within the translator's scriptorium, one of these correctors may be the translator himself. The evidence justifying detailed inclusion of G-correctors' work in the critical apparatus is as follows.

A binocular microscope reveals the order in which the manuscript was written and decorated: (1) text (2) blue paragraph marks (covering text on f. 9^v/32, for example) (3) two of the early correctors' work, over blue paragraph marks on f. 10^r/11 and f. 10^v/33 but under rubrication in the places listed on p. lxxvii (4) rubrication (including ornamentation of paragraph marks on ff. 3^v, 12^v, 22^v, 42^v, 43^r) (5) by f. 39^v and 44^v (top left) the rubricator appears to have caught up with the user of the 'arabic' hand, rubrication being under it thereafter, though other marginalia continue to be covered by it. The marginalia very often lengthen vowels, usually inserting *e*, *o* or *a* (see e.g., f. 21^r).

Several hands appear (at least four on f. 48^r for example). Identifying them is perilous, often demanding a decision on a single caret, cross or inserted vowel. I therefore call all annotators' and correctors' hands G^3 in the critical apparatus. A brief account of them here merely directs the reader to examples of each. I call the first hand 'roman' because it is responsible for the earliest roman *capitulum* numbers (*xviii* on f. 6^v to *lxxxxv* on f. 24•) though they are not the only ones in roman numerals, as we shall see. It is characterised by a light, hesitant touch apparent in marginalia on f. 7^v, three of which are under rubrication, a fact confirmed by ff. 9^v, 11^r, 19^r etc., where *capitula* in this hand (whose gloss *scilicet pylgrym* remains) were erased before the rubrication, and written in a clear space by 'fourth hand' (see below)—perhaps therefore, that of the rubricator. The 'arabic' hand uses arabic numbers (the first, *51*, on f. 14^v though earlier examples may be hidden by the binding). It is later than the 'roman', since on ff. 20^r and 20^v it cancelled *lxxij* and *lxxiiij* inserting *72* and *74* respectively; but it can only be a little later, since it is apparently under rubrication on f. 32^v. From the beginning it provides many glosses and corrections. On f. 32^v its spelling of *haaue* and *taaken*, and on f. 31^v its alteration of *shake* to *shaake* in a marginal note, suggests that this is the hand responsible for the frequent insertion of additional vowels, as on f. 22^v. Numbering of the *capitula* confirms the evidence in the Relation of the Manuscripts suggesting that G^3 and C worked from the same manuscript: *capitula* on ff. 6^v, 10^r 10^v run parallel with those in C, but are not marked by ornamented capital letters or new pragraphs in G. Instead, the 'roman' hand has put the numbers in the margin, and marked the relevant medieval 'paragraph-marks' in the text by an L-shaped frame.

The only other significant hand, which is small, firm and compact, wrote for example *haue* f. 6^v, *he* f. 10^r and a long insertion at the foot of f. 90^v. I have not found it under rubrication, but it looks s.xv. A fourth hand writes *lv* and *lvi* on ff. 16^r, 19^r and elsewhere; a fifth adds *capitula* numbers on ff. 9, 11^r, 12^r, 14^r, 15^r, 16^r and elsewhere; a sixth writes glosses (*strenkthe* and *glouen*) on f. 29^v and elsewhere; a crude hand writes *thus* on f. 16^v, *his* on f. 27^r, *58* on f. 15^v and other notes. There may be marginalia in other hands.

Notes on flyleaves: f. iv^r a rough s.xviii hand *Romance of the Monk of the Pilgrimage of the life of Manhood*; f. 102^v a s.xvi hand *Nota. He that in youthe to Sensualite | Applythe his mynde to Lust & Idelnes | To Lyve in ease, he of necessite | myst Lyve in age in woo & werchydnes, | Ease will not be bothe yonge & olde doubtles, | therfore flee ease, and ease will Folowe the | And Folowe ease & ease wyll from the Flee;*[30] f. 104ʳ fifteen lines of writing indecipherable under ultra-violet light; f. 104ʳ a s.xvi–xvii hand, *parcit virga lupis et oues censoria plectit | preteritis crassis miseros grassamur in Iros.*

J. ST JOHN'S COLLEGE, CAMBRIDGE: MS. G.21 [James, *A Descriptive Catalogue . . . St John's College, pp. 15–16*].

s.xv². Explicits and Incipits of the four parts: ff. 51ʳ, 90ʳ, 114ʳ. ff. ii 136 ii. 258 × 174 mm. Written space 183 × 110 mm. 29–33 lines (measurement of a 33-line p.). Collation: ii 1⁸–17⁸ ii. Quire signatures: (i)–xvii top right of every eighth verso. Script: f. 1ʳ, the first five lines of f. 1ᵛ, and f. 136ᵛ colophon red, in Textura-based script not that of the text, which occurs unaccountably (in black) in *Quod*, ff. 43ʳ, 118ʳ, as well as in proper names on ff. 29ʳ, 29ᵛ, 30ᵛ, 34ʳ, 36ʳ. Initials: crude 1–9 line red, ornamented in black ink not used in the text. In most cases (eg. ff. 6ʳ, 11ʳ, 11ᵛ) ornamentation apparently preceded formation of the red letter (though on f. 6ᵛ the reverse is the case), perhaps being sketched in by the scribe? On f. 42ʳ ornamentation in the letter takes the form of a crude 'Tudor' rose, and on f. 114ʳ of a 'ragged staff'. Capitals sometimes marked by a red stroke. Binding: s.xv brown leather over bevelled boards, two thongs. Secundo folio *is full nedfull.*

Provenance: Thomas, Earl of Southampton A.D. 1635 gave the manuscript from the library of William Crashaw, M.A. of the College. Inside back cover: *ROBERTUS* in a rough pen hand, *VILLEMVS* in decorative, crudely painted capitals. The verso of the last flyleaf has in s.xv hands, *Luke the,* and at the bottom, upside down and cropped *Wylleam polle the hermetes* [? *hermet of*] *my god master Ryche* and (partly over the doubtful *-es*) *Be the grete* and *Wylleam Ryche Wylleam Ryche Blake.* On f. 71ᵛ the same hand wrote *Be my willeam Ryche thes boke thes boke was mad.* This, apart from the alteration of *shyn-/ende* to *shynynge* on f. 3ᵛ (text 126), *gracia deo* under *Grace deu* on the last line of f. 4ʳ (text 178), and the occasional curious alteration of *a* to *o* (not noted in the Variants), is the only annotation or correction not in the scribe's hand.

Transcription. The hand is very clear, but in addition to the usual unambiguous abbreviation marks there are many ambiguous horizontal strokes over words or parts of words. For example, f. 1ᵛ/25 *groūn* apparently for *grounde,* f. 26ᵛ/24 *mūn* for *munde,* f. 28ʳ/20 *herȳn* for *herynge.* Sometimes this stroke is otiose: f. 19ᵛ/25 *chaūmberere,* f. 22ᵛ/1 *Achaūn berere.* Often it may or may not be otiose, as at f. 8ᵛ/7 *custōmere,* f. 8ᵛ/16 *gāmen.* Where possible, expansion warns of ambiguity: final strokes over

---

[30] Robbins and Cutler, No 1151·5.

n, *r*, and after *d* are also expanded to *-e* since this scribe (unlike that of M) is not given to flourishes.

M. STATE LIBRARY OF VICTORIA, MELBOURNE, AUSTRALIA: MS. *096 G94 [Sinclair pp. 364-8, No. 217 Manion and Vines, pp. 110-12, no. 45]. Mr. M. B. Parkes kindly dated the hand to s.xv[1]. Mr John Bromwich finds the armour in illuminations on ff. 28[r], 174[r], 182[v] no earlier than 1376 or later than 1433. Contents: f. 36[r] *þe Pilgrimage of þe Lyfe of þe Manhode*, Books 2-4 begin on ff. 36[v], 63[r], 79[v]. F. 96[r] *Pilgrimage of the Soul* and Hoccleve and other poems. Collation: *pace* Sinclair, also Manion and Vines (i + 1-9¹⁰10⁵11-22¹⁰23² + i): i + 1-9¹⁰10¹⁰ wants 6, 7, 8 before f. 96 and 10 after it probably blank 11¹⁰ wants 1 before f. 97 12-22¹⁰23² + i.

The 10th quire consists of ff. 91-6. Ff. 91-4 are signed *k{ j}, kij, kiij, k{iiij}, k.v*, being cropped from f. 95. Ff. 92 and 96 are conjugate. The stub opposite f. 93 (*k.iij*) is clear. Ff. 94, 95 appear to be separate, but it is not possible to be sure. Either quire 10 is made up of scraps, or parts of it (*k.vi–viii* and *x*) were cut away. The latter is more likely, for the following reasons. Quire 11 consists of ff. 97-105, the first five folios signed *l.ij–v*: the first leaf is missing and the last detached. The first would have carried the beginning of *The Pilgrimage of the Soul*. In fact, f. 96 (unsigned *k.ix*, as it were, of the previous quire) carries the beginning of the new work, but in a different hand, the regular scribe's hand reappearing on f. 97. The fifteenth-century note at the bottom of f. 95[v] (sig. *k.v*, cropped) is therefore misleading in saying: [*here endeth ye*] *first part of yis buke, and ye secund part bigynnes in yis next qware.* But then, *pace* Sinclair, the hand

Quire 10

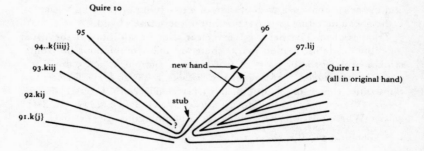

95

96

94..k{iiij}

97.lij

93.kiij

new hand

92.kij

Quire 11
(all in original hand)

stub

91.k{j}

?

is not that of the main scribe, nor of the scribe of f. 96, so the note may have been written after binding, its author (like Sinclair) expecting f. 96 to begin a quire.

Perhaps some disaster was suffered by the first leaf of the 11th quire before binding, and it was removed, the contents being transferred to the best leaf of the five blanks still at that stage forming the end of the 10th quire. Four otiose leaves were then cut away (perhaps all five, coming at the end of þe Pilgrimage of þe Lyfe of þe Manhode, were originally meant to go, or f. 96 may have been intended for a blank final folio). This hypothesis is supported by there being a space for an illumination at the beginning of the replacement folio, f. 96, never filled though all subsequent illuminations are present. The leaves of the 10th quire which are now missing may well have been too bad to use.

The skin is poor, with stitched splits in ff. 35, 72 (two), 77, 82 (two), 83, 89, 95, 147, 216, 217, unstitched splits in ff. 54, 63, 74, natural holes in ff. 5, 59, 63 (four), 72 (two), 76, 84, 97, 110, 112, 116 (two), 132, 133, 141, 142, 154, 204, and cuts which may indicate removal of other damaged skin on ff. 7, 35, 55, 68, 139, 164, 169.

In addition to the main scribe and the one whose hand appears on f. 96, a third wrote the last seven and a half lines of f. 56ʳ: though similar to the main scribe's hand it shows, among other differences, a quite distinct formation of g. A fourth hand wrote f. 158ʳ's last line.

The illustrations and their relationship to those in MS. O are described in Henry, Scriptorium, 37ii (1983), 264–73. Their positions and rubrics, omitted from the Critical Apparatus, are listed below. Rubrics are sometimes related to the text rather than the illustrations, which they sometimes precede and sometimes follow. Line references in the list below are to the word in the main text immediately after the illustration, but are followed by the folio on which the rubric appears.

19	1ʳ	*The vision of þe cite of Jerusalem shewid to a pilgryme · of whilk cite Cherubyn with his flawmyng swerde was made porter*
110	2ᵛ	*þe descripcion of grace dieu · apperyng to þis pilgryme in hir aray ·*
206	4ʳ	*How grace dieu ledd þis pilgrime in to hir howse · whilk hang on hight in þe ayer · and þer in was a watir ·*
434	7ʳ	*How þe officiall ordeyned first þe sacrament of matrymone ·*
452	7ʳ	*How þe sacrament of ordres is giffyne · and what it is ·*
536	8ʳ	*Here is ordayned þe worthy ordre of prestehede · and tellis what it is ·*
776	11ᵛ	*How Moyses went to dyner callyng þe officiall þer to · and changyng brede in to flessh · and wyne in to blode · and how Reson meruailes gretely of swilke mutacyon ·*
897	13ʳ	*How grace dieu · answeris to nature · and tellis how scho*

haues power ouer nature in wirkyng · and is hir maistres
in all thynges ·

Secundo folio *Chanons · and of.*

To the names scribbled by successive hands, noted by Sinclair and by Manion and Vines, add the *francys franc* (in two hands?) f. 148ᵛ. There are small corrections and additions to be made to the account of other scribbles. On f. 216ʳ the list of virtues should read *Merci Abbes, Obeyence prioresse, Discipline prioress, Poverty Stuerd, Chastity Chambrerer or Chastelan, Lession or studie pitancer, Orison harbinger, Invocation trumpeter* (my punctuation). This refers to the inhabitants of the monastery near the end of Book 4, where it is in fact Worship who is trumpeter, her horn being Invocation. On f. 215ᵛ at the foot, *y Explicit* can be seen under u.v., over *x Explicit* erased. F. 217ᵛ *mara* [sic] *gracia plena dominus tecum* is followed by scribbles and unintelligible words, then by an uncomprehending and corrupted copy of the prayer; below that in a ?s.xvii hand, perhaps *Mark Reeues.*

Provenance of the manuscript ought to be traceable between the Cliffords of Chudleigh and its purchase for the Victoria State Library under the Felton Bequest in 1936 on the advice of Sydney Cockerell.[31] Sinclair says the purchase was made from Messrs. W. H. Robinson, but they have no record of the sale. The British Library Cockerell papers,

---

[31] Lindsay, pp. 41–2; *The Times*, 31 October, 1936, p. 11. I am indebted to Rosemary McGerr at Yale for advance information from her forthcoming edition of Book 1 of the ME *Pilgrimage of the Soul*, showing that the Cliffords had the manuscript from the Rouclyff family with whom they intermarried (John Roucliffe's name is on f. 215ᵛ, as Sinclair notes).

which might indicate earlier provenance, are reserved, and the archives of Chudleigh offer no apparent help.[32]

Blots and smudges of a whitish substance (yellow under ultra-violet light) may be wax, as if the manuscript was read by candlelight. They appear on ff. 2^r, 3^r, 4^v, 8^v, 11^v, 18^v and on thirty-seven other pages up to f. 178^v.

Transcription. The manuscript shows y/þ confusion. Although its scribe's y is clearly distinguishable from his þ by a diagonal descender ending in a forward return stroke, þ is often used where y or ȝ is to be expected, or vice versa. Perhaps misguidedly, I retain his forms in the Variants. Examples of þ for y occur on f. 12^r/8 *þnowgh*, f. 26^v/5 *þouth*, and of the less common y for þ on f. 4^v/16 *yin*, f. 17^v/14 *yem*, f. 19^r/12 *yairs*, f. 31^r/7 *oyer*. This confusion occurs also at the end of Book 4 in the 'Pilgrim's Lament' found only in this manuscript, for example f. 93^v/22–3: *I beseke þow to graunt me space of þour gentresse*: however, in the Appendix presenting it I standardise to the letter expected. This confusion of forms may be an idiosyncrasy of the M scribe, since MO are close, and O is so literal and inaccurate that had ε shown this peculiarity one would expect O to reflect it.

This is the most difficult of the manuscripts in abbreviations and final flourishes, though medial marks of abbreviation (with the exception of the otiose superior horizontal discussed below) are usually unambiguous. I sometimes expand *-m'*, *-n'*, *-r'* (where the final stroke is swept up and back over the letter) to *-me*, *-ne*, *-re*. Other final flourishes are usually ignored, with the result that M's forms commonly run parallel with O. Perhaps it is evidence of their redundancy that most of the final flourishes have at some stage been erased on ff. 40^v, 184^r, 209^r, 215. Otiose horizontal strokes over a word or part of a word are common, as at ff. 15^v/6 *holdynge*, 16^r/17 *a leggeance*, 26^v/28 *ensaumple*, 31^r/10 *bounte*, 31^r/26 *daungerous*, 33^v/24 *foundement*, and have been ignored.

O. BODLEIAN LIBRARY, OXFORD: MS. LAUD MISC.740 [Coxe, col. 525; see also Hammond (1933), p. 340.].

s.xv. Contents: Books 2–4 begin on ff. 48^r, 86^r, 109^r respectively. ff. i + 128. Foliation (?s.xviii) 1–129 begins on i: references in the edition are to this. 257 × 190 mm., heavily cropped. Written space 165 × 114 mm. 31 lines. Collation: i + 1^8 + 16^8. Catchwords on all quires except the last. Three scribes: the second begins on f. 44^v, the third on f. 109^r. In addition to that of the rubricator also apparent in earlier corrections, and identified in the critical apparatus by O^2 where necessary, various other hands appear in marginalia and corrections.

Decoration: twenty fine miniatures, also borders and initials, all resembling those in Deguileville's *Pèlerinage de l'âme*, New York Public

---

[32] I am grateful to Lord Clifford for allowing me to examine records at Ugborough.

Library, Spencer MS. 19 which are probably from the same shop.[33] In Laud Misc. 740 however, the illuminator did not use the 'perspective' floor-pattern apparent in Spencer MS. 19: his floors are two-dimensional patterns. Some of the miniatures (without their borders) are reproduced in black and white in Tuve, as indicated in the list below.

The illustrations, and the two rubrics within the body of the text which are omitted from the critical apparatus, are briefly listed below (marginal rubrics are in the critical apparatus). Description of the illuminations, and their relationship to those in M, are published separately (see p. xxxix above). Line references are to the word following the illustration.

1	2^r	The Dreamer and his audience (Tuve, Fig. 28).
110	3^v	*hic gratia dei apparenȝ primo homini nato.*
206	5^r	Grace Dieu's 'house' (Tuve, Fig. 30).
226	5^v	*Baptismus*
536	10^v	A bishop gives sword and keys.
776	14^v	The Pilgrim receives sealed keys.
1083	19^v	Penitence and Charity (Tuve, Fig. 42).
1440	25^v	Communion.
1835	32^r	The Pilgrim receives the Satchel of Faith (Tuve, Fig. 78).
2759	47^v	Memory carries the Pilgrim's armour.
3787	66^r	Sloth (Tuve, Fig. 34).
3947	69^r	Pride rides Flattery (Tuve, Fig. 32).
4392	77^v	Envy ridden by Treason and Detraction.
4711	83^r	Lust, Pride, Treason and Detraction attack (Tuve, Fig. 80).
4853	85^v	Avarice.
5472	97^r	Gluttony (Tuve, Fig. 83).
6043	107^r	The vat of Penance.
6136	109^r	The Sea of the World (Tuve, Fig. 86).
6393	113^v	Youth.
6691	118^v	The Ship of Religion (Tuve, Fig. 89).

There is a marginal drawing of *Rude Entendement* on f. 49^r. Initials, and sometimes capitals, coloured. Letters by the first scribe have often been extended into marginal ornamentations or grotesques, as at f. 30^v, where two beast-heads say *haue at; haue at ye.* Binding: early seventeeth-century pasteboard in a suede chemise; probably by R. Badger, printer.[34] Secundo folio (f. 3) *grete wondre*).

[33] Pächt and Alexander, p. 81, item 925; one of its miniatures is reproduced in *Illuminated Books*, Pl. LX, No. 156. For information on the illuminations I am grateful to Dr Kathleen Scott.

[34] Coxe (1858), p. lx.

Provenance: Archbishop Laud's autograph and '1633' on f. 2ʳ shows that he owned the manuscript in 1633 when he became Archbishop of Canterbury, or acquired it between 1633 and 1635, when he gave it to the Bodleian as part of the First Donation, of 22 May 1635.[35]

The tradition that the archbishop received the manuscript from a William Baspoole rests on the tantalising colophon to Cambridge University Library MS. Ff.6.30, one of two surviving seventeenth-century abridgements of the *Pilgrimage* (the other being Cambridge, Magdalene College, Pepys MS. 2258). The colophon in Ff.6.30 is: *Written according to þe first copy. The originall being in St. John's Coll. in Oxford, and thither given by Will. Laud Archbishop of Canterbury, who had it of Will. Baspoole, who, before he gave to ye ArchBishop the originall, did copy it out. By which it was verbatim written by Walter Parker, 1645, and from thence transcribed by G G 1649. And from thence by W. A. 1655. Desiderantur Emblemata ad finem cujusque capitis, in Originali apposita.*[36]

It has long been assumed that Baspoole's gift was Laud Misc.740.[37] Indeed, Tuve showed that Pepys MS. 2258 derives from Laud Misc.740 (though showing the influence of some French Manuscripts as well),[38] several of whose peculiar errors it inherits,[39] both manuscripts clearly showing the same annotator's hand,[40] the miniatures of Laud Misc.740 being echoed in the Pepys manuscript's pictures,[41] and its marginalia occasionally being incorporated.[42] If its colophon is to be believed, Ff.6.30 therefore derives (at some three removes) from the Pepys manuscript.[43]

However, the colophon remains tantalising. As Tuve notes, Laud Misc.740 was not in St John's but the Bodleian during the 1640s and 1650s. She observes that 'it may quite well have been in St. John's Library first, between the time when Laud wrote his name and "1633" on the first page, and 1635'.[44] She also remarks that 'one has no right to be surprised that twenty years later, a man who had never seen the original (the colophon writer) did not know it had left one library for another'.[45] But it

---

[35] Coxe (1858), pp. xxxv, lx; *Summary Catalogue* (1953), pp. 128–30.

[36] Also in Tuve, p. 155.

[37] *A Catalogue of Manuscripts Preserved in the Library of the University of Cambridge*, II, p. 596; W. A. Wright (1869), p. x; Locock, p. lxiv.

[38] Tuve, p. 208, figs. 76, 77.

[39] Tuve, p. 164, n. 13; p. 196, n. 28; pp. 201–2. The Variants do not record O (f. 5ᵛ) as reading *stephys*, which Miss Tuve thought gave the Pepys reading *steppes*, because O probably reads *stepliys*, though the Pepys scribe may, as easily as Miss Tuve, have read it as *stephys*.

[40] Tuve, p. 202.

[41] Tuve, Figs. 27–30, 31–4, 42–3, 78, 79, 80–3, 86–9.

[42] Tuve, p. 202.

[43] I hope I have correctly understood Miss Tuve to imply that Pepys 2258 is Baspoole's copy (pp. 214–15): her unrevised, posthumously published book is not always easy to follow.

[44] Tuve, p. 214.

[45] Tuve, p. 214, n. 338.

does seem unlikely that the Archbishop's *gift* to the College was revoked in 1635 when he gave the manuscript to the Bodleian. Indeed, neither St John's College *Registrum Benefactorum* nor any other St John's source appears to record this gift from Laud, though others are assiduously noted. Was Laud Misc.740 simply part of a library of Laud's at St John's instead of being actually given to the college? There is another faint possibility. St Bernard's College, which was on the site before White's rebuilding in 1555, was a Cistercian House of Studies.[46] Could the College have owned Laud Misc.740 (a Cistercian text) and instead of receiving it from Laud, have given it to him in recognition of his benefactions (he built the second quadrangle and Library building)? Tuve conjecturally identified Baspoole as son of Richard Baspoole of Potter Higham, Norfolk, d.1614. Could William Baspoole have belonged to St John's?

Earlier provenance of Laud Misc.740 is suggested only by a s.xvi autograph on f. 129ᵛ: *This is Amb{r}os Suttones Booke*[47] beneath a tantalisingly cropped line (or passage) in the same hand; by f. 128ᵛ *William Buk*[. . .] visible under ultra-violet light, and by f. 63ʳ *Wb,Arc'bish.y.Th.* (?). Relevant also, perhaps, is the illuminator's known contribution to Spencer MS. 19,[48] made for Sir Thomas Cumberworth of Somerby, Lincs., in about 1430. We have other evidence that he owned a *Pilgrimage*, though which of the three is not stated.[49] This suggests a north-eastern original for Laud Misc.740 too.

Marginalia, etc. The hands identified here are not distinguished in the Variants: I name them here simply so that they may be more easily referred to in any future identifications of these hands in other manuscripts. One hand wrote before the rubricator worked on f. 66ʳ, where it is carefully surrounded by rubrication of the illumination's frame, which itself is under part of the illumination (as one would expect). It seems to be the hand of Scribe 3, whose text begins at f. 109ʳ. If the three scribes of the text are Hands A, B and C, this is therefore Hand C.

The next earliest hand in the marginalia is probably that of the rubricator, which may logically be designated Hand D. One of his marks is under part of the illumination on f. 66ʳ, so it was before the illuminations were put in that he read the text, marking the places of omission and error with red in both text and margin. Scribe 3 then rectified these mistakes. On f. 123ᵛ one of the rubricator's marginal corrections (*I*) is on top of a correction in black (probably in Hand C). Several of his marginalia are on f. 82ᵛ. He identifies some sacraments and many other items, and often uses arabic numerals, for example on ff. 6ᵛ (*2. confirmacio; 3ᵃ vnguenta*). Other hands in the marginalia, in the order in which they first occur, are as follows. On f. 1ᵛ is a s.xvii list: *Doubtfull words, and letters signifijng* —

[46] Ker, "Oxford College Libraries", p. 487.
[47] Tuve, n. 40, notes that the lordship of Sutton was connected with the parish of Potter Higham, Norfolk.
[48] *Illuminated Books*, p. 57; De Ricci and Wilson, II, p. 1339.
[49] Deanesly, p. 356; Andrew Clark, p. 48.

y — th | sweuen — dreame | syne — Afterward; so or then | hyrne — corner | saule — delight | Algatiȝ — although | Gab — prate | yerdis — rodds | mowe — maye o me [. . .] | *leue — beleeue | recch — care | hate — call | sygh — sawe or see | hele — couer | Araine — a spider | behight, or hight — promise.* This hand (Hand E) wrote the gloss on *obley* (Variants 1460; f. 26ʳ), on *relef* (1489; f. 26ᵛ) and elsewhere. It is the 'Italian' hand which Tuve finds in marginalia on ff. 65ʳ, 119ᵛ and often elsewhere, and which she shows to occur also in captions and chapter headings in Pepys 2258.[50]

Also on f. 1ᵛ in Hand F, which Tuve calls the 'fake (or pseudo) Gothic',[51] is *whoe-euer (after I am dead) doe chaunce this Booke to vew, | with patience read, þen after Judg. some good þer maye ensew*: this hand has more notes and marginalia than any other, and has often overwritten words in the text.[52] On f. 26ᵛ it dates itself *c.* 1630 (*A monkes opinion of þe Sacrament, 300 years since*).

There are several other hands in marginalia: I may not have distinguished them all. Hand G is on f. 3ʳ, 7ᵛ (*nota*), 9ᵛ (*Resoun*), 13ᵛ, 14ʳ, 30ᵛ, 50ʳ, 58ᵛ, 61ᵛ, 62ʳ, 66ʳ (*sleuthe*), 69ʳ, 80ʳ, 83ᵛ, 87ʳ, 90ᵛ, 91ʳ, 96ᵛ, 101ᵛ (*quasi mortuus*), 115ᵛ, 116ʳ. I list all the occurrences I could see, since they are very faint (usually invisible on microfilm). This writer uses Latin and English, occasionally (f. 80ʳ) copying words from the text without apparent reason. On f. 32ᵛ is one of the rare examples of Hand H: a small Court hand, and on f. 34ᵛ a probably fifteenth-century hand (Hand I) makes a long comment.

On f. 129ʳ in a 'gothic' hand (Hand J) is *God made a Buylding* [with *man* over it in another hand] *rare on earth, without the help of any · | þe frame composedf wonderous art, xxxx & gaue it vnto many: to keepe þeir cheifest treasur in, þat envy might not blast it | which, saufly kept from synn & shame; o happy if þou hast it | thy blessed buylding was not v{a}yne & kepers ware all true | but keepers oft proues trecherous which makes þe owners rue* (see Crum, I, 279 on the poems); under that in Hand K, a cursive script: *a good conscience*; and in another 'gothic' hand (Hand L): *The sowle that takes delight in syhing | is gayn'd vpon by custome.* Hand M, on f. 129ᵛ, gives *Sow Be it know* (in a 'gothic' style).

Transcription Comprehensive transcription has not been possible, so frequent are minor tamperings (overwriting, erasure, additions of punctuation etc.) in a text already more corrupt than the others. In addition, O's own spelling is too inconsistent to facilitate correct expansion of abbreviations. For example, f. 2ʳ/4 *thoþ'* is expanded to *thoþir* since *othir* appears on f. 6ʳ/25, but see f. 6ʳ/26 *othyr*, f. 5ᵛ/17 *othire*.

[50] Tuve, pp. 202, 203, 212; figs. 63, 64, 90 (upper marginal note).

[51] Tuve, pp. 201, 213–14; fig. 90 (lower marginal note).

[52] Mr M. B. Parkes once suggested to me that this might be the hand of Stephen Bat(e)man but not surprisingly I cannot identify it with the latter's ordinary hand (i.e. not 'fake-Gothic') in, for example, Cambridge University Library MS. o*.14.23.G.A.1528 (which has his signature), or Oxford, Bodleian Library MSS. Bodley 155, Auct. F.5.29, Digby 171.

There is the usual proportion of cryptic horizontal abbreviations marks, as in *benyḡ*, *crōmyd*, *āght*. Sometimes the stroke is otiose, as at f. 6ᵛ/16 *lambē*. In examples like the latter I am unable to warn the reader of ambiguity. There are a few idiosyncratic abbreviation marks, for example f. 40ᵛ/21 *coŕte* for *corecte*, f. 12ᵛ/3 *subîtes* for *subiectes*, f. 8ᵛ/7 *p̂gyng* for *purgyng*. Whereas in M the forms for *þ* and *y* are distinct, though often used in the wrong places, in O they are indistinguishable, so I transcribe *þ* or *y* as expected. The case of *ȝ*, however, is different: it is used for initial *þ* (f. 3ᵛ/5 *ȝorghe*, f. 3ᵛ/23 *ȝoghte*, f. 8ᵛ/16 *ȝof*), for *y* (f. 5ᵛ/5 *ȝere*, f. 6ʳ/21 *mēȝe* for *menye*), sometimes appearing in a *z* form with this function (f. 2ʳ/4, 7, 8), and for final *s* (f. 6ᵛ/17 *seruantȝ*). I retain *ȝ*.

S. SION COLLEGE LIBRARY LONDON: MS. ARC.L40.2.E.44

[Ker (1969), pp. 290-1].

As Ker observes, this was once part of Cambridge, Trinity College, MS. R.3.20: see Walls (1977), Green (1978) for discussion of the original make-up. Brusendorff implies that this John Shirley manuscript was written between 1426 and 1446.[53] Furnivall, *Autotypes* (n.pag., four plates from the end) dates it 1440 and offers a page in facsimile.

'Chapter headings' by Shirley in a larger script, appearing darker than the text, are in the critical apparatus. Running titles (which are very varied) are in different ink, and though Brusendorff assumes they are Shirley's,[54] they may be in the hand which on f. 14ʳ (modern pencil foliation) wrote *To the* {. . .}. Shirley's guide-letters to initials are usually visible, for example f. 29ʳ. Though crude, the initials resemble those in other Shirley manuscripts: indeed the 'crowned A' such as is found on f. 24ᵛ has been the object of scholarly argument (Hammond, *English Verse* pp. 192-3)—so they would seem to be his.

Shirley's numbering of the *capitula* marked by these capitals is wrong. At f.24ᵛ he makes no allowance in numbering or capitalisation for *capitulum lxxx*, and remains one behind until f.28ᵛ where at *Certayne quod sheo* he misses *capitulum xcviii*, so is two behind. He misses a number again on f.30ʳ and two on f.30ᵛ; by *A quod sheo* on f.30ᵛ he is therefore four behind at his *Capitulum Civ* (MS *Ciiij*). This might be expected to suggest the intervention between G and S of a manuscript less legible than G (if S does in fact derive from G, see pp. lxxii-lxxv). But Shirley is notoriously careless, and in any case G's *capitula* at the points above (G ff. 22ᵛ, 25ᵛ, 27ʳ twice) are so small and faint, as is often the case, that they might easily have been missed.

Provenance: Ker cites 'the 1720 catalogue'.[55] It is in fact of 1724. It is in this catalogue, sig. Ppppp, that former ownership of the manuscript

[53] Brusendorff, p. 213.
[54] Brusendorff, p. 280, n. 1.
[55] Ker, (1969), p. 29. The error probably arose because one Sion copy of this catalogue, *Bibliothecæ Cleri Londiniensis in Collegio Sionensis Catalogus, Duplici Forma Concinnatus*, classmark L26.1/SI 7 MSA, has part of the title-page date torn away, leaving only AD. MDCC. The other copy, at L26.1/SI 7(2) is complete.

(which it misnames *The Pilgrimage of the Soule*, as does the manuscript's present binding) is ascribed to 'Berkley'.[56] I find no earlier evidence that the manuscript ever belonged to the First Earl of Berkeley—and if it did, it is difficult to see how it could show 'the injuries which it received by fire and water in the great fire of London'[57] when the Sion College Library was 'at its former site'[58] which was in London Wall.[59] Berkeley did make a bequest to the College, but in 1682 (1681 *DNB*), and even that was not effected until Berkeley died, in 1698: 'having assigned the books to our College, [he] retained them at the Durdans during his life'.[60] The Durdans was in Epsom,[61] which even the Great Fire did not reach! The bequest is listed in the Book of Benefactors,[62] but no mention is made there or elsewhere in the benefactions of a *Pilgrimage* or of any manuscript which might reasonably be the *Pilgrimage* under another name. Perhaps there is a clue in 'The catalogve of the books in Dvrdens Librarie'.[63] The second of these vellum-covered books (in a quire of fourteen leaves, of which one forms the cover, which I have called f. 1) has on f. 2ᵛ a note in a seventeenth-century hand not that of the catalogue:

> Note] *That all those Bookes wᶜʰ have þᵉ Letter S either before or after them, are remooved to Sion college,* and below that Note. *That half the Manuscripts, and all the Mapps in Folio, except Mercator's Atlas, & Speed's Theatre of Great Britain, are remooved to Sion College, although they are not marked in the Catalogue.*

The *Pilgrimage* is not in this catalogue, but this note might imply that it was sent to Sion before Berkeley's formal bequest, since 'marked' is ambiguous, and might mean 'noted' as well as 'distinguished by an S', and since the annotator's hand cannot be dated with such accuracy as to prove that he did not write before 1666 and the Great Fire.

Whether the manuscript came from Berkeley or not, one would expect it to be listed in one of the pre-1724 college catalogues. I have searched all the manuscript and printed ones listed in the bibliography, without success. Hammond's statement that the manuscript shows damage due to the Great Fire, which rests on the assumption that the manuscript was already in the library of Sion College by 1666, is without foundation. The damage it shows might be due to damp. The provenance of the manuscript before 1724 is unproven.

---

[56] It is to this entry, under *Libri manuscripti in Folio. A. Libri Manuscripti & nonnulli variores impresse, sub arctiori custodia in Archivis adservati No. 15* that a modern 'A.15' on the manuscript f.1 refers us.

[57] Hammond, *Chaucer*, p. 333.

[58] Hammond, *Chaucer*, p. 182.

[59] Pearce, p. 232.

[60] Pearce, p. 259.

[61] *DNB*; Pepys, *Diary*, 26 July 1663. Even the Berkeleys' town house in St John's Street, Clerkenwell, was outside the Fire's range.

[62] MS. Arc.L40.2.564 under 1682.

[63] MS. Arc.L40.2.EC2(1,2,3).

To Ker's reference to E. P. Hammond's *Chaucer* may be added Brusendorff, pp. 207–36, 453–83., and A. I. Doyle.

Transcription. Shirley's hand is clear in principle, ambiguous in detail. Its commonest peculiarity is the otiose horizontal stroke, not recorded in the Variants. For example, at 120 *on*] *vpon* S, there is a long stroke over *vpon*, as there is at 253, 520, etc, etc. The stroke is frequently over *beon*, as at 170, 675, etc; over *some* as at 502, 528, 529, and is over 165 *longe*, 2228 *gloven*, 2251 *attemperaunce* among many others. Doubtless some of these were meant to indicate doubled vowels or nasals. Where over a final nasal, the stroke has sometimes been expanded to *-e*, for example in *myne* since *þyne* occurs in full. Where modern use suggests it, the stroke over final *-ou* has been expanded to *-ioun*. In addition to the usual unambiguous marks of abbreviation, Shirley uses many final flourishes, especially after final *-d*, *-f*, *-y*, *-g*, *-t*, and cutting the ascender of *h*, *l*, or the descender of *þ*. These have been ignored, as have the swung dashes which fill over-large spaces between words, and a variety of line fillers.

THE STEMMA

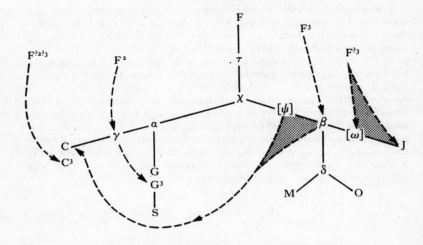

C   Cambridge: University Library, MS. Ff.5.30
G   Glasgow: University Library, MS. Hunter 239
J   Cámbridge: St John's College, MS. 189 (G.21)
M   Melbourne: State Library of Victoria, MS. *096 G94
O   Oxford: Bodleian Library, MS. Laud Misc.740
S   London: Sion College Library, MS. Arc.L.40.2.E.44

All six manuscripts are available on microfilm in their respective libraries; J and M are also in Edinburgh University Library, M558 and M325 respectively.

THE RELATION OF THE
MANUSCRIPTS

Only in the critical apparatus can all the substantive variants be found which provide evidence for the relation between the manuscripts. The following demonstration is therefore not comprehensive, though it is complete. Most of the evidence below is selected from that available in Book 1, which offers more than enough proof of the Stemma: but some important examples are from Books 2–4. In outline, the Stemma is as follows. The six manuscripts CGJMOS derive from one translation τ of the French F. The Stemma shows their common descent from the archetype χ, but τ and χ may be physically identical, representing different stages in the translator's autograph. Thereafter, two branches, α and β are apparent, α closely echoing the French. β, though often in error, is occasionally unique in preserving the original reading: unambiguous examples of this are found only in Books 2–4 (perhaps indicating α's declining concentration). Relations within the β-branch are clear. There is some evidence of a manuscript $[\psi]$ between the archetype and β. From β descend JMO. J is characterised by free treatment of its lost exemplar $[\omega]$, which J's misreadings suggest was written in a poor hand. In the subgroup MO descended from δ, O is notable for corruption. M, though often adding material, remains the best descendant of β. The β-branch shows evidence of reference to a French manuscript F^3 not that of the translator.

Relations in the α-branch are complex. Evidence for the independent physical existence of α itself is sparse, and like that for χ may only represent a further level of correction to the archetype. The influence of a French manuscript F^2 (not that of the translator, unless his copy itself carried marginal or interlinear variations) appears in γ, transmitted to C, and to G's corrector(s) G^3; γ may not be physically distinct either, again representing a level of correction to the archetype.

Even C and G are not simple in themselves. Essentially similar, and close to the archetype, they both show a great deal of early erasure, correction and glossing. In addition, C shows (in the original scribe's work and that of his main corrector) contamination by the β-branch, and one of the C correctors made independent reference back to a French manuscript.

Maas has observed that 'where contamination exists, the science of stemmatics breaks down',[64] and even in the light of West's treatment of contamination as if it were the norm rather than the exception,[65] it is

[64] Maas, p. 48.
[65] West, pp. 35–47.

possible that some evidence cited below has been misinterpreted. Nevertheless, the overall picture is clear. The α-branch seems to have been produced in a scriptorium very close to the translator: probably that of his own community. It used a single very correct manuscript, which it modified from time to time (perhaps the ψ, α, and γ states). It is even possible that some or all of the alterations at these different stages were made by the author himself, 'improving' his own work after he had forgotten why he had written what he did in his original translation. If the scriptorium was that of the translator's community, it would explain why there was evidently such interest in the text, as revealed by the painstaking corrections not only in the varied stages of τ, but in G and C. There is room for research into the scriptorium involved.

C's transcription and subsequent correction in the light of a β-type manuscript (perhaps β itself) is also consistent with the idea of a community specially interested in this translation. If β had been written for some allied or neighbouring community, it might have been possible to borrow it, or one of its descendants, for consultation when C was being made.

The procedure adopted in demonstrating the Stemma is essentially the classical one described by Maas.

THE TRANSLATION No special proof is offered of the fact that all the extant English manuscripts derive ultimately from one translation: the entire critical apparatus clearly manifests their basic similarity. The nature of the translation is not directly relevant to proof of the Stemma, and so is discussed below, pp. lxxxiii–lxxxix.

THE ARCHETYPE On some occasions its scribe appears to have misread an English word (the Notes give a full account of alternative explanations, and of resulting editorial emendations). The archetype χ may, as already explained, be the translator's fair copy of the first stage of his corrections to the original translation. It is not credible that χ should be a physically distinct manuscript and produce so very few errors. At 511 it is just possible that the translator first wrote *porters* for *huissiers*, and on reading his text altered it to *priuees*, but is unlikely, and misreading of *porters* seems more unlikely still. At 1413 perhaps he misread *resited* (*recite* F) as *rested*; at 1512 *leene on* (*apuies* F) may have been misread as *leeue in*; at 1924 perhaps his *lachese* or *lechese* (*remis* F) became *lestest*, at 2245 *his ordene* (*sordenee* F) may have become *his ardene*; at 2294 *armurers be named* (*des armeurieurs sont nommes* F) may have become *armurers ben armed*, and at 2737 *pyer* (*pierre* F) perhaps became *preyer*. In the case of 2294 and 2737 the corruption may have been in the French.

HYPARCHETYPE β AND THE β-BRANCH

The existence of β is indicated by the frequency with which JMO share (1) omissions, (2) additions and (3) non-original readings as against CGS and the French. Evidence is abundant, and so will not be discussed in detail.

(1) JMO very often share omission of material present in CGS and the French. It is both accidental, whether due to eyeskip or other factors, and apparently deliberate.

(a) Omission due to eyeskip is technically no proof of genetic relation, but frequent coincidental omission by both J and δ (MO's ancestor) is unlikely. At 123 *and in . . . amelle* β's eye leaped ahead to *and in the middes þerof a sterre*, causing the omission of the first of the two similar phrases. At 171–2 *and . . . him* the eye leaped from the end of the first clause to the end of the second: *and who hath not me, alle thinge faileth him*. At 541–2 *and*[2] *. . . me* the eye might have moved either from the beginning of *and wente* in the preceding clause to *And þanne* in the following clause, or from the beginning of the omitted clause to the beginning of that following. Further examples occur at 707–8, 1008–10, 1035–7, 1219, 1271–2, 1364, 1404–5, 1544–56, 1608, 1895–7, 1942, 1986, 2124–5, 2174, 2246, 2273.

Other omissions appear to be due to carelessness. Four examples occur before line 114 (where S is missing as a witness): 16 *wyilde* (but perhaps this was confused with the next word *worlde*), 61 *grete*, 70 *stiked*, 104 *faire*. S is present when at 204 *goodliche* and at 2579–80 *þilke . . . couenable* are omitted.

(b) Omission due to refusal to retain difficult readings probably occurs at 114 *withouten any ysinge*: at 1129 β again had difficulty with this verb, corrupting *ysen* to *I Sent(e)*. Similar examples occur at 595–6, 884–5, 1082, 1287.

β often omitted with good reason, finding his exemplar corrupt. At 1851 he left out the meaningless *nature*, the result of the translator having misread French *navre* 'wounded'. Similarly at 1947–8 *and . . . scrippe* where the English is inadequate, β omitted a whole clause. Other examples are at 1479, 1619, 2245, 2322–3, 2666, 2737–8.

Omission of what the scribe of β probably regarded as otiose occurs at 429 *lettede hem not* which β seems to have thought unnecessary in front of *ne oppressed hem ne greued hem of nothing*. At 721 he may have thought *and withholde* unnecessary after *cleerliche vndirstande, and wel lerne*. Similar omissions occur at 683–4, 1008–10, 1027–8, 1183, 1532, 1546, 2383. A large number of small omissions may be deliberate attempts to smooth the text, or may be unconscious, for example 291 *þat*, 345 *now*, 400 *þat*, and examples 405, 485, 499, 513, 555, 641; 664, 780, 1076.

(2) Additional material making the text more explicit occurs at 423 *hornes*, where *of A Snayle* is added. At 1268 *it* is explained as *the worm of conscience*. β also made small additions at 1149, 2684, 2686.

(3) Non-original readings include those made in error and those apparently deliberate.

(a) β often had difficulty with the syntax or grammar of his exemplar. At 45–6 *þat entre þere* he misunderstood the verb *entre* as a noun, the phrase therefore appearing as *the entre whare* in JMO. At 80–1 *maden . . . clymbe þider* β did not realise that *maden* was followed by an accusative and infinitive construction, and so substituted *thedyr they clambe* (so JMO) for *clymbe þider*. At 552 β mistook *take him Grace herself* for *take him herself*, with resulting confusion in meaning. Further examples occur at 1374, 1503, 2138, 2726.

Misreading is commoner still. Sometimes, as in the first four examples below, variations in JMO's readings at first obscure the issue. At 40 *alþouh*, β's dialectal *þof al* was corrupted to *of al* (and then *yf al* in O), but misread as an abbreviation of *þereof al* by J. At 77 *enoynted*] *sare* J, *noyed* MO is due to β's having written something like *enoyeed* or *noyeed*, for which J substituted. At 324 *levinge* β's exemplar, which I call [ψ] since evidence for it is so scant, must have had something like *leuȳg it*, to have been mistaken by β for *benygnite* (so JMO). At 2112 β took *armed* (*arme* F3876) for *anueld*—understandably since anvils, mentioned at 2093, 2116, 2159, 2166, fit the context. In all these places the substitution of *stithy* in one or more of the β-branch witnesses obscures the issue. Simpler examples are at 1129 *ysen*] (*issir* F) *I Sente* JMO, 1293 *I wole keepe*] (*veul je garder* F) *es welle kepede* JMO; 1397 *Alle ben dedlich*] (*touz sont mortex* F) *alle to be Ilyke* JMO; 1805 *men*] (*on* F) *mete* JMO; 2094 *hameres*] (*martiaus* F) *harmes* JMO; 2126 *moneyden him*] neu*ere he moued hym* J, *moued hym* MO.

(b) Deliberate substitution is not always easy to identify. Where the French is unhelpful, it is always possible that instead of substitution by β we have preservation of τ's reading, as at 1 *whiche*] *the whilke*, and 149, 173, 190, 213, 246, as well as 670 *shette*] (*clorre* F) *spere* JMO; 1706 *kyte*] (*escouffle* F) *glede* (also a bird of prey) JMO; 1959 *bineme*] (*ostast* F) *refe* JMO; 2702 *al be it*] *þouȝ alle* JMO.

It is, however, usually clear when substitution occurs. Some examples from a mass of possible evidence are: 320 *rudesse* (F590) gives us *rudeshipe*] *reddour* JMO; 392 *issir* (F722) *ysen*] *prese*; 503 *appercoit* (F922) *apperceyuen*] *persayves*; 569 *delitable* (F1044) *delitable*] *delectabille*; 618 *le* (F1128) *þe*] *ȝoure*; other examples are at 636, 701, 713, 767, 778, 781, 849, 881, 904, 985, 1071, 1164, 1172, 1263, 1288, 1320, 1430, 1910, 1985, 2671.

Substitution is not always obvious. At 2729 β apparently did not understand *whan I wole yelt invisible* and substituted something like *whan I wole I wil seme inuisible*, giving MOS's *I wil seme inuisible* and J's *maketh me . . . nouȝt be Sene in in visible when I wille*.

Alterations to word-order by β are not uncommon, for example 805 *flesh quik* (*char vive* F1488), and 1141 *likour foul* (*liqueur ordre* F2105) each transposed in JMO. At 1290-1 *and departede to hise freendes* (*et departi / A ses amis* F2369-70) becomes *to frendes and depertyd*; at 1407 *signed and marked* (*seigniez . . . et merchiez* F2579-80) becomes *merkede and Signede*; at 1519 *wyn ne bred* (*vin ne pain* F2788) becomes *breede ne wyne*.

THE RELATION BETWEEN J, M AND O. None of the manuscripts in the
β-branch can be the ancestor of any of the others: each shows (1) separative
omissions, (2) additions and (3) non-original material.

The J Manuscript cannot be the origin of M or O.

(1) Omissions, both accidental and deliberate, are plentiful.

(a) Eyeskip explains omissions at 194–5, 1300–1, 1575–6, 1758–9, 1760–
3, 2023–4, 2352–4, 2380–2, and at 91–2 and 166–7 is the result of J's
misunderstanding.

(b) Exclusion of what J regarded as otiose may explain omission at 8–9
of Now cometh neer and gadereth yow togideres alle folk, and herkeneth wel.
Smaller examples occur at 91, 112, 479–80.

(2) Additional material makes the text more explicit or emphatic. At 36
β's of the bokelere becomes of the swerd and the bokelere: similar additions
are at 68, 91, 204, 222, 224, 231, 296, 407, 1121, 1353, 1589, 1603, 2002.
Addition for emphasis is at 11, where sitte and herkne becomes herkyn it
ententyfly, and at 47–8 where Eche was agast becomes I was wondere sare
agaste. Other examples are at 51, 73, 111, 170, 177, 265, 1066–7 and 1985
where the mild to hewe þee becomes to be hewyne als smalle as flesche to the
pote.

(3) Non-original readings in J include those due to error and deliberate
substitution.

(a) Error accounts for 34 skirmynge] schymerande; 248 ministre] My
Iustere; 263 sithe ledde me] syn he led O, seynede J. Sometimes nonsense
results, as at 601 meselrie] mesehy; 839 nouelries] monethes; 1043 rude
vnderstondinge] mede vnde fraudynge. Since MO did not have difficulty at
these points one suspects the existence of an intermediate ancestor [ω]
between β and J, in a difficult hand; see also 1293, 2022, 2034, 2069, 2163,
2212, 2370.

(b) Substitution is no less common. Examples are 10–11 putten hem
forth] take good tent þerto; 28–9 þer hadde iche wight shortliche to passe me]
Schortely to saye thare hadde ilke a wight; 40 payage] paymente; see also
49, 55, 72, 77, 95, 122, 145, 197–8, 202, 256, 1158, 1278, 1313, 1645, 1995,
2113, 2162, 2173, 2193.

Alteration to word-order is at 162–3 bi day as bi nihte, and bi niht as bi
day] be nyghte as by day and by daye as by nyght; 800 and my wit al
outerliche] alle vttyrly and my witte; 1057–8 right litel is woorth yowre
argument] ȝowre argument is litille worth; see also 1074, 1077–8, 1122. Two
lines are transposed at 1308–10.

This demonstration that J cannot be the origin of M or O has shown
also that it is a free adaptation of β. A few readings, however, are so close
to variant French readings that they can hardly be accounted for merely
by the twin operation of free transcription and coincidence. It is possible
that all these examples belong on p. lxi, among glosses found originally in β, but in the cases cited here not passed on to either M or O.
Alternatively, J or J's hypothetical exemplar [ω] made occasional reference to a French manuscript F³ (not the translator's but not, of course,

varying from his at all points) and bore marginal or interlinear glosses occasionally incorporated in J's text. Two examples occur where the text requires explanation, so that such cross-reference might be expected. At 2236 Grace tells the pilgrim that without the helmet he would run the risk of being shot through the eye *if þe viseer ne were streyt*. Stürzinger's ten collated manuscripts read *se n'estoit l'euilliere estroite* (F4093) and manuscript *A* reads *se nestoit loilliere estroite*. Now J has *ware ne the viser ware strayte olierde*, and unless one postulates derivation from a gloss, the last (unrecorded) word is hard to explain. It looks as if the French was reconsulted, resulting in the glossing of *viser* by [*an*] *olierde*, J then incorporating noun and gloss in his text. Though unrecorded, *olierde* is plausible: *-erde* for *-ere* forms are cited by *OED vizard* and *visor*, which both derive from OF *viser* and exhibit the same relationship as *olierde* / *oilliere*, based on the use of *-ard* (*-erd*) as a formative of an English derivative noun (*OED -ard*). At 1097 *courreyinge* (*couroians* F2028, from *cuivrier* 'hurt') is the reading in CMOS (G's *courveyenge* being a corruption): *MED curreien* 2b gives the meaning 'to punish by beating', which fits the sense well. But J has *wele plyande*, echoing the *bien ploians* variant in Stürzinger's MS. *A*. Reference was apparently made to a French manuscript not that of the translator. Other examples are less convincing, and may be due to coincidence. At 18 all the witnesses except J translate *J'estoïe* (F34) by *I was in*; but J has *I was Sclepinge in* and Stürzinger's *A* has *ie dormoie en*. At 20 to *þe citee of Jerusalem* is followed in J by *the whilke I hadde sene by fore*, and where the edited French has *En Jherusalem la cite* (F38), Sturzinger's *P* apparently has *Laquelle monstree mestoit* added. Two other readings in J may indicate independent reference to the French, although in each case it does not differ from that referred to at these points by the translator. At 118 *of hir fairnesse* is *whase bewte did* in J, which is nearer in vocabulary though not structure to the French (*Qui*) *de sa biaute* (F232), and *la dite* (F482) is 260 *the forsayde* in J but *þe same* in the other manuscripts. Whether or not J received influences from a French manuscript not that of the translator does not essentially affect the Stemma, but if such influence occurred it is part of a pattern showing how all the English witnesses were in one way or another modified by an elaborate process of cross-reference and checking: evidence of the availability of both French and English manuscripts of this text, and the importance attached to their accurate transmission.

The M Manuscript cannot be the origin of J or O.

(1) Omissions from M are mainly but not exclusively small.

(a) Eyeskip explains three of the longest, at 296-7, 1351-2, 2710-11. Others appear to be due to misunderstanding or carelessness, as at 75, 143, 392, 586, 1615, 2119-20.

(b) Deliberate excision of small words is hard to differentiate from carelessness but probably accounts for examples at 156, 170, 394-5, 406, 695, 744, 1193, 1771, 1926, 2021, 2091, 2574, 2757.

(2) Additional material, sometimes of unusual length, is common in M. Three examples suggest that M's exemplar was illustrated, and that M's layout was designed in accordance with it, before the scribe began work. At 206 *I pray yow* is followed in M by *for þe luff of god*, the text continuing correctly for two words *tarieth nouht*, and then adding the forty-two words cited in the critical apparatus. The addition seems to be nothing more than a space-filler: the next page, f. 4^r, began with an illustration, so the scribe filled up f. 3^v. The same is true at 535 and 1340-1. Another long addition, perhaps prompted by the scribe's feelings about extravagance in dress, occurs at 4033.

The 'chapter headings' and illustrations are not considered here since they are not strictly addition to the text. There are however numerous small additions within the text, making it more explicit, as at 57, 317, 384-5, 752, 898, 1798, 2562, or to add emphasis, as at 1464, 1614. At 1317 *þe languishinge] lanquyse and þem þat morneʒ*, M's addition is clearly connected with the misdivision of the preceding *þe languysand* (cf. *þe langwyschande* J) into *þe languyse and*, though it may be questioned whether the addition caused or was the result of the misdivision. Perhaps M's exemplar had *languysand* glossed by *þem þat morneʒ*.

(3) Non-original material in M is included in error or deliberately substituted.

(a) Misreading and misunderstanding of the exemplar produce a large number of errors peculiar to M, as at 12 *withouten any owttaken] with outyn any doute takynge*, 101 *swich a dwellinge] þe sygeʒ ay dwellynge*, 342 *hurtle] hurt ill doars*. Further examples occur at 110, 304, 443, 494, 654, 1163, 1327, 1539, 1673, 1823, 2123-4, 2300, 2350, 2695.

(b) Substitution is common. On two occasions, for example, M rejects *abash*: 213 *abashed me] was aferde somwhat*, 227 *Art abasht] Art þou aferde*. Other substitutions are at 242, 271, 348, 369, 400, 544, 573, 574, 671, 774, 880, 899, 2193, 2354, 2356, 2453.

Alteration of word-order, cited here although the alteration may not be conscious, is found on a few occasions, as at 757, 888, 1363, 1670.

The O Manuscript cannot be the origin of J or M.

(1) Omissions are less common in O than errors, and are hard to analyse, so careless is the scribe. Indeed the prevalence of gross error suggests that he might have been working at speed (perhaps even, on occasion, from dictation). No attempt will be made to classify omissions, beyond distinguishing those due to eyeskip.

(a) The largest eyeskip is at 1177-80: the eye leapt from *astone it* immediately before the omission to *astone it* at the end of it. Other examples occur at 83-4, 1025, 1321-2, 1616, 2362-3.

(b) The difficulty of distinguishing between accidental and deliberate omission in O is well illustrated by 318-20, where a hand not the scribe's, though similar to it, wrote *instrument* over erasure of the last word on the page, and inserted at the bottom of the page *& softe soft he schuld be þat* *hase it, for oft grete reddo*ur *mys*, perhaps omitted because it caused difficulty (as it clearly did to other scribes). All the corrector's efforts fail to rectify the original mistake, since the next word, forming a new paragraph at the top of the next page, was *Fallys*, the original scribe having treated this as if it were a word in itself instead of part of one. Lines 1321-2 may represent rejection of a difficulty but it is also a good example of the difficulty of distinguishing omission from substtution: J and O independently misread abbreviated *oopere* in *misseyde of oopere* as *othe* "oath". In addition, O did not understand the admittedly obscure remark by Charity, that she *ne misdide oopere, and nouht þanne I haue maad doo sum harm withoute misdoinge* so he contracted it to *ne doynge*, fabricating the ungrammatical *mysseyd of the othe ne doynge* 'spoke ill in word or deed'. Small omissions occur at 66, 374, 375, 433, 657, 720, 807, 843, 874, 900, 930, 995, 1027, 1108, 1122, 1283, 1286, 1414, 1575, 1849, 2235, 2259, 2362-3, 2631 and (the scribe having changed at 2559) at 2639, 2682, 2744.

(2) Like M, O has illuminations and captions not echoed in other English manuscripts. These are again excluded from this demonstration. True additions, as distinct from minor ones made in the course of error or substitution, are not found in O: one would not expect a scribe so careless of his copy to bother to contribute to it.

(3) For the same reason, non-original material in O is usualy accidental.

(a) Errors are legion, indeed their frequency goes a long way to explaining the rarity of rejection of difficult readings or excision of otiose material: normal symptoms of intelligent if misguided scribal activity. The scribe of O Sometimes retains and distorts what he does not understand, often producing nonsense: at 715, 731, 773 he fails to understand *Ad Aliquid* (or the abbreviation for it in his exemplar), and writes *ad* (followed at 731 by a paragraph mark) a second *ad* being supplied each time in a different hand; at 2189 he changes what appears in JM as *he waxeth wood* 'he goes mad' to the nonsensical *he wa\xi/s hys wode* 'he waxes his wood'. Similar misunderstandings are at 105-6, 296-7, 696, 2344.

Simpler misreadings abound, whether due to visual confusion, as at 90 *thoruh*] *ȝorghe*, 1007 *conferme*] *conserue* or 1097 *teeth*] *toche*, or to other carelessness. Examples are at 40, 64, 102, 108, 121, 167, 208, 210, 229, 264, 318, 411, 468, 522, 532, 610, 687, 689, 692, 708, 714, 718, 760, 766, 791, 792, 807, 830, 837, 850, 878, 889, 899, 900, 903, 906, 918, 923, 955, 960, 962, 979, 1001 and more than thirty other places in Book 1 alone. At 2559 the scribe of O changes, and there are fewer errors, which do, however, occur at 2620 *hem*] *þan* and at 2644, 2652, 2659, 2697, 2710.

(b) Deliberate substitution such as 1012 *bylde*] *hewe* is naturally rare in the work of such an unthinking scribe. Variations in word-order are hardly more common: four are at 66, 1042, and in the work of the second scribe at 2685 and 2690-1.

In spite of all this omission and non-original work O has its uses as a witness, occasionally being the only manuscript in the β-branch to agree with the French and α-branch, and so provide valuable evidence of the correct reading. At 13, Guillaume naturally speaks of having written in French. Only G and O echo this, in an unthinking retention of their exemplar's reading which for different reasons is typical of each of them. CSJM, more alert (or less fastidious) scribes, have altered the word to *englische* in order to avoid anomaly. Further examples occur at 74–5, 255–6, 1539, 2711. On at least five occasions O's witness is still more important, being at points where the French is little or no guide, and the English variants are either synonyms, as at 2093, 2116, 2122, or analogous phrases, as at 2193.

The MO Subgroup

The next step is to demonstrate that MO must derive from a proximate common ancestor δ, since in addition to the peculiar errors discussed above, they show omission, errors and non-original material in common as against the other witnesses. Excluded from this place in the argument are glosses, often identical in M and O. These are dealt with elsewhere, and logic demands that at this stage attention is drawn to the existence of conjunctive errors which are also separative: shared by M and O where CGS and J are right, and where J is unlikely to have removed by conjecture what was error in β. J's propensity for elaboration complicates matters. At 15, for example, one might think that *forsake and leue*] *forsake* MO is evidence of their derivation from a common ancestor, but J's *refuyse and forsake* might mean that β only had *forsake*, which J independently elaborated.

(1) No omissions peculiar to MO can definitely be attributed to eyeskip or the deliberate rejection of material. They do, however, share many small omissions, each of which might in isolation be supposed the result of independent smoothing. Only the high incidence of such occurrences suggests that even these are evidence for the derivation of M and O from a common ancestor. As the least conclusive evidence they will be treated first. At 493 is one of the more complicated cases. What appears in CGS as *youre god ye haue chosen* is in J and presumably β *ʒowre godde has ʒe chosen ʒow*, where *ʒow* is reflexive; MO or their ancestor took *ʒow* as accusative and so omitted *ʒe*, reversing the sense, to *þour god has chosen þow* (the *þe* for *y* are M's). At 726 is a simpler and more typical example: *þe lordes*] *lordes* MO: without the supporting evidence of similar examples it might well be thought that M and O independently omitted an otiose word. The same is true at 741–2 where only MO omit *of* from *of þe keyes also*, in MO's omission at 930–1 of *for* from *for it boundeth*, in the following omissions: 954, 1132, 1917 *and*; 1190 *þe*; 1263 *to*; 1265 *him*; 1763 *in*; 1861 *in*[2] from *in bodi and in soule*; 1952 *þee* (where *comforthe the* in J suggests the omission may be due to eyeskp); 1972 *þat*; 2078 *And*; 2090 *for*; 2129 *þe*; 2163 *bi swich*; 2447 *to*; 2594.

Equally small, but less easy to attribute to independent omission, are the following. At 154 *lord* is omitted from *is lord aboue alle*. At 173 the omission of *alle* from *alle harmes* may be due to a desire to avoid a phrase too similar to *alle thinge* in the previous line; it seems more likely that this desire was in δ's scribe rather than having been felt independently by M and O. At 655 *of* is omitted from *ful of kunnynge*: it seems unlikely that M and O independently misunderstood *kunnynge* for an adjective, and so turned *ful* into an adverb. At 741 *naked and vnsheped*] *vnschetid and nakid* J, becomes merely *naked* in MO. At 757 *hid þan vnhyd* becomes in J *hidde than vnkouerid*, but MO have only *hidd*. At 1115 the omission of the first *it* from *I softe it and make it weepe* is still less likely to be independent omission, as it spoils the construction. The same is true at 1133, *inne* being left out of *to putte inne and bowke*, and at 1159 where the sense is obscured by the omission of *thinkinge* (*thinkande* in J). At 1850 J's reading *and man borne of amaydene* is his variation on CG's *mad man, and of a mayden born* and MO are unlikely to have arrived independently at *made man of maden born*. Similar omissions are at 1204, 1306, 1483, 1686, 1812, 1947, 2119, 2220, 2381–2, 2619. At 2205–6 omission of *ne* from *shulde not be heled* reverses the meaning.

It will be obvious how rare are longer omissions shared by M and O. However, at 160 *þow seye neuere noone fairere* is omitted only in MO. That there is no mechanical reason to account for it is all the more evidence for the existence of δ.

(2) Unlike M, the ancestor of MO shows little inclination to add to the text. All additions are minor, for example 487 *sheweth*] *shewis wel*; 831 *I intermeted*] *I þere entermetyd*; 1401 *hole, grete and smale*] *hole : both grete and small*. Other small examples are at 1968, 2005, 2013, 2071, 2354.

(3) Non-original material is both accidental and deliberately substituted.

(a) Accidental error is often the result of misunderstanding which can only be interpreted in the light of J's reading. For example, at 301 *neede þei haue at here eedinge* seems already to have been corrupted by β, since J has *þayme nedes to have at thayre endynge*; but δ corrupted further, giving MO's *þei nede to haue it at þer endynge* (where M noticed and cancelled the intrusive *it*). At 1327 β had not introduced corruption: *I made him bounde*] *I made hym be boundene* J, *I made hym bow* MO is the result of MO's ancestor having failed to recognise the causative construction 'I had him bound', with consequent substitution of the active *bow*. As a result, *corowned* no longer has a participial adjective to which to be parallel, and is read by MO's ancestor as an active past tense so that *hym* must be added. At 2181 *afforce me I wole to bere*] *bifore me I will do bere it* MO is the result of MO's ancestor having initially misread *afforce* (*aforce*) as *afore*: it was then natural to change *to bere* to *do bere*. At 2195 *deyne*] *dy* MO, it is clear, although J omitted the word, that he did not have MO's reading in front of him: J omitted *deyne to* because it is otiose in *For drede of deth he shulde not deyne to turn ayen*: it could not have been regarded as otiose and given MO's *For drede of deth he shuld nouȝt dy*. Other errors peculiar to MO are found at 62 *begunn en*] *be ganne* J, *become* MO; 299

þei] *þo* MO; 407 *hem*] *hym* MO; 1199 *places*] *place* MO; 1300 *þe*] *hire*
MO; 1531 *þe*] *þi* MO; 1539 *straunge*] *strange* J, *strong* MO; 1540 *fanned*]
thresched J, *band* MO; 1628 *aresoned*] *aunswerde* J, *reseyued* MO; and at
2137, 2277, 2334, 2415, 2686.

(b) Substituted material peculiar to MO cannot always be easily distinguished from accidental error, for example at 1308 *neiþer*] *noon* MO
may be the result of *neiþer* having been taken for a pronoun (though this
error is not possible at 2097, where the same variation occurs). However,
the following appear to show substitutions by *δ*, since they are shared by
MO: 100 *þat he ne may*] *þen he may*; 260 *bi þat on*] *by þe*; 262 *nothing*]
nouȝt; 269 *þat I ne*] *þen I*; 457 *quod she*] *scho saide*; 504 *heerde*] *hirdman* M,
herdiman O; 590 *deserueth*] *seruys*; 775 *sheþed*] *in sheth*; 840 *þouh*] *if*; 903
hastyf] *hasty*. Similar examples occur at 1139, 1142, 1241, 1308, 1501,
1737, 1817, 1911, 1967, 1975, 2194, 2215, 2544, 2562, 2632, 2655.

Word-order variants include 199 *no lengere be*] *be no langere*; 577 *be*
freend (transposed); 691 *I hadde al*] *al I had;* and examples at 742, 1205,
2567.

Glosses in β, and the influence of F³

Though not strictly part of the proof of the Stemma, this is an appropriate place for evidence that some disagreements between M and O
are due to transmission of glosses, present in *β* (whence they pass to J)
and retained in *δ* (whence they pass to M but are omitted by O, which in
each case retains the text of *δ*). Those appearing only in J are listed on
pp. lv–lvi. At 138 *excited*] (*excite* F269), *excut* O, *excitede and stirrede*
J, *stirred* M, might be accounted for by *β*'s having had *excited* glossed
stirrede: it is typical of J, which has few marginalia, that the gloss has been
absorbed into the text (as apparently happened at 2236 *streyte olierde*,
discussed on p. lvi). The same is true at 255, in O's retention of the
original reading *þu schall price at a budde* (*un grant bouton | Tu ne prises*
F474–5) where J has *þowe schalle nouȝt sette by* and M has *þou shal sett at*
nouȝt. At 3822 *of abbotes* appears in J as *prioures*, M adding *and priors*,
suggesting that *β* carried the gloss *priors*. At 1148 it is clear that some
glosses in *β* derive from consultation of F³, which may or may not be
identical with the French manuscript that influenced J (pp. lv–lvi), not that
used by the translator. CGS and O have *knewe*, following *connissoie* (of
Stürzinger's manuscript *A⁷*) but J has *knokkid*, and M has *knokk* written
over *know*, which suggests that *β* had *knew* with a marginal or interlinear
correction *knokk(ed)* made after consultation of a French manuscript carrying Stürzinger's accepted reading *contrisoie*. This correction in *β* was
then adopted by J and transmitted to *δ* as a marginal or interlinear annotation which O rejected but M eventually accepted. There is a similar
case at 2991, where *τ*'s corrupt source gives his *walkere*, as shown by
CGMS; JO 'correctly' have *churle* (*paisant* F). *β* and *δ* had *walkere* glossed
by *churle* as a result of consultation of F³: M rejected, JO accepted the
gloss. This completes the proof of the *β*-branch of the Stemma.

HYPARCHETYPE α AND THE α-BRANCH

That CGS derive from α and not directly from χ can only be proved by their sharing of 1) omissions and 2) errors as against JMO and F. Since omissions are rare, and the errors arguable, one may doubt the independent physical existence of α altogether: is possible to explain all the evidence for it in other ways (the common ancestor of JMO had access to a French manuscript, and may have rectified omissions in χ which now appear only in α). The strongest evidence for α occurs in Books 3 and 4.

(1) Three small and four large examples of omission imply α. At 1832 only CGS omit *bar* from *Neuere I trowe man ne womman so fair a scrippe bar ne lenede to*: in the text it is supplied from MO, J having the slightly modified *ther was neuere man ne woomanne bare a fayrere scrippe ne bourdoun lened to.* The archetype seems therefore fully to have translated *Onques, je croi, fame no hon | Si belle escherpe ne porta | Ne a bourdon ne s'apuia* (F3364-6). It does look as if α omitted *bar*, leaving us with the nonsensical image of the pilgrim leaning on his satchel. But it is possible, if unlikely, that both C and G (assuming for the moment that S does derive from G as corrected, see below pp. lxxii-lxxv) independently omitted *bar* under the influence of *burdoun's* following so closely. It is perhaps still more possible that the omission was made by the archetype, and nonsense resulting, β correctly emended by intelligence or by reconsultation of the French which, as will be suggested, was to hand in the scriptorium where C and G[3] worked, and where β may have worked too, since C shows early contamination from the β-branch. This hypothesis would presuppose either the unlikely independent physical existence of χ, or τ's making his own fair copy, and being subject to the eyeskip. Nonsense also results from CGS's omission of the negative at 2727. In *to þat entente þat þou do no harm, no* is supplied from JMO which, though their corruption of some parts of the passage at first obscures the fact, essentially give the meaning of *A fin que tu ne faces mal* (F5007). But here too the omission might have been made in the archetype or even by C and G (or their ancestors), because of the juxtaposition of *do* and *no* (or *na* and *ha-* if the translator used the *na* for *no*). In the former case β might have correctly emended, perceiving the illogicality. In either case this evidence for independent α would evaporate. At 4274 *led* (*amenee* F) is omitted by CGS, but it is possible that C and G independently left it out, especially if faced with *hadde ledde.*

Some omissions, however, are substantial. They are less easy, though not impossible, to attribute to independent omission, and since they do not result in nonsense, it is unlikely that JMO's source was prompted to consult F[3]—though it is just conceivable that he was making a more systematic check of the whole, at this point. At 3480-3 α suffered eyeskip from *with me* in 3480 to *with me* in 3483. At 5019 α omitted a whole line by eyeskip from *Auarice* to *Auarice*, then found *I am cleped* in 5020 redundant, so left it out. At 5311-12 eyeskip from *she vseth* resulted in omission of one, and at 6382–4 eyeskip from *bere þee* resulted in omission of two lines (F11,859–63).

(2) There are no examples of clear addition to the text by hypothetical α, but on one occasion it looks as if a gloss in χ (though not one I can explain) was built into α, though not into β: at 3365 *stike* is an acceptance, made in the light of F *tronc* (on which JMO's *strare* is surely a variation), of the subpunctated word in G's *stykię blast of wynd*, which appears in CS as *blast of wynd*. There being no certain examples of addition by α, the next step is to examine those occasions when it is possible, though in few cases is it certain, that β alone preserved the original readings (as shown by JMO), CGS showing non-original readings as against JMO and the French.

(a) There are only two examples which may be due to accidental error. At 1197 *crookede cornere*, JMO's equivalent of *cornet* (F2202) has been accepted in place of CGS's *crook or cornere*, and at 1240 so has *swept*, which represents an acceptance in place of CGS's *kept* of JMO's reading as the equivalent of *baliee* (F2278), on the assumption that the French is a form of *balayee* 'swept' (as apparently at 1237) rather than a form of *baillier* 'to guard'. At 2994 only JMO's *ordinaunce* reflects the French singular. Smaller examples are at 3465, 4927 (where only JMO's *ve* echoes F *ve*), 5784, 7119 (where only JMO's *wel ofte* echoes F *bien souvent*). In a class of its own, because in Chaucer's *A.B.C.*, is 5939, where only JMO's *rest* (CGS *lust*) reflects F11,050 *repos*.

(b) On six occasions there has been substitution by CGS's or JMO's ancestor, but it is not certain which. At 955 *firmament* (*firmament* F1767) is JMO's reading accepted in place of CG's *walkene*, but JMO's echo of the French may be the accidental result of substitution. At 1210 *felthe goth* (*ordure . . . va* F2224) is an acceptance of JMO's construction which unlike CGS's *felthes gon* is singular like the French: again either reading might be substitution. At 1232 all the English manuscripts are corrupt, but the question is whether *sans . . . deception* (*sans . . . excepcion* in τ's source?) was initially corrupted to *with owtene exepcioun of* (so JMO) or to CG's *withoute outtakinge* (+ *of*, S). At 1692 *apparence* the reading of JMOF is accepted, but perhaps CGS's *apparisaunce* should be retained as the more difficult reading in spite of the fact that it is unrecorded in *OED, and MED* cites only this example. (If *apparence* was the original reading this is of course an example of error in α rather than substitution by β.) At 1746 *maxime* is again JMOF's reading, in place of CGS's *gretteste principle*: this case is analogous, in its choice between native and latinate readings, to that at 955.

THE RELATION BETWEEN C, G AND S.

The next step is to show, as far as is possible, that none of the manuscripts CGS can derive from any of the others in its group. As far as the uncorrected forms CGS are concerned (as opposed to C as corrected and G as corrected) there is no shortage of evidence. The relation of the corrected forms is another matter, greatly complicated by three factors: contamination, the ambiguity of the evidence relating S to G as corrected, and the fact that two most important witnesses, C and G, are heavily glossed and corrected by several hands, some so early that in C marginal corrections suggested by C³ are usually written in the original scribe's hand over erasure in the text, and in G marginal corrections suggested by the two main G³ hands themselves occur under rubrication. It will be best, therefore, initially to demonstrate the relation to each other of the α-branch manuscripts by using only examples where correction, gloss and contamination are absent. It is of course unlikely that either of the manuscripts corrected very early should have acted as an exemplar before their correction, but the possibility cannot be quite excluded if C, G and β were in the same scriptorium. The line of descent of the uncorrected forms will therefore be traced first.

The C Manuscript cannot be the ancestor of G or S.

By definition, all examples of omission, addition and non-original material in C are the subject of Notes or are self-explanatory in the critical apparatus.

(1) Omission is rare in C. The longer examples are due to eyeskip. There are a few small examples.

(a) All four passages omitted in Book 1 as a result of eyeskip are in the last nine hundred lines or so, as if due to scribal boredom. At 1846-7 *in þe thre I sigh þat* was omitted when the scribe's eye leaped from *þat* preceding the omission to *þat* at the end of it. At 1974-5 *to preyse for þer is non so litel drope þerof þat nis michel* is similarly omitted (*michel | michel*). Similar examples are at 2153-4, 2476.

The above omissions would in themselves be sufficient proof that neither G nor S can derive from C, but some little omissions support this conclusion. They are so minor that their causes are not differentiated. At 772 *subiectes also* (*aussi subjes* F1421) only CJ omit *also*; C clearly cannot be the exemplar of G or S, which have it. At 37 *þat ded oþer wounded he ne shulde be* only C omits *ne*, reversing the sense. In all the following examples only C omits, and F shows that C is unlikely to preserve the original reading: at 810 *is* (*est* F1496) is omitted, at 977 *to* from *to displese* (*desplaire* F1811), at 1374 *wel* (*bien* F2521), at 1622 *an* from *an al* (*un tout* F2977), at 1648 *þee* from *tauhte þee* (*t'apris* F3027), at 2665 *ne hidous* (*ne hideuse* F4894).

(2) C does not add to the text, but non-original material due both to error and substitution is found.

(a) Errors due to misreading or carelessness occur at 40 *payage*] (*paiage* F75) *parage* C; 537 *hauteyn*] (*haultaine* F987) *haunteyn* C, *hye* JMO; 644 *saue*] (*garantir* F1173) *haue* C; 655 *deuyne*] (*devine* F1192) *demyng* C; 1278 *yow*] (*vous* F2347) *youre* C, where only G retains the original reading. Other examples are at 1072, 1084, 1336, 1337, 1342, 1483, 1586, 1766, 1781, 1819, 2165, 2192, 2249, 2302, 2477, 2619, 2620, 2710.

(b) Deliberate substitution by C is rarely to clarify the text, as at 37 (S being missing as a witness, as in all examples before 114) where C replaces an awkward *nouht*-construction by *In so michel þat*; 2630 *light*] (*lumiere* F4824) *sight* C is either clarification or substitution of the expected word. Many substitutions are anglicisings. C's rejected reading follows the French in the examples that follow: 39 *passage*] (*passage* F73) *passinge*; 79 *sure*] (*seurs* F156) *siker*; 243 *surer*] (*plus seur* F452) *sikerere*; 392 *ysen*] (*issir* F722) *goon*—where β also substitutes, using *prese*; 945 *of*] (*de* F1749) *in*; 1129 *ysen*] (*issir* F2084) *gon*; 1131 *ysed*] (*issues* F2088) *ronnen*—where β again substitutes or omits. Further examples are at 1073, 1428, 1530, 1946, 2098. Many substitutions may reflect preference for the commoner word: 582 *goodshipe*] *goodnesse*; 2510 *vnlikynge*] *vnliknynge*. Other small examples are at 815, 1073, 1406, 1654, 1919, 2069, 2192, 2249. Some substitutions reduce or distort the meaning: 531 *he*] *þei*; 1586 *hire*] *me*; 1610 *hep*] *hopp*.

Variation of word-order occurs at 333 *crueltee any time*] (*ja mais cruaute* F614) *any crueltee*—resulting in omission as well; 367 and 2404 *to þee woorth*] *woorth to þee*; other examples are at 825, 1497, 1662, 2544, 2602.

The relation of C to the β-branch

CJMO may often agree merely as a result of independent normalising in Cβ. Those examples must be carefully distinguished which unambiguously show contamination of C by the β-branch. We look, therefore, for examples where G (and S, though that is not significant) agree with the French but CJMO agree in error not explicable by normalising.

Since it is not easy for a scribe to give two exemplars (γ and a β-manuscript) his whole attention, one expects to find reference made to the β-branch at points where C's exemplar was difficult. This proves to be the case, but the picture which emerges is not tidy. Both C and his corrector appear to have used a β-branch manuscript, since not only do alterations echoing β occur over erasure in C where erasure in the margin indicates the influence of C³'s work, but they occur where no such guide exists, and one or two borrowings from the β-branch even occur in the text of C itself, not over erasure, indicating that C consulted the β-branch during his initial transcription.

The first three examples show C³'s intervention and are in themselves inconclusive. At 530 *þerwith* (*avec* F973) is clearly original, but JMO have *þerto*, and under ultra-violet C³'s *to* can be seen in the margin, though C never incorporated it in his text. The confusing ambiguity of *þerwith* in context (*OED therewith* illustrates its breadth of meaning) may have prompted C³ to correct independently, or he may have consulted the β-branch. At 643 *maketh many times leue sinne* literally renders *Fait mainte foyz pechie laissier* (F1172) 'often causes sin to be abandoned', but it appears in CJMO as *maketh men many . . . .* This looks like contamination of C by β, but *men* in C is over erasure and is followed by a C³ caret: it is not clear what has erased, unless C had had *maketh many many times*, having instinctively tried, as he transcribed, to normalise the awkwardly literal use of the passive infinitive to *many* (people) *many* (times). In that case, the corrector might have thought *many many* was a mere dittography, and independently substituted *men* for the first occurrence of it. Similar independent action might explain 2548 *lerne*, where C has *to bere* added, not over erasure but by insertion, in accordance with {*to*} *bere* visible under ultra-violet light in the margin, and echoing J: contamination was not, it seems, from δ, M or O.

However, among examples where C's alterations do not appear to have their origin in the work of C³, the first alone might serve as proof of contamination from the β-branch, since conjecture could hardly explain the agreement of CJMO. At 511 *priuees* (*huissiers* F938) is a crux: one expects *porters*. CJMO have *princes*, C being over erasure, apparently in the scribe's hand. It looks as if, puzzled by his exemplar's reading (probably represented by G's *priues* (S's *pryuee* as an adjective) C referred to the β-branch, which was unfortunately corrupt. At 679 *make* (*faire* F1237) is GS's reading whereas CJMO have *lete*, C being over erasure, again apparently in the scribe's hand. Normalisation might have been achieved in other ways, such as by the use of *have* or *suffer*, so it looks very much as if C himself referred to the β-branch when correcting his transcription. At 1059 is some more evidence of the part of the β-branch consulted. The text's *filthe* is an editorial emendation; C probably had something like GS's *fulthe*, but perhaps puzzled by the undoubtedly intentional force of the author's noun (*laidure* F1962) consulted the β-branch and over erasure wrote *folye*, echoing, be it noted, rather J's *fole* than MO's *fule*, so that contamination is unlikely to have come from δ, M or O. At 1215 CJMO again agree in gross error: SG have *peyne* (*paine* F2233)—S's form is adopted as nearer C's normal spelling—but CJMO have *time*, C over erasure. At 2367-8 *but þat* (*Mais que* F4334) is G's reading: CJMO have *if þat*, with *if* in C written over the erasure of *but*, visible under ultra-violet light. S's substitution of *so* perhaps indicates the kind of dissatisfaction with the original which C felt, and indeed C might well have used *so* or *if* as a substitute, his agreement in *if þat* all the more strongly suggesting consultation of the β-branch.

In a few examples, C's agreement in error with JMO is not over erasure in C. In these cases there are three possibilities: either reference was made at difficult passages to the β-branch during C's initial transcription, the many examples of C's agreement over erasure (where not due to C³'s intervention) being the result of noticing difficulties too late to avoid erasure, or there is coincidental substitution in both C and β, or perhaps γ had been collated with a β-manuscript whose variants had been written into it, to be occasionally adopted by C. Four examples are noted; 255-6 *þou shalt not preyse at a bodde* (*un grant bouton | Tu ne prises* F474-5) has already been mentioned on p. lxi, O's retention of the French idiom against JM's *nouȝt sette by* and *sett at nouȝt* being explained by a gloss in β. Perhaps the un-English idiom prompted C to check his exemplar against a β-manuscript, and C's *sette at nouht* as against GS's *preeyse at a budde* is the result of C's accepting the gloss given to a β-manuscript reading. Coincidental agreement of Cβ is surely hard to credit. There is no shortage of ME idioms to express contempt: the 'enemies' might have been not worth a rush, or a bean, or (like Chaucer the Pilgrim's first rhyming) a turd. At 2098 *pile* (*pel* F3850) is SG's *pyle*/*pyll*, CJMO having *pileer*, C as before not over erasure. There are three possible explanations for this agreement of CJMO (see Note 2098), but the weight of other evidence suggests that it is due to C's reference to β at points of obscurity. At 1697 *deuynale* is GS's reading (*adevinement* with a variant *devinement* F3118) where CMO have *denyinge* and J has either *dynynyg* or *dyuynyg* (it looks as if [ψ] had *dyuyȳg*—cf. [ψ]'s possible *leuȳg* at 324, p. liv). Since at 1059 (p. lxvi) the readings suggest that C cannot be contaminated by δ, M or O, and since J's corruption here at 1697 shows that C can hardly be contaminated by J, we must assume its contamination from β itself or a manuscript between the archetype and β. The main point is that C's agreement with the β-branch's -*ing*(*e*) ending, let alone its change of *deuynale* 'divination' to *denyinge* 'objection, rejection', is unlikely to be coincidence. The final example noted is rather surprising: at 2216 *Lady*, CJMO add *quod I*, there being no parallel in F. Here there is no obscurity to have prompted C to consult the β-branch, so either the archetype wrote it and GS's exemplar omitted it as superfluous, or C and β added it independently.

It would create a wrong impression to ignore the numerous occasions when alterations have been made in C (sometimes with and sometimes without origin in C³'s marginalia) which bear no relation whatever to readings in G³, the β-branch or anywhere else. Alterations made in the absence of G³'s marginal suggestions occur at 98 *thing* (*chose* F195), mysteriously altered over erasure to *citee* in C; at 470 *wole* (*wulleþ* GS) became *wol eyþer*, the second word over erasure; at 673 C altered *men*[1] to *þei* over erasure the first time it occurred, but did not write *men* the second time, simply substituting *þei* for *men*[2]. Further examples of alterations made over or by erasure, without there being any marginal guide, occur at 884, 1106, 1232 (erasure), 1494, 1554, 1607 (erasure).

Such corrections in C made in accordance with a marginal guide occur at 542 *me*, where C obviously altered *hym* (which survives in GS) to *me*, with *id est pilgrim* over it, either correction or gloss being in accordance with a now illegible marginal erasure. It looks as if the corrector acted independently, by the sense of the passage. This seems to have been the case at 616 *þat*, which is GS's reading, omitted by JMO and altered by C over erasure to *as michel as*, in accordance with a note now erased from the margin. Similar again is 638 *avisement*, glossed interlinearly *id est techinge* in response to an erased marginal note. Further examples occur at 695, 1352, 1785, 1946, 1947, 2503, 2652. At 1656 *ye* there is a caret following in the text of C, but no insertion in accordance with the *had* in the margin, erased but visible under ultra-violet light.

Consideration of C's descent from γ must be postponed until G³ is considered (p. lxxv), since evidence for both is interdependent.

The S Manuscript

Paleographical evidence alone may be sufficient to show that S cannot be the origin of C or G: John Shirley's hand appears to be later than either. Plenty of textual evidence supports this.

(1) Omission in S is both accidental and deliberate.

(a) Omission caused by eyeskip is common, as one might expect in a careless scribe. A small example occurs at 197–8. Most are longer. At 1038–9 *For whan I spak of þe ax* is left out by eyeskip from *ax* immediately before to *ax* at the end of the omission. Similar examples are at 1095–9, 1159–60, 1171–3, 1351–2, 1356, 1556–7, 2278–9, 2364–5. At 2055–8 a kind of double eyeskip (*þanne | þan* and *vnyrened | yrened*) may account for an unusually long omission.

(b) Carelessness appears to be the only explanation for the omission at 284 of *bi* from *bi which*, but accidental omission other than that due to eyeskip is curiously rare in S. The other examples of omission noted appear to be deliberate: the rejection of otiose or difficult matter. The former may account for omissions at 132, 171, 180, 308–9, 484–5. At 488–92 a long passage seems to have been left out because it is difficult, and shorter omissions occur for the same reason at 1360–1 and 2098.

(2) Added material in S (probably Shirley's own, since addition is characteristic of his work) includes a great many 'chapter headings' and comments on the text. Though cited in the critical apparatus, these are excluded from the argument as they are not strictly additions to the text. In any case, they are in a large and slightly differing script, easily visible, as are scribal comments marked *nota per Shirley* in the margin. There are several additions not so distinguishable. At 117 misunderstanding led S to add *suche a scrippe and bourdoun*, and other examples occur at 151, 153, 254, 258, 2528. A number of large additions immediately preceded 'chapter headings', as if Shirley felt free to expand concluding material: examples are at 146, 1298, 1321, 1322, 1420–1, 1465.

At 433 after *grettere*, which should be the end of a section, there is a long dittography, which might, but only with difficulty, have been corrected by any descendants. S repeats with only two minor variations (*phareon* for *Phareon* and *thraldome* for *thralledome*) the passage he had already written seven lines earlier at the beginning of his f. 6ʳ *weel phareon seying him þat he suffred · þy folk serue god with outen thraldome | and þat he letted hem nought ne oppressed hem ne greued hem of no thing.* It is just possible that the passage began a page in his exemplar too, lending itself to dittography after interruption. If this were true, it would be evidence against S's deriving directly from any of the witnesses, none beginning a page at this point. The passage on examination of conscience beginning at 1157 is treated very freely by S, who makes omissions as well as additions. At 1161 *gret was þat sinne] which was horryble and gret synne* clearly includes

addition for emphasis; the same seems to be true at 1163 *mistooke þee*]
mistooke þee so to done | and longe to perseuer vnrepentant contryt ne confessed
and at 1164 *or þe stiringe þow purchasedest*] *but by þy sordyble and voluptuous
thoughtes purchasedest þe an apetyt of yuell doyng so leues þou þe potte al
hoole.* Together these additions almost constitute evidence of particular
personal reaction to the matter of indulged 'sin in thought'. At 1170 *pot*]
potte of conscience and 1179 *forbere it nouht*] *forbere not þe potte of þe
conscience,* addition makes the text more explicit.

(3) Non-original readings are as usual due both to accidental error and
deliberate substitution. Sometimes the first results in the second.
   (a) Accidental error is clear at 129 *seechinge*] *seeke* 143; *bifel*] *beon felle*;
167-8 *fader þe grete kinge*] *fader Grace*; 219 *bregge*] *bote*; 261 *thryes*] *þer*;
269 *Sithe*] *sauf*; 395 *dediedest*] *dyedest*; 1040 *me with yow*] *moeveþe you*;
1102 *beesme*] *besynesse*; 1109 *Penitence*] *pytaunce*; further examples are at
1120-1, 1402, 1478, 1536-7, 1884, 2448, 2480. At 1495 there is evidence
(relevant to the later demonstration that S is likely to derive from G as
corrected) that S was working from a manuscript which if not G had G's
forms: *to whom I helpe*] *to hom i h\e/elpe* G, *to mannes help* S suggests that
S read *hom i* as Lat. *hominis* (G retained foreign words in other places, for
example 2666).
   (b) Deliberate substitution is apparent at 140 *þat*] *howe*, S seeking to
avoid *þat . . . þat* in 139-40. It accounts for 319 *a softe; softe*] *a pleyne |
sofft* where repetition of *sofft* has been avoided. At 850-1 the charming
explanation of Nature, who strips the trees in winter *for to kerue hem ooper
robes and kootes seemynge alle newe* is reduced to *and þus affter þe saysouns
I prouyde him þayre vesture.* Less damaging are 990 *I wolde*] *me list*, 1626
looketh] *beoþe avysed*, and 2049's explanatory *suich*] *so vnryveted*, but at
2013 *al þe world þerinne mired is nouht as greet as aas in a dee* becomes the
clumsy *al þe worlde þer Inne is als myche or lasse in comparysoune as is · þe
poynt of aas · in a dees.* Addition and substitution combined at 2554-5
again precedes a 'chapter heading': Shirley's pen runs away with him,
giving 2554 *hors*] *swyfft coursier*, and *go sharplich*] *stert and prykke smertlych* and 2555 *þan þe mule þat goth roundliche her wey*] *by þe smert vnavysed
weye þane by þe eesely passage weel avysed.* Last in deliberate substitutions
is 2619-20 *nought it is worth*] *nought it avayllepe.* Substitution the result
of misunderstanding is only partially deliberate: at 1321-2, for example,
and nouht for þanne I haue maad doo sum harm withoute misdoinge] *Ne ellys
neuer did I · ne made doo harome | for any misse doyng to me,* and at 2012's
extraordinary *mire him wel and considere him*] *heele and leeche hem of hir
disayses · and beholde hem self,* which seems to be the result of misreading
mire as *make*, with consequent reading of adverb *wel* as adjective.
   Alteration to word-order, not easy to notice in the work of such a
cavalier scribe, is at 150 *al I wolde fain in sooth wite*] *al þis in sooþe wolde I
fayne wytt.*

G's closeness to the French

Having shown by C and S's peculiar omissions and errors that they
could not have been the ancestors of G, this can be shown in another way,
by citing some of the many occasions when G is uniquely close to F. It is
undoubtedly closer to the archetype than the other witnesses (see p. xxxv
for reasons why it was not used as the base manuscript). Sometimes
this closeness to the French is apparent only in spelling, and so does not
appear in the critical apparatus: for example 90 *camele*] *chameylle* G (*ch-
amel* F176); 2486 *Souprised*] G (*Souspris* F4557).

Examples where G is the only member of the α-branch to preserve the
original reading are at 777 *was redy* and 1127 *how*, both cases where
'correction' has corrupted the other manuscripts. In the following examples only G is original, a fact of which we should be unaware but for
F; 490 *him*, perhaps 876 where only G follows the French in omitting *of*;
880 *noces* (*noches* F), a modification of the unique *noses* G; 1144, 1152 and
2494, where only G has, like the French, *ne ne*; 1374 *wel a poynt*; 1538 *of
sunne*; 2300 *ennuye*; 2661 *þis . . . Memorie*; 2666 *mugoe*] *mugos* G; 2728
and.

The G Manuscript

The ubiquitous work of correctors complicates proof of G's sep-
arateness. In view of the very early stage—before rubrication—at which
many corrections were made to G, it is most unlikely that the uncorrected
manuscript could be the exemplar for C or S, but the possibility, however
remote, must be considered. Examples might be drawn from points where
G is wrong as against all the other manuscripts and the French, and the
work of the corrector G³ is not present. This evidence will be cited later,
however, to show how G as corrected relates to C and S (G as corrected
carrying, of course, the uncorrected readings too). For the moment evidence will be drawn from points where G itself is wrong, though the error
or omission has been corrected by the meticulous G³. There is abundant
material in this category alone to show that uncorrected G could not
possibly be the ancestor of C or S.

(1) Omissions in G (made good by G³) are accidental results of eyeskip
or other carelessness. Eyeskip accounts for 725–6, where *and lordschypynge
whan he had seruauns thanne he was lord*, is supplied by G³ (the 'roman'
hand) in the right margin. Passages omitted through G's eyeskip are also
supplied by G³ at 1398–9, 1735–6 and 1985–6, while at 2450–1 *fore ther
fore y haaue Raught hem and vnfolden hem and taaken hem thee do hem on
faste* is supplied in the margin, partly under rubrication.

Other omissions from G are rectified by G³ at 49 *swerd* (*glaive* F93),
100 *ne* (*ne* F198). At 113 *I ysede*] *y sede* G, G³ supplied *y ysede*, and though
S is missing as a witness, here as in all examples before 114, the other
readings show clearly that G omitted. Other examples occur at 209, 864–
5, 997, 1053, 1249, 1260, 1881, 1927, 2023–4, 2033, 2194, 2273, 2407,
2460, 2551, 2692.

(2) No additional material by G's meticulous scribe has been noted. Non-original readings are also accidental rather than the result of deliberate substitution. Examples noted include 136 *banere*] *boonere* G, with *baneere* (*baniere* F265) supplied as a correction by G³; 393 *hanginge*] *hongyn* G, *hangynge* G³ (*pendans* F723) where JMO have *that hynges*; 641 *lyth þe*] *by the* G with *by* corrected to *lyth* by G³; 680 *seeche*] *teche* G, *seeche* G³. At 727 *þis*] *t/his*, the *t-* is inserted into G, probably by G³, who wrote *thys* in the margin. Simpler examples, all corrected by G³ in accordance with F, are at 756 *swerd*] *spere* G, *swerd* G³ (*glaive* F1388); 898 *answerede*] *answere* G, *answerede* G³ (*respondi* F1659); 1035 (where JMO omit) and 1372 *whoso*] *he so* G, *ho* G³ (*qui* F1918, 2517) where G³ is under rubrication; 1285 *truwauntes*] *tyreauns* G, *trywans* G³ (*truans* F2360); 1286 *releef*] *reelef* G, *Releef* G³ (*relief* F2363); 1431 *ye hadden*] *he hadde* G, *ʒee* G³ (*aviez* F2625); 2284 *on*] *of* G, *on* G³ (*es* F4179 presumably for *en les*); 2306 *Achimelech*] *acbimelech* G, *achimelech* G³ (*Achimelech* F4219); 2386 *publican*] *bublycann* G, *publikan* G³ (*publien* F4365), 2729 *yelt*] *ʒitt* G, *ʒyllt* G³ (*rent* F5012); 2745 *al*] *acc* G, *all* G³ (*Tout* F5044). These examples are important only to disprove the unlikely hypothesis that G was the exemplar of C or S before its correction by G³. The next examples are more significant.

The corrected G manuscript (G plus G³)

Though CG and S are separate, G as corrected is related to S and to C in different ways which will be considered in turn. First, however, consideration must be given to the occasions on which G as corrected appears to show unique error as against the other ME manuscripts and F. This would preclude its being the ancestor of S or C. In fact, it is in every case possible that G preserves χ's reading. At 243 only G, and in the β-branch MO, omit *for* from *for þou shalt passe no surer wey*; but it is impossible to say whether *for* was independently supplied by C, J and S—G having preserved τ's translation of *Pas plus seur ne pues trouver* (F452)—or whether the translator wrote *for*, having the variant French *Quar pas . . .* in front of him, and G and δ omitted it, perhaps affected by *foorth* immediately preceding. At 899 *fersliche*] (*fierement* F1661) *feerleche* looks like error in G (particularly since at 1074 G has *feersleche*) but G might be original, CβS independently substituting the commoner word; so too at at 1006 *bore*] *bere* CS (*nee* F1864) and at 1112 *yerde*] *ʒerdes* G (*verges* F2054) where, however, Stürzinger's *H¹L* have *verge*, so the evidence cannot be conclusive. At 1178 *til*] *for**te/(-te* an insertion apparently in G's hand) translates *Que* (F2168) and looks like G's error against the other manuscripts' forms of *til* or *to*, but CβS may have substituted the synonym, as they may at 2220 have rectified omission of *and* (*et* F4065). At 2289 *bi þe hondes*] *hy the hondes* (*par les mains* F4188) G's unique confusion of *b/h* is perfectly clear in the manuscript (f. 30ᵛ): CS may have corrected by conjecture, as CβS may have done at 2569 *Etiques*] *ecyqves*, clear on G f. 34ᵛ: three words earlier is the clue that this work is Aristotle's.

At 2418 *þat it ne is covenable*] *nys couenable* G (*qui convenable | No . . . soit* F4427–8) G either smooths or preserves the original reading, expanded to varying equivalent negative clauses by CS*β*. At 2515 *of armures ye speken to me* (*d(es) armes me parlastes* F4611) only G omits *to*, which C*β*S might independently supply or G omit. At 4454 *þat* (*Que* F) is omitted only by G, but might easily have been inserted by C*β*S. The same is true at 4641, where only G omits *þe* (*le* F8666) in *ouer þe see*. None of these is a fully separative error, since each might have been rectified by CS, as in *Moyseses* at 278 and 1803, 1408 *testamement*, and 1912 *is* for *his*.

In addition to noting the ambiguity of these readings, it is important to remember that the G manuscript has been cropped, so that all the above errors (if such they are), apparently uncorrected by G³, may have at one time carried marginal corrections and so deserved no mention here. In practice this is unlikely, since words in the text so corrected are usually marked by a small cross or other distinguishing sign, and marginal corrections are rarely at the edge of pages (but see f. 23ʳ for an exception).

In two cases, the fact that G³ glosses incorrectly might seem to be evidence that neither C nor S (who have the correct reading) could have derived from G as corrected. At 619 CS have *þat oon* (*L'une* F1129) but GJMO have *the to*, presumably *that o* with final -*t* transferred, as in the dialect form, to the second word (*OED* under *T* 7). G³ glosses *to* interlinearly as *ii*. If C or S derived from G as corrected, they or their ancestor would have had to ignore the conspicuous gloss written not in the margin but over the line. But G³'s uncharacteristically stupid gloss is so manifestly wrong, *the to* being followed in the next line by *the tother*, that it is likely to have been ignored. The same is probably true at 3847, where *neuer recchinge* (*nonchalance* F) appears in G with *rechynge*, glossed by G³ as *Prechchynge*.

Having disposed of those occasions which if presented in the critical apparatus without comment might suggest that neither S nor C could derive from G as corrected, it is time to turn to the relation between G as corrected and the individual manuscripts in the α-branch.

S's derivation from G as corrected

S should perhaps be excluded as a witness, since it seems to be derived, though not immediately, from G as corrected, at least in the first part of the work (possibly to 3213, certainly thence to 5083: its exemplar thereafter appears to have been C—see below). It has been retained as a witness because of its intrinsic interest as a Shirley manuscript and because of the complex pattern of influence it displays. On first sight one or two readings appear to disprove its derivation from G as corrected, seeming to show S uniquely preserving the original reading as against C, and G as corrected. These turn out to be no more reliable than the ambiguous ones just cited in the previous section. At 623 *Hy*] *hiegh* S (*haut* F1135), *bi* CG looks like the result of *h/b* confusion in CG, but it might have been α's error, corrected by S or itself misread as *hi* with the accidental effect that S regained the translator's original. At 1177 *rounge* is an acceptance of S's reading *rovnge* (*rungier* F2167 'gnaw'), which though accurately represented by JM's *frete hit*, is quite corrupted in G's *Renge* and even in CG³'s *raunge*. There is no doubt about this marginal reading in G³, as comparison with G's ff. 16ʳ and 32ᵛ (*Raunge*/*Raught*) will show: G³'s *o* is never joined to the following letter as his *a* is, and both are in the hand which at 32ᵛ is under rubrication. But S clearly did not understand what he had in front of him, altering G³'s *neuere stinte to raunge so michel til it hadde slayn* into *neuer stint to rovnge it is so michel til hade slayne*; that he shows the correct infinitive may simply be due to his misreading G³'s marginal (and very tiny) *Raunge* as *Rounge*, expected in the familiar context of the gnawing conscience (*MED conscience* 2.c).

There being only these two, inconclusive examples which might prove S independent, it seems likely that it derives from G as corrected. If this were so, we should expect a number of omissions and errors to be shared by the corrected G, and S. That these too are all to some degree ambiguous is another reason for S's not having been eliminated as a witness. The following readings are ambiguous not only because they might often be shared preservation of the original reading rather than shared error, but because occasions where S agrees with G³ (and, incidentally, with C as a rule) might conceivably have been due to GS's being a subgroup derived from a common proximate ancestor, the corrector of G then entering his corrections and glosses back in that ancestor as marginal or interlinear corrections occasionally but not invariably inherited by S. Economy of hypothesis suggests that S derives from G as corrected.

(1) G and S rarely share omissions of material unambiguously present in CJMO and F, but at 164 and 2412 *þat* (*Que* F315 and 4414) is omitted only by GS; at 2068 *þat cause* (*ceste cause* F3797) only GS omit *þat*. A little less certain is 2090 *but if*] *butt* (*s'* . . . *ne* F3835). On at least four occasions it is impossible to tell whether GS omit in error or preserve the original reading: at 365 *made . . . to passe*] *made . . . passe* GS (*passer* / *Fist* F671–2); 472 *þat it ne shal come*] *þat ne schalt come* GS (*Qui ne viengne* F868); 935 *to medle*] *medle* GS (*Mesler* F1730); 1369 *tobreken it and vnmaken it*] *to brekyn and on maken it* GS (*le despiecent et deffont* F2512). At 4675 GS's shared omission of *Fiat Dan coluber in via* (with a conspicuous gap in G, the quotation supplied by G³ in the margin) is not necessarily significant, as S often omits Latin.

(2) In citing errors and substitutions shared only by GS it is important that examples are drawn from points where C is not over erasure (which might mean that it once shared their reading) and where, if error is apparent, the French is translated by CJMO. Otherwise there is always the possibility that GS preserve the original reading. Such examples are rare, and only one (2382) cannot be explained by independent substitution or omission in C and β. The doubtful situation, where F is no guide, is very common, as these examples of minor error or substitution show: 161, 168 and 292 *þo*] *thilke* GS; 169 *folk*] *folkes* GS, where G has *-es* abbreviated

but S does not: similarly at 342-3 *folk*] *folkes* GS; 259 and 320 *he*] *thylke*; 278 *of Aaron*] *of aarones*; 311 *mayden*] *mayde*; 316 *two*] *twey*; 356 *þouh*] *all thowgh*; 439 *togidere*] *togideres*; 588 *þei*] *thilke*; 674 *in makinge*] *a makynge*; 759 and 1582 *þat*] *thilke*; 942 *of heuene*] *of the heuene*; 1512 (and ten other occasions, see Note 86-7) *trist(e)*] *trust(e)*; 1593 *bifore*] *to fore*. One example is technically word-order variation: 995-6 *I wolde*] *wolde I*; 1102 and 1809 *ful*] *well* GS (*mont* F2036 and F3325); 2391 *feebelnesse*] *feeblesse* GS, *freylnesse* O (*enfermete* F4376); 2509 *feebelenesse*] *feeblesse* GS (*debilite* F4599) The choice is between similar English words or forms: G³ offers no correction to any of them.

The French is some guide, suggesting GS are in error, at 1604 *my seyinge*] (*mondit* F2940) *my seyenges* GS and at 1822 *þi*] (*t'* F3347) *þe* GS where it is true there is a French variant *l'* which might indicate preservation of the original reading by GS. 2382 shows a distinctive form rather than error: *hyde it*] (*Mucier le* F4359) *huded* G, *hyded* S where G appears to have a northern form of the two words. At 2436 *þis*] *his* GS (*ceste* F4457) is corrected to *thys* by G³ in G's margin, but S or his exemplar apparently did not notice. In the absence of evidence conclusively to prove S separate, these small agreements of G and S as against the other manuscripts do, even though we cannot be certain whether they agree in being correct or in being in error, suggest in sum that S derives from G as corrected.

The main difficulty in the path of this conclusion is C's contamination from the β-branch, which in theory might account for all these apparent deviations of GS and CJMO, especially since, as we have seen, C sometimes consulted the β-branch actually during transcription. But contamination of C from the β-branch either during transcription or in subsequent correction tended to show, not in the *minutiae* I have been listing, but in major differences, and often at points of difficulty (p. lxv above). In addition most of the significant agreements between C and the β-branch (but see pp. lxvi-lxvii) are at points where C is written over erasure — points specifically excluded from the examples above. The paucity of major omission and error shared by GS is a measure of their ancestor's accuracy, also indicated by the number of occasions when GS apparently preserve the original reading as against all the other manuscripts, which on these occasions (unlike those just cited) do not agree with each other. Since these are apparent in the variants and explained in the Notes they are referred to briefly (in the forms adopted in the text to agree with C's practice): 245 *ne*²; 392 *ysen*; 463 *on*; 537 *hauteyn*; 719 *ne ne*; 1047 *cometh me to*; 1129-30 *ysen out*; 1243 *and*; 1483 *soothliche*. At 2245 only GS have *ardeyne*, just possibly preserving the erroneous original reading which led β to omit the word. At 2325 only GS correctly have *Ogiers*.

An important group of original readings shared by GS consists of examples in which CJMO may agree as a result of independent expansion, omission or normalisation in Cβ. This group must be set against that in which there is evidence of direct relationship between C and the β-branch (pp. lxv-lxvii). Examples are: 154 *suspeccionous*] GS (*souspeconneuse* F) *suspeccious* CJMO; 175 *forveied*] GS (*Fourvoiez* F) *forfeted* CJMO; 502 *OF*] GS (*Du* F) omitted by JMO, erased in C; 637, 641, 646, 657 *platte*] GS (*plat* F) *flatte* CJMO; 653-4 *is right*] GS (*est droiz* F) *it is right* CJMO, where *it* is inserted by C; 861 *for þat for* CGS, where the first *for* is cancelled in C, J has *for Afore*, MO have *for*; 1027 *ne*] GSF, omitted by CJMO; 1248 *of*] *by* CJMO; 1290 *cene*] GS, *sopere* CJMO and *ceened*] SG, *suppede* CJMO; 1495 *to*] omitted by CJMO; 1714 *falsed*] *fals* JMO, *-d* erased C; 1930 *þis*] *it* CJMO; 2195 *ne ne*] *ne* CJMO; 2392 *þan*] *and* CJMO; 2526 *feeblesse*] *febilnesse* CJMO; 2717 *þat*] omitted by CJMO. At 1506, *þis knoweth* is GS's reading (*Cetui connist* F), and G³ has *scilicet herynge* in the margin; C's *þis heeringe* (*heeringe* added over erasure and extending into the margin) might be an independent alteration or derive from the β-branch *In herynge thowe knaweste* J, *bot in herynge he knowes* MO.

In some cases where the GS reading has not been accepted, perhaps it should have been: 2314 *confused*] *confus* GS; 2601 *suich on*] *such* GS; 2650-1 *nygh þee*] *nygh to thee* GS. If these readings are original, Cβ agree coincidentally or by contamination.

That S derives indirectly from G as corrected is also suggested by the many occasions when G³ and S agree in error which is hard to attribute to independent alteration. In one group of such shared errors, agreement is in fact between C as well as G³ and S. This last group of examples, showing the closeness of G as corrected and S, will be described after consideration of the relation between C and G³. In this way repetition of evidence from the CG³S group — first in the context of CG³ agreements and then in the context of G³S agreements — will be avoided.

The relation between C and G³

First, it is clear that C cannot derive from G as corrected. There are several occasions on which C is either unique in preserving the original reading, or is closest to the archetype where all witnesses are corrupt. The first three examples are minor. At 66 *þat I seygh*] *y sygh* (*que veue ay* F128) is admittedly at a point where S is missing as a witness and O omits the whole phrase, but JM as well as CF include *þat* or its equivalent, so it looks as if G omitted it in error. At 113 *I ysede me* (*m' ... issi* F221) G omits *me*. It is true that JMO's *I passede* is no help, and S is missing as a witness, but it looks as if C preserves the original reading. At 158 (*Vois tu* F305) I suspect that the archetype had *Seeste*, with enclitic pronoun. If so, this form is preserved clearly in C, though G's incomplete *seest* may represent it; βS then normalised, adding *þowe*. This is more likely than C's substituting an enclitic for an independent pronoun. There is one doubtful occasion on which C, disagreeing with all the other witnesses, may yet preserve the awkward original which Gβ smoothed: at 979-80 *al were þe flaume þeron*, [*and*] *þerof* it is possible that C should be accepted and *and* omitted, there being no precedent for it in *Comment que la flambe i fust. /De ce* (F1816-17): Gβ might well have inserted *and* to separate *þeron* and *þerof*. Perhaps 1378 is equally tenuous: only C's *aperceyue* echoes *apercevoir* (F2528), GJMOS having *perseyue*.

The best example is at 1342 where the French (2459) begins a paragraph with *Je Jhesus*, for which Stürzinger records no variant. Only C has *I Ihesus*, the pronoun being omitted in GJMOS. This seems to be the result of independent omission in Gβ, for such omission is very likely here: *I Ihesus* is easy to misread as if the two *I*s were a doubling to indicate capitalisation of the first letter of *Ihesus*. The readings here are clear: all the manuscripts begin a paragraph, and the first *I* (of *Ihesus* in GJMOS) is accordingly capitalized and enlarged as well as being decorated or illuminated. Only in C is the first illuminated *I* the pronoun: there is no possibility therefore of the repeated capital *I* being a doublet for the first letter of *Ihesus*. Independent error on the part of G and β is much more likely than C's having under these circumstances noticed the omission of the pronoun and supplied it (but see n. 1342).

Some examples suggesting that C cannot be derived from G (corrected or uncorrected, since they too are drawn from places where G³ is not present) are cited on p. lxxiv, where GS are shown to share error as against CJMO and F. The most important examples, which belong here too, are at 1604, 1822, 2382, 2436. See also p. lxxxix for conflicting CG³ glosses.

C cannot derive from G as corrected, then, and we have already seen that G cannot derive from C (pp. lxiv–lxv). But neither can G³ derive from C. G³ is not so common, or C so often in error, that G³ is likely to be often present and 'correct' where C is wrong. One example must suffice: it is discussed in detail in the Note. At 2245 G³'s *dysordene* (*MED disordeine* adj.) is very close to the variant *desordenee* at F4109, and is unlikely to derive from C's *disordeyned*, which looks like a substitution of the later word (*MED disordeined* under *disordeinen* v.3 cites this unemended line).

C and G³, therefore, must derive from a common source if they share readings against GJMOS. Most though not all of the similarities between C and G³ are between words or passages fully incorporated into C's text and not merely present as glosses or insertions, so we must suppose that the source of G³'s work was also the origin of C, unless we are to postulate the steady use by C of two exemplars at once, in addition to his occasional reference (p. lxv) to a β-branch manuscript. Parallels between G³ and C's main text which agree with F but not the other witnesses, are as follows: 113 *y ysede*] *y sede* G, *y ysede* G³ (S being missing as a witness); 393 *hanginge*] *hongyn* G, *hangynge* G³; 1170 *þat*] *þat* G, *thylke* G³, which C also has; 1254 *smerte*] omitted by G, supplied by G³ though not in JMOS; 1754 all the witnesses except C have *þat*, subpuncted in G in agreement with F, which has no equivalent for it; 1998 *ayen*] omitted in G, supplied by G³ in accordance with F (J also happens to have it); 2729 *yelt*] *ʒitt* G, *ʒelit* G³. It must be said that at 1998 G³ is in the 'arabic' hand, not that of the other corrections cited here. This need not affect the essential argument. Both hands are so early that each is on occasion under the rubrication. The hand of most of these examples wrote the *capitulum* numbers in roman numerals, and it appears under rubrication on G's ff. 4^v (3 times), 13^v, 15^v, 18^v, at f. 22^v *C^m lxxx*, f. 33^v *pilgrym*. The example at 1998 (f. 26^v) is in the hand which begins adding or substituting arabic *capitulum* numbers from f. 19^v: it is under rubrication at f. 32^v, in the long supplied passage in the bottom of the left margin. It looks as if two scribes collaborated on checking G.

The manuscript γ common to G^3 and C cannot have been α because on some occasions α passed the original reading to G while C and G^3 differ from this, being 'wrong'. At 1290 *cene*] *Cene* GS, (*cena* F), *sopere* C, scilicet *souper* G^3, it is true that JMO have *Sopere* too, and it is an obvious substitution, but it is still clear that α read *cene* and so was not CG^3's common source, unless α was perhaps glossed *sopere* here, and Cβ accepted the gloss—indeed it was suggested at the outset (p. li) that γ might simply represent a level of correction to the archetype.

Several pieces of evidence suggest not only that manuscript (or 'stage') γ existed, but also that it was influenced by reference back to a French manuscript, in some cases clearly not that used by the translator. The readings of this F^2 may have been entered in γ as marginal glosses, making their transmission to CG^3 easier. In most of the following evidence, all the witnesses except CG^3 (but including G) show words based on a given French reading, whereas C and G^3 have a word translating a recorded variant of the French. Perhaps in other cases where C and G^3 agree this is also true, but the fact cannot be detected as the variant is not recorded by Stürzinger. In one instance the case is a little different. At 1254 the fact the GJMOS do not translate *cinglans* (variant *cuillans* MS. L, F2302) suggests that τ or χ omitted it. But CG^3 read *smerte*. It looks as if their common source γ had acquired *smerte* by reference back to a French manuscript — though in this case we cannot say whether or not it was that used by the translator. Again at 1844-5 we cannot be sure that the French referred back to is not that used by the translator. GJMOS's readings make it clear that the archetype had something very like *But þese thre thinges weren to me michel wunderful and gretliche dredinge* for (*Mais*) *ces trois choses mervelleuses* / *Mont* [*recte: Mout*] *me furent et (fort) douteuses* (F3389-90, citing *choses*, the variant recorded for *BM^{1}LM*, rather than *cloches*, Stürzinger's accepted reading, which was clearly not in front of the translator). Only C and G^3 have *But þese thre thinges weren to me wunderful · & hard · & dowtows* (G^3 with an otiose *and* and an erasure before *and hard*). The *dowtows* cannot be coincidence: it must surely be due to reference back to the French *douteuses* (see Note for why this was necessary). At 2245 it is however quite clear that the French used for checking carried a variant reading different from that in front of the translator (see Note). The fact that JMO omit the word suggests that β was puzzled by the archetype's *his ordeyne* or *his ardeyne* (*s'ordenee/sordenne* F4109), which gave GS's *his ardeyne*. C's *disordeyned* and G^3's *dysordene* are due to γ's having been so puzzled by the archetypal reading that he made one of his references to a French manuscript, which at this point happened to carry the variant *desordenee* recorded in six of Stürzinger's manuscripts.

The evidence for CG³'s common descent from γ with its glosses derived from F² must not be allowed to obscure the fact that on many occasions C and G³ share unique readings for which no parallel in the French variants is recorded. These occasions might prove an invaluable guide to the eventual tracing of the manuscript I have called F², if it exists to be traced. Alternatively they may simply represent occasions when γ was glossed or corrected in the margins or when γ just varied from all the other witnesses (in which case we must assume a very complete check from it by G³ against G). Examples are mostly small. One, where the French is no guide, is somewhat longer: at 2117-18 (see Note) *for to resseyue and endure* is supported by GJMO, and misread by S, as the translation of *Pour recevoir ... et endurer* (F3885-6); CG³'s *but resseyueth & endureth* suggests that γ smoothed. Shorter examples include 760-1: at 760 CGS's *he mai vnbynde þee þe keyes* renders *Les clefs te puisse deslier* (F1397), but at 761 *and vnsheþe þe swerd*, which accurately renders *Et le glaive desgainer* (F1398), is *and vnsheþe þee þe swerd* in CG³. At 811 *she maketh hire* is *for she maketh hire* in CG³ without any precedent in F: it looks as if γ smoothed here too. At 1482 there is again no precedent in F for CG³'s *now* before *sumwhat*. Other examples suggesting CG³'s relation to γ are at 2165 *þat] whiche* CG³ (*Qui* F3969); 2186 *olde time] þe olde time* CG³ (*anciennement* F4002) and *fighte] fighte with* CG³ (*bateillier* F4003); 2241 *harde] strongliche* CG³ (*fort* F4102); 2257 *and of outrageous spekinge] and woodshipe of outrageous spekinge* CG³ (*Et d'outrageusement parler* F4132); and 2261 *maisterman] mister man* (*pautonniere* F4139) where the initial error in translation remains uncorrected. Interesting also is 2292 where, as at 1844-5, C makes sense but G³ does not, indicating the less completely assimilated nature of G³'s reference to γ: only CG³ have *is* before *vnderstonde*, but C omitted the *is* before *alle* in the previous line, avoiding unnecessary repetition. Here as in 2261 it is significant that erroneous translations remain uncorrected, suggesting that these particular agreements between C and G³ follow alterations made in their common source without reference by that source to another French manuscript. At 2344 *punished] so punished* looks like a smoothing in γ since there is no precedent in F4288 *puni*; so too does 2561-2 *þe armures] considere þe armures* where F4693 shows no precedent but the translation is awkward; smoothing may also account for 2677 *As] And as* (*Aussi* F4917).

A common ancestor for C and G³ is also suggested by the many examples where interlinear glosses apparently in C's hand (though hard to identify, being distorted) are echoed by those in G³ (both the 'roman' and 'arabic' hands). At 419 *he* is glosed *id est ambrose* interlinearly by C, and *sanctus ambrose* by G³. Other examples (all, except 1890, 2229, 2339, personal pronouns glossed by proper nouns) are at 471, 540, 556, 576, 587, 636, 637, 691, 810, 811 (twice), 1049, 1268, 1890, 2229, 2252, 2339,

2341. C's scribe apparently left true glosses in, as glosses in his own text, instead of incorporating them like the alterations made in γ, where the corrected word may have been cancelled.

Sometimes G³'s glosses have no parallel in C. If C were derived from G³ or if γ carried these glosses, and G³ but not C received them, we should have to assume a remarkably selective or haphazard approach by C to his model, whichever it was. It is possible that C missed all these glosses in γ, but it is simpler to assume that G³ often glossed on his own account: his method is altogether officious (or painstaking, depending on one's point of view) as the critical apparatus's account of his alterations to spelling shows. Examples of these solitary glosses in G³, in the 'roman' hand unless otherwise stated, are (the gloss following the lemma): 773 *noone*] scilicet *sugys*; 1772 *capacitee*] scilicet *desyr*; 2100 *victour*] scilicet *concourere* in the 'arabic' hand; 2327 *pilke*] *swerd* (where S also has *swerd* in its text); 2333 *She*] *swerd;* 2356 *swerd*] scilicet *Iustice* in the 'arabic' hand; 2549 *me*] scilicet *grace dieu*; 2588 *noon*¹] scilicet *armure* in the 'arabic' hand; 2592 *she*] scilicet *grace dieu*; 2671 *she*¹] scilicet *memorie*; 2679 *pou*¹] *the pylgrym*; 2691 *hire*] scilicet *memorie*; 2692 *she*²] scilicet *grace*; *I*] *pilgrym*; 2729 *pilke*] scilicet *ston* in the 'arabic' hand.

There are also examples, best mentioned here, where over erasure or interlinearly C writes a correction or gloss in accordance with a now erased marginal entry, but where no parallel gloss appears in G³. As in the reverse case, this evidence weighs against direct relationship between G³ and C. Indeed, at 1026 C's gloss and G³ actually conflict, G³ correctly glossing *she* by scilicet *nature*, while C has interlinear *Grace*; they differ also at 2486 *Souprised* where G³ has *superysed* over an erasure in the response to a now erased marginal gloss, but C has interlinear *ouercome*. At 542 *me* is over erasure in accordance with a correction by C³ erased from the left margin, and *id est pilgrim* is added interlinearly by C: GS have *hym*, which in G is interestingly marked by G³ for a gloss never apparently supplied, and unlikely to have been cropped, since the corresponding mark is in the margin, and there is plenty of room by it. This would suggest that C's corrections were not from G³. It is also important, in view of examples considered on p. lxv, that at this point C's correction cannot derive from the β-branch, which omits this passage.

The very variety of corrections and glosses given by C (with or without C³) as well as by G³ makes it very unlikely that either derives from the other: C and G³'s agreements, though numerous and impressive, are a small proportion of the total. It is more likely that C incorporated γ's variant readings and retained its glosses as glosses, that G³ copied both from γ, and both C³ and G³ made additional, individual additions and corrections (but note the exact correspondence of a twelve-word correction at 4017 by C³ and G³).

It is perhaps worth mentioning here that the process of correcting C seems to have gone on independently of the work of the usual corrector, who as far as we can tell made no direct use of F. At 1508 (F2765–7) a passage apparently omitted by the translator is made good only in C's margin, in a fifteenth-century hand. Conceivably a corrector referred back to the French at 2737, but the case is curious. In *of þe same pyer* (*De la dicte pierre* F5028), *pyer* is an editorial emendation. The β-branch has no equivalent to F's phrase. G as corrected, and S, have the corrupted *of the same preeyere* (due to corruption in the French or misreading of the Gallicism *pyer* by χ, α or G) G³ having inserted the *of* in the margin, and subpuncted *same*. C, surprisingly, has *after my stone*; it is over erasure, and perhaps imitating the scribe's hand. Since the guiding correction has been erased from the margin, it is hard to say which corrector is involved. He may have referred independently to the French; on the other hand he may have recognised a reference to the *stoon* of 2729, and intelligently emended the obscure reference to prayer. This would explain his omission of *the same*.

The relation of C, G³ and S

We come now to examples of further variations inherited by C and G³ from γ which have also been passed on to S; thus while continuing to demonstrate the CG³ link, we return to evidence of S's descent from G as corrected (and its possible descent, in part, from C). Typical of these examples of CG³S agreement against the other witnesses and F is 568 *neuere oon dar neighe approche* (*un seul approchier n'ose* F1042) where to *neighe* CG³S add *ne*, G³ inserting it in the margin with a caret in the text. τ seems to have translated *approchier* in such a way as to clarify *approche*, which could mean 'come nearer' or ' come near'. It looks as if γ mistook *neighe* for a verb and so added *ne*: this time GC³S acquire error from γ. At 777 however, the error inherited from χ is corrected with the help of γ (who had access to another French manuscript, see pp. lxxvii–lxxviii above). Agreement of GJMO shows that for *Moyses vout aler disner | Et son mangier vout aprester | Tout autrement que il n'estoit* (F1433-5); τ mistakenly wrote *Moyses wolde go dine and his mete was redy al ooperwise þan it was*, taking *mangier* as a subject, and not recognising *aprester* as an infinitive. CS have, and G³ inserts, *haue* after *and*; CS omit *was redy* and G³ subpuncts it. At 1127 CG³S are again in error as against GJMO and F: *how* (*comment* F2080) is glossed *though* by G³, and CS have *þouh*. This might be accounted for by independent substitution of *þouh* by S, G³ and C, but taken with other examples linking G³ and S, the influence of γ is the more economical explanation. At 1585 we have strong evidence that S absorbed G³'s marginal corrections: *hire* has *nature* over it in C, *scilicet nature* glossing it in G³, but S has *nature hire* in its text, having incorporated the gloss *nature*, not noticing the tiny *s.* indicating *scilicet*. At 1640 the case is more complex because F was corrupt or misread, causing corruption in all the ME manuscripts (see Note). GMO indicate that χ erroneously had *þee I tauhte þe vnderstondinge*. In γ this appears to have become *þere I taught þee vnderstondinge*, as in CG³S. At 2661 long and complex alterations are transmitted to S. Full details are in the Note, but it is clear from GJMO the *þis wenche hatteth bi her name riht and is cleped Memorie* became *þis wenche is nempned & bi hire rihte name cleped* in GC³S, under the influence of γ, which here carried the variant French word-order.

At 1844 the variants are interesting. That *muchull (Mont* [recte: *Mout*] F3390) in GMO should be subpuncted by G³ and absent from CS fits the pattern under consideration: G³ and S acquired the effects of cancellation from γ. S seems to have rejected the rest of G³'s correction, but G³ muddled it, and had to write out the whole clause at the bottom of the page, leaving an erasure and nonsense even in that. S chose to follow G's original reading. In one place it looks as if S actually absorbs and misplaces a marginal gloss in G³: at 3034-5 *þis staf is enemy to þilke þat she [wole] haue freendes*, G³ correctly glosses *staf* by scilicet *obstynacioun*, and *she* by *gracedieu*; S, however, has the nonsensical *...to þilke þat is obstynacioun*. A comparable reflection of S having G and G³ in front of him seems to occur at 4437, where *he þat* is in G as *he hath*, with *hath* corrected in the margin to *that* by G³. S wrote *haþe* then altered it to *þat*, as if he did not at first notice the marginal correction.

We are left with the question of why C and G³ so often show glosses (p. lxxviii) not in S. Doubtless Shirley or intervening scribes paid only patchy attention to glosses and corrections in their exemplars. The lateness of S's hand compared to those of C and G as corrected suggests the intervention of more than one manuscript between G as corrected and S.

The Relation between S and C.

I have already mentioned (p. lxxx) the variant readings shared by CG³S. It is remarkable that in the latter part of the *Pilgrimage* S ceases to be closely related to G³, and begins to be closely related to C. This evidence is important to our understanding of Chaucer's *A.B.C*, for it virtually eliminates S as a witness to several disputed readings. This association between S and C may begin as early as 3213, where *kyng oþer erle (conte ne roy* F5938) is, in CS only, *kyng oþer elles*. After 5087 examples abound: 5083 *Larescyne] (Larrecin* F9492) *Latrosynie* CS over erasure in C); 5096 *bineme] byen* CS; 5097 *hole makere] (pertuiseresse* F) *vnmakere* CS; 5098 *vnhelere] and* add. CS; *a¹*] om. CS; 5103 *þat¹*] *al* CS; 5133 *brode] (couver* F) CS, *breede* GJMO, with no gloss from G³ (a rare rejection of G); 5139 *kyne] (vaches* F) *koyn* CS; 5188 *þe] here* CS; 5243 *russet] lyuerey* CS (over erasure in C); 5255 *trewaundes] trewauntise* CS; 5264 *his] (son* F) *þis* CS; 5273-4 *doon so michel] so doon with hem* CS; 5276 *throne] tresore* CS; 5319 *stenderesse] (estenderresse* F) *steynowresse* CS; 5370-1 *wronge and haltinge] haltinge and wronge* CS; 5401 *stiringe] stuting* ('stuttering') CS; 5629 *Allas, allas] Allas, allas, allas* CS; 5770 *releeue] deliuere* CS; 5833 *Incipit carmen secundum ordinem litterarum alphabeti.*] (in CS only); 6026 *he] she* CS; 6839 *seyn] seyn alle* CS; 6854 *she*] om. CS; 6884 *It] þer while* CS; 7069 *couple] compleyne* CS. A final example may properly belong in the previous section on the relation of CG³S: at 6491 τ apparently left a gap; the gap appeared in G, with *vacat* ('there is a gap') written over it by G³ — but in CS *vacat* appears as part of the text.

ANOMALIES

Of course, there are anomalies which do not appear to fit the Stemma at all. None is intractable: I mention them only in order to avoid over-simplification. The most common anomaly is agreement between JMOS, but such agreement, when the French shows that the error cannot be in C and G with JMOS correct, is always attributable to S and β's independent error. When F is indecisive, JMOS may perserve the original reading, as at 214 *as þouh*] *as* JMOS (*com* F405); 834 *me and yow*] *ȝowe and me* JMOS where *moi et vous* (F1541) has the variant *vous et moi; 2639 þe*] *thy* JOS, *þin M*, where *Les* (F4842) has the variant *Tes*.

As a rule F indicates that JMOS are in error. Independent error caused by S and β misreading their exemplars is the rarest cause of their agreement, but at 2250 *throte hool* (*gorge entiere* F4118) becomes *throte bolle* in JMOS by expectation of the common English phrase (O added *bolle* to *throte* at 2253, for example). Independent alteration of word-order is hardly more common as a cause of JMOS's agreement. Examples are 1089 *of a chambre comen out*] (*d'une chambre issirent* F2015) *come owte of a chaumbre* JMOS, and similar normalisations at 1330 and 1519. Independent omission is a litle more common. Two examples due to eyeskip are 707-8 and 2372-3. At 730 *þe* was left out to smooth a generalisation and at 1150 *hachees* was omitted, no doubt because of its unfamiliarity. Minor substitutions are of the expected kind: 273 *þilke*] *þat* JMOS; 751 *men*] *thay* JMOS; 954 *leese*] *haue loste* JMOS; 1306 *þilke*] *Scho* JMOS. Predictably, in view of the characteristics of S and β revealed earlier, the commonest cause of coincidental agreement between JMOS is addition. *Grace* becomes *Grace dieu* at 262, 264, 781, 783, for example; and other small smoothing additions occur at 263, 360, 452, 599, 645, 774.

Surprising numbers of agreements in error between J and S occur, most of them obviously due to independent action. Misunderstanding by J and S of their exemplars has produced 1177 *astone*] *stane* JS. The apparent omission at 1521 of *and hanged* is in fact due to smoothing: the phrase occurs earlier in both J and S. At 1300-1 omission in both *in hire hande wolde also telle hire tale and red hire scripture* is due to eyeskip from *scripture* before the omission. Independent substitution explains JS's agreement at 134 *she*] *it*; 604 *doo*] *giffene* J, *I gyven* S; 737 *to*] *tille*; 1291 *grete Thursday*] *schire Thursday*. Normalising addition accounts for 365 *Israel*] *þe childer of Israel*; 731 *þat oon and þat ooþer*] *bath the tane and the tothere*; 1153 *ne weeneth*] *ne wene nouȝt*. However, at 3800 it is hard to avoid the implication that S had J in front of him: for *mossy* J has *mossebe groun*, and S adds *and mosse bygroven*. Did he briefly use J as exemplar (as he may have first used G, the moved to C)?

Not only JMOS and JS, but also JM sometimes agree in error. Of the five occasions in Book 1 noted, 83, 97 and 134 are insignificant. At 1026 *quod she* becomes in J: *Quod nature I hafe sayde that I wille saye at this tyme*, and in M: *quod nature I wil say nouȝt elles. And perfor say þhe what þow likes · and I shal gladly here þow ·* Their general similarity is due to the cryptic text. Grace-of-God has told Nature that if she has finished complaining, Grace will answer her: *But if ye wole sey noon ooþer thing, I wol answere*, which is followed by the ambiguous *Nay quod she.* J and M also agree in some additional material at 1628, where *aresoned him* has become *reseyued hym* in MO, *aunswerede hym* in J, to which M adds *honestly · and answerid on þis Wyse*, and J adds *on this wyse*. The additions soften the abruptness of β's reading.

There are several other infrequent anomalous groupings. M and S agree in error at 1351-2, where both omit *and comen into þis world* apparently through eyeskip from *chyld* before the omission to *world* at the end of it. MOS appear to be related by their reading *what sees þou* in 226 for *þou what seiste*] (*Tu que dis* F423), but they have only regularised word-order, while J simplified to *whate*. Even CJ share error at 2212 *werre ne torment*] (*guerre ... ne tourment* F4049-50) *werre ne tournament* — independent error reinforced by the association with *werre*, and by the correct *werre and in tournament* at 2201-2. Finally, CS share error on some occasions. At 997 *al*] (*tout* F1846) *on* GS is due to independent substitution of the expected idiom *sei on* for *sei al*. At 997-8 *today more game* GMO is correct, as *a gieu ... hui mais* F1846-7 (literally 'game ... henceforth') shows. How then are we to explain C's *today but game*, J's *to daymare but gamene*, S's *þis day but for gaame*? In spite of their superficial similarity, they must be independent alterations to express the sense 'only a joke'.

The complexity of relationships in the α-branch, and between C and the β-branch, may have misled me. Even the existence of the French has not precluded the many occasions on which the correct reading remains uncertain, and must be accounted for in Notes. Nevertheless, the broad lines of the Stemma are not in question, and 'anyone who is afraid of giving an uncertain text had best confine himself to dealing with autograph manuscripts'.[66] The contamination of C can easily be detected; it is otherwise close to the accurate G, except for a normal number of scribal errors and its happy use (in contrast to G) of a familiar southern dialect in an unambiguous hand.

THE TRANSLATION

The evidence cited in this section is not comprehensive, and is exclusively from Book 1. A complete listing of the Translator's neologisms, omissions, errors and substitutions would be wearisome, and all but the smallest are dealt with in the Notes. Since we do not know which French

[66] Maas, p. 17.

manuscript was the source it is in any case impossible to assess the translation accurately: many apparent errors must be due to unrecorded corruption in the French.[67] There is a second reason why it is difficult accurately to assess the translation. It is all too easy to assume that its extreme literalness is entirely due to lack of skill or imagination. Even Workman thought the *Pilgrimage* showed less sense of style than contemporary translations,[68] though he pointed out that in fifteenth-century English translations from Latin or French the usual intention (whether due to timidity, to the dictates of a lost school of criticism, or to reverence for the model) was to keep as close to the sentence structure of the original as English permitted. The relationship between French and the rapidly developing English of the period is such that it is hard to know whether literalisms in diction and syntax were the result of clumsiness or experiment with fashionable neologism.

Certainly the translator used many words whose first recorded usage is later than or contemporary with the *Pilgrimage*. Most are mentioned in the Notes. An example is 803–4 *barlich corn*: *MED barli-corn* gives the earliest instance as 1500 — about a hundred years later. 1246 *chastisere* (*chastierresse* F2288) is first cited by *MED chastisour* in 1400, its occurrence in the *Pilgrimage* being dated 1450 instead of the first quarter of the fifteenth century, as the paleography of G suggests; 1159 *hachees* (*haschies* F2138) *MED hache* n.2 'anguish' is similar. At 1287, *daungerous* (*dangereus* F2364) meaning 'the dangerously ill' is a substantival use of the adjective not recorded at all by *MED daungerous* or *OED dangerous* 4, though the latter records the adjective meaning 'dangerously ill' from about 1616. Though not an example of literalism this does illustrate the translator's occasionally pioneering use of language. The case of 880 *noces* (*noches* F1630) 'wedding' is a little different. Strange enough to survive among the English witnesses only in G's *noses*, it might easily be mistaken for mere uncomprehending Gallicism, yet *OED noces* (which does not record the *Pilgrimage* example of the word, having had access only to Wright's edition, in which only C's readings appear) cites the *Ancren Riwle* as well as the *Castle of Love*, the reference in each case being to the feast at Cana. This would seem to be an example of a loan-word of short life-span, as is 1697 *deuynale*, *MED divinaille* and *OED divinail* showing few examples (this one not included) and none later than Caxton. One wonders whether the more obvious Gallicisms, such as 2666 *mugoe*, 2737 *pyer*, were attempts at the fashionable flourish.

[67] It is possible, though unlikely, that the source is among the fifty-five potentially relevant manuscripts known to Stürzinger. By the variants he cites, all but twenty-six or twenty-seven can be eliminated. For evidence of the nature of the source see Henry, "The French Source Manuscript of the Middle English Prose *Pilgrimage of þe Lyfe of þe Manhode*", *University of Ottawa Quarterly*, 54iv (1984), 26–33.

[68] Workman, pp. 84–96. The paucity of medieval theorising about translation is discussed by Amos, Ch.1., and the development of contemporary secular styles is discussed by H. S. Bennett, "Fifteenth-Century Secular Prose".

That the translator's respect for his model was high is clear not only from his literal method but from the rarity and insignificance of additional material in his translation. Typical examples occur at 144 *heere* for which there is no precedent in F280; 152 *she answerede me and seyde* (*elle me respondi* F293), where an English tag is employed; 226 *quod she* for which there is no precedent in F423; 274 *peynted reed* (*Paint* F506) where *reed* simply clarifies the image of the cross painted with blood. These additions, if not explained by unrecorded variants in the French, might indeed have been introduced by γ (whether completely distinct from the translator's work or a stage in its correction, as suggested above p. lxxvii). The same is true of the following examples: 297 *trewe leeche and suer* (*loial mire* F548); 307 *withholde to myself* (*retien* F567); 339 *answerde hire and seide* (*respondu li a* F625), and in those cited in the Notes for 399, 442, 568, 954, 1017, 1714–15, 1974, 2212, 2275, 2365, 2608, 2659.

A few readings, if not due to corruption in the French, may be due to deliberate substitution: 11 *þis* (*la vision* F21); 233 *or* (*et* F436); 252 *a* (*la* F470); 445 *þat þei so shulden* (*ce* F817); the untypical 1708-9 *with how michel his desire may be fulfilled* (*sa capacite* F3139); 2035 *hyere* (*pass si bas* F3738) a rare avoidance of literalism; 2330 *herte* (*pensee* F4269); 2412 *oon* (*vestues* F4415).

Errors are more numerous (Book 1 shows there are 78: about one in every four hundred and twenty words, which is a 0·24 per cent rate of error) but most of these are minor, and some as already stated may be due to corruption in the French, or to awkwardness in the French even as recorded. Examples of the latter occur at 43, 79, 196, 1268-9, 2729. Corruption in the French may explain 216 and 509 *his(e)* (*ces*); 275 *seruauntes* (*sergens*); 594 *execucioun* (*discution*, with variants *distinction*, *dissention*).

Minor errors, that is to say those which have comparatively little effect on the meaning, are of the kind which follow. At 49, *en sauf* 'in a place where it will do no harm' is taken to mean *in safetee* 'in a place where it would come to no harm'; at 102 *saulee* 'satisfaction' turns the adjective *saoul* into a noun; at 112 *walkinge* is supposed to render *errant* 'wandering'. Similar trivial examples occur at 211, 305, 311, 356, 426, 466, 468, 499, 605, 632, 1026, 1132, 1140, 1200, 1243, 1607-8, 1640, 1737, 1750, 1969, 2290-1, 2522, 2528, 2668, 2689, 2735.

Errors in syntax occur at 116-17, 150, 770-1, 861, 1011-12, 1523, 2216, 2263, 2402, 2467, 2507. Some more serious errors, leading to real confusion, occur as follows (all the others are discussed in Notes). At 46 *entrer a force y convenoit* 'one could not enter without suffering violence' (literally 'it was necessary to enter with violence') becomes *entre þere I muste needes*, the function of *a force* being misunderstood. At 47 *Nul mais passer* 'no-one at all pass' becomes *non but passe*, the intensive negative *mais* being misunderstood. At 106 *voir, si com songoie* 'indeed, as I dreamed' becomes *see as I mette*, *voir* having been misunderstood. Other serious mistakes are found at 109, 175, 426, 431, 598-9, 610-11, 674, 730,

752, 776-7, 841, 865, 998, 1088, 1110-11, 1164, 1243, 1268, 1296, 1430, 1730, 1901-2, 1941-2, 1962 (and 1972-3, 1982-3, where *esbouciee* mysteriously becomes *aproved* or *preeued/preeved*), 2080, 2161, 2257, 2284, 2312, 2334-5, 2490, 2497, 2519, 2624, 2647, 2733. With the exception of *esbouciee | aproved*, these are understandable errors: it is not surprising to find *mes* 'messenger' mistaken for *mes* 'food' at 431; *pas* the negative mistaken for the noun 'step' at 610, giving *paas; fais et faissiaus* 'big bundles and little bundles' mistaken for parts of *faire* at 674, giving *maad and in makinge; nee* 'born' confused with *niee* 'knotted in' at 730, giving *knyt; tortue* 'tortoise' ingeniously interpreted as the curly-horned ram at 841; *paine* 'trouble' becoming *bred* at 865, or *emolument* 'reward' becoming, by an error in etymology, *gryndinge* at 2161. Such rather endearing errors show that awkwardness in the translation is due to the translator's being an Englishman working literally rather than a Frenchman unfamiliar with English. The percentage of serious errors of this nature is approximately 1.4.

In the examples above, 674 *fais et faissaius* was mistranslated partly as a result of misreading *faissiaus* as *faissians*. Misreading might also account for 730 *knyt* where *nee* was mistaken for *niee*. Some twenty-five examples of error are quite clearly due to misreading, probably by the translator, though the possibility of corruption in F accounting for them cannot be ruled out. At 56 *enmieles* 'honeyed' was mistaken for *en mietes* giving *croumede* 'in crumbs'; at 142 *Biaus* 'fair' was mistaken for *Miaus* giving *My;* at 152-3 *entens i* was mistaken for *en tens*, giving *In time;* at 191 *uns* was taken for *nus*, giving *naked;* at 220 *lieu* was taken for *l'eaue*, giving *þe water*. Similar examples occur at 286, 356, 375, 507, 515, 579, 622-3, 791, 1232, 1249-50 (?), 1260, 1552-3, 1851, 2165, 2676.

Minor errors are absent between 790-1232, misreadings absent between 632 and 1026, although major errors are made in the 800s and 900s. If this means anything at all, it might point to better condition of the source manuscripts in this area (perhaps to a change of scribe) or merely to a fresher state of mind in the translator.

Major omissions are extremely rare. Six may be due to the translator's having found the French difficult — but here again omission or illegibility in the source might be the cause. At 843 *impressions* 'effects (of the elements)' is omitted; at 1333 *pour ces maus* may have appeared in the variant form *Par ces maus* and so have made no sense; at 1902 two lines of French are left out, possibly because the translator misunderstood the preceding construction and so failed to make sense of them; at 2552 *St Joce* may not have been recognised, as the name *Cis* for Saul's father may not at 2563, where confusion in meaning resulted; at 2730 a rare usage of the verb *repondrai* seems to have led to omission of a phrase.

Some omissions appear to be due to eyeskip, as in the case of 72 where *Mains moines* may have led to the omission of the equivalent of *Mains* 'many' and 1540 where *Pluseurs bateurs* may have resulted in the omission of the equivalent of *bateurs*. More commonly, the equivalent of a whole

French line as been omitted, eyeskip being all too easy when reading couplets — indeed eyeskip in the French itself may explain 293, 378, 482, 550, 686, 1379, 1976, 2595, 2630.

A few omissions are so minor that it is difficult to distinguish in their causes between carelessness and deliberate exclusion of material which though effective in verse is superfluous in prose. Among the most ambiguous examples possibly due to carelessness are 101 where the equivalent of *bel* 'pleasant' is omitted before *dwellinge*, 744 where the equivalent of *et grant desroi* 'and great disorder' is omitted after *folye*, 1074 where the equivalent of *De parler* 'to speak' is omitted after *folilich*, and in further examples at 1141, 1249, 1254 (an omission corrected by the common ancestor of C and G³), 2015, 2207, 2240, 2397, 2518, 2533, 2545, 2553.

By far the largest category of 'errors' in the translation may well be the result of the translator's pruning, since the meaning is not radically altered by their omission; but it is hard even here to be sure that carelessness or corruption is not the cause, so small are the French words concerned. The equivalent of *y* or *i* is left out at 1966, 1994, 2547, 2559, 2726, 2735, while the equivalent of *en* is left out at 156, 389, 685 (?), 1504, 1515, 1518 and seventeen other places.

Other examples which may be omissions of the otiose are numerous. The translator frequently omitted a word from a pair or series in parallel (or it was cancelled at the γ stage), as at 44-5 where *De sanc rougis, tains et vermaus* became only *steyned red with blood*, or at 824 where *remuer ... et muer* became simply *remeve*, or at 958 where *perdu | Et expire et abatu* became *ylost and abated*. Similar examples in which the omitted word is sometimes genuinely otiose as in the first example above, and sometimes expresses what is strictly speaking a new idea, as in the second example, occur at 55, 229, 393, 689, 775, 860, 905, 991, 1096, 1117, 1130, 1135, 1165, 1179-80, 1198, 1225 and 1229 (where, in view of 1237 where the equivalent of *housse* 'brushed' was omitted, *housse* may have been left out because it was not understood), 1228 (where error as well as omission is found), 1262-3, 1284, 1455, 1546, 1574, 1644, 1748, 1968, 1985, 2020, 2287, 2310, 2405, 2429 (but see note), 2451, 2550, 2595, 2613, 2630 (if not due to eyeskip, since it is the equivalent of a whole French line which is omitted), 2684.

Most omissions of the otiose concern small words or phrases not part of such series. At 5 the equivalent of *en dormant* 'sleeping' is presumably omitted as unnecessary after his *sweuene*. At 92 the equivalent of *assez tost* 'very soon' was apparently thought unnecessary as a modification of *pere men mihten fynde*. Similar small examples are at 135, 285, 288, 323, 330, 368, 436, 446, 519 and 657 (both showing omission of the equivalent of *sans mentir* 'without lying'), 710, 776 (if not due to eyeskip), 1055-6, 1104, 1419, 1479, 1486, 1885, 1933, 2029, 2068, 2091, 2279, 2345, 2372, 2386,

2435, 2580, 2597, 2641. This does not include scarcely avoidable omissions such as that at 2439 where *perdus et perdues* refers to masculine *escus* and feminine *targes*, both being covered by English *lost*.

We are so disinclined to attribute any skill to the literal translator that we may do him injustice by not recognising his own skill with the limited prose he has chosen to employ. Even the large number of omissions easily attributed to pruning may suggest a man careful of style. It may be that the translator first rendered his text complete, and only at the γ stage trimmed it or allowed it to be trimmed. That he was not insensitive to the rhythm and music of prose is apparent from 2101, where the balanced antitheses of the French are preserved in the English by judicious modification of the literal method. In rendering

> Son profit fait dont autre gent
> Font leur mal preu et (leur) domage;
> Croistre (li) font ses bles orage
> Et tempeste emplir ses guerniers
> Et pestilence ses celiers,
> De grans durtes il a mol lit
> Et de tourmens son grant delit,
> Sese dainties fait de povrete
> Et son soulas d'adversite.
> Jëunes le font encraissier
> Et maladies enforcier
> Pointure et tribulation
> Li font sa recreation (F3858–70)

the translator turned *orage* 'storms' into *clowdes*, to alliterate with *corn*, and cleverly underlined the paradoxes of F3867–8 by creating the alliteration of *fastinges maken hym fat, and syknesses strengthe*. This is a delicate use of words in an otherwise severely literal approach. That translation was not merely mechanical is shown by the number of occasions when successful transpositions of the French word-play are made. The best example is perhaps at 2120–1 where, unable to play on the equivalent of *point*, he transposes the punning to the equivalent of *droit*, so that *Sur li fu pointoie et point | Et mesure a son droit point* (F3889–90 where Deguileville himself seems to have invented a verb *pointer* with the sense 'to make right' (*a point*)) becomes, with no distortion of Middle English idiom, *vpon him it was rihted and prikked and mesured aright at his rihtes*. A similar, though somewhat less successful attempt to retain the original word-play occurs at 2136–9, where once again play on *point* is transposed to play on *riht*:

> Certes, dist elle, le pourpoint
> Si te fust bine taillie a point,
> Se tu a point fusses taillies;

Mais a toi qui apointiez
N'es pas a doit selonc son point (F3917-21)

becomes: "*Serteyn*," quod she, "*þe purpoynt were shape for þe ariht if þow were ariht shape: but on þee it holt þat art not rihted ariht after his riht.*" Between 499-501 play on *departe* 'separate', *parte* 'go away with', *partye* 'portion', *parte* 'to share' etc., competently echo the French punning:

Quar de li vous faut departir,
S'a vostre Dieu voulez partir;
Ne pouez pas tous ·II· avoir
Ensemble, ce pouez savoir,
Quar vous meismes avez dit
Que vostre Dieu avez eslit
A heritage et partie . . . (F901-7 and on to 920).

But this is not the place to attempt a full-scale appreciation of the translation. The evidence cited above is intended only to indicate the painstaking if fallible method of the translator, to point to the extraordinary number of small excisions, which may indeed have been made at the γ-stage of the English tradition, and to suggest that the translation is worthy of further attention, so that peculiarities of style which are due to Deguileville, and inadequacies in our critical response which may be due to his mode and style being currently unfashionable shall be correctly attributed, and not laid in error at the anonymous translator's door.

On the other hand, his frequently sensitive adaptation of rhythms within literal constructions deserves due recognition: a process begun by Rosemond Tuve, who observed how frequently the "beautiful rhythm of the early prose" was flattened in the seventeenth-century Pepys Manuscript version, which for example reduced to *This Myll was made by the wynde of Envy, and naughtiness* the lovely *þilke mille was maad to þe wynd, and with þe wynd of envye grounde* (1546-8), rhythmically superior to *Ce moulin fait a vent estoit | Et au vent d'envie mouloit* (F2837-8).[69]

EDITORIAL METHOD

TEXT

The spelling of C is retained, and so is its orthography, including distinction between *u* and *v*, and between *þ* and *th* in spite of the fact that such distinction does not mark any difference of function (witness f. 12ᵛ where the catchword *And þilke* is followed at the top of f. 13ʳ by *And thilke*)[70] beyond the invariable use by C of *Th* rather than *þ*. Distinction

[69] Tuve, p. 164, and n. 13.
[70] References are to the modern pencil foliation.

of *j/i* is retained, even where modern use would require *j*, for example in *justice / iustice*, except where each represents the personal pronoun *I* (for example 1360 *y*, 1888 *i* and 1899 *j*) when they are standardised to *I*, and on rare occasions when *j* clearly represents *i*: 596 *jre* becomes *ire*, 755 *jt* becomes *it*, 1420 *Wjte* becomes *Wite*, for example. Initial *ff*- is transcribed *F* or *f* according to modern use. After a decorated initial, where scribal practice is to follow the initial with a capital letter, -*ff*- is transcribed only as *f* (e.g. *Of*, not *Off* at 2283).

Modern practice has been followed in word-division, punctuation, capitalisation and paragraphing. Punctuation of speech presents a particular problem, direct speech often occurring with the speech of a second person whose words are themselves being recounted by a third: for example at 1644 ff., the *maister*'s words are being recounted by Sapience in her dialogue with Aristotle, all of which has been described by Grace since line 1488. The sequence in such cases is double quotation marks for the initial speaker, single for the second, and double again for the third. Underlinings in the manuscript (usually marking proper nouns) have been ignored, and where absent but necessary according to modern convention they have been supplied, for example at 2569 *Etiques* the title of Aristotle's *Ethics*.

Acceptance of an alternative reading, or the rare editorial emendation is indicated by [ ], enclosing whole words even when only part of a word is in question. Emendations usually follow C's precedent in form, but sometimes a form untypical of C is used either because there is no precedent in C or because use of the form likely to have been in the archetype more clearly reveals the process by which C's error arose, for example at 1924. Square brackets also enclose folio numbers, for example [f.10ᵛ]: these sometimes occur in the middle of a word, as in the manuscript. Letters or words erased or obscured in the manuscript but distinguishable under ultra-violet light, and those supplied, but not visible because totally erased, obscured or cropped, are contained by { }. Insertions by the scribe, in the margin or above the line in C are indicated by \/; deletions are indicated only in the critical apparatus, and decorated capitals only in general terms in the Description of Manuscripts.

Abbreviations are clearer and more consistent than those of the other scribes. Unless otherwise stated in the Notes, expansions follow precedents in C. Most are common: *þᵘ*, *wᵗ*, *þᵗ*, *þᵗ*, *qd'*, ·*i*· become *þou*, *with*, *þat*, *quod*, *id* est, respectively. Ampersand is silently expanded to *and*, except where a rejected reading is cited in variants. Superscript *a*, *i*, *u* become *ra*, *ri* (*ui* in *aliqⁱd*), *ru* respectively. Superscript *s*, rarely used, becomes simply *s* (363 *whos*, 1104 *Lordinges*). There are the usual *ro*, *ar*, *er* strokes on *þ*. The commonest form of abbreviated 'Jesus Christ' is *ihū* (sometimes *jhū*). The initial letter is standardised to *I*. At 2119 and elsewhere *ihc̄* is for *Ihesus* (in full at 1341); at 2200 *cⁱst(es)* becomes *Crist(es)* in spite of *cryst* at 1848. A few abbreviations are ambiguous. The second letter in *ll* sometimes has a short bar not through it but extending to the right, as at 1346 and 1348 *jewell*, 2643 *all*. It may represent final *e*, but this is unlikely in view of the fact that C uses *iewell* once, *jewel(l)* ten times but does not end the word in *-e* once.

The superior comma-like curl has a wide variety of meanings. Following *qd* it indicates *quod*, but when final it usually indicates *-e*, as at 363 *debonaire* (twice in Book I in the unabbreviated form); 490 *cure*, used on three other occasions, always with final *-e*; 494 *youre*, never spelled otherwise by the scribe. At 902 *elles* it indicates final *-es*. Medially it may mean *er* (30 *euere*, 77 *neuere*) or *re* (429 *oppressed*, 434 *prechede*, 697 *preyinge*).

The abbreviation sign over vowels is expanded to *m* or *n* (but at 376 it may be over *e* in *peple*, though it has not been expanded to *o*, if that is what it means). Sometimes when over nasals it seems to indicate the omission of a nasal, as at 1451 *ammynistrade*. Where over a final nasal as a firm stroke and not a mere flourish, it is expanded to *e*, as at 491 *mowne*. In one respect the scribe's habit is idiosyncratic. A two-minim letter with an abbreviation mark over it would normally be taken as *un* or *um*, the nasal being indicated by the abbreviation mark. It is in fact frequently *n* with a mark of abbreviation over it which indicates expansion to *un*, the abbreviation mark standing for the vowel. There is clear evidence for this idiosyncrasy. First, the C-scribe usually distinguishes *u* from *n* with unusual clarity. Second, on a number of occasions this scribe, who does not normally employ otiose marks or decorative flourishes, uses *m* with the mark of abbreviation over it, at points where he cannot have meant m*m*, or use the mark to identify as a nasal an ambiguous two-minim letter next to a *u*. Examples, in alphabetical order, are 923 *chaumberere*; 1239 *chaumbre* and eleven other occasions; 70 *cloumben;* 1952 *coumforte*; 1898 *coumforteth*; 865 *croume;* 56 *croumed*; 2072 *discoumfyte*; 400 *discoumfyted*; 1951 *discoumforte*; 1948 *discoumforted* (in spite of 2016 *discomfort*); 468 *doumbe*; 980 *flaume* (*flawme* at 667). As is already apparent the use of *o/ou* or *a/au* is inconsistent: 1685 *champyoun*; 293 *champouns*; but 41 *chaumpiouns* and 255, 2525 *chaumpioun*.

This brings us to the many occasions when the abbreviation mark is over not *m* but a two-minim letter: *n* or *u*. The use of *m̄* for u*m* suggests that contrary to convention the scribe has also indicated expansion to u*n* by placing the mark over the nasal. It looks as if the C-scribe or the tradition to which he belonged took the mark to indicate expansion to *u* when used over the two-minim letter he took for *n*, and by analogy extended its use to *m*. It will be noticed that over both nasals it is used where *o/ou* or *a/au* forms are possible: 1527 *aungeles*, 467 *avaunte*, 95 *avauntage*, 835 *bounde(d)* (also in *bounden, boundes, boundeth*), 133 *bountee*, 1430 *bourdoun* and twenty-six other occasions as well as *burdoun* in full at 2076; at 296, 2536, 2623 *counfort*, 2639 *counforte*, 578 *counforted*, 1897 *counforteth*, all in spite of *confortouresse* at 2637. That word appears in both *coum-* and *coun-* forms; so does *discounfited* 2636, 2715, and *discounforted* 30, 217, 561, 2608. Other examples of the abbreviation mark over *n* are *founde(d)*, *founden*, *foundement*, *marchaunt*, *masounrye* (compare *masowned* in full at 210), *penauntes, raunpen, raunsome | raunsoum, wound(es), wounded(e).* Similar strokes are found in sixteen words ending -*aunce*, only one of which, *aqueytaunce*, also occurs in C with an -*ance* ending in full (if not simply a case of abbreviation mark omitted in error). There is only one other example of -*ance*: at 1714 where an alternative reading is accepted. The *a/au* words all varied in ME between a pronounciation with the diphthong *au* and one with either ME short *a* or late ME long *a* (or both). There is, in the rarity of his use of the written-out form, some suggestion that spellings with *a* (or *o*) are natural to him, and that he puts in the abbreviation mark as a sop to those who use *au* or *ou*.

Associated with this problem is the familiar one of correctly expanding final -*ou* (or in this scribe's case -*on*) with an abbreviation mark over it. Sometimes it can only be for -*oun*: *bourdoun, canoun, coroun.* The scribe has often included *i* or *y* where we expect it, as in *administracioun, affeccioun, championun(s), champyoun.* In cases where he gives unabbreviated precedent for -*ioun* I have normally followed modern practice. In one case, however, modern practice echoes a corrupt form which appeared only in the sixteenth century, so *i* is not introduced in 2568 *staloun.*

VARIANTS

The sigla are normally listed in the order CGJMOS: S, though belonging to the α-branch, should perhaps be eliminated as a witness, so it is cited last. Sometimes, however, it might be cited first: 2098 *pile] pyle* S, *pyll* C reflects the fact that S has been accepted, though modified in accordance with C's practice. All substantive variants are recorded. Those due merely to dialect, orthographic or minor grammatical differences are included only if significant. Words are usually but not invariably regarded as variants if they have separate entries in *OED*. Exceptions include some common dialect variations: *hem | them, to | tille, sterre | sternes*, and variations on *þo | thilke | thay[m] |thase.* In addition, lack of distinction between forms of the same word conceals a good deal of variety, for example between *a | an, o | oon, as | also* adv., *be | been* pp., *bicumen | bicome, cloped | cledde, church | kirk, cloumben | clymmyd, come | comen* pp., *cowth | could* 3 per. pret. subj., *deth | deede | dede, doone | do* pp. Some obvious slips and errors are cited simply to show a manuscript's level of unreliability: for example '569 *profitable] prorofitable* O' records one of O's frequent mistakes. In addition, the variants include a few instances of spellings not represented in *OED* (or *MED* up to letter N). Many readings, such as corrector's work (which is particularly important in G), which are not variants are recorded because they offer other evidence. Marginalia are recorded because they offer evidence of the relation between manuscripts. Under one line reference and after one lemma are all marginalia which are significantly similar in different manuscripts (even though the position in some manuscripts may differ). I retain *þ ð ȝ u v i j* and manuscript word-division and punctuation, even in C's readings where they occur after the lemma, and even in M's confusion of *þ* and *y* (though these are normalised in the 'Pilgrim's Lament' in the Appendix). French cited is Stürzinger's.

Manuscripts in substantive agreement with the lemma are not noted, but it is important to remember that the absence of citation of S before line 114 does not signify its agreement: in 1-114 S is absent as a witness. The spelling of a variant is that of the first manuscript cited after it.

Details such as brackets and underlinings (including those indicating expansion) in the text are omitted from the lemma, but italicising to indicate expansion is retained in citations after it, to avoid misleading the reader: abbreviations in GJMOS are much more ambiguous than in C.

Rubricator's hands are indicated by 'rub' only if they used red, otherwise by superior 2. Hands other than those of the scribe or rubricator are indicated by superior 3 without further differentiation.

Abbreviations describe the lemma or variants they follow, thus:

mar. annotation in the margin; the lemma in this case and the next two is the word ending the line nearest the marginal note in the manuscript first cited (see, e.g. 122).

add. mar. additional to the text, and in the margin, e.g. '503 *heerdes*] *men* add. mar. O³.'

rub. mar. annotation in the margin (in red in the first manuscript cited): e.g. '278 *Moyses*] *Episcopus* rub. mar. MO.'

marked mar. the lemma is at the beginning or end of a line which is marked in the margin (e.g. 1515): but many such marks are omitted from the variants (see p. xxxiii).

ins. mar. written in either margin, but belonging to the text, which usually bears a caret to indicate the omission.

ins. inserted in the text over a caret. Letters inserted are, if necessary, numbered consecutively through the whole lemma, e.g '1670 *save þee*] *saaue thee* (1st *a* and 2nd *e* ins. G³) G.' means that G's corrector inserted the first *a* in *saaue* and the first *e* in *thee*. Bracketed comments such as '(2nd *a* ins. G³)' mean either that the second *a* in the lemma is inserted by G's corrector or, if there is no second *a* in the lemma, that one was inserted by the corrector immediately before or after the first.

add. ins. additional to the text, inserted over a caret or other omission mark, e.g. '239 *but*] *it* add. ins. C' means that C erroneously inserted *it*.

add. additional to the text, e.g. '10 *drawe*] *þaym* add. J' means that only J has a form of *drawe þaym*.

add. into mar. additional to the text and extending from the end of a line into the margin so as to suggest late addition.

add. rub. red subheading additional to but incorporated in the body of the text and not associated with an illumination, e.g.

'411 *it*] *how curates shuld kepe þere kirkes* add. rub. *M*.'

can.   cancelled.

add. can.   additional to the text and cancelled. Scribal designations refer only to the cancellation: '2227 *whan þou*] *the helme* add. can. O³, means the addition was made by O's main scribe and cancelled by one of his correctors.

If *over, under, alt., trs., om., o. er., erased, u.v., lost, cropped,* {cropped}, *em. ed., rub.* follow material it means that it is: above the line, below the line, altered to the material following the abbreviation, transposed, omitted, written over erasure, erased but visible, visible under ultra-violet light, destroyed by friction or other damage, cut away by a binder, an unidentified word cut away by the binder, an editorial emendation, in red.

An erasure is indicated by *er.* (e.g. 1844-5). A hyphen precedes a variant suffix and follows a variant prefix, e.g. '679 *fardelle*] *-s* J' indicates that J has *fardelles*.

Two abbreviations describe the material they 'contain': *prec. . . . mar.* and *with . . . mar.* mean: in the left margin, preceding the lemma e.g. '815 *As*] prec. *Capitulum xxix* mar. CGS' means that in C the line beginning *As* (and a line nearby in GS) is preceded in the margin by the *capitulum* number; in the margin and related to the text as correction or gloss by a distinguishing mark: '1127 *how*] (with *thowgh* mar. G³)' means that G's corrector put a mark over *how* in the text, and after a similar mark in the margin wrote *thowgh*.

Line references are not always simply consecutive: when a long passage itself containing variants is a lemma (usually to indicate its insertion or omission), it is first cited as a whole, then return is made to variants within the long passage. For example, at 7264-8 a long omission from M is recorded, then other variants in 7264, 7265, 7266, 7268 are noted. Difficulty is often caused by the frequency with which scribes modify syntax and meaning — especially by varying punctuation. This cannot be conveniently revealed by variants.

Minor variations (insertion, erasure) affecting only part of a variant already cited are in brackets before the siglum: 419 *haue*] *ʒhave* (*h* ins.) J means that the *h* of *ʒhave* was inserted in J. Illuminations and their captions have not been included since they occur only in MO and there is no direct link between the illustrations in the two. They are listed on pp. xxxix and xli-xliii. 'Chapter headings', however, are noted. The fact that these headings are sometimes distinguished from the rest of the text by the use of a larger or different script is not recorded, but additions to the text which are not chapter headings are distinguished from chapter headings themselves, with the result that where a real addition is immediately followed by a chapter heading, the same siglum appears twice under one line reference in the variants. For example, at '704 *leue*] *and comaundement* add. S, *Takeþe hede howe þat þe pilgryme · was abaysshed · of moyses rule* add. S', the words *and comaundement* are a genuine addition to the text, followed by a chapter heading, recognisable by its imperative construction.

Catchwords are omitted, as are coloured letters and paragraph marks unless they form part of a variant passage. Scribes' guide-letters under coloured capitals are recorded only if significant, e.g.: 1420 *Wite*] om. J, *3It* with scribe's guide *y* visible S.

Liberties have been taken in recording *capitulum* numbers. No attempt has been made to distinguish the hands (very various in G) in which they are written, or to indicate variety or abbreviation of numbers, e.g. 1917 *propir*] *twelfe Sere* J, *xii Apostoli* rub. mar. M, M's scribe in fact wrote *xii^{cim}* for *duodecim*. I also standardise *iiii* to *iv* throughout, and silently complete partially cropped numbers where the sequence of numbering indicates the lost material: e.g. at '434 *As*] prec. *Capitulum xvii* mar. CS' the last three digits are in fact cropped in S, whose next capitulum is clearly marked *xviii;* but where there is no evidence apart from the preceding and following *capitulum* numbers that any existed, no number is supplied: for example 1727 *Yit*] prec. *Capitulum lxxxiv* mar. CG where on f. 25ᵛ Shirley (out of step with the numbers in CG) would have had *lxxxiii*, his next number being *lxxxiv*. No account has been taken, either, of the fact that where two manuscripts are cited together since they share the same capitulum number, one shows it in roman and other in arabic letters: e.g. '273 *First*] *Capitulum ix* rub. mar. MO' disguises the fact that O wrote *Capitulum 9*.

Expansion of abbreviation marks is consistent only within each manuscript: it was not possible to be consistent throughout them all, so varied is their practice. Further details are given in the Description of Manuscripts. The French and its variants are given if relevant, but are cited more fully in the Notes.

PLATES

And whan wow and nature thus hauen ben
under my cure. yat han lerned in my scooles
bope faire dedis and faire woordis. wow pe seyen
me now erre : pit pe childen forbere me ¶ pe childen haue in mynde of pe champyon pat hadde
tauht his kunynge to a poore man . and hadde no
thing talke of his . for whan pei weren in pe feeld
at pe requeste of tweyne dukes. pat wolden defende
bi hem eche of hem lier owen . for which pei hadden
gret strif . pe maist pit which was muche wisere
pan pe prentys : bi gan to speke to his prentys ⁊
aresone him . ¶ What is pis qd he . come pe tweyne
apens me pat am aloone : pis was neuere of gret
mannynesse ne of wurpi corage. And pane whan
pilke lookede bihynde him who was pere : pe maist
pat him twich a strook : pat led to pe cerpe he sente
him . ¶ pit haue I nouht qd he tauht al my wyt
to my prentys ¶ It is euele bifalle pee to day whan
pow come apens me .

O I sey pee . So god saue pee . weeneft pow
pat I haue tauht pee now al my wit ⁊ al
myn art. and pat al myn I haue piuen pee. wi-
oute withholdinge any thing ? Euele wow wolden
awurpe with me. if I hadde no thing to defende
me with. bi sum wey. for comge to me vplepynge :
wow arguest me of sophistrie. of fraude ⁊ of gile.
bi defaute of discretioñ ¶ Now sey me. if I were
autere ⁊ shewed pee a purs. pe which I wolde piue
pee. and seyde pee. loo pis I haue piuen pee. bere
it with pee. for it is bi my wille ¶ If it so were pat
wow bere it forth . and sithe pou fonde per inne

hem her owne for whech they hadden gret stryf/ the maister whech
was 3itt wysore than the prentys began to speke to his prentys and
aresne hym what is this q^d he come 3ee tweyne a3ens me that am
allone. this was neue of gret worthynesse ne of wurthy corage and
thue whan thilke lookede be hynde hym ho was there the maister
3aff hym suche a strok that ded to the erthe he sent hym 3it haue
y no3ght q^d he talk3ht all my wit to my prentys it is euell be
falle the to say whan thow come a3enst me·

So y sey the· so god saue the sweeneste that y haue to3ght
the now all my wit and all myn art/ and that all myn y
haue 3eue the with out with holdyng any thing/ euell thou wol
dest a worthe with me 3iff y hadde nothing to defende me with by
som wey/ for doynge to me vylenye thou arge west me of sophistrie
of fraude and of gyle by defaute of distresonn/ now sey me 3iff y the
re a mercer and sheewede the a pinn· the whech y wolde 3yue the and
seyde the loo this y haue 3eue the beer it with the/ for it is by my wille
3iff it so were that thow beer it foorth and outye thow forsende the
3yue foure floryns other fyue other syxe scholde it seeme the that y
hadde any thing deserued the· other that y were ther fore a sophistre
serteyn q^d aristotell nay. butt me scholde thenke such a 3ifte full of
gret fredom and of wurship and of gret contesye·

Certeyn q^d she oo it is of the bred that i haue mad so subtill
for with oute y haue not sheewed the grete tresour that i ha
me put with yime· butt y haue ry3ht prynyly hidd it forte enry
chesse with the poorne folk· for 3iff it were sheewed with oute ther
scholde non dorre resseyue it/ charyte ordeygned it so· that hath of
the poorne gret pitee/ and ther yine is no gyle· butt deede of mercy

butt 3iff with oute y hadde sheewed gret apparysannce· and put
with yime thing that were lytell to preyse· other that hadde not
gret quantite/ thanne thow my3htest arge we me of gyle and blame me
yt y answere the oother weye for it is no deseyte thow3h y
sheewe it lytell to the eye and it is gret with yime· and y
wull that oo it be beleeued stedfastliche with oute makynge any
nayle/ but 3iff y wolde no3ht this· other 3iff y deede it oother

in my ꝑoꝉes hath fayre dedes and fayre wordes powꝛ
ze bade me erie zit ze schulde forbere me · ze schulde
have in mynde of the champion that hade taught his
kunynge tille a poꝛ man and nathynge had taken of
hy ꝑsoꝛe and when thay ware in the felde at the reqͧ
este of twa dukes that walde defende by thay aythere
there awne · ffoꝛ owille twa had grete stryse betwene
thay · The maystere whilke was zit the wisere than
the prentice began to speke to his prentice and aresonͤ
de hym whate es this qͧod he cōi ze twa ageyn me
allane · this come nenͤ of grete worthynes ne of w
orthy curage · And than when the ꝑrynce liked be
hynde hym wha was thare with hy · the maystere
gaue hym swilke a strake that dowue to the erth he
wente · zit qͧod he hase I nought taught the alle
my witte · Jt befelle the asaiy grace to day when powꝛ
come agayne me · So I say the w god me saue wene̅
ꝑ that I hase taught the alle my witte nowe and alle
my craftes and that alle artes and my kunynge I haue
giffen to the with owten witͤhaldynge of any thynge
ꝑuilke walde ꝑ fare with me zif I hade nought to defe
nde me witͤ hy sum othere waye · ffoꝛ thow argueth
me and rephendes me na felaiy woande · by sophistrie
fraude and gyle for defawte of distression · Saue me
nowe and I were a mercere and schewede the a puꝛse
whilke I walde gyffe the · and sayde to the · lo this
I gyeue the bere hit with the · for it is my wille ꝑat
thow haue it · zif hit ware sew that pow bare it furth
and wyne thowe fande ꝑin foure florenes or fyfe or
sex · schulde it seme that I had any thynge dessaysed
the or that I ware ꝑfoꝛe a sophistere · certaynly qͧod

yer other. for suche two had grete stryfe. The maister is milk was yit ye
þysiþen ye prentyse bigan to speke vnto his prentyse and areson hym.
What is þis þo he. come þe two agayn me. yat am allone. þis was neu
of grete worthynesse. ne of worth curage. And þen when ye prentyse loked
byhynd hym. who was per. ye maister gafe hym stille a strooke. yat deed
to ye erth he sent hym. yit haue I nouзt qd he taught al my witt to my
prentyse. It is euel bifallen ye to day. When þou come agaynes me. So
I say ye. so god ye saue. Renys þou þat I haue taught ye al my witt now.
and al myne aute. And yat al myn I haue tiзforo to ye witt outord with
holdyngs of any thynge. Euel þou wolde þirke with me. if I had no
thynge to defende me with. by some other way. for no vilany doynge
þou arзuys me. of saphistrye. of fraude. and of style by faute of distru
cion. Rob say me if I were a mercer and shabid ye a purse while I
wold gife ye. and syde to ye. lo þis I haue tiзforo to ye. bere it worth
ye. for it is by my wille. If it so were yat þou bere it forth. and sithen
þou fynde perin four florentes or fyue or sex. shuld it seme ye yat
I had any thynge disslayned ye. or yat I were perfor a sophister. Cer
tayn qd Aristotle. flay. Bot me shuld thynk stille a thift. fift of grete
fredom. and of worsship. and grete curtesy. Certayn qd sho so it is
of ye brede yat I made so sotil. for withoute I haue nouзt shewid ye
tresorio yat I haue privit within. bot I haue riзht ppurely hid it. for
to enrych with ye pure folks. for if it were shewid withoute. þer
shuld noon drue rerdise it. I sherite ordeynes it so. yat hath of ye ppy
grete pite. and perin is no style. bot dede of mercy. Bot if withoute
I haue shewid grete apparence. and prit within thynge yat wer
litel to preise. or yat hase nouзt grete quantite. þan þou myshtst
arзu me of style and blame me. yit I answer ye otherwyse. for it is
no deceyte. yof I shew it litel to ye eeзh. and is grete within. And
I wil yat it so be trisied and bileuyd stedfastly. with outen makyng
demynynge. Bot if I wold nouзt þis. or did otherwyse. þen paunte þou
myshtst arзu me of mystakynge. Rob say me yit I prey ye yat
arзuys me. of my mystoynynge. yat sayse it is nouзt reson. yat ye
vessell. or ye house be lesse. þen yat that is perin. saw þou neuer.
nowdur in no outer ye quantite of ye hert of man. Certayn qd he

and fayre worde yoȝht ȝe saiþ me noiþ eiie . ȝyt
ȝe schulde forthir me . ¶ ȝe schulde haue in mynde
of þe schampion þt had taȝht hir rymyng to
a puir man and no thyng had takyn of hys þ for
¶ when þan wer in þe feld at þe request of two
dukys . þ wold defende by hym eche of þam þam
alone for syche two had grete stryfe . ¶ þe maþt
syche was ȝyt wyser þan þe prentyse he gan to spke
to hys prentyse and a rejon hym . ¶ what es þis qd
he coune ȝe two a ȝeyne me þt am allone . ¶ y is
was neu of grete worthynes ne of worthi cnage .
¶ and þan qwan þe prentyse lukyd by syriud hym
who was yer . ¶ þe master ȝaf hym syche a strouie
þt dide to þe erthe þe sent hym . ¶ ȝit haue y not qd
he taȝht all my skylte to my prentys . it es eise le
fallyn þe to day when þ com a ȝeus me . ¶ So
y say þe so god saue me weny s þt þt y haue taȝht þe
all my skylte noiþ . and all myn cnre and þ all myn
y haue ȝeuyn to þe þt oþte holdynge of any thynge
oyþt y wold worthe kt me . ¶ yf y ne had to defend
me kit by syn othir wey . ¶ for no vilany doynge
þ argury s me of sophystry of siriud and of gyse by
faute of dyscesspon . ¶ z Dow sey me if y wer
mccu and scheusyd þe a puire syche y wold ȝyue þe
and seyde so þis y haue ȝyuyn to þe . ¶ kere yt kit þe
for it es le my skyll . ¶ yf it so wer þt y kere it
forthe and syn þt fond þt foure florente or fyue or
sett schuld it seme me . þt y had any thynge dysseyuid
re . yof þt y wer yir for a sophystry . ¶ Certane qd
ayt . nay . for me schuld thynke syche a ȝyfte full
of grete fredom and worschipe and grete curtasy

... and for nought y schuld travell me ...
... mmnows o none is tyme to leue armys
... ostyn any abydynge yf y" leue me a while ye y"
schall hald yam and kep yam to yᵗ ende yᵗ when yᵗ
schall be nede yai may lechr yᵉ yf yai be heuy.
go faire, for softe men far gos. ¶ ... ouer ys yᵉ
mule som tyme at sernt Jame yᵗ gose wildly, yan
is he yᵗ smytys hys hors, and spurs it and makys
hym go scharply, for myche soner he frudys encom
brans, yan ye mule yᵗ gos wildely thre wey.
Of yᵉ y" strlys of D. yᵗ yᵉ armr somtyme sayd
down y say yᵗ yf of hym y" wyll take ensawmppll
y wyll not vndyrtake yᵉ. ¶ 3ot y wold y" vn
dyrstond me how y" schall make yr foundement for
furst you shuld consydr his childhode for chyld he was
yᵗ tyme and lytill as ye story sayth. Also on ye toyer
syde ye armos wer not made for a popet, for yai wer
for ye sone of Saul ye grettest of ye contre. Wherfor
you shuld wele wnk yai were grete stuffed & rght
heuy. So yat yes two ynms behold and yam diligent
ly wyth grete syght & 3ys of ye armo & lerd yam
count. ¶ ffor Saul yai were gode but for 33 yai were
no ynmg worth. ffor yat yat is gode for a colt is not
gode for a stalonet & this is y Ar sers in ethis. but
if 33 had ben as grete as you and as he was syne
and yan he had onarmed hym certanly you were
yan caused for to take ensawmppll of hym and to
as he dyd but pus 3d he neu ne yus to do taght
he neuer. ¶ffor when he was becomyn a man he was
Armed in all wer, it nedis not to suppose yat he
onarmed to wer went, for if he had so gon on lyf

O. Oxford: Bodleian Library MS. Laud Misc. 740, f.44ᵛ; (Hands A, B).

Now I telle you lordyng how I fond myrch
ment in my wey. And I woll telle you it þat
more þat þan is grettest to me. And touchis me
moste. for in valeyes and in hillys, I se many
þyngys ynow of which I shuld neuer make ende
If I wold telle you all. And all so it shuld anoye to me
and to yo þat shuld here it. Now I say yow all, I went by
a wey þat I was takyn be for me I fond a see, wheþer in was   our life in worlde a
myche to be hole tempest, it was grelly of tempest, gret   sea of many aduersitees
and of wyus, men and women þer wer þat all clothys be
whan þer in. som has þer fete a botkne no more I see of þam.
oþer stode up ryghtis, I semes þay wolde haue stolkne for
some of þam has þeug þo, ne saw þe see letys þam. some oþir
I se a restis by þe fete and fast bone wyth long herbys þat
wer in þe see þat myche anoys þam. some oþir I se blyrses
be for I yeue I muck þuf farays of myche I helse me styll
at þis tyme. When I se siche þyngis, I afrays, I was
and grelly abaysshit sore god, mios I what þyng is, mє siche,
a se ght sait, I neuer þer sett, no siche, syditis, in my contre
ne se siche fyshe as me þynk, I se se se, now goo furthe may
I not me moste, torne agayne or her abyse in abysyng.

ÞE LYFE OF ÞE MANHODE

[f.5r] To þilke of þis regiown whiche han noon hows (but alle,
as seith Seynt Poul, be þei riche, be þei poore, be þei
wise oþer fooles, be þei kynges oþer queenes, alle þei ben
pilgrimes) I wole shewe yow a sweuene þat bifelle me þe
tooþer day. I hadde in wakinge rad and considered and wel   5
seyn þe faire romaunce of þe Rose, and I trowe wel þat þat
were thing þat most moovede me to mete þis swevene which I
wole after shewe yow. Now cometh neer and gadereth yow
togideres alle folk, and herkeneth wel; let þer be no man
nor womman þat drawe bakward: alle þei shulden putten hem   10
forth, alle þei shulden sitte and herkne, for þis towcheth
alle, boþe grete and smale, withouten any owttaken. In
[Frensch] I haue set it so þat lewede mowe vnderstande it;
and þerinne may {ic}he wight lerne whiche wey men shulden
taken and which forsake and leue: and þat is thing þat miche 15
nedeth to þilke þat in pilgrimage gon in þis wyilde worlde.
Now vnderstandeth þe swevene þat bifelle me in religioun at
þe abbey of Chaalit, as I was in my bed.
Me thowhte as I slepte þat I was a pilgrime and þat I
was stired to go to þe citee of Jerusalem in a mirour: and   20
me thouhte it was gret withoute mesure. I hadde aperseyued
and seyn þilke citee from ferre, and me thouhte it of riht
gret aray: þe weyes and þe aleyes of þilke citee boþe
withinne and abowte weren paved with gold, þe foundement
and þe masounrye of þe citee was set on hy and of newe stones 25
it was mad, and an hy wal enclosede it aboute. Many þer were
with[f.5v]inne of howses, of places and of dwellinges: [þere]
was al gladshipe, ioye withoute sorwe; [þere] hadde iche wight
(shortliche to passe me) generalliche of alle goodshipes
more þan euere þei cowde aske or thinke. But it discounforted   30
me michel þat eche wyght entred not at his wille, for þe
entre whiche was right strongliche kept. Cherubyn was
porter þerate, which heeld in his hand a foorbushed swerd
wel grownden with two sharpe egges, al skirmynge and
turnynge. Wel he coude helpe him þerwith for þer is noon,   35

kan he neuere so miche on þe bokelere, þat [þere] mighte passe
þat ded oþer wounded he [ne] shulde be; [nouht] þat þe
prince of þe cite, for he hadde manhode, [ne] receyuede deth
at þe [passage], and hadde þe spere in his side and left his
blood in [payage] alþouh he ouhte no raunsome; and so diden
also hise knyhtes, hise chaumpiouns, his sowdiours: alle
þei drunken of his chalys, and alle þei resseyueden deth
at þe passage. At þe kernelles ouer þe yate of whiche þe
porter forbereth noon, I seyh þe penselles hanginge steyned
red with blood. Whan I hadde aperceyued al þat, I sih þat
entre þere I muste needes, if þer were noon ooþer passage:
and algates bi thilke wey I seyh non but passe.* Eche was
agast whan he hadde seen Cherubyn, but hennesforthward
he may wel putte his brennynge swerd in safetee.

But right as I lyfte myne eyen an hy and biheeld,
a wol gret wunder I sigh, wherof I was gre{t}liche abashed:
Seint Austyn I sigh an hy on þe kernelles and sat and wel
semede a foulere oþer a [f.6r] feedere of briddes. With him he
hadde many ooþere grete maistres and doctours þat holpen to
feede þe briddes, for for þe feedinge þat þei hadden and þe
seed þat þei shadden bi croumede morcelles and here swete
[seyinges] and faire, many folk bicomen briddes and after flyen
euene upright. Many certeyn I seigh of Jacobines, of
Chanownes and of Augustines and of alle manere of folkes
lewed and seculere, clerkes and of [religious], and of beggeres
and of needy þat gadered hem feþeres and maden hem grete
wynges and sithen bigunnen to flee and for to clymbe hye into
þe citee. Aboue Cherubyn þei flyen, wherfore þei tooken n{o}
keep of his dawngere. Als soone as on þat ooþer side I turnede
my sight and my biholdinge, yit more I wundrede me
of a thing þat I seygh: aboue þe walles of þe citee I seygh
ooþere folk of auctoritee þat holpen here a{q}ueyntees and
bi sleyghtes putten hem in. First I seih Seynt Beneyt þat
on hy ayenst þe walles hadde a gret ladder dressed wherinne
weren stiked twelve degrees of humblisse bi whiche cloumben
wel swiftliche into þilke citee þilke þat weren of hise folk:
monkes blake and [white and greye], withoute vndertakinge of
any. After I seyh Seint Fraunceys þat wel shewed hym freend to
þilke of his religioun: for as I hadde in metinge, a corde
wel wriþen þat bi places was knet he hadde set dounward
þe wal, bi which eche þat was his aqueyntee ran up; þer was
noon, were his handes neuere so enoynted, þat he ne ran up

soone inowh and he gripede faste to þe knottes. Many ooþere
on þe walles I seih, of which I am not sure to telle yow
alle þe names nor how þei maden [f.6v] here aqueyntes
clymbe þider on alle sides, for only my lookinge was upon
þe side þat was to meward: ferþere miht I not see, wherfore
me forthouhte sore. But so miche I sey yow shortliche, þat
in þe wal þat was to meward I seih a dore litel and streyt,
which þe kyng of þe citee made keepe in equitee. þe keye
þerof he hadde taken to Seint Peeter, in whom he wel triste
and certeyn wel mihte triste in him, for þerbi he suffrede
noon to passe but oonli poore folk: for þilke þat lyeth nouht
hadde seyd þat þe riche mighte not entre þere no more þan a
camele miht passe thoruh þe eye of a nedele. þe entre was
wunder subtile, and eche wight oncloþed him and naked him at
þe entringe. þere men mihten fynde olde robes gret plente,
for þerbi passede non cloþed (but if he hadde o{f} þe kynges
robes, and þilke passeden al dai whaneuere þei wolden). Miche
likede me þis passage for þe commune avauntage þat alle folk
hadden þere if þei bicumen verrey poore. þer was no daungere
so men wolden despoile hem, and here olde robes leue withoute
for to haue newe withinne þe cloos. þis [thing] ouhte wel to
like, for [þer] is not miche to doone: þer was neuere noon
so riche þat he ne may be poore if he wole; and certeyn good
it is to be it, for to entre þerbi into swich a dwellinge, and
good it were to faste a litel for to haue ful saulee at þe
sopere. Now haue I seid yow shortlych inowh of þe faire citee,
how in þe faire mirour I aperceyued it, and þerfore to go I
meeved me, for þider I wolde be a pilgrime if I mihte elleswhere
see as I mette.* Noon [f.7r] reste I seygh, but wel me
thouhte þat gret reste I shulde haue had if I hadde be withinne
þe cloos. Neuere thouhte I to departe þens if I mihte
fulliche come þider.

As I hadde. thouht þis, anoon after I bithouhte me þat
me failede scrippe and bourdoun, and þat me needed to haue
hem: for it is thing wel sittinge to eche walkinge pilgrime.
þanne I ysede me out of myn hous in whiche I hadde ben ix
monethes of þe sesoun withouten any ysinge. A bordoun I bigan to
seeche, and a scrippe, necessarie to þat [þat] I hadde to doone.
And as I wente wepinge and bimenynge me, seechinge where I
mihte fynde a marchaunt þat mihte helpe me þerof, I seygh
a lady in my wey: of hire fairnesse she dide me ioye. She
seemede douhter to an emperour or to a king or to sum ooþer

gret lord. She hadde on a rochet beten with gold, and was
gert with a grene tissue þat was, as me thouhte, al along
arayed with charbuncles. On hire brest she hadde a broche
of gold, and in þe middes þerof þer was an {a}melle, and in þe
middes þerof a sterre, wherof certeyn I hadde gret wunder.
Hire hed was corowned with gold, and al aboute envirowned
with gret foisoun of shinynge sterres. Wurþi he was
certeyn þat hadde yive it hire and so arayed hire. Curteis
she was as me thouhte, for she saluede me first, and askede
me goodliche what I wente so seechinge. And þanne I was al
abashed, for I hadde not lerned þat a ladi of so gret aray
shulde deyngne to caste hire chere to meward. But anoon I
avisede me þat as I hadde lerned and woot wel, þat who þat
hath in him [f.7v] most bountee hath in him most humblesse,
and þe mo appelen þe tre bereth þe more she boweth to þe
folk. Humblesse is þe signe of goode hertes and of
benyngne, and ho þat bereth not in him thilke banere, hath
not in him hool bountee. þanne I answerde hire, and tolde
how it was bifalle me: þat I was excited to go to þe citee
of Jerusalem but þat I was sori bi as miche as I hadde
neiþer scrippe ne burdoun, and þat I wente seechinge hem,
and askinge hem heere and þere. And she answerde and seide:
"My freend," quod she, "if þow wolt heere goode tidinges
of þat þat þou seechest, come with me: for þer bifel þe neuere
so gret a good as þat þou hast founde me and met with me heere
today, for I wol helpe þe anoon of al þat euere þou hast
neede."

And þanne anoon I miht no lengere holde me þat
whateuere bifel me I ne wolde wite al: boþe hire name and what
she was. "Ladi," quod I, "youre name, youre cuntre and
youre regioun, and who ye ben, al I wolde fain in sooth wite,
and praye yow ye wole telle [it] me; and I trowe I shal be
þe gladdere." And þanne she answerde me and seyde: "In
time* I wole telle it þee: I wol noþer be to þee doutows ne
[suspeccionous]. I am douhter to þe emprour þat is lord aboue
alle ooþere. He hath sent me into þis cuntre for to gete him
freendes: nouht for þat he hath neede, but for þat
it were him riht leef to haue þe aqueyntaunce of alle folk
and þat oonliche for here owen profite. Seeste", quod she,
"how I am arayed and dight queynteliche with charbuncles and
with sterres, þow seye neuere noone fairere? And þat is for
to yive light to alle þo þat wolen take þe weye bi nyghte [f.8r]

and it is þat eche wight fynde me as wel bi day as bi nihte,
and bi nihte as bi day, so þat þei doo no folye. I am thilke
þat þou shuldest seeche whan þou gost into straunge londe:
for \as/ longe as þou hast me in cumpanye, þou miht haue no
better freend. If þou gost withoute me in þis cuntre, it
may not be þat þou ne be bihated boþe of my fader þe grete
kinge and of alle þo þat ben with him. þer may no wight do
wel withoute me: I am needeful to alle folk. þe world hadde
ben lost er þis ne hadde I mayntened it. Whoso hath me
with him, nothing faileth him, and who hath not me, alle
thinge faileth him. I am gouernouresse of alle thinge, and
of alle harmes I am leche: I make þe blynde see, and yive
strengthe to þe feeble; I reise þo þat ben falle; I
redresse þilke þat han [forveied], and I wole withdrawe me
fro no folk but from hem þat sinnen dedly, and of swiche
I haue no cure as longe as þei ben in swich unclennesse.

Grace Dieu I am cleped, ne ooþerwyse am I not nempned.
Whan þou shalt haue neede of me, so þow shalt clepe me: and
certeyn þat shal be riht ofte er þou come fulliche* to þe
citee þat þou hast seyn, for þou shalt fynde lettinges
and mischeeves of aduersitees and encombraunces which þou
miht not passe withoute me (noþer þou ne noon ooþer),
leeue me right wel. And þouh þou mihtest passe foorth or
eskape without me (which thing may not be) yit I sey þee
þat into þe dwellinge of Jerusalem þou shalt not entre
withoute me, ne sette þi foot þerinne: for alþouh þou
haue seyn many thinges and aperceyued þat summe entren
al naked, [f.8v] and þat summe fleen in bi aboue, and þat
summe entren bi sleyhtes, and summe ooþere bi Cherubyn,
þer entreth noon but bi me, be þou riht siker: for þilke
þat ben naked* I make hem uncloþe hem withoute, for to
cloþe hem þe bettere ayen withinne; ooþere I make feþere
with my vertues for to flee wel, and þanne afterward þei
flee as I wole. þis þou hast wel seyn at eye. Ooþere I
putte in þe beste wise I can to assaye, so þat alle I
make hem passe in and entre. Now þou miht wite withoute
dredinge wheþer myn aqueyntance be good. If þee like it,
sey it anoon, and let þi speche no lengere be hyd."

And þanne anoon I answerde: "Lady, I crye yow mercy
for þe loue of God þat with yow ye wole aqueynte me and
þat ye wole neuere leue me: þer is nothing so necessarie
to me to þat þat I haue to doone. And gretliche I thanke

165

170

175

180

185

190

195

200

yow þat goodliche ben come first to me for my goode. I
[hadde] of nouht elles neede. Now ledeth me wher ye wole:
I pray yow tarieth nouht." Thanne she took me in þilke
same houre and taryede me no lengere but ledde me into
an hows þat was hires [as] she seide, and tolde me þat
þere I shulde fynde al þat I hadde neede of. She hadde
founded þilke hous and masowned it, as she seyde, xiii C
yer and xxx bifore þat time as she wiste wel. I seyh
þilke hows with good wille, and yit at þe sihte I
abashed me, for it heeng al on hy in þe eyr, and was
bitwixe þe heuene and þe eerþe riht as þouh it hadde come
þider and alight from þe heuene. It hadde steples and
faire toures, and his aray was right fair—but it
discounforted me riht michel þer was a water bifore it
and þat needes I muste passe [f.9r] it if I wolde entre into
þe hous. Ship ne bregge ne plaunke was þer noon, and yit
þe water was deep, as I aperceyued wel after whan I was
al plounged þerinne. And þanne I bigan to speke to
Grace, and askede how I miht askepe, and whi þer was
suich passage, and if þer were owher elles any ooþer, and
þat bi ordre she shulde say me what good þat water shulde
do me.

Thanne she answerde: "þow what seiste!" quod she,
"Art abasht for so litel? þou wolt go into Jerusalem and
þou shuldest passe þe grete see (þe grete see is [þis] world
heere which is right ful of gret anoye of tempestes, and
of tormentes, and of grete wyndes) and how mihtest þou
passe it whan þou hast gret drede of so litel? Heere þou
shuldest haue no drede, for as þou ouhtest wel to wite
þer passe heere mo litel children þan grete men or olde:
heere is þe firste passage of alle goode [pilgrimage]. þer
is noon ooþer wey bi noon ooþer place, saue onliche bi
Cherubyn (þerforth hauen somme passed, and in here owen
blood han wasshen hem); and neuerþeles þouh þou woldest
take þi wey bi Cherubyn, yit i{s} not þis wey contrarie
{to þe}e, but is to þee certeyn right nessessarye:
for if þou loo{ke} whenes þou comest, and þe hows [ful] of
dunge in whiche þow hast be ix monethes, þou hast miche
neede to washe þee. And þerfore I rede þee to passe heer
foorth, for {þ}ou shalt passe no [surer] wey. Heerbi passede
a king sumtime þat assurede wel þe paas (and þat was thilke
þat made þe paas, which was nouht foul ne [ne] misdede not). If

þow wolt passe it, sey it now and I wole do come þee [hider]
a special sergeaunt of myne þat of God is official. He is
keepere of my meyne, and ministre of thilke passage. þilke
shal [f.9v] helpe þee to passe, to baþe þee, to washe þee;
þilke shal also crosse þee, for he shal see anoon þat þou
wolt go ouer þe see and conquere Jerusalem: and for þat þow
shalt þe lasse drede þine enemyes he shal sette a crosse
upon þi breste, anooþer bihynde þee and also anooþer upon
þin heed for þou shalt þe lasse drede alle mischeues. He
shal enoynte þee as a chaumpioun, so þat þou shalt not preyse
at a bodde alle þine enemyes. Now answere anoon what is þin
avys." And þanne I seyde: "It is my desire þat anoon ye
make him come to me." Thanne cam to me at hire comaundement
þe official of whiche I haue spoke bifore; and he took me
bi þat on hand and put me into þe same water: þere he wesh
me, þere he bathed me, and thryes he plounged me þerinne.
Grace gabbed me of nothing: he crossede me, and enoyntede
me wel, and sithe ledde me into þe hows, where þer is riht
noble and fair herberwh. And þere Grace made me fayr
semblaunt: fairere þan she hadde do bifore. þere she seide
she wolde shewe me many thinges and teche me, and þat I
shulde do riht gret wysdom, if I wolde vnderstonde it. Riht
as she spak þus I sigh many merueyles anoon, of which I wol
not holde me stille þat I ne wole sumwhat seye. Sithe
afterward whan my time cometh I wole telle yow of my skrippe
and \of/ [my] burdoun which I desirede (for I shal haue leiser
inouh).

First I seih in þilke place as in þe middes þerof þe
signe of Thau which was peynted reed with þe blood of þe
white lamb: þat is þe signe with which Goddes seruauntes ben
marked amyddes þe forhed. And þis I sigh apertlyche, if my
meetinge gabbe me [f.10r] nouht: a maister I sigh faste by þat
seemede to be a vicarie of Aaron or of Moyses, for I sigh him
holde in his hand a yerde crooked at þe eende, and his hed he
hadde horned. He was cloþed with a robe of lynene, and I trowe
wel of sooth þat he were thilke of which Ezechiel speketh of in
his ix chapitre, for in þe folkes forhedes he sette þe holi
Tahu with whiche he blissede hem. It was, as he seide, þe
tokne bi which God shulde be to hem benigne, for he wole þat
alle hise folk be marked [with] swich a tokne in þe forhed. With
þilke tokne Grace Dieu made blisse me, and marke me in þe
forhed: and þerof I was miche þe gladdere, for I hadde wel

250

255

260

265

270

275

280

285

neede þerof, nouht of necessite but of sittinge congruitee.

Afterward I sigh þat þilke maister made oynementes þat he took to þe forseide officiall, in seyinge swiche woordes: "Lo heere iii wurþi oynementes þat I take þee for alle folk. With þe firste tweyne þou shalt enoynte alle þo þat shulen be pilgrimes and wolden be champiouns. þe thridde shal be for þe woundede, for þe hurte, and for þe brusede and for þilke þat shulen ligge in here dede beddes withoute havinge counfort: with þis oynment þow shalt enoynte hem, and be to hem trewe leeche and suer, enoyntinge hem oueral bisyliche þat han neede. þerof certeyn hauen gret neede alle pilgrimes and alle walkers þat passen bi þis eerþe, for alle þei be euere more in werre: wherfore it may not be þat þei ne beeth ofte yuele iled and hurte, and perfore neede þei haue at here eendinge of þis oynment. Now enoynte hem withoute failinge, for perfore I take þee þe oynment. Of summe oynementes [f. 10v] to meward (to enoynte þe newe kynges, for Moyses vicaryes, and for leches as þow art, and for þe boord on whiche we eten, and for Tahu þat I make in þe forhedes) I withholde to myself þe execucioun, þe vse and þe administracioun. Now keep þe þat þou mistake þe not to meward, ne misdoo nouht."

As þei speken þus bitwixe hem tweyne and ordeyned here oynementes, anoon a mayden cam doun of a tour toward hem, þat was cleped Resoun as Grace hadde tolde me. She bigan to speke to hem, and seyde withoute flateringe: "Lordinges, þat þus diuisen and speken of youre oynementes, and holden heere youre parlement of enoyntinge of ooþer folk: vnderstondeth now tw{o} litele woordes þat I wole soone haue vnclosed yow. Oynement is softe thinge boþe to opne wounde and to shitte. Softe it shulde be leyd with an {euene} instrument and a softe; softe he shulde be þat hath it, for to gret rudeshipe mysbifalleth: he þat is hurte hath noon neede to be rudeliche treted (for sumtime rudeshipe mihte hurte more þan þe oynement shulde helpe). þilke ben rude þat ben felle and cruelle as lyouns þat wolen thoruh vengen hem, withoute anything [levinge] or sparinge: and swiche ben no goode surgiens, ne leches, ne fisiciens, for þei wolen take here oynementes to rudeliche to hem þat ben hurte. And perfore I am descended and come to avise you, þat þer be in yow no rudeshipe, ne crueltee, ne felnesse: but beeth pitous to yowre woundede folk, and merciable, and softe.

Treteth hem alle sweteliche, and þanne shal youre oynement   330
stonde in stede. Ye shulde ofte bithinke yow þat ye were
enoynted for to bicome [f.11r] softe, pitowse and debonayre,
withoute doinge [crueltee any time]: and þat ye be not rigurowse
bi felnesse no day in yowre live, and þat ye shulde foryive
alle harmes and stonde to God. For if þe prophete gabbe   335
not, he hath withholde to him alle [vengeaunce]: and þerfore
whoso wole bineme it him, to yuel ende he may come." Whan
Resoun hadde þus spoken, þe vicarie of whiche I seide
bifore answerde hire and seide: "Sey me I praye you if
ye can: whi I haue þus myn hed horned, and þe yerde sharp   340
at þe eende? Is it not for to do punishinge and correccioun
of yuel dedes? I trowe I shulde putte and hurtle þe yuel
folk with myne hornes, and prikke hem with þe sharpe ende
raþere þan enoynte hem with þe oynement." "Mi faire swete
freend," quod Resoun: "now vnderstonde me yit a litel.   345
þow knowest wel what þou hast seyd, but þou hast not yit
lerned al. þow shuldest haue manere, as þow ouhtest wel to
wite, to prikke and to hurtle. First þou shuldest softeliche
avise hem and teche hem þat þou seest erre, and sithe if
þow seest hem obstinat þou hast good leeue to prikke hem: 350
it longeth wel to þin office to do iustice of wikkede folk,
but first be softe er þou be oþer prikkinge or rigurowse.
And yit I sey þee a poynt ferþere: if þou haue rigurowsliche
hurtled any wyght oþer prikked for his misdede, looke þou
haue not doon it withoute þe sweete oyle of compassioun   355
and of pitee; for þouh þou be horned for iustice, algates in
þin herte þou shuldest haue pitee of þilke þat þou hast
iuged. Bithinke þee þat þou were enoynted er þow were
horned, and er þow haddest any prikke, and er þow haddest
any yerde oþer staf: and þat ouhte michel softe þee whan   360
þow wolt correcte any wyght. [f.11v] þow shuldest not also
foryete of whom þow doost þe vicariship. For þer was
neuere noon more debonaire þan þilke whos vicary þow art:
þat was he þat seemed horned and was not horned (þat was
Moyses þat made Israel to passe thoruh þe see) þat with þe   365
yerde he held he made hem good passage. Now vndirstonde
þis lessoun, for it is to þee woorth a gret sermoun. þouh
þou seme horned withoute, lat þin herte be al naked withinne;
and be merciable withinne, whateuere þow be withoute. Fallas
þou miht make heerinne withoute misdoinge. Haue þin herte   370
tretable and debonayre after þin ensample: þouh þou haue a

yerde sharp at þe eende, bihold also how it is crooked and
stowpeth toward þat ooþer ende. Dowte not þat þat \ne/
tokeneth þer shulde be in þee humblesse whan þou chastisest
bi equitee. Now vnderstond why þilke yerde is taken
þee and graunted þee. It is to gouerne with þi peple, and
make hem passe thoruh þe foorde of þis world. With þi yerde
þow shuldest assaye if it be to deep or if þer neede oþer
brigge or plaunke; for if þer failede eiþere brigge or
plaunke it shulde longe to þee to make it: and þerfore þi
name is Pontifex. Now vnderstonde it: þis is þi lessoun.

Now I wule sey þee yit, if þow wolt vnderstonde to me a
litel, whi þou hast þis faire yerd, and whi horned hed þou
hast. Sumtime in þis place riht heere enhabited þe hornede
of helle, and long time bi possessioun he hadde maad heere
his dwelling. But for it displesed to Grace Dieu, þat hadde
mad þe hous for to dwelle þerinne hirself, she made arme
þee with þese hornes, and made take þee þe [f. 12r] yerde: so
þat bi þee wente out þe vntrewe dwellere þat wolde be lord.
þow hurtledest him with þine hornes whan þou puttest him
out of þe place, and þow beete him with þi yerde whan þou
madest him [ysen] out of þe place. þe tweyne faire labelles
hanginge at þi tweyne hornes þou conqueredest at þe
clensinge and sweepinge and poorginge of þe place: and þat
was whan þou dediedest and halwedest and blissedest þe
place. And for þat þou were a good champioun in þe
dedicacioun Grace Dieu wole þat þou arme þe ofte in þe armes
þat þou were victour inne, in tokne þerof \and/ warnynge þat
it falle þee not in foryetinge, and to þat ende also þat
þilke vntrewe þat þou hast discoumfyted and hurtled and
beten doun be no customere to come þereas þow art, and
also to þat eende þat þou be nih and fresh to fighte newe
in alle times and in alle sesouns ayens þilke þat wolen
exile þe hous of Grace Dieu and dispoile it of hire
goodes bi dymes and taxes, bi violences and bi extorciouns.
But þerof, as I wot wel of sooth, þow doost not wel þi
deuoir: for þiself grauntest hem and shewest þe weyes to
haue hem, þe which thing Grace Dieu halt no game. And
þerfore I sey þee withoute flateringe þat it is but a jape
of þine hornes and of þi staf: þine hornes ben of a snayl
þat hyden hem for a straw anoon as þei haue felt it.

Seynt Thomas hadde none swiche hornes, which
strongliche defended þe king þe entre and þe wey into his

hous: for wrongfulliche and withoute cause he wolde make it
thral þer it shulde alwey be free. þe wurthi man hadde   415
levere dye þan suffre [f.12v] it to be thral. Of Seint Ambrose
also I sey þee, þat defended his hous ayens emperoures and
emperises, so þat he was lord þerof alone. 'Youre paleys',
quod he, 'ye haue: youre toures, youre castelles and youre
citees, þe reuenewes of þe empire; wel ouhte þis to   420
suffice yow. Of myn hous medle ye nouht: leueth it me—ye
haue nothing þerinne. In my tyme it shal neuere be thral:
I hadde leuere leese þe lyfe.' þese hadden not hornes ne [ne]
beren hem nouht withoute resoun. If þou were also wel
horned in defendinge þe fre vsages of þin hous þat þow hast   425
wedded [and] with þe ring which þou hast on þi fynger,* and if
þow vsedest wel þi yerde, and argudest wel Pharaon, seynge him
þat he suffrede þi folk serue God withoute thraldom, and
þat he lettede hem not ne oppressed hem ne greued hem of
nothing, þanne were þou goode Moyses, and seruedest Grace   430
Dieu with hire goode mes;* and michel shulde plese hire alle
times þat she wiste þee armed. Now do so hensforward and
þi wurshipe shal be þe grettere.''

As Resoun spak þus to Moyses and prechede, þe official
turned him and bar with him þe oynementes, and putte hem in   435
saaf. And sithe I sigh as me thouhte a wommam toward þe
west, and a man toward þe est, þat comen boþe to þe
official anoon. And eche of hem took him his hand, and he
took hem and ioyned hem togidere and sithe seide hem,
as me thouhte: "Ye tweyne shule be boþe oon, and iche   440
of yow bere trowthe to ooþer. Neuere dayes of youre lyue
shal þer departinge be maad of yow tweyne, but þer be
certeyn cause, and bi Moises þat is þere. Now keepeth wel þis
sacrament, and loueth yow togideres trewelich.'' [f.13r] And
thilke tweyne biheighten þat þei so shulden; and þanne þei   445
departeden .þens. þe official turnede ayen and wente to
Moises, þat was yit at þe sermoun þat Dame Resoun made him.
But as þei weren alle togederes and speken, a gret cumpany
of folk maden cesse here parlement anoon: bifore Moises
þei comen, and maden him requeste þat sum seruice in his   450
hous he wolde yiue hem and graunte hem.

And þanne he took a peyre sheren, and made summe of
hem come neer him, and clippede hem anoon, in seyinge
hem þat God shulde be here part and here heritage: suffice
it shulde if þei weren wise. Whan Moyses hadde þus doon,   455

Reso*u*n droowh hire anoon towardes hem, and bigan to speke
to hem, and seide: "Lordinges," quod she, "entendeth
hider. It is gret wysdom, what any man saye, su*m*time to
feyne folye: þouh ye be shoren and clipped as fooles upon
þe hed þis folie is gret wysdom, for þerfore I p*r*esente
me to be alwey youre freend, whosoeu*er*e hath þerto envye.
Forsaketh nouht þis loue, for ye shole haue it bifore alle
folk. If it ne be long on yowre folie,* and if ye wol not
haue me, ye shule neu*ere* haue good freend in youre lyue.
I am Reso*u*n bi whom ye been [discerned] from ooþere bestes:
and oonliche as longe as ye shule haue me ye shule be men.
And whan ye wole go w*ith*oute me ye shul wel mown ava*u*nte
yow—ye be but as do*u*mbe bestes and as coltes þat ben
cloþed. Withoute me ye shul neu*ere* haue wurshipe, be ye
neu*ere* so grete lordes. If ye [wole] make jugementes,
silogismes o*þ*ere argumentes withoute me, shul ye neu*ere*
haue conclusio*u*n þat ne shal come to confusio*u*n. [f.13v] Now I
wule telle yow, if ye wite it nouht, how ye shule keepe my
loue. Ye muste ete and drinke more sobirliche þan ooþer
folk, for drunkenesse and glotonye maken me soone t*u*rne to
flight. Ire þat is vnmesured and felonye þe woode maken me
voide þe hous in which þei haue here habitac*i*o*u*n. Fleschliche
loue driueth me al out and soone maketh me voide þe place:
and þat withoute glose ye mowen se in þe roma*u*nce of
þe Rose. Now I pray yow", quod she, "þat ye keepe yow fro
alle þese vices if ye loue me, and fro alle ooþere also,
for I holde not him to freend þat aba*u*ndoneth him to vices.

Yit I wole telle yow", quod she, "tweyne shorte woordes of
þe shorne place which is enclosed al aboute ro*u*nd with a
seercle as þouh it were a castel or a towr*e*. A gardyn it
seemeth wel enclosed with a heygh wal. þe place withinne
vnheled sheweth *þat* yowre hertes shulden ben opne al
holliche to God, w*ith*oute any mene empechement. þe
ro*u*nde sercle maketh þe closure aboute *þat* ye haue
no cur*e* of þe world; for from [him] ye muste departe if
with youre God ye wole parte: ye mow*e*n not haue boþe
tweyne togideres, þat mown ye wel wite, for ye haue seyd
youreself þat youre God ye haue chosen to heritage and to
your*e* p*a*rtye (bi whiche seyinge I se nouht þat ye shulden
reioyse of þe world, for whan any wight wole parte, I
vnderstonde not he may haue al, but taketh þat oon and
leueth þat ooþer.) Now taketh þat þat ye haue chose: a

better part mown ye not haue. Suffice it oughte, for I
doute not þat þilke part ne is worth al þe remenaunt.
Fair to yow [f.14r] þanne is [þe] closure þat closeth yow and   500
walleth yow in disseueringe yow from þe world, and
departeth wel yowre part. {Of} þe place shorn is also fair
to yow, for þerbi men apperceyuen þat [ye] been goode heerdes.
It is wel right þat þe goode heerde take sumtyme flees
of hise bestes for his labour. Shere yow [yowre] shepherde   505
may at his neede, but to skorche yow is not yiue him
leeue: for men han not taken him al,* but oonliche sheres
for to shere yow with dueliche.''

Whan Resoun hadde þus spoken to hise shorene, and
preched to ooþere þat weren þere, Moises yaf seruices   510
gladliche as þei askeden: for summe he made [priuees] of
his hous and chamberleynes, and ooþere he made sergeauntes
for to areste and putte out þe enemyes þat ben in þe
bodyes. To ooþere he dide gret wurshipe, for to alle he
yaf leue to be rederes of his paleys, and to preche   515
Goddes lawe. Summe ooþere he made holde candeles to
serue to þe grete boord þat was set þer he shulde ete. To
ooþere he took his gilte cuppe void, with which his
bord is wurshiped, for to serue him þerwith. To ooþere
he made bere þe bodi of Ihesu Crist upon here oo shulder   520
þer he sette it: and was upon þe lifte shulder, þat to
bere with shulde be þe strengere. þilke he wolde bi
especial weren ministres and serueres to him and to þe
official at þe boord and coadiutowres.

Whan al þis was ordeyned as it is aboue diuised,   525
eche of hem bigan to serue to deserue his office. þe
bord þei wenten and maden redy, for it was time to dine.
Summe spredden þe cloþes, ooþere leyden þe bred aboue,
ooþere brouhten þe wyn and casten it in þe cuppe (and
þerwith, as me thouhte, a litel water þei dide). [f.14v] But   530
bifore [he wente] to dinere, Moises wolde deliuere him
of summe þat yit abiden him and weren not yit deliuered;
and þilke he wolde make special officialles of his hous,
to helpe þat ooþer official (which hadde wel neede, for
as he seide, he mighte nouht aloone gouerne swich an hows).   535

Now I wole telle yow how he dide. First he clepede
Grace Dieu with an [hauteyn] vois al were it she was not
fer. She sat in hire trone and of alle she took keep,
and I sat at hire feet, wherof I was ioyeful and glad.

Whan she herde hire cleped, she ros hire up withoute
abidinge and wente hire to Moyses, and with hire she
ledde me. And þanne whan Moyses sigh hire nyh him he*
bigan to wexe more hardy, and fulliche dide þat þat I
wole telle yow shortlyche. First he [anoynede] þe handes
of hem and ioynede hem togideres, sithe took a swerd
wel kervinge, cleer and furbished, and brennynge, with
tweyne egges, and handsom, turnynge and variable.
Wel me thouhte it was þilke þat I hadde seyn Cherubyn
holde: and þilke it was treweliche, wel propirliche
figured. þilke swerd he took hem and þerof made hem
present with a keye þat he heeld, þat Grace Dieu hadde
take him. Grace hireself (whiche was þere þat to do
þis halp him) he yaf hem, and seyde hem: "Loo heere
Grace Dieu:" quod he, "taketh hire to yow; I yive
hire yow \in/to cumpany, to þat ende þat ye make of hire
youre freend." Whan I herde þilke woord I was wroth
and abashed, and seyde: "Allas, what shal I do if I
haue þus lost Grace Dieu? þilke hornede hath yive hire
to þese newe officialles: I hadde leuere to be ded þan
he hadde doon me swich wrong." [f.15r] Whan Grace Dieu
sigh me þus discounforted, faste she lowh of me, and
sithe clepede me and seyde: "Fool, wherto gost þou þus
thinkinge? Wenest þou for to haue me aloone to freend?
þow ouhtest wite þat commune profite is þe beste. And
þe profite of a commune welle is miche grettere þer
eche man and womman may drawe water at here wille and
haue þerof here esement: þan is a welle closed þer
neuere oon dar neighe approche; and yit I sey þee
þat profitable, so good, ne so delitable þe water þow
hast alone ne shal be as þilke shal be þer eche man goth.
I am welle of alle goodnesses. Neuere holde I me
enclosed: I wole profite to alle folk, and alle I wole
loue peramowres. And þerinne mihte þou leese nothing,
but it may encrese þi good, for alle þilke þat I wole
loue I wole make þi freendes, and þe mo goode freendes
þow hast, þe bettere þow shalt be, me thinketh. Now haue
noon envye þouh I be freend to oopere."

    Whan I was þus counforted ayen of Grace, þat hadde
avised me, anoon I sygh Dame Resoun go to þe chayere
to preche. "Lordinges," quod she: "vnderstondeth me:
youre profyite lyth þerinne, I trowe. Biholdeth wel þe

grete benefet and þe grete [goodshipe] þat Grace Dieu
hath doon yow, þat þis day is comen and descended for yow.
Considereth what yiftes bi hire Moises hath departed
yow: for þe swerd he hath take yow þat God hadde forged   585
for him for to keepe with þat no sinnere entrede into
þe cuntre of whiche he is lord. Now vnderstondeth what
swerd it is: how it is perilouse to fooles, how miche þei
shulden drede it þat shulden vse it. þe swerd serueth of
iii thinges, for whan any deserueth peyne he smiteth   590
with þe poynt oþer with þe egge, oþer elles with þe
flat in spa[f.15v]ringe. þe poynt yiueth techinge
þat þer be neuere do jugement withoute gret discrecioun
in þe doinge of þe execucioun* of cause nouht yknowe,
but hid and vnknowe. Michel is he of foolhardiment and   595
of surquideoures þinkinge þat bi ire wole venge him or
juge bi suspeccioun. Michel is a swerd yuel sittinge
to blynd man and to purblynd man þat wole smyte at
þe tastinge* and kannot cheesen good from yuel. þer
shulde no man bere þilke swerd þat cannot wel discerne   600
bitwixe helthe and sikenesse, bitwixe þe grete meselrie,
and þe mene and þe [lasse]. A juge shulde wel vnderstonde
þe circumstaunces of a misdede, bifore þat any jugement
were doo. Swerd, as I fynde writen, is clepid departinge
of throte. Wel aughten alle juges þat wolen wel iuge   605
departe þe throte, and wel discerne þat men seyn: for
right after þat he hath herd allegge he shulde do his
jugement, and non ooþerwise.

Now I wole telle yow of þe tweyne egges for whiche
þe swerd is cleped kervinge (wherto oo paas alone   610
sufficeth not to telle),* and what techinge lyth
þerinne. If ye haue yowre swerd poynted and sharp
bi discrecioun, it is wel riht þat ye haue justice
in youre lond aboue alle vices: þat alle misdedes
and alle sinnes ye haue leeue to correcte, excepted   615
þe cas withholden þat þe grete horned hath withholden.
And for [þat] youre lond is departed in doble partye,
þerfore it needeth þat þe swerd haue tweyne kervinges as
answeringe to hem. þat oon partye is þe bodi of þe
manhede, þat men clepen man withoute; and þat ooþer is   620
þe gost, þat is cleped man withinne. þat is youre lond
þat is in tweyne: departed [f.16r] it is withoute beinge
tweyne. þese tweyne as [Hy] Justice ye mown whan it is time

iustifye: to þe bodi for hise sinnes ye mown yiue trauaile
and peyne inouh, and charge it with penaunces for to
driue without þe sinnes; to þe gost for diuerse cas, as
whan it is obstinate in his sinne and wol not amende for
amonestinge, ye mown turne to þe kervinge withoute any
sparinge. Hurte hym ye mown dedliche bi þe strok of
cursinge: and þer is no wounde so cruelle, for withoute
remedye it is dedlych; and þerfore he auhte michel drede
him þat feeleth swich a strok perce on him. Wel auhte he
also bithinke hym þat shulde smite with þe egge; and wel
I telle yow þat dueliche þerwith smyt noon but if he haue
first smite with þe flat of þe swerd, oþer þat he hath
avised first þilke þat he wole so smyte and make deye bi
þilke strok. Bi þe [platte] of þe swerd I vnderstonde good
and trewe avisement, trewe amonestinge and liueliche
prechinge, whiche smit þe euele dedes in sparinge, and
spareth hem in wel smytinge: þat is þe woord of Ihesu
Crist, in whom lyth þe respyt of þe deth. With þe
platte ye shulden vsen whan ye seen youre subiectes
erre: sermonynge and prechinge maketh many times leue
sinne, and if ye mown so saue hem it is bettere þan to
smite with þe sharpe. Now ye hauen þanne how ye mown
and shulden after diuerse cas vse boþe of þe [platte] and
of þe kervinge oþer of þe poynt in wel juginge: for oo
time ye shulden iuge, anooþer time ye shulden punishe,
anooþer time preche; and þerfore it is cleped withoute fable
sharp on boþe sides, and varyinge. þilke swerd is taken
yow to þat ende þat ye haue it alwei redy to [f.16v] turne it
and to varie it at youre wille, and remeve it after þat þe cas
asketh, and right and euenenesse is; and þerfore is
right þat ye hatten, as wel bi effect as bi name, Cherubyn
ful of kunnynge and of [deuyne] wisdom. For if ye weren
not Cherubyn, many harmes ye mihten doo, as whan ye shulden
smite with þe [platte] perauenture ye wolden turne youre
swerd and smite with þe kervinge; oþer whan ye shulden
iuge, ye wolden correcte bifore, doinge al þe contrarie of
þat þat were to doone. And þerfore in vnkunnynge hand is
not þis swerd wel sittinge, and also in irows mannes
hand þis swerd is riht perilous, for brenninge it was take
and graunted bi Grace Dieu: þe cause is (if ye wole wite it)
for, howeuere ye turne it, be it in prechinge or in iuginge,
in punishinge or in correctinge, ye shulden shewe it

brennynge of verrey loue and charite, for loue is þe
brennynge fyre þat maketh it flawme.

Now I wole telle yow (if ye witen nouht) whi ye haue
þis swerd. Porteres ye ben, as me thinketh, of þe kyngdom of
heuene. þe keyes ye haue, withoute lesinge, for to shette þe   670
doore and for to opne it; withoute yow may no wight passe.
Ye keepen þe pas of þe entre in. To yow men muste shewe
what [men] bringen, bifore [men] passen þe yate. Alle manere of
fardelles, smale and grete, maad and in makinge, bifore yow
musten be vntrussed and al vnfold and al shewed. þer is   675
nothing so wel closed þat it ne shulde be vnclosed bi
verrey shewinge of hol shrifte. Now looketh wel þat ye
haue take þilke swerd and þilke keyes bi avisement. Ye shulden
[f.17r] [make] noon passe þat wole not shewe his fardelle:
ye shulden seeche þe sinneres and make hem discharge hem   680
of here misdedes. Alle ye shulden weye wysliche, and
iuge hem discreteliche, keepinge wel þe verrey interpretacioun
of youre name, to þat eende þat men mown bi riht clepe yow and
nempne yow Cherubyn. And þanne whan ye haue al iseyn and al
biholde and knowe and iuged þe misdedes, and charged þe peynes   685
and enioyned wurthi penaunces, þanne ye mown vnshette þe
doore and make youre penauntes entre in. þis is þe tokne of
þe swerd, and þe shewinge of þe keyes, and þe lernynge and
þe techinge. Now keepeth yow wel þat ye vse discreteliche
with hem as ye shulde.''   690

Whan Resoun hadde þus spoken, and I hadde al seyn and
herd, lust took me and gret desire for to haue þis brennynge
swerd and þe keyes þerwith for to be vsshere of þilke passage,
and porter. But to what ende I shulde come þerof I hadde
nowht yit thouht. It is \thing/ bifalleth ofte: for of [þat]   695
þat wil taketh men seen nouht allwey þe eende. As I hadde þus
ythouht, I wente me to Moyses, preyinge him þat he wolde yiue
me þilke faire swerd and graunte me þat I mihte haue þe
vsage of þe keyes for to keepe þilke forseyde passage. Moyses,
whan he hadde herkned me, he sheþede þe faire swerd and bond   700
faste þe keyes, and enseled al wel wyseliche, and sithe took
me and graunted me boþe þat oon and þat ooþer benigneliche,
in seyinge to me þat I lookede wel þat I vnbond not þe
keyes, ne þat I stired not þe swerd forto I hadde leeue.[f.17v]

Whan he hadde seide me þis I was abashed, for I hadde   705
seyn noon to whom he hadde þus idoo neiþer of woord ne of
dede. Faste I bithouht me what I shulde do, or what I

miht do with þilke swerd ysheþed, seled, wrapped, and with
þe keyes þat he had take me also enseled and wel ybounden.
I wende ful wel he had desceyued me, whan I apperceyued
Grace Dieu; she led me to Resoun þat spak to me: "My
faire freend," quod Resoun þe wise, "what thinkest in þi
corage? Where lernedest þou at scole? þi thouht is wel
foolliche. I see wel þou hast not lerned þe predicament
of Ad Aliquid. þilke predicament hath reward elleswhere
þan to himself: he maketh his edifyinge upon ooþeres ground
wol wisliche; al þat he hath, he hath of ooþere, and yit
dooth wrong to no wight. If ooþere ne were, þer shulde
nothing be of it, ne [ne] miht be. Ensaumple I wole take þee
so þat þou mowe see þat at eye, cleerliche vndirstande,
and wel lerne and withholde. Whan God had mad þe world,
bifore þat man was foormed he was onlich cleped God (if
Genesis ne gabbe). But whan man was foormed þanne was God
cleped Lord, in tokne þat whan he hadde seruauntes he was
lord and lordshipinge. Whan he hadde seruauntes þanne he
was Lord, and yit he was neuere þe grettere. But þe lordes
of þis cuntre ben not swich, as me thinketh, for þe mo
seruauntes þei haue so miche þei make hem þe grettere:
here seruauntes and here meyne yiuen hem lordshipe. Lordship
was knyt in subgis and engendred, and if þe subgis ne were,
lordshipes shulden perishen. þat oon and þat ooþer Ad
Aliquid may be seid as me thinketh, for þat oon hath his
comyng out and his hanginge of þat ooþer: for whan þat oon
is, þat ooþer is also; and whan þat oon faileth, þat ooþer
faileth also. [f.18r]
    Now vnderstond wel þis lessoun þow [þat] art in subiectioun:
bihold wel þat þou art subiect to ooþere and þou hast no
subiect. þi souereyn, whateuere he be, hath jursdiccioun,
miht and lordship ouer þee. But oo thing disceyveth þee:
þou hast no subiect as he hath; for þerbi þou hast failed
to haue þe faire swerd vnheled, naked and vnsheþed—and of
þe keyes also, to haue hem vnwounden and vnseled. With þe
swerd naked what shuldest þow do, and with þe keyes vnheled,
þouh þou haddest hem? Nothing, þat I see, but gret folye. If
I bere a knyf vnsheþed and naked, and hadde nothing to kerue,
I shulde make þe folk to weene þat I were a fool or þat I
wolde wounde or sle sum wight. If I bere keyes also naked
and wente thoruh þe strete þer I hadde neiþer dore ne lok,
sum men mihten weene perauenture þat I bere false keyes, or

þat I wente to robbe þe folk: and lightliche men mihten
thinken, whan men seyen my keyes liche þe keyes þat ooþer   750
men hadden, þat with hem I vnshette here dores.* Serteyn þi
keyes han wardes, as þe straungeres han, and þerfore I sey
þee, sithe þou hast nothing to shette ne to vnshette, and
sithe þow hast nothinge to kerue ne to kutte, it is bettere   755
þi swerd be sheþed þan vnsheþed, and it is bettere þe keyes
þat þou hast ben hid þan vnhyd, for al bitimes may men come
to vnkeuere boþ[e] þat oon and þat ooþer. þus Moises took
hem þee wysliche and dueliche, to þat ende þat whan þi
souereyn wole, and seeth time, he mai vnbynde þee þe keyes   760
and vnsheþe þe swerd: and þat shal be whan he wole take
þe of his subgis to helpe him, whan he wole take þee matere
wherupon þou miht werche; and elles þou miht nothing doo,
if þou ne wolt misdoo. Perile of deth oonlich he outtaketh
þee, if it be euident: for þanne þou miht vnsheþe þe swerd   765
and vnbynde þe keyes: [f.18v] necessitee yiueth þee leeue and
abaundoneth þee \þe/ vsage, so þat þer be noon ooþer to whom
þe dede longeth to. Thilke to whom þis office longeth to is
he þat holt his swerd naked, and hath þe keyes vnbownde,
naked and vnseeled—þat is þilke þat hath iursdiccioun   770
and lordshipe and is his curat for he is put under him.* If
þou haddest subiectes [also], as he þou mihtest do: þi miht were
Ad Aliquid; but þou hast noone, as me thinketh, wherfore þou
shuldest not abashe ne wrathþe þee, þouh þe swerd be taken þee
sheþed, ne þouh þou haue þe keyes enseled, bounden and   775
wrapped."

Whan Resoun hadde þus preched me, Moyses wolde go dine
and his mete [was redy] al ooþerwise þan it was,* for þer was
nothing but onliche bred and wyn: but it was no{t} mes at his
wille, for he wolde haue flesh to ete and blood þerwith for
to deface þe olde lawe þat hadde seid þat no blood ete þei   780
shulde. To helpe him he clepede Grace, and she wente to him
anoon. And þanne I sigh a gret wunder, to which þer
is noon lich: þe bred into quik flesh he turned, as Grace
ordeyned it; þe wyn he turnede into red blood þat seemede
wel be of a lamb. Sithe as curteis he wolde clepe þe   785
officialles to dynere, in techinge hem his kunnynge,
yivinge hem his power for to make swich conuersioun as
turneth to wundringe. And sithe he yaf to ete to alle
of þilke newe mees withoute daunger: and he eet with hem
and drank of þe blood, I seeinge it with myne eyen. Bi   790

ouht þat I haue herd speke þer shulde noon kunne telle of
non swich mutacioun þat hath so wunderful a renown.

Whan I hadde biholden þis mete, I turned me to
Resoun for to preye hire þat she wolde preche me of þilke
dynere and teche me. But riht as I turned me ayen, I
fond her al [f.19r] abashed. "Ladi," quod I, "what is þis? What
eyleth yow? Al abashed me thinketh yow. Techeth me of
þilke mete and precheth me þerof I prey yow." "Serteyn
I wole not," quod she, "for I can nothing [heeron]. Heere
lakketh me myn vnderstondinge and my wit al outerliche: I
am blynd, I see nothing, I haue lost al my sighte. I was
neuere so abashed in al my live. For þouh þilke hornede
Moyses hadde of an ey imaad a fair brid, or of a barlich
corn a pipe, I wolde haue holde me in good pees ynowh.
But al abashed he hath maad me: for flesh quik of bred
he hath maad, and of wyn blood for his drink, ayens
nature and ayens vsage. And treweliche I wol sey it to
Nature whan I see hire: and I wole sende after hire to
come speke with Grace Dieu, withoute taryinge, for al
þis she maketh do, and ofte [is] riht contrarious to hire;
she maketh hire, bi hire hynesse, leese hire custome and
hire vsage." And anoon as she hadde seid þis she lefte
me and to hire tour she goth; and sorweful in þe place she
lefte me and sorweful into hire tour she wente.

As I was alone and thouhte on þese thinges, I sigh
toward þe tour an old oon þat cam and neihede me. She
hadde nouht þe cheer glad, but right wroth. She hadde
hire handes vnder hire sides, and hire eyen glowynge as
gleedes. I thouhte wel it was Nature, bi þat þat Resoun
had seid me: and she it was soothliche, as I wiste wel
after. Redi me thouhte hire to chide miche more þan to
preche, for toward Grace Dieu she wente and rudeliche
spak to hire: "Lady," quod she, "to yow I come to chide,
for to defende myn owen. Wennes cometh it yow for to remeve
myne ordinaunces? It ouhte suffice [yow ynowh] [f.19v] þe party
þat ye haue, withoute medlinge yow of myn, and withoute
cleymynge maistrye þerof. Of þe heuene ye haue þe lordshipe,
withoute any ooþer havinge part þerof: ye maken þe
sterres turne and þe planetes varien, and þe speeres as ye
wolen, laate or rathe, ye gouerne. And wol loth certeyn
wolde ye suffre, and loth wolde ye be þat I entermeted me
anything þerof. And so wolde I treweliche be riht weri if

ye in my part cleymede hynesse, or medlede yow: I wolde
dye as soone as suffre it. Bitwixe me and yow was sette
a bounde þat divideth us so þat noon of us shulde mistake   835
ayens ooþer: þat is þe wheel in whiche þe moone gooth
alwei aboute. þilk wheel departeth us, and yiueth eche of
us hire part. Withoute is youre partye; þere haue ye þe
lordshipe; þere ye mowe, if ye wole, make nouelries ynowe.
For þouh ye made of Venus an horned beste, or of Mercury a   840
ram* I wolde wel holde me stille ne neuere speke þerof, for
þere I cleyme nothing. But withinne al is myn. I am
maistresse of þe elementes and of þe wyndes: for to make
varyinges in fyr, in eyr, in eerþe, in see I lete nothing
stonde stille in estaat. Al I make turne and drawe to ende.   845
Al I make varye erliche and late. I make newe thinges
come and olde to departe. The eerþe is of my robes and in
prime temps alwey I cloþe it. To þe trees I yeue cloþinge
and apparamens ayens somer, and sithe I make dispoile hem
ayen ayens winter for to kerue hem ooþer robes and kootes   850
seemynge alle newe. þer is neiþer brembel ne broom ne
ooþer tre þat I ne cloþe ayen: was neuere Salomon cloþed
with suich a robe as is a bush. þat þat [f.20r] I do, I do bi
leysere, for I am not hastyf, and al mutacioun þat is
doon in haste I hate. And þerfore is myn werchinge þe   855
more woorth: witnesse on Resoun þe wise. I slepe nouht,
ne I am nouht ydel, ne I am not precious to do alwey my
deveer after my wit and my powere. Men and wommen I make
speke. I make briddes flee, bestes go, fisshes swymme,
dragowns raunpen, cornes growen. I am lady and maistresse   860
of al togidere. But me thinketh euele [for] þat for a wenche ye
wolde holde me whan my wyn ye make bicome blood, for to
make a newe beuerege. Litel lakketh þat I ne were wood.
Of þe bred I am not so wroth, for I entermeted me neuere to
make cruste ne croume, ne neuere bred I sette. But sooth   865
it is þat I deliuerede and took þe matere of whiche men
maken it: þat ye witen wel. And þerfore I haue wrethe [to]
myn herte whan ye remeeven it into quik flesh, and
nakenen me of my right. Whennes cometh it yow to do þus?
It liketh [me nouht], I telle yow wel, but I haue to   870
miche forbore yow and to miche suffred yow in my cuntre
whan ye haue er þis, I ne wot bi what auctorite, remeved
myne vsages and myne ordinaunces, my dedes and my customes.
    I remembre wel of þe brennynge fyr þat ye setten in my

greene bush withoute *bre*nnynge it, and al passinge my
wille. I bithinke me wel also of þe yerdes of Aaron and
Moyses: for þat oon ye maden \bicome/ an addere, and þat
ooþer þat was drye and withoute humo*ur* ye maden wexe
greene ayen, and bere leues, floures and frute. Of
water also ye maden wyn, at þe [noces] of Architriclyn—
and many ooþere remeevinges, of which were to longe to
holde [f.2ov] parlement. Also, me luste not to foryete
of þe v*ir*gines chyldinge which ye maden co*n*ceyue withoute
man (wherof ye diden miche ayens me) and whan ye maden
hir*e* [chylde] v*ir*gine, wit*h*oute clepi*n*ge me. Swiche
thinges I haue suffred longe, wherof I sorwe gretliche,
and neu*ere* erst spak I ne made noise þerof, wherof me
forthinketh. For men mowe ofte suffre to miche and be to
longe stille and slepe to miche; for bicause I haue holde
me stille, ye ben now come ayen for to make newe thinges,
bi whiche ye exite me right now to chide w*ith* yow bi
right gret ire and wratthe. And wel I telle yow þat ne
were ye so gret a ladi, ye shulde right soone haue þe
werre, and at yow I wolde sette: and sithe I wolde teche
you to remeeve so myne vsages withoute warnynge and
clepinge of me."

Whan Nature hadde þus yspoke, Grace, þat hadde al
yherd, answerde hire in þis man*ere*: "Nature, ye be to fers,
þat so fersliche and so prowdliche speken to me. I trowe
ye ben drunken of your*e* wynes. And dru*n*ken and wood ye
semen wel, bi þe grete ire þat ye shewen. I wot neu*ere* if
ye be neewe wexe a fool or elle*s* þat ye ben doted. It is
not longe ago þat ye seyd ye weren not hastyf: but I see
þe co*n*trarye in yow, for wit*h*oute avys ye speke to me
hastiliche and niceliche. And I telle yow wel þat I wolde
speke to you riht foule and bete yow also, ne were myn
owen wurshipe, and for þe wratthe I see in yow: for
irowse folk ben to forbere, for þei mown not discerne
cleerliche a sooth for here trowblede vnderstondinge. Now
seith me, Dame Nature, þat þus of youre owen forfeture
vndertaken me, and blamen [f.2ir] me, and arguen me of bo*u*ndes,
and seyn þat I haue michel mistaken me whan I entrede into
youre gardyn: so God saue yow, of whom holde ye, and
whe*n*nes cometh yow þat þat ye haue? Ye be lich þe wylde
swyn þat eteth þe mast in his busch, and hath no reward
whe*n*nes it cometh him ne of what side. þe hed and þe eyen

he hath [in] þe eerþe, and looketh not an hy toward þe
heuene fro whennes it cometh, but [halt him oonliche] to þe
mast. Also I trowe ye knowe not me or elles ye deygne not
to knowe me, for I am debonaire, and am no chidere.   920
Openeth a litel discretliche þe eyen of youre vnderstondinge,
for if ye vndo wel þe liddes, me for maistresse and yow for
chaumberere ye shule fynde al apertliche: and þanne ye shule
speke to me softeliche, and do to me homage of al þat ye holden
of me. Sumtyme of my curteisye I took yow a gret partye of   925
þe world for to ocupye yow with and to werche treweliche
with so þat ye weren not ydel, and þat of al ye [yolden] to me
[trewe] acounte, as chamberere shulde alwey do to hire
maistresse. And þerfore if ye were riht wys ye wolde not
speke of bounde þat is set bitwixe yow and me; for it   930
boundeth yow, not me: it forshetteth yow from passinge
ouer, for so I wole bounde it. But to þat ende þat I
shulde not entre weene not þat I bounded it, for I may entre
whan I wole, and neuere \wil/ speke to yow þerof. Yit more:
if me likede it shulde not neede yow to medle no more, for   935
I wolde wel al aloone do þat þat is to doone if I wolde;
but I wole not do so, for it longeth not to me: it is not
riht þat a maistresse ne haue alle times a chaumberere. Now
ye ouhte þanne to wite þat [withoute] me ye haue no powere: and
þat wole I prooue inowh bi þat þat ye haue seid bifore.   940
Wel ye knowe þat I make þe sterres [f.21v] to uarie and to turne
and þat þe gouernaunce of heuene longeth freeliche to me.
    Now seith þanne, so God keepe yow, if I made a neewe pley,
þat I dide awey þe sunne from þe heuene, and þat I meeued
it so wel þat [of] an hundreth winter it were not seyn ne   945
founden ne aperceyued, what faire thinges wolde ye make?
And how wolde ye eche yeer yiue robes to yowre bushes?
And how mihte ye make meyntene generaciouns þis hundreth
winter withoute failinge? Aristotle þat was an heþene
þat bi argumentes kneew weel soothnesse, I make myn   950
aduocat ayens yow in þilke debat. He seith and proueth
bi resoun þat generacioun is mad bi my sunne of whiche I
haue spoke: and þerfore if I had don it awei ye shulde
leese yowre powere, and riht nothing shulde ye mown do.
Right so it is of þe [firmament], and of þe planetes also: 955
for if I made al cesse or elles þat I wolde do al awey,
ye mihten wel go slepe and reste yow al at leisere, for
youre power were al ylost and abated. And þerfore it

miht not be þat al þe lordshipe ne were myn, al to remeeve
or to meyntene as it come to my lust. And þerfore ye
shulde not grucche ne chide to me so sharpliche: for as
Isaye seith, it is gret pride and gret despyt whan þe
axe wole dresse him ayens þe carpenteere, and whan þe pot
wole argue þe pottere and blame him, and asketh him his
shap, or pleyne him þerof. And þerfore ye shulde wel wite,
if þer were in yow any kunnynge, þat ye doon me despyt
riht gret, þat ye gon þus arguinge me, and vndertaken me
þus of my doinge—and hauen no powere withoute me. For
ye ben nothing but oonliche my tool and instrument þat
I made sumtime to helpe me, withoute any neede þat I
hadde: [f.22r] ne nouht þat I shulde alwey haue yow with me,
but oonliche whan þat I wolde. For alle times þat me liketh
and þat it be my wille, many thinges I wole do, and neuere
clepe yow þerto: and wole remeve þe wyn into blood, and into
quik flesh þe white bred and þe browne also if I wolde. For
I were elles not maisteresse, but if I dide my wille alwei
at my lust. So it ouhte not [to] displese yow whan yit in
helpinge yow I do þat þat ye mown not do: as of þe
brennynge bush, þat I kepte þat it was not brend al were þe
flaume þeron, [and] þerof ye shulde soonere thanke me þan chide
and crye. And of þe yerdes I sey yow þe same, and of þe
virgine mooder. Of þe water I turned into wyn also, and of
alle þat euere I haue doon withoute yow, me thinketh þat ye
shulde more glade yow þan wrath yow: for þe chaumberere
shulde glade hire of þe faire deedes of hire maistresse,
and nameliche whan she leeseth nothing, and also for
abetter þe commune profyte. Now dooth al þat yow liketh,
for litel or nouht it is to me. Gladeth yow or wrattheth
yow if ye wole, or chideth, for for yow [wolde] I nothing
leue to do of þat þat I wolde doo."

Whan Grace Dieu hadde þus argued and spoke, Nature
answerde: "Ladi," quod she, "I haue wel vnderstonde
yow, and wel I see þat to argue with yow I mihte not
endure. Bettere me is to yow obeye þan anything to sey
ayens yow. But neuerþeles if I durste a litel yit I
wolde argue to yow." "Hardiliche", quod Grace Dieu: "sei
[al] for I holde al þat euere ye mown seyn and arguen today
[more] game. And þerfore leueth nouht a del, þat ye declare
wel youre herte." Quod Nature: "Sithe [f.22v] I haue leeue,
yit wole I arguen, and of youre woordes I wole arguen, for I

sorwe gretliche þat ye haue so argued me of my seyinges, and
rebuked me. Ye haue seid þat þe maistresse shulde not be
withoute a chaumberere, and me for chaumberere ye haue
holde: for which thing I argue þat if ye be maistresse,
with yow as chaumberere I shulde alwey be cleped, and withoute   1005
me ye shulde remeeve [nothing] ne make nothing [bore]. And
þat ye wolden yit conferme bi þe ax which ye seiden shulde not
dresse him ayens þe carpentere: as þouh ye wolden sey, or al
withoute seyinge vnderstonde, þat ayens yow þat ben
carpentere I shulde not ben so fers. Bi þis confirmacioun   1010
me thinketh I haue myn entencioun: for as men mown not
werche ne þe carpentere bylde a good hous withoute an ax,
riht so ye shulde do nothing withoute me if ye wole nouht
misdoo. In alle times ye shulden lede me with yow and clepe
me; and bettere it were, as me thinketh, þat I were with yow   1015
alwey þanne þese neewe officialles þat doon with yow alle
heer needes. Ye yiven hem al youre powere, and for to yiven
hem ye binemen me; and neuer þe lattere I miht neuere haue
non suich powere of yow þat I kowþe make flesh of bred, and
þat I mihte remeeve wyn into blood : and yit I haue alwey   1020
doon my deueir in alle times, after my powere."
    "Serteyn," quod Grace, "in no wise I pleine me nouht
of youre service: I wot wel þat ye haue doon wel ynowh.
But if ye wole sey noon ooþer thing, I wol answere yow soone
ynowh, ne I wole seeche noon ooþer counseil." "Nay" quod   1025
she. "I answere", quod Grace, "þat þat confoundeth yow: [f.23r]
þat is þat ye vnderstonde nouht aright my seyinges, ne [ne]
thinke nouht; for whan I seide þat a maistresse shulde
alle times haue a chamberere, it was wel seyd—I meynteen
it; but in þat winne ye nothing, for I seyd not in alle   1030
places, but in alle times: and þat is not oon, for if in
alle places she hadde a chaumberere, it shulde turne þe
maistresse to more thraldam and vnwurship þan to hire
freedam and to hire wurship. But in alle times she shulde
haue it (and þat is hire wurship, whoso wel seeth) so   1035
þat she may comaunde hire, and ordeyne hire what þat she
wole. þis hadde ye not wel vnderstande as ye shulde; also
ye vnderstonde not wel þe manere of þe ax. For whan I spak
of þe ax it was not to þat ende þat I shulde also helpe
me with yow in alle times (as þe carpentere with his ax,   1040
to howse and to hewe) but for þis certeyn I spak it: for
I fond in yow feerstee, wherfore I took þerof liknesse for

to enfoorme with youre rude vnderstondinge. For if þe ax shulde nouht dresse him ayens þe carpentere, yit lasse shulde ye don it, ne were ye of yuel doinge ayens me þat haue maad yow, forged yow, shape yow and portreyed yow for to wurshipe me and serue me whan it cometh [me] to my lust. þis may not þe carpentere sey to his ax, for anooþer maister made it, and he hath þe vsage þerof, withoute more. Necessite maketh him keepe it, so þat he haue no defaute of breed: but of yow I haue no neede. Haue youre herte neuere þe more feers: withoute ax I may wel werche, and forge, and shape and carpentere withoute tool and withoute instrument; of al I may do at my lust: {to me shulde} no wiht compaare him, neiþer carpentere {ne ooþer}, for I haue singulere miht to do al at my wille. And þerfore I sey yow shortliche þat [f.23v] right litel is woorth yowre argument, litel is woorth also youre murmur; and also a gret [filthe] me thinketh whan ye gon þus grucchinge of my yiftes and spekinge and murmuringe, for I shulde be euele serued if I mihte not yive of myn owen as wel to ooþere as to yow. It is not matere of wratthe; it shulde not hevy yow of nothing: for it is not good þat þe good go alwey on oo side, þat wite ye wel. It ouhte suffice yow ynowh, þe miht þat ye holden of me, which is so fair þat neuere king mihte haue noon swich, neiþer for siluer ne ooþer avoir. If I yive any special yifte to myne officialles, I looke þat of nothing ye leese: it is foly if ye wrathe yow.''

Whan Grace hadde þus yspoken, Nature, þat hadde herd it, bisiliche kneeled at hire feet and humbleliche: "Ladi," quod she, "I pray yow [þat] on me ye haue merci. Argueth no more ayens me, for pleynliche I [see] my defaute. I haue stired me folilich to yow and fersliche. Ye ben my maistresse, I see it wel: ouer alle I ouhte obeye to yow. Of nothing it shulde displese me of thing þat ye wol doo. I thinke neuere to speke but þat ye wolen at þis time foryive me al benigneliche, withoute withholdinge any yuel wil." "Serteyn," quod Grace, "and I wole it. But keep yow wel, upon yowre eyen, þat ye neuere ageynseyn my faire werkes, ne my dedes: for anooþer time I miht not suffre so miche, ne wolde not suffre.''

Whan þis parlement was ended, and Moyses hadde dyned, he wolde departe of [his] releef, and yive almesse, and

enlargise it to poore erraunt pilgrimes of whiche þer was   1085
gret plente þerinne; but bifore þat he miht yive anything
þerof, tweyne la[f.24r]dyes of fair beringe, þat weren fair
withouten filthe, of fair manere withoute mistakinge, I
sigh, þat of a chambre comen out: and wel curteysliche
þei putten hem bitwixe Moises and þe folk. þat oon   1090
heeld a testament: a gret chartre and a scripture
wherinne was miche lettere writen. Al vnfold it she
hadde for to rede it, as \ye/ shule heerafterward
heere seye. But first of þat ooþer I wole seyn, of which
serteyn I wundrede miche. In oon of hire handes she   1095
heeld a mailet, and in þat ooþer she hadde a good yerde,
smal and greene and courreyinge. Bitwixe hire teeth and
hire mowth she heeld a beesme þat more toucheth me; wel
curteisliche she heeld it, and she seemede neuere þe
lasse wys: if anooþer hadde holden it so, men wolden   1100
haue holden hire for out of wit. She þis spak first to
þilke folk ful wysliche: hire beesme letted hire nothing
to speke ne to preche.

"Lordinges," quod she, "I wot wel þat ye biholden
[myn array], but I trowe wel þat ye witen neuere what   1105
myn array bitokeneth yow. But cometh neer: I wole
telle it, and of nothing I wol gabbe yow. I am þe faire
litel-biloued, þe debonaire ydred, þe riht wurþi litel
ypreised, þe graciowse litel plesaunt. Penitence I
am cleped: wardeyn of þe yle hyd. Alle filthes I make   1110
ley doun bifore þat any wight entre in, and þerfore I
bere with me mailet and yerde and beesme: with þe
mailet I breke and brose bi contricioun and angwich þe
herte of man: whan it is fulfilled with old sinne and
harded I softe it and make it weepe, compleyne, sighye   1115
and sorwe. And riht as þe chyld bi betinge maketh þe
juse come out of þe harde appel, [f.24v] and softeth it with
smitenge, riht so bi my smytinge I make teres come out
and crye: 'Allas, what I haue forfeted! I repente me.
A, a! mihte I haue allegeaunce!' With þilke mailet I   1120
brosede so sumtime Peeter, and softed him þat so hard
ston hadde been þat his goode maister he hadde forsake:
I beet so michel and smot hym þat tendre and softe I
yelde him. So michel I dide in hym bi my smytinge þat
bi hise eyen I made come out þe juse and þe teres of   1125
weepinge, in bitternesse and in sorwe. Of þe Magdaleyne

I dide riht so, for [how] þat hir herte were harded in
sinne bi long time, algates bi betinges I made so many
teres come out of hire, and so michel of hire juse [ysen]
out, þat I wesh hire al þerinne and purgede hire. For
whan teres ben comen out and [ysed] of an herte wel
contrite, I gadere hem ayen withoute abidinge, and
sithe of hem I made a bowkinge for to putte inne and
bowke and wasshe alle filthes. þilke tere is so riht
strong þat þer is no sinne so fowl, so defamowse, þat is
put þerinne þat it ne is wasshe: and for þat I kan so
wel washe, so wel laþere, and so wel bowke hath God maad
me his chambrere and his principal lauendere.

Now vnderstondeth yit whi I bere þe mailet with me. þe
herte of a sinnere is a gret pot of eerþe filled with a
likour foul and stinkinge, þat men mown not voide, for
as miche as men mown not turne it at here wille ne
remeve it: þat is þat bi his hardnesse and his grete
obstinacioun wole not amende, ne [ne] may not repente. þilke
vessel I smite riht harde and sharpliche with my mailet.
Peeces I make þerof and contrite, and alle þe gobettes I [f.25r]
make riht smale, to þat ende þat þe grete filthe þat was
þerinne be shed: for if I knewe hem not wel and made
not riht smale peeces of hem, þer mihte leue and abide
filthe ynowh in þe peeces.

Now vnderstondeth þis lessoun, ye þat verray
contricioun wolen make of youre sinnes. Thinketh not ne [ne]
weeneth þat it sufficeth to biholde and thinke þe sinnes
in gret, for lookinge so in gret is but leue þe pot hool;
and suppose it were brosed, yit were not þat inowh, for
eche gobet shulde be to gret, and in eche of hem mihte
leue to gret filthe. And þerfore ye shulden breke al,
and brose bi smale gobbettes and parties, in grete
syhinges and gret hachees, in thinkinge swich a tyme
þow didest þus, swich a Sonedai, swich a Moneday, þanne þou
didest þat, and þanne þat; gret was þat sinne, and
grettere was þat; so oftetimes þou dist þat sinne, and
in þat manere þou mistooke þee; litel þow were tempted,
or litel þow were stired, or þe stiringe þow purchasedest.
þis is þe manere to breke þilke foule uessel, to make of
it contricioun bi swich consideracioun. þus do I, witeth
it wel, with my mailet þat I holde in myn hand: I breke
al, withoute anything levinge, and make al contrit withoute

any sparinge.

Yit a litel woord I telle yow of [þat] foule pot   1170
filled with filthe. Withinne for his grete filthe a
worm maketh his norture; withinne it is engendred and
born, and withinne norished and reised: þat is þe worm
of conscience, þat seemeth to haue þe teeth of yren, for
it is so cruelle and so prikinge, so remordinge and so persinge,   1175
þat if þer were [f.25v] not who to sle it and smite it
and astone it, it wolde neuere stinte to [rounge] so michel
til it hadde slayn his maister. And þerfore I bere
mailet, to þat ende þat I forbere it nouht but þat I sle
it and smite it and astone it: þat is whan þe pot is wel   1180
contrite and wel brosed, as I haue seid, for but [if] it were
contrite bifore, my mailet mihte neuere touche it ne sle
it ne make it dye. Now suffreth þanne youre pot ful of
filthe to be wel contryte, and þanne I wole venge yow of
þe worm, and sle it bifore yow. þis is þe verray exposicioun   1185
and þe significacioun of my mailet þat ye seen, þat Contricioun
is cleped.

Now I wole telle yow of þe beesme þat I haue
bitwixe my mouht and my teeth. Bifore I haue seyd yow,
and yit I sey yow, þat I am chaumberere to God þe Fader   1190
almihty; and certeyn it is wel sittinge \to/ a chaumberere
and to a wenche to haue a beesme. But so miche þer is
þat þe manere of þe holdinge may meeue yow, and þerfore
ye shulde wite þat to þilke place bi whiche men shulden
caste out al þe filthe and sweepe, þider men shulden   1195
turne þe beesme: for elles þer mihte be gret suspeccion
þat in sum anglet or in sum heerne or [crookede] cornere
þe filthe were heled or heped. In Scripture I haue seyn
in diuerse places and haue red it, of diuerse yates diuerse
names: for þat oon is seyd of fisshes, þat ooþer of heuene,   1200
þat ooþer of helle, þat oon of bras, þat ooþer of iren,
and manye ooþere of which I holde me stille, for it were
longe to telle. But among alle, oon þer is of whiche is
seyd in Neemye þat it is cleped þe yate of felthe: for
þer[f.26r]bi men curen and putten out alle filthes. It is   1205
better þat þilke paas be foul þan al þe remenaunt weren
foul. Now beth eche oon wel vnderstondinge: in þe hous of
whiche I am chaumberere, of whiche Grace Dieu is þe
maistresse, þer ben vi yates, of whiche þer ben v bi
whiche þe [felthe goth] in. þat oon is þe yate of smellinge,   1210

þat ooþer is of herkeninge and of heeringe, þat ooþer of savowringe, þat ooþer of feelinge, þat ooþer of lookinge. Bi þese v yates, drede nouht, þer entereth ofte filthe ynowh, but bi hem mown nouht ysen ne comen out ayen þilke filthes: and þerfore I shulde leese my peyne if I turnede my beesme þiderward.

That ooþer yate þat is þe sexte, whiche is needeful to saluacioun, is þe yate of filthe, bi which eche wiht purgeth him and cureth him, bi whiche eche wiht putteth out al if he wole not leue foul: þis is þe mouth of sinneres, whiche of þe yates is þe beste for she putteth out alle þe misdedes in þe fourme þei ben doon, and seith hem to his confessour in waymentinge and in weepinge. Toward þis yate I haue turned and conuerted and born me beesme [al] to sweepe, poorge and clense: for as longe as I am chaumberere to Grace Dieu my maistresse, I [wole] holde clene hire hous withoute withholdinge of any filthe. My beesme is my tunge and my palet,* with which I sweepe alle filthes, and remeeve and clense: þer is nothing þerinne up ne doun, neiþer in corner ne in hole, þat al I ne wole remeeve and seeche and caste out bi hol shrifte withoute fraude and withoute outtakinge anything. Al I putte out {bi} [f.26v] þe foule yate; þer is nothing withinne þat I ne bere out with my tunge and with my beesme, for I wot wel it is þe wille of Grace Dieu my maistresse, which wole abide in no place but it be riht wel swept and clensed: þat is to sey þat she hath no cure of conscience in whiche filthe is inne, for conscience is þe hous, þe chaumbre and þe dwellinge in whiche she maketh hire abidinge whan it is wel swept.

Now ye haue herd whi I holde þus þe beesme in my mouth: how also I make confessioun bi certeyn exposicioun; and I wole telle yow also shortliche þe tokenes of my yerdes: why I holde hem, and what I do with hem (and ye shule not holde it in ydel). Of grete scooles I am maistresse, and chastisere of children: I correcte þe yuel-doeres, þouh þei be of xx^{ti} yeer old or of an hundreth, for euel-doere chyld is cleped [of] þe lettere þat courseth hem. Whan any þanne hath misdoo, I ley me in awaite to wite þe sooþe: if he be passed bi my mailet of whiche I haue spoke, and if he haue put him vnder my beesme, and if he be swept þerwith. And whan I see him so contrite and

wel shrive as I haue seid, þanne to chastise him \wel/ with
my yerdes I smyte him, peyne and betinge I yive him
for his goode and his amendinge. Oon houre I make hym   1255
remembre his olde sinne, and sey 'Allas, whi assented I
to þat, to be now a wrecche?' Anooþer time I make him
sey ayen: 'Sweete lord God, faire sweete lord, I bihote
þee amendement: I wole no more be so hardi þat I dar wratthe
þee, ne þat I dar sinne for þee.' Oon hour þus I make to   1260
preye, anooþer to sighe, [f.27r] anooþer to weepe, anooþer
time I make him yiue and departe þat þat he hath to þe needy
and to mendivauns, and do almesse. Anooþer time I make him
go and trauaile in pilgrimage, or in sum ooþer long wey and
anooþer time faste and do sum abstinence to withdrawe him   1265
fro his sinnes. þus vnder yerde I holde him and punishe
him, and bete him wel and smyte him, and chastise him to
þat ende þat it bite him nouht, ne turne ayen to his
sinne* of whiche he is cast out and purged; and to þat ende
also þat þe olde sinnes þat he hath doo ben punished, for   1270
þer shulde no trespas passe withoute punishinge: with yerdes
shulde þilke be beten þat hath consented to sinne. Heerfore
I holde hem. Now ye wite it, fro misdoinge keepeth yow;
if ye wole wite þe name of þe yerdes, þei ben cleped
satisfaccioun: for satisfaccioun is as michel to sey as to   1275
do as michel peyne or more withoute ayenseyinge, as þer was
delite in þe sinne.

Now I haue seid yow and maad [yow] sermoun of my
craftes and of my name: but why I am come hider bitwixe
Moyses boord and bitwixe yow þat abiden and asken of his   1280
releef, I haue not yit seid yow. But herkeneth and I wole
telle yow. Ye shulde wite þat I am partere and porter of
þis releef. Withoute me ye shulden not come þernyh, but if
ye [wole] mysdo. It is no releef to yive to fooles, ne to
yive to truwauntes. It is not to yive to womman gret (but   1285
if she be gret with þe grace of God). It is a releef for
hem þat ben in langour, for syke and for daungerous, of
whiche whoso taketh it digne[f.27v]liche may not be
þat he ne haue allegeaunce. þis is þe releef þat lefte of
þe gret [cene], þer God [ceened]: þilke he brak and   1290
departede to hise freendes þe grete Thursday, with which
al þe world is fed and quikned and susteyned. þis releef
I wole keepe streitliche and cheerliche: ne þider I wole
þat no wight go but if þat he be beten with [my] yerdes,

and but [if] he be passed bi my mailet and maad clene with my
beesme. Now eche wiht keepe him wel as for himself, for I
do þat þat I ouhte. And þis is þe cause for whiche I am in
swich wise comen hider."

Whan þis lady hadde spoke and told hire doinge, þat
ooþer ladi þat was þere and heeld þe scripture in hire
hande wolde also telle hire tale and rede hire scripture
bifore alle folk. "Lordinges," quod she, "wel it is
sooth þat withoute lesinge and disceyte Penitence hath
told yow and divised yow hire grete office: and þerfore
I wole telle yow also wherof I serve, and who I am. I am
þilke þat hadde neuere in despyte neiþer grete ne smale;
þilke þat loueth alle folk with hol herte, withoute yuel
wil; þilke þat seecheth no vengeaunce, ne neiþer showveth
ne smyteth; þilke þat hath set hire entente to forbere
hire enemyes. I am þe mooder of vertues: þilke þat
[cloþeth] þe naked folk, þilke þat made Seint Martyn vncloþe
himself for to cloþe þe poore man. I am norishe of
orphanynes, osteleer to pilgrimes, þat of þe harmes of
oopere I make myne: and to alle, my goodes ben commune.

My name if ye wole wite it, Charite ye shule clepe me:
for charitee holt in cheertee þat þat oopere holden [f.28r]
in vilitee. I feede þe hungri and visite þe languishinge.
I am þilke þat of ooperes good am as glad as of myn owen:
þilke þat debonairliche suffreth al pacientlich, þilke
þat keepith not heere bakbitinge ne murmur, þilke þat
neuere misseyde of oopere ne misdide oopere, and nouht
for þanne I haue maad doo sum harm withoute misdoinge.
If ye haue ouht herd speke of þe king Ihesu and told how
he wolde bicome man and suffre deth for þe men, ye shulde
wite þat I am she þat made him haue swich annoye: for I
made him come doun from heuene, and made him take flesh
of mankynde. I made him bounde to þe pileer and corowned
with thornes; I made him sprede hise armes in þe cros,
dispoile him and opene his side; þe feet and þe handes
I made tacche of him, and perce hem with grete nailes.
Sithe I made his blood come out of his tendre body, and
his gost yelde. But witeth wel, I made hise harmes
turne yow to gret good: for I made him descenden doun
into helle for to fecche yow alle, for to caste yow out
of þe deepe pit and lede yow into Paradise, to yive yow
and [leue] yow a yifte þat he hadde riht cheere—þat is

pees, [with] which þe heuene shyneth, and of whiche
Paradise gladeth. þe fourme how he yaf þis yifte and
graunted it is writen in þis testament þat I holde
heere present bifore yow: Testament of Pees it is cleped.   1340
Now heereth, I wole rede it:

'I, Ihesus þe sone of Marie, weye, soothnesse and lyf: in my
deth þat is [nyh] and þat is to me al certeyn I make my laste
testament, in whiche I leeue freeliche to hem þat ben in þe
vale of weepinge and in þe lond of labour, þe yifte of pees   1345
þat is my jewell—þe moste [f.28v] gracious and [þe] faireste
þat is in heuene or in eerþe, or þat men mown fynde or seeche.
þat is þe jewell with whiche I pleyed me sumtime in
Paradise: of whiche I made my solace whan I was in my
cuntre. But with it I pleyede no more sithe I entrede into   1350
þis world, for whan I was bicomen chyld and comen into þis
world, whan time was I shulde pleye and þat I [hadde] had my
jewel, my ministres of Paradise beren it into þis cuntre,
and maden present þerof to þilke for whiche I shulde haue
turment, with whiche jewell þei haue pleyed euere sithe   1355
þe time þat I was born, nouht for it was hers, ne for it
shulde be hers (for my seruauntes þat kepten it mihten not
yiuen it hem, ne þei weren not wurþi to resceyuen it ne to
have it in havinge): þei haue had it oonliche to repele it
at my lust, for saue I may no wyht yive it ne shulde yive   1360
it. But alleweys þe grete maistresse Charite, my ledere þat
ledeth me as a chyld and dooth with me at hire lust, bi
hire rihtes hath þerto brouht me þat I haue yiven to hem
þilke faire jewell and yit freeliche yive it hem and
abaundone it hem. A fairere yifte yaf I neuere, but if I   1365
yaf myself. It is a iewell þat was fourmed, forged and
maad and carpentered of my fader, withoute smytinge of
strok and withoute heeringe of makinge noise: for noyse and
strokes maken it nouht but tobreken it and vnmaken it.
If þer were any þat wolde wite of his facioun, I wolde   1370
wel take þe patroun propirliche to hem of good vnderstondinge.
Whoso tooke a carpenteres sqwire, and sette upward þe first
ende, if he sette þat ooþer doun, with þe cornere in þe euene
lyne: if it were so þat [wel a] poynt [f.29r] in þe cornere
þat ioyneth þe lynes were fastned and sette an 'a', and in þe   1375
endes were sette 'p' and 'x' so þat 'x' were on hy, and
'p' alowh, as it is heere figured:

	x
p	a

lightliche he mihte wite his facioun, and aperceyue þere
his name right wel writen. These thre letteres heere doon
to wite þat to thre thinges shulde þilke haue pees to   1380
whom is left and graunted þis faire jewel: þat is þat first

on hy þere 'x' is set in scaffold, bi which I am in short
vnderstonde and tokened, he shulde haue perfite pees in
swich manere þat alle dedes don ayens my wille ben
restreined and amended. Afterward in þe anglet wel sett
and where she is sett and nestled, 'a', bi which is
vnderstonde þe soule þat in þe bodi of þe manhode is,
shulde also haue good pees bi destroyinge of misdedes
whiche shulden be defaced and arased bi penaunce: for
þilke may not be in pees þat is werred with sinne, and alle
ooþer pees is nouht for him if he apese not þe werre
bitwixe him and conscience bi þe instrument of penaunce.
Afterward yit to his neihebour, þat bi þe 'p' of þe laste
ende is vnderstonde, he shulde haue pees; which to haue
ouhte to meeve him þe same degree þat he is inne,* for it
is noþer hyere ne lowere: boþe in oo degree I sette hem
whan þe scripture I fourmede and maade. Alle ben dedlich,
boþe þat oon and þat ooþer: worm is þat oon and worm is
þat ooþer. It is nothing woorth dispitous herte and fers
ne nouht is woorth noþer pride ne daunger. Alle we shule
passe bi oon hole, grete and smale, michel and litel. Now
let hem do so miche þat þei leesen not my jewel bi here
pride. Eche wiht haue pees with his neyhebour, and so
shal þe patroun [f.29v] be ful maad of þe squyre of whiche
I haue spoke, and þe pees whiche I haue figured.

    Þis figure and þilke patroun is a [notarye] signe with
whiche shulden be signed and marked alle goode testamentes:
and with þilke signe openliche I haue signed my testament.
To alle folk I haue yiven pees and graunted and confermed.
Now eche wight keepe it as for himself, after þe loue þat
he hath [in] me: for after þat men louen me, þerafter eche
wiht wole keepe it.' "

Whan Charitee hadde al rad þis testament and rested,
þanne she bigan ayen hire parlement, and suiche woordes she
seyde afterward: "Lordinges, now ye haue herd bi þis
scripture þat I haue rad heere how Ihesu hath loued yow,
and yiven yow his jewel, and also how he grauntede and yaf
it yow at my request. Now wole I \yit/ telle yow shortliche
whi I haue sett me with þilke testament bitwixe yow and Moyses
boord. Wite ye shulden þat I am awmenere and dispenser of
þe releef; and as Penitence hath preched you and told yow
þat withoute hire ye shulden not go þerto but ye wole misdo,
riht so I telle yow þat withoute misdoinge ye shulden not
withoute me drawe yow þider, ne withoute me ye shulde not
come þer nygh if ye ne wole offende me. þe testament of þe

yifte of pees and þe jewell which þe sweete Ihesu lefte
bifore his deth with me perfore I bere to þat ende þat I
[avise] yow so þat to þe releef in no wise ye approche ne come
but ye haue þe jewel of pees. For in þe anglet of þilke
jewel, bicause it \is/ priuee and fair, wole þilke holi releef   1430
be put and resseyued and gadered. And perfore if ye hadden
it not ye mihten be punished [f.3or]; perfore I rede yow
in good feith þat ye beren pees and þat ye passen bi me,
þat am departere and yivere of þe releef: for if ye comen
nouht bi me and passeden bi ooþere weyes, thefte it shulde   1435
be holde, and harm mihte come yow þerbi. Now keepeth
yow wel, offendeth nouht; for I do wel inow my devoir,
and þat is þe cause for which I am come hider fro my
chambere."

Whan Charite hadde al ful seid and preched withoute   1440
ayenseynge, þanne I sigh many pilgrimes þat were [encline]
to obeye: bi Charitee evene þei wenten and þe jewel of pees
beren, sithe passeden bi Penitence withoute havinge
drede of hire. þei vnderputten hem to hire mailet, and
with þe beesme þei swepten hem; with yerdes I sigh þei   1445
weren bete; and afterward of þe releef þei resseyueden, þe
which Moises yaf hem as Charitee ordeyned it. Sithe I sigh
summe cursede þat priueliche bi ooþere weyes hydinge hem
fro Charite and fleeinge Penitence withoute any shame [þei]
wenten to þe releef and resseyueden it. Moises, withoute   1450
any exceptinge and ayenputtinge, þis releef ammynistrede
hem, and curteysliche took it hem. But I wole telle yow
how it bifel of hem and \how it misbifel hem/ whan þei hadden
had þis releef: riht as þouh þei hadden be comen out of a
riht blac colyeres sak, oþer out of a foul dong-hep, al   1455
blac þei bicomen and salwh, foul and stinkinge and elded.
And yit more, [alle] hungry þei kamen ayen, and needy—
þei weren na more sauled þerwith þan if þei hadden fleeinge
passed bi þe doore of an obley-makere withoute anything
havinge [þere] to ete. Of þe ooþere it was not so: but whan   1460
þei hadden resseyued þe releef of whiche þei hadden, alle
þei [f.3ov] weren so fulfilled and sauled þat ooþer
thing þei wolden noon, ne nothing of þe world þei preyseden.
þei bicomen so faire, so gentel þat as to regard of hem me
thouhte alle folk foule, as wel þe clerkes as þe lewed.   1465

Now [I wole] telle yow withoute lesinge þat þat made me
michel abashed. Wunder it is þat litel thing may fulfille

a gret thing, but þe wundres ben grettere whan many thinges
þat ben grete mown haue, of þat þat is not gret, fillinge
sufficiaunt. Alle þe releef þat I sigh yive was so litel
to my seemynge, þat þouh swiche ten I hadde had to a dyner,
I hadde not be fed sufficientliche; and algates not fulliche
oon, but þei eche on weren fulfilled and suffised: a litel
to eche of hem suffised, and ful of a litel eche of hem was.
This made me gretliche thinke and trouble myn vnderstondinge,
and to whom to speke I ne wiste if to Grace Dieu I ne speke;
and nouht for þanne to hire durste I not speke ne come nyh
hire for she [was] lened hire at þe ende of þe arayed bord where
she biheeld þe releef yiven and [almused]. Algates I hardied
me, and went wel nyh to hire. Whan she sigh me, anoon she
turnede hire towardes me and goodliche seide: "What seechest
þou heere? I see wel þer lakketh þee sumwhat." "Serteyn,"
quod I, "[soothliche] ynowh me lakketh, for I vnderstonde nouht
how þis releef þat is so litel sufficeth to so michel
folk, for to me aloone it shulde not suffice, þouh þer were
swich ten: wherfore I preye you þat ye wule teche me þerof
a litel and preche me." [f.31r]

"Goode freend," quod she, "now vnderstonde, and anuye
þee nouht þouh I holde þee longe to teche þee, for I see
wel þou hast neede. þis releef heere þat is yiven, oon houre
it is flesh and blood cleped, anooþer it is cleped bred and
wyn, whiche is mete to pilgrimes. Flesh and blood it is in
sooth, but bred and wyn it is figured. And sooth it is þat
sumtime it was bred and wyn, but þou [seye] þat into flesh and
into blood it was remeeved bi Moyses [to] whom I helpe: wherfore
Nature chidde to me, and yuele wratthed hire. Bred and wyn
þouh þow clepe it, [I] avise þee and charge þee þat flesh
and blood it be vnderstonden of þee, and stidfastliche leeved of
þee. Ne þat shulde not meeve þee þat at þe taast and at þe
sighte, at þe smellinge and at þe savouringe bred and wyn
it may seeme þee: for þilke foure wittes disseived þei ben
thoruhout, and fooles holden. þei kunne nothing. Doted þei
ben, let hem go ligge: fonned þei ben. But þe witt of
heeringe oonliche enfoormeth þe vnderstondinge more þan
þilke of taaste heerayens, oþer of smellinge, savouringe
or sighte. þis knoweth more subtylliche and apperceyueth
more cleerliche. And er þis it was figured in Ysaak and
Esau:* for þe foure wittes wolden haue disceyued him al
vtterliche, as þow shalt see pleynliche, whan þow hast

rad Genesis; but of þe heeringe he was nothing disceyued,   1510
for þerbi he kneew his sone Jacob and apperceyued. Right so
I sey þee, þat if þou triste and leeve in þese foure
wittes, þou shalt al vtterliche be disceyued: for foolliche
þou shalt weene þat of þe flesh it be white bred, and þat þe
blood þerfore be wyn, so þat [f.31v] þe sooþe þou shalt   1515
neuere haue ne wite bi þilke wittes. To þe herynge þou mostest
leeue thoruhout and triste þee: bi it þou shalt wite þe
sooþe, and by it þou shalt be enfoormed. It shal teche
þee al at þe fulle þat it is no more neiþer wyn ne bred,
but it is þe flesh þat was sprad on þe cros for þee and   1520
hanged, and þat it is þe blood with which þilke cros was
\bi/dewed and spreynt. And if þis bred þou wolt nempne and
clepe wel and wurþilyche, I sey it is bred of lyf of which
al þe world hath his lyf: also I haue in myn vsage to
clepe it bi swich langage. Bred I clepe it and bred I   1525
nempne it þat from þe heuene cam for to feede man. It is þe
bred with whiche ben fedde alle þe aungeles þat ben in
heuene. It is þe bred which pilgrimes shulden putte in
here skrippes. þouh in litel quantitee þou hast seyn it,
wel I haue [avised] þee þat to þi lokinge ne to þi sighte   1530
þow shuldest no trist haue: þe heeringe techeth þee oonliche,
and taketh þee þe lernynge, and þerfore þou mihte wel lerne
of þat þat þou shalt heere me seyn.

Charitee, þat þow hast herd speke and preche nouht
longe ago, was cause of þilke bred, and bi hire it was   1535
contrived. She brouhte þe greyn from heuene to eerþe and
seew it. þe eerþe þer it was sowe was neuere ered ne
labowred: bi heete of sunne it wex, and bi dew þat fel
þeron. Charite made berne it and in straunge berne putte
it. Manye founden it þere, and throsshen it and fanned   1540
it. So michel beten it was, so michel fanned it was þat
from þe straw it was disceuered. His cloþinge was doon
of him so þat he was naked, and naked [f.32r] afterward to
þe mille he was born, and disgisyliche grounden: for in þe
hoper of þe mille, in whiche þer was no lynene cloth, he   1545
was grounden, broken, brused and tormented. þilke
mille was maad to þe wynd, and with þe wynd of envye
grounde; and nouht for þanne þis mille hadde stones þat
weren nouht softe: stones of yuel rownynge, stones of
bakbitinge, with which it was frusht bifore þat it was   1550
taken to þe hoper. Whan it hadde þus be grounde, þanne

putte hire foorth Charite, and wolde bicome baker*e* for to
bulte and make þerof bred. Hire oovene al hot was bifore,
whiche she wolde bake it inne. But [so] it is þat she
cowde not turne it ne moolde it at hire wille, whiche
forthouhte hire: but of nothing she abashed hire, for I
wole telle þee what bifel þerof. She bithouhte hire on a
maistresse þat was þe moste subtile þat was in burgh or in
toun. Sapience she was cleped ou*e*ral þere men kneewen hire.
þer was nothing þat mihte be thouht þat she ne cowde doon it
anoon. Bifore þat time she hadde lerned þilke wit in þe
scooles of hire cuntre. Al þe world if she wolde in a box
she [shulde] wel doo, oþer in þe shelle of an ey she shulde wel
putte an hool oxe; and for þis subtilitee Charite was
bithouht of hire: for þe bred þat she wolde make of þe
groundene corn þat was redy, she wolde it were so wysliche
moolded and so subtylliche þat bi seemynge it were litel,
and þat to alle it mihte suffice so þat of a riht litel
eche wer*e* ful sauled and wel sufficed. Whàn Charite hadde
þus ythouht, to fulfille hire wille to Sapience she wente
and dide so michel [f.32v] þat she fond hire. She was in
hire chayere, and took keep of al. So michel Charite
preyede hire þat to bake with hire she made hire come.
Sapience þis bred turnede, and book it: and riht as Charite
seyde hire, riht so of al she dide; and yit more subtylliche
she dide it and more wysliche, for she turnede it gret
*with*oute mesure, for to yive þerof feedinge to alle, and þat
eche mihte þerof be sauled and sufficed. And how wel how
gret þat eu*e*re she made it, bi seemynge she made it litel;
and vnder litel closure she made it haue his mesur*e*. And
yit more subtylliche she made anooþer exp*e*riment: for of
eche of þilke p*a*rtyes þat of þat bred shulden ben broken,
wheþer it were litel or gret, she made eche of hem as gret
as þouh alle hadden be togideres, whiche thing plesede nouht
to hire þat chidde with me, but certeyn michel it heviede
hire, for she can nothing but hire riot, for eelde þat
hath doted hire. But þere algates cam she nouht, for of
me she bithouhte hire: for wel she dredde hire þat yit she
mihte be blamed and rebuked. But I wole telle þee what
she dide: a clerk of hires, Aristotle, she souhte, and
sente him to speke to hire and to blame hire and to argue
hire.

Whan Aristotle was come bifore hire he seyde hire

þe greetinges, and sithe seyde hire bi likenesse: 'To
yow, Dame Sapience, sendeth me Nature to speke, to shewe   1595
yow yowre mistakinges. Michel it displeseth hire þat ye
quassen þus hire ordinaunces and remeeven, and also it
pleseth nouht me, for alþouh ye ben my freend, I wole neuere
leue for yow þat I ne wole seye þat þat I woot. Wel ye
witen [f.33r] þat \it/ is no resoun þat þe vessel or þe hous   1600
be lasse þan þat þat is þerinne. On þat ooþer side, if I make
folk weene bi argumentes of a gret paleys oþer of a chirche
þat it were a torell litel, soothliche litel þei wolden
preyse my seyinge, þe wise folk, and wolden skorne me
and holde me for a sophistre. These thinges heere haue ye   1605
doon in þilke bred þat is disgise: for þe feedinge withinne,
with which alle folk ben ful fedde, þat [in] þe world miht nouht
—ne þe heuene miht not—suffice it,* ye haue enclosed and put
bi a disgise wise in so litel a closure, vnder so litel an
[hep], þat þouh þer were suiche foureteene, in myn hond I   1610
wolde wel holde hem. þis may I nouht wel suffre, ne resoun
may not weel preeve it, ne is it not riht gret wunder þouh
Nature merveile hire. But þouh ye hadden so michel doon,
and þat ye mihte haue doon it þat þe dwellinge were as gret
as þe feedinge is gret, oþer elles þat þe feedinge were as   1615
litel as þe hous is litel, wel inouh I wolde suffre it, and
Nature wolde it wel. On þat ooþer side, it were youre
wurshipe þat withoute desceyte men wisten how gret þe
feedinge were withoute goinge divinynge. And yit more me
misliketh (and Nature halt hire not stille) þat ye haue   1620
preeued my maxime fals and repreeved. For certeyn I herde
neuere speke ne in my lyve sih þat [an] al, whatsoeuere it
were, ne were grettere þan a part þerof. But ye witen wel
þat ye haue mad þe partye as gret as þe al, which is a gret
mistakinge ayens me and ayens Nature. þis is þat I am come   1625
hider fore, and wherfore I was sent hider. Now looketh what
answere she shal haue þat hath sent me.' [f.33v]

Whan Aristotle hadde spoken, Sapience aresoned him:
'Freend,' quod she, 'þat cleymest me freend for þat þou
louest me (and þerinne þou hast nothing lost, for þerbi   1630
is al good bifalle þee): wel þou shuldest avise þee if þow
woldest, and bithinke þee þat tweyne scooles I heeld sumtime,
in whiche þee and Nature I tauhte. For Grace Dieu wolde it,
and hadde ordeyned me þertoo, to teche in þat oon to werche
diuerse artes and excersise, to make wunderful thinges, and   1635

subtile and gracious. And in þilke was first Dame Nature
my scoleer. þere I tauhte hire and lerned hire noble craftes
and riht subtile, as to make floures—lilyes, gaye roses and
violettes—and ooþere graciouse craftes wherof to seye it is
no neede. In þat ooþer scoole, [þee] I tauhte [þe]
vnderstondinge and enfoormed þee to argue* and to dispute and
to juge and discerne bitwixe þe goode and þe wikkede, and
to make canoun and lawe: for þerfore was þilke scoole
ordeyned. And þere was my wise douhter, Science, þat is so
subtile, whiche heeld þere þe parlementes and foormed þere þe
argumentes: for þe loue of whom þou come and were in þe
scooles—and so michel þow didest, what up what doun, þat to
mariage þow haddest hire. In þilke scoole I tauhte [þee], and
þere þou were my prentys, and þere weren shewed þee alle þe
secrees of Nature, for al þat euere I tauhte to Nature,
riht soone after I told it to þee, nouht þat þou shuldest
mown make anything þerof, but þat þou shuldest wel kunne
juge. Swich wurshipe and swich curteysye shewed wel þat I
was freend to þee. [f.34r] And whan þow and Nature [þanne]
hauen ben vnder my cure, þat han lerned in my scooles
boþe faire dedes and faire woordes, þouh ye seyen me now
erre, yit ye shulden forbere me. Ye shulden haue in mynde
of þe champyoun þat hadde tauht his kunnynge to a poore
man, and hadde nothing take of his. For whan þei weren in þe
þe feeld at þe requeste of tweyne dukes þat wolden defende
bi hem eche of hem here owen, for which þei hadden gret
stryf, þe maister, which was [yit] wisere þan þe prentys,
bigan to speke to his prentys and aresone him. "What is
þis," quod he, "come ye tweyne ayens me þat am aloone?
þis was neuere of gret wurþinesse ne of wurþi corage."
And þanne whan þilke lookede bihynde him, who was þere, þe
maister yaf him swich a strook þat ded to þe eerþe he sente
him. "Yit haue I nouht", quod he, "tauht al my wyt to my
prentys. It is euele bifalle þee today, whan þow come ayens
me." So I sey þee: so God save þee, weenest þow þat I haue
tauht þee now al my wit and al myn art, and þat al myn I haue
yiven þee, withoute withholdinge anything? Euele þow woldest
awurþe with me if I hadde nothing to defende me with bi sum
wey: for doinge to me vyleynye þow arguest me of sophistrie,
of fraude and of gile, bi defaute of discrecioun. Now sey me:
if I were a mercere, and shewed þee a purs þe which I wolde
yive þee, and seyde þee "Loo þis I haue yiven þee, bere it

with þee, for it is bi my wille," if it so were þat þow bere
it foorth and sithe þou founde þerinne [f.34v] foure
floreynes or fyve or sixe, shulde it seeme þee þat I hadde   1680
anything disceyued þee, or þat I were þerfore a sophistre?'
'Serteyn,' quod Aristotle, 'nay. But me shulde thinke suich
a yifte ful of gret fredom and of wurship and of gret
curteysye.'

'Serteyn,' quod she, 'so it is of þe bred þat I haue   1685
maad so subtile: for withoute I haue not shewed þe grete
tresore þat I haue put withinne, but I haue riht priuely
hid it for to enrichesse with þe poore folk. For if it were
shewed withoute, þer shulde noon dore resceyue it. Charite
ordeyned it so, þat hath of þe poore gret pitee; and   1690
þerinne is no gile, but dede of mercy. But if withoute I
hadde shewed gret apparence, and put withinne thing þat
were litel to preyse, or þat hadde not gret quantite, þanne
þow mihtest argue me of gile and blame me. Yit I answere
\þee/ ooþerweys, for it is no desceyte þouh I shewe it litel   1695
to þe eye and [it] is gret withinne. And I wole þat so it be
bileeved stidfastliche, withoute makinge [deuynale]. But
if I wolde not þis, or if I dide it ooþerweys, þanne
perauenture þow mihtest argue me of mystakynge. Now sey me
yit I prey þee (þat arguest me of my doinges, þat seist it   1700
is not resoun þat þe vessel or þe hous be lasse þan þat þat
is withinne): seye þou neuere neyþer inne ne oute þe
quantitee of þe herte of man?' 'Serteyn,' quod he, 'in
sooth I haue wel seyn it treweliche.' 'Now sey me', quod
she, 'bi þin oth: how gret it is to þi seemynge?' 'Serteyn,'   1705
quod he, 'a kyte a litel enfamined shulde skarsliche be ful
sauled þerwith, for litel it is and nouht gret.' 'Yit', quod
she, 'I aske [f.35r] þee if þou wite ouht with how michel
his desire may be fulfilled, and with how michel it mihte
be ful esed and sauled, or what thing [shulde] suffice it?'   1710
'Serteyn,' quod he, 'fulfille it and saule it and staunche
it mihte not al þe world, þouh al at his wille he hadde it.'
'Now needeth it þanne,' quod Sapience, 'þat [fillinge] to
[suffisance] þow fynde it, oþer þat false{d} [be] þi commune
auctoritee þat is wide spred, bi whiche þow hast preeued and   1715
seyd þat in þe world þer is nothing voyd, for of sumthing it
shal be filled oþer it shal be empty.' 'þerof', quod he, 'I
wole sey my seyinge, for I haue wend, and yit weene, þat oo
god þat is sovereyn shulde make it al ful.' 'Soothliche,'

quod she, 'þow seyst wel, and of nothing mistakest þee þerof, but it needeth þat þilke god be grettere þan þe world is gret, and so enclosed in þe world it may not be þat it ne shulde ouerflowe it.' 'Serteyn', quod he, 'I may not to þat of nothing wel withseye.' 'And how shulde it', quod she, 'be put in an herte þat is so litel? þanne muste þe hows bi resoun be lasse þan þe good þat is put þerinne, and so shal þi seyinges be false. Yit I wole shewe þee þis apertliche al ooþerweys: Grece and Athenes þow hast seyn, and many tymes ben þere. Now sey me sooth if it be in þi mynde, how michel þat oon is from þat ooþer,* and if þer been manye studyauntes, and how grete þe citees ben?' 'Serteyn,' quod he, 'I mynde me wel þat þei ben grete, and þat þer comen ynowe of studiauntes þider, and of scoleeres and of folk of diuerse craftes.' 'Now sey me', quod she, 'where hast þow put alle þese gretnesses þat þou seist [me]?' 'In my memorie I haue [f.35v] [put] hem:' quod he, 'certeyn I wot it riht wel.' 'Oo,' quod Sapience, 'and shalt þou þerfore conclude me, if memorye be in þin hed, þat in lasse place þan is þin hed þou hast enclosed tweyne grete citees with alle here studiauntes? In þe appel of myn eye I wole shewe þee þis also: biholde it how it is litel, and algates þer enhabiteth þerinne holliche al þi visage, as þow miht see apertliche. Also looke in a mirour, þou shalt se þi visage and his shap. And if þow wolt do ooþerweys, for to assoile better þine argumentes (þat seist I haue falsed and repreved þi maxime, in as michel as eche partye \þat/ may be broken of þe bred I make as gret as al) make þat al þe mirour be tobroken in diuerse partyes, and if þi biholdinge be to eche of hem, þer shal not be þilke in which þow ne shalt see þi visage al apertliche, and apperceyue as wel and as holliche as þou didest first in þe mirour whan it was hool, wherinne þer ·was but oon visage.' 'Now, lady þat hauen þe engyn so subtil,' quod he, 'vnderstonde ye þat localliche, virtualliche or ooþerwise \þat/ alle þese thinges ben put in þe places ye haue seyd and enclosed? For þerafter I wolde answere, or þerafter I wolde holde me stille.' 'Serteyn,' quod she, 'localliche I vnderstonde not, but ooþerweys: vertualliche I vnderstonde summe, and ymaginatyfliche summe, and representatyfliche summe of þe thinges I vnderstond, and it thurt not recche to wite of þis anoon, for I haue taken þee ensaumples onliche for avisement, for to make þee

soone vnder[f.36r]stonde and soone [to] teche þee and lerne þee
how vnder litel figure is hid þe grete feedinge. For as in
diuerse wises in þe litel places þese thinges ben put, riht
so withinne þis bred al þe souereyn good is put, soothliche   1765
nouht ymaginatyfliche, nouht [representatyfliche], nouht
vertualliche withoute more, but it is put þerinne and
contened bodiliche and rialliche, presentliche and verreyliche
withoute any similacioun, and withoute ooþer decepcioun.

The cause why it is put þere, in partye it is told   1770
tofore: for þe herte is litel, þe bred as litel is maad
also; and for his grete capacitee, þe good souereyn I haue
put withinne: þe litele to þe litele, þe grete to þe grete I
haue euene maad as answeringe. For after þat þe herte is,
right soo þe feedinge is maad. If it be litel, litel bred it   1775
hath; if it wole ynowh, it shal fynde withinne þat þat may
saule it and fille it and suffice it, and þerinne is no
mistakinge, þouh þe hous for suich cause is michel smallere
and lasse þan þe good þat enhabiteth þerinne. And suppose
þat to þi seemynge I hadde maad thing missittynge and þat   1780
þou were not wel apayed of þat þou hast herd me [seyn]: yit
I sey þee þat if I ne [wole], I shulde not answere to þee,
for if I cowde not make or sumtime dide [summething]
more notable and wunderful þan ooþere, for nouht shulde
I be maistresse and techere of ooþere. So þat see heere   1785
myn answere; if þow wolt, shewe it ayen to Nature,
chaumberere to Grace Dieu and my scoleer, for for hire I
wole nothing leue to do of þat þat I wolde do: for Charitee
I wole alwey do [f.36v] and plese hire þat þat I can. She
shal nothing kunne diuise me þat I ne wole do it withoute   1790
abidinge.'

Aristotle, whan he herde þis, al dedliche he answerde
hire: 'Serteynly I apperceyue weel þat of yow shal I
nothing winne. It is michel better for me go my wey þan
more argue ayens yow. I go. Dooth whateuere ye wole: good   1795
leeue ye haue.' Thus þilke wente and tolde ayen to Nature
þe wit he hadde founde in hire, for whiche he was departed.
Nature þanne suffrede it: she mihte no more; and þat hevyede
hire."

Whan Grace hadde þus told me þis faire tale of hire   1800
goodnesse, I hadde gret wille and gret hunger to haue of
þilke bred to ete. "Lady," quod I, "with herte I pray yow
þat of þis releef of Moyses ye wole make yive me for to ese

with myn empty herte: longe it hath be empty ne it was
neuere sauled, for it wiste neuere yit of whatt men shulden
fille it." "Serteyn," quod she, "þi requeste I holde not
dishoneste. Michel is þis bred necessarie to þee to þe viage
þou hast to doone: for bifore þou mowe come to þe place þer
þou hast þi desire, bi ful wikkede pases þou shalt go, and
wikkede herberwes þou shalt fynde, so þat ofte þou shalt haue
misese if þou bere not þis bred. And my leeue þou hast to
take it whan þou wolt. But alweys it is riht (as I fynde
in my lawes) þat þou haue first þat þat þow hast asked
bifore: þat is þe scrippe and þe burdoun of þe whiche I
seide þee þat in myn hous I wolde purueye þee of hem al
bitymes, þat shulde be [f.37r] whan I hadde shewed þee þe
faire thinges of withinne, whiche alle folk seen nouht.
Now I haue in partye shewed þee þe thinges and opned hem to
þee, I am redi to holde þee [þi] couenauntes. Withoute
failinge, þe scrippe and þe burdoun þou shalt haue alle þe
tymes þat þow wolt: and sithe if þou wolt þou miht putte of
þe bred in þi scrippe, and after as good pilgrym sette þee
to þi wey." "Lady," quod I, "miche graunt mercy: þat is my
wish and my desire. Dooth me soone to haue it, for I haue
gret lust to stire me. Me thinketh riht longe þat I ne
were forthward and set in þe wey: for it is fer þilke citee
to whiche I am exited to goon."

And þanne into a place þat she hadde where þer weren
many faire iewelles she ledde me withoute dwellinge, and
of an hucche whiche she vndide, rawhte þe scrippe and
þe burdoun. Neuere I trowe man ne womman so fair a scrippe
[bar] ne burdoun lenede to, in whiche he mihte bettere assure
him, and in a wikkede pas triste. þe fairnesse and þe
goodnesse of hem bisiliche I lokede: wherof I wole not
holde my pees, þat sumwhat þerof I ne wole seye. þe scrippe
was of greene selk, and heeng bi a greene tissu. Lysted it
was wel queynteliche with xii belles of siluer. Whosoeuere
forged hem, a good maister he was, for eche of hem was
enameled, and in eche enamelure þer was propre scripture,
þe whiche right as I sigh it at eye I wole telle yow. [f.37v]
In þe firste þer was writen **God þe Fader** as me thouhte, **þe
heuene and þe eerþe made of nouht, and sithe foormede man;**
in þe secunde **God þe Sone**; in þe thridde **God þe Holi Gost**. But
þese thre thinges weren to me [michel] wunderful and [gretliche
dredinge], for of so nyh þei ioyneden togideres þat þei seemeden

[alle be] oon; and specialliche þis I sey: þat [in þe thre I sigh þat] þer was but oonliche oon claper þat to alle þe thre servede. In þe feerþe belle writen þer was **Goddes Sone Ihesu Cryst from heuene into eerþe descendede, bi þe Holy Gost conseyued, mad man, and of a mayden born**; in þe fyfthe **He was tormented for sinneres and on þe crosse doon,** [nature]* **ded and buryed**; in þe sixte **descended doun into helle for to caste out alle hise freendes and lede hem into Paradys**; in þe sevenþe **sussited**; in þe eyhtþe **steyn into heuene and on þe riht half of his fader sett, for to iuge þe quike and þe dede.** In þe nynthe was set **þe holi Cristene Cherche with þe holi sacramentes þat ben solempnysed þerinne**; in þe tenþe **þe oonhede and þe communioun of þe seyntes, and þe indulgence of sinne bi cristenynge and penaunce**; in þe elevenþe **risinge of alle þe dede þat shulen come to þe iugement in bodi and in soule, and þere shulen heere here sentence**; in þe twelfthe **guerdoun of alle goode dedes, and punyshinge of hem þat þe yuel dedes haue doon and nouht repented hem.** þis is of þe belles þe scripture þat writen is in þe enamelure, bi which (if ye wole) þe bewtee of þe scrippe seen ye mowen.

Now I wole telle yow also of þe burdoun þat was of anooþer facioun. It was liht and strong and euene, [f.38r] and was maad of tre of Sethim þat in no time mai rote, ne perishe for cause of fyr. On þe ende an hy was a pomelle of a round mirour, shynynge and fair, in whiche cleerliche men mihten see al þe cuntre þat was fer. þer was no regioun so fer þat þerinne men ne mihten seen it, and þere I sygh þilke citee to whiche I was exited to gon: riht as I hadde seyn it and aperseyued it bifore in þe mirour, also in þe pomelle I syh it, wherof I was fayn. þe better I louede þe bordoun in sooth, and þe more I preysede his facioun. A litel bineþe, anooþer pomel þer was (a litel lasse þan þat ooþer) þat was maad riht queynteliche of a charbuncle glistringe. Who þat euere it made and cumpasede, and þat to þe burdoun ioyned it, he was not of þis lond: in anooþer place he muste be souht. Ryht wel it was sittinge to þe burdoun, and ryht auenaunt. Nothing þer mislikede me in it but þat it was not yrened; but afterward, she þat shewed it me appesed me wel.

Whan þese iewelles weren drawen out, þanne seide me Grace Dieu: "See heere þe scrippe and þe burdoun þat I

1850

1855

1860

1865

1870

1875

1880

1885

haue bihyght þee: I make þee yifte of hem. In þi viage
þou shalt haue neede of hem. Keep hem wel, and so þou shalt
be wys. þe scryppe Foy is cleped, withoute which þow
shalt neuere do jurney þat ouht shal availe: for þi bred
and þi vitaile þow shuldest in alle times haue þerinne,
and if þow wolt wite þis bi ooþer seyinge þan by myn, Seynt
Poule shal wel enfoorme þee, þat telleth þat it is writen
þat þe iuste liveth bi his scrippe (þat is to seyn, whoso
wel vnderstonde, þat he liueth of þe good þat he taketh
þerinne). þis scryppe is of greene colour, for [f.38v]
riht as greenesse coumforteth þe eye and þe sight, riht so
I sey þee þat sharp feith maketh sighte of vnderstondinge:
ne neuere shal þe soule perfytliche see, if þis greenesse
ne lene him miht and strengthe. And perfore she shal neede
þee for to redye þee in þi wey." "Lady," quod I, "seyth me
for þe loue of God, of þese belles so litele, why þei ben
þus [atached] and stiked in þe skrippe: of þe thre also þat
han but oon claper, whiche to hem is commune." "Serteyn,"
quod she, "in þe time bifore (þat was in þe time þat I
made þe scrippe) it sufficed al sympilliche to leeue in
God perfyteliche: and þanne was þe scrippe withoute ringeres
and withoute belles. But I telle þee þat many erroures
sourdeden sithe, and many harmes. Eche wolde leeue in God
as him likede: oon leeued in oo wise, anooþer in anooþer
wise, at his devys, as þou shuldest wel wite if þow haddest
seyn here erroures. And so was þis scrippe elded and
defouled; but for to recouere þe bewte, and for to do awey
alle erroures, and for oon bileeue shulde be to alle, and
withoute desceite, þe twelve Apostles setten þeron þese
twelve belles þat þer ben, and in eche of hem propir
writinge þat propirliche techeth and seith in what manere
and how men shulden [leeue] in God stedefastliche. þese
twelve belles heere maken þe twelve articles of þe feith,
þat ben þe which þow shuldest stedefastliche bileeue
and haue in þi memorie. Ofte þei shulde awake þee and ringe
at þin ere; for nouht be þei not maad belles ne ringeres:
for if þow were to slowh oþer leftest to looke þe writinge,
at þe leste with ringinge of summe of hem þou mihtest
remembre þee. On þat ooþer side [f.39r] Seint Poul seith
and to þe Romayns he hath writen, þat bi heeringe swich
ringinge men haven þe feith perfytliche so þat he putte
not þe ringinge in þe scryppe: but it exiteth þe memorie

in what manere men shulden bileeue. Nouht þat [þis] sufficeth   1930
onliche to bileeue stidefastliche, for þer ben mo ooþer
thinges þat ben to bileeue stidfastliche, as of þe wyn and
bred þat ben remeeved into flesh and blood; of God also in
Trinite, thre persones in oonhede, wherof þou hast seyn þe
ensaumple in þe belles of whiche þow askedest. For riht as   1935
oo claper serueth to thre belles wel and faire, riht so is
þe Trinite but oo God alone in soothnesse. God alone and
thre it is, and eche of þe thre is God: þat þow shuldest
bileeue stidefastliche, and many ooþere of ringinges of
whiche as at þis time I wole holde me stille, and for to   1940
lasse ennuye leue it: for of þe twelve alle þei hangen, whoso
wel at here rihtes al wel vnderstant."*

Ryght as Grace Dieu spak and · diuisede of þese belles
I, þat biheeld þe scrippe and alwey hadde myn eye þeron,
sygh dropes of blood sowen and dropped þeron, whiche thing
michel displesede me and meevede al my corage [of] þat I   1945
hadde not seyn it bifore, [and þat] I hadde seyn and apperceyued
þe scrippe. "Lady," quod I, "newe I am discoumforted euele.
I se blood shed on þe scrippe, þat neuere er I apperceyuede.
Eyþer apeseth me of þilke blood or elles taketh me anooþer
scrippe." "Haa," quod she, "discoumforte þe shuldest þou   1950
nouht, but coumforte þee: for whan þow wost þe cause, þou
shalt loue þe scrippe þe bettere. þer was sum[f.39v]time
a pilgrym þat highte Steuene, þat in yowþe bar þe scrippe
in alle places þer he wente. But he was aspyed with
theeves for þe scrippe þat was fair: michel þei peyneden   1955
[hem] to bineme it him, and michel peyne þei diden him.
But he defended him so wel þat he wolde for nothing men
shulden bineme him suich a scrippe, but leeuere he hadde
men sloowen him. Algates þei sloowen him and mordred him   1960
and stoned him, and of his blood was þus þis scrippe
bidropped and aproved. But þat time it was fairere for
þe blood þat was al neewe, for colour þat is red upon
greene chaumpe it is wel fair: and þat apperede openliche,
for after his bleedinge it was boren more þan bifore, michel   1965
more, and more desired. Many folk comen after, and so
michel diden þat þei hadden it, and afterward for to defende
[it] and keepe it þei suffreden to dismembre hem, and
suffreden peynes and tormentes to þe deth. Whoso wolde
nombre þe martyres þat for it suffreden deth, þer is neiþer   1970
tunge coude [seyn] it ne herte thinke it ne hond write it,

so þat þouh þilke scrippe were bidropped with þilke blood
and preeued, it is [not] thing þat is to wundre upon, but
it is thing michel [to preyse for þer is non so litel drope
þerof þat nis michel] more woorth þan a margerye, and
more precious. And I sey þee wel þat if þe dropes weren
neewe þow woldest holde hem riht faire. But it is long
time gon þat no wiht bledde of his blood þeron: þe
bleederes ben passed and alle agoon. But þerfore ben þe
dropes of blood þat ben elded neuere þe lasse worth. Of
þe bewte recche þee neuere whan þou hast thing þat is as
michel worth; so þat þe scrippe þus dropped with þis blood
[f.40r] and so preeued I take þee in ensaumple, to þat
ende I sey it þat if men wolden withdrawe it þee oþer
bineme it þee, raþere þow shuldest suffre to hewe þee
and sle þee þan suffre to bineme it þee. Now take it
þanne anoon, for it is sittinge to þee." "Ladi," quod I,
"wel it sufficeth me of þis blood which ye haue seyd me,
but me thinketh riht hevy þat ye take me þis scrippe
bi couenaunt, for I wot neuere how I shal heerafter vse
it. Algates she liketh me, and nothing misliketh me
þerinne, so I wole take it withoute taryinge, sithe I haue
graunt of yow." And þanne withoute lettinge I took it,
and abowte me anoon I dide it, and Grace Dieu halp me þat
arayed it me at hise rightes. Wel glad was I whan I seyh
it aboute me and felte it, for longe bifore it was þat I
hadde desired it michel and asked it.

Now I wole telle yow ayen of þe burdoun of which
Grace Dieu made me sermoun. "After", quod she, "þat I
haue seyd þee of þe scrippe whiche gladeth þee wel, I
wole also telle þee of þe burdoun at þe shorteste þat
I may. þe burdoun hatteth Esperaunce, whiche is good
in eche sesoun: for þilke þat leneth \him/ sikerliche
þerto may not falle. þe wode of sechim of which it is
maad sheweth ful wel which it is. To it þou shuldest
lene þee in alle euel paas wher þou shalt go. In wikkede
paas holde it riht euene, and looke wel on þe pomelles,
for þe pomelles shulen holde þee up and nouht suffre
þee to falle. The hye pomel is Ihesu Crist þat is as þe
lettere seith a mirour þat is withoute spot, in [f.40v]
whiche eche wyght may see his visage: in whiche al þe
world may mire him wel and considere him, for al þe world
þerinne mired is nouht as greet as aas in a dee. In thilke

pomel þou shuldest mire þee and ofte looke þerinne. Lene
þee þerto, and strongliche clyue to þe poyntes, for whan   2015
withinne þou seest wel, þou shalt neuere haue discomfort of
nothing, and as longe as þou lenest þee þerto þow shalt
neuere falle in wikkede paas. Now think heeron if þou be
wys, and þe bettere þow shalt do þi viage. That ooþer pomel
is þilke of whom he was born, þat is þe Virgine Marie   2020
mooder þat conseyuede and bar hire fader; þat is þe
charbuncle glisteringe þat enlumineth þe niht of þe world,
bi þe which ben brouht ayen to wey alle þat ben distracte
and forveied, bi þe which beth enlumined alle þilke þat
beth in derknesse, bi þe which beth reised þe fallen doun   2025
and þe ouerthrowen. And þerfore she hath be graffed bi
subtile art, and ioyned to þis burdoun þat is so fair,
to þat ende þat she be oo pomel, for first þer was but
oon allone whiche sufficed not: eche miht not come þerbi
þerto ne holde it; but bi þis, men comen and lenen   2030
þerto anoon, so þat þis is necessarie to eche wight þat
is pilgrym. þerfore I rede þat þou lene þee þerto and
triste in alle times, for bi it þow shalt be meyntened
and susteyned in alle wikkede paas, and bi it þou shalt
mown come to þat ooþer þat is hyere, so þat whan þou art   2035
lened and afficched to twey pomelles, wel I telle þee
þat sureliche and sadliche þou miht go, and þerfore in þe
burdoun þou miht wel triste þee and assure [f.41r] þee,
for þe pomelles þat ben set þeron shulen susteyne þee in
alle euele paas. þis is a good burdoun. Keep it wel. I   2040
haue yive it þee so þat þyn it is." Thanne in þe hond
she put it me wherwith to myn herte she dide gret ioye,
for wel I seyh þat [redy I was] in al to putte me to my weye.
    But algates it mislikede me of þe burdoun þat it was not
yrened. "Lady," quod I to Grace Dieu, "I may not holde   2045
me, bi God, þat I ne sey yow my thouht of þilke burdoun þat
is not yrened. It mislikeþ me michel, witeth it wel: for
alle ooþere I see yrened, þerfore if ye wole, seith me whi
suich ye haue take it me." "Haa," quod she, "what þou
art a fool! It needeth þee not a belle at þi nekke! Haue   2050
I not right now seyd þee (if þow woldest a litel remembre
þee) þat to þe eende aboue þou shuldest triste þee, and
lene þee to þe pomelles, for þe pomelles shulen holde
þee up and not suffre þee falle? þe eende bineþe dooth þee
nothing, and nouht for þanne wel þou wost þat a burdoun yrened   2055

weyeth more þan þilke þat is vnyrened. Vnyrened I took it þee for to my weenynge þou shuldest bere it þe bett*er*e. And on þat ooþer side, yrened burdo*u*n stiketh deppere in þe fen and in þe dunge þan þilke þ*at* hath noon yren: and þe deppere it stiketh, þe more is þilke empeched þat bereth it ov*er* þilke þat bereth it vnyrened; {and} þ*er*fore I haue take it þee suich, for I wol not þat þou be empeched, neiþer in forwh ne in mire, ne þat þou haue noon encombra*u*nce."
"Haa lady:" q*u*od I, "yit oo woord. Me thinketh I am not a fool: nouht for þat þat ye haue seyd, but [f.41v] for þat of which ye speken nouht. If ho*u*ndes assaile me oþer theeves, and my burdo*u*n be not yrened, trowe ye þei wole drede it so michel as if it were yrened bifore? And for þat cause onlich I [speke] þis, and noon ooþerweys." "þerto" q*u*od she, "I make þee answere, for burdo*u*n is not to smite with ne to fyghte with, but withoute more to lene [þee] to. And if þou seye þou wolt withoute more defende þee, armures with which þou shalt wel defende þee withoute offence, and with which þou shalt wel discou*m*fyte þin enemys riht anoon I wole take þee: for I wot wel wher*e* I shal fynde hem." "Haa lady," q*u*od I, "bi swich condicio*u*n þe burdo*u*n liketh me wel, wherfore I pray yow þat ye fecche þese armures and taketh hem me."

And þa*n*ne Grace Dieu entrede into hire curtyne, and clepede me: "Now bihold", q*u*od she, "an hy to þilke p*er*che. I muste go to fecche armure to go fer with.* Ynowh þow seest to arme þee with: þer beth helmes and haub*er*gouns, gorgeres and jakkes, taarges and al þat needeth to þilke þat wole defende him. Now take þere þat þat þou wolt haue, and arme þee: þow hast leeue." Whan I syh þese faire armures, michel I reioysede me of þe bewtee of hem: but algates I wiste not wel with which I shulde do me profyt best, for I hadde neuere vsed armes, ne I hadde nouht ben armed. "Lady," q*u*od I, "sheweth me now I pray yow, if ye [f.42r] wole, whiche armures I shulde take, and how I shulde arme me: for but if ye helpe to arme me ye hadden do nothing."

And þa*n*ne she took a doublet of a diu*er*s facio*u*n; I sigh neu*er*e noon swich, ne neu*er*e herde speke of noon swich, for riht euene bihynde on þe bak was set an anevelte þat was maad to resseyue strokes of ham*er*es. Of it at þe firste bigynnynge she made me yifte and present: "Loo heer*e*" q*u*od she, "a doublet, þe beste þat eu*er*e man sigh: for whoso hadde neiþer handes ne feet, and were [tached] to a

[pile], [but] þat he hadde þat upon him withoute more he shulde neuere be venquished, but he shulde with gret wurship be victour of alle hise enemys. And ouer I sey þee (and be not abaasht) whoso hath on þilke garnement, he dooth his profyt with þat þat oopere doon here vnprofyt and here harm: clowdes maken his corn growe, and tempestes fylleth hise gerneeres, and pestilence hise seleeres; of grete hardshipes he hath a softe bed, and of tormentes his grete delite; hise deyntees he maketh of pouerte and his solas of aduersitees; fastinges maken hym fat, and syknesses strengthe; pouerte and tribulacioun maken him his recreacioun. þe more men prikken it þe hardere it is: and riht as þe doublet is maad with poynynges (for whi it is cleped a purpoynt) riht so whoso hath it on, of prikkinges he bicometh armed. Bi prikkynges it is worth þat þat it is, and withoute prikkinges it is nothing woorth. If þou wolt wite what it hatteth, Patience men clepe it, whiche is maad to suffre peynes and to susteyne [f.42v] grete prikkinges, for to be as [an] anevelte þat stireth not for þe strok of a feþer, [for to resseyue] and [endure] al with good wille, withoute murmurynge. This doublet wered on Ihesus whan in þe crosse for þee he was hanged: vpon him it was rihted and prikked and mesured aright at his rihtes. Al he suffrede and al endurede, and no woord seyde ne sownede: an anevelte he shewede him and was to alle þe strokes of whiche he was smite, and þerfore on him was forged and moneyed þi raunsoum. þe wikkede smiþes fo\r/geden him on his bak and moneyden him; so þat þou schuldest wel suppose þat whan þe kyng wolde arme him with þese armures þei been goode, and þat þei ben not to refuse: wherfore take hem and do hem on, and so þou shalt be miche þe rediere to do on þat ooþer armure þat upon þese shulden be, for bineþe goth þe dowblet whoso wole arme him bi resoun."

And þanne I took þe garnement and cloþed me: I ne wot how; hevi me thouhte it, and streyt, and to bere it michel it greeuede me. "Lady," quod I, "youre purpoynt was not a poynt shape for me: swich mihte I not bere it withoute greevinge me to michel." "Serteyn," quod she, "þe purpoynt were shape for þe ariht if þow were ariht shape: but on þee it holt þat art not rihted ariht after his riht, for þou art to fat and haste to miche grees vnder

þe wynge and art to boistous, to ryotous and to michel
fed. Swiche thinges maken þee so gret þat withoute
grevaunce þow miht not bere þe purpoynt on þi bak, and
þerfore in al þou muste confoorme þee to it, not it to
þee, doynge awey þat þat is to michel [in] þee: [f.43r]
michel smallere þou moste be if þou wolt be wel cloþed."
"Lady," quod I, "techeth me now how ye vnderstonden þis:
to wite soothliche wheþer me neede ouht a carpentere to
hewe me, how I mihte be rihted and shape to his riht."
"Serteyn," quod she, "ryotous þou art inowh and envyous.
Wite þow shuldest þat þe purpoynt wole rihte þee if þow
wolt bere it withoute dispoylinge; þee needeth noon ooþer
carpentere: it shal hewe þee to his riht, and after it
rihte þee. [þouh þee thinke sore þerof at þis firste tyme,
it nis but for to rihte þee:] but after whan þou art rihted
it shal be to þee neiþer greevous ne harmful. If þer be
any þat [missey] þee, or þat dooth þe vileynye, turne þe
bac towardes him: lawhe in þin herte, and sey no woord. It
shulde nothing recche þee to haue þe berkynge of howndes:
turne þe anevelte, and lat him smyte al at his wille, for bi
þe strokes he shal yive þee he shal rihte þee þe purpoynt.
And also I sey þee þat þerbi þow shalt haue þe gryndinge
of corownement:* for bi swich smytinge and forginge and
bi swich knokkinge shal be forged þee þe corown þat no
man kowde make; þat is þilke with whiche ben corowned
[þe] martires þat þe purpoynt loueden, [þat] upon þe
anevelte suffreden to knokke so michel and strokes to
yiven þat bi þe strokes was forged hem and arayed hem
þe coroun. And þerfore in good feith I rede þee þat þe
purpoynt withoute lettinge þow bere, for in oo tyme
þat hastliche shal come it shal neede þee: þat shal be
whan Tribulacioun shal aspye þee, and assaile þee in
feeld, in wey and in hous, and shal sende þee hire
seruauntes þat so grete strokes shulen smyte upon þee,
and so michel [f.43v] shulen knokken upon þee þat if
þou haddest not on þe doublet, in gret perile of deth þow
shuldest be. Now do þerof þi pleyn wille, for of þe
seyinge I do my devoyr." "Ladi," quod I, "michel it
liketh me þat þat ye seyn, ne of nothing I ayensey yow,
but of so michel þat my powere is not so gret, as I trowe,
þat it mowe suffice and susteyne þe doublet: algates
afforce me I wole to bere it as longe as I may. If ye

wole take me more, looketh wherof I haue neede: I wole be sufficientliche armed þouh I shulde berste."

Thanne she rauhte an haubergeoun of a fair and plesaunt facioun, and seyde me: "Take þis garnement, whiche was maad in olde time, for to fighte ayens deth and ayens alle thilke of his ost: þat is, ayens peynes and tormentes and alle here dredes. For deth is a beste so wylde þat whoso seeth it he woodeth: he leeseth purpos and cuntenaunce, and þe burdoun of Esperaunce. He is yuele bitaken and lost þat is not þanne cloþed with þese armures; but [who] þat with þilke haubergeoun is cloþed preyseth it nouht at a bodde: he gooth suerliche in alle werres to haue loos and conquere prys. For drede of deth he shulde not deyne to turne ayen, ne [ne] wolde not. þis garnement forgede sumtime þe smith of þe hye cuntre, þat forgede þe light and þe sunne withoute tonges and withoute hamer. In þilke time þer was appreeued ne alowed noon ooþer armure: ne yit he is not wel armed þat þerwith is not armed ne cloþed. This haubergeoun hatteth Force whiche Ihesu Cristes champiouns wereden in old time, whiche [f.44r] weren so stable in werre and in tournament, and so stronge, þat þei setten þe deth at nouht; and þat was for þe haubergeoun which was of so strong a shap þat for \no/ wepene ygrounden þer was neuere mayl ybroken: but cause þer was al preeued, whiche shulde not be heled, for with þe nailes with whiche was nayled þe sone of þe smith and ryven, þe mailes were enclowed and rivetted. þe yren was also tempred in þe blood þat com out of hise woundes, wherfore þe haubergeoun was michel þe strengere and þe more sure. And alle þilke þat weren þat time þerinne cloþed, weren so riht strong þat þer was no mortal werre ne [torment], were it neuere so strong ne so cruelle, þat þei dredden a straw. And þerfore þow shalt do it upon þe purpoynt if þou leeue me, and se if þou be meete þertoo."

And þanne þe haubergeoun I took, and anoon after seide here: "Lady, I pray yow þat goodliche er ye make me don on þis garnement, þat ye wole shewe me al þat þat ye wole arme me with, for after þat þat I sigh I wold redye me to be armed." And þanne a gorger, an helme, a targe, a peyre glooves and a swerd she rauhte me withoute any tarynge, and seyde: "With alle þese armures it needeth þou arme þee at þe leste: and if þou kunne defende þe wel þei shule suffice þee ynouh, al be it I wolde take þee

2185

2190

2195

2200

2205

2210

2215

2220

ooþere if I founde gret miht in þee; but I wole keepe hem
to ooþere þat I shal fynde strengere þan þee. With þe
helme and with þe gorger for to keepe hool þin hed þou
shalt first arme þee, whan þou hast doon on þin haubergeoun,
and sithe þe glooves þou shalt take with which þou shalt
[f.44v] glooven þin hondes: for if in hem þou hiddest hem
nouht, þou were not wel armed. This helme as þow shuldest
wite is Attemperaunce of þe sighte, of þe heeringe and
of þe smellinge: thinges þat mown greeve þee, for riht as
þe helme keuereth and refreyneth his wittes, and restreyneth,
riht so Attemperaunce serueth to keepe \þe/ eye þat it be not
to open and to miche abaundoned to folye and to vanitees.
For if þe viseer ne were streyt þer mihte entre in swich
arwe þat euene to þe herte it mihte go, and withoute
remedye wounde it to þe deth. To heere also murmurynge,
bakbitinge, fool speches þilke helme stoppeth so holliche
þat to þe herte ne to þe thouht no dart may misdo, al be
it þat þe wikkede neyhebore can [harde] sheete his arwes
and his springaldes: to þe posternes þei mown wel casten
but þei shulen no fre entree haue in. Of þe smellinge
also I sey þee, for þe helme keuereth it so þat bi his
[ordeyne] smellinge þe herte is nothing hurt. So þus
for to keepe þee þis helm is good to arme þee with, for it
is þilke þat sumtime was cleped Helme of Saluacioun, of
whiche Seint Poul amonesteth þat men don it on here hedes.

Now I wole [sey] þee of þe gorgeer, which [shulde] keepe
[þe] throte hool. Sobirtee it hatteth in þis cuntre and also
ouer see. It is a party of Attemperaunce which was maad
for to restreyne Glotonye: for she taketh folk bi þe
throte and ouercometh hem. But þow shuldest wite þat þis
armure is maad of double mailure for it shulde not be
strong inowh if it ne were so doubled, and þe cause is for
Gloto[f.45r]nye hath double woodshipe: woodshipe of savouringe
and of outrageous spekinge. Bi þe savouringe stiren
þe goomes with which she wolde sle hireself. Bi þe
spekynge maketh þe sleyghtes with which she sleth hire
neighebores, as þow shalt after wite more pleynlyche
whan þou shalt seen it, so þat ayens suich a [maisterman] it
is good to haue a gorgeer, for it is a thing wel sure,
al be it litel armure. And þerfore I rede þee þat goodliche
and bisiliche þou arme þee þerwith; of þi mete and of þi
drink be þou neueremore daungerous: what þou fyndest, take

it gladliche, and of litel hold þe wel apayed. Of spekynge
riht so I sey þee: keep þi mouth, and missey of no wight, and
in alle times spek to alle folk resonableliche. With þis
gorgeer was sumtime armed þe abbot of Chalyt þi goode
patroun Seint William: for þouh he hadde had but bred   2270
and water, as wel he hadde be payed as þouh he hadde had
ooþere mes ynowe, wherof þou miht fynde in his lyf þat he
cowde faste wel among grete mes, and also haue thirst. And
þere þou miht se also þat of spekinge to alle folk he was
not oonliche himself atempree, but he attemprede also þe   2275
euele-spekeres whan he herde hem: 'Sey,' he wolde seyn, 'to
þilke þat is in a feeuere whan he trembleth þat he tremble
nouht, and ye shul see how he wole cesse. Riht so' (he
wolde seyn) 'þilke þat ye speken of wolde cesse if he
mihte, wol gladliche.' So þat whan suich a man armede him   2280
with swich a gorgeer, and gorgered him soo, þou shuldest also
fastne on gladliche þi gorgeere and arme þee þerwith. [f.45v]
Of þe glooues also I sey þee, wherof is good þou be
mynged: for if on þine hondes þou were hurt, with þe remenaunt
þou shuldest litel doo. þe hondes, þat shulden be armed   2285
and glooved with þe glooves, ben touchinges and handlinges
and tastinges: for al be it þat men mown fynde bi al þe bodi
withoute tastinge, algates it is most wist and knowen
bi þe hondes, for þei maken most þe touchinges and þe
tastinges, and þerfore it is more leeued of folk þan ooþere 2290
tastinges ben. þerfore [is] alle [tastinge] generalliche
vnderstonde bi þe hondes. þe glooves with whiche þilke
tastinge and þilke hondes þow shuldest arme ben þese þat
I haue shewed þee, þat with [armurers be named] þe thridde
part of Attemperaunce which men clepen Continence: þe which 2295
seyinge in singuler may wel be seid equipolle to a plurelle,
for of dede and of wille his name shulde be doubled, for þe
dede shulde not suffice if þe wille ne were þerwith. With
oo glooue shulde no wiht be wel glooved ne wel armed, so
to be withoute [ennuye] tweyne needen, for dede and wille   2300
muste boþe be had: goode þei ben boþe þo tweyne togideres,
as me thinketh, and couenable. Swich [continence] þus
doubled is cleped of summe gaynpayn, for bi it is wunne
þe bred bi þe whiche is fulfilled þe herte of [man];
and þat was figured heerbifore in þe bred þat Dauid askede: 2305
for Achimelech wolde neuere graunte it him ne take it him
bifore þat he wiste he was glooued and armed with gaynpaynes.

þis þou miht fynde if þou wult studie in þe Book of Kynges. þese [f.46r] glooues hadde sumtyme Seynt Bernard whan þe womman was leyd bi him in his bed al naked: for howeuere she tastede him and stired him and exited him, neuere turned he him towardes hire, ne to hire taste assentede. She fond hise hondes so armed þat she wende him a man of yren, wherfore confused she departede, and wente out of his bed withoute hurtinge him; and þat maden þe gaynpaynes with whiche he hadde armed hise hondes, and þerfore I rede þee þat goodliche þou arme þee lich: for þerfore I haue brouht hem þee hider, and presented hem.

Of þe swerd þou shuldest wite þat bettere armure þou miht not haue: for if þou kowdest wel helpe þee þerwith and haddest noone ooþere armures, þow shuldest be more dred certeyn þan if þou were armed with ooþere armures and haddest noon, oþer cowdest not helpe þee þerwith. þis swerd Justice is cleped: amonges alle þe most chosen and þe beste þat euere girde or handelede kyng or erle. Neuere was [Ogiers] swerd ne Rowlondes ne Olyueeres so vertuowse ne so mihti, ne hadden so michel bountee. þis is þilke þat whan time is, yildeth to eche þat þat is his. þis is a swerd to an emperour, a regent, a gouernour, bi whiche alle þilke of his hous ben gouerned withoute mistakinge. For in alle times she manaseth þat þer be noon þat misdo. She keepeth þe bodi fro rebellinge, and constreyneth þe herte to loue God. She maketh þe herte conuerte from fraude, and forsake baret. þe will, þe affeccioun, þe vnderstondinge and þe entente, þe soule and alle hire meyne so arayeth hem and [f.46v] chastiseth hem* þat þer is noon of hem þat durste misdoon hire, on peyne of drawinge out of boþe here eyen; for anoon withoute abidinge it shulde be corrected with þe swerd. Ensaumple þou hast in Seint [Beneyt] þat with þis swerd was girt (þe king had girt him þerwith whan he made him lord of lawes), for whan he sygh þat his body þat was tempted wolde not obeye to him as good emperour and as good gouernour, with þe swerd he smot it so cruelliche, and punished it, þat wel nygh he hadde slayn it: wherfore it was neuere afterward rebelle ne inobedient to his comaundement. This swerd þou shalt bere and bi it þou shalt defende þee from alle þilke þat I haue seyd þe bifore, whiche been [þi] priuee enemyes: for enemy more daungerous, more shrewed ne more perilous þow ne miht haue þan [þi]

*pri*uees and þilke þat ben nigh þee. So whan þou feelest   2350
any rebelle and go ayens þi saluacio*u*n, smite him so harde
þat he be no more so fers ayens þee. And whan þou seest
any of hem forueyne and ap*er*ceyuest it [and] þou seest þe
herte erre and thinke to any baret, whan þou seest þe
thouht gon out of good wey and ordeynee, whan þou seest þe   2355
wille encline to dede disordeynee, þa*n*ne lat þe swerd be
shake and put bifore: bi it lat eche be redressed and
driven ayen *in*to his place. Now do it þus wysliche, for I
passe me shortliche."

"Ladi," q*u*od I, "it were wel sittinge, as me thinketh,   2360
þat sum sheþe I hadde of yow wherinne I mighte putte þe
swerd: for I mihte not alwey bere it þus, withoute þat it
greeuede me. On þat ooþ*er* side, Seynt [Beneyt] bar it not
þus naked [f.47r] but he hadde it girt aboute him as þe
king hadde girt it; and þat haue ye wel tauht me, bi which   2365
thing me thinketh þat su*m*time þe swerd hadde a gerdel and a
sheþe in whiche she was put. And þat wolde I haue, [but]
þat it were youre wille." "Sertes ful wel þou seist," q*u*od
she, "and wel me liketh þat ententyf to my woordes þou hast
ben; and þ*er*fore al at þi wille þe scauberk to þe swerd   2370
þou shalt haue, and gerdel with which þou shalt gerde it."
And þa*n*ne anoon I sigh hire gon toward þe noble perche þat
is toward þe perche on whiche þat ooþ*er*e armures weren and
hongen. From þennes þe scauberk she vnheeng, and brouhte
it, and seyde: "Loo heere þilke þat Seynt Beneyt putte   2375
in þe swerd and bar it. A good thong þ*er* is for to wel
gerde þee, and a good bocle for to [streyne] it. Now take
it and keepe it wel, and leese it for nothing. þilke
scauberk is cleped Humilitee bi his riht name, in whiche
þow shuldest þi swerd herberwe and þi justnesse hide: for   2380
if any good þou seest in þiself, and þat þou hast done þat,
and þat, hyde it þou shuldest in þilke scauberk which is
maad of dedliche skyn, mynginge þiself and thinkinge, in
alle times biknowinge þat þou art dedlich and þat of þiself
þou hast not doon it, but þat it is bi me. Bithinke þee of   2385
þe publican and þe [pharisien], þat diu*er*sliche hadden here
swerdes and beren hem: for þilke þat in þe sheþe hadde it,
and bikneewe himself a sinnere, was preysed and hyed; and
þat ooþ*er* for he hadde his swerd vnsheþed and vnscauberked
was lowed. It is michel more worth oon accuse himself and   2390
biholde his feebelnesse, [f.47v] entende to þe scauberk and

to þe leþer, þan to diskeuere his iustice, [þan] to sey 'Bihold
my swerd which I haue vnsheþed yow': for so doon þe prowde
folk ful of wynd, and vauntynge folk þat ne seecheen but
veynglorie and þat þer be alwey mynde of hem. þow shalt
not do so. Raþer þou shalt hyde þe swerd in þe sheþe, lowinge
þee and humblinge: for causes þou shalt fynde ynowe whan
wel þou hast biholden þiself. And þanne whan þou hast [þus] put
it in and sheþed it, with þe girdel þou shalt girde þee:
and with it þine armures þou shalt [streyne], to þat eende þat
þou bere hem þe more sureliche and þe fastere; for þere is
noon, be he neuere so wel armed, but it be fastned aboue
eiþer with girdel or with baudryk þat shulde sey he were
wel armed. So þat þe girdel shal be [to þee worth] a baudryk
whan it is wel girt aboute þee and with his bocle wel fastned.

þe girdel hatteth Perseueraunce, and þe bocle is cleped
Constaunce, whiche shulden in alle times holden hem togideres
withoute any departynge: for at þe neede and at þe assaut
þat oon withoute þat ooþer is wel litel woorth. þe girdel
for þe grete lengthe holt þe armures in miht. She holt hem
vertuous, with þe swerd þat she susteyneth. She holt hem
alwey oon, keepinge hem þat þei ben not doon of for noon
enchesoun in no time ne in no sesoun. þe bocle holt and
keepeth faste þe girdel, þat it vnfastne nouht. Al it holt
in estat stedefastliche and keepeth al sureliche, for þat
is þe riht fastnynge and þe surenesse of þe armure, so þat
whan þow askedest þese thinges it liked me wel, for þer is
nothing þerof þat it ne is covenable to þee and [f.48r]
riht profitable. Now vse hem as þou shuldest, and þou
shalt doo þi wurshipe gretliche." Whan þese woordes I herde,
I bicom thouhti and abashed, for of þis exposicioun was litel
myn entencioun. Scauberk and girdel lasse greevinge I wende
wel haue had withoute fable: and al were it þat I wolde þat
þe purpoynt whiche I hadde on hadde be doun, always I suffrede
at þat time and nothing answerde.

Whan of þe scauberk she hadde þus seid me, she took
hire woordes ayen anoon. "Now I wole sey þee", quod she, "yit
a woord of þe targe. Withoute targe is no wiht wel ne ariht
armed, ne wel kept, for þe targe defendeth þat ooþer armure
from [empeyringe]: bi it been þe ooþere kept þat þei ben not
atamed. And as longe as it is put bifore, so longe ben þe
ooþere saaf. þis targe hatteth Prudence, whiche þe kyng
Salomon bar sumtime customableche for to do riht and

iugement. þis targe was more woorth to him þan two hundreth
sheeldes and thre hundreth targes of gold þat he putte in
his neewe hous; for bi þis targe he was wurshiped and   2435
preysed in his time, and whan he hadde afterward lost it
al his wurshipe fel: alle hise targes of gold and hise sheeldes
weren neuere woorth to him a red hering, for lost þei weren.
þis targe targede him as longe as he bar it with him but   2440
soone was he lost whan þe targe was lost, so þat þerbi þow
miht see and apperceyue, if þou wolt, þe woorth of his targe
whiche was more þan fyve hundreth of gold. þerfore I rede þee
bere it, [f.48v] þee and þin armure to keepe and for to pleye
þerwith and scarmushe whan þow seest enemyes come; þouh þou   2445
kunne not pleye at þe bokeler or kunne not wel helpe þiself,
she shal teche þee to pleye: ooþer maister shal þee noon
neede. Now take it whan þow art armed with [þe tooþer]
armures þat þou hast. It were wel time, if þow woldest, þou
tooke hem to doon hem on: for þerfore I haue rauht hem and   2450
vnfolden hem and taken hem þee. Do hem on faste, for þou
hast neede of nouht elles."

   Whan þese woordes I vnderstood, myn herte al afrighte,
for as I haue seyd, I hadde not customed to be armed. And
on þat ooþer side michel I bisorwede þe purpoynt þat I hadde   2455
on. Algates for to hire plesaunce doon and fulfille, to arme
me I assayede, and at þe haubergeoun I began. Vpon þe
purpoynt I dide it on: but þat it was wel sey I nouht. Whan
I hadde doon it on, anoon I took þe double gorgere and dide
it aboute my nekke, and sithe shof myn hed in þe helm and   2460
hid it. After I took þe gaynpaynes and þe swerd, with
whiche I girte me. And sithe whan I was þus armed I putte
þe targe to my side. Al I dide as she hadde seyd me, al
were it it liked me litel. Whan armed þus I sih me, and
þat I felte þe armure upon me greevous and hevi, and   2465
pressinge me as me thouhte: "Lady," quod I to Grace Dieu,
"mercy I pray yow þat of nothing ye displese yow, þowh I
shewe yow my disese. þese armures greven me so miche þat
I may not go foorth. Eiþer I muste heere abyde or alle I
muste doon hem of. þe helme alþerfirst dooth me so gret   2470
encumbraunce þat I am þerinne [f.49r] al astoned and blynd
and def. I see nothing þat liketh me, ne heere nothing
þat I wolde. Bi þe smellinge I feele nothing, þe whiche me
thinketh gret torment. Afterward þilke shrewede gorgeer (þat
yuele passioun smyte it) bi þe throte maistrieth me soo,   2475

[þat me thinketh it shulde strangle me, it streyneth me so]
þat I may not speke às I wolde, ne [auale] nothing þat
deliteth me, ne þat profiteth me anything to þe bodi.
Afterward with þe gaynpaynes wel I wot I shal neuere winne
my bred; youre glooues ben not for hem þat han tendre   24
handes, and tendre I haue hem, and þat forthinketh me. And
þei ben harde out of mesure: I mihte not endure hem longe
swiche withoute sheendinge myself. Riht so of þe remenaunt:
I sey, shortliche to deliuere me, al greeueth me so riht
gretliche þat neuere at shorte wordes I mihte telle it, but   24
I hadde grettere wit þan I haue. [Souprised] I am as Dauid
was, þat hadde not lerned armes. Armed he was, but bisiliche
and hastiliche he leyde hem doun. And perfore as he dide
wole I doo, for his ensaumple liketh me wel: alle þe
armures I wole ley doun, and with þe burdoun I wole passe   24
me. I haue leeuere go lightliche þan abide heer sureliche.
Go foorth miht I nouht if I ne leyde doun þe armure, and so
shulde I be letted to go [into] þe faire citee. Wherfore I pray
yow it anoye you nouht; ne [ne] holdeth it not for a despyte."

"Sertes," quod she, "now sheweth it wel þat   24
withholde þou hast nothing of al þat I haue seyd þee, or
wel litel þou thinkest þeron; oþer þou weenest perauenture
þat in me be so gret vnthrift þat my wordes ben fables oþer
þat þei ben disseyuable. Wenest þou it, so God keepe þee,
sey it me raþere bitimes [f.49v] þan to late!" "Lady,"   25
quod I, "for þe loue of God, mercy: weeneth it neuere soo. I
wot wel þat ye seyn nothing þat ne is ordeyned for wele.
But my miht streccheth nouht to þat, þat armour mowe
longe be bore of me. Nouht for þat I haue foryete youre
woordes of anything, for certeyn I bithinke me wel þat ye   25
haue seyd me, þat þouh at þe firste þei doon me encumbraunce
þei shulden not so whan I were \longe/ lerned of hem. But I
sey yow þat I may not lerne hem, for I fynde in me to gret
feebilnesse and in hem to gret hardnesse: þese ben thinges
gretliche [vnlikynge] and discordinge." "And whi", quod she, 25
"hast þou put me to trauaile, and wherto hast þou required
me þe armures whan þou miht not bere hem (oþer wolt not
bere hem?" "Lady," quod I, "I thouhte not þeron whan ye
setten me in þe wey. Burdoun yrened I hadde asked yow al
onliche. But whan of armures ye speken to me, and   2
amonested me of hem, þanne I required hem, for wel I
wende my strengthe hadde ben for to haue boren hem.

But ooþerweys it is, for in me no strengthe is, I se it
wel, for I am wery as soone as I am armed." "Strengthe
þou hast not" quod she, "for herte in þee þou hast noon.   2520
It is nouht for þat þou ne art sholdred ynowh and boned:
strong and mihti ynowh þou art, if any good herte in þee
þow haddest. For of þe herte cometh þe strengthe of man,
as þe appel of þe appel tre. What mihte seye a litel man,
whan þow þat seemest a chaumpioun refusest to bere þese   2525
armures, and excusest þe bi [feeblesse]? [f.50r] What
shuldest þou also doo, I prey þee, if þou mostest be armed
to keepe þee from ooþere? þou maist not bere hem, as þou
seist. Yit also I prey þee what shalt þou do whan þi wey
þou shalt go vnarmed, and þat þine enemyes shulen assaile   2530
þee and enforce hem to sle þee? Serteyn þanne þou \shalt/
seyn 'Allas, whi woldest þou evere vnarme þee? Whi leeuedest
þou not Grace Dieu? Now þou art all disceyued. Now þou wost
what mischeef it is, and wost also wel þat so gret
greevaunce was it not of beringe of þe armure as it is to   2535
endure þese harmes. Now weren þe armures gret counfort to
me if I hadde hem. Allas wheþer euere I shal mown fynde
Grace Dieu ayen, þat she wole arme me?' Whan þou hast þus
icryed, and þat þou art wounded to þe deth, weenest þou, so
God saue þee, þat I wole þanne gladliche drawe me þiderward   2540
whan þou hast of nothing leeued me and for þi goode? And on
þat ooþer side, þouh I wente so God kepe þee what shulde I
do þeere? þou shuldest be now michel strengere þan þou
shalt be þanne, for þou shalt [þanne be] feeblished with
woundes þat þow shalt haue. So þat whan þou miht not now   2545
bere þe armures ne endure hem, at þat time \to come/ I shulde
go for nouht, and for nouht I shulde trauaile me. Now
anoon is þe time to lerne armes withoute any more abidinge.
If þou leeue me, aboute þee þou shalt holde hem and keepe
hem, to þat eende þat whan it shal be neede þou mowe helpe   2550
þee with hem. If þei ben hevy, go faire: for softe men fer
goth. [f.50v] Soonere is þe mule ofte-times at Seynt James
þat goth roundliche, þan is þilke þat smiteth and sporeth his
hors and maketh him go sharpliche: for michel soonere he
fyndeth encombraunce þan þe mule þat goth roundliche [her] wey.   2555

Of þat þou spekest of Dauid, þat þe armure sumtime leyde
doun: I sey þee þat if of him þou wolt take ensaumple, I
wole not undertake þee. But I wole þou vnderstonde how þow
shalt make þi foundement: for first þou shuldest biholde

and considere his chyldhode, for chyld he was þat time, and
litel, as þe story seith; also on þat ooþer side, þe
armures whiche weren nouht for a [poopet] but þei weren for þe
sone of Saul, þe gretteste of þe cuntre. Wherfore þou shuldest
wel thinke þat þei weren grete and stuffed and right hevy.
So þat (þese twey thinges biholden and thouht diligentliche)
with gret riht Dauid dide of þe armure and leyde hem doun. For
Saul þei weren goode, but for Dauid weren þei nothing woorth:
for þat þat is good for a colt is not good for a staloun.
þis is þat Aristotle seith in *Etiques* where it is writen.
But if Dauid hadde ben as gret as þou as he was sithe,
and þanne he hadde vnarmed him, serteynliche þou were
þanne caused for to take ensaumple of him and do as he
dide; but þus dide he neuere, ne þus to do tauht not þee,
for whan he was bicomen a man, he was armed in alle werres.
It needeth not to suppose þat he vnarmed into werres wente:
for if so he hadde gon, onlyue hadde he neuere turned ayen.
þe armures in alle times he louede, and þat time þat he
vnarmed him of þe armure of Saul, he [f.51r] took ooþere
with whiche he sloow Golias: þilke þat time weren to him
couenable. If þou were a chyld as he was, þow mihtest do as
he dide. I wolde wel suffre þat in þi chyldhode þou haddest
not so gret penaunce. But þou art gret ynowh to bere þese
armures if þou wolt preeue þiself wel, and shame þou
auhtest to haue if þou forsake to bere hem."

"Ladi," quod I, "I see ful wel þat I shulde nothing
winne to resiste, ne to argue, ne to despute ayens you. But
I telle you þat doun I moste ley al togideres withoute more
abidinge. þer is noon þat of I ne wole do, for þer is noon
of whiche I haue ioye: alle þese armures han frushed me and
pressed me and defouled me." And þanne þe bocle I vnboclede
and þe armures I vnlacede, sithe leyde doun girdel and swerd,
with þe targe litel-biloued. Whan she sygh me so doo,
anoon she areynede me and seyde: "Sithe þow wolt þus vnarme
þee, and al þin armure do awey, þou shuldest at þe leste
biseeche me to fecche þee oon (whoso it euere were) þat were
mihty, þat mihte bere þe armure, and þat trussede hem on
þe shulder and bere hem after þee, to þat eende þat þou mihtest
take hem alle times þat þou haddest neede." "Ladi," quod I,
"so michel I haue offended you þat I durst not aske yow
þat: but now I require it yow in biseechinge." "Now a litel"
quod she, "abide me, and I wole [lede] þee suich on I trowe

þat shal [wel susteyne] þe armure and þat wel shal bere hem
with þee." And þanne Grace Dieu wente hire (I wot not wel
into what place) and I al aloone abod þere where I vnarmede
me of alle poyntes. I dide [f.51v] of gorgeer and haubergeoun   2605
and helm and doublet. Oonlich I withheeld þe scrippe and þe
burdoun for pilgryme. Whan I sih me þus vnarmed þanne I was
al discounforted. "Aa, goode swete God," quod I, "what shal I
doo, whan so michel peyne I haue do to Grace Dieu my
maistresse and my goode procuresse? She hadde now arayed me   2610
queynteliche and nobleche: as an erl arayed me she hadde, and
as a duke. Nothing failede me: but I ayens hire techinge and
hire swete amonestinge haue al doon of and haue nothing
withholde. Faire swete God, why haue I my vertu lost, and
where haue I doon it? Whi am I not more mihti, more strong,   2615
more hard, more vertuows, so þat I mihte susteyne and suffre
wel þe armures? Michel I were þe more worth certeyn, and Grace
Dieu wolde loue me þe bettere: alle folk wolden [also] preyse
me þe more and loue me þe more and drede me þe more. But [nouht]
it is [worth]. I mihte not endure hem bi no wey. To Grace Dieu   2620
I committe me, and al in hire I wole abide: yit I trowe she
wole helpe me, and þat she wole not yit faile me; and þerof
she hath maad semblaunt (wherfore my counfort is þe grettere)
for (for to make me ashamed)* she is gon bisyliche to fecche
sum wight and bringe, þat mihte bere þese armures."   2625

As I was in þis plyt and diuisede þus myself aloone,
cam Grace Dieu, þat ledde a wenche þat hadde noone yen as me
thouhte at þe firste whan I syh hire; but whan she was nyh
comen to me and þat I hadde wel apperceyued hire, I sigh þat
hire [light] was set in hire haterel bihynde, and bifore she   2630
sigh nothing. þis was thing [f.52r] riht hidous as me
thouhte, and riht dreedful, and I was þerof wunderliche
abashed and thouhti. As heerof I thouhte and strongliche
wundrede me, Grace Dieu spak to me: "Now I se wel," quod she,
"now I see how þow art a wurþi knyght, and whan þou shuldest   2635
fihte þou hast leyd doun þin armure and art discounfited
withoute smitinge of strok. þee needeth a bath to bathe þee
and a softe bed to ley þee inne; a surgien to sounde and
counforte ayen þe senewes þat ben brused." "Ladi," quod I,
"þerof shule ye be leche and confortouresse: for soothliche   2640
I am so wery þat I mihte no more susteyne þe armure, ne I
hadde no more strengthe; wherfore I pray yow ye ben not wroth
ne euel apayed, for yit I haue trist and hope to yow of all."

"Now," quod she, "I haue founden þee þis wenche, and led
hire þee from a cuntre þat is ferre, for to socure þee at þi
neede: for wel I see but I helpe þee soone þou woldest go a
shrewede wey. þis wenche þou shalt see, and þine armures þou
shalt take hire, and she with þee shal beren hem, to þat ende
þat alwey whan it is neede (as I haue seyd þee) þou fynde hem
redy and do hem on. For but if þou haddest hem alwey nygh
þee, and didest hem on at þi neede, þou shuldest be ded and
slayn, and euele betaken." "Lady," quod I, "of þis monstre
whiche ye haue maad me a shewinge of wolde I fayn wite
þe name, and whi it is of swich facioun. It is a thing
disgisy to me and nouht acustomed. On þat ooþer side I
wende as I hadde lerned of yow þat a seruaunt ye wolde
haue led me light and strong for to helpe [f.52v] me: for
þe craft of swich a wenche is but to bere a pot—swich a
wenche mihte neuere endure to bere swiche armures." "Therof"
quod she, "I wole sey þee shortliche ynowh and answere þee.
þis wenche [hatteth bi her name riht and is] cleped Memorie,
whiche apperceyueth nothing ne seeth of þe time comynge, but
of þe olde time she can wel speke, and diuise to þe time
passed. And bihynde ben sette hire yen and hire light. It is not
thing riht dreedful [ne hidous] as þow weenest, but it is thing
riht necessarie to alle þilke þat wolen make here [mugoe]
and here prouidence of any wit or science. Er þis hadden
clerkes of vniuersitees fallen to pouerte if here havinge
or kunnynge þat þei geten bifore ne kept hem: for litel is
woorth thing ygoten if after þe getinge it ne be kept. So
she hath þe eyen bihynde, and þerbi wite wel þat she is
tresorere and keepere of science and of gret wysdom. And
after þat þou shuldest wite þat al þe wit and þe kunnynge
she keepeth: she bereth it so and in alle places she hath
it with hire, so þat if þou make hire bere and keepe þese
armures with þee, she shal norishe hem,* ne neuere daunger
shal she make þerof. As strong as she is to bere hem,
as mihti she is to keepe hem. And þerfore haue hire not in
despyt as þou hast seyd bifore, þat þou holdest hire for a
wenche þat shulde but bere a pot; but þiself þou shuldest
despise and litel preyse if so miche good þow coudest: for
þat þat þou maist not bere she shal wel bere withoute
greevinge hire. And [f.53r] þat shal be a grettere
confusioun to þine eyen þan if a seruaunt bere hem þat were
strong and mihti. And þerfore avisiliche and witingeliche

I haue brouht hire to þee, to þat ende þat whan she hath þe
armure and shal bere hem, þat þou assaye to bere also, or
elles þat þou haue gret confusioun." "Ladi," quod I, "sithe
it is þus, I wole to yow neiþer sey ne ayensey. Ne also
ayensey yow miht I nouht wel of nothing. Now lat hem þanne   2690
alle be houen upon hire and trussed, and sithe I wole go
bifore and she shal sewe me." And þanne she and I hoven hem
up, and to Memorye tooken hem. And she took hem gladliche,
as it was gret neede. Whan þei weren trussed Grace Dieu, God
yilde hire, wel goodliche spak to me in seyinge me swiche   2695
woordes: "Now þou art", quod she, "arayed to go into þe
faire citee. þou hast Memorie [þi] soomeer þat after þee
shal come bihynde, whiche shal bere þin armure to arme þee
whan it shal be time; þou hast þe scrippe and þe burdoun, þe
faireste þat euere man bar; of alle thinges þou were redy if   2700
of Moises bred þou haddest. Go and take it; leeue þou hast,
al be it þou hast not deserued it. But keep þee wel þat of
þat þou shuldest do passe þee nothing as þou hast seyn and
knowen þat men shulden doon."

And þanne to Moyses I wente and of his bred I asked   2705
him, þat was of þe releef þat he yaf and grauntede to þe
pilgrimes. He yaf it me and I took it, and sithe in [my]
scrippe I putte it. [f.53v] Sithe to Grace Dieu I turnede
ayen, and of hire goodshipes I thankede hire, preyinge hire
þat she wolde not leue me, ne alonygne hire, and   2710
biseechinge hire þat at my neede she wolde not be fer fro
me; for wel I wiste (as I seyde hire) þat withoute hire I
mihte nothing. "Serteyn," quod she, "soothliche withoute
me þou miht nothing do, and soone þou shuldest be
discounfited if of me þou ne haddest keepinge. þerfore   2715
þou doost as þe wise whan þou requirest þat þat þou wost
is needeful to þee. And for [þat] I fynde þy requeste in
nothing dishoneste, þerfor to go with þe is myn entente as
at þis time, and nouht to departe fro þe I thinke, if it
ne be by þin offence." "Lady," quod I, "michel graunt mercy: 2720
now I haue ynowh as me thinketh." "Now vnderstonde,"
quod she, "how gon with þee I thinke. þer ben summe þat
hauen in here freendes so gret trist and hope þat þei ben
miche þe wurse, for þei thinken þat þei [shulen] be forborn
and kept bi hem, þouh þei hauen doon, or doon, yuele. So   2725
for þat þou shalt not triste to michel to me or lene þee,
to þat entente þat þou do [no] harm in trist of a susteynour,

of þi sight [and] of þin eye I wole not be seyn. I haue a
stoon þat to þe folk (whan I wole) yelt invisible. Bi þilke
I wole hyde me from þine eyen so þat whan þou shalt weene
þat I be with þee, þanne perauenture I shal be ago bi sum
ooþer wey sumtime, and turned from þee; and þat shal be
whan þou puttest þee ooþerweys þan [f.54r] dueliche: as
whan þou wolt not deingne to aske þi wey, oþer wolt not
go; and whan þou wolt leue þe goode weyes and go bi þe
wikkede weyes. þerfore be avised to go wysliche hensforthward;
for from hensforth I vse and wurche [of þe same pyer]: and
anon I parte fro þi siht and þi biholdinge." As soone as
she hadde þat seid, more sih I hire not, wherof loowh not
myn herte, which sorweful was, but more mihte it not do.
Algates to go my wey as I hadde purposed it I wolde not leue,
but I wolde anoon take my wey. To Memorie I bad þat she
shulde come after me and þat she sewede me: þat she brouhte
myn armure and þat she foryete noon. She soothliche dide it
so; al she brouhte, nothing she loste. And it was gret neede,
for after I fond so gret encumbraunce þat I hadde be ded
sumtime if I ne hadde be wa\r/nished of armure. Nouht þat I
dide hem on, ne took hem alwey at my neede, for many times
bi my slouthe I suffrede strok of dart of arwe þat I hadde
not suffred if I hadde be wel armed.

Now I haue seid yow al withoute lesinge oon partye of
my swevene. þe remenaunt I shal telle yow heerafter whan I
haue time. And ye þe more gladliche shulen heere it whan ye
ben rested awhile. Withoute interualle alle thing enoyeth,
boþe þe faire weder and þilke of reyn. Anooþer time ye
shule come ayen, if more ye wole heere: and þerwhiles I wole
avise me to telle ariht as I mette.

Heere endeth þe firste partye of þis book.
And heere biginneth þe secunde partye. [f.54v]

After þat I haue seyd bifore of þat I sigh in slepynge,
ooþere wundres þat I sigh [sithe], as I haue bihyght yow, I wole
shewe yow, for it is not resoun to hele it. As I hadde
ordeyned me at alle poyntes to go my wey, I bigan michel to
thinke whi it was þat I miht not þus bere myn armures, or whi
þat I hadde not as gret power as þilke wenche hadde þat bar
hem after me. "Now I am a man", quod I, "þat seemeth a
chaumpioun (for mayme wot I noon in me, but am hool of alle
lymes) and þat am maad ynowh to bere boþe þis wenche and hire

berdene, whens cometh it þat I am þus failed of miht þat I may
not endure an hour þat þat I see hire bere? Shame and
confusioun it is to me when she is strengere þan I."

As on þis I thouhte, and þat allewey thinkinge wente, I
mette in my wey a gret cherl euele shapen, grete [browed] and
frounced, þat bar a staf of crabbe tree, and seemed to be a
wel euel misterman and an euel pilgrim. "What is þis?" quod
he, "Whider goth þis pilgrim, Lord whider goth he? He weeneth
he be now ful wel arayed and queyntised, but anoon with me he
shal lette, and to questiouns he shal answere." Whan þus I
herde him speke, I bicom wunder sore abashed, for I wende he
wolde haue ronne upon me withoute more abidinge. Algates
curteisliche I spak to him, and humbliche: "Sire," quod I,
"I require yow þat ye wole not enoye me ne enpeche me of my
viage, for I go fer in pilgrimage, and a litel [f.55r]
lettinge wolde greve me gretliche." "Serteyn," quod he, "þe
disturbaunce comet{h o}f þin ouertrowinge. Whens cometh it
þee, {so G}od saue þee, and whi art þou swich and swich þat
þou da\r/st passe þe lawe þat þe king hath [wold ordeyne]? A
while ago þe kyng made defence þat non took scrippe, ne þat
noon bare it with him, ne [ne] handelede burdoun: and þou
ayens his ordinaunce bi þi foolliche surquidrye hast vndertake
to bere boþe þat oon and þat ooþer, as me thinketh. Whens
cometh it þee, and how hast þou dorre be so hardi? Euele þow
come, and euele þow wentest, and euele hider þou brouhtest
hem. Neuere day in þi lyve ne didest þow a grettere folye."

Whan þese woordes I vnderstood, more þan bifore I was abashed,
for what to answere I ne wiste, ne [answere] hadde I noon.
Gladliche an aduocat I wolde haue hired me if I mihte haue
founden him, for gret neede I hadde of oon if I hadde wist
where to haue purchaced him. Algates [as] I studyede how I
mihte escape, as I lifte up myne eyen I sygh [comen þat after
which I hadde gret desire—þat was] Dame Resoun þe wise whiche
men mown wel knowe by þe langage, for she wole nothing sey but
sittingeliche and wel ordeyned. Bifore I hadde seyn hire,
wherfore she was þe more knowen to me. I was riht ioyful whan
I syh hire, for wel I thouhte þat bi hire shulde þilke crookede
cherl be maat which harde hadde grucched me: and so he was at
þe laste, and I pray yow vnderstondeth how.

Resoun cam euene to him, and seide him: "Cherl, sey me,
now God keepe þee, wherof þow [f.55v] seruest and whi þou

seemest so diuers. Art þou a repere or a mowere, or an
espyour of weyfareres? How hattest þou, and where gaderedest
and tooke þi grete staf? þe staf is not auenaunt ne sittinge
to a good man." And þanne þe cherl lened him on his staf, and
seyde hire: "What is þis? Art þou [mayresse] or a neewe
enquerouresse? Shewe þi commissioun and at þe leste þi name I
shal wite, and þe grete powere þat þou hast, þat bi semblaunt
þou shewest me: for if I were not suer þerof, I wolde to þee
answere nothing." And þanne Resoun putte hire hond into hire
bosum bi a spayere, and took out a box of which she drow a
lettere, sithe seyde him: "Serteyn my poowere I wole wel do
þe to wite. Hold, see heere my commissioun: rede it, and þou
shalt wel wite my name and my power, and who I am, and whi I
am come hider." "Serteyn," quod he, "I am no clerk, ne I can
nothing in þi leves; rede hem as þou wolt, for wite wel I
preyse hem litel." "Beawsire," quod she, "alle men ben not
of þin opynioun. Of michel folk þei ben wel preysed and
loued and auctorised: and nouht for þanne þou shalt heere hem
but my clerkes failen me alle. I wole putte þee out of
suspessioun, and shewe þee what powere I haue. Come forth
clerk," quod she to me: "vndoo þese letteres out of plyt,
rede hem bifore þis bachelere þat weeneth he be a lord. Whan
he heereth hem red, if God wole he shal answere me." And
þanne I took hem and redde hem, wherof þe cherl was nothing
wel apayed, for alwey he grummede and alwey [he] shook his
chyn, And [f.56r] at euery woord I redde, I sygh his teeth
grynte. If ye wole wite þe tenure of þe lettere, heerafter
ye shule heere it.

'Grace Dieu (bi whom gouernen hem þei seyn þe kynges, and
regnen) to Resoun oure goode louede freend, and in alle goode
dedes wel proued, gretinge: and of þat we sende, dooth pleyn
execucioun. Of neewe we haue vnderstonde (wherof us is not
[fair]) þat a cherl shrewede, prowd and daungerous, þat bi his
name maketh clepe him and nempne him Rude Entendement, hath
maad him an espyour of weyes, and a waytere of pilgrimes, and
wole bineme hem here burdouns and vnscrippe here scrippes,
bigylinge hem with lyinge woordes. And for he wolde be þe
more dred, he hath borwed of Orgoill his wikkede and cruelle
staf, þat men clepen Obstinacioun (þe whiche michel more
displeseth me þan dooth þe frouncede cherl): for þe which
thing, maundement we yiven you nouht* in comaundinge, þat ye go
þiderward, and amoneste þilke musard þat his staf he ley

[doun], and þat he cesse of þe surpluis. And if anything he withstond, oþer wole not abeye, yiueth him day competent at þe assyses of jugement. Of þis pleyn power we yiven yow and maken you commissarye. Yiven in oure yeer þat eche wiht clepeth M¹CCCXXXI.'   2855

Whan al was rad, Resoun took ayen hire letteres and putte hem in saaftee, and sithe areynede þe cherl, and seyde him swiche wordes: "Beausire," quod she, "now þou hast herd my power, and whi I come heere, wolt þou more answere to me of þat I haue asked þee?" "Who art þou?" quod þe cherl. "Who   2860 am I?" quod Resoun, "For Seint Germeyn, hast þow not herd riht [f.56v] now what men han red heere? Thinkest þou on þi loues, oþer to take toures or castelles?" Quod he: "I haue wel herd, bi Seint Symeon, þat þou hattest Resoun. But for it is a name defamed, þerfore I haue asked who þou art (and with   2865 good riht)." "Nouht defamed, bi Seint Beneit!" quod Resoun, "But where hast þou founde þat?" "At þe mille" quod he, "þer I haue be, þere þou mesurest falsliche and stelest folkes corn." "Beausire," quod she: "heere now tweyne litel woordes, and vnderstonde. Misseyinge is no wurþinesse, ne þou   2870 spekest not as þe wise. At þe mille perauenture ye haue seyn a mesure þat is cleped 'resoun' [for to hele with his gret vnresoun] but þerfore it is not 'Resoun' but it is fraude and desceyt. Bitwixe name and beeinge I wole wel make difference. Oon thing is to be Resoun, and anooþer thing haue his name.   2875 Of þe name men mown maken couerture for to hele with here filthe. þis thing is falle many a time in many a strete: þat who þat is not fair make him queynte, and who þat is not good make him simple. Alle vices gladliche doon it, and ofte-times maken hem kouerynge with þe name of þe vertu contrarye, for to   2880 lasse displese þe folk. And yit is not þe vertu þe lasse woorth bi a straw, but it is signe þat it is good, whan þe vice appareth him and clopeth him þerwith. So þat if with my name þilke mesure [hath wold] queyntise him and hele him, þerfore am I not defamed, but wurshiped shulde be þerby of   2885 alle folk of vnderstondinge." "What is þis?" quod he. "þat God haue part! þou wolt be preysed of þat þat ooþere shulden [f.57r] be blamed. If I kneewe not a flye in mylk when þou toldest it me I hadde gret wrong. Weene not þat whan I heere nempne a kat or an hound, þat I ne wot wel it is noon   2890 oxe ne kow, but þat it is an hound and a kat. Bi here names I

knowe wel eche of hem, for here names and þei be al oon. So
þat if þou hattest Resoun, I sey also þou art Resoun; and if
'resoun' stele þe corn, I sey þat of þee it is stolen: al þe
water þat maketh þe mille turne ne mihte wasshe þee þerof, for
alle þine slye woordes and fallaces. Weene not þat euere
ooþerweys þou make me [to] vnderstonde."

And þanne Resoun, smylinge and al turnynge it into jape,
seyde him: "Now I see wel þat of art þou hast lerned, and
subtiliche [þou]   kanst   argue   and   bringe   foorth   faire
ensaumples; [and] if þou haddest a grettere bely,* þou woldest
weel seeme wurþi." "O!" quod he: "þou scornest me!" "þat I
do, certeyn," quod Resoun, "wite it wel: and yit more wole
scorne þee, forto I wite þi name as þou wost myn. And wite
wel þou hast no wurshipe of þe helinge: I ne wot what þou
shalt haue of þe tellinge." "Wurshipe?" quod he: "What
seyst þou? þe vnwurshipe is þin. þou hast my name in þi
leues, and askest it! þou art lich him þat sit on his asse
and yit seecheth it oueral. I ne wot what it tokeneth but
\if/ it be scornynge." "Aa!" quod Resoun: "Art þou þilke
þat art set in my leues? þe name withinne wel I wiste, but
þee knew I not. I heeld an oppinyoun þat I and my name is not
oon: for with my name may appare him eche theef þat goth to
stele, and þerfore I wende soo [f.57v] of þee, for hadde I
not yit lerned þat þou and Rude Entendement weren oon
[ioyngtliche]—but now I see wel withoute suspecioun þat ye
ben oon withoute distinctioun. þine ensaumples han tauhte it
me, and þine seyinges þat ben so subtile. I wot bi þi woordes
þat þou propirliche art Rude Entendement: more miht þou not
argue, but oonliche so be þou nempned, for bi existence þou
art it withouten difference, wherfore I foryiue þee þe
vileynee þat þou hast seid me bi felonye, for I see wel þou
wendest þat of me it were as it is of þee. But Rudeness tauht
þee soo to weene, for rude þou art, as eche wight seeth wel
(and euel willed), and þerfore set þee was þis name." With
þese woordes þe cherl was ateynt to þe herte. Nouht he seyde,
for he cowde not, but oonliche grinte with [þe] teeth.

Resoun stinte not, but song him of anooþer song. "Now,"
quod she, "sithe I woot þi name, gret neede haue I nouht to
aske more of þe remenaunt: in my letteres it is al cleer, for
an espyour þou art of weyes, and an assaylour of pilgrimes.
þou wolt bineme hem here burdouns and vnscrippe here scrippes.
Why doost þou it, by þi soule, ayens þe wil of my lady?" "For

þat þei" quod he, "witingliche passen þe gospel þat I haue
herd seyd in oure toun, and keepen it shrewedeliche þer it is 2935
defended to alle as I haue [wel] vnderstonde: þat no man bere
out of his hoom neiþer scrippe ne burdoun—so whan þat I see
hem bere hem ayens þe defence of þe kynge, gladliche (for to
keepe þe lawe) I do peyne to make hem to leve hem." [f.58r]
"Oo," quod Resoun: "ooþerweys it goth. þilke defence was 2940
longe agon al ooþerweys turned and remeved to þe contrarie.
Wel it is sooth þat it was defended, but afterward it was
recomaunded. Cause [couenable] þer was, for whiche þer needed
wel chaunge. It is not vnwurshipe to þe king þouh he chaunge
his lawe for cause honeste. þe cause of þe chaunginge ayen, 2945
shortliche I wole telle þee if þou wolt. Whoso is at þe ende
of his wey hath [no] neede to be pilgrime, and he þat were no
pilgrime shulde litel do with scrippe or with burdoun. Jhesu
þe kyng is þe eende to whiche alle goode pilgrimes thinken:
þat is þe eende of good viage and of good pilgrimage. To þat 2950
terme and to þat ende weren comen hise goode pilgrimes bi his
clepinge. Whan he defended hem þat no þei beren scrippe
ne burdoun, but leften hem and leyden hem doun, sufficient he
was and mihty to deliuere hem plentivowsliche al þat hem
needede, withoute beeinge in any ooþeres daunger. On þat 2955
ooþer side, he wolde þat whan he sente hem to preche, þat here
herkeners aministreden hem, and founden hem here vitailes, for
euery werkere is wurþi to haue and resseyue hyre. And eche
wight dide þerof so michel þat þe turnynge ayen no wiht
pleyned him: wherof þou hast herd þat he askede hem oones, 2960
whan him thouhte good: 'Hath you' quod he, 'anything lakked,
whan I haue þus sent yow withoute scrippe to preche to þe folk
and to shewe þe woord of God?' And þanne þei answerden him:
'Serteynliche sire, nay. Sufficientliche we haven hadde, and
nothing [is] faylede us.' [f.58v] 2965
    Lo heere þe cause for whi was defended þat þei beren no
scrippe and þat þei vseden not of þe burdoun. But whan he
shulde afterward gon and passen bi þe brigge of deth, whan he
sigh þat he, þat was þe eende of here wey, departede from hem,
þanne wolde he chaunge his lawe as a softe and [a] tretable 2970
kyng, and seyde hem þat þei tooken ayen here scrippes and
diden hem on ayen. 'Whoso hath' he saide, 'any sak, take it
and a scrippe þerwith': as þouh he seyde apertliche and
cleerliche: 'þouh I (for ye weren comen to þe ende of youre
wey) defendede yow þat ye hadden ne bere no scrippe, now I 2975

muste alonygne me from yow and leue yow, I wole þat ye taken
ayen al, as ye hadden bifore, for I wot wel whan ye han lost
þe sighte of me, a scrippe shal be needeful to yow, and a
burdoun to lene yow to. Pilgrimes ye musten ben ayen, and
sette yow to [þe] wey ayen, elles [shule] ye not mown folwe me
ne come to me. On þat ooþer side, whan I am gon ye shule
[nouht] fynde þat gladliche shal do yow good, ne þat with
good herte speke anything to yow. To youre scrippe ye shule
holde you [forto] ye come ayen to me. Now taketh it, for I
graunte it yow for þe neede I see þerof.' So see heere al in
apert þe cause, which is sufficient, to bere scrippe and
burdoun: wherfore þou shuldest not medle þee to areste þilke
þat hauen it, ne þat beren it where þei gon—leeue þei hauen,
and cause þer is, into þe time þat eche cometh to þe ende of
his viage and of his pilgrimage."

"What is þis?" quod þe walkere:* "What gost þou þus
jangelinge me? Wolt þou holde þe gospel at fable and lesinge?
þow seist it vncomanded, þat þat [f.59r] God hadde ordeyned;
whiche thing, if it so were, riht so alle hise ordinaunce
shulden \be/ put out of þe book and defaced and scraped."
"Nouht so," quod Resoun: "for it is riht to wite þe time
passed: how men diden, how men seiden, whi þat was, what cause
þer lyth, whi þer weren mutaciouns of doinges. And þerfore
is not þe gospel reprooved ne defaced, but to goode
vnderstonderes it is þe more gracious and þe more pleasaunt.
þe mo diuerse floures ben in þe medewe, þe more is þe place
gracious, and þe more þat here facioun is diuerse, þe more
gladliche men biholden hem." And þanne blissede him þe cherl
with his rude crookede hond. "What is þis?" quod he: "þou
wolt amase me and enchaunte me! Al þat I sey, þou turnest and
stirest \al/ to þe contrarye: falsnesse þou clepest
fairnesse, and of fairnesse þou seist falsnesse. þat þat was
of þe kyng defended, þou seist was comaunded, turnynge þe
gospel al upsodoun bi disgisy woordes and lyinge. þou ne art
but a bigilouresse of folk. Lat me stonde, for I preyse not
þi woordes ne þi dedes at thre verres. In my purpos I wole
holde me, and of nothing seeche þee."*

"At þe leste," quod Resoun, "þilke staf þou shalt ley
doun, for þou wost wel Grace Dieu hath comaunded it and
ordeyned it." "To Grace Dieu", quod he, "of what it may
greeue I see not. On þat ooþer side, necessarie it is to me
to þat þat I haue to doone: I lene me þerto and I defende me

þerwith, and sette þe lasse bi alle folk—and me thinketh I
am michel þe more dred—and þerfore if I leyde it doun, a
gret fool I were and a gret cokard." "Oo," quod Resoun: 3020
[f.59v] "þou seist not wel. þou hast neede to haue oopere
frendes.* Grace Dieu shulde neuere loue þilke þat bere swich a
staf. It was neuere leef to hire: she hateth it more þan þe
goot þe knyf, so þat if þou leidest it not doun, þow were not
wys." "Oo!" quod þe cherl: "How þou art a fool to seyn   3025
swiche woordes! If þe staf greevede hire not, whi shulde it
displese hire?" "I wole sey þee", quod Resoun, "rudeliche,
for ooþer mete I se wel þi rude throte asketh not. If þou
haddest a freend to whiche any wight dide disese, it shulde of
nothing greeue þee but of as michel as it shulde displese þee.   3030
Grace Dieu loueth alle folk, and wole þe avauncement of alle,
and þerfore whan any [wight] hath mischeef, or þat men don
[it] any disese, albeit she hath no greuaunce yit hath she
displeasaunce. þis staf is enemy to þilke þat she [wole] haue
freendes. Ne were it, þe Jewes wolden come to hire and   3035
conuerte hem; alle heretikes wolden also leue here errour,
and amende hem. Bi it weren put to confusioun Nabal and
Pharao, for to it þei leneden so, þat þei purchaseden here
deth. If it ne were, Obedience shulde regne ouer al and
comaunde. Eche shulde do þat þat he comaundede, and of   3040
nothing disobeye. If it ne were, alle rude wittes wolden ben
enclyn, and humble hem—þiself, þat hattest Rude Entendement,
if þou ne lenededst so faste to it [wolde] leeue me and amende
þee—and þerfore I rede þee ley it doun, and lene þee no more
þerto." "Haa God!" quod he: "What I preyse litel woordes   3045
þat ben of þis manere. I wole to þee of nothing obeye, ne I
wole not leue þe staf. I wole lene [me] þerto, [f.6or] wolt
þou oþer [ne] wolt þou, wite it wel." "Now," quod Resoun,
"now I se wel þat þer is no more to speke with þee, but
oonliche to cite þee to þe assises of jugement. I somowne   3050
þee, withoute more taryinge. Come þider withoute sendinge any
ooþer."
      Thanne Resoun turnede hire ayen to meward, and clepede
me: "Go", quod she, "hardiliche, withoute dredinge Rude
Entendement. Sey him nothing ne [ne] answere him not, for þe   3055
techinge of Salamon is þat men answere no woord to him þat men
seen and fynden a fool." "Lady," quod I, "suinge he seith
ooþerweys, for he seith men shulden answere him for to shewe
him his shame." "Serteyn," quod she, "þou seist sooth, but

þou shuldest vnderstonde and wite þat þilke woord was
dispenced me for to answere whan it were tyme, and þerof haue
I doon ynowh (albe my trauaile lost, for he is of nothing
amended ne ashamed). A feþere shulde as soone entre in an
anevelte as woordes shulden entren in him or profiten. He is
as hard as [ayemaunt] oþer dyamaunt, for þat þat he conceyueth
first he wole for nothing leue, so þat with swich a cherl to
speke þou miht no pris conquere. Go þi wey withoute chidinge
with him, and lat him grucche ynow, shake his bridel and his
chin, and gnawe on his staf." "Lady," quod I: "I thanke yow
of þat ye teche me þus, but I telle yow certeynliche þat I
durst not passe forth for þe cherl hardiliche, but I hadde
whateuere it were* of yow: wherfore I pray yow þat with me
ye come, and þat passinge him ye lede me, for I haue also to
speke with yow and wole aske yow of sumf.6ov]thing nedeful,
longinge to my bisinesse." And þanne withoute taryinge bi þe
hond she took me, and til I was passed þe cherl, ladde me,
[and] in my wey she sette me, wherof I hadde gret ioye. þe
cherl bilefte þere grucchinge, lenynge on his staf, grummynge:
but þerof roughte me nothing. Resoun loowh faste þerof.

    Whan þus I sigh me ascaped and was wel gon forth, of
Resoun I bigan to aske þat of which ye haue herd me speke.
"Lady," quod I, "michel I haue ben in gret thouht, and yit
am, why I may not endure ne susteyne noon armure. A wenche I
see bere hem, whiche is shame to me whan I may not bere hem
also, þat shulde be more mihti bi þe half and more strong, if
any herte were in me. Wherfore I pray yow and biseeche yow
þat ye wole teche me þe cause whens it may come, for gret
desire I haue to wite it." Thanne answerde me Resoun: "What
is þis?" quod she. "In þe hous of Grace Dieu not longe agoon
I sigh þee, and many times þou speke to hire. How hast þou be
so michel a fool þat of hire þou ne hast asked þis? And not
for þanne I trowe not þat sumwhat she ne haue seyd þee bi
which þou miht apperceyue and wite þat þou askest."
"Lady," quod I: "I wole telle yow. Many of hire seyinges
foryeten I haue: of þis wel I mynde me withoute more, þat she
seide me I was to thikke. But if I made me smallere or dide
myself any harm, a feloun men wolden clepe me: ne on þat
ooþer side, I myhte neuere bere myn armure so wel as if I were
gret and strong. But swiche thinges maken me abashed, for þei
ben nouht in [f.61r] vsage. I enquerede not þe sooþe of Grace
Dieu, for I dredde I hadde ennoyed hire or mistake me to hire:

wherfore I prey yow þat ye wole lerne [it] me and make me
vnderstonde it." "Wost þou", quod she, "who þou art, wheþer
þou be aloone, or double þou be: if þou haue noon to norishe
but þiself, ne to gouerne and arraye?" And þanne al abashed I
seide hire: "Ladi, in feith me thinketh þat I haue noon but
myself to gouerne, ne I haue noon ooþer to thinke on. I am al
aloone, ye seen wel. I wot neuere whi ye aske it." "Now
lerne", quod she, "and vnderstonde and herkne bisyliche, for
ooþer thing I wole sey þee, and of þe contrarie I wole teche
þee. þow norishest þilke þat is þi grete enemy. Of þee he is
euery day fed, yiven drinke, hosed and cloþed: þer ne is mete
so precious, so costlewe ne so [delitous] þou ne wolt yive
it þilke, how miche þat euere it shulde coste þee. Bitake þee
it was for to serue þee, but þou art his seruaunt bicome:
wantounliche þou wolt hose him, and take him noble robes,
queyntise him with iewelles, with tablettes, with knyves, with
girdelles, with purses, with disgisye lases of silk medled red
and greene; queynteliche þow wolt eche day aray him, and eche
niht [wel softe] ley him and do him his ese. Oon day þou
chaufest him þe bath, and sithe stiwest him. On þe morwe þou
kembest him, þou polishest him, and seechest him mirthes and
disportes as michel as euere þou miht, day and niht. Swich as
he is, þou hast norished him, and michel more bisy þou hast
ben aboute him þan a womman aboute þe chyld she yiveth souke
and feedeth. A gret while it is þat þou [bigonne] and [f.61v]
neuere sithe stintedest (þouh I seide xxxvi^{ti} winter I
failede, I trowe, but litel): and albeit he hath þus
[his likinge, and þat þou hast þus serued] him and
forbore him, þou shuldest wite þat he bytrayeth þee and
desceyueth þee and dooth þee harm. þat is þilke þat suffreth
þee not to bere ne to endure þin armure. þat is þilke þat is
þin aduersarye all þe times þat þou wolt doon wel."
     "Lady," quod I: "I am awundred of þat ye tellen me
heere. If ye ne weren so wys, and hadden in yow so gret wit,
I wolde weene al were lesinge, or elles þat it were meetinge.
But in yow I wot so michel good þat gabbe wolde ye not for
nothing, wherfore I pray you þat ye sey me who is þilke
wikkede traytour, what is his miht and his shap, where he was
bore, how he hatteth, to þat ende þat I know him and do him
disese ynowh: for þouh al quik I dismembrede him, wel were I
not venged." "Sertes," quod she: "þou seist sooth, for
þerwith þou shuldest wite þat ne were þou, of him were

3105

3110

3115

3120

3125

3130

3135

3140

noothing, or litel thing it were. þer wolde no wiht biholde
it ne deyngne to preyse it, for it is an hep of rotennesse, a
buryelles maad of filthe, a restinge for a coluer.* By itself
it may not remeeve ne nothing doo ne laboure, for he is
impotent and contract, deef and blynd and counterfeted. It is
a worm diuerse and cruelle, þat was bore in þe eerþe of
wormes: an herte withinne him breedinge wormes, and
norishinge wurmes withinne it—a worm þat in þe laste eende
shal be mete to wormes and shal rote. And albeit of swich
makinge and of swich condicioun, yit þou makest him ligge bi þee,
and in [þi] bed slepe with þee, [f.62r] and gost aboute to gete
him al þat is good for hym, as I haue seid þee bifore. And
yit more, whiche is a vyle thing: whan he hath eten and is to
ful, þou berest him to priuee chambres or to feeldes, to voide
hys wombe. Now looke wheþer þou be verriliche a [serf] and a
wrecche, for of al þat he can þee neuere thank, but is þe more
haunteyn and þe gladdere to do þee harm, so michel he is of
shrewede doinge." "Ladi," quod I: "his name whi telle ye me
not anoon withoute taryinge, for rediliche I wolde venge me
and anoon go sle him I wolde!" "O," quod Resoun: "leeue
hast þou nouht to sle him, but wel þou hast leeue to chastise
him and to bete him and to abate his customes, to yive him
peynes and trauailes, and ofte to make him faste, to
vnderputte him to Penitence, withoute þe whiche good
vengeaunce of him shalt þou neuere haue, ne neuere in no time
be wel avenged, for as while erst þou seye (if wel þou
vnderstoode) Penitence is his maistresse and oonliche his
chastiseresse—þilke þat hath þe rihte iugement of him whan
time and [sesoun] is present. þerfore take him to hire, and she
shal bete him and chastise him so wel with hire yerdes þat a
good seruaunt he shal be to þee from hens forthward: and þat
shuldest þou raþere desire, and more wilne and procure, þan
þou shuldest do his deth, for he is to þee taken to lede
to þe hauene of lyf and of saluacioun. It is þe bodi and þe
flesch of þee: ooþerweys can I not nempne it."
    "Lady," quod I: "what sey ye? Haue I met, oþer mete
ye? Mi bodi and my flesh ye clepen ooþer þan myself, and yit
ye seen þat with yow I am alloone, ne noon þer is heere but we
tweyne. I wot not [f.62v] what þis tokeneth, but if it be a
fairye!" "It is not so," quod Resoun, "for of my mouth cam
neuere out lesinge ne fairye, ne nothing þat men shulden clepe
meetinge. But sey me bi [þe] feith þou owest to God, if þou

were in a place þere þou haddest þine mirthes—good mete,
softe bed, white cloþes, ioye, reste and gret disport, and þi
willes boþe day and niht—þat I mowe wite sooth if þou woldest
make þer any taryinge and abidinge." "[Serteynliche]," quod I:
"ye!" "Aha," quod she: "what hast þou seid? þanne þou   · 3190
woldest leue þi pilgrimage and þi viage!" "Ladi," quod I:
"þat shulde I nouht, for al bitymes afterward I shulde go."
"Al bitimes, wrecche?" quod she: "þer nis man in [þe] world
lyvinge þat euere may come bitimes, renne he neuere so faste.
And suppose þat after þe mirthes and eses, þou thinkest go   3195
þider al bitymes bi trauaile and bi labouringe: I aske þee if
þou woldest ouht sette þee to [þe] wey as longe as þou founde
swich ioye and swich solace?" "Allas lady," quod I, "allas!
þerto can I not answere, but þat oonliche I wot wel fayn I
wolde abide, and also fayn I wolde go." "þanne", quod she,   3200
"þou hast double wil and double thouht: þat oon wole abide,
[þat] ooþer wole go; þat oon wole reste, þat ooþer werche; þat
þat oon wole, þat ooþer ne wole. Contrarie þat oon is to þat
ooþer." "Ladi," quod I: "certeynliche as ye seyn I feele in
me." "þanne art þou not sool:" quod she, "þou and þi bodi   3205
ben tweyne, for tweyne willes ben not of oon but þei ben of
tweyne: þat wot eche wiht."

"Ladi," quod I: "I pray you þat ye sey me who am I,
sithe my bodi I am not. I shulde neuere be in ese if sumwhat
heerof I ne wiste." "Haa," quod she: "what hast þou lerned?   3210
þou canst not michel, as me [f.63r] thinketh. It is miche
more woorth oon to know himself þan who is emperour, kyng oþer
[erle—þan] can alle sciences, and haue al þat is of þe
world. But sithe þou hast not lerned it, þou art wel avised
to aske it, and I wole shortliche ynowh telle þee sumwhat þat   3215
I vnderstonde. The bodi shet withoute, of whiche I haue
spoken to þee, is in alle degrees out shet. þow art of God þe
portreyture and þe ymage and þe figure. Of nouht he made þee,
and foormede þee to his liknesse. A more noble facioun mihte
he not yive þee: he made þee fair and cleer-seeinge, lightere   3220
þan brid fleeinge, immortal withoute euere deyinge, and
lasting withoute endinge. If þou wolt wel biholde þiself,
but þat þou haue forfeted nothing, to þi noblesse may compare
heuene ne erþe, ne se, brid ne ooþer creature, except þe nature
of aungeles. God is þi fader, and þou his sone. Weene not   3225
þat þou be sone of Thomas of Guileuile, for he hadde neuere
sone ne douhter þat was of swich condicioun ne of so noble a

nacioun. þi bodi ([þat] is þin enemy) þat þou hast of him,
of him it cam þee: he bigat it as kynde ordeyned him. Riht
it is þat þe tre bere swich fruyt as kynde techeth it. Riht
as thornes mown not bere ne caste figes, riht so þe bodi of þe
manhode may not bere fruyt but foul and veyn, vyle filthe and
corrupcioun, rotennesse and stinkinge dunge. But swich thing
art not þou, for þow hast not þi comynge foorth of dedliche
man, but it is come þee of God þi fader. God made neuere with
hise handes in þe world but twey bodies of manhode, to whiche
tweyne he committede to make þe oopere after þe ensaumple.
But þe facioun of þe gost he withheeld bi certeyn avys. Al he
wolde [f.63v] were maad of him withoute medlinge of any wyht
elles. He made þee, for a gost þou art, and putte þee in
þe bodi þat þou art: þerinne he putte þee for to enhabite a
while, and for to preeve, to wite soothliche if þou woldest be
vertuous and knyghtliche, to wite wheþer þou woldest venquise
þe body or yelde þee to him. Bataile þou hast to him in alle
times, and he to þee: if þou ne yelde þee, bi flateringe he
ouerthroweth þee doun and desceyueth þee and maketh þee yelde
þee ouercome. Vnder him he holt þee if þou leeue him, þereas
þou shuldest venquise him bi miht. He shulde neuere haue
power ouer þee if it ne were bi þi wille. þou art Sampson he
is Dalida: þou hast strengthe in þee, he hath noon. He can
nothing do but flatere þee, to delyuere þee to enemyes. He
wole bynde þee if þou wolt, and shal shere al þin her—and þi
priuytees, whan he wot hem, to [þe] philistyens shal shewe
hem. þat is þe frendshipe þat he hath to þee, and þe trouthe
and þe feith. Now looke if þou wolt assente to him withoute
smytinge of strok, if þou wolt be desceyued as Sampson was,
and holde a fool." "Ladi," quod I: "wundres I heere: I
meete verryliche, I trowe. A spiryt ye clepen me (þat am
shoven heere in my bodi) þat ye seyn am cleer-seeinge, and yit
I see neyþer more ne lasse. And of my bodi ye haue seyd it is
blynd, þat seeth wel—and manye oopere grete wundres whiche
ben fleen in myne eres. Wherfore I pray yow ye wole teche me
and lerne me more cleerliche, for aske can I not wel, of þe
baishtnesse þat I haue." [f.64r]
    And þanne Resoun bigan ayen. "Now vnderstond", quod she,
"hider. Whan þe sunne is shadewed, and at time of midday is
shoven vnder a cloude and may not be seyn ne apperceyued, I
aske þee, for my loue, þat þou sey me whens cometh þe day?"
"It cometh," quod I, "to my seemynge, of þe sunne þat is hid,

þat maketh his lightnesse passe thoruh þe cloude [and avale] 3270
—as" (quod I) "men seen it thoruh sum glas, oþer as men mown
seen fyre in a lanterne." "Serteyn," quod Resoun: "if
þat þat þou hast seid þou haue vnderstonde, [bi þe sunne
þou shalt vnderstonde] þe soule [þat] þou hast in
þilke dedliche bodi. þe bodi is a cloude and a lanterne 3275
bismoked, thoruh þe whiche, how it euere be, þe brightnesse
withinne men seen: þe soule þat enhabiteth in þe bodi
spredeth his brightnesse outward, and maketh weene to
foolliche folk þat al þe light be of þilke poure cloude with
whiche þe soule is shadewed. But if þe cloude ne were, þe 3280
soule shulde haue so gret light þat she shulde see al
pleynliche from þe est to þe west. She shulde also see and
knowe and loue hire creatour. The eyen of þe bodi ben not
swiche,* but þei ben as glasses bi þe whiche þe soule yiueth
light to þe bodi withoute. But heerfore þou shuldest not 3285
weene þat þe soule haue neede of þese eyen and þese glasses,
for bifore and bihynde, withoute bodilyche fenestralle, he
seeth his gostlich good, and sumtime he shulde þe bettere see
it if þe bodi hadde noon eye. Tobye a time was blynd as to þe
body, but þerfore was he not blynd as to þe soule, for bi him 3290
was his sone tauht how he shulde meyntene him, and what wey he
shulde holde. Neuere shulde he haue tauht it him if with
[f.64v] þe soule he ne hadde yseye. þe soule sigh al
cleerliche, and knewe þat þat he seide him. So if I sey þou
seest cleerliche, yit I wole conferme it, for þou seest, nouht 3295
þi body [which] is blynd boþe withinne and withoute. Neuere
shulde he see sighte if bi þi liht it ne were: and riht as I
sey þee of þe sight, right so I sey þee of þe heeringe and of
hise wittes, for þei ben but instrumentes bi þe which he
resceyueth of þee þat þat he hath. For he ne heereth ne seeth 3300
if it ne be oonliche bi þee: and I sey þee vtterliche, if þou
ne bere him wel or susteyned him strongliche, as a donge hep
he shulde be, ne neuere shulde he stire him."

"Lady," quod I, "now I aske and I pray yow how is it þat
þe soule, whiche is withinne, bereth \so/ þe bodi, and he 3305
withoute? Me thinketh bettere þat þat is bore þat is contened
withinne; and bettere me thinketh berere and susteynour þat
þat is withoute, for þilke bereth þat conteneth, and þilke is
bore þat halt him withinne." "Now vnderstonde", quod she, "a
litel. þi cloþinge and þin habite, it conteeneth þee, and þou 3310
art withinne: þow woldest make gret wundringe if I seyde it

bere þee or gouerned þee in any wyse." "Is it þus
Lady?" quod I. "Ye," quod she, "but þis in difference I
sette þee, þat þe soule bereth and is born. She principally
bereth þe body, but he bi accident bereth him, and in
resortinge him to his vertu is entendaunt.* If euere þou seye
gouerne a ship in a ryueere and leede, þere [þou] mihtest take
ensaumple withoute harmynge þee on any wyse. þe gouernayle
whiche is withinne ledeth it, and so led it is and leedeth:
for if he withinne [f.65r] ledde it nouht, his ship wolde not
leede him. þi soule is þe ledere and þe gouernowr of þi bodi.
She ledeth it, she bereth it, and in ledinge so bereth it. þe
bodi bereth it at his wille, and after þat she concenteth. þe
bodi shulde not bere here but if she bere þe bodi, and þerfore
þou shuldest peyne þee to gouerne so ariht þi bodi, þat in
ledinge him he mowe lede þee to sure hauene after þe deth."

"Ladi," quod I: "certeynliche I trowe þat youre speche
shulde be to me riht necessarie. If ye wolden doo so michel
for me þat ye dide me [of] of my [ship], and dispoiled me of þe
body, and shewed me þilke vnthrift, þilke blynde (þat so miche
hath misdoo me as ye seyn, so ofte-times, and yit mai not be
stille) so þat I mowe preeve and fynde þat þat ye seyn: nouht
þat I drede of anything þat ye ne seyn riht wel, but I
vnderstonde nouht certeynliche ne cleerliche youre woordes,
wherfore I pray yow þat ye wole entende þerto for to teche me
a litel." And þanne Resoun seide: "I trowe riht wel þat
litel þou vnderstondest me—and wost þou whi? It is for þe
bodi maketh an obstacle bifore, gret and thikke. Ooþer thing
can he not doon but aldai be to þee contrarious. But for þou
hast bisouht it, I wole do it of þee if I may—and þou shalt
also laboure þerto, and do peyne with me, for litel I shulde
do bi myself if of þee helpe I ne hadde. Algates trusse him
ayen þou shalt moste [and] haue him ayen on þi bak, for it is
not in my powere to sequestre him longe from þee—and yit it
is hard to make þe forberinge oon sool moment. To þe deth þis
longeth, whiche cometh ofte withoute sendinge after. Now take
on þat side, and I on þis, and [f.65v] entende nouht neiþer
hider ne þider." And þanne Resoun sette hond to me, and I
putte me in hire baundoun. She drowh and I shof. So miche we
dide, she and I, þat þe contracte was ouerthrowe fro me and I
vncharged. Whan vntrussed þus I was, I was rauished into þe
eyr an hygh. Me thouht I fleih, and þat nothing I weyede. At
my wille oueral I wente, and up and doun, and fer I seyh.

Nothing in þe world (as me thouhte) was heled ne hid fro me.
Gladed I was gretliche. þis mislikede me oonliche: þat yit I   3355
moste þerinne enhabite and herberwe and dwelle, for nothing or
litel I seigh þerinne but þe empechement of my wey. Wel I
seigh þat it was sooth al þat Resoun hadde preched me: wel I
seigh my bodi þat it was dunge, and to preise it was nothing.
Wel I seigh þat alwey it shulde abide in oo place, but it were   3360
doon awey. At þe eerþe streiht it lay þere: neiþer it herde
ne seigh. His contenaunce was tokne þat no vertu in him he
hadde. I wente and cam al aboute him to wite sooth if he were
aslepe, and I tastede his [pouce]—but wite wel I fond nouht
in sinewe ne in condyt ne in veyne more þan in a [stike],   3365
in pouce ne breth. It was nouht, I seigh it wel. Fy on him,
and on alle hise [doinges].

    When I hadde considered al þat, Resoun after arened me.
"Loo heere", quod she, "þou seest wel þin enemy. Now þou
knowest him wel: þis is he þat suffreth þee not to bere ne   3370
endure þin armure; þilke þat bi flateringe beteth þee doun
and ouercometh þee, and yildeth [þee] venquised; þilke þat
empecheth þee to clymbe and flee an hy to þi creatour. I haue
spoke þee inowh heerof bifore: it ouhte suffice þee so
michel. With[f.66r]inne him þou moste entre, charge him and   3375
trusse him ayen. Bere him into þi viage and into þi
pilgrimage." "Ladi," quod I, "myn entencioun and my deuocioun
was þat with þe armure I armede me, and þat þus I wente armed
a while for to preue wheþer I mihte bere hem þus: for me
thinketh veriliche now þat þei weye nothing." "Sertes," quod   3380
she, "þou seist sooth. Litel þei weyen, wherfore þou shuldest
wite þat þouh þus þou vsedest hem, þou shuldest no merite
haue. þou shuldest do hem on whan þou hast on [þi] contracte,
blynd and naked: wel he ouhte susteyne þi dedes,* for [wele]
he wole at þe goode parte. þou shalt neuere haue [wele] at þe   3385
laste, of whiche he ne wole be þerof [parcenere]. Now trusse
him ayen and take him [ayen], and sithe entende to arme þee."

    Whan she hadde seyd me þis, withoute taryinge I fond me
trussed. Al þe miht I hadde and þe welþe of whiche I
rejoycede me, oo for to seye, in oo moment al was shadewed   3390
vnder þe cloudy cloude vnder whiche þer is [noon] wel
cleer-seeinge. þilke cloude þat I hatede so miche bifore and
preysed so litel, I bigan to loue ayen and to bimeene and
thinke þat to him I wolde assente, and þat his wille I wolde
doo. But whan I apperceyued afterward ayen þat so I [shulde] be   3395

disceyued, I bigan to tere and to weepe and to sighe:
"Allas!" quod I, "þou what shalt þou do? To whiche of þese
tweyne shalt þou acorde?" And þanne seide me Resoun: "What
eyleth þee? Whi art þou discoumforted? Weepinge longeth to
wommen, but to men it becometh not wel." And þanne I seyde
hire: "Heerfore I weepe, for riht now withinne þis houre,
bifore þat I hadde trussed ayen þis poore [f.66v] bodi, I was
so mihti þat I wende wel haue ben worth tweyne. I fly aboue
þe skyes hyere þan eyþer heroun or egret. I sigh and
vnderstood, and found no contrarie. Now is þe game so turned
[ayenward] þat my contrarye I haue founden ayen. þe bodi
oppresseth me and beteth me doun, and halt me vnder him
venquised. I haue no vertu bi whiche I may resiste him ne
contrarye him. Mi wille I haue vtterliche lost. I ne wot
where it is bicome. Mi strengthe ne is but of þilke þat quik
into þe eerþe is flowen.* As an ape is tyed to a blok and is
atached þat he may not stye an hy (þat in styinge he ne cometh
soone doun ayen) so is to me an hevy blok þe bodi, and a gret
withholdinge. He felleth me ayen whan I wolde flee, and
withholt me whan I wolde clymbe: for me as me thinketh was seid
\þat/ þat I sigh writen a while ago—þat þe bodi (which is
corrupt and shrewed and hevy) greeueth þe soule, and so
oppresseth it þat in wrecchednesse he holt it. So am I put
bineþe, so holden, so serued, þat no wunder it is þouh in
weepinge I sey 'allas', so discoumforted I am gretliche,
and riht sorweful."

Thanne seide Resoun: "Seest þou," quod she, "wel þat I
haue of nothing gabbed þee: þat þe bodi is þin aduersarie of
al þe good þou woldest do." "Sertes," quod I: "it is so, I
see it wel, God yelde yow. But seith me oo woord: whi is he
strengere þan I, and whi I am not, ne may not be, as strong as
he?" "Strengere", quod she, "is he not, but þou miht not
ouercome him in his cuntre. In þin owen þou shuldest, if þou
were þerinne. Eche wight is strong on his owen dung-hep, and
tristeth to his cuntree. He is heere in his cuntree, on his
dung[f.67r]-hep and upon his dunge set, and þerfore he is þe
strengere ayens þee, and þe more fers and of þe grettere
beringe; but if in ooþer places þou haddest him in þi
cuntree, þou shuldest be strongere: þere he shulde not mown
withsitte þee ne ayensstonde þee. Not þat I sey þee þus for
to putte þee into faitourye, ne þat I wole sey þat þou ne miht
mate him and supplaunte him: for if þou wult, upon his

dung-hep (if þou canst anything of þe cheker) þou shalt make
him chek and maat, make he neuere so michel debaat. Litel
drinkinge, litel etinge, litel restinge, trauaile goode,   3440
disciplines and betinges, orisouns, and weylinges—þe
instrumentes of penaunce—[shulen] do þee riht and vengeaunce.
þei shulen make þee victour, to gret wurshipe of þee, wule he
oþer noon; and þanne whan he is þus adaunted vnder þee, þanne
þou shalt wel mown arme þee with armures: for sooth to seyn,   3445
þou hast noon so gret lettinge ne so gret encombraunce as of
þat he is so slugged, to wilful and to miche fed—and þat it
was þat Grace Dieu seide þee whan she spak to þee." "Ladi,"
quod I: "certeynliche now first I vnderstonde [it] but þat time
I vnderstood it nothing, al were it she spak me of þe bodi. I 3450
wende it and I hadde ben al oon, but it is not so. Bi yow þe
sooþe I haue lerned, after þat I haue enquered." "Certeyn,"
quod she, "al þe sooþe bi hire þou mihtest wel haue wist if þou
haddest bisouht hire, for of hire haue I [al] lerned. Nothing
cowde I, if she ne were, ne nothing of me were. Al þat I sey   3455
þee, it is bi hire. If I clepe þi bodi þin enemy, heerafter
þou shalt wel wite it is so, for whan þou woldest go [f.67v]
any good wey, he shal turne þee amys and make þee go anooþer
wey. And suppose þat sumtime he suffre þee go bi þere þou
shuldest, yit I sey þee þat slough þou shalt fynde him, and   3460
[slugged]. Longe he wole reste, and turne upon þat ooþer
side. Whan at þe mete þou hast set him, late he wole rise and
with euele wil. Al he wole do slowliche, for to make þee
lettinges. His good he shal wel kunne espye, and whan it is
tyme to flatere þee; and [þou] þanne shalt take no [gret] keep, 3465
[but] disceyued þou shalt fynde þee, wherfore I rede þee wel þat
upon þi warde þou keepe þee, and nouht trist þee on him ne in
hise flateryes: for whan þou dost his wille, þou shuldest in
soth wite þat ayens þiself þou strengthest him, and ministrest
him his tool with whiche he werreth þee and turneth þee out of 3470
þi wey. So if þou haue wel vnderstonde me, he may wel be
knowen to þee, and wel þou miht see þat he is þilke þat is þi
mortal enemy, þat suffreth þee not to bere ne endure þin
armure."

"Ladi," quod I, "God yilde yow: I see riht wel þat it   3475
is þus. Ye haue my bodi wel distincted from me, and al
cleerliche shewed me how alwey he is contrarious to me,
to alle þe [goodes] þat I [wole] doo; so þat for I wot yow
wys, and þat I shal alwey haue neede of yow, gladliche I

wolde ye heelden þe wey to þe citee with me [where I am
stired to go, for I trowe riht wel þat I shal fynde
many an enemy in my wey, for þe shrewede paas which I know
nouht, wherfore if ye weren with me] gret counfort ye shulden
do me, so þat I prey yow þat ye wole come with me, bi yowre
wille." "Grace Dieu," quod she, "if þou haue hire with
þee it sufficeth wel: þou shalt neuere in þi live haue more
profitable companye. Nouht þat I wole [f.68r] excuse me þat I
ne wole go with þee. [I wole go with þee] sithe þou wolt it,
but I telle þee wel þat bitwixe us tweye shal be sumtime cloudes
oþer vapoures arisen, oþer mistes oþer smokes, thoruh whiche I
shal be hid fro þee. Sumtime þou shalt see me thikkeliche and
derkliche, and sumtime neiþer more ne lasse þou shalt se me, ne
litel ne michel; and sumtime cleerliche þou shalt se me wel
apertliche. After þe wey þou gost, þerafter þou shalt see me;
but algates if þou hast neede of me, seeche me aboute þee, for
if þou seeche me bisiliche, þou shalt fynde me rediliche. Now
alwey go, for þou hast no neede to tarye ne to abide. Tak
good wey, and leeve not þi bodi, whiche is to þee of euele
feith." And þanne thankinge hire of hire goodshipes, I sette
me upon my wey, foorth to go withoute abidinge. Ofte I fond
al þat she tolde me, and aperceyued al þat she tauhte me.
Seelden it was þat I sih hire, but if I dide gret peyne þerto.
þe cloude hidde hire from me, þat þe bodi made bitwixe us
tweyne. "Now God keepe me from lettinge, for I can neiþer wey
ne path bi which I may sureliche go to þe cite I thinke to:
wel I thinke þat I shal haue to doone, for whan I fynde myn
aduersarie (þilke þat I haue softe norished) me thinketh þilke
þat I neuere sygh wole not do me more despyte."*

Thus alwey as I wente and þus in goinge studiede, I sygh
þat my wey [fourchede] and departede in twey weyes: nouht þat
þei twinneden fer it seemede, þat oon from þat ooþer, but
[f.68v] bitwixe tweyne an hegge riht wunderful I sigh þat was
set, whiche seemede streighte fer. þer grewen þerinne bushes
and bramberes: bushes thorny, ful of prikkes, thikke plaunted
thoruhout, and thikke entermedled. þat oon of þe weyes costed
[it] on þe lift half, and þat ooþer on þe riht half: wel it
seemede þat oo wey it were if þe hegge amidde ne were. On þe
lifte side þer sat and lenede hire on a ston, a gentelwomman
þat hadde hire oon hond vnder hire spayere, and in þat ooþer
hond she heeld a glove whiche she vsede pleyinge: aboute hire
fynger she kaste it and turnede it in and out. Bi hire

countenaunce I sigh wel she was nouht of gret care, for litel
rouht hire of spinnynge or to laboure ooþer labour.

On þe wey on þe riht half, a makere-ayen of [mattes] and
arayour I sigh sitte, þat arayede and made ayen hise olde   3525
mattes; and more yit, wherof abashed I was, for þat þat he
hadde maad I sigh him al tobreke ayen, and sithe araye it
ayen. Wel me thouht a fool he was, and þat no witte in him he
hadde. Litel I preisede him, but a fool I was, as I
aperceyuede wel sithe. Algates first to him I spak, al were   3530
it was me not leeuest, and seide him: "Sey me now I pray þee
frend, which of þese weyes is þe bettere? I wente neuere
heerbi. Teche me bi which I shal go." "Whider", quod he,
"woldest þou rihtliche go?" "Go?" quod I: "I wule ouer see
into þe citee of Jerusalem, of whiche þe bisshop is born of a   3535
maide." "Come", quod he to me, "[heer, for] I am rihtliche in
þe wey. Right bi me þe wey of innocence, and þe euene wey,
biginneth. þis is þe wey bi whiche þou miht go to þe citee of
[f.69r] biyounde see." "Fain", quod I, "wolde I wite if þat
þat þou seist me is sooth, for þi werk seith me þat litel wit   3540
in þee þer is: I see þou art set to make mattes, whiche is a
foul craft and a poore—and I see þat ofte þou vndoost þat
þat þou hast wel doon, and makest it ayen, and þat thinketh me
is no gret wit, but if þou teche me þe cause."

And þanne answerde me thilke: "þouh of poore craft I be,   3545
it is no cause to blame me fore, ne to argue me of folye. Eche
wiht may not forge corownes of gold, ne chaunge gold. Oon
hath oo craft, anooþer anooþer; þat þat oon dooth, anooþer
dooth not. If alle weren of oo craft, pooreliche þei shulden
chevice hem, and I telle þee wel þat þe craft þat is most   3550
poore, is most neede of, and ofte is more necessarye þan þilke
þat is riche and gret. þat oon bi þat ooþer is meyntened and
gouerned and sustened. þer is neuer oon þat is wikked but þat
it be treweliche vsed. It [thurt] not recche, but þat þe man
be not idel whereuere he be. More is woorth poore craft trewe   3555
þan idel of court ryal. þouh I breke and make ayen to þat
ende þat I be not idel, þou shuldest not þerfore blame me:
for if I hadde ooþer thing to laboure, I wolde ocupye me
þeron, and nouht tobreke þat þat I haue maad for to make it
ayen. But þou seest wel þat I haue nouht to doone but if I   3560
rente my werk and made \it/ ayen. þis ouhtest suffice þee if þou
louedest me [to þi rihtes]." "Loue!" quod I, "And who art þou?
And whennes is swich thouht come þee? þou didest me neuere

good, ne miht doo, as me thinketh. Men mihten holde me a fool
if I yeue þee my loue, but I knewe þee ooþerweys: I see in
þee but folye and cokardye, þat preysest more [f.69v] þe
laboreres þan þe idel folk. I wot neuere who hath tauht þee
þis, ne who hath maad þee sey [it] neiþer, for wel I wot þat
reste is michel bettere þan labour, and were bettere for
oon holde him in ese þan eiþer werche or diche—and as longe
as þou holdest þe contrarie, for a fool þou shalt be holde
alweys." "Oo," quod he: "my faire sweete frend, litel þou
knowest me, as me thinketh, and litel also þou knowest [Oiseuce]
and hire perilous countenaunce. I aske þee—answere me now—
for what cause is it and for what resoun þat yren þat is cleer
and foorbushed waxeth rusty and foul, and holt not alwey his
fairnesse?" "If it be so", quod I, "of þat þat þou seidest
me bifore, I haue wrong to argue more with þee: for at þilke
woord þou hast ouercome me." "Serteyn," quod he: "it is
riht so þerof, for riht as þe yren with whiche men doon
nothing is in perile þat it wole soone ruste, riht so þe man
also þat is ydel and nothing dooth is in perile þat he ruste
soone bi vice and bi sinne. But whan he wole ocupie him and
bisye him in labour, þat keepeth him from sinne and from
spottinge of rust. þis is woorth to him a foorbishour and a
file and filour."

"I prey þee", quod I: "þat þou sey me where swiche
woordes þou hast drawe, and also þi name and who þou art, for
gretli I am abasht þat þou þat I wende a nice man, answerest
me so wel." "Grace Dieu," quod he, "whiche þou seest not,
speketh to þee, nouht I. She putteth me in myn ere, and
counseileth me, al þat euere I sey. Be neuere abasht, for þou
shuldest wite þat I am þilke þat yiueth þe bred to þe folk,
withoute which þe kinrede of Adam hadde er þis ben [f.70r]
dede for hunger ne nouht hadde be woorth elles þe arch of
Noe. I am þilke þat shortliche maketh þe time passe, withoute
enoyinge—þilke for whiche alle men ben born, for þe bitinge
of þe appel. Cleped I am bi my riht name Labour, or
Ocupacioun. Clepe me as þou wult: I ne recche wheþer of þese
tweyne. Bi me þei passe, þilke þat gon into þe citee of
biyounde \þe/ see, of whiche þou speke \to/ me at þe
biginnynge. Now do þou as is in þi thouht. Come bi me, or on
þat ooþer side tak þi wey: but keep þee wel þat bi þe
cheesinge of þi wey þou [be holde] no fool."

Whan [he] hadde [þus] seid me þe mattere who he was and what

name he hadde, I thouhte I wolde go bi his wey. But in þat
time my sory body bigan to flatere me, and to glose me,
seyinge to me: "Fool! What gost þou þus thinkinge? Leevest
þou þis fool, þis cokard? Leeue him nouht. Go from him. He
ne is but a turmentour and a trauailour of folk. Go spek with   3610
þe dameselle þat hath hire hond vnder hire spayere: aske hire
þe wey also, as þou hast doon of þis. She perauenture shal
telle þee swich woord þat þou shalt neuere recche of þis wey
þat is on þe riht half, but shalt go bi þat ooþer on þe lift
half." "Oo," quod I to þe bodi: "ful wel, ful wel knowe I   3615
þee. I wole not þerof, for I woot wel if I leevede þee I
shulde soone go an yuel wey." "And if I sey sooth," quod he,
"wolt þou þanne leeue me?" "Ye" quod I. "þe wey on þis
side", quod he, "is not fer from þe wey on þe yonder side. Al
is oon, but þat bitwixe tweyne is þe hegge of thorny wode. An   3620
hegge is no wal with kernelles for to close with toures
[f.70v] ne castelles: þer is noon hegge ne is perced in
sum place and tobroke, or þat men ne mown perce it and breke
it in sum place; so þouh þou were forveyed oþer ferred from
þi wey, soone inowh þou mihtest passe þe hegge and turne ayen   3625
to þi wey withoute any withseyinge—wherfore if þou
vnderstonde my seyinge, it may not michel greeve þee to go
speke with þe faire þat sit yonder upon hire ston." And þanne
I seyde him: "Go we now þilke wey, wel I see pees shulde I
noon haue, but in sum poynt I leeuede þee."   3630

To þe damiselle I com me, þat at þe eende of þat ooþer
wey sat, and seide hire gretinges; and she seide: "God looke,
freend." "Damiselle," quod I, "treweliche ye [do] me a gret
curteysie and ye tauhten me my wey if ye coude it." "Of þe
wey", quod she, "þou miht not faile if bi me þou wolt come,   3635
for I am porter and vussher of many a fayr wey. I lede þe
folk to greene wode to gadere þe violettes and þe notes. I
lede hem to þe places of delite, of pley and of disport: þere
I make hem heere songes, roundelles and ballades and swete
sownes of harpes, of simphaunes, of organes and of ooþere   3640
sownes whiche were wel longe to telle al. þere I make hem see
pleyeres at þe bal, pleyes of iogelours, pleyinge at þe
tables, at þe chekeer, at þe bowles, at dees, at merelles and
manye ooþere museryes. If into swich place þou wolt go, bi me
þou muste passe. Now loke wheþer þou wolt come, for with þee   3645
þi counseil þou hast." "Counseyl", quod I: "(allas) sorweful!
Counseil I haue, but he hath no wil to counseil me treweliche.

A[f.71r]yens me, to werrye me, he is bicome aduocat. Wel was
I desceived whan I acorded me to yive him a pensioun to
counseile me; and yit I am more desceyued, for alwey boþe
yisterday and today haue he wole þilke pensioun, and take it
him I muste. I wot neuere wheþer euere I shal haue riht of
him, or wheþer euere I shal see me venged." "Why so?" quod
she: "Seist þou so? þou art a fool. See I not wel þat he
hath yiven þee good counseil whan he hath brouht þee to me?"
"Serteyn," quod I, "fayn I wolde it were soo: but I ouhte
make a crosse þanne, for it shulde be þe firste time þat euere
he hadde wel counseiled me." "Sey me now", quod she, "how he
hath counseiled þee, and bi what woordes he hath mad þee come
hider to me, and what he seide þee—and I wole telle þee
anoon if his counseil be good and trewe." "He seide me", quod
I, "þat aloyngne me ne forueye me fro my wey michel mihte I
nouht, þouh I come to speke with yow: and þat þouh I were
forueyed or out of my wey bi yow, yit (he seide me) þe hegge
shulde soone be perced and broke, wherbi I shulde soone mown
[turne] ayen to my wey. Swiche wordes haue brouht me hider:
God leeue I be wel aryued." "Now þou maist", quod she, "see þat
he wole not disceyue þee. He wole suffre for to saue þe and
for to keepe þee from harm: for whan he speketh to perce þe
hegge to redresse þee, wel þou miht see þat he seecheth nouht
to his disport ne to his solas, for if any peyne þer be,
soonest shal he haue it allone, nouht þou. He shal be
scracched and prikked and bebled. Leeue him þerof al
sureliche: in þat [f.71v] miht þou nothing leese. Come bi
me. It is þi wey. þou art not þe firste pilgrime: þer haue
come summe er now—þe wey is al forbeten."

"Ladi," quod I: "sithe ye wole and rede þat I go bi
yow, seith me þe condicioun of yow, and how ye hatten: þis
wolde I fayn witen biforn I wente yowre wey." "Therof", quod
she, "needeth þee nouht gretliche recche to wite if þee like,
for many þer haue passed bi me þat þis haue not asked. I was
so plesaunt to hem þei speken not þerof neiþer more ne lasse.
Neuerþeles, sithe þou wolt knowe þis, wite in certeyn þat I am
oon of þe popettes þat Dame Peresce (whiche þou shalt see and
fynde heerafter) [made and] sette heere. Hire douhter I am, and
am cleped Oiseuce þe tender sister.* I loue better to strike
my glooues, to keembe myn hed, to shode me and to biholde me
in a mirour þan do any ooþer labour. I wisshe after festes
and Sonedayes for to rede vanitees, to gadere lesinges

togid*eres* and make hem seeme soothe, and for to telle trifles   3690
and fables, rede roma*u*nces of lesinges. I am þe freend of
þi bodi: whan þ*ou* slepest and whan þou wakest I keepe him þat
he haue no peyne, and þat þer be no wales in þe hondes. Ofte
I yive him greene garla*u*ndes, and ofte I make him biholde his
skin, if it be fair, and if [he] be wel arayed, wel cloþed and   3695
wel hosed, and su*m*time I make wormes come in þe hondes for to
digge in hem, to tile and to ere hem withoute any sowinge.
Now looke what þow wolt doone—what þou thinkest, what co*u*nseil
[þou] hast. If þou be leef to come bi me, sey it anoon,
and withoute taryinge tukke þi lappes in þi girdel and set þee   3700
in [þe] wey." [f.72r] Whan she hadde so seide me, anoon I
seide hire: "Sithe my bodi is youre frend, if ye loue him
treweliche, ye shulden not desceyue him: and wel ye witen, if
[he] weren forueyed, he were desceyued—for I wolde sharpliche
and shrewedliche passe. Soone ynowh I wolde make me swich an   3705
hole þat I wolde fynde ayen my wey. Litel I wolde bipleyne
him, þouh he were prikked and scracched!" "Go," q*u*od she:
"spek no more. Of himself þe wey is chosen. Blame not me, ne
argue me not of fals loue." And þa*n*ne bi Oiseuce I passede,
and into hir wey entrede me. þat ooþer wey I sette al in   3710
negligence and into foryetinge, þis I took bi my folye. It
may not be it ne is þe wers for me. Forueyed I am, but I wot
nothing þerof but riht soone I shal see it wel ynowh. Now God
yiue me grace [so] to go, and þe shrewede pases so to passe þat
su*m*time er I come to þe ende of þe shrewede wey I mowe come   3715
ayen to þe goode wey, and passe þe hegge."

Thus as I wente [alwey] costinge þe hegge, a vois I herde
on þat ooþer side þat clepede me and seide: "Musard, what
doost þou þere, and whider gost þow? Why hast þou leeved þe
counseil þilke berkinge lyere Oiseuce, þe grete   3720
jangeleresse? þe co*u*nseil þat she hath yiven þee shal lede
þee \to/ pou*er*te. It shal lede þee euene to þe deth, albeit
þe wey is wrong. In litel time she hath desceyued þee. Seint
Bernard clepede here not for nouht stepdame of vertu, whan he
kneew hire and was avised of hire. She is more stepdame to   3725
pilg*ri*mes þan kyte to chekenes—wel I trowe þou shalt fynde
it soone ynowh, and þat swich þou shalt fynde hire [f.72v]
anoon, if þou ne come hider and leue þe wey of biyounde." And
þa*n*ne al abasht I was, and as who seith al out of myself, for
who spak I sigh not, and who it was I wiste not. Algates I   3730
answerde: "Sey me now", q*u*od I, "[I] pray þee, who þou art þat

[areynest] me and þat þus spekest to me? I shulde neuere be at
ese but I wiste sumwhat." And þanne answerde þilke þat spak:
"þou owhtest wel wite who I am, for I hadde doon þee michel
good (if anything þerof þou haddest withholden): I am þilke
þat ledde þee into myn hous and shewede þee many a fair iewel,
and made þee yifte of hem. Grace Dieu men clepen me."

Whan I herde þat, þanne I seide hire: "Goode ladi, sithe
it is ye, I thanke yow, and wel I ouhte, þat ye deyne to speke
to me. I haue had gret wille to speke with yow, of þis wey
for to aske yow who maketh þis hegge þat is heere amidde.
Wherfore I pray yow þat ye lerne me and teche me þe sooþe, and
sithe afterward to my powere I wole do my devoyr to passe it,
þouh my bodi haue to suffre. I thinke wel to suffre it. He
hath be my counseilour—þouh he haue sorwe, I ne recche!"
"Serteyn," quod she: "forth þou shuldest passe it thoruh, if
any herte þou haddest, for after þat þou gost ferþere, þou
shalt haue þe hegge thikkere." "Ladi," quod I: "þerof I am
glad, for bi so michel shal þe bodi þat [hath] wold bitraye me
in makynge me come on þis half, be punyshed þe more." "Now
vnderstond," quod Grace Dieu þanne: "þe hegge þat is amidde
þe twey weyes is þe ladyes whiche þou seye haue a maylet and
smerte yerdes, and þe beseme [f.73r] bitwixe þe teeth.
Penitence she maketh clepe hire in heuene, in eerþe and in
see. She plauntede þe hegge for þilke þat gon þe wey
biyounde, to þat ende þat þei mown not passe to þis half
withoute enduringe of peyne. She plauntede it also for to
take þerof yerdes and baleys, and for to hafte þerwith hire
mailettes alle times þat it be neede: for in many places she
hath to doone with hem, for to withdrawe with sinneres from
yuel. Þe hegge at þis biginnynge is not riht thikke. I rede
þou passe it anoon, for soone heerafter þou miht fynde swich
thing þat shal lette þee, and shal not suffre þee passe
hider."

And þanne I bigan to biholde hider and þider, and to
muse, to wite if I mihte fynde any hole bi which I mihte
passe. But in musinge I sygh Resoun on þat ooþer side, wherof
I was michel abasht. Wel I knewe hire bi hir visage. "Ladi
riht wys," quod I: "how haue ye left me on þis half, þat
wende foot bi foot with me ye hadde allwey come and nouht left
me?" "On me" quod she, "it is not long, for þou hast first
left me. If þou haddest come on þis half, yit þou haddest had
me with þee. But weene not þat I wole go wey þat be

blameworthy. I wole holde me to þe goode wey, bi which goon
þe goode pilgrimes. Come hider, and leeue Grace Dieu, for she   3775
hath profred þee þe faireste of þe pley, and fool þou shalt be
if lengere þe wey on þat ooþer half þou go." Whan she hadde
þus seid me, yit I bigan to muse and to koleye, to biholde
where þe leste thikke of þe hegge were, and þe leste sharpe—
for I hadde pite of þe bodi, more þan I shulde. Now God for   3780
his pitee [f.73v] keepe me, for I am nygh a shrewed market:
while þe brid goth coleyinge hider and þider turnynge þe
nekke, ofte it bifalleth þat in þe strenges he is take whiche
is set in his wey, oþer it happeth þat he is slayn with a
bolt, oþer bilymed. He is a fool þat doth not whan he may,   3785
for he shal not whan he wolde.

Now I wole telle yow how it bifel me, wherof michel
[misfel] me. As I wente musinge, seechinge an hole in þe hegge,
þer weren in my wey strenges and cordes whiche I sigh not.
Withinne hem I felte me teyed sodeynliche, and bi þe feet   3790
arested, wherof I was gretliche abasht and sori to myn herte.
I lefte spekinge to Resoun, and haluelinge I foryat Grace
Dieu. Of þe hegge I made no fors, ne to fynde neiþer hole ne
gap. I hadde inowh to doone and to thinke, to [vnknytte] þe
cordes. Breke hem mihte I nouht wel, for I was not so strong   3795
as Sampson. A vile old oon, [foul] and maugracious and hidous
(þat I sih not bifore, for she com seuynge me) helde þe cordes
and þe streenges with þat oon hand, and gripede hem. Whan I
turnede me ayen and sigh hire, abasht I was more þan bifore,
for I sigh hire al mossy, and of mosse al rouh—foul and old,   3800
vile and blak, salwh. She hadde be foul in an halle, whoso
hadde seyn hire daunce. A boucheres ax she hadde vnder hire
side for to kille with swyn, and she bar cordes in a fardelle
bounden to hire nekke. Wel I wende, whan I sigh þe manere,
þat a takere of wulues she hadde ben, or of otres, for to kinges   3805
huntes [for] þe wulf and for þe otre longen swich trusses.

"What is þis?" quod I: "þou olde stinkinge! What comest
[f.74r] þou þus folwinge me? What art þou, and bi what riht
arestest þou me heere? þou shuldest not come þus withoute
spekinge oþer koughinge: wel it sheweth þou come neuere out   3810
of good place. Flee hens, and let me don of þese strenges
from aboute my feet: I am neiþer gerfaucoun ne faucoun ne
sperhauk ne a merlyoun ne noon ooþer faucowners brid, þus for
to be bownde with gessis." And þanne þe olde answerde me.
"Bi myn hed," quod she: "þou askapest me not as þou weenest.   3815

Euele þou come heere. Of me *þou* shalt haue it! 'Olde
stinkinge' þou hast cleped me. Old I am, but miscleped me þou
hast of þat stinkinge þou hast seid me, for stinkinge am I
not, I trowe. In many a fair place haue I be, boþe in winter
and in somer, leyn in chambres of empro*u*res, of kynges and [of]
oo*þere* grete lordes: leyn in corteynes of bishopes, of
abbotes, of prelates and of preestes, þat neu*ere* was cleped
stinkinge erst in no time, ne nempned. Whens cometh it þee
how durst þou speke þus? þou art in my strenges arested and
teyed: I trowe þou woldest be riht fers, and speke riht euele
to me if þou were ascaped me—and *þer*fore sithe I holde þee,
I trowe þat I shal wel venge me. I wole putte þee into swich
place where I wole make þee leeue in my god."

"Thow olde!" q*u*od I. "Who art þou, þat hast þe herte so
stout? þi name þou shuldest sey, sithe þou manasest me so."
"Serteyn," q*u*od she, "I wole it wel þat it be nothing heled
to þee mi name, who I am, wherof I serue. I am wyf to þe
boucher of helle, þat lede hy*m* bi cordes þe pilgrimes þat I
may a[f.74v]reste and bynde bi þe feet as þouh it were swyn.
Manye I haue led him er now, and yit I shal lede him ynowe, of
whiche þou shalt be þe firste, if þou ne ascape me out of my
strenges: þerfore I come to bynde þee þus pr*i*ueliche and
stilleliche, for if I hadde ooþerweys comen, I wende wel haue
lost my trauaile, for *þou* woldest haue passed ou*er* and go þi
wey. I am þe olde þat ly bi children in here beddes: þat
make hem turne on þat ooþer side, and be loth to rise. I am
boren for to ley hem in cradel and to make hem slumbre, and to
shitte þe liddes of here eyen þat þei see nouht þe light. I
am þilke þat maketh þe gou*er*nour slepe amiddes þe ship vnder
þe mast whan he hath lost oþer broken þe [steere], þouh it be
amiddes þe see, and þat he see wyndes risen. Whan he hath
lost cheuisha*u*nce, I make him putte al in neu*ere* recchinge,
and al suffre perishe and go to nouht, and þe ship go in
perile. I am þilke *þat* make thisteles come into gardynes
withoute delvinge, and make brambres and netles to rise. Ofte-
-times it hath bifalle me þat þat was redi to make [bi] þe morwe,
I slewthede it and dide no more þertoo. Gladliche of alle
thinge gen*er*alliche I abide þe time to come, and wel ofte bi
me hath be many a good werk slewthed.

I hatte Peresce þe goutous, þe encrampised, þe boistous,
þe maymed, þe foollich, þe fo*u*nded, þe froren. And if
ooþerweys þou wolt nempne me, Tristesse þow miht clepe me:

for all þat I see, it annoyeth me, and riht as a mille þat
hath in him nothing to grynde maketh poudre and bren of
himself, riht so go I gryndinge myself and wastinge myself,   3860
and al for anoye. For þer pleseth me nothing but it be doon
[f.75r] at my lust and at my wille, and for alle [thinge]
annoyeth me soo, I bere þis ax which men clepen Annoye of Lýf,
þat astoneth and dulleth þe folk riht as a gobet of led. þis
is propeliche þe ax with whiche I dullede sumtime Helye, vnder   3865
þe [genievre]. Ne hadde be þe hye [honged] bi whiche he was
twyes excited, he hadde not escaped me for miht he hadde.
With þis ax I dulle and lede þe clerkes at cherche. So hevy
and so leded I make hem þat if þei were weyen, men mihten
selle hem bi peys, and oon shulde [wel weye] two or thre. I   3870
spare noon þat I may dulle, and þat I fynde.

These strenges heere and þese cordes with wiche þou art
bounden, ben maad of my bowelles, and þerfore þei ben stronge.
þow miht drawe: þei wolen not breke. þei ben not cordes of
Cleeruaus, but þei were made of synewes al blak and twyned and   3875
out of my wombe drawen. If þou wolt wite how þei hatten, þat
oon hatteth Negligence, þat ooþer is Werynesse and Letargie þe
sownere. Leþie þei ben and softe: suiche I made hem for to
bynde with þe folk, and for to wynde faste aboute hem to make
þe folk abide withoute reendinge of here robes. If I sey   3880
sooth, þou wost, for bi hem tweyne I holde þee.

Of hem þat þou seest trussed and fardelled at myn nekke,
as at þis time I holde me stille, and leue it [for] til anooþer
time: al bitimes þou shalt fynde þee in hem and feele þee
bounden. Of oon withoute moo I wole telle þee, for I wole   3885
more enforce me to bynde þee and areste þee þerinne þan in þe
ooþere: þilke corde bi his rihte name is cleped Desperacioun.
It is [f.75v] þilke þat Judas heeng bi whan he hadde bitrayed
þe kyng Ihesu. þis is þe hangemannes corde of helle with
wiche he draweth and hangeth on his gibet þilke þat he taketh.   3890
I bere it aboute in þe cuntre for þe hangeman hath committed
it to me to þat ende þat if I fyndẹ any fool, I make him a
knotte aboute þe nekke, and þat I drawe him and lede him, and
þat he haue euele sorwe. Now looke wheþer to good hauene þe
wynd of þe north haue brouht þee, and wheþer Oiseuce, þat   3895
seith she is my douhter, haue wel serued þee of gyle? She
made þee come on þis half, and heere þou shalt dye, if I ne
dye."

Whan þe olde hadde þus spoken and sermowned of hire

craft, with gret despyte I seyde hire ayen: "þou olde mossy! Me thinketh þin acqueyntaunce nothing woorth. Lat me go, for þou doost me lettinge, and hast er now doon." And þanne she drow hire ax from vnder hire side, and smot me so gret a strok þat doun she ouerthrewh me. If myn hawbergeoun I hadde had, wel it hadde þanne be me in sesoun, for þe strok which I was smyten with was dedlich, ne hadde I had with me in my scrippe of þe oynement þat þe kyng maketh, þat is þe gostlich oynement þat no dedlich man kan make. þat hadde Grace Dieu put in my scrippe whan I took it. Wel she wiste I shulde haue neede þerof, and þerfore she hadde þerinne put it. "Harrow!" quod I, whan doun I sih me. "Goode Lord God, Ihesu, mercy! þis olde hath ouerthrowe me and slayn me with hire ax: if of you I ne haue socoure þe sonere, I see nothing of tomorwe in me. Help me and socoure [f.76r] me, and out of þis peryle caste me."

As I compleynede me, and in compleyninge lay doun, þe olde leyde doun hire fardell, and wolde vnfolde þe hangemannes corde for to tye me aboute þe nekke—wherof me thouhte not wel. "Weenest þou", quod she, "for to eskape for þi waymentinge and for þi cryinge? þe hangemannes corde I wole putte aboute þi nekke and fastne, and sithe afterward I wole be [drawestere] and [hangestere] of þee. In þat dede wole þe hangeman avowe me wel: it shal like him wel." Whan I herde swich manassinge and sigh wel þe redyinge, on my burdoun I bithouhte me. To him I cleuede, and myn herte com ayen. With boþe handes I gripede it, and lenede me þerto, and so miche dide þat as who seith I ros ayen on my feet and dressede me. I wolde haue flowe toward þe hegge, but þilke olde was neiþer slowh ne slepy, but after me she com with hire ax, and with hire cordes she withheeld me, of which I was not vnenpeched. "Ayen! Ayen!" quod she: "þou gost not yit, I trowe. It stont þee in no stede to drawe ayen þiderward: þe hegge þou mostest foryete. To myn ax and to my cordes þou mostest of alle thinge acorde þee." þus she drof me ayen with hire ax, and droowh me bi þe streenges þat I bar and þat I droowh after me. Sorweful I was, and gretliche dredde me þat with þe false Judas corde she made any knotte aboute my nekke. Neuerþeles, for I obeyede to hire al to al, she trussede it ayen on hire nekke as it was first, and forbar me. þat ooþer she leet doun and [drawe] doun bi þe eerþe, seyinge þat if I drowe me (were it [f.76v] neuere so litel) to þe heggeward, she wolde anoon take hem ayen and to hire she wolde drawe me ayen. So she dide as she seide, and wel heeld þat she bihyghte, for alle times þat I wolde go toward þe hegge and [rekeuer] it, she fered me with manasses, and heff up hire ax to me, and took hire cordes and drowh, and from þe hegge aloyngned me. 3945

As I wente aloygnynge me so from þe hegge (as þilke olde made me go wher she wolde) upon þe pendaunt of an hidous valey, foul and dep and derk, tweyne olde, riht hidous and þat to me weren riht wunderful, I sigh come euene to me. þat oon 3950 bar þat ooþer in hire nekke, of whiche þilke þat was born was so gret and so swollen þat hire gretnesse passede mesure. It was not werk of nature as argued hire shap. At hire nekke she bar a staf, and an horn she hadde in hire forhed, bi which she shewed hire riht fers. In here hand she heeld an horn 3955 and bi a baudryk she bar a gret belygh; and she was arayed with a white mantelle. A peyre spores she hadde on *with* longe rewelles wel arayed. Wel it seemede she was maistresse of þe olde, hire berere: go she made hire where hire likede, and she heeld hire a mirrowr wherin she lookede 3960 hire face, hire semblaunt and hire visage. Whan I sih þus þese tweyne olde, "What is þis?" quod I. "Swete God, mercy! In þis cuntre ben but olde? Olde heere, and olde þere! I wot neuere wheþer I be in Femynye þer wommen hauen þe lordship. If I be slayn bi hem me were bettere haue ben ded [f.77r] 3965 born, and michel soriere I wolde be soo þan if I dyede in mortal werre." And þane a vois cam to me þat was (as I trowe) of Grace Dieu, þat seide me an hygh: "To disconfort þee is nothing woorth. Bataile þou shalt haue with þese olde, oþer withoute bataile þou shalt yilde þee. þou art entred into 3970 here cuntre, and þer entreth noon þat ne is assailed of hem and werred, be it on horse oþer on foote. Be not abasht for tweyne or thre, for þou shalt fynde heerafter ooþere ynowe þat wolen holde þee riht nigh; and I telle þe wel þat if þou ne bee ooþerweys armed and arayed, þou shalt neuere keepe þee so 3975 wel þat þou ne shalt be vileynesliche treted." And þanne I seide here: "I pray you þat ye seyn me who ben þese heere þat I see comen nygh, and maken me abasshe soo." "þou shalt" quod she, "al bitimes aske hem whan þou wolt. Right as þilke þat leedeth þee bi here cordes hath seid þee who she is, riht 3980 so shule þese heere withoute lesinge seyn þee who þei ben, for I haue so ordeyned hem and comaunded hem."

Ryht as I entended to þilke noys þat I herde hye, þe olde

þat hadde þe horn, and rod on þat ooþer, cam prikinge euene to me, sporinge upon þat ooþer olde. Hire horn she took and bleew, and after she seide me: "Abide me þere! Euele come þou heere. Yilde þee anoon, oþer at a strok see þi deth." "Who art þou", quod I to hire, "to whom I shulde yilde me þus? But if I wiste þi name, I wolde neuere yilde me to þee." "And I wole", quod she, "teche it þee. þow shuldest wite", [f.77v] quod she, "þat I am þilke þat of olde am cleped and alosed þe eldeste. þer is noon so old as am I. I avaunte me þerof: I forsake it not. Bifore þat þe world was maad or þat þe heuene were ful maad, in þe nest of heuene I was bred and conceyued and engendred. A brid þat men clepeden sumtime Lucifer bredde me: was þer neuere of brid so euele a bredinge bred, for anoon as I was disclosed, and þat I sigh and aperceyuede my fader, so harde I bleewh him with þese belyes þat I haue with me, þat from þe hye nest I made him falle doun and plounge into helle. He was bifore a whyt brid, noble, gentel, brightere shynynge þan þe sunne at ful midday. Now he is bicome so blecched, so salt, so foul, þat [it] is werse þan þe deth. In þe see he is waxe a fysshere, and a takere of briddes and of bestes. Heerafter þou shalt wel see him, whan [after] þe see þow shalt go. Now I sey þee, whan I hadde þus put him and shoven him out of his nest, I fel doun with him, ne in heuene I dwellede no more. Into eerþe I com, whiche was neewe maad, of whiche me thouhte not riht fair, for I sygh þere a werk which was maad to clymbe an hy to þe nest from which I was fallen, and from which I hadde maad my fader falle into derknesse. Whan I sygh þat, in me þer was but wretthe, wherfore I bithouhte me þat if I mihte, I wolde withoute tariynge make him falle also, and lette him to clymbe. As I thouhte I dide: I com to him, my belyes I took, and so bleewh him in his thouht, and so made his wombe [f.78r] to swelle, þat him thouhte if he eete of þe fruyt whiche was defended, he shulde be [as God his souereyn, al ful of wisdom]. Be þis wey he was suprysed and from al to al desceyued; and þerfore he was driven out of Paradys and straunged þertoo. He loste also his avauntage to clymbe and go to þe nest.

Whan I hadde don þese tweyne chyldhodes, while I had soukynge teeth, and þat I was yit in chyldhode, I bithouhte me þat I wolde yit do harmes inowe. Manye I haue don, and alwey doo, and wole do. I make and purchace þe werres, and make þe lordes of cuntres haue discensiouns bitwixe hem, and discordes

and indignaciouns, þat oon ofte deffye and despise þat
ooþer for euele wil. I am ladi and condyeresse, cheuentayn
and constablesse of alle stoures in chevachyes þeras baners
ben displayed, þeras ben basenettes and helmes, and
garnementes of velewet beten with gold and siluer and ooþere   4030
queyntisinges, and alwey þei ben neewed bi me. I make hoodes
purfyled with silk and ribaned with gold aboute; hattes,
cappes, and hye crestes, streyte cotes with hanginge sleeves
bi þe sides, to white surcotes rede sleeves, to nekke and
breste white a coote wel decoloured to be wel biholde.   4035
Garnementes to longe or to shorte, hoodes to litel or to
grete, bootes litel and streyte or so grete men mihte make
of hem tweyne or thre, a girdel smal or to brod with whiche
queintisen hem as wel þe halte, þe boistouse, þe spaueynede,
þe blynde, þe embosede, þe maymede and ooþere—swiche thinges   4040
I make, for I wole þat euery wyght haue to me his eye, and þat
of me be seid 'withoute peere' and 'singuler of aray' to þat
ende þat I [f.78v] haue prys of alle and þat noon be paringall
to me. For of peere ne felawe I keepe noon in no time, and
soone wolde myn herte clyve if any comparede him to me.   4045

Al þat I seye, I wole susteyne, be it good or yuel, and
mayntene it, and neuere wolde I repele thing þat I hadde euele
seid. I wole haue noon vndertakere, no maister, no techere,
for riht as a scabbed beste hateth hors comb, and sor hed a
comb, riht so hate I techinge and counseil and avisement. þe   4050
wit of ooþere I preyse nothing: me thinketh my owen bettere,
and þat I can more þan any ooþer, and þat þer is no time
nothing wel doon ne wel seid ne ariht ordeyned but it be
forthouht bi my wit; and suppose þat any wiht dide anything
wel or seyde, be it neuere so wel seid or doon, sithe bi me it 4055
was not doon, myne herte so disdeynows þerof I haue, þat litel
lakketh it ne bresteth on tweyne. I wolde aloone haue þe
loos, þe wurshipe, þe prys, and wel I dar sey þat sori I am
whan any is wurshiped or preised but I. If any haue lasse þan
I, anoon I haue him ·in despyte. I sey anoon he is nouht or   4060
þat he is an asse cristened. If I heere þer be any wiht þat
preyse me, I make semblaunt þat I heere it nouht, or elles I
sey him: 'þou skornest me: þou shuldest not so do. I wot wel
I am nouht so sufficient as ye gon seyinge of me. Mi fame I
knowe wel and see, but I kan nothing and þat forthinketh me.'   4065
And wost þou whi I sey it, and why I humble me þus? Weene not
þat I sey it to þat ende þat men seyn ayen to me: 'Ye seyn

sooth, ye ku*n*ne nothing—ye haue knowinge of youreself' for
if men seiden me soo, myn herte shulde breke of sorwe and
anoon I shulde [f.79r] be slayn with þe spere I hadde forged.
But I sey it for [þat] I wole þat þe tale be turned ooþerweys:
þat is to sey þat it turne as bifore is seyd, wryinge to my
wurshipes so þat at þe eende my preysinge be brouht ayen and
confermed, þat men seyn: 'Lady, saue youre grace, from hens
to Boloyne-[þe]-Grace is noon þat cowde ne mihte do as ye;
youre wit is singuleerliche to alowe and to preyse: I sey it
yow withoute scornynge and withoute any flateringe.' And
þánne whan I heere swiche beringes up and swich avau*n*tinge
blastes, myn herte hoppeth for ioye, and lepeth and trippeth.
Swollen and wombed þanne I bicome as þou seest, and of gret
beringe. þei maken me place more þan I hadde: large chayer,
large   benche,   sitte   allone   as   pri*n*cesse,   go   bifore   as
duchesse, be with folk envirowned aferre withoute beeinge
empressed, for anoon I shulde breste if I wer*e* anything
empressed.

Feers   I   \am/   þa*n*ne   as   leopard,   and   thwart   my
lookinge. Asquynt I biholde þe folk, and for feerstee I
strecche my nekke and heve up þe browen and þe chin, makinge
þe countenau*n*ce of þe lyou*n*. I go with my shuldren spaulinge
and with my nekke coleyinge, with alle myne ioyntes stiryinge
and with alle my sinewes I make it queynte. I am þe scume þat
wole flote aboue [þe] good water and [swimme]. Of ooþeres
wel doinge I wole make a scaffold and sitte aboue as an ape.
I am as a swollen bladd*ere* þat hath in yt but stench whan a
man breketh it or vnbyndeth it. I see nouht my feet ne my
goinge for my gretnesse and my swellinge, ne neu*ere* apperceyue
ne see defaute þat is in me. þe defautes of ooþ*ere* I see
[f.79v] wel, [but of here goodshipes I see nothing, and
þerfore] I am japere and scornere of alle folk: [swich shulde
noon be founde at þe Castell Landoun for no peny.] In old
time I was cleped queen, and corowned; but Ysaie, whan he sih
me, anoon he cursede my corou*n*. Sorweful he was whan I bar
it, and whan queen I was cleped.

I hatte Orgoill þe queynte, þe feerce hornede beste,
whiche haue take horn and set amydde my forhed, þe folk to
hurtle. It is an horn þat is cleped Feerstee and Crueltee—
an horn of vnicorn, which is more cruelle þan biscorn or
chisel of carpent*er*. In þe world þer is no steel, be it
neu*ere* so wel tempred ne grou*n*de, so wel poynted ne sharp, þat

SECOND PART 99

mihte perce ne entre withinne þe herte of man withoute 4110
reboundinge ayen if þis horn ne helpe and made þe wey. I make
þe wey to daggeres, to swerdes and to alle ooþere yrenes whiche
ben made to sle men with. I hurtle on þe riht half and
þe left half withoute sparinge preest [ne] clerk, [and
more cruelliche I smite þan a riht wylde bore,] and wite 4115
wel þat [þilke þat hauen poorged hem of here sinne to
here power I hurtele harder and more cruelliche þan
ooþere.] With me I bere a payre belyes, spores, staf
and horn, and am cloþed with a mantelle to shewe myn
estaat þe fairere. 4120

My belyes hatten Veynglorie, maad to quykene with coles,
for to make folk þat ben blacked with old sinne weene þei
ben shynynge and most wurþi of alle ooþere. þese belyes hadde
Nabugodonosor in his forge, þat seide he hadde founded
Babiloyne in his beautee and in his strengthe. þe sparcles 4125
þat he caste sheweden wel þat he hadde withinne gret quiknynge
of cole þat was maad bi instrument. As wynd looseth and
felleth doun þe fruit of trees, [f.8or] riht so þe wynd of
þilke belyes leith alle vertues doun to þe eerþe. Al he
bloweth doun þat he ouertaketh. He leeueth no goodshipe 4130
bifore him. He vnnestleth þe hye briddes, and ouerthroweth
doun here feedinges. He maketh hem leese bi here folye þe
sustenaunce of here lyvinge. If euere þou herdest speke of þe
rauen þat sumtime heeld a cheese in his mowth, to whom þe fox
seide: 'Rauen, so God keepe þee as sey me a song. I haue 4135
desire to heere þe sweete soun of þi faire polished throte,
which is more woorth þan of a symphanye. Leuere I wolde heere
it þan soun of organe or of sautree, wherfore faile me not
I prey þee, for I come hider þerfore.' þe whiche whan he felte
swich wynd, and was ouercome with suich blowinge, þe cheese he 4140
mihte no lengere susteyne, but leet it falle. To singe
he took him up withoute taryinge, as þilke þat hadde þe herte
gay, for he wende þat þe fox hadde seyd treweliche. But nay—
of his song he ne rouhte: þe cheese withoute more he wolde
haue. He bar it awey as him likede, and þus desceyuede þe 4145
rauen. Bi þis ensaumple þou miht cleerliche apperceyue þat þe
wynd of þe belyes maketh hem þat ben best feþered leese and
ley doun þat þat þei haue, þat is to seye þat whan I see any
haue vertu in him, eiþer goodes of grace \or/ of fortune, to
þat eende þat I drawe for oon and þat I doo awey his merelle, 4150
with þese belyes heere I whistle him and blowe him soo þat þat

he holt he leeseth and cometh doun. The wynd of þilke belwes
shulde neuere powder ne asshen abide (þat is dedliche man,
which is seid þat asshen and powder and dunge is). þis
[f.8ov] powder whan it is blowen, it is with litel wynd
reysed, soone gon in disparpoylinge and cast into perdicioun.
þese blastes maken reedes and floytes and shalmuses [often],*
and þilke þat ben voide of goodnesse and han no wit in hem. I
blowe with þilke belyes þe herth to þilke þat of his soule
wole make a wastel to þe maister deuel; and yit I sey þee
þerwith þat whoso hath light in his bosum, with þilke belyes I
fanne* it, and wheþer it be greyn or chaf, thing þat ouht be
woorth or nothing woorth, I preeue it bi faste blowinge: for
if it be chaf soone I make it rise, but if it were greyn it
wolde nothing do for my belyes.

    Bi þese belies I can wel drawe and gadere ayen wynd, for
whan any goth blowinge me and whistlinge in myn ere, seyinge
me þat I am fair and þat I haue a fair cote, þat I am noble
and riht mihty, wys, curteys and wurþi, þanne I drawe þat wynd
to me, and in my wombe I make it place. Gret I bicome, as þou
seest: I haue seid it þee er now. þilke wynd þanne maketh me
araye me as a pecok, heue up my tail hye to þat ende þat men
mown apperceyue my confusioun. To hem þat seen nothing, I
haue an hundreth eyen of Argus þat ben shed in my tail (beter
to here jugements þan to myn owen) with whiche I see myself
cleerliche. Of þe wynd of þese belyes I am swollen so þat if
I ne were avented I shulde soone breste, or withoute brestinge
dye for sorwe. And þerfore in stede of an aventour I haue a
special horn bi whiche I caste and vapoure out þe wynd [f.81r]
þat I haue [in] my bodi. þis horn bi his name shulde be cleped
Vantaunce oþer Void Paunche: it is þilke bi which I abashe
alle þe bestes of þe cuntre—bi þe whiche I make hem heue up
here hedes whan I [wole] blowe harde. I blowe prise ofte-time
whan I haue nothing take, neiþer in feeld ne in wode: for
ofte I avaunte me of þat þat I haue of neiþer more ne lasse,
and seye þat I haue in time passed doon þat þat neuere com in
my thouht. I sey I am of gret kyn, of hygh and noble auncestrye:
þat I was bore in gret hous, to which longeth grete
possessiouns, and wel kan do þat and þat, [and þat] þe kyng
knoweth me wel, and inowe of ooþere [tournements] whiche ben but
bostinges; and þe fooles weenen þat it be prise, þat kunnen
nouht þe gise. I blowe also whan I haue take a pray, oþer þat
I haue to my thinkinge doon any wurþi dede, for to þat entente

þat I wolde haue wurshipe I wole neu*ere* hele it, ne to be ded
holde it stille. As an henne þat hath leyd kakeleth anoon, so   4195
to eche wiht I telle it anoon: 'Tprw! Tprw!' I sey, 'Tprw!
Tprw! Haue ye herd, haue ye seyn, how I haue [seyd, how I
haue done]? What sey ye þerof? Is it wel idoo? Thinketh
yow I haue pr*o*perliche ydoon it, and subtilliche? Trowe ye
þat þilke or þilke hadde doon it þus? Whan I wole studye   4200
or thinke on a thing, I am not agast þat þer be any þat kan
bettere do, ne may, þan I.'

  Of þilke horn cometh out gret breth whan it is blowen
with ful bely, and a wrecche is he with*o*ute drede þat bloweth
al þat he heereth, and þat bi no wey wole herkne ne heere noon   4205
horn. Alwey wole swich a musard (þat for þe horn is cleped
a fool) þat men herden him alwey speke, and þat no man seide
[f.81v] nothing but of him. Who þat wole alwey holde
p*ar*lement of himself, resembleth þe kockow þat can nouht singe
and iangle but of himself. Swich a fool, swich a blowere þat   4210
of his wynd is cleped avau*n*tour, seith þat he wot wel and
vnderstant what folk wolden seye, and recoupeth here woordes,
and holt hem as fooles. To alle he answereth withoute
askinge, and maketh his sentences flee abrod. He argueth, he
assoileth, he concludeth, and of swich cloth maketh ofte   4215
clout þat who þat seide it is nouht of swich colo*u*r, soone he
shulde be redi to chide and to rebuke, and to make poudre*
flee. Soone shulde he make eerþe-dene and sturinge of thunder.
Swiche folk kan wel blame vices, and magnifye fastes and
v*e*rtues and penau*n*ces, al be þer noon in here pau*n*ches, for   4220
þer is nothing in hem but wynd and blowing to make þe folk to
wundre upon hem. This horn maketh a shrewede hunte for seelde
it bifalleth þat he is a takere; he driveth al awey with his
horn, and riht as þe pye with hire cryinge and chateringe
suffreth no brid nestle nygh hire but maketh hem flee awey,   4225
and maketh hireself to be hated of hem alle, riht so eche wiht
goth to flihte whan þei heeren þe noise of þilke horn: [þer]
[wole non] nestle nyh him for his iangelinge and his cryinge.
This horn was not Rolandes, .with whiche he bleewe in his
deyinge. It is not maad of þe horn of an oxe; and longe   4230
it is sitthe it was not neewe: it hath be maad eu*ere* sithe I
was born, and of him I was hansellid, and as longe as I live I
shal not [f.82r] leue it ne stinte to blowe it. By it eche
wiht shal mown knowe me and be avised of me if þei wolen.

  Of þe spores I sey þee also, for bi hem knowen I am. þei   4235

shewen þat I ride faire palfreyes oþerwhile gladliche, for I
shulde not deyne to go on my feet but I hadde hors [bi] me.
þei seyn I am more redi for to reuerse and do ennoye þan for
to go. To go bacward myn heeles ben most redy: þat
oon hatteth Inobedience, and þat ooþer is cleped Rebellioun.
þe firste Adam took on him whan he eet of þe frute bi Eeue: he
mihte bi no wise taste it but he wente reuersinge, and reuerse
mihte he nouht but he hadde first þe spore. þe wey was nouht
haunted: withoute mo Eue hadde gon it, and after here wente
he. Sorwe cam þerof and yit shal. þe spore whiche made him
hardy, hooked him and to deth putte him. Of euel time was he
gentel man þat for to ete hadde a spore, and in sori time he
hadde a steede whan for him he moste vse it, for ne hadde þe
steede been þat of his riht side was foormed, hadde he neuere
deyned to haue vsed it ne had it to his mete. That ooþer
spore sette sumtime on his heele þe kyng Pharao: þat was whan
þe souereyn kyng of his miht wolde deliuere þe peple of Israel
out of his powere and of his hond, and caste hem out of his
lond. But for ayens a strengere þan himself he wolde doo his
miht, his spore was a lettinge to him and a gret encumbraunce:
for whan he hadde longe spored, in þe ende he reuersede so
harde þat in þe see he ouerthreew. Swich þer is þat
weeneth assaile ooþere, þat with his owen strok ouerthroweth.
Men seyn he is not wys þat hurteleth ayens a sharp poynt. But
[f.82v] what þat euere shal bifalle, þe prowde may not
withholde him, but trusteth so in his spore þat at þe ende he
leeseth his lyf.

Now I wole telle þee of þe staf þat I bere in stede of a
burdoun. I sustene me þerwith and lene me þerto whan I fynde
any wyht þat wole tarie me, and whan any wole ouerthrowe me bi
his sermoun and preche me. I skirme þerwith and defende me
whan any ayens my lust wole bi resoun ouercome me and bineme
me my condiciouns. I defende vices and sinnes: þer is noon,
old ne neewe, þat deyneth to yelde him as longe as I wole
defende him. þis is þe staf þat Rude Entendement þe cherl
heeld in his hand, as þou seye whan Resoun desputede with him.
Obstinacioun it is cleped, as it was told þee þat time. þis
is þilke on whiche Saul lenede him whan Samuel vndertook him of
þe pray þat he hadde [led] and kepte from Amalech. It is a staf
for a cowheerde whiche may in no time [bowe], for it is hard
and knorred and writhen. In þe wodes of Egipte my fader fond
it þat brouhte it me. In euele time [was] it [founde] for þilke

þat þerwith shal be beten. The cherliche hertes I bete, and
smite þerwith with gret wille for to harde hem and make me be
bihated of folk of good vnderstondinge. I make flee and drive   4280
awey Grace Dieu [of] alle places and make a stumblinge to hem
þat ben bisy to turne ayen to þe hegge of Penitence; and to
þat eende þat þe lettinge be þe grettere, I haue maad a stake
for to tye too þe laces of Peresce, þe bettere to withholde at
my lust þilke þat I wole. Now bihold wheþer þow ouhtest wel   4285
to crye 'Allas!' whan þou hast founde me. I wole shewe þee
anoon þe pley þat [f.83r] I can pleye. But first, sithe I
haue þus miche seid þee, I wole sey þee of my habite.

This mantelle with whiche I am arayed as þow seest, it is
longe ago þat it was maad, for to couere with þat þat I haue   4290
of felthe, and for to mantelle with my defautes and consele
myne vnthriftes. Riht as þe snow embelisheth and whiteth a
dong hep withoute, or þat peynture maketh shynynge a buryell
þat is foul and stinkinge, riht soo þis mantelle hath
mantelled me and seith to þe folk þat I am fair, and þat I am   4295
an holi thing; but and I were wel disclosed and were seyn
withinne, I shulde of neuer oon be preysed. If euere þou seye
an enchauntour pleye with an hat, how he maketh þe folk to
weene þer be sumwhat vnder (and ofte it is þer is nothing),
[þerfore] þou miht wel vnderstonde þat albeit I be mantelled and   4300
wel hatted withoute, whoso seye me wel withinne shulde mown
seye 'Blow! Heer is nothing!' A brid þat hatteth ostrich
bereth þe significacioun of þe mantelle þat I haue, and of me,
whiche hath þe feþeren aboute him, and algates flee may he
nouht, ne reise himself into þe eir. Summe þat [knewen] him   4305
nouht shulden weenen he shulde fle. Riht so þe folk leeuen,
after þe habite whiche [þat] þei seen withoute, þat I be a brid
hye raueshed, heuenlich, contemplatyf, þat I be a gostliche thing
and þat I shulde flee to heuene. But algates in eerthe I habite
and al þere delite me. Flee may I nouht, [flee can I nouht].   4310
Mantelle and wynges I haue for nouht. Ypocrysie bi his rihte
name þis mantelle I clepe. It is furred with fox skynnes in
lengthe and in brede, albeit withoute woven, maad and worpen
[f.83v] of wulle of white sheep. Ofte I bere it to cherche,
and do it on whan I go [to] preye to God, and [I] araye   4315
me þerwith whan I drede me þat any wolde putte me out of þe
estate and of þe dignitee [which] I haue a while be inne. I
do it on also whan I am al put out and deposed, and make þe
sanctificatur to recouere sum hap. I do as Renard dide, þat

made him ded in þe wey for to be cast [in] þe carte and þanne
haue of þe heringe. Bi it I haue ofte ben in gret estate and
gret degree, and as an ape clomben an hy and be as a goddesse
biholden. An ape I am, and apes ben þei þat vsen it, for it
maketh do and counterfete ooþere craftes þan men kunnen do.
And it is but an apeshipe to make þe folk muse so. Ape was þe
pharisee þat withoute shewede him cloþed with bountee,
counterfetinge þat he was iuste and livede wel, and as he
seyde, fastede tweyes in þe woke, and was no sinnere as þe
publican þat shewede to God his mayme. þe ape þat made him
sumtime a cobelere bitoknede him, for he medlede him so michel
of þe craft þat at þe laste he kitte his owen throte. He is a
fool þat medleth him of craft he hath not lerned. I were not
þis mantelle aloone: it is maad for alle olde. Eche borwith
it [to] his [aray], for to be of þe fairere aray. Peresce
maketh hire wurþi and I make me humble. Alle þe ooþere also
coueren þe viletee of hemself þerwith. þe more it is vsed, þe
more strong it is, and þe lasse wered. I wole anoon do it þee
on, for I wole make þee assaye it, and sithe after, if I haue
leisere, of þee I wole do at my wille."

Whan Orguill hadde þus told me of hire aray, yit my wille
was to wite who þat ooþer was [f.84r] þat bar hire and
susteyned hire. "Oolde," quod I: "who art þou þat
susteynest Orguill upon þee, and þat suffrest so þat so euel a
beste be set upon þyn hed? I trowe þow be nouht wurþi, whan
þou berest hire þus upon þee." And þanne she answerde me:
"Sithe", quod she, "þou wolt wite who I am, I wole sey it þee
withoute taryinge. Wel þou seist", quod she, "withoute
flateringe me, whan þou seist I am nothing woorth: for soo it
is. I am þe olde fool þat to eche wiht sey faire woordes, and
intermete me to salue þe grete lordes, doinge awey þe fetheren
of hem þat þei haue nouht on hem. I preyse hem boþe in
riht and in wrong, in servinge hem of *Placebo*. I sey nothing
ayens here wille, for wel I haue lerned to lye. To fooles I
sey þei ben wise, to hem þat ben hastyf I sey þei been
atempree, to hem þat ben negligent I sey þei ben diligent, and
to tirauntes I sey þei ben pitowse. I can wel russhe a dungy
place and coife a [sore hed] and I can with good oynture enoynte
a shrewede wheel þat cryeth, þat it shal crye more after and
communeliche be þe werse. I am welcome alwey to princes courtes
and [wel] resceyued: þer is neiþer jogelour ne jogelouresse
þat maketh grettere solas þere þan I doo; but þei ben fooles,

for alle I desceyue hem with þe floyte. I am þe mere mayden
of þe see, þat often make drenche and perisshe þilke þat wolen
heere my song. Flaterye I am cleped bi my name, Tresouns
cosyn, eldere douhter to Falsetee, norice to Iniquitee.   4365
Alle þe olde þou hast seyn bifore, and alle þilke þou shalt
see after, alle [f.84v] þei ben fed, norished and susteyned
with my brestes, and albeit I am þus norishe to alle bi my
vice, I am to Orguill an vndersettere and a susteynour by
especial. Hire I bere, hire I holde up, as þow seest, and   4370
mayntene hire. Ne were I, she wolde falle anoon, for she
shulde not kunne go on foote.''

    "Sey me now,'' quod I, "wherof serueth þilke mirrour þat
I see?'' "Herdest þou'' quod she, "neuere speke ne telle of þe
vnicorn, how in þe mirrour she leeseth al hire feerstee of þe   4375
wildernesse, and how she holt hire stille whan she hath seen
hire hed þerinne?'' "I haue wel herd speke it'' quod I. "I
wole'' quod she, "bi good riht likne Orguill to þe vnicorn,
for if she mirrede hire not ofte, eche wight shulde wundre
in hire manere, and for loue she wolde nothing do. But whan   4380
she hath wel mirred hire, and biholde hire visage, she
bicometh more debonayre to þilke þat holt þe mirrour. This
mirrour is [Resonance] and Acordaunce To þat þat Men Seyn, for
whan þe prowde seith anything, he wole þat men seyn: 'þou
seist sooth, it is so; I am a good mirrour, mirre þee in me.'   4385
But if he founde no mirrour, he shulde not hele his feerstee,
but anoon he shulde haue up þe horn, and anoon hurtle as
vnicorn—and þerfore to þat eende þat I be forboren and nouht
hurtled I bere þe mirrour, and graunte al þat I here or see.
I am Ecco of þe hye wode, þat answere eche wiht by my [folage], 4390
and sey al þat I heere wheþer [euere] it [shal] helpe or ennoye.''

    And riht as Flaterye heeld me þus with talinge, and spak
to me and tolde me hire doinges, and þe craft þat she cowde
do, anooþer old com upon me, wherof com gret afray to myn
herte. Tweyne [f.85r] speres she had ficched and tacched in   4395
hire tweyne eyen. She wente upon þe grounde with foure feet
as a dragoun, and witeth wel þat she was so leene and so drye
þat she hadde in hire flesh ne blood. Alle hire ioyntes and
hire sinewes seemeden as vnheled. Upon hire bak þer seeten
ooþere tweyne olde þat weren as gastlich as she, or more, and   4400
dreedful and horrible. þat oon sat musselled with a fauce
visage, and so she hadde hid hire foorme and hire visage þat
no man shulde see hire. A daggere she hadde in hire riht

hond, and a box she held in hire left hond, but þe daggere she
hidde bihinde hire, and conseled it. Þat ooþer olde heeld in
hire hond a spere þat was al ful of eren of men perced, [þat]
weren spited þeron. Þat oon ende extendede to meward, and þat
ooþer bitwixe hire teeth she hadde, with a red bon bloodi
rounginge as she com. Þe yren of a barbede spere was ymped
þerinne. It was maad swich an yren for to perce with and
hooke þe pilgrimes. Þe olde shrewe made hire riht fiers (þat
euele passioun come to hire).

Whan I hadde wel seyn þese olde, and wel apperceyued here
aray, I bithouhte me þat I wolde wite here names, if I mihte.
"Þow olde," quod I to þe firste, þat was berere of þe ooþere:
"sey me wherof þou seruest, and þi name, if þou wolt. Gret
hidouschipe and gret drede ye doon me, þou and þese ooþere
foule olde." And þanne she answerde me: "Serteyn,
þouh þou be abasht, it is not withoute cause, for soone
wolde I deliuere þee to þe Deth. I am Envye, which Orguill
conceyuede sumtime whan Sathanas lay bi hire, to whom I am
douhter. In þe world þer ne is castel ne toun þat I ne haue
doon [slauhter] inne of many a man and many a womman. I am þe
wylde beste þat sloowh sumtime Joseph, which Jacob seide þat a
wylde [f.85v] beste hadde deuowred him. Soothliche," quod
she, "I am þe riht wylde beste whom to see shulde no wight
haue ioye ne yiue peny þerfore; þat which I live with is
bitter, and I shulde neuere be at ese if I savowrede swete
thing. Ooþeres lennesse norisheth me, and ooþeres wrathe
reioyseth me. Ooþeres ioye teeneth me, ooþeres sorwe is my
[tete]: and if of swich mes I hadde ynowe, I shulde be gret and
fat ynowh anoon; but for I may not haue ofte swich mes at my
wille, I am lene and pale, and discolowred. Þe prosperite of
ooþere sleth me and maketh me lene and pale. Þe ese of ooþere
eteth my blood and souketh it as leches. I leeue [wel] and I
were in Paradise I shulde anon dye [of] sorwe: þe goodshipe þat
is þerinne shulde sle me, and þerfore he þat putte me þerinne
dide me wrong, for Deth hath assured me and couenaunted me þat
I shal neuere deye bifore þe time þat al þe world be ended.
And yit [leeue I] nouht þat I shal þanne leese þe lyfe: þe Deth
bihight it me for þat bi me in þe world he sette him. Bi me
he come þider in and entrede, and bi me he regneth and shal
regne. I am þe beste serpentine þat chewe al shrewednesse: I
hate alle folk þat wel doon, and to my power I confounde hem.
þer is nothing þat I can loue in heuene, in eerthe, ne in see.

I do despite to Charite, and werrye þe Holy Gost.

With þese tweyne speres þat þou seest departe and come out of my tweyne eyen, I pursue and werrye eche wight. þat oon hatteth Wrathe of Ooþeres Ioye, and þat ooþer is cleped Ioye of Ooþeres Aduersitee. Of þe firste, Saul strengthed him to smyte Dauid whan he harpede, for he hadde despite and gret wratthe whan he was more preised þan he. Of þat ooþer kyng Ihesu had[f.86r]de þe side perced: more harm dide him þe skorninge þat þe Iewes maden of his torment þan dide þe spere þat [Longis] putte in his side. These speres ben rooted and plaunted deepe in myn herte, but bi myne eyen þei haue here issue, for to make [me] beste horned, and for to make me caste venyme bi myne eyen, and envenyme my neghebores bi oonliche oon lookinge. Myne eyen ben eyen of [baselique], whiche slen þilke þat nestlen or enhabiten nygh bi me. Dede þei ben as soone as I see hem. Mo of ooþere shrewednesses I do ynowe whiche my douhtren mown wel telle þee, if þou wolt aske hem: þei mown more esiliche speken þat ben on horse upon my bak, þan I þat haue no reste. In askinge hem and and seechinge who þei ben, and in heringe what þei shulen sey þee, þou shalt mown wite if þou wolt of sooth who I am."

"And I wole," quod I, "withoute taryinge gladliche aske hem. Who art þou", quod I, "þat sittest first upon Envye þe fierse, þat hast þi visage and þi facioun hid vnder þis fauce visage, þat berest box and oynement, and knyf ydrawe in hideles, wherof no good I may thinke, if sum ooþer thing þow ne sey me." And þanne she answerede me and seyde: "If euery wiht wiste who I am, þer wolde noon neyghe me ne acqueynte him with me. I am an executrice and a fulfillere of my moderes wille, Envye. And bicause she mihte not greeve eche wiht as she wolde, she sette me sumtime to scole, and preyede me þat I lernede suich an art and swich a malice wherbi I putte hire euele affeccioun into execucioun. Now I telle þee I wente me to a scoole [f.86v] and þere I fond my fader þat was maister þerof, and þere tauhte my sister to ete mennes flesh raw, and to rounge bones as þou seest. Whan my fader sigh me, 'Hider now, my douhter,' quod he: 'wel I see þat sum gile or sum malice þou wolt kunne for to desceyue with þe folk. I wole teche it þee with good will, and gretliche I shal be gladed þerof.' And þanne my fader vnshette an hucche, and droow out þerof þis box and þis fauce visage, and took me þis knyf priueliche, whiche I bere stilleliche and in hideles.

'Douhter,' quod he: 'who þat wole desceyue briddes, he may
not sette þe wacches in þe thikke þer þei ben, ne in þe
pathes, for if þei seyen a wacche þere, anoon þei wolden flee.
þis, my douhter, I sey þee for þus michel, for if þou wolt
desceyue anooþer it needeth nouht þat þi foule face make to
him a wacche, ne þat þi misshapen visage hidous and derk and
foul þou shewe him, for so þou shuldest leese al þe labour
þou settest þeraboute. But it needeth, deere douhter, þat þou
haue manere more subtile—þat þou shewe him fair semblaunt
and fair cheere bifore, [oþer] þat þow doo as þe scorpioun
þat maketh bi dissimulacioun fair semblaunt and fair
cheere, and stingeth with þe tail bihynde; and þerfore,
so þat þou accomplise and do þat withoute failinge, knyfe and
box and oynement and fauce visage I presente þee. þese ben
instrumentes and tooles bi whiche manye han ben perished.
Joab, whan he slowh Amason and Abner sumtime halp him þerwith.
Judas also was not vnwarnished of hem whan he [solde] þe kyng
Ihesu—Triphon also, and manye ooþere whiche ben not wery to
haue hem. I rede þee douhter to haue hem to counforte [f.87r]
with þi mooder, to helpe hire to fulfille þat þat she may
not doon allone. With þe oynement þou shalt enoynte hem
whiche þou darst not smyte with þe knyfe; and with þe fauce
visage peynted, to þi visage þou shalt make a kage: þat is to
seye þat þi thouht þou shalt hele with falsnesse, and bifore
shewe ooþer þan þou shalt be withinne, and sithe þou shalt
haue woordes þat shulen be softe and enoyntinge. þis is þe
oynement with whiche ben enoynted ofte þe kinges and þe
prelates. þer is neiþer duk, erl ne baroun þat ne wilneth þis
oynement, for þei wolen alwey þat men seyn hem þat þat shal
not anoye hem. Wherfore, douhter, hardily enoynte hem with
þilke sweete oynement, and sithe after þe oynture, smyte hem
so þat þei mown not be cured.'

Now I telle þee whan my fader hadde þus seid me, out of
þe scoole he wente. Upon my mooder I am sett in þis wise, as
þou seest. Maistresse I am as me thinketh, of al þat hath be
tauht me. Wel I can sette my fauce visage, and in alle poyntes
entermete me of þe box and of þe oynement for to lawhe with þe
mouth, and bite with þe tooth [I can wel] withoute abayinge, and
make my cheere simple: on þat oon side frote and enoynte, and
on þat ooþer side smite and stinge. I am þe addere þat holt
him vnder þe gras til sum wiht cometh þat I sle whan he is
sett bi me on þe gras. Withoute þou seest me arayed, but

þerfore þou knowest me not treweliche. Men knowen nouht wyne   4530
bi þe hoopes, ne folk bi þe clothinge. Many a wilowh is ofte
cloþed with faire leues þat is withinne al holowh and al ful
of wormes. I am a wormy wilowh: whoso leneth to me is lost;
and þouh he [f.87v] triste me nouht, yit may noon askape me,
for fro me may no man keepe him—neiþer strengthe of folk, ne   4535
gret foysoun, ne here wittes I preyse not at a budde: so þat I
haue set on my fauce visage and cast on hem a fals lawghinge,
alle þei ben perished and disceyued, and alle fallen into my
mercy. I am Tresoun, þat haue maad many times many a shrewede
drauht. I pleyede neuere at game of merelles ne of chekeer   4540
þat bi my art I ne took which þat I wolde: þer is neuer oon,
neiþer rook ne king, þat whan I wole I ne drawe to me; and
for þi lyfe hath longe enoyed my mooder Envye, she hath
comaunded me and seide me þat I drawe þee to me withoute
respite, and þat ded I presente þee to hire, so þat now riht I 4545
crye 'A la mort!' and sey þat of me þou shalt haue it. Euele
come þou heere. Seint Nicolas þat suscited þe ooþere* shal
neuere haue þee out of myne hondes."

   And þanne as she neihede me, and þat to deth she wolde
haue smyte me, þat ooþer þat sat with hire areyned hire and   4550
seide hire þus: "Sister, be nouht so hastyfe. Suffre þat he
lyve, I prey þee, til so miche þat he wite my name, and sithe
togidere we shule assaile him. I shulde dye for sorwe and
wreththe if as wel as þou I ne greuede him." "And I" quod
she, "graunte it wel. But I preye þee [avaunce] þee. I   4555
wole þat anoon we haue þe wurshipe to don him vnwurship ynow."
And þanne þe bicchede shrewe ([þat] euele passioun come to
hire) areyned me, berkinge on me, rounginge on þe bon þat she
heeld. "How?" quod she, "Art þou so hardy þat þou hast
brouht hider a staf? I hate [f.88r] boþe euene stafes and   4560
crokede þat ben sharpe at þe ende bineþe. Alle þilke þat
beren hem I loue not, but gladliche whan I see my time I berke
on hem and bite on hem bihynde, albeit þat fair cheere and
fair semblaunt I counterfete hem bifore hem, as mi sister
dooth. And for þou hast a staf (albeit nouht croked), bicause   4565
my mooder Envye louede neuere þee ne þi fader, of me þou shalt
haue it. Euele come þou heere: I wole ete þee anoon al quik.
To þe bon I wole ete þee, and drawe þi [skin] of þi body.
þow seye neuere in þi lyfe mastyf ne bicche in bocherye þat so
gladliche wolde ete raw flesh as I ete it: I haue þe throte   4570
bloodi as þe wolf þat hath strangeled þe sheep in þe folde,

and hath rounged his chekes. I am of þe lynage of \þe/ raven
þat hath mad his nest in helle: I loue to ete caraynes—þe
more stinkinge þei ben, þe more cheere I haue hem. I wolde
neuere bite good morcelle while I mihte haue a shrewede. þouh
I hadde appeles to keepe, I wolde neuere sauoure hem bifore
þat I seye hem sumwhat roten or foul: but if I founde in hem
rotennesse, þanne anoon I wolde bite hem, and gladliche assaye
hem and sauoure hem and chewe hem. þis is my lyfe and my
norture, as it is to my mooder Envye." The whiles she tolde
þis, al were I abasht, a litel I bigan to smyle, and seyde:
"þow olde, þow were good to keepe and to cheese myne appellen.
And [so] þow wolt forbere to bite me, I wole take þee rotene
and shente appelen ynowe, and if þis wole not suffice þee, I
wot where lyth michel filthe: I wolde fynde þee ynowh þerof
raþere þan þou go grucchinge to me." [f.88v] And þanne anoon
she took ayen hire woordes, and seide me þus: "Me needeth
nouht go to fer if I wole fynde swich filth: in my mouth I
haue þe instrumentes with whiche I haue maad þe forginges.
þouh þer were noon in þe world, bitwixe my teeth þei shulden
be forged ayen, as þe maister tauht me whiche tauhte my
sister." "I leeue wel", quod I, "þat if þou haddest mateere
þou woldest forge: but withoute matere forgeth no wiht, for
kunne a smith neuere so wel forge, withoute yren and withoute
steel he may noon ax forge." "I fynde matere", quod she,
"ynowh, for alle þe goodshipes þat I may fynde I can turne þe
goode into euel, and interprete hem falsliche. I can wel
turne wyn into water, and fyn triacle into venyme. I can wel
sheende þe goode appelen, and diffame þe wurþi folk—and
sithe I deuowre hem as raw flesh and ete hem."
    "How hattest þou?" quod I to hire. "Detraccioun," quod
she, "þat todrawe and topulle þe folk with my teeth, for to
make colys for my mooder which is syke, þat she may soupe it
in stede of potage. She hath mad me a makere of mete and hire
maister cook. I serue hire of [eren percede] þat ben put and
spited thoruh with my spere with þe sharpe yren, in wise of
smale hastelettes. Mi tunge I clepe my spere, for his [wounde]
whiche he maketh [cruelle]: it perceth and smiteth sorere
and more cruelliche þan any spere or any kervinge thing—þer
mihte no barbede arwe make a more cruelle ne a more perilouse
wounde, þouh it were cast of an arblast. þe eren þat þou
seest spited and shoven on þilke spere ben þe eres of [f.89r]
hereres and herkeneres of þat þat I seye. þilke þat heeren

gladliche my seyinges, putten here eres upon my spere for to
serue with my mooder which þei seen languishe."   4615

"And wherfore", quod I, "hath it a crook hooked to þe
yren of þe spere?" "I wole telle þee" quod she. "Whan I
haue perced an ere or manye, and cast my spere thoruh hem at
my wille, þanne gladliche I hooke to me þe name of anooþer,
and crooke it: with bettere wille I stele a good name þan a   4620
theef dooth tresoure." "þanne," quod I, "þou art a theef, for
good name is more woorth þan richesse." "Serteyn," quod she,
"wel sooth þou seist (but Salomon hath tauht it þee): a
proued theef I am of al good name. Fairere thing may I not
stele in þis cuntre, as me thinketh: wherfore but I make   4625
restitucioun þerof, I may haue no foryifte þerof (but þerto
wolde I be ful loth, for þe gret shame I shulde haue þerby).
Orguill also, whan she wiste it, she wolde neuere acorde hire
þerto." "And what doost þou" quod I to hire, "whan þou hast
hooked a good name bi þe ere þat [herde], and dispoiled sum   4630
worthi man þerof?" "Serteyn," quod she, "þe noueltee*
I tolde þee er now: I turne good name into venyme and so I
norishe my mooder." "Me thinketh", quod I to hire "þat
neuere of al þis yeer I ne sih a shrewedere beste þan þee."
"Serteyn," quod she, "I leeue it wel. Werse þan helle I am,   4635
for helle may not enoye to hem þat ben not in his clos, or þat
ben of holy lyvinge: for þouh Seint Johan were withinne
helle, he shulde noon harm haue—þe grete perfeccioun of him
shulde make him shadwe. And [f.89v] I telle þee I greeue as
wel þe absente as þe presente: no more it greeueth me to   4640
caste my spere ouer þe see þan a myle or tweyne, and I telle
þee, as wel I annoye hem þat ben of good lyvinge as hem þat
ben it nouht. If Seint Johan were in eerþe, yit of my spere
he shulde haue. In heuene, and I wolde, anoon I shulde smite
him (I haue assayed it er þis); and summe oopere I haue   4645
smiten þerinne, and yit I shal. And I telle þee þat [also] I
wole no lengere now holde me þat I ne wole smite þee and make
þee falle doun." And þanne answerde Tresoun: "Sister," quod
she, "doo we togidere. Smite on þat oon side, and I wole
enoynte him, and sithe on þat ooper side I wole smite him, and   4650
so shal he not mown escape if he ne haue riht excellent
phisician." "I wole it wel," quod þat ooper, "but I preye
þee þat of þe sadel we make him first ouerthrowe, so þat
he mowe no more ride."

Whan þese woordes I herde, thouhty I bicom and abasht,   4655 for I wende nouht ne thouhte to haue had hors. "þou what?" quod I to Tresoun: "Haue I hors? Detraccioun, whi hath she seid þis? If þou wite it, telle it me." "Resoun" quod she, "tauht it me whan she spak with me and seide me þat on horse he is wurþen up þat of good name is [renomed]. þis hors shulde haue foure feet, as eche wiht shulde wite, for if he hadde thre or tweyne or oon withoute mo he shulde halte: þer were no wiht [wel] wurshiped þat on swich an hors were wurþen uppe. That oon of þe feet of þilke hors is þat a man haue in him noon evell, but þat he haue [f.90r] holi fame. þat ooþer is þat he be not of condicioun of thraldam. þe thridde is þat he be engendred in legittime mariage. þe feerþe þat he haue no rage ne tecche of woodshipe, ne neuere haue had in his lyfe. þese ben foure feet couenable to hem þat beren witnesses, and for þat þou feelest þee wurþen up upon þilke hors, mi sister hath spoken to ouerthrowe þee doun, and I wole also helpe þertoo." And þanne she spak ayen to hire sister and seyde: "Sister," quod she, "bi whiche partye is it þat we shule first assaile him? Kanst þou" quod she, "þe song þat Israel of Daan song: 'Fiat Daan coluber in via'? I am Cerastes þe hornede, and Daan þe crookede addere þat go nouht [bi] euene wey, and þat bite folk in stelth. I wole go al stilleliche and bihynde bite þe nailes of þe hors þat he hath, and þus I trowe he shal falle—þat is to seye þat þeraboute as he shal nothing apperceyue of me, I wole bite him priueliche and do him lettinge, for if I made me felt of him, and þat in apert I bite him, anoon with his yrened foot he shulde yiue me in þe visage. Thinges þat hauen no feelinge doon so.* He shal nothing apperceyue þat my tooth biteth bihynde [forto] he falle al bacward þat he mowe not rise, and þat þe hors shal halte." And þanne answerde Tresoun: "Now hider þanne, assaile we him. It liketh me wel þat þou hast þus [exposed] þe seyinge of Jacob."

And þanne Detraccioun caste upon me hire spere and hurte me and sithe ran with open throte toward me, as a wood womman, with þe teeth took þe hors bi þe nailes, and made him halte sore. Me also spared [f.90v] she nothing: with þe teeth she took me. Wel she shewede hire þat of dragownes kynde she was. Doun she beet me, wherof I was sorweful—but þerfore askapede I nouht. Euene to meward com Envye: with hire tweyne speres she smot me, and in my bodi [putte] hem. Tresoun feynede hire nouht, for as longe as hire sister bot

me, and wente rounginge my sides, she heeld hire oynement,
with whiche on þat oon side she enoyntede me, and on þat ooþer
side in þe wombe she shof me with hire knyf and hire daggere.   4700
þe olde with þe gret staf with alle hire instrumentes neighede
me and seide: "Yilde þee! þou seest wel þou miht not
escape." And þanne she bigan to wrastle with me, to bete me
to smite me and to make me [to] suffre peyne ynowh. Whan I sih
me þus bitrapped, if gretliche I were discounforted it needeth   4705
not to aske: wel I mihte crye "Allas!". Peresce hadde
respyt ynouh to peyne hire to areste me, for arested I was at
alle poyntes, ne helpe myself mihte I nouht. Algates my
burdoun I heeld euene, and it was not falle fro me; and gret
triste I hadde þat þerbi I shulde afterward escape.   4710

As I was in þis plyte and þat I biheeld hider and þider,
toward an hullock I sigh renne and come an old oon. "Hold him
faste!" quod she to þe ooþere: "Hold him faste, for I come.
Looketh he ascape yow nouht bi þe burdoun whiche he gripeth
too!" þilke olde was disguysee, for with poyntes she was   4715
armed al aboute as an irchoun. Bi a baudrike she hadde a
siþe, and in hire handes she hadde twey caliownes greye.
As me thouhte, fyre come out of hem bi hire visage. [f.91r]
And wel I telle yow, al were it þat withoute woodshipe she
was, it seemede not soo. In hire mouth she hadde a sawe, but   4720
what to doone with I ne wiste if first I ne askede hire.
"Thow olde," quod I whan she was come nygh me: "Sey me whi
þou hast swich countenaunce and array, and what þou hattest.
Gabbe me of nothing: fayn I wolde wite it, albe I haue ynowh
to suffre." And þanne hire tweyne caliowns she smot togideres   4725
so þat she made þe flawme lepe into my visage. "Serteyn,"
quod she, "of my craftes I wole anoon make þee feele, and my
name I wole divise þee. I am þe olde angry, þe euele kembed,
þe evele tressed, þe irchownes douhter, rownded togideres,
wiche roundeth him for vertu.* With his broches he hath armed   4730
me for I shulde be dred, and to þat ende þat if any wiht
neighe me, þat he shal haue of sum broche. Vengeaunce I
seeche and wole haue, of alle þilke þat I may wite haue misdoo
me, in kindelinge ayens God and alle hise halwen.* I trowe wel
þat I shal amende it, for I wot wel vengeaunce is taken in his   4735
hond as in souereyn hond. I haue seyn þerof siker writinge.
I am prikkinge and hateful, impacient and ryght bisy—more
sharp þan brambere or thorn or greisiler: whoso wolde close
his gardyn with a strong hegge and subtile,* he shulde sette me

þere, for þer shulde noon hegge do so miche as I. I hatte
Noli Me Tangere, þat haue anoon [*carmen in ve*], þat with
a litel enchesoun make a cast of a broche upon þe poynt* \in/
levinge þilke þat bifore was my freend. I make of men
howlinge cattes* at ful midday [f.91v] and nouht seeinge, and
bleende hem and make hem bestial, and trouble hem \in/ al here
avys. I serue of vinegre and of vergeous, and of greynes þat
ben soure and greene, and yive hem to hem þat ben coleryk
raþer þan to hem þat ben flewmatyk......................
...................................* in þe litel world þis
thing þat is so round is cleped, reise þe wyndes and
thundres and make tormentes, and I make resoun withdrawe, and
vnderstondinge shadewed.

I hatte Ire þe rivelede, þe toode envenymed, þe chidere,
mooder of houndes, þat of swetnesse hath in hire nothing. I
am more hastyf þan coles, and more soure þan wurmode. I am [þe]
[kyndlinge] of whiche þe fyre lepeth out whan any wiht assaileth
me be it neuere so litel. þer may noon so litel wynd blowe toward
me þat anoon I [ne] muste caste smoke, hurtele my caliouns
and smyte and make þe flawme lepe out. If drye tunder I hadde
ynouh, I wolde putte anoon þe fyre þerinne. Despyte hatteth
þat oon of þe caliouns, and þat ooþer is cleped Chidinge—
þilke þat sumtime smiten togideres þe twey wommen þat askeden
iugement of Kyng Salomon, whiche of hem hadde þe qwik chyld.
With þese caliouns I forgede sumtime þe sawe which I haue in
my mouth. þe hamer þerto was þilke þat is cleped Chidinge,
and Despyte was þe anevelte. Impacience is þe yren þerof
which was taken and maad in helle: þe more men smyten it,
þe lasse it platteth, and þe more men heten it þe hardere it
waxeth. I made sumtime endente it subtiliche: now herkene
how.

Dame Justice, þe smyþiere of vertues and þe forgeresse,
hath a file [f.92r] þat bi name is cleped Correccioun—þat is
þe fyle þat alwey fyleth sinne to þe roote. It ne may suffre
neiþer rust ne filthe þat it ne fyleth awey and clenseth; and
for she wolde sumtime haue fyled me and don out my rust, I
sette ayens hire þe shrewede yren of which I haue spoken þee.
She, whan she wende haue fyled me, fyled myn yren and endented
it. A sawe I haue maad þerof: þou seest it wel. Hise teeth
ben grete as of an hound. þe sawe is cleped Hayne, bi [whom]
disioynct þe onhede of breþerhede and þe trouthe of [vnite is
sawen]. In Iacob and Esau þou hast seyn þe figure. I sawede

hem and vnioyned hem, and boþe þat oon and þat ooþer I sente
fer—and so haue I many anooþer doo, of which were to longe
to telle. I bere þis sawe with my teeth to þat ende þat whan
I sey my Pater Noster I be sawed and disceuered from God þe   4785
Fader, for whan I preye þat he haue mercy on me and foryive me
my misdedes as I foryive þilke þat hauen misdoon to me, and [of]
hem I foryive nothing, I wot wel þat ayens myself I preye, and
turne þe sawe to meward. Ther is in þis sawe so riht litel of
wurshipe, prys or wurþinesse þat who þat be maister þerof, he   4790
putteth him vnder þat þat he saweth (þat is, in þe pit bineþe,
in whiche dwelleth þe Sathanas). I thinke þat þou shalt assaye
it, and þat þou shalt be mayster þerof anoon, and sithe
afterward I wole gerde þee with þe syþe I haue aboute me.
It is þilke þat I gerde murdreres with whan I make hem my   4795
knyghtes. Barabas hadde it gert sumtime whan he was take and
put in prison. Ho[f.92v]micidye it is cleped bi his riht
name, and Occisioun. It is þilke þat moweth þe lyfe and þe
gost out of þe bodi: þilke with whiche þe tyrauntes targeden
hem sumtime whan þei slowen þe seintes. He is not man but   4800
beste, þat vseth swich a siþe. þe siþe maketh him wylde, and
seeche pray in many wodes. Swiche bestes ben perilous for
hem þat gon bi cuntre: to hem shulde þe kyng raþere hunte þan
to hert or buk or bor. And for þou art pilgrime, I [am] set
me in [þi] wey: with þe siþe I wole girde þee, with whiche I   4805
wole now mowe þi lyfe."
    As I was in þis plyte, and þat I abod oonliche þe deth,
Memorie I syh faste bi me, þat seide me: "Sey me [whi]
swich armures þow wolt not of: excuse þee miht þou nouht,
for I am faste bi þee, and þou shuldest alwey haue þin armure   4810
redi, if þou woldest. Lo hem heere, as Grace Dièu seide
þee. Make not heere þi bed, for þou shuldest haue shame þerbi
and þou abide lengere. It is shame þou hast so longe abide,
and profyte hast þou noon had þerbi. If þou haddest er now
had hem on, þou haddest nouht now be deliuered to þilke olde   4815
þat hauen þus withholden þee and surmownted þee and felled
þee." Whan I sigh þat þus mi wenche argued me and vndertook
me, sorweful I was and a careful herte I hadde þat lengere I
shulde ligge. To my burdoun I gripede, and as who seith aroos
ayen. Slowliche it was, for I was feebele for I hadde leyn   4820
longe. I wolde haue doon on myn armure, but I hadde no time
ne leisere. Peresce putte hire bifore, and manasinge me seide
þat if I neighede þe armure, of hire ax I shulde haue.

[f.93r] Hire I dredde, and nothing dide. Hire pley I hadde
lerned bifore: now God keepe me from havinge werse, for
powere haue I in me no more. I haue in me nothing more wherin
I triste but þe burdoun to which I lene me. Mi scrippe
\serueth/ me of riht litel: to þe bred þat is þerinne I dar
not touche to my profyte as longe as I am on þis half in þe
wronge wey. If I ete it Grace Dieu wolde holde it no game. I
am hungry biside þe bred. Euele leevede I Oyseuce at þe
firste time: she desceyuede me whan I leeuede hire, for bi hire
I am holde a wrecche; bi hire I am deliuered to þese olde
theeves, espyowresses of pilgrimes. In hire hondes I shulde
dye, if of Grace Dieu I ne [haue] socowr.

As I wente þus waymentinge, rounginge on my brydel, a
valye deep, ful of busshes, hidous, horrible and wylde I sigh
bifore me, bi which passe I muste if I wolde go forth, wherof
I was abasht, for bi wodes hauen men lost al here wey, and
many periles ben in hem to pilgrimes þat goon alloone:
theeves, murderes, wylde bestes duellen in hem in hydeles, and
many disgise thinges þer ben ofte-times founden in hem. Swich
thing as I fond whan I passede þerbi [as] I wole telle yow, but
bifore þat I sey yow more heerof, to þat ende þat it enoye yow
nouht I wole heere yive yow good niht, and heere I wole make a
restinge. Tomorwe if ye wole, come ayen [and] þanne ye shule
heere þe remenaunt: ynowe I wole telle yow of mischeeves and
encumbraunces þat I fond—pitee ye shule haue þerof, as I
trowe, and taketh keep eche as ayens himself, for of þe
mischef of anooþer eche [maketh] a mirrowr for himself.

Heere endeth þe secunde partye of þis book. [f.93v]
Heere biginneth þe thridde partye of þis book.

Now herkeneth now sweete folk, myne auentures, and how I
was euele welcomed and euele led in þe wode of whiche I haue
spoke. Als I descendede and aualede into þe deepe valey,
anooþer olde, of ooþer figure, of ooþer manere, of ooþer
foulnesse þan I hadde seyn bifore, I sigh hadde sette hire
in my wey. Disgised shrewedliche she was, and it seemede þat
avisiliche as hire pray she abod me, and þat upon me renne she
wolde. Swich thing in Daniel, ne so maad in Ezechiel, ne
foulere in þe Appocalipsis I bithinke me nouht þat euere I
sigh. Boystows she was and wrong-shapen and enbosed, and
cloþed with an old gret bultel, clouted with cloutes of old
cloth and of leþer. A sak she hadde honged at hire nekke:

wel it seemed þat make flight wolde she nouht, for she putte   4865
þerinne bras and yren, and sakked it. Hire tonge whiche she
hadde [drawen] out halp hire þerto faste. Hire tunge was mesel
and foule defaced. Sixe hondes she hadde, and tweyne stumpes.
þe tweyne hondes hadden nailes of griffouns, of whiche þat oon
was bihynde in straunge manere. In oon of þat ooþere handes   4870
she heeld a fyle as þouh she shulde fyle brideles, and a
balaunce wherinne she peisede þe zodiac and þe sunne in gret
entente to putte hem to sale. A disch in þat ooþer hand she
heeld, and a poket with bred. In þe fifte she hadde a
crochet, and upon hire hed a mawmet she bar, which made hire   4875
eyen biholde downward. þe sixte hand [f.94r] she hadde
lenynge upon hire brokene haunche, and sumtime she haf it hye
to hire tunge and touchede it. [Whan swich] an old oon so foul
I sigh, and þat bi hire passe I moste, abashed ynowh I was,
for I was [al] wery bifore for to haue anoye as I haue seid.   4880
"Harrow!" quod I, "God, what shal I doo? I am ded if
þis foule beste areste me heere in þese busshes. She hath so
many handes þat if she gripe me I drede me I shal neuere
askape. Counseile me faire sweete Ihesu, or elles I am lost."

    In þilke poynt I sygh þe olde come toward me for to   4885
assaile me and seide me: "Bi Mahoun", quod she, "(þat is my
god in whom I leeue) þe abod I. Of me þou shalt haue it.
Euele come þou heere. þou shalt dye heere. Ley doun þi
skrippe and þi burdoun and do omage to my Mahoun: it is he bi
whom I am alosed and cleped wys and wurþi and wurshiped—   4890
þilke withoute whom no wiht is preysed in eerþe ne autorised,
þilke bi whiche ben wurshiped many grete fooles and cleped
wise. To him needeth þou submitte þee, and him to serue
sette þee, and sithe afterward [shamefulliche I shal make þee]
vileynesliche dye." Whan þe olde took swiche woordes to   4895
sey, þer took me no lust to lawghe, but wel I wolde of sooth
wite hire name and who she were. "þow olde," quod I, "sey
me þi name and who þou art: wherof also þou seruest, of what
linage, of what nacioun þou art, and of what regioun, who is
and wherof serueth þin ydole to whiche þou woldest I putte me   4900
to serue. It is not resoun þat to a marmoset þat is blynd and
deff and dowm I serue and do omage, þat am of noble fre
lynage; [f.94v] and if so be þat I shulde to him serue for
drede of deth, yit I sey þee I wole wite who he is and also
wite soothli I wole who þou art, and whens, wherfore I prey   4905
þee answere me anoon." And þanne þe olde answerde: "Sithe

þou wolt wite who I am anoon, soone ynowh I wole sey it þee;
but first I wole shewe þee of my chyldhode and of my pley, so
þat þou leeue me þe bettere. Come after me þer þou seest me
go and crye faste 'Allas, I shal now see þe sorwe of weepinge
and of weylinge ful of sorwe: þe sorweful sighinges ful of
lamentacioun.' þer seeth it noon þat ne cryeth 'Harrow, which
gret woodshipe'."

And þanne þe olde made me gon upon a gret hassok, and
[biholde] a fair chirche in a pleyn, founded bisides a
chekeer wher þer weren ches, boþe grete and smale, of which I
sigh rookes and knyghtes and þe king [þat] ledden gret
estaate.* Eche of hem hadde his swerd gert, which was to me
disgisee thing, for ooþer times I hadde pleyed at þe ches, and
hadde seyn noon þat was of swich manere. Here countenaunce
was right fiers, for to þe chercheward þei wenten and bete it
doun þei wolden. þe kyng first bifore wente, and mynede þe
foundement. Of a bisshopes croos he made his howwe and his
pikoyse. Pikoise was þe sharpe ende, and howwe was þe
krookede ende. "What is þis?" quod I whan I sigh þat þat I
see þere: "Am I abasht? Is þis meetinge or faireye or
fantome or woodshipe? Is þis þe [ve] and þe [heu] of
which þow speke me [of]? It is þis, cer[f.95r]teyn;
soothliche þis \is/ [heu] and [ve] ioyn\t/liche, þis is
interiectioun sorweful, werinne is nothing þat lusteth." And
þanne þe olde seide me: "It is, treweliche, þis þat I haue seid
þee. See þere þe king of þe cheker and hise rookes and hise
knihtes whiche hauen alle \þe/ poyntes limited hem and
ordeyned hem in þe cheker. Ynowh þei hadden of here owene
lond, withoute getinge of ooþeres, ne were I. But I may not
suffre þat þei haue sufficience withoute binemynge of ooþere,
and þerfore I sende hem to þilke cherche, þat is nygh here
cheker, for to delue and bineme. To þe kyng þat shulde founde
cherches and defende hem and gouerne hem I haue take a tool
ful of wurshipe, for to do cherles werk: þat is \a/ bishoppes
croos, to make þerof an howwe and a pikois. A bisshopes cros
is wurshipful, but to a king it is thing reprouable to diche
and to delue and to vnfounde foundaciouns þat hise auncestres
hauen founded and ooþere noble lordes. A cherl he bicometh
whan he dicheth and delueth and he maketh an howwe of þe staf
þat bicom crooked for holi cherche whiche he shulde susteyne.
Cherl is also þe hornede whan þe staf with which his cherche
is susteyned and gouerned and with whiche he is wurshiped taketh

[it] to þilke þat maketh þerof pikoys and howwe, to þat ende
þat his cherche be beten doun and fordoon for it is nygh þe   4950
cheker. þat oon is cherl and þat ooþer more: but I sey not
which is þe more. þe kyng holt pike and howwe and delueth,
wherof þe cherche sorweth—and þe hornede deliuereth him tool
whan he deliuereth him dimes. His croos to his burdoun he
yiveth him whan þe cherche [f.95v] he abaundoneth him. þerof   4955
prophesied sumtime Jeremie, and wepte for he sigh þat folk
howweden and doluen aboute þe cherche, þat she payede
subsidies, dimes and extorciouns: he seide, wundringe him and
compleyninge him sorwefulliche, how she, þat was princesse of
alle folk and [þe] maistresse, was bicomen tributarie—and who   4960
dorste doo þat, as þouh he wolde seye he ouhte wel to weepe.
Now weepe" quod she, "and make gret sorwe as I haue seide
þee bifore. þe chirche is mined aboute: litel lakketh it ne
is ouerthrowe. To destroye it eche wight setteth too þe hond,
boþe rook and pown. Al þe cheker folweth þe king, but all   4965
þat þei don, þei don bi me: I make hem do al þat þei do, for
of bifore þis time þei ben my scoleres. Strengthe hath neiþer
kyng ne rook þat þei ne obeye to me alle. Alle þei studyen in
myn art, come þei raþe, come þei late. Jeremye (and þou leeue
not me) witnesseth it, þat is woorth thre."   4970
    "Michel abasht", quod I to hire, "þou makest me if þou
sey me nouht who þou art, for I [may] not see þat þou miht haue
swich power. I see þee poreliche cloþed, misshapen, crooked
and embosed, and mawgre nature engendred and forthouht as I
trowe: and how shuldest þou haue lordshipe ouer kynges and   4975
erles, and be lady to hem þat ben engendred bi nature, and
nobleliche [born]?" "And I wole telle it þee": quod she, "þow
shuldest wite þat I am þilke þat haue þe sorseryes bi whiche I
biwicche þe folk. Whan I wole, I make me plesaunt, graciowse
and lusty, and whan I am [f.96r] biloued and plese, þat þat I   4980
comaunde is þe soonere doon. I biwicche erles, dukes,
princes, kynges: þer is noon þat bi my sorceryes ne doon my
[comaundemente]. I am þe douhter of Besachis, Apemendeles, þat
haue set þe king soo þat he lawheth whan I lawhe, and is
sorweful whan I am it—þat suffreth þat I do of his corowne   4985
and make him yive it me (þus ywriten þou shalt fynde \it/ in
þe secunde Esdras). Sumtime þe king hadde a lemman which was
longe in his cumpanye, and so michel he louede hire þat al his
tresore he took hire \to dispende/ to þe needy, to þe poore
religious: Liberalitee she hyghte, and was sumtime of gret   4990

name, and þilke þat louede þe kyng michel. And often she wolde purchace þat þe king yaf so michel of his tresore þat þer fel him þerof riht gret wurshipe. He gete him þerbi michel wurshipe and prys, and his tresore was neuere þe lase, but encresede ynowh, for riht as þe corn sowen dooth more good and profyte þan þilke þat lyth in þe gerner, riht so þe goodes þat ben yiven ben more worth þan þe hepede. Now I telle þee, whan I sigh hire þat þe kyng wurshiped þus, I bithowhte me þat if I mihte, of alle poyntes I wolde withdrawe hire. So I dide as I thouhte. Into þe kinges chaumbre I entrede: so miche I dide bi sorcerie þat þe porter leet me entre in. To þe kinges bed I wente. His lemman I fond biside him, and þere I withdrough [him] hire and stal him hire, and out of þe chaumbre I drouh hire. In prisoun vnder keye I putte hire, þer she is and alwei shal be. Afterward into þe kinges bed I entrede, and in hire place I leyde me. He wende I hadde ben his lemman, but I was it nouht: I biwicchede him and desceyuede him so þat [f.96v] his tresorere I was. I keepe al his tresore and al his siluer and his gold. He weeneth I do him wurshipe, but I do him gret vnwurshipe, and al his lyfe shal doon him, while of me he maketh his lemman, for a more defamed lemman miht he not haue for al his auoir.

If þow wolt wite mi nacioun, whens I am and what is my name, þou shuldest wite þat I was born in þe vale of þe derke helle. þe Sathanas [engendred] me, and þens he brouhte me to vsereres þere he norishede me, wherfore vserere I am cleped: summe clepen me Coueytise, and summe ooþere clepen me [Auarice. Couetise I am cleped for I coueyt ooþeres goodes, and] Auarice [I am cleped] for I keepe my goodes to miche. Clepe me as þou wolt, and be nouht abasht þouh þou see me þus toragged and toclouted and euele cloþed. þou shuldest wite þat I wole neuere yive of myn to doo good with: I haue robes ynowe to doon on, but I wolde raþere late hem alle roten and alle to be eten with wurmes þan I or any ooþer shulde be esed with hem. I hadde [good] freendes ynowe if I cowþe ariht departe myn which serueth me of nouht, but I am lich þe hound þat lyth on þe hep of hey, to which if any sette hand he abayeth and berketh and cryeth, albeit þat he ete noon þerof. I haue handes ynowe to gripe with, but I haue none to yive with: þe hondes of my yivinge ben kitte and doon from here stumpes—[þou seest wel I haue but þe stumpes]—a fool he is þat asketh me yiftes. I

desire but for to gadere hepes of pens, þat is myn office
and my craft. Sixe handes I haue for to gripe [hem] with
in sixe maneres and to glene [hem], for to sakke [hem] in   5035
my sak to peise me and charge me to þat ende þat if I falle
adoun I mowe no more ryse ayen. þe more I haue, þe more
I wolde haue. Vnstaunchable is my wille; [f.97r] my thouht
and my affeccioun may haue no fulfillinge. I am þe grete gulf
of þe see þat all resceyueth withoute anything castinge out   5040
ayen, þat al gadereth and al sweleweth, and nothing yeldeth ne
nothing cometh out ayen. I make me hard and trusse me and
peise me of swich metalle as I see peiseth most—þat is, gold
—of which I make me a blok and a stake and tye me þerto, for
rihtfulliche I may be cleped an ape clogged. It seemeth þat I   5045
kepe þe clogge, but it keepeth me michel bettere: it keepeth
me þat I go nouht hye, and doun it holt me, and doun it
peiseth [me]. To Judas þat bitrayede þi kyng, þis blok sumtime
I heeng so in hise purses and putte so miche bras in hise
sakkes þat from hye to lowe I made him shamefulliche falle   5050
doun and plounge into helle.

Now I wole telle þee of myne handes with whiche I gripe
þe metalles and þe bras as I haue told þee. Werse handes, as
I trowe, in þi lyfe founde þou neuere. Riht soone þou shalt
assaye it. þe firste, which is armed with nailes of griffoun,   5055
is cleped Rapyne, whiche maketh him gentel, and seith þat his
pray suffreth him to take him where he mowe fynde him, [þer] as
he goth ofte and robbeth þe pilgrimes in þe wodes, and sleth
hem in þe weyes. 'I haue' quod she, 'þe nailes crokede.
Gentel I am, drede me not. þer is nothing it wole forsake,*   5060
and hool it is þat it mowe graspe al and oueral take my pray;
whosoeuere grucche, þe thing is myn.' þus þis hand pleyeth him
and dooth manye harmes boþe day and niht. þis is þe hand of
þe puttok þat kaccheth and gripeth þe chikenes: she taketh
hors and kartes, [f.97v] and þe puruiaunces þat goode folk   5065
hauen maad for here owen vsage. If a poore man haue oxe or
swyn to keepe for his store, she taketh it and neuere reccheth
hire þouh þe poore man selle his cote for his lyflode, but þat
[his]* lust be fulfilled. With þis hond so I kerue and shere
þat at þe kervinge it araseth and breketh, and at þe clippinge 5070
and at þe sheringe I skorche al withoute anything levinge. I
do as þe yrayne doth, for as longe as any blood or marigh [be]
in þe flye, al she souketh it and pulleth it. þis hand is a
skorcheresse and [baconresse] of poore folk. She seecheth

þe lous vnder þe skyn,* for to haue and bineme þe more, and
whan þe poore ben skorched þus and topulled, and þat alle her
goodes ben þus shaken and drawen out and arased, whoso wende
fynde lyflode þere mihte wel be holde a fool. þus thinke I to
pulle þee and make of þee my dispense: souke þi marigh and þi
blood and drawe to me þat which þou shuldest live with. But
of þe ooþere fyve handes I wole sey þee first, as I haue
bihight þee.

That ooþer hand which I bere bihynde at my bak in
straunge manere is þe hand with which I gadere to meward
priueliche and in hydeles [ooþeres] goodes. It is þe hand þat
maketh. þe feet to wagge, and þe eren to be kitte. [Coupe
Bourse] it is cleped, and [Larescyne] þe defamede. It is þe
hand þat dar aske no glooves of þe glouere to gloove hym with,
for it sheweth him nouht but bi nihte and whan þe moone shineth
nouht. Crookede nailes [f.98r] it hath as þat ooþer hath, for
[she accroches] whan she hath time, as miche as þat ooþer
[dooth]; but it is so þat hire drauht cometh nouht so to
knowleche, wherof it is sorwe and gret mischaunce. Manye þer
ben now of accrocheres and kaccheres aboute þe kyng, þat if
þei weren apperceyued, þei ouhte haue ynowh to doone to paye
ayen to þe king. Swiche folk maken him to [bineme] ooþeres
for he may nouht reioyse his owene. þis hand is an [hole makere]
of howses and an vnhelere, [a] brekere of cofres and a roungere
of floreyns and counterfetere of seles, and a graueresse of
false seles: a fals lokyere and a fals monyere, and a fals
tellere of pens. þis hand dispoileth þe dede, and holt clos
wyndowes and dores into þe time þat she haue griped and glened
[þat] þat she wole. þilke is executrice and dispendere of þe
residue of þe testat, wherof I telle þee þat to hireself she
wole drawe and accroche þe faireste. Of þis hand ben nouht
exempt folk þat gon and stelen bi [nihte]; ne false forsters þat
ben assentinge to swiche dedes; ne false seruauntes also þat
seruen folk vntreweliche and labowren falsliche; millewardes
also, þat filleth here resoun withoute clepinge of Resoun;
false tailowres also and ooþere folk þat [ooþeres] goodes taken
so largeliche þat if it were wist, þe [hand selfe] wolde hange
hem—and nouht for þanne hanged þei shule be at þe laste,
whan þei haue abide longe ynowh. At þe laste I wole hange hem
myself as I haue hanged many anooþer.'' ''[How],'' quod I: ''art
þow an hangestere?'' ''Ye, cer[f.98v]teyn'', quod she.
''Peresce'', quod I, ''tolde me it was she.'' And þanne she seid

me: "Certeyn, she it is treweliche, but þat is oonliche of þe
soule; but I am boþe of þe bodi and of þe soule." "So God
keepe þee," quod I: "sey me now, who heeng þe bodi of Judas,
wheþer þou or she? Gabbe me nouht." "Neuere, God keepe me,"   5120
quod she, "but I sey þee we boþe putte on him þe knotte
togideres, and bi assente heengen him. But ne hadden myne
handes holpen, Peresce hadde neuere drawen him hye, for his
bodi peysede, and þat longeth nouht to hire—and þerfore
principalliche myn hand made þe hanginge. If þou leue me,   5125
keepe þee from swich an hand, for she maketh þe rerewarde:
she taketh þe folk subtilliche, and sithe whan she may she
hangeth hem.

Of þe hand þat holt þe file, I wole telle þee, for it is
my lust. It is þe hand with whiche I gripe and putte togidere   5130
and hepe þat þat ooþere hauen laboured and conquered with here
swetinge. She is maad ayens Nature, for in alle times she
dooth bisinesse to sette bras and yren to brode for to
engendre ooþer pondre. Ooþere handes maken it ammenuse with
handlinge, but þis maketh it encrese al maugre Nature. An   5135
enchauntouresse she is gret, for alwey bi enchauntementes she
maketh it conuerte into paresis, and of fyve maketh bicome
sixe. She maketh and forgeth (withoute smitinge of strok) [kyne]
þat mown not dye, and bi þe longe enduringe of hem, [Kyne]
of Yren she maketh clepe hem; and she hath corn in gerners,   5140
and abideth til þe greyn be deere, and þanne hire corn she
selleth to þe dubble, and taketh þerfore dubble payement. She
holt [f.99r] a fyle for to fyle with ooþeres substaunce and
waste it: litel and litel it goth rounginge ooþere in comynge
and goinge. þer is nothing þat biside it mihte endure, þat al   5145
to vsure it ne muste go.* Vsure bi name it is cleped, for bi
hire is þe lyf vsed of þilke þat in here vsage vseth his time
and his age. If so in vsage it ne were as it is, eche wiht
wolde be agast of it; but soo in vse bicomen it is, þat in
feyres knowen it is: into þe feires þe folk gon \vsinge it/   5150
bifore alle folk and fylinge also, but [þer] is noon meyr ne
provost þat ayensseith to here dooinge."

"Sey me", quod I, "of þe balaunce in which with so gret
entente þou peisest þe zodiac and þe sunne, for it is thing of
whiche I wundre." "Lerne", quod she, "and vnderstonde wel,
for I wole gabbe of nothing. Grace Dieu aboute þe zodiac
sumtime sette þe sunne to shyne to eche wight and for to be
commune to þe world. To alle she wolde it were general, and

þat noon hadde defaute þerof. Now I telle þee þat þat
displesede me for my profyte which lay not þerinne, for I sigh
[þat] if I hadde not þe time, and appropred it not to me, right
litel I myghte werche with my fyle, and riht litel fylen; and
*þer*fore I approprede to me þe zodiac: þe time and þe sunne I
made myn owen, and in my bala*u*nce I putte hem. Bi myn outrage
I haue maad myself weyere þerof and sellere. I selle it bi
dayes and bi wookes, bi [vtaues] and bi quinzimes, bi monethes
and bi yeeres al hol; and þe pound I selle for twenty pens,
þe moneth I selle for nyne shillinges or for ten. After [þat]
eche wight taketh þerof, þerafter I weye it and selle it." [f.99v]

"Now sey me", qu*o*d I, "I preye þee, of a wodyere þat
solde me a while ago wode in his foreste, and seid me: 'þe
wode is þin for thretti shillinges if *þou* wolt anoon make me
þe payment, and if to þe yeer ende *þou* wolt abide, for fourti
shillinges I moste selle it.' I wolde wite forsooth if þilke
peysede þe zodiac and solde it." "þerof", qu*o*d she, "I wole
telle þee as I haue herd speke. Su*m*time þe wodieres solden
here wode upon þe stok, and seyden: 'If þou wolt haue my wode,
anoon *þou* shalt yive þerfore swich prys, and if þou wolt
abide to þe yeer, for grettere p*r*is I moste selle it:
for bi þe yeer my wode shulde wexe, and þerafter it shulde be
þe more worth.' If þus he selde þee þe wode, þilke, I sey þee
as bi myn avys þat he weyede not þe time; but if þe wode were
dou*n* and hewen and kitt, I trowe þe time were weyen of þe
thing which mihte not amende ne multiplye. Whan for long time
þe thing is sold, þe zodiac is peysed, but whan þe thing may
of himself multiplye, I weene and leeue þat þe waxinge is
oonliche peysed and mesured." "þe wodyeres", qu*o*d I, "sellen
seelde [þe] wodes but on þe stokkes: þei liggen longe dou*n* er
þei mown ben sold; and algates deere it maketh he*m* whan þei
ben not payed in hande." And þa*n*ne she answerde me and seyde:
"I wole sei þee þat þat lyth me on herte, availe what availe
may. If þe wodyeres of þe wode diden nouht þe hewinge of þe
wode bifore þat þe biggeres comen to hem, wel long time þei
mihten abiden er þei shulden selle here wodes, for þe
marchau*n*tes whan þei [f.100r] seyen þe wode nouht hewen ne
kitte wolden seye: 'To longe we shulden abide. Passe we ou*er*
and go we hens; oure thing wolde be hasted, we haue no neede
to tarye.' And þerfore as I trowe it was ordeyned for co*m*mune
profite þat er þe marchau*n*tes camen, þe selleres shulden felle
here wodes, and make kitte hem and araye hem: and þat was a

good ordinaunce and a gret fortheringe to hem þat of timber
hadden neede or þat wolden brenne wode; and þerfore ouhten
þei not leese þat doon here curteysye, if for ooþere þei haue
hewe here wode which wolde haue amended withinne a yeer. I
trowe þe derrere þei mown selle it withoute mistakinge, so þat   5205
þei doon it nouht ne thinke it nouht for no treccherie ne
bigilinge, for in swich wise þei sellen þe zodiac and peisen
it. And perauenture summe doon it soo, but koueringe þei haue
bi þat þat it is acustomed, and þat þe vsage is approued. Now
vnderstonde it wel and [expose] it as þou wolt, boþe þe texte   5210
and þe glose.

Of þe hand with þe dysh I wole telle þee ooþere tidinges.
This hand heere is cleped Coquinerie. Trewaundrie bi name I
cleyme it, and Maungepayn I clepe it. It is þilke þat hideth
brybes in his sak; and so manye þer ben þat mowled þei waxen,   5215
and doon good to no wiht. þat is þilke þat biseecheth bred
for þe loue of God, and wole in no place paye scotte for
nothing þat she dispendeth, and hath no desire þat any wight
amende bi hire curteysye þat she wole do. With þe dish she
purchaceth hire lyflode riht shamefulliche, albeit þat if she   5220
wolde she [f.100v] mihte amende it, [if she wolde] laboure and
peyne hire to winne. þat is þilke þat hath þus toragged me
and toclowted me as þou seest. It can nothing doo but make
loutes and pauteneers and bagges, and bere bribes and clawe
me in þe busshes. She leedeth me into þe grete weyes þere þe   5225
weifareres and þe pilgrimes or grete lordes shulden passen
to asken þere here almesse; and to þat ende þat þei haue
þe grettere pitee of me, and þat þei mowe with ſſiþe] bettere
wille yive me þe more of heres, she maketh me more feeble bi
þe thridde part, and more poore þan I am, and þerwith I sey   5230
þee þat bi art she maketh me counterfete and withdrawe with
feet and handes, and go crooked on a staf and crye 'Allas'
withouten resoun; and albeit I haue noon harm and my
wombe ful, yit oþer hye or lowe I curse hem þat failen me.
This hand borwen ofte to trewaunde with þese gentel folk: 5235
in here grete haukinge glooves þei kunne putte it and hide it,
it and wel þei kunne glooven [it] whan þei wolen trewande
þerwith. To þese religious þei st\r/ecchen it withoute
hauynge shame in askinge. 'Now hider skinnes for haukes
hoodes,' and 'yif me a loyne if þou wolt, and a peyre   5240
gessis' and 'I haue gret neede of a brod gerdel, and of a
coler to my grehound. Make yive me of youre cheeses, I prey

yow' and 'Faile me nouht þat I [ne] haue a gowne of þe [russet]
of yowre abbeye. Lene me eighte dayes a soomeer and an hors for
to ride on, I prey yow, a carte for to lede with my wode, and
twey plowes or thre for to ere my lond: ye shule haue hem
ayen with[f.101r]inne þe moneth.' And þus from hand to hand
þei helpen hemself shamefulliche in sparinge of here owene
þere þei haue ynouh of here owene; and it seemeth þat þei
weene not þat poore folk of abbeyes hauen anything but for
hem, wherof þou hast seyn, if þou woldest, þat whan þei hauen
nouht þat þat þei asken, þei taken noon excusacioun, but hauen
gret indignacioun and haten hem of þe hous. Now looke wheþer þei
ouhten wel to loue me, whan I make hem þus to bere þe dish of
[trewaundes] and putte [hem] my hand in here glooues whan with
my sak and with my dish at here elbowes I shame hem. It is [a]
neewe manere þat noblesse seecheth þus his bred, and þat þus
it is bicome thral to me þat am old and hoor."

"Of þe hand with þe crochet", quod I, "sey me a litel if
þou wolt, for as of þis it sufficeth me." And þanne she
answerde me and seide: "þe hand with þe crook was sumtime
fisshed in þe derk helle. Simon Magus and Giesy brouhten it
me hider and maden me yifte and present þerof, but þe crook yaf
hire Simon, of þe firste figure of his name and cheuenteyn.
As a crochet it is figured, þou wost it wel: [.S.] it is nempned
þis crook. þis crook and þis .S. shewen wel þat I am abbesse,
but it is of a blak abbeye þereas folk liven shrewed lyf. Of
þis crochet [et ce] Simon þis hand hatteth Symonye: it is an
hand þat entreth into þe hous of Ihesu Crist bi false breches
and holes as theeves,* and whan withinne it hath led hem, and
with hire crook hooked hem, [f.101v] of hire crochet crooses
she maketh hem, and pastores of sheep she maketh hem.
Pastores, I sey, but þilke it ben þat so feeden hem and doon
[so michel] þat bettere men mihten clepe hem wulues þan
keeperes of sheep: with here croses bi strengthe þei
withdrawen and disencresen Grace Dieu of þe [throne] of hire
rialtee bi yifte of temporalitee. Oon hour þei ben biggeres,
anooþer time þei ben selleres, and often þei wagen hemself to
hem þat taken hem þe monye. Grace Dieu is wroth þerwith, for
hire thinketh wel she is litel preysed whan she is waged and
leyd for so litel thing. Also she is not wel apayed, ne it
lusteth hire not wel whan þilke þat she hath sette in
lordshipe doon hire þilke velenye. This hand with al hire
crochet is of swich maneere and swich gise þat oon houre it

biggeth, anooþer it selleth, þerfore whoso wole propirliche   5285
speke, whan it selleth 'Giezitrye' and whan it biggeth 'Symonye'
it is seyd; but communeliche Symonye comprehendeth þe names.
Of swich hand ben nouht exempt þilke þat maken synge masses
for bihotinge and yivinge of siluer. þe preestes also ben
nouht exempt þerof þat taken þe siluer, but ben lich þe false   5290
Judas þat solde Ihesu for pens: and þerwith I sey þee yit þat
werse þan Judas þei ben, for whan he sigh þat he hadde don
euele, he yelte ayen þe pens—but þei wole not doon so: þer
shal no silogisme of resoun, ne predicacioun, neuere make hem
yilde it ayen, ne lede hem to swich ende. And if þe cause þou   5295
wolt wite, [f.102r] I sey þee (wite it forsooth) þat þe sak
which at [my] nekke I bere hath so subtile a yate þat what is
cast þerin may not out ne be doon awey. It is maad as a
were for fysh: entree þer is, but issue nouht, and [for þat]
myne handes and alle þilke þat [hauen] hem or borwen hem mosten   5300
caste þerinne al þat þei mown conquere, [for þat] þer may
nothing come out of þe sak: it moste roten þerinne."

Whan she hadde þus tolde me and seid of þis hand,
which dooth to God gret despyte as me thinketh, after I
preyede hire and seyde hire þat she wolde telle me of þat   5305
ooþer hand which she hadde leyd upon hire mayme. "þat ooþer
hand" quod she, "is cleped Baret, Treccherie, Tricot,
Hazard, and Disceyuaunce, whiche alwey avaunceth hire to bigile
þilke þat ben symple and withoute malice, or þat ben nyce to
marchaunde. False weihtes and false balaunces and false   5310
mesures she [vseth: and after þat she biggeth or selleth,
of eche] she vseth doubleliche. With þe grete metyerde she wole
mesure þat þat she biggeth, and þat þat she [wole selle] with
þe smallere mesure she wole mete. Right so with balaunces she
dooth, and with þe weyhtes þat she dooth in hem, for wel she   5315
can make chaunge of hem after þat she deliuereth or
resceyueth. Neuere mesurede she ariht ne iustliche weyede
weyghte. Swich thing dooth to God despite: I haue seyn it
writen in Prouerbe. This hand is a [stenderesse] of corteynes
and a makere. She maketh curteynes to draperes for þe   5320
coloures of þe cloth shulde seeme þe more fyne to þe folk: and
I telle þee also þat riht ofte she sheweth goode penywoorþes,
but afterward whan [f.102v] þei ben bouht she hath ooþere of
þe same colour, which she deliuereth þe biggere. Manye [dooth]
þis hand [of harmes]. O time she marchaleth hors and maketh þe   5325
badde seeme good to hem þat wolen bigge hem, anooþer time bi

þe cuntre selleth false gerdeles and swiche ooþere thinges, and sheweth hem to þe symple folk for to haue siluer falsliche; anooþer time taketh ymages in [þese] cherches þat ben olde, and maketh hem holes in þe hed, and for to make þe preest winne she dooth oyle or water or wyne (whiche she hath rediest) in þe hole þat she hath maad, to þat ende þat whan þe licour descendeth doun, it mowe be seid þat it swet, and þat þe olde ymage mowe be named to do miracles. Þanne I go speke with þe trewaundes and make hem to seeme embosed or contract or deff or dowm, and in swich wise I make hem come bifore þe ymage, and crye '[Las], holi ymage, hele me! After God in yow I haue grettest feith!' And þanne al hool I reise hem and in short time with myn hand I shewe hem hol. But wunder is it nouht, for harm hadden þei noon ne sykenesse: al oonliche myn euel þei hadden. But þe folk weenen it nouht: þei arretten it to þe ymage, and þus þe preest winneth and þe folk maken a fals feste. Many anooþer harm hath þe hand doon, and alle [þe] dayes yit dooth, but I wole sey þee no more now, for I haue ynowh to sey þee yit."

"At þe leste", quod I, "þou shalt sey me, if þou wolt, for what cause þou hast þe hand upon þe haunche þat halteth, and whi it approcheth so ofte and toucheth to þe me[f.103r]sel tunge." And þanne she answerde me: "Serteyn, my tunge whiche is mesel is cleped Periurement, and my mouht I clepe [Mensonge] for it draweth of þe spaueyne. To þese tweyne thinges Treccherie is familier and freend: to hem she draweth gladlich for it cometh hire of kynde. Bi hire was maad Menterye, and bi hire I am spaveyned. Bi Menterye is also Periurement born and engendred, for Periurement may not be but if [Mensonge] make him come foorth, and in [Mensonge] and in Periurement may not be þat þer ne is sum Baret. þese ben thre thinges of acord, albeit þei haue gret wrong. þis is þe cause for whiche þe hand is lened on þe haunche, and for which she entermeteth hire to taste and to visite so ofte þe tunge."

"Now sey me", quod I, "how þou seist þi tunge Periurement, and whi þou clepest þi spaueyned haunche Menterye." "I mette sumtime", quod she, "with Verite and Equite, þat souhten here bred and weren riht poore. þei hadden none freendes, ne yit ne hauen, as me thinketh. Whan I sih hem, I wolde haue turned aweyward, for wel I wiste winne of hem mihte I nothing. At þe laste I lefte here wey and bigan to fle bi þe feeldes withoute holdinge wey. At a molle

hill I stumblede and fil doun and spaveyned me: yit I am not
hool ne [ne] shal be day of my lyfe. Boistows I am and [wronge]   5370
and haltinge. To þe virly I go hippinge. My mayme and my
spaveyne I clepe Mentirye, for þer is noon haltinge so foul as
lyinge, but algates to me it is necessarie to þat þat I haue
to doone. Soneste my sak is filled [f.103v] þerwith, and
soonest I fynde cheuesaunce þerwith. If riht I were and riht   5375
wente, I shulde not fynde so mychel, ne ynowh, for swiche
comen bi me þat wolden gon here wey and keepe hem fro my wey.

Now I telle þee þat whan I go þus haltinge, þus lyinge and
hippinge, þer goth out of me so gret hete, so stinkinge and so
gret brennynge and so gret desire of wilnynge to haue yit more   5380
þan I haue of auoyr, þat out I moste drawe my tunge, as an
hound þat is to hoot. To þe kinges court I go me after þat I
haue herd of þe lawes, and sey þat an aduocat I wole be, and
þat of ples I wole medle me. þere I make þe ooth þat my tunge
I ne wole drawe for no folk but if þei haue good riht, but   5385
whan I wole, þe style I haue and hippe a while bi lesinges and
lyinge, but wheþer euere it be riht or wrong, my tunge I may
not forbere þat I ne drawe it out whan I see I shal haue
moneye. And I telle þee þat riht so I doo as þe balaunce
which enclineth his tunge to þilke part þat of þe peys hath þe   5390
grettere part, for þere I see greteste winnynge, þider I
conuoye my tunge, þiderward I drawe it most gladliche as I
see þer ben most pens. Ofte-times it hath befalle þat summe
hauen come to me preyinge me þat I [helpe] hem of here cause,
and þat I [witnesse] hem a trewe riht, and þat I [swere]   5395
þerfore. And wost þou what I dide þanne? Be riht siker þat
whan moneye þei tooken me for to caste in my sak, anoon I
swoor lightliche þat in [f.104r] þe cause þei hadden riht, and
þat with good riht þei pleydeden (and wel I wiste veriliche
þat it was al ooþerweys).   5400

Swich manere of langwetynge and of [stiringe] and turnynge
upsodoun þe wrong into þe riht for to drawe with and for to
bringe with to my sak sum siluer, sheweth whi þe tunge is seid
and cleped Periurement, and also I telle þee þat mesel she is
bi sweringe and bi lyinge, and for þe brennynge þat she hath   5405
to assemble ooþeres goodes bi false languetinges and vntrewe
sweringes. So michel I haue gabbed and forsworn and so
falsliche languetted, þat I shal neuere be bileeued if canoun
or lawe ne chaunge. Bi it men mowe knowe me, for swich tunge
is not yifte of Nature. Nature wolde wretthe hire if man or   5410

womman drowe to hem with þe tunge yren or bras, and do þerwith
as with an hand, and þerbi þou miht wel see þat I longe
nothing to Nature, ne þat I am not of hire linage, ne neuere
was of hire werchinge, and bettere þou shalt wite it whan þou
hast herd of my bowche."

"It is wel", quod I, "myn entencioun þat þou make me
þerof collacioun, and after þat foryete nouht þe mawmete of
which þou hast spoken me." "My bowche", quod she, "is þilke
bi which ben bowched þilke þat shulden ordeyne hemself after
riht rule, and also rulen oopere. It is a thing superflue
whiche maketh alle rules bowchede and enpecheth al þat riht
is. þou shuldest wite þat þilke it is þat maketh þe riche be
[f.104v] likned to a camaile þat may not passe at þe yate of
heuene for his bouche. Whan man entreth naked into þe world
bi þe posterne which is streyt, if he shulde bi þe same wey
recouere ayen, and bitwixe þe tweyne he maketh him bouche, he
ouhte wel to wite þat if þe hole ne be woxe, he may not passe,
oþer he muste do awey his bouche. Man \þat/ entreth into
religioun bi a vow or bi professioun and gadereth þat þat he
hath left and þat whiche he hath renounced, bi þe posterne of
Paradys (which is streyt, as þou seye) passe may he nouht at
þe deth as longe as he bereth with him swich a bouche. This
bouche is Propertee, which dredeth Pouerte hire phisician so
michel þat she dar nouht abide hire, for she wolde tobreste
hire and cleue hire and shende hire. þis is nouht thing to
hele, for riht as a soor hed maketh no ioye of a good comb, no
more keepeth Propertee þat Pouerte take him in cure. She
hateth it—and I also, for in as michel as I am bowched, þe
bouchede and þe enbosede þat ben comen into þese cloistres
ben my kyn and cosyns, and manye oopere of myn affinitee ben
bouched biside here rule, and gon biside þe rihte wey
wrongfulliche: and of redressere ne of vndertakere þei taken
no keep. Whan þou art heerafter of [my bouchede], þou shalt wel
see hem, and þat shal be riht soone if I may.

But first I wole telle þee a woord of myn ydole mawmet
which is my lord and my god, and þyn shal be also as I trowe.
Now keepe þee wel, for al haue þou refused him, þi god he shal
be boongree mawgree. [f.105r] Myn ydole and my mawmet is þe
peny of gold and of siluer wherinne is enpreented þe figure of
þe hye lord of þe cuntree. It is a god þat wole ofte be
swaþed and bounden: þat wole þat men cowchen him ofte and
vncowche him, þat wole ligge in cofres, in hideles and in

corneres, and be hid in eerþe wel ofte with wormes. þat is þe
god þat bleendeth hem þat turnen here eyen toward him; þat
maketh fooles stowpe here eyen into þe eerþe and waite þe   5455
moldewerp; þilke þat maketh þe folk bouched as I am, or more;
þilke þat hath difigured me and defamed me as þou seest. He
made me foul and vnthryfti, and algates so michel he haunteth
me and so michel he pleseth me and so hath my loue, þat in
eerþe I wurshipe him as god. þer is nothing þat I mihte do   5460
þat I ne wolde do it for to drawe him to me and to lede him
into myn hous. Sumtime I made roste Laurence upon þe coles
for he hadde binome it me and turned it fro me. I loue him
so michel þat I waxe a fool, and ofte leese my cote. For him
I haue many pleyes as þou seest, boþe at þe merelles and at þe   5465
dees, and go dispoiled and naked as a wafrere doun þe strete:
and for I loue him so michel, I wole þat also þou make him
fair semblaunt, and þat he be serued of þee and bi þi lord.
Now looke what þou wolt doo, for trewes of me þou shalt no
more haue. Wurshipe him anoon, and in alle degrees yilde þee   5470
to him."

As Auarice prechede me and constreyned me to wurshipen
hire false [ydole], lowe I herde crye bihynde me with hye voys
and with hye teene: "Harrow, felawe, is þat [þe] man þat I see
þere, with [f.105v] which Auarice holt ple, and nothing dooth   5475
to him? Go we þider and assaile we him, and do we him shame
ynowh. Auarice hath spared him to miche. She ouhte wel to be
holden nice." "Serteyn," answered hire felawe, "þou seist
sooth. Now do we peyne þat of oure handes he askape [nouht us],
and þat he leue ded in þe place." Whan swich woordes I herde,   5480
more I was abasht þan bifore, and gladliche I wolde haue take
þe flyght if I ne hadde dred þe folwinge. A litel aside I
turnede me, and biheeld and sigh come a gret old oon with a
long nose and grete eyen and euele-shapen, þat a foul sak deep
and perced heeld with hire teeth, and hadde withinne it a   5485
tonell. To strangle me she shoop hire manere, and ayens me
strauhte hire handes and swoor me bi alle halwen and trowthe
she ouhte to Seynt George þat she wolde take me bi þe throte.
Anooþer I sigh come after þat michel more made me [affraye]. A
fauce visage of a ladi wel ifigured in hire left hand she bar,   5490
and as with a targe dide þerwith. She rod on a swyn, and
arayed she was wel faire: but hire array was michel blakked
and defouled of dunge, wherfore she shadwede hire visage and
hire facioun vnder hire hood. A darte she hadde þat smot me

al bifore þat I spak to hire. Bi þe eye it entrede. To þe
herte it com me, wherfore michel misbifel me þat I hadde nouht
on myn helm and þat I was not armed upon myne eyen. Afterward
she smot me [on] þe handes, wherfore me hadde [f.106r] needed
my gaynpaynes to haue glooued me with and þat I hadde hem on.
But sooth it is þat þe folk seyn: "þe fool abideth nouht til
he honge".* Whan I sygh me þus yhurt and þat I was not yit
assured of þe firste, for wel she made me cheere þat (for I
hadde no gorgere on) bi þe throte I shulde be holde—I ne
wiste what to thinke ne what to doo. So michel I see wel, þat
to crye and braye shulde nouht be woorth to me a def note.
"Wrecche," quod I, "what shalt þou do? Michel euel it is
bifalle þe certeyn, þat euere þou come heere alowh. It hadde
michel bettere bifalle þee if at þe firste þou haddest leeued
þe mattere. Now þow hast wratthed Resoun, and Grace Dieu is
goon, and þou art so hurt in þine handes for defaute of
gaynpaynes þat þou miht not bere þi burdoun. At þe leste þou
shuldest aske who þei ben þat hauen doon þee þat."

    "þou olde", quod I þanne, "þat berest with þi teeth þe
[foule] sak perced, sey me þi name, and gabbe me nouht, if in
ernest withoute smytinge strook þou wolt þus make me dye."
And þanne þe olde answerde: "If þou wost who ben Epicurie,
þou shuldest wite þat I am here mooder, whosoeuere haue be
here fader." "Who ben", quod I, "Epicurie?" "It ben", quod she,
"a folk þat of here persede sak maken here god: þat in alle times
hauen here thouht to fille it for to uoyde it. In þe kichene
þei wolden rouken an hol day [and more] gladliche for to roste
a smal hastelet or to make a steike or sum ooþer disgisee
thing. þei hauen no delite but if in mete and drink þei hauen
it: þat [f.106v] þei holden a delite oonliche and a mirthe."
"How hattest þow?" quod I to hire. "Glotonye," quod she,
"þat in my percede sak putte so michel þat it bicometh foul
and stinkinge. I sakke as michel sumtime as tweyne or thre
poore men mihten wel fille here sakkes with. If þou wistest
wel þe wast, þe outrages and þe los þat I do of metes in þe
yeer, Castrimargye þou woldest properliche sey I were, and
clepe me." "And what is", quod I, "Castrimargye?" "It is",
quod she, "plounginge and drenchinge of morcelles þat men mown
fynde in goode housholdes. Alle goode lopyns I plounge and
drenche: þer is neuere noon þat I sende anything too, and yit
I telle þee þat I haue sakked many oon þat I haue needes cast
out ayen and put out and left trases of dunge after me as a

snayle." "Fy!" quod I: "þou olde stinkinge! Go no more
spekinge to me þerof: it is thing abhominable and foul and
reprouable." "Serteyn," quod she, "þou seist sooth: but
whan þou wolt wite þe soothe, it is resoun þat I sey it þee.   5540
If men clepen me Glotonye and þat I ete to michel and drinke and
[swelwe] michel, it is not thing þat I shulde hele. I am þe
wolf of þe wode þat alwey haue raage in my teeth: for alwey I
muste make þe chyn trotte and þe throte gaape. I am Beel þat
al deuowreth, and þat putte my nose into kichenes bi þe   5545
wyndowes for to smelle and seeche and trace as dooth an huntes
hound, to wite which mete is þe beste. My nose is long:
oueral I putte it in smellinge, but myn entente is al to wite
if I myhte fynde thing þat I mihte showve in my sak."
[f.107r] "Sey me", quod I, "if þou fille it ouht with metes   5550
of litel prys, if with benes or with gret bred þou madest
euere þi wombe gret?" "Wite wel", quod she, "þe trouthe:
þat as wel I haue customed to sakke gret brown bred as to ete
grete metes. As wel þe [rudesse] as þe curiowstee maketh me
glotoun, but þe longe nose was yiven me of my fader, to þat   5555
ende þat I made me fisshinge to þe guste of my grete
leccherye."

"And what thing", quod I, "is guste?" "It is þat", quod
she, "bi which passeth al þat I swelwe and þat wherinne is
myn delite withoute more. It is þe bouchinge of my sak which   5560
it maketh bi towchinges, and yit it hath not twey fyngres of
lengthe if it were mesured. Fayn I wolde it were lengere and
þat it were as þe nekke of an heroun, and I wolde wel þer
were eueremore þere passage of sweete morselles—þat with
lopyns it were wel froted. Were I on horse or on foote* I   5565
rouhte neuere what peyne þe persede sak hadde, but þat it were
ful. þe eyen ben grete, [brennynge my guste]: þat oon and þat
ooþer wolen al; as michel or more as þe guste may gusten, þe
eye wole deliuere him. þe eyen ben more vnmesurable þan þe
sak is eiþer long or brod. As longe as anything may into þe   5570
paunche, þei haue of nothing sufficience. It is a thing þat
michel hath shorted my lyfe bi my folye: þer is noon more
perilowse knyf þan is a superflue morselle." "And whi", quod I,
"puttest þou in [morselle þat is] soo pestilencial?" "I bere",
quod she, "so pestilencial a touche in my mouth þat whan it   5575
hath touched to þe morsell, it taketh swich reuelle in it þat
if [f.107v] to þat ooþer it ne touchede, as out of witte it
shulde be. þat oon after þat ooþer I wole touche withoute

stintinge. It reccheth him neu*ere* of my p*ro*fite, but þat withoute more he haue his delite." "Sey me", q*uo*d I, "how it is nempned and cleped, þilke touche." "It is", q*uo*d she: "a wichche,* a fleinge messanger þat seith and telleth to alle þat þat þe herte hath comaunded. Maleschique and Malevoysigne þe folk clepen hire þat ben hire neighebowres, for gladliche she misseith, and soone seith vileynye whan she hath towched goode morselles and filled hire with goode wynes." "Is she þanne", q*uo*d I, "a vintere, þat to assaye wynes entermeteth hire? What is she?" þanne she seide: "þere she taketh hire grete disport. Bi hire I am vnmesurable, and bi hire I am cleped Glotoun. She putteth me to [vnwurshipe], and binemeth me boþe prys and wurshipe. She hath left me þe [tonell] þat in my sak þou seest bouched. It aualeth and tunneth þe wyne, and thoruh outrage so michel it yeueth me þat I haue neiþer wit ne resoun, ne can fynde my hous, ne leyn me in my bed."

"þou art þanne," q*uo*d I to hire, "thing þat hast no techinge ne gou*er*nement in þee." "þat is sooth", q*uo*d she: "if þou wistest riht wel al myn gou*er*naunce, for whan I haue tunned my wynes and chewed my metes, I wolde þanne sey veleynye to God and to Oure Lady, Seinte Marye. If Resoun come to me I wolde anoon sey 'Fle fro me!'; þouh Justice, þouh Equite, þouh Pr*u*dence, þouh Soothnesse comen alle to me þei shulden be shouen out and putte ayen. Sobernesse and Attemp*er*aunce shulden haue of me [f.108r] but mischaunce. I haue skorn of hem and make drive hem out. Whan þe wyne is entred into myn horn þanne I am as fers as vnicorn; þanne I wole hurtle eche wight, chide oon, blame anooþer, and roile myne eyen as a bole. It is not for nouht þat I haue twey wombes as a butour, [for butour] I bicome, and þis bifalleth ofte."* "How?" q*uo*d I: "Hast þou twey wombes?" "Ye," q*uo*d she, "þat ben genderes of Dame Venus þat folweth me heere, of which Yueresce is þat oon seid, and þat ooþer þe Gulf, þat to ete is euere redy. Whan þe firste hath stinte etinge,* and þat ooþer hath apperseiued it, he seith he wole ete also; and if it bifalle þat he drinke first, þat ooþer wole drinke also, and seyth anoon 'I reuye it': and oones sufficeth hem nouht, no certeyn, ne twyes ne thryes, but wolen alwey withoute ende pursue þat þat þei haue bigunne. Eche wole take last, and eu*ere* it is to biginne as longe as þer is wyne in þe pot and til þe mete be put to þe ende. þese twey wombes maken Dame Venus reuelle: bi hem she is most ryottous and to doon euele

lest shameful. Bi hem most gladliche she holt hire nygh me,
and cometh after me. Bi whereeuere I go, she goth gladliche,
for she thinketh wel þat she shal haue in subieccioun þilke
whiche I haue seised bi þe throte. I thinke it shal be þou,
sithe þou art come hider."   5625
    And \þanne/ she took me bi þe throte with boþe handes,
and seide me þus: "Sithe þou hast no gorgeere, wite wel in
certeyn þat michel þe more feers and more cruelle þou shalt
fynde me." "Har[f.108v]row!" quod I: "Allas, allas!
Let me speke to þilke þat I see go bihynde þee. She hath   5630
smiten me with hire darte. Euele I shal be bitake and lost if
of sooth I ne wite who she is." And she seide me: "In þee it
is. I wole wel þat she sei it þee; but þow shalt not askape
me—I wole holde me seised of þee sithe I haue þee so nigh
me." And þanne I askede to hire þat hadde smiten me: "Who   5635
art þou? Niceliche þou gost bi þe cuntre upon þilke swyn, as
me thinketh: and niceliche bronnched and hid vnder þyn hood."
"Serteyn," quod she: "I am þilke þat make my subgis dwelle
and enhabite in fennes as frosshes, þere I amase manye boþe of
sighte and of speche and of here countenaunce also. I am   5640
Venus, of which þou hast herd Dame Glotonye speke (þat
maistryeth þee bi þe throte). Longe agon I putte and drof
Virginitee \out/ of þe world. þe aungeles which she was
sister too hadden me neuere sithe wel in herte. þei stoppen
here noses whan þei seen me, which thing þei wolden nouht doon 5645
for a stinkinge karayne but if grettere vice were þerinne. I
pursue Chastitee oueral withoute stintinge eiþer winter or somer.
Ne hadde she withdrawe hire [and hid hire in] religioun I hadde
er [now] put hire to deth; but I fynde þe castel soo strong þat
harm may I noon doon, but if any come muse at þe dore as was   5650
of oon* þat corrupt hadde he not be if out he hadde not goon.
Also I may not anoye Chastitee but if he go out at þe dore."
    "What haue þei tweyne misdoon þee," quod I, "þat
[f.109r] þou wolt hem so litel good?" "Virginitee", quod she,
"wolde neuere lye in bed ne in chaumbre þat I lay inne. It   5655
was neuere þat I ne was hateful to hire and abhominable for my
stinkinge, which may not be binome me: Chastitee hateth me
also, and whan she seeth me, seith 'Fy! I haue leeuere lace*
my mantelle þan ly any time bi þee; I haue leeuere yilde me
into an abbeye þan anything be in þi cumpanye'." "How?" quod   5660
I, "May þis be sooth, þat þese monkes (white, greye or blake)
hauen resceyued Chastitee, and þat she is yolden to hem?"

"Yis", quod she, "sikerliche, but it displeseth me gretliche. She is dortowrere þere and maketh here beddes as chamberere." "She hath office þanne?" quod I. "Sooth," quod she, "and for þat I haate hire þe more and pursue hire—I am þe more sharp ayens hire." "Whi", quod I, "hast þou smiten me?" "Whi," quod she, "weenest þou sithe I am so nyh þee þat þou shalt nouht feele of me? Bi myne hed þat is wel kembt, þou hast not yit al assayed. Whan I assaile any—whoeuere it be—I parte nouht so soone from him."

"Art þou", quod I, "so wel kembt and arayed as þou seist? If þou were it, þou woldest not, as I trowe, hide þee from me." "Now vnderstonde", quod she, "a litel. It is wel sooth þat if I were fair, I wolde not þus shadewe me vnder myn hood. It folweth nouht þat þouh I be þus kembt and a litel make þe queyntrelle, þat for swich cause I am fair. I am foul, old and slauery, foule stinkinge and dungy: more vile bi ynowh þan I dar seye, for it is nouht for to speke. I shadewe me þat men [f.109v] seen me nouht, albeit I am riht queynte, and recche neuere of [ooþer] sihte. In place þer no sighte is I go bi turnynges and bi corneres, and seche hydinges and corneres, and se no sighte at ful midday, and haue peyne and thouht ynowh, and ofte putte me in perile to doo a litel of my lust. If þou wistest how ofte, and bi which place I go ofte, I trowe þou woldest michel abashe þee, and þat riht litel þou woldest preyse me.

I ride a wunderful hors,* for þereas þe pas is wurst and is as most filthe, þere, of his kynde, he leith him. þe hors is Euele Wil þat bereth me, and is redy as a sowe to ley hire þere þe dunge is and bidunge hire. It is figured as a swyn þat in þe eerþe hath his [musell]. þereas he leith himself he leith me, but it is more in foul place þan in clene. Bi him I am þus soiled and bidunged and defouled, and he also; þus *in* [*abstracto*] foul I am but *in* [*concreto*] I am michel foulere and þerfore I bere a peynted fauce visage, for to make þerof [a] couertour to my visage ful of filthe. þis fauce visage is cleped Fardrye, with which whan I am eelded and bicome riueled and frounced and discolowred I make me shynynge in despite of nature, in chaunginge of my feture; þanne I make me a pryue chaumbre for alle þilke þat passen þe wey: a verrey dung-hep in a weylate, þer eche at his time may come to make filthe." "Fy!" quod I. "I recche neuere now of þi knoweleche ne of þee. I see wel now and knowe þat to haue parlement with þee is nouht but gret diffamacio*u*n."

"Serteyn," q*u*od she, "if þou haddest seyn þe   5705
instru[f.11or]mentes þat I haue hid vnder my cote, if þow ne
were michel out of [þe] wey þou sholdest preise me michel
lasse, and lasse speche holden with me." "Shewe me hem,"
q*u*od I to hire, "and telle me how þei ben nempned." ["þat
oon", quod she, "hatte *raptus*, þat oo*þer* *stuprum*, þat   5710
oo*þer* *incestus*, þat oo*þer* *adulterium*, and þat oo*þer*
fornicacioun—of þat oo*þer* is nouht] for to speke of.
þis may wel suffice þee: vnderstonde hem now as þow wolt,
and wite wel þei ben *p*erilouse. þou shalt not see hem at
þis time, for I shewe hem neu*ere* more ap*er*tliche for here   5715
vnthrifty feture and here foulnesse; and yit algates wel
I kan smite su*m*me with hem whan I haue leiser. I wole smite
þee but þou flee fastere or go þan tigre: but sithe Glotonye
holt þee, of þi flight I drede me nouht. Of me þou shalt   5720
haue it. Heere *þou* shalt dye, and neu*ere* go fer*þer*e."
And þa*n*ne þe olde smot me with a darte to þe herte and
fellde me. Glotonye halp hire michel. Bi þe throte do*u*n she
shook me. Auarice and alle þe oo*þer*e, [þei] sheweden nouht þat
þei hadden [gowtes]: eche of hem smot me at here cours with   5725
swich armure as she hadde. Binome me þa*n*ne was my bordo*u*n
but my scrippe þei leften me. þei thouhten wel recou*ere* it whan
at alle poyntes þei hadden slayn me. Whan I sigh me þus
bitrapped, beten do*u*n, smyten, hurt, whan I hadde my burdo*u*n
lost bi which I was wont to reise me ayen, neu*ere* man as I   5730
trowe was more desolat þan I. "Allas!" q*u*od I, "What shalt
þou do, sorweful wrecche? What shalt þou sey? Now art þou
comen til þin ende. Why were þou eu*ere* pilgrime? Whi tooke
þou eu*ere* burdo*u*n for to leese it in þis cuntre? It hadde ben
bett*ere* for me [f.110v] þou haddest be ded born. Who may   5735
eu*ere* helpe þee? Who may visite þee? Who may counseile þee?
þow hast lost Grace Dieu þi goode freend. Aa! Penitence,
Penitence, whi made I eu*ere* drede to passe þe thorny hegge?
Ye shulden now be me ful sweete and deere, ne were I so
aloyned and strau*n*ged from yow. Youre yerdes and youre   5740
disciplines, youre pr*i*kkinges and youre thornes weren to me
oynement now, to my riht grete misaduentures. [He], armes of
chiualrye, I ouhte biweyle you al my lyfe þouh I livede
lengere. I was oones arayed and enoorned with yow riht
queynteliche, but allas, wrecche, for longe was it nouht but   5745
anoon I leyde you do*u*n. Many harmes haue bifalle me sithe

þerbi, and now riht withoute any forberinge I am deliuered and put to þe deth. [He], sacrament of holi cherche, I drede me I preyse þee litel. I drede me I haue resceyued þee in veyn, sithe I haue lost my burdoun bi whiche I was wont to reise me when I was falle. [He], citee of Jerusalem to which I was excited to goo, how shal I excuse me to þee, and what answere shal I make þee? I hadde bihight þee in my corage þat I wolde do þe viage to þee, for þat I sigh þee in \þe/ faire mirrowr cleer and polisshed. Now I am beten, now I am hurt soo þat on my sides it is seene. In euele time forueyed I: I trowe I shal neuere seen þee."

As I compleyned me and biweyled my losses, I sigh a cloude passe whiche was nouht michel reysed, of whiche þe wynd com also. She com from þe midday. Ouer me she tariede and þere abood a while, but gret fors made I nouht þerof [f.111r] for þe sorwes þat I felte: I was as half ded, and litel lyfe hadde in þe bodi. Now vnderstondeth (so God keepe yow) how loth Grace Dieu departeth hire from hem þat she hath socoured bifore, whan misaduenture hath bifalle hem, and how gladliche she socowreth hem whan neede is. Of þilke cloude descendede a vois þat seide me þus: "Now up, wrechche coward, now up! To michel þou hast crept up and doun. þou hast euele proued þi craft,* for þou art a shrewede knyght. I haue brouht þee þi burdoun ayen, to [releeue] þee from orphanitee. Entende to me. I reeche it þee and yilde it þee and stablisshe it þee: I wole nouht yit þi deth, albeit þou hast don wrong ayens me, but I wole þou conuerte þee and þat þou amende þee and þat þou lyue." Whan swiche woordes I vnderstood, a litel I opened myn eyen, and sigh an hand on hy þat heeld my burdoun, and arauhte it me. I thouhte it was þe hand of hire þat at þe firste time hadde taken it me—and she it was. "[Haa], God," quod I, "goode tidinges! Neuere deseruede I to yow þat ye shulde þus thinke on me. Now riht I hadde be lost if ye ne hadden socoured me. Sithe my burdoun ye yilden me and of youre pitee ye areechin it me, ye don me counfort of my sorwes, and respiten me of þe deth. Graces and thankinges I yelde yow, sweete Ihesu Crist. [He], Grace Dieu my sweete lady, now I see wel þat [yit] ye louen me, ye hauen not at alle poyntes forsaken [me]: ye hauen at þe neede shewed yow redy to helpe me, if it ne be [long] on myself. I wot neuere whens þis cometh yow but of youre debo[f.111v]nayrtee, for in me haue ye not founden it. Youre counseil I leeuede neuere: with good riht

it is euele bifalle me. With boþe myne handes I crye yow
mercy, and weepinge sey my gilt. I shal amende it I bihote   5790
yow, my ladi, bi my soule. Withoute more foryiueth me þis
time: I wole anooþer time leeue yow. Redresseth me and
releeueth me, for þe abidinge greeueth me riht michel. To þe
hegge euene I wole go if bi yow I haue deliueraunce. And if
ye wole ye shule lede me þider, whan ye haue reised me hens."   5795
    And þanne Grace Dieu answerde: "I wole sey þee riht a
fair game. If þilke þat is awmeneer wolde do so michel toward
my fader (which is hire sone—she is his mooder) þat he wolde
yive me ayen to þee, yit þou shuldest not go to wast, yit þou
shuldest wel turne ayen to Penitence. I wolde gladliche lede   5800
þee þider if þou woldest, and doo from þee [þe] torment." "And
who", quod I, "is þilke ladi þat [to ordeyne] of yow is lady?
A gret lady she is whan she is ordeynowr and awmeneer of yow!"
"Serteyn," quod she, "þou seist sooth, and þerfore þou
mostest first haue þin herte to hire, and crye hire mercy. If   5805
she wole, I wole helpe þee, and socowre þee at þis neede: and
also I haue wil þerto, as I haue er now shewed þee. If þou
wite nouht who þe lady is, gret defawte and gret shame it is
to þee. She hath ooþer times kast þee and releeued þee out of
many an yuel paas. It is þe charbuncle and þe pomelle of þin   5810
burdoun þat is so fair. I haue spoken þee [f.112r] þerof er
now: þou art a fool whan þou hast foryete it." "Lady," quod
I, "I wiste nouht ne [ne] took no keep þat of hire ye speken,
but I wende of sum ooþer ye hadden spoken, unknowen to me, þat I
hadde neuere seyn bifore: but sithe it is to my charbuncle, I   5815
wole gladliche opene myn mowth and with good herte preye as I
can to hire. But if ye wolden yive me þe foorme and shewe me
þe manere how I shulde biseeche hire, right gladliche I wolde
doon it."
    And þanne of þe clowde a scripture she caste me, and   5820
seide me þus: "Loo heere how þow shuldest preye hire, boþe at
þis neede and alwey whan þou shalt haue semblable neede, and
whan in swiche olde hondes þou shalt bee. Now rede it anoon
apertliche, and biseeche hire deuowtliche, and with verrey
herte bihoote hire þat þou wolt be good pilgrime, and þat þou   5825
wolt neuere go bi wey þere þou weenest to fynde shrewede
paas." Now I telle yow þe scripture I vndide, and vnplytede
it, and redde it, and maade at alle poyntes my preyeere in þe
foorme and in þe maneere þat þe same scripture conteenede, and
as Grace hadde seyd it. þe foorme of þe scripture ye shule   5830

heere. If 'A.B.C.' wel ye kunne, wite it ye mown lightliche, for to sey it if it be neede.

Incipit carmen secundum ordinem litterarum alphabeti. [f.112v]

Almihty and al merciable queene
To whom þat al þis world fleeth for socour
To haue relees of sinne of sorwe and teene:
Gloriowse Virgine, of alle floures flour,
5 To þee I flee, confounded in errour.
Help and releeue þou mihti debonayre.
Haue mercy [of] my perilous langour:
Venquissed me hath my cruelle aduersaire.

Bountee so fix hath in þin herte his tente
10 þat wel I wot þou wolt my socour bee:
þou canst not warne him þat with good entente
Axeth þin helpe, þin herte is ay so free.
þou art largesse of pleyn felicitee,
Hauene of refute, of quiete and of reste.
15 Loo how þat theeves sevene chasen mee—
Help, lady briht, er þat my ship tobreste.

Comfort is noon but in yow, ladi deere,
For loo, my sinne and my confusioun
Which ouhten not in þi presence appeere,
20 Han take on me a greevous accioun
Of verrey riht and desperacioun,
And as bi riht þei mihten wel susteene
þat I were wurþi my dampnacioun,
Nere merci of you, blisful queene.

25 Dowte is þer noon þou queen of misericorde
þat þou nart cause of grace and merci heere:
God vouched saf thoruh þee with us to accorde,
For certes, Crystes blisful mooder deere, [f.113r]
Were nowe þe bowe bent in swich maneere
30 As it was first of Justice and of Ire,
þe rihtful God nolde of no mercy heere:
But thoruh þee han we grace as we desire.

Euere hath myn hope of refuit been in þee,
For heer biforn ful ofte in many a wyse

35 Hast þou to misericorde resceyued me;
    But merci, ladi: at þe grete assyse
    Whan we shule come bifore þe Hye Iustyse   5870
    So litel shal þanne in me be founde
    þat but þou er þat day [correcte vice],
40 Of verrey riht my werk me wole confounde.

    Fleeinge I flee for socour to þi tente,
    Me for to hide from tempteste ful of dreede,   5875
    Biseeching yow þat ye you not absente
    þouh I be wikke. O help yit at þis neede:
45 Al haue I ben a beste in wil and deede
    Yit ladi, þou me cloþe with þi grace.
    þin enemy and myn—ladi, tak heede—   5880
    Vnto my deth in poynt is me to chace.

    Gloriows mayde and mooder which þat neuere
50 Were bitter, neiþer in eerþe nor in see,
    But ful of swetnesse and of merci euere,
    Help þat my fader be not wroth with me.   5885
    Spek þou, for I ne dar not him ysee
    So haue I doon in eerþe (allas þer while)
55 þat certes, but þou my socour bee,
    To stink eterne he wole my gost exile. [f.113v]

    He vouched saaf, tel him, as was his wille,   5890
    Bicomen a man to haue oure alliaunce,
    And with his precious blood he wrot þe bille
60 Upon þe crois, as general acquitaunce
    To euery penitent in ful criaunce;
    And þerfore, ladi briht, þou for us praye: 5895
    þanne shalt þou boþe stinte al his greuaunce
    And make oure foo to failen of his praye.

65 I wot it wel þou wolt ben oure socour
    þou art so ful of bownteé in certeyn:
    For whan a soule falleth in errour   5900
    þi pitee goth and haleth him ayein.
    þanne makest þou his pees with his souereyn,
70 And bringest him out of þe crooked strete.
    Whoso þee loueth, he shal not loue in veyne:
    þat shal he fynde as he þe lyf shal lete.   5905

Kalendeeres enlumyned ben þei
þat in þis world ben lighted with þi name;
75 And whoso goth to yow þe rihte wey
Him thar not drede in soule to be lame.
Now queen of comfort, sithe þou art þat same   5
To whom I seeche for my medicyne,
Lat not my foo no more my wounde [entame]:
80 Myn hele into þin hand al I resyne.

Ladi, þi sorwe kan I not portreye
Under þe cros, ne his greevous penaunce   5
But for youre boþes peynes I yow preye
Lat not oure alder foo make his bobaunce [f.114r]
85 þat he hath in hise lystes of mischaunce
Conuict þat ye boþe haue bouht so deere.
As I seide erst, þou ground of oure substaunce,   5
Continue on us þi pitous eyen cleere.

Moises þat sauh þe bush with flawmes rede
90 Brenninge, of which þer neuer a stikke brende,
Was signe of þin vnwemmed maidenhede:
þou art þe bush on which þer gan descende   5
þe Holi Gost, þe which þat Moyses wende
Had ben afyir, and þis was in figure.
95 Now ladi, from þe fyir þou us [defende]
Which þat in helle eternalli shal dure.

Noble princesse, þat neuere haddest peere,   5
Certes if any comfort in us bee
þat cometh of þee, Cristes mooder deere:
100 We han noon ooþer melodye or glee
Us to reioyse in oure aduersitee,
Ne aduocat noon þat wole and dar so preye   5
For us, and þat for litel hire as yee
þat helpen for an Aue Marie or tweye.

105 O verrey light of eyen þat ben blynde,
O verrey [rest] of labour and distresse,
O tresoreere of bountee to mankynde,   5
þee whom God ches to mooder for humblesse:
From his ancille he made þe maistresse
110 Of heuene and eerþe, oure bille up for to beede.
þis world awaiteth euere on þi goodnesse,

For þou ne failest neuere wight at neede. [f.114v]   5945

Purpos I haue sumtime for to enquere
Wherfore and whi þe Holi Gost þee souhte
115   Whan Gabrielles vois cam [to] þin ere:
He not to werre us swich a wunder wrouhte,
But for to saue us þat he sithen bouhte;   5950
þanne needeth us no wepene us for to saue,
But oonly þer we diden not as us ouhte
120   Doo penitence, and merci axe and haue.

Queen of comfort, yit whan I me bithinke
þat I agilt haue boþe him and þee,   5955
And þat my soule is wurthi for to sinke,
Allas, I caityf, whider may I flee?
125   Who shal vnto þi sone my mene bee?
Who but þiself þat art of pitee welle?
þou hast more reuthe on oure aduersitee   5960
þan in þis world miht any tunge telle.

Redresse me, mooder, and me chastise,
130   For certeynly my faderes chastisinge
þat dar I nouht abiden in no wise
So hidous it is [rihtful] rekenynge.   5965
Mooder of whom oure merci gan to springe,
Beth ye my juge and eek my soules leche,
135   For euere in you is pitee haboundinge
To eche þat wole of pitee you biseeche.

Soth is þat God ne granteth no pitee   5970
Withoute þee, for God of his goodnesse
Foryiveth noon but it like vnto þee:
140   He hath þee maked vicair and maistresse [f.115r]
Of al [þis] world, and eek gouernowresse
Of heuene, and he represseth his iustise   5975
After þi wil, and þerfore in witnesse
He hath þee corowned in so rial wise.

145   Temple deuout þer God hath his woninge
Fro which þese misbileeued depriued been:
To you my soule penitent I bringe;   5980
Resceyue me—I can no ferþere fleen.
With thornes venymous, O heuene queen,

150   For which þe eerþe acursed was ful yore,
       I am [so] wounded as ye may wel seen,
       þat I am lost almost, it smert so sore.

       Virgine þat art so noble of apparaile,
       Ledest us into þe hye tour
155   Of Paradys; þou me wisse and coun{sei}le
       How I may haue þi grace and þi so{co}ur
       Al haue I ben in filthe and in er{ro}ur:
       Ladi, vnto *þat* court þou me aiou{rn}e
       þat cleped is þi bench, O fresh flour,
160   þeras þat merci euere shal soiourne.

       Xpc þi sone þat in þis world alighte
       Upon þe cros to suffre his passioun,
       And eek suffred *þat* Longius his herte pighte:
       And made his herte blood to renne adoun,
165   And al was þis for my saluacioun,
       And I to him am fals and eek vnkynde,
       And yit he wole not my dampnacioun:
       þis thanke I yow, socour of al mankynde. [f. 115v]

       Ysaac was figure of his deth certeyn,
170   þat so ferforth his fader wolde obeye
       þat him ne rouhte nothing to be slayn:
       Riht soo þi sone lust as a lamb to deye.
       Now ladi ful of merci I yow preye
       Sithe he his merci mesured so large,
175   Be ye not skant, for alle we singe and seye
       þat ye ben from vengeaunce ay oure targe.

       Zacharie yow clepeth þe opene welle
       To wasshe sinful soule out of his gilt,
       þerfore þis lessoun ouht I wel to telle:
180   þat nere þi tender herte, we weren spilt.
       Now ladi, sithe þou canst and wilt
       Ben to þe seed of Adam merciable,
       Bring us to þat palais þat is bilt
       To penitentes *þat* ben to merci able. Amen.

       Explicit carmen.

Whan   þus   I   hadde   maad   my   preyere   to   hire   *þat*   is

dispensere to Grace, hye I heef myn hand and drowh my bordoun   6020
to me. Grace, as I haue told you, of hire goodshipe raught it
me. Whan I hadde it, to Grace I seide: "As me thinketh riht
now, I fynde þat if ye wolde helpe me I shulde be reised ayen,
and þat anoon I shulde haue hele if with youre oynement ye
enoyntede me. Wel I wot þat my charboncle hath so wel   6025
vnbocled þe bocle vnder which ye weren bocled, þat freedam [he]
yiveth yow to helpe þilke þat ye wolen, þouh þei ben dede or
hurt. Excuse yow of dispenseer ne of awmeneer mown ye not,
she wole ye ben delt aboute, þat no wight haue [f.116r]
defaute of yow but þat it be youre wille, so þat if of you I   6030
haue no socour, it holt not of hire but of yow. Helpeth me.
She wole helpe me: I truste and alwey þertoo I lene me." And
þanne Grace Dieu rauhte oon hand and seyde me þus: "Sithe þou
hast gret triste to me I wole helpe þee. Tak hider þi fynger.
Rys up, and lene þee to þe bordoun, and looke þou feyne þee   6035
nouht. þou shuldest for nouht reche me þi finger but if þou
helpe to reise þiself." And þanne my fynger I took hire, and
to þe burdoun I gripede. So michel I strengthede me and so
michel she halp me þat to þe foule olde it forthouhte. Eche
wente into here regioun, to here confusioun; but neuerþeles   6040
sithe I sigh hem and sithe þei diden me gret annoy (and þouh I
seide allwey, I trowe I shulde not gabbe).

    And þanne Grace Dieu shewede \me/ a gret roche in an hy
place. An eye upon þilke roche þer was, þat droppede dropes
of water—and a kowuele þer was binethe þat resceyuede alle   6045
þe dropes. "Seest þou", quod she, "þe kowuele?" "Ye" quod
I. "þerinne", quod she, "þou mustest baþe þee for to hele þi
woundes and for to wasshe þee." "Seith me now," quod I to
hire, "whens þe water cometh, I preye yow: þilke eye þat I
see abasheth me, and þe water also þat I see come out þerof."   6050
"Now vnderstonde a litel," quod she, "and turne to me þin
ere. þilke roche þat þou seest þeere is þe herte of þilke þat
witingeliche hath left þe wey of saluacioun, as þou hast: þat
is harded in his errour as roche. Now I telle þee þat whan I
haue left [f.116v] [it] þus a gret while in his sinne, I am   6055
sumtime take with pitee of him, and with his eye I make him
conuerte and turne to himself, for he shulde biholde hise
owene dedes; and þanne whan þe eye hath wel seyn þe hardshipe
of þe herte, anoon it is stired harde to weepe and to droppe
teres. A welle gladliche he wolde be for to make it softe if   6060
he mihte: but for he may nouht, to þat ende þat he lese not

his labo*ur*, þis kowuele I haue set vnder for to take þe droppinges. I wole not þat þe teres þat I see so shed ben lost: þei ben goode to make þe bath, to þilke þat hath mayme in þe herte. It is a secund cristeninge, with [which] Penitence can wel make hire lye and hire bowkynge. þerinne was baþed and stiwed þe Magdaleyne su*m*time. Seint Peet*er* also bathed him þerinne—þe Egipcian Marie \also/ and manye ooþere þat I sey nouht. Of Penitence þou herdest it seid if þou woldest, whan þou seye hire: and þerfore if þou wolt be heled, þerinne þou mustest be wasshen. It is a gret purginge." "Ladi," qu*o*d I, "if it were youre wille to lede me to þe place I wolde gladliche go þider: withoute yowe I shulde nothing do þere." And þa*n*ne she seide: "It liketh me wel. Go bifore: þou shalt fynde me þere, go þou neu*ere* so faste."

Now I telle yow þider I wente, pas for pas, and þere I fond hire—but vnder þe clowde she was hid and shadewed as she was bifore. Whan I come þider, þe kowuele I sigh, which was not ful ne half ful. "Ladi," qu*o*d I, "heer is not water ynowh wherinne I may be wasshe: þer is wel litel to make of a bath." And þa*n*ne Grace Dieu lowe abeescede a yerde [f.117r] [þat] she heeld in hire hand. Where she hadde take it I wot neu*ere*: I hadde not seyn it bifore, wherof I abashed me michel. I thouhte þat Moiseses it were, with which he smoot þe roche in deserte. Soone he made water come out þerof for to hele þe thrist of Israel: and it was þat treweliche, as I sigh bi dede euident: with þilke yerde she smot þe roche, and anoon þer cam water out þerof into þe cowuele þat was þervnder it ran, and euene cam, but alwey took his cours thoruh þe eye, as I haue seyd yow. "Now", qu*o*d she, "*þou* hast water ynowh to be wasshe if þow wolt. Entre þerinne and wasshe þee þerinne, for a poynt I haue maad it þee warm. To þe cheekes put þee þerinne, and þe wasshinge shal be good for þee."

And þa*n*ne withoute taryinge I entrede in and bathed me and wesh me. It hadde al heled me, I trowe, if I hadde endured it ynowh; but soone I wente out þerof, for of suich baþinge I hadde not lerned: I was not lych to Dauid, þat seide he made him bath alle þe nihtes of his teres, and shedde hem upon his bed. Whan I was þus comen out of þe bath, Grace Dieu seide me: "Weenest þou þou be so soone hool? If into thornes I hadde put þee and into prikinge netles al naked (as þou haddest wel deserued) how woldest þou haue suffred hem, þat a litel water, of which þou shuldest reioyse þee for þin

hele, þou miht not suffre a litel while? How mihtest þou also
suffre þe hegge þat þou hast desired, whiche þou shalt fynde
more thorny and more sharp and dangerows withoute comparisoun
þan þou didest at þe firste time, þat suffrest not to bathe
þee? Go [f.117v] now, and do as þou wolt. I shal see how
wurþi þou shalt be to þat þat is to come, for bifore þou hast
not ben it. But a good knight, whan he is hurt in þe stour and
[eschawfed], he is michel þe more corageows after, and þe more
knightlich. If þou so doost, I wole be glad þerof, and with
þe bettere wil I wole helpe þee: but algates at þis time þou
shalt no more see me. I go. I wole see what þou wolt do yit
and what wey þou wolt take."

Whan I herde þat þus she seide me and þat in swich wise
she dide, sorweful I bicome and abasht. "Allas!" quod I,
"What shalt þou do? Allas wrecche, allas: which side shal I
go whan I wot not where I shal take my wey? I trowe þat
neuere pilgrime was more abasht þan I. Goode Lord God, help
me: þou art þe hye pomelle of my burdoun. I crye to þee and
biseeche þee þat in þee I mowe see where is my wey, and þat
þou gide me. Holi charbouncle shinynge, of which my burdoun
is maad shinynge, lighte me bi where I shal go. þou art oon
pomel in which I haue gret suretee and trist and haue had al
my chyldhode. To þee I holde me; to þee I lene me. But if
þou helpe me, lost I am." So as I spak þus to my pomelles and
preyede hem, I bithouhte me on which half I hadde left þe
hegge. Bi gesse I thouhte I wolde go, and þat litel or
nothing I shulde faile þerof. To þe wey I sette me soone
ynowh, but I dide not my iorney, for I fond empechement. If
ye wole heere how, cometh ayen anooþer day, for heere I wole
make a restinge.

Heere eendeth þe thridde partye of þis book. [f.118r]
Heere biginneth þe feerþe partye of þis book.

Now I wole telle yow lordinges, how I fond empechement in
my wey, and I wole telle yow withoute more of þat þat is
grettest to me and toucheth me most: for in valeyes and in
hilles I sigh manye disgisy thinges of whiche I shulde neuere
make eende if I wolde telle you al, and also it shulde anoye
to me and to þilke þat shulden heeren it. Now I sey yow, as I
wente bi a wey þat I hadde take, bifore me I fond a see
wherinne was michel to biholde. Tempested it was gretliche
of grete temptestes and of wyind. Men and wommen þer

weren þat al cloþed swommen þerinne. Summe hadden here feet
aboue: I sigh no more of hem. Ooþere stooden upriht, of
whiche summe hadden wynges and seemeden þei wolden haue flowe
ne hadde þe see empeched hem. Summe ooþere I sih arested bi
þe feet and faste bounden with longe erbes þat weren in þe
see, þat michel anoyed hem. Summe ooþere I sigh bended bifore
here eyen, and ooþere ynowe diuerseliche arayed, of which I
holde me stille as at þis time. Whan I sigh swiche thinges,
afrayed I was and gretliche abasht. "Lord God," quod I:
"what thing is þis? Swich a see sigh I neuere: þer is noon
\swich/ see in my cuntree, ne suich fish as me thinketh. I
see wel now go foorth may I nouht. I muste turne ayen or I
muste heere abide in abidinge þi merci. If I putte me þerinne
I am dreynt. If I go bi þe coste [f.118v] I shulde go mis
anoon if I ne founde who þat yeue me sum good avyis. Lord
God, I wot neuere what I shal do if I ne haue avys bi þi
Grace." At þe laste I avised me to myself and bithouhte me þat
if þere I abide, winne mihte I nouht þerbi, and of þe turnyng
ayen I was siker þat yit lasse I shulde winne, and thouhte þat
upon þe stronde I wode go to see if I miht fynde ship or boot
bi which I mihte passe and go ouer withoute perile.

On þe wey I sette me withoute taryinge, and bigan to
coste þe see al after þe stronde, but I made nouht riht gret
viage. O what I sih—sweete folk, blisseth yow—a foule
beste þat alle þilke þat wel hadden biholden it shulden neuere
ben assured. I sey for me my soule dredeth it alle þe times
þat I bithinke me þeron. þilke beste was disgised soo
vileliche, and so foule figured, þat of þe speche I shulde
haue gret affray if I speke yow longe þerof. Ordeyned I haue
þat peynted it be heere and figured, to þat ende þat who þat
wole mowe see it: ooþerweyse chevice me cowde I nouht.
Alweys, so michel I sey you þat in þe see I sigh him fisshe.
þerinne he hadde cast hise angles, and his lyne he heeld with
hise handes. An horn he hadde hanged at his nekke, and he bar
a trusse of cordes, and a nette fleinge he \had/ hanged upon
þe see bineþe þe cloudes. Whan he sigh me come, anoon he
bigan to blowe and to houpe and to strecche his cordes in my
wey so þat I shulde not askape. Whan I sigh suich redyinge,
abasht I was gretliche, for wel I sigh þat if I passede bi
him, anoon taken shulde I be. "Sweete God," quod I, "what
shal I do? Shrewede wey I fynde: [f.119r] whider shal I go?
I shal neuere out of þis place if I ne haue helpe of þi

Grace."

In þis poynt I sigh come an olde oon rennynge. A fagot
of wode she bar, and bakward she ran, and thwartouer and
asqwynt she biheeld me for she was purblynd. Whan she was
nygh, "Now hider," quod she, "yilde þee to me." "And who
art þou", quod I, "to whom I shulde yilde me?" "I am", quod
she, "in fair wey a stumblinge, and a lettinge to folk on
foote and on horse. I hatte Heresye þe purblynde, þat anoon
as my fader bloweth, I come areste pilgrimes for to
vnscrippe hem of here scrippes. I hate scrippe ouer alle
thing. I thinke to shewe it þee wel, for I wole bineme þee
þyn if I may, and tobreke it. I see scripture in þe belles,
þat as to my biholdinge, it is nouht a poynt ne ariht writen."
"Hold þi pes, þou olde cursede!" quod I. "þe scripture is
writen aright, but þou lokest not ariht: with purblynde eyen
and thwartinge may not be hool lookinge." "Me reccheth
neuere" quod she. "Wel I wole þat after þat I see with eye
þe scriptures ben corrected thoruhout and torent. As I go al
contrarye, and bacward myn heeles, and sewe not oopere ne go
not bi here paas, no more haue I not biholdinge to þe
scripture as oopere hauen. Brent I shal be yit as I trowe,
and put into þe fyir, and þerfore I bere with me þis fagot
heere al redy for to sette fyir þerinne." "Sey me sooth now,"
quod I, "art þou þe olde þat madest brenne þe Templeres?"
"Ye, soothliche," quod she, "and þou shuldest also wite þat I
am þilke þat stirede ayens Augustyn in þe time þat he was
pilgryme—but I mihte neuere bineme him his scrippe ne
vnscrippe him. With my shame [f.119v] I departede from him.
A fool I was whan I assailede him." "And whi", quod I,
"assailest þou me?" "What?" quod she. "Weenest þou þat þou
be as strong as he was?" "Nay, certeyn," quod I, "but I sey
þee þat sithe þat man hath ouercome þee, þou shuldest not
afterward be so boistous to manward." "Haa!" quod she.
"Alle hauen not euene strengthe. I haue sithe founde manye
þat I haue vnscripped mawgre hem, and so wole I doo of þee.
Hider now," quod she, "take me þi scrippe withoute
taryinge." "I wole not certeyn!" quod I. And þanne she
sette at me, and swich time þer was þat she made me agast þat
she shulde haue binome me þe scrippe or broken it or doon sum
þerof awey. Neuerþeles I bleynte, and with my burdoun smoot
hire so þat I made hire uoyde þe place. And þanne Grace Dieu
appeerede to me and seyde þat I hadde wel doon þat I hadde

defended me, and þat þerfore she wolde shewe me my wey and
wolde come with me. "Ladi," quod I, "I thanke yow gretliche
of þat ye be comen hider and of þat þat ye bihoten me and
counforten me þus ayen. I hadde ben lost in þis hour if ye
hadden dwelt lengere: þilke wylde beste þere hadde al
discomforted me. þis wylde see hadde also maad me al abasht,
and yit I wot neuere what it is if of yow it ne be tauht me,
wherfore I preye yowe þat ye wole teche me and lerne me of
þese thinges." "Men mown", quod she, "wel speken goinge, and
gon spekinge. Go we, and I wole teche þee and seyn þee
shortliche þese thinges."

Now I telle yow þat biside þe cordes þat þe wylde beste
hadde stended in my wey we wenten, [f.120r] and mawgre him
passeden forth. How it euere were he durste not grucche, were
it neuere so litel, for Grace Dieu whiche he dredde. After þe
see costynge, Grace Dieu com spekinge to me and seyde: "þis
see", quod she, "þat þou seest, is þe world, þat no time is
þat þer ne is torment þerinne, for Veynglorie whiche bloweth
þerinne (þat is þe beligh þat Orguill bereth). It is not
longe agoo þat þou seye it at eye. Bi þis see swimmen and
gon diuerse folk diuerseliche. Summe goon þe feet aboue, and
þat ben þilke þat ben charged with þe beringe of þe sak of
Auarice which is nouht couenable in see for þe grete weihte of
it ploungeth þe heed of þilke þat bereth it, and maketh him
foundre doun so þat he may not swimme. Swiche folk I holde
lost forto þe time þei ley al doun. Of oopere þat goon al
upriht, of whiche summe ben weenged, wite wel þat þei ben a
folk þat keepen nothing of þe world but oonliche here
sustenaunce, and hauen here trist in God al oonliche. In þe
see þei ben for þei mihten not elles liue bodiliche, but þei
seechen not þe gostly lyfe in þe see: wel þei witen þat in
ooþer place þei shule haue it, and þerfore þei swimmen and gon
upriht. þe wynges ben wynges of vertues for to flee with to
þe cuntree aboue. Swiche folk ben lich a brid þat Ortigometra
I clepe, for whan he shulde passe þe see and is trauailed of
fleeinge, to swimme in þe see he taketh him; but in swimmynge
he streccheth his wynge and maketh þerof a seil and a steere
soo þat he sinke not doun and so þat he mowe flee ayen aboue
þe see as he dide bifore. Right so of þilke whiche [f.120v] I
speke to þee: onliche in þe see þei ben forcause of
necessite—but here willes elleswhere þei haue.

Of hem þat bi þe feet ben bounden and arested with þe

erbes, wite wel it ben folk þat be michel biloued, þat hauen alle here affecciouns to delite hem in vanitees and ydel seculer thinges. þei louen better wordliche needes þan children to go to mariages—and with suiche thinges þei ben wounden bi legges and bi feet. How þei shulden flee, I wot 6275 neuere: þei haue ynowh to doone to swimme.

Of hem þat han here eyen blyndfelled and ben as blynde, wite wel þei been foollish folk þat leeuen but in kyn and in thing þei seen withoute. Albeit þe world is foul and al þat is þerinne, neuerþeles blyndfelled þei maken hem þe fooles 6280 of a fairnesse it hath, of which Salomon spak sumtime and seide þat it was veyn (in þe Pistel of þe Magdaleyne), and þerwith þei haue bended hem, þat þou seest þere, and blynded hem. Eyen þei haue with which þei seen nothing for vanitee þat stoppeth hem and for fortune and prosperitee þat thoruhout 6285 blyndeth hem. In perile þei been, þou seest it wel. I wole nothing sey þee more of hem.

But if þou wolt anything heere of þe wylde beste þat þou seest fisshe on þe stronde, I wole telle þee shortliche withoute lesinge. þilke beste hatteth Sathan, which dooth 6290 al his entente to haue alle þilke þat ben in þe see bi his fysshinge and bi his hookinge with his lyne and with hise temptacioun with which he tempteth man and womman, to whiche whan any consenteth, anoon with þat oon he ta[f.121r]keth him and anoon he pulleth him and draweth him to him for to bere 6295 him with him. But for he may not haue alle so at his wille, þat is to seye, for þat with þe ees ne with þe feedinge of temptacioun he taketh not as he wolde, þerfore he hath lerned to make cordes and breide thredes and to make nettes to fishshe with, for to drive awey feþeren* and for briddes fleeinge. For 6300 hem þat þou seest haven wynges and ben goode contemplatyf folk he is bicome a fowlere and hath stended his nette upon þe see, þat þei beten not here wynges ne askape him: for hem þat him thinketh wolden flee and gon out of þe see, an hunte he maketh him and hath stended hise strenges and hise cordes bifore here 6305 wey.

þer shal noon goon out þat he ne arresteth if he may, or bi feet or bi hed—þou seye neuere yrayne þat made so manye nettes and snares for þe flyes, ne þat sette so gret bisynesse as þis beste bisyeth him for to bynde creature of mankynde; 6310 and alwey he werpeth temptaciouns and breideth hem and weueth hem and alwey stercheth his werk, and alwey putteth thredes in

þe reedes.* But certeyn, whoso were wys and hadde a litel
strengthe, þouh it were but þe strengthe of a flye þat he
hadde, of alle hise strenges he shulde not recche. Hise   6
cordes ben but copwebbes: þei ben rent and broken with þe
flyght of a gret flye, wherfore Seint Jerome seith þat þer is
noon discomfyt of him ne withholden in hise bondes but if he
wole, for feeble þei been boþe he and hise strenges. But
þerfore I sey þee nouht þat þou riht bisyliche and wysliche ne   6
keepe þee, for he hath a thowsand artes for to desceyue folk
with, and a thowsand and a thowsand [f.121v] þat þou seest
not. He taketh gladliche a fauce visage and falsliche
dissimuleth þat he is a briht aungel and þat he seecheth not
to do harm. Bithinke þee how he desceyuede an heremite to   6
whom he appeerede with a fauce visage, in liknesse of a good
messanger and of a good aungel. þe deeuel seide to þe
heremite þus: 'þe deeuel', quod he, 'is subtile. Be war þou be
not supprised of him. He wole come to þee tomorwe, and shal
seeme þi fader. I rede þee þou hindre him and smite him   6
first.' On þe morwe his fader com to him, wherof michel
misbifel him: his sone sigh him and smot him and fellede him
doun to þe eerþe ded. Subtilliche Sathan desceyuede him, but
to late he apperceyued it. Keep þee from him if þou leeue me
—from hise settinges and from hise nettes. It is þilke of   6
which Seint Peeter seide þat he seecheth day and niht what he
may take and deuowre. If I wolde telle þee in how many wises
and maneres he hath slayn many sheep, and how many lambren he
hath departed fro þe brest and strangled, I trowe it shulde
not plese þee, for I see riht now it anoyeth þee. Keep þee   6
fro him. I passe me shortliche þat I werye þee nouht to
michel þerof.''

  As Grace Dieu spak to me, I sigh bifore me a damisele þat
bar a bal. Nice she seemede: rouh and feþered on þe feet she
was as a dowve. To hire I wolde speke, and seide   hire: 6
Damisele, me thinketh þat niceliche ye beren yow. I wot
neuere wherof ye serue.'' "If", quod she, "þou wost wherof I
serue, of my manere þou shuldest not speke more ne lasse, but
agast of me þou shuldest be.'' [f.122r] "Who be ye, gentel,''
quod I, "which if men made of you saale, mihte no man livinge   6
ouerbigge yow ne loue yow to michel.'' "þou gabbest of
nothing'', quod she, "but þat men vsed me wel; but it is riht
hard to doone to folk þat ben of wikkede doinge. I hatte
Jeonenesse þe lyghte, þe tumbistere, þe rennere, þe fonne,

þe lepere þat sette nouht alle daungeres at a glooue. I go, I   6355
come, I lepe, I flee, I springe, I carolle, I trippe, I daunce,
I trice goinge to þe reuelle, I strogle and lepe diches
joynpee, and caste þe ston with þe ferþeste. I abasshe me
neuere more to passe dych, hegge ne wal; and of my neyghbowres
apples in here gardynes I wole haue, I am lopen in an appel   6360
tre lightliche anoon—I am not for nouht rouh on þe feet, ne
feþered for nouht. Mi feet beren me where I wole: þei hauen
wynges, þou seest it at eye. Azael bar hem sumtime, but he
abouhte it sore. To gret lightnesse sumtime is not good for
þe lyfe. Oon with hevy feet, wys, is more woorth þan foure   6365
fooles with fleeinge feet, and þerfore er þis Holicherche hath
ordeyned þat þer were no persone set þerinne for to gouerne it
þat ne hadde feet of led for to go with, so þat þerof I am
priued as longe as I am þus rouh-footed.

A crooked staf me lakketh for to cholle with and a bal to   6370
pleye me with. Ooþer croce needeth me non: if I hadde, it
were folye, for my feet mihten not holden hem from stiringe,
ne ne wolden not. I haue not yit my fulle of pleyinge at þe
boules, to gadere floures, to bigile, to pleye at þe merelles,
to heere songes and instrumentes and seeche [f.122v] my   6375
disport. In my bal day and niht I haue more ioye þan in al
þat euere my fader tauhte me, or in al þat euere my mooder
seyde me. I posse it, I handele it, I pleye þerwith. þis is
my studye: I haue no thouht but to pleye me and procure my
merthes." "Serue ye", quod I, "of anything more?" "þat þou   6380
shalt see wel," quod she, "for anoon I wole trusse þee and bi
þe see bere þee." "Shal ye bere me? What haue ye seyd,
Damisele?" quod I. "Ye wolen nouht bere litel, whan ye speke to
bere me." "Yit I wole bere þee," quod she, "oþer þou shalt
soone fynde þilke þat shal do þe soule from þe body whiche in   6385
Latyn men clepe Mors." "And what thing", quod I, "Is Mors?"
"þou shalt", quod she, "wite, whan þou hast seyn Vilesse, and þat
she shal bicomen in þee." "And where is Vilesse," quod I,
and where dwelleth she, and what thing is it?" "In time",
quod she, "þou shalt wite, but þat shal not be yit. Yif hider   6390
þin hand: I wole flee, and bi þe see I wole bere þee þere þou
shalt see many merueyles, if þou ne slepe or slombre to
michel." And þanne withoute more taryinge she took me bi þe
hand, and anoon sette me in hire nekke, and sithe took hire to
flee aboue þe see. Wel assured was I nouht, for þe grete   6395
wawes þat I sigh and for þat she plounged me þerinne whan she

wolde. In gret perile she putte me ofte bi hire nice, foolisshe man*ere*. Cyrtim, Caribdim and Cillam, Bitalasson and Sirenam and alle oo*þere* p*er*iles of þe see she made me feele and endure. And if ye witen not what is Cirtes, Caribdis and þe oo*þere* thre, I wole shewe it þou riht shortliche, for I think mo*re* to oo*þer* eende.

Cirtes is prop*re* wil, þat as sond assembled maketh an hil in þe see, bi whiche whan a [f.123r] wawe cometh* it muste make a stintinge. If I sigh man or wo*m*man þat gad*er*ede and hepede his willes to michel, and þat kepte not to doo as oo*þere*, I wolde sey þus: 'It is sond, it is grauel þat hepeth to michel togi̯deres þat maketh þe botme of þe see bouched, and binemeth þe weye of þe see to swimme'. Þat is Cirtes þe perilous— keep þee from hi*m*. He is dredful.

Caribdis is þe wysdom and þe ku*n*nynge þat is in þe world: secul*ere* implicacio*u*n and worldliche ocupacio*u*n, alle swiche thinges gon aboute alwey, alday turnen, alday varyen, alwey in her*e* *idem* comen ayen and not in oo point holden hem. It is a meevinge sercelich, suich in þe ende as at þe firste. It hath noon abidinge ne eende, no more þan is in þe wheel of a mille as longe as it dureth and water cometh þerto. If of Salomon ye bithinke yow—how he souhte aboute, how he assaiyede of alle, and how he heeld it thing veyn, and torment and peyne—ye mown wite and bi his ensa*u*mple if ye wole, þat al þe ocupacio*u*n and þe marcha*u*ndise of þe world is a verry Caribdis and a wrong perile.

In Cilla and Bitalasso also but shrewednesse I sey you noon: Cilla is seid adu*er*sitee, Bitalassus p*r*osperitee. It ben sleyhtes with whiche Fortune maketh hire wheel turne. Bitalassus maketh it gon up, and Cilla maketh it avale do*u*n. Ye haue seyn it peynted on walles: ye knowe it wel. I holde me stille with þis. Aduersitee dooth as Cilla, for whan any wight [f.123v] goth bi him, he is hurtled and tempested, and with þe wawes of þe see possed. Howndes gon abayinge upon him, m*ur*muringe with here teth of his doinges. It is a perile þat many folk dreden, and loth ben to putte hem þerinne; but þat oo*þer* is not lasse to drede whoso cowde wel biholde it, for withholdinge and cleyey and arestinge and glewy is þilke of wordlich richesse, of wurshipe, of strengthe, of idel fairnesse, þat wonder it is þat þilke ne is p*er*ished þat passeth bi it. Sirena is wordliche solas, þe which with hir*e* singinge and idel desport draweth þe shipmen to hire. Þat is

a perile to which Joenenesse ledde me and bar me ofteste. I
trowe she louede it wel, or elles þat she haated me to þe   6440
deth.

Now I telle yow whan I was a riht gret while born þus, on
þe lift side I sigh an old oon þat rood þe wawes of þe see,
and hadde a skin gert aboute hire as a smythiere, and in hire
hand a gret hamer, and a peire tonges she bar with wich she   6445
manaced me harde fro fer. "Hider now," quod she, "lighte
doun. þou shalt ne more be þus bore: þou mustest lerne to
swimme bi þe see as ooþere doon." þanne wolde I wite hire
name and who she was and wherof she seruede. "Sey me", quod
I, "wherof þou seruest, how þou hattest and who þou art, and   6450
why þou manasest me, þat nothing haue misdoon to þee, I wot
wel." And þanne she answerde me: "Mi skin, my tonges and
myn hamer shewen wel ynowh my craft, for þei been [f.124r]
tooles to forge with. Me faileth nothing but an anevelte:
wel is it bifalle þee if þou haue oon, for if þou haue oon, I   6455
wole forge þeron þi corown and make it; and if þou hast it
not, euele welcomed shalt þou be anoon, wite it wel. Mi strook
shal not be in idel: upon þee or upon þe anevelte it shal
falle." And þanne of þe noble gambesoun þat Grace Dieu in hire
hous hadde yiven me (wheron þe anevelte was set bihynde) I   6460
bithouhte me—but to laate it was, for I hadde it nouht on.
To laate he cometh to arme him þat first is entred into
tournement.

Soone ynowh she tauht it me. But þe surplus she seide me
first: "I am", quod she, "þe goldsmithesse and þe forgeresse   6465
of heuene, þat make and forge in þis cuntree þe corownes of
Paradys. þe metalle of which I wole werche, I bete and smite
to preeue it and in a brennynge oovene I putte it to se of
what metalle it is. Oon hour with þe tonges I take it and
platte it and strecche it, and anooþer I hepe it ayen with þe   6470
hamer with whiche I bete it; þe goode metalle I make bettere,
þe wikkede I make wurse. Tribulacioun I am cleped, bi alle
scriptures approoved. My hamer Persecucioun is seid, with
which I pursue many oon and smite hem (whan I see my time) so
gret a strok, þat if þe purpoint which Memorie hath he haue   6475
not on, he is lost and confounded. To Job sumtime it needede,
and to alle þilke of þe kalender and to many ooþere þat ben not
writen þerinne for it is to litel—for if þei ne hadden   take
þe purpoynt and þe anevelte at riht time, þe grete strokes þat
[f.124v] I smot hem hadde confounded hem withoute delay.   6480

My tonges ben þe distresse and þe anguishe þat so harde
presseth troubel herte þat it thinketh it is streyned in a
pressour shet with a vys and loken, as   drestes defouled, of
which men haue seyn wel ofte þat bi þe condyt bi which teres
descend, a gret pressinge which of þe sorwe is messangere.*
The skyn of whiche I make my barm-fell I clepe Hountee and
Confusioun, for whan I haue acloyed any wyght and so beten
and hamered (be it   rihtfulliche or wrongfulliche) þat he
shulde be put to þe deth or þat he shulde be maymed on þe
bodiliche bodi, anoon his skin abiggeth it bi þe shame þat I
doo it, for bi þe ..... and bi þe skin (which is al oon)
þilke knoweth wel who I am. And to whom þat I wole doo annoye
men mown wel knowe bi his visage, for mawgre him is my
strok: confusioun he hath þerof and shame, but I sette litel
acounte bi hise doinges. I make a barm-fell þerof for to
forge with, for to make him more encumbred. þe more shame þe
man hath, þe more persecucioun he fyndeth. If þou haue of
swich a skin, I wole wite it and make my barm-fell þerof, and
afterward I wole smyte þe more hardliche and þe fastere upon
þee: if þou be void, þou shalt breke oer sowne hye. In
voydnesse is but murmure whan men smyte it with an hard thing.
I wot it wel—I haue assayed it. þe lawe was committed to me
er now: Adonay committed it to me whan he made me smythiere
of heuene."

"Shewe me þi commissioun", quod I, "if þou sey sooth,
and also þi power, for I wole leeue þee today no more of
no[f.125r]thing if I ne see it and rede it." And þanne anoon
she putte hire hand in hire bosum and drowh out þe
commissioun, and seide me: "If þis sufficeth þee nouht, I
haue anooþer of anooþer maister which I wole yit shewe þee
afterward." "þilke", quod I, "I wole haue also." She took it
me and I sigh hem boþe, of whiche þe firste was writen in þis
manere:

> 'Adonay kyng of iustice which hath þe power in þe eclips,
> þe grete emperour of nature, whos rewme dureth alwey:
> Greetinges to Tribulacioun, suich as we ouhten to sende hire.
> Of neewe we haue vnderstonde þat Prosperitee þe stepdame of
> Vertu hath set hand in oure wordliche kingdom, and hath put
> hoodes bifore þe visages of oure soudyours, and hath doon of
> here armures and binome hem here swerdes and bokeleres and
> withoute abidinge wole lede hem to hange hem with instrumentes
> of ioye; and yit more—þat she hath uoided þe garnisonis þat

I and my Grace sette sum time in diuerse regiouns,
where we hadden goode castelles in which we hadden
goode vesselles wherinne we hadden put fulfillinge   6525
of þe grete tresores of Paradys, þat was þe sweete shedinge of
oure grace and þe oynture (it is michel more noble tresour
þan is siluer, gold or stoones). And for oure macier þou art
and oure sergeauntesse, we senden þee and comitte þee þat þou
go bi alle houses and þat þou seeche Prosperitee soo þat þou   6530
fynde hire, and þat þou smyte hire soo þat she durre no more
be so proud ne rebelle ayens us. And also we sende þee and
committe þee þat afterward þou hurtle alle þilke so cruelliche
þat hauen here [f.125v] hoodes wrong turned, and þat
Prosperitee hath blyndfelled, þat þei take avisement and þat   6535
þei vnblyndfelle so here eyen þat þei mown biholde to þe
heuene, for þus capped ne bended shulden þei not be but if þei
wolden. And after þat here armure and here mailes ben
tobroken, þou shalt forge hem and make hem ayen and soone make
hem cloþe hem ayen: of Paradys we haue maad þee smithiere and   6540
goldsmithesse þerfore. Afterward we sende þee þat þou take in
þin hand and holde alle disportes and solaces and alle ioyes
and pleyes þat ben wordliche, and þat þou go not out of þe
place bifore þat þou haue buried hem alle. We wole not þat
oure knyghtes ben hanged with suiche craftes. We yiuen þee   6545
also power þat þou go see oure vesselles, if anything be in
hem. If þei ben voide, þei wole sowne whan þou smitest hem.
If þei be not ful, þou shalt heere murmure: it is þe tokne bi
whiche þou shalt knowe hem. To do þis we yiuen þee pleyn
power, and commaunde to alle grete and smale þat to þee þei   6550
ben obeisaunt withoute ayenseyinge. þis was maad þe day and
þe yeer þat Adam was out into exill.'

þat ooþer commissioun ye shule heere if ye wole, which is
not swich.

'Sathan þe amyrall of þe see, enemy to þe kynrede of   6555
Adam, kyng and lord of iniquitee and persecutour of equitee:
Gretinge to Tribulacioun suich as we mown sende hire.
Vnderstonde we haue of neewe (wherof us thinketh not fair) þat
þe seruantes of Adonay ben so pryded ayens us þat þei wolen be
resceyued to þe place from which we [f.126r] ben fallen—and   6560
eche of hem hauen taken a scrippe and a burdoun, men seyn,
seyinge þat þei wolen do þe pilgrimage þider and þe viage;
wherfore maundement we yiuen þee and comaundinge þat þider þou
go withoute taryinge and þat þou smyte withoute manasinge alle
þilke þat þou seest clymbe þider, and as michel of heres as   6565
þou myght fynde. Do more to hem þan þou didest to Job, from
whom þou tooke hise temporal goodes. Bineme hem here scrippes

and here burdouns, and put þi tonges to þe bodi, to þe lyuere
and to þe lunges, so þat here hertes and here entrailes comen
out as of Judas, and þat þei hangen hemself with hise cordes.
Of þis pleyn power we yiven þee. þis was maad in þilke sesoun
þat þe king of Jewes maade þe theef stye into heuene.'

Whan þese commissiouns I hadde diligentliche red, seyn
and herd, I foolded hem and took hem ayen; and þanne
seide hire: "So God keepe þee," quod I, "sey me now if þou
wolt vse of boþe, or elles of wheþer þou wolt vse. þei
strecchen nouht to oon ende, no more þan triacle and venym."
"Whan I shal", quod she, "smite þee and knokke upon þee, þanne
þou shalt wite if þou wolt, of whiche of þe tweyne I shal vse,
for if þou sey ne sowne no woord but in yildinge thankinge to God,
þanne þou miht wel wite of sooth þat I sergeaunte with þe power
and with þe vertu of þe firste; but if þou wolt haue þi manere
in grucchinge to God and to hise seintes, and vnscrippinge
þee of þi scrippe, and castinge doun þi burdoun, as dide
Theophile, þanne [f.126v] þou miht wite also þat I do it bi þe
enemy, so þat on þee it holt withoute more of which I shal
vse—for I werche al after þat I fynde in hertes of men. As
þe sunne bi fayrnesse hardeth þe dunge and softeth wex or
suette, riht so of me I may sey þat after þat þe matere is
disposed and ordeyned, þerafter I shal sergeaunte and werche
diuerseliche. Now keep þee from me: I may no lengere holde
me þat I ne smyte þee." Anoon as she hadde so seyd, she com
euene to me and wel dide hire couenaunt, and smot me þat doun
into þe see she felled me. Joenenesse leet me falle and wente
hire wey and flygh. Ne hadde my burdoun be, I hadde be
dreynt withoute taryinge. To it faste I heeld me, for swimme
cowde I nouht (and yit I miht wel haue lerned it if I ne hadde
to michel aslewthed it).

Many I sigh certeyn þat swommen wel, and wel strauhten
here handes to poore folk whan þei hadden neede—and many
ooþere þat stireden here feet and gladliche wenten bi
Penitence into grete viages and into grete pilgrimages. þis
is þe manere of swymmynge þat I sigh do in þilke see; but I
swam not soo, for I tristede oonliche to my burdoun which sank
not to þe botme but swam aboue. Now I telle yow, as I wente
þus swymmynge, þe smithiere ledde me, alwey knokkinge upon me,
and so faste heeld me in presse with hire tonges þat me
thouhte I was put in a pressour. So michel sorwe I hadde in
herte þat for litel I hadde lete my burdoun go dounward þe see

where it go wolde.   6610

Whan in swich perile I sigh me, þanne I preyede to God
merci: "Mercy", quod I, "sweete creatour! [f.127r] Be not
failinge to me in my mischeef and in my sorwe, þouh I haue
bi Joenenesse my lyf foliliche vsed a while. Sweete
creatour, I repente me, and certeyn, wel I auhte repent   6615
me þerof, for whan I sih Joenenesse bifore me, and þat
she was a sotte, þi Grace which ledde me and condyed me I
lefte, and suffred hire bere me. To þe forge she hath brouht
me. Now she hath bore me, now I am falle, now is it
soothliche misbifalle me. If þou redy ne make me a refute as   6620
þou didest bi þi Grace to Noe in þe time of þe Diluvie, þou
seest, sweete God, þat I am peresshed. Lord, make me of þee a
shadwe and a restinge in which I may go showve me and dwelle,
for þi smithiere; and if of þee I may not make it, at þe
leste, sweete God, þat it be þi wille þat þi Grace mowe be   6625
it as it was wont to be me."

As I made þus my preyere, þe smithiere anoon herde me,
and seyde me sithe I hadde not leyd doun my burdoun and þat I
cryede to God mercy, she wolde leede me and conduye me to
Grace Dieu. "I am", quod she, "riht as þe wynd þat ledeth   6630
leves into shadewes and into corneres. Whan any wole flee
into þe skyes, and afterward hapneth him to falle (oþer
mishapneth), he hath neede þat withoute tariyinge he fynde
refute and cornere to keepe him, and þat he be turned into
place þer he be not defouled. I am þilke þat gladliche dooth   6635
þilke craft whan it is neede: I chastise þilke þat ben
dissolute, and bete þilke þat I see to dulle. þilke þat ben
forueyed, I putte hem into wey, and neuere shulde I be at ese
bifore I hadde [f.127v] founden hem a cornere where I mihte
hyde hem. Summe I drawe to þe pitee of þe ryal magestee of   6640
God; ooþere I leede to þe Grace, summe ooþere to þe Sterre
Tresmountayne. Summe I leede holdinge up here handes to summe
of þe ooþere seintes. þider as any hath vsed to hide hem,
þider I lede hem—and for þat Grace Dieu is þilke shadwe
which alwey þou hast founden redy at alle þi needes, I leede   6645
þee þider. Recche þee neuere þouh þou haue peyne."

As Tribulacioun made me þus hire narracioun, I biheeld
þat I was nyh þe ryuaile þat I wolde go too. Grace Dieu I
sih, þat heeld hire stille and hadde not stired hire. Whan I
was nyh, "Hider," quod she, "where hast þou be? Whens   6650
comest þou? I wende I hadde lost þee, for I sigh þee nouht

longe. þou leftest me wel niceliche. I wot neuere how þou
hast take hardement to turne ayen to me. Sey me, so God saue
þee, whi þou leftest me soo, and who hath led þe þus ayen to
me on þis side." Whan I sigh she argued me so, anoon I seyde
hire: "Merci, Ladi: soothliche, niceliche I departede fro yow
and foliliche. Deere I haue sithe abouht it; but algates I
confesse and biknowe þat þe grete goldsmithesse hath led me
ayen to yow: loo hire heere where she holt me and cometh with
me mawgre me. Driveth hire fro me I prey yow and beth me a
cornere for hire. Þat þat she hath doon sufficeth me wel
sithe she hath maad me turne ayen to yow. Yit haue I gret
hope ye wole not fayle me." In makinge þus my preyere, þe
goldsmithesse drouh hire ayen and bar awey hire instrumentes,
wherof [f.128r] I was not sori; but michel weryere she lefte
me þan I hadde be longe bifore.

And þanne Grace Dieu seide me: "Now þou seest þat riht
so man to bisy lyth euele as a got þat scrapeth to michel.
Þou hast alwey wold so michel medle þee þat þou haddest neuere
reste: þou hast ben up and doun, and in þe feeld of þi
flowinge* left me þat am þi refute. Sorweful wrecche, whider
woldest þou flee? Whider woldest þou go, and what shuldest
þou doo whan men wolden do þee annoy, if I ne were þi shadewe?
Wrecche sorweful, what haddest þou doon riht now, whan
Tribulacioun tormented þee soo, if þou ne haddest founde me in
þis cuntree? Certeyn she hadde led þee and aryued þee to a
shrewede hauene, and þat shulde haue be to þilke fishere þere,
of whom she hath a commissioun. It is not longe þat þou seye
him strecche hise angeles for to take with þe folk.

Neuerþeles, and þou wolt come and holde þee with me, yit I
wole not faile þee, but I wole yit be þee a freend, and I wole
lede þee in riht short time euene to þe hegge þer þou menest;
and if þou woldest abbrigge þi wey and shorte it wel, to go to
þe faire citee to whiche þou art stired to go, yit I wolde wel
leede þe þider withoute goinge bi þe longe wey. But nouht for
þanne equipollence þer shulde be of Penitence. Penitence hath
put hire yerdes and hire maylettes in diuerse places, and yit
most effectuelliche in þe wey of which I holde þee speche she
hath set hire instrumentes. But þe wey is lasse and michel
shortere to go bi to þe citee þer þou woldest go to: so þerof
þou shalt answere me—my wil þou hast herd." [f.128v] Whan
þese woordes I herde, of ioye I was al fulfilled: michel
liked me þe abbregginge of my wey and þe shortinge, and

nothing it mislikede me of þat \she/ bihight me þat yit she
wolde helpe me. "Lady," quod I, "short wey is good for a   6695
recreaunt pilgrime, and recreaunt I am, and trauailed. þe
shorte I wole gladliche go. Leedeth me þider I pray yow, and
sheweth it me. I am nothing aferd þouh þer be equipollence of
þe hegge of Penitence."

In þilke poynt, a ship riht gret and wunderful I sigh   6700
flotinge in þe see, wel nygh þe arryuaile, al redy to make
passage. She was bounden with hoopes al aboute, and faste
fretted; but summe of þe hoopes weren slaked for defaute of
oseres, summe weren to slakke and summe weren to broken—þe
bindinge was þe lasse strong. But þe hoopes hadden not þe wrong,   6705
for þei weren stronge ynowh if þei hadden be bounden. In þilke
ship weren many howses and many dwellinges, and weren riht noble
and seemeden wel kynges houses. þer weren toures and castelles,
walles with arches and kernelles—and aboue was þe mast of þe
ship dressed, wherupon heeng þe seyl ystreight, whiche   6710
ooþerweys is cleped veyle, al redy to seyle but þat it hadde
good wynd and þat it hadde noon encumbraunce. "Seest þou
þilke ship þere?" quod Grace Dieu to me. "Ye, parde," quod
I, "but I am abasht, for I sigh neuere erst noon swich."
"Yit", quod she, "þou shalt be more abasht whan þou shalt be   6715
withinne, þere þou shalt see þe faire thinges if þou dorre
entre with me þerin." "Seith me now", quod I, "how þe ship
hatteth, and who gouerneth it, and if I muste entre þerinne to
passe þe see?" [f.129r] "þe ship", quod she: "bi his name is
cleped Religioun. She is bounden and bounden ayen, fretted   6720
with obseruaunces. As longe as it is so bounden, it may not
perishe ne faile. To Bynde Ayen it is cleped, to þat ende þat
in it ben bounden ayen þe dissolute and defouled soule of
þilke þat putteth him þerinne. If þe grete hoopes and þe
olde,* whiche þe goode religiows setten þeron sumtime, weren   6725
wel kept and wel bounden ayen at here rihtes, þe ship shulde
neuere faile in no time for harm þat mihte come þertoo; but
þer ben summe folk þat recchen so litel of þe smale oseres þat
bynden hem, þat þe ship is in perile—for it is knowen thing
þat þe hoopes seruen of nouht but if þe oseres fastne hem. þe   6730
oseres I clepe þe smale comaundementes whiche ben restreynynge
and keeperes of þe grettere, wherfor I seye þat who þat
breketh hem or looseth hem to michel, al þe ship is to michel
loosed, and neuere shulen þe grete olde* ben wel kept but \if/
þei ben bounden with summe lighte comaundementes in wise of   6735

smale oseres. Now wolde God my fader þe kyng þat Religioun
were swich as it was whan at þe biginnynge she took hire
byndinge; but of bynderes ayen ben almost noone, for alle þei
hauen lost here instrumentes, þe smale oseres ben broken, þe
grete hoopes ben þe lasse strong—and þerfore þe ship is
michel þe more perilowse and þe more dredful. Nouht þat I
wole blame it ne despreise it ne disalowe it for yit þer ben
goode bynderes and of religious* ynowe þat hauen non neede þat
men putten on hem neewe oseres. Of it am I gouernowresse,
maistresse and conduyeresse, and þe [f.129v] mast which is
dressed hye with þe seyl crossed amidde helpeth me wel to lede
it whan þe wynd wole blowe þerinne. þe mast is þe cros of
Ihesu Crist, and þe wynd is þe Holi Gost, þe which, as
Gildenemouth seith, mown lede þe ship to hauene. If into
Jerusalem hastliche þou wolt go, þou mustest entre hider in and
logge in oon of þe castelles, eiþer of Cluigni or of Cistiaus
or in anooþer þat to þi lust shal leede þee þidir bettere at
þi wille. Alle ben defensable and stronge for to keepe
þerinne boþe body and soule: þer may noon enemy þere do
harm, kunne he neuere so michel caste or sheete, if it ne were
so þat men opened hym þe castel and þat a man yolde him. Go
we now þider, I rede þee. It is bettere þan bi swymmynge: þei
ben in perile, þilke þat passen bi swymmynge, and vnneþes
askapen."

And þanne Grace Dieu ledde me into þe ship, and þere
shewede me þe faire castelles of whiche I haue spoke, and
seide me þat I wente where I wolde go al at my wille, and she
wolde make me entre. As she seide, I chees, and to entre I
stirede me anoon. þe porter I fond at þe entree, which bar an
hevi maace. "Porter," quod I, "let me go: I wole entre into
þis castel. Grace Dieu hath ordeyned me soo, which hath led
me euene hider." "Frend," quod he, "if I wiste þat it
plesede þe kyng I wolde wel suffre þee entre in, but I wot it
nouht." "Is þanne þe king þerinne?" quod I. "Ye,
certeynliche;" quod he, "I were not heere elles. I wolde
neuere helde me at þe dore if I ne wiste þe king withinne.
Whan I holde me at þe dore it is tokne þat withinne is þe kyng
of [f.130r] Paradys." "How art þou cleped?" quod I. "Paour
de Dieu", quod he, "I hatte, and am þe biginnynge of wisdam
and foundement of goodshipe, and I haue out sinne also þat he
be not logged in þilke castel, ne I suffre him not entre into
þis ship to enhabite þerinne. If he entre herinne, it is

maugre myn, priuiliche, in hideles. My grete maace is cleped
þe Vengeaunce of God and þe Gryselichhede of Helle, of whiche
alle auhten haue drede. I bete and smyte and chastice þe folk   6780
þat þei doon no folye. If þis maace ne were, eche wolde
preyse me to litel."

"What!" quod I. "Shalt þou smite me?" "Ye," quod he,
elles þou shalt not entre into þe castel." And þanne I bigan
to biholde Grace Dieu, and seide hire þus: "Goode sweete   6785
lady, me thinketh þe entre is not so abaundoned to me as ye
seyden me." And þanne she answerde and seide me: "Hast þou
foryete þat I haue seid þee þat þou shuldest fynde
equipollence of þe hegge of Penitence? \Stroke/ of porter
is no deth: he shal not smite þee so harde þat þou ne   6790
shalt yit mown endure oopere peynes. Refuse not to entre in
for þe maace. A knyght oweth wel to suffre colee er he entre
into stour or haue dignitee of wurshipe." "Is it so?" quod I
to hire. "Ye!" quod she. "And I wole entre þerinne
gladliche", quod I, "but þat I entre not first. Goth bifore: 6795
I wole sewe yow and go anoon after yow." Thanne entrede she
and I after; but þe porter þat was nygh foryat nouht to smyte
me. Swich a strok he yaf me þat he made me quaake, and doun
hadde gronded me ne hadde my burdoun [f.130v] be. Alle
knyhtes þat hauen swerdes resceyuen not swiche colees: gret   6800
joye it were and profyte I trowe if þei hadden swiche.

Now I telle yow, whan I was passed forth bi þe porter
þat I haue nempned, I sigh manye merueyles in þe castel,
whiche me thouhte riht faire. þer was þerinne cloystre and
dortour, chirche, chapitre and freytour: and I sigh also   6805
ostelrye þerinne bi þat oon side, and fermerye. To þe
ostelrye I wente at þe firste, thinkinge to herberwe me þere.
þere I sigh Charitee, þat seruede and herberwede þe pilgrimes,
and ofte wente to þe yate to feede þe poore folk, þat I haue
spoke you of heerbifore. It is she þat heeld þe scripture of   6810
pees, whan Moyses yaf and departede þe releef. Foorth I
passede. Into þe cloystre I wente and to þe chirche, and þere
I fond a fair cumpanye of ladyes, of whiche I wot not þe names
of alle (for withoute mo of hem þat sitten me most at herte
and of which I wundrede most I askede þe names of Grace).   6815
Tweyne I sigh þat cloumben þe degrees of þe dortour and wenten
togideres: and þat oon hadde a gambisoun and þat ooper bar a
staf. þilke with þe gambisoun was at þe grees, and þere she
abood me. Of oopere clopes she was al bare saue as michel

as she was cloþed inne, and þat ooþer was armed on þe handes
and glooued with glooues, and with a rochet riht whyt she was
arayed wel nobleliche. Tweyne ooþere I sigh speke togideres
and go toward þe chapitre, of whiche þat oon bar cordes and
byndinges, and þat ooþer heeld a fyle steled [f.131r] bitwixe
hire teeth, and was armed with a targe. Anooþer I sigh þat
wente bi þe cloistre, and as me thouhte she bar mete croumed*
upon parchemyn, and þer sewede hire a whyt culuer in þe eyr
fleeinge after hire. Anooþer yit I sigh go euene foorth
toward þe freytour, whiche as it seemede me hadde a gorgiere
aboute hire throte. Anooþer I fonde at þe chirche, þat bar a
messangeres box, and hadde wynges redy streiht for to flee to
þe skyes, and in hire hand she bar an awgere and heeld it hye.
With þat ooþer hand (wherof I abashed me michel) she serued
dede folk þat I sigh þerinne; and it seemede þat bi hire
seruice she made hem bicome onlyue ayen. Anooþer þer was yit
þerinne þat in hire hand bar an horn, and made þerinne a gret
soun of organes and of sawtree. I thouhte she was a
jowgleresse and a disporteresse to folk.

Whan I hadde wel seyn þese thinges I was stired to
aske of Grace Dieu wherof þese ladyes serueden, and who þei
weren. "Lady," quod I to hire, "I preye yow, techeth me who
ben þese ladyes, and wherof þei seruen, for I am abasht for
hem." And þanne she seide me: "I wole þat þou see first
apertliche at eye how men seruen in þe freytour, and þat
þou see þe dortour." "Go we now þider" quod I to hire. Into
þe dortour we wenten, and þere I sigh hire with þe staf, þat
maade þe beddes and leyde on hem white cloþes; [f.131v] and
hire felawe with þe gambisoun sang swich a song: 'I wole
singe; I ouhte wel doon it: I bere nothing with me. At þe
litel wiket I shal not be withholde, for I am naaked'. In þe
freytour afterward I sigh þat of whiche I was michel more
abasht. Many dede folk alle buryed yeven mete to þe quike,
and serueden hem sweeteliche and deuowtliche on knees—and þe
lady with þe gorgier was fretoreere, she viseted hem þat
eeten, and filled hem here defautes.

"Now I wole telle þee", quod Grace Dieu, "of þe noble
ladies of þis place, and of þat þou hast seyn heerinne. þe
ladi þat bereth þe strenges and þe cordes and þe byndinges,
she is þe maistresse of heerinne: next me she is Prioresse,
whiche leedeth alle þe cloystreres in les bounden bi hondes
and bi feet, and maketh hem prisoneeres with opene dores. Bi

name she is nempned and cleped Obedience. Hire cordes and
hire byndinges been hire diuerse comandementes whiche bynden
propre wille þat it doo nothing of his owen lust. Heerafter
þou shalt wite it wel, whan þou shalt be holden in hire   6865
laaces.

The ladi þat bereth þe file—she is cleped bi name
Discipline. She is þe ladi þat keepeth þe ordre, þat þei be
not hardy to do euele. þe fyle þat she bereth in hire mouht,
it is Vndernemynge of Euele. She leueth nothing þat she ne   6870
correcteth and skowreth and forbisheth, and to þat ende þat
she do alle thinge a poynt, and þat ooþere misdoon not hire,
she is targed with þe targe þat þou hast left, and þat þou
took to Memorie. þe name I haue [f.132r] seid þee: to
reherce it were litel woorth.   6875

She with þe gambesoun (which hath seid þe song) is Wilful
Pouerte, þat hath bi hire goode wille left alle þe goodes þat
she hadde in þe world, and as michel as she mihte haue
þerinne. At alle poyntes she hath vncloþed hire: riht now
þou haddest seyn hire naked, ne hadde I put on hire þe   6880
purpoynt þat bi lachesse þou took to Memorie to bere. þow
wost wel how men clepen it. She singeth, þou hast herd it,
þat she hath nothing aboute hire þat shal withholde hire to
passe to þe citee þere she wolde go to. It needeth þee wel
þou acqueynte þee with hire, and þat þou preye hire, holdinge   6885
up boþe þine handes, þat she wole comforte þee to þat ende
þat þou mowe singe soo.

Of hire felawe I sey þee also (þat bereth þe staf and
maketh þe beddes) I rede þou make þi freend al þi lyue,
þat she make þi bed alle nihtes, and þat þou make hire a place   6890
with þee. Gladliche she wole ligge with þee alle times þat þe
liketh. She lith and resteth hire ofte with þat ooþer al
niht. Good it is to haue swich dortorere, swich wenche and
chaumberere. þouh Venus come \in/to þe dortour she wolde
drive hire out with hire staf, and wolde suffre hire ligge   6895
in no bed þat þer were for no peny; and if þow wite not why
it is, þe cause and þe resoun is swich: for Venus, as she
seith, drof hire and putte hire sumtime out of þe world,
wherfore it is riht þat she drive hire ayenward and do hire þe
same. þis ladi is cleped Dame Blaunche þe wasshene—þilke   6900
þat ` of no wiht hath [f.132v] cure if he ne be whyt and
withoute filthe; and if ooþerweys þou wolt nempne hire,
Chastite þou miht clepe hire, chasteleyne of þis castel. þer

is noþer archere ne querelle þat she ne wole defende, and þat
neiþer arwe ne darte entre. She is not for nouht armed with
þe gloouen and glooued: whoso is at þe dore bi whiche þe
assaute cometh, with hand armed he is ofte michel more hardi
ayens þe dartes þat ben cast. Weel þou wost þe name of
þe gloouen: I tauht it þee in myn hous. A fool þou were whan
þou vngloouedest þee of hem: it wole be hard to haue hem ayen
afterward.

The ladi þat þou hast seyn goo bi þe cloistre and bere
mete upon parchemyn is pitaunceere of heerinne, and
suthselerere. She yiveth mete to þe soule, and feedeth it þat
it hungre nouht. She filleth þe herte, with hire goode and
sweete mete, nouht þe wombe. She is also cleped Lessoun and
Studie bi hire rihte name, and hire mete is nempned Holi Writ
þat is putt þeron, and vessel maad of parchemyn for it shulde
not shede bi þe wey: it mihte not be kept soo wel ne so faire
in ooþer vessel. With hire I rede þou acqueynte þee, for bi
hire (if þou wolt) þou shalt lightliche haue þe acqueyntaunce
of þe ooþere; and þe loue and þe knoweleche and þe grace of
þe Holi Gost, þat folweth hire as a whyt culuer, shal shewe þee
and sey þee al þat þei doon in þe londe of biyonde. He is
messanger, and cometh to speke with þilke þat he seeth studie,
and þat taken here feedinge bi þe hand of Lessoun.

Now I wole telle þee yit after of þat þou hast seyn in þe
freytour. She þat hath þe gorgiere is ladi [f.133r] and
freytoureere. Abstinence þou shalt clepe hire whan to hire
þou shalt speke. Hire gorgiere is Sobrietee: þou ouhtest
wite it if þou ne haue foryete it—I seide it þee er þis.
þe dede þat seruen and feeden þe quike deuoutliche, withouten
lesinge ben þe goode folk þat ben gon out of þis world, þat
han yiven so michel of here goodes to þe quike þat þei ben
susteyned þerwith and sufficientliche fedde. Serteyn þilke
were riht nice þat wiste nouht he hadde seruice of dede and
eete of heres, and withoute heres shulde dye of hunger
—and þerfore seruice men taken of hem, riht as þouh þei weren
present, and in preyinge for hem men shulden thanke hem, and
þerfore þei ben sette on knees as þouh þei seiden: 'Preyeth
for us. With owres ye liven: with boþe youre handes* preyeth
for us'. Now", quod she, "þat is wel doon; heerinne þou
hast seyn it in dede.

þe ladi þat is at þe cherche, which bereth a
messangeres box, it is þe ladi þat serueth hem ayen, after

þat eche deserueth—and with þe augere þou hast seyn, she
perceth þe heuene so þat she maketh þe goodshipes descende þat
yilden hem here lyfes. þis awgere is seid bi name Feruaunt
Continuacioun þat bi his goode continuaunce maketh þe heuene
an hygh perce, and also yiueth hem mete and sweeteliche   6950
abaundoneth it hem. Halfpeny ne peny haue þei nouht yive þat
it ne is guerdoned hem an hundrethfold, for þei haue þe lyf
þat shal neuere faile—so þouh þei hauen serued þe quike, þei
ben also serued ayen bi hem: here messangeere rediliche
serueth hem ayen and apertliche maketh hem rise from deth bi   6955
þe grete [f.133v] goodes þat she dooth hem, and purgatorie she
abbreggeth hem, and here peynes she alleggeth hem. If of þe
lady þou wolt wite þe name, she hatteth Orisoun, and sumtime
she is cleped Preyere in ooþer manere. She hath wynges for to
flee faste and for to soone stye into heuene for to soone   6960
doo hire message bifore God for mankynde, and is procuresse
whan time is to see him. Messangere she is and rediliche
presenteth him bifore þe kyng, and in good feith sheweth þat
þat is bihight him—and bi hire is noon put in defaute but
þat here procuracioun be seled with deuocioun. To hire I rede   6965
þat þou go, and þat þou sende hire bifore from þee to þe citee
to which þou wolt go. She shal wel kunne redye þee a place
and a couenable dwellinge þereas þou shalt make habitacioun.
It is not resoun þat þi comynge þider ne be wist bifore: þer
sette neuere man þe foot withinne þat ne hadde sent bifore.   6970
Of þe theef it was customed þat was hanged with Jhesu: he
sente Orisoun bifore. He was þe bettere and euere shal be:
so shalt þou do and þou leeue me, for þou hast neede as he
hadde.

The ladi þat þou hast herd pleye with instrumentes, and   6975
bereth an horn, þat is þe waite þat awaketh þe king alle times
þat he slepeth, bi hire blowinge. Bi hire cryinge, if he ly
to michel, she maketh him rise. In Latin, Latria she is
cleped bi name and nempned. Hire horn is þe Inuocacioun of
Dieu 'In adiutorioun' at euery hour withoute weeryinge: so she   6980
bloweth at þe biginnynge, and sithe to hire organes she
aplyeth hire, and deliteth hire to þe melodye, and to þe
sawtrye she taketh hire, enter[f.134r]medlinge þerwith, and
þanne þer is gret melodye of sweete song and of psalmodye.
þus þe instrumentes ben cleped and nempned bi here names: 6985
þese ben þe instrumentes þat ben plesaunt to my fader þe king
almihti. Michel he loueth swich organe and swich song and

swich jogelorye, and for þat it liketh him wel, he maketh of
þilke þat pleyen *with* hem and doon it hise principal pleyeres,
and hise special jogeloresses. Swich thing longeth wel to a
kyng for his disport, as whan þei blowen."

As Grace Dieu spak þus to me I sigh hire bifore me þat
heeld þe byndinges, and þat she come to me euene. "Hider
now," qu*o*d she, "who art þow? What seechest þou in
cloistre? \Whider gost þou/? I wole þou sey it me anoon: I
wot neu*ere* wheþer þou espye us." "Lady," qu*o*d I, "espye yow
wole I nouht, but I shulde go in into Jerusalem þe citee,
wherfore Grace Dieu hath led me hider for to abbregge my wey
and for to shorte it." "Hath she not seid þee", qu*o*d she,
"þat heerinne þou shalt fynde hard bed, hard lyfe and hard
passage, albeit þat it seemeth not swich?" "Yis," qu*o*d I,
"but I wolde fayn do hire wille if I mihte." "þer is nothing",
qu*o*d she, "þou ne shalt do wel if þou ne be to lache. Al
holt in good wille, and wheþer þou hast it good, to proof
I wole putte þee anoon. Hider now, cum forth," qu*o*d she,
"take hider þine handes and þi feet; I wole sette þee \as/
fauco*un* in gesse." Whan swiche woordes I herde, riht
gretliche I was abasht, for I hadde not be wont to be bou*n*den
ne corded. Flee durste I nouht for [f.134v] Grace Dieu þat
hadde led me to þe place. "Hider now," qu*o*d I, "dooth what
ye wole, I am abau*n*doned to yow. I durst not be contrarious
to thing þ*at* ye wolden doo. Grace Dieu hath wel avised me þat
I shal fynde in þis place cou*n*terpeis and equipollence of þe
hegge of Penitence." And þan*n*e she vnfolde hire byndinges and
bi þe feet bond me so, þat me thouhte I was sette in stokkes
oþer take with grinnes. þe byndinges with whiche she hadde
bou*n*den me she heeld with hire handes bi þat oon ende, and
seide me þat whan I wolde gon oo wey, I shulde go anooþer.
Afterward I wiste it wel, but of þat strof I nothing—I haue
leu*ere* sey it anooþer time þan write it heere in my book.
Afterward she bond myne handes and seyde me þat alle þe
werkes I dide shulden be bareyn but if I dide hem bi hire. My
tunge yit she made me drawe out, and aboute it a byndinge she
putte me, and seyde me I shulde nouht speke if bi hire I ne
speke. "þis byndinge", qu*o*d she, "is cleped Silence:
Benedicite, þis is þilke þat oonliche vnbynt it. Of Grace
Dieu I sey nouht (ne of hem þou hast seyn, ne of ooþere
þou shalt se) þat to hem þ*ou* ne miht speke whan anything þou
wolt aske hem."

Whan þus þe Prioresse hadde sette me and bounden me as
hound leced, a gret while afterward I sigh tweyne olde, wherof
michel I abasshed me. Þat oon bar tweyne potentes on hire
nekke, and she hadde feet of led, and a box she hadde bihynde
hire as a messangeere. Þat ooþer was also a messangere, and
upon hire heed bar a bed, and hadde trussed hire lappes in
hire girdel, redy as me thouh[f.135r]te for to wrastle. To me
þei comen togidere and seyden me: "þe Deth sendeth us to þee
for to tourneye, for she cometh to þee withoute taryinge, and
hath seid us and enioyned us þat from þee we departen nouht
bifore þat we haue ouerthrowen þee and to þe eerþe felled þee.
She wole fynde þee tormented and maat so þat she mowe sey
þee 'Chek and maat'." "Who ben ye?" quod I anoon. "I knowe
neiþer yow ne þe Deth. I wole wite who she is, and if Deth be
youre maistresse; and I wole also wite if boþe tweyne ye ben
with hire, wherfore seith it me if ye wole, and youre names and
wherof ye seruen." And þanne þei seiden me: "þe arguynge ne
þe thuartinge is nothing worth ayens us ne ayens Deth neiþer,
for þer is noon þat may be so strong þat we ne abaaten him of
alle poyntes as soone as we come. Þe Deth hath þe lordshipe
in þe world ouer þe lyfe of þe bodi, and kynges and dukes
dreden hire more þan doon smale poore folk. Riche and poore
she maketh euene, and neuere spareth no wight, and in many
places entreth ofte þere she hath not sent bifore, soo þat she
hath don curteysye to þee whan she hath maad us come bifore.
Þis is a certeyn warnynge þat she cometh to þee hastliche. Of
hire we ben messangeres, and special currowres. Eche of us
shal sey þee hire owen name."

And þanne þilke spak þat bar þe bed upon hire heed and
þat seemede a wrastlere: "I hatte", quod she, "Infirmitee,
þat oueral þer I fynde Hele sette me to wrastle with him for to
venquishe him and ouertrede him. Oon houre she felleth him,
and anooþer time I felle [f.135v] him; but fewe as I trowe
shulden felle me ne were Medicine, þat dooth sum coumfort,
whiche was bore to dryue me awey. Ofte it bifalleth þat I
fynde hire lened or sette at þe dore bi whiche I shulde passe
for to go do my message, and so I muste turne ayen or soiourne
long time withoute; and neuerþelees mawgre alle þe boxes and
hise emplastres and hise oynementes and hise empassionementes,
sumtyme I entre in and couple me to þilke anoon which Deth
hath sent me to. Down I bete him and doun I ouerthrowe him.
He hath no mary þat I ne souke. His blood I drinke, his flesh

7030

7035

7040

7045

7050

7055

7060

7065

7070

I ete, so þat he hath neiþer strengthe ne vertu—and þanne in
þe bed þat I haue I ley him, so þat Deth fynde him al redy his
lyfe to drawe withoute havinge to michel to doone." "Thou art
not", quod I, "messangere to which men ouhten make good
cheer." "Yis, þat I am," quod she, "for þou shuldest wite
þat I am þilke þat make remembre on Penitence whan she is put
in foryetinge: þilke þat bringeth folk to þe wey whan þei ben
out þerof, and setteth hem ayen in þe rihte wey. Sumtime
þilke þat made Nature, for he sigh þat summe ne reccheden
nouht of him and hadden foryeten him and litel dredden him,
clepede me and seide me: 'Go into þilke wordliche cuntree and
wrastle with hem and bete hem doun þat þou fyndest boistous
ayens me; for þei haue hele, þei preysen me litel, and
hauen put me in foryetinge. Correcte hem and chastise hem and
bynde hem so faste in here beddes þat þei [f.136r] mowe not
arise ne turne hem at here wille, and þat þei leese savour of
etinge and al þe appetite of drinkinge—to þilke ende, I sey
it þee, þat I wole þei preye me of mercy, and þat þei amenden
hem and entenden to saue here soules, so þat þe Deth mowe
fynde hem in swich plyt þat eche of hem mowe sey to hire:
"Deth, I drede þee nouht a straw; I haue sette al myn herte
and al my thouht to my creatour. Smyte whan þou wolt, my
soule is al arayed for to gon out of his bodi: Penitence þe
lauendere hath maad it be so miche in hire bowkinge þat it is
porged and wel wasshen".' Now I telle þee þat whan he hadde
þus seyd me, soone I obeyede to him. Mi lappes I put in my
girdel, and wente me bi þe cuntree; and so michel I haue doon
þat manye I haue discounfited and ouerthrowe with wrastlinge.
In bedde I haue maad many ligge, and of þee wole I do no
lasse. Make þee redy. I wole wrastle with þee and soone leyn
þee doun in þi bed."

"That ooþer", quod I to hire, "shal first as couenaunt
is, sey me who she is." "I wole it wel" quod she. And þanne
þat ooþer seide: "I am þilke þat whan þou were bore with
Jeonenesse, þou wendest neuere haue seyn. þou seidest of
me: 'She is ferre; she shal not come a good while. She goth
softe, she hath feet of led, she may not go: I haue tyme
ynowh to pleye me.' Now I telle þee, soothliche feet of leed I
haue, and go softe, but ferre men gon litel and litel ful wel
—er þis men hauen seid it. þouh I be comen softe, algates
[f.136v] ouertake þee I haue, and tidinges I bringe þee þat þe
Deth whiche forbereth nouht cometh to þee. Hire messangere

I am: she may haue no messangere þat may speke þerof more
verryliche. My felawe gabbeth sumtime for sumthing contrarye
þat suffreth hire not to do hire message, but me may nothing
empeche to shewe it certeynliche. Vilesse þe dotede I hatte:
þe leene, þe rivelede, þilke þat hath þe hed hoor and wel
ofte al bare of her—þilke of whom folk shulden aske
counseil, and bere gret wurshipe too, for I haue seyn þe time
passed, and michel good and yuel preeued. þis is þe glose of
science, and þilke bi which men kunnen þe thinges. þer shal
neuere noon kunne no science if he ne haue seyn and preeued.
Neuerþelees, ofte it bifalleth (and needeth nouht to hele it)
þat albeit þat I haue seyn ynowh and preeued ynowh and cowde
ynowh, and albeit I haue wel an hundreth winter, I am sette in
þe rewe of children and at þe laste dote and haue no wit to
counseil. þis is þe cause for which Ysaie cursede me sumtime
whan he sigh me."

"Sey me", quod I, "of þe potentes, and þanne anoon go
hens sithe þou hast doon þin erande: me liketh nouht þi
presence." "Like or nouht like," quod she, "so shal it not
be. Deth shal first come to þee er I departe fro þee. I wole
anoon bete þee so michel þat gret ioye shalt þou neuere haue.
Courbe and impotent I wole make þee with þe grete strokes I
shal yive þee. Neuerþeles so michel auauntage þou shalt haue
of me if þou be wys, þat þe twey potentes þat I haue to lene
me too [f.137r], I wole take þee: nouht þat I wole for þis
enchesoun bineme þee þi burdoun, for with þe spiritual staf,
þe temporal is good. My potentes ben bodiliche, and for to
susteyne þe body ben: for þis cause I dide make hem, and
took hem and trussed hem. Curteys I am, for hem þat I bete, I
ouerthrowe hem nouht soo soone þat on þat oon side þei \ne/
ben susteyned, if on þat ooþer side þei ben smiten, wherfore so
lightliche fallen þei nouht, ne so soone misbifallen—so þat
now take hem if þou wolt. þei shule neede þee wel, boþe
tweyne: mi strokes ben sore to bere (soone þou shalt wite it,
if I ne deye). Hider now," quod she to hire felawe, "it is
time þat we doon him annoye; wrastle with him and make him
ligge in þi bed, and on þat ooþer side I wole helpe þee and
annoye him to my powere." And þanne boþe togideres þei tooken
me and maaden me anoon falle doun, and bi þe throte þei tooken
me to streyne me and harde to pinche me. Crye and braye I
mihte riht wel: ooþer solas hadde I noon. In þe bed at þe
laste þei leyden me, and bounden me and seiden me: "Araye

7115

7120

7125

7130

7135

7140

7145

7150

7155

þee, þe Deth cometh. If she take þee sodeynliche, it is not
long on vs: we haue wel warned þee, and yit we warnen þee."

As I was holden in þis plyte, and þus lay on þe bed, I
sigh a lady come þat made myn herte glade. She hadde a symple
biholdinge, and a visage benigne and plesaunt, and hadde
drawen out hire oon brest bi þe vente of hire cote; and she
hadde a corde in hire hand as þouh she wente to hey. To me
she com hire and vnfolded hire corde, and þanne seyde me:
"Hider now, come to þe fermorye, for þou [f.137v] art not wel
heere." And þanne I seide hire: "Sweete lady, I bihoote yow
bi my soule and swere yow þat with yow I wolde gladliche go,
but for I wot not who ye be, I biseeche yow þat ye wole teche
me." "And I wole", quod she, "sey it þee. Wite of sooth þat
I am þilke þat after sentence yiven in alle jugementes I
shulde be resceyued but if wrong be doon me. Whan þe
souereyn kyng sumtime hadde doon jugement of mankynde and put
to deth bi here folye, þanne I maade him leue of his hand, and
for to haue in sum bileevinge I maade him sette a bowe
withoute corde in þe heuene for cause of accord. With þe
corde which þe bowe was corded (and þat I haue vncorded) I
drawe and bringe out þe wrecches of miserie whan I fynde hem
þerinne, and þerfore accordeth hire Resoun þat I hatte
Misericorde—þat is to seyne, Corde of Wrecches, for to drawe
hem out of foul wrecchedness. My mooder Charitee was cordere
and thredere of þis corde. As soone as it breketh, shal
neuere noon mowe stye into heuene."

"Why", quod I, "haue ye drawe youre brest? Is þere milk
þerinne with whiche ye wole yive me souke?" "Ye," quod she,
"þou hast more neede þerof, and yit shalt haue, þan of gold or
of siluer. Pite it hatteth: it needeth wel to yive souke
with to þe poore folk. I yive þerwith sowke to þe hungrye and
I werne it not to þilke þat in time passed hauen misdoon me.
Aristotle seith þat milk is noon ooþer thing but blood þat is
remeved and maad al whyt bi decoccioun of heete þat blyndeth
his rednesse. If þou wost not what it is to seyn [f.138r] þou
shuldest wite þat man ful of ire hath nouht in him but red
blood þe whiche shulde neuere be whyt but if Charite boiled it
and turned it into whitnesse: whyt milk it bicometh whan it
is soden, and þe rednesse goth al awey: and þanne þilke þat
hath swich milk foryiveth al þat men han misdoon him. To him
is wel sittinge swich a brest and wel auenaunt.

My fader, þat was put on þe cros, was not vnwarnished

of swich a brest, al were it nouht neede. To shewe it he maade
perce and kerue his riht side, þe side of his manhode. þer
dide neuere no mooder ne ne norice so michel for hire chyild.   7200
þanne his brest shewede wel—to eche it seide: 'Come forth!
Haue! Whoso wole souke, come forth! In me is no more blood
of ire: Charitee hath remeeved it and soden it into whyt milk
for commune profite.' þer sook neuere noon non swich milk, ne
droouh noon swich brest. Now I telle þee þat þus I yive sowke   7205
to þilke þat I wot hauen neede, and so I am lich my fader and
also Charitee my mooder; and þerwith þou shuldest wite þat in
alle places þat I may see any poore þat hath hunger, anoon I
yive him bred. Mete and drink I yive after þat I haue foysoun
of good. If I see any discomforted, any naked, any vncloþed, I   7210
cloþe hem ayen and coumforte hem, and stire hem and counseile
hem to pacience. þe pilgrimes I resceyue in myn hous, and
whan any is in prisoun, I go visite hem ones in þe moneth at
þe leste. þilke þat ben dede I burye hem, and þilke þat lyen
in bedde bi eelde or bi syknesse I serue hem in humblesse;   7215
and heerfore hath Grace Dieu maad [f.138v] me enfermerere of
þis place. I serue þe grete and þe smale, and ofte make hem
ayen here beddes and suffre hem endure no defaute þat I may
amende. If with me þou wolt come I am redy to serue þee."
"Gret wil", quod I, "haue I þertoo, but how it shal be I ne   7220
wot: þese messageres holden me so nih þat I may not goon
after yow. If ye diden hem from me, gret bountee ye diden me."
"Doon hem awey", quod she, "may I nouht, but with my corde I
wole lede þee with me, if I may, into þe fermerye to reste.
þe messangeres shule come þider also, and I trowe wel nouht   7225
leue þee bifore þat þe Deth come, ne forbere þee." And þanne
hire corde she bond to þe bed, and ledde me forth. þe olde also
foot bi foot comen þider, wherof I was nouht glad. þe power
was nouht myn, and amende it mihte I nouht.

Whan in þe fermerye I was and hadde leyn þere a while,   7230
sodeynliche and a soursaut I sigh an old oon þat was clumben
an hy upon my bed, wherof I was gretliche abasht. She afryght
me soo þat speke to hire mihte I nouht ne nothing aske of
hire. In hire hond she heeld a siþe, and she bar a cheste of
tree, and anoon she hadde sett oon of hire feet upon my brest   7235
for to streyne me. "Ho, ho!" quod Grace Dieu þanne, þat was
not fer fro þat place. "Abide a while. I wole sey him twey
woordes þat I haue to sey him." "Sey now þanne anoon:" quod she,
"longe taryinge anoyeth me—I wolde deliuere me anoon for I

haue to go elleswher*e*." And þa*n*ne com Grace Dieu to me and
sweetelich seide me: "Now I see wel þat þou art at þe streyte
passage of þi pilgr*i*mage. Loo heere þe Deth þat is comen,
which is þe ende of alle eerþeliche thinges [f.139r] and þe
termininge. She thinketh to mowe þi lyfe and putte it al in
declyn, and sithe in hire coffyne þi bodi she wole putte, for
to take it stinkinge to wormes. þis thing is al co*m*mune to
eche man and womman. Man in þis world is ordeyned to þe Deth
as þe gras in þe medewe to þe siþe, for þat þat is today
greene and tomorwe drye is hey. þou hast now be greene a long
time, and hast had reynes and wyndes; but now þou mostest be
mowe, and tobroke in twey peeces: þat oon is þe bodi, þat
ooþer þe soule. þei mihten nouht passen togideres. þe soule
shal first go, and sithe afterward þe bodi shal go. But þat
shal nouht be so soone—þe flesh shal first be roten and
neewe geten ayen at þe gen*era*l assemblee. Now looke wheþer
þou be wel apoynted and arayed: if it ne \be/ long on þiself,
þou shalt anoon come to þe citee to whiche þou hast ment. þou
art at þe wiket and at þe dore þat þou seygh sumtime in þe
mirro*ur*. If þou be dispoiled and naaked, *þou* shalt be
resceyued withinne. þou haddest wel chier þilke entree at þe
first whan þou seigh it, and algates so michel I sey þee þat þou
crye mercy to my fader in biheetinge to Penitence þat þouh *þou*
haue nouht doon hire sufficience, gladliche þou wolt don it
hire in purgatorie þere þou shalt go too." Now I telle yow, if
I mihte haue spoke I hadde maade hire many dema*u*ndes of whiche
I hadde doute and kneewe nouht. It is folye for to abide to
þe neede. Whan men weenen þat Deth be riht fer, he abitte at
þe posterne. Wel I wiste þat: I was supprysed. þe Deth leet
þe siþe renne, and maade [f.139v] þe soule departe from þe
bodi.

þus me thouhte as I mette, but as I was in swich plyte
and in swich torment, I herde þe orlage of þe couent þat rang
for þe Matynes as it was wont. Whan I herde it I awook, and
al swetinge I fond me, and for my meetinge I was gretliche
thouhti and abasht. Algates up I ros me and to Matines I
wente, but so tormented and weery I was þat I mihte nothing
doo þere. My herte I hadde so fichched to þat I hadde met þat
me thouhte, and yit do, *þat* swich is þe pilgrimage of dedliche
man in þis cuntre, and *þat* he is ofte in swich periles—and
þerfore I haue sett it in writinge in þe wise þat I mette it.
Nouht *þat* I haue sett al, for þe writinge shulde be to long.

If þis metinge I haue not wel ymet, I preye þat to riht it be
corrected of þilke þat kunne bettere meete, or þat bettere
mown make it. þus michel I sey also, þat if any lesinge þer
be þerinne, þat to meetinge it be arretted, for bi meeting   7285
may nouht alle sooth be shewed. Errour wolde I noon meynteene
bi noo wey, but gladliche I wolde and haue wilned þat by þe
meetinge þat I haue seyn, alle pilgrimes ryghteden hem and
kepten hem to forueye. Faire he chastiseth himself, men
seyn, þat bi ooþere is chastysed. þe errour and þe forueyinge   7290
of ooþere shulde ben warnynge þat eche take his wey soo þat he
mowe come to good eende—þilke eende þat is þe guerdoun and
þe rewarde of þe ioye of heuene whiche God grawnte [f.140r] to
alle quike and dede. Amen.

Heere endeth þe romaunce of þe monk, of þe Pilgrimage of   7295
þe Lyfe of þe Manhode, which is maad for good pilgryme þat in
þis world swich wey wole holde, þat he go to good hauene and
þat he haue of heuene þe ioye. Taken upon þe Romaunce of þe
Rose, wherinne þe art of loue is al enclosed. Preyeth for
þilke þat maade it, þat hath maad make it, and wrot it. Amen.   7300

VARIANTS

(see p. xcii for the editorial conventions used below.)

1 S *is missing until* 114; To] *prec.* Capitulum 1 *mar.* C, *prec.* Here begynnes þe prolouge opon þe buke whilk is named · Grace dieu · *translate* oute of Fraunch in to ynglyssh as it folowes *rub.* M (Grace dieu *has* Cawsod *over* M³); þilke] folke J; whiche] the whilke JMO; hows] dwellynge Place here J, -es M. 2 seith ... Poul] seynt paule saies M; poore] pore (*with* poure *mar.* G³) G. 4 yow] *om.* J; sweuene] dreme M; bifelle me] *trs.* J. 4-5 þe tooþer] this othere J. 5 in] *om.* J. 6 þat þat] that JMO. 7 were] was JMO; thing] the thynge JMO; most] *om.* JMO; swevene] dreme M; which] the wylke JMO. 8 after] -warde J. 8-9 Now ... wel] *om.* J. 9 folk] ? -*es* G; let þer be] loke that J; no] The pilgrimage of man. wherin *þe* authore doth discouer *þe* manifoulde miseries of *þis* lyfe. And the great loue of God, to such as call vppon hyme in tyme of their trouble, faithfully. *add. mar.* O³. 10 þat] *om.* JM, to O; drawe] þay*m add.* J; bakward] abak J, o bakward M, a bakeward O. 10-11 putten hem forth] take good tent þerto J. 11 alle ... sitte] *om.* J; herkne] it ententyfly *add.* J; þis] it J. 12 alle] to alle JO; any] *o. er.* O³; owttaken] excepcioun J, doute takynge M, owt takynge (owt *o. er.* O³) O. 12-13 In Frensch] In Englishe CM, I hafe Seitt it J. 13 I ... it] in ynglische J; lewede] me*n add.* J, þe lewde men M. 14 þerinne] *þere* J; wight] man J; whiche] whate J; men] he J; shulden] scholde J. 15 which] he schulde refuyse and *add.* J; and leue] *om.* JMO; thing] athynge JMO. 15-16 miche nedeth] is full nedfull J. 16 in ... gon] gase in Pilg*ri*mage J; in²] Of J; wyilde] *om.* JMO. 17 Now vnderstandeth] *trs.* J, 3he *add.* MO; þe] þis M; swevene] dreme M; bifelle] mette J. 18 Chaalit] Chalice J; was] Sclepinge *add.* J; bed] Pars Prima *add.* J, Liber Guilielmi Laud Archiepiscopi Cantuar*ensis*: et Cancellarii Vniuersitatis Oxon*iensis.* 1633. *at foot p.* O³. 19 Me] *prec.* Capitulum ii *mar.* C, capit*ulum* i *rub. mar.* M; slepte] was Sclepande J. 20 to¹] for to J; go] wende J; to²] in to GMO; in] the whilke I hadde sene by fore as in J. 21 thouhte] that *add.* JMO; it] I O. 21-2 hadde ... and¹] Perseyfed I hadde J. 22 þilke] that JMO; from] fra JMO (*o. er.* O³). 23 þilke] that JMO. 24 and] *ins. mar.* O; abowte] with owtene J; gold] And *add.* M; foundement] gru*n*de J. 25 and¹] of JMO; masounrye] masonynge GMO; þe²] *ins.* O; hy] height JMO; newe] the newe J. 26 enclosede] closedde J; it] alle *add.* J; Many] Grete Plente J; were] was J. 27 and] *om.* O; dwellinges] dwellyngstedes J; þere] þer C (*see note*). 28 gladshipe] and *add.* J; þere ... wight] þer ... wight C, Schortely to saye J; iche] icht O; wight] *om.* O. 29 shortliche ... me] thare hadde ilke a wight J, schortly to passe O; generalliche] *with* generally ? *etiam mar.* O³; goodshipes] goodeschyp O. 30 But] *prec.* Capitulum iii *mar.* C; discounforted] myscomforthed J. 31 wyght] man J; his] owne *add.* J; for] of *add.* JMO. 32 whiche] the whilke JMO; right] *om.* J. 33 þerate] *om.* J; which] and he JMO (he *ins.* O); a] newe *add.* J. 34 skirmynge] schymerande J. 35 turnynge] and *add.* J; he] *om.* J; him] selfe *add.* J, *ins.* O; is] was JMO. 36 on] of MO, of the swerd and J; þe] *om.* O; þere] þer C. 37 þat] þen MO; ded ... wounded] Ne he schulde awey J; he ... be] he shulde be C, be dede or sare woundede J, shuld he be MO; nouht þat] Jn so michel *þat* C, nouht þan MO, 3e nought J. 38 for] Afore J, *þe* waye to lyfe. is death. then happye is that death. that bring*es* imortall life *mar.* O³; hadde] takene *add.* J; ne] he C, and JO, and 3hit M; deth] the deede J.

39 passage] F, passinge C. 40 payage] parage C, paymente J; alþouh] þereof
alle J, þof al M, yf all O. 41 chaumpiouns] and *add.* J. 42 resseyueden]
Suffrede J. 43 þe¹] his JO; kernelles] kyrnell O; ouer] of MO; of
whiche] {of} whech *ins. mar.* G³, whilke J. 43-4 þe porter] *om.* JMO. 44 þe]
om. JMO. 45 red with] *trs.* M; aperceyued] perseyuyd and Sene J, perseyued
MO; þat¹] þis JMO; I sih] and behaldyne J; þat²] the JMO. 46 þere]
whare JMO; I] me JMO; muste] behouede J; needes] entir *add.* JMO; if
þer were] for þere was JMO, bi christ's meritt*es* þe sword was done awaye &
enterance made more easye. *mar.* O³. 47 bi ... wey] I sawe nane passe Inne J,
I see noon passe MO; I ... passe] butte by that waye JMO; Eche] I J, Ilkon M;
was] wondere sare *add.* J. 48 agast] and aferde *add.* M, and namely *add.* J;
he] I J; but] fra *add.* J; hennesforthward] hennes forward GM, heyne forwarde
J. 49 wel ... safetee] safly putte vppe his swerde J, How saynte Austyn and
odir*e* diu*e*rse doctoures satt abowen þe Citee of Jer*u*salem and fedd folk *with* þere
doctryne *add. rub.* M; his] *om.* O; swerd] *ins. mar.* G³. 50 But] *prec.*
Cap*itulum* iv *mar.* C, Cap*itulum* ii *rub. mar.* M; lyfte] vp *add.* M; and biheeld]
om. J, I biheld M, and I be held O. 51 wol gret] I Sawe J, a right grete MO;
I sigh] a wondirfulle sight J; was] right *add.* MO; gretliche] astou*n*dede and
add. J. 52 sigh] stande *add.* J; hy] hight JMO; on] in J, opon M; þe] a J;
kernelles] kernelle J; and¹] *om.* J, he *add.* M; sat] *om.* J. 53 semede] hit
semede hym to be J, hym semyd MO. 54 þat] whilk M. 55 for²] by M,
ins. O; þat] *ins. mar.* G³; hadden] fedde thaym J. 56 þei] *om.* O;
croumede] crommes and by J. 57 seyinges] songes C, sayinge JMO, diz F;
bicomen] and ermade *add.* M; after] -wardes J. 57 flyen] flowe JMO.
58 upright] -ys MO; certeyn] Settys J; I seigh] sawe I there J. 59 of²] *om.*
J; folkes] folke MO, folke of lerede of J. 60 and¹] of J; clerkes] *om.* J, clerk
O; of religious] de religieux F, of religiouns CO, regulere J; and³] *om.* J.
61 þat] the whilke J; maden] *ins.* O; grete] *om.* JMO. 62 sithen] *om.* J;
bigunnen] become MO; to¹] atte J, for to M; for] *om.* J. 63 wherfore] and
þerfore J, þerfor MO; token] take J. 64 Als ... as] Also O; on ... side] on
the toother syde GM, I turnede J, on þe oþer syde O; I turnede] on the tothir
Side J, (tornde *o. er.* O). 65 more] *om.* J. 66 þat I seygh] y sygh G, *om.* O;
walles] walle J. 67 þat] the whilke J. 68 bi sleyghtes] Putte thay*m* in to
the cete J; putten hem in] alle by Sleyghtes J. 69 on hy ayenst] to J; walles]
wall J; dressed] vp *add.* J. 70 stiked] *om.* JMO; degrees] grees J;
humblisse] mekenes JMO; whiche] the whilke J, wche O; cloumben] thay
clambe J. 71 wel] *om.* J, ful MO; þilke¹] the JM, þat O; folk] -es G, that is
to saye *add.* J. 72 monkes] monk C; white and greye] blans et gris F, greye
and white C; vndertakinge] chalange J. 73 any] How saynt Francyse helpid
þem of his religion · and how þe kay of þe cite of Ier*u*salem was bitakyn vnto saynt
petire *add. rub.* (þe kay *ins.*) M; After] *prec.* Cap*itulum* v *mar.* C, Cap*itulum* iii
rub. mar. M, this *add.* J; wel] *om.* J; freend] frendely and ȝeede J; to] vnto
M. 74 þilke] þem MO, thay*m* that ware J; I hadde] me thought J; metinge]
swefnynge J; a corde] he hadde acorde in his hande J, he hadd *add.* M. 75 wel]
om. M; þat] the whilke J; bi places] *om.* J; knet] knettede full of knottes ·/
This ilke corde J; hadde] *om.* J; set] hange J, it *add.* M; dounward] downe
by J, by *add.* MO. 76 bi which] *om.* J; eche] alle J, ilk man M; was] ware
J; aqueyntee] -s J. 77 enoynted] sare J, noyed MO, ointe F; þat] þan MO;
he ne] *trs.* J, he MO. 78 and] if MO; he] *om.* J. 79 walles] wall O;
am] can*n*e J; sure] siker C, *om.* J; to] *om.* J. 81 clymbe þider] thedyr they
clambe J, Thedir*e* clam many folk M, þider clam þa O; for] but gaf I J, *om.* MO;
lookinge] sight J; was] *om.* J; upon] telle J, of MO. 82 þe] that JMO;

not] wele add. J.   82-3 wherfore me] and that J.   83 sore] ryght sare JM;
so] this J.   83-4 shortliche ... meward] om. O.   84 wal] -lys J.   85 made]
gerte J.   86 hadde] om. J; taken] be toke J, bitakyn M; to] vnto M; wel
triste] tristede mykille J, trs. MO.   87 certeyn] -ly J; wel miht] soo he myght
wele J, wele he myght MO; triste in him] om. J; þerbi] om. J; suffrede] ne
suffrede C.   88 to passe] passe in þere by J; poore] pore (with poure mar. G³)
G, poure J, pure MO; folk] -es G; þilke] he JMO; lyeth] lyede J; nouht]
neuere J.   89 hadde] om. JMO.   90 miht] may JMO; thoruh] ʒorghe O;
þe ... nedele] a nedylle eyʒe J.   91 eche] ilke a J; wight] that thare wente in
add. J; oncloþed him] om. J, marked mar. M³; and²] om. J; naked] naknede
JMO.   92 men] om. J.   93 þerbi] thare J; non] in add. J; cloþed] cladde
J; of] (f erased C).   94 passeden] passede in J; al dai] euer al day MO;
whaneuere] whan J.   95 þis] that J; commune] grete J.   96 þere] om.
JMO; bicumen] com M; was] (w o. er. C).   97 so] that add. JM; and] late
add. JMO; leue] be JMO.   98 thing] chose F, citee o. er. (with er. mar. C³) C.
99 like] yow add. ins. o. er. (with er. mar. C³) C; þer] þere o. er. C.   100 þat]
þen MO; ne] ins. mar. G³, om. MO; if] and yf O.   101 it²] om. JMO;
swich] þe sygeʒ M; a] ay M; dwellinge] place add. J; and] Right as J.
102 good it were] it ware goode J; to¹] so O; for] om. MO; haue] a add.
JMO; saulee] saule GM, sawle J, sowle O; þe] om. GMO.   103 seid] tolde
J.   104 in] as in J; þe] a JMO; faire] om. JMO; I¹] hadde add. J, haue
add. MO; aperceyued] perseyfed JMO; to go] I mevede me J.   104-5 I ...
me] to goo J.   105 wolde] thought J, and add. O; elleswhere] for ellys where
O.   106 see] om. O; mette] dremed J.   107 þat] om. J; gret reste] I
schulde hafe hadde J; I¹ ... had] grete reste J.   108 departe] parte J; þens]
fro þens C.   110 As] prec. Capitulum vi mar. C, capitulum iv rub. mar. M;
hadde] was J, om. MO; thouht] thynkande J; þis] y thowghte add. can. G, On
this wise J, þus M.   111 me¹] i with mee mar. G³; failede] lakkid bath J;
needed] gretly add. J.   112 thing] a thynge JM; eche] ilke a J; walkinge]
om. J; pilgrime] forto have add. J.   113 I ysede] y sede (with y ysede mar.
G³) G, I passede JMO, our first being ·9· monthes in our mothers wombe & þen,
we begin our pilgrimage mar. O³; me] m' F, om. GJMO; in ... ben] whilke I
had bene in JM, natiuitas hominis rub. mar. M.   114 withouten any ysinge] om.
JMO, S begins at any.   114-15 I ... seeche] and Ascrippe J.   115 and a scrippe]
I be gan to seke J; necessarie] whilke were necessary J; þat²] at O, om. CJ; to
doone] adoo J, howe þe lady Grace dieux mette with þe pilgryme. and coumforting
him add. S.   116 And] SO S, prec. Capitulum vii mar. CS; and] om. S;
bimenynge] makande my mane J; me] om. J, my self S; seechinge] om. S.
117 þerof] suche a scrippe and bourdoun add. S; seygh] was ware of J.   118 in
my wey] om. J; of ... fairnesse] whase bewte J, de sa biaute F; she] om. J; me]
grete add. J.   119 seemede] weel add. S; to¹] vnto M; to²] om. J.   120 On]
opon hir M, vpon S; beten] overe betyne J; and] scho add. JMO; was] om.
O.   121 gert] Abovene add. J; grene] greene (2nd e ins. G³) G; along]
endelange J.   122 arayed] hernaiste J, note mar. O³; on] Opon M; brest]
me thought add. J.   123 and ... an] om. JMO; amelle] (partly er. C), emall G,
om. JMO, Emayle S, esmaile F; in²] in a add. O.   124 certeyn] for soth J.
125 hed] me thought add. J; aboute] it was add. M.   126 foisoun] Plentee J;
shinynge] schynande (-nde can. with -ynge mar. J³) J; Wurþi] Aworthy lorde J.
126-7 he was certeyn] -ly J, certeine he was S; hadde] om. J; yive] gave J;
hire] to hir MS.   128 she was] me thought J; as me thouhte] sche was J;
saluede] Saluste J, salute M, salud O.   129 so] to S; seechinge] seecke S;

al] *om.* O. 130 þat] behold *per* Shir{ley} *mar.* S (so *Ker: Brusendorff, p. 212, suggests* behold{eth}...). 131 to¹] for to S; meward] -es S. 132 and... wel] and wist wele J, *om.* S; þat³] soo J. 133 hath¹] hadde JS; in him¹] *om.* S; hath²] hade S; in him²] *om.* S; humblesse] mekeness JMO. 134 þe²] that the JM; she] it JS. 135 Humblesse] For mekenesse J, Mekenes MO; hertes] hert M; of²] *om.* M. 136 ho] wha *alt.* who J; þat] soo J; thilke] that JMO; banere] boonere (*with* baneere *mar.* G³) G, baniere F. 137 him] þat *add.* M; hool] hale *alt.* hole J; þanne I] y þan I (y *ins.* O³) O; tolde] talde *alt.* tolde J, hyr *add.* O. 138 me] to me O; excited] and stirrede *add.* J, stirred M. 139 þat] *om.* J; bi] for M; as²] that JO. 140 ne] nor MO; þat] howe S; seechinge] to seeche S. 141 askinge] spirande eftere J; hem] burdon, betokins fayth . vnto which, whoe soeuer leaneth shall neuer fall *per*petually *mar.* O³. 142 tidinges] tydyng O. 143 þat²] at O; þer] þe M; bifel] beon felle S; þe] *om.* M. 144 a] *om.* C; þat] *om.* MO; þou] nowe *add.* J. 145 helpe] purvaye J. 146 neede] of ne doute þee not ne dispeyre þee nought in no wyse *add.* S, how grace dieu enfo*ur*mes þis pilg*ri*me of hi*r*e bewtes · and also of hi*r*e name *add. rub.* M, Beholde howe · þe pilg*ry*me spekeþe to · dame Grace dieux · humbully beseching and hertely desyring for to knowe hir name *add.* S. 147 And] *om.* O, *prec.* Cap*itulum* viii *mar.* CS, cap*itulum* quintu*m rub. mar.* MO; me] stille *add.* J; þat] þan MO. 148 whateuere] ne whate Soo eu*ere* J, what þat euere S; bifel] of *add.* J; ne] *om.* JMOS; wolde] desyred S; wite] to knowe S; al] *om.* S; boþe] *om.* S; and] to knowe *add.* S. 149 Ladi] A lady S; I] bath *add.* JMO; name] and *add.* JMO. 150 regioun] *alt.* relgiou*n* O³; who] whate JS; ye] *om.* S; al ... fain] *ins. mar.* O³, al þis in sooþe S; in sooth] wete J, *om.* O³, wolde I fayne S; wite] in sothfastnes J, *ins. mar.* O³. 151 and praye] And I praye JM, & I p*r*ay *ins. mar.* O³; yow] that *add.* JM, that *add. ins. mar.* O³; ye ... telle] *ins. mar.* O³ it] al \to/ C, *om.* MO³; me] *ins. mar.* O³; and²] as *add.* J; trowe] fully *add.* S. 152 þe] mykil M; and] hic grat*ia* loquit*ur* ad *per*egrinum (*final* m *minim short* O) *rub. mar.* MO. 153 time] comynge *add.* J; þee¹] for *add.* S; to þee] *om.* O; doutows] dredefulle J. 154 suspeccionous], souspecionneuse F, suspeccious CJMO; þe] þat MO; lord] *om.* MO. 155 cuntre] *with* worlde *mar.* O³. 156 þat¹] *om.* M, þat *add.* S; neede] to hem *add. ins.* (*with* u.v. to hem *mar.* C³) C; þat²] *om.* M. 157 him] to hym M; folk] -es G. 158 oonliche] anelye *alt.* onelye J; Seeste] þowe *add.* JMOS. 159 how] þat *add.* M. 160 þow seye] *trs.* J, *om.* MO; neuere ... fairere] *om.* MO. 161 light] Grace our light, vnto life euerlasting *mar.* O³; to] vnto M; take] *om.* J. 162 is] not *add.* S; eche] ilke a J; day] nyghte J; as²] or *alt.* os O; nihte] day J. 163 nihte] daye J, þe nyght MO; day] nyght J; thilke] scho JMO, þat ilk S. 164 þat] *om.* GS; gost] gase *alt.* gose J; straunge] stronge O. 165 miht] maye J; no] -t O. 166 gost] ga *alt.* go J. 167 be] but *add. can.* C; þat] þen MO; ne] *om.* JMO; be] base S; bihated] hated MO; fader] and *add.* O. 167-8 þe ... kinge] Grace S. 169 folk] ? -es GS. 170 ben] be *ins. mar.* S; lost] lange *add.* J; er þis] *om.* M; Whoso] Wha Soo *alt.* Who Soo J. 171 with him] *om.* S. 171-2 and ... him] *om.* JMO. 171 who] so *add.* S. 172 am] ham O; gouernouresse] gouernowre J, gou*er*nesse M, þe gouerneresse S; thinge] -s S. 173 alle] *om.* MO; leche] the leche JMO; see] to see JMS; yive] -s J, I gife M. 174 reise] areyse S; ben] buþ (*with* beeþ *mar.* G³) G. 175 redresse] dresse S; þilke] thay*m*e JMOS; forveied] fourvoiez F, forfetid CJMO. 175-6 and ... and] *ins. foot þ.* O. 176 fro] -m G, fra *alt.* fro J; folk] -es G; and] for M. 177 cure] ne rekke I nought of thayme *add.* J.

178 Grace Dieu] Grace deu (*with* gracia deo *at foot p.* J³) J;   I am] *trs.* JS;
cleped] callede JMO;   ne] and JMO, noon *add.* S;   ooþerwyse] other weys G;
am I] *trs.* MO;   not] *om.* S.   179 Whan] Soo eu*er*e *add.* J;   shalt haue] Has
J;   so] swagatis J;   þow shalt] *trs.* JS;   clepe] calle JMO.   180 certeyn]
sothly J, -ly S;   fulliche] *om.* S;   þe] þat M.   181 fynde] many adu*er*site *add.*
J;   lettinges] lettynge JMO.   182 and¹] *om.* JMO;   mischeeves] myschefe J;
of] *om.* J, and MO;   aduersitees] *om.* J;   encombraunces] encomberau*n*ce JMO.
183 miht] maye JMO.   184 leeue] beleue (be *ins.* O³) O;   þouh] alle ȝif J, þof
M, oyf (o *ins.* O³) O;   mihtest] myght JMO.   185 eskape] scappe MO;   thing]
om. O.   186 into] in J;   dwellinge] mansiou*n* J.   187 ne] nor MO;   þi] na
J;   alþouh] ȝif alle J, þof al M, of all O.   188 aperceyued] p*er*sayfed JMO;
entren] entrede JMO.   189 al] *om.* JMO;   naked] by scleyghtes J;   þat¹] *om.*
JMO;   summe] othere *add.* J;   fleen ... aboue] by nakid entridde in J, flowe in
abowue MO;   þat²] *om.* M.   190 entren bi sleyhtes] flowe in abovene J, entred
by sleghtes MO, entren by sleght S;   Cherubyn] and ȝit *add.* J, ȝhit *add.* MO.
191 entreth] entrede JMO, entren S.   192 vncloþe] to vnclethe J.   193 þe]
om. JMO;   ayen] *om.* S;   feþere] federd J, fedres MOS.   194 flee ... þei] *om.*
J;   afterward] -es S.   195 I¹] o. *er.* C;   þis] þat *add. can.* O.   196 in] *add.*
S;   wise] waye that J, wyse þat M;   to] *ins. mar.* G³, *ins.* O³;   assaye] hem *add.*
S;   I] *om.* J.   197 hem] redy *add.* J;   passe] to passe JMO;   miht] maye
baldely J;   wite] with oute dreding S.   197-8 withoute dredinge] at J (dredyng
o.er. O), wit *ins. mar.* S, The pilgrims happye acquaintance w*it*h grace *mar.* O³.
198 good] or nought *add.* J;   it] *om.* J.   199 sey] aske J;   it] me J;   no
lengere] be MO;   be] no langere MO;   hyd] ehydde fro me S, Loo nowe howe
þat I aqueynted me with þe feyre lady Grace dieux and cryed hir mercy *add.* S.
200 And] SO S, *prec.* Cap*itulum* ix *mar.* CS;   answerde] and sayde *add.* JS, and
saide to hire þus *add.* M.   202 ye] *om.* J;   necessarie] nedefulle J.   203 to
doone] at doo J.   204 goodliche] *om.* JMO;   ben] ȝe first J, ȝhe MO;   first to
me] to me are I to yowe and alle J;   I] for I M.   205 hadde] haue C;   of ...
elles] nede J;   neede] of nouȝt ellys J;   now ... me] lede me now J;   wher]
whidyr JMO.   206 yow] for þe luff of god *add.* M;   nouht] for I wil obey to
þow at þo*ur* owne commawndement · And I thank þow lowly with all my spiryte ·
þat þus playnly ȝhe haue tellyd me þo*ur* bewtes and þo*ur* name · for it dose me
right grete gladnesse · and alwey schall do *add.* M, hic duci*tur* ad ecclesiam ad
bap*t*ismum *rub. mar.* MO, Nowe maye yee seo howe Grace dieux tooke me by þe
hande leding me on pilgrimage *add.* S;   Thanne] *prec.* Cap*itulum* x *mar.* CS,
Cap*itulum* vi *rub. mar.* MO;   in] *om.* JO;   þilke] The JMO.   207 me¹] *om.*
JM, noght O;   into] to G, til S.   208 an] a *o. er.* O;   þat¹] the whilke sche
sayde J;   as] si F, And CO, *om.* J;   she seide] *om.* J.   209 þere] I schulde
fynde J;   I ... fynde] thare J;   hadde] *ins. mar.* G³;   She] And scho M, As sche
þat O.   210 þilke] that JMO;   she] *o. er.* C;   seyde] deyd O.   210-11 xiii
... xxx] xxxi ȝere · and xxx J, xiii C · and xxx ȝere M;   bifore] twoo hondrithe and
xxxvij year synce ye maikyng of this booke *mar.* M³, an*n*o 1330 *mar.* O³;   þat] þe
S;   as ... wel] *om.* J;   seyh] behelde J.   212 þilke] that JMO;   sihte] þ*er*e of
add. J.   213 abashed me] was gretly abaschede J, was aferde somwhat M;   hy]
height J;   and] hit *add.* JMO.   214 bitwixe] betwene GJOS;   þouh] *om.*
JMOS;   hadde] *om.* M;   come] fallene J.   215 alight] lightede J, lyght MO;
from] fro JMO;   þe] *om.* O.   216 his] the JMO;   aray] þerof *add.* J.
217 discounforted] myscomfortede J;   michel] that *add.* J.   218 þat] *om.* J;
needes] nedelynges J;   I¹] me M;   muste] mot OS;   it] that watere J, to MO.
219 þe] that J;   ne¹,²] nor M, no O;   bregge] bote S;   noon] ryght nane J.

220 aperceyued] P*ersayfede JMO; wel] *om.* M; after] -warde JMO. 221 al]
bedouen*e add.* J; to] vnto J. 222 Grace] deu *add.* J, dieu *add.* MOS;
askede] aske G, hir *add.* JS; askepe] that watere *add.* J. 223 if] *om.* J;
owher] ouerwher*e* M, owr where O, ought S. 224 þat bi ordre] fayre I prayede
hir that sche walde telle me J, by þat ordre S; she … me] by ordir J. 225 me]
How þepilgrym was aferd of þe forsaide wat*ir* to be wasshyn *þer* in. *add. rub.* M,
howe þat þe lady Grace dieux aunswerd þe pilgryme *add.* S. 226 Thanne]
Ande J, *prec.* Cap*itulum* xi *mar.* C, Cap*itulum* vii Baptismus. *rub. mar.* M, Baptismus
rub. over black mar. O; she[1]] þe lady Grace dieux S; answerde] and sayde vnto
me *add.* J, saide MO, and sayde *add.* S; þow … seiste] whate J, what sees þou
MO. 227 Art] þowe *add.* JMOS; abasht] aferde M; litel] for if *add.* S;
wolt] wolde JMOS; into] to JS; and] *om.* S. 228 þou shuldest] thare
behofes the to J, þou shal MO, þee most S; þis] ce F, þe C. 229 which] the
whilke J; right] *om.* J; of[1]] angres and *add.* J; gret] *om.* J; anoye] noyes J,
angwysch O; of[2]] grete *add.* J, and M, *om.* O; and] *om.* JO. 230 of[1]] *om.* O;
of[2]] *om.* MO; grete wyndes] wyndes grete and many J; mihtest] schalle J,
myght MO, þou S; þou] *om.* G, mihte S. 231 whan] Sene JMO; hast] soo
add. JMO; so] this J, *om.* MO; litel] watere *add.* J. 231-2 þou shuldest]
aught þe to J. 232 ouhtest] maye J, aught MO; to wite] see J. 233 þer]
om. J; passe heere] *trs.* J. 234 pilgrimage] JMO, -s CGS. 236 þerforth]
thare a waye J; somme] some (*3rd minim ins.* O[3]) O. 237 han] hase J, watere
add. J; neuerþeles] natheles GS, *om.* J, ʒit MO; þouh] ʒif JMO; woldest]
wolde JMO. 238 yit] *om.* J; is not] (s *erased* C), this way J; þis wey] is not
J, þat wey S. 239 to þee] (*blotted* C); is … certeyn] in certayne hit is to the J,
certain it is to þee S; but] it *add. ins.* C; certeyn] & *add. ins.* C; right] *om.* J.
240 looke] (*blotted* C); whenes] whene JM; ful] plaine F, foul CS.
241 whiche] the whilke J; hast be] was J, in *add.* MO; þou] þe necessity of
baptisme, to wash vs from originall synne *add. mar.* O[3]. 242 rede] counseil M;
þee to] that þou J. 243 foorth] forrth *alt.* foorth G[3]; for] *om.* GMO, wit it
weel *add.* S; þou] (*er.* C); surer] plus seur F, sik*er*ere C. 244 a … sumtime]
sum tyme a kinge J, a worthi kynge somtyme M; þat[1] … thilke] *om.* J; paas]
passage MO; þat[2]] Christ *þe* righteouse *add. mar.* O[3]; thilke] he MO. 245 þe]
this J; paas] Passage JMO; which] and ʒit he J, worthi kynge *add.* O; ne[2]] F,
neu*e*re J, *om.* CMO; misdede] did amysse J; not] *om.* J. 246 it[2]] me JM;
now] tite *add.* J; wole] schalle J; do] gerre J; come þee] come to the JMO,
trs. S; hider] þider C. 247 of God] is þe official M, (gode *ins.* O); is
official] of god M. 248 ministre] my Iustere J, mynisterer S; thilke] that
JMO; passage] The pre*est mar.* O[3]; þilke] he JMO. 249 þee[2]] and *add.* S.
250 þilke] He JMO. 251 go] passe J; ouer] ewyr O; þe] *om.* G; þat] *om.*
JMO. 253 breste] and *add.* S; also] *om.* S; upon] on GO. 254 þin] thy
JMO; for] And J; þe] *om.* M; drede] þyne enemys / and frome *add.* S.
255-6 not … bodde] un grant bouton … ne prises F, price at a budde O, sette at
nouht CM, nouʒt sette by J. 256 enemyes] apere stert *add.* J; Now answere]
trs. J, me *add.* M; anoon] bylyve J. 257 þanne I] I Aunswerde and J;
seyde] Lady *add.* J. 258 make] þe offyscyall *add. can.* G; him] *ins.* M[3];
come] to come J; me[1]] How grac*e* dieu made þe pilg*ri*me ben wasshyn in þe
forsaide watir*e add. rub.* M, howe þofficial of Grace dieux / by hire comaundement
· plunged me in þat water · and wesshe me cleene *add.* S; Thanne] *prec.* Cap*itulum*
xii *mar.* CS, Cap*itulum* viij *rub. mar.* MO; cam] þere *add.* J; hire] þe S;
comaundement] of þe lady dame Gracedieux *add.* S. 259 whiche] the whilke
J; haue spoke] spake of J, of *add.* M; he] thylke GS. 260 þat on] þe MO;

þe] þat S;   same] forsayde J;   water] and *add.* JM;   he] *prec.* hic baptiȝatur *rub.*
mar. MO.   261 me²] þare *add.* J;   thryes] þer S.   262 Grace] dieu *add.*
JMS, Gracia dieu O;   me¹] *om.* J;   of] *ins.* (*and ins. mar.* G³) G, *om.* JMO;
nothing] nouȝt MO.   263 sithe] seynede J, sithen MO;   ledde] he ladde
JMOS;   þer is] was JMO.   264 noble] fayre J;   and] in O;   fair] nobille J;
Grace] dieu *add.* JMOS;   me] *om.* MO.   265 semblaunt] ȝe mekille *add.* J.
266 many ... me²] and teche me many thinges J;   many] grete *add.* M;   me²] *om.*
MO.   267 riht] *om.* J.   268 þus] þis S;   I¹ ... anoon] Anone I sawe many
mervayles J.   269 þat I ne] that ne I J, þen I MO;   seye] of *add.* J;   Sithe]
puis F, *om.* JMO, sauf S.   271 my] -n C;   leiser] space M.   272 inouh]
ryght I nowe J, how þe pilgrym saw þe signe of tav · paynted with reede blode in
the temple *add. rub.* M, Of þe sightes wheche I seghe in þe hous where dame Grace
dieux ledde me to *add.* S.   273 First] *prec.* Capitulum xiii *mar.* CS, Capitulum ix
rub. mar. MO, hic describit templum *rub. mar.* MO;   þilke] that JMOS;   as] hit
were *add.* J.   274 Thau] *followed by the sign* J.   275 which] the whilke J.
276 amyddes] amydde G, ymyddes JMO.   277 meetinge] metayle J;   þat] hit
S.   278 Aaron] -es GS;   Moyses] -es GS, Episcopus *rub. mar.* MO;   him]
hem S.   279 in his hand] ayerde S;   a yerde] in his hand S;   his²] *om.* J.
280 he hadde] *trs.* J;   lynene] clath *add.* J;   trowe] -de J.   281 of sooth] *om.*
JMO;   þat] *om.* J;   he] hit J;   were] was JMO;   thilke] that JMO³ (*ins.* O³);
of which] *om.* JMO;   speketh] spake JMO.   282 his] the J;   ix] ij J, nyenteþe
S;   chapitre] of his prophesye *add.* J;   folkes forhedes] forhedys of the folke J,
forhede of þe folk M, forhededis of þo folke O;   holi] signe of *add.* J.
283 whiche] the whilke J;   It] 2 confirmacioun *rub. mar.* M, 2 confirmacio *rub.*
mar. O.   284 bi] *om.* S;   benigne] benyngne (*3rd* n *ins.*) J.   285 with] bi C.
285-7 With ... forhed] *ins. mar.* G³.   286 þilke] that JMO;   made] hym *add.*
JMO;   marke] -d S;   me²] *om.* J.   287 þe] *om.* MO;   wel] grete J.
288 congruitee] Of specialle oynementes whilk was bitakyn to an Officiall *add. rub.*
M, howe þe hoolye · oynementes were taken to þe officyale · for þe general heele of
alle þoo *þat* wolde · lyve affter þe doctrine of þe fayre lady Dame Grace dieux *add.*
S.   289 Afterward] AFter S, *prec.* Capitulum xiv *mar.* GS, capitulum x *rub.*
mar. MO;   þat¹] *om.* JMO;   þilke] that JMO, þe S;   maister] or vicare over C³;
made] make J;   þat²] the whilke J, whilk MS.   290 in] *om.* JMO.   291 þat]
om. JMO;   take] betake J;   folk] ?-es G.   292 With] tria vnguenta *rub. mar.*
MO;   tweyne] twa JMO.   294 woundede] woundes J;   þilke] alle tha J.
295 havinge] any *add.* S.   296 counfort] of the lyfe here *add.* J;   oynement]
-es MO;   shalt] do *add.* S.   296-7 and ... hem²] *om.* M.   297 suer] *partly*
erased (with er. mar. C³) C;   enoyntinge] enoygnt O;   oueral] *om.* JM, and O.
298 þerof] þere for *alt.* þere of M;   certeyn] Sothely J;   gret] *om.* JMO;   neede
... pilgrimes] alle Pilgrimis nede J.   299 walkers] that walkis JMO;   þat ... bi]
in JMO;   þei] þo MO.   300 more] *om.* O;   þat þei] that ne thay J, þen þei
MO;   ne beeth] moste nedes be J, be MO.   301 ofte] -tymes J, offten S;
iled] ledde JMO;   neede þei] þayme nedes J, *trs.* MO, extrem vntion *add. mar.*
O³;   haue] to have JMO, it *add.* MO (*can.* M).   302 Now] Loke thowe J.
302-3 withoute failinge] on alle wise J, withouten faile MO (with *ins.* O³).
303 for] *om.* O;   þe] this JMO.   304 meward] I kepe *add.* JO, my warde I
kepe M;   þe] with alle J, to O.   305 art] hurte *add.* J.   306 on] opon M;
whiche] þe whilk MO;   we] *ins.* O³;   for] the Signe of *add.* J, þe *add.* MO;   þat]
whilke JMO;   make] made J;   forhedes] forhede M.   307 execucioun] of
thise *add.* J, and *add.* MO.   308 Now ... þe] kepe the nowe wele J;   to ... ne]
ne to mewarde J, to me warde nor M, (no *alt.* ne O), *om.* S.   308-9 misdoo

nouht] *om.* S, Here Resou*n* techis officialles and vicares to be mercifull to þere subgett*es*, And also what bitokenes a bisshopp*es* Miter*e* · and whi his staff is crokyd *add. rub.* M, Howe þe lady resoune as þey speken þus to gedire of þeyre oynementes · came adovne and comuned *with* hem of dyuers matters *add.* S. 310 As] *prec.* Cap*itulum* xv *mar.* CS, ca*pitulum* xi *rub. mar.* MO; speken] ware this spekande J, spak MO; þus] *om.* J, to gedirs *add.* S; bitwixe] betwene GS; tweyne] twa JMO. 311 mayden] mayde GS; doun] adovne S; toward] -s GS. 312 þat] the whilke J, which S; cleped] callede JMO; as] and J; Grace] dieu *add.* JMOS; me] bifore and *add.* J; bigan] Lady Reason, the handmayd to grace. *add. mar.* O³. 313 speke] no*ta per* Shir{ley} *add. mar.* S; withoute] *om.* J, any *add.* MO; flateringe] on this wise J. 314 and holden] Vnderstandis JMO. 315 youre] the J; parlement] spekynge J. 316 now] *om.* J; two] MO, (o *erased* C), twey GS, *om.* J; þat ... haue] *om.* J; vnclosed] *om.* J, enclosyd O; yow] *om.* J, to þowe M. 317 softe] a soft M; to¹] forto C; wounde] a wounde J, vnguentu*m rub. mar.* M, N*ota bene* istud capit*ulum* vnquentum *rub. mar. and marked* O. 318 shitte] close J; Softe] -ly J, -yd O; it] *om.* O; euene] *erased* C; instrument] *o. er.* O. 319-20 and ... mysbifalleth] (and ... mys- *on additional line* O³. 319 a] *om.* O; softe¹] pleyne S; to] *em. ed.* of to GCS, ofte Sithis ou*er* J, oft to M, oft O. 320 rudeshipe] reddour JMO; mysbifalleth] *em. ed.* mys bifalleth CG, fallith amisse J, mys fallis MO, yt befalletþe offt amisse S; he] thylke GS. 321 rudeshipe] ruydnes J. 321-2 sumtime ... helpe] (time ... helpe *ins. mar.* O³), of *add.* O; hurte more] *trs.* S. 322 þan] þe medecyne of *add.* S; shulde] wolde S; þilke] Thaye J, þoo MO; ben¹] buþ (*with* beeþ *mar.* G³) G. 323 lyouns] lyoune S; thoruh] thurghly J; hem] alle *add.* C. 324 anything] Ony JMO; levinge] letinge C, benignite JMO; no] not O. 325 ne leches] *om.* JMO; ne²] nor MO. 326 to¹] ou*er* J. 327 þerfore I] *trs.* J; descendid and comen] com*men* and descende MO; avise] teche *over* C, warne J; you] and to conseile þowe *add.* M. 328 ne¹] nor M, no O; ne felnesse] *om.* JMO; beeth] luke ȝe be J, ȝhe *add.* MO. 329 folk] -es S; softe] trete thayme alle J. 330 Treteth hem alle] softly and J, entreteth hem alle S; oynement] -es JMO. 331 bithinke] vm- J; were] offt *add.* S. 332 and] eke *add.* S. 333 crueltee any time] ja mais cruaute F, any crueltee C; not] to *add.* J. 335 harmes] -se M; to] ? noat *add. mar.* O³. 336 him] selfe wreke and *add.* J; alle] *om.* J; vengeaunce] JMO, -s CGS. 337 bineme] reve JMO; him] fro hym MO; to] tylle ane J; he may] schalle he J, he shal MO; come] tourne S. 338 spoken] y spoken G; þe] hic e*piscopus describitur rub. mar.* O; whiche] whame JMO; seide] spake of J, haue saide MOS. 339 bifore] *illegible word o. er. add.* O³; hire] *om.* J, hym O; if] and O. 340 can] deeme *add.* S; hed] thus *add.* J. 341 Is it] I Suppose hit is J; not] but *add.* JO, quod scho bot *add.* M; for to] til *add.* S. 342 dedes] doers JMO; shulde] Schalle JMO; putte and] *om.* J; hurtle] hurtille J, hurt ill doars M, hurt yll O; þe yuel] and ill M. 343 folk] -es GS; hornes] hondes S; hem] raþer *add.* S; ende] of my ȝerde *add.* J. 344 þe] *om.* J; oynement] -es JO. 345 now] *om.* JMO. 346 wel] *om.* J; hast²] *prec.* Reason in religion, or þe duty of a Bishope *mar.* O³. 347 shuldest] schalle JMO; þow] the JMO; ouhtest] awȝte JMO. 348 wite] bath *add.* J; to¹] forto J; hurtle] hurtille JO, hurt M. 349 hem¹] the JM, þe *alt.* þem O; erre] here O; sithe] then JMO. 351 þin] ane J, of *add. can.* O; office] Officiale JMO; to²] for til S; iustice] correcceiou*n* J; of] to J; wikkede] ill M. 352 be¹] þou *add.* S; oþer] eyther G, ovyr J, owthir MO. 353 ferþere] Overe J, firþermore S. 354 hurtled] hurtyd M, ehurtled *with* S; wyght] with J.   356 þouh] all thowgh GS, ȝif alle JMO;   for²] forto J;   iustice] doo ryght J.   357 þin] thy JMO;   herte] Noat. mar. O³ *and in other hand:* þe councell of grace, by Reason hir handmayd deliuered to þe Ministerye. mar. O³; hast] haues MO.   358 iuged] in gyde MO;   were¹] was JMO;   anoynted ... þow] *om.* J;   were²] *om.* J, was M.   359 and² ... haddest²] or JMO.   360 any] eyther GS, othir*e add.* MO;   softe] to Softe JMOS.   361 wolt] schulde J; wyght] man J;   þow ... not] Also soo J, Also MO;   also] þow scholde nouȝt JMO.   363 more] Soo JMO;   þan] as J;   þilke] he JMO;   whos] was JO; art] and *add.* J.   364 horned²] and *add.* JMO;   þat] which S.   365 made] þe childer of *add.* JS;   to] *om.* GS;   thoruh þe see] þe see thoroughe S;   þat²] for S.   366 yerde] whilke *add.* J, þat *add.* MO;   held] in his hande *add.* J; he] *om.* J;   Now vndirstone] *trs.* J.   367 to þee woorth] woorth to þee C, nota *per* Shirle{y} mar. S; þouh] Of J.   368 al] smethe and *add.* J.   369 withinne] in *add.* O; whateuere] whate Sum eu*ere* J;   Fallas] and feynynge behufes *add.* J, Deceyte M, -s S.   370 þou] the J;   miht] *om.* J;   misdoinge] and *add.* JMO; þin] þi MO.   371 and] *om.* J;   debonayre] *om.* J, þin *add. can.* M;   þin] in O.   372 yerde sharp] *trs.* MO;   also ... is] how it is al so GJMO;   and] *om.* S.   373 stowpeth] stowpande JMO;   toward] -es S;   Dowte] the *add.* J, But S; þat(2) ... ne] that ne that J, þen · þat MO.   374 tokeneth] bitokenethþ at (bi*can.*) C, bitokenes MO;   in þee] mekenesse J;   humblesse] in the J, mekenes MO;   whan þou] *om.* O.   chastisest] chastise JO, chastysed S.   375 Now vnderstond] *trs.* J;   þilke] the JMO.   376 þee¹] to the J;   þi] *om.* O.   377 make] to make S;   passe] to Passe J;   thoruh] þee *add.* S;   foorde] See J; þis] (is *o.er.* O);   world] (ld *o. er.* C).   378 shuldest] schall O;   þer] þou S; oþer] eyther G.   379 eiþere] owþere JMOS.   380-1 þi name] is JM (is *ins.* M).   381 is] thy name JM;   Now vnderstonde] *trs.* J;   it] *om.* J.   382 Now] ȝit J, Why pontifex. *and in another hand:* Note mar. O³, pontifex i*d est* mar. S;   I wule] *trs.* J;   þee yit] alitelle J;   vnderstonde to me] take tente vnto me J, to me take tent MO.   382-3 a litel] *om.* J.   383 whi²] an *add.* S.   383-4 horned ... hast] thyne heued is hornede J, þou haues a hornyd hede MO.   384 Sumtime] Com tyme *with scribe's guide* c *visible* O;   in þis place] right here J; riht heere] in this howse J;   enhabited] wonnyd M;   hornede] deuyll *add.* M.   385 helle] feonde *add.* S;   bi possessioun] *om.* J;   hadde] *om.* J, he hade *add.* S; heere] by Christ our head, & captain, we haue gott, a good possession mar. O³.   386 his] *om.* O;   to] *om.* JO.   386-7 þat ... þerinne] *om.* JMO.   387 made] gerte J, mayd (d *ins.* O³) O.   388 þese] *om.* JMO;   made] gerte J, mayd (d *ins.* O³) O;   take] deliu*ere* J;   yerde] (*2nd* e *ins.* G³).   389 vntrewe] vtruwe S; þat²] which S.   390 hurtledest] hurtellest S;   puttest] putte JM, puttyd O.   391 place] dedica*c*io templi *rub.* mar. M, hic dedecacio templi *rub. mar.* O;   þow] *om.* J;   þi] thyne G.   392 madest] gerte J;   him] *om.* M;   ysen] issir F, goon C, prese JMO;   tweyne] twey GS, fayre J, two MO;   faire] twa J, *om.* S.   393 hanginge] pendans F, hongyn (*with* hongynge mar. G³) G, that hynges JMO; þi] -ne C, the J;   tweyne] twey G, twa JMO;   hornes] betakenes that *add.* J, bitokenys *add.* MO.   394 and¹] the *add.* JMO;   and²] the *add.* J;   þat] *om.* M.   395 was] *om.* M; whan] *om.* M;   dediedest] *om.* JMO, dyedest S;   and¹] *om.* JMO.   396 þat] *om.* JM;   were] was J.   398 þat¹] *om.* G, in the whilke J, whilk M, in wyche O;   were] was JMO;   victour] *om.* O;   inne] *om.* J, and *add.* MO;   tokne] takynge J, tokenynge M.   400 þilke vntrewe] þou discumfitede J, þe vntrew MO;   þat] *om.* JMO;   þou ... discoumfyted] the vntrewe J;   and¹] *om.* M;   hurtled] hurtid M.   401 beten] betyd O;   be] to be JMO (*u.v.* to *alt. illegible* O);   customere] custume S;   þereas] thare whare JMO.   402 to¹]

in S;   nih] redy J, new M.   403 in alle¹] *om.* J;   ayens] ageyne JMOS;
þilke] alle þay J.   404 and] *om.* S.   405 bi¹] thurgh J;   violences] violence
JOS; bi³] *om.* JMO.   406 þerof] þer þe self grauntest hem S;   as] *om.* J, os O;
I wot wel] wille I wete J;   of] *om.* J, for MO;   sooth] *om.* J;   wel] *om.* M.
407 þiself] was the firste that *add.* J, þou *add.* O;   grauntest] grantede JMO;
hem] hym MO;   shewest] schewede JMO.   410 þi] *Episcopi cornua similia
testudini spatiantur (? spaciantur ? spaciosa) rub. mar.* O;   staf] ȝerde J;   þine]
Thy JO;   a] *ins.* O.   411 for] fro O;   straw] sta O;   felt] fled O;   it] touche
hem *add.* S, how curates shuld kepe þere kirkes *add. rub.* M, Loo here howe saint
Thomas with þe right of his horned mytre and his staffe defended þe Right of the
chirche ageynst þe kynge *add.* S.   412 Seynt] *prec. Capitulum* xvi *mar.* CS,
capitulum xii *rub. mar.* MO;   Thomas] of Cauntirbery *add.* J;   which] that J,
hornys *add.* O, whane he S.   413 strongliche] stalworthly J, *ins. mar.* O³;   þe¹]
þe *add.* S.   414 wrongfulliche] wrangwysely J;   make it] have made hit JS,
makyd O, *Sanctus Thomas cantuarensis rub. mar.* MO.   415 þer it shulde]
whare alle waye JMO, þer as hit schoulde S;   alwey] it schulde JMO;   be]
holden *add.* S;   wurthi] *ins. mar.* O³.   416 thral] a thral S;   Of] *om.* J.
417 also] I seye þee S;   I sey þee] *om.* J, also S;   þat] *om.* J, which S;   ayens]
Agayne JMO;   emperoures] the emperour JMO.   418 emperises] the emperice
JMO;   was ... þerof] Alane was lorde J, was lorde þer MO;   alone] þerof J;
paleys] Place JMO,   419 he] *id est* ambrose *over* C, sanctus ambrose *add. mar.*
G³, *Sanctus Ambrosius rub. mar.* MO;   toures] castelles J;   castelles] towres J;
and] *om.* J.   420 citees] wíth *add.* C, and ȝour townes and *add.* J;   þe] hoole
add. S;   reuenewes] reuenant J, retenews OS;   wel] this J;   þis] welle J.
421 yow] and *add.* JMO;   of myn hous] nouȝt to entermete ȝowe J, of my hows
MO, ne *add.* S;   medle ye nouht] of myn howse J, entermett þow nouȝt MO;
me] for *add.* J, to me S.   422 In my tyme] *om.* MO.   423 leese] to leese S;
þe] my JMO;   þese] This mann JMO;   hadden] hadde JMO;   not] no M;
hornes] of A Snayle *add.* JMO;   ne ne] ne CJ, nor MO.   424 beren hem
nouht] he hadde nouȝt his hornes J, he bare þem noȝt MO;   resoun] cause J, skell
MO;   also] on the same wise J.   425 horned] meaneing ye church, *and in a
later hand not mar.* O³, ehorned S;   defendinge] of *add.* JMO;   vsages] vsage
JMO.   426 and¹] Et F, can. C, *om.* J;   on] opon M.   427 vsedest] vsede
JMO;   argudest] repriued J;   Pharaon] Pharoon *alt.* Pharaon C;   seynge]
biddande J.   428 suffrede] Suffre JMO.   429 lettede hem not] *om.* JMO;
ne¹] opresse thaym, nouȝt MO;   oppressed] nouȝt J, opresse M;   ne²] nor MO;
greued] greve JM;   of] on J.   430 nothing] na kynne wise J;   þou] *om.* S;
seruedest] Servede JMO.   431 hire¹] a J;   shulde] þowe *add.* JMO.   432 þee]
Soo *add.* J;   armed] harmede J;   Now do] *trs.* J;   hensforward] heynforwarde
J.   433 þe] *om.* O; grettere] weel phareon seying him þat he suffred · þy folk
serue god withouten thraldome and þat he letted hem nought ne oppressed hem ne
greued hem of nothing *add. repeating a line above* S, Loo howe þofficyall by *vertu*
of his oygnementz · knytt man · and woman to gedirs lawfully whyles þey lyve *add.*
S.   434 As] *prec. Capitulum* xvii *mar.* CS, *capitulum* xiii *rub. mar.* MO,
Matrimonium rub. mar. MO, þAnne S;   resoun ... þus] (spa *o. er.* C), spake dame
Resoun þus S.   435 in] *ins.* O³.   436 saaf] warde *add.* JM, sauftee S;
sithe] than JMO, afftir þat S;   toward] commande fra J, -es S.   437 toward]
fra J, -es S;   est] and *add.* J;   þat] thay J, whilk M; boþe] *om.* S.   438 anoon.
And] *trs.* M;   eche] aythere JM;   his] thaire JMO, right *add.* J.   439 and¹]
om. J;   ioyned] ioynande J;   togidere] -s GS;   sithe] Seyne JMO, *om.* S;   hem]
þus *add.* M, *om.* S.   440 tweyne] twa JMO;   iche] aithere JM.   441 bere]

be JMO; trowthe] trewe JMO; Neuere dayes] Neueraday J, Neuerday MO.
442 shal] shal add. S; departinge be maad] be made depertynge J, be departynge
made MO; tweyne] twa JMO; but] 3if add JMO. 443 cause] -s M; and]
that schalle be discussede and demede add. J, foundyn M, om. S; bi ... þat] om.
S; is] be O, om. S; is þere] o.er. it be so add. o. er. C, om. S; Now] om. J.
444 sacrament] made þer by Moyses add. S; loueth] lyevys J; yow] om. J, to
add. O; togideres] to gedir JMOS; And] so add. S. 445 tweyne] bathe J,
two MO, om. S; beheighten] heyght JMO; so shulden] shulde do soo J, schuld
O. 446 departeden] so add. S; þens] theym ·/ than J. 447 yit] ryghte J.
448 togederes] to gedyr JMO; and] om. J; speken] Spekande sammene J, spake
MO. 449 maden] þayme add. JMO; cesse] to ceesse J; here ... anoon]
anane of theyre speche J. 450 þei] alle add. S; maden him requeste] besought
him J, made hir request S. 450-1 sum ... hous] he Wolde grawnte thaym J.
451 he ... hem²] Sum Office or sum Servise in his hous J; hem¹] to þem MO,
how þe sacrament of ordres is giffyn and what it is add. rub. M. 452 And] om.
JMO, prec. Capitulum xviii mar. CG, capitulum xiv rub. mar. M, ordo rub. mar. M,
Ordination Sunday o. er. of rub. mar. O³; he] Moises JMO; peyre] of add.
JMS; made] gerte J. 453 neer] telle J; in] om. JMO. 454 hem] to
hem C; God] om. JMO. 455 wise] Howe Raysoune þanne vpon hir langage
speke to hem add. S; Whan] prec. Capitulum xix mar. CG, Capitulum xviii mar.
S. 456 Resoun] Anane J; droowh] resoun J; hire] drewe J, nere M;
anoon] hir J; hem] him S. 457 quod she] scho saide MO; entendeth]
herkynneth J, 3he add. MOS. 458 hider] me and taketh hede to my wordys J;
what] o. er. C, so add. J, prec. Resoun mar. O³. 459 þouh] If al M; shoren]
schavyne J, eshore S; fooles] om. M. 460 for] And S. 461 to be alwey]
alwey to beo S; freend] ageynes add. J; whosoeuere] all tha þat J; hath] haue
GMOS, þerto J; þerto] has J. 462 þis] my J; alle] othere add. J. 463 If]
but 3if J; ne] om. JO; on] in C, of JMO; yowre] awne add. J. 464 haue]
ins. mar. G³. 465 whom] whilk MO; discerned] (with disseueryd mar. G³),
disceuered CJ, Discerne (variants Dessepares GM¹, Departis A) F; from] fra
JMO. 466 and] om. JS; oonliche] Namlye J, om. S; shule²] should S, prec.
nota de racione rub. mar. MO. 467 wole] wolden GS; mown] Mowe ins.
mar. G³, mow MO, om. S; avaunte] a want O, avaunce S. 468 ye be] bot 3e
er JM, bot 3e O; as¹] om. S; doumbe bestes] trs. JM, bestys doyn O. 468-
9 þat ben cloþed] om. JMO. 469 shul] shoulde S. 470 wole] wulleþ GS,
wille JMO, wol eyþer (eyþer o. er.) C; jugementes] om. JMO. 471 me] id est
resoun over C, with scilicet Resoun mar. G³; shul ye] trs. JMO. 472 þat] it
add. C, om. JMO; ne ... confusioun] om. JMO. 472-3 I wule] id est resoun
over C, with scilicet Resoun mar. G³, trs. J. 473 yow] om. O; wite] wate
JMO; it] om. J; keepe] prec. nota rub. mar. O³. 475-6 turne to flight] to fle
J. 477 voide] to voide C; which] the whilke J. 478 al] waye add. J;
soone] maketh me J; maketh me] sone J; voide] to voide JMO. 479-
80 and ... Rose] om. J. 479 se] it mare open add. S; þe] faire add. C.
480 fro] -m GS. 481 þese] þiere M, þe O, om. S; ye] wole add. o. er. into
mar. C; loue] o. er. into mar. C; and ... also] om. S. 482 not him] trs. J;
to] my J; abaundoneth] gyevis J, bewys MO; vices] vice MO, prec. nota quid
significat tonsura rub. mar. MO, Yit 3ee may see firþermore howe raysoun spekeþe
to hem add. S. 483 Yit] prec. Capitulum xx mar. CG, Capitulum xix mar. S;
I wole] trs. J. tweyne ... woordes] of 3owre crowne that es schavene J, of þe schorn
place MO, twey short wordes S. 483-4 of ... place] twa Schorte Wordes JMO.
484 which] It JMO; round] om. S. 484-5 aboute ... seercle] om. S.

485 þouh] *om.* JMO.   486 enclosed] *om.* JMO.   487 vnheled] vn coverde J, vnhilled MOS;   sheweth] wel *add.* MO;   yowre] owre O.   487-8 al holliche] *Om.* O.   488 any] *om.* J;   mene] moien F, me*n*nes J, *om.* M, men O; empechement] impedyment M.   488-2 þe ... wite] *om.* S.   489 sercle] þat *add. o. er.* C;   aboute] sheweth *add. o. er. (with u.v.* sheweth *mar.* C³) C; þat] *o. er.* C;   ye] *o. er.* shuld *add. o. er.* C.   489-90 haue no cure] *o. er.* C, rekke nou3t J (cure *alt.* care O).   490 from] fra JMO;   him] *(with* hytt *mar.* G³), it CJMO.   491 with ... god] 3e wille have parte J;   ye¹ ... parte] with godde J, ye wil haue part M;   not] inded ye Minstres, are, or shoud be, god*es* heritage *mar.* O³;   boþe] *om.* O.   492 tweyne] *om.* J, two MO;   togideres] to gedyr J;   þat ... wel] wete 3e wele forsoth J;   haue] *om.* J.   493 ye haue] hase 3e J, had MO;   chosen] 3ow *add.* JM, schosyn 3ow O, *om.* S;   to¹] be 3o*ur add.* J;   to²] *om.* J.   494 bi] þe M;   se nouht] can nou3t See J, say nought M.   495 reioyse] 3ow *add.* JMO;   world] *om.* O;   wole] have *add.* J.   495-6 I ... al] he may nou3t have alle as I vndirstande J.   496 not] þat M, þat noght O;   taketh] take JMO.   497 leueth] lefe JMO;   Now taketh] *trs.* J.   498 mown] myght JMO;   Suffice it oughte] It aught to suffise yowe JM, It a*u*ght to suffice O.   499 doute] hit *add.* JMO;   þat] ne *add.* J, þan MO;   þilke] that JMO;   part] may 3ee not haue and it *add.* S;   ne] *om.* JMO.   500 Fair] *(with* fayerer *mar.* O³);   to yow þanne] than to 3owe J;   þe] la F, þis C.   500-1 and ... in] alwaye JMO.   501 from] fro alle JMO.   502 departeth] depertande J;   Of] Du F, *er.* C, *om.* JMO;   shorn] Schavene J;   is also] *trs.* J.   503 men apperceyuen] p*er*sayves men J, men p*er*ceyues MO;   ye] þe C;   goode] godde es J, goddis MO;   heerdes] men *add. mar.* O³.   504 wel] goddes es J, gude MO;   heerde] hirdman M, herdiman O;   flees] fleces J.   505 bestes] schepe J.   505-6 for ... may] *om.* J.   505 his] for hys *add. can.* O;   yowre] þoure C, þe MO.   506 at] as O;   his] is O;   skorche] fla JM, sla O;   yow] thay*m* J;   is] he J, it is M;   not yiue] has no J;   him] *om.* JMO.   507 men] þere J, al MO;   han] ar J, is MO;   al] *om.* JMO;   sheres] schris O, þe shereres S.   508 shere] clippe J;   yow] *om.* J, lawfully rightfully and *add.* S;   with] *om.* MOS;   dueliche] Howe diu*er*se offices where distribute to diu*er*se men in holy kirke *add. rub.* M, Howe Moyses · sone affter þat Raysone hade þus spoken · made and ordeyned diuers officiers here filowing *add.* S.   509 Whan] *prec.* Cap*itulum* xxi *mar.* CGS *(? xx* S), cap*itulum* xv *rub. mar.* MO;   hise] *o. er.* C, thayme that ware J;   shorene] *o. er.* C, schavene J.   510 to] tille J;   weren] was MO;   yaf] þay*m add.* J, gaf gaf O;   seruices] servise JM, se*r*uce O.   511 gladliche] *om.* J;   he] be J;   priuees] pryuee S, huissiers F, p*r*inces CJMO;   of] in S.   512 and¹] some he made his *add.* S.   513 putte] to putte J;   þe¹] *om.* JMO;   þe²] *om.* J.   514 to alle] *om.* J.   515 yaf] thay*m*e *add.* J;   to¹] for to MO;   paleys] place JMO.   516 Goddes] godde is J;   lawe] worde S;   made] forto *add.* JMO, til *add.* S.   517 þer] whare JMO;   To] vnto M.   518 took] gave J;   which] þe which C;   his] is S.   519 þerwith] with J;   To] *om.* J.   520 bere] to bere JMO;   oo] *om.* J.   521 þer] as *add.* S;   was] that J;   þat] the whilke J;   to] forto J.   522 with] þei *add. o. er.* C, he *add.* M, we *add.* O;   þilke] þere J, þoo M, Too O;   he wolde] *trs.* J;   bi] in JMO.   523 serueres] Seruandis J, se*r*uant3 MS.   524 coadiutowres] coadjuteurs F, coadiusteurs G, coadmynistroures S, Howe þe officiers maden redy · by þe comandement of Raysoun *add.* S.   525 Whan] *prec.* Cap*itulum* xxii *mar.* CGS;   aboue diuised] *trs.* J.   526 eche] ilkane JM; to serue] *om.* MO;   to deserue] *om.* J;   office] and *add.* M;   þe] To þe CJMOS *(into mar.* C).   527 maden] alle *add.* J.   528 Summe] of hem *add.* S; ooþere] some S;   aboue] vpon the Burde J, opon MO.   529 ooþere] some S;

þe¹] *om.* JS;   casten] putte JMS.   530 þerwith] *with u.v.* to m*ar.* C³, þerto
JMO;   a litel water] thay did J;   þei dide] a litille watere J.   531 he] þei C;
wente] -n C;   him] *om.* S.   532 of] *om.* S;   abiden] habade J, a dydid O;
yit] fully *add.* J.   533 þilke] thase J, þo M;   officialles] official O, officiers S.
534 wel] mekille JMO.   535 nouht] *om.* J;   hows] with outen more helpe ·
And all þis I biheld and mykill more whilk we*re* tediouse for me to tell · and also
somwhat noyuse to þe herers *add.* M, Now take heede · howe Moyses cleped Grace
dieux *add.* S.   536 Now] *prec.* Capitulum xxiii *mar.* CGS, ca*pitulum* xvi *rub.*
mar. MO, Sacerdociu*m rub. mar.* MO;   I wole] *trs.* J;   clepede] callede JM.
537 hauteyn] haultaine F, ha*unteyn* C, hye JMO;   al ... it] ʒit alle J, þof al þat M;
was] ware J.   538-9 and¹ ... feet] *om.* S.   539 feet] face J;   was] fulle *add.*
J;   and²] fulle *add.* J.   540 she¹] *with scilicet* grace dieu *mar.* G³;   hire] *o. er.*
grace dieu *over* C³;   cleped] *o. er.* C, callede JMO;   ros] reysede J.   541-
2 and² ... ledde] *om.* JMO.   542 me] *o. er.* id est pilgrim *over* (*with er. mar.* C³)
C, me F, hym GS (*marked for gloss* G³), *om.* JMO.   543 þat þat] þat O.
544 shortlyche] Howe Grace dieux tooke hem · þe keyes · and þe swerde · þat
cherubyne · hade *add.* S;   First] *prec.* Capitulum xxiv *mar.* CGS;   anoynede] *em.*
ed., ioynede CGJOS, tuke M (*see note*).   545 and ... hem] *om.* J;   togideres] to
gedere JMO;   sithe] and Seyne J, he *add.* JMO.   546 kervinge] trenchau*nt* J;
cleer] bright J;   and¹] *om.* JMO, wel *add.* S.   547 tweyne] twey GJMO;
and¹ ... variable] turnande and Variable and ryght hansum J.   548 thouhte]
that *add.* JMO;   was] *ins.* M;   þilke] þat Swerde J, that MO;   hadde seyn]
Sawe JMO.   549 holde] have in his hande by alle manere of figure and schappe
J;   þilke] So J, þat MO;   it] is O;   treweliche] *om.* JS;   wel] *om.* J, full MO;
propirliche] *om.* J.   550 figured] *om.* J;   þilke] that JMO;   hem¹] *om.* JMO;
þerof] made thay*me* a p*re*sente J.   550-1 made hem present] þe*re* of J.
551 þat¹] he *add. can.* C;   þat²] whilke J, which þat S.   552 take] *prec.* Claues
rub. mar. MO;   Grace] *om.* JMO, dieux *add.* S;   hireself] *prec.* ? accusence *mar.*
C³;   whiche] that J.   552-3 þat ... him] to helpe hym at do this J.   553 hem¹]
þen M;   hem²] on this wise J.   555 into] in JMO;   of] *om.* JMO.   556 I¹]
pilgrime *over* C, *with scilicet* pylgrym *mar.* G³;   þilke] that JMO.   557 what]
I *add.* S.   558 haue þus lost] thus hafe loste J, haue lost þus M;   þilke] ʒone
JM, ʒow O;   hath] have J;   hire] *om.* J.   559 þese] þie*re* MO;   officialles]
officialle O;   to be ded] have diede J, be dede O.   560 he] to S;   had] haue S;
me] any *add.* S;   swich] þis J, slilk M;   wrong] awronge S, Reson p*re*ches vnto
p*re*stes and telles more of a threfolde swerde *add. rub.* M, Loo here may yee seo
howe Grace dieux · reproueth þe pilgryme of his lewed opynyoun*e add.* S;   Whan]
prec. Capitulum xxv *mar.* CGS, ca*pitulum* xvii M.   561 discounforted]
myscomfortede J;   of] atte JS, on M.   562 sithe] than JMO, *om.* S;   clepede]
Scho callede J, callid MO, *om.* S;   me] *om.* S;   and] *om.* S;   Fool] quod cho
add. J.   563 Wenest] wenys (*with* weenest *mar.* O³) O;   for] *om.* JMO;   aloone
to freend] to frende al by thyne ane J.   564 þow] the J;   ouhtest] awht JMO;
wite] to wete JMOS;   commune] the comen JMO, conune S.   565 welle]
wille J;   grettere] bettere JMO;   þer] whare J.   566 wille] welle J.
568 oon] dare S;   dar] noone S;   neighe] ne *add.* CS, ne *ins. mar.* G³;   approche]
come nere JMO.   569 þat] so *add.* CJMOS, so *ins. mar.* G³, que (*variant* si *L*)
F;   profitable] p*ro*rofitable O;   delitable] delectabille JMO.   569-70 þe ...
alone] schalle neu*ere* the watere be J, shal be þe wat*er* MO.   570 ne ... be] that
þowe has alane JM, þu has allon O;   þilke] that JMO;   be²] that *add. can.* .G;
þer] whare JMO;   goth] to *add.* CJ (*o. er. with er. mar.* C3).   571 am] þe *add.*
M, þe *add. ins.* O³;   goodnesses] goodschepes GOS, goodnesse JM;   Neuere] I

halde me JMO; holde I me] neue*re* JMO. 572 enclosed] closede J.
573 loue] as *add.* M; peramowres] *prec.* waters of lyfe, grace þe fountayne *mar.*
O³; þerinne] in that JMO; mihte þou] I maye J, þou may MO; nothing] no
gude M. 574 it] (t *ins.* O³); good] gudnes M; þilke] *om.* J. 574–5 I ...
loue] *om.* S. 575 I wole] *trs.* J; freendes²] þat *add.* M. 576 be] thynke
JMO; me thinketh] grace dieu *over* C, *with scilicet* grace dieu *mar.* G³; Now]
Luke thowe J. 577 þouh] ȝif JMO; be freend] *trs* .MO; to] tille JS.
578 I] pilg*ri*m *over* C, *with scilicet* pylg*ry*m *mar.* G³; I ... Grace] Grace hadde thus
comfortid me Agayn J, dieu *add.* MOS; þat] and I J, þus *add.* M. 579 avised] *id
est* tauht *over* C, saide to M; anoon] *om.* J; þe] *om.* MO. 580 to] and
JMOS; preche] and þus she seyde *add.* S, Takeþe heede heere howe dame
Raysoune · entreþe þe chayer to preeche *add.* S; Lordinges] *prec.* Cap*itulum* xxvi
mar. CGS, Racio p*ra*edicat sacerdotibus *rub. mar.* MO; me] for *add.* J. 581 þer-
inne] there as J; Biholdeth] ȝhe *add.* MO. 582 goodshipe] lordship S,
goodnesse C. 583 descended] to yowe and *add.* S; for] fro O. 584 Con-
sidereth] ȝhe *add* MO; bi hire] þat *add. ins.* C, Moyses haþe dep*ar*ted S; Moises
... departed] by hir S. 585 yow¹] to þowe MS; for] fro O, *om.* S; þe ...
yow²] *om.* S; hadde] *om.* JMO. 586 for¹] fro O; him] selfe *add.* J; with]
om. M; entrede] entre JMO. 587 of whiche] whare of J, where M; Now
vnderstondeth] Resoun *over* C, *with scilicet* Resoun *mar.* G³, *trs.* J. 588 it is
perilouse] perylous it es J. 589 shulden²] *om.* JMO; vse] vsith JMO; þei]
thilke GS. 590 iii] Gladius triplex *rub. mar.* MO, ?ȝ×.ȝᵗ. gladio parcutitur *rub.
mar.* O; deserueth] seruys MO. 591 egge] -s O. 593 þat] *om.* GOS;
be] shal be S; do] *om.* J; jugement] gyffyn*e add.* J. 594 þe doinge]
execucioun J. 594 of þe execucioun] doynge J; cause] -s J; yknowe]
knawyne JMO. 595 vnknowe] nought knawen M, *om.* S; of¹] a M;
foolhardiment] fule hardynesse J. 595–6 and ...þinkinge] *om.* JMO.
597 juge] gyffe iuggemente J, do Iugement S; bi] with JMO; Michel ... swerd]
Fulle vnsittande hit es J; yuel sittinge] a Swerde J. 598 to¹] tille a J, to a
MOS; and ... man] *om.* OS; purblynd] apurblynde J, a pure blynde M; man²]
also *add.* J. 599 good] the gude JMOS; from] fra JMO; yuel] the ille J, þe
euyll MOS. 600 bere ... swerd] þilk swerde bere S; þat] *o. er. (with er. mar.*
C³) C, ȝif þat he J; cannot] *o. er.* C; wel] *o. er.* C, *om.* JMO. 601 bitwixe¹,²]
betwene GJMOS; helthe] Hele JMO; meselrie] mesehy J, miserye S.
602 lasse] leste J, mendre F, litel C; A] þe S. 603 circumstaunces]
circumstau*n*ce JMOS; þat] ar JS. 604 doo] giffen*e* J, I·gyven S; as] *o. er.*
O; clepid] *om.* JMO; departinge] a dep*ar*tynge JMO. 605 throte] the
throte JMO; þat] *om.* J; wolen wel] *om.* J, *trs.* S; iuge] *om.* JS. 606 departe
... and] *om.* S; wel] *om.* MOS; þat] Whate JMO, *þat* þat S. 607 þat] *þat*
þat S; hath] *om.* JO; allegge] So *add.* JMO; do] giff J. 608]ooþerwise]
other weys G, for no thing *add.* S, Nowe take hede what thing verrayly betokeneþe
þe twoo egges of þe swerd *add.* S. 609 Now] *prec. scilicet* Resoun *mar.* G³,
prec. Cap*itulum* xxvii CGS; I wole] *trs.* J; þe] *om.* MO; tweyne] tweye G,
twa JMO. 610 cleped] callede JM. 610–11 wherto ... telle] *om.* J.
610 wherto] wher til S; paas] place S; alone] (e. *o. er.* O), aboue S. 611 s-
ufficeth] suffice M. 613 wel] *om.* JMO. 613–14 justice in youre] *o. er.* O.
614 lond] handis that is atte Saye rightwisnes J, *o. er.* O; misdedes] mysdede
MO. 615 sinnes] Synne JMO; to] for to S; excepted] owte takyn*e* J,
except MOS. 616 þe¹] *om.* J; cas] -es J; withholden¹] reseruede J, *with*
holdyng O; þat] whilke J; horned] Saluo honore dei *mar.* O³; withholden²]
tille hym selfe *add.* J. 617 And for] *o. er. into mar.* C; þat] as michel as *o. er.*

(*with er. mar.* C³) C, *om.* JMO;   lond] handis J.   618 þe] 3oure JMO;   tweyne]
tweye G, twa JMO;   kervinges] keruyng O;   as] *om.* JMO.   619 þat oon] the
to (ii *over* G³) G;   of] and J.   620 manhede] man S;   men clepen] is callede
J, men calles MO;   man] the man JMO;   withoute] forth *add.* JMO;   and] *om.*
J.   621 is cleped] men calles JMO;   þat] this JMO.   622 in ... departed]
dep*ar*tede in twa JM, in two O;   departed] and yit *add. into mar.* C.   622–3 it
... tweyne] *om.* JMO.   623 þese] Thier MO;   tweyne] twa JMO;   Hy] haut
F, bi CG;   Justice] iugges JMO.   624 for his sinnes] *into mar.* C.   625 charge]
chastyse J;   penaunces] penau*n*ce JMOS.   626 without] out JMO;   þe¹] *om.*
J;   sinnes] And *add.* M;   cas] causes J.   627 his] *om.* J;   for] nane *add.* J.
628 amonestynge] monyschyng O.   629 bi] *o. er.* (*with er. mar.* C³) C, with
JMO.   630 and] Sothlye *add.* J;   for] *om.* S.   631 it is] is it *marked for
reversal* M;   he] it J;   drede] to drede JMO.   632 feeleth] hym hurte with
add. J;   perce] *om.* J;   on him] *om.* J;   he] hym JMO.   633 bithinke] to be
thynke J, for to bethenk S;   hym] Noat *mar.* O³;   þat] shulde *add. can.* C;   egge]
-s MO;   wel] *om.* J.   634 yow] Sothely *add.* J;   dueliche ... noon] þere can
nane Dewly Smyte *þere with* J, dewly smyte þerwith can no man MO;   haue] *om.*
M.   635 oþer] that es J: þat] *om.* S, is *add. ins.* M.   636 avised] *id est*
warned *over* C, a vised (*with* s*cilicet* warned *mar.* G³) G, first J, wernyd hym M,
warnyd O;   first] Smetyn*e* and so warnede him J, hym *add.* O;   þilke] *om.* JMO;
so] Sogatis J;   make] hem *add.* S;   deye] deede JMO.   637 þilke] that JMO;
platte] plat F, flatte CJMO;   I] *id est* resoun *over* C, *with* s*cilicet* Resou*n mar.* G³.
638 and trewe] *om.* S;   avisement] *id est* techinge *over* (*with er. mar.* C³) C.
639 smit] smytes JMOS;   þe] þere J.   640 hem] hy*m* JMO;   wel] goode
JMO;   smytinge] and *add.* J.   641 lyth] *o. er.* (*with er. mar.* C³) C, by (*with*
lyth *mar.* G³) G;   deth] drede J;   With] *om.* JMO.   642 platte] plat F, flatte
CJMO;   vsen] to smite *add. o. er.* (*with er. mar.* C³) C;   whan ... youre] *o. er.* C;
subiectes] substaunce S.   643 erre] er *alt.* or *with* x *mar.* O³, For *add.* J;
maketh] men *add. o. er.* (*with er. mar.* C³) C, manytyme J;   many times] makis
men J, many tyme men MO;   leue] to leue J, þere *add.* M.   644 and] þerfore
add. J;   so] Sogatys J;   saue] garantir F, haue C;   to] forto J.   645 sharpe]
of þe swerde *add.* M, How Reson telles whiþe swerde is called versatilis, and odire
tyme flammeus *add. rub.* M, Nowe filoweþe here · howe Grace dieux techeþe
Cherubin, whanne he shal smyte with þe flatte and wha*n*ne with þe egge of þe
swerd *add.* S;   Now] *prec.* Cap*itulum* xxviii *mar.* CGS, cap*itulum* xviii *rub. mar.*
MO;   ye hauen] *trs.* J, avez (*variant* sauez *A*, oyez *A⁴L*) F, herde *add.* JMOS;
þanne] *om.* JMO;   how] *o. er.* O.   646 cas] -es J;   of] *om.* JMO;   platte]
plat F, flatte CJMO.   647 of¹] *om.* JMO;   kervinge] egge *add.* J, eggis *add.*
MO;   of²] *om.* JMO;   wel] goode JMO; *prec.* tria iudices facient *mar.* MO;
juginge] iuggemente JMO;   oo] I *over* G³.   648 shulden¹] shoule S;   time]
om. J;   punishe] pynche O, and *add.* S.   649 anooþer] *om.* S;   time] *om.* JS;
preche] *om.* S;   cleped] callede JMO;   withoute] versatil *quare dicitur rub. mar.*
MO.   650 sides] the Sides J;   varyinge] variable and pliable J, and plyable
add. MO;   þilke] That JO;   swerd] that *add. can.* G;   is] cleped kerving and is
add. S.   651 yow] to 3owe JMO.   652 at] a O;   þat] *om.* JMO;   þe] *om.*
G.   653 and¹] as *add.* JMO;   right] euenehede JMO;   and²] *om.* S;
euenenesse] right JMO;   is¹] askes M, it O;   is²] it is CJMO (it *ins.* C).
654 hatten] haue M.   655 of¹] *om.* MO;   deuyne] devine F, demynge C,
Cherubyn sunt iudices *rub. mar.* MO.   656 not] wisdame and *add.* S.   657 þe]
om. O;   platte] plat F, flatte CJMOS.   658 kervinge] egge J.   659 correcte]
þe *add.* O.   660 in] *om.* J, mannes *add.* J.   661 not] no S;   þis] *om.* S;   in]

ane *add.* JM, a *add.* O, þe *add.* S.   661-3 and ... ye] S *repeats.*   662 is] *om.*
O; riht] wele O;   brenninge] keruyng O, cur gladius flamme*us* d*icitur rub. mar.*
M; it] was J, þat O;   was] it J;   take] to ȝowe *add.* J, takyng O.   663 is] ȝif
ȝe wille wete J;   if ... wite] is J;   it] *om.* J.   664 for] is that J;   howeuere]
howe so euere J, euer how M;   be] *om.* JMO;   it²] *om.* JMO.   664-5 or ...
punishinge] *om.* JMO.   665 in²] *om.* MO;   shulden] schulle J.   666 loue
and charite] charyte and luf O.   667 flawme] to flawme C, flawmande JM,
flawmyg O, How prestes er named porters of heuene and haues powere to here
confession *rub.* M, Nowe Grace dieux telloþe hem why she haþe given hem þis
swerd *mar.* S.   668 Now] *prec. Capitulum* xxix *mar.* CGS, c*apitulum* xix *rub.*
mar. M;   I wole] *trs.* J;   witen] wate JMO.   669 thinketh] semeþe S;   of¹]
for O.   670 keyes] saundouthe *add.* J;   withoute lesinge] *om.* J;   shette] spere
JMO.   671 wight] man M.   672 in] *om.* JMO;   To] In S;   men] me O;
muste] nedis *add.* J.   673 men¹] þei CJ (o. er. C);   bifore] are J;   men²] þei
CJ;   passen] in at *add.* J.   674 fardelles] fardell MO;   in] a GS.   675 musten
be] busbe J.   676 þat ... vnclosed] *om.* S;   it ne] ne G, *trs.* J, bot it MO, how
ye Ministery ought to be taken, and vsed *mar.* O³.   677 Now looketh] *trs.* J.
678 haue] *om.* JMO;   þilke¹] that JMO;   þilke²] thay J, þe M, þo O;   shulden]
schulle J.   679 make] faire F, lete CJMO (o. er. C);   fardelle] -s J.
680 seeche] teche (*with* seeche *mar.* G³) G, serche and seke M, serche O;   dis-
charge] to discharge JMO.   681 weye] wey (*with* weye *mar.* G³) G, and pondire
add. M.   682 iuge] deme JMO;   hem] *om.* JMO.   683 men] ȝe J;   mown]
myght JMO;   bi riht] rightly J, right MO;   clepe] calle JMO (a cross *mar.* O³).
683-4 and ... yow] *om.* JMO;   iseyn] sene JMO.   685 knowe] knawhy J;
misdedes] mysdede JO.   686 enioyned] engioyned (*with* enioyned *mar.* O³) O;
wurthi] *om.* MO;   penaunces] penaunce JMO;   ye mown] maye ȝe do J;
vnshette] vndo JMO.   687 penauntes] penytentis M, penaunces S;   entre] to
entre J;   þis] per O;   þe] no O.   689 Now keepeth] *trs.* J;   yow] *om.* JMO;
vse discreteliche] them J, viselyand dyscretly O.   690 with hem] discretely J,
þem MO;   shulde] How powere of preestes was giffen to þis pilgryme vndir seale
add. rub. M, Loo howe þe pilgryme desyred for to haue þe brennyng swerd and þe
keyes of Raysone *add.* S.   691 Whan] *prec. Capitulum* xxx *mar.* CGS, cap*itulum*
vicesimum *rub. mar.* M;   þus] al þis M, all þus O;   spoken] y spoken G;   I]
pilgrim over C, *with* s*cilicet* pylgrym *mar.* G³, al MO;   hadde al] I had MO.
692 herd] grete *add.* J;   took me] I hadde J, was to me M, to me O;   desire] I
was *add.* O.   693 þerwith] *om.* JMO;   of ... passage] and Portere J, of þat
passage MO.   694 and porter] of þat passage J;   shulde] schall *alt.* schuld O;
þerof] *om.* JMO.   695 yit] *om.* M;   thouht] be thought me JMO;   thing] a
thynge that JM, þat *add.* S;   bifalleth] fallis M, be fall O;   þat] hem *o. er.* (*with*
er. mar. C³) C.   696 þat] atte J;   wil ... men] men wyll take O;   men] we S;
As] And whane S.   697 ythouht] thouȝt JMO;   to] til S.   698 þilke] that
JMO;   and graunte] (and gra- *o. er.* (*with er. mar.* C³) C);me²] þat *add. can.* G;
þe] *om.* MO.   699 keyes ... keepe] *partly erased* C;   þilke] that JM, þo O;
forseyde] same S;   passage] Nowe feloweþe how Moyses deliuerd boþe þe swerd
and þe keyes enseled to þe pilgryme *add.* S;   Moyses] *prec. Capitulum* xxxi *mar.*
CGS.   700 sheþede] schotte J;   swerd] in the Scawberke *add.* J.   701 keyes]
to gedyr *add.* J;   wel] fulle JMO.   701-2 and² ... benigneliche] *om.* S.
702 me¹] theym J;   graunted] gafe J.   703 in] *om.* JMO;   lookede] scholde
luke JM.   704 stired] drowe J;   forto] be fore JMO, vn to þe tyme / þat S;
hadde] firþer *add.* S;   leeue] and comaundement *add.* S, Takeþe hede howe þat
þe pilgryme · was abaysshed · of Moyses rule *add.* S.   705 Whan] *prec.*

Ca*pitulum* xxxii *mar.* CGS;   me] to me S;   þis] thus J;   was] gretly *add.* J.
706 þus idoo] done þus before J, þus done MO;   neiþer] *om.* J;   of[1,2] in J.
707 Faste] than *add.* J;   what[1]] *þat add.* S.   707–8 or ... do] *om.* JMOS.
708 þilke] that JO, þe M;   ysheþed] Scawberkyd J, schet O;   seled] *om.* J;
wrapped] and wrappede JMO.   709 also enseled] *trs.* J;   ybounden] bou*n*dyne
JMO.   710 me] Bot a*dd.* M, And þus astonyed *add.* S.   710–11 whan ...
to[1]] *om.* J.   710 apperceyued] *per*seyued MO, hade a*per*ceyued S.   711 she]
that GMOS;   Resoun þat spak] Than spake resoun J, Reson þan spak MO, þane
Raysou*n* spak S;   to[2]] vnto J;   me[2]] and Sayde on this wise *add.* J, in þis wyse
and seyde *add.* S, Loo howe Raysoun spekeþe to þe pilgryme · and repreyueþe his
thought *add.* S;   My] *prec.* Ca*pitulum* xxxiii *mar.* CGS.   712 thinkest] þowe
add. JMOS.   713 corage] mynde JMO;   scole] the Scole JS;   wel] fulle
JMO.   714 lerned] lern O.   715 of] in sophisterye cleped S;   Ad Aliquid]
ad ¶ ad (*2nd* ad O[3]) O;   þilke] that JMOS;   predicament] -*es* O.   716 edifyinge]
edificac*i*oun J;   upon otheres ground] fulle wisely J, vp on othire grounde M, a
pont othir grownd O.   717 wol wisliche] apo*n*e anothere grownde J, ful wysely
MO;   he hath[2]] of othere J, *ins. mar.* O[3];   of ooþere] he hase it J, -s S.
718 dooth] he duse J;   wrong] no worng O;   If] of O.   719 nothing be] *trs.*
JS;   ne ne] ne ... ne F, ne C, *om.* JMO;   miht be] *om.* JMO; take] schewe J.
720 þou] *om.* O;   see] *prec.* ? Ex*em*plu*m* (? *Genesim*) *mar.* O[3];   þat[2]] it J, *om.*
MO;   eye] & *add. ins.* C;   cleerliche] *om.* J;   vndirstande] hit wele *add.* J, to
vnderstonde S.   721 wel] *om.* J;   lerne]it *add.* J;   and witholde] *om.* JMO, it
add. C;   Whan] not*a* ? {*per* Shirley} *cropped mar.* S.   722 cleped] callede JM.
723 ne gabbe] gabbe nought J; was God] *trs.* JMO.   724 cleped] callede JMO;
in] and O;   seruauntes] *add.* GMO (*can.* G);   he was] *trs.* JMO, cleped *add.* S.
725–6 and ... Lord] *ins. mar.* G[3], *om.* JMO.   726 he was] *trs.* JO;   þe[2]] *om.*
MO.   727 þis] this (t *ins.* (*with* thys *mar.* G[3]) G);   not] nane J;   þe] *om.* MO.
728 seruauntes] þat *add.* M;   so] *ins.* O;   þe] more *add. can.* G, þo *o. er.* O.
729 lordshipe] -s MS.   729–30 Lordship ... engendred] *prec. om.* O.   730 was]
es JM;   þe] *om.* JMOS.   731 lordshipes] lordschepe JMO;   perishen] bath
add. JS.   731–2 Ad Aliquid] may be Sayde J, ad ¶ ad (*2nd* ad O[3]) O.   732 may
be seid] ad Aliquid J;   thinketh] thynk MO;   for] *om.* J.   733 of] on J.
734 also] *om.* JMO;   þat oon] that ton (*with* the *mar.* G[3]) G.   735 also] Nowe
beholde and see þat þou þat art heere in subieccioun moste neodes be subiect til
oþer *add.* S.   736 Now vnderstond] *prec.* Ca*pitulum* xxxiv *mar.* CGS, *trs.* J,
also *add.* M;   þat] qui F, *om.* C.   738 subiect] for *add.* S;   whateuere] whate
sum euere J;   he] *ins. mar.* G[3].   739 oo] I *over* G[3].   740 for] and JMO;
þerbi] þere fore JMO.   741 vnheled] *om.* J;   naked] vnschetid J, *om.* MO;
and[1] *o. er.* C, *om.* MO;   vnscheþed] *o. er.* (*with* vnsheeþed *mar.* C[3]) C, onschethed
(*2nd minim erased*) G, naked JMO;   of] *om.* MO.   742 þe keyes] also MO;
also] þe keyes MO;   vnwounden] vnbou*n*dyne JM, vnwondyd OS.   742–
3 With ... do] whate schulde thowe do with the swerde nakyd J.   743 shuldest
þow] scholdeste G;   do] þo O;   vnheled] vnbou*n*dyne J, vnseled S.   744 þouh]
ȝif JM;   haddest] hadde JMO;   þat] *om.* M;   see] can see J;   If] For ȝif J.
745 naked] not*a mar.* O[3];   hadde] *om.* M;   kerue] þere with *add.* J.   747 wight]
þerwith *add.* J;   If ... keyes] (*with* beere *mar.* G[3]), Also J;   also] ȝif I bare kayes
J.   748 þer] I *alt.* and *add.* S.   749 sum men] somme GOS, *per*aventure J;
mihten... perauenture] Sum myght wene J, myght suppose *per*auento*u*r M;   I]
ware fals & *add.* J.   750 to] for to M;   lightliche] ryghtilly J;   men mihten]
trs. J.   751 men] thay JMOS;   liche] tille a*dd.* J.   751–2 þe ... hadden]
thayres J.   752 with hem] *om.* JMO;   vnshette] opende JO, purposid to opyn

M;   dores] doeyrs M, How Raysoun spekeþe to pilgrime of þe keyes & swerd
add. S;   Serteyn] *prec.* Cap*itulum* xxxv *mar.* CGS, -ly J;   þi] tez F,the GMS.
753 han] swilke a*dd.* J;   þe] þire J;   straungeres] othere J.   754 sithe] Seyne
JMO;   shette] kerfe J;   ne] no J, nore O;   vnshette] openeJ.   755 sithe]
seyn JMO;   hast] al so *add.* S;   ne] no O;   to²] tu O;   bettere] þat *add.* S.
756 swerd] spere (*can. with* swerd *mar.* G³) G;   sheþed] schet O;   vnscheþed]
vnscheted JO;   þe] thy JO.   757 þat] que F, *om.* GJOS;   þou] *om.* J;   hast]
om. J;   þan] *om.* MO;   vnhyd] vnkouerid J, *om.* MO;   bitimes] be tyme J;
may men] *trs.* M.   758 to] forto *add.* J.   759 þee] (*2nd* e *ins.* G), *om.* O;
wysliche] wise leeche S;   þat¹] thilke GS.   760 seeth] See J;   time] his tyme
J, þe tyme S;   þee] *om.* JMO.   761 vnsheþe] þee *add.* C, þe *add. ins.* G³,
vnschette JO;   whan] þat *add.* O;   wole] shal S.   762 þe] *om.* J;   he] ȝe O;
þee] there J;   matere] matyrsJ.   763 miht¹] maye JMO;   if] bot ȝif J, bot
MO;   ne] *om.* JMO.   764 Perile of deth] He outakes alle anely J.   764-
· 5 oonlich ... þee] þerill of dede J, he oonly outetakes þe MO.   765 be] may beo
S;   euident] euuydyd O;   for] fro O;   miht] may J;   vnsheþe] vnschet O;
þe] þi O.   766 vnbynde] vmbynd O;   þe] thy JM.   767 abaundoneth]
grauntes JMO;   þee þe] the JMO.   768 dede] -s MO;   to¹] Loo howe þe
lady Raysoun declareþe þe pilgryme / to whas keeping · þe naked swerde and þe
keyes vnseled · longen to *add.* S;   Thilke] *prec.* Cap*itulum* xxxvi *mar.* CGS, Tylke
(*with* thylke *mar.* G³) G, he JMO.   769 he þat] thilke that GS, þat MO;   þe]
his M.   770 þilke] hee JMO.   771 and lordshipe] in hym J;   is¹] *ins.* M;
put] depute S;   If] and ȝif J.   772 haddest] hadde JM, has O;   also] *om.* CJ;
he] duse *add.* J, hafes *add.* M;   þou mihtest] myght þou J, þou myght MO;   do]
and *add.* JMO.   773 Ad Aliquid] ad ad (*2nd* ad O³) O;   noone] *with* scilicet sugys
mar. G³;   thinketh] thynke JMO;   wherfore] me thynke *add.* J.   774 abashe] be
abayste JMO;   þee¹] þerof *add.* J;   þouh] þowe have *add.* J, if M;   be] *o. er.* C,
om. J;   þee²] to the JMOS.   775 sheþed] in sheth MO;   þouh] of MO;
enseled] boundene J;   bounden] wapped J;   wrapped] enselyd J, wappyd M,
How affter þis seying of Raysoun · Moyses wolde go dyne · *add.* S.   776 Whan]
prec. Cap*itulum* xxxvii *mar.* CGS, cap*itulum* xxi *rub. mar.* MO;   preched] declared
S;   dine] to dinere JS.   777 and] haue *add.* CG³S (*ins.* G³);   was redy] (*can.*
G³), *om.* CS;   al] nane J;   ooþerwise] oother weys GO;   was¹] by fore *add.*
JMO.   778 nothing] no no thyng O;   but²] and J, for S;   it] that JS;   not] (t
erased C), nowght GJMO;   mes] mete JMO.   779 haue] *prec.* Eukaristia *rub. mar.*
MO;   þerwith] al *add.* S.   780 hadde] *om.* JMO;   seid þat] comawndede J.
780-1 no ... shulde] thay schulde ete ne blude J.   781 To] Than to J, Forto M,
þat shoulde S;   clepede] callede JM;   Grace] dieu *add.* JMOS.   783 noon]
othere *add.* J;   bred] bered O;   into ... turned] he turnyd into qwyk flesche J;
Grace] dieu *add.* JMOS.   784 it] þat O, and *add.* JM;   wyn] also *add.* S.
785 be] to be JM;   a] þe S;   Sithe] Seyne JMO;   as] of S;   curteis] the
curtaise J, curteyse S;   wolde] *om.* J;   clepe] callid J, call M.   786 officialles]
Officiale JMO, officiers S;   dynere] with þe officialles *add.* S;   in] *om.* J;   hem]
hym JMO;   kunnynge] conmyg O.   787 yivinge] (ing *o. er.* C);   hem] hym
JMO.   788 And] *om.* M;   sithe] Seyne JMO, siche S;   to²] at J.   789 þilke]
that JMO;   newe] *o. er.* C;   mees] mete J;   he] *om.* M.   790 I] me J;   it]
om. J.   791 I] harde and *add.* J;   kunne] cum O.   792 non] any JMO;
so] to O;   renown] Howe þe pilgryme · desireþe of Raysoun · to knowe of þis
mete and of þys drynk þe hoole intencioun *add.* S.   793 Whan] *prec.* Cap*itulum*
xxxviii *mar.* CGS;   hiholden] by holde (e *ins.* G³) G;   I²] and S.   794 for to]
and J;   preye] prayede J.   794-5 of ... me¹] and teche me of þat dynere J.

794 þilke] þis MO.   795 me¹] *om.* O;   I²] & S.   796 abashed] and gretely
aferde *add.* M;   is] menes J.   797 Al abashed] me thynketh ȝowe J, al aferde
M;   me ... yow] alle abaiste J, me thynke þow MO;   Techeth] Thech M.
798 þilke] this JMO;   Serteyn] -ly J.   799 I ... not] quod Scho JMO;   quod
she] I wille not JMO;   for] *om.* JMO;   nothing] Racio deficit in sacr{amento}
eukaristie *rub. mar.* MO (defecit O);   heeron] þeron (þ *o. er. with er. mar.* C³) CS.
800 and my wit] alle vttyrly J;   al outerliche] and my witte J.   802 þouh] alle
ȝif J, if M, *om.* O;   þilke] *om.* J, þat MO.   802-3 hornede Moyses] *trs.* J.
803 hadde] haþe S;   of an ey] (of an *o. er.* C), made JMO;   imaad] mad GS, of
an egge JMO;   of²] *om.* M.   804 pipe] -n M.   805 flesh quik] *trs.* JMO;
of bred] he had made me J.   806 he ... maad] of breed J;   of wyn blood] blude
of wyne J;   for his drink] *om.* JMO;   ayens] agayn MO.   807 ayens] (a *ins.*
G³), agayn MO;   And] *om.* O;   sey] schewe J;   to] es O.   808 whan] als
sone as J.   809 come] to *add.* J, and *add.* S.   810 þis] *om.* O, geres *add.* J;
she] *id est grace dieu over* C, *with scilicet* grace dieu *mar.* G³, geres J;   maketh]
scho J, may S;   do] be done JMO;   ofte] -n S;   is] it is (it *into mar.* M³) M, she
is S, *om.* C;   hire] *id est* nature *over* C, *with scilicet* nature *mar.* G³, nature J, for
add. CG³ (*ins. mar.* G³).   811 she] *id est grace over* C, *with scilicet* grace dieu
mar. G³;   maketh] *om.* S;   hire¹] *om.* JMOS, *id est* nature *over* C, *with scilicet*
nature *mar.* G³, *om.* J; hire²] *om.* J;   hynesse] nature *add.* JMO;   leese] leeseþe
S.   812 vsage] ymage S.   813 and²] al S;   sorweful] -ly J;   in þe place]
scho left me M, *om.* S.   813-14 she ... me] in þe place M, *om.* S.   814 and]
om. S;   sorweful] -ly J, soryful O, *om.* S;   into ... wente] how Nature arguys and
chidys with grace dieu · for þis forsaide mutacion *add.* M, *om.* S.   815 As]
prec. Capitulum xxxix *mar.* CGS, capitulum xxii *rub. mar.* M, Capitulum xxiii *rub.*
mar. O, Howe nature came to þe pilgryme semyng wroþe *add.* S;   was] all *add.* G,
this *add.* J;   on] upon C;   þese] this JMO;   thinges] thynge JMO.   816 toward]
-es S;   oon] 1 *over* G;   and] *om.* J;   neihede] beside J.   817 cheer] chyere
(*2nd* e *ins.* G³) G;   wroth] wrathelatene J.   818 eyen] full *add.* S.   819 gleedes]
glede J;   wel] by þat / þat *add.* S;   bi þat þat] be þat O, which S.   820 seid]
spoken S;   me] *om.* J, to me of S.   821 Redi] already S;   miche] *om.* J.
822 for] *om.* J;   toward] -es S;   and] ful *add.* S.   823 spak] Scho spakke JS;
to¹] vn to S;   hire] Howe · my lady nature þe olde arresouneþe · dame Gracedieux
in rude maner *add.* S;   Lady] *prec.* Capitulum xl *mar.* CGS, hic natura loquitur de
sacramento eukari{stie} *rub. mar.* MO, hic natura loquitur gracie *rub. mar.* O;   she]
nature *over* C, *with scilicet* nature *mar.* G³;   to³] forto J.   824 for to¹] to J,
owen parte *add. into mar.* M³;   Wennes] wheine JMO, Of whennes S.   825 or-
dinaunces] ordynaunce JMO;   suffice] to Suffise JMO;   yow ynowh] jnowh to
you C;   þe] nota per Shir{ley} discord of n{ature and} grace dieux *mar.* S;   party]
pert O.   826 medlinge] mellynge JMO;   yow] *om.* J;   and withoute] or J.
827 þe¹] *om.* J.   829 turne] to turne J;   speeres] spere J.   830 laate] let yee
S;   or] and J, oþer S;   rathe] arely JMO, *om.* S;   ye] *om.* S;   And] and *add.* O;
wol] right J;   loth] late J;   certeyn] -ly J.   831 wolde] ware J;   suffre] to
Suffyr J, be M;   and] fulle *add.* JMO, wel *add.* S;   loth] wrath J;   be] suffire
M;   þat] ȝif J;   I] þere *add.* MO.   832 be] *om.* O;   weri] eville a payde J,
wroth M.   833 medlede] mellede JMO.   834 as²] I wolde *add.* J;   it] me
S;   Bitwixe] betweene GJOS;   me and yow] moi et vous (*variant* vous et moi *H*)
F, ȝowe and me JMOS;   sette] *o. er.* C.   835 noon] nowthere J.   836 þat]
And that bownde J;   wheel] Sercle J;   whiche] the whilke J.   837 alwei] a
way O;   þilk] That JMO;   wheel] Cercle J;   yiueth] *prec.* A discource between
grace, & Nature. the gret loue of god, by grace. þe great power of god, by Natures

invisible workeing, of hir most visible workes (*1st* r *ins.*) *mar.* O³ *and in another
hand* Noat *mar.* O³.   837-8 eche of us] aithere JM, ethe O.   838 hire] her
G, there JO, his MS;   partye] parte JMO.   839 ye mowe] *trs.* J;   wole]
wolde MO;   nouelries] monethes J, neuelrys *alt.* meeuelrys (*minim and 2nd* e *ins.*
O³) O.   840 þouh] if MO;   of¹] Of *add.* J;   Mercury] Mercur*i*us M;   a] of
G.   841 ne] and JMO;   neu*ere*] nathynge J.   842 I cleyme] *trs.* J;
withinne] the Cercle *add.* J;   myn] for *add.* S.   843 of¹,²] *om.* O.   844 va-
ryinges] varyinge JMO;   in²] and JO;   eerþe in see] water and in erthe J.
845 turne] to turne J;   to] tille an J.   846 make] garre J;   varye] verray J;
newe] alle J;   thinges] thyng O.   847 come] *om.* JMO;   olde] newe J;   to]
om. S;   departe] Loo howe þat dame nature sheweþe hir power *add.* S;   The]
prec. Cap*itulum* xli *mar.* CGS;   my] me S;   robes] roobed S.   848 temps]
tymes M;   I¹] y *ins. mar.* G³;   þe] *om.* J.   849 apparemens] araye JMO;
ayens] agayne JMO;   sithe] Syne JO, siche S;   make] garre J.   850 ayen]
om. JMOS;   ayens] agayne J, nat*ure* spe{keþe] *mar.* S;   winter] þe wynter
GJMO.   850-1 for ... newe] and þus affter þe saysouns I prouyde hem þeyre
vesture S.   850 kerue] keu O;   robes] clathes JMO;   kootes] robes JMO.
851 seemynge] (*2nd* e *ins.* G³);   brembel] brambre G, brambir*e* MO;   broom]
brere JMO;   ne²] nane *add.* J.   852 I ne] *trs.* J;   cloþe] thayme *add.* J.
853 a²] the J;   þat þat] þat at J, þat O.   854 hastyf] hasty JMO;   mutacioun]
-s J;   is] er J.   855 þe] *om.* MOS.   856 woorth] -ye J;   witnesse] I take
wittenes J;   on] of JMO;   I] *with* scilicet *nature mar.* G³.   857 ne¹] ner S;   I
am not] *om.* J;   preciows] for seyinge JMO³ (*o. er.* O³).   858 and¹] affter *add.*
S;   I] *with* scilicet *nature mar.* G³.   859 speke] to Speke JS;   I make] *om.* J;
flee] to flee JS;   go] to goo J;   swymme] to Swym*me* JS.   860 raunpen]
raumpaunde JO, rawpand M;   growen] to growe J.   861 togidere] -s S;
thinketh] thynke right J, thynk MO;   þat] *om.* JMO.   861-2 for ... me] ʒe
walde halde me for AFore A wensche J.   861 for] (*can.* C).   862 my wyn] ʒe
make J;   ye make] my wyne J;   bicome] to be com*me* J.   863 beuerege] (ge
o. er. with er. mar. C³), veuerage O;   lakketh] it lakkes JMO;   þat] þen MO;   I
ne] *trs.* J, I ner M.   864 wroth] worthe O;   I²] *om.* J.   864-5 to make] *ins.
mar.* G³, forto make nowþere J, for to make M, of S.   865 ne¹] nor M, or O, of
add. S;   sette] ne sewe *add.* J, ett M.   866 took] thay*m add.* J;   whiche] þe
wyche O.   867 þat] *om.* S;   ye witen] witte ʒe *alt.* wate ʒe J;   wrethe] grete
wreth J;   to] in *o. er.* (*with er. mar.* C³) C, in J.   868 into] to M, þe O.
869 nakenen] nakes J;   right] Loo howe dame nature / spekiþe greuously to dame
Grace dieux of many thinges · þat she did with oute hir knowing *add.* S;   Whennes]
prec. Cap*itulum* xlii *mar.* CGS, fra wheyne J, fro whyns MO;   þus] *o. er.* C, on
this wise J.   870 me nouht] me right nouht C, *trs.* J;   to] so S.   872 whan]
wene J, Weyen M;   ye] *om.* J, *prec.* {Nature s}pekeþe to · {Gra}ce dieux · *mar.* S;
haue] *om.* JMO;   er þis] *om.* JMO;   ne wot] wat neu*ere* J;   auctorite] ʒhe *add.
ins.* M³.   873 vsages] vsage JMO;   and¹] *om.* JMO;   myne] *om.* S;
ordinaunces] ordynaunce JMO, *om.* S;   my dedes] *om.* JMOS;   my²] myn M.
874 remembre] me *add.* JMO;   ye] *om.* O.   875 it] þereof J.   876 bethinke]
vmbethynke J;   of²] *ins. mar.* G³.   877 bicome] to become J;   þat²] the
GJM, þo O.   878 humour] humd*ur* J, honor O;   maden] gret J.   879 floures
and frute] and fruyt with floures S.   880 wyn] and *add.* O;   noces] noses G,
noches F, feste CJ, necessite M, messe O, wedding S;   Architriclyn] archedeclyn*e*
G, Archedreclyn*e* S, Archedecline (*variant* Archetreclin *TL*) F.   881 ooþere]
wondirfull *add.* M;   remeevinges] mutaciouns ʒe make J, mutacions MO;   of]
om. J;   were] it wer*e* MO;   to¹] *om.* J.   882 holde parlement] telle J;   luste]

lyste JMOS;   to] *om.* J, for to S.   883 of] *om.* J;   þe] no*ta* ne v*i*rgine Mar*i*a
rub. mar. M;   which] wham J;   conceyue] *om.* J, *with* conceiue *mar.* O³;
withoute] *om.* J.   884 man] *om.* J, sede of man M;   wherof ... maden] *om.* J.
885 hire] *o. er.* C, *marked for gloss* G, *om.* JMO;   chylde] enfanter F, bere a chyld
o. er. C, *om.* JMO, bere chylde S;   virgine] & she v*i*rgine *o. er.* C, *om.* JMO, sheo
beyng virgyne S;   withoute] *o. er.* C, *om.* JMO;   clepinge me] *o. er. and* to
counseil *add. o. er.* C, *om.* JMO, wittyng S, Howe nature spekeþe yit to Gracedieux
in þe same mater *add.* S;   Swiche] And when 3e had done Swilke J, *prec.* Cap*itulum*
xliii *mar.* CGS.   886 I¹] *with* s*cilicet* nature *mar.* G³;   I sorwe] me for thynkes
J.   887 erst] ar nowe JMO;   spak] ne herde S;   I] worde *add.* J;   made
noise] *trs.* J;   wherof] and þereof J;   me] I J, soore *add.* S.   888 forthinketh]
hafe grete sorowe J;   mowe ... suffre] oft soffi*re* may M.   889-90 and ... stille]
om. S.   889 to] ouere J;   I] to O.   890 now] onewe J, new O;   ayen] me
add. J.   891 whiche] the whilke J;   me] him and me S;   right] *om.* J;   bi²]
with JMO.   892 right] *om.* J, *ins. mar.* O²;   wel ... yow] I telle 3owe Wele J.
892-3 ne ... ye¹] ware ne 3e ware J, yee ne were S.   893 soone] (*lst* o *ins.* G³).
894 werre] wers O;   wolde¹] wil M;   and ... wolde] to J;   sithe] -n MO.
895 to] at J;   so] atte J, muche *add.* S;   vsages] vsage JMO.   896 clepinge]
callynge JM, slepynge O;   me] Takeþe heede nowe I beseeche yowe howe
ma dame Gracedieux aunswerd to dame nature · to alle hir compleyntes *add.* S.
897 Whan] I hane þat (*with scribe's guide* I *visible*) S, *prec.* Cap*itulum* xliv *mar.*
CGS, ca*pitulum* xxiii *rub. mar.* M, Grace dieu *rub. mar.* O;   yspoke] Spokyn*e* JO,
spoken holdynge hir*e* handes right fiersly vndire neth hir sydes · and hir eyen
glowynge M;   Grace] dieu *add.* JMOS;   þat ... al] that J, *om.* M, can. (*with* hard
over O³) O, þat all hade S.   898 yherd] herde alle hir speche J, herde hir wele
and M;   answerde] answere (*with* answerede *mar.* G³) G, & sayde *add.* J;   manere]
matere JO, mat*er* on þis wyse M;   Nature] q*u*od scho *add.* M;   to] *ins. mar.* G³,
ouer J.   899 fersliche] fierement F, feerleche G, fresly O;   speken] Spekis
JMO, h*i*c gra*cia* loqu*i*tur nature *rub. mar.* M;   me] yit natu*re* to {gr}acedieux *mar.*
S;   trowe] suppose M.   900 drunken¹ ... wynes] *om.* S;   And] for J, *om.* S;
drunken and] *om.* O.   901 wel] to be *add.* J.   901-2 I ... be] Er 3e J.
901 if] *prec.* that *mar.* O³.   902 neewe wexe] nowe waxyn*e* JM, waxyn now O;
elles] *om* J;   þat] *ins. mar.* G³, *om.* J.   903 ago] gone JMO;   þat] seyne J;
seyd] hadde saide J, þat *add.* O;   hastyf] hasty MO;   but] nowe *add.* J, Lo O.
904 in yow] *om.* J;   avys] a visement JMO;   speke] spake O.   905 niceliche]
vnwyselich S;   þat] *om.* J.   906 speke] with yowe and *add.* S;   also] wele O;
were] it for *add.* J.   907 wratthe] that *add.* J;   I] *prec.* nota *mar.* G³.
908 folk] men O;   forbere] be for borne JMO;   discerne] Man cannott *over at
top p.* O³.   909 a] the JMO;   here] þaye arre J;   vnderstondinge] Loo howe ·
Gracedieux yit spekiþe to dame nature · in þis same mater eesing hir compleyntes
add. S.   909-10 Now ... me] *prec.* Cap*itulum* xlv *mar.* CGS, Saye me nowe J.
910 me] *o. er.* C, *with* s*cilicet* grace dieu *mar.* G³, ma S;   þus] þat S;   owen] *om.*
JMO.   911 blamen] blamyd J;   and²] *om.* S;   arguen] reprevede J, *om.* S;
me³] *om.* S.   912 into] in O.   913 holde] I halde J.   914 whennes]
wheyne JMO;   cometh] it *add.* M;   yow] 3ow yt (3ow *can.*) O;   þat þat] that
JOS;   haue] þat *add.* S.   915 his] the JMO;   hath] take J.   916 whennes]
wheyne JMO;   him] *om.* J, hym hym (l*st* hym *can.*) M;   þe eyen] þanne S.
917 in] -to CJ;   eerþe] -warde J;   toward] to J, -es S.   918 fro] for O;
whennes] wheyne JM, when O;   halt him oonliche] oonliche halt him C, haldeth
hym haly JMO.   919 trowe] nou3t *add. can.* M.   920 to] for to M;   am¹]
meke and *add.* J;   am²] I am M.   921 Openeth] 3he *add.* MO;   þe] *o. er.* C,

om. S. 922 wel] wisely J; liddes] of ȝour eyȝhy*e add.* J; maistresse] þe maystresse S; for²] *om.* GJ. 923 al] *om.* J. 924 softeliche] alle softely JMO; do] make J; of] for J. 927 with] alle *add.* J; þat²] *ins.* O; of al ye] ȝe of alle to gedyr schulde J; yolden] ȝelde JMO, rendissiez F, wolde C; to] *om.* MO. 928 trewe] treweli C; acounte] -s J. 929 if] and J. 930 of] no *add.* S; bounde] -s J; is] are J; set] *om.* O; bitwixe] betwene GJOS; for] *om.* MO. 931 boundeth] byndeth JMO; yow¹] and *add.* JM; me] to me S; forshetteth] for barreth JM, for berys O; from] *o. er. (with u.v.* f{r}om *mar.* C³) C, of J. 932 I wole] wolde I J; it] so *add. can.* O; But] nat *add.* JMO; þat¹] the JO. 933 shulde] shoulne S; entre] in when*e* me lyste *add.* J; bounded] be bounde J; it] so *add.* J, it so yt (it *ins.*) O. 934 þerof] ne aske ȝowe leve J; Yit more] *om.* J. 935 likede] lykþ O, lyke S; to] *om.* GS; medle] melle J, mell þow MO. 936 I¹] alane *add.* J; wolde] schulde J; al aloone] Inow J; þat²] at J. 937 but] byde S; wole] wold MOS. 938 þat] but ȝif J; a … ne] a maystresse J, ne maistres M, ne a maystres O; chaumberere] Yit beholde howe dame Gracedieux alleyþe moo Resou*n*s a geynst þoppynyonable seyinges of dame Nature *add.* S; Now] *prec. Capitulum* xlvi *mar.* CGS. 939 þanne] (e *ins.* G), *om.* J; withoute] sans F, with CGMOS. 940 inowh] wele J; þat²] at J, þe O; ye] he J. 941 þe] *prec.* {d}ame Gracedieux {speke} þe ageinst nat*u*re *mar.* S; turne] abowte *add.* J. 942 heuene] the heuene GS; longeth] belongeþe S. 943 Now seith] Saye nowe J; a neewe] anowe J. 944 þat¹] So that J; from] fra JMO. 944–5 and … wel] *om.* J. 945 þat] Soo that J; of] *om.* J, in C. 946 aperceyued] p*er*seuede JMO; ye] *om.* O. 947 eche] yche a S. 948 make] *om.* JMO. 949 failinge] -s S; Aristotle] *with* Aristotil *rub. mar.* M; heþene] man *add.* JMOS. 950 þat] whilke JS; weel] *om.* JMO; soothnesse] the soth J, þe sothnesse MO, -s S; I make] *trs.* J. 951 ayens yow] *om* .J; þilke] this JMO; debat] caase J; He] with *scilicet* arystotell *mar.* G³; proueth] it *add.* S. 953 if I had] I had J, I hade if I wolde haue S. 954 leese] have loste JMOS; and] *om.* MO; riht] *om.* JMO; shulde ye] *trs.* J; mown do] haue mo doone S. 955 of¹ … and] *om.* S; firmament] walkene CG; of þe] othere J; also] moeving S. 956 made] thaym *add.* J; cesse] to ceesse J; þat I wolde] *om.* J; do] did thay*m* J; al awey] *trs.* J. 957 wel] also wele J. 958 ylost] lost JMO; it] I S. 959 miht] may J, myghe O; þat] ne *add.* J; ne were] es J. 960 meyntene] maynte O; come] -s JMO; lust] wille JMO; þerfore] for thy J. 961 to] with J. 962 Isaye seith] I say O; gret¹] agret C. 963 ayens] agayne JS; carpenteere] carpentary M. 964 argue] repyne J; blame] To the *cropped mar.* S³; asketh] aske JMO; him²] of *add.* J. 965 ye shulde] *trs.* S. 966 if] and J. 966–7 despyt … gret] grete despite J. 967 arguinge] reprovande J; me¹] *om.* J; vndertaken] reprenez (*variant* reprouues *A*7) F, vndirtakande J, reprouynge M, vndirtakyng OS. 968 doinge] -s J; and] Seyne ȝe J. 969 nothing] *om.* JMO; tool] truyle O; and] myne *add.* JMO; instrument] -is S. 971 hadde] þat I had *add. can.* O; ne] and J. 972 whan] *scribble mar.* S; þat¹] *om.* JO. 973 þat it be] is JMO; many … do] I wille do many thynges J; wole] wolde S. 974 clepe] calle JMO; wole] I wille JMO; remeve] chau*n*ge when me lykes J, chaw*n*ges O; þe] *om.* J; and²] brede *add. ins.* M³. 974–5 into … flesh] with white brede J. 975 þe¹ … bred] into qwikke flesche J; and þe] in to M. 976 I¹ … not] els I ware not J, I wer noght ell O; alwei] *om.* JMO. 977 lust] lyste JMO; to] *om.* C; yit] it J. 978 yow] of ȝowe J; þat þat] that JMO; of] towchande J. 979 þat I kepte] I kepyd hit JMO; þat²] as O. 979–80 al … flaume] ȝif alle the flawme ware J,

al þof it were þe flawme M, all with þe flame O. 980 and] om. C; þerof] þer fore
O; soonere] rathere J, þe sonere MO; me] om. G; þan] for to add. S.
981 and¹] with me or J, or MO; crye] blame me J. 982 virgine mooder] trs.
J; Of] and of JS, and MO; water] also that add. J, þat add. M; also] om. J;
and] 13 þen-trial hs mar. S³. 983 haue] hadd M; thinketh] thynke JMO.
984 chaumberere] chambre O. 985 maistresse] lady JMO. 986 leeseth]
(leeseeth 4th e can. C), hyr Selfe loste J, lese MO; nothing] þereby add. J; for]
to add. M. 987 abetter] & for (for ins. with er. mar.) add. C, þe better / and for
S, to add. J; Now dooth] trs. J. 988 or] ellys add. J. 989 yow¹] om. M;
if ye wole] or chyde J, om. S; or chideth] 3if 3e wille J, 3he add. MO; for¹] om.
JOS, as add. M; wolde] wil JO, wole C; nothing] leue S. 990 leue] lese J,
no thing S; do] þo O; of] om. J; þat] at J; I wolde] I wil J, me list S; doo]
Nature arguys to grace dieu · and sais scho shuld be to hire as chamberere add. rub.
M. 991 Whan] prec. Capitulum 24 and xxiv rub. mar. M, þat þis feyre lady dame
add. S; þus] on this wyse J; spoke] to nature · Than add. JMO, made hir
resouns by goode avyse / þe lady S. 992 answerde] on this wyse add. J, on þis
wyse answerede MO, as yee may here add. S, Now takeþe goode heede I beseeche
yowe howe Nature answerd add. S; Ladi] prec. Capitulum xlvii mar. CGS; she]
with scilicet nature mar. G, nature S; vnderstonde] vndyrstandynge J. 993 see]
wot S; to] for to S; mihte] maye J. 994 me is] it is to me JMO; to yow obeye]
for tille obey vnto 3owe J, vnto þow obeye M, obeye to yowe S. 995 ayens] agayn
M; But ... durste] om. O; neuerþeles] natheles GS, 3it JM; if] and J; a ...
yit] om. JMO. 995-6 I wolde] om. O, trs. GS. 996 argue to yow] om.
997 al¹] tout F, whate þowe lyste J, on CS; al²] ins. mar. G³; þat] þat add. S;
euere] om. S; mown ... arguen] maye argue or saye J, may arguy and say MO,
cane or may sey S; today] þis day S. 998 more] mais F, but add. J, but C,
but for S; ye] ne 3e JM, ne add. OS; declare] open J. 999 Nature] natura
J; Sithe] Seyn JMO. 1000 yit] om. S; wole I] trs. S; and of] om. O;
youre] awne add. JS, om. O; woordes ... wole] om. O; arguen²] om. O, begynne
myne argument S. 1001 sorwe] swore O; so ... me] reprouyd me So J, so me
arguyd MO (arguyd o. er. O³); of my seyinges] of my seying O, and ... rebuked
me S. 1001-2 and ... me] and so rebukede me J, or my seyinges S. 1003 me]
om. J; chaumberere] chambre O; for] youre add. S; haue] om. J. 1004 for
... thing] wharfore J. 1005 with yow] I schulde alwaye J; as] a O;
chaumberere] chambrere (-re O³) O; I ... alwey] be with · 3owe J, alwey I should
MO; be] om. J; cleped] om. J, called M. 1006 remeeve nothing] neuere
remove J, renuwe no thing S, remeeve C; ne make] ins. mar. G³ and marked for
replacement of nothing¹; bore] nee F, bere C, om. JMO, encresse and bere S.
1007 þat] thare J; wolden yit] trs. J, may yit S; conferme] þis add. J, conserue
O; þe] om. O. 1008 ayens] agayn M; carpentere] carpantary M. 1008-
10 as ... fers] om. JMO, yit dame nature · affermeþe hir power ageyns Gracedieux ·
add. S; By] prec. Capitulum xlviii mar. CGS; confirmacioun] om. JMO.
1011 thinketh] thynke JMO; entencioun] entente J, sayde þis fayre lady dame
Nature add. S. 1012 bylde] bigge J, hewe O; hous] and of feyre entayle add.
S. 1013 ye shulde] trs. JMO; wole] walde JMO. 1014 misdoo] do
amysse J; clepe] calle JM. 1015 me] when 3e schulde aught do add. J; it]
þat O; thinketh] thynke JMO. 1016 þese] thyr JM, þis O; officialles]
Officialle JO; þat] yt J; doon] dos JMO; with] o. er. under rubrication C.
1017 hem] to hem S. 1017-19 and ... powere] om. S. 1018 binemen] take
fra JMO. 1019 non] om. JMO; suich] slike M; and] ne J. 1020 remeeve]
Soo chaunge J, chaunge so MO; into] to S; I haue] trs. M. 1021 powere]

and my kunnynge *add.* J, Grace dieu enfo*u*rmes Natur*e* · how scho haues power
w*ith* oute hir*e add. rub.* (power *ins.*) M, Nowe takeþe heede howe Grace dieux
answereþe *add.* S.   1022 Serteyn] *prec.* Cap*itulum* xlix *mar.* CGS, -ly JS;
Grace] dieu *add.* JMOS;   in no wise] I playne me J;   I pleine me nouht] on na
wise J, I pleyn me MO, compleyne I me S.   1023 wel] and knawe *add.* J.   1024–
5 thing ... ynowh] *ins. bottom of p.* O² (? O³).   1024 thing] -es O² (? O³).
1025 ynowh] *om.* J;   ne] and J;   I ... ooþer] *om.* O;   Nay] *om.* J.   1026 she]
Grace *over* C, *with* s*cilicet* nature *mar.* G³, nature I hafe sayde that I wille saye at
this tyme tha*n* J, natur*e* I wil say nou3t elles · And þerfor say 3he what þow likes ·
and I shal gladly here þow · þan M;   answere] 3owe *add.* J;   Grace] dieu *add.*
JOS, dieu on þis wyse *add.* M;   þat¹] and M;   þat²] thynge þat *add.* J.
1027 þat¹] *om.* JMOS;   is] *om.* O;   ye] ne *add.* S;   seyinges] sayinge J.   1027–
8 ne¹ ... nouht] *om.* JMO.   1027 ne²] *om.* C.   1028 nouht] on hem *add. ins.*
C.   1029 alle ... haue] hafe alwey J, alwey haue MO, at alle tymes haue S;
chamberere] chambrer (*last* r O³) O;   seyd] I sayde J.   1030 þat] poynte *add.*
J;   winne ye] schalle 3e wynne J.   1031 places] place O;   and þat] J *repeats*;
is] *om.* J;   oon] alle ane JMO.   1031–2 if ... she] 3if scho in all places J, in al
places if scho M.   1032 places] place O.   1034 to] *om.* J.   1035 haue it]
favere hir J;   whoso] he so (*with* ho *mar.* G³) G, *om.* JMO, and who so S.   1035–
7 whoso ... shulde] *om.* JMO.   1038 vnderstonde] vndyrstode J.   1038–
9 For ... ax] *om.* S.   1039 þat²] *om.* J.   1040 me with] moeveþe S.
1041 howse] have makynge J;   certeyn] cause J;   spak] speke S.   1042 I
fond] in 3ow O;   in yow] I fownd O;   feerstee] fyrste J, first MO;   þerof] þere
in M, heer þer of S.   1043 with] *erased* O;   rude vnderstondinge] mede vnde
fraudynge J.   1044 ayens] agayne JMO;   yit] wele J.   1045 it] *followed by*
caret *with* er. *mar.* C³;   ne] but 3if JM, but þt (þt *can.*) O;   were ye] *trs.* JMO;
þat] And þat O.   1046 haue] *om.* J;   yow¹] yowre O;   forged] for godde J;
yow²] and *add.* M;   shape] shaped (d *erased*) G, shope J;   yow³] *om.* J.
1047 cometh me to] me venra a F, cometh to C, is JMO;   lust] er. *add.* C, lyste
JMO.   1048 þis] Thus JMO.   1049 he] carpenter *over* C, *with* s*cilicet*
carpe*n*ter *mar.* G³;   withoute] *om.* S.   1050 keepe] to kepe JS;   haue] hase J.
1051 I haue] hase I J;   neede] and þerfore *add.* J, þerfor *add.* M, þer of *add.* O;
Haue] yee *add.* S.   1052 feers] forse J;   ax] *om.* S;   I may] *trs.* J;   wel]
worship *add.* S.   1053 and¹] *om.* JMOS;   carpentere] be carpyntere JMO;
withoute] (oute *ins. mar.* G³);   tool and] *lost* C.   1054 of all] alle thynges J;
I may] *trs.* J;   lust] lyste JMO.   1055 to me shulde] *lost* C;   wiht] man*n* J;
compaare him] make comp*a*rysou*n*.   1055–6 ne ooþer] (*partly lost* C), ne nane
othere J.   1057 shortliche] *om.* J.   1017–8 right ... argument] 3owre
argument is litille worth J.   1058 litel ... also] and also lityll worth es J;   youre]
awne *add.* J;   murmur] memou*r* J.   1059 filthe] fulthe GS, laidure F, folye *o.*
er. C, fole J, fule MO;   thinketh] me thynke JMO;   þus] *om.* MO;   grucchinge]
so *add.* MO;   of my] *om.* J.   1060 yiftes] *om.* J, wittes S;   and¹] *om.* J;
murmuringe] of my gyftes and of myn*e* werkys *add.* J;   shulde be] ware J, wol
and shoulde beon S;   euele] ill M, apayed and *add.* S.   1061 to] *om.* J.
1062 not¹] na JMO;   wratthe] ne *add.* J, wreche O;   it ... not] ne hit schulde J;
hevy] heuyee (*2nd* e *ins.* G³) G.   1063 of] *om.* JMO;   nothing] any thynge
MO;   þat] *om.* J;   þe] *om.* JMO;   good²] goud (*with* good *mar.* G³) G, *om.* J;
go] gange J.   1064 oo] 1 *over* C, a J, o M, *om.* O;   þat] *om.* J;   wite] waite M;
wel] forsoth *add.* J, enoughe *add.* S;   It ouhte] *om.* S;   suffice] to Suffyse JMO.
1065 holden] have J;   fair] *o. er.* C.   1066 king] thynge J;   swich] slike M.
1066–7 ooþer avoir] for golde Ne naen noþere gude J, for any hauynge M, for any

oþre O.   1067 officialles] Officialle JMO.   1068 I] and JS;   looke þat] *om.*
J;   of] *om.* JMO;   nothing ye leese] þerfore *add. ins.* C, ȝe lose no thynge þeron
J, ȝhe nothynge lose MO;   is] grete *add.* J;   if ye] for to J.   1069 yow] How
nature askes me*rcy* of grace dieu *add. rub.* M, Takeþe hede howe Nature askeþe
mercy lowly of Gracedieux of þat she haþe presumed ageynst hir *add.* S.
1070 Whan] *prec.* Cap*itulum* i *mar.* CGS, cap*itulum* xxvi *rub. mar.* M, þat *add.* S;
Grace] dieu *add.* JMOS;   yspoken] Spokene to JMO, spoken S;   þat hadde]
whilke J.   1071 it] hir JS;   bisiliche] Scho *add.* JMO;   kneeled] down *add.*
MO;   and] *om.* MO, Alle S;   humbleliche] mekely tille hir Sayde J, mekely MO.
1072 pray] Be seke JS;   þat] þa*n*ne C;   on ... merci] ȝe have me*rcy* on me J.
1073 see] voi F, knowe C;   defaute] (*2nd* e *ins.* G[3]).   1074 I ... me] and folily
and to fersly J, stired me M, and stird me O;   folilich ... fersliche] I sterede me
agaynes ȝowe J;   and] *om.* G;   fersliche] fresly O.   1075 ouer] eu*ere* J;   I[2]]
me JS;   ouhte] oweþe wel S;   obeye] forto obey J, to obeye MO (*2nd* o *ins.* O[3]);
to] vnto J.   1076 Of] *om.* JMO, and S;   nothing it shulde] It Schulde nathynge
J, noo thing shoulde S;   of] þe J, *om.* MOS;   thing] *om.* S;   wol] list S;   doo]
to doone S.   1077 neu*ere*] mare *add.* JMO;   speke] agaynes ȝowe *add.* J,
agayn þow M;   but] So J;   þat] if S.   1077-8 at ... me] for giffe it me at this
tyme J.   1078 benigneliche] that I have giltede agaynes ȝowe J;   withholdinge]
of *add.* J, holding of S.   1079 Serteyn] For Soth J, sooþely S;   Grace] dieu
add. JMOS;   and] *om.* JMO;   I wole] that wille I gladly do J;   it] *om.* JMO;
But] luke ȝe *add.* J.   1080 upon] Opayne of JMO, open S;   eyen] heued J;
ageynseyn] me of *add.* JMO.   1081 faire] fader S;   ne] of *add.* J, and S;   I
miht] wille I J, I wil MO.   1082 miche] of ȝowe *add.* J;   ne ... suffre] *om.*
JMO, how þat Moyses whane he hade dyned dep*ar*ted · þe releef of his mete · vn
to þe poore pilgrymes *add.* S.   1083 Whan] *prec.* Cap*itulum* li *mar.* CGS (*a
cross and* 51 G[3]), cap*itulum* xxvii *rub. mar.* M;   parlement] Spekynge JMO.
1083 dyned] edyned S.   1084 of] *om.* J;   his] son F, þis C.   1085 enlargise]
enlarge JMO.   1086 þerinne] *om.* J, in MO;   þat] ar J, *om.* MO;   he] *ins.* O[3].
1087 tweyne] two JMO, tweye GS;   þat weren] and of J, and MO;   fair] chere
add. J.   1088 filthe] and *add.* S;   of fair] *om.* JMO;   manere] *om.* JMO,
maners S.   1089 þat] whilke JS;   of ... out] come owte of a chaumbre JMOS;
wel] fulle JMO.   1090 bitwixe] betweene CJOS;   þat oon] than J.
1091 heeld] in hir hande *add.* J.   1092 writen] and *add.* J;   Al] *om.* S.
1092-3 it she hadde] Scho had it JS.   1093 for to] redy forto J;   it] *om.* S.
ye] I J.   1093-4 heerafterward ... seye] schewe ȝowe afterwarde J, eftir here
see MO.   1094 seye] *prec.* penitencia *rub. mar.* M;   seyn] telle ȝou J.
1095 serteyn] Sothly J;   wundrede] wou*n*dre me J, wonder S;   miche] howe
add. S.   1095-9 In ... curteisliche] *om.* S.   1095 In] For in J;   of]
Penitenc*ia rub. mar.* MO;   hire] *om.* J.   1097 and[2]] *ins. mar.* G[3];   courreyinge]
courveyenge G, wele plyande and J;   Bitwixe] betwene GJO;   teeth] toche O;
and[3]] in *add.* J.   1098 heeld] hadde GMO;   more ... me] me m*er*veylede
maste of J;   wel] and ryght J.   1099-100 she[2] ... wys] neu*ere* the lasse wyse
scho semede J.   1100 if] and if J.   1101 for] *can.* C, a foole and J, fer S;
of] her *ins. mar. u.v.* C[3], *add.* J.   1102 þilke] the JMO, þis S;   ful] well GS;
beesme] besynesse S.   1103 ne] nor MO;   preche] Loo howe þe lady Grace
dieux precheþe and declareþe vn to þe peple · þe signefycaunces of hir arraye *add.*
S.   1104 Lordinges] *prec.* Cap*itulum* lii *mar.* CGS;   þat] *om.* J.   1105 wel]
om. JMO;   þat] *om.* JMO; ye] *o. er., followed by partly erased caret* C;   witen]
wate JMOS;   neuere] nouȝt JMOS.   1106 myn array] it *o. er.* C;   yow] *om.*
JMOS;   neer] neere (*2nd* e *ins.* G[3]) G *with* neer *mar.* G[3], for *add.* JS, and *add.* M.

1107 telle] *into mar.* O²; it] ȝowe *add.* JMS, *into mar.* O²; of] *om.* S; I wol]
trs. J; þe] a O. 1108 ydred] dredde JMO, I dreed S; riht] *om.* O.
1109 ypreised] praysede JMO; Penitence] pytaunce S. 1110 cleped] callyd
JMO; þe] nota de penitencia *rub. mar.* M; yle] lyle S; hyd Alle] *trs.* S;
make] gerte J. 1111 bifore] to fore S. 1112 and¹] *om.* JMOS; yerde] -s
G, rod *over* O³. 1113 angwich] angwysh (h O³) O. 1114 sinne] *om.* J.
1115 harded] hardnede JMO; softe] Softene JS; it¹] *om.* MO; weepe] to
wepe J, soffte / weepe S; compleyne] to compleyne J; sighye] to Sigh J, syght
O. 1116 sorwe] to sorowe J; bi] thurgh J; þe] *om.* JMO. 1118 bi] þorowe
J. 1119 what] what *add. can.* O; haue] hiely *add.* J. 1120 allegeaunce] *with*
or foryeuenes *mar.* C³, repentaunce & allegeaunce S; þilke] that JO, þis M.
1120-1 I brosede] ebrused S. 1121 so¹] *om.* J; sumtime] some tyme (*2nd
minim and 1st e* O³) O; Peeter] the Apostille *add.* J; and] *om.* S; þat] nota de
sancto Petro *rub. mar.* M; so] a *add.* J, *om.* O. 1122 his ... maister] he
forsoke J; he ... forsake] his good maystere J; he] *om.* O; hadde] did S.
1123 I beet] hym *add.* J, it be O; tendre and softe] I made hym J. 1123-4 I
... him] tendyr and softe J. 1124 in] tille J; bi] þorow J. 1125 bi] owte
of J; come out] the Iuys J; þe iuse] coume J. 1126 þe] *om.* MO;
Magdaleyne] Magdalene F, Maudeleyne GJMOS. 1127 riht so] the same J,
also M; how] (*with* thowgh *mar.* G³), comment F, þouh CS; þat] euere *add.* J;
harded] hardnede JMO; in] with JMO, de Magdalena *rub. mar.* M. 1128 bi
long] Olange J; betinges] betynge JMO; made so] *into mar.* (*with er. mar.* C³)
C. 1129 hire¹] eyen *add.* J; of²] *om.* J; hire iuse] Iuys J, Iuysse of her S.
1129-30 ysen out] issir F, gon out C, I Sente oute of here J, I sent oute MO.
1130 al] *om.* MO. 1131 and] *om.* JMO; ysed] issues F, ronnen C, *om.* JMO;
of ... wel] weel of an hert S. 1132 hem] þem JM, þan O; ayen] sammen J;
and] *om.* MO. 1133 sithe] Seyne JMO; inne] *om.* MO; and] for to *add.* S.
1134 þilke] Tha JMO; tere] -s JMO; is] ar JMO; riht] *om.* JMO. 1135 so²]
no so J. 1136 it ne is] ne it es J, þen it is MO; wasshe] and purgyd *add.* J;
þat²] *om.* JMO. 1136-7 so wel washe] *om.* S. 1137 so wel laþere] *om.* JS;
and] *om.* S; hath God] *trs.* J. 1138 lauendere] lavandiere F, laundere JMO,
Loo howe dame Gracedieux declareþe why sheo bereþe þe maylet with hir *add.* S;
Now] *prec.* Capitulum liii *mar.* CGS (*and* 53 *mar* G³), *om.* J. 1139 yit] wel yit
C; þe] þis MO. 1140 is] as *add.* O, but *add.* S. 1141 likour foul] *trs.*
JMO; men] *ins.* O; voide] be voyd O. 1142 as²] þat MO; mown] myght
MO; not turne] *trs.* J. 1143 þat¹] And þat J; þat²] he that J; his¹] had
add. can. M; hardnesse] hardynesse J, harnies (i *ins.*) O; and] *om.* MO; his²]
om. J, of MO. 1144 obstinacioun] obstynacy J; wole] he wole (he *ins.*) C;
ne²] F, *om.* CJMOS; þilke] that JMO. 1145 my] *illegible word over* C³.
1146 Peeces] Smale Pecis J; and ... and] *om.* J, *illegible word over* C³, as for
contrycioun S. 1147 þat¹] þo O. 1148 shed] out *add.* JM; if] *ins.* M;
knewe] knokkid J, know *alt.* knokk M, contrisoie (*variant* connissoie *A*⁷) F; hem]
it J; and] I S. 1149 not] hit J; riht] þem M; smale] þere myght leve *add.*
JM, þer myght bene *add.* O; of hem] þerof J, of it MO; þer] of one pece þere J.
1150 in þe peeces] *om.* J, Penance tellis of contricion with his maylette *add. rub.*
M, Takeþe hede howe dame grace dieux sheweþe þe maner of verray contricioun ·
by open ensaumples *add.* S. 1151 Now] *prec.* Capitulum liv *mar.* CGS (*and*
54 *mar.* G³), capitulum xxviii *rub. mar.* M, Vndyrstandeth J; vnderstondeth]
nowe J; lessoun] doctryne S; ye] alle yee S. 1151-2 verray ... sinnes] for
synnes wille hafe verraye contricyoun J. 1152 ne²] F, *om.* CJMOS.
1153 weeneth] nouȝt *add.* JS; sufficeth] suffice MO; biholde] beon holde

contryte S;   and ... sinnes] ȝowre synnes generaly So J, þe synnes and thynk MO;
thinke] on add. S.   1154 for ... gret] for þat J, sorow þat add. o. er. M³,
forlookyng S;   is] nys (n can.) G, and S;   but] om. S;   leue] ye lefe J, to leue
MO, not add. S.   1155-6 and ... and] ne in gret sherdes / for oþer in þe potte
or S.   1155 yit] om. J;   were not þat] that ware nouȝt J;   for] þaim add. J.
1156 eche²] ylke ane J;   of hem] a sherde S;   mihte] prec. Contricio rub. mar. M.
1157 to] om. JS.   1158 brose] om. J, buse hem S;   bi] al by M, in S;   smale]
sherdes add. S;   gobbettes] morseles J;   parties] partys J, partes MO, pieces /
þat is to sey S;   grete] forthyngkynge and add. J, thynkyng and add. MO, sore S.
1159 syhinges] Syghynge JMO;   and] o. er. with er. mar. C, om. JMOS;   gret]
om. JMOS;   hachees] om. JMOS;   in] om. JMO;   thinkinge] on this wyse add.
J, om. MO.   1159-60 swich ... þus] om. S.   1159 swich] (sw o. er. C).
1160 þow didest] (w o. er. C), trs. JMO;   Sonedai] þou dydist þus add. S;
Moneday] mononday O.   1161 þat¹] þis S;   þanne] om. MS;   gret was þat]
which was horryble and gret S. 1162-3 so ... manere] om. S.   1162 þou dist]
did þou soo J, so add. MO.   1163 þee] so to done / and longe to perseuer
vnrepentant contryt ne confessed if add. S;   litel þow were] litille was þou J, Litil
þou was MO, þowe were lytell S;   tempted] tempid M.   1164 or litel] om.
JMO;   þow were] om. JMOS;   stired] om. JMO;   or²] om. JMO, but S;   þe ...
þow] by þy sordyble and voluptuous thoughtes S;   purchasedest] made JMO, þe
an apetyt of yuell doyng so leues þou þe potte al hoole add. S.   1165 þilke] that
JMO;   to²] For to J;   of] into mar. O².   1166 it] cleene add. S;   swich]
parfyt S;   witeth] with J.   1167 þat] which S.   1168 al¹] þe hoole potte
add. S.   1169 any] thing add. MOS, Yit dame Grace dieux declareþe moore
openly of þe foule potte of conscience ful of filthe add. S.   1170 Yit] prec.
Capitulum lv mar. CGS;   a ... woord] wille I telle ȝowe J;   I telle yow] a litille
worde J, I wil tell þow M;   þat] (with thylke mar. G³), þilke C;   pot] of conscience
add. S.   1171-3 for ... withinne] om. S.   1171 with] of S;   for] with add.
M;   grete] om. JMO.   1172 norture] nurryschynge JMO;   withinne] thare
add. J;   engendred] genderid M.   1173 born] borne (e ins. G³) G;   norished]
nuryschit alt. nuryschid O.   1174 seemeth] (1st e ins. G³);   þe] hir S;   teeth]
teche JO;   for] prec. vermis conscientiae rub. mar. M.   1176 if þer] om. J;
not] ne J;   who] I ware J, I MO.   1177 astone] stane JS.   1177-80 it² ...
it³] om. O.   1177 rounge] raunge C, Renge (with Raunge mar. G³) G, frete hit
ȝa J, frete it M, rovnge it is S.   1178 til] forte (te ins.) G;   it] om. S;   his] þe
JM;   þerfore] þere M.   1179 mailet] the maliet JM, a maylet S;   þat¹] the J;
it] om. S;   nouht] þe potte of þe conscience add. S;   sle] smyte J, fleey S.
1180 and¹] om. S;   smite] stane J;   astone] Slae J, stoon S;   wel] fulle JMO.
1181 brosed] ebrused lyche S;   haue] here to fore add. S;   but if] trs. J, but C;
it] þe conscyence S.   1182 contrite bifore] trs. S;   it] worme J.   1183 ne
... dye] om. JMO;   Now suffreth] trs. J;   youre] o. er. (with er. mar. C³) C.
1184 I wole] trs. J.   1185 sle] ins. mar. O³.   1186 þe] om. S;   þat²] & it J,
which S.   1186-7 Contricioun is cleped] is callid contricioun J, is contricien called
MO, Here Penaunce tellis of confession whilk beris a besom in hire mowth add.
rub. M, Howe þat Gracedieux openeþe to vs þe tokein and þe signefyaunce of hir
besome add. S.   1188 Now] prec. Capitulum lvi mar. CGS, capitulum xxix rub.
mar. M;   I wole] trs. JS;   þe] my JMO;   þat] which S;   haue] holde S.
1189 bitwixe] be tweene GMOS (2nd e ins. G³), in J;   mouht] Confessio rub. mar.
M, Confessioun rub. mar. O;   and] be twene J;   Bifore ... yow] I sayde ȝowe
before J.   1190 chaumberere] chambrer (final r ins. O³), O Chaumborer S;
þe] om. MO.   1191 certeyn] -ly J;   wel] om. J, ful MO;   sittinge] þat add.

can. C;   a] *om.* O.   1192 to¹] *om.* J, *ins.* M;   a¹] *can.* G, *om.* O;   wenche]
hande maydene J, for *add.* S;   so] Sum J;   miche] thynge J.   1193 þe¹ ...
holdinge] myght resonabely move ȝowe J;   may ... yow] and that es the man*ere* of
the haldynge of the besume J;   may] myght MO;   and] *om.* M.   1194 shulde]
schalle JMO;   þilke] that JMO;   bi] of J, to M, þo O.   1195 al ... sweepe]
and Swepe alle the filthe J;   þider] -wardes S;   men shulden] *trs.* J.   1196 elles]
ell O;   gret] agrete JMO.   1197 þat] þer O;   anglet] angle J;   sum²] angel
or in sum *add.* (angel or in *can.*) O;   heerne] (*1st* e *ins.* G³);   or²] sum aþer *add.*
JO, in som odire *add.* M;   crookede] crukede JMO, crook or CGS.   1198 heled]
hidde JMO;   heped] kept S.   1199 diuerse¹] *prec.* 2⁰ *paralipomenon* xxxiii
capitulo rub. mar. O;   places] place MO;   haue] *om.* S;   it] *om.* JMO;   diuerse²]
porte diuerse rub. mar. M.   1200 þat¹] *om.* JMO;   seyd] callede the ȝate JMO;
fisshes] fisches (with fyssches *mar.* G³) G, suches J;   þat ooþer] the toother (*2nd* o
ins. G³) G, Anoþere the ȝate J, an nothir*e* MO.   1201 þat ooþer¹] the toother
(*2nd* o *ins.* G³) G, Anoþere the ȝate J, an nothir*e* MO;   þat oon] anoþere J;   þat
ooþer²] the toother (*2nd* o *ins.* G³) G, anothere J.   1202 of] *om.* J;   holde me
stille] Speke noȝt of at this tyme J.   1203 longe] to lange JMO;   to] forto J;
telle] reherce thay*m* alle J, dwelle S;   among] (? -s G);   alle] othere *add.* J;   oon]
(1 *over* G³), þere es J;   þer is] ane J, of which oon þer is *add.* S;   of] the J.
1203-4 is² ... Neemye] Neemyas Spekes J.   1204 in] of O;   it] *om.* JMO;
cleped] callede J, *om.* MO.   1205 curen] *om.* JMO;   and] *om.* JMO;   out ...
filthes] oute all fylthe J, al filth oute MO (fylthe *into mar.* O³), *prec.* Neemie 2° *rub.
mar.* (*and* Nehemiah O³) O.   1206 þilke] this JMO;   paas] place JMO, -es S;
be] -on S.   1206-7 weren foul] befule JMO.   1207 Now] *om.* J;   beth ...
oon] ȝe schalle J;   wel] *om.* S;   vnderstondinge] vnderstande · that J;   of] *om.*
JS.   1208 chaumberere] Chaumbourier S;   of whiche] and J.   1209 ben¹]
es J;   whiche] weche (*2nd* e *ins.* G³) G;   v] fyue (v *over* G³) G.   1210 whiche]
þe wheeche S;   þe¹] *om.* JMO;   felthe] filthe JMO, -s CGS;   goth] gas JMO,
gon CGS;   þat oon] (1 *over* G³) Ane J, þe first S;   smellinge] swellyng O.
1211 þat ooþer¹] the toother (*2nd* o *ins.* G³) G, anothere J, þe secound S;   is] *om.*
JMO;   of¹] *om.* J;   herkeninge ... heeringe] tastynge J, sauourynge MO;   þat
ooþer²] the toother (*2nd* o *ins.* G³) G, the thrid JS.   1212 savowringe] felynge
JMO;   þat ooþer¹] the toother (*2nd* o *ins.* G³) G, the ferthe JS;   feelinge] (*1st* e
ins. G³), hyerynge JMO;   þat ooþer²] the toother (*2nd* o *ins.* G³) G, the fyfte JS;
of²] *prec.* ye v. sences by which synn enters *mar.* O³.   1213 þese] thyr JMO;
drede nouht] with owtyne drede J;   ofte] tymes *add.* JM, tyme *add.* O.
1214 hem] þa same ȝates J;   ysen ne] *om.* JMO.   1214-15 ayen ... filthes] the
fylthis agayne J.   1214 þilke] þe MO.   1215 and] *om.* JMO;   peyne] paine
F, time CJMO (*o. er.* C);   turnede] lete tourne S.   1216 þiderward] -s S,
Howe þe yate of þe sight is eopened takeþe heede I prey yowe (eepened *alt.* eopened)
add. S.   1217 That ooþer] *prec.* Capi*tulum* lvii *mar.* CGS, {n}ota *mar.* G³, The
JMO;   þe] *om.* J;   sexte] sight S.   1218 saluacioun] þe saluac*ioun*;   which]
the whilke JS;   eche] *o. er. into mar.* C, ilk a J.   1219 purgeth] doþe purge S;
cureth ... wiht] *om.* JMO;   whiche] þe which S;   putteth] putte S.   1220 al]
felthe *add.* J;   if ... foul] *om.* JMO;   þis] ȝate *add.* J, þat M.   1221 sinneres]
þe synners S;   of ... beste] es the beste of thir Sex ȝates J;   þe²] *om.* M;   she] it
JMO.   1222 out] *ins.* M;   fourme] that *add.* JMO, as *add.* S;   ben] ware
JMO.   1223 confessour] -s S;   waymentinge] (men- *o. er. into mar.* C), *with*
lament *mar.* O³;   in²] *om.* O;   weepinge] Lo nowe howe þe besome is borne
by þis Chaumborier towardes þis yaate of þe mouþe here may yee seo *add.* S.
1224 Toward] -es S;   yate] *om.* J;   and born] *om.* S.   1225 al] -so C;

poorge] to purge J; clense] to clense J.   1226 I¹] nature add. S;   chaumberere] Chaumbourier S;   wole] wolde CO.   1227 withoute] any add. S;   withholdinge] holdynge G.   1228-9 My ... filthes] om. JMO.   1228 palet] of my mouthe add. S.   1229 remeeve] it add. J;   clense] it add. J.   1230 þerinne] þere M;   corner] (1st r ins. O³);   ne²] neyþer S.   1231 þat ... ne] that ne alle I J, þen al I MO;   wole] seche and add. O;   and¹] serch and add. M, om. O;   seeche] om. O;   and²] also add. M;   bi] thurgh J.   1232 outtakinge] (out erased C), of add. S, exepcioun of JMO, of add. S.   1233 bi] erased C.   1234 withinne] þerin JMO;   bere] it add. J.   1236 which] that J;   wole] wolde S;   but] ȝif add. JMO;   riht] om. J.   1237 and] and add. S;   þat] om. O;   she hath] þere be JM, om. O.   1238 cure] herne J;   of] thy add. J;   in whiche] where any S; is] be J;   inne] lefte J.   1239 chaumbre] schambreer (er ins. O³) O;   dwellinge] a wellyng O.   1240 swept] swepede JMO, bailee F, kept CG, ekepte S, Penaunce tellis of Satisfaccioun with hire ȝerdes add. M, Nowe shoule yee here howe þis Chaumbourier and why sheo holdeþe hir yerdes and what sheo doþe with hem add. S.   1241 Now] prec. Capitulum lix mar. CGS, capitulum xxx rub. mar. M, thus mar. G³;   ye haue] trs. J;   holde] bere MO;   þus] om. JMO.   1242 also I make] I make also JS.   1243 and] And nowe J, Now CMO (o. er. C);   I wole] trs. MO;   yow] nowe add. S;   also] om. JMO;   tokenes] betakynnynges J.   1244 holde] Satisfaccio rub. mar. M, Satisfaccioun rub. mar. O;   what] (h ins. O³);   and²] than add. J, yif yee lust to here add. S;   ye] sche O.   1245 not ... it] see that I halde thaym nouȝt J;   Of] o. er. O³, þees add. S.   1246 chastisere] chastysere J, chaistesere M, schasteser O, chastysiere S.   1247 xxⁱᵗᵗᵀ] xxx MO;   yeer] wynter M;   of²] fourty or add. J.   1248 euel-doere] -s JO;   chyld] er callede J, is called MO, is cleped O, a chylde S, maledictus puer centum annorum rub. mar. M;   is cleped] childer J, a childe MO;   of] De F, by CJMO;   courseth] cursede JMO.   1249 þanne] Of thayme JMOS;   misdoo] mys do (do ins. G³) G;   me] om. JMO;   awaite] Wayte J.   1250 my] any J.   1251 spoke] spooke (e ins. G³) G;   and¹] om. JMO.   1253 shrive] scherwyn (r ins. O³) O, eshryven S;   haue] om. J;   seid] before add. J;   to] wol I S;   chastise] schasty O.   1253-4 with ... him¹] and Smyte hym with me ȝerdes J.   1254 my] smerte add. CG³ (ins. mar. G³), cinglans (variant cuillans L) F;   yerdes] ȝerde M;   him¹] with add. S;   him²] to hym O.   1255 and] for add. J;   Oon] And J, and on O;   houre] -s J, þat add. O;   make] þat I make add. can. O.   1256 remembre] to remembre J;   sey] on this wyse add. J.   1257 to²] for to S.   1258 sey] to say J;   faire] and add. J;   sweete] swete add. can O;   bihote] hete J.   1259 þat I] to J.   1260 þee¹] ins. mar. G³;   þat I dar] to do na mare J;   for] tofor (to ins.) C;   þus] om. J, I make þee þus S;   I make] hym add. mar. can. G³, hym add. JM (ins. M), þus S.   1262 yiue] to gyffe JM, om. S;   departe] parte S;   þat²] at J.   1263 to] om. MO;   mendivauns] (vauns subpuncted with er. mar.) C³, beggers JMO;   do] to do J, a noþer tyme to do S;   almesse] Almesdedys J.   1264 go] to goo J;   and¹] sore add. S;   pilgrimage] -s S;   in²] om. J.   1265 anooþer] Sum J;   faste] to faste JS;   and] or O;   do] to do JS;   sum] om. J;   to] for to S;   him] om. MO.   1266 þus] gates add. J;   yerde] my ȝerd MS.   1267 him¹] & chastise him add. (can. rub.) C, weel add. S;   bete] smyte S;   wel] om. S;   and²] om. S;   smyte] beete S;   and³ ... him] om. JMO;   to] þat S.   1268 it] conscience over C, with scilicet consyence mar. G³, the worm of conscience JMO, so add. S;   nouht] and remoorde S;   ne turne] ne that he turne nouȝt J, þat he tourne not S;   ayen] -s O.   1270 sinnes] synne J.   1271 passe] om. J.   1271-2 with ... sinne] om. JMO.   1272 þilke] þey S;   beten] ebeete S;   hath] haue S;   Heerfore] and þer fore S.   1273 holde] kepe S;   hem] and *add.* S; Now ye] *om.* J; wite] *om.* J, wote MO; it] *om.* J, þis S; fro misdoinge] from mys dooynge G, kepeȝ ȝowe nowe J, for mysdoyng O, from misdoing · I prey yowe S; keepeth yow] fra mysdoynge J. 1274 if] And if CS (*o. er. into mar.* C); ye] *prec.* {nota per} Shirley *mar.* S; þe²] my JS; yerdes] ȝerd M; þei] it M; ben] is M; cleped] callede JMO. 1275 to¹] at J; as] for *add.* S. 1276 peyne] penau*n*ce J,a peyne S; withoute] *om.* J, grouchching or *add.* S; ayenseyinge] a ȝens seyenge GS, *om.* J, gayn saynge MO. 1277 in] doyng of *add.* S; sinne] Here penaunce tellis more of þe holy sacrament *add. rub.* M, Nowe þe Chaumbourier openeþe to hem / why sheo is commen betwene Moyses bord and hem wheeche abyden · on þalmesse of his releef *add.* S. 1278 Now] *prec. Capitulum* lx *mar.* CGS, ca*pitulum* xxxi *rub. mar.* M; I haue] *trs.* J; yow²] youre C, alonge J, *om.* MOS; sermoun] moyses burd or the lawe grace by Christ our helpe *mar.* O³; my] myn S. 1279 craftes] ocupaci*o*uns S; but] and MO; bitwixe] betweene GJMOS. 1280 bitwixe] betweene G, entre F, *om.* JMOS. 1281 seid] y seyd G, tolde S; yow] alle *add.* JMO. 1282 telle] seye S; yow] þe sooþe *add.* S; shulde] shoul S; wite] with J, vnderstande S; am] booþe þe *add.* S; partere] Portere JMO, þe partier S; porter] partere MO, þe portier S. 1283 þis] þe M; Withoute] for with oute S; shulden] shoule S; come þernyh] nere hit J; if] *om.* O. 1284 wole] wolden C, walde J; to¹] forto JS. 1284-5 to yive to¹] *om.* J. 1285 truwauntes] tyreauns (*with* trywans *mar.* G³) G; to²] forto J; to³] *om.* O, þees *add.* S; womman] wynmene þat beon S. 1286 she] þey S; be] *om.* O; a] *om.* MO; releef] reelef (*with* Releef *mar.* G³) G. 1287 for¹] and in JMO; syke] Sekenesse JMO; and] *om.* JMOS; for²] *om.* JMO; daungerous] *om.* JMO. 1288 taketh] makith J, heede *add.* S; digneliche] worthyly it JMO; may not] ne may not JS. 1289 þat he ne] þat ne he J, þen he M, þam he O, but þat he S; allegeaunce] legeaunce M. 1290 cene] F, (*with scilicet* souper *add.* G³), sopere CJMO; þer] þat *add.* S; ceened] him self *add.* S, cena F, suppede CJMO; þilke] this in the relefe J, þis is þe breede (breede *o. er.*) M, þis es O, þat S. 1290-l and departede] to his frendes JMO (to *ins.* O), *om.* S. 1291 to ... freendes] and depertyd JMO; þe on þe JMO; grete] schire JS. 1292 þe world] cristen mén S; is] Beon S; and¹] alle þe worlde *add.* S. 1293 I¹] es JMO; wole] welle JMO; keepe] kepede JMO; cheerliche] clerely J; ne] and JS; I wole] *trs.* J. 1294 þat¹] *om.* M; go] come S; þat²] *om.* JMOS; my] -n C; yerdes] ȝerde M. 1295 if] *om.* CMO. 1296 keepe him wel] as for hym Selfe J; as for himself] kepe hy*m* wele J. 1297 þat þat] þat JO; I ouhte] me awe to do J, to doone *add.* S; And] wateþe weel verrayly þat *add.* S; is] *om.* J, þe pryncypal and al *add.* S; for whiche] why JMO, why at þis tyme S. 1297-8 in ... wise] þus S. 1298 swich] slike M; hider] and þer for vnderstondeþe and bere it awey I prey yowe *add.* S, Takeþe heede now / howe þe Lady dame Charite telleþe hir offyce *add.* S. 1299 Whan] *prec. Capitulum* lxi *mar.* CGS, ca*pitulum* xxxii *rub. mar.* M; told] alle *add.* J; doinge] -s J. 1300 heeld] had J; þe] hire MO. 1300-1 in ... hande] *om.* J. 1301 wolde ... scripture] *om.* JS. 1302 bifore] for fore S; folk] the folke J; she] Caritas *rub. mar.* M, Charitie *rub. mar.* O; wel] *om.* JO, whyle S; is] alle *add.* J. 1303 lesinge] Charitie *mar.* O³; and] or S; withoute ... disceyte] penytence J; Penitence] with owtene lesynge ad desayte J, þat penitence MO. 1304 yow²] of *add.* J, leving *add.* S; and²] yow S. 1305 wole] wolde nowe S; yow] *om.* S; also] wherfor and *add.* M, *om.* S; who] whate J, þat *add.* S; am¹] For *add.* S. 1306 þilke] Scho JMOS; hadde neuere] *trs.* J; in] *om.* J; neiþer] *om.* MO. 1307 þilke] Scho JM, *om.* O, and sheo S. 1307-8 þat ...

þilke] om. O.   1307 hol] alle J;   herte] and add. JM.   1308 þilke] Scho
JM, I am sheo S;   seecheth] seechet G.   1308-9 seecheth ... smyteth] has
sette hir entente to forbere her enmyes J.   1308 neiþer] noon MO.   1309 þilke]
Scho JM, siche O.   1309-10 hath ... enemyes] Seketh no vengaunce ne nane
purseweth ne smyteth J.   1309 hath] has o. er. O³;   to] for to MO.
1310 vertues] I am add. S;   þilke] scho JMO, same add. S.   1311 cloþeth]
revest F, cloþed C;   folk] om. J, -s S;   þilke] Scho JMO (sche has e ins. O);
vncloþe] to vncleth J.   1312 cloþe] hym add. can. M;   norishe] þe Noryce S.
1313 orphanynes] the faderlesse J, orphanys MO, þe Orphanynes S;   osteleer]
hostellier S;   to] of J, pore add. S;   þat] Scho þat J, and S;   of¹] om. JMO;
þe] alle J, om. MO.   1313-14 harmes of ooþere] othere men harmes JMO.
1314 I] om. J;   make] -th J;   alle] folke add. J, men add. M, mankynde add. S;
commune] And yif yee desyre / to knowe add. S.   1315 if ... wite] om. S;   it]
es J, is add. MO, is cleped add. S;   Charite] and soo add. S.   1315-16 ye ...
for] om. JMO.   1316 charitee] I S;   holt] holde S;   cheertee] cheerte (3rd e
ins. G³) G, chere J;   þat þat] that J;   ooþere] men add. M, folkis add. S.
1317 visite] -th J;   þe²] om. M;   languishinge] languyse and þem þat morneȝ · I
comforte M.   1318 þilke] scho JMOS;   ooþeres] othere JMO;   good] -s
JMO, with others good mar. O³;   am²] es JMO.   1319 þilke¹] Scho JM, sch
O, I am scheo S;   debonairliche] & add. J;   suffreth al pacyently Suffres J, and
add. MO, thing add. S;   pacientlich] alle J;   þilke²] Scho JMO, I am sheo S.
1320 þat¹] om. O;   keepith not] neuer kepeþe S;   heere] o. er. C, to hire JMOS;
murmur] grucchynge JMO;   þilke] Scho JMO, I am sheo S;   þat²] was add. ins.
M.   1321 of] thurgh J;   ooþere¹] athe JO;   ne] neuer add. S;   ooþere²] tille
othere J.   1321-2 misdede ... withoute] om. O.   1321 and] om. S;   nouht]
om. S.   1322 for þanne] forthy J, om. S;   I ... maad] Ne ellys neuer did I · ne
made S;   doo] Sum JM;   sum] to do J, tak o. er. M, om. S;   withoute] for S;
misdoinge] any misse doyng to me S.   1323 If] prec. Yit þis fayre lady dame
Charite declareþe more of hir ocupacioun S, prec. Capitulum lxii mar. CGS;   ouht
herd] trs. S;   þe] om. J;   and] om. J, I S;   told] om. J, yowe first add. S.
1324 bicome] be come (be ins. and mar.G³) G;   deth] þe deeth S;   þe] om. J;
men] mankynde J, -s soules S;   ye] now thus mar. G³;   shulde] shul S.
1325 haue] to hafe and to suffyr J;   swich] slike M;   annoye] am I J, and peyne
add. S.   1326 made¹] was þe causer of S;   him come] his komyng S;   from]
fra JMO.   1327 of] and M;   bounde] be boundene J, bow MO;   corowned]
hym add. MO.   1328 thornes] þe thornes S;   in] on JMOS.   1330 I
made] of him JMOS;   tacche of him] I made be tuchede J, I made tach M, I mad
take O, I made tachche on the crosse S;   and] sithe add. S;   perce] persede J;
hem] om. J.   1331 Sithe] Seyne JMO.   1332 his ... yelde] yeelde his gooste
S;   witeth] ȝe add. JMO;   wel] þat add. C;   harmes] armes S.   1333 turne]
to turne J.   1335 doo] om. O;   deepe] -s S;   to] for to M;   yow²] om. J.
1336 leue] to lefe J, laissier F, lene C;   þat¹] whilke J;   is] om. J.   1337 with]
bi ins. C.   1339 þis] the JO;   þat] whilke J.   1340 present] in my hande J;
Testament] þe testament S;   cleped] callyd JO, called and named of cristes own
mouth M.   1341 Now heereth] heres it for nowe J, Now here ȝhe it MO;   I ...
it] vnto þow at þis tyme add. M, and take hede S, there follow Here is þe testament
of pees · and tellis what it is add. rub. M, Howe þe feyre lady dame charite redeþe
you here þe testament of pees add. S.   1342 I] om. GJMOS, Je F, prec.
Capitulum lxiii mar. CGS, capitulum xxxiii rub. mar. M;   þe] that es JMO;   sone
of Marie] mary Sonne JMO;   soothnesse] Sothefastnesse JMS;   lyf] and add. J.
1343 nyh] prochaine F, niht C;   I make] maketh J;   laste] om. J.

1344 testament] and my laste wille *add.* J.   1345 in] *ins.* M;   of²] Testa*mentum*
pacis *rub. mar.* M, Testamente of pece *rub. mar.* O.   1346 þe] *om.* C.
1347 fynde] Seke J;   seeche] fynde J.   1348 whiche] þe whilke MO.
1350 sithe] Seyne JMO.   1351 for ... bicomen] *om.* M;   chyld] achilde J, *om.*
M.   1351-2 and ... world] *om.* MS.   1352 was] that *add.* J;   shulde] shuld
(d *ins.* O³) O;   and] *o. er.* C;   þat] *o. er.* C, *om.* J;   hadde] shulde haue *o. er.*
(*with er. mar.* C³) C.   1353 cuntre] atte the tyme of my birthe *add.* J.
1354 present þerof] þere of a presente J, a presand þer of MO;   for] of JMO.
1355 sithe] seyne JMO.   1356 þe] *om.* OS;   time] *om.* S.   1356-7 ne ...
hers] *om.* S.   1357 for] bot for MO;   kepten] kepeth JMOS;   mihten] I
myght O.   1358 hem] to hem S.   1359 it in havinge] possessioun J;   had]
er. add. C, *om.* JMO.   1360 lust] lyste J.   1360-l for ... it] *om.* S.
1360 may] þere may J.   1361 alleweys] alwey JMO.   1362 ledeth] ledde
JMO;   and] *om.* O;   at] *om.* JMO;   lust] lyste JMO.   1363 rihtes] ryghte
JM;   hath] sheo haþe S;   þerto] brought me M, *om.* O;   brouht me] þer to M.
1364 þilke] that JMO;   yive] I gyffe JM, I gafe O.   1364-5 and² ... hem] *om.*
JMO.   1365 abaundone] habounde S.   1366 forged] *om.* JMO.   1367 of²]
or J.   1368 of] or MO, en (*variants* ne *LH²* ou *A*) F;   makinge noise] *trs.* J.
1369 tobreken] breketh JMO;   it²] *om.* GS;   vnmaken] vmmakys O;   it³]
followed by er. C, Nowe dame Charite enfourmeþe vs of þe setting vp of þe Iowayle
add. S.   1370 If] *o. er.* C, *prec.* Capitulum lxiv *mar.* CGS (*with a cross mar.* G³);
þer] *o. er.* C;   were] *o. er.* C, be JS;   any] *o. er.* C, man *add.* J;   þat] *o. er.* C;
wolde] wille JS;   wite] with J;   of] *om.* J;   his] sa F, the J, þis MOS;   facioun]
farcioun þerof J;   wolde] wille J.   1371 take] hym here *add.* J;   þe ...
propirliche] the proper patron therof J, þe patrone properly þer of MO, proprely
þe patroun S;   to hem] *om.* J;   of] by J.   1372 Whoso] he so (*with ho under
rubrication mar.* G³) G, And soo S;   a] *om.* G, þe S;   carpenteres] carpentere
JMO, carpentiers S;   sqwire] swier (i *ins.*) O;   upward] -es S.   1373 if he
sette] and JMO;   doun with þe] *om.* S;   cornere] that ioyneth the lynes *add.* J,
dovne *add.* S.   1374 þat] *om.* J;   wel] A were weel S, *om.* C;   a] F, in þe C,
om. JMOS;   poynt] point F, payntede that J, poynted MS, payntyd O.
1375 were] and were Ioyned and S;   and sette] *om.* JS;   a] *rub.* G;   þe²] *om.* J.
1376 p] *rub.* G, a P S;   x¹] *rub.* G, an X S;   x²] *rub.* G, þe x S;   hy] hyght M.
1377 p] *rub.* G;   alowh] lawe JMO, lich *add.* S;   heere] in þis margyne *add.* S;
figured] and Sette *add.* JMO, *diagrams follow* GJM, ¶ p ¶ a *follows* O.
1378 lightliche] soo *add.* S;   wite] with J;   aperceyue] apercevoir F, perseyue
GJMOS.   1379 his] is JS;   name] nane J;   right] *om.* JMO;   writen] y
wryten G, Loo here filowing declareþe þauctour þe tokeninge of þeos thre lettres ·
P · A · and x : takeþe heed *add.* S;   These] *prec.* Capitulum lxv *mar.* CGS, þire J.
1380 to²] of J, þoo MO;   þilke] þay JO, *om.* M.   1381 þat²] *om.* J, þe MOS.
1382 þere] whare JMO, *om.* S;   x] *rub.* G;   in¹] an J, on MO, in his S;
scaffold] scaffaldede J;   I am] *om.* S;   in short] vnderstandyne J, it is *add.* S.
1383 vnderstonde] schortly J;   tokened] onbetaknede J.   1384 swich] slike
M;   ben] schuldebe J.   1385 amended] Yit Charytee redeþe forþe of þe
testament and descryve þe lettres *add.* S;   Afterward] -es S, *prec.* Capitulum lxvi
mar. CGS;   anglet] cornere J;   wel] *om.* J;   sett] *om.* JS.   1386 and¹] *om.*
JS;   where] *om.* S;   she] A J, *om.* S;   is¹] *om.* S;   a] *rub.* G, *om.* J.
1387 vnderstonde] Anima That es *add.* J;   þat] whilke JMO;   in] is in J;   þe³]
om. O;   manhode] man herde O;   is] *om.* M.   1388 shulde] he schulde J, þe
schuld O;   destroyinge] restreynynge JMO, þe destroying S;   misdedes] (mis *o.
er.* C *with er. mar.* C³).   1389 be] destruyede *add.* J;   arased] racede JMO.

1390 þilke] thay J, þo MO;   is] er JMO.   1391 nouht] worth *add*. J;   for] to
J;   him] thay*m* JMO;   he] thay J;   apese] pese J;   þe] they J;   werre] were J.
1392 bitwixe] betwene GJMOS;   him] thay*m* J;   bi] thurgh J;   instrument] -ʒ
MO.   1393 yit] *om*. J;   þe¹] *om*. J;   p] *rub*. G.   1394-5 to ... haue ouhte]
hy*m* awght to hafe J.   1395 to] alle J;   meeve] *om*. MO;   him] *om*. S;   þe] in
the J;   is] hes O.   1396 hyere] heyegher S;   boþe] for bath J;   sette] se O;
hem] *om*. M.   1397 þe scripture] I fourmede J, I þe scripture S;   I fourmede]
the scripture J, fourmed S;   ben] to be JMO;   dedlich] Ilyke JMO.   1398-
9 worm¹ ... ooþer] *ins. mar*. G³.   1398 þat oon²] 1 *over* G³.   1399 woorth] a
add. J;   herte] and felle *add*. J.   1400 noþer] *om*. M;   we] *om*. J.   1401 oon]
a J;   hole] both *add*. MO.   1401-2 Now let hem] latte thay*m* nowe J.
1402 so] lytell and *add*. S;   miche] *om*. J;   jewel] goode wille S;   bi] thurgh J.
1403 Eche] Ilke a J, ilk M, euery S.   1404-6 squyre ... þis] *om*. JMO.
1406 þilke] that JMO, þis S;   notarye] notaries C.   1407 whiche] þe whiche
CJ;   shulden] it schulde J;   signed] merkede JMO;   marked] Signede JMO.
1408 þilke] that JMO;   openliche I haue] I have openly JMO;   testament]
testamemte G.   1409 confermed] conseruyd O.   1410 eche] ilk a J, ilk M.
1411 in] to CJ;   þat] that *add*. MO;   þerafter] eftere that JMO;   eche] ilke JM.
1412 wiht] wele *add*. M;   keepe] (*3rd* e *ins*. G³);   it] how charite is awmnere and
dispensere of relefe of Moyses denere *id est* holy sac*r*ament *add. rub*. M, Loo þus
Charite eondeþe hir testament and affter sheo bygynneþe hir p*ar*llement *add*. S.
1413 Whan] *prec*. Cap*itulum* lxvii *mar*. CGS, cap*itulum* xxiv *rub. mar*. M;   þis]
hys O;   rested] hir a litille *add*. J.   1414 ayen] *om*. O;   parlement] Sermoun
J;   suiche] slike M.   1415 afterward] *om*. JMO;   Lordinges] slike *add. can*.
M, *om*. O, quod sheo *add*. S.   1416 haue rad heere] here hafe redde J.
1417 his] worthi *add*. M;   grauntede] ʒowe *add*. J, haues graunted M.
1418 Now] And nowe J;   wole I] *trs*. JMO.   1419 sett] *om*. J;   with] *om*. O;
þilke] that JMO;   bitwixe] betwene GJOS.   1420 boord] þis tyme of þe fest
add. S, Yit dame Charite declareþe here more of hir office and ocupacioun *add*. S;
Wite] *om*. J, ᛠIt *with scribe's guide* y *visible* S, *prec*. Cap*itulum* lxviii *mar*. CGS;
shulden] schalle wele vnderstande J, shoullen S;   awmenere] awner O, amoignnier
S;   dispenser] Spensere J.   1421 Penitence] penau*n*ce JMO.   1422 shulden]
shoule S;   but] it *add*. J, if *add*. S;   wole] wolde J.   1423 yow] *om*. O;   þat]
om. J;   withoute] with J;   ye] ne *add*. S.   1425 þer nygh] nere it J;   ne wole]
wolde nouʒt J, wol not S;   þe] *om*. J.   1426 þe²] that JMO.   1427 bifore
his deth] with me J;   with me] before his deede J;   þerfore] *om*. J;   I bere] to
that ende J, it *add*. MOS;   to þat ende] I bere J;   I²] ʒe JMO.   1428 avise]
F, teche C;   to þe releef] onna wyse ʒe approche J;   in] *om*. S;   in ... approche]
to the releefe J;   come] nere it *add*. J, nygh *add*. M.   1429 but] ʒif *add*. JM;
anglet] Angles J;   þilke] that JMO, þe O, þe ilke S.   1430 jewel] *om*. S;
priuee] p*re*cyous JMO;   wole] I *add*. J;   þilke] that JMO;   holi] iewell *add*.
can. M.   1431 and¹] *om*. S;   gadered] kepede JMO;   if] and JO;   ye] he
(*with* ʒee *mar*. G³) G.   1431-2 hadden it] had it JM, hadyd O.   1432 mihten]
mun*d*e J.   1433 ye¹] *om*. O.   1435 and] but JMO;   passeden] passe JMO;
shulde] schalle JMO.   1436 holde] *om*. S;   and] grete *add*. JM;   mihte] there
myght J;   yow] to yow C, *om*. J;   Now] *om*. J.   1437 wel] that ʒe *add*. J, weel
add. S;   offendeth] Offende J, offende ʒhe me MO;   inow my devoir] my deuere
Inowe J.   14-38 þat] it S;   for which] why S;   fro] -m GO.   1439 chambere]
Nowe takeþe heed my freondes howe þe pilgrymes passen by penytaunce · with þe
iuwayle of pees *add*. S.   1440 Whan] *prec*. Cap*itulum* lxix *mar*. CGS (*and*
69 G³), cap*itulum* xxxv *rub. mar*. M;   al ful] -ly J.   1441 many] monye (e *ins*.

G³) G; þat] *om.* J; were] *into mar. (with u.v.* were *mar.* C³) C, *om.* J; encline] enclins F, -d CMOS (ined *small o. er.* C), enclynande J. 1442 to] and J; obeye] Obeyande J; bi] to JMO; and] *ins.* O³, to *add. can.* O; þe ... pees] beren with hem S. 1443 beren] they bare JMO, þe Iouwayle of pees S; sithe] Seyne JMO; passeden] thay passede JMS; havinge] any *add.* C, drede J. 1444 drede] havynge J; vnderputten hem] putte thay*m* vndir J. 1445 with] *om.* J; hem] and *add.* J; yerdes] the 3erdys JMO. 1446 of þe releef] thay ressayvede J; þei resseyueden] of the releefe J. 1446-7 þe which] that J, whilk MOS. 1447 Sithe] Seyne JMO. 1448 cursede] cursse S; priueliche] pryvelegge S; hydinge] hied JMO; hem] *om.* M. 1449 fro] -m GS; and] *om.* JMO; shame] or drede *add.* J; þei] *om.* C. 1450 it] And *add.* J. 1451 exceptinge] excepciou*n* J; and] or J; ammynistrede] he mynistrede JMO. 1452 curteysliche] certaynly J. 1453 hem²] of hem S. 1454 had] taken*e* JMO; riht as þouh] they be coom as blakke as J; be] *om.* JMO; a] *om.* O. 1455 riht blac] *om.* JMO; sak] seke (*last* e *ins.* O³) O; donge-hep] dunge J. 1456 and¹] al S; salwh] Sulwy J, *om.* M, soloug he O; foul] passynge foule M, black *add.* S. 1457 alle] ouer *ins.* C; kamen] bi kamen (bi *ins.*) C; ayen] *om.* JS. 1458 sauled] Sowlede ne fillede J, soulyd O; if] *om.* JMO; þei²] þan O. 1459 obley-makere] oblyt- M, vmbleye- S. 1460 havinge] obly · a wafer · wafer bread, w*hich* in spayne is vsed in the Sacram*ent add. mar.* O³; Of] On J, For O; oo*þere*] toothere (*2nd* o *ins.* G³) G, syde *add.* J; so] of þe o*þere add.* J. 1461 alle] *caret followed by* ete ÷ alle *with er. mar.* C, eten *add.* S; sauled] Sowlede JO. 1463 þei wolden] *trs.* J; þei²] ne *add. can* G; preyseden] prisyde M. 1464 bicomen] be becomen S; faire] & *add. ins.* C, gentylle J; gentel] fayre J, and so gladd *add.* M; as to] in JO (*o. er. of* to O), as M; regard] reward M, rewarde *alt.* regarde O. 1465 alle] (e *ins.* G³), oþer *add.* S; folk] -es S; þe¹] *om.* O; clerkes] lerede J, and þe letterd men *add.* S; þe lewed] hem þat beon vnlettred cleped lewed men S, How þe pilgryme wondres of þe relefe · and prayes grace dieu to enform him more *þer of add. rub.* M, Nowe listeneþe and hereþe howe þe pilgryme was sore abasshed *add.* S. 1466 Now] *prec.* Capitulum lxx *mar.* CGS (*and* 70 *mar.* G³), ca*pitulum* xxxvi *rub. mar.* M; I wole] wole I CJ (*id est* pilgrime *over* C); withoute] any *add.* S; þat¹] athynge J; þat²] which S; made] (*2nd* a *ins.* G³); me] (*2nd* e *ins.* G³). 1467 michel] gretly J; abashed] a baysche G; it is] me thought J; þat] þat *add.* JMO; litel] a litil M; may] myght J; fulfille] fille J. 1468 þe] mare J; wundres] wondyr me thought J; ben] *om.* J; grettere] *om.* J; whan] that J. 1469 mown] myght J; haue] (*2nd* a *ins.* G³); of ... gret] (not *o. er.* C, *2nd* that *ins.* G³), Sufficiau*nt* fillynge J. 1469-70 fillinge sufficiaunt] of that that es nou3t grete J. 1470 sufficiaunt] suffisaunt G, sufficiaunce M, souffisaunce S. 1471 þouh] þerof J, þof MO; swiche ten] (x *over* G³), I hadde had J; I ... had] (had *with* hadde *mar.* G³), Slyke ten J; a] *om.* JMO. 1472 sufficientliche] suffisantleche G. 1473 þei] *om.* JMO; on] of þem *add.* M; weren] was JMO; fulfilled] fillede JMO; and suffised *om.* JMO. 1473-4 a ... hem¹] and a lytille Suffycede J, and suffisyd a litil MO. 1474 suffised] to ilkane of thay*m* J, to ilk of þem MO, *om.* S; and] *om.* S; ful ... litel] of a litille J, *om.* S; eche] ilkane JM, *om.* S; of hem] *om.* S; was] fulle *add.* J. 1475 This] *prec.* Howe þat þe pilgryme was gretlych troubled and adowted S, *prec.* Capitulum lxxi *mar.* CGS; thinke] for to thynke J; trouble] troubler F, trublede JMOS. 1476 to whom] I ne wyste J; to speke] to wham for to Speke J, I shuld speke M, speke O; I ne wiste] or forto Spirre the cause J, it *add.* O; if] Bot 3if it ware J, bot if I shuld speke (bot if I *o. er.*) M, *om.* O; I ne speke] *om.* JM. 1477 for þanne] thy J;

durste I not] speke MO;   speke] I ne durst MO.   1478 was] *can.* C;   lened]
lenande J, seatyd O, lefft S;   hire] *om.* JMO;   arayed] (d *o. er.* C).   1479 yiven]
om. JMO;   and] *om.* JMO;   almused] GS, aumosner F, al musede C, *om.* JMO;
Algates] Atte the laste J, yit I *add.* S;   hardied] auntrid JMO.   1480 wel nyh]
nerehande JMO;   Whan] and when J;   me²] (*2nd* e *ins.* G³).   1481 towardes]
towarde JMO;   goodliche seide] *trs.* JO, sayde me gudely M.   1482 þou] *om.*
G;   heere] quod scho *add.* J;   þee] now *add.* C, now *add. ins. mar.* G³, *om.* J, *ins.*
M;   Serteyn] -ly J.   1483 soothliche] voirement F, softeliche C, Soth it is J,
om. MO;   ynowh] Sumwhate J, now MO;   lakketh] nowe *add.* J.
1484 sufficeth] suffice MO;   so²] *om.* MO.   1485 folk] of folk C;   to] *om.* J;
þer] it J;   were] *ins.* O³.   1486 ten] x *over* G²;   preye] beseke J.   1487 me]
Loo nowe howe Grace dieux techeþe þe pilgryme *þat* þat he desyreþe *add.* S.
1488 Goode] *prec.* Cap*itulum* lxxii *mar.* CGS;   now vnderstonde] *trs.* J;   anuye]
greue J.   1489 þee¹] Sacra*ment* caled relef *mar.* O³;   to] forto J;   þee³] (*1st* e
ins. G³).   1490 wel] þat *add.* S;   hast] grete *add.* JMO.   1491 flesh and
blood] callede J, no*ta* de pane & vino *rub. mar.* M;   cleped¹] fleshe and blude J,
called MO;   anooþer] houre *add.* M;   it²] *om.* J;   cleped²] callede JMO.
1492 to] vnto M, No*ta rub. mar.* MO;   it is] in sothe O.   1492-3 in sooth] in
Sothfastnes J, it es fygured (fygured *o. er.* O³) O.   1493 but] of *add.* J, *o. er.* O³;
bred ... is] *o. er.* O³;   is] hase J;   figured] the figure J, *om.* O.   1494 sumtime]
prec. A Monkes opinion of þe Sacrament, 300. years since *mar.* O³;   þou] *om.*
JMO;   seye] sigh *o. er.* C, *om.* JMO;   þat] *om.* JMO.   1495 into] *om.* JMOS;
to] a F, *om.* CJMO;   whom] hom G, I helped J, Hym MO, mannes S;   I helpe]
(heelpe *1st* e *ins.* G³), hym J, -d MO, help S.   1496 to] with S;   yuele] *om.* J;
wratthed] I *add.* S;   hire] gretly *add.* J.   1497 þouh] þof (*with* though *mar.*
O³) O;   clepe] calle JMO;   it] a vise þee *add. can.* C;   I] *om.* CJ, I bidde þee S;
þee¹] (*1st* e *ins.* G³), wele *add.* J;   and] I *add.* C;   þee²] (*2nd* e *ins.* G³).   1497-
8 flesh and blood] þou vndyrstande hit J.   1498 it ... þee] flesche and blode J;
vnderstonden] *prec.* Reade wi*th* diligence *mar.* O³;   stidfastliche leeved] leve it
stidfastly J, (*with* beleeued *mar.* O³);   of²] *om.* J.   1499 þee¹] (*1st* e *ins.* G), *om.*
J;   Ne þat shulde] And loke it J, Ne þat shal MO;   not ... þee] move the nou3t J;
taast] (*2nd* a *ins.* G).   1500 bred and wyn] it seemeth to the J.   1501 it ...
þee] (þee *1st* e *ins.* G³), brede and wyne J;   seeme] be seme MO;   disseived þei
ben] es dessayvede J.   1502 thoruhout] *scribble and* ¶ Owte O;   fooles holden]
trs. S;   Doted] fules J.   1503 ben¹] and doted *add.* J;   go] *om.* JMO;   ligge]
alane J;   fonned þei ben] *om.* JMO.   1504 heeringe] þe herynge MO;
vnderstondinge] *om.* JMO.   1505 þilke of] *om.* JMO;   taaste] doth *add. into*
mar. (*with* u.v. do{the} *mar.* C³) C, *om.* J, þe taast MO;   heerayens] *om.* JMO;
oþer] to the J, *om.* MO;   of²] *om.* MO;   smellinge] syght MO;   savouringe] the
Sight J, smellynge MO.   1506 sighte] the sauo*u*rynge J, sauo*u*rynge MO;
þis] heeringe *add. into mar. o. er.* C, *with* sc*i*licet herynge *mar.* O³, In herynge J,
bot in herynge MO;   knoweth] thowe knaweste J, he knowes MO, Isack & Esau
mar. O³;   subtylliche] (i *alt.* y C), sothely M, sutthly O;   apperceyueth] p*er*sayfes
JMO.   1507 And] that lange *add.* J;   it] *om.* J.   1508 Esau] For y sak ful
wiel wende of jacob *þat* fedde hym · that hit hadde been his sone Esau *add. ins.*
mar. C³, videte {*cropped*} *mar.* S;   foure] forsayde *add.* J;   wolden haue] *om.* J;
him] Isaak J.   1509 shalt] maye J;   see pleynliche] opynly See J.   1509-10
hast rad] redyste J;   Genesis] the boke of genese J;   of] in J, *om.* MO;   þe] *om.*
J;   nothing] Heareing noate, that bred, and wyne are the visable sygnes of an
invisable grace *mar.* O³;   disceyued] deceyued *add.* S.   1511 þerbi] þe hering
add. S;   apperceyued] p*er*sayfede it was he J, perceyued MO, hit *add.*S, Howe þat

dame Grace dieux gyveþe pleyne instruccioun vnto þe pilgryme of þe sacrament of oure cristen byleue *add.* S; Right] *prec. Capitulum* lxxiii *mar.* CGS (*and* 73 *mar.* G³). 1512 sey] sawe S; þee] *2nd e ins.* G³), *om.* O, þer S; þou] þo O; triste] truste GS; leeve] *2nd e ins.* G³); in] *om.* O. 1513 foolliche] þorowe tha Wittes J. 1514 weene] (*2nd e ins.* G³); of] *om.* J; it] *om.* J; þat²] *om.* JO. 1515 þerfore] *om.* JMO; be] *om.* J; þe] *2 lines marked mar.* C³; sooþe] þerof *add.* J; þou shalt *trs.* J. 1516 þou mostest] the behoues J. 1517 thoruhout] and tryste J; and triste] and truste GS (e *ins.* G³), alle vtterly for J; þee bi] (*1st e ins.* G³), þerby JMO, for by S; it] *om.* JMO, alloone *add.* S. 1518 sooþe] (e *ins.* G³); by] þorowe J, *om.* S; it] *om.* S; þou] *om.* S; shalt] *om.* S; be] cleerly *add.* S. 1519 þee] (*2nd e ins.* G³); al at] atte J, *trs.* MO; þe] Nota *rub. mar.* O; no more] *om.* J, ne nought ellys *add.* S; wyn] breede JMOS; bred] wyne JMOS. 1520 but] þat *add.* S; sprad] spredde and hyngede J, hanged and spradde S; on þe cros] apon the crosse JMO, for þe S; for þee] (*1st e ins.* G³), on þe crosse S. 1520-1 and hanged] *om.* JS. 1521 þat] tat (*1st t ins.* O³) O; it] *ins. mar.* G³, *om.* S; which] þe which S; þilke] the JMOS. 1522 bidewed] dewyd O; spreynt] Sprynglede J, sprenkelid MO; And] *om.* JMO; þis bred] þowe wille name J; þou ... nempne] this breed wele J, wele *add.* MO. 1523 clepe] calle it JM, it *add.* O; wel and] *om.* JMO. 1524 hath] hafe J; also] And also S; haue ... vsage] (haue *2nd a ins.* G³), vse J; to] so to C. 1525 clepe¹,²] calle JMO; it¹] breede *add.* J, *om.* MO; swich] trewe J, soth M; and] *ins.* O³. 1526 from þe heuene] coom J, fro þe heuen MO; cam] fra heuene J; þe²] *om.* J. 1527 whiche] the whilke J; ben¹] is MO. 1528 bred] with *add. can.* C, with *add.* O; pilgrimes] *into mar.* O³ *and* Nota *rub. mar.* O, þe pilgrymes S. 1529 in ... þou hafe Sene it J; þou ... it] in litille quantite J. 1530 wel ... þee] (haue *2nd a ins.* G³), I hafe declarede the wele J; avised] avise F, tauħt C; þee] (*1st e ins.* G³); to¹] *om.* M; lokinge] lookynge (*2nd o ins.* G³) G, lykynge J. 1531 trist] trust G; haue] to haue S; þe] þi MO; heeringe] (*2nd e ins.* G³); þee] it GJO. 1532 and ... lernynge] (þee *ins.* G³), *om.* JMO; mihte] do *add. can.* G, may J, mygh O; lerne] lere J. 1533 þat²] at J; seyn] How charite was bakester and Sapience muldere of þis brede *add. rub.* M, Howe Charite was þe verray cause of þis bred *add.* S. 1534 Charitee] *prec. Capitulum* lxxiv *mar.* CGS (*can. and* 74 G³), capitulum xxxvi *rub. mar.* (*for* xxvii) M; hast] hath M. 1535 ago] Seyne gane J; þilke] that JMO; and] and *add. can.* O; was] *caret add. with er. mar.* C³. 1536 contrived] contreeued (*2nd e ins.* G³) G; þe] it O; greyn] greene O; from] fra JMO; eerþe] (*2nd e ins.* G³), serche S. 1537 seew] dewe S; þe] *om.* JMO; eerþe] (*2nd e ins.* G³), *om.* JMO, serche S; was¹] Christ ye bread of lyfe note *mar.* O³; was²] it was OS; ered] ernd S. 1538 labowred] by man *add.* J; heete] þe hete S; sunne] þe sunne CJMO (þe *ins.* C *with u.v.* {þ}e *mar.* C³); dew] þe dewe S. 1539 þeron] þer opon M; made] (*2nd a ins.* G³), gerte J; berne] repe J, bery M; straunge] estrange F, strange J, a strong M, stronge O. 1540 founden it þere] *om.* JMO; and¹] *om.* JMO; throsshen] bande J; fanned] thresched J, band MO, *om.* S. 1541 it¹] *om.* S; So ... michel²] *om.* S; fanned] vanneden (en *can.*) G; þat] And S. 1542 from] fra JM, for O; it was] *om.* S. 1543 of] on S; naked¹] nakned GM. 1543-4 to þe mille] he was borne J. 1544 he was born] to the mylne J. 1544-6 disgisyliche ... was] *om.* JMO. 1545 whiche] þe which S; no] o. er. C. 1546 broken] and *add.* CJM; and tormented] *om.* JMO; þilke] that JMO. 1547 maad] (*1st a ins.* G³); to] for J, of S. 1548 grounde] groonde (e *ins.* G³) G, grundene he was J, growndyn MS, *om.* O; þanne] thy J; stones] (*2nd o ins.* G³).

1549 softe] stonys *add.* MO;   stones[1]] (*2nd* o *ins.* G[3]), stany J;   yuel] ille J;
rownynge] grynding S.   1550 frusht] freschede J;   þat] *om.* M.   1551 taken]
taake (*2nd a ins.* G[3]) G, takynge O;   to] in to MO;   hadde] had (*with* hadde *mar.*
G[3]) G, was JMO;   be grounde] growndene JMO;   1552 putte ... charite J;
Charite] putte hir furth J;   bakere] baxter*er* J, þe baker S.   1553 bulte] it *add.*
JS;   make] (*2nd a ins.* G[3]);   al hot] was J;   was] alhete J, it was S.   1554 so]
soth *o. er.* C;   it[2]] *o. er.* C;   is] was J.   1555 turne] molde MO;   ne] *om.* J;
moolde] turn MO;   whiche] and that JM, þat O.   1556-7 but ... hire] *om.* S.
1556 hire[1]] Sare *add.* J, *ins. and ins. mar.* M[3].   1557 þee] (*1st* e *ins.* G[3]);
bithouhte] vmbethought J;   on] of JMO.   1558 þe] *prec.* Sapience *rub. mar.*
MO;   þat was[2]] *om.* S;   burgh] borowgh G.   1559 cleped] callede JMO.
1560 she ne] *trs.* J.   1561 þilke wit] *om.* JMO.   1562 scooles] scole O;   Al
þe world] that scho wolde J;   if she wolde] alle the werlde J;   she] *id est* sapience
over C *with er. mar.* C[3], *with scilicet* sapience *mar.* G[3].   1563 shulde] wolde C;
doo] it *add.* M;   þe] a M;   an ey] an naye M, a ney O;   wel] do and *add.* J.
1564 an] a JM;   þis] hir JMO.   1566 so] *om.* S.   1567 moolded] mylded
J;   bi ... were] hit semede JMO;   were] was S.   1568 and] ȝit *add.* JMO;
þat] *om.* J;   to alle] it myght Suffice J, it myght M, I myght O;   it ... suffice] tille
alle tho J, to al suffice MO.   1569 eche] ilkane JM;   ful] -ly J;   sauled]
sowlyd O;   and wel sufficed] *om.* JMO, Loo nowe howe dame Charite secheþe
dame sapience for to declare hir hir entent and menyng *add.* S;   Whan] *prec.*
Capi*tulum* lxxv *mar.* CGS (*and* 75 *mar.* G[3]), Then J;   hadde] *can. rub.* J, *om.* O.
1570 þus] *can. rub.* J;   ythouht] thought JMO;   hire wille] *om.* S;   to[2]] vn to
M, -wardes S;   to Sapience] sche wente J;   she wente] to Sapience J.   1571 dide
so michel] So it schope J;   hire] Sapience JMO;   She was] whare scho satt J,
where scho was MO, *om.* S.   1572 of al] thynges *add.* J, for *add.* S.   1573 to
... hire[2]] (baake *1st a ins.* G[3]), scho made hir to come with hir J;   she ... come]
forto bake hir breed J, com O.   1574 Sapience] *with scilicet* sapyence *mar.* G[3];
þis ... turnede] turnede hit and mylded it J;   þis] þe MO;   and[1]] N*ota rub. mar.*
O;   it] to þat S;   and[2]] *om.* S.   1575 riht] *om.* O;   of al] in alle thynges J;
yit] *om.* O.   1575-6 subtylliche ... more] *om.* J.   1576 wysliche] wilfullych
S.   1577 þerof feedinge] *trs.* J;   to[2]] for S;   and] to *alt.* and O[3];   þat] *ins.*
O[3].   1578 eche] ilke ane J, ilk M;   mihte] (e *ins.* G[3]);   þerof be] fully *add.* J,
be þer of full MO;   sauled] soulyd O;   and sufficed] *om.* JMO;   how[1]] *om.* O;
wel] and *add.* J.   1579 þat] So J;   made[1]] (*2nd a ins.* G[3]);   seemynge]
semelyng O;   made[2]] (*2nd a, and* e, *ins.* G[3]).   1580 vnder] wonder S;   haue]
to hafe J.   1581 she made] *ins. mar.* G[3], *om.* JMO;   of] *om.* J, al MO.
1582 eche] eeche one (*3rd* e *ins. and* one *can.* G[3]) G, ilkane J, on *add.* MS;   þilke]
the JMO;   of þat bred] schulde be brokyne J;   þat[2]] thilke GS;   shulden ben
broken] (been *1st* e *ins.* G[3]), of þat breed J, schuld brokyn O.   1583 eche]
ylkane JM.   1584 þouh] ȝif J;   togideres] to gedyr JMO;   plesede nouht]
was na thynge plesande J.   1585 to] *om.* M;   hire] nature *over* C, *with scilicet*
nature *mar.* G[3], nature hir S;   þat] thow sawe *add.* J;   chidde] chide J;   me]
(*2nd* e *ins.* G[3]);   certeyn] -ly J;   michel] right mekill J.   1586 hire[1]] me C;
for[2]] grete *add.* J.   1587 hath] es O, hade S;   þere] þat S;   cam] coomes (?
commes) M.   1587-8 of me] (*2nd* e *ins.* G[3]), scho vmbethought hir J.   1588 she
bithouhte hir] of me J, sche thoght hir O;   wel] Sare J.   1589 blamed] (*2nd a
ins.* G[3]);   rebuked] ȝif scho oght mellede hire *add.* J;   þee] (*1st* e *ins.* G[3]).
1590 a ... Aristotle] Scho sought J;   she souhte] a clerke of hyrs þat hight ·
Aristotle J.   1591 to[2]] *with* JM;   hire[1]] sapience *over* C, *with scilicet* sapyence
mar. G[3], Sapience JMO;   to[3]] *om.* O;   toT4XT] *om.* J;   argue] reproeve S.

1592 hire] Howe þat daun Aristotle · was sent by nature to sapience add. S.
1593 Whan] prec. Capitulum lxxvi mar. CGS, capitulum xxxvii alt. capitulum xxxviii
rub. mar. M;   bifore] to fore GS;   he] Aristotil rub. mar. O.   1594 þe] fyrste
J;   sithe] Seyne JMO;   seyde] he syde JMOS;   hire] om. JO;   To] Aristotill
rub. mar. O.   1595 Nature] dame nature S;   speke] & add. CMS (ins. C), with
30we add. J;   to²] forto J, om. S;   shewe] scheewe (1st and 3rd e ins. G³) G.
1596 yowre] (e ins. G³);   mistakinges] mystakynge JMO;   Michel] It displeseth
hir J;   it ... hire] mekille J, it mysplesith hir M, it mysplese hyr O.   1597 quassen]
þus MS;   þus] vndoes M, qwassen S;   hire] here (2nd e ins. G³) G;   ordinaunces]
ordynaunce JMO;   and¹] hem add. S;   remeeven] (2nd e ins. G³).   1598 pleseth]
plese MO;   me] (2nd e ins. G³);   alþouh] þow3 alle JMO;   neuere] nou3t J.
1599 for] ins. G;   þat¹] þen MO, but þat S;   ne] om. MO;   þat³] Atte J.
1599-1600 Wel ye witen] 3e wate wele J, wele · ðhe wote MO.   1600 þat¹] om.
J;   or] ne S.   1601 þat¹] thing is add. S;   þat²] þe which S;   is] conteynyd
add. J;   þerinne] sithen add. MO;   On] om. O;   if] þat yif S.   1602 folk] -es
S;   weene] to wene J;   paleys] place JMO;   a²] greete add. JMO.   1603 torell]
litill JMOS;   litel¹] tourelle or alitille chapelle J, towre M, torell O, tourrette S;
litel² þei wolden] they walde litille JM, lytel wold wolde þey S.   1604 seyinge]
dit F, seyenges GS;   folk] -es S;   and] om. JM;   me] (caret before e G³).
1605 me] (2nd e ins. G³);   sophistre] Takeþe hede nowe of Aristotles wordes to
dame sapience add. S;   These] prec. Capitulum lxxvii mar. CS, Capitulum lxxxvii
for lxxvii mar. G (and 77 mar. G³), þis MO;   thinges] thynge M;   heere] that J,
om. MO;   haue ye] trs. JMO.   1606 þilke] this JMO;   þat] om. J;   is] are
woundere J;   disgise] -d CMO.   1607 with] om. O;   ful] -ly J;   in] ou
(variant au H) F, er. C, alle JMO;   world] worlde (with wordle mar. G³) G, wolde
S;   miht] mygh O, ne might S.   1608 ne ... not] om. JMO;   ne] in add. S;
miht] om. S;   not suffice] trs. S.   1609 bi] on J;   closure] and add. J.
1610 hep] masure F, hopp C;   foureteene] fourteene (2nd e ins. G³) G, fortune O;
hond] alt. hand C.   1611 wolde] Schulde J;   wel¹] weel (1st e ins. G³) G;
hem] hit J, om. MO;   wel²] om. MO.   1612 preeve] (2nd e ins. G³);   ne] om.
JMO;   not²] na JO;   riht] om. J;   þouh] 3if J.   1613 hire] here G, here of J,
þere of add. MO;   ye] he O.   1614 þat¹] at O;   þat²] 3if J;   were] had bene
JO, om. M.   1616 ne ... litel] om. O, þane add. S;   wel inouh] wolde I S;   I
wolde] I wil M, weel enoughe S.   1617 it¹] om. J;   wel] Asente þerto add. J.
1619 feedinge] (2nd e ins. G³);   withoute ... divinynge] om. JMO.   1620 misliketh]
myslykyd J;   stille] payed J;   haue] ins. mar. G³, om. S.   1621 preeued] om.
J;   certeyn] -ly J.   1622 neuere] yit add. o. er. C;   sih] seeyn M;   an] ne ane
J, om. C, and S.   1623 were¹] be JMO;   ne were²] es J, þan it is MO;   a] the
JMO;   ye witen wel] wele þe wate J.   1624 ye] (2nd e ins. G³);   haue] (2nd a
ins. G³);   þe partye] (2nd e ins. G³), deperte alt. þeperte O, þe part S;   as²] om. J;
þe²] om. JMO.   1625 ayens¹] agayn MO;   me] nature S;   and] om. J;
ayens²] ins. G³, a 3eyne O, om. S;   Nature] me S;   þat] it that J, þat · þat S;
am] om. M.   1626 and] om. JMO;   wherfore] om. J, þat add. S;   hider] atte
this tyme add. J;   Now] Luke J;   looketh] nowe J, beoþe avysed S.   1627 hath
... me] can. G³, Sente me JMOS, How Sapience answeris vnto þe clerk Aristotle
add. rub. M, Howe dame sapience · aunswerd daun · Aristotle add. S.
1628 Whan] prec. Capitulum lxxviii mar. CGS (and 78 mar. G³), capitulum xxxix
rub. mar. (another in other mar. erased) M;   Aristotle] -s S;   spoken] þus add. M,
soo spoken S;   Sapience] dame sapience S;   aresoned] aunswerde J, reseyued
MO;   him] can. with hym mar. G³, on this wyse add. J, honestly · and answerid
on þis Wyse add. M.   1629 me] (2nd e ins. G³), for thy add. J;   þat] þat · þat

O.   1630 and] *om.* O;   þerinne] þerof J.   1631 is] er*e* M;   good] goode (*1st* o *ins.* G³) G, -s JMO;   wel þou shuldest] thowe schulde wele J;   if] and JO. 1632 woldest] walde JMO;   þee] (*1st* e *ins.* G³);   tweyne scooles] twey skooles G, two scoles MOS, Sum tyme I helde J;   I ... sumtime] twa Scoles J.   1633 þee and nature] (*2nd* e *ins.* G³), I tawht J;   I tauhte] the and nature J;   For] *om.* J. 1634 me] (*2nd* e *ins.* G³);   to¹] *om.* S;   þat oon] the ton GJMO, þe tovne S; to²] forto J.   1635 excersise] -s JMS;   wunderful] wondir*e* M.   1636 þilke] þat JO, þat scole M;   was first] *trs.* S.   1637 tauhte] Sate J;   hire¹] *om.* JMO; hire²] thare *add.* J.   1638 to] forto J;   make] (*2nd* a *ins.* G³);   gaye] *om.* J; and²] *om.* J.   1639 ooþere] (*2nd* e *ins.* G³) G;   to seye] it es no nede J, to lye M, to tell O.   1639-40 it ... neede] to lye J.   1640 þat ooþer] the thoother GJMO (*1st* o *ins.* G³);   þee I tauhte] (the *with* there *mar.* G³), þere I tauhte CS, I tawht the J;   þe] þee CGS (*1st* e *ins.* G³), L' F, *om.* JMO.   1641 þee] (*1st* e *ins.* G³);   to¹] for to S;   to²] *om.* J, for to S;   and³] *om.* JMS.   1642 discerne] to discerne JS;   bitwixe] be tweene GJMO (*2nd* e *ins.* G³);   wikkede] ille J. 1643 to] forto JMO;   make] (*2nd* a *ins.* G³);   canoun and lawe] rewles of policy JMO;   for] *om.* JMO;   þilke] that JO, þe M.   1644 þat] whilk MS. 1645 heeld ... parlementes] was Submaystere thare J;   foormed] enfourmed S; þere] *om.* J.   1646 loue] tane JMO;   and] in O.   1647 scooles] scole O; to] in J.   1648 þilke] that JMO;   þee] (*1st* e *ins.* G³), þere I enfourmed þe *add.* M, t' F, *om.* C.   1649 were] was JMO;   prentys] Apprentise M;   weren] was JMO;   þee] (*1st* e *ins.* G³).   1650 secrees] priuetees J, secrete₃ MO, secreet S; for ... euere] *om.* S.   1651 riht] *om.* J;   told] taught M;   it] *om.* M;   þee] (*1st* e *ins.* G³);   shuldest] *om.* O.   1652 mown] *om.* JMO;   make] (*2nd* a *ins.* G³); wel] *om.* J;   kunne] *om.* JM, ken O.   1653 juge] and discerne *add.* J;   Swich] Slike M;   and] *om.* J;   swich] *om.* J, slike M.   1654 was] ay *add.* S;   to] vn to S;   þee] (*1st* e *ins.* G³), yit howe sapience taught firþermore *add.* S;   And] *prec.* Capitulum lxxix *mar.* CGS (*and 79 mar.* G³);   whan] Sey*n* J;   þanne] donques F, thus C, thusgates J, *om.* S.   1655 þat] and J;   han] has JM, *ins.* O³;   scooles] scole MO.   1656 woordes] (*1st* o *ins.* G³), worde O;   þouh] þoght O;   ye] *caret add. with u.v.* had *mar.* C³;   me] (*2nd* e *ins.* G³);   now] *om.* JS.   1657 me] (*2nd* e *ins.* G³).   1658 his] hir M;   kunnynge] rynnynge M; to] tille JS.   1659 hadde nothing] *trs.* JMO;   take] (*2nd* a *ins.* G³);   his] w *add. can.* G, hym J;   For] þerfore · and J.   1660 tweyne] tweye GS, twa JMO. 1661 eche of hem] aythere J, ilkon of þem MO;   which] swilke JM, syche O; þei] twa JMO.   1662 stryf] be twene thay*m add.* J;   maister] yit *add.* C;   yit] encore F, miche C, *om.* S;   wisere] the wisere JM.   1663 to²] vnto M; aresone] aresounde J.   1664 tweyne] twa JMO;   ayens] ageyne JMO;   me] (*2nd* e *ins.* G³);   þat] *om.* J;   am] *om.* J.   1665 was] come J;   corage] (*2nd* e *ins.* G³).   1666 þilke] the Prynce J, þe prentyse MO;   who] he S;   þere] with hym *add.* J.   1667 ded] downe J;   eerþe] (*2nd* e *ins.* G³) G;   sente] wente J. 1668 him] *om.* J;   haue I nouht] quod he J;   quod he] hafe I nought J;   tauht] the *add.* J.   1668-9 to my prentys] *om.* J;   is euele] befelle the J;   bifalle þee] (*2nd* e *ins.* G³), asary grace J;   ayens] agayne J.   1670 So] *prec.* Capitulum lxxx *mar.* CG (*and 80 mar.* G³);   þee¹] (*1st* e *ins.* G³);   save þee] (*2nd* a *and 2nd* e *ins.* G³), me Saue J, *trs.* M, saue me O;   þow] *om.* G;   haue] (*2nd* a *ins.* G³). 1671 tauht þee ... wit] (*1st* e *ins.* G³), taught the alle my witte nowe JMO, nowe taught þee al my witt S;   art] craftes J (ho alt. a O);   þat] at S;   myn²] artes and my kunnynge J.   1672 yiven] ₃eue (*with* ₃yue *mar.* G³) G;   þee] (*1st* e *ins.* G³), to the JMO;   withoute] (e *ins.* G3);   withholdinge] of *add.* JMO;   þow woldest] walde þou J, þou wolde MO.   1673 awurþe] fare J, wirke M, worthe

O;   me[1,2]] (*1st e ins.* G[3]);   hadde nothing] hadde nought J, ne had O;   to] for to
S;   sum] othere *add.* JMO.   1674 doinge ... vyleynye] thow argueth me and
reprehendes me J, no vilany doynge MO;   þow ... me] na velany doande J;   me[2]]
(*2nd e ins.* G[3]);   of] by J.   1675 of[1,2]] *om.* J;   bi] for J;   Now sey me] (me
2nd e ins. G[3]), Saye me nowe J.   1676 if] and J;   a[1]] *om.* O;   þee] (*1st e ins.*
G[3]);   þe which] whilke JMO.   1677 þee[1]] (*1st e ins.* G[3]);   þee[2]] (*1st e ins.*
G[3]), to the JM, *om.* O;   haue] *om.* J;   yiven] ȝeue (*with* ȝyue *mar.* G[3]) G;   þee[3]]
(*1st e ins.* G[3]), to þe MO.   1678 þee] (*1st e ins.* G[3]);   bi] *om.* J;   wille] þat
thow haue it *add.* J;   so were] *trs.* J.   1679 sithe] Syne JMO;   þou] *om.* S;
foure] iv *over* CG[3].   1680 floreynes] florences M, florente O;   fyve] v *over*
CG[3];   sixe] vi *over* CG[3];   þee] (*1st e ins.* G[3]), *om.* J, me O.   1681 þee] (*1st e
ins.* G[3]);   or] o *alt.* þof o. er.* O[3].   1682 Serteyn] -ly J;   me] o. er.* C, (*2nd e
ins.* G[3]).   1683 ful] *om.* S;   fredom] (*2nd e ins.* G[3]);   of[2]] *om.* O;   of[3]] *om.*
JMO.   1684 curteysye] Howe *þat* dame sapience declareþe hir entent by
symilitude *add.* S.   1685 Serteyn] *prec.* Cap*itulum* lxxxi *mar.* CG (*and* 81 *mar.*
G[3]), Cap*itulum* lxxx S, Sothly J;   so] sooþe S;   haue] *om.* JMO.   1686 maad]
(*1st a ins.* G[3]);   for] the vertu of ye Sacrament inwardly · not outwardly *mar.* O[3];
I haue] y haaue (*2nd a ins.* G[3]) G, *trs.* J;   shewed] scheewed (*1st e ins.* G[3]) G;
grete] *om.* MO.   1687 tresore] tresouurr G (? -s J);   haue[1,2]] (*2nd a ins.* G[3]).
1688 enrichesse] enriche J, euery rych o. er.* M[3], encrese (en o. er.* O[3]) O;   with]
om. J;   þe] *om.* S.   1689 shewed] scheewed (*1st e ins.* G[3]) G;   Charite] N*ota*
rub. mar. O.   1690 ordeyned] ordeyneþe S;   hath ... poore] of þe pou*er* hafe J.
1691 if] and J.   1691-2 withoute I hadde] I had put with owtene and J, mercy
and *add.* S.   1692 shewed] scheewed (*1st e ins.* G[3]) G;   apparence] aparisaunce
CGS;   withinne] with S;   thing] ? -es G.   1693 hadde] hasse J.
1694 mihtest] myght JMO;   me[1]] (*2nd e ins.* G[3]);   blame] (*2nd a ins.* G[3]);   me[2]]
yit takeþe heed howe dame sapience · makeþe hir resoun in þe same *add.* S;   Yit]
prec. Cap*itulum* lxxxii *mar.* CG (*and* 82 *mar.* G[3]), Cap*itulum* lxxxi *mar.* S.
1695 þee] (*1st e ins.* G[3]);   ooþerweys] other wyse JMOS;   þouh] þerof J, þof
MO;   shewe] scheewe (*1st e ins.* G[3]) G.   1696 it is] is CJMO;   þat] *ins. mar.*
O[3];   so it be] it be soo J, it so be tristed and M.   1697 makinge] maakynge (*1st
a ins.* G[3]) G;   deuynale] adevinement (*variant* devinement *A, L*) F, dyuynyg (?
dynynyg) J, denyinge CMO.   1698 not] do J;   if I[2]] *om.* JMO;   it] *om.* JMO;
ooþerweys] oþere wyse JMOS;   þanne] (e *ins.* G[3]).   1699 mihtest] myght
blame me and J, myght MO;   me[1,2]] (*2nd e ins.* G[3]);   mystakynge] Howe dame
sapience spekeþe to nature in þis mater *add.* S;   Now] *prec.* Cap*itulum* lxxxiii
mar. CG (*and* 83 *mar.* G[3]), Cap*itulum* lxxxii *mar.* S.   1700 þee] (*1st e ins.* G[3])
G;   me] (*2nd e ins.* G[3]);   doinges] mysdoynge JMO;   þat[2]] þere þow J;   seist]
sayde J;   it] that J.   1701 þan] o. er.* C;   þat þat] þat J.   1702 is]
contenede *add.* J;   withinne] þerin JMO;   seye] n*ota* per Shir{ley} *mar.* S;   ne]
no MO.   1703 Serteyn] *om.* J;   quod he] ȝis forsoth J.   1703-4 in sooth]
quod he J.   1704 haue] (*2nd a ins.* G[3]);   treweliche] *om.* JMO;   me] (*2nd e
ins.* G[3]).   1705 þin oth] *om.* JMO;   Serteyn] -ly J.   1706 kyte] glede
JMO;   a[2]] un F, *om.* JMOS;   litel] *om.* J;   enfamined] that ware hungrye J,
enhowngerid MO;   ful] o. er.* (*with u.v.* ful *mar.* C[3]) C, -ly J.   1707 sauled]
fedde J, sowlyd O;   þerwith] with hit S.   1708 þee] (*1st e ins.* G[3]);   þou] þo
O;   wite] wate JM.   1709 and ... how] S *repeats*;   michel] his desyre *add.*
can. M.   1710 ful] -ly J;   sauled] sowlyd O;   shulde] mihte C.   1711
Serteyn] -ly J;   fulfille] fille JMO;   saule] stanche JMO;   staunche] saule JM,
soule O.   1712 mihte] myghte (e *ins.* G[3]) G, it *add.* M;   al[2] ... wille] he had it
J;   he ... it] alle at his wille J.   1713 þanne] thay*m* J.   1713-14 fillinge to

suffisance] fulfillinge to sufficience C, þou fynde it J, sufficiaunt fillynge M, suffisaund fyllynge O.   1714 þow ... it] Suffyciaunt fillynge J; oþer] elles *add.* J;   falsed] (d *erased* C), fals JMO, falshede S;   be] bi CMO;   þi] þe M. 1715 spred] espredde S.   1716 voyd] ne empty *add.* J.   1717 filled] fulfillede JMO.   1718 sey] maynteyne J;   weene] wenes J, weneth M;   oo] 1 *over* G³, a J.   1719 sovereyn] gude *add.* J;   ful] *om.* O;   Soothlice] No*ta rub.* *mar.* O.   1720 seyst] sayde J;   wel] sooþe S;   of] *om.* JMO;   mistakest] *þou* mistakest S;   þee] (*1st* e *ins.* G³).   1721 it needeth] nedelynges it be houes J; þilke] that JMO;   is] *om.* M;   gret] *om.* M.   1722 enclosed ... world] it may nouȝt be J;   it ... be] enclosede in the werlde J;   þat it ne] for than hit J, þen it MO.   1723 Serteyn] Sekerly J;   I may not] here a gayne J;   to þat] maye I nouȝt J, of þat M;   of] *om.* J, to M.   1724 nothing] *om.* J;   withseye] saye J; how] than *add.* J;   it] be *add.* J;   be] he S.   1725-6 þat ... good] *om.* S. 1726 þat] þat *þat* S.   1727 seyinges] sayinge JMO;   false] yit howe dame sapience declareþe to þe pilgryme by symylytudes / þe mat*ere* of þe sac*r*ament *add.* S;   Yit] *prec.* Capi*tulum* lxxxiv *mar.* CG (*and* 84 *mar.* G³);   shewe] scheewe (*1st* e *ins.* G³) G;   þee] (*1st* e *ins.* G³), *om.* M;   apertliche] properly JMO.   1728 al] in M;   ooþerweys] oþ*ere* wyse JMO;   þow hast] *trs.* J, No*ta rub. mar.* O. 1729 tymes] atyme J, tyme O;   þere] thare (*with* there *mar.* G³) G, in *add.* JMO, Inne and þeer S;   Now sey me] Saye me nowe J.   1730 þat oon] 1 *over* G³; from] fra JMO;   ooþer] (*2nd* o *ins.* G³);   been] bee (*2nd* e *ins.* G³) G. 1731 studyauntes] studyand J;   Serteyn] Sothely J.   1732 mynde me wel] (mee *1st* e *ins.* G³), have wele in mynde J.   1733 studiauntes] studience J; of³] *om.* M.   1734 Now sey me] (mee *1st* e *ins.* G³), Say me nowe J.   1735 hast] haste (e *ins.* G³) G;   þow] *om.* G;   put] *om.* S.   1735-6 alle ... haue] *ins. mar.* G³.   1735 þese] this JMO;   gretnesses] grettenesse JMO;   seist me] of *add.* J, (se *cropped mar.* G³), seyst CS, me dit (*variant* dit *L, T*) F.   1736 memorie] mynde certaynly J, mynde MO;   I haue] *trs.* J, *prec.* nota O³;   put] *om.* C; quod he certeyn] quod he J, certayn quod he MO.   1737 it] *om.* JM;   Oo] A ha JMO;   quod] saide MO;   and] þ*ann*e J;   shalt þou] schalte G, shalt S; þerfore] *om.* J, þ*er* of for (of *can.*) O.   1738 me] (*2nd* e *ins.* G³), *om.* J;   þin] thy JO, mynde *add. can.* M.   1738-9 þat ... hed] *om.* S.   1739 is þin hed] (thyne *has* e *can.* G), thy heued es J, ys *þi* hede O;   tweyne] twa JMOS. 1740 studiauntes] Yit dame sapience declareþe þis mater · by a noþer ensaumple *add.* S;   In] *prec.* Capi*tulum* lxxxv *mar.* CG, Capi*tulum* lxxxiv *mar.* S, Also in J; shewe] scheewe (*1st* e *ins.* G³) G.   1741 also] *om.* J;   it¹] *om.* J;   algates] neu*er*theles J.   1741-2 þer ... þerinne] þerin in habiteȝ J, þ*ere* inhabit*es* MO. 1742 holliche] *om.* S;   þow] No*ta rub. mar.* O;   miht] maye JO, *om.* M. 1743 apertliche] prop*y*rly J;   mirour] and *add.* J;   se] þerin *add.* J.   1744 his] þy S;   ooþerweys] oþ*ere* wyse JM.   1745 þat] for *þou* J, þou MO;   haue] (*2nd* a *ins.* G³);   falsed] *om.* JMO;   and] *om.* JMO;   repreved] inproued J. 1746 þi] þe S;   maxime] gretteste principle CGS.   1747 make¹,²] (*2nd* a *ins.* G³).   1748 tobroken] brokyn*e* JMO;   if] thy visage and *add.* J;   þi] they (e *can. with* thy *mar.* G³) G, þin C, þai O.   1749 eche] ylke ane JM;   not be þilke] be na p*ar*ty J, nouȝt be þat party MO;   in which] that J, *om.* MO;   þow ne] *trs.* J, þen þou MO.   1750 see] þerin *add.* J;   apperceyue] persayfe JMO. 1751 holliche] hooleeche (*1st* o *ins.* G³) G;   whan] þat] *add.* S.   1752 þer] *om.* J;   was] seemed S;   oon] 1 *over* G³; a J;   visage] Here þe pilgryme spekeþe ageyne to dame sapience *add.* S;   Now] *prec.* Capi*tulum* lxxxvi *mar.* CG, Capi*tulum* lxxxv *mar.* S.   1752-3 þat ... he] quod he þat ha*s* ȝo*ur* eghtȝ So Sutille J. 1753 engyn] eyene MO;   he] ariystotyl *over* C³;   localliche] or *add.* JMO.

1754 þat] *(can.* G), *om.* C;   þese] þis MO;   thinges] thynge M;   ben] þei *add.*
ins. C;   þe] a JMO.   1755 places] place JMO;   ye] *þat* ye CJMO;   haue]
om. J;   I wolde] *trs.* J.   1756 þerafter] *om.* S;   I wolde] *trs.* J, I wole S;
holde me] be JMO;   stille] NOwe dame ˙sapyence aunswerþe to þe pylgrymes
seying in þis wyse *add.* S;   Serteyn] -ly J, *prec.* Cap*itulum* lxxxvii *mar.* CG *(and*
87 *mar.* G³), Cap*itulum* lxxxvi *mar.* S.   1757 I vnderstonde] vndirstande I it J,
it *add.* MO;   but] bo O;   ooþerweys] oþere wise JMOS.   1758 and] *om.* J;
ymaginatyfliche] ymagyneleche *(with* ymagynatyfleche *mar.* G³) G.   1759
summe¹ ... vnderstonde] *om.* J.   1760 recche] me · to make the *add.* J;   of]
om. J.   1760-3 for ... feedinge] *om.* J.   1760 haue] *(2nd* a *ins.* G³).
1761 taken] taake *(2nd* a *ins.* G³) G, takyng O;   þee] *(1st* e *ins.* G³), *om.* MOS;
ensaumples] þensaumples S;   avisement] þavisem*ent* S;   for to] to S;   make]
(2nd a *ins.* G³);   þee²] *(1st* e *ins.* G³), þo O.   1762 to] *om.* C;   þee¹] *(1st* e *ins.*
G³), *om.* MO;   þee²] *(1st* e *ins.* G³).   1763 litel] a litel M;   in] *om.* MO.
1764 wises] wyse JMO;   places] place JMO;   þese] þier M, þis O;   ben] he O.
1765 þe] *om.* JS.   1766 representatyfliche] presentatyfliche C;   nouht²] Nota
rub. *mar.* O.   1767 withoute] (e *ins.* G³);   and] *om.* O.   1768 contened]
contenu F, conceeued *(2nd* c *alt.* t *to read* conteened) G, *om.* O, contrened S;
verreyliche] virtually JMO.   1769 similacioun] dissimulaci*oun* S;   and] or J,
om. O;   ooþer] any JM;   decepcioun] *(with* gyle *mar.* G³), or gile *add.* C, Inmensis
pater inmensis filius inmensus spiritus sanctus *add.* S, yit dame sapience declareþe
of þe sacrament more to hir entent *add.* S.   1770 The] *prec.* Cap*itulum* lxxxviii
mar. CG *(and* 88 *mar.* G³), Cap*itulum* lxxxvii *mar.* S;   þere] therin JMO;   partye]
-s S;   it²] *om.* J.   1771 tofore] fore G, before J, *om.* M, for O;   for] be cause
add. JM;   þe¹] *ins.* O;   as ... maad] alle so I made J;   is²] I MO.   1772 also]
als litelle J;   capacitee] *(with scilicet* desyr *mar.* G³), capate J;   þe] þerfore the
JMO;   good souereyn] *trs.* JMO, seyþe *add.* S;   haue] *om.* JMO.   1773 withinne]
þerin JMO, Nota rub. *mar.* O;   litele²] and *add.* J.   1774 haue] *(2nd* a *ins.* G³);
euene maad] *trs.* J;   as] *om.* J.   1775 right soo] o. er. *(with mar. u.v.* {ri}ght so
C³) C;   maad] *(2nd* a *ins.* G³);   it²] es O.   1776 hath] has (s o. er.) O;
ynowh] nouȝt J;   withinne] it *add.* JMO;   þat²] at J;   saule] soule O.
1778 þouh] of J, For MO;   smallere] *om.* JMO.   1779 and] *om.* JMO;   þan]
gooþe · and *add.* S;   þerinne] with in it J.   1780 þat¹] as S;   to] *om.* JMO;
I] *om.* JMO;   maad] *(1st* a *ins.* G³);   thing] -es JMO;   missittynge] missetting
S;   þat²] ȝit J.   1781 apayed] payede JMO;   þat] as *add.* J, þat that MO;
me] *(2nd* e *ins.* G³);   seyn] seyd C.   1782 þee¹] *(1st* e *ins.* G³), *om.* MO;   if]
and J;   ne wole] ne wolde C, walde J, wil nouȝt MO;   þee²] *(2nd* e *ins.* G³).
1783 dide] nouȝt *add.* J, doo S;   summething] aucune chose F, -es C, som tyme
O.   1784 ooþere] a noþere JS.   1785 So þat] þou maist *(þou o. er.* maist
ins.) (with mar. u.v. þow mayste C³) *add.* C, And J, se þat O;   see] loo J, so ȝe O.
1786 if] þat *add.* M;   wolt] sewe it and *add.* S;   shewe] scheewe *(1st* e *ins.* G³) G;
ayen] *om.* M;   to] in to S.   1787 chaumberere] Chaumbourier S;   for²] feere
of S.   1787-8 I wole] *trs.* J.   1788 nothing leue] (nothing has otiose -es G),
trs. JO;   þat²] at J;   wolde] wil J;   do] & *add. ins. (with mar. u.v.* And C³) C.
1789 þat þat] in that J, in þat that M, þat at O.   1790 kunne] kene O, doo ne
konne S;   me] *(2nd* e *ins.* G³);   þat] þen MO;   ne wole] wil MO, wol nat S;
it] *om.* O;   withoute] (oute *ins. mar.* G³).   1791 abidinge] how Aristotle went
his way · And pilgrime askes of þat brede *add. rub.* M, Howe Arystotle aunswerd
to sapyence *add.* S.   1792 Aristotle] *prec.* Cap*itulum* lxxxix *mar.* CG *(and*
89 *mar.* G³), Cap*itulum* lxxxviii *mar.* S, cap*itulum* xl *rub. mar.* M, when O;   whan]
om. M, aristotill O;   he herde] he hadde herde J, herynge M, herde O;   þis] al ·

þis S. 1793 hire] *om.* J; Serteynly] quod he *add.* JS, Vraiement dist (il) (*variant* Vraiement *B, M*) F; apperceyue] Persayve JMO, haue ap*er*ceyued S; þat] to Argue *add.* J; of] with J; shal I] *trs.* JMO. 1794 michel] *om.* J; for] to J; me] (*2nd* e *ins.* G³); go] to go JMS. 1795 ayens] ayen CM; go] wil go M. 1796 þilke] he JMO; ayen] *om.* J. 1797 hire] Sapience J; for ... departed] *om.* J. 1798 it] For *add.* J; no more] na noþere do J, agayn say *add.* M; þat] than J; hevyede] hir J. 1799 hire] forthought J, Howe þat Aristotle desyred to ete of þat breed *add.* S. 1800 Whan] *prec.* Cap*itulum* lxxxx *mar.* CG (*and* 90 *mar.* G³), Cap*itulum* lxxxix *mar.* S; þus] *om.* JMO; me] (*2nd* e *ins.* G³). 1801 gret¹] *om.* JMO; haue] (*2nd* a *ins.* G³). 1802 þilke] that JMO; to] forto J; with] alle myn*e add.* J; pray] preye (*2nd* e *ins.* G³) G. 1803 þis] the JMO; Moyses] -es G; make yive me] (mee *1st* e *ins.* G³), do me to hafe J. 1804 with] alle *add.* J; herte] body M; longe] (e *ins.* G³); ne] and J. 1805 neuere] 3it *add.* J; sauled] sauleed G, sawled MS, sowled O, fellede J; yit] are now *add.* J; of] *om.* JMO; men] mete JMO. 1806 it] Howe dame Gracedieux aunswerd *add.* S; Serteyn] *prec.* Cap*itulum* lxxxxi *mar.* CG (*o. er.* C, *and* 91 *mar.* G³), Cap*itulum* lxxxx *mar.* S, -ly J; she] Grace dieu J; not] right S. 1807 Michel] for my wille J; þee] (*1st* e *ins.* G³); to²] for J; viage] þat *add.* M. 1808 doone] (*2nd* o *ins.* G³), make J; bifore] ar J; mowe] *om.* JMO; þe] þat JMO; place] (*2nd* a *ins.* G³); þer] whider J, wher*e* MO. 1809 hast þi desire] desyres JMO; bi ... pases] þow schalle goo J; þou shalt go] by many wikked path J; ful] well GS, many *add.* MO; pases] pathes MO. 1810 herberwes] herbergeries JO, herber*e* M; þat] *om.* J; ofte] tymes *add.* J; haue] (*2nd* a *ins.* G³). 1811 misese] disese J; not] of *add.* J; bred] with the *add.* J; to] forto *o. er.* M. 1812 take] make O; riht] gude J, *om.* MO. 1813 lawes] (*2nd* a *ins.* G³); haue] (*2nd* ains. G³); þat²] at J; hast] *ins.* G³. 1814 þe whiche] whilke JMO. 1815 þee¹,²] (*1st* e *ins.* G³); hem] it MO. 1815-16 al bitymes] Off the breed alle be tyme J, al by tyme MO. 1816 þat] þow JMO; shulde] schalle JMO; be] sekyr *add.* JMO; hadde] hafe JMO. 1816-17 þe faire] *trs.* (þe *ins.*, fayr *o. er. and prec. caret*) O³; be ... faire] *scribbles over* O³. 1817 of] *om.* JMO. 1817-18 withinne ... thinges] *om.* J. 1817 seen nouht] has nou3t seeyn MO, Loo nowe howe þat dame Gracedieux spekeþe to þe pilgryme *add.* S. 1818 Now] *prec.* Cap*itulum* lxxxxii *mar.* CG (*o. er.* C, *and* 92 *mar.* G³), Cap*itulum* lxxxxi *mar.* S; in ... þee] schewyd þe in perty O; þe] *om.* S. 1819 þee¹,²] (*1st* e *ins.* G³); þi] þine C; couenauntes] cownande JM. 1820 haue] (*2nd* a *ins.* G³); þe³] *om.* M. 1821 sithe] Seyne JMO; miht] may JS. 1822 in] and O; þi] t' F, the GS; after] -wardes J; as] *om.* M; good] a good JS; pilgrym] I shal *add.* M; þee] (*1st* e *ins.* G³). 1823 to] in M; þi] þe M; wey] Howe þe pilgryme answereþe Gracedieux *add.* S; Lady] *prec.* Cap*itulum* lxxxxiii *mar.* CG (*o. er.* C, *and* 93 *mar.* G³), Cap*itulum* lxxxxii *mar.* S; graunt mercy] thanke to 3owe J, gra*r*amtt m*er*cy · For M, -s S. 1824 and] of J, in O; me] (*2nd* e *ins.* G³); it] þaym J, quod I *add.* O. 1825 lust] liste J; me] (*2nd* e *ins.* G³); Me] (*2nd* e *ins.* G³); thinketh] thynke JMO; longe] that *add. can.* G. 1826 forthward] forward GMOS; for] and JMO; it] that JMO; fer] to *add.* C, For JMO; þilke] the J, þat MO. 1827 exited] stirryd M; goon] to *add.* S, Howe dame Grace dieux · delyuerd to þe pilgryme þe scrippe & þe b*ur*done *add.* S. 1828 And] *prec.* Cap*itulum* lxxxxiv *mar.* CG (*o. er.* C, *and* 94 *and a cross mar.* G³), Cap*itulum* lxxxxiii *mar.* S; a] the J, þat M; þat she hadde] *om.* JMO; þer weren] many fayre iowelles J, wer*e* MO. 1829 many ... iewelles] ware J, many Iewell O; withoute dwellinge] Onane J. 1830 of] out of CJ; hucche] whechche G;

rawhte] Scho raught JMO, sheo raught me S;   þe] a JMO.   1831 þe] a J;
Neuere] I trowe J;   I trowe] ther was neuere J;   man] manne (*2nd* n *ins. o. er.*
O³) O, no man S;   ne] *om.* O;   womman] *om.* O;   so ... scrippe] bare J.
1832 bar] porta F, a fayrere scrippe J, *om.* CGS;   ne] and S;   to] ne *add.* S;
assure] ensure J;   1833 a] al S;   triste] truste G, hym *add.* J, trust too S.
1834 lokede] be helde J.   1835 my] me J;   pees] stille J;   þat] ne *add.* J, þen
MO;   þerof] þat *add.* S;   I ne wole] I will JMO;   seye] speke JO, speke at þis
tyme M;   þe] *prec.* Capi*tulum* xli *rub. mar.* M.   1836 was] al *add.* S;   a] *om.*
O;   Lysted] bystidit O.   1837 wel] fulle JMO.   1838 forged] (*final* e *ins.*
G³);   good] grete J;   eche] ilkane JM;   was²] wele *add.* J.   1839 in eche]
euerych S;   enamelure] of þe sayde belles *add.* S;   þer] hade S;   was] his S.
1840 as] þat *add.* S;   it] *om.* JMO;   at] *with* myne JS;   eye] -ne J;   telle]
declare S;   yow] with outen any addicioun or dyminnyshhyoun *add.* S, Howe þe
pilgryme devyseþe þenamaylling of þe belles *add.* S.   1841 In] An *with scribe's*
guide a *visible* S, *prec.* Capi*tulum* lxxxxv *mar.* CG (*o. er.* C, *and* 95 *mar.* G³),
Capi*tulum* lxxxxiv *mar.* S;   God þe Fader] as me thought J;   as me thouhte]
godde the Fadire J, which *add.* S.   1841-2 þe² ... made] made heuene and the
erthe J.   1842 and¹] in O, an S;   made] (e *ins.* G³);   sithe] Syne JMO.
1843 secunde] belle *add.* S.   1843-5 But ... dredinge] *with* but thyse thre
thynges weren to mee wonderffull and (*er.*) and hard and doutous *foot of p.* G³.
1844 þese] thir JM, þer O;   to] *om.* J;   me] (*2nd* e *ins.* G³), *om.* JMO;   michel]
(*can.* G³), fulle J, myche O, Mont F, *om.* CS.   1844-5 gretliche dredinge]
(*marked for gloss* G³), full dredfulle J, hard and dowtows C, fort douteuses F.
1845 of] *om.* JMOS;   so] als S;   nyh] nere J;   þei¹] were *add.* JMO, the
12 articls of the Creed *mar.* O³.   1846 alle be] (*1st* e *ins.* G³), to be alle C, alle
but JS;   oon] 1 *over* G³;   in þe thre] belles *add.* JS, *om.* C.   1846-7 I ... þat¹]
G, I sawe JMO, *om.* CS.   1847 þer was] *om.* JMO;   oonliche] *om.* JMOS;
oon] 1 *over* G³, a J, o O;   þat²] whilke J;   to ... thre] serued S.   1848 servede]
to alle þoo three S;   þe] *om.* S;   writen þer was] ther was writen J, wryten was S;
Goddes] godde J;   Sone] the Sonne J.   1849 Cryst] þat *add.* S;   from] fro
(o *o. er.* O³) O;   bi ... Gost] consayvede J, *om.* O.   1850 conseyued] by the
haly gaste J;   mad] (*2nd* a *ins.* G³), and J, and made S;   and] *om.* JMO;   of a
mayden] of a mayde G, borne J, of maden MO;   born] of amaydene J;   fyfthe]
hit was enamaylled howe *add.* S.   1851 sinneres] synnes S;   and] *om.* S;
crosse] corsse O;   nature] Navre F, naturelly CS, *om.* JMO.   1852 sixte] vi
over C, belle / howe *add.* S;   descended] he descended JMOS.   1853 caste]
take J;   in] rose again from the dead *mar.* O³.   1854 sevenþe] vii *over* G³,
belle *add.* S;   sussited] rayse fra deede to lyfe on the thridde daye J, frome deeþe
to lyf *add.* S;   eyhtþe] viii *over* G³, aghtene J, *o. er.* S;   steyn] He Steyede J,
stiuyd (? stinyd) O, steyng S;   into] in tille J.   1855 on ... fader] Sittes J;
sett] on the right hande of his fadere J;   iuge] deme J;   quike] wylke O.
1856 nynthe] ix *over* G³, nyenteþe belle S;   set] enamaylled *add.* S;   holi
Cristene] *trs.* S.   1857 solempnysed] Solempnede J.   1858 tenþe] x *over*
G³, tenteþe belle S;   oonhede] vnyed M, houed O;   þe³] *om.* GMO.
1859 indulgence] forgyfnesse J;   bi] thurgh J;   and] by *add.* MOS.
1860 elevenþe] xi *over* G³, eleventeþe belle S;   risinge] þe arysing S;   dede] deth
M;   shulen] schollen (*with* schullen *mar.* G³) G, should S;   þe²] *om.* O.
1861 iugement] dome J;   in²] *om.* MO;   here] þair *alt.* þam O.   1862 sentence]
(sen- O³);   twelfthe] xii *over* G³, twelteþe belle enamayled S;   guerdoun]
rewardynge J, reward MO, þe guerdouns S;   goode] (e *ins.* G³).   1863 þe] *om.*
JMO;   yuel] eeuelle (*2nd* e *ins.* G³) G;   haue] haauen (*2nd* a *ins.* G³) G.   1864 of

þe belles] the Scripture J, of *þe* bell O, (þe *alt.* of S);   þe scripture] of the belles J, -s O.   1864-5 writen is] was written*e* J, *trs.* S.   1865 ye] (*2nd* e *ins.* G³). 1865-6 þe³ ... scrippe] ʒe maye See J.   1866 seen ye mowen] þe Bewte of the Scrippe J, ʒhe may see MO, Here þe pilgri*me* tellis of his burdou*n* · and grace dieu enfourmeʒ hym of xii bells *add. rub.* M, Takeþe heed of þe fasoun of þe bourdoun *add.* S.   1867 Now] *prec.* Cap*itulum* lxxxxvi *mar. o. er.* C, 96 *mar.* G³, Cap*itulum* lxxxxv *mar.* S;   I wole] *trs.* J;   also] of the Burdoun J;   of þe burdoun] also J, of my burdon MO;   was] Burdon *rub. mar.* O *and* a pilgrims stafe *and in another hand u.v.* betokens fayth read *mar.* O³.   1868 facioun] *with* fasioun *mar.* G³; and¹] *om.* JMO.   1869 was] it was J;   maad] (*1st* a *ins.* G³);   tre] the tree JMO;   Sethim] Sethyra J, sechym S;   in no time] neuer*e* J.   1870 for ... of] by JMO;   þe] o*þ*ere *add.* J.   1871 and] ryght J, *om.* MO.   1872 was¹] ware J.   1873 þat] þen MO;   þerinne men] ne *þ*ere in men J, *trs.* S;   ne] *om.* JMOS;   and] *om.* JMO;   þere] Inne *add.* S.   1874 þilke] that JMO, þe S; whiche] the whilke J;   exited] stirred M.   1875 and ... before] and per*s*ayfed it before J, bifore and per*c*eyued it MO;   also] So J;   in²] of S.   1876 pomelle] *o. er.* M;   was] right *add.* JM;   fayn] and ioyfulle · *add.* J.   1876-7 þe ... bordoun] Sothly J.   1877 in sooth] the better I luffed the burdoun J;   preysede] luffed J;   his] þe M;   facioun] farsioun J.   1878 bineþe] þat *add.* J;   anooþer ... was] ther was a no*þ*ere pomelle J;   a litel] Sum whate J.   1879 þat ooþer] the toother (*2nd* o *ins.* G³) G, þe first S;   þat²] whilke J;   maad] (*2nd* a *ins.* G³). 1880 glistringe] alle glitri and alle schynande J, gliterynge MO;   Who] (o *ins.* G³); þat¹] so J;   euere it made] (t *ins.* O³), it eu*er*e maade (*1st* a *ins.* G³) G, eu*er*e made it J;   cumpasede] it *add.* J;   þat²] *om.* JMO.   1881 ioyned] *ins. mar.* G³, applied JMO;   it] *ins. mar.* G³, *om.* O;   þis] þat M.   1882 he] hym MO. 1883 auenaunt] accordynge M.   1883-4 Nothing ... me] (mee *1st* e *ins.* G³), Thare was Nathynge myspayede me J, þer*e* mysliked me nouʒt MO.   1884 in] *om.* J;   it¹] *om.* J, þis MO;   but¹] anely *add.* J;   þat] at O;   it²] the burdou*n* J; yrened] hupyd ne pyked J, yryved S;   afterward] -es S.   1885 shewed] scheewed (*1st* e *ins.* G³) G;   me¹] to me JM;   appesed] apposyd O;   wel] Howe Gracedieux techeþe þe pilgryme howe he shal gouerne him by þe weye *add.* S. 1886 Whan] *prec.* Cap*itulum* lxxxxvii *o. er. mar.* C, 97 *mar.* G³, Cap*itulum* lxxxxvi *mar.* S;   þese] þier*e* M, *þ*er O;   iewelles] Ieuell O;   out] of the hucche *add.* J; þanne] *om.* J.   1886-7 seide ... Dieu] Grace Dieu Sayde vnto me J.   1886 me] (*2nd* e *ins.* G³), to me M, dame *add.* S.   1887 See] loo JS, schew O;   heere] quod Scho *add.* J, her O.   1888 haue] *om.* J;   bihyght] hight J;   þee¹] (*1st* e *ins.* G³);   make] (*2nd* a *ins.* G³);   þee²] (*1st* e *ins.* G³);   of] to O;   In] for in J; viage] visa J.   1889 and] Scripp *id est* fides *rub. mar.* M, þe scripe *rub. mar.* O *and* what it meaneth *mar.* O³.   1890 wys] fun*d*e *add.* J;   þe] *om.* S;   scryppe] it *add.* J, I *add. can.* O, of *add.* S;   Foy] feyth *over* C³, *with scilicet* feyth *mar.* G³, called J, feith MO;   is] *om.* J;   cleped] faith J, called M, *u.v.* the fa{i}r scrip *mar.* O³.   1891 neuer*e* do] make na J;   availe] the *add.* JO.   1892 þi] thyne other J;   vitaile] -s J;   in ... times] alwaye J.   1893 wite] *with* O;   þis] or *add.* O.   1894 þat¹] þe whilke J;   telleth] tell O;   ·þat² ... writen] *om.* JMO. 1895 iuste] ryghtwys JM, ryghwys O, man *add.* S;   bi] thurght J, thurgh MO; scrippe] fayth JMO.   1895-7 þat² ... þerinne] *om.* JMO.   1897 þis] þe O; of] *om.* JMO;   colour] -ed J.   1898 sight] also *add.* J.   1899 þee] (*1st* a *ins.* G³);   sharp feith] faith maketh JMO;   maketh] (*2nd* a *ins.* G³), Scharpe JMO; sighte] the sight J.   1900 ne] and J;   neuere ... soule] the Sawle schalle neu*er*e J;   perfytliche see] *trs.* J;   if] but ʒif JM, bot O.   1901 ne] *om.* JMO; strengthe] strenghe J;   þerfore] (*2nd* e *ins.* G³);   she] it J;   neede] be nedefulle

J. 1902 þee[1]] (*1st* e *ins.* G[3]), to the J, redy *add. can.* M, nede þe *add. can.* O, *om.* S; þee[2]] (*1st* e *ins.* G[3]); wey] Loo nowe howe Gracedieux telleþe þe pilgryme · why þe belles ben tached to þe scrippe *add.* S; Lady] *prec.* Cap*itulum* lxxxxviii *o. er. mar.* C, 98 *mar.* G[3], Cap*itulum* lxxxxvii *mar.* S; me] (*2nd* e *ins.* G[3]). 1903 for ... of[1]] *om.* J; þese] þier*e* M, *þis* O; belles] bell O; so] a JMO; litele] þat I may vnderstonde *add.* S. 1904 þus] *om.* S; atached] atachies F, tacched CS; and] *om.* S; stiked] *om.* S; in] to S; skrippe] (*1st* p *ins.* G[3]), and *add.* S; þe[2]] first *add.* S; also] *om.* S. 1905 oon] 1 *over* G[3]; whiche] þe which S; to hem] es comou*n* J, alle *add.* S; is commune] to thay*m* J; Serteyn] *prec.* Cap*itulum* lxxxxix *o. er. mar.* C, 99 *mar.* G[3], -ly J. 1906 þe[1]] *om.* J; bifore] here before J; þat[1]] yt O; in þe time] *om.* S; þat[2]] when JMO, er S. 1907 made] (*2nd* a *ins.* G[3]); þe] this JMO; al] *om.* J; sympilliche] symple MO; to] *om.* GMO; leeue] be leve JMO. 1908 perfyteliche] *om.* JMO; þanne] þat O. 1909 belles] bell O; þee] (*1st* e *ins.* G[3]); þat] tyme *add.* J, *om.* MO. 1910 sourdeden] felle JMO; sithe] *om.* JMO; many] er *add. can.* M; Eche] For ilke a man J, Ilkon M. 1911 oo] 1 *over* G[3], in[2]] of MO. 1912 his] is G, awene *add.* J; wel] *quincunx mar.* G[3]. 1913 so] *om.* J. 1914 for[2]] *om.* J. 1915 oon] 1 *over* G[3]; and[2]] *om.* J. 1916 twelve] xii *over* G[3]; þeron] opon MO, þer vppon*e* S. 1917 þat þer ben] *om.* JMO; and] *om.* MO; eche] ilkane JM; propir] twelfe Sere J, xii Apostoli *rub. mar.* M. 1918 writinge] -s J; þat] þe which S. 1919 and] *om.* JMO; how] *om.* JMO; leeue] bileeue C; þese] thir JMO. 1920 heere maken] (*2nd* a *ins.* G[3]), *trs.* JO, makes þier*e* M; þe[1]] *ins.* G[3], thir JMO; feith] xii articlo fidei *rub. mar.* M; þat] *om.* J; ben] *om.* J. 1922 þi] *om.* JMO; memorie] mynde J; awake] wakene J, wake MO; þee] (*1st* e *ins.* G[3]). 1923 ere] -s M; nouht] they er nought J; be þei not] for nought J, be þei MOS; belles] bell O; ne] and JMO; ringeres] witt þou wele *add.* M. 1924 oþer] and JMO; leftest] lested (*with* leftest *ins.* G[3]) C, lyste JMO, listed S; to[2]] nou3t JMO; looke] to *add.* JMO. 1925 at þe leste] of Su*m*me þay*m*e J; with ringinge] at the leste J, with þe ringing S; of[1] ... hem] with rynggynge J; mihtest] myght JMO. 1926 þee] *om.* M. 1927 and] *om.* J; to þe Romayns] *ins. mar.* G[3], *om.* JMO, haþe wrytte S; he ... writen] *om.* J, to þe Romayns S; heeringe] of *add. ins.* (*with u.v.* of *mar.* C[3]) C, and *add.* JMO. 1928 ringinge] thing S; haven] haaue (*2nd* a *ins.* G[3]) G, maye hafe J; he] thay J. 1929 þe ringinge] in the scrippe J; in þe scrippe] the rynggynge J; but] *om.* J; exiteth] and stereth *add.* J. 1930 manere] (*2nd* e *ins.* G[3]); þis] ce ci F, it CJMO; sufficeth] suffi3e O. 1931-2 for ... stidfastliche] *om.* S. 1931 ben] er *ins.* M, es O; mo] no O; ooþer] nothir O. 1932 þat] *om.* J; ben to bileeue] to be leued J, are to bileue M, ar to beleuyd O. 1933 bred] the breed JMO, notta *both mar.* O[3]; flesh] the flesch J. 1934 in] and O; oonhede] on hede O; þe] *om.* JMO. 1935 þe] *om.* MO; belles] bell O; askedest] are *add.* J. 1936 oo] 1 *over* G[3]; serueth] þer *add.* S; belles] bell O; is] in *add.* JMO. 1937 Trinite] Triniee *alt.* Trinite C; oo] 1 *over* G[3]; alone[1]] *om.* JMO; soothnesse] Sothfastnes J; alone[2]] alle ane J. 1938 thre[1]] iii *over* G[3], persones *add.* J; it] *om.* J; is[1]] *om.* J; and] Anch S; eche] ilkane J; þe] *om.* MO; God] a *add.* J; þow] *om.* M; shuldest] schalle J. 1939 of[1]] *om.* JO; ringinges] ryngynge M. 1940 whiche] wheche (*2nd* e *ins.* G[3]) G; as] *om.* J; wole] *om.* J; to] *om.* O. 1941 lasse] lese J, lassen S; ennuye] ennuier F, irksomnesse J, anoye MO, envye S; it] thay*m* J; of] on J; þe] thir*e* J, þies M; twelve] xii *over* G[3], thre J; þei] þe oþere J; hangen] hynges J. 1942 wel[1]] *om.* JMO, wil S; at ... al] *om.* JMO; wel[2]] wyll O; vnderstant] vnderstands þis (*s* O[3]) O,

vnderstonden S, how þe pilgryme saughe dropes of bloode vp on þe scrippe · of
whiche he merveylled add. S.   1943 Ryght] prec. Capitulum c mar. C, Capitulum
100 mar. G³, Capitulum lxxxxviii mar. S;   as] dame add. S;   þese] thise (e ins.
G³) G, þis O;   belles] bell O.   1944 biheeld] beholde O;   alwey] -es S;   eye]
eyhene JMO;   þeron] þere appone J.   1945 sygh] I saw O;   sowen]
Spryngklede J, om. O;   dropped] drope O.   1946 me] (2nd e ins. G³);   of] de
F, for (o. er. with u.v. for mar. C³) C, om. JMO;   þat] þat add. S.   1947 it] om.
MO;   and þat] (that can. G³), Et de ce F, and than JMO, And S, caret after (with
er. mar. C³) C;   hadde seyn] Sayde JMO.   1947-8 and ... scrippe] om. JMO.
1948 quod I] om. M;   newe] nowe JO, om. M;   discoumforted euele] trs. J.
1949 I¹] for I J;   on] apon J;   þat] whilke J, yt (alt. þat O³) O;   neuere er] I
persayfed J, nowe add. M;   I apperceyuede] neuere are J, I perceyued MO.
1950 apeseth] queme J, ese alt. apese O;   me¹] (2nd e ins. G³);   þilke] that JMO;
or] eyþer S;   elles] ell O;   taketh] (2nd a ins. G³), gyffe JM, get O.   1951 scrippe]
How dame Grace dieux aunswereþe þe pilgryme of þe blody scrippe add. S;   Haa]
prec. Capitulum ci mar. C, quincunx and Capitulum 101 mar. G³, Capitulum lxxxxix
mar. S, om. J, A·a MO, Aha S;   quod she] Discomforte the J;   discoumforte þe]
(thee 2nd e ins. G³), quod scho J, dysconfor þe so O;   shuldest þou] scholdeste G,
trs. S.   1952 þee] (1st e ins. G³), om. MO;   wost] wate JMO.   1953 loue
þe scrippe] þe scrype lyk O.   1954 þat²] whilke J;   yowþe] his 3ough J;   þe]
this J.   1955 alle places] alle plaaces (2nd a ins. G³) G, aplace J, all place O;
þer] that J;   with] of O.   1956 fair] marked mar. C, So Fayre J.   1957 hem]
him C;   bineme] refe JMO.   1958 him] þam O;   he²] be (alt he O³) O;
nothing] þat add. MOS.   1958-9 men shulden] latte thaym J, (meen alt. men
S).   1959 bineme] reve it J, reue MO;   suich a scrippe] om. J;   he hadde]
hym J, þat add. S.   1960 men ... him] ware to be dede J, (? soowen S);   Algates]
Atte the laste J, so þey dyden for add. S;   mordred] martyrred J.   1961 him]
to dede add. J;   þus] his scrippe S;   þis scrippe] his scrippe J, þus S.
1962 fairere] than it es nowe add. J.   1963 þat¹] om. J, þan MO (ins. mar. O³);
was] than add. J;   al] fairere and M, om. S.   1964 it] om. JM;   wel] right J,
ful MO;   apperede] apeerede (2nd e ins. G³) G.   1965 bleedinge] (2nd e ins.
G³);   boren more] mare brym J, trs. MO;   þan] þam O;   michel] om. JMO.
1966 more¹] om. JMO;   and¹] mykille add. JMO;   after] ward add. O.
1967 diden] thay dyd J;   afterward] -ys J, after MO;   defende] -d G.   1968 it¹]
ins. G³, om. CMO;   suffreden] þem add. MO;   to] for to S;   dismembre] (dis
O³).   1969 peynes ... þe] ins. mar. O³.   1969-70 Whoso ... deth] ins. mar.
O³.   1970 nombre] noum J;   deth] þe deþe S;   neiþer] na J.   1971 seyn]
telle C.   1972 þat] om. MO;   þouh] 3if alle J;   þilke¹] the J, þat MO;
þilke²] that JMO.   1973 and] om. JMO;   preeued] om. JMO;   not thing] no
thinge CJO;   þat is to] forto J, to O.   1974 to ... so] om. C;   litel] sotil M,
om. C;   drope] a droppe J, om. C.   1975 þerof] om. C;   þat nis] þat it ne es J,
þen it is MO, om. C;   michel] om. C;   þen a margerye] and mare precious J, þen
a margaryte MO, perlle add. S.   1975-6 and ... preciows] than a margery J.
1976 þee] (1st e ins. G³);   if] and J;   weren] more add. can M.   1978 wiht]
wythe alt. wyght O³;   þeron] for add. J.   1979 agoon] gone JMO;   þerfore]
neuerþeles J;   ben²] the dropes of blude that are alde JMO.   1979-80 þe ...
elded] er JMO.   1981 þee] þey S;   þou] þat O;   þat] om. JMO;   is] om.
JMO.   1982 so þat] Off J;   scrippe] i add. can. G;   dropped] bedroppede J;
þis] the J, his S.   1983 preeved] approuede J, poruyd O;   þee in] the JMO,
þeyme S.   1984 I sey it] om. J;   withdrawe] (2nd a ins. G³);   þee] (1st e ins.
G³), fra the J, om. S.   1985 bineme] reue JM, reuyd O;   it] om. O;   þee¹] om.

S;   raþere] *ins. mar.* G³, þe raþer S.   1985-6 þow ... þee²] *ins. mar.* G³.
1985 shuldest] so *add. can.* O;   hewe þee] be hewyn *e*als smalle as flesche to the
potte J, to pieces *add.* S.   1986 and sle þee] *om.* JMOS;   þan ... þee²] *om.*
JMO;   suffre] *om.* S;   to] for to S;   Now take] *trs.* J, not take O.   1986-7 it
... anoon] belyfe J, þou onoon it to þe M, þam o non O.   1987 is] *om.* J;   to]
for S;   þee] (*1st e ins.* G³), ie *alt.* þe O, howe þe pilgryme spekeþe to þe lady
Grace dieux of þe scrippe *add.* S;   Ladi] *prec.* Cap*itulum* cii *mar.* C, 102 *mar.* G³,
Cap*itulum* c *mar.* S.   1988 wel] *om.* S;   sufficeth] Suffice JMO;   me¹] (*2nd e*
ins. G³);   which] þat at J, of which MO;   haue] (*2nd a ins.* G³);   me²] (*2nd e ins.*
G³).   1989 me¹˒²] (*2nd e ins.* G³);   take] taaketh (*2nd a ins. and* th *can.* G³) G,
haue take C, taken S.   1990 neuere] not S;   shal] shoulde S;   heerafter] here
afterwarde J.   1991 Algates] neu*er*theles J;   she] it JMO;   me¹˒²] (*2nd e ins.*
G³).   1992 I wole] wolde god · and so I S;   take] (*2nd a ins.* G³);   sithe]
Seyne JMO;   haue] (*2nd a ins.* G³).   1993 yow] howe þe lady Gracedieux ·
arrayed þe pilgryme · with þe scrippe *add.* S;   And] *prec.* Cap*itulum* ciii *mar.* C,
103 *mar.* G³, Cap*itulum* ci *mar.* S;   withoute lettinge] I tuke M;   I took] with
outen lettynge M;   it] þis scripp M.   1994 and¹] *can.* G;   abowte me] a
bowtme (t O³) O;   me¹˒²] (*1st e ins.* G³) G;   anoon ... it] I did it Onane JMO;
þat] Qui F, and JMOS.   1995 arayed it] arayded it G, atyred J, *trs.* MO,
dressed it S;   me] (*2nd e ins.* G³), *þer*with *add.* J, aboute me S;   at] *om.* OS;
hise] alle J, *om.* S;   rightes] right MO, right weel S;   Wel] Fulle JMO;   glad] I
add. O;   was I] *trs.* J, þer of *add.* S.   1995-6 seyh it] was S.   1996 aboute
me] and feled it J, sure þer with girde S;   me] (*2nd e ins.* G³);   and ... it] aboute
me J, And flede it O.   1997 hadde] *om.* OS;   michel and] *trs.* JMO;   it²] *with*
lowly preyer *add.* S, þe pilgrime spekes more of his burdou*n* and of þe ii pomellis
add. rub. M, Nowe Gracedieux declareþe to þe pilgryme þe vertu and þe nature of
þe bourdoun *add.* S.   1998 Now] *prec.* Cap*itulum* civ *mar.* C, 104 *mar.* G,
ca*pitulum* xliii *rub. mar.* M, Cap*itulum* cii *mar.* S, þe burdon *rub. mar.* O;   I wole]
trs. J;   ayen] *ins. mar* G³, *om.* JMOS;   of þe burdoun] *om.* JO;   of which] whate
J, þe lady *add.* S.   1999 made] (*2nd a ins.* G³), sayde J;   me] (*2nd e ins.* G³), to
me J, *om.* O;   sermoun] aft*er*warde J, a sermon M, in sarmon O;   After ... she]
Quod scho Seyn J;   þat] *om.* J.   2000 þee¹] (*1st e ins.* G³), *om.* JMO;   of] *om.*
J;   whiche] þat S;   gladeth] (*2nd a ins.* G³);   þee²] (*1st e ins.* G³), me þe O;
wel] mekille J.   2000-1 I wole] now wille I J, nowe *add.* S.   2001 also] *om.*
JMO; þee] (*1st e ins.* G³);   of þe] of þee of þe S;   at þe] als J, at S;   shorteste]
Schortely J;   þat] as J.   2002 Esperaunce] hope *over* C³, *with* scilicet hope
mar. G³, that esperaunce that es als mykille at Saye on Inglische as hope *add.* J,
P*er*esperaunce MO.   2003 eche] euery S;   þilke] þa JM, *þe* O, he S;   him]
tham JMO;   sikerliche] þer to S.   2004 þerto] sikurlych S;   falle] fayle O;
sechim] Sethym JMO;   of which] that J.   2005 maad] (*1st a ins.* G³), of *add.*
J;   sheweth ful wel] (scheeweth *1st* e *ins.* G³), whate it es J;   it *add.* MO;   which
it is] scheweth fulle wele J, what it is MO;   þou] *om.* O, *illegible mar.* S.
2006 euel] and paraylous *add.* S;   paas] pathis JM, place O, -es S;   wher ...
wikkede] *om.* S.   2007 paas] pathe J, passeȝ M, pace O, *om.* S;   euene] and
add. can. G;   wel] *om.* S;   on] vpon S;   pomelles] pomell S.   2008 þe ... up]
þer þou shouldest haue yyne handelyng (? yyue) S;   shulen] shuld MO;   þee]
(*1st e ins.* G³).   2008-9 nouht ... þee] (*2nd e ins.* G³), Suffyr the nouȝt J;   and
... falle] for to kepe þee surelych frome fallyng S, Loo what si*n*gnefyen þe twoo
pomelles of þe bourdoun *add.* S.   2009 The] *prec.* Cap*itulum* cv *mar.* C,
105 *mar.* G³, Cap*itulum* ciii *mar.* S;   hye] ouermast S;   pomel] -ys O;   is¹] of
þe bourdou*n* betookeneþe S.   2009-10 is² ... seith] as the letter Sayse es J.

2010 þat] *om.* J, which S; is] *om.* J. 2011 eche] ilke a J, euery S; whiche²] þe whiche S. 2012 mire] wounder JMO, heele and leeche S; him¹] þaym JMOS; wel] of hir disayses S; considere] beholde S; him²] thaym JMO, hem self S; al þe world] þerin JMO. 2013 þerinne] alle the werlde JMO; mired] wondrede JMO, *om.* S; is] It is MO; nouht as greet] als myche or lasse in comparysoune S; aas] |·|over G³, ane aas JMO; dee] · *over* G³; thilke] that JMO. 2014 pomel] mirrour JMO; þou shuldest] *trs.* J; mire] wondyr JMO, beholde S; ofte] of S; looke þerinne] looking S. 2015 þee] (*1st* e *ins.* G³), *om.* O; and] *o. er. with er. mar.* C, ofte luke þerin and *add.* J; clyue] *ins. mar.* G³. 2016 withinne] thowe See₃ wele J; þou ... wel] with in J; haue (*2nd* a *ins.* G³). 2017 nothing] thynge JMO; þee] (*1st* e *ins.* G³), *om.* J. 2018 paas] path J, place O; Now think] *trs.* J; heeron] here of O; þou] þe S. 2019 þow shalt] *trs.* J; do] in alle *add.* J, haue S; That ooþer] The toother (*2nd* o *ins.* G³) G, *prec.* Cap*itulum* cvi *mar.* C, 106 *mar.* G³. 2020 þilke] scho JMO. 2021 mooder] the modere JMO; and bar] *om.* M; þat] *prec. þen trials mar.* S³. 2022 charbuncle] carboncle (*with* charboncle *mar.* G³) G, stone *add.* O; glisteringe] gliter J, gliterynge MO, glistennyng S; þat] and J; enlumineth] the lightnys J, lightnessh M, lyghtnesse O; niht] lyght J. 2023-4 bi ... forveied] *om.* J. 2023 þe which] whilk MO; wey] þe way MOS. 2023-4 þat ... and] *ins. mar.* G³, *om.* MO. 2023 ben²] lyen S; distracte] distraught S. 2024 forveied] erraunte₃ M, errant O; þe] *om.* M; þilke] tha JM, to *alt.* þo O. 2025 fallen doun] fallande J, fallynge MO. 2026 þerfore] that J, þere MO; hath be] es JMO; graffed] grafted JO. 2027 burdoun] burdon *and otiose -us* J. 2028 oo] 1 *over* G³. 2029 oon] 1 *over* G³; whiche] by it ane *add.* J; not¹] For *add.* J; eche] man *add.* J; þerbi] ne *add.* JMO. 2030 bi] wight *add. can. rub.* O; þis] *ins. mar.* O³; comen] þere to *add.* M; lenen] lenet J. 2031 eche] ilke a J, euerych S. 2032 rede] þee *add.* S. 2033 triste] truste (e *ins.* G³) GS; in ... times] þerin alwaye J, þer to in ale tyme S; bi] þorowe J; be] *ins. mar.* G³. 2034 wikkede] and parayllouse *add.* S; paas] paasso₃ J, pace O, -es S; bi] thurght J. 2035 mown] *om.* S. 2036 afficched] afichie F, fychede JS, fastened M, fyschid O; twey] the twa JMO, two S; wel] I telle the J; I telle þee] (*3rd* e *ins.* G³), wele J. 2037 þat] þane S; þou miht] maye þou J, þou mightest S. 2038 miht] may J; triste] truste GM, treste O, *om.* S; þee¹] (*1st* e *ins.* G³), *om.* S; and] *om.* S; assure] sure S; þee²] (*1st* e *ins.* G³). 2039 þe] three *add.* S; shulen] schuld O; þee] (*1st* e *ins.* G³), and vphalde *add.* J; in] and O. 2040 alle] (e *ins.* G³); paas] paasse₃ JS, pace O. 2041 haue] (*2nd* a *ins.* G³); it þee] (*1st* e *ins.* G³), *trs.* J; Thanne] *prec.* Cap*itulum* cvii *mar.* C, 107 *mar.* G³, And than J; þe] my J. 2042 it] þe bourdoun S; me] (*2nd* e *ins.* G³), *om.* JS; wherwith] whare þurght J, wherby MO; to myn herte] scho dyd grete ioye J; to] in S; myn] my O; she ... ioye] to my herte J. 2043 redy I was] I was redy C; al] thynges *add.* J; to²] forthe on S. 2044 algates] ₃it neuerþeles J, all₃it algates MO, yit a lytel S; it¹] *om.* S; me] (*2nd* e *ins.* G³); þe] my JMO; þat] for that J; not] *om.* S. 2045 yrened] y yrened G, pykede J, I ryueted S; holde] contene J, restreyne S. 2046 me] (*2nd* e *ins.* G³); bi God] par Dieu F, *om.* JMOS; þat I ne] that ne me J, þen I MO; sey] muste nedes telle J, tell MO; my thouht] what I thenk S; of] touchande J; þilke] this J, þat MO, þe S. 2046-7 þat² ... yrened] witte ₃e wele it myslyketh me mykille J. 2047 It ... wel] that it es nou₃t pyked J; is] hit is S; yrened] y yrened G, yryueted S; it] I O; wel] wol M. 2048 alle ooþere] I See J; I see] alle other*e* J; yrened] y yrened G, er pyked and J, ryueted S; if] I pray ₃owe that J; ye wole] it lyke yowe S; me] (*2nd* e *ins.* G³). 2049 suich] ₃e hafe take me J, oon *add*. MO, so vnryveted S; ye ... me] Swilke ane J; take] (*2nd* a *ins*. G³); it] *om*. MO; me] (*2nd* e *ins*. G³), to me MOS, howe dame Gracedieux aunswereþe þe pilgryme to his demaunde why þe bourdoun is not ryveted *add*. S; Haa] Oo J, Aa MOS, *prec*. Cap*itulum* cviii *mar*. C, 108 *mar*. G³, Cap*itulum* civ *mar*. S; what] *om*. J, þat S. 2049-50 þou art] *trs*. J. 2050 a fool] styrde with folye S; þee] (*1st* e *ins*. G³); at] aboute JM; þi] þin M; Haue] (*2nd* a *ins*. G³). 2051 þee] (*1st* e *ins*. G³); if] and J; a] *om*. J, beo a S; litel] *om*. J; remembre] -d S. 2052 þee¹] (*2nd* e *ins*. G³), *om*. S; to] in JMO; aboue] a bowte O; triste] truste GS; þee²] (*1st* e *ins*. G³). 2053 þee] (*1st* e *ins*. G³); pomelles¹] pomelle JM; for] *om*. S; þe pomelles²] the pomelle JO, wheeche S; shulen] shoulde S. 2054 þee¹,²] (*1st* e *ins*. G³); not ... þee] Suffyr the nouȝt J; falle] to falle JS; þee³] (*1st* e *ins*. G³), *om*. J. 2055 þanne] thy J, þam O. 2055-8 wel ... side] *om*. S. 2055 wost] wate JMO; yrened] y yrened G, hupid & piked J. 2056 þilke þat] that J, þat that MO; vnyrened] oniyrened (i *ins*. G³) G, Vnpiked J; Vnyrened] on y yrened G, I tuke it the JO, I tuke þe M. 2056-7 I ... þee] (þee *2nd* e *ins*. G³), vnpiked J, vnyrned MO, *marked mar*. C³. 2058 yrened] y yrened G, a piked J, an yrned MO, þilk þat is vnryveted S; burdoun] *om*. S; stiketh] gase J, stylk*es* (-*es* O³) O. 2059 dunge] and fastyr stekketh þerin J; þilke] þat JMO; noon] na J; yren] y yren*e* G, pike J; and²] ay *add*. J. 2060 stiketh] gase the faster it stikketh and J; more] iron *mar*. O³; þilke] he JMO, it S; empeched] lettede JMO; bereth] beþeþe *alt*. bereþe S. 2061 over] than JMO; þilke] he JMO, part *add*. S; it²] *ins*. G³; vnyrened] on y yrened G, vnpiked J, vnyreveted S; and] *u.v*. And C³; þerfore] þere J; haue] (*2nd* a *ins*. G³). 2062 take] (*2nd* a *ins*. G³); it] *om*. J; þee] (*1st* e *ins*. G³), to the J; suich] on this wyse J, in swilk wyse M; empeched] letted JMO. 2063 forwh] frure O; ne¹] nor MO; haue] (*2nd* a *ins*. G³); encombraunce] emcomberaunce M. 2064 Haa] A·A JMOS; lady] *om*. S; yit] hyeres me J, *om*. MO; oo] I *over* O³; thinketh] thynke JMO, semeþe S; not a] na J. 2065 fool] as yee rehersen *add*. S; haue] (*2nd* a *ins*. G³). 2066 of which] that J, which S; ye ... nouht] of *add*. J; assaile me] or theues J; me] (*2nd* e *ins*. G³); oþer theeves] assayle me J. 2067 and] *marked for gloss* G³, in O; yrened] y yrened G, pyked J, yreveyted S; ye] that *add*. J; it] *om*. O. 2068 yrened] y yrened G, piked J, eryveyted S; bifore] *om*. J; þat] ceste F, *om*. GS. 2069 speke] spak CO; þis] *om*. J, it MO, þus S; and] on *add*. J, of *add*. MO; ooþerweys] oþer wise JMO; þerto] Here to J. 2070 make] (*2nd* a *ins*. G³); þee] (*1st* e *ins*. G³); for] this J; not] ordeyned *add*. J, made *add*. S. 2071 but] *om*. J; þee] toi F, þer C; seye] will say MO. 2072 þou wolt] þou wolde J, with outen more MOS; withoute more] *om*. J, þou wil MOS; defende þee] (*4th* e *ins*. G³), have whare wi*th* þou myȝt defende the J. 2072-4 armures ... anoon] I schalle take the J. 2072 armures] armo*ur* JMO. 2073-4 wel ... shalt] *om*. M, also *add*. S. 2074 I ... þee] armo*ur* wi*th* whilke þou schall wel defende the · with oute offence and with whilke þou schalle wele discommfyt thyn*e* enmys onane J; take] (*2nd* a *ins*. G³). 2075 hem] this armo*ur* J; Haa] A JMOS. 2076 bi] on J; swich] þis burdoun] me liketh J, þis burdon M; liketh me wel] the burdou*n* wele J; me] (*2nd* e *ins*. G³); wherfore] (*2nd* e *ins*. G³). 2077 yow] me M; þese] this JMO; armures] armo*ur* JMO, Grace *and in another hand* presenteth armore for the bodye, in this our earthlye pylgrimage · as Helmett, gorgett, Haburgion, gauntlet, sworde & targett. of it selfe good, yet not fitting y*e* body without tyes, & a gyrdle to keepe it close thertoe . so patience, temperance, constanty, Justice & purden*ce etc* profitts little (being the Armore for y*e* sowle) except they haue the tyes of fayth. & gyrte by the hand of grace. not with standing dame natures help. read xii leaues *mar*. O³; hem] it J; me] (*2nd* e *ins*. G³), to me M, Loo here howe dame Gracedieux shewed hir perche honging ful of armures to þe pilgryme *add*. S. 2078 And] *om*. MO, *prec*. Ca*pitulum* cix *mar*. C, 109 *mar*. G³, ca*pitulum* xliv *rub*. *mar*. M, Ca*pitulum* cv *mar*. S; þanne] thus JO; into] with in JS. 2079 clepede] called JM; me] (*2nd* e *ins*. G³), tylle hir *add*. J; Now bihold] *trs*. J; hy] heght J; þilke] ʒone JMO; perche] perke þedyr J, perke MO. 2080 I] me JMO; muste] by hofeth J; to¹] *om*. J; armure] the armo*ur* J; to go fer] *om*. JMO; with] *ins*. G³, *om*. JMO; Ynowh] fo J, for ynowgh MO; þow seest] þ*ou* Seeʒ I now J, *om*. S. 2081 þee] (*1st* e *ins*. G³); haubergouns] (*1st* u *ins*. G³). 2082 and¹] *om*. J; jakkes] dowbelettys and *add*. J, and *add*. MO; al] þay*m* *add*. J, hoole herneys to þilke *add*. S; needeth] they nedeth J; to þilke] *om*. J, þam MO, *om*. S; þat²] or S. 2083 him] thay*m* JMO; Now take] now taake (e *ins*. G³), *trs*. J; þat þat] that atte J, þat MO, suche as S; wolt] desyrest S; haue] (*2nd* a *ins*. G³), to have S. 2084 þee] (*1st* e *ins*. G³), for *add*. S; hast] Schalle haue J, now *add*. M; leeue] goode leve J, licence M, liu *alt*. leue O, of me *add*. S; Whan] *prec*. Ca*pitulum* cx *mar*. C, 110 *mar*. G³; þese] this JMO; armures] armoure JMO. 2085 michel] in my herte J; reioysede me] was reioysed J; me] (*2nd* e *ins*. G³); algates] neuerþeles J. 2086 with] wyth (h O³) O; do me profyt] beste J; best] do my pro*fi*t J. 2087 neuere] before *add*. J; ne I] ne JMO, ner S; hadde] *om*. JS; nouht] *om*. J, neuer MS; ben] was S; me] (*2nd* e *ins*. G³). 2088-9 ye wole] it be ʒo*ur* wille J, hit lyke yowe S. 2089 armures] armo*ur* JMO; shulde¹] Schalle J; and] N*o*ta over C³; shulde²] schalle J. 2090 me¹,²] (*2nd* e *ins*. G³); for] *om*. MO; if] *om*. GS; helpe] not *add*. *ins*. O³; ye²] *om*. J, I OS; hadden] *om*. J, haue M, kan OS; do] *om*. J, done M; nothing] it es nouʒt alle þ*at* I have done J, howe dame Gracedieux cheseþe his armures *add*. S. 2091 And] *prec*. Ca*pitulum* cxi *mar*. C, 111 *mar*. G³, Ca*pitulum* cvi *mar*. S, *om*. M; a²] *om*. JMO. 2092 swich¹] byfore *add*. J, slike M; noon swich²] swilke ane oþere J. 2093 riht] ryghe O; was set] *ins*. M³; an] a J; anevelte] stithe JM, I*d est* a stethi *add*. O. 2094 maad] (*1st* a *ins*. G³); to] forto JO; Of] and JMO; hameres] harmes JMO; of] *prec*. Paciencia *rub*. *mar*. O, *om*. JS; it] *om*. JS. 2094-5 at ... present] *om*. J. 2095 firste] (e *ins*. G³); made] (*2nd* a *ins*. G³); me] (*2nd* e *ins*. G³). 2096 quod she] a doublet J; a doublet] q*u*od scho JMO; beste] (*2nd* e *ins*. G³). 2097 neiþer] noon MO; ne] ner S; and] in *alt*. and O³; tached] atachiez F, teyed C. 2098 pile] pyle S, pyll G, pel F, pileer CJMO; but] Mais F, If CJ, *om*. S; þat¹] *om*. JS; he¹ ... him] *om*. S; þat²] doublet *add*. J; more] doute S. 2099 venquished] conqueste O, descoumfyted S; with] be O. 2100 be] *om*. S; victour] *with* s*ci*licet ? concou*re*re *mar*. G³, discoumfyt S; of] *om*. S; ouer] this *add*. J, þat *add*. O, more S; þee] (*1st* e *ins*. G³). 2101 and] luke þ*ou* *add*. J; hath] haue M; on] that garment J, vpon S; þilke garnement] apone hy*m* J, þat garment M, þis garmente O. 2102 þat²] at J. 2103 and¹] in O; growe] to growe J, grow *alt*. graw O³. 2104 fylleth] (y *o*. *er*. C); hise] garnementes and *add*. S; pestilence] -s S. 2105 seleeres] celliers S; grete] (*2nd* e *ins*. G³); hardshipes] hardschepe JMO; à] *om*. S; bed] -des S. 2106 tormentes] tournamentes is S; his] *om*. J; maketh] (*2nd* a *ins*. G³). 2107 his] of S; of] his S; adue*r*site] adue*r*site JOS; fastinges] Fastynge JM; maken] (*2nd* a *ins*. G³), makes JM. 2108 syknesses] Sekenesse JMOS; strengthe] strenkthen (n *can*. G³) G, athendeʒ hy*m* J, strengthys hym MO, strenkeneþe him S, N*o*ta *rub*. *mar*. O; pouerte and] *om*. JMO. 2109 maken] (*2nd* a *ins*. G³); him] *om*. JM; his] *om*. O; more] (*2nd* o *ins*. G³), *ins*. *mar*. O³; it] him S. 2110 it] he S;

and] for S;   maad] (*2nd* a *ins.* G³).   2111 poyninges] poynynge JMO;   whi] which S;   cleped] called JMO;   a] *om.* O;   so] *om.* J.   2112 prikkinges] prykkynge JMO (*1st* k *ins.* O³);   armed] a stithy J, an aneueld i*d est* a stithy M, an aneueld O;   Bi] with JMO;   prikkynges] prikkynge JMO (*1st* k *ins.* O³]. 2113 worth] wrought J;   þat²] at J;   withoute prikkinges] with oute p*r*ikkynge J, with prikk oute prikkynge (prikk *can.*) M, with prykkynge owt (*1st* k *ins.* O³) O. 2114 If] And if M;   wite] oght *add. o. er.* O³.   2115 clepe] calleth JMO; maad] (*1st* a *ins.* G³);   to²] forto M.   2116 prikkinges] p*r*ikkynge JMO;   as] *om.* JMO;   an] a J, *om.* C;   anevelte] annefelde (*3rd* e *can.* G³) G, stithy JM. 2117 of] *ins.* G;   a] *o. er.* O³.   2117-18 for² ... endure] (forte, reseyue, endure *marked for gloss,* forte, reseyue *can. with* butt Reseiueþ and endur{eþ} *mar.* G³), Pour recevoir ... et endurer F, but resseyueth and endureth C, for to reysen and endure S.   2118 wille] and *add.* J;   murmurynge] grucchynge JMO. 2119 This] *prec.* Cap*itulum* cxii *mar.* C, 112 *mar.* G³, same *add.* S;   on Ihesus] on Ih*esu* GMOS, ih*esu* c*r*iste on hy*m* J, cryste *add.* O.   2119 whan] *om.* MO;   in þe crosse] he hynged on the crosse J.   2119-20 for ... hanged] for the J, for he was honged M.   2121 mesured] (esu *o. er. with er. mar.* C³);   aright] ryght JMO;   at] *om.* J;   his] *om.* J;   rihtes] *om.* J, right M;   al] *om.* S. 2122 endurede] he endured J;   seyde] agayn seide M;   sownede] sewnyd O; an] A JM, þam O;   anevelte] stethy JM.   2123 shewede] scheewed (*2nd* e *ins.* G³) G;   was¹] so he was J, bewand *add.* M;   to] tille J;   strokes] stroke O;   of] *om.* J, with M;   whiche] þat J;   he] *om.* O.   2124 smite] with *add.* J, þerfore] *om.* J;   on] *om.* JO;   him] *om.* J;   was] that ware J, it *add. ins.* M; and²] *om.* JMO;   moneyed] *om.* JMO, coyned S.   2124-5 þi ... forgeden] *om.* JMO.   2125 smiþes] smethes (*with* smythes *mar.* G³) G;   him] *om.* JMO, it S.   2126 moneyden] neue*r*e he moued J, ? moued M, meuyd O;   so þat] Tharfore J;   schuldest] *om.* J;   wel suppose] *trs.* S.   2127 þese] this JMO; armures] doublet J, armou*r* MO, *þat add.* S;   þei] it J;   been] es J;   goode] and fyne *add.* J.   2128 þat þei ben] *om.* JMOS;   to] *om.* J;   take] taak (*2nd* a *ins.* G³) G;   hem¹] it J, *om.* S;   hem²] it J.   2129 þe] *om.* MO;   rediere] (e *o. er.* C);   on] þee *add.* S.   2130 armure] *om.* S;   upon þese] schulde be J; shulden be] a bovene vpon*e* this J;   bineþe] þe neþemast S;   þe] na *add.* J. 2132 And] *prec.* Cap*itulum* cxiii *mar.* C, 113 *mar.* G³;   garnement] vpon *add.* S; me] (*2nd* e *ins.* G³);   ne wot] wat nouȝt J, wote neue*r* O.   2133 me] (*2nd* e *ins.* G³);   it¹] *om.* O;   to ... it] gretly it greued me J.   2133-4 michel ... me] (me *2nd* e *ins.* G³), to bere it J.   2134 youre] N*ota rub. mar.* O;   purpoynt] purposynge O.   2134-5 not a poynt] nathynge J.   2135 shape] schaape (*1st* a *ins.* G³) G;   for] O³;   me] (*2nd* e *ins.* G³), *ins.* O³.   2135-7 swich ... shape²] *ins. mar.* O³.   2135 swich] ane *add.* J;   mihte] (e *ins.* G³), may J;   I] *ins.* O³; it] *om.* JMO.   2136 greevinge] grete greuaunce J;   me] (*2nd* e *ins.* G³), to me J, mykil to me MO³;   to michel] *om.* JMO;   Serteyn] -ly J.   2137 were¹] was MO;   shape¹] schaape (*2nd* a *ins.* G³) G, ryght welle J, *om.* O;   for þe ariht] I Schapyne for the J, for þe ful right MO;   if] and J;   ariht²] of ryght JMO; shape²] schaape (*1st* a *ins.* G³) G.   2138 on] *om.* J;   þee] right *add. can.* M, *om.* J;   it] *ins.* M, *om.* J;   holt] to hold MO, *om.* J;   þat] thow JMO, þou *add.* S; rihted] schapyne ne rithed J, aright S;   ariht] of right MO, arighted S;   after] *om.* J, at O.   2138-9 his riht] forto halde it on the J.   2140 þe] l' F, thy JO, þin M;   wynge] -s O;   art] þou erte JMO;   boistous] and *add.* C;   and²] to fatte and *add.* S;   michel] weel S.   2141 fed] efedde S;   maken] (*2nd* a *ins.* G³);   þee] (*2nd* e *ins.* G³);   gret] N*ota rub. mar.* O;   withoute] grete *add.* J. 2142 miht] may JMO;   on] opon M;   and] *om.* JMO.   2143 al] thynges *add.*

J; confoorme] comforte (me ins. mar. O³) O; þee] (2nd e ins. G³); to¹,²] tille
J; it¹] and add. J.   2144 away] alwey S;   þat²] as J;   in] en F, on C, to S;
þee²] (2nd e ins. G³).   2145 be¹] (2nd e ins. G³);   if] yt O;   wel] om. JS;
cloþed] þere with add. J, howe þe pilgryme askeþe counsell of dame Gracedieux ·
howe he might be clooþed · with þis pourpoynt add. S.   2146 Lady] prec.
Capitulum cxiv mar. C, 114 mar. G³, Capitulum cvii mar. S;   me] (2nd e ins. G³);
how] how add. can. O.   2147 wheþer] wheþe S;   me] (2nd e ins. G³);   neede]
nede (de ins. mar. O³) O;   ouht] any J, om. O.   2148 me] (2nd e ins. G³), and
J;   and] right add. J;   shape] schaape (1st a ins. G³) G;   his riht] hym J.
2149 Serteyn] -ly J;   ryotous] to riotous J;   inowh] om. J;   envyous] to enuyous
J.   2150 Wite þow shuldest] thow scholde wit J;   þe] þis S;   if] yt if (if ins.
mar. O³) O.   2151 noon] na J, not O;   ooþer] noþere J, nothir O.
2152 carpentere] carpentary M;   hewe] (2nd e ins. G³);   þee] (1st e ins. G³);
riht] -s J.   2153 þee¹] it schalle add. J, Nota rub. mar. O.   2153-4 þouh ...
þee] om. C.   2153 þee²] ye O;   sore þerof] trs. J;   þis] the J;   firste] furste (e
ins. G³) G.   2154 nis] (n can. G³), is J, is nouȝt MO;   after] -warde J;   þou]
þat O.   2155 þee] (1st e ins. G³).   2156 missey] -th CJ;   þee] (1st e ins.
G³);   þe²] þi O.   2157 towardes] towarde JMO;   him] and add. O;   þin]
thy JO;   It] I J.   2158 nothing] na mare J;   recche] dere J, o. er. M;   þee]
(1st e ins. G³), o. er. M, for add. S;   to haue] than J, o. er. M.   2159 þe] þin M,
þi O;   anevelte] stethy JM;   al] om. J;   at] om. O.   2160 strokes] þat add.
CJ (ins. with er. mar. C), strokk þat MO;   yive] ȝeue (ȝyue over G³) G;   þee¹]
(1st e ins. G³), om. J;   he shal] om. JMO;   rihte] (e ins. G³), om. JMO;   þee²]
om. JMO;   þe²] þi M;   purpoynt] be commeth als harde as a stethy add. J, shal
be þe strangere add. M.   2161 sey] prey S;   þerbi] therefore J;   haue] (2nd a
ins. G³);   þe] om. J;   gryndinge] graant J, grauntynge MO, emolument (variant
molument L) F.   2162 corownement] the crowne of lyfe J;   swich] the whilke
J;   forginge] forgevynge J.   2163 bi] om. MO;   swich] whilke J, om. MO;
knokkinge] fightynge and forgynge J, fyghtyng MO;   þee] om. JMO;   corown]
coroune (with scilicet {coro}wne mar. G³) G.   2164 kowde] can J;   þat] And
that J;   þilke] the corowne J, þat MO;   with] om. J, by MO;   whiche] that J;
ben corowned] om. J.   2165 þe] -se C, om. J;   martires] had add. J;   þe
purpoynt] loveden J;   loueden] this purpoynt J;   þat] (with wheche mar. G³),
whiche C, they J.   2165-6 upon þe anevelte] Suffred so mekille to be knokked
J.   2166 anevelte] stethy M;   suffreden ... michel] on the stethy J;   and] So
many add. J.   2166-7 to yiven] þeron ressayfed J.   2167 bi] thurght J;
strokes] (r ins. O es O³);   and ... hem] om. J.   2168-9 þe purpoynt] with outen
any lettynge þow bere J.   2169 withoute ... bere] the purpoynte J;   oo] 1 over
G³.   2170 neede] be fulle nedefulle J;   þee] to the J;   þat²] and that J.
2171 þee¹] (1st e ins. G³);   þee²] (1st e ins. G³), om. O.   2172 feeld] þe felde
CO;   and ¹]om. M;   in²] ins. O³.   2173 seruauntes] Sergaunte J, seruand
MO, sergens F;   þat] and S;   upon] on M;   þee] (1st e ins. G³).   2174 and
... þee] (þee 1st e ins. G³), om. JMO;   if] and J.   2175 on] apon the JO, on þe
M;   þe] this JMO.   2175-6 þow shuldest] trs. J.   2176 Now do] trs. J;
þerof] om. M, þer wythe O;   þe] my M.   2177 do] haue done J;   Ladi] prec.
Capitulum cxv mar. C, 115 mar. G³.   2178 me] (2nd e ins. G³);   þat þat] that
at J, þat O;   ye] (2nd e ins. G³);   seyn] have seyde J, me add. S;   ne] and JMO;
of] on J;   ayensey] a ȝens sey G.   2179 so¹] thus J;   þat] om. JMO.
2180 it] I O;   suffice] to bere add. J;   algates] Neuerþeles J.   2181 afforce]
enforce J, bifore MO;   me] (2nd e ins. G³);   to] thowe J, do M;   If] Sayde
Grace dieu loke ȝif J.   2182 take] (2nd a ins. G³);   me] any J, of me MO;

looketh] Lady quod I luke ʒe J;   haue] (*2nd* a *ins.* G³);   I²] For I J;   be] als *add.*
JMO.   2183 armed] as I maye *add.* J;   I] habirioune fortis *rub. mar.*
O;   berste] howe þe pilgrime desyred of dame Gracedieux more herneys *add.* S.
2184 Thanne] *prec. Capitulum* cxvi *mar.* C, 116 *mar.* G³, Cap*itulum* cviii *mar.* S;
rauhte] forth *add.* J, me *add.* MS;   an] a O.   2185 plesaunt] a plesaunt JMO;
facioun] farsioun J;   me] (*2nd* e *ins.* G³), vnto me J;   garnement] quod Scho *add.*
J.   2186 whiche] the whiche J;   maad] (*1st* a *ins.* G³);   olde] þe olde CG (þe
ins. mar. G³);   for to] *om.* J;   fighte] with *add.* C, with *add. ins. mar.* G³, Feith J;
ayens] a gayne J.   2187 ayens¹] agayne J;   alle] (e *ins.* G³);   thilke] þa JM,
om. O;   of] *om.* O;   ayens²] agayn M.   2188 here] his JO;   dredes] dreedes
(*1st* e *ins.* G³) G, dedys O.   2189 wylde] felle and so cruelle J, wyll O;   whoso]
who O;   woodeth] waxeth wood JM, waxis hys wode (xi *ins.*) O;   leeseth] loses
M, lose O.   2190 Esperaunce] *with* hope *mar.* G³;   yuele] eeuelle (*2nd and 4th*
e *ins.* G³) G.   2191 bitaken] be taaken (*1st* a *ins.* G³) G, takyne JM, takynge O;
þese] this JM;   armures] armour JM.   2192 who] he C;   þat] So J;   with ...
haubergeoun] is cledde J;   þilke] þat MOS;   is cloþed] with that haubergeoun J.
2192-3 preyseth it nouht] he Seteth by þe deed nouʒt J, he settis nouʒt þer by MO,
preyse him at nought S.   2193 at a bodde] a bene J, a rech M, a bud O, *om.* S;
he] for who haþe it, he S;   haue] (*2nd* a *ins.* G³), wynne J.   2194 loos] fame
MO;   prys] the pryse JMO;   of] *ins. mar.* G³);   deth] N*ota rub. mar.* O.
2194-5 shulde not deyne] schulde nouʒt J, shuld nouʒt dy MO, deigneþe not S.
2195 to] *om.* J;   ne ne] F, ne CJMO;   wolde] he *add.* M, it *add.* O;   not] *om.* O.
2196 þe²] to gods seruants Death brings life *mar.* O³;   hye] of *add. can.* G³;   and]
of O.   2197 tonges] tonge O;   withoute²] *om.* M;   þilke] that JMO.
2198 þer] ne *add. ins.* (*with u.v.* ne *mar.* C³) C;   was] noon *add.* MO;   appreeued
ne alowed] nane oþere Armur J;   noon ooþer armure] Approued ne alowede J.
2199 is¹] it O;   þat] *om.* S;   þerwith] es nouʒt armed and cledde J, *om.* S;   is² ...
cloþed] þere with J, *om.* S;   This] *prec. Capitulum* cxvii *mar.* C, 117 *mar.* C³.
2200 hatteth] hath J, had O;   Force] strengthe *over* C, *with scilicet* strenkthe *mar.*
G³, & strenght *add.* JMO, faith feares not Death *mar.* O³;   whiche] When JO;
Ihesu] *om.* J;   Cristes] cryste O;   champiouns] lorica fortitudo *mar.* M.
2202 in] soo stedefaste in J, *om.* MO;   tournament] tourmentynge J, torment MS,
turmiente O.   2203-4 of so strong] So strange of J.   2204 ygrounden] ware
it neuere so scharpe grundene J, grondyne MO.   2205 mayl] nayle O;   ybroken]
marked mar. C³, brokyne JMO;   but] gret *add.* J;   al preeved] *om.* J;   shulde]
awe J.   2206 not] *om.* MO;   be] to be J;   heled] consiled J;   with¹] *om.* S;
was nayled] the Smyth sonne J, were nayled S.   2206-7 þe ... smith] was nayled
J.   2207 and ryven] vnto the crosse J;   þe² ... were] ware the mayles J, þe
nayles war OS;   enclowed] ? enclened O.   2208 was also] *trs.* J.
2209 wherfore] þerfore S.   2210 weren] weeren (*1st* e *ins.* G³) G.   2211
þerinne cloþed] *trs.* JMO, þer Inne eclooþed S;   weren ... strong] (weeren *1st* e
ins. G³), ware clethede So strangly J, clothid were so stronngly MO.
2212 mortal] metelle J;   werre] were J;   torment] tourment F, tournament CJ;
were it] þof it were M.   2213 straw] strau (*with* straw *mar.* G³) G.   2214 if¹
... me] (me *2nd* e *ins.* G³), *om.* J;   se] luke J;   þou] it J.   2215-16 And ...
here] *om.* J, *prec. Capitulum* cxviii *mar.* C, 118 *mar.* G³.   2215 abd] *om.* O;   after]
-warde MO.   2216 seide] (*2nd* e *ins.* G³), I saide MS;   here] to hir*e* M;
Lady] quod I *add.* CJMO;   goodliche] *om.* J;   ye] (*2nd* e *ins.* G³), I S.
2218 make] (*2nd* a *ins.* G³), *om.* S;   me¹] (*2nd* e *ins.* G³), *om.* S;   þat] *om.* J;
wole] goodly *add.* J;   shewe] scheewe (*2nd* e *ins.* G³) G, me²] (*2nd* e *ins.* G³);
al] *om.* J.   2218 þat þat¹] þat at J;   ye] she S;   me] (*2nd* e *ins.* G³), *ins.* M;

þat þat²] (2nd that ins. mar. G³), that JMOS. 2218-19 I wold] trs. J. 2219 redye] (2nd e ins. G³) G; me] (2nd e ins. G³); be] beon S. 2219-20 a ... swerd] with out any taryinge Scho raught me J. 2219 an] a O. 2220 peyre] of add. MOS; and] om. G; a³] om. MO. 2220-l she ... tarynge] agorgere a helme · atarget · a payre of gloues · and a swerde J. 2221 seyde] vnto me add. J; With] om. J; þese] theese (1st e ins. G³) G, this J; armures] armour J. 2221-2 it ... þou¹] the nedeth J. 2222 arme] to beon armed S; þee] (ins. mar. O³), om. S; þe¹] om. O; leste] beste J; þou²] I J. 2223 shule] schuld O; ynouh] at the fulle J; al be it] þat add. C, ȝif alle J; I] ins. mar. G³. 2224 if] and J. 2225 þat] whilke J; þee] þou ert J. 2225-6 With ... hed] Thow schall fyrste arme the J. 2226 hool] with S. 2226-7 þou ... þee] (penultimate e ins. and with add. can. G³), with the helme and the gorgere forto kepe thy heued hale J. 2227 whan þou] ins. mar. and the helme add. can. O³; on] vpon S; haubergeoun] habergoun (with haubergoun mar. G³) G. 2228 and] om. JO; sithe] Seyn JMOS; þe glooves] (2nd o ins. G³), þou Schalle Take J, þi glouys MOS; þou ... take] thy gloues J, om. S; take] (2nd a ins. G³). 2229 glooven] arme S; for] bot add. J; in ... hem²] they ware coverde and hylded with þaym J; in] o. er. M; hem¹] glooves over C, with scilicet glouen mar. G³, þi handes o. er. M, þan O; hiddest] had o. er. M, hyd O; hem²] marked for gloss G³. 2230 nouht] om. JS; armed] howe þat Gracedieux declareþe to þe pilgryme þe signefyaunce of alle þeos pieces of his hernys add. S; This] prec. Capitulum cxix mar. C, 119 mar. G³, Capitulum cix mar. S; shuldest] wele add. J; Attemperaunce] temperaunce JMO; sighte] and add. MO, temperancia rub. mar. MO; þe²] om. J; heeringe] (1st e ins. G³). 2232 þe] om. JMO; mown] myght J, note mar. O³. 2233 helme] o. er. M; refreyneth] defendeth J; his] þe O; wittes] sight JMO; and restreyneth] om. JMO. 2234 riht] om. M, and O; Attemperaunce] serueth J, temperance MO; serueth] temperaunce J, seruyce M; to] forto M. 2235 to¹] ouermekel J; and¹] ne J, om. O; to miche] om. O; abaundoned] habundande JM, om. O; and²] ne M, om. O; to³] om. O. 2236 if ... streyt] ware ne the viser ware strayte olierde J. 2237 arwe] an arwe CJM (o. er. C), a rew O, arowes S; þe] thy J, þin M; go] passe J; withoute] the eye · and eare, the inletts to many euills mar. O³. 2238 it] the JMO; þe] thy J; To ... also] Also to hyere J; heere] (2nd e ins. G³), heryng M; murmurynge] and add. O. 2239 bakbitinge] and add. J; fool] fowle JMO, -ishe S; speches] Speche JMO; þilke] the JMO; so holliche] the eres J. 2240 herte] (2nd e ins. G³). 2241 harde] (with strongleche mar. G³), strongliche C; arwes] arow O. 2243 no ... in] not have na ferrere entree J, no ferrere haue entre in MO. 2244 for] that J. 2245 ordeyne] em. ed., ardeyne GS (with dysordene mar. G³), disordeyned C, om. JMO, ordenee F (variant desordenee TAM¹LMH); herte] (2nd e ins. G³); nothing] nouȝt J; þus] on this wyse J. 2246 for ... þee¹] om. JMO; þis] the JMO; to²] forto JMO; arme] kepe JMO; þee²] the heued J, om. O. 2247 is] om. O; þilke] that JMO, the helmett of saluation mar. O³; cleped] called JMO; Helme] the helme JMO; of¹] om. J; Saluacioun] om. J, hele MO; of²] om. JMO. 2248 amonesteth] amonysch MO; men] þat add. J; hedes] Nowe dame Gracedieux enfourmeþe þe pilgrime of þe might of þe Gorgier add. S. 2249 Now] prec. Capitulum cxx mar. C, 119 can. 120 cropped mar. G³, Capitulum cx mar. S; I wole] trs. J; sey] telle CJ; þee] of þe add. can. M; shulde] shal C; þe] þi C. 2250 hool] entiere F, bolle JMOS; Sobirtee] Sobernesse JM, sobynesse O; hatteth] Sobrietas rub. mar. M, Sobyrnesse rub. mar. O. 2251 ouer] beȝonde J; see] the see JMOS; is] ins. with es ins. mar. O;

Attemperaunce] temperaunce JMO; maad] (*1st* a *ins.* G³). 2252 for¹] *om.* O; she] glotonye *over* C, schee (*1st* e *ins. with* scilicet gloutonye *mar.* G³) G; taketh] (*2nd* a *ins.* G³). 2253 throte] bolle *add.* O; But] what O; wite] do *with* O. 2254 is] *om.* O; maad] (*1st* a *ins.* G³), *om.* O; mailure] mayle J, vaylour O. 2255 if it ne] warne it J; so] Sogatys J; doubled] dowble O. 2256 woodshipe²] that is atte Saye J, *om.* MO; savouringe] tastynge J. 2257 and] woodshipe *add.* C, woodschype *add. ins. mar.* G³; of] *om.* S; outrageous] outrage JMO; savouringe] tastynge J; stiren] scho sterith J. 2258 with] whith M; which] wheche (*2nd* e *ins.* G³) G; Bi] with S; þe²] *om.* O. 2259 maketh] make J; þe] scho J; sleyghtes] slyght O; sleth] *om.* O. 2260 neighebores] neghtbore JOS; after] -warde J; wite] it *add.* MO. 2261 ayens] agayne JO, *om.* M; maisterman] (*with* mystermann *mar.* G³), mister man C, maystrefulman S; 2262 haue] suich *add.* C, (*2nd* a *ins.* G³); wel] fulle JMO. 2263 it] but *add.* J. 2264 arme] (*2nd* a *ins.* G³). 2265 neueremore] neuere J; what] but whate So J; take] (*2nd* a *ins.* G³), þou *add.* S. 2266 it] goodly and *add.* J; apayed] payde JMO. 2267 of] *om.* J; no wight] nathynge JMO. 2268 in ... times] to alle folkes S; spek ... folk] in alle tymes speke S. 2269 Chalyt] chalys GS, Chalice JMO; þi] the J; goode] (e *ins.* G³). 2270 hadde had] had JS. 2271 as¹ ... payed] he walde hafe haldyne hym alse wele payed J; payed] apayed S; hadde] er. *add.* C. 2272 mes] metes JMO, messes S; wherof þou] *o. er.* C; miht] *o. er.* (*with er. mar.* C³) C, maye JMO. 2273 faste] wele J, and thrist *add.* MO; wel] faste · and thryst J; grete] (*2nd* e *ins.* G³); mes] meesse₃ JS; and ... thirst] *om.* JMO; also] *ins. and ins. mar.* G³. 2274 miht] may J; was] *om.* J. 2275 not] alle *add.* J; atempree] temperante J, temperat MO; he ... also] also he tempred J, he tempered also M, be temperid allso O. 2276 Sey] *om.* JMO. 2277 þilke] thaym it is by hym that ȝe speke of · as it by a man J, þem MO; is] it is MO; in] *om.* MO; whan he] that J; trembleth] trembleth and schaketh (l *ins.*) J; þat²] when JMO; he²] schulde *add.* JMO. 2277-8 tremble nouht] *trs.* J. 2278 shul] schulde JMOS; wole] wolde JMOS; cesse] ȝif he myght *add.* JM; Riht so] *om.* S; he²] I J, *om.* S. 2279 wolde seyn] Say ȝow J, *om.* S; þilke] he JMO, *om.* S; þat] *om.* S; ye] *o. er.* otiose caret *add.* C, *om.* S; speken ... cesse] *om.* S. 2280 wol] fulle JM, *om.* O; So] Se J; þat] *om.* J, þan M; whan] seyne J; suich] Continencie *rub. mar.* O. 2281 gorgered] gorged JMOS. 2282 gladliche] *om.* S; þerwith] Nowe dame Grace dieux telleþe him of þe gloues *add.* S. 2283 Of] *prec.* Capitulum cxxi *mar.* C, 121 *mar.* G³, Capitulum cxi *mar.* S; þe] *om.* J; is] it is S; good] þat *add.* S. 2284 mynged] munged G, remembrede JMO; for] *om.* JMO; on ... hondes] þou ware hurte J; on] of (*with* on *mar.* G³) G; þine] þi M, þe O; þou ... hurt] on thy handes J. 2286 þe] Iren J, þiere M, þer O; touchinges] tactus & gustus *rub. mar.* M, towchyyng O; and²] *om.* M. 2287 tastinges] felynges J, tastyng O; al] of all O; fynde] felynges *add.* J. 2288 withoute] *om.* JMO; tastinge] *om.* J; algates] neuertheles J; wist] vist *alt.* wist O. 2289 bi] hy G, and *add. ins.* O³; þe¹] he O³; touchinges] touchynge JMO. 2290 tastinges] felynge J, tastynge MO; þerfore] (*2nd* e *ins.* G³); more] moost S; folk] the folke J, -es S. 2291 tastinges] felynges J, tastynge O; is ... tastinge] -s M, er alle felynges J, alle tastinges C; generalliche] is *add.* C, is *add. ins.* G³. 2292 whiche] þe wyche O; þilke] that JMO. 2293 tastinge] felynges J, -s M; þilke] the J, þat MOS; arme] (*2nd* a *ins.* G³), the *add.* JMO; ben] *om.* J, by S; þese] tha JMO. 2294 shewed] scheewed (*1st* e *ins.* G³) G; armurers be named] *em. ed.*, armures ben armed CGJMOS. 2295 part] party J; Attemperaunce] temperaunce JMO; which¹]

that J;   clepen] calleth JMO, abstynence and *add.* S;   Continence] continence
rub. mar. M.   2296 in] cleer and *add.* s;   equipolle] -nt J.   2297 dede] þe
deed S;   wille] þe wille S.   2298 ne were] (nere *alt.* were C), ware nought J;
þerwith] *om.* O;   With] *þat with* O.   2299 oo] 1 *over* G³;   no] not (*u.v.* t) O;
glooved] egloued S.   2300 ennuye] envier (*variant* ennuier *G*) F, annuy COS,
nuy J, ? enmy M;   tweyne needen] hym nedeth twa J, two nedis MO;   and] for
add. J.   2301-2 muste ... couenable] *om.* JMO.   2301 goode] gloouen *add.*
S;   þei] gloouen *over* G³.   2302 Swich] *prec.* Cap*itulum* cxxii *mar.* C, 122 *mar.*
G³;   continence] continenence C.   2302-3 þus doubled] of dede and of wille
J, of dede and will MO, þus double S.   2303 is cleped] oft es called J, of somme
MO;   of summe] men *add.* C, of *add. can.* G, *om.* J, is called MO;   bi] thurgh J.
2304 bi] w*ith* JMO;   þe²] *om.* JMO;   man] (*with* mankynde *mar.* G³), -kynde C.
2305 heerbifore] byfore JMO;   þe] þat O;   askede] of Abimalech *add.* J.
2306 Achimelech] F, acbimelech (c *can. with* achimelech *mar.* G³) G, abymalech
JMOS;   it¹] to J.   2307 þat he wiste] he wyste that J, he wyst MO;   he²] he
add. S;   and] *om.* M;   armed] *om.* JMO;   gaynpaynes] gayn
payne JMO.   2308 þou¹] maye J;   miht] þou J, *om.* M, may O;   þou²] the
JMO;   wult] lyste JMO.   2310 his] þe S.   2311 and exited] *om.* JMO;
him³] *om.* JMOS;   neuere] he turnyd hy*m* J.   2311-12 turned he him] neu*ere*
J.   2312 towardes hire] to hirwarde J, toward hir MO.   2313 him] he had
bene J.   2314 departede] dep*er*te O.   2315 him] of him J;   maden] (*2nd a*
ins. G³);   gaynpaynes] gayn payne O.   2316-17 þerfore ... for] *om.* J.
2317 lich] him *add.* C, *om.* MO;   for] (*final* e *ins.* G³), and M;   I] have J;   haue]
(*2nd a ins.* G³), I J;   hem þee] *trs.* JM, *om.* O.   2318 and] am *alt.* and J, an O;
presented] þee of *add.* C, thee of *add. ins. mar.* G³, made p*re*saunt J;   hem] of
þay*m* to þe J, to þe *add.* M.   2319 Of] yif of S;   shuldest] schalte JO, gladi*us*
iusticie *rub. mar.* MO.   2320 miht] mygh O;   not] nane J;   if] and J, þe *alt.*
yf O³;   þou] *ins. mar.* O³;   kowdest] cowth JM, cowthe *ins. mar.* O³;   wel]
swerde wele (swerde *can.*) O.   2321 noone] na J;   armures] armou*r* J;   dred]
dredd (*3rd* d *ins.* G³) G.   2322 certeyn] in certayne J, *om.* O;   armed] (*2nd a*
ins. G³);   armures] armou*r* J.   2322-3 and ... þerwith] *om.* JMO.   2323 noon]
i*d est* swerd *over* C³;   cowdest] þou koudest S;   Justice] es called J.   2324 is
cleped] ryghtwysnes J, is called M;   amonges] amonge MO;   alle] othere *add.* J;
þe ... chosen] choysest J;   beste] swerd *over* G³.   2325 girde or] *om.* JMO;
erle] cayser J;   Neuere was] *trs.* J;   Ogiers] Ogrers C, *om.* JMO.   2326 swerd]
om. JMO;   ne¹] *om.* JMO;   Rowlondes] Swerde *add.* JM, rowland swerde O;
Olyueeres] olueris O.   2327 is þilke] *with* swerd *mar.* G³, is it J, it is MO,
swerd *add.* S;   þat] *om.* OS;   is²] *can.* O³·   2328 to¹] *om.* J;   eche] ilkema*nn*
JM;   þat þat] that JMOS;   is his] *trs.* S;   a] ane J.   2329 a regent] *om.* JO,
or M;   agouernour] *om.* J;   þilke] þay þat er J.   2330 his] þis S;   gouerned]
(*2nd* o *ins.* G³);   mistakinge] mys taakynge (*1st* a *ins.* G³) G;   alle] (e *ins.* G³).
2331 she] justice *over* C³, it JMO;   manaseth] menace F, ammonyscheth J,
monyshith M, monysch O;   misdo] (s *ins.* O³);   She] it J.   2332 fro] -m GS.
2333 God] goode O;   She] *with* swerd *mar.* G³, It J, þis MO;   maketh] (*2nd a*
ins. G³), garres J;   herte] (*2nd* e *ins.* G³);   conuerte] to conuert M, couert S;
from] fra JM, for O;   forsake] to forsake MS.   2334 baret] all deceytes M;
þe] *er. mar.* C;   will] and *add.* S;   þe¹] of MO;   affeccioun] and *add.* S.
2335 so] it J;   hem] *om.* J.   2336 chastiseth] chastise JMO;   is ... durste]
dare noon of hem (h *alt.* of) S; durste] dar*e* M.   2337 hire] *om.* JMO;   on] O
JS, of MO;   drawinge out] drawynge GO, booþe hir eyeghen S;   of² ... eyen]
drawing oute S.   2338 shulde] schall O;   þe] þis M.   2339 swerd] justice

over C³, *with* scilicet Iustice *mar.* G³;   Ensaumple þou hast] Of Seynte Benet J; in ... Beneyt] ensaumple þou hafe J;   in] of MO³;   Beneyt] Beneynt C;   þis] þe S.   2340 swerd] þat he *add.* S;   had] *om.* JS;   he] had *add.* MO;   made] (*2nd a ins.* G³), made *add.* O.   2341 lawes] (*2nd a ins.* G³), the lawes JMO; he] beneyt *over* C, *with* scilicet bennet *mar.* G³;   þat¹] *om.* JMO;   þat was] *om.* J. 2342 tempted] tempyd O;   wolde] he walde J;   him] bot *add.* J;   as¹] a J;   as²] a J, *om.* MO.   2343 þe] þis M;   swerd] swerde (*2nd e can.* G³) G;   and] so *add.* C, so *add. ins. mar.* G³.   2344 wel nygh] nerhande JM;   slayn] hym *add. can.* O.   2345 afterward] -s J, affter S;   inobedient] disobedient (dis *ins.* O³) O.   2346 This] *prec.* Capitulum cxxiii *mar.* C, 123 *mar.* G³;   þou shalt] *trs.* J; bi] with J;   þou²] *om.* O.   2347 shalt] *om.* O;   defende] fende S;   from] fra JMO;   þilke þat] that at J, þat MO; haue] (*2nd a ins.* G³);   seyd] syde S;   þe] (*2nd e ins.* G³), *om.* M.   2348 whiche] wheche (*2nd e ins.* G³) G;   þi] -ne C; enemyes] enmy O;   more] *ins. mar.* O³.   2349 shrewed] parayllous S; perilous] shrewed S;   þow ne miht] myght þou nou3t J, þou might not S;   þi] -ne C.   2350 priuees] enmyes *add.* M;   þilke] *om.* J, þo MO;   ben] ar *ins.* O³; nigh] I neghe O;   þee] *om.* O;   So] that *add.* GJMO (*can.* G).   2351 and] ang S;   ayens] agayne JMO;   him] *om.* J.   2352 ayens] agayn MO. 2352-4 whan ... baret] *om.* J.   2353 forueyne] it *add. can.* G, forfett MO; aperceyuest] perceyues MO;   and þou] as whan þou o. er. (*with er. mar.* C³) C; seest] se O;   þe] þere MO.   2354 herte] -s M;   baret] baratt (*with* barett *mar.* G³) G, vnthrifte M;   whan] and when MO;   þe] thy JM, þi *ins. mar.* G³. 2355 thouht ... seest] *ins. mar* O³;   gon] gange J;   good] þe goode S;   and] in to M;   ordeynee] ordenee F, ardenee (*with* ordene *mar.* G³) G, ordynaunce or J, foly and M, *om.* S;   þe] thy JMO.   2356 encline] -d S;   dede] -ly M, that es *add.* J; disordeynee] synne M, deordeynate O, disordeyned S;   swerd] *with* scilicet Iustice *mar.* G³.   2356-7 be shake] *with* schaake *mar.* G³, schakyne owte of the schethe J.   2357 put] *ins. mar.* O³;   bifore] hit *add.* JMO;   bi] *ins.* JMOS; it] *om.* S;   lat] and lat S;   eche] ilke ane of þaym J, ilkone M;   redressed] dressed M.   2358 into] to JMO;   Now do] *trs.* J;   it þus] þis JMO. 2359 me] *om.* JMO;   shortliche] fro þis matire *add.* M, Loo nowe howe þe pilgryme desyreþe a sheeþe for þe swerd *add.* S.   2360 Ladi] *prec.* Capitulum cxxiv *mar.* C, 124 *mar.* G³, Capitulum cxii *mar.* S;   wel] fulle JMO;   thinketh] thynke JMO.   2361 sum sheþe] I hadde J;   I hadde] sum schethe J;   of] o O;   yow] *cross mar.* O³;   wherinne ... putte] to putte J, to putt in MO.   2361-2 þe swerd] in *add.* J, þis swerd M.   2362-3 for ... me] *om.* O.   2362 mihte] maye J;   þus] open *add.* S;   withoute þat] but 3if J, þat *add.* M, þat S;   it²] I S. 2363 greeuede] do me J, ne greued S;   me] (*2nd e ins.* G³), greuaunce J;   þat] þe O;   Beneyt] Beneynt C.   2364-5 aboute ... it] *om.* S.   2365 it] *om.* O; haue ... tauht] (haue *2nd a ins.* G³), taughte 3our selfe J;   me] (*2nd e ins.* G³), right nowe *add.* J;   which] wheche (*2nd e can.* G³) G.   2366 me] (*2nd e ins.* G³); thinketh] thynke JMO.   2367 she] it JMOS;   haue] (*2nd a ins.* G³);   but] if o. er. of u.v. but C, mais F, if JMO, so S.   2368 þat] *om.* JMOS;   ful ... seist] quod scho J.   2368-9 quod she] þowe Says ryght wele J.   2369 wel] *om.* J; me] (*2nd e ins.* G³);   þat] þow erte *add.* JMOS;   ententyf] entendaunt JMO. 2369-70 þou ... ben] þowe has leue J, and hidir to ward has ben M, (bene O³). 2370 þe scauberk] to the swerde þou schalle haue J;   þe²] þi M.   2370-1 to ... haue] (haue *2nd a ins.* G³), the Scawberke J.   2371 gerdel] the gyrdelle J; which] þe which S;   þou²] þat O;   it] the JMO.   2372 And] *prec.* Capitulum cxxv *mar.* C, 125 *mar.* G³;   gon] than *add.* J;   toward] to O, -es S.   2372-3 þat ... perche] *om.* JMOS;   armures] armour J;   weren] was J;   and] *om.* JMO.

2374 hongen] hunge*n* J, hongyn*e* M, hongyng O;   From þennes] and of the perke
J, Fro þens MO;   þe scauberk] scho toke J;   she vnheeng] the Scawberke J,
scheche vnhenge O.   2375 it] me *add.* J;   seyde] me *add.* C;   heere] quod
Scho *add.* J;   þilke] the Scawberke J, that MO;   Beneyt] (yt *o. er.* C).   2376 in
þe swerd] the swerde in J;   þer is] also J;   for to wel] forto J, wele forto MO.
2377 þee] with *add.* JMO;   a] *om.* O;   streyne] estraindre F, strengthe C;   Now]
take it J.   2377-8 take it] (*2nd* a *ins.* G³), nowe J.   2378 keepe it] kepyd O;
wel] it *add.* O;   leese] (*2nd* e *ins.* G³), loke that þou lose J, lose M;   it³] nouȝt
add. J;   nothing] no thynge (y *ins.*) O;   þilke] the J, That MO.   2379 cleped]
called JMO, *prec.* humilita*tis* vagi*na* *rub. mar.* M, vagina humilita*tis* *rub. mar.* O;
name] (*2nd* a *ins.* G³).   2380 þi¹ ... herberwe] herbere thy swerde J;   þi²] þerin
J;   justnesse] ryghtwysnys J.   2380-2 hide ... þat] *om.* J.   2381 if] *om.* O;
þat¹] *o. er.* (*with er. mar.* C³) C.   2382 and] *om.* MO;   hyde it] huded G,
hyded S, hyde MO;   þou shuldest] *om.* J, *trs.* MO (schulde *ins.* O³);   þilke] that
JMO.   2383 maad] (*1st* a *ins.* G³);   dedliche] a deedly JMO;   mynginge]
remembrande J, Rememoryng M, I remembrynge O;   thinkinge] *om.* JMO.
2383-4 in ... times] euere mare J.   2384 þat²] *om.* JMO.   2385 þou] þat *alt.*
þou O;   hast] naste S;   not] nathynge J, noȝt *ins.* M;   bi] alle þurgh J;   me]
gr*ac*e dieu *over* C, (*2nd* e *ins. with* s*c*ilicet gr*ac*e dieu *mar.* G³);   Bithinke]
Thynke JMO, *prec.* de publicano et phariseo *rub. mar.* M;   ᵖee] *om.* J, þou MO.
2386 publican] bublycann (*with* publikan *mar.* G³) G;   and] of *add.* JMO;   phar-
isien] pharisee C.   2387 hem] diuersly *add.* J;   þilke] he JMO;   in þe sheþe]
had hit J;   hadde it] in a scheth J.   2388 bikneewe] knew M;   himself] hem
selfe S;   and²] commendyd of godde and *add.* J, receiued *add. ins. mar.* O³;   hyed]
enhyed JM, enhyned O;   and³] *om.* S.   2389 and vnscauberked] *om.* JMO.
2390 lowed] made love J, made lawe MO;   It] *o. er.* C;   oon] aman J;   accuse]
to Acuse J.   2391 feebelnesse] feeblesse GS, freylnesse O;   entende]
entendaunde JMO;   scauberk] schawbert *alt.* schawberd O.   2392 þan] than
(*with* thanne *mar.* G³) G;   iustice] rightwysnes J;   þan] and CJMO, Que (*variant*
Et *A*) F;   to³] *om.* JMO.   2393 haue] (*2nd* a *ins.* G³);   vnsheþed] vnschetethid
(te *can. rub.*) O;   yow] nowe J, to þowe M.   2394 vauntynge] ay vauntynge J,
of avauntyng M, auauntynge (aun *lacks a minim*) O;   ne seecheen] scheweth JMO,
not *add.* S.   2395 þat] *om.* JO;   þer] fore *add.* O;   alwey] þi *add. ins.* M, in
add. O;   mynde] *o. er.* (*with u.v.* mynd *mar.* C³) C.   2396 so] bot *add.* J;
þe¹] thy JMO;   þe²] thy J.   2397 þee] (*1st* e *ins.* G³);   humblinge] mekande
the JMO;   causes] cause JO, þat *add.*M.   2398 wel þou hast] þou hase wele
JM;   And] *prec.* Capi*tulum* cxxvi *mar.* C, 126 *mar.* G³;   þus] *om.* C.
2399 sheþed] schethe O;   with þe girdel] thou schalle gyrde the J;   þou ... þee]
with the gyrdell J.   2400 þine armures] þou schalle streyne J, þin armo*ur* MO;
þou ... streyne] thyne armou*r* J;   streyne] strengthe *o. er.* (*with er. mar.* C³) C.
2401 hem] that M;   þe¹,²] *om.* JMO.   2402 but] ȝif *add.* J.   2403 or]
eyþer S.   2404 to þee worth] (*1st* e *ins.* G³), worth to þee C.   2405 þee] (*1st*
e *ins.* G³);   fastned] fested JMO.   2406 þe] This JM;   hatteth] hatte GJMO
(e *ins.* G³), hatte at alle tymes S;   Perseueraunce] p*er*se perseuerans O;   bocle is]
boclers S;   cleped] cloped G, called JMO.   2407 whiche] p*er*seuera*n*cia et
constancia *rub. mar.* M, Perseuerance Constancia *rub. mar.* O;   times] tyme M;
hem] *ins. mar.* G³, *om.* JMO;   togideres] to geddyr JM.   2408 at þe¹] atte J, at
S;   þe²] *om.* J;   assault] sawte O.   2409 wel] weell (*2nd* e *can.* G³) G, but J,
ful MO.   2410 lengthe] lenche O;   holt þe] haldeth the JMO, holdeþe S;
armures] armou*re* to geddyr JMO;   She] syche O.   2411 vertuous] -ly O;
she] *with* s*c*ilicet gurdell *mar.* G³.   2412 alway] -s S;   oon] apon*e* J;   þat] *om.*

GS. 2413-14 holt ... girdel] kepeth the gyrdil and heldit it faste J.   2414 faste]
(e *ins*. G³);   it¹] ne *add*. *can*. G³, þat O;   vnfastne nouht] (not *ins*. *mar*. G³), ne
vnfestyne MO.   2414-15 holt in estat] *o.er*. (*with er*. *mar*. C³) C.   2415 estat]
astat GJ, one state M, o state O.   2416 fastnynge] festynge JMO;   þat] *om*. J.
2417 þow] þat *alt*. þou O. askedest] askes MO;   þese] this JMO;   thinges]
thynge JMO.   2418 þerof] of thyne askynge J, *om*. MO;   þat ... is] nys G, þat
ne it es J, þen it is MO, nyse it not þat S;   covenable] couable (? conable) O.
2418-19 to ... profitable] it is and profytable vn to þee S.   2419 Now vse hem]
vse theym nowe J.   2420 þi] self *add*. M;   Whan] *prec*. Cap*itulum* cxxvii *mar*.
C, 127 *mar*. G³;   þese woordes] I herde J, I þies wordes M;   I herde] these
wordes J, herd M.   2421 bicom] ryght *add*. J;   was] fulle *add*. J.
2422 entencioun] entent J;   Scauberk ... greevinge] I wende fulle wele have hadde
J;   Scauberk] schawberte *alt*. schawberde O, þe skawberd S;   girdel] þe girdell
S.   2422-3 I ... had] ascawberke and a girdille lesse greuande J.   2422 wende]
u.v. wele *add*. *erased* M.   2423 haue] (*2nd a ins*. G³);   withoute] *om*. J;   fable]
(*2nd a ins*. G³), *om*. J;   al ... it] ȝif alle it ware J;   þat¹] So that J, *om*. MO;   þat²]
om. J.   2424 on] vpon S;   doun] done of J, done O;   alweys] ȝit J;   suffrede]
(*2nd e ins*. G³), it *add*. MO.   2425 answerde] þan *add*. J, I aunswerd S, Loo
nowe howe dame Grace dieux spekeþe to þe pilgryme of þe targe *add*. S.
2426 Whan] *prec*. Cap*itulum* cxxviii *mar*. C, 128 *mar*. G³, Cap*itulum* cxiii *mar*. S;
of þe scauberk] scho hadde on this wyse talde me J;   she ... me] of þe Scauberke
and the gyrdelle J, þus scho had saied me MO;   she¹] dame Gracedieux S;   seid]
tolde S;   me] (*2nd e ins*. G³), *er*. *add*. O.   2426-7 she² ... anoon] Onane scho
toke hir wordys a gayne and Sayde J.   2427 I wole] *trs*. J, I wolde S;   sey]
telle J;   yit] *om*. O.   2428 targe¹,²] (*2nd a ins*. G³), -tte J;   Withoute targe]
þer S;   ne] *om*. OS;   ariht] ryght J, *om*. OS.   2429 wel] aright defended ne S;
kept] with owten taarge *add*. S;   targe] (*2nd a ins*. G³), -tt J, *with* target *mar*. O³.
2430 from] fra JM, For O;   empeyringe] emperyringe (*1st* r *can*., u *or* n *alt*. y) C,
enpáyrynge J;   been] is S;   þe ooþere] booþe þe body and þe tooþer herneys S;
kept] ekepte with outen enpeyring and S.   2431 atamed] a taamed (*3rd a ins*.
G³) G, entamees F, attained JMO, ne perced *add*. S;   it] *with* targe *mar*. G³;
bifore] a for O.   2432 saaf] *prec*. targe *mar*. G³;   þis] this *under* O³;   targe]
(*2nd a ins*. G³), -tt J;   hatteth] hatte GMOS, hight J;   þe] *om*. JMO;   kyng] *om*.
O.   2433 customableche] prudencia *rub*. *mar*. MO;   and] *om*. J, right *add*. M.
2434 iugement] to vse *add*. M;   þis] Thit O;   targe] (*2nd a ins*. G³), -t J;   two]
ii *over* G³.   2435 thre] iii *over* G³;   targes] targetis J.   2436 þis] ceste F,
his GS (*with* thys *mar*. G³);   targe] (*2nd a ins*. G³), -tt J;   he was] *trs*. J;
wurshiped] worschipe O.   2437 whan ... afterward] efterwarde when he J, -es
S;   it] *with* targe *mar*. G³, this targett of prudence J.   2438 wurshipe] -s S;
alle] al (*with* alle *mar*. G³) G;   hise¹] iiie *mar*. O;   targes] targettys J, (s *ins*. O³);
of gold] and sheldes S;   and] alle *add*. JO;   his sheeldes] of golde S.
2439 weren¹] was O, ne were S;   neuere] nouȝt JS;   red hering] rede herynge
(*with* redd hering *mar*. O³) O, myte S.   2440 targe] *into mar*. (*with er*. *mar*. C³)
C, -tt J;   him¹] well *add*. J;   but] caret *add*. O.   2441 soone] (*2nd o ins*. G³),
was *followed by* caret O;   was¹] sone O;   whan] fra J;   þe] this J;   targe] -tt J.
2442 miht] maye J;   apperceyue] persayfe JMO;   wolt] that*add*. JMO;   þe]
þee S;   woorth] value J, taarge S;   of] with S;   his] this JMO;   targe] -tt J.
2443 whiche] *om*. JMO;   was] worth *add*. S;   þan] þe *add*. M;   fyve *with* v
mar. *and over* G³;   þee] (*2nd e ins*. G³).   2444 it] *marked mar*. C³;   þee] to
kepe the J, *om*. O;   to keepe] and for to pleye þerwith *add*. *can*. C, with J.
2445 enemyes] thyne Enmyes JO, þenmys S.   2446 kunne] cowth MO;   helpe]

kep OS, aidier (*variant* garder *T*) F.   2447 she] the targett J;   to] *om*. MO, for
to S.   2448 Now ... it] Take it nowe J;   þe tooþer] the *opere* J, þe to odire
MO, þee til þyne oþer S, þat ooþere C.   2449 armures] armo*ur* J;   wel] good
JMO;   woldest] that *add*. J.   2450 to] for to S.   2450-1 for ... on] *ins. o.
er. mar.* G³.   2450 for] And J, *om*. MO;   I haue] *trs*. JMO;   rauht] taken
JMO;   hem²] to the *add*. JMO.   2451 and] *om*. JMO;   taken] *om*. JMO,
betaaken S;   hem²] *om*. JMO;   þee] *om*. JMO;   on] vpon S;   faste] *with* faste
erased at end of insertion mar. G³   2453 Whan] *prec.* Cap*itulum* cxxix *mar.* C,
129 *mar.* G³;   þese woordes] I vndyrstode JS, I þies wordes M, I þir wordys O;
I vnderstood] (w *alt.* d C), this wordes JS, vndirstode MO;   herte] (*2nd* e *ins.*
G³), wax *add*. J, was *add*. MOS;   afrighte] a ferde M.   2454 haue] (*2nd* a *ins.*
G³);   seyd] byfore *add*. J;   hadde] was JMO;   not] vn O, beon *add*. S;
customed] (t *alt.* d C), vsed J, acustumed S.   2455 michel I bisorwede] I hadde
grete sorowe and disese of J.   2456 on] opon me M, vpon S;   Algates]
Nau*ertheles* J;   hire ... doon] do hir plesaunce JMOS;   and] for to *add*. S;
fulfille] fulw fylle hir wille J, fulfill hir will MO.   2456-7 to ... me] I assayed J;
arme me] armee (ar *with* arme *mar. o. er.* G³) G, hic armat se peregrinus *rub. mar.*
MO.   2457 I assayede] to arme me J, I assyd O;   began] and *add*. J.
2458 on] *om*. JMO;   but ... nouht] *om*. JMO;   sey I] I sey it S.   2459 on]
apone JMO;   dide] deede (*3rd* e *ins.* G³) G.   2460 it] *ins. mar.* G³;   aboute]
opon MO;   sithe] than JMO;   myn] my JO;   in] to *add*. M.   2461 hid]
bukled J;   After] -warde J.   2462 me] (*2nd* e *ins.* G³);   sithe] than JMO;
putte] toke JMO.   2463 targe] -tt J;   to] and put it be JMO;   she] he S;
seyd] byddyne J;   me] (*2nd* e *ins.* G³).   2463-4 al ... it] ȝif alle J, al þof M, þat
add. S;   me¹] (*2nd* e *ins.* G³);   litel] but litylle J, Howe þe pilgryme spekeþe to
Gracedieux howe his armures disesen him *add*. S;   Whan] *prec.* Cap*itulum* cxxx
mar. C, 130 *mar.* G³, Cap*itulum* cxiv *mar.* S;   armed þus] I Sawe me JS, *trs*. MO;
I sih me] thus armedde JS;   me²] (*2nd* e *ins.* G³).   2465 þat] at J, *om*. S;
felte] *o. er.* O³;   upon ... hevi] *o. er.* C, this greuouu*s* apon me heuey J, þus greuou*s*
· heuy MO;   me] (*2nd* e *ins.* G³), so *add*. S;   hevi] heuye (*2nd* e *ins.* G³) G.
2466 me¹] (*2nd* e *ins.* G³), adovne *add*. S;   me²] (*2nd* e *ins.* G³);   thouhte (e *ins.*
G³).   2467 mercy] I crye ȝow J;   I pray yow] m*ercy* J;   nothing] hic excusat
se q*uod* no*n* potest portare arma *rub. mar.* MO;   ye] *ins. mar.* G³, it JMO.
2468 disese] dyshese O.   2468-9 þese ... foorth] *om*. JMO.   2469 Eiþer]
Certeynly o*þere* J;   I²] me J;   heere abyde] *trs*. J.   2469-70 alle I muste]
ellys I muste S, I most doon S.   2470 doon hem of] do Off this armoure J, hem
alle of S;   alþerfirst] aythyr fyrste O;   me] (*2nd* e *ins.* G³).   2471 þerinne al
astoned] all astonyed þerin J.   2472 def] for *add*. S;   me] (*2nd* e *ins.* G³);
heere] hieres JO, I here M;   nothing] nowþere J.   2473 þat I wolde] *om*.
JMO;   þe¹] *om*. M;   þe whiche] bot þat: whilke to fele J, to whilk M;   me] (*2nd*
e *ins.* G³).   2474 thinketh] thynke JMO;   þilke] this J, þat MO;   shrewede]
om. JM;   þat] þere J.   2475 bi þe throte] maystres me So J, it *add*. MO;
maistreth me soo] (me *2nd* e *ins.* G³), by the þrote J;   soo] *om*. MO.   2476 þat
... so] *om*. C;   thinketh] thynke JMO;   shulde strangle] worowes M;   me²,³]
(*2nd* e *ins.* G³).   2477 ne] Me JMO;   auale] a vaale (*3rd* a *ins.* G³) G, avaler F,
a vayles JMO, avaleþe S, haue *o. er.* C.   2478 me¹] (*2nd* e *ins.* G³);   me ²] (*2nd*
e *ins.*G³), me *add*. O;   anything] many tymes prayed the profitt dauid. Lord teach
me to walke in thy wayes · in thy lawes · in thy commandemente · how harde for
synfull flesh to beare ye armor of righteousnesse *mar.* O³.   2479 Afterward]
prec. Cap*itulum* cxxxi *mar.* C, 131 *mar.* G³, Also J;   with þe gaynpaynes] weel I
wot · þat S;   wel I wot] I wate wele JMO, with þe gaynepaynes S.   2480 youre]

(e *ins.* G³);   glooues] (*2nd* o *ins.* G³), grlouen S;   hem] hym JMO;   han] haauen (*1st* a *ins.* G³) G, hath JMO.   2481 I haue] *trs.* J;   hem] *om.* J;   forthinketh me] *trs.* J.   2482 þei] *with* s*cilicet* gloouen *mar.* G³, the gloves J;   out of] oute of (e *ins.* G³) G, with owtyn*e* JMO (o *ins.* O).   2483 swiche] *om.* J, so syche O; withoute] bot ȝif J;   sheendinge] I schente J, schedynge O;   so] on the same wyse J, *om.* MO;   of þe remenaunt] I Say J.   2484 I sey] of the remenant J; me[1,2] (*2nd* e *ins.* G³);   greeueth] thay greve J, (r *ins.* O);   riht] *om.* J.   2485 neuere ... wordes] at schorte worde J;   wordes] worde MO;   I mihte telle] I may neu*e*re telle J;   mihte] (e *ins.* G³), may MO;   but] ȝif *add.* JM.   2486 haue] (*2nd* a *ins.* G³);   Souprised] G, Souspris F, Sup*e*rysed *o. er.* (*with* er. *mar.* C³) *and* id *est* ouercome *over* C, Suppr*e*ssed J, Supprisid MOS.   2487 lerned] vsed to bere J.   2488 hem] his armys J.   2489 wole I] *trs.* MO, (he *alt.* I S);   me] (*2nd* e *ins.* G³).   2489-90 þe armures] þ*ere* armys J, þe armes M, þis armys O, þarmures S.   2490 I wole[1,2] *trs.* J;   doun] adoune S;   þe] my JMO.   2491 me] (*2nd* e *ins.* G³), forth on my way J, *om.* MO;   I ... sureliche] *om.* J;   haue] (*2nd* a *ins.* G³), hadd MO;   heer] heere (*1st* e *ins.* G³) G;   sureliche] durlych S.   2492 Go] For gange J;   if] bot ȝif JMO;   ne] *om.* JMO.   2493 I[1] *ins. mar.* O³;   into] in C;   Wherfore] therefore JMO;   pray] preye (*2nd* e *ins.* G³) G.   2494 it[1]] that ȝee J, þat it MOS;   anoye] displese J, greue MO;   ne ne] F, ne CJMO;   a] na J;   despyte] howe þe lady dame Grace dieux · replyeþe sore agayns þe pilgrymes seying *add.* S.   2495 Sertes] *prec.* Capi*tulum* cxxxii *mar.* C, 132 *mar.* G³, Capi*tulum* cxv *mar.* S;   she] Grace dieu J;   sheweth] scheeweth (*1st* e *ins.* G³) G, Semeth J.   2496 withholde] *þou* hase J;   þou hast] with haldyn*e* J, *trs.* MO;   al] þat S;   haue] (*2nd* a *ins.* G³);   seyd] tolde S;   þee] to the JMO;   or] els *add.* J.   2497 wel] fulle JMO;   þeron] þer vpon S.   2498 þat[1]] *om.* J;   in me] (*2nd* e *ins.* G³), So grete vnþryfte J;   be] *om.* J, is MO;   so ... vnthrift] in me J, suche vnthryfft S;   fables] fable JMO.   2499 þat þei ben] *om.* JMO;   ben] *prec.* s*cilicet* grace dieu *mar.* G³;   þou] *om.* G;   it] soo J;   þee] (*1st* e *ins.* G³).   2500 it] *om.* J;   me] (*2nd* e *ins.* G³);   raþere bitimes] bytyme · For bet*t*er it es betyme J, by tymes · rathire M, be be tymys O;   to late] (*2nd* a *ins.* G³), ouerlate J, late M;   Lady] A·A· lady J.   2501 quod I] *with* s*cilicet* plgrim *mar.* G³;   God] good O;   weeneth] Suppose ȝe J, Wene ȝhe MO;   it] *om.* J;   neuere] noȝt J;   soo] for *add.* J.   2502 wel] weell (*2nd* e *ins.* G³) G;   seyn] say me O;   þat ne] þat it ne CS (it *o. er. with* er. *mar.* C³), þat ne it J, þen it M, bot yt O;   ordeyned] full wele O;   for wele] fulle wele JM, ordeynd O.   2503 þat[2]] þat þis *o. er.* (*with* u.v. þis *mar.* C³) C, *om.* JMO;   armour] *o. er.* C.   2503-4 mowe ... me] *om.* JMO.   2504 longe be] *trs.* S;   me] (*2nd* e *ins.* G³);   Nouht ... haue] (haue *2nd* e *ins.* G³), I hafe nathynge JMO;   youre] of ȝo*ur* JMO.   2505 of anything] *om.* JMO;   bithinke] vnbethynke J;   me] (*2nd* e *ins.* G³);   þat] of that at J, of þat þat S;   ye] (*2nd* e *ins.* G³).   2506 haue] (*2nd* a *ins.* G³);   seyd] *o. er.* O³;   me[1]] (*2nd* e *ins.* G³), to me M, *o. er.* O³;   þouh] of O;   þe] *om.* O;   firste] tyme *add.* J;   me[2]] (*2nd* e *ins.* G³).   2507 so] se G (*with* so *mar.* G³), do so J, see S;   whan] fra J, what S;   were] had JMO;   longe] (*with* er. *mar.* C³).   2508 lerne] bere M;   me] (*2nd* e *ins.* G³);   to] So J.   2509 feebilnesse] feeblesse GS, debilite F;   to] So J;   þese] thir J, þiere M, þer O.   2510 vnlikynge] dessemblables F, vnliknynge C;   And] *prec.* Capi*tulum* cxxxiii *mar.* C, 133 *mar.* G³.   2511 þou[1]] *om.* G;   me] (*2nd* e *ins.* G³);   hast þou required] haste Reqweered (*1st and 3rd* e *ins.* G³) G, asche þou J, hast þou askid MO.   2512 þe] of S;   armures] arm*our* JMO;   wolt] walde J, þowe wolt S.   2513 thouhte] towght O.   2514 setten] sed O;   me] (*2nd* e *ins.* G³);   wey] ȝe wate wele *add.* J;   Burdoun yrened] I asked þowe anely J.

2514-15 I ... onliche] a burdoun piked with yrene J.   2514 Burdoun] þe
bourdoun S;   yrened] ·I· yerned which S;   al] *om.* MO.   2515 of armures] ȝe
spake J, of armo*ur* MO;   ye speken] of armo*ur* J;   to] *om.* G;   me] (*2nd* e *ins.*
G³).   2516 me] (*2nd* e *ins.* G³);   required] reqweered (*2nd* e *ins.* G³) G, asked
JMO.   2517 ben] Sufficient *add.* J;   for] *om.* O;   haue] (*2nd* a *ins.* G³).
2518 ooþerweys] oþerwyse JM;   in me] þer is na strength J;   no ... is] in me J;
se] parceyue S;   it²] *om.* M.   2519 Strengthe] *prec.* Capi*tulum* cxxxiv *mar.* C,
134 *mar.* G³, No*ta rub. mar.* O, þowe has na J.   2520 þou ... not] (hast *followed
by erased caret with u.v.* noght *mar.* C³), strenthe J, *quod* sche O;   quod she] þu
has not O;   herte in þee] þou hase na J;   þou ... noon] herte in the J.   2521 þat]
þat *add.* JS;   þou ne] *trs.* J, þan þou M, þam þu O, þou S;   art] herte O;
sholdred] weel *add.* S;   ynowh and boned] and and baned Wele I nowe and J.
2522 art] hart O;   any ... þee] þou had J.   2523 þow haddest] any good herte
in the J.   2524 appel²] *om.* J;   seye ... man] alitille man Say J, is say in a lytell
man O, þe lytel man sey S.   2525 þese] this JM.   2526 armures] armo*ur*
JM;   feeblesse] flebece (*variants* feblece G, feiblece L, foiblesse A) F, febilnesse
CJMO.   2527 þou¹] *om.* GJ;   þou²] þe JMO;   mostest] muste nedys J, must
MO, shouldes algates J.   2528 from] fra JMO;   þou] and þou J, and S;
hem] armures for feoblesse S.   2529 shalt] shuld MO;   þou] *om.* GJ;   þi
wey] þou schalle goo J.   2530 þou ... go] thy wa J;   shalt] schuld MO;   þat]
when JMO.   2531 and] enforme and *add. can.* O;   enforce] the *add.* J, inforse
(in *o. er.* O³) O;   hem] *om.* O;   Serteyn] -ly J;   þou] schalle J;   shalt] (*with u.v.*
shalt *mar.* C³), þou J, schuld O.   2532 Allas] *om.* J;   woldest] walde JMOS;
þou] *om.* G, I JS;   þee] me JS;   leeuedest] trowid JMO.   2533 þou¹] *om.* G,
I J;   Grace Dieu] dame Gracedeiux S;   þou art] am I J;   þou wost] wate I, þou
wote MO.   2534 wost also] also I wate J, wit also M, wote allso O.   2535 of
beringe] to bere J, of þe berynge M;   of²] *om.* J;   þe armure] þarmures S.
2536 þese] ther*e* J, þier*e* MO;   weren] ware JO;   armures] armo*ur* JO.
2537 me] (*2nd* e *ins.* G³);   if] and J;   wheþer] whedere J, whidir*e* M, wedyr O,
where S;   euere ... mown] I schalle nowe eu*er*e J;   euere] *om.* M;   I²] shoulde
S;   shal] shuld M, I S;   mown] nowe S;   fynde] my lady dame *add.* S.
2538 ayen] *om.* S;   þat she] *o. er.* C, *om.* J;   wole] in wille forto J, wolde ageyne
S;   me] (*2nd* e *ins.* G³);   Whan] *prec.* Capi*tulum* cxxxv *mar.* C, 135 *mar.* G³, And
whanne þat S.   2539 icryed] cried JMO;   þat] at O.   2540 God] good O;
saue] (*2nd* a *ins.* G³);   þat I] *with* grace dieu *mar.* G³;   drawe] (*2nd* a *ins.* G³);
me] (*2nd* e *ins.* G³).   2541 hast ... me] walde nouȝt leue me of nathynge that I
sayde the J;   þou] þat O;   me] (*2nd* e *ins.* G³);   and] *om.* J.   2542 wente]
thiddyr *add.* J;   so ... þee] *om.* J;   kepe] saue S.   2543 be now] *trs.* JMO.
2544 þanne be] *trs.* C, bene JMO;   feeblished] feblysch J, febelid MO.
2545 þat¹] whilke J;   haue] (*2nd* a *ins.* G³);   whan] Sene J;   miht] may J.
2546 armures] armes J, armo*ur* M;   at þat time] to come J;   to come] (*with u.v.*
to come *mar.* C³), at tyme J.   2547 and] AAnd O;   for nouht] in Vayne J;   I
shulde] *trs.* J;   me] (*2nd* e *ins* G³);   Now] For to en arme the Nowe J.
2548 anoon] *om.* J;   þe] *om.* JMO;   lerne] to bere *add. ins.* (*with u.v.* {to} bere
mar. C³) C, lere forto bere J;   withoute] (e *ins.* G³);   more] *om.* O.   2549 If]
And J;   leeue] *om.* S;   me] (*2nd* e *ins. with scilicet* grace dieu *mar.* G³);   aboute
þee] þou schalle halde þaym J;   þou² ... hem] apone the J.   2550 þou] þai O.
2551 þee] thy selfe J;   with hem] *ins. mar.* G³, *om.* JMO;   faire] -ly J, -ly and
softly M;   softe] -ly JM;   fer] fayre M.   2551-2 for ... goth] *underlined, with*
pro*uerbium mar.* S.   2552 is þe mule] offt tymes S;   ofttimes] ofte tyme G,
Sum tyme JMO, komeþe þe slowe Mule S;   at] to S;   James] Iame J.

2553 roundliche] sofftlych S; is] *prec.* softely, and saufly *mar.* O³; þilke] he
JMO; smiteth] *om.* S. 2553-4 and ... hors] his hors with sporres J, hys hors,
and spurres it O, sporeþe his swyfft coursier S. 2554 maketh] (*2nd a ins.* G³);
go] to go J, stert and prykke S; sharpliche] smertlych S; michel soonere]
offtymes S. 2555 fyndeth] more *add.* S; þan ... wey] by þe smert vnavysed
weye þane by þe eesely passage weel avysed S, yit takeþe heede howe david Grace
dieux resouneþe towardes þe pilgryme *add.* S; her] his C, *om.* J; wey] *om.* J.
2556 Of] *prec.* Cap*itulum* cxxxvi *mar.* C, 136 *mar.* G³, Cap*itulum* cxvi *mar.* S, IF
(*with scribe's guide* o *visible*) S; þat¹] that *add.* JM. 2557 þee] *om.* JMO; if]
þow₃ J; of him] þou wille take ensaumple J; þou ... ensaumple] of hym J;
take] (*2nd a ins.* G³). 2558 undertake] chalange J; wole²] wold O, þat *add.* S;
vnderstonde] me *add.* JMO. 2559 make] (*2nd a ins.* G³), *scribe changes here* O;
shuldest] wolde S; biholde] *om.* JMO. 2560 and¹] *om.* JMO; chyld] a
childe J. 2561 seith] telleth J; side] considere *add.* C, Concidere *add. ins.*
mar. G³. 2562 armures] armo*ur* J; whiche] *om.* JMO; weren¹] was JM;
nouht] made *add.* JMO; poopet] poupart F, popot *alt.* popat C, puppet J, childe
or a litill man M; but] for MO; þei weren] made *add.* J, ordeyned and made
add. M, *om.* S. 2562-3 þe sone of] *om.* J. 2563 Saul] hym selfe that was J;
gretteste] maste man J, man *add.* S; 2564 and¹] welle *add.* J, *ins.* O; hevy] (e
ins. G³) G. 2565 þat] ₃if þou J; þese ... thinges] be halde J; twey] two MO;
biholden] be holde GOS, there twa thynges J; and] *om.* J; thouht diligentliche]
diligently þou schall See that J, diligently considerid M, þaim diligently O.
2566 þe armure] þarmures S; For] for *add.* J. 2567 for] marked *mar.* C;
weren þei] *trs.* MO; woorth] For for Saule thay ware good *add.* J. 2568 þat¹]
thing *add.* S; a¹] young *add.* S; is²] nys S; a²] an olde S. 2569 þat] it J, it
þat S; in] the buke of *add.* J, his *add.* S; Etiques] ecyqves G; where ...
writen] *om.* JMO. 2570 if] *om.* J; hadde] *om.* J; þou] art and *add.* M, and
add. JOS; sithe] -ne JMO. 2571 he hadde] *om.* S; him] hem S.
2571-2 þou ... þanne] than had þou J. 2572 caused] cause J; take] (*2nd a ins.*
G³). 2573 not þee] nou₃t he J, he neuer O, he not þee S. 2574 a] *om.* M.
2575 vnarmed] hym when he *add.* J; into ... wente] wente to werres J, to any
werrys went M, to werreswent O, went in to þe werres S. 2576 so he hadde] he
had J, he hadd so MO, he so hade S; gon] vnarmed *add.* J; hadde he] *trs.* JM.
2577 armures] armo*ur* J; in] *om.* M; times] tyme M. 2579 þilke] *om.*
JMO, þowe S. 2579-80 þat ... couenable] *om.* JMO. 2580 mihtest] myght
JMO. 2581 wolde] myght J. 2582 not] noon S; þese] this JMO.
2583 armures] armoure JMO; wolt] *into mar.* (*with er. mar.* C³) C; preeue] it
add. M; shame] schaame (*2nd a ins.* G³) G; þou²] the JMO. 2584 auhtest]
awht JMO; haue] (*2nd a ins.* G³), thynke J. 2585 Ladi] *prec.* cap*itulum* cxxxvii
mar. C, 137 *mar.* G³; ful] *om.* JMO; shulde] schalle JMO. 2586 winne] *om.*
S; resiste] *with* stande ₃owe J, withstande MO; to³] *om.* J; ayens] ageyne
JMO. 2587 þat] *om.* J; doun ... ley] me bus nedes laye downe J, me must lay
MO; al togideres] this armo*ur* ilke dele J, al to gidere MO. 2588 noon¹] *with*
scilicet armure *mar.* G³, of thaym *add.* J; þat ... do] that ne I wille do thaym of J,
þen I wil do of MO, þat þer of I ne wol do S; noon²] of thaym *add.* J. 2589 of
whiche] that J; ioye] of *add.* J; alle ... armures] this armo*ur* J, Al þis armo*ur*
MO; han] hase alle J, has MO; frushed] to frusched J, thrusshid M; me]
(*2nd e ins.* G³); and] *om.* J. 2590 me¹] (*2nd e ins.* G³), *om.* MS; me²] (*2nd e*
ins. G³); And] *prec.* Cap*itulum* cxxxviii *mar.* C, 138 *mar.* G³; bocle] gyrdille J.
2591 armures] armo*ur* JMO; sithe] and syne J, -n MO; doun] the girdille J, I
downe M, adoune S; girdel] downe J, þe gurdel S; swerd] the Swerde JS.

2592 targe] (*2nd* a *ins.* G³), -tt J;　　Whan] And when J;　　she] *with* scilicet grace
dieu *mar.* G³;　　me] (*2nd* e *ins.* G³);　　so doo] *trs.* JMO.　　　2593 me] (*2nd* e *ins.*
G³);　　Sithe] Syne JMO;　　þus] þou O.　　　2594 þee] (*1st* e *ins.* G³);　　shuldest]
scholde JMO;　　þe] *om.* MO.　　　2595 biseeche] pray JMO;　　me] (*2nd* e *ins.*
G³);　　fecche] gette J;　　þee] *om.* MO;　　oon] 1 *over* G³;　　it] *om.* J, eu*er* OS;
euere] *om.* M, it OS;　　were¹] where (*with* weere *mar.* G³) G.　　　2596 þat mihte]
forto J, to O;　　þe armure] it S;　　þat²] *om.* JMO;　　trussede] trusse JMO.
2597 hem] *om.* J;　　mihtest] myght JMO.　　　2598 take] (*2nd* a *ins.* G³);　　alle
times] aye J;　　þat] when*ne* J;　　haddest] had JMO.　　　2599 I haue] (*2nd* a *ins.*
G³), *trs.* J;　　durst] (*final* e *ins.* G³).　　　2600 require] requeere (*2nd* e *ins.* G³) G,
aske JMO;　　in biseechinge] and I be seke ȝowe there of J, besekyng MO;　　Now
a litel] Ha byde me here J.　　　2601 abide me] alitille while J;　　me] (*2nd* e *ins.*
G³);　　wole] schalle J;　　lede] amerrai F, leue *or* lene (ue *or* ne *o. er. with er. mar.*
C³) C, brynge JM;　　þee] to þe MO;　　suich] *om.* J, sith S;　　on] *om.* GS;　　I
trowe] that J.　　　2602 þat¹] as I · trowe J;　　wel susteyne] wele bere JMO,
susteyne wel C;　　and þat] *om.* JMO;　　wel²] *om.* JMOS;　　shal ... hem] *om.* JMO.
2603 And] *prec.* Capitulum cxxxix *mar.* C, 139 *mar.* G³, *om.* JMO;　　hire] *om.*
JMO;　　wot not] ne wotte M, (wott *ins.* O³).　　　2604 al aloone] a bade thare J;
abod þere] by my ane J.　　　2605 me] (*2nd* e *ins.* G³).　　　2606 and¹] *om.* JMOS;
doublet] and alle *add.* J;　　withheeld] halde JMO;　　scrippe] hic deponit arma *rub.*
mar. MO.　　　2607 pilgryme] my Pilgr*i*mage J, a pilgryme S;　　me] (*2nd* e *ins.*
G³);　　þanne] *om.* J.　　　2608 Aa] Haa G, Ha·ha O;　　goode] (e *ins.* G³);　　swete]
sweete (*3rd* e *ins.* G³) G.　　　2609 peyne] *om.* J;　　I] *o. er.* C;　　haue] (ha *o. er.* C),
(*2nd* a *ins.* G³);　　Dieu] my lady *add.* S.　　　2610 me] (*2nd* e *ins.* G³).　　　2611
me] (*2nd* e *ins.* G³).　　　2612 Nothing] þere *add.* J;　　me] (*2nd* e *ins.* G³).
2612-13 I ... haue¹] agayn hir techyng and hire swete amonysshyng · haue I M.
2612 ayens] geyne J, agayn*e* O;　　techinge] *rub. mar.* O³.　　　2613 haue¹,²] (*2nd* a
ins. G³), I haue M.　　　2614 withholde] with (*2nd* o *ins.* G³);　　haue] (*2nd* a *ins.*
G³);　　my ... lost] lost my vertue J.　　　2615 I¹] *ins.* M³;　　not] nowe J;　　more²]
and JMO;　　strong] and *add.* JMO.　　　2616 more hard] *om.* S;　　more²] and M,
and more O;　　mihte] myghte (e *ins.* G³) G.　　　2616-17 susteyne ... wel] wele
Suffyr and Susteyne JMO.　　　2617 armures] armes J;　　I were] the worthier J;
þe ... worth] I ware than J;　　worth] -i O;　　certyen] -ly J.　　　2618 bettere] and
add. J;　　alle ... also] Also alle folk wolden C, alle folke also wolde J.　　　2619 me¹,²,³]
(*2nd* e *ins.* G³);　　me²] *om.* MO;　　þe more²] *om.* JMO;　　nouht] now C, it J.
2620 it] nouȝt J;　　is worth] is wurs C, worth J, avaylleþe for S;　　mihte] maye J;
not] *om.* MOS;　　endure hem] endure þan O, in no wyse S;　　bi no wey] endure it
S;　　To] In JMO.　　　2621 me] (*2nd* e *ins.* G³);　　wole] *om.* S.　　　2622 helpe] (e
ins. G³);　　me¹,²] (*2nd* e´ *ins.* G³);　　þat] *ins. mar.* G³, *om.* MOS;　　she wole] *om.* S;
yit] *om.* S.　　　2623 she hath] *trs.* J;　　maad] (*2nd* a *ins.* G³);　　grettere] mare J.
2624 make] (*2nd* a *ins.* G³);　　me] (*2nd* e *ins.* G³);　　ashamed] a schaamed (*3rd* a
ins. G³) G;　　fecche] Seke J.　　　2625 bringe] to me *add.* J, kyng M;　　þese] this
JMO;　　armures] armoure JMO, Beholde howe · þat dame Gracedieux · ledde a
wenche þat hade noone eyeghen *add.* S.　　　2626 As] *prec.* Capitulum cxl *mar.* C,
140 *mar.* G³, Capitulum xlv *rub. mar.* M, Capitulum cxvii *mar.* S, *prec.* hic memoria
introducitur & portat arma *rub. mar.* O;　　þus myself] *trs.* JMO;　　aloone] alone
(*with* allone *mar.* G³) G.　　　2627 cam] coom (*2nd* o *ins.* G³) G;　　þat ledde]
ledande J;　　þat²] marked *mar.* C³;　　me] (*2nd* e *ins.* G³).　　　2628 þe] *om.* MO;
firste] (e *ins.* G³), tyme *add.* J;　　whan] *om.* S;　　nyh] *om.* J.　　　2629 to] nere J;
me] (*2nd* e *ins.* G³);　　þat¹] *om.* JS;　　apperceyued] persayved JMO.　　　2630 light]
sighte C, eyen J;　　was] ware J;　　in ... haterel] be hynde J;　　bihynde] hire hatrelle

J; she] Sawe J.   2631 sigh] I J;   hidous] hedous (with hydous mar. G³) G;
as] om. O;   me] (2nd e ins. G³).   2632 thouhte] (e ins. G³).   2632-3 þerof
... abashed] woundyr a baist þerof J.   2632 wunderliche] wondirfully MO.
2633 thouhti] right thoghtfulle J, thoughtfull MO;   As] Capitulum cxli mar. C,
141 mar. G;   heerof I thouhte] I was thus thynkande J, of hire I thoght MO;
strongliche] om. J, gretely MO.   2634 wundrede] muysande J;   me¹] (2nd e
ins. G³), of hire J;   me²] (2nd e ins. G³), and sayde add. J, prec. nota rub. mar. O.
2635 now I see] om. JMOS;   how] om. J;   and] þat JO, for S.   2636 þou]
om. J;   doun] advone S;   art] so add. S.   2637 þee] (1st e ins. G³), Thou O;
needeth] nedis MO;   to] for to S;   bathe] (2nd e ins. G³);   þee] (1st e ins. G³),
in add. JM.   2638 inne] and add. J;   sounde] the add. J, coumfort S.
2639 counforte] sovnde S;   þe] Les (variant Tes L) F, thy JOS, þin M;   þat]
om. O;   ben] þou erte J, om. O;   Ladi] prec. Capitulum cxlii mar. C, 142 mar. G³.
2641 mihte] maye J;   no] (otiose stroke over C);   susteyne] Suffre JMO.
2642 hadde] have J.   2643 euel] iuelle (with eeuell mar. G³) G;   apayed]
payde JMO;   haue] (2nd a ins. G³);   trist] trust GS, hope J;   hope] tryste J;
to] in JMO;   all] to geddyr add. J.   2644 Now] prec. Capitulum cxliii mar. C,
143 mar. G³.   I] hafe J;   haue] (2nd a ins. G³), I J;   founden] for O.   2645 þee¹]
to þee (to ins. with u.v. to mar. C³) C, om. JMO;   from] fro JMO;   a] om. JM, þe
O;   cuntre] fir JM, contre O;   þat is ferre] countre JM;   for] om. J.   2646 wel]
I wele J;   but] 3if JMO;   soone] þowe wolde J;   þou woldest] Sone J, þou
wolde MO.   2647 armures] armoure JMO.   2648 take] (2nd a ins. G³);
hire] to hire M;   with þee] (1st e ins. G³), schalle bere thaym J;   shal ... hem]
with the J.   2649 alwey] -s S;   þou] maye add. J, shuld add. O.   2650 haddest]
had JMO;   nygh] nere J, om. S.   2651 þee] to thee GS;   didest] dyd JMO.
2652 euele] wyll O;   betaken] faryne with alle J, taken MS;   Lady] prec.
Capitulum cxliv mar. C, 144 mar. G³;   monstre] with u.v. mon{stre} mar. C³.
2653 whiche] of whilk MO;   haue] (2nd a ins. G³);   maad] (2nd a ins. G³);   me]
(2nd e ins. G³);   wolde I] trs. JMO.   2654 þe] hir JMO;   it] scho JMO;
facioun] farsioun alt. fassioun J.   2655 disgisy] disgysyd MO;   acustomed]
customable J, custumyd MO;   þat ooþer] the toother (1st o ins. G³) G;   side] it
es a thynge digisy to me · For add. J;   a seruaunt] 3ee walde have brought me J.
2656-7 ye ... me¹] a Seruant J.   2657 haue] (2nd a ins. G³);   me¹] to me MO;
light] legier F, lysty JMO;   strong] strenkeþe S;   me²] (2nd e ins. G³).
2658 craft] offyce J;   is] nys S;   to] forto JMOS.   2659 armures] armour J,
armes ne armures S;   Thereof] prec. Capitulum cxlv mar. C, 145 mar. G³, Therfor
O.   2660 she] schee (1st e ins. G³) G;   I wole] trs. J, I S;   þee¹] om. M.
2661 þis ... Memorie] þis wenche is nempned & bi hire riht name cleped Memorie
CG³S (foot p. G³);   þis] can. G³;   wenche] can. G³, ilke wenche J;   hatteth]
hatte can. G³;   bi ... riht] (by naame ryghte each marked for gloss and 2nd a ins.
G³), memorye J, by hire right name MO;   and] marked for gloss G³, om. JMO;
is] his (marked for gloss G³) G, om. JMO;   cleped] om. JMO;   Memorie] by hir
ryght name J.   2662 apperceyueth] persayfe3 JMO;   nothing] nou3t J;   þe]
om. JMO;   comynge] (2nd o ins. G³).   2663 þe¹] Memoria rub. mar. M;   and
diuise] ins. mar. O³.   2664 bihynde] be kynde J;   sette ... yen] hir eyen Sette
J;   light] sight J;   is] (t alt. s C);   not] na JM.   2665 thing ... dreedful] fulle
dredfulle thynge J, thynge ful dredefull MO;   ne hidous] ne So hedous J, om. C;
as] o. er. C;   thing] athynge J.   2666 þilke] om. JMO;   make] maaken (1st a
ins. G³) G, have J, om. MO;   here] om. JMO;   mugoe] em. ed., mugos (marked
for gloss G³) G, ordinaunce C, om. JMOS.   2667 and] o. er. C, om. JMOS;
here] om. JMO;   prouidence] F, purueaunce JMO;   Er] Lange are J.

2668 clerkes] the clerkes JM; fallen] al *add.* M. 2669 or] of GJMOS, et F; geten] geeten (*2nd* e *ins.* G³) G, gate JMO; ne ... hem] keped thaym nou3t J, ne kepeþe hem S. 2669-70 is woorth] *trs.* J. 2670 ygoten] getyne JMO; ne be] be nou3t J, not weel *add.* S; So] See M. 2671 she¹] *with* scilicet memorie *mar.* G³; eyen] eye MO; þerbi] therfore JMO; wite wel] it wele wit J. 2672 tresorere] tresour J; science] -s S. 2673 after] *om.* J; þat¹] *om.* J; þe²] *om.* O. 2674 keepeth] it *add.* JMO; and] þat J; places] plaases (*2nd* a *ins.* G³) G, place MO. 2675 if] *om.* J; make] (*2nd* a *ins.* G³); bere] to bere J; and keepe] *om.* J; þese] this JMO. 2676 armures] armour JMO; ne] and J; neuere daunger] scho schalle neuere J. 2677 shal she make] make daungere J; As] And as CG (and *ins. mar.* G³). 2678 haue] (2nd a *ins.* G³). 2679 þou¹] *with u.v.* the pil{grym} *mar.* G³; hire] so *add.* S. 2680 but bere] *trs.* M. 2681 if] and J; so ... good] þou couthe JMO; þow coudest] so mekille goode JMO. 2682 þat²] at J; bere²] *om.* O, it *add.* S. 2683 greevinge] grevaunce JM; hire] of hir J, *om.* M; a] *om.* J; grettere] greuaunce and a gretter *add.* M. 2684 þine eyen] the J; a] thy JMO; hem] *with* the *add.* JMO; þat] whilke J. 2685 strong] myghty O; mihti] stronge O; witingeliche] wittely and O, purpose J. 2686 haue] (*2nd* a *ins.* G³); hire] here *add.* JMO; þat²] And MO. 2687 to bere] þaym *add.* J, also S; also] to bere S. 2688 elles] ell O; þat] *om.* J; haue] (*2nd* a *ins.* G³); gret] schame and *add.* J; Ladi] *prec.* Cap*itulum* cxlvi *mar.* C, 146 (145 *over erased*) *mar.* G³; sithe] Sen JMO. 2689 to yow] nowþere JMO; neiþer] to 3owe JMO; ayensey] *om.* S; Ne] And JMO, *om.* S; also] *om.* S. 2690 miht I nouht] nyl I nou3t J, ne may I not S; miht] myghte (e *ins.* G³) G; wel] wille J; Now] *om.* J; hem] vs J; þanne] *om.* JM, all O. 2691 alle] lyfte vp J, þan O; be houen] alle this armour J; upon] *om.* J, uppe S; hire] *with* scilicet memorie *mar.* G³, *om.* JO, bak *add.* M; and¹] *om.* M; trussed] trusse it on hir J, on here trussed O; sithe] Syne JMO, þanne S; I wole] *trs.* J. 2692 sewe] seewe (*2nd* e *ins.* G³) G, follow JM; me] (*2nd* e *ins.* G³); þanne] *ins. mar.* G³, *om.* MOS; she²] *with* scilicet grace *mar.* G³; I] pilgrym *over* G³; hoven] lifted J; hem] *om.* S. 2693 to Memorye] (yd *alt.* ye C), toke tham J; tooken hem] to Memory J. 2694 neede] howe þat Gracedieux counseylled þe pilgryme on his wey *add.* S; Whan] *prec.* Cap*itulum* cxlvii *mar.* C, *illegible word and* 147 *mar.* G³, Cap*itulum* cxviii *mar.* S, And when M; þei] alle hire armures S; weren] þus *add.* M. 2695 yilde] it *add.* J; wel goodliche] Spakke to me J, full gladly M, ful godely O; spak to me] fulle goodly J; me¹,²] (*2nd* e *ins.* G³); in] *om.* JMO; me²] *om.* JMO; swiche] þise J. 2696 þou art] *trs.* J; quod she] armed JMO; arayed] quod Scho JMO; to] for to S; into] to J. 2697 faire] grete JMO; Memorie] *with* memorie *mar.* G³; þi] -n C, a JM, O O, to þy S; soomeer] so mery O; þat] whiche S; after þee] (*2nd* e *ins.* G³), schalle comm after the J. 2698 shal come bihynde] behynde J; whiche] þat S; armure] and *add.* MO; to] for to S. 2699 shal be] es JMO. 2700 faireste] (*2nd* e *ins.* G³); þou were] *trs.* J. 2700-1 if ... bred] had þou J, (of *ins.* O³). 2701 þou haddest] of Moyses brede J, þou hadd MO; Go] nowe *add.* J; leeue þou hast] for þou has leue J. 2702 al be it] þou3 alle JMO. 2703 þat] þat at J, þat · that M, all O; do] þer *add.* S; passe þee nothing] nathynge passe þe J. 2704 þat] what S. 2705 And] *prec.* Cap*itulum* cxlviii *mar.* C, 148 *mar.* G³; his] the J. 2706 þat²] whilke J; yaf and] *om.* JMO; þe²] *om.* O. 2707 pilgrimes] and *add.* J, And soone *add.* M; me] (*2nd* e *ins.* G³); and¹ ... it] *om.* JMO; sithe] *om.* J, sithen MO; in] to *add.* MO; my] -n C. 2708 it] and *add.* J; Sithe] *prec.* Cap*itulum* cxlix *mar.* C, 149 *mar.* G³, seyne JMO, So S;

to] þe lady *add.* S.   2709 goodshipes] gudeshipp MS.   2710 she ... me¹]
om. M;   ne] *om.* M;   alonygne] alone J, *om.* M, alonge O;   hire] fro me *add.* CJ,
om. M;   and] *om.* JMO.   2711 biseechinge ... neede] *om.* JM.   2711–
12 she ... me] (me *2nd e ins.* G³), *om.* J.   2712 as ... hire ¹]*om.* M;   þat ... hire]
if scho left me in my nede M.   2713 mihte] do *add.* CM;   nothing] do *add.* J;
Serteyn] *prec.* Capi*tulum* cl *mar.* C, 150 *mar.* G³, -ly JS;   soothliche] *om.* JMO,
þat S.   2714 me] (*2nd e ins.* G³);   miht] may JMO;   nothing] ryght nought
JMO.   2715 of] þou J, on S;   me] (*2nd e ins.* G³), of J;   þou] me J;   ne
haddest] had na J, ne had MO.   2716 requirest] askes of me J, askes MO,
requerdest S;   þat²] at J, þen *add.* M, *om.* S;   wost] wate wele JO, wote M.
2717 is] nedful *add. can.* M;   þat] ce que F, *om.* CJMO;   requeste] askynge J;
in] *om.* S.   2718 dishoneste] vnhonest O;   to ... þe] it es myne entent J;   is
myn entente] (myn *final* ecan. G), to gae with the J;   as] *om.* J.   2719 fro] -me
S;   I] *om.* J;   thinke] *om.* J, ne thenk S.   2719-20 if it ne] bot ȝif it J.
2720 by] þurgh J, *om.* S;   þin] awne *add.* J, þi O;   offence] defawte J;   mercy]
No*ta* qu*are* gra*cia* vadit cum homine *mar.* O.   2721 me] (*2nd e ins.* G³);
thinketh] thynke JM, þinkes O;   Now] *prec.* Capi*tulum* cli *mar.* C, 151 *mar.* G³,
Vnderstande quod Scho J, þanne S;   vnderstonde ... she] nowe J.   2722 how]
who S;   gon ... þee] (*1st e ins.* G³), I thynke J, is myn entent · and as *add.* M, goo
with þee S;   I thinke] to gae with thee J, and thenk þat S;   summe] men *add.* C.
2723 hauen] (*2nd a ins.* G³), in thayre frendes J;   in ... freendes] hase J;   trist]
trust GS.   2724 þei¹] tham J;   thinken] thynke JMO;   shulen] shulden CM.
2725 kept] couerde J;   bi] *om.* S;   þouh] wheder J;   hauen doon] *om.* J;   or
doon] do J, *om.* MO, ouerdoone S;   yuele] or wele *add.* J, gude or euyll MO.
2726 þat] *om.* JMO;   not] nowght (t *alt.* w) G;   triste] truste (e *ins.* G³) GS;
me] (*2nd e ins.* G³);   or] tille oþere J, to othir*e* MO;   lene] I leve J, (? I leue
MO).   2727 þou do no] tu ne faces F, þou do CGS;   trist] trust GOS.
2727-8 of ... and] *om.* J.   2728 and] (*with* ne *mar.* G³), et F, ne CMOS;   eye]
-n JO;   a] *precious add.* J.   2729 to þe folk] maketh me to the folke J;   whan
I wole] nouȝt be Sene in in visible J, *om.* MO;   yelt] ȝitt (*with* ȝyllt *mar.* G³) G,
om. J, I wil seme MO, leene (? leeue) it S;   invisible] when I wille J;   þilke] *with*
scilicet ston *mar.* G³, that JMO.   2730 me] (*2nd e ins.* G³), *om.* S;   from] fra
JMO;   whan] *om.* JMO.   2731 þat] whenne JM, *om.* O;   be] am JMO;
þanne] þat JM;   ago] gane JMO;   bi] *om.* J.   2732 sumtime and] *trs.* S;
turned] am tourned S;   from] fra JMO.   2733 þee] forth J, in *add. ins.* M;
ooþerweys] oþere wise J, odire way MO.   2734 deingne] dyne J;   þi] the
JMO;   wolt²] *with* J, þou wolt S.   2735 go] to ga the ryȝt waye J;   leue] not
lene (? leue) S;   goode] (e *ins.* G³);   bi] *om.* J.   2736 be] ȝe wele *add.* J;   to]
þat þow J;   wysliche] fra *add.* JMO;   hensforthward] heyne forwardes J, hens
forwarde MO.   2737 from] fra JMO;   hensforth] heyne forwarde J, hens
forwarde OS.   2737-8 I ... anon] *om.* JMO.   2737 of ... pyer] *em. ed.,* of the
same preeyere G (of *ins. mar.* same *can.* G³), of þe same preyer S, aft*er* my stone *o.*
er. (*with u.v.* after my stone *mar.* C³) C.   2738 parte] wille gae J, go MO;   fro]
-m GS;   and] fra *add.* JM;   As] *prec.* Capi*tulum* clii *mar.* C, 152 *mar.* G³.
2739 þat] sayde J, þus MO;   seid] y seyd GS (I *alt.* y S), thus J;   more] I Sawe
hir J;   sih ... not] na mare J.   2739-40 loowh ... was] I was fulle Sorowfulle in
herte J.   2740 mihte it] I myght J.   2741 Algates] Neuerþeles J;   to ...
wey] I wolde not leue J;   as ... it] my vyage J;   I² ... leue] þat I was purposed
forto make J;   I²] *om.* S;   wolde] wull (*with* wolde *mar.* G³) GO.   2742 I
wolde] y wull (*with* wolde *mar.* G³) GO, anane J;   anoon take] (take *2nd a ins.*
G³), I wente J;   wey] and *add.* J;   To Memorie] bade J;   I bad] memory J.

2743 shulde] *om.* GMO; come] (*2nd* o *ins.* G³). 2743-4 come ... she] *om.* J. 2743 þat she¹] *into mar.* O³; me²] and *add.* O. 2744 foryete noon] and *add.* J, *trs.* O; soothliche] *om.* J; it] my biddynge J, *om.* O. 2745 so] *om.* J; al] acc (*with* all *mar.* G³) G, and S; brouhte] and *add.* J; And] for so S; it] that J. 2746 after] -wardes J; I¹] sheo S. 2747 if ... hadde] had I nouȝt J; warnished] garnysch J; of] with J. 2748 alwey] away *o. er.* M, -s S; at] al atte J. 2749 bi] thurgh J; strok] strakes J; dart] -es J; of²] and J; arwe] -s JMO; þat] whilke J. 2750 if I hadde] had I J; armed] Takeþe hede nowe howe þauctour telleþe þat oþer part of his sweven here filowyng *add.* S. 2751 Now] *prec.* Capitulum cliii *mar.* C, 153 *mar.* G³; I] have JM; haue] (*2nd* a *ins.* G³), I JM; seid] tolde J, all O; yow] seyd O; al] *om.* J, you O; oon] 1 *over* G³, as S. 2752 swevene] sweeuene (*2nd* e *ins.* G³) G, dreme M, sweunynge (un *a minim short*) O; I shal] *trs.* J; heerafter] efterwarde JMO. 2753 haue] (*2nd* a *ins.* G³); þe ... gladliche] schalle also here it J; shulen ... it] the mare gladly J. 2754 thing] -es MO; enoyeth] er nuyfulle J. 2755 weder] wedir (edi *o. er.*) M; þilke of] þe JMO. 2756 if] and J; more] ȝe schalle here J; ye wole heere] mare J; þerwhiles] the whiles GOS, in the mene tyme J. 2757 me] (*2nd* e *ins.* G³); ariht] ryght JO, *om.* M; mette] dremydde J, Heere endeth þe firste partye of þis book, And heere biginneth þe secunde Partye *add. rub.* C, heere endeth the furste partye of thyse bookes *mar.* G³, Explicit pars Prima *add.* J, lo þus endeþe here þe first partye of þe booke & folowing begynneþe here þe secounde partye takeþe hede and reed *add.* S. 2758 And] *prec.* Capitulum i *mar.* CGS, *prec.* Capitulum 1 ijᵉ partes *mar.* M, *om.* CJMO, filowing *add.* S; heere] *om.* JMO, begynneþe S; biginneth] INcipit J, *om.* MO, here S; þe ... partye] Pars Secunda J, *om.* MO, takeþe hede and reed S. 2759 After] *prec. rub.* Here þe pilgrime metys with Rude entendement · and of þer disputacion · and how þat Reson spekis to rude entendement M, SEtheyne J; þat¹] *om.* J, þat *add.* S; haue] had MO; seyd] talde ȝow J, before O; bifore] seyd O; þat²] certayn thynges whilke J, þat *add.* MOS; in] my *add.* S. 2760 ooþere] nowe wille I telle ȝowe of oþere J; sithe] siche C, Seyne JMO; haue] *om.* J; bihyght] hight JMO. 2760-1 I³ ... shewe] *om.* J. 2761 yow] *om.* JMO; not] na JS; hele] layne J; it] them fra ȝowe J; As] *prec.* Capitulum ij CG *mar.*, Right as S. 2762 to¹] forto J. 2763 whi¹] what O; miht not] had no myght M; þus] *om.* JO; armures] armour JMO; or] other GS, and JMO; whi²] *ins. mar.* G. 2764 þat¹] *om.* JMO; not] *ins. mar.* G; þilke] that JMO; hadde] *om.* JMO. 2765 me] mee (*2nd* e *ins.* G³) G; am] *om.* MO; þat] þe O. 2766 mayme] (yme *o. er.* C), mare harme J; wot] feel S; me] mee (*1st* e *ins.* G³) G. 2767 maad] (*1st* a *ins.* G³), strange *add.* JM; to] for to S. 2768 whens] wheyn JM; am þus] *trs.* J. 2769 þat¹] to bere that J; þat²] *om.* MO. 2770 whan] that J. 2771 As on] *prec.* Capitulum iij CG *mar.*, Allane JMO; þis] þus O; þat] thus JMO, what S; wente] I wente JMO; I²] AT the laste I J. 2772 mette] Rudē entendement *rub. mar.* O; browed] browes C. 2773 frounced] in the face *add.* J, frounted MO; þat] He J; crabbe] a crabb MO; and seemed] a grete and a lange and J, for *add.* S; to be a] *om.* J. 2774 wel] *om.* J, full MO; misterman] he Semede wele to be *add.* J; euel²] ille J. 2775 goth¹] he *add.* M; He weeneth] *with* cherll *and scilicet* cherll *mar.* G³. 2776 queyntised] quayntely JMO; but] *om.* O; me] (*2nd* e *ins.* G³). 2777 shal¹] shalle *alt.* shalbe O; lette] a byde J, speke M, and a

byde *add*. S;   Whan] *prec. Capitulum* iv *mar*. CG;   And whanne S;   þus]
I herde hym speke J, I herd him þus S.   2777-8 I ... speke] thus J, speke S.
2778 wunder] *om*. S;   abashed] agaste M.   2779 wolde] schulde J;   haue]
(*2nd a ins*. G³);   me] (*2nd e ins*. G³);   abidinge] taryinge J;   Algates]
Neuerþeles J.   2780 humbliche] mekely JMO.   2781 require] requeere
(*2nd e ins*. G³) G, beseke J;   wole ... me¹] (mee *2nd e ins*. G³), do me na disese
na nuy J;   ne ... me²] ne enpeeche mee (*4th and 6th e ins*. G³) G, ne that ȝe lette
me noȝt J, ne lett me MO.   2782 go fer] wende J, fair MO.   2783 wolde]
wol S;   me] (*2nd e ins*. G³);   Serteyn] *prec. Capitulum* v *mar*. CG *and scilicet*
cherll *mar*. G³;   þe] thy J.   2784 disturbaunce] disturblaunce C, discomber-
aunce O;   þin] awene *add*. JMO;   Whens] wheyne J;   cometh it] commeste
J, come it O.   2785 swich and swich] So balde J, swilk M, such O, et tex et
quiex F.   2786 lawe] (*2nd a ins*. G³);   wold ordeyne] *em. ed*. a voulu ...
ordener F, wull ordeingne G, wel ordeyned C, ordayned JMO, ful ordeynd S;
A] It es but a J.   2787 ago] gane sene J;   made defence] (*2nd a ins*. G³),
defendyd J;   took] schulde take J.   2788 bare] schulde bere J;   it] *om*. J;
ne ne] ne CJMO;   handelede] handill JMO.   2789 ayens] agayn M;
foolliche] foly and thy J, foly MO;   surquidrye] witt M, surquydaunce S.
2790 þat oon] Scrippe J;   þat ooþer] burdoune J;   me] (*2nd e ins*. G³);
thinketh] thynke JMO.   2791 hast þou dorre] haste dorre G, durste þowe J,
has þou durst MO, hast dure S.   2792 come] (*2nd o ins*. G³);   hider þou]
þou J, *trs*. S.   2793 hem] hider *add*. J;   ne] *om*. JMOS;   didest þow]
dedeste G, *trs*. S;   a grettere] so grete JMO, gretter S.   2794 Whan] *prec*.
Capitulum vi CG; þese woordes] I herde J;   I vnderstood] thise wordes J;
more] I was wele mare J;   þan bifore] abayschid J;   I was abashed] than I was
byfore J.   2795 what to answere] I wyste neuere J;   I ne wiste] whate I schulde
saye J;   answere²] answerere C.   2796 Gladliche] Ane aduoket J;   an ...
wolde] wolde I fayne J;   haue¹] (*2nd a ins*. G³);   me] (*2nd e ins*. G³);   haue²]
(*2nd a ins*. G³).   2797 for] so O;   hadde] haue S;   wist] wetyne J.
2798 to] y myght JMO;   haue] (*2nd a ins*. G³);   purchaced] gotene J;   him]
oon M;   Algates] ANde J;   as] *om*. CM, com F, howe S;   studyede] Stude
thus Studiand J.   2798-9 how I mihte] for to S.   2799 als] *om*. J, and
MO;   I¹] *om*. MO;   comen þat] venir Ce F, *om*. C, ane come after me J, come
after oon M, come after me O.   2799-800 after ... was] *om*. C.   2800 Dame]
Reson *rub. mar*. O;   whiche] whome S.   2801 mown] myght JMO;   þe]
here J;   but] right wel *add*. S.   2802 sittingeliche] fittyngly O;   Bifore]
I haue J;   I ... hire] hir bifore J.   2803 wherfore] and þerfore J;   þe] *ins*.
G;   more] moore þe (*1st o ins*. G³, þe *subpuncted and can*.) G;   me] (*2nd e
ins*. G³);   I ... ioyful] (ioyefull e *ins*. G³ *in* G), when I Sawe hire J.
2803-4 whan ... hire¹] I was ryght ioyfulle J;   wel] I Supposed J.   2804 I
thouhte] wele J;   shulde] that cruked churle J.   2804-5 þilke ... cherl] schulde
J, that crukid churle MO.   2805 maat] matt (*with* maatt *mar*. G³) G;   which]
þe whilke J;   harde hadde] *trs*. JMOS.   2806 þe] *om*. MO;   and] *om*.
J.   2807 Resoun] *prec. Capitulum* vii CG, Takeþe heede howe dame Raysoune
· speketh with þe pilgryme in þis mater *and mar*. {capitulum} ii S;   him²] *om*.
JS, to hym M;   me] (*2nd e ins*. G³).   2808 keepe] helpe JMO.
2809 repere] Reepere (*2nd e subpuncted*) G;   or¹·²] other G.   2809-10 an
espyour] a spiere JMO.   2810 weyfareres] wayferynge menn JMO;   hattest]
hatte JMO;   where] ou F, when JMO;   gaderedest] gadereste (*with* gadredeste

mar. G³) G.   2811 tooke] gatte J;   Þe] That J;   auenaunt] conuenient
M.   2812 And] *prec. Capitulum* viii CG;   him] *ins. mar.* G³.   2813 hire]
with scilicet Resoun *mar.* G³, tille hire J, to hir M;   þis] *quod* he *add.* J;
mayresse] mairesse F, meystresse CJM;   or] other GS;   a neewe] *om.*
JMO.   2814 enquerouresse] enqueresse S;   leste] last M.   2814-15 I
shal] *trs.* J.   2815 þe] (*2nd e subpuncted* G), þi M;   þat²] whilke J;   bi]
þi *add.* O.   2816 þee] (*1st e ins.* G³), nathynge answere J.   2817 answere
nothing] to the J;   *drawing of Rude Entendement mar.* O³;   And] *prec.*
Capitulum ix CG;   into] in JMO.   2818 drow] toke J, oute *add.* M, tooke
out S.   2819 sithe] Puis F, & sithe CS (& *o. er. with erasure mar.* C³), and sithan
MO, *om.* J (*see note*);   him] tille hym J.   2819-22 Serteyn ... hider]
J.   2819 my] by my S.   2820-1 Hold ... wite] *om.* MO.   2821 wel]
om. MO;   my¹] and my MO;   and ... power] *om.* MO.   2822 Serteyn]
prec. Capitulum x CG, Certaynly J.   2822-3 I² ... nothing] of thy leves J.
2823 in þi leves] can I nathynge J, of þi leuys M, of þe leuys O, in þe leeues S, en
voz feulles F;   rede] of bookes reed but looke S;   þou wolt] þee list S;   wite]
wit þou J.   2824 litel] bot litille J.   2826 for þanne] for thy J.
2827 but] 3if *add.* J;   me] (*2nd e ins.* G³), not *add. ins.* O³.   2828 suspes-
sioun] (ss *o. er.* C);   haue] (*2nd a ins.* G³).   2829 þese] this JMOS, ces F;
letteres] letter JMOS, letres F;   out of plyt] and vnfalde it J, and vnplyte it MO,
of his plytes & S.   2830 rede] *om.* J;   hem] *om.* J, it MOS;   bifore] to fore
S;   Whan] and whenne.   2831 if God wole] with goddes grace S;   And]
prec. Capitulum xi CG, *om.* MO.   2832 I] *with scilicet* pylgrym *mar.* G³;
hem¹] the letteres J.   2833 apayed] (*1st a ins.* G³), payed JMO;   for] *om.*
JMO;   alwey¹] -s S;   grummede] gruyned JMO;   he²] *om.* C.   2834 at]
om. J;   euery] euere ilke a J;   I¹] that I JM;   sygh] herde J;   teeth] *ins.*
mar. G.   2835 grynte] gnaste JMO;   wole] wulle (e *ins.* G³) G;   heerafter]
heere after (*3rd e ins.* G³) G, here J.   2836 it] nowe *add.* J.   2837 Grace]
prec. Capitulum xii CG, þe lettyr *rub. mar. and* from grac to Reason *another hand*
mar. O³;   gouernen] is gouernid (is *ins.*) O, yee gouernen S;   hem] *om.* O;
þei] as þei CJ, all waye O;   þe] bath JO;   kynges] þe kynges S.
2838 regnen] regner F, regions JMO;   to] vnto J;   goode¹] wel J;   louede]
be louede (be *subpuncted*) G, beloued JMO.   2839 we] (*2nd e ins.* G³), atte
we J;   sende] you *add.* O³.   2840 Of neewe] Nowe on newe J, *with* a late
mar. O³;   we haue] wee haaue (*1st e, 2nd a ins.* G³) G *with* a *mar.* G³.
2840-1 whereof ... fair] *om.* O.   2840 wherof] whate of J;   us is] we er J.
2841 fair] bel F, fayn CJM;   a] *ins. mar.* G³;   cherl shrewede] *trs.* S;   prowd]
om. J;   and daungerous] and aungerous J.   2842 name] (*2nd a ins.* G³);
maketh] (*2nd a ins.* G³), gars J;   clepe] calle JMO;   and nempne] *om.* JMO;
him²] *om.* JMOS.   2843 maad] (*1st a ins.* G³);   him] Rude intendment þe
Churle *mar.* O³.   2844 bineme] tene theym and reue J, refe M, bereue (be
subpuncted) O;   hem] hem of *ins. mar.* G³;   burdouns] Scrippe J, burdoun
MO;   vnscrippe] hem of *add.* C, *om.* JMO;   here] *om.* M;   scrippes] burdoun
J, scripp MO.   2846 Orgoill] pride *over* C, arguyll (*with* pride orguyll *mar.*
G³) G, Dame pride J, sir Pryde MO;   his] hir J.   2846-7 and ... staf] staffe
and cruelle JMO.   2847 clepen] calleth JMO;   Obstinacioun] obstinacy
JMO;   michel] *om.* O.   2848 dooth] *om.* O;   cherl] chell (*with* cherll *mar.*
G³) G;   þe] *om.* JMO.   2849 we] (*2nd e ins.* G³) G;   nouht] *can.* G³,
om. S;   in comaunding] *om.* J.   2850 þiderward] thedyre J, to giderward
O;   þilke] that JO, *om.* M.   2851 doun] a doun CS;   of] remenaunt and

add. J; anything he] *trs.* J. 2852 day competent] *trs.* J. 2853 assyses] assise JMO, assises F; power] the year of grace. 1331. admonish: and vpon repentance, absolue *mar.* O³. 2854 maken] (*2nd a ins.* G³); oure yeer] the ʒeere of vs J; eche] euerych O. 2855 clepeth] calleth JM, called O. 2856 Whan] *prec. Capitulum* xiii CG, And þen when M; Resoun] Sche J; letteres] letres F, letter JMO. 2857 hem] it JMO; in] in to J; saaftee] saauete (*2nd a ins.* G³) G; the boxe and Syne in to hir bosum J; sithe] than J, -n MO; areynede] Scho areined J. 2858 hast] (*2nd a ins.* G³), *om.* J. 2859 come] coom (*2nd o ins.* G³) G; heere] hider J; more] now J. 2860 þat I] *o. er.* C, þat þat I S; haue] (ha *o. er.* C), (*2nd a ins.* G³); Who¹] why whate J, *prec. Capitulum* xiv CG; Who²] whate J. 2861 not] nouʒt JM. 2862 what] þat *add.* S; men] this man J; han] haauen (*1st a ins.* G³) G; heere] (*2nd e ins.* G³); Thinkest þou] *trs.* S; on] of MO. 2863 loues] luffe J, lothnesse *o. er.* M; oþer] or JOS, *om.* M; to] þou thynkis forto J, forto MO; or] and J; he] *with* cherll *mar.* G. 2863-4 I ... herd] (haaue *1st a ins.* G³), be Saynte Symeoun J. 2864 bi ... Symeon] I hafe welle herde J; hattest] hatte JMO. 2865 name] (*2nd a ins.* G³); defamed] (*2nd a ins.* G³); haue] (*2nd a ins.* G³); who] that *add.* J; and] that *add.* J. 2866 Nouht] *om.* J; defamed] (*2nd a ins.* G³); quod Resoun] thare sayes þou amisse J. 2867 where] I pray the *add.* J; þer] whare JMO. 2868 I] haue S; haue] (*2nd a ins.* G³), I S; mesurest] mesured JMO; and] *om.* J; stelest] *om.* J, sellid MO; folkes] folk (*with* folkes *mar.* G³) G, mennes M. 2869 corn] and salde hit *add.* J; Beausire] *prec. Capitulum* xv CG; now] þou S; tweyne] twey G, twa JMO, þeos S; litel] *o. er.* C, *om.* J. 2870 woordes] (woo *o. er.* C); vnderstonde] thaym *add.* J; Misseyinge] my saying O. 2871 ye] hafe J; haue] (*2nd a ins.* G³), ʒe J. 2872 cleped] called JMO; resoun] ther's many naught that semmeth good and many slipps, wher other's stood. *mar.* O³. 2872-3 for ... vnresoun] *om.* CS, forto couere with the mylneres grete vnresoun J, forto couer with his grete vnresoun MO, Pour sa grant desraison celer F. 2873 but ... Resoun] *om.* S. 2874 Bitwixe] be tweene GJMOS; name] (*2nd a ins.* G³); make] (*2nd a ins.* G³). 2875 Oon] oo (1 *over*) G; is] it is J, is it M; anooþer] (*2nd o ins.* G³); thing] *om.* J; haue] (*2nd a ins.* G³), to hafe JMO; his] the J; name] þere of *add.* J. 2876 name] (*2nd a ins.* G³); men mown] *trs.* J; maken] maake (*1st a ins.* G³) G, þaym *add.* J; hele] couere JMO. 2877 filthe] falshede J; þis] theose S; thing] -es S; is falle] falleth J, fallen S; a¹] *ins.* G, *om.* MOS; time] tymes S, bathe *add.* J; many²] townes and in J; *prec.* good accomying or altercacion *top of p.* O³; townes and in J; a²] *om.* JMO; strete] -s J. 2878 who¹] he S; þat¹] so so J, so MO; fair] good J; make] maak (*1st a ins.* G³) G, maketh J; queynte] symple J; who²] So *add.* JMO; þat²] *om.* JMO; good] fayre J. 2879 make] (*2nd a ins.* G³), maketh J; simple] qwaynte J; vices] vises (with vyc{e}s *mar.* G³) G. 2880 maken] (*2nd a ins.* G³); name] (*2nd a ins.* G³); vertu] that es *add.* J. 2881 lasse¹] displese JM, *prec. by caret rub.* G³; þe¹] to the JMO (þe *can. rub. with* ye *mar. after rub. caret* O³); yit] it *add. subpuncted* C; is not] the vertu J; þe vertu] es nouʒt J. 2881-2 þe³ ... woorth] wors J, lesse worth MOS. 2882 straw] ne the lesse worthy *add.* J; sign] a signe J. 2883 vice] visce (with vyce *mar.* G³) G, wise J, *om.* S; appareth] apparaileth JO, apparissh M; þat] *om.* J. 2883-4 with my name] all mesour make hym qweynte J. 2884 þilke mesure] with my name J, þat

mesure MO;   hath wold] hath wull G, haþe wol S, Sest voulu F, wole C, *om.*
JMO;   queyntise] *om.* J, aquaynteȝ M, quayntes O;   him¹] *om;*   hele] coueres
JMO, heeld S.   2885 defamed] (*2nd a ins.* G³);   wurshiped] þerby Schulde
I be J;   shulde be] wirscheped J, shuld I be O;   þerby] *om.* J.   2886 folk]
-es S;   What] *prec. Capitulum* xvi *mar.* CG;   he] sche (*with* cherll *and he mar.*
G³ *2 hands*) G.   2887 Þat] So J, as MO;   part] of me add. JMO;   F *line*
om. see note;   Þou] *I Se wele* þou J;   wolt] wille JM, wold O;   þat ooþere]
oother (*with* that oothre *mar.* G³) G, oþer men (men *subpuncted*) O, oþer S.
2888 blamed] (*2nd a ins.* G³), of add. J.   2889 Weene] ȝe add. J, þou add.
O.   2890 nempne] neuened JM, nempnyd O;   or] other GS.   2891 ne]
na add J.   2891-2 but ... knowe] *ins. mar. with caret in text and markings in*
mar. rub. O³, *with the following variants.*   *2891* þat] *ins. mar.* G³, *om.* MO;
names] (*2nd a ins.* G³).   2892 wel] thaym J;   eche] *om.* J, ilkon M, eluerych
O;   · of hem] wele J;   names] (*2nd a ins.* G³);   be] er JM.   2893 hattest]
hatte JMO;   also] that add. JMO.   2894 þee] (*1st* e *ins.* G³).
2895 maketh] (*2nd a ins.* G³), gerres J;   turne] a bout add. J;   ne mihte] myght
nouȝt J, myght not (not *ins.* O³) O;   þee] (*1st* e *ins.* G³).   2896 þine] by (*with*
thy *mar.* G³) GS;   slye] Schleyght J;   and] thy add. J;   fallaces] sotill M,
fals O;   euere] euery S.   2897 ooþerweys] þou schalle make me J;   þou
make me] (*2nd a ins.* G³), oþerwyse J, þou shal me make M, þou shalt make me
O;   to] *om.* C.   2898 And] *prec. Capitulum* xvii *mar.* CG;   Resoun] alle
J;   al] *om.* JS;   into] to JMO.   2899 seyde] I Sayde J, smyled and sayde
S;   him] *om.* J, to hym M;   of art] þou hase lernede J;   þou hast lerned] arte
J.   2900 subtiliche] Sutelte J;   þou] *om.* C;   foorth] (*2nd* o *ins.* G³).
2901 ensaumples] ensaumple MS;   and] *ins. mar.* G³, *om.* CJMO (*see note*);
if þou haddeset] had þou J;   grettere] grete J;   woldest] scholde J.
2902 weel] ful wele M;   wurþi] to be a grete clerke J;   he] I knowe add. J.
2902-3 Þat I do] For Sothe J.   2903 certeyn] *om.* J;   quod] she add.
subpuncted C;   it] *ins. mar.* G³, þou J, *om.* MO;   wel] that I do add. J;
more] I wille scorne the J.   2903-4 I ... þee] mare J.   2904 forto] tille JO,
to M;   name] (*2nd a ins.* G³);   wite] it add. J.   2905 hast] getes J;
of þe helinge] forto layne it J;   ne wot] whate neuere wheder J.   2906 shalt]
shouldest S;   haue] (*2nd a ins.* G³), any add. J;   Wurshipe] wurschipp (wur
o. er. with scilicet wurschyp *mar.* G³) G.   2906-7 What ... þou] *om.* S.
2907 vnwurshipe] wirschepe JMO;   name] (*2nd a ins.* G³).   2908 askest]
þou ascheȝ J, ȝit þou askes MO.   2908-9 þou ... it¹] *om.* J.   2908 on] opon
M.   2909 oueral] eueralle J;   ne wot] wate neuere J;   tokeneth] meneȝ
J;   but] *marked for gloss* G³.   2910 þilke] he JMO;   Art] is MO.
2911 withinne] wytt O.   2912 knew] kenne J;   I²] ȝee (*with* y *mar.* G³)
GS;   heeld] halde JMO, hard O, heelden S;   an] *om.* MO;   is] nys S.
2913 oon] (*with* scilicet Resoun *mar.* G³);   with] which S;   appare] apparayle
J, clothe M, appere O, enpayre S;   him] *om.* O;   eche] ilke a J, ilk M, euerych
OS;   to] *ins. mar.* G³.   2914-5 hadde I not] ȝit J.   2915 yit] had I nouȝt
J.   2916 ioyngtliche] ioynyngeliche C, Joygnliche S, conjointement F;   wel]
om. JMO;   suspecioun] suspeccioun *alt.* suspecioun *with er. mar.* C.
2917 oon] (1 *over* G³), alle ane J;   withoute] wyþ OS;   Þine] awne add. J;
han] haauen (*2nd a ins.* G³) G.   2918 seyinges] seyinge O;   þat ben] þou
art O;   I wot] By thy wordes JMO, propreliche add. S;   bi þi woordes] I wat
JMO.   2919 þou¹] properly JMO;   propirliche] þou arte JMO, *om.* S.
2920 nempned] neuende and named J;   existence] (*with* beynge *mar.* G³).
2921 foryiue] forȝeue (*with* gyue *mar.* G³) G.   2922 þou¹] according to the harte

such be the thoughts *mar.* O³;   me] (*2nd e ins.* G³), to me CM;   bi] thurght thy J;   þou] þat þou S.   2923 wendest] wenest S;   þat] *om.* JMOS;   of me] (*2nd e ins.* G³), it ware JMO (were *can.* O);   it were] of me JMO. 2924 as] and S;   wight] man J;   seeth] maye see J.   2925 and¹] et F, *om.* G, and fulle J, full O;   set þee] was thy name J;   was þis name] giffen*e* the J, was þi name M, was þe name O;   With] *prec.* Ca*pitulum* xviii *mar.* CG, Ca*pitulum* te{rtium} *mar.* S;   *prec.* Loo howe þe fayre lady dame Raysoun yit spekeþe to þe Cheorlle clepid Rudeentendement S.   2926 þe¹] li F, this GS;   Nouht] bot nouȝt J.   2927 for ... not] *om.* O;   grinte] gnasted JMO, he grimtte S; with] *ins. mar.* G³;   þe] hise C.   2928 of] *om.* JS.   2929 sithe] Seyn JO;   name] (*2nd a ins.* G³).   2930 in my letteres] it es alle clere J, In my let*ter* MO;   it ... cleer] *2 lines marked in mar.* C, in my let*ter* J.   2931 an²] *om.* J.   2932 bineme] beneeme (*2nd e ins.* G³) G, reue JM, bereue O;   hem] *ins. mar.* G³;   vnscrippe] take fra thay*m* J.   2933 þou] *om.* G;   it] Swa J; þi] my M;   ayens] agayn M;   lady] Grace dieu *add.* J, dame Gracedieux *add.* S.   2934 þat¹] *om.* JMO;   þei] he JMO.   2935 herd seyd] p*r*eched J, harde redde S;   it¹] *with scilicet* gospell *mar.* G³.   2936 wel] *om.* C;   bere] schulde bere J.   2937 hoom] (*1st o ins.* G³) G;   þat] *om.* JMO;   see] Sawe JS.   2938 hem] thys *add.* J;   defence] defendynge JMO;   þe²] defendyng *add. can.* M.   2939 lawe] (*2nd a ins.* G³);   peyne] me *add.* J;   make] (*2nd a ins.* G³), ger J;   to] do (*with* to *mar.* G³) G, *om.* JMO.   2940 Oo] *prec.* Ca*pitulum* xix CG, Do (*with* oo *mar.* G³) G;   Resoun] dame Raysoun S; ooþerweys] oþerwyse JM;   Þilke] that JMO;   defence] defendynge JMO. 2941 agon] syne JO, sithen M;   ooþerweys] oþerwyse JM;   turned] it is turnyd M.   2942 Wel] *om.* J;   sooth] quod he *add.* S;   afterward] aft*er* MO. 2943 recomaunded] co*m*maunded JMO;   Cause] And couenable J;   couenable] convenable F, cause J, resonable C;   þer²] it JMO.   2944 wel] *om.* JMO; chaunge¹] chau*n*gynge JMO;   not] name JO;   to þe king] for þe kyng *repeated, 2nd can.* M.   2945 cause¹] honeste J;   honeste] cause and resounable J; Þe] his J;   ayen] *om.* JMO.   2946 I wole] *trs.* J;   telle] say MO;   þee] (*1st e ins.* G³);   wolt] hyere it J, wil here M.   2947 hath] he has JMO; no¹] noon C;   neede] langere *add.* J;   be] lenger *add.* S.   2948 do] hafe at do J;   or] other GS.   2949 þe²] *om.* J;   whiche] the whilke J, whilke M;   goode] (e *ins.* G³).   2950 is] it is O.   2950-1 To ... terme] *om.* M.   2951 terme] eende S;   to] *om.* J;   ende] terme S;   weren] where O;   comen] twoo men S.   2951-2 bi his clepinge] *om.* JMO.   2952 no more] they schulde J;   þei beren] na mare J, þey were S.   2953 leften] lefe J;   hem²] all *add.* MO;   sufficient] For Sufficiaunt J.   2953-4 he was] and mighty S.   2954 and mihty] he was S;   to] for to S.   2955 needede] nedes O;   ooþeres] othere JMOS.   2957 herkeners] herers J;   aministreden] minystrid JMO;   founden] founded S;   vitailes] vitayll O. 2958 euery] euerilke J;   werkere] laburrere J;   and resseyue] *om.* JMO; And] that tyme *add.* J;   eche] euerilke J.   2959 þerof] So thayre deu*e*re J, so moch O, so miche S;   so michel] to thay*m* J, þer of O (the laborer worthy his hyer *mar.* O³);   þe] þayre J;   no wiht] þer was nane of þay*m* that J. 2960 oones] on a tyme J.   2961 thouhte good] *trs.* J;   yow] nowe *add.* S; he] J;   anything] lakked JMO;   lakked] any thynge JMO.   2962 þus] sent yowe S;   sent yow] þus S;   to¹] *om.* J.   2963 shewe] scheewe (*1st e ins.* G³) G;   woord] wordes S;   him] (*2963-4* wherof ... good *add. dittography* S).   2964 Serteynliche] Certys J;   sire] quod thay *add.* J;   nay] but *add.* J.   2965 is] est F, ne C, *om.* J.   2966 Lo] *prec.* Ca*pitulum* xx CG;   for]

om. JO;   whi] which S;   was] thay ware JMOS;   beren] scholde bere J, bar
M.   2967 vseden not of] schulde vse na J, vsid no M, vsed not O;   þe] *om.*
JM.   2967-8 whan he shulde] efterwardes J.   2968 afterward] when þou
scholde J, -es S.   2970 a²] *om.* C.   2971 seyde] bade J;   tooken] schulde
take J;   here] þe MO.   2972 diden] bere J, do MO;   on ayen] *om.* J;
he saide] a Sacchelle J, any sekk MO;   any sak] quod he J, he saide MO.
2973 þouh] ȝif J, *ins. mar.* O³ *after rub. caret in text and mar.*;   he] I J, he he
O.   2973-4 and cleerliche] *om.* J.   2974 for] wham *add.* JMO;   þe] þat
M.   2975 hadden] *om.* J;   ne] schulde J.   2976 me] *ins. mar.* G³;
I] tharfore I J;   ye] (*2nd* e *ins.* G³);   taken] (*2nd* a *ins.* G³), it *add.* J.
2977 al] *om.* J;   whan] fra J, þat S, when Christ died, he then left vnto vs a token
of his goodness *mar.* O³;   han] haaue (*2nd* a *ins.* G³) G.   2979 ye musten]
behufe ȝowe J.   2980 sette] putte J;   þe] youre C;   ayen] *om.* J;   shule]
shulden C;   mown] *om.* JMO.   2982 nouht fynde] fynde noon C, nowght
fynde not (nowght *ins. mar.*, not *subpuncted* G³) G, fynde þaim J, fynde MO, no
wight fynde S;   gladliche] schalle nouȝt J;   shal] gladly J, not *add.* MO;
þat²] *om.* JMO.   2983 speke] wol speke S;   anything] any gode þing O.
2984 forto] til C, to JMO;   Now] Take it J;   taketh it] nowe J.   2985 see¹]
ȝe hafe *add.* J;   So see] Loo J.   2987 wherfore] for which S;   þilke] hym
JMO.   2988 hauen] (*2nd* a *ins.* G³), *om.* J;   it¹] *om.* JS;   ne] *om.* J, and
MO;   þat] *om.* JMO;   beren] beres JMO;   it²] *om.* O;   where] when
JMO;   leeue] they have J, licence M;   þei hauen] leue to bere þaim J.
2989 cause] the cause J;   into] vnto J;   þat] (þat *add. at end of line?* G³);
eche] ilke man JM, he O;   cometh] come JMO.   2990 his²] viage *add. can.*
C, hool *add.* S.   2991 What] *prec. Capitulum* xxi *mar.* CG;   walkere] churle
JO, paisant F (*see note*);   gost þou] gost G.   2992 me] (*2nd* e *ins.* G³);
Wolt þou] wulte G;   at] a JMO;   lesinge] a lyeesynge J.   2993 it] (*with*
hyt *mar.* G³) is *add. ins.* M;   þat þat] that JMO;   hadde] has JMO.
2994 so¹] *om.* JMO;   riht] alle J;   so²] in *add. subpuncted* G;   alle] *om.* J,
in al MO;   ordinaunce] -s CGS.   2995 scraped] of *add.* J.   2996 Nouht]
Nathynge J.   2997 how²] & how O, þat *add.* S;   what] *om.* J.   2998 þer
lyth] thirlleþe S.   2999 but] *om.* J.
3001 ben] that er J, er M, *om.* O;   þe¹] A JMO;   is þe place] gracious J.
3002 gracious] is þe place J;   þat] *o. er.* C, is *add. subpuncted* G, þere JMO;
here] *o. er.* C, er J, is M, ar of O;   facioun is] (is *ins. mar.* G³), dyuerse JMO;
diuerse] fawsiouns JMO.   3003 gladliche] *om.* S;   And] *prec. Capitulum* xxii
mar. CG;   blissede him] the chorel J, blyssed here O;   þe cherl] blessed hym
J.   3004 his] here I, þe S;   rude] rudy J;   is] deuylle is J;   he] me thynke
add. J.   3005 amase] amaase (*3rd* a *ins.* G³) G;   me¹,²] (*2nd* e *ins.* G³);
enchaunte] enhaunce S;   Al] of al S;   I] euere þou J;   turnest] it *add.*
JMO;   and²] *om.* J.   3006 stirest] *om.* J;   þe] *om.* J.   3006-7 falsnesse
... fairnesse²] *om.* S.   3006 clepest] callyste JMO.   3007 of] *om.* JMO;
þou seist] es *add.* J, falsnesse S;   falsnesse] þou sayest S;   was] of the kynge
J.   3008 of þe kyng] was J;   was] it was J, is S.   3009 al] *om.* S;
disgisy] Sutille J, desgisid M;   lyinge] -es M;   ne] *om.* JMO.   3010 bigil-
ouresse] begylere JMO;   not] neyþer S.   3011 ne] ȝit *add.* J;   þi²] *om.*
S;   dedes] deedes (*1st* e *ins.* G³) G;   verres] benes J, resshes M, barrys O, neres
F (*see note*);   I wole] *trs.* J.   3012 me] (*2nd* e *ins.* G³);   of] *om.* JMO;
nothing] aske þe J;   seeche þee] seche thee (*with* seeche *mar.* G³), neuere leve J,
biseke þe MO, serche þee S.   3013 At] *prec. Capitulum* xxiii *mar.* CG;   leste]
laste J;   þou shalt] *trs.* J.   3014 it] *om.* J.   3015 he] (*with* cherll *mar.*

G³); of] *om.* JS. 3015-6 what ... greeue] can I nouȝt se J. 3015 it²]
(*with scilicet* staff *mar.* G³). 3016 I see not] whate it maye greve J; On]
And on JMO; necessarie] it es J; it is] necessary J, it was S. 3017 haue]
(*2nd a ins.* G³); to] forto JMO; I³] *om.* J; defende] -th J. 3018 sette]
I Sette JMO; me] (e *ins.* G³) G; thinketh] think JMO, semeþe S.
3019 michel þe] *trs.* JMO. 3019-20 a gret fool] I ware J. 3020 I were]
a mykille fule J; cokard] cowarde J; Oo] Mafaye J. 3021 haue] (*2nd a
ins.* G³). 3022 shulde] schalle JMO; loue] haue S; þilke] the JMO.
3023 hateth] (*2nd a ins.* G³); þe] þou O. 3024 goot] gayte J, gate gaite (gate
can.) M, gat O; it] hytt *ins. mar.* G³, doun*e* O, not doun S; not doun] down
nouȝt down (*1st* down *can.*) M, it not O, hit S. 3025 Oo] *prec. Capitulum* xxiv
mar. CG; How] *om.* JMO. 3026 greevede] greues S; hire] her (*with*
grace dieu *mar.* G³) G. 3028 ooþer mete] I See wele J; I se wel] thy ruyde
throte ascheȝ J; þi ... not] nane oþere mete J. 3029 a freend] ascende J;
of] *om.* M. 3031 loueth] loved J; avauncement] fortherynge J.
3032 and] *om.* JMO; wight] man C, (*with* man *mar.* G³); hath] any *add.* J;
men] me J. 3033 it] him C, (*with* hym *mar.* G³), *om.* JMO; any] *om.*
JMO; disese] to *add.* J; hath¹] hafe JMO. 3034 staf] (*with scilicet*
obstynaciou*n mar.* G³); þilke] tha JMO; þat] is obstynacioun *add.* S; she]
(*with grace* dieu *mar.* G³); wole] wull GS, wolde CJMO, veut F; haue] (*2nd*
a *ins.* G³). 3035 Ne] I warne J; were it] *trs.* J; come] *om.* MO; to]
om. JMO; hire] *om.* JMO, hit S; and] *om.* M. 3036 conuerte hem] turne
to the crysten feith J; wolden] also S; also] *om.* J, wolden S; errour] -s
JMO. 3037 hem] ȝif it ne ware *add.* J; Bi] thurgh J, so þat S; confusion]
confessioun J; Nabal (*rub. underline with* nabal & pharao *rub. mar.* O²).
3038 for] *om.* S. 3039 it] hitt (*with scilicet* obstinacioun *mar.* G³) G.
3040 comaunde] have his commaundmente J; Eche] and ilke a man J, Ilkone
M, euerych O; shulde] to O; he] wer *add. ins. mar.* C³, (*with scilicet* obedience
mar. G³). 3041 nothing] na wyse J; it] (*with scilicet* obstinacioun *mar.*
G³. 3042 enclyn] -ande J, -ed MOS; humble] obeyande J, bowh MO;
hem] *om.* J; hattest] hatte JMO. 3043 ne] lened J; lenedest] nouȝt J;
to] þere J, vn to O; it] (*with* obstinacioun *mar.* G³), to J; wolde] *om.* C, þou
woldest S; leeue] trowe JM, be enclyned and trow M; me] *om.* O, þee S.
3044 þee²] þou J. 3045 Haa] *prec. Capitulum* xxv *mar.* CG, {Capitulu}m
quartum *mar.* O; God] *om.* JMOS; he] in fayth *add.* J; What] *om.*
JMO. 3045-6 I ... manere] thowe Spekis in vayne J. 3045 litel] þi *add.*
MOS. 3046 of¹] on S; to þee] nathynge obey J; of²] *om.* JMOS;
nothing obeye] vnto the J; ne] *om.* MO. 3047 staf] bot *add.* M; me]
om. C, (*2nd e ins.* G³). 3047-8 wolt ... þou²] wit it ryght wele J; wolt þou]
wult G, whedir þou will MO, woltowe S. 3048 oþer] or MO, *om.* S; ne
wolt þou] ne wulte G, wolt þou not C, þou wil nouȝt M, nyll O, niltowe S; wite
it wel] whethere þou wille or nouȝt J. 3049 now] *om.* JMOS; more] bute
add. M. 3050 to²] to aper at, vn to S; þe] *om.* C; assises] assise JMO;
of] þe grete *add.* M; I] þerfor I M. 3051 þee] come þider *add.* S; þider]
in proper person *add.* J; withoute²] any essoyne *add.* S. 3052 ooþer]
attourney and þer to answer for þi self *add.* S. 3053 Thanne] *prec. Capitulum*
xxvi *mar.* CG, capitulum tercium *mar.* O²; *prec.* Here Reson byddis þe pilgrime
go fro Rude entendment. and also sett*es* hym in his right way. ledyng hym by þe
hand O²; meward] (*with* pilgrim *over* C³), (*2nd e ins. with* pilgrim *mar.* G³), -ys
Jo, me M; hic recedet peregrinus arustic*atione rub. mar.* O²; clepede] Sayde
vnto J, called MO. 3054 Go] Oo S; withoute] nathynge J. 3055 ne

ne] F, ne CJMOS.   3055-6 þe ... is] Salamoun bidde J.   3056 answere]
schalle aunswere J;   woord] thing S.   3057 and fynden] *om.* O;   suinge]
Efterwardes J, semynge M;   seith] bidde3 J.   3058 men] me S;   shulden]
I shulde do S;   him] (*with* scilicet fooll *mar.* G³);   for²] *om.* O.
3059 shame] (*2nd a ins.* G³);   Serteyn] -ly J.   3060 wite] knaw M, it *add.*
O;   þilke] that JMO.   3061 dispenced me] (*with* scilicet Resoun *mar.* G³),
putte in my disposicioun J;   it were tyme] tyme es J;   haue] (*2nd a ins.* G³).
3062 albe] 3if alle J, þof al be M, albe it þat S;   lost] be loste J, were lost S;
of] *om.* J.   3063 ashamed] aschaamed (*2nd a ins.* G³) G;   in] in to C.
3064 anevelte] stithy JMO (*with* a stithe or anuile *mar.* O³);   woordes] of profit
add. J;   in] tille *add.* J, to *add.* MO;   or] other G, *om.* J, of MO, and S;
profiten] *om.* J, profite MO, him *add.* S.   3065 ayemaunt] aimant F, adamaunt
CS, the adamaunde J, a dyamant O;   oþer] *om.* J, or MS, or *ins. mar.* O³;
dyamaunt] *om.* J, adamant *ins. mar.* O³.   3067 þou miht] wirschippe J;   no
pris] myght þou nane J, not pryce O;   conquere] wynne J, ne conquer (ne *ins.*,
and whi Arc bish{ } *illegible* O³).   3068 shake] and schake J.   3069 chin]
cheyne S;   Lady] *prec.* *Capitulum* xxvii *mar.* CG.   3070 þat¹] þat at
JMO;   me] (*2nd a ins.* G³).   3071 durst] doorste (e *ins.* G³) o. *er.* G, darre
J;   not ... forth] o. *er.* G, (*with* forthe *foot* p. O³);   for þe cherl] hardelych S;
hardiliche] *om.* J, for þe Cheorlle S;   but] bot 3if J;   hadde] hafe J.
3072 whateuere ... were] Sumwhate of 3owe J, some what S;   of yow] whate so
euere it be J;   pray] preye (*2nd e ins.* G³) G;   with me] (*2nd e ins.* G³), 3e
come JS.   3073 ye come] with me JS;   þat] *om.* S;   passinge him] 3e lede
me J;   ye lede me] 3ee bede mee (*with* leede *mar.* G³) G, tille that I be paste hym
J;   haue] (*2nd a ins.* G³).   3074 sumthing nedeful] Summe nedfulle thynges
J, some thynges nedfull M.   3075 longinge] that langes J;   And] *prec.*
Capitulum xxviii *mar.* CG;   withoute] any *add.* M.   3075-6 bi þe hond] scho
ledde me J.   3076 she took me] by the hande J, scho MO;   and ... cherl] *om.*
JMO;   til] forte JS;   ladde me] (mee *2nd e ins.* G³), *om.* J.   3077 and]
om. C, *ins. mar.* G³;   me] (*2nd e ins.* G³).   3078 bilefte] lefte JMO;
grucchinge] and groynande & *add.* J;   lenynge ... staf] *om.* S;   grummynge]
om. JS, gronyng and gnaistyng M, groynyng O.   3079 me] (*2nd e ins.* G³), I
JO;   nothing] not of þe which S;   Resoun] and resoune J;   þerof] there atte
J.   3080 Whan] *prec.* *Capitulum* xxix *mar.* CG;   *prec.* *Capitulum* iv *mar.*
M;   *prec.* Þe pilgryme askes Reson why he may nou3t bere þe armoures, & also
of þe birthyne of flessh (also ... bi- o. *er.*) *rub.* M;   *prec.* hic inquirat quare non
potest portare arma *rub. mar.* O²;   þus] I Sawe me JS;   I sigh me] thus JS.
3080-1 of Resoun] I be gan to aske J.   3081 I ... aske] of resoun J;   þat] *om.*
JMO;   haue] (*2nd a ins.* G³);   me] (*2nd e ins.* G³).   3082 I haue] (*2nd
a ins.* G³), *trs.* J;   ben] *om.* S.   3083 am] I am S;   ne susteyne] to bere
J.   3084 is] gret *add.* J;   to me] *om.* J.   3085 strong] -ere J.
3086 and ... yow] *om.* O.   3087 whens] Fra wheyne J, fro whens MO.
3088 Thanne] *prec.* Capitulum xxx CG;   answerde me] resoune J;   Resoun]
aunswerde me J;   what] that (*with* what *mar.* G³) G.   3089 In ... Dieu] it
es nou3t lange Seyne gane J;   not ... agoon] Þat I Sawe the J.   3090 I sigh
þee] in the hous of Grace dieu J;   times] thare *add.* J;   þou speke] *trs.* MO;
How] many tymes *add.* J.   3091 of hire] of here (*with* grace dieu *mar.* G³)
G, þou asked nou3t this J;   þou ... asked] of hir J;   þou askid nought MO.
3092 þanne] thy J;   I trowe not] *om.* O;   þat] þan M, *om.* O;   sumwhat]
ne Sumwhate J;   ne haue seyd] (*2nd a ins.* G³), has sayde J, haues said MO, ne
haue not sayde S.   3093 apperceyue] persayfe JMO;   wite] wryte S;

askest] asked JMO. 3094 I wole] telle ʒowe J; telle yow] I wille that J. 3095 foryeten] I haue JMO; I haue] (*2nd a ins.* G³), forgetene JMO; of] bot of J; wel] *om.* J, is weel S; I mynde] menes J, in my mynde S; me] (*2nd e ins.* G³), *om.* S; withoute more] *om.* J. 3096 me[1,2]] (*2nd e ins.* G³); to] so S; if] and J; made] (*2nd a ins.* G³); or] other GS. 3097 a feloun] men walde calle me J; The 7 leaues following doe declare the manifould miserys of ye sowle, through ye contynuall tentation of þe flesh. Reade *with* patience, þen Judg. *mar.* O³; men ... me] A grete fole J; clepe] call MO; ne] And JMO. 3098 myn armure] so wele M; so wel] myne arm*our* M. 3099 thinges] (*with* armures *mar.* G³); maken] (*2nd a ins.* G³); me] (*2nd e ins.* G³); abashed] aferde M. 3100 sooþe] (e *ins.* G³); of] dame *add.* S. 3101 dredde] me that I Schulde hafe greued J; hadde] werin thou mayst, much profitt fynde both for thy sowle, and for thy mynde *mar.* O³; or] other GS, and or M; mistake] mystaake (*1st a ins.* G³) G; to] agaynes J. 3102 lerne] lere J; it] *om.* CO; me[1,2]] (*2nd e ins.* G³); make] (*2nd a ins.* G³). 3103 vnderstonde] to vndyrstande J; quod] (*with* scilicet Resoun *mar.* G³); she] resoune J; who] whate J. 3104 double] þou be J; þou be] double J, *ins. mar. after rub. caret mar. and text* O³, *om.* S; haue] (*2nd a ins.* G³); noon] norisch M. 3105 ne to gouerne] *om.* J; and arraye] *om.* JMO; abashed] aferde J. 3106 seide] (*2nd e ins.* G³), answerde J; Ladi] quod I *add.* JMOS; me] (*2nd e ins.* G³); thinketh] thynke JM; þat] *om.* JMOS, Que F; haue] (*2nd a ins.* G³). 3106-7 but myself] to gouern M. 3107 to gouerne] bot my self M; haue] (*2nd a ins.* G³). 3108 it] this J; Now] *prec.* Capitulum xxxii *mar.* CG. 3109 lerne] *om.* JMO; and[1]] *om.* JMO; vnderstonde] herkyne graythely J; herkne] vndyrstande J; bisyliche] wele J. 3110-1 teche þee] telle the and teche J. 3111 þilke] þat JMO; þat] þat is þat (þat is *partly erased*) O; Of] and of J; þee[2]] *om.* J; he] it J, *om.* MO; is[2]] *om.* J. 3112 euery] euere ilke a J; fed] and *add.* MO, efedde S; drinke] at drynke J; hosed] *om.* J; cloþed] cledde J; ne is] *trs.* J; mete] noon *add.* S. 3113 costlewe] costfull JMO; delitous] delicate C, delicious JMO (*see note*); þou ne] *trs.* J; wolt] walde J; yive] ʒeue (*with* ʒyue *mar.* G³) G. 3114 þilke] *om.* JO, hym M, to þilk S; shulde] *om.* JMO; Bitake] taken JMO; þee[2]] to the JM, it was O. 3115 it was] to þe O; for] *om.* JMO; his seruaunt] becommene J; bicome] his Seruau*nt* J. 3116 wantounliche] qwayntely J, Wantoun M; take] (*2nd a ins.* G³); noble] nobil (*with* noble *mar.* G³) G. 3117 queyntise him] make hy*m* qwaynt JMO; iewelles] Jeuell O; tablettes] with hornes Siluered *add.* J, taglet*tes* O; knyves] with nowches *add.* J. 3118 lases] (*2nd a ins.* G³). 3119 eche[1]] ilke a J, euerych O; eche[2]] eu*erych* O. 3120 wel softe] wol softeliche C, fulle Softe JMO, mont molement F; him his] *om.* S. 3121 him[1]] *om.* J; þe[1]] in JMO; and sithe] anoþere day J, and sithen MO; stiwest] þou stewes J, stewis MO. 3121-2 On ... him[1]] *om.* J. 3122 kembest] tomlys M, comlys O; þou ... him[2]] *om.* M; mirthes] myrth JMO. 3123 euere] *om.* J; miht] maye J; day] nyght M; niht] day M. 3123-4 as ... þou[1]] *ins. mar. after rub. caret mar. and text* O³. 3124 hast[1]] þou *add.* (*can. rub.*) O; hast] had M. 3125 him] *om.* MO; a] the J; woman] is *add.* J; she] that sche JO, þat M; yiveth souke] fedeth J, giffes hym souke M. 3126 feedeth] gyffeʒ atte Souke J; it is *trs.* J; þat] Sene JMO; bigonne] biginne C. 3127 sithe] sene JMO; stintedest] þou stynted JMO, þou doest stint S; seide] sey O; xxviti] syx and thritty (*with* xxxvi *mar.* G³) G. 3128 failede] trowe J; trowe] fayled J; he] that he

J.   3129 his ... þus] *om.* C;   serued] kept C, *om.* J;   him] *om.* J;   and]
om. J.   3130 bytrayeth] betraysshed S.   3131 desceyueth] desceyued S;
þee^2] (*1st* e *ins.* G^3);   Þat] And þat J;   þilke] he J.   3132 bere] be J;
to^2] *om.* G;   þilke] he JMO.   3133 þe] *om.* JMO;   wolt] walde JMO;
doon] done (*with* done *mar.* G^3) G.   3134 Lady] *prec. Capitulum* xxxiii *mar.*
CG;   am awundred] woundre me J, am wondrid MO;   of] þis *add.* CJ (*can.*
C), þat *add.* MO.   3135 and] *om.* J;   hadden] ʒe ne hadde J, hadd nought
MO;   wit] as ʒe have *add.* J, a witt S.   3136 weene] þat *add.* S;   or] other
GS;   it] I O;   meetinge] (*1st* e *ins.* G^3), a dreme J, (*with* dreming *mar.* O^3).
3137 wot] knawe and wate J, wote wele M;   gabbe] ʒe walde J;   wolde ye not]
gabbe J, ʒhe wolde M, wold ye O.   3138 me] (*2nd* e *ins.* G^3);   þilke] þat
JMOS.   3139 he was] *trs.* M.   3140 how] and how O, and what S;
knowe] may knowe J, knewe O;   do] to do O.   3141 þouh] ʒif alle J, of O;
al quik] I dismembred hym J;   I^1 ... him] all qwek J;   wel] ʒit ware I nouʒt
J.   3141-2 were I not] welle J, were I nowe S.   3142 Sertes] *prec. Capi-*
tulum xxxiv *mar.* CG.   3143 shuldest] efft *add.* S;   ne were þou] ʒif þou
ne ware J, it ne were þou S;   were] ne were S.   3144 noothing] lytelle atte
rekke off J;   litel ... were^2] elles nought J.   3145 an] han (h *subpuncted*)
G.   3146 buryelles] buryell GJOS, barell M, similacre F (*see note*);   maad]
(*1st* a *ins.* G^3), (*nota de carne rub. mar.* M);   coluer] colliere JMO.   3147 not]
nathynge JMO;   ne^2] me S.   3148 contract] contrarie O.   3150 an] *om.*
J, and MOS;   herte] *om.* J, herto M, þerto O;   withinne ... wormes] *om.* J.
3050-1 and ... wurmes] *om.* JS.   3151 withinne it] *ins. mar. after rub. caret*
mar. and text O^3, *om.* S;   a worm] *om.* S;   laste] lasse S.   3152 And] *om.*
C;   albeit] ʒif alle it be J, þof all þat it be M.   3153 ligge] to ligge CJO.
3154 þi] þe CJ;   slepe] to slepe O;   gost] þou gase JMO.   3155 haue] (*2nd*
a *ins.* G^3).   3156 whiche is] swilk MO;   to] *om.* J.   3157 priuee cham-
bres] the *priuee* JMO;   feeldes] þe feldes JO;   to^3] for to S.   3158 Now]
luke J, and S;   looke] nowe J;   wheþer þou be] varrayliche S;   verriliche]
verrriliche C, wheþer þou be S;   serf] thral C, Servande JMO;   and] or S.
3159 al þat] this J, al þe S;   neuere] no O.   3160 gladdere] redyer J.
3163 Ladi] *prec. Capitulum* xxxv *mar.* CG, *prec. Capitulum* qui{ntum} *mar.* S;
his name] his naame (*1st* a *ins.* G^3) G, I beseke ʒowe that ʒe wille telle me J.
3161-2 whi ... not] why telle ʒee mee not (*3rd, 5th* e *ins.* G^3) G, his name J, wil ʒhe
tell me MO, why telle yee not to me S.   3163 anoon] scla J;   go sle] hym
J, slo M;   him] anane J;   I wolde] *om.* J, *trs.* O;   O] *om.* J;   leeue] þou
hase J.   3164 hast þou nouht] na leve J, hastowe noon S;   wel] *om.* J;
hast^2] good *add.* J;   to^2] for to S.   3166 make] (*2nd* a *ins.* G^3).
3167 vnderputte] putte J;   Penitence] penaunce JMO;   þe] *om.* JMOS.
3168 of him] *om.* J;   shalt þou] schalte (e *ins.* G^3) G, *trs.* J, shal S;   haue] *om.*
M;   ne neuere] *om.* M;   in no time] *om.* JMO.   3169 avenged] venged
JMO;   as] o. er. C, A JMO, si F;   while] litil J;   erst] before JMO;   wel
þou] *trs.* JMO.   3170 vnderstoode] vndyrstonde MO.   3171 chastiseresse]
chastiere J, chastiser MO;   þilke] Scho JMO;   þat hath] is J, haues MO;
rihte] (e *ins.* G^3).   3172 and^1] sithene þat *add.* M;   sesoun] resoun C;
take] (*2nd* a *ins.* G^3);   hire] *with* scilicet penytaunce *mar.* G^3.   3173 and
...him^2] *om.* S;   wel] *om.* O.   3173-4 a good seruaunt] he schalle be J.
3174 he shal be] a goode Seruaunt J;   hens] heyne J;   forthward] forward
GJMO, forwardes S;   þat] *ins.* J.   3175 raþere] more JMO;   more] *om.*
JMO.   3176 to þee] (*1st* e *ins.* G^3), takyne J;   taken] taake (*1st* a *ins.* G^3)
G, to the J;   lede] þee *add.* C, hym *add.* JMO.   3177 hauene] (a *ins.*

G³).   3178 ooþerweys] Oþere wise JMO.   3179 Lady] *prec. Capitulum xxxvi mar.* CG;   I²] ʒe JMO;   met] dremed J.   3179-80 oþer mete ye] of J.   3180 flesh] whilke *add.* J;   clepen] calle JMO.   3181 noon þer] na noþere J;   heere] (*2nd e ins.* G³).   3182 tweyne] twa JO;   tokeneth] menes J.   3183 of] oute of JO.   3184 out] *om.* JO;   clepe] calle JMO.   3185 meetinge] dremynge J;   me] *with scilicet* resoun *mar.* G³;   þe feith] þi feith CGMS (*with* the feyth *mar.* G³), foi F;   þou¹] that þow JMO;   if] and J.   3186 þere] whare JMO.   3187 reste] (*2nd e ins.* G³).   3188 willes] wille JMO;   þat I] *om.* J;   mowe] *om.* J, myght MO;   wite] *om.* J;   sooth] *om.* J, þe soth MOS;   if] whedere J.   3189 make þer] maake there (*2nd a ins.* G³) G, *trs.* J, make þee S;   abidinge] or nought *add.* J;   Serteynliche] Serteyn C.   3190 what] *with scilicet* pilgrim *mar.* G³;   hast þou] hast G, hastowe S;   þou²] walde J.   3191 woldest] þou *add. can.* C, þou J.   3192 þat] *ins. mar. after rub. caret mar. and text* O³;   al bitymes] efterwarde J;   afterwarde] alle be tyme J;   shulde] myght J, *ins. mar. after rub. caret mar. and text* O³.   3193 bitimes] by tyme MO;   wrecche] wreche (*2nd e ins.* G³) G;   she] (*with scilicet* resoun *mar.* G³);   þe] þis C.   3194 bitimes] betyme JMO.   3195 þe] þa JMO;   eses] ese JMO;   go] to ga J, *om.* O.   3196 bitymes] be tyme JMO;   trauaile] -s MO.   3197 sette] putte J;   þe] thee (*2nd e subpuncted* G) þi C.   3198 lady ... allas] *o. er.* G.   3199 Þerto] here to, to þat S;   þat] alle *add.* J;   oonliche] *o. er.* C;   wel] Ful JMO.   3199-200 I wolde] *trs.* J.   3200 also] als S;   I wolde] *trs.* J;   Þanne] wele J.   3201 þou hast] hafe þou J;   abide] *with* and *add.* J.   3202 reste] and *add.* JMO;   ooþer²] wille *add.* JMOS;   werche] travayle J.   3202-3 þat⁴ ... oon¹] þat þat oon CMS.   3203 ne wole] wille nouʒt JMO;   Contrarie] the tane is J;   þat oon is] contrarye J, alwey *add.* S.   3204 I feele] *o. er. with er. mar.* C.   3205 sool] þe soule MO;   she] bot *add.* J.   3206 tweyne] twae JMO.   3206-7 for ... tweyne] *om.* O.   3206 ben²] buth (*with beeth mar.* G³) G;   oon] (1 *over* G³);   þei] tweyne S.   3207 tweyne] twa JM;   eche] euerych O.   3208 Ladi] *prec. Capitulum* xxxvii *mar.* CG, (L *extended to grotesque* O³);   quod I] I prey yowe S;   I pray you] quod I S;   þat ye] *om.* S;   sey] telle J, *om.* S;   me] þere *add.* J, *om.* S;   who] howe S;   am I] *trs.* JS.   3209 sithe] Syn JO, sithen M;   my bodi] I am nouʒt J;   I am not] my body · For J, am not I S;   neuere] *om.* S;   ese] here of *add.* S;   if] bot ʒif JM;   sumwhat] I wiste J, I here M, I here not (not *ins.* O³) O.   3210 heerof] Sumwhate J, of somwhat MO, *om.* S;   I ne wiste] here of J, þat I ne know M, ne wyst S.   3211 Þou canst not] me thynke J;   michel] þou can nouʒt J;   as me thinketh] (mee *1st e ins.* G³), fulle mekyll J, as me thynk M.   3212 who is] to be JMO;   kyng] duke *add.* J, Nota *rub. mar. and* & learne to know / þi selfe · a royall conquest, to master thy affections *mar.* O³;   oþer] or JMOS.   3213 erle] elles CS;   þan] Or þat C, other than (other *ins. mar.* G³) G;   alle] (e *ins.* G³);   sciences] scyence JMO;   haue] (*2nd a ins.* G³);   þat is] the welthe J, þat þat is O;   of] in MO.   3214 sithe] Syn JO, sithen M, þat *add.* S;   it] ʒit *add.* J, *om.* S;   wel] *om.* J.   3215 wole] Schalle J.   3216 The] *prec. Capitulum mar.* xxxviii CG.   3217 is] lat it be JMO;   alle] (e *ins.* G³);   shet] sett M.   3218 porteyture] portature J;   made] (*2nd a ins.* G³).   3219 þee] (*1st e ins.* G³).   3219-20 to ... þee¹] *om.* S.   3219 mihte] (e *ins.* G³), he O.   3220 he¹] myght O;   þee¹] *om.* O.   3221 brid] the bridde JMO;   immortal] *om.* J;   and] ye state of ye inward man / good *mar.* O³.   3222 wolt] wille JM.   3223 but ... haue] (haaue *2nd a ins.* G³), hadde þou J;   forfeted] nouʒt J, þi self *add. can. rub.* O;   nothing]

forfetted J;   þi] þin M;   may] myght na ma*nn* J, may no man M, may ne (ne
ins. mar. after rub. caret in mar. and text) O;   compare] make co*mpar*ison off
nowther in J.   3224 ne[1]] in J;   ne[2]] *om.* C;   brid] ne brid C;   except]
oute takyne J;   nature] kynde J.   3225 of] *om.* J;   þi] þin M;   þou] art
add. O;   his] is (*with* hys *mar.* G[3]) G;   Weene not] wened S.   3226 one]
þe sone S;   of[2]] or J, or of M, & O;   Nota *rub. mar.* O[2];   Guileuile] Guilelme
(*with* Guileuile *mar.* G[3]) G, will*i*am JMO, Deguileville F;   he] þey O.
3227 a] *om.* JMO.   3228 nacioun] kynde J, natur MO;   þat[1]] which *ins. with*
er. mar. C;   þou] *om.* J;   hast] has bene J, haues MO;   of him] ofte and
J.   3229 cam] come (*with* coom *mar.* G[3]) G;   bigat] gate JMO;   it[2]] *om.*
J, þe O;   kynde] kynge J;   Riht] It is J.   3230 it is] ryght J, *om.* S;
þat ... Riht] *om.* S;   techeth] hym *add.* J.   3231 caste] brynge forth J;
riht] *om.* J.   3232 and[2]] of J.   3234 not[1]] þ*ou* J;   þou] nou3t J;   not
þi] nathynge JMO;   comynge] co*m*mande J, connyng S;   God made only twoe
Read *mar.* O[3];   dedliche] synne *add. can.* O.   3235 þee] *om.* J;   made]
(*2nd a ins.* G[3]).   3235-6 with ... handes] in þis worlde S.   3236 in þe world]
in this werlde JMO, with his handes S;   twey] -ne (ne *subpuncted and* ij *over*
G[3]) G;   whiche] the whilke J.   3237 make] (*2nd a ins.* G[3]).
3238 facioun] ensau*m*pille JMO;   gost] spirit J;   withheeld] (*1st e ins.*
G[3]).   3239 of[1]] *om.* S;   him] þem M;   withoute] with S;   medlinge]
mellynge JMO.   3240 made] (*2nd a ins.* G[3]);   gost] Spiritte J;   and] *om.*
S;   putte] he putte CG (he *and 2nd e ins.* G[3]), in *add.* O, *om.* S;   þee] (*1st*
e ins. G[3]), *om.* JMS;   in] *om.* S.   3241 þe] thy J, *om.* S;   bodi] *om.* S;
þat] *om.* JMOS;   þou art] *ins. mar. after rub., also in text* O, *om.* S;   þerinne]
and thare J, and þerin (and *can.*) O;   putte] (e *ins.* G[3]);   enhabite] it *add.*
J.   3242 preeve] the *add.* J;   to[2]] and O;   soothliche] sootleche G;
woldest] walde JMO.   3243 knyghtliche] kyndely J;   woldest] walde
JMO.   3244 or] other GS;   þee] (*1st e ins.* G[3]);   him[1]] *with* s*cilicet* body
mar. G[3];   hast] hase JMO.   3245 times] tyme J;   ne yelde þee] 3elde the
nou3t J, to hym *add.* M, woldest not yeelde þee S.   3246 þee[2]] (*1st e ins.* G[3]);
and[2]] *om.* MO;   maketh] gers J, *om.* MO;   þee[3]] (*1st e ins.* G[3]), *om.* MO;
yelde] 3eldid M.   3247 þee[1]] & *add. ins.* C, and M;   leeue] (*2nd e ins.* G[3]);
þereas] (þere *with mark over and in mar.* C).   3248 haue] (*2nd a ins.* G[3]).
3249 ouer] of J;   if ... were] *om.* M;   wille] witterynge J, witt MO.
3250 hast] hase JMO, Sampson *mar.* O[3].   3251-2 to[1] ... þee] *om.* J.
3252 wolt] wille late hym J, will MO;   shal] *om.* J;   shere] Schafe off J;
her] her*tes* J.   3253 whan he] *with* s*cilicet* body *mar.* G[3];   hem] and *add.*
M;   to þe philistyens] to þilke philistyens C, he schalle schewe tha*i*m J.
3253-4 shal shewe hem] (scheewe *1st e ins.* G[3]), to the philistenes J, he shal shewe
hem S.   3254 þat he] *with* s*cilicet* body *mar.* G[3], *om.* S;   hath to þee] *om.*
S.   3255 þe] *ins. mar.* O;   Now] luke J;   looke] (*2nd o ins.* G[3]), nowe
J.   3255-6 if ... strok] *om.* J.   3255 wolt] will MO.   3256 wolt] will
JMO.   3257 Ladi] *prec.* Capitulum xxxix *mar.* CG;   wundres] grete wondres
J, wonder is O;   heere] (*1st e ins.* G[3]);   in my body · 3e say that I am clere
add. J.   3258 meete] trowe J, dreme MO;   trowe] dreme J;   A spiryt] 3e
calle me J;   ye clepen me] a spirit J, yee clepen here S.   3259 shoven] Sette
JMO;   heere] verrayliche S;   þat] *om.* J;   ye] I 3he MO;   am] þat I am
J.   3260 see] (*2nd e ins.* G[3]), ne se S;   haue] (*2nd a ins.* G[3]);   seyd] that
add. JS.   3261 ooþere] oother (*with* oothre *mar.* G[3]) G;   grete] (*2nd e ins.*
G[3]);   wundres] hafe 3e saide *add.* J, 3he say *add.* M.   3262 eres] eeres (*2nd*
e *ins.* G[3]) G;   pray] preye (*2nd e ins.* G[3]) G;   ye] (*2nd e ins.* G[3]), that 3e

JMO.   3263 lerne] lere J;   me] mee (*2nd* e *ins.* G³);   aske] I can no3t wele J;   can ... wel] aske J;   of] by cause of J.   3263-4 þe baishtnesse] þe abaistnes J, þabaysshednesse S.   3264 haue] (*2nd* a *ins.* G³).   3265 And] *prec. Capitulum* xl *mar.* CG, Capitulum vj *mar.* S;   Reason *mar.* O³.   3266 hider] and herkyne wele whate I Saye J;   and ... is] *om.* J.   3267 shoven] *om.* J, shewid MO;   apperceyued] persayfed JMO.   3268 þee] (*2nd* e *ins.* G³);   whens] fra wheyne J;   cometh] the daye J;   þe day] commeth J. 3270 maketh] (*2nd* a *ins.* G³);   passe] to passe J;   þe] a MO;   and] *om.* CJ; avale] *om.* CJ, a valy M.   3271 as¹] and as S;   quod I] *om.* J, men seyne S; men seen] quod I;   it] as it is seen S.   3272 in] thurgh M;   Serteyn] *prec. Capitulum* xli *mar.* CG;   -ly J.   3272-3 if ... þou¹] *om.* J.   3273 hast] *om.* J, has MO;   seid] *ins. mar.* G³, *om.* J;   haue] (*2nd* a *ins.* G³);   bi þe sunne] *om.* CJ.   3274 þou shalt vnderstonde] *om.* CJ;   þat] *er. with er. mar.* C.   3275 þilke] that JMO;   a¹] the JMO;   a²] þe J.   3276 þe¹] *om.* JMOS;   how] so *add.* J;   it euere] *trs.* J.   3277 men] may be J;   þat] *om.* J;   in] *om.* J.   3278 brightnesse] lyghtnesse O;   weene] fonned folke and fulische J.   3278-9 to ... folk] to wene J.   3279 þe] that JMO;   be] *om.* S;   þilke] that JM, þe O.   3279-80 cloude ... were] *ins. mar.* G³. 3279 cloude] *with* body *mar.* G³.   3279-80 þe¹ ... shadewed] *om.* S. 3280 But if] Bot JMO, *om.* S;   þe cloude] warne J, ne wer MO, *om.* S;   ne were] the clowde ware J, þe clowde MO, *om.* S.   3281 haue] (*2nd* a *ins.* G³); she] it M;   shulde] wolde S.   3281-2 see ... shulde] *om.* S.   3282 She] *with* sowle *mar.* G³;   also] *ins. mar.* G³, *om.* JMOS;   see] knawe JMO. 3282 knowe] luffe JMO;   loue] See JMO.   3283-4 creatour ... ben] *om.* J.   3283 The] *prec. Capitulum* xlij *mar.* CG.   3285 heerfore] there for (t *ins.* O³) O;   þou] schulde J;   shuldest] þowe J.   3286 haue] has JS; þese¹] thise (*with* theese *mar.* G³) G, the JMO;   and] *om.* J;   þese²] thise (*with* theese *mar.* G³) G, *om.* JMO;   glasses] (*2nd* a *ins.* G³), of the body J. 3287 fenestralle] -ys OS;   he] *with* sowle *mar.* G³.   3288 seeth] seketh JMO;   good] fode and See3 it J.   3289 eye] -ne JOS;   Tobye] the body J;   a] Sum J;   time] Note *mar.* O³.   3290 body] Jo *mar.* G³. 3291 his] *om.* J;   shulde] holde *add. can.* M.   3292 Neuere] He Schulde J;   shulde he] neuere J;   haue] (*2nd* a *ins.* G³);   if] *om.* J.   3292-3 with þe soule] had he no3t Sene J.   3293 he ... yseye] with the sawle J, he hadd nou3t seeyn MO.   3294 þat þat] þat S;   I] þou JMO.   3295 seest¹] nou3t *add.* J;   cleerliche ... seest²] *repeated* G.   3296 which] þat C;   Neuere] He schulde J.   3297 shulde he] neuere J;   bi þi liht] it ne ware J;   it ne were] by thy light J.   3297-8 I ... right] *om.* J.   3298 so I] *trs.* J.   3299 hise] *with* scilicet body *mar.* G³, oþere J;   ben but] ne beeth but GO (ne *subpuncted* G), er nou3t bot J;   instrumentes] Instumens G;   þe] *om.* M.   3300 þat þat] þat MO;   he¹] *with* scilicet body *mar.* G³;   ne heereth] herith nou3t J. 3301 if¹ ... be] bot JO, not M;   if²] that 3if J;   þou] he JMO.   3302 ne bere] hyere J;   wel] no3t wele J;   or] other GS, þou scholde chastyse hym JMO;   susteyned him strongliche] And but 3if þe Spirite · Supporte hym and borowe hym J, And bot if þe goste supporte hym MO;   as ... hep] he schulde be J.   3303 he shulde be] as a dunge hepe J;   ne] and JO;   neuere] he scholde J;   shulde he] neuere J, *trs.* S.   3304 Lady] *prec. Capitulum* xliij *mar.* CG;   now] *om.* J;   I aske] *om* J;   and] *om.* JS;   I²] *om.* MOS;   pray] *om.* S;   yow] *om.* S;   how] telle me now J;   is it] *om.* JS, *trs.* MO;   þat] *om.* JS.   3305 withinne] in the body J;   so] *om.* J;   and he] *with* scilicet body *twice mar.* G³, that es JMO, for he S.   3306 withoute] with Inne S;

thinketh] thynk MO;   bettere] bere *add.* S;   þat²] it J;   þat is] be MO, þane
þat þat is S;   contened] *om.* JMO.   3307 and¹ ... berere] And bett*er* me thynk
þat þe berer*e o. er.* O³;   me] (*2nd* e *ins.* G³);   thinketh] thynke that the JMO,
semeþe might beo S;   and²] the *add.* J, *om.* O;   susteynour] es *add.* JMO (*mar.
with rub. caret in text* O).   3307-8 þat þat is] *ins. mar.* O.   3308 þilke¹]
that JMO;   þilke²] þat JM, þat þat O.   3309 him] *om.* M;   Now] *prec.*
Capitulum xliv *mar.* C;   Vndyrstand J;   vnderstonde] nowe J;   she] i*d est*
resou*n over* C;   *with* scilicet *resou*n *mar.* G³.   3310 cloþinge] (e *ins.* G³);
it] is O.   3311 withinne] it bot *add.* J;   woldest] wolde JMO;   make] (*2nd*
a *ins.* G³);   if] and J.   3312 bere] beere (*2nd* e *ins.* G³) G, -s MO;
gouerned] gou*er*nede (de *ins.* G³) G, gou*er*nys MO;   þee] (*1st* e *ins.* G³);   þus]
em. ed., quod she *add.* CGJMOS.   3313 quod she] *with* scilicet Resou*n mar.*
G³, Bot in this J;   but þis in] quod Scho J, bot in þis MO;   difference] I Sette
J.   3313-4 I sette] the J.   3314 þee] difference J;   soule] bath *add.* J;
and] eeke *add.* S;   She] *with* scilicet soule *mar.* G³.   3315 but] not M;
he] *with* scilicet body *mar.* G³, the body J;   accident] auccidence J;   him] *with*
scilicet sawle *mar.* G³, the sawle J.   3316 him to] *trs.* JMO;   his] is M;
vertu] his M;   is] vert*u* M;   entendaunt] A good si*m*milly · reade *mar.* O³;
If] ᴣuye (*with* ᴣyff *mar.* G³) G;   euere] þowe sawe J;   þou seye] euere J.
3317 gouerne] Schippe J;   a ship] gou*er*ned J, shipp*e* O;   leede] ledde JMO;
þou] -h C;   mihtest] myght JMO;   take] (*2nd* a *ins.* G³).   3318 ensaumple]
an ensa*u*mple C, sample O;   gouernayle] gou*er*naunce JMO.   3319 withinne]
demisel *mar.* O³;   ledeth] gou*er*nit it and ledeth J, *om.* S;   it¹] *with* schippe
mar. G³, *om.* S;   and¹] *om.* S;   so] *om.* S;   led] it es J, *om.* S;   it is] ledde
J, *om.* S;   and leedeth] and it ledeth J, *ins. mar.* O³, *om.* S.   3320 for ...
withinne] *om.* S;   it] *with* scilicet schyp *mar.* G³, and *add.* S;   his] þe S;
wolde not] it self S.   3321 leede] ledeþe S;   him] it S.   3322 ledeth]
leedeth (*1st* e *ins.* G³) G;   ledinge] leedynge (*1st* e *ins.* G³) G;   so] scho J, *om.*
O.   3322-3 Þe ... it] *om.* JMO.   3323 his] *with* scilicet soule *mar.* G³;
and] wonderfull are þe workes / of þe Lord. & his wayes / paste finding out. *mar.*
O³;   þat] *ins.* O³;   she] schee (*2nd* e *ins.* G³) G, consentis O;   concenteth]
she O.   3324 bere²] beere (*3rd* e *ins.* G³) G.   3325 peyne] pyne S.
3326 ledinge] legynge J;   mowe] might S;   lede] leede (*1st* e *ins.* G³) G, *om.*
S;   þee] (*1st* e *ins.* G³);   hauene] (*2nd* a *ins.* G³), heuene J;   þe] thy JM.
3327 Ladi] *prec. Capitulum* xlv *mar.* CG;   certeynliche] *om.* JMOS;   speche]
speeche (*1st* e *ins.* G³) G.   3328 me] (*2nd* e *ins.* G³);   riht] *om.* M;   If]
and J.   3329 þat] as to enfou*r*me me redily as S;   me¹] (*2nd* e *ins.* G³),
om. S;   of¹] out CJM (*o. er. with er. mar.* C), *om.* O, by þensaumple S;   my]
þe S;   ship] shap C, nef F;   dispoiled] spuled J;   þe] my JMO.
3330 me] (*2nd* e *ins.* G³), *om.* M;   þilke¹,²] that JMO;   vnthrift] blyndenesse
S;   blynde] vnthrifft S.   3331 be] *om.* J.   3332 fynde] sooþe *add.*
S.   3333 þat¹] For that J;   drede] dreede (*2nd* e *ins.* G³)G, doute J;   þat
ye ne] þat ne ᴣe J, þen ᴣhe M, but þat ye O;   but] for *add.* J.   3334 ne] and
MO.   3335 pray] preye (*2nd* e *ins.* G³) G;   me] (*2nd* e *ins.* G³).
3336 And] *prec. Capitulum* xlvj *mar.* CG;   seide] vnto me *add.* J, me *add.* S;
riht] Reason *mar.* O³, *om.* S;   wel] quod Scho *add.* JS.   3337 litel] þou
vnderstandis me J, *om.* O;   þou ... me] litille J;   wost þou] woste G, wat þou
JMO;   It is] *om.* J.   3338 maketh] (*2nd* a *ins.* G³);   bifore] the *add.*
J.   3339 he] it JMO;   þee] *om.* M.   3340 it¹] me JS, *om.* MO;   do
it] *with* scilicet body *mar.* G³;   of] can. O³, to S.   3341 do] *om.* JMO;
me] (*2nd* e *ins.* G³).   3341-2 for ... hadde] *om.* J.   3342 do] *om.* O;

Algates] Neuer*þeles* J;   trusse him ayen] the muste nedes J, trusse him S.
3343 þou shalt] (t *ins*. G³), & *add*. C, & *add*. *ins*. G³, trus hym ageyne J, *om*. MO,
ageyne *add* S;   moste] *om*. J, þou must MO, most þee S;   and] *om*. C;   haue]
(*2nd* a *ins*. G³) G.   3344 my] þy S;   him] *with* s*cilicet* body *mar*. G³;
þee] *with* soule *mar*. G³.   3345 make] (*2nd* a *ins*. G³);   forberinge] for bere
J;   oon] oo GJM (j *over* G³), þi O;   sool] a *add*. *ins*. O³;   þis] it JMO.
3346 ofte] of J;   take] þou *add*. JMO.   3347 on¹] *om*. O;   þat] the ta J;
þis] the to*þere* J;   entende] luke *þou* tente J;   nouht] *om*. JMO.
3348 þider] Take hede howe dame Raysoune sette honde on þe pilgryme and he
abaundonne*þe* him to hir *add*. S;   And] *prec*. C*apitulum* xlvii *mar*. CG, {cap-
itulum} vij *mar*. S;   sette] putte J;   to] vn to J, to to O, on S;   I] *om*. J.
3349 putte] (e *ins*. G³);   me] (*2nd* e *ins*. G³), hooly *add*. S;   She] *with* s*cilicet*
Resou*n mar*. G³;   I] *with* s*cilicet* pylgrym *mar*. G³;   we] (*2nd* e *ins*. G³), sheo
S.   3350 she] *om*. S;   contracte] *with* s*cilicet* body *mar*. G³.
3351 vntrussed] I was thus J;   þus I was] vntrussed J.   3352 Me] (*2nd* e *ins*.
G³);   þat] *om*. S;   nothing] I weied J;   I weyede] na thynge J.
3353 and¹] *om*. JMO;   fer] for MO.   3354 as] *om*. JMO;   was] it was JMO,
þat \it/ was S;   heled] hilled S;   ne] *om*. JMO, ? *can*. S.   3355 Gladed]
(*2nd* a *ins*. G³);   gretliche] and bot *add*. J, but *add*. *can*. O;   mislikede me]
(mee *1st* e *ins*. G³), anely J;   oonliche] mysliked me J.   3355-6 I moste] me
muste JMO, þer Inne S.   3356 þerinne] *with* s*cilicet* body *mar*. G³, in habite
J;   enhabite] inhabite (*with* enhabite *mar*. G³) G, þerin J;   and¹] *om*. O;
herberwe] herbege *ins*. *mar*. *after rub*. *caret also in text* O;   nothing] litell J;
or] other GS.   3357 litel] nathynge J;   þe] *om*. J;   empecehment]
impediment JMO.   3358 al] *om*. JM. and *can*. O;   me] *with* truly *mar*. O³.
For *add*. J.   3359 to preise] it was nathynge J;   it was nothing] to p*r*ayse
J.   3360 oo] i *over* G³, oone OS;   but] ʒif *add*. JM.   3361 doon] born*e*
J;   streiht it lay] streit it lay (*with* streighte *mar*. G³) G, thare JS;   þere] streight
it lay J, streight it lay where S.   3362 seigh] it sawe JO;   tokne] token (*with*
tokne *mar*. G³) G;   no ... him] he had J.   3362-3 he hadde] na vertue in hym
J.   3363 sooth] the Soth JMOS, mon F.   3364 aslepe] on slepe JMO;
pouce] -s C, pounse O;   wite] ʒe *add*. J;   nouht] now*þere* J.   3365 in¹]
can. M;   ne¹] *om*. M;   condyt ne in] *ins*. *mar*. *after rub*. *caret also in text* O³;
veyne] -s S;   stike] stykie blast of wynde (stykie *subpuncted, cross over*) G, blast
of wynd CS, st*r*are J, straw MO, tronc F.   3366 in] a *add*. subpuncted G, *om*.
JMO;   It was nouht] was þere nane J, it was M;   I ... wel] *om*. M;   Fy] *om*.
MO.   3366-7 on ... after] *om*. M.   3367 doinges] dunges C, doynge J, dong
O, maintien F.   3368 Whan] *prec*. C*apitulum* xlviij CG;   considered al þat]
al considerd · þat S;   after] -wardes J, -ward O, *om*. S;   arened] hade anfou*r*med
S.   3369 þou seest] *om*. J;   wel] *om*. JS;   þou²] knawth J.
3370 knowest] þou J;   þee] (*1st* e *ins*. G³).   3371 endure] to endure JM;
þilke] He JMO.   3372 þee¹] *ins*. *mar*. G³, *om*. MO;   yildeth þee] yildeth þe
C, (*2nd* e *ins*. G³), makes the to ʒelde the J, ʒeldis þe MO, yeldeþe S;   venquised]
venquisch J;   þilke] He JMO.   3373 empecheth] letteʒ JMO;   clymbe] flye
on hye J;   flee an hy] clymbe J, fleeghe vp on hy S;   haue] (*2nd* a *ins*. G³).
3374 þee¹] *om*. JMO;   inowh] here of JMO;   heerof] marked *mar*. C³, I nowe
JMO;   bifore] *om*. S;   suffice] to Suffice JS, suffre O;   þee²] (*1st* e *ins*.
G³);   so] *om*. J.   3375 michel] *om*. J;   Withinne him] bot nowe *þou* schalle
entre agayne J, with in MO;   þou moste entre] in telle hym and J;   charge] (*2nd*
a *ins*. G³), the with *add*. J.   3376 ayen] and *add*. J;   into¹] in J;   into²]
om. J.   3377 pilgrimage] Reson techis þ*at* þe pilg*r*ime may nouʒt bere þe armo*u*r.

for þe birthyn of his flessh. *add. rub.* M;   Ladi] *prec. Capitulum* xlix *mar.* CG, *capitulum* v *rub. mar.* M;   entencioun] entente J;   my] myne (-ne *subpuncted*) G.   3378 þat[1]] Forto J;   with þe armure] arme me J;   I armede me] with the arm*our* J;   þat[2]] for to J;   þus] *om.* J;   I wente] wende J.   3379 for[1]] *om.* J;   bere] preoue S;   þus] armed *add.* J;   me] (*2nd* e *ins.* G[3]). 3380 thinketh] thynke JMO.   3381 weyen] hic sup*er* corp*ore* portat arma *rub. mar.* O.   3382 þus] þou CO, *om.* J;   þou[1]] þus CO;   no merite] have na mede ne J.   3383 haue] (*2nd* a *ins.* G[3]), na meritte J;   on[2]] *om.* JMO; þi contracte] (þin C), *with* s*ci*l*ice*t b*o*dy *mar.* G[3].   3384 ouhte] hy*m add.* J; susteyne] to susteyne JS;   wele] welþe *o. er. with er. mar.* C, bien F.   3385 at[1]] the laste *add.* J;   goode] (e *ins.* G[3]);   parte] departe JMO, partir F;   haue] (*2nd* a *ins.* G[3]);   wele] welþe *o. er. with er. mar.* C;   þe] *om.* M.   3386 of whiche] that J;   he] *om.* O;   be] *om.* J, þer of S;   þerof] thare JMO; parcenere] p*er*ceyu*er*e C, pa*r*seneer G, at the depa*r*tynge J, at partyng MO, p*er*seuerer S, parconnier F;   Now] Trusse hy*m* J.   3386-7 trusse him] nowe J. 3387 ayen[2]] *om.* CO;   sithe] Syne JMO;   entende] buske the J. 3388 Whan] *prec. Capitulum* lj *mar.* CG;   she] *with* s*ci*l*ice*t resou*n mar.* G[3]; me[1]] *om.* J;   þis] thus JMS.   3389 miht] that *add.* J, mirthe S;   and] alle JM, and all O;   whiche] (e *subpuncted* G).   3390 rejoycede] reioyed MO; oo[1]] O GS, as wha J, of MO;   for to] *om.* J;   oo[2]] a J, oon MS. 3391 cloudy] *om.* J;   cloude] þere es nane *add.* J;   whiche] þe whiche CS; noon] noo CS, nul F.   3392 cleer-seeinge] se and þey clerely J;   Þilke] That JMO.   3393 bimeene] beo þe meene S.   3394 and] to thenk *add.* S; þat[2]] at JMO.   3395 apperceyued] p*er*sayfed JMO;   afterward] -es J; shulde] wolde C;   be] so *add.* S.   3396 disceyued] *twice, 1st can.* M;   and[1]] *om.* OS.   3397 Þou] *om.* JMO;   þou] I J.   3398 tweyne] *marked for gloss* G[3], twa JMO;   shalt] þou M;   þou] I J, shall M;   And] *prec. Capitulum* lij *mar.* CG;   seide me] seyde mee (*3rd* e *ins.* G[3]) G, resou*n*e J;   Resoun] Sayde vnto me J.   3399 þee] quod seho and *add.* J;   þou] so *add.* JMO;   longeth] and p*er*tineʒ *add.* M.   3400 becometh] es nouʒt Semande ne be co*m*meth þame J;   seyde] Answerde J.   3401 hire] *om.* J;   Heerfore] quod I *add.* J, therfor O;   withinne] in JMO.   3402 hadde] *om.* JMO.   3403 haue] (*2nd* a *ins.* G[3]), to haue J;   tweyne] oþere twa J, two MO.   3404 skyes] clowdes J; hyere] heyere (*1st* e *subpuncted*) C;   or] other G;   egret] Egle JMO, grues F.   3405 vnderstood] vnderstonde S;   Now] bot J, Bot now M;   game] (*2nd* a *ins.* G[3]).   3406 ayenward] ayend ward C;   haue] (*2nd* a *ins.* G[3]). 3407 me[1,2,3]] (*2nd* e *ins.* G[3]).   3408 whiche] þe which O;   resiste] ageyne stande JM.   3409 haue] (*2nd* a *ins.* G[3]);   lost] i lost G.   3410 where] (h *ins.* G[3]);   ne] *om.* JMO;   of] as JMO;   þilke] a thynge J, þat thyng MO; þat] es *add.* J, þe O;   quik] whilk O.   3411 into þe eerþe] flowene J, is flowyn O;   is flowen] in to the erth JO;   is[2]] that es JO;   to] tille J, vn til S; blok] clogge JMO;   is[3]] so es J.   3412 atached] taithed J, tachid M, festynd O;   he[1]] *ins.* G[3];   may not] ne may MO;   stye] clymbe J;   hy] height JMO;   þat[2]] þan M, but þat O;   in styinge] ne in clymbynge J;   he ne cometh (he *ins. mar.* G[3]), he co*m*meth JMO.   3413 soone] (*2nd* o *ins.* G[3]);   is] it is MS, is it O;   me] (*2nd* e *ins.* G[3]);   blok] clogge JMO.   3414 me] (*2nd* e *ins.* G[3]) G;   wolde] will JMO.   3415 me[1]] (*2nd* e *ins.* G[3]) G, *om.* J; me[2]] (*2nd* e *ins.* G[3]) G;   thinketh] thynke JM.   3416 I] corp*us* quod sorum peccat*orum* aggra*u*at ani*m*am *rub. mar.* O;   ago] gane Seyne J, agone O;   which] the which O.   3417 and[1]] *om.* J.   3418 he] *o. er. with er. mar.* C;   am I] I am *ins. mar.* G[3], *om.* CJMOS, sui je F.   3419 so holden] and O;   serued]

followed by otiose caret G³;   þouh] 3if J, þat MO;   in] *om.* J.
3420 weepinge] I wepande J;   I sey] Say J.   3422 Thanne] *prec. Capitulum*
liij *mar.* CG, Sees thow J;   seide] quod J;   Seest þou] than J;   quod she]
om. J;   wel] *om.* JMO.   3422-3 I haue] (*2nd a ins.* G), of no thyng MO.
3423 of nothing] gabbedde the J, I haue M, *om.* O;   gabbed þee] of nathynge J,
I gabbys þe O;   þe] ne the J, þi M;   of] in J, for O.   3424 þe] *om.* JM;
þou] that þou J;   woldest] schalte J, wolde MO.   3425 yelde] it *add.* JM;
seith] I Praye 3owe Say me J, say 3he MO;   oo] oon MS;   he] *with scilicet* body
mar. G³.   3426 I am] I name S.   3427 miht] may JMO.   3429 Eche]
Ilke a J, Everych O;   on] in M;   dung-hep] dunghylle JS.   3430-1 tristeth
... and¹] *om.* J.   3430 tristeth] triste M;   He] *with scilicet* body *mar.* G³;
on] vpone S.   3432 ayens] agayn M;   þe¹] Noat *mar.* O³.   3433 if] and
J;   in ooþer places] þou hadde hym J, in odir place MO;   þou haddest him] in
other place J;   þi] -n M.   3434 strongere] than he *add.* J, þer for *add.* S;
mown] *can.* O.   3435 withsitte] withsett MO, withstonde S;   ne ... þee¹] *om.*
S;   þee²] (*1st e ins.* G³);   þus] this JMO.   3436 þee] (*1st e ins.* G³);
þou ne] *trs.* J.   3437 and] ne M;   supplaunte] marked *mar.* C³;   wult]
wille JMO;   upon] euene vp on hym on J.   3438 dung-hep] dunghille J;
if ... of] assayle him or pley with him at S;   þe cheker] (ch *o. er. with erased* cheker
u.v. mar. C³), þeschesses S;   shalt] schalle JM;   make] (*2nd a ins.* G³), seye
to S.   3439 and] *om.* JMO;   make he] (*2nd a ins.* G³), and þer fore make
S.   3440 drinkinge] drynke J;   trauaile] good J, -s MO;   goode] weell (*with*
goode *mar.* G³) GMOS (*ins. mar. after rub. mark also in text* O³).
3441 weylinges] wepynges J, wakynges O.   3442 penaunce] (*2nd e ins.* G³),
-s S;   shulen] shulden CS;   þee] (*1st e ins.* G³).   3443 þei] that J;
shulen] schalle J, do þee right and *add.* S;   make] (*2nd a ins.* G³);   of] to J,
om. MO;   þee²] *om.* MO;   wule] *om.* JMO;   he] *with scilicet* body *mar.* G³,
om. JMO.   3444 oþer] *om.* JMO, or S;   noon] *om.* JMO;   he is] þou has
JMO;   adaunted] dauntyd hym JMO.   3445 shalt] schalle JM;   mown]
om. J;   arme] (*2nd a ins.* G³);   armures] the armour JO, armour M;   to seyn]
I Say the J.   3446 hast] (*2nd a ins.* G³), hafe J, has MO.   3447 þat¹] that
add. JMO;   so] to mekille J, to O;   slugged] Sluggy J.   3448 þat] dame
add. S;   þee¹] *om.* J;   Ladi] *prec. Capitulum* liv *mar.* CG.   3449 certeyn-
liche] *om.* OS;   first] *can.* O;   it] *om.* C.   3450 vnderstood] vnderstand
(*marked for correction* G³) G;   it¹] *om.* MO;   al were it] þof all M;   she spak]
grace dieu *mar.* G³;   me] to me JMOS;   bodi] the flesh, is contrary / to the
spirit. *mar.* O³.   3451 it¹] *with* body *mar.* G³;   al oon] al loone S;   Bi yow]
the soth O.   3451-2 þe sooþe] by you O.   3452 þat] *om.* JMO;   haue]
(*2nd a ins.* G³);   Certeyn] Sekerly J, Certe ne S.   3453 al þe sooþe] by hir
J;   bi hire] *with scilicet* grace dieu *mar.* G³, þou myght haue wittene J;   þou
...wist] all the sothe J, þou myght haue wist MO, þowe mightest knowe and haue
weel wist S.   3454 haddest] had JMO;   al] *om.* CGS, tout F.   3455 me]
of mee ne (*1st e ins.*, ne *can.* G³) G, were S;   were] of me S.   3456 hire]
with grace *mar.* G³;   clepe] calle JMO.   3457 is] *om.* J, þat it is S;   woldest]
walde JMO.   3458 amys] anes J;   make] (*2nd a ins.* G³), gerre J;   þee²]
(*1st e ins.* G³);   go] to go S;   anooþer] (*2nd o ins.* G³).   3459 And] *ins.*
mar. after rub. mark also in text O³;   suppose] sppose (*with* suppose *mar.* G³)
G, I Suppose JMO, I *add.* S;   sumtime] 3if *add.* J, he souffre þee S;   he suffre
þee] he suffreth thee GMO, some tyme S;   bi] *om.* JMOS;   þere] whare JMO,
as *add.* S.   3460 þat] *om.* J;   slough] slow (*with* slowgh *mar.* G³) G, thowe
schalle Fynde hym J, þowe slowe S;   þou ... him] (hym *with scilicet* body *mar.*

G³), slawe J.   3461 slugged] slugginge C, Sluggy J, sluggyssh MO;   he] *with*
body *mar.* G³;   upon] vp JMO.   3462 at þe mete] þou hase Sette hym J;
þou ... him] (hym *with* body *mar.* G³), atte the mete J;   he wole] *trs.* J.
3463 Al] thynge *add.* J;   he wole] *trs.* J;   make] (*2nd a ins.* G³);   þee] (*1st*
e *ins.* G³).   3464 lettinges] lettynge JMO;   wel kunne] *trs.* MOS.
3465 and] *preceded in error by caret which should follow it* G³, *ins. mar. after rub.*
mark also in text O³;   þou ... keep] thanne wha*n*n thow schallt taak no keepe *ins.*
mar. G (*see note*);   þou] þanne CG³S, *subpuncted* G;   þanne] whan CG³S,
schalle JMO;   shalt] þou shalt CG³S, *cross over* G, than JMO;   take] *cross over*
G;   no] *cross over* G, *om.* O;   gret] *om.* CG³S, *cross over* G;   keep] *cross*
over G.   3466 but] *om.* CG³S, *subpuncted* G;   þee²] *om.* J.
3467 warde] (*2nd a ins.* G³), word O;   nouht triste] *trs.* J;   þee²] *om.* J;
ne] *om.* JMO.   3468 flateryes] flaterynge JMO;   dost] wate JMO.
3469 him] *with* scilicet body *mar.* G³.   3470 werreth] varreyes O;   þee²] (*1st*
e *ins.* G³).   3471 haue] (*2nd a ins.* G³).   3472 to þee] *om.* S;   miht]
maye J;   þilke] þat JM, *om.* O;   þat] *om.* O;   þi] -n M.   3473 suffreth]
ne souffre S.   3474 armure] Howe þat þe pilgryme thankeþe dame Raysoun of
hir doctryne *add.* S.   3475 Ladi] *prec. Capitulum* lvj *mar.* CG, Capi*tulum* v{iij}
mar. S;   yilde] it *add.* S.   3476 is] right *add.* J;   haue] (*2nd a ins.* G³);
distincted] distinged JMO.   3477 alwey] he is J, -s S;   he is] alle waye J.
3478 goodes] good CJ;   wole] wolde CS.   3479 alwey] haue S;   haue] (*2nd*
a *ins.* G³), alwey S.   3480 wolde] that *add.* JMOS;   to þe citee] *with* me J;
with me] to the cetee J.   3480-3 where ... me] *om.* CGS.   3480 where]
whither J, þer MO.   3481 to] *om.* J.   3482 paas] pathes J.   3483 if]
and J;   ye²] it JMO.   3484 þat¹] *om.* J;   yow] *om.* M;   þat²] *om.* S;
bi] ȝif it be ȝoure J.   3485 Grace Dieu] *prec. Capitulum* lvij *mar.* CG;   ȝif
þowe J;   quod she] *with* scilicet Resoun *mar.* G³;   if ... hire] (haaue *1st* a *ins.*
G³), hafe Grace dieu J.   3486 wel] the J;   haue] (*2nd a ins.* G³).
3487 Nouht] þat O;   I²] ne J.   3488 ne] I J;   þee¹] *with* resoun *mar.*
G³;   I ... þee²] *om.* CJMOS, *can.* G;   sithe] Sene JO, sithen M;   wolt] couetȝ
J.   3489 telle] wille telle J;   tweye] twa JMO, tweyne S.   3490 oþer¹]
or JMO, and O;   arisen] rysande J, ryse M, rysiour O;   oþer²] or JM, *om.* O;
oþer³] or JMO;   I] *with* resoun *mar.* G³.   3491 þee] and *add. ins. mar.*
G³;   see] *ins. mar.* G³;   me] see *add. can.* G.   3492 derkliche] & *add.*
C;   þou shalt] *trs.* J.   3493 litel] mekille JMO;   michel] litil JMO;
cleerliche] schalle þou See me J, *om.* M;   þou ... me] (mee *1st* e *ins.* G³), clerely
J;   wel] *om.* JMO.   3494 apertliche] *om.* JMO;   þou] es that þou J;
þou shalt] *trs.* J, reason the hand mayd / to grace *mar.* O³;   me] *om.* M.
3495 algates] neu*er*þeles J;   hast] haue JMO.   3496 if] and J;   me¹] (*2nd*
e *ins.* G³), *om.* O;   Now] Gae J.   3497 alwey] nowe J;   go] always J;
hast] (*2nd* a *ins.* G³);   to²] *om.* J.   3498 not] to *add. ins.* O³.   3499 And]
prec. Capitulum lviij *mar.* CG, *om.* M;   þanne] *o. er.* M;   thankinge] I thankyd
J, thankid I MO;   goodshipes] and *add.* JMO.
3500 upon] on JMO;   foorth] to wende J;   to go] forth J;   Ofte] tymes *add.*
J;   *prec. capitulum* vj *rub. mar.* M.   3501 al¹] *om.* J;   she¹] resoune J;
aperceyued] p*er*sayued JMO, in our earthly pilg*ri*mage / the flesh, our greatest / Enemy
and dymms / the sight of the sowle *mar.* O³, weel *add.* S.   3502 Seelden] seelde
GS;   I²] *om.* J.   3503 hire] *with* resoun *mar.* G³.   3504 tweyne] twa
JMO;   neiþer] pilgrym *mar.* G³.   3505 cite] þat *add.* JM.   3506 I¹]
with pylgrym *mar.* G³;   thinke] Suppose JS.   3506 haue] (*2nd a ins.* G³),
mekille *add.* J;   to] at J;   fynde] hym *add.* J.   3507 þilke¹] *om.* J, hym

MO; haue] (*2nd* a *ins.* G³); softe] maste loued and J, moste MO; norished] enorysshed S; me] (*2nd* e *ins.* G³); thinketh] thynke JMO; þilke²] he JMO. 3508 neuere] ne *add. can.* G; not] *om.* J; despyte] Wille Crane *follows* C³. 3509 Thus] *prec. Capitulum* lix *mar.* CG; as] *om.* JMOS, comme F; wente] furched waye *add.* J; studiede] I Studied and at the laste J, I studyed MO, hic caro cogit peregrinum deuiare *rub. mar.* O. 3510 fourched] disseuerede C, varyed M; twey] twa JMO. 3511 it seemede] for the tane J, to me *add.* O; þat oon] Semed bot a litille J, *om.* O, þat S; ooþer] bot litill *add.* MO. 3512 bitwixe] tham *add.* J, þe *add. ins.* O³, hem *add.* S; an hegge] on height JO; wunderful] -ly J; þat] *om.* J, þar *o. er.* O; was] *om.* J. 3513 set] an hegge *add.* JO, on heght M; streighte] streyt (*with* streighte *mar.* G³) G, and *add.* J; þerinne] þer nine C, booþe *add.* S. 3514 and] of J; bramberes] brembeles JS; bushes thorny] *trs.* S; prikkes] ware *add.* J, þei wer *add.* MO; thikke] *om.* JMO. 3515 thikke] they JO, þei wer M; entermedled] entermelled JS; oon] j *over* G³. 3516 it] *can.* C, *om.* JO; half¹] of the hegge *add.* J; riht] lifft S. 3517 oo wey] j *over* G³; they hadde be bathe bot J, an weye MS; it were] a waye J, it was M; if] and of M, þogh O; amidde] a myd (*with* a mydde *mar.* G³) G, hadde nouȝt bene J, in myddis M, in þe myddys (ij ways *mar.* O³) O; ne were] by twene þam J, was nouȝt M, were noght O; On] *prec. Capitulum* lx *mar.* CG. 3518 side] halfe J; gentelwomman] gengyll womman G. 3519 oon] a J. 3520 vsede pleyinge] (*2nd* e *ins.* G³), whyrled abowte hire fyngere J. 3520-1 aboute hire fynger] playande hir J. 3521 it¹ ... it²] *o.er.* C; in and out] *ins. mar. after rub. caret also in text* O³. 3522 nouht of] of na JMO; care] (*2nd* a *ins.* G³). 3523 rouht] scho J; hire] rought J, labor *rub. mar.* O; or] other GS; to laboure] of J, any *add.* S; ooþer] *om.* MO; labour] -s J, *om.* MO. 3524 On] *prec. Capitulum* ixj *mar.* CG, In J; on] of JOS; a makere-ayen] maakere (*2nd* a *2nd* e *ins.* G³) G, I Sawe Sit J; of mattes] of maites C, a bichere J, of old mattes MO. 3524-5 and arayour] and an arayor G, or areparalere J, *ins. mar. after rub. mark also in text* O³, *om.* S. 3525 I sigh sitte] of mattes J, I sigh M, *om.* S; þat] *om.* S; arayede] bocched J, *om.* S; and] *om.* S; made] (*2nd* a *ins.* G³), *om.* S; hise] *om.* S; olde] (e *ins.* G³), *om.* S. 3526 mattes] *om.* S; whereof] of which S; abashed] I was JS; I was] a baist J, more abaysshed S. 3527 al] *om.* J; tobreke] breke it J; sithe] Syne JMO; araye] (e *ins.* G³). 3528 thouht] thowth (*with* thowghte *mar.* G³) G; a fool] he schulde be J; he was] a foole J; no ... him] he had J. 3528-9 he hadde] na witte in hym J. 3529 but] for JMO; a fool] I was; I was] a ful J, he was MOS. 3530 aperceyuede] persayued JMO; sithe] Syne JMO; first] to hym JS; to him] *with* matter *mar.* G³, first J. 3531 it was] that he ware J; me¹] (*2nd* e *ins.* G³), nouȝt JMO; not] leue J, me M, to me O; leeuest] to me J; and] tille I *add.* J; him] *om.* J; me²] (*2nd* e *ins.* G³). 3532 which] whedyr J; þese] thir J; neuere] are *add.* J. 3533 heerbi] here a waye J; bi] JMO; which] waye *add.* JM. 3534 woldest] walde JMO; rihtliche] ryght JMO; Go] I walde J; quod I] ga J, quod he S; I wule] quod I J, I wold MO; ouer see] *om.* JMO; ouer þe see S. 3535 into] to J; of²] in MO; bisshop] kynge J; is] was J. 3536 maide] -ene JMO; quod he] *with* scilicet matter *mar.* G³, right *add.* JMO; heer for] Heerfore C; rihtliche] ryght euen J. 3537 Right] *om.* JMO; me] (*2nd* e *ins.* G³); þe² ... wey²] begynnes J; innocence] innocentes MO; and] *om.* O. 3538 biginneth] the waye of innocence and the euen waye J; miht] may JMO. 3539 see] the See JMOS; quod I]

264   ÞE LYFE OF ÞE MANHODE

with pylgrim *mar.* G³;   if] whedere J.   3540 seist] Sayse JMO, hast sayde
S;   is] be JMOS;   seith] shewys O;   litel wit] thare es J, lytel what S.
3541 in þee] litelle wit J;   þer is] in the J;   see] that *add.* JMO.   3542 craft]
werk M;   vndoost] vndose JMO.   3543 wel doon] *trs.* S;   makest] (*2nd*
a *ins.* G³), maketh JMO;   it] efte *add.* J;   thinketh] thynk M.   3545 And]
prec. Capitulum lxiij *mar.* CG, *om.* JMO;   answerde me] he J, answerid he
MOS;   thilke] aunswerde me J, me MO, me þus S;   of poore craft] I q*u*od he
be J;   I be] of pouer crafte J.   3546 no] na resonable J, nou3t MO;   blame]
(*2nd* a *ins.* G³);   argue] repreove S;   Eche] Ilke JM, Euerych O.
3547 wiht] man J, ne *add.* S.   3547-9 Oon ... not] *om.* JMO.   3548 oo]
i *over* G³, oon S;   anoober¹] haþe *add.* S;   anoober²] crafft *add.* S;   þat þat]
þat S.   3549 alle] (e *ins.* G³), folkes *add.* S;   oo] a J;   pooreliche] thay
schulde J;   þei shulden] pouerly J.   3550 þe] þat JMO;   is] men haue
S.   3551 ofte] types *add.* J;   more] maste JS;   þilke] that JMO.
3552 riche] grete J;   gret] riche J;   bi þat ooþer] is maynteyned J;   is
meyntened] by the tothere J;   and²] *om.* MO.   3553 neuer oon] *with* s*cilicet*
kraft *mar.* G³, na crafte J;   þat is] *om.* J;   wikked] euylle J;   but þat] 3if JMO,
so be þat S.   3554 be] the greatest trade least / needfull *mar.* O³;   thurt]
thruste C, þat OS.   3554-5 but ... idel] of whate crafte that a man ware J.
3554 þe] a M.   3555 whereuere he be] So þat he ware nou3t ydel J;   poore]
no*ta mar.* G³O³.   3556 idel] -nes JMOS;   court] þe moost ryal S;   ryal]
court S;   breke] my mattes *add.* S;   make] (*2nd* a *ins.* G³), hem *add.* S.
3556-7 to þat ende] soo þat S.   3557 idel] wher euer he bee more is worth
ocupacioun honest þanne ydelnesse *add.* S;   þerfore] blame me M;   blame me]
þerfore M.   3558 if] *om.* J;   hadde] none *add.* J;   me] (*2nd* e *ins.* G³);
tobreke] breke J;   haue] (*2nd* a *ins.* G³);   make] (*2nd* a *ins.* G³).
3560 haue] haaude (*2nd* a *ins.* G³) G;   nouht] elles *add.* J.   3561 rente]
reende S;   made] it *add.* CJMOS (*ins.* C);   suffice] to Suffice JMOS.
3562 to þi rihtes] ariht CJ, *with* a Ryghtes *mar.* G³, to þi right O, a ton droit F;
Loue] *prec. Capitulum* lxiv *mar.* CG, *marked mar.* C³, Luffed the J;   And] *om.*
JMO;   who] wheyne J.   3563 whennes] wheyne J;   þee] to the JS.
3564 thinketh] thynke JM, semeþe S;   mihten] myghte (e *ins.* G³) G;   a] grete
add. J.   3565 yeue] gave J;   þee¹] (*1st* e *ins.* G³);   my] myn (n *subpuncted*)
G;   but] 3if *add.* JMO;   ooþerweys] bettere J, odirwyse MOS.   3566 and]
nyce *add.* J;   preysest] prayseth JMO;   þe] *om.* J.   3567 þee] (*1st* e *ins.*
G³).   3568 maad] maade (*2nd* a *ins.* G³) G;   it] þis C;   þat] *can. and*
*subpuncte*d O.   3569 reste] ydelnesse *can. rub. and subpuncted* O;   and] it
add. ins. C;   were] better J;   bettere] ware it J.   3570 oon] 1 *over* G³, a
man J, an olde man M;   holde] to halde J, be M, (h *ins.* O¹³);   werche] to dyke
J;   or] other G;   diche] delfe or oþere werkes do J, according to þe flesh *mar.*
O³.   3571 þou shalt] *trs.* J;   holde] (*2nd* o *ins.* G³).   3572 sweete] (*2nd*
e *ins.* G³);   frend] quod he wel *add.* S;   me²] (*2nd* e *ins.* G³);   thinketh]
thynke JMO;   and] wel *add.* S.   3573 also] *om.* S;   Oiseuce] ydelshipe
CJM, *with* ydelscipe *mar.* G³, ydilesse O.   3574 I] *with* s*cilicet* mattere G³;
þee] quod he *add.* J.   3575 and ... resoun] *marked mar.* O³, *om.* S;   cleer]
clene J, forged and fourbisshed S.   3576 and foorbushed] furbisched J, cleer
S;   waxeth rusty] resteþe S;   foul] wexeþe foule S;   not] *ins.* M;   alwey]
om. J, alweys stille S.   3577 so] *om.* O;   quod I] *with* s*cilicet* pilgrym *mar.*
G³;   seidest] sayes MOS.   3578 me] (*2nd* e *ins.* G³);   haue] (*2nd* a *ins.*
G³), do J;   þilke] that JMO.   3579 þou hast] *trs.* J;   Serteyn] -ly J;
quod he] *with* s*cilicet* mattere G³.   3580 so] *om.* M;   þe] *om.* J;   men] *om.*

O.   3581 þe man] also M.   3582 also] *om.* J, þe man M;   ruste] ne rouste
S.   3583 vice] *-es* O.   3584 þat] it J.   3585 of] or O;   Þis] *with*
scilicet labou*ur mar.* G³, it J;   and] *om.* O.   3586 and] a *add.* CMS, *om.* J;
filour] *om.* J, Loo heere howe þe pilgryme raysouneþe ageynst þe matte maker of
his teechinges and seyinges *add.* S.   3587 I¹] *prec. Capitulum* lxvj *mar.* CG,
Cap*itulum* ix *mar.* S;   quod I] *with scilicet* pilgrym *mar.* G³.   3587-8 swiche
woordes] þow had J;   þou hast drawe] thise wordes J;   name] (*2nd* a *ins.*
G³).   3588-9 art ... wende] *om.* S.   3589 a] had bene a J, *om.* S;   nice]
nyne O;   man] had ben*e add. can.* O;   answerest] answere M.   3590 wel]
and So wisely *add.* J;   quod he] *with scilicet* Matt*ere mar.* G³.   3591 þee]
and *add.*   me] *om.* JMO, it S;   myn] my J;   ere] mowth J.
3592 Be] þou *add.* M;   neuere] noȝt J.   3593 shuldest] labour giues bread
to the / back and belly, but ydle/ness brings both to / distruction *mar.* (bread *alt. to*
illegible word O³) O³;   þilke] he JMO;   yiueth] ȝeeueth (*with* ȝyueth *mar.* G³)
G;   þe¹) *om.* JMO.   3594 hadde] lange *add.* J;   þis] tyme *add.* M.
3595 ne] and J;   hadde be woorth] elles J, hade beon S;   elles] had nouȝt the
schippe J, *om.* S;   þe arch] Aarche (*2nd* a *ins.* G³) G;   bene wrought J, þe Shipp
M;   of] *om.* J.   3596 Noe] *om.* J;   I am] Schortly to Saye J;   þilke þat]
I am J;   shortely MO, þilke S;   shortliche] he that JMO;   shortlich þat S;
maketh] (*2nd* a *ins.* G³);   passe] to passe JO.   3597 enoyinge] nuyng J;
þilke] He JO, I am he M;   alle] (e *ins.* G³);   þe] *om.* JMO.   3598 Cleped]
I am J, Callid MO;   I am] called J;   name] (*2nd* a *ins.* G³);   or] other GS,
labor *et* occupacio *rub. mar.* O.   3599 Clepe] Calle JMO;   me] *ins. mar.*
G³, *om.* MO;   ne] rekke J;   recche] neu*ere* J.   3600 tweyne] twa JMO,
þou call me *add.* M;   Bi me] *with* labou*ur mar.* G³;   þilke] þay JMO;   into]
to M;   of] *om.* M.   3601 þe¹] *ins.* (*with erased* þe *u.v. mar.* C³) C;   to]
ins. C (*with erased* to *u.v. mar.* C³) C, *om.* G.   3602 is] *om.* J, I O;   in þi
thouht] þou thynke best J;   Come] *-es* M;   or] other GS.   3604 cheesinge]
(*1st* e *ins.* G³) G;   þi] *-n* M;   be holde] biholde C, (*2nd* o *ins.* G³);   fool]
How þe body of þe pilgryme is besy to counseile hym. to go by ydelnesse. and forsake
labou*r add. rub.* M.   3605 Whan] *prec. Capitulum* lxvij *mar.* CG, *capitulum*
vij *rub. mar.* M;   he] þus C, *with* thus *mar.* G³, *ins.* O³;   þus] *om.* CS,
subpuncted G, on this wise J;   me] (*2nd* e *ins.* G³), vnto me J;   þe mattere]
om. J.   3606 name] (*2nd* a *ins.* G³);   bi] *om.* JMO.   3606-7 in þat time]
Sone J.   3608 seyinge] and sayde J;   to] vnto J;   me] (*2nd* e *ins.* G³);
What] wharto JMO, *om.* S.   3608-9 gost ... fool] *om.* S.   3608 gost þou]
goste (e *ins.* G³) G;   Leevest] trowes M.   3609 þou] þus *add.* O;   þis²]
nise *add.* J;   cokard] *with scilicet* Matt*ere mar.* G³;   Leeue] Trow M.
3610 ne] *om.* JMO. |3611 dameselle] dayoyselle (*2nd* e *ins.* G³) G;   hire²] þe
M.   3612 also] *om.* JMO;   of] of hym JM, hym O;   She] schee (*1st* e *ins.*
G³) G, Perauenture J;   perauenture] Sche J, shall telle þee S.   3612-3 shal
telle þee] perauenture S.   3613 swich] Sum J;   recche] *with* think *mar.*
O³.   3614 shalt] *om.* JMO, þou shalt S;   þat ooþer] þe wey O;   on²] that
is on JMO.   3615 Oo] *prec. Capitulum* lxviij *mar.* CG;   ful wel²] *om.*
JMO.   3616 not þerof] *om.* O;   if] that ȝif JO;   leevede] trowe M;   þee²]
to þin wordes M.   3617 soone] (*2nd* o *ins.* G³).   3617-8 And ... Ye] *om.*
J.   3617 sooth] þe sooþe S;   quod he] *with scilicet* body *mar.* G³.
3618 leeue] trow M;   me] (*2nd* e *ins.* G³);   Ye quod I] *with scilicet* pilgrim
mar. G³;   Quod he J.   3619 quod he] *with scilicet* body *mar.* G³;   is not]
nys not S;   on] that es on J;   yonder] ȝonde J.   3620 bitwixe tweyne] the
hegge of thornes J, bitwen þem two MO, bytweene þe tweyne S;   is ... wode] es

by twene þaim J, -s O; An] and G, And a M. 3621 no] not S; wal] -led
S; kernelles] kirnell MO; close] vs add. JMO; with²] in add. JMO;
toures] om. JMO. 3622 ne castelles] om. JMO; þer] ne þer S; noon]
no M; hegge] -es M; ne is] þat ne is C, that ne it es J, þen it is M, but þat
it is O, aperceyued wel neghe in some place ne S; in] om. JS. 3623 sum]
om. J; place] (2nd a ins. G³), om. J, ne S; and¹] om. J, ne S; tobroke]
om. J, broken MO; or] other GS, om. J; þat] om. J; men] om. J; ne]
om. JMOS; mown] om. J; perce it] om. J, perchid M; breke] brokene
J. 3624 place] (2nd a ins. G³); forveyed] om. M; oþer] om. M;
ferred] ferpassed J, ferr M, faryn O, feered fer S. 3625 passe] thurgh add. J;
hegge] -es MO. 3626 wherfore] (2nd e ins. G³), For JMO. 3627 michel]
muche GS; to] For to JMOS. 3628 with] marked mar. C; faire]
damyselle add. JM; yonder] om. O; hire] his S; þanne] (e ins. G³).
3629 I¹] Otium rub. mar. O; him] with scilicet body mar. G³; now] quod
I than add. J; þilke] ʒone JMO; wel] wille J, I MOS; I²] wil MO, see S;
see] weel S. 3630 haue] (2nd a ins. G³); but] ʒif add. J; in sum poynt]
I J; I] in Sum poynte J, om. M; leeuede] trowed M. 3631 To] prec.
Capitulum lxix mar. CG, capitulum viij rub. mar. M; damiselle] vide mar. O³;
me] om. O. 3631-2 at ... wey] sat J. 3632 sat] at the begynnynge of the
toþer way J; and¹] om. J; seide¹] I hailesed J, I Sayd O; gretinges] om.
J. 3633 do] diden C, with dede mar. G³, done S; a] om. MO.
3634 tauhten] tawghte (e ins. G³) G, wille teche J; coude] knaw J, knew
MO. 3635 þou miht] maye þou J; bi me] þou wille com J; þou wolt come]
by me J. 3636 a fayr wey] fayre wayes JMO; lede] leede (2nd e ins. G³)
G. 3637 folk] -es S; to¹] the add. JS; greene] om. S; notes] myntys
O. 3638 þe] om. JMO; places] (2nd a ins. G³), place MO; delite] -3
M; of²] and J, om. S; pley] om. S; of³] om. M; disport] -es M.
3639 make] (2nd a ins. G³); hem] þeim (with theme mar. O³) O; heere] om.
JMO; roundelles] roundenʒ J, redels MO; and ballades] om. MO.
3640 of harpes] and Sethelys add. J, om. S; of simphaunes] om. S; of³] and
J, om. S; organes ... ooþere] om. S. 3641 sownes] melodyes J, om. S;
whiche] of whilke JMO; were] to lange, al add. S; wel longe] it ware J;
see] to See JMO. 3642 pleyes] players J. 3643 tables] (2nd a ins. G³);
þe chekeer] þe chesse and J, at þexchequer S; þe²] om. O; dees] the dice JS;
merelles] the merellys JS; and] at M. 3644 museryes] miseries JS,
mustaryes M; into ... place] (2nd a ins. G³), þou wille ga J, -s S; þou wolt
go] in to Swilke place J, with me and add. S; bi] om. M. 3645 muste] go.
and add. M, neodes add. S; Now loke] trs. J; wolt come] wille ga J, or þou
nyll add. M; for] -th S; with þee] þou has thy counselle J. 3646 þi ...
hast] with the J, counsell þou hast S; Counseyl] prec. Capitulum lxx mar.
CG. 3647 I] hafe J; haue] (2nd a ins. G³), I J; but] for JMO.
3648 Ayens ... me²] he is be comene a uoket J; he ... aduocat] agaynes me to
with stande alle eville and J, he has become aduocat O; Wel] also J; was] I
J. 3649 I¹] was J; acorded] (final e ins. G³); yive] ʒeeue (with ʒyue
mar. G³) G; him] ins. O. 3650 counseile] (2nd e ins. G³); am] om.
J. 3651 today] þis day S; haue he wole] (2nd a ins. G³), he has wilned and
crafed J, haues he well M, he desired O; þilke] that JMO. 3652 I¹] me
M; muste] nedes add. J; wheþer] whidere J; euere] I Schalle J; I shal]
euere J; haue riht] see me vengid M; of] on M. 3653 or] other GS;
wheþer] ins. mar. after rub. mark also in text O³; euere] I schalle J; I shal]
euere J; see me venged] &c add. G, on hym add. J, haue right of hyme add.

O, see him venged S; Why so] *prec. Capitulum* lxxj *mar.* CG, Why JMO.
3653-4 quod she] Sayse þou So J. 3654 seist þou so] quod scho J; wel] *cross
mar.* O³. 3655 yiven] 3eue (*with* 3yue *mar.* G³) G. 3656 Serteyn] Nowe
certis J; fayn] I walde J; I wolde] fayne J; ouhte] scholde J.
3657 make] (*2nd a ins.* G³), hakke J, for to make M, to make O; a crosse] *om.*
J; þanne] in the poste J; euere] he M. 3658 he] euer M; hadde] *om.*
M; Sey] Telle J; now] *om.* O. 3659 hath] he *add. can.* C, had O;
mad] (*2nd a ins.* G³); come] to com*e* JMO. 3660 wole] schalle J.
3661 quod] *om.* S. 3662 I¹] *om.* S; aloyngne me] I myght nou3t J, to be
withdrawen M, *o.er.* O³; ne forueye me] mekille aloyne me J, *om.* M, *o. er.* O³;
fro ... michel] ne Porvey ferre J, for my way moche (for *o. er.* O³) O.
3662-3 mihte I nouht] fra my way J. 3663 come] came S; þat] *om.* JMO;
þouh] if M. 3664 forueyed] f*o*uruueyed (*2nd u subpuncted*) G, *om.* M; or]
other GS, *om.* MO; out] putt out M; bi] wey *add. can.* C, cawse of *add.* J;
hegge] -s MO. 3665 shulde¹ ... I] *om.* S; soone] mow MOS (*can.* O);
mown] turne J, sone MOS. 3666 turne] *om.* CJ; ayen] to my wey S;
to my wey] ageyne S; Swiche] wyþ such O; haue] (*2nd a ins.* G³), he has
O. 3667 leeue] þat *add.* S; aryued] armyd and aryuyd M, armed O;
Now] *prec. Capitulum* lxxij *mar.* CG, Mafay nowe J; þou maist] *trs.* J; quod
she] *om.* J, see MOS; see] q*u*od scho MOS. 3668 þee] bot *add.* J; suffre]
harde thynges *add.* J; saue] (*2nd a ins.* G³). 3669 for to] *om.* J; to²]
for to S. 3670 hegge] -s MO, þane he spekeþe and meneþe *add.* S; wel]
þou may J; þou miht] welle J; nouht] nathynge J. 3671 any peyne] þere
be J; þer be] ony payne J. 3672 shal he] *trs.* MO; haue] (*2nd a ins.*
G³); allone] alle lane and J, and *add.* O; þou] 3owe J, but *add.* S; shal]
schall (h *ins.* G³) G. 3673 scracched] scrated JMO; and¹] *om.* O; and²]
alle *add.* J; bebled] bled O; Leuue] trow M; him] *with* body *mar.* G³;
þerof] þerfore J. 3674 in þat] For þerin J; miht] may J; leese] (*2nd e
ins.* G³); Come] to come J. 3675 me] for *add.* J; firste] (e *ins.* G³);
haue] (*2nd a ins.* G³). 3676 summe] *om.* S; is] by me. it is þi way. and
þis way *add.* M; al] welle J; forbeten] treded J. 3677 Ladi] *prec.
Capitulum* lxxiij *mar.* CG; sithe] Sen JMO. 3678 me] (*2nd e ins.* G³);
þe condicioun] youre S; of yow] condycyouns S; ye hatten] *trs.* J.
3679 wente] ga JMO; wey] Howe þat þe pilgryme askeþe of dame ydelnesse what
is hir name · and howe men cleep hir *add.* S; Therof] *prec. Capitulum* lxxiv *mar.*
CG, {Cap}*itulum* x *mar.* S. 3680 þee¹] *om.* J; gretliche] ne *add.* J, to *add.*
S; to ... like] whedere that wit it es noght J, *ins. mar. after rub. mark also in text*
O³. 3681 many] ane *add.* J; þer] *om.* JMO; haue¹] (*2nd a ins.* G³);
þis ... asked] Spirred me neu*e*re my name J. 3682 hem] that *add.* JM; þei]
þer S; not] neu*e*r MO; more] lesse J; lasse] mare J. 3683 sithe] sen
JMO; wolt] desirest to JS; knowe] wit S; þis] it O, *om.* S; wite] þou
schalle wele wit J, þis *add.* O, þowe shalt knowe S; in] *om.* J, for S; certeyn]
om. J; am] *ins.* M. 3684 oon] i *over* G³; þat] of O; Peresce] slewthe
over C³, *with* slewthe *mar.* G³, Slewth JMOS; whiche ... s*e*e] sette here S;
and] *om.* JMOS. 3685 fynde] *om.* JMOS; heerafter] as þou shalt knowe
S; made] *trs.* GC, and S; sette] *om.* S; heere] *om.* O, after *add.* S;
douhter] Idleness bringeth Mysery. diuersly. *mar.* O³. 3686 cleped] called
JMO; Oiseuce] idelship *over* C³, Huiseuse (*with* ydelschipp *mar.* G³) G, Idilnes
JMO (*with* ydilshipp *rub. mar.* M). 3687 to²] *om.* O; shode] *om.* O;
me¹] myn*e* hare J, *om.* O. 3688 do] to do CJM, for to do S; ooþer] *om.*
M. 3689 Sonedayes] halydayes S; lesinges] *marked mar.* C³.

3690 togideres] to gedyr JMO;   make] (*2nd* a *ins.* G³);   seeme] to Seme J.
3691 fables] & *add.* C, and *add. ins. mar.* G³, & to *add.* O;   romaunces] romans
MO.   3692 bodi] bath *add.* JMO (*ins. mar.* O³);   whan²] *om.* JMO;   þou²]
om. JMO;   wakest] doste awake S.   3693 haue] (*2nd* a *ins.* G³);   wales]
blaynes J;   þe] his J.   3694 yive] ȝeue (*with* ȝyue *mar.* G³) G;   garlaundes]
chapellettes S;   I²] *om.* JM;   make] (*2nd* a *ins.* G³), *om.* JMO;   him²] *om.*
JMO;   biholde] he be haldys J, to beholde S.   3695 he] it CM;   cloþed]
I cladde J, cledd MO;   and²] *om.* JMO.   3696 make] (*2nd* a *ins.* G³);
come] to come JMOS;   in] in to S;   þe] his J;   for to] and M, to O.
3697 digge] bigg M, pyke hem oute S;   in hem] at þam J, *om.* S;   tile] hem
add. CGS (*ins. mar.* G);   sowinge] (*2nd* o *ins.* G³).   3698 Now looke] *trs.*
J;   thinkest] and *add.* O.   3699 þou] þu C;   it] *om.* J, me *add.* S.
3700 withoute taryinge] tary noȝt J;   tukke] vp *add.* J, take vp MO;   in] vndyr
JMOS;   set] avaunce S.   3701 þe] þi CS;   Whan] *prec.* Capitulum lxxv
mar. CG;   so] thus J, *om.* S;   me] *om.* J.   3702 hire] tille hire agayne J,
to hir M;   Sithe] Sen JMO;   my bodi] ȝe J;   is] er J;   youre] *om.* J;
loue] -d S.   3704 he¹] ye CGS, il F;   forueyed] gone owt of his way M;
desceyued] diffamed J;   sharpliche] passe O.   3705 and] *om.* JMO;
shrewedliche] *om.* JMO;   passe] sharply O;   Soone] *om.* O;   ynowh] I
thought J, for *add.* O;   make] (*2nd* a *ins.* G³).   3706 wey] and *add.* J;
bipleyne] playne JMO.   3707 him] *with* scilicet body *mar.* G³;   scracched]
Scratted JMO, cracched S;   Go] forth *add.* J;   she] and *add.* J.
3708 Blame] (*2nd* a *ins.* G³).   3709 argue] repreeue S;   loue] How grace
dieu info*ur*mes hym of þe hegge whilk is called Penitence *add. rub.* M;   And] *prec.*
Capitulum lxxvj *mar.* CG, ca*pitulum* ix *rub. mar.* M, vj cap*itulum rub. mar.* O;
om. JMO;   bi Oiseuce] by huyseuse (*with* ydelschippe *mar.* G³) G, I Passed J,
by ydilshipp MO, by dame ydelnesse S;   I passede] by Idilnesse J.
3710 entrede me] I entred J, I entrede me MO;   ooþer] hic deuiat p*er* ocium *rub.*
mar. O;   wey] wey *add.* subpuncted G.   3711 into] in J;   þis] way *add.*
J.   3712 it ne is] that ne it es J, þen it is MO;   Foruēyed] Bigiled M;   I¹]
with pilgrym *mar.* G³.   3713 it wel] *om.* O;   God] presumtion *mar.* O³.
3714 yiue] ȝeue (*with* ȝyue *mar.* G³) G;   G;   me] (*2nd* e *ins.* G³);   grace]
om. J;   so] for C;   to¹] do and *add.* S;   pases] pase JMO;   so²] *om.* J.
3715 come¹,²] (*2nd* o *subpuncted* G);   wey] þat *add.* J.   3716 goode] (e *ins.*
G³);   hegge] -s O.   3717 Thus] *prec.* Capitulum lxxvij *mar.* CG;   alwey]
-s C;   hegge] -es GMOS (es *subpuncted* G), and atte the laste *add.* J;   a vois]
I herde JO;   I herde] a voys JO.   3718 clepede] called JM.   3719 and]
om. JMO;   hast þou] hast G;   leeved] trowed M, herde S.   3720 counseil]
consell (*with* conseyll *mar.* G³) G;   þilke] that JMO;   Oiseuce] huiseuse (*with*
idelschippe *mar.* G³) G, ydil schepe JMO.   3721 jangeleresse] ianglere JMO;
þat] *om.* GS;   þee] for þe J;   shal] shall *add. can. subpuncted* O;   lede] be
JMO.   3722 þee¹] to JMO;   to¹] the JMO;   lede þee] even S;   euene]
leede þee S;   albeit] ȝif all J.   3723 is] be JM;   she hath] *trs.* GS.
3724 Bernard] Idleness stepdame to vertu. Bernard *mar.* O³;   clepede] called
JMO;   for nouht] *with* owten cause J, noght all for noght O;   of] to JMO;
vertu] the vertuȝ J.   3726 kyte] glede JMO;   to] is to þe M.   3727 swich]
with steppdame *mar.* G³, þou schalte fynde hire J;   þou ... hire] swilke J.
3728 ne come hider] lese nouȝt that way beȝonde and J;   and ... biyounde] come
hedyr J, and leue þe way biþonde MO, þat hegge *add.* S;   And] *prec.* Capitulum
lxxviij *mar.* CG.   3729 as] *om.* MS;   who] way J, *om.* M;   seith] Say J,
om. M;   al²] -most M.   3730 spak] to me *add.* JS;   sigh] wist M, ne saughe

hem S;   and] ne J;   was] shuld be M;   wiste] see M;   Algates] neuertheles J.   3731 quod I] (I *ins. mar.* G³), I prey þee S;   I pray þee] pray þee C, (i *ins.* J), quod I S;   þou art] *trs.* M;   þat] thus *add.* J.   3732 areynest] arguest C, arayneth JM, is ayens O, reproeuest S;   þat] *om.* J;   spekest] Spekes JMO.   3733 but] ȝif *add.* JMO;   wiste] wit J;   sumwhat] þerof *add.* J;   And] *prec. Capitulum* lxxix mar. CG;   þanne] (ne *ins.* G³);   answerde] the voyce J;   þilke] that spake J, þat MO;   þat spak] aunswerde and sayde J.   3734 owhtest] aght JMO;   wite] to wete J;   hadde] haue JMO;   þee] for þee S.   3735 anything þerof] þou haue with halden J;   þou ... withholden] any thynge þere of J;   þilke] Scho JMO.   3736 ledde] (*1st* d *ins. with* ledde *mar.* G³) G;   þee²] (*1st* e *ins.* G³), thare *add.* J;   iewel] *o. er.* C.   3737 made] (*2nd* a *ins.* G³);   Grace Dieu] Men calles me J;   men ... me] Grace dieu J.   3738 Whan] *prec. Capitulum* lxxx *mar.* CG;   hire] vn till hire J;   Goode] (e *ins.* G³);   sithe] Syn JMO.   3739 and] as J, *om.* M;   wel I ouhte] me awht J, with all myn hert *o. er.* M³, weel aught S;   þat] *om.* S.   3740 to¹] with JMO;   me] for *add.* S;   haue] (*2nd* a *ins.* G³);   with] to S;   yow] and *add.* S.   3741 maketh] (*2nd* a *ins.* G³), made JS;   þis] þes O;   hegge] -s O;   is] ar O;   amidde] be twene thire wayes J, in myddis MO.   3742 lerne me and] *om.* J;   me²] *om.* M.   3743 sithe] Syne JMO;   afterward] aftere JMO;   to my powere] schalle I J;   I wole] at my Powere J;   do my devoyr] enforce me J, do my besynesse M.   3744 Þouh] If M;   bodi] enmy JMO;   haue] (*2nd* a *ins.* G³), wille nouȝt JMO;   to¹] *om.* JMO;   suffre] it *add.* J;   wel to] forto J;   it] *om.* O;   He] *with* body *mar.* G³.   3745 haue] (*2nd* a *ins.* G³);   ne recche] rekke neuere J.   3746 Serteyn] *prec. Capitulum* lxxxi *mar.* CG, -ly J;   quod she] *with* grace *mar.* G³;   forth] *om.* JMO;   shuldest] nouȝt *add.* J, shall M;   it] *om.* J, thurgh MO;   thoruh] *om.* J, it MO.   3747 any herte] þowe had J;   þou haddest] any witte in þe J;   after þat] ay J;   þou gost] the lengere J;   ferþere] þou gase J.   3747-8 þou shalt haue] (haaue *2nd* a *ins.* G³), the thikkyr J.   3748 þe hegge] schalle þou fynde J;   thikkere] the hegge J, þe thykker O.   3749 bi] *om.* O;   hath] *can.* C;   wold] wull G, *om.* J, wele MS, þus O, voulu F;   bitraye] betrayse G, betrayed JMO, betraysshed S.   3750 in] *om.* JMO;   makynge] (*2nd* a *ins.* G³);   come] to come JO;   þis] his S;   Now] *prec. Capitulum* lxxxij *mar.* CG.   3751 quod Grace Dieu] þen MO;   þanne] *om.* J, quod grace dieu MO;   hegge] -s O;   is] ar O;   amidde] be twene J, in myddis M, amyddys OS.   3752 þe²] þat J;   whiche] þe which O;   haue] (*2nd* a *ins.* G³);   and] þe *add.* S.   3753 þe teeth] hir teth J, *ins. mar.* O³, þen *add. can.* O.   3754 Penitence] *with* penitencia *rub. mar.* M;   maketh] (*2nd* a *ins.* G³), gers J;   clepe] calle JMO;   heuene] erth M;   in²] and in J;   eerþe] heuen M.   3755 þe¹] *om.* M;   hegge] -s O;   þilke] thase JMO.   3756 þat²] *om.* O;   þei] *om.* J;   not] *om.* S.   3757 She] *with* penytaunce *mar.* G³;   it] *om.* O.   3758 take] (*2nd* a *ins.* G³);   and baleys] *om.* JMO;   and²] *ins. mar.* G³, *om.* S;   þerwith] þerof M;   hire] *ins. mar.* G³, *om.* S.   3759 mailettes] maliet JO;   alle times] (*1st* e ins. G³), ay J, altyme MO;   þat] when JMO;   be] is JMO;   many] monye (e *ins.* G³) G;   places] (*2nd* a *ins.* G³);   she] has J.   3760 hath] scho J;   to doone] (*2nd* o *ins.* G³), nede to note J, nede to do MO;   with] *om.* J;   withdrawe] (*2nd* a *ins.* G³);   with] hem *add. can.* (*with* ȝerdes *mar.* G³) G, þem *add.* M, *om.* O.   3761 at] þat at O;   þis] the JMOS;   thikke] þer fore *add.* J;   rede] (*2nd* e *ins.* G³).   3762 anoon] sone J;   swich] suche (e *subpuncted*) G.   3763 þat] *ins. mar.* G³, *om.* JO;   shal¹] schulde JS;   shal²] schulde J;   þee²] (*1st* e *ins.* G³);   passe] to passe M.   3765 And] *prec. Capitulum* lxxxiij *mar.* CG;   to[1]] forto JMO.   3766 muse] mase M; mihte[1,2]] (e *ins.* G[3]);   hole] or muysse *add.* J.   3768 michel] gretly J; visage] (s *ins.* J);   Ladi] A lady M.   3769 riht wys] quod I JMO;   quod I] that es so wise J, right wise MO;   haue] (*2nd a ins.* G[3]);   half] Syde JMO; þat] I J.   3770 wende] went M;   foot bi foot] alle way JMO;   with me] ȝe had come*n* J, foote by foote MO, I wende þat *add.* S;   ye hadde] with me J, by me as I supposyde M;   allwey come] fute by fute J, and come M, comen O. 3771 On me] It es noȝt lange J;   quod she] *with* s*c*ilicet resou*n mar.* G[3], on me J;   it ... long] is it not long GS, quod scho J.   3773 If þou haddest] Had þou J;   yit] þ*ou* had J;   þou haddest] ȝit J.   3773 wey] the way JS; be] is JMO.   3774 blameworthy] (*2nd a ins.* G[3]);   to] in J, by MO;   þe] (*2nd* e *subpuncted* G);   goon] good J.   3775 þe goode] Pil*g*rimes J; pilgrimes] gase J;   leeue] triste M.   3776 hath] *om.* S;   profred] p*re*ferid M;   fool] ane abbe*re* fole J, a folle MO;   þou] shalt O;   shalt be] erte J, þou be O.   3777 if] gyve S;   lengere] þ*ou* ga J, þou len*ger* MO;   þe wey] *om.* JMO, wey S;   on ... half] any lengyr J, on þe tothir syde O;   þou go] on that Syde J, go MO;   Whan] *prec. Capitulum* lxxxiv *mar.* CG.   3778 to koleye] to Spie J, *om.* M, to ley O;   to biholde] and luke J, and to behold O, for to beholde S.   3779 leste[1]] leeste (*1st* e *ins.* G[3]) G, left M;   of þe hegge] was J;   were] of the hegge J;   leste[2]] (*2nd* e *ins.* G[3]), left M.   3780 þe] my JMO. 3781 keepe] helpe J;   nygh] ny (*with* nygh *mar.* G[3]) G, nere JM.   3781 while] -s J;   coleyinge] spiande and lokande J, mouyng M, colyng O;   þider] and *add.* J;   turnynge] too*ur*nynge (*2nd* o *subpuncted*) G;   þe[2]] (*2nd* e *ins.* G[3]). 3783 ofte] hit befalleȝe S;   it bifalleth] offt S;   in þe strenges] he is takyn*e* JS; he is take] (*2nd* a *ins.* G[3]), in gildres J, with strengis S.   3784 is[1]] er JMO, beon S;   wey] (*final* e *ins.* G[3]);   oþer] or JMO;   happeth] hapneth JMS;   he] (*ins.* G[3]);   is[2]] *om.* O;   a] an M.   3785 oþer] or JMO;   bilymed] *with* Sum oþ*ere* gynne. or elles reste Sum lym J, his wynges belymed S;   He] nota *mar.* G[3].   3786 for] p*er* chaunce afftterwardes *add.* S;   shal] sleuthe *mar.* O[3];   wolde] Nowe takeþe heede of þaventures þat byfel þe pilgryme in his wey *add.* S.   3787 Now] *prec. Capitulum* lxxxv *mar.* CG, *capitulum* x *rub. mar.* M;   I wole] *trs.* J;   how] *ins. mar.* G[3];   whereof] (wher *ins. mar.* O[3] *with rub. caret in text)*;   for of S.   3788 misfel] mis bifel C, myssauenture felle J, mysse be fell (be fell *ins. mar.* O[3] *with rub. caret in text*) O, mishappe bytide S, mesavint F;   me] to me M, *ins. mar.* O[3];   As] Right as S;   musinge] and *add.* JS;   an] a J;   þe] (*2nd* e *subpuncted* G).   3789 my] the JMO; whiche] wheche (*2nd* e *ins.* G[3]) G, that J;   sigh] p*er*sayued J;   not] and *add.* S.   3790 hem] me S;   me] hem S;   þe] my S.   3791 to] in JM. 3792 to] with S;   haluelinge] *om.* J, half MO, haluedeel S;   I[2]] *om.* JMO, al so I S;   foryat] speeche with *add.* S.   3793 Of] and of (and *ins. mar.* G[3]) GJ;   made] (*2nd a ins.* G[3]);   ne to fynde] neyþer O;   neiþer] to fynde O. 3794 hadde] (e *ins.* G[3]);   to[3]] howe I myght J, how to O;   vnknytte] vnknyite C, and knytte (*with* on *mar.* G[3]) G.   3795 Breke] (*2nd* e *ins.* G[3]) for breek S; I[1]] he J;   so] *om.* S.   3796 A] And so a S;   foul] *om.* CO;   and[1]] *om.* J;   maugracious] vng*ra*cious JMO;   hidous] to by halde *add.* J, an hydous O.   3797 þat] whilke J;   com] alwey *add.* S;   seuynge] (seu *o. er. with er. mar.* C), Folowande J;   me] & *add.* CO.   3798 with þat] wyth in hir (*with* with hir *mar.* O[3]) O;   and[2] ... hem] *om.* J;   Whan] *prec. Capitulum* lxxxvj *mar.* CG.   3799 me] *om.* M;   abasht] I was J;   I was] mare J;   more] a baist J;   þan] I was *add.* JO.   3800 mossy] mossebe grou*n* J;   of mosse] alle rowe J, mosse S;   al rouh] of mosse J, bygroven S;   foul] vile J;   and[2]] *om.*

S.   3801 vile] foule J;   blak] and *add*. CS;   halle] on þe hye benche *add*.
S.   3801-2 whoso ... hire[1]] and fouler in þe S.   3802 vnder] at J.
3803 side] vndyr hir girdyll *add*. J;   kille] sla JMO;   with] Swyne J;   swyn]
with alle as it Semed J, beestis S;   bar] (*2nd a ins., final subpuncted* G[3]);   cordes]
(*2nd o ins.* G[3]).   3804 to] in J;   manere] maneere (*1st e ins.* G[3]) G.
3805 a ... wulues] scho had bene J;   takere] (*2nd a ins.* G[3]);   wulues] fooles
S;   she ... ben] a takere of wolfes J;   or] other GS;   to] vnto J.
3806 for[1]] fo C;   and ... otre] *om.* J;   trusses] thynges to be trussed J.
3807 What[1]] *prec. Capitulum* lxxxvij *mar*. CG;   stinkinge] trotte *add*. J, creature
add. S;   What[2]] whare to JM;   comest] come J.   3808 riht] power S.
3809 þus] Sodaynly vpon me *add*. J.   3810 oþer] or JMO;   koughinge]
hostynge J;   wel] þow Schewes J;   it sheweth] (scheeweth *1st e ins.* G[3]), wele
J.   3811 Flee] Ga J;   hens] heyne fra me J.   3812 gerfaucon] faukoun
J;   ne[1]] *ins. mar. after rub. caret also in text* O[3];   faucoun] gerfaucoun J, *ins.
mar. after rub. caret also in text* O[3]; ne[2]] *om*. J.   3813 a merlyoun] merlioun
JO, Emerlyoun S;   noon ooþer] nowþer J;   brid] -dis J;   þus] forto J.
3813-4 for ... bownde] be bun*de* thus J.   3814 gessis] chesse M, cordes as I
weere gyved S;   And] *prec. Capitulum* lxxxviij *mar*. CG;   olde] tratt *add*. J,
vecke *add*. S.   3815 hed] faith J;   askapest me] passes J;   not] so lightly
add. J;   weenest] for *add. ins. mar*. O[3].   3816 þou come] *trs*. JMO;   heere]
hedyre JMO, and so *add*. s;   þou[2]] *om*. J;   haue] (*2nd a ins.* G[3]);   Olde]
and *add*. S.   3817 stinkinge] tratte *add*. J;   cleped] called JMO;   am] alde
I gra*u*nte hit wele *add*. J;   miscleped me] þou has J, myscalled me MO.
3817-8 þou hast] called me amysse J.   3818 of þat] thar*e* J;   stinkinge] þou
called me J, þou clepes me S;   þou ... me] stynkande J, stinking S;   am I] *trs*.
M.   3819 not] as *add*. M;   I trowe] *om*. S;   a] *om*. M;   haue] (*2nd a
ins.* G[3]).   3820-1 leyn ... lordes] *ins. mar. after rub. caret also in text* O[3].
3820 leyn] liggande J;   of[3]] *om*. C.   3821 ooþere] *om*. M;   lordes] and
add. S;   in] with in JS;   corteynes] þe courtyns S;   bishopes] (o *ins*.
G[3]).   3822 abbotes] pri*o*ures J, and priors *add*. M;   of[2]] oþere *add*. J, in
chambers of M;   and] *om*. O;   of[2]] *om*. J;   þat] and ʒit J;   neuere was]
was I neu*e*re J;   cleped] called JMO.   3823 erst] *om*. J, or now M;   in
no time] *om*. J;   ne] *om*. J, or M;   nempned] *om*. J;   þee] to calle me So
add. J.   3824 speke] þus MO;   þus] Swilke wordes Syn J, speke MO.
3825 woldest] walde JMO;   riht] full M.   3826 if] and J;   ascaped] (*3rd*
a *ins.* G[3]), fra *add*. JMO;   sithe] Sen JMO;   holde] (*2nd o ins.* G[3]), haue
the thus in my bandou*n*e J.   3827 þat] *om*. JMO;   shal] *ins. mar*.
G[3], wille JMO;   wel] weell (*with* weell *mar*. G[3]) G, *om*. JMO;   venge] avenge
S;   I wole] and J;   into] *om*. J.   3828 place] a place MS;   wole] schalle
J;   make] (*2nd a ins.* G[3]);   leeue] to leue JS, trow M;   god] &c *add*. G;
goode S.   3829 Thow] *prec. Capitulum* lxxxix *mar*. CG;   olde] tratte *add*.
J;   hast] (*final e subpuncted* G), thus *add*. J;   þe] thy JMO.   3830 name
(*2nd a ins.* G[3]);   sey] telle me J;   sithe] Sen JMO;   manasest] manasches
JMO.   3831 Serteyn] -ly J;   quod she] I will M;   I wole] q*u*od scho M;
it wel] *om*. JMO;   heled] layned J.   3832 to[1]] fra JMO;   þee] (*1st e ins.*
G[3]) G, nowþere *add*. J;   mi name] *om*. J, þy name S;   am[1]] ne *add*. J, & *add*.
OS;   þe] gret *add*. S.   3833 lede hym] lede to hym CO (to *ins*. O[3]), leede
hym (*2nd e ins.* G[3]) G, with my cordes J, ledis hym MO;   bi cordes] (*2nd o ins.*
G[3]), ledes tille him alle J.   3834 feet] fote ryʒt J;   þouh] *om*. J, if M;   it]
thay J;   swyn] or suche beestis *add*. S.   3835 Manye] (e *ins.* G[3]);   I haue]
(*2nd a ins.* G[3]), *trs*. JO;   lede] leede (2nd e *ins.* G[3]) G;   ynowe] y nowgh (*with*

nowe *mar.* G³) G.   3836 whiche] (e *ins.* G³);   shalt] schaalt (*1st* a *ins.* G³)
G;   be] by J, see S;   ne ascape] eschape nouʒt J;   me] *om.* JMO.
3837 strenges] And *add.* JMO.   3838 ooþerweys comen] *trs.* C, oþere wyse
commen*e* JMO;   wende] was ferde J;   wel] *om.* J;   haue] (*2nd* a *ins.* G³),
to haue JO (Be my wylle*am* Byche thes boke / thes boke was / mad *mar.* J³), þat I
hade S.   3839 woldest] walde JMO;   passed ouer] gane þurgh the hegge to
the toþere waye J, goon ower MO.   3839-40 go þi wey] lefte this J, passed þi
way MO.   3840 I] *prec. Capitulum* lxxxx *mar.* CG;   þe] þat O;   olde] (*2nd*
o *ins.* G³);   ly] lyes JMO;   bi] the *add.* J, my *add.* MO.   3841 make] -s
JMO;   turne] to turne tha*i*m J, þem *add.* M;   be] *om.* M, þe *add.* O;   loth]
-er O;   to] for to MS.   3842 boren for] scho that J;   to ley] layes J;
to²] *om.* JM;   make] -s J;   slumbre] to Slom*e*re J;   and²] *om.* J;   to³] I
JMO.   3843 shitte] Spere J;   see nouht] may noʒt See J.   3844 þilke]
scho JMO;   maketh] (*2nd* a *ins.* G³);   gouernour] of the schippe *add.* J;
slepe] t sclepe JMO;   amiddes] a mydde G, *om.* J, in myddis M, in þe myddys
of O;   þe ship] *om.* J.   3845 lost] broken S;   broken] lost S;   steere]
steerne C.   3846 amiddes] a mydde G, myddes J, in myddis MO;   þat] ʒyf
þat J;   wyndes] wynde S.   3847 I] and J;   make] -s J;   putte] to putte
JM;   recchinge] *with* Prechchynge *mar.* G³.   3848 al] Suffyre J, to suffre
O;   suffre] alle JO, I make suffir M, to suffre S;   perishe] to perishe CJ;
go²] to go OS;   in] to JMO.   3849 þilke] scho JMO;   make] -s JMO;
gardynes] and feldes *add.* J.   3850 withoute] *om.* J;   delvinge] *om.* J;
make] (*2nd* a *ins.* G³), *om.* J, -s M;   brambres] brembils JS;   rise] for fawte
of delfynge and tillynge *add.* J, aryse S.   3851 þat²] thynge that J;   bi þe
morwe] on þe morwe C, *with* on *mar.* G³, I Slew*the*d J, at morwe O.   3852 I
slewthede] by the morn*e* J, I haue aslewid M, Iaslowed S;   it] *om.* J;   þertoo]
And *add.* J.   3853 abide] haue list to abyde M;   time] thing S;   wel] fulle
JMO.   3854 be] many A goode werke JOS;   many … werk] bene JS, sleuþed
(*with* slothed *mar.* O³) O;   slewthed] be S.   3855 hatte] hade S;   Peresce]
slowthe *over* C, pereste (*with* slowthe *mar.* G³) G, Slewth JMO;   goutous] Sleuth
rub. mar. MO.   3856 maymed] mathymed J;   þe²] *om.* J;   founded]
affounded J;   froren] frosene JMO, foreyne S.   3857 ooþerweys] þou wille
name me J, odir way M, oþer wyse O;   þou … me¹] other*e* wyse J;   Tristesse]
with sorowfull *mar.* G³, þou may calle me J, tristicia MO;   þow … me] Tr*i*sticia
J, þou myght call me M, þou may clepe me S.   3858 it] *om.* J;   annoyeth]
nuyse J;   a] the J.   3859 in him] nathynge JMO, *om.* OS;   nothing] in
hy*m* JM;   maketh] (*2nd* a *ins.* G³).   3860 go] may J, *om.* MO;   myself¹]
am M, *om.* O;   wastinge] (*2nd* a *ins.* G³), *om.* J;   myself²] *om.* J.
3861 anoye] envy and angyre J;   pleseth] (*2nd* e *ins.* G³);   but] ʒif *add.* J.
3862 and] *om.* S;   alle] (e *ins.* G³), Sloth · lyf*es* anoyance *mar.* O³;   thinge]
-s C.   3863 annoyeth] nuyes J;   soo] *ins.* O³, and also S;   clepen] calles
JM;   Annoye] *e*nniy G, envy or Irkes*um*nesse J, envye S;   Lyf] the lyfe J.
3864 and dulleth] *om.* J;   gobet] lu*m*pe J.   3865 whiche] þe whilk (n*o*ta de
hely *rub. mar.*) M;   I dullede] sumtym*e* JMO;   sumtime] I dulled JMO;
Helye] Helyas J, he lyþe S.   3866 genievre] juniperyn CJO (*with* Plumbum *rub.*
mar. O), *with* juniperyn *mar.* G³, Iunipir tree MS, genevre F;   Ne … be] Had
noʒt J, ne had it be O, ne hade he by S;   hye honged] hye hunger C, aungil J,
hegge honged S.   3867 twyes] *om.* J;   excited] and wakande *alt.* wakynge
J;   he¹] *with* helye *mar.* G³;   for] *om.* J;   miht] þat *add.* C, *om.* J;   he²]
om. J, I MOS, hadde] *om.* J, haue MO, haue hadde S.   3868 I dulle] ydulle
S;   lede] with plu*m*bu*m mar.* G³, leeded S;   cherche] the kyrke JS.

3868-9 So ... leded] & make þaim O.   3869 I make hem] (*2nd a ins.* G³), so
heuy and so ledyd O;   weyen] & *? add.* S.   3870 selle] fele JMO;   bi] *om.*
O;   and] *om.* S;   oon] i *over* G³;   wel weye] *trs.* CO, weye M;   two] tweyne
(ii *over* G³) G, *om.* S;   or] other G;   thre] iii *over* G³, *om.* JMO.
3871 spare] (*2nd a ins.* G³);   noon] not (*with* non *mar.* G³) GS;   and] ne S;
fynde] in my strynges *add.* J.   3872 These] *prec. Capitulum* lxxxxj *mar.* CG;
wiche] wheche (*2nd e ins.* G³) G.   3873 bounden] tyed J;   bowelles] bowell
O;   ben²] ryght *add.* J.   3874 Þow miht drawe] drawe þou neuere So faste
J, þou may draw M, þowe might weel drawe hem but S;   breke] bryste J;   cordes]
stryngis J;   of] made of S.   3875 Cleeruaus] cleeuaus (*with* cleeruaus *mar.*
G³) G, cleruaunce MO, þentraylles S;   were] beoþe S;   synewes] Fyneux J;
al] ydlenes, and negligence./ þe cordes of sloth *mar.* O³;   and²] *ins.* G³, *om.*
JMO.   3876 of] *ins.* G³;   wombe] and *add.* CJMO (*subpuncted* G), þey
beoþe S;   hatten] hate I Schalle telle the J, hate MO;   þat] necligencia *et* fatigacio
rub. mar. M.   3877 oon] I *over* G³, hatteth] hatte GJMOS;   Negligence]
and *add.* JMO;   is] *om.* JS, hate MO;   Werynesse] weerynesse (*1st e ins.* G³)
G;   and] or J;   Letargie] loyterer O.   3878 sownere] the routere *add.* JM,
vnlusty and þe Router O;   Leþie] Lyþer O.   3879 bynde] blynde J;   with
þe folk] folke with J;   wynde] thaim *add.* J;   þaim wyþ *add.* O;   hem] *om.*
O;   to²] forto JMOS.   3880 reendinge] rentynge and ryfynge J, rentyng
MO.   3880-1 If ... sooth] þou wate J, If I say þe soth M, I I say soth O.
3881 þou wost] 3if I Say soth J, þou wote MO;   bi] *with* JMO;   tweyne] twa
JMO.   3882 Of] *prec. Capitulum* lxxxxij *mar.* CG.   3883 I ... it] *om.* J;
for] *om.* CJ;   til] *om.* JMO;   anooþer] *om.* J.   3884 time] *om.* J;   al]
For alle J;   þou shalt] *trs.* JM, shall I O;   þee²] (*1st e ins.* G³).   3885 Of]
with J;   oon] i *over* G³, of tham *add.* J;   I ... þee] *om.* J.   3886 bynde]
areste J;   areste] bynde J;   þee²] (*1st e ins.* G³).   3887 þilke] that JMO;
corde] *om.* J;   name] (*2nd a ins.* G³);   cleped] called JMO;   Desperacioun]
desperacio *rub. mar.* M, disparation *mar.* O³, despacyoun S.   3888 þilke] that
corde J, þe same M, þat O;   whan] efter þat J.   3889 þe] his J, *om.* MOS;
kyng] cryst S.   3890 draweth] hanges JMO;   hangeth] drawes JMO;
þilke] þa JMO;   taketh] (*2nd a ins.* G³).   3891 in] by JMO.   3892 it]
ins. mar. G³;   to¹] *om.* GS;   þat¹] þe J;   fool] folk (*subpuncted with* fooll
mar. G³) G, þane *add.* S;   make] (*2nd a ins.* G³), may make J.   3893 þat]
om. J, þerby S;   I] *om.* J;   him¹] *om.* J;   and³] *om.* JO.   3894 haue]
(*2nd a ins.* G³), may haue S;   Now looke] *trs.* J.   3895 wynd] northrune J;
of þe north] wynde J;   haue] (*2nd a ins.* G³);   Oiseuce] idelshipe *over* C³, *with*
ydilschippe *mar.* G³, ydilschepe JMO;   þat] þowe J.   3896 þee] (*1st e ins.*
G³);   of] By S;   she] þat J.   3897 made] (*2nd a ins.* G³), gerte J, makeþe
S;   þee] me M;   come] to come M;   and] *om.* J;   þou] schalle J;   shalt]
þou J, shouldest S;   if I ne] Olesse þan I J.   3898 dye] were S.
3899 Whan] *prec. Capitulum* lxxxxiij *mar.* CG, And than when J, And when MO;
þe] this J;   olde] (*2nd o ins.* G³), tratte *add.* J;   spoken] sermoned S;
sermowned] talde me J, spoken S.   3900 craft] -es J;   olde] (*2nd o ins.*
G³);   mossy] mysbegrowyne quod I J.   3901 Me] (*2nd e ins.* G³);
thinketh] thynke JM, semeþe S;   acqueyntaunce] es *add.* JMOS.   3902 er
now] done JMO;   doon] or nowe JMO;   þanne] than (*with* thanne *mar.* G³)
G.   3903 side] gyrdille J;   smot] gafe J;   me] with *add.* M;   so ... strok]
om. S.   3904 þat doun she] *om.* S;   ouerthrewh] felled J, *om.* S;   me] *om.*
S;   If myn hawbergeoun] (habergoun *with* houbergoun *mar.* G³ *in* G), Hadde I
than had J;   I hadde had] my hauberioun J, I hade S.   3905 wel it hadde]

wele had J, þanne hadde S; þanne] *om.* J, wel it hade S; be] me J; me]
bene J, *om.* MO; in sesoun] *om.* J; which I was] *om.* JMO. 3906 smyten]
om. JMO; with¹] *ins. mar.* G³, *om.* JMO; was] had nouȝt bene to me J, hadd
ben to me MO; ne] or J; with²] *om.* M; me] (*2nd* e *ins* G³), *om.* M;
in] *om.* J; scrippe] (e *ins.* G³). 3907 maketh] (*2nd* a *ins.* G³); is] to sey
add. O. 3908 þat] whilke J; no] faiþe *mar.* O³ *and* faith *mar. different hand*
O³; man] *ins.* M; kan] maken S; make] (*2nd* a *ins.* G³), can S; hadde]
Grace dieu JS; Grace Dieu] bade J, hade S. 3909 it] For *add.* J; haue]
(*2nd* a *ins.* G³). 3910 she] bade J; hadde] scho me J; þerinne] putte it
J; put it] þerin J; Harrow] *prec. Capitulum* lxxxxiv *mar.* CG.
3911 doun]I saw me J; I sih me] downe J; God] *om.* O; mercy] quod I
add. S. 3912 olde] tratte *add.* J; If] bot ȝif J; of you] y hafe Socoure
J. 3913 I ... socoure] (haaue *1st* a *ins.* G³ *in* G), of ȝowe J, of yowe *add.* S;
sonere] tittere *alt.* sonere J; tomorwe] comforth M, me help S; in me] to
morowe S. 3914 Help me] Swete lorde *add.* J; and ... me] (*1st* e *ins.* G³),
om. JS; and ... þis] *om.* J, sorowe and *add.* S; peryle] *om.* J; caste] *om.*
J, to caste S. 3915 me] *om.* J. 3916 As] *prec. Capitulum* lxxxv *mar.* CG,
ANd as S; compleynede] lay complaynande J; me] on this manere *add.* J;
and in] *om.* J, my *add.* S; compleyninge] *om.* J, compleynt S; lay doun] laye
doune (*1st, 2nd* e *subpuncted* G³) G, *om.* J, lay me doune (me *subpuncted* O³) O,
adovne S. 3917 olde] (*2nd* o *ins.* G³), tratte *add.* J; doun] adowne S;
wolde] be gan to J; vnfolde] haue vnfolded OS; þe] hir M; hangemannes]
gret mannes S. 3918 tye] bynde JMO, haue tyed S; me] it J, *om.* MO;
þe] my JMO; me²] (*2nd* e *ins.* G³); thouhte] (e *ins.* G³); not] nathynge
J. 3919 Weenest þou] Weenest G; eskape] (*2nd* a *ins.* G³); þi] gret *add.*
S. 3920 waymentinge] lamenting *mar.* O³, for] *om.* JMO; corde] (*2nd* o
ins. G³); I] *om.* J; wole] Schalle J. 3921 putte] *om.* J, it *add.* S;
fastne] be festnyd faste a boute it J, it *add.* MOS; sithe] Seyn JMO; afterward]
-es S. 3922 drawestere] drawere CJMO, trahinerresse F; hangestere]
hangere CJMO, caryer S, penderresse F; þee] and *add.* JMO. 3923 him]
me S; Whan] *prec. Capitulum* lxxxxvj *mar.* CG. 3924 wel] *om.* S; on
my burdoun] I be thouȝt me J, of my bourdoun S. 3924-5 I ... me] (bethowghte
last e *ins.* G³ *in* G), on my burdoune J, and *add.* S. 3925 him] it JMO;
cleuede] clymed O; and] *ins. mar.* G³, *om.* MOS; herte] (*2nd* e *ins.* G³);
ayen] and *add.* JS; With] in my J; boþe] both myn MO, my booþe S.
3926 dide] I didd JMS. 3927 þat] *om.* S; who] so M; ros] vp *add.* J,
aroose S; me] forto ga *add.* J. 3928 haue] (*2nd* a *ins.* G³); flowe] fledde
J; þilke] the JMO; olde] (*2nd* o *ins.* G³), tratte *add.* J. 3929 com] coome
(*2nd* o *ins.* G³) G, good Spede *add.* J. 3930 cordes] (*2nd* o *ins.* G³); she]
om. J; withheeld] helde J; me] agayne and faste scho cryed on me *add.* J;
of ... not] *om.* J; vnenpeched] *om.* J, empeched S. 3932 stont] schalle stande
J; þee] *om.* MO; ayen¹] *om.* MO; ayen²] *om.* J; þiderward] -es S;
þe hegge] þow muste for gete J, *om.* S. 3932-3 þou ... foryete] the hegge J,
and to forgeten S. 3933 To] and to JM, *om.* S; to] *om.* JS; my] myn
(n *subpuncted*) G; mostest] neodes *add.* S; of] ouer J, for S. 3934 alle
(e *ins.* G³), any S; thinge] -s JO; me] (*2nd* e *ins.* G³). 3935 droowh
me] with hire cordes J; bi þe streenges] drewe me J; and² ... after] *om.* J.
3936 me¹] *om.* J; dredde] I dreded JMO. 3937 corde] (*2nd* o *ins.* G³), -s
O; made] (*2nd* a *ins.* G³), schulde haue made J; any] an *followed by* er. O.
3938 to¹] vntille J; on] in J. 3939 first] be fore J; me] bot *add.* J;
leet] drew M. 3940 drawe] drawn C, tham *add.* J, lete M; seyinge] and sayde

J, to me *add*. M;   if] *ins*. M³.   3940-1 were ... litel] towearde the hegge
J.   3941 to þe heggeward] ware it neu*ere* so litille J.   3942 hem] him S;
ayen¹] *om*. S;   and] *om*. S;   hire] ageine *add*. S;   she wolde] and S;   drawe
me] *trs*. O;   ayen²] *om*. O, to hir S;   So] *prec. Capitulum* lxxxxvij *mar*.
CG.   3943 heeld] heelde (*1st* e *ins*. G³) G, scho helde J;   þat] as J;
bihyghte] hight JMO;   alle] (e *ins*. G³), like a J.   3944 times] tyme J;
go] haue go CJO;   toward] -s S;   and] *om*. J;   rekeuer] -ed CO, recou*ere* (*with*
Rakeeu*ere* mar. G³) G, *om*. J;   it] hem O.   3945 with] fell *add*. M;
manasses] manace J, manasshyng*es* M;   heff] lifte J;   hire] grysely *add*. M.
3946 took] bigan to take M;   and²] *om*. J, ay *add*. S;   hegge] & *add*. J, -*es*
M; me] and þat was to me grete discomforte. as ȝhe shall after vndirstonde in þis
next chapiter *add*. M;   *then* How Pryde apperis to þis pilgrym · and hir aray. and
also of hir gen*era*cion, þat is to say, veynglory. Avawntyng. disobeyng. rebellyon.
and ypocrisy *add. rub*. M.   3947 As] *prec. Capitulum* lxxxxviij *mar*. CG,
capitulum xi *rub*. M, And as J;   aloygnynge] *o. er*. C, So JMO;   me so] so mee
(*with* mee so *over* G³) G, aloynande me JMO;   þilke] that JMO, hic describit
superbia *rub. mar*. O;   olde] (*2nd* o *ins*. G³), tratte *add*. J.   3948 made] (*2nd*
a *ins*. G³);   go] to go JS;   wher] when J;   she] *o. er*. C, þat she S;   þe]
om. O;   pendaunt] pendaunce O;   an] *om*. J.   3949 and¹] *om*. S;   derk]
mirke J.   3949-50 tweyne ... wunderful] I Sawe come even to mewarde J.
3949 tweyne] two MO;   olde] *2nd* o, *and* e *ins*. G³).   3950 riht] pride &
flatterie *mar*. O³;   I ... me] twa alde ryght hidous that to me Sight ware right
wondirfulle J;   Þat oon] the ton (i *over* G³) G.   3951 whiche] wheche (*2nd*
e *ins*. G³) G;   þilke] scho JMO.   3953 not] na J;   argued] hire schappe
J, agreed S;   At] and on S.   3954 bar] (*2nd*
a *ins*. G³).   3955 shewed hire] semed JO, shewed M;   fers] and felle *add*.
J;   heeld] had *ins*. M;   horn] to blow with *add*. C, *add. ins. mar*. G³.
3956 a¹] hir S;   she bar] þer hong S;   gret] peyre of O;   belygh] *o. er*. C,
payre of bellewes JO, grete belowes M, to blowe with *add*. S.   3957 with] in
J;   peyre] of *add*. JMOS;   hadde] (e *ins*. G³);   on] vpone S.   3958 wel]
þei wer MO;   Wel] It Semed J, and weel S;   it seemede] þat *add*. C, wele J.
3959 olde] (*2nd* o *ins*. G³), hire JMO;   hire berere] that bare hire JMO;   go]
Scho gerte J, She made her O;   she made hire] sche maade here (*1st* a *ins*. with
berere *mar*. G³) G, ga JO.   3960 hire²] (*with* here *mar*. G³).   3961 visage]
chere JMO, Howe þat þe pilgryme was agaste of þeos two horryble olde hydous
creatures *add*. S;   Whan] *prec. Capitulum* lxxxxix *mar*. CG, *Capitulum* {xij} *mar*.
S.   3962 tweyne] ij *over* G³, twa JMOS;   olde] anes *add*. J;   Swete] sweete
(*1st* e *ins*. G³) G, lorde J.   3963 ben] buth (*with* beeth *mar*. G³) G, noȝt *add*.
J; olde¹] anes *add*. J;   olde²] (*2nd* o *ins*. G³);   þere] chere S.   3964 in]
nygh O;   Femynye] Furenuye S;   þer] whare JM;   wommen] þe wymmen
S;   hauen] (*2nd* a *ins*. G³);   lordship or none *add*. O.   3965 slayn] here
add. S;   bi] wyþ O;   were] hade beon S;   haue] (*2nd* a *ins*. G³), to haue S.
3966 soriere] gladdyre J;   I wolde] *trs*. J;   soo] *om*. JO;   if] *om*. J.
3967 werre] batayle J;   And] *prec. Capitulum* C *mar*. CG;   þane] thanne
(ne *ins*. G³) G;   þat was] *om*. JMO;   as] *om*. J.   3968 þat] whilke J;
seide] *om*. MO;   me] *om*. J, to me (to *ins*.) M;   an] *om*. J, oonly MO;   hygh]
om. JMO;   To] was *ins. o. er*. M, for to S;   þee] quod the voys *add*. J, sayd
þe O;   is] it es J.   3969 nothing] nouȝt J;   haue] (*2nd* a *ins*. G³);
this JMO;   olde] (*2nd* o *ins*. G³), delle *add*. J;   oþer] or els J, or MO.
3970 bataile] bataylle (e *ins*. G³) G.   3971 þat ne] þan he M, but he O;   is]
be O.   3972 it] he JMO;   horse] *with* horsse *mar*. G³;   oþer] be he J;

Be] Bot be he J.   3973 tweyne] ii *over* G³, twa JMO;   or] other G, ne for
S;   thre] iij *over* G³;   ooþere] *om.* JMO;   ynowe] y nowgh (*with* y noowe
mar. G³) G.   3974 holde] (*ist* o *ins.* G³);   nigh] *o. er. with er. mar.* C, hate
and assayle the fellye J;   wel þat] bot J, þat MO;   ne] *om.* J.
3975 ooþerweys] *opere* wise JMO.   3976 þou ne] *trs.* J;   be] villaynsly J;
vileynesliche] be J, vilansly (*with* villainously *mar.* O³) O;   treted] entreted S;
And] *prec. Capitulum* Cj *mar.* CG;   þanne] (ne *ins.* G³).   3977 here] *with*
grace dieu *mar.* G³;   you] quod I *add.* J;   þat] *om.* JMO;   ye seyn] *om.* J;
me] to me C, *om.* JS;   þese] twa *add.* J;   heere] (*ist* e *ins.* G³).   3978 nygh]
nere J;   maken] (*2nd* a *ins.* G³);   abasshe] So J, -d MOS;   soo] a baiste J;
Þou] Knowe þou O.   3979 she] *with grace mar.* G³;   bitimes] be tyme
JMO;   hem] selfe *add.* J;   Right] For right J;   þilke] scho JMO.
3980 bi] with J;   seid] talde J;   she is riht] *om.* J.   3981 so] *om.* J;
shule] schulle (e *ins.* G³) G, *om.* J;   þese ... seyn] *om.* J;   þee] (*ist* e *ins.* G³),
om. J;   who] *om.* J;   for] *om.* JMO.   3982 I] *om.* JMO;   haue] (*2nd*
a *ins.* G³), *om.* JMO;   so ... hem²] *om.* JMO.   3983 Ryht] *prec. Capitulum*
Cij *mar.* CG, And right J;   entended] *o. er.* C, tentid JMO;   þilke] this JMO;
hye] *om.* J, on hy MO;   þe] *om.* J;   olde] (*2nd* o *ins.* G³), *om.* J.   3984 þat¹
... ooþer] *om.* J.   3985 sporinge] sparynge (*with* spoorynge *mar.* G³) G,
spornyng M;   upon] *om.* J, vpone me and vpone S;   olde] (*2nd* o *ins.* G³), and
add. J.   3986 after] that *add.* J;   seide] cried J;   me¹] to me C, on me
J;   Abide] quod scho *add.* J;   me²] *om.* J;   þere] þat O;   come] to me
S.   3987 oþer] or JMO;   at] *ins.* M;   a] *ins.* G³;   see þi] þou schalle
be J;   deth] dede J.   3988 to hire] *om.* JMO;   I shulde] *trs.* O;   yilde]
ins. M.   3989 wiste] witte J;   name] (*2nd* a *ins.* G³);   wolde] wille J, wol
S;   And] *om.* J.   3990 I wole] my name O;   teche] I woll teche O;   it]
ins. O;   shuldest] schalte J;   wite] *o. er.* C.   3991 quod she] *ins. mar.*
erased O³;   þilke] scho JMO;   olde] (*2nd* o *ins.* G³), eld M, þe oolde S;
am²] I am MO;   cleped] called JMO;   alosed] losed CS.   3992 am I] *trs.*
J, for *add.* S;   me] my Selfe J;   I³] and S.   3993 or] other G, *om.* J;
þat] *om.* J;   þe²] *om.* JMO;   heuene] *om.* J.   3994 were] *om.* J, was M;
ful maad] *om.* J;   heuene] pride, and the effects thereof. noat *mar.* O³.
3995 men] sumtyme O;   clepeden] calledd J, men O;   sumtime] *om.* J, called
O.   3996 þer] *om.* J;   of] *om.* JMO;   euele] ille J;   a] *om.* JMO;
bred] brid *marked mar.* CO, *om.* JMO.   3997 þat I] *om.* S;   aperceyuede]
Þer sayfed JMO.   3998 harde] faste J;   þese] thire J;   belyes] (yes *o. er.*
C);   þat] whilke JS;   haue] (*2nd* a *ins.* G³).   3998-9 with me] by my side
J, here *add.* S.   3999 nest] of heuen *add.* J.
4000 whyt] wight (*with* whytte *mar.* G³) G;   noble] and *add.* JS;   gentel] *om.*
O.   4001 brightere] & bryght J, bryght O;   þe] a S;   ful] be fulle S;
Now] and nowe J;   he is] *trs.* S.   4002 blecched] Blak and J;   so²] *om.*
JMO;   salt] *om.* JMO, fast S;   so³] and so JMO;   it] he CS;   is] *ins.*
M.   4003 þe see] þis S;   a²] *om.* M;   takere] (*2nd* a *ins.* G³).   4004 of]
om. JMO;   wel] *om.* JO;   whan] *om.* J.   4005 after] over C, *om.* J;
þe see] *om.* J, þies MOS;   þow ... go] *om.* J;   Now] *prec. Capitulum* Ciii *mar.*
CG, *om.* J;   I sey þee] *om.* J.   4006 ne] and J, so O.   4007 I dwellede]
myght dwelle J;   more] langer J.   4008 maad] I made J;   whiche] whech
(*with er. mar.* G³) G;   me] (*2nd* e *ins.* G³);   a] *marked mar.* O.
4009 which¹] that J;   to²] vn to S.   4010 and ... maad] *o. er. with er. mar.*
C, *om.* S;   my ... falle] *om.* S   4012 wherfore] *ins. mar. after rub. mark also*
in text O;   me] *om.* O.   4013 make] (*2nd* a *ins.* G³);   falle] to falle J;

As] And as J.   4014 dide] whanne *add*. S;   to] tille J;   my belyes] and toke
J;   I took] my belwes J;   bleewh] I blewe J.   4015 made] y made J, hym
and his *add*. M;   to] for to S.   4016 him] he M;   defended] hiym *add*.
JM.   4016-7 he² ... wisdom] he shulde be as ful of ku*nn*ynge as god his soue*r*eyn
(*with* he scholde be as full of wysdon \and/ konnynge as god hys soue*r*eigne *foot of*
page C³)|C, (*with* he scholde be as full of ~~wysdon~~ konnynge as god hys soue*r*eigne
G³).   4017 al] as *add. ins.* G³, as S;   of] witte and of *add*. J.   4018 was]
enpressed and *add*. S;   from ... al²] vttyrly J;   desceyued] note *mar. and marked*
mar. O³;   and²] *om*. S;   þerfore] wherfore S.   4019 straunged] Strange
Made J, straunge make M, straunger made O;   also] alle JMO.   4020 go] to
ga JOS.   4021 Whan] *prec. Capitulum* Civ *mar*. CG;   tweyne] twa JMS, *om*.
O;   while] -s JMOS;   had] So *add* J.   4022 bithouhte] (e *ins*. G³).
4023 do] ma *add*. JM;   inowe] *om*. J;   I²] hafe J;   haue] (*2nd a ins*. G³),
I J.   4024 make] (*2nd a ins*. G³), also *add*. S;   þe¹] *om*. J.   4025 of]
dyuerse *add* J, þe *add*. MO;   haue] (*2nd a ins*. G³), to haue M;   and] *om*. O,
hir *add*. S;   discordes] indignaciou*n*s O.   4026 indignaciouns] in dignaciou*n*
JM, discordys O;   þat oon] i *over* G³, ilkane with othere J;   ofte] to *add*. C,
tymes and *add*. J, of þaim to O;   deffye] defyeþe S;   despise] to despyse O,
despyseþe S.   4026-7 þat ooþer] anoþere J.   4027 condyeresse] ledere J,
cowntase M.   4028 constablesse] constabilresse JM, Constable S;   of alle]
om. J;   in] and J;   chevachyes] chevaunces as bareresse or S.   4029 ben]
basynettys J, *om*. MO;   basenettes] es J.   4030 and²] with *add*. S.
4031 queyntisinges] qwaynte gyses J;   neewed] newe J, *marked mar*. O³;   I
make gownes to be wele plityd bifor and bihynd and depe iaggid of þe fresshest wyse
and of þe gay gailaunt man*er*. ilk moneth to be of new shapp *add*. M;   make] also
add. M;   hoodes] (*1st* o *ins*. G³).   4032 with gold] aboute J;   aboute] with
golde J.   4033 cappes] with hye crestes *add*. J;   and hye crestes] cappes of
dyuerse gises J;   ȝit in women I haue fonden a new gyse. I make þem to haue two
hornys wele atyred and standynge vp right. as it shuld be a yonge bull, to putt. whilk
hornys makes þem to stoupe at þe dore and to entre in o syde. for þei be so brode.
And euen in þe myddis of swilk hornys is my fadir Lucifer sittynge in man*er* of soft
and an esy sadull. I am also scho þat makes þer colers of þer serk*es* to hyng down
and to be prikkid bihynd þem þer belt*es* endes to haue knott*es* to þe grownd*e*. to haue
bair brestes and bair pursees I make also *add*. M;   cotes] pynched gownys *add*.
J;   with] *om*. J.   4034 sides] syde J;   to¹] *om*. M;   surcotes] garmentes
J;   sleeves] wele paynted with leuys and lett*ers* · wele lynyd colers · with an non
sequitur *add*. (non sequitur *underlined rub*.) M.   4034-5 to² ... white] gar-
mentys lawe colerde J.   4035 a ... biholde] forto schewe the white nekke & the
white halse oþere with standande colers wele enbrowdede and Sette with perle or
wi*th* Spanges of Silu*er* or of golde J;   brest] þe brest M;   white] wyþ O;
decoloured] decooled GS, Voyded · colerid M, voyded wyþ a voyde coler O;
biholde] I make *add*. M.   4036 longe] and to syde *add*. M, syde and O;   or¹]
other GMOS;   shorte] to wyde or to Strayte. Sum reve*n*e in many Jagges. Sum
cutted and corven strayte of dyuerse coloures. with resons and poyses *add*. J;   or²]
oþer S.   4037 grete] Sum with mare cleth in the tepet than in alle the hude ef*ter*
add. J;   bootes] and shoes *add*. M;   or] other GJMS;   grete] þat *add*. CMOS,
mekille J;   mihte] myghte (e *ins*. G³) G;   make] (*2nd a ins*. G³).
4038 hem] oon S;   tweyne] twa JMO;   or¹] other G;   smal] to Smale JS;
brod] hornes and wiscles harnaiste with Silu*er* and golde and alle oþere Swilke newe
gyses *add*. J.   4039 queintisen hem] thay make tham qwaynte J, þey queyntyse
þaim (*with* note *and marked mar*. O³) O.   4040 þe embosede] and *add*. J, *om*.

MO; ooþere] þat haues mykill riches *add*. M.   4041 euery] euerilke J, eche O;   haue] (*2nd a ins*. G³);   to me] his eye O;   his eye] to me O.   4042 be] it be J;   seid] I am *add*. J;   peere] *ins. mar*. G³, felaw MO;   of²] in JMO. 4043 ende] *om*. O;   þat¹] *ins. mar*. G³, *om*. S;   haue] *prec. scribbles* C³, (*2nd a ins*. G³);   alle] (e *ins*. G³), at alle suche thynges *add*. J;   and] *om*. S; paringall] paringe C.   4044 ne] of *add*. JS;   nor M;   I keepe] *trs*. J. 4045 herte] (*2nd e ins*. G³);   clyve] cleue (*with* clyue *mar*. G³) G, bryste and clefe in Sundyre J, and brist *add*. M;   comparede] compaared (*1st a ins*. G³) G, ware like and made comparisoun J, or likkyn *add*. M.   4046 susteyne] vphalde J; be ... yuel] and maynteyne J.   4046-7 and ... it] be it good or ille J. 4047 wolde I] *om*. J, repent ne *add*. M, repele (n *alt*. 1) O;   hadde] hafe J. 4048 haue] (*2nd a ins*. G³);   noon] no M;   no¹] ne J, nor M, *om*. O;   no²] ne JMO.   4049 beste] hors J, *o. er*. O;   hateth] the *add*. JS, an *add*. MO.   4049-50 and ... comb] *om*. JMO.   4049 a²] þe S;   4050 hate] (*2nd a ins*. G³);   and¹] *om*. M;   and avisement] *om*. O;   Þe] *with* ho *mar*. O³. 4051 thinketh] thynke JM;   owen] witte JMO;   bettere] the beste J. 4052 þat²] *o. er. with er. mar*. C, *om*. O;   þer] *o. er*. C;   no time] neuere mare J, in no tyme O.   4053 nothing] any thynge JMO;   doon] saide M;   ne] nor M;   seid] I Seyde J, done M;   ariht] right JMO;   but] ʒif *add*. JMO. 4054 forthouht] before thogh J, bifor thoght MO;   bi] of O;   wit] wille JMO; þat] if O.   4055 or¹] other GS;   seid] done J;   or²] other G, ne J;   doon] Sayde J;   sithe] Olesse than J, sithen M, Sen þat O;   bi me] it be done J. 4055-6 it² ... doon] by me J.   4056 so disdeynows] y hafe J, is OS;   þerof] *o. er. with er. mar*. C, So denyous JMO;   I haue] (haaue *1st a ins*. G³), þerof JOS.   4057 lakketh] that *add*. JS, but þat *add*. O;   it] ne J, myne herte O; ne] it J, *om*. MO;   on tweyne] in twa JMO;   aloone] note *mar. and marked mar*. O³;   haue] (*2nd a ins*. G³).   4058 wurshipe] and *add*. JO;   wel] I dare J;   I dar] well J;   sori] I am J;   I am] Sory J.   4059 wurshiped] praisid M;   or] other GS, and J;   preised] worsshippid M;   but] all oonly *add*. M;   haue] (*2nd a ins*. G³);   lasse] more *o. er*. O³.   4060 haue] (*2nd a ins*. G³);   anoon²] þat *add*. C;   nouht] -es J;   or] other GS.   4061 cristened] ecristened S;   heere] (*1st e ins*. G³);   þer be] *om*. J, þat M, þer, þat þere beo S;   wiht] man J.   4062 preyse] *prayses or com*mendes J, preiseʒ MO; þat] as J;   heere] herde J.   4063 skornest] skornedest S;   me] and tha *add*. J;   þou shuldest] *trs*. J;   do] so M;   so] *om*. J, do M.   4164 gon seyinge] saye J.   4066 And] *prec. Capitulum* Cv *mar*. CG, bot J;   whi] *om*. J;   sey] sayde S;   it] this J, *om*. S;   why I] *om*. S;   humble me] make it J, meke me M;   not] *om*. S.   4067 þat I sey] note *mar*. O³, *om*. S;   seyn] schulde Say J;   ayen] to me J;   to me] agayne J.   4068 nothing] for *add*. J; haue] na *add*. J.   4069 herte] (*2nd e ins*. G³);   shulde] wolde CO;   of] for CJMO;   and] *om*. CJ.   4070 spere] (*2nd e ins*. G³), þat *add*. CJMOS.   4071 þat¹] *om*. CJMO;   þat²] *om*. JMO;   ooþerweys] oþer wise JMO.   4072 þat²] *om*. S;   bifore] it es sayde J;   is seyd] before J; wrynge] writhande JM;   wyrchyng O.   4073 wurshipes] worschepe JM; eende] of *add*. J.   4074 saue] (*2nd a ins*. G³);   hens] heuene J, here S. 4075 þe] de C, *om*. JS;   is] haþ S;   noon] nouʒt MO;   cowde] do *add*. O, might S;   ne] or M, and also S;   mihte] koude S;   ye] do *add*. J. 4076 to¹] for to S.   4077 scornynge] glosing S;   and ... any] feynynge or *add*. J, or S;   flateringe] slaterye S;   And] *prec. Capitulum* cvj *mar*. CG. 4078 beringes up] vpberynge J, beryng vpp MO;   avauntinge] blastes J. 4079 blastes] of a vauntynge J;   herte] (*2nd e ins*. G³);   lepeth] leepeth (*2nd* e *ins.* G³) G.   4080 Swollen] note *mar.* O³;   and¹] grete *add.* J, *erasure* O; þanne] I become O;   I bicome] þan O;   seest] may se O.   4081 Þei maken me] (maake *1st* a *ins.* G³), mare place J, þei make my O;   place more] thay make me J;   chayer] cheer S.   4082 sitte] to Sitte JS;   allone] a bouen*e* J, al abown MO;   go] to ga J.   4083 be] to be J;   with folk] enviround J; envirowned] with folke J;   afeere] after S;   withoute beeinge] that I be noȝt J.   4084 empressed] opp*r*essed ne thru*n*gene J;   anything] any J. 4085 empressed] pressedde J.   4086 Feers] For JMO;   thwart] I haue *add.* C, I haue *add. ins. mar.* G³, loketh J.   4086-7 my lookinge] out warde and J.   4087 I¹] *om.* J;   feerstee] fersness*e* J, fers MO, ferst S. 4088 makinge] maakynge (*1st* a *ins.* G³) G.   4089 þe²] a MO.   4090 stiryinge] sturyenge (*1st* e *subpuncted* G³) G.   4091 with] *om.* J;   scume] flewe S.   4092 þe] *om.* CJ;   good] (*final* e *ins.* G³);   swimme] swunne C; ooþeres] othere men J, odir M.   4093 wel] wille J, me *add.* C;   make] (*2nd* a *ins.* G³);   and] I sett (sett *can.*) M;   ape] (*2nd* a *ins.* G³).   4094 as] *om.* JMOS;   yt] *o. er.* C;   stench] stynke JMO.   4095 breketh] vnbyndes J; or] other GS;   vnbyndeth] brekes J;   my¹] myne awne J.   4096 gretnesse] *prec.* Inmyb *top of* p. C³;   apperceyue] persayfed JO, p*er*ceyue M.   4097 þat] *om.* JO;   is] *om.* JO;   me] my Selfe J, self *add. ins. mar.* O³;   Þe] bot the J;   defautes] defaute S.   4098-9 but … þerfore] *om.* C.   4098 goodshipes] godeshippe OS;   nothing] neu*ere* adele J.   4099 þerfore] *followed by misplaced caret* G³;   I … folk] y GS, *ins. mar.* G³;   japere] Skornere J, *om.* MO;   and] *om.* MO;   scornere] de mar*e* J;   folk] *om.* JM, such O;   swich] *om.* CGJS, Swilk oon M;   shulde] *om.* CGJS.   4100 noon] *om.* CGJS; be founde] *om.* CGJS, fynde M;   at þe] *om.* CGJS;   Castell] *om.* CGJS, of *add.* M;   Landoun] *om.* CJ. *cross over* G³, London M, (e *ins. over* a O³), labour S;   for no peny] *om.* CJ, *crosses over* G³;   old] (*2nd* o *final* e *ins.* G³). 4101 cleped] called JMO.   4102 me] my corowne JMO;   anoon] *ins. mar. after rub. caret in text* O³;   cursede] weried J, cursseþe S;   my coroun] it JO; he²] *with* isaye *mar.* G³.   4103 it] *with* corowne *mar.* G³;   queen] I was called J;   I was cleped] qwene J, I was called M;   Loo heere howe þe foule olde horned beest beknoweþe to þe pilgryme hir name *add.* S.   4104 I] *prec.* C*apitulum* Cvij (*i erased* C) *mar.* CG, C*apitulum* xiij *mar.* S;   Orgoill] pride *over* C, *with* pride *mar.* G³, þat is to say · Pride *add.* M, *with* pryd the quainte *mar.* O³; queynte] þe galante *add.* M.   4105 haue] (*2nd* a *ins.* G³);   horn] þe horn C, a horne JMOS;   set] it *add.* J, has sette O;   amydde] ymiddes JMO, amiddes S;   þe folk] to hurtille J.   4105-6 to hurtle] the folke þ*er*with and to put J, and putt *add.* M.   4106 þat] which S;   cleped] called JMO;   Feerstee] Ferse JMO;   Crueltee] cruell JMO.   4107 vnicorn] the vyncorne J;   more] fers and *add.* JMO;   cruelle] fell O;   biscorn] twybille J;   or] other GS. 4108 of] of M.   4109 ne¹] and JMO;   so²] ne so S;   poynted] ne So scharpe J;   ne sharp] poynted J, and sharp MO.   4110 mihte] my (*with* Myghte *mar.* G³) G, may JMO;   herte] (*2nd* e *ins.* G³);   man] a man*e* J.   4111 if] bot ȝif J;   ne helpe] (heelpe *1st* e *ins.* G³), be helpande J;   and] ne Se;   made] make (*with* maade *mar.* G³) GJMOS;   make] (*2nd* a *ins.* G³).   4112 wey to] *om.* S;   daggeres] daggere JM;   to²] þe S;   swerdes] Swerde J, *with* note *mar.* O³, speres and axses *add.* S;   to³] *om.* S;   alle] (e *ins.* G³);   whiche] wheche (*2nd* e *ins.* G³) G, that J.   4113 made] and ymagyned *add.* S. 4114 half] *om.* J;   ne] or CJMO, ne F;   and] *om.* C.   4115 more] *om.* C; cruelliche] *om.* C, cruell O;   I … a] *om.* CGS;   riht] *om.* CGJS;   wylde] *om.* CGS;   bore] *om.* CGS, bare J;   and wite] *ins. mar.* G³, it *add.* JMO, *om.*

S.   4116 wel] *ins. mar.* G³, *om.* S;   þat¹] *ins. mar.* G³, *om.* OS.
4116-7 þilke ... power] I hurtele most cruelliche C, *om.* G, y hurtle most crewelleche
ins. mar. G³, *om.* S.   4116 þilke] thase JMO;   hauen] hadde JM;
sinne] -s JMO;   to] atte J.   4117 I ... cruelliche] þilke þat to here power
hauen poorged hem of here sinne C, *om.* G, thylke that to ther power haaue
puurged hem of her synne *ins. foot of page.* G³, *om.* S;   hurtele] Smyte
JMO;   þan] *om.* C, hem þane S.   4118 ooþere] *om.* C;   With] *prec.*
Capitulum Cviij *mar.* (vii *o. er.* C) CG;   me] (2nd e *ins.* G³), also *add.* J;   payre]
of *add.* JMOS;   belyes] *o. er.* C, *om.* J;   staf] a staffe J.   4119 horn] a
horne J;   am] cledde J;   cloþed] I am J;   a] white *add.* J;   shewe] scheewe
(1st e *ins.* G³) G;   myn] (final e *subpuncted* G).   4121 belyes] *o. er.* C, vayn
glory *mar.* O³;   hatten] hatte JMO;   Veynglorie] vaynglory *rub. mar.* O;
with coles] *trs.* J.   4122 make] (2nd a *ins.* G³);   weene] to weene CJ, whane
þay weene S.   4123 alle] *om.* S;   Þese] Thyre J.   4124 seide] (2nd e *ins.*
G³).   4125 sparcles] sperkes JMO.   4126 wel] nabugodonosor *mar.*
G³;   withinne] hym *add.* JMO.   4127 cole] -s J;   was] ware J;   instru-
ment] -es JMO;   As] *prec. Capitulum* Cix (ix *o. er.* C) *mar.* CG;   wynd] þe
wynde S.   4128 þe¹] *om.* JM;   riht] *om.* JMO;   þe²] *om.* MO.
4129 þilke] the JM, þo O;   belyes] *o. er. with er. mar.* C;   leith] felleth down
J, down *add.* MO;   alle ... doun] alle *vertues* JMO.   4130 He] *marked mar.*
C³.   4131 hye] *om.* O;   ouerthroweth] thrawith them J.   4132 here¹]
om. J;   feedinges] that he ou*er* takes · He leues na goodschepe before hym · He
vnnestlys the hye briddes and thrawys tham downe þare Fode J;   maketh] geres
J;   here²] fedyng *add. can.* M;   folye] and *add.* J.   4133 lyvinge] this
maye þou See by ensau*m*ple *add.* J;   euere] *om.* MO;   herdest] have herd
O.   4134 mowth] nebbe the J, n*o*ta de coruo · *et* de vulpe *rub. mar.* O, heere
þe {fable of} þe Raven {and þe} Fox *mar.* S.   4135 Rauen] quod he *add.* J;
þee] N*o*ta *rub. mar.* O;   as sey] Synge J, say M;   a] some S;   haue] (2nd
a *ins.* G³), grete *add.* JS;   soun] The tale of the fox suttle, and Ravyne þe symple.
mar. O³.   4137 woorth] melodyous S;   þan] noise *add. ins.* M;   of a]
owthere J;   symphanye] or harpe *add.* J;   I wolde] me ware J;   heere] to
hyre J.   4138 soun] the sowne JMO;   organe] -s JMO;   or] other GS;
sautree] a sawtry M;   faile me not] I pray the J.   4139 I prey] fayle me nouȝt
J;   whiche] *with* Rauene *mar.* G³, Rauen J.   4141 susteyne] halde J;   To
singe] and tuke vp J, and to syng OS.   4142 he ... up] atte Synge J, he tuke
vp MO;   þilke] he JMO;   þe] his J.   4143 wende] that *add.* J;
treweliche] soth J;   But] *repeated* J;   nay] *om.* JMO.   4144 he¹] *with*
scilicet fox *mar.* G³, the Foxe J;   ne rouhte] rought nathynge for J;   withoute
more] alle anelye J.   4144-5 wolde haue] (2nd a *ins.* G³) covayted J.
4145 He] *with* fox *mar.* G³, and J;   as him likede] atte his liste J;   desceyuede]
the fox *add.* J.   4146 Bi] *prec. Capitulum* Cx (*followed by* i *erased* C) CG;
miht] may JS;   apperceyue] persayfe JMO.   4147 maketh] (2nd a *ins.*
G³);   þat ... feþered] *om.* M;   leese] to leese CM, (2nd e *ins.* G³), to leve J.
4148 þat þat] þat O;   haue] (2nd a *ins.* G³), if þei by right wele federid *add.*
M;   þat³] *om.* JM;   any] wight *add.* J.   4149 haue] (2nd a *ins.* G³), vertu
M;   vertu] -s J, haue M;   eiþer] or JMO, oþer S;   goodes] good J, godnes
O;   or] other G;   fortune] I besy me so *add.* O.   4150 I drawe] *om.* J;
for oon] i *over* G³, *om.* J, -s M, *ins. mar. after rub. caret in text* O³;   and] *om.*
J;   þat I²] *ins. mar. after rub. caret in text* O³, *om.* S;   awey] fro hym *add.*
O;   merelle] m*e*ryte J, meritys and O.   4151 with þese belyes] *om.* J;   I]
wis *add. can.* M;   whistle] whiltel S;   him¹] *om.* O;   soo] þat *add.* J.

4151-2 þat¹ ... holt] (þat² *with* vertu *mar.* G³), he loses J.   4152 he leeseth]
he seseth (*with* leeseth *mar.* G³) G, that atte he haldeth J;   The] *prec. Capitulum*
Cxi *mar.* CG;   þilke] the J, þat M, tho O.   4153 shulde] schalle J;   neuere]
no O;   ne asshen] abyde J;   abide] ne asches J.   4154 seid þat] called J,
saide man*ne* (manne *can.* M) MO;   and¹] *om.* O;   and²] man *mar.* G³;   is²]
om. JO.   4154-5 Þis powder] and O, þis power S;   with ... wynd] raysed
J.   4156 reysed] with litille wynde J, areysed S;   in] to *add.* JMO;
disparpoylinge] despoylling S;   cast] -yng O;   perdicoun] *with* loss *mar.*
G³.   4157 maken] *2nd a ins.* ofte *add.* C, ofte *add. ins.* G³, in *add.* O;   and¹]
om. O;   often] *om.* CS, *can.* G, tymes *add.* J.   4158 and¹] ryght so *add.* J;
þilke] thay J, þo MO;   han] haauen (*2nd a ins.* G³) O;   no] (*final* n *subpuncted*
G);   I] *with* pride *mar.* G³.   4159 þilke] the J, þo M, no O;   þe] of J;
herth] erthe JM, hert O;   to] So JM, is so O;   þilke] thykke to thay*me* J, thikk
to þo MO;   of his soule] they make J.   4160 wole make] (*2nd a ins.* G³), of
theyre Sawle J;   þee] (*1st* e *ins.* G³).   4161 þat] *om.* M;   light] ought
JMO.   4162 fanne] wane S;   be¹] *ins. mar.* G³, it *add.* O;   greyn]
corne;   or] other GS, of M;   thing] that est at saye thynge J;   ouht] corn
mar. O³;   be] is O.   4163 woorth] wrout3 J;   or] other GS;   nothing]
noght O;   woorth] worght J, is worth *ins. mar. after rub. caret in text* O³;   faste]
(e *ins.* G³).   4164 make] (*2nd a ins.* G³);   rise] to ryse J;   if²] and J;
greyn] corn*e* J.   4165 belyes] blowyng O.   4166 Bi] *prec. Capitulum* Cxij
(i *erased* C) CG, *om.* J;   þese belies] *om.* J;   drawe] (*2nd a ins.* G³);   ayen]
om. J.   4167 any] men J;   goth] gase J;   and] or JMO;   ere] eere (*2nd*
e *ins.* G³) G.   4168 me] (*2nd* e *ins.* G³);   haue] (*2nd a ins.* G³) G;   cote]
(*2nd* o *ins.* G³) *with* skyn*e* mar. G³, skynne JO, *id est* skynn *add.* M.
4169 mihty] wight *add.* J;   wys] and *add.* S;   and wurþi] *om.* S;   þanne]
(e *ins.* G³), and droughe I S;   I drawe] *with* draawe *mar.* G³, þanne S.
4170 and] *om.* J;   in] to *add.* J;   I make it] (maake *1st* a *ins.* G³ in G), *om.*
J;   place] *om.* J, a place M;   Gret] and thane I be co*m*m J;   I bicome] grete
J.   4171 seest] & as *add.* J;   it] *om.* J;   wynd] (*final* e *subpuncted* G);
maketh] (*2nd a ins.* G³).   4172 araye] to aray J;   me] and *add.* S;   a] *om.*
S;   haue] to heve S;   hye] onn hygh O;   þat] the J.   4173 apperceyue]
per*s*ayfe JMO.   4174 haue] (*2nd a ins.* G³).   4175 owen] *with* eyen *u.v.*
mar. G³;   with] witte JM;   myself] *om.* JMO.   4176 Of] *prec. Capitulum*
Cxiij (*1st* i *erased* C) CG;   swollen so] *trs.* J;   if] bot 3if J.   4177 ne ware]
ware J;   avented] vented JMO;   or] other GS.   4178 And] *prec. Capitulum*
Cxiiij (*o. er.* C) CG;   þerfore] (*final* e *ins.* G³);   aventour] ventous JMO;
haue] (*2nd a ins.* G³).   4179 whiche] wheche (*2nd* e *subpuncted*) G;   caste]
(e *ins.* G³).   4180 þat] *prec.* In me begynde god me spede *top of p.* C³;   heue]
(*2nd a ins.* G³);   in] *om.* C;   name] (*2nd a ins.* G³);   be] lyeing & boasting
mar. O³;   cleped] called JMO.   4181 Vantaunce] *id est* bostinge *over* C³,
with vauntynge *mar.* G³, a vauntynge (*with* Avayntyng *rub. mar.* M) JMO;   oþer]
or JMO;   þilke] it JS;   which] þe which S;   abashe] aferde M, avoyde S.
4182 bestes] beste JM, bo*s*te O;   þe²] *om.* M;   make] (*2nd a ins.* G³), gere
J.   4183 wole] wolde C;   harde] pride *mar.* G³, *om.* J;   I blowe] *om.*
J.   4184 haue] (*2nd a ins.* G³);   nothing] takyn*e* J;   take] (*2nd a ins.*
G³);   feeld] (*final* e *subpuncted* G).   4185 haue] (*2nd a ins.* G³);   of²]
om. MOS   4186 I haue] (*2nd a ins.* G³), in tyme past O;   in ... passed] þat
I haue O;   þat þat] þat MO;   com] (*2nd* o *ins. and final* e *subpuncted* G³).
4187 I sey] *with* pride *mar.* G³;   of¹] so O;   gret] of *add.* O.   4188
þat] and þat S;   grete] hugge S.   4189 and¹] *ins. mar. after rub. caret also*

in text O³, *om.* S;   wel kan do] that I can*e* wele do J, *om.* S;   þat¹] *om.* OS;
and² þat²] Et que F, *om.* JOS; ·   and³ þat³] *om.* CG.   4190 inowe] other*e* grete
lordes J, *om.* O;   of ooþere] I newe I Say I hafe bene atte many J, ʒat I haue bene
in many O;   tournements] arayes C, *with* arayes *mar.* G³, and batayles *add.* J,
tourmentis S;   ben] ne ben Cs, breth *(with* beeth *mar.* G³) G.
4191 bostinges] bostynge J;   þe] *(2nd* e *subpuncted* G), *om.* J;   it] I S.
4192 I¹] *prec. Capitulum* Cxv *mar.* CG;   blowe] *with* pride *mar.* G³;   haue]
(2nd a *ins.* G³);   a pray] *om.* S;   oþer] or JMO.   4193 haue] *(2nd* a *ins.*
G³);   for] *om.* S.   4194 wolde] wil M;   haue] *(2nd* a *ins.* G³);   ne] no
(with ne *mar.* G³) G;   to be ded] halde hit Stille J.   4195 holde it stille] to
be dede þerfore J;   As] but as O;   leyd] ane egge cries and J;   kakeleth] cakyll
O.   4196 to] tille J;   eche] ilke JM, everych O;   anoon] belyue J;   Tprw
Tprw] *om.* J, trowe ye O;   I sey] *om.* S;   Tprw³] *om.* JOS   4197 Tprw]
om. JS, true O;   Haue] *(2nd* a *ins.* G³);   haue¹] *(2nd* a *ins.* G³);   how I haue]
om. S;   seyd] leyd C, *om.* S;   how I²] *om.* C.   4198 haue] *om.* C, *(2nd*
a *ins.* G³);   done] *om.* C;   idoo] done JMO.   4199 yow] nouʒt *add.* J;
haue] *(2nd* a *ins.* G³);   properliche] done J;   ydoon it] properly J, done
MO.   4200 þilke¹] he that JM, he O;   or] other G, *om.* S;   þilke²] he that
J, þat MOS;   hadde] schulde have J;   wole] wolde J.   4201 or] other G;
agast] ferde JMO;   þat²] *om.* M.   4202 bettere do] *trs.* J.   4203 Of] *prec.*
Capitulum Cxvj *mar.* CG.   4204 bely] bellowes JMO;   and] *om.* J;   a] *ins.*
G³, *om.* M;   drede] tell not all thou heare *mar.* O³.   4205 heereth] canne J;
bi] *om.* O;   no] þe S;   heere] no thing ne *add.* S.   4206 wolde] wol S;
for þe horn] es called J;   is cleped] a fole J.   4207 a fool] For the horne J;
herden] heerden *(2nd* e *ins.* G³) G.   4208 but] byleue *add.* J.
4208-9 holde parlement] a vaunt J;   of] *om.* J;   resembleth] es lyke JO, is like
to M;   þe] a O;   can] *om.* J.   4210 and] ne JMO;   but] a vaunter *mar.*
O³, ay *add.* S.   4211 wynd] *(final* e *subpuncted* G);   cleped] called
JMO.   4212 what] þat S;   woordes] *(1st* o *ins.* G³).   4213 as] but
JMO;   alle] thynges *add.* JMO.   4214 maketh] *(2nd* a *ins.* G³);   sentences]
sentence JMO;   abrod] note *mar.* O³;   argueth] and *add.* J.
4215 assoileth] assailes MOS;   he] and J;   swich] white J;   maketh] *(2nd* a
ins. G³);   ofte] *om.* J.   4216 clout] clut *(with* a cloutte *mar.* G³) GF, a clout
C, blakke J, -es O;   þat¹] and J, and þat O;   þat²] So J;   is] ware JMO;
of … colour] Soo J.   4217 to²] forto MO;   to make] *(2nd* a *ins.* G³), ger J.
4218 flee] flyes J;   shulde he] *trs.* J, shuld me M, he wol S;   make] *(2nd* a *ins.*
G³).   4219 Swiche] suche (e *ins.* G³) G;   magnifye] *with* preyse *mar.* G³;
fastes] fastynges JMO;   and²] *om.* JMO.   4220 penaunces] penaunce
JMO;   al] ʒif alle J;   be þer] *trs.* J;   paunches] paunchere J.
4221 wynd] *(final* e *subpuncted* G);   make] *(2nd* a *ins.* G³);   þe] *om.* J
4222 This] *prec.* cxvij (i *erased* C) CG;   maketh] *(2nd ins.* G³);   a] *om.* J;
hunte] huntynge JMO;   seelde] Seldom JMO.   4223 bifalleth] Falles
JMO;   al awey] away M, alwey O.   4224 and¹] For J;   þe] a J, a iay or
a M;   and²] hir *add.* J;   chateringe] claterynge JMO.   4225 nestle] to nestle
COS, bigge J;   nygh] ner*e* J, *om.* O;   maketh] *(2nd* a *ins.* G³), garres J;   flee]
fly MS;   awey] *ins. mar.* G³, *om.* JMO, firþer more S.   4226 maketh] *(2nd*
a *ins.* G³);   hireself] þay*me* selfe J;   hated] *(2nd* a *ins.* G³), haded S;   hem]
om. J;   eche] ilke a J, ilk M, euerych O.   4227 goth to flihte] *(final* e *ins.*
G³), flees J;   heeren] *(2nd* e *ins.* G³);   horn] *(final* e *ins.* G³);   þer] þei
CS.   4228 wole] -n C;   non] not C, *om.* S;   nestle] bigge J;   nyh] ner*e*
J;   cryinge] and clateryng *add.* M.   4229 This] *prec. Capitulum* Cxviij (viij

o. er. C) *mar.* CG.   4230 longe] yit it is S.   4231 it is] long S;   sitthe]
Sen JMO;   not neewe] made J, mad newe (mad *o. er. of* not) O, nuwe S;   sithe]
Sene   JMO.   4232 hanselled]   haxselde   J.   4233 ne]   nor.   O.
4233-4 eche wiht] schalle J, ilk wight M, euerych wyght O.   4234 shal] ilke
wight J;   mown] *om.* J;   be] to beo S;   þei] he J;   wolen] Of þe spore dame
Grace dieux declareþe vn to þe pilgryme þe tokennynges *add.* S.   4235 Of] *prec.*
C*apitulum* Cxix (ix *o. er.* C) CG, Cap*itulum* xiv *mar.* S;   I sey þee] also J;
also] I Say the J;   for] that J;   knowen] I ham J;   I am] knawen*e* J.
4236 oþerwhile] gladly JMO;   gladliche] other*e* while JMO.   4237 to] *om.*
GO;   feet] fote JMO;   but] ʒif J, if *add.* S;   hadde] *ins. mar.* G³;   hors
bi me] hors biside me CS, *with* hors be syde me *mar.* G³.   4238 seyn] that *add.*
JM;   do] to do S;   ennoye] envye S;   þan] *o. er.* C, *om.* J;   for] *o. er.* C.
4239 to go] forthward *add.* (*all o. er.*) C;   To go] *o. er.* C, *om.* J;   bacward myn heeles] *o. er. and into mar.* C.   4239-40 þat oon] *with* sporre *mar.* G³,
sporre *add.* JMO.   4240 cleped] called JMO.   4241 Þe firste] *with scilicet*
spore *mar.* G³, sporre *add.* JM;   Adam took] toke Adam *trs.* J, disobeying and rebellion *rub. mar.* M, prides toe spurrs. inobedience: Rebellion *mar.* O³;   þe]
for boden*e add.* J;   bi] thurgh the eggynge of J.   4242 mihte] myghte (e *ins.*
G³) G;   bi] *om.* MS;   taste] (*2nd a ins.* G³), faste S;   but] ʒif *add.* JS.
4243 hadde first] *trs.* J.   4243-5 Þe ... spore] *om.* J.   4243 hadde]
inobedience *mar.* G³, be *add. ins.* O³.   4244 it] hir S.   4245 he] *with* Adam
mar. G³;   made] (*2nd a ins.* G³).   4246 hardy] and *add* J;   deth] þe deeþe
S;   Of] In J.   4247 he] had J.   4248 hadde] he J;   moste] nedes *add.*
J;   it] the spurr*e* J;   ne hadde] hadd he nouʒt J.   4249 þat ... side] that
was fourmed J, of his right side S;   was foormed] of his ryght Syde J;   hadde
he] *trs.* J.   4250 haue] (*2nd a ins.* G³) *om.* J;   vsed] vse J;   it¹] *with* spore
mar. G³;   That] *prec.* Capitulum Cxx (*final* j *erased* C) *mar.* CG.
4251 spore] was *add. ins. mar.* O³;   on] opon M;   his heele] kynge pharao J,
(hys *can.* O);   þe kyng Pharao] hele J, of kyng pharao (of *o. er.*) O;   þat] and
that J.   4252 of¹] thurgh J;   þe²] his JMO;   peple] the childyr*e add.*
J.   4253 of²] *om.* J;   hond] thraldom*e* J.   4254 for] pharao *add.* J;
ayens] agayn*e* JMO;   a] hym that was J, *om.* MO;   he] *om.* J.   4255 spore]
sporys O.   4256 longe] (e *ins.* G³), *om.* S.   4257 harde] hardde (de *ins.*
G³) G;   see] high O;   he ouerthreew] was ouerþrawyn*e* and drowned J, he
ouerthrowen was M, ouerþrowen he was O;   Swich] folk *add.* C;   is] er
JM.   4258 assaile] to assayle J;   his] thayre J;   ouerthroweth] þaym*e* Selfe
add. J.   4259 seyn] that *add* J;   hurteleth] spurnes J, hurlleþe S;   ayens]
agayne JMO;   poynt] prikke J.   4260 þat] not*a mar.* G³, so JO;   shal] *om.*
J;   prowde] poudre (*subpuncted with* prowde *over* C³) C, man *add.* JMO;
may] wille JMO.   4261 spore] -es O;   ende] laste J.   4262 lyf] thus *add.*
J, Take hede howe þat Gracedieux declareþe to þe pilgryme of þe bourdoun *add.*
S.   4263 Now] *prec.* C*apitulum* Cxxj (Cxxii *alt.* Cxxi C) *mar.* CG, Cap*itulum*
x{v} *mar.* S;   I wole] *trs.* J;   þee] (*1st* e *ins.* G³);   staf] bourdoun S;
I² ... of] which is S;   a] my S.   4264 burdoun] staffe S;| sustene] prids
staff. obstina*cion mar.* O³;   and] a S.   4265 and] or JM;   bi] with
JMO.   4266 sermoun] wordes J;   and¹] or JMO;   skirme] Skyrmuyse
J.   4267 ayens] agayn M;   wole] by resou*n* O;   bi resoun] wyll O;
bineme] refe JM.   4268 condiciouns] c*o*ndicioun JMO;   defende] þer*with*
add. J;   noon] *with* synne *mar.* G³.   4269 to] bowe ne *add.* J.   4270 þat]
of M.   4271 heeld] had JO, whilk he hadd M;   as þou seye] *om.* JMO.
4272 Obstinacioun] Obstinacy JMO;   it¹] es J, *om.* S;   is] it J;   cleped] called

JMO; þee] at *add.* M, of *add.* O; þat] obstinacy *rub. mar.* M, late O.
4273 þilke] it JMO, þe staff S; whiche] kyng *add.* J; lenede him¹] *om.* J;
vndertook] reproued J; of] for J. 4274 led] *om.* CGS, amenee F; and
kepte] (*2nd e ins.* G³), Fra amalech J; from Amalech] and keped on lyfe J.
4275 in] *om.* JMO; bowe] blowe (burioyne *over*) C. 4277 þat] and J;
was] greewh *o. er. with er. mar.* C; founde] *om.* C; þilke] thayme J, *om.* M,
þo O. 4278 The *om.* J; cherliche] Churles J. 4279 smite] ysmitte
S; make] (*2nd a ins.* G³), to make S; me] *alt.* theme O³; be] *om.* JMO.
4280 bihated] hatene JMO; I] It J; make] garres J; flee] Grace dieu
J. 4280-1 and ... away] flee J. 4281 Grace Dieu] and dryfes hire a waye
J; of] fro CJ; places] place O; make] (*2nd a ins.* G³). 4282 to¹] vn
to S; Penitence] penaunce JMO. 4283 þe¹] *om.* J; haue] (*2nd a ins.*
G³); maad] of the staffe *add.* J; stake] stok O. 4284 laces] cordes J,
louses MO; Peresce] slowthe *over* C, *with* sleuthe *mar.* G³, Slewth JMO, to tye
vnto the lasses of Sloth *mar.* O³. 4285 þilke] þa JMO; Now bihold] (*final
e subpuncted* G), *trs.* J; þow] the JMO; ouhtest] aught JMO; wel] *om.*
O. 4286 Allas] or nouȝt *add.* J; whan] Sen J; founde] folwed O;
shewe þee] onane J. 4287 anoon] schewe the J; þat] *om.* O; sithe] Sen
that J, sithen MO. 4288 haue] (*2nd a ins.* G³); þus miche] sayde the JM,
so moch O, þis mich S; seid þee] thus mykille J; sey] telle J; þee²]
firþermore *add.* S; of] *om.* J. 4289 This] that of the J, þat is þe MO;
am] þus *add.* S; as] pryds Mantle hipocrisye *mar.* O³. 4290 ago] tyme
passed J; þat¹] Sen J; it] this mantelle JMO; maad] (*1st a ins.* G³);
haue] (*2nd a ins.* G³). 4291 for to] *o. er.* O; consele] hide JMO.
4292 vnthriftes] vnthryfte JMO; embelisheth] bleches JMO; whiteth] doþe
whyte S. 4293 hep] hille J; þat] as J; peynture] a payntouur JMO;
maketh] (*2nd a ins.* G³); shynynge] a berielle fayre and J; a buryell] schynande
J. 4294 stinkinge] with in *add.* J; þis] þe O; mantelle] *om.* J, Nota *rub.*
mar. O; hath] *om.* J. 4295 seith] sheueþ O. 4296 an] *om.* O;
thing] *ins. mar. after rub. caret also in text* O³; and¹] if M; I] if I *add* S.
4297 of ... oon] (1 *over* on G), be praysed J; be preysed] of neuere a mann J;
If euere] *om.* J. 4298 an enchauntour] a iugillour J; maketh] (*2nd a ins.*
G³). 4299 vnder] þer vnder S; and] *om.* J; ofte] ofttymes J; it is]
when J, is MO, hit happeneþe S; is] *om.* O; nothing] vndyr *add.* J.
4300 þerfore] Per bi C, there fore (*2nd e ins., fore with by mar.* G³) G, So J;
miht] schalle J; wel] *om.* J; albeit] ȝif alle J, þat *add.* S. 4301 withoute]
(oute *with* owte *mar.* G³) -ne J; seye] sees M, þat seye S; mown] *om.* J.
4302 Blow] lowe O; brid] fowle J; ostrich] an ostrich CM, Strucio J.
4303 bereth] Has J; haue] (*2nd a ins.* G³). 4304 whiche] also he J; hath]
with bridd *mar.* G³; þe] *om.* J; aboute] opon J; and] bot J, *om.* MO;
algates] ȝit J; flee] he may noȝt J. 4304-5 may he nouht] (*with scilicet*
ostrysch *mar.* G³), flye J. 4305 knewen] knowen C. 4306 shulden] walde
J; weenen] þat *add.* S; so] as (*subpuncted with* so *mar.* G³) GOS; leeven]
þat *add.* C, þat *add. ins. mar.* G³, supposes M. 4307 whiche] I bere *add.* J;
þat¹] *om.* C, *subpuncted* G; withoute] and weenen S. 4308 contemplatyf]
and *add.* C, and *add. ins. mar.* G³. 4309 and] ane J; algates] netherlese
J; eerthe] þe erth M; habite] dwelle J, abyde S. 4310 al þere] þerin J,
all þing O; delite me] es alle my delyte J, delytes me O; nouht¹] ne *add.* S;
flee ... nouht] *om.* CM. 4311 Mantelle] *om.* S; haue] (*2nd a ins.* G³);
Ypocrysie] *prec.* Capitulum Cxxiij *mar.* CG, *with* ypocrisy *rub. mar.* O.
4312 name] (*2nd a ins.* G³); þis mantelle] calle I J; I clepe] this mantille J,

I call M, is called O.   4313 in] *om.* J;   brede] breede (*2nd* e *ins.* G³) G;
withoute] (e *ins.* G³);   maad] warpe*n* JS;   worpen] made JS.   4314 of¹]
þe *add.* C, þe *add. ins. mar.* G³;   bere] haue born M;   cherche] the kyrke
JM.   4315 and¹] I *add.* C;   on] The outsyd lambe / fox within *mar.* O³;
to¹] *om.* C;   to²] *om.* JMO;   I¹] *om.* CS.   4316 drede] dreede (*1st* e *ins.*
G³) G;   me²] *om.* MO;   wolde] & wulde (*with* wolde *mar.* G³) G;   putte]
(e *ins.* G³).   4317 estate] state JM;   and] oute *add.* M;   of] *om.* JO;
þe] *om.* O;   which] þat C;   haue] (*2nd* a *ins.* G³).   4318 al] -s S;   make]
(*2nd* a *ins.* G³).   4319 as] þat *add.* S;   Renard] *with scilicet* fox *mar.* G³,
the fox *add.* JMO, Bernard S.   4320 made] (*2nd* a *ins.* G³), layde J, did MO;
him] in *add. subpuncted* G;   ded] (*final* e *subpuncted* G), *om.* JMO;   in¹] to
add. M;   in²] to *add.* CJMO;   þanne] so JMO.   4321 haue¹] (*2nd* a *ins.*
G³), to hafe JMOS;   of] *om.* S;   þe] *om.* MO;   heringe] that was þere in
add. JMO;   it] this mantelle JMO;   haue²] (*2nd* a *ins.* G³);   ben] putte *add.*
J;   and] N*ota rub. mar.* O. in *add.* S.   4322 ape clomben] hape clomben (*with*
aape cloumben *mar.* G³) G, hepe clu*m*byn (1 *alt.* h) O;   be ... goddesse] be *add.*
subpuncted G, bene behalden J, as a goddesse MO.   4323 biholden] as a
goddesse J, be bihaldyn MO;   apes] apysche JMO;   ben þei] þey ar O;   it¹]
mantelle *over* C, *with scilicet* Mantyll *mar.* G³.   4324 maketh] (*2nd* a *ins.* G³),
tham to *add.* J, to *add.* MO;   counterfete] counterfetys O;   men] man J.
4325 apeshipe] apisch craft M, Apisshe thing S;   make] (*2nd* a *ins.* G³);   muse]
to muyse JMO;   Ape] Ane ape JMO, Þe Aape S.   4326 bountee] the pharisye
mar. O³.   4327 iuste] goode and rythwyse J;   he²] n*ota* de pharisee *et*
publicane *rub. mar.* M.   4328 in] *om.* GS, En F.   4329 þat¹] whilke J;
mayme] gilte and be knewe hy*m* Selfe a synnere J.   4330 him¹] the pharisene
J;   medlede] melled JMO, did medle S.   4331 laste] (e *ins.* G³);   throte]
in Sundyre *add.* J.   4332 medleth] melles JMO;   craft] þat *add.* C, A Crafte
that JM, a craft O, þe which *add.* S;   hath] was O;   I] *prec.* Capitulum Cxxiv
mar. CG. (*marked mar.* C).   4333 mantelle] *with* ? ypocryse *mar.* G³;
aloone] alle anely on my Selfe J, all on my self MO;   maad] þe Mantle of pryde,
often / vsed, and made olde, and / I would it w*ere* ma*de* vseless *mar.* O³;   for]
om. JMO;   alle] (e *ins.* G³);   olde] (*2nd* o *ins.* G³);   Eche] for ilke a J, for
ilk M, for euerich O.   4334 to his aray] at his time C, *with* att hys tyme G³;
be] Seme J;   þe] *om.* J;   Peresce] slewth *over* C, Sclewth JMO.
4335 maketh] (*2nd* a *ins.* G³);   I] *with scilicet* ypocrysye *mar.* G³;   make] (*2nd*
a *ins.* G³);   humble] meke JMO;   þe] *om.* J;   ooþere] *with scilicet* vyces *mar.*
G³, vyces *add.* JMO.   4336 viletee] vilness M, -s -S;   more] (*2nd* o *ins.*
G³).   4337 more] (*2nd* o *ins.* G³), *om.* J;   strong] stranggere J;   þee] on
JMO.   4338 on] the JMO;   make] (*2nd* a *ins.* G³);   þee] (*1st* e *ins.* G³);
assaye] to assaye J;   sithe] seyne JM;   if] that J;   haue] (*2nd* a *ins.* G³).
4339 of þee] I wille do me wille J;   I ... wille] of the J, þer er many þat vsis and
beris / þis mantyll opon þem of ypocrisy ~~opon þem~~ and specialy in Religion. of whom
/ Jhesu spake to his disciples and saide þus Take3 entente vnto fals prophe*te*s and /
ypocrite3 whilk coomes to yow in shepis clothyng · for þei er like to symple / shepe
owteward ⸳ bot withinforth þei er like to rauysshynge wolfes . Bot / of þer fruytes
and of þer werkes ⸳ 3he shall know what þei er . Bot ye must / know me and go with
me . for I haue tolde of myne office ⸳ and myne aray / and why I were þus my mantyll
and haues wynges ·/ *add.* M³ *and* Here þe pilgryme spekis to Flat*er*yng . whilk beris
vp Pryde . in hir nekk . *add. rub.* M, I wyll do all my wyll O.   4340 Whan]
prec. Capitulum Cxxv *mar.* CG, capitulum xij *rub. mar.* M;   Orguill] pride *over*
C, *with scilicet* pride and pride *mar. under rubrication* G³, and pride *add.* M;

yit] my *add. can.* M. 4342 Oolde] Olde (*final* e *ins.* G³) G, thow alde delle J, Þou olde M. 4343 susteynest] beres J; Orguill] pride *over* C, with pride *mar. under rubrication* G³, pryde M; þat¹] *om.* JMO; so þat] *om.* O. 4344 wurþi] worth JMO. 4345 And] *prec. Capitulum* Cxxvj *mar.* CG. 4346 Sithe] Sen JM, Sone O; quod she] þou wille wit J; þou ... wite] quod scho J; who] *om.* J, what MO. 4346-7 I¹ ... she] *om.* J. 4348 flateringe] faytynge J; me] of me J; nothing] noȝt JMO, Flattery. prydes Supporter *mar.* O³. 4349 olde] (*2nd* o *ins.* G³); eche] ilke JM, euerych O; sey] Sayse JMO. 4350 me] (*2nd* e *ins.* G³); salue] nota bene *mar.* O³; þe¹] *om.* JMOS; grete] *om.* S. 4351 hem¹] and the motes ȝa ofte tymes *add.* J; þat] whene J; haue] (*2nd* a *ins.* G³); hem²] *ins. mar. after rub. caret also in text* O³, ariht *add.* CGS; boþe] in ryght JMO, in trouthe S. 4352 in¹] *om.* O; in²] *om.* JS; of] with S. 4353 ayens] agayn M; haue] (*2nd* a *ins.* G³); To] Vnto M. 4354 sey¹] þat *add.* O; sey²] that *add.* JO. 4355 atempree] tempery M; sey] þat *add.* MS; and] *om.* J. 4356 sey] that *add.* JS; russhe] reche JMO, strewe greene risshen and floures vpone S. 4357 place] (*2nd* a *ins.* G³); coife] *with* couer *mar.* O³; sore hed] forhed (*with* soor hed *mar.* C³) CM; oynture] *with* oygnture *mar.* G³. 4358 shrewede] drye S; crye] nomore S; more] na mare J, note *mar.* O³, gyge S; after] *om.* S. 4359 be] he es J, for S; alwey] *om.* S. 4360 wel] *om.* C, fayre J; jogelour] -s O; jogelouresse] Jonglouruesse (*2nd* u *subpuncted*) G, menstralle JMO, Jangeleresse S. 4361 maketh] (*2nd* a *ins.* G³). 4362 hem] *om.* MO; þe floyte] flaterye S; mere mayden] Mermayde O. 4363 make] (*2nd* a *ins.* G³), gers J, makes MO; drenche] drowne J, be drowned M, perisshe S; perisshe] drenchen S; þilke] þay J, þo MO; þat²] Flaterynge *rub. mar.* M; wolen] *om.* JS. 4364 heere] (*1st* e *ins.* G³), heres J, vnbyheren S; Flaterye] Flaterynge JMO; cleped] called JMO; my] ryght *add.* J. 4365 eldere] the eldere J; to¹] of J; Falsetee] marked *mar.* C, *with scilicet* falssnesse *mar.* G³, Falshede JMO; norice] nutrice J, trefoil *mar.* O³; Iniquitee] *with* oneeuenesse *mar.* G³, wikkydnesse J. 4366 olde] þat *add.* CJM, (*2nd* o *ins.* G³); þilke] þat *add.* C, thay that J, þo þat M. 4367 after] here aftere J; alle] (e *ins.* G³); and] note *mar.* O³. 4368 brestes] breste JM; albeit] þat *add.* CJ, þof all M; þus] *om.* MS; alle] þilke *add.* S. 4369 to ... susteynour] in Specialle J; Orguill] *with scilicet* orguyll L, pride R *mar.* G³, pride M. 4369-70 by especial] tille Orgule ane vndirsettere and a susteynour J, in speciall MO. 4370 holde] (*2nd* o *ins. and* pride *mar.* G³). 4371 Ne were] warne J; I] ware *add.* J. 4372 not] *om.* M; on] a G, no *add.* M, a F. 4373 Sey] *prec. Capitulum* Cxxij (Cxxiij *1st* i *erased* C) CG; þilke] þat JMO. 4374 see] the bere *add.* J; Herdest þou] herdest G; quod she] neuerspeke J, never O; neuere speke] quod scho JO; ne telle] *om.* J, here telle O. 4375 in þe mirrour] he loses J, he is þe myrour O; she leeseth] (*2nd* e *ins.* G³), in the myrrour J, lesys O; hire] his JM, þe O; feerstee] fellenesse J, ferce M, fyrst O; of] and J; þe] his JMO. 4376 wildernesse] wildenesse JMO; she¹,²] he JMO; hire] hym JMO. 4377 hire] his JMO; hed] liknesses J; haue] (*2nd* a *ins.* G³); herd] (*final* e *subpuncted* G); speke] telle J. 4377-8 I wole] Quod scho J, Þen will I M, I wold S. 4378 quod she] I wille J; Orguill] pride M. 4379 she] *with scilicet* orguyll *mar.* G³, he JMO; mirrede] *o. er. with er. mar.* C, wondred JMO, attyred S; hire] hym JMO; ofte] þerinne *add.* C, by þe myrrour *add.* S; eche] ilke a J, ilk M, euerych O. 4380 in] on JMOS; hire] his JMO; loue] (*2nd* o *subpuncted* G); she] he JMO, I S; wolde]

wil J.   4381 she] he JMO;   hath] was J;   mirred] *o. er. with er. mar.* C,
wondrede JMO;   hire¹] of hym J, hym MO;   hire²] his awen J, his MO;
she] þere fore he J, he MO.   4382 þilke] thay*me* J, *om.* MO.   4383 Reson-
ance] F, Resouenance CGS (*with* rememoringe *over* C³, *with* reme*m*brynge *mar.*
G³), aunswerynge agayne *add.* J;   and] or J;   Acordaunce] acordynge JMO;
Men] he J;   Seyn] sayse J.   4384 prowde] man *add.* J;   þat] *om.* G, seyne
S;   seyn] agayne *add.* J.   4384-5 Þou seist] Soth JMO, *om.* S.
4385 sooth] say ȝe J, þou sayes MO.   4385-6 mirre ... mirrour] *om.* J.
4385 mirre] *o. er. with er. mar.* C, wondir MO;   þee] (*1st* e *ins.* G³);   in me]
o. er. with er. mar. C.   4386 no] my S;   hele] hide JMO;   feerstee]
fersenesse J, ferce M, hede O, furst S.   4387 anoon¹] als sone J;   he shulde]
ins. mar. O³;   haue] (*2nd* a *ins.* G³), hefe JO;   þe] his JM;   anoon²] *ins.*
mar. O³;   hurtle] putte J;   as] an *add.* CJMOS.   4389 hurtled] ne diseased
add. J;   bere] be M;   here] heere (*1st* e *ins.* G³) G, bere J.   4390 answere]
-se JMO;   eche] a *add.* subpuncted G, ilke JM, euerich O;   folage] folye (*o.*
er. with er. mar. C) CJ.   4391 sey] sayse JM;   heere] (*1st* e *ins.* G³);   euere]
om. COS;   subpuncted G, so J, þat eue*r* M;   shal] shulde C;   helpe] do good
J;   or] oþer G;   ennoye] skath J, in tyme to come *add.* M, Nowe take hede here
/ of þe wounderful sightes filowing wheche þe pilg*r*ine seeghe *add.* S.   4392 And]
prec. C*apitulum* Cxxviij *mar.* CG (viij *o. er.* C), *om.* JMO, *prec.* {C*apitulum* x}vj
mar. S;   riht] Xhitt M, Descripcio invidie *rub. mar.* O;   Flaterye] flattrynge
JMO;   talinge] talkynge JMOS;   spak] *om.* J.   4393 to me] *om.* J;
doinges] typinges S.   4394 anooþer] And oþer S;   old] (*2nd* o *ins.* G³), ane
add. J;   wherof] of þe whiche S;   com ... afray] myn*e* hert S.   4394-5 to
myn herte] was gretliche agrysed S.   4395 Tweyne] twey GMOS, Tha J;
had] *o. er. with er. mar.* C;   ficched] *o. er. with er. mar.* C, fochid MO.
4396 tweyne] two J, eyen MO;   eyen] two MO;   upon] vp J;   foure] *with*
iiij *mar.* G³.   4397 dragoun] griffoun J;   witeth] it *add.* MO;   þat] *om.*
J.   4398 hadde] nowthere *add.* J;   hire¹] nowdir *add.* MO.   4399 hire¹]
here (*2nd* e *ins.* G³) G;   seemeden] bare *add.* J;   as] and J;   vnheled] vnhidd
JMO;   Upon] On JO.   4400 tweyne] *with* ij *mar.* G³, twa JMO;   olde]
(*2nd* o *ins.* G³), anes *add.* J;   gastlich] gostely M;   or] other GS.
4401 oon] 1 *over* G³;   sat] that (*with* satte *mar.* G³) GS;   musselled] mused
S.   4401-2 a ... visage] *with* visur *mar.* G³.   4401 fauce] faucefleeme
S.   4402 visage] visure *over* C;   and¹ ... visage² *om.* S;   so] scho hadd hid
M;   she ... hid] hadd hid so M, she had O.   4403-4 she ... daggere] *om.*
O.   4404 held] heelde (*3rd* e *ins.* G³) G.   4405 olde] (*2nd* o *ins.* G³), and
add. J.   4406 al] *om.* J;   eren] men JMO;   of men] eres JMO;   perced]
parkkyd (*1st* k *ins., with* pikked *mar. after rub. caret also in text* O³) O;   þat²]
whiche C, *with* wheche *mar.* G³, *om.* S   4407 weren] and JS;   spited] aures
mar. G³;   oon] I *over* G³;   extended] reched J, entendid M, esteemed S;
meward] -es J.   4408 bitwixe] betweene (*2nd* e *ins.* G³) GJMOS;   red] *om.*
O.   4409 rounginge] (*o. o. er. with er. mar.* O³), rounged JMO;   barbede] (*2nd*
a *ins.* G³);   ymped] (y *o. er. with er. mar* C³), nipyd O.   4410 an] any J;
yren] yre J;   and] *o. er. with er. mar.* C, forto *add* J.   4411 hooke] (*1st* o *ins.*
G³);   þe] *om.* J;   þat] þare J.   4413 Whan] *prec.* C*apitulum* Cxxix (xxix
o. er. C) *mar.* CG;   þese] this JMOS;   olde] (*2nd* o *ins.* G³);   wel] *om.* S;
apperceyued] persayfed JMO.   4414 bithouhte] be thowghte (*final* e *ins.* G³)
G;   wite] þeir names O;   here names] (*2nd* a *ins.* G³), knowe O.
4415 Þow] Two O;   olde] wiche *add.* J;   berere] (*final* e *ins.* G³), breoþer
S.   4416 me] by þy fader kyn *add.* S;   and] what is *add.* S;   name] (*2nd*

a *ins*. G³); if þou wolt] also J, *om*. MO, for *add*. S. 4417 hidouschipe] drede J, hidous M; drede] dreede (*1st* e *ins*.. G³) G, hydousnesse J; doon] make J; me] to me to hafe bath J; þese] this GMOS, ces F. 4418 foule] alde J; olde] holde (*with* oolde *mar*. G³) G, fowle thynges J; þanne] (e *ins*. G³); Serteyn] quod she *add*. C, -ly quod scho J. 4419 þouh] if M; cause] (*2nd* a *ins*. G³); soone] Onane J. 4420 wolde] wille J, Envye . begotten / by the diuell vpon pryd *mar*. O³; Orguill] *with* pride *mar*. G³, pride my modere J, pryde M. 4422 In] alle *add*. J; ne is] *trs*. JM; castel] kasteell (*2nd* e *ins*. G³) G, Reade this agayne *mar*. O³; ne²] na *add*. J; toun] (*final* e *ins* G³); I ne] *trs*. J; haue] (*2nd* a *ins*. G³). 4423 slauhter] shauhter C, þerin J, sleyghte O; inne] sclaw3tter J, þerin OS; many²] *om*. S; a²] *om*. OS. 4424 beste] beest (*1st* e *ins*. G³); sloowh] flogh O; sumtime] wyþ *add*. O; Jacob] his fadere *add* J. 4426 riht] *om*. S; shulde] na with3 J; no wight] schulde J. 4427 haue] (*2nd* a *ins*. G³); ioye] to see *add*. S; ne] *marked mar*. C, me S; þat] thing *add*. C, fude *add*. J; which] that JM, þe wech *ins*. *mar. after rub. caret also in text* O³, *with* which S; I live with] *ins*. *mar. after rub. caret also in text* O³, I leue S; is] his *ins*. *mar. after rub. caret also in text* O³. 4428 bitter] *ins*. *mar. after rub. caret also in text* O³; ese] eese (*2nd* e *ins*. G³) G; savowrede] fafourd J. 4429 Ooþeres] Othere folke J; ooþeres] othere mennes J. 4430 Ooþeres] Oþere mennes J; ooþeres] Othere mennys J; my] me O. 4431 tete] mete C, teete (*with* mamilla *mar*. G³) GS, tethe J, ioye M, leef O; of ... mes] I hadde I newe J, if of such mesys O; I ... ynowe] of swilke messes J, inowe I had O. 4431-2 I² ... mes] *om*. J. 4432 ynowh] *om*. O; haue] (*2nd* a *ins*. G³); ofte] *om*. O; mes] -ys O, ynoughe *add*. S. 4433 lene] leene (*2nd* e *ins*. G³) G; and²] A true discipcion of / an envious man *mar*. O³; discolowred] ille coloured J. 4434 sleth me and] *om*. S; pale] (*2nd* a *ins*. G³). 4435 leches] (*2nd* e *ins*. G³) G, hors leches J, a leche O, in þe marras on mennes legges *add*. S; leeue] trow M; wel] *om*. C; and²] if MS. 4436 of] for CJMS, for for (*1st* for *can*.) O, de F. 4437 þerfore] *om*. J; þat] hath (*with* that *mar*. G³) G, haþe *alt*. þat S; putte] (e *ins*. G³); þerinne] *with* paradise *mar*. G³. 4438 me¹] grete J; couenaunted] *o. er*. C, made cowuaunte with J, couenaunt O. 4439 al þe world] the werlde JMO; be ended] be atte ane ende J, be all at an ende MO. 4440 leeue I] *trs*. C, trow I M, I O; nouht] þat I shall þen M; þat ... þanne] nou3t M; leese] (*2nd* e *ins*. G³). 4441 bihight] beheighte (*final* e *ins*. G³) G, hight JMO; it] *om*. J; þat] thy J, *om*. M; bi me] he thorowe me J. in ... him] was putte in to the worlde J, *om*. S; Bi me] *ins. mar. after rub. caret also in text* O³. 4442 in] *om*. S, by me *add. can. rub*. O; shal] derelyche *mar*. G³. 4443 chewe] -s JM, shewes O. 4444 to] atte J. 4445 þat] Enuye an enemy to all / things good *mar*. O³; in²] ne in O; eerthe] (*2nd* e *ins*. G³). 4446 werrye] werrays JM. 4447 þese] thire JM; tweyne] twa JMO, twey S; departe] (*final* e *ins*. G³), *om*. J; and] *om*. J. 4448 tweyne] twa JMO; eche] ilke a J, ilk M, euerych O. 4449 oon] 1 *over* G³, spere *add*. J; Ooþeres] oþeremen J; Ioye] welefare J; and] *om*. O; cleped] called JMO. 4450 Ooþeres] othere mennes J; Of] with J; firste] furste (e *ins* G³) G, kynge *add*. J; strengthed] enforced J. 4451 whan] as J. 4452 whan] that J; he¹] dauid *over* C³, *with* dauid *mar*. G³, dauid J; preised] epreysed S; he²] saul *over* C³, *with* saull saull *mar*. G³; Of] with JMO. 4453 þe¹] his JMO; perced] ryght to the herte · And *add*. J. 4453-4 him ... dide] *om*. S. 4454 þat] *om*. G, Que F; þe¹] *om*. MO; maden] hym *add*. O. 4455 Longis] F, longius CJOS, Longinus M; These] *prec. Capit-*

ulum Cxxx (*final* j *erased* C) *mar*. CG, þir JM;   ben] *om* J;   rooted] plantede
J, ratyd O.   4456 plaunted] rutid J;   deepe] (*2nd* e *ins*. G³);   bi] thurth
J, *om*. S;   myne] (e *subpuncted* G);   haue] (*2nd* a *ins*. G³).   4457 me¹]
om. C;   beste] beest (*1st* e *ins*. G³) G, ahornedde J, a beest S;   horned] beste
J, hornys MO;   caste] kaste (e *ins*. G³) G, to caste oute J.   4459 oon] 1 *over*
G³, *om*. O;   baselique] basiliske CJS, Basiliscus MO, basilique F;   whiche]
wheche (*final* e *ins*. G³) G, that JM, þat *add*. S.   4460 þilke] þa JMO;   nygh
bi] nere J;   Dede] deede (*2nd* e *ins*. G³) G, thay er J;   þei ben] dede J;   as]
also J.   4461 of] *om*. J;   shrewednesses] schrewydnes JMOS.
4463 mown] more esily O;   more esiliche] may O;   horse] (*with* horsse *mar*.
G³) G.   4464 haue] (*2nd* a *ins*. G³);   seechinge] in sperynge J.
4465 and] *om*. O;   heringe] heerynge (*2nd* e *ins*. G³) G;   shulen] wille JMO,
om. S;   þee] nowe *add*. J, *om*. S.   4466 mown] *om*. JO.   4466-8 if …
hem] *om*. JMO.   4467 withoute taryinge] gladlich S;   gladliche] with outen
tarying S.   4468 Who … I] *prec*. Capitulum Cxxxj (*penultimate* i *erased* C)
CG, Than I aschyd hir that satte fyrste apon envye J.   4468-9 þat … fierse]
wha erte þow quod I J.   4469 þat] þou M;   hast] so *add*. J.   4469-70 and
… visage] *om*. J.   4469 and þi facioun] *om*. MO;   þis] þi MOS;   fauce]
faus (*with* fals *mar*. G³) G.   4470 box] þe box S;   and¹] with J, *om*. MO,
of S;   oynement] -ys JMO;   ydrawe] drawene JMO.   4471 no good] I
may thynke J;   I may thinke] na gude J;   if] Bot ȝif J, *om*. M;   sum … thing]
þou saye me JK, -es MO.   4471-2 þow … me¹] Sum othere thynges J, þou may
say me MO.   4472-4 If … me] *om*. M.   4472 euery] ilke J, euerych
M.   4473 noon] com *add*. *ins*. O³;   him] hem S.   4474 moderes] *o. er*.
with moderes *u.v. mar*. C³.   4475 bicause] by caause (*2nd* a *ins*. G³) G;
mihte] myghte (e *ins*. G³) G;   not] the executrix of envye *mar*. O³;   greeve]
(*2nd* e *ins*. G³);   eche] ilke JM, euerych O.   4476 sette] (*final* e *ins*. G³);
me¹] (*2nd* e *ins*. G³);   scole] scool (*2nd* o *ins*. G³) G, the scole J;   þat I] *om*.
JMO.   4477 lernede] (*3rd* e *ins*. G³), to lerne JMO;   putte] may put J, myght
put MO.   4479 a] *om*. JMO.   4480 þerof] þer þer of S;   þere] taught
my Sistere J;   tauhte my sister] thare J;   raw] (*final* e *subpuncted* G).
4481 and] for *add*. S;   rounge] (o *o. er*. C).   4482 Hider] Come hider COS,
comm nowe J;   now] hidere J;   quod he] *om*. S;   wel] I SeeJ;   I see] wele
J;   or] other GS.   4483 sum] *om*. O;   wolt] walde J.   4484 teche]
(*2nd* e *ins*. G³);   and … be] *om*. S.   4485 gladed þerof] *om*. S;   And] *prec*.
Capitulum Cxxxij (Cxxxiij *1st* i *erased* C) *mar*. CG;   þanne] (e *ins*. G³);
vnshette] opned J;   an hucche] a Cheste S.   4486 þerof] *om*. S;   þis¹] his
O.   4488 Douhter] *marked mar*. C³;   he¹] *om*. S;   þat] sa J.
4489 þe²] that JM;   thikke] place JMO;   þer] whare JMOS;   þei ben] *with*
briddes *mar*. G³, *om*. JMO.   4489-90 ne … pathes] (*2nd* a *ins*. G³), thayre pathes
er J, er þer pathes MO.   4490 seyen] se O;   þere] stir S;   wolden] woll
O;   flee] a waye *add*. J.   4491 þee] (*1st* e *ins*. G³);   for²] *om*. O.
4492 anooþer] any body J, ony oþer;   nouht] ne spedeth nowþere *add*. J;   face]
(*2nd* a *ins*. G³);   to] *om*. JS.   4493 him] thayme JMO;   wacche] whache
(e *ins*. G³) G;   þat] in *add*. M;   and¹] *om*. JMO.   4494 þou shewe]
beschewed to J;   þe] thy JMO;   labour] þat *add*. CJM.   4495 settest] duse
J.   4496 haue] (*2nd* a *ins*. G³);   manere] mare Sutille J, a maner MS;
more subtile] maneres J, more subtylytee S;   þat] and þat (and *ins. mar*. G³)
CG;   him] thayme J;   fair] goode J, *om*. MO.   4497 bifore] *om*. J;   oþer]
ooþer thing C, *om*. J, and *add*. M;   þat] *om*. J, al thing lefft *add*. S.   4497-9
þow … cheere] *om*. J.   4497 scorpioun] does *add*. M.   4498 dissimula-

cioun] (*final* e *add.* G³), simulacioun M.   4499 cheere] chere (*with* cheere *mar.*
G³) G;   and stingeth] *om.* O.
4500 so] *om.* JMO;   accomplise] i*d est* fulfille *over* C³, do that JMO, þat *add.*
S;   do] fulle fille JMO;   þat²] it JS;   and²] *om.* OS.   4501 and¹] with
J, *om.* S;   þee] here *add.* J, to þee S.   4502 instrumentes] the instrumentys
JS;   whiche] wheche (*2nd* e *ins.* G³) G;   han] haauen (*1st* a *ins.* G³) G, ane
hase J;   perished] perchid and perisshid M, percyd O.   4503 Amason] F,
Amasa JMO;   sumtime] thay *add.* J;   þerwith] *ins. mar.* G³, *om.* JMOS.
4504 not] negh M;   vnwarnished] vngarnyschyd J, warnyssht O;   hem] him
S;   solde] *em. ed.* slowh CGJMOS, vendi F;   þe] *om.* J.   4505 ooþere]
þer ware *add.* J;   whiche] that J;   ben] ware J;   not wery] (*2nd* e *ins.* G³)
G, gladde J;   to] forto J.   4506 haue hem¹] *o. er. subpuncted* C, (*2nd* a *ins.*
G³);   rede] reede (*2nd* e *ins.* G³) G;   þee] *om.* JM, my O;   to¹] that þou
J, þou MO;   haue²] (*2nd* a *ins.* G³);   counforte] þee · and to coumfort *add.*
S.   4507 mooder] and *add.* CJ, and *add. ins. mar.* G³.   4509 whiche]
wheche (*2nd* e *ins.* G³) G, wyþ whych O, þar with S;   and] that *add. subpuncted*
G;   fauce] faux (*with* falss *mar.* G³) G.   4510 peynted] *om.* J;   to¹] *om.*
J, vn to S;   þi visage] *om.* J.   4511 hele] hyde JMO;   bifore] with outene
þowe schalte J, þou shall *add.* MO.   4512 sithe] Syne JMO.   4513 haue]
(*2nd* a *ins.* G³).   4514 whiche] the whilke J;   ben enoynted] ofte tymes kynges
and prelates J.   4514-5 þe¹ ... prelates] er enoynted J, þe Knyghtes and also
Prelates M, þe kynges knyghtys, and prelatys O.   4515 þat ne wilneth] that ne
thay wille be gladde of J, þen he wil haue M, but he woll O.   4517 hardily]
enoynte thayme J;   enoynte hem] hardily J.   4518 sithe] syne JMO;
oynture] vnctur JMO.   4519 cured] couered O.   4520 Now] *prec.* Capit-
ulum Cxxxiij *mar.* CG;   me] to me J.   4521 he] *with* fader *mar.* G³, I MO;
wente] and *add.* GJMO (*subpuncted* G);   mooder] (*2nd* o *ins.* G³).   4522 think-
eth] thynke JM.   4523 I] *om.* S;   can] kanne (ne *subpuncted*) G, *om.* JS;
sette] (*2nd* e *ins.* G³), besette S;   fauce] faux (*with* fals *mar.* G³) G.   4524 to]
I can J, *om.* MO.   4525 bite ... tooth] wel I can CS, weel y kan *ins. mar.* G³,
bite with the teethe JM, byte wyþ to teth O;   I can wel] bite with þe tooth
(*dittograph* with þe tooth *subpuncted* C) CS, byte with the tooth I kann weell (I
...weell *subpuncted*) G, *om.* J;   abayinge] baying or brekynge J, lagh teth *mar.*
O³.   4526 cheere] chere (*2nd* e *ins.* G³) G;   þat oon] the to (1 *over to* G³)
G;   frote] for *o. er.* O;   and¹] to JMO.   4527 side] *om.* O;   stinge] stange
JMO.   4528 vnder] -neþe O;   til] forte GS, to M, *o. er.* O³;   wiht] men
J;   cometh] cum JMO;   I] may *add.* JMO.   4529 on] apone JO.
4530 þou knowest] *trs.* J.   4531 hoopes] cercle J;   ne] þe O;   Many] (*final*
e *add.* G³);   ofte] *om.* J.   4532 withinne] hol J;   al holowh] with in J.
4534 may] he may J, may he O;   noon] nouȝt JO.   4535 no man] nane
JMO;   neiþer] be *add.* O;   strengthe] fewe S;   of] *om.* S.   4536 at] *om.*
S.   4537 haue] (*2nd* a *ins.* G³);   on¹] hem *add. can.* C;   fauce] faux (*with*
fals *mar.* G³) G.   4538 ben] *om.* J;   perished] perisch J;   my] *om.* S.
4539 I] *prec.* Capitulum Cxxxiv *mar.* CG;   Tresoun] Treson *rub. mar.* M,
Perdicioun *rub. mar.* O;   haue] (*2nd* a *ins.* G³), has JMO;   many¹] monye (e
ins. G³) G;   many a] ful S.   4540 drauht] draughtes S;   pleyede] pley
O;   chekeer] the chekere J.   4541 þat¹] þen MO;   bi my art] (*2nd* a *ins.*
G³), be by myne arte J, by myn hert art (hert *can.*) M;   I ne took] I tuke JMS,
I take O;   which] man *add.* J, Treson *mar.* O³;   þat²] *om.* O;   wolde] woll
O;   oon] nane J, *om.* M.   4542 neiþer] *om.* M;   þat] ne *add.* J, but S;
ne²] *om.* JS;   drawe] (*2nd* a *ins.* G³), hit *add.* S.   4543 enoyed] nuyd me

J, enoyed me MO;   she] *om.* J.   4544 seide] bidden J;   þee] (*1st* e *ins.*
G³).   4545 respite] taryinge J;   ded] I presente the J;   I ... þee] (*4th* e *ins.*
G³), deed J, I present to þee S;   to hire] heere S;   now riht] *trs.* J.   4546 A
la mort] *with* to þe deth *mar.* G³, all a morte J, ale morte M;   sey] Syne JO, sithen
M;   þat] þou J, *om.* MO;   þou shalt] schalle J, a la Mort *mar.* O³;   haue]
(*2nd* a *ins.* G³);   it] with deth *mar.* G³, the deed JMO.   4547 come] came
S;   heere] hiddyr JMO;   suscited] *with* reised *mar.* G³, raysed J;   þe ooþere]
þe thre dede C, the man fra deed to lyfe J, three oþer S.   4548 haue] (*2nd*
a *ins.* G³);   þee] (*1st* e *ins.* G³).   4549 And] *prec. Capitulum* Cxxxv *mar.*
CG;   neihede] come nere J;   þat] *om.* J;   to deth] walde have smeten me J,
to þe deeþe S.   4549-50 she² ... me] (*2nd* a *ins.* G³), to deed J.   4550 with]
by S;   areyned] reproued J, arguyd MO.   4551 hire] *om.* JS;   þus] on this
wyse J;   hastyfe] hasty MOS.   4552 til] forte G, *om.* J, for MO;   miche]
om. J;   wite] may witte J;   name] (*2nd* a *ins.* G³);   sithe] seyne JO, sithen
M, þanne S.   4554 if] þat I *add.* S;   as¹ ... þou] I greved hym nouȝt J;
I¹ ... him] als welle as þou J, ne greeued him S;   And] *om.* J.   4554-5 quod
she] graunt it welle J.   4555 graunte it wel] quod the tothere J;   preye] (*2nd*
e *ins.* G³);   avaunce] þat þou haste *o. er.* (*with* haste *erased u.v. mar.* C³) C;
a vaunte J, avaune O.   4556 haue] (*2nd* a *ins.* G³);   wurshipe] wurschippe
(e *ins.* G³) G;   to] for to S;   ynowh] Take heede heer howe þeos twoo arreyned
ful despitously · þe poure cely pilgryme *add.* S.   4557 And] *prec.* Capitulum
Cxxxvi *mar.* CG, Ca*pitulum* xvij *mar.* S;   þat] *om.* C, þere J, with S.
4558 me¹] hir S;   berkinge] herkande J;   me²] and *add.* S;   rojunginge]
ruggande JMO.   4559 quod she] erte þou so hardy, artowe quod sheo S;
Art ... hardy] quod scho J, so hardy S;   þat þou hast] to J.   4560 brouht]
brynge J;   stafes] staaues (*2nd* a *ins.* G³) G.   4561 þilke] tha JMO.
4562 loue] (*2nd* o *subpuncted* G), thayme *add.* JMO;   berke] wreke me J, breke
O.   4563 bite on] betes JMO;   albeit] þof al M.   4564 hem¹] *om.*
JMO.   4656 albeit] al þof it M;   bicause] by caause (*2nd* a *ins.* G³) G.
4566 louede] (*2nd* o *subpuncted* G), luffeth J;   neuere þee] the nouȝt J;   of
me] þou shalt S;   þou shalt] of me S.   4567 haue] (*2nd* a *ins.* G³), *ins.* M;
it] *with* deth *mar.* G³, euille dede JMO;   heere] hedyr · For J;   ete] eete (*2nd*
e *ins.* G³) G.   4568 I wole] *om.* OS;   ete] eete (*2nd* e *ins.* G³) G, *om.* OS;
þee] *om.* OS;   drawe] (e *ins.* G³);   skin] *em. ed.*, soule oute CGJMOS.
4569 mastyf] dogge *add.* J, mastice M.   4570 wolde] wille JMOS;   ete¹] eete
(*2nd* e *ins.* G³) G;   raw] rawgh (gh *subpuncted*) G;   I¹) wol *add.* S;   haue]
(*2nd* a *ins.* G³).   4571 þat] the lynage of ravine *mar.* O³;   strangeled]
swalowed M;   folde] (e *ins.* G³), flokk J.   4572 rounged] (o *o. er. with er.*
mar. C), rugged JMO;   chekes] cheekes (*2nd* e *ins.* G³) G, cheke O;   of²] *o.*
er. (*with erased* þe *u.v. mar.* C³) C;   raven] Raauene (*2nd* a *ins.* G³) G.
4573 hath] (*2nd* a *ins.* G³);   loue] (*2nd* o *subpuncted* G)   4574 þei] *with* scilicet
karoygnes *mar.* G³;   þe] in þe M;   I haue hem] (*2nd* a *ins.* G³), þey beon to
me S.   4575 while] -s MOS;   mihte] myghte (e *ins.* G³) G;   haue] (*2nd*
a *ins.* G³);   shrewede] shreude (e *ins.* O³) O.   4576 neuere] *om.* O;
sauoure] saue O;   hem] ne ete þayme *add.* J.   4577 þat] *om.* JM;
sumwhat] *om.* JS;   roten] *om.* S;   or] other G, *om.* S;   foul] *om.* S;   if]
and J;   hem²] somme *add.* S.   4579 hem²] *om.* MO, byforne þat I seghe hem
add. S;   and chewe] *om.* O.   4580 Envye] Here is þe descripcion of detraccion
and bakbytyng · what it is *add. rub.* M;   The] *prec.* Ca*pitulum* Cxxxvij (Cxxxviij
1st i *erased* C) *mar.* CG, capitulum xiv *rub. mar.* M, *om.* J;   whiles] while GS,
When J;   tolde] me *add.* O.   4581 al] ȝif alle J, al þof M;   were I] I ware

JM.   4582 olde] delle quod I *add.* J.   4583 so] if Cj;   wole] wel M; take þee] *(2nd e ins.* G³), schewe the J, gif þe *ins.* M;   rotene] and take þe J. 4584 and shente] roten*e* J, and chew þe M, and shewe þe O.   4585 lyth] (i *alt.* y C), is O.   4586 raþere] *(2nd a ins.* G³);   go] ga thus J, shuld go M; me] -warde J;   And] *prec. Capitulum* Cxxxviij (viij *o. er.* C) *mar.* CG. 4588 nouht] quod scho *add.* J;   go to] *trs.* JMO, goo so S.   4589 haue[1,2]] *(2nd a ins.* G³);   þȝ¹] *om.*, J;   maad] *(1st a ins.* G³);   forginges] forayns J.   4590 bitwixe] betweene GJMOS.   4591 ayen] *om.* J;   whiche] þe which S.   4592 I¹] *prec. Capitulum* Cxxxix (xxxix *o. er.* C) *mar.* CG; haddest] had JMO.   4593 woldest] walde JMO;   forgeth no wiht] þou myght nouȝt JMO.   4594 kunne] þowȝ JMO;   neuere] can neu*ere* JMO; withoute²] *om.* JO.   4595 noon ax] forge J, nouȝt ax M;   forge] nane axe J; matere] matiere *(2nd e ins.* G³) G;   quod she] (schee *1st* e *ins.* G³), I nowe J. 4596 ynowh] quod scho J;   goodschipes] goodschippe JO.   4596-7 þe goode] thay*me* J.   4597 euel] þe euyll M;   hem] þaim thay*me* J;   wel] *om.* JMO.   4598 into¹] to J.   4599 goode] (e *ins.* G³);   and²] *om.* M. 4600 sithe] Syne JMO;   I] *om.* J.   4601 hattest] hate JMO;   hire] detraccio *rub. mar.* M, Detracciou*n* pr*in*ceps Coquor*um* invidie *rub. mar.* O; Detraccioun] is my name *add.* M.   4602 þat] enforces me in alle that I may *add.* J, is *add.* M;   todrawe] forto drawe J.   4603 colys] koolys *(2nd o ins.* G³), a colice JO;   for] to JMO;   mooder] *(1st o ins.* G³).   4604 mad] *(2nd a ins.* G³).   4605 cook] cukeȝ M;   hire] *marked mar.* C;   eren] percede C, *with* aures *mar.* G³;   percede] eren C;   þat] detraction Envys cooke *mar.* O³.   4606 spere] sperys O;   wise] man*ere* JMO.   4607 I clepe] is JMO;   my] sp *add. can. rub.* M;   spere] *ins.* M;   his] the J;   wounde] cruelle C, crewell *ins. mar.* G³.   4608 whiche] that JMO, he] it J;   maketh] *(2nd a ins.* G³);   cruelle] *om.* C, *subpuncted* G, es cruell and felle J, cruelly O; it] *with* tonge *mar.* G³;   sorere] soore *(1st o ins.* G³) G, *om.* JMO.   4609 and] *om.* JMO;   cruelliche] cru*e*ly cruelly J;   spere] *(2nd* e *ins.* G³). 4610 mihte] myghte (e *ins.* G³) G;   barbede] huked J;   make] *(2nd a ins.* G³);   a²] *om.* J.   4611 of] out of CJ;   arblast] awblastyr J;   Þe] At þe O;   eren] aures *mar.* G³;   þat þou] *om.* O.   4612 seest ... of] *om.* O; þilke] this J, þe M.   4613 and] þe *add.* S;   I] *with* detracioun *mar.* G³; Þilke] thay J, þo MO;   heeren] *(2nd* e *ins.* G³).   4614 gladliche] Note of Detraction *mar.* O³;   my¹] *with* de{tracioun} *mar.* G³;   seyinges] seying O; eres] eeren *(with* aures *mar.* G³) G.   4615 mooder] *(1st* o *ins. with* envie *mar.* G³), Enuy *add.* JMO;   which] that GS *(with* whech *mar.* G³), *om.* JMO;   þei ... languishe] *om.* JMO.   4616 And] *prec. Capitulum* Cxl *(final* j *erased* C) *mar.* CG;   hath it] has þou JMO;   a] this JMO.   4617 yren] *(final a ins.* G³).   4618 haue] *(2nd a ins.* G³);   or] other G;   manye] two M. 4619 to me] *with* det{raccioun} *mar.* G³;   name] *(2nd a ins.* G³). 4620 crooke it] croked O;   bettere] bitt*er* M;   good] *o. er. (with* gud *mar. after rub. caret also in text* O³) O, þeyre goode S;   name] *(2nd a ins.* G³);   þan] as *add.* JM, þat is as O.   4621 þou art] *trs.* J;   for] Detraction is worse þan a / theefe *mar.* O³.   4622 name] *(2nd a ins.* G³);   more woorth] better O; Serteyn] Certaynly J;   quod she] þou says J.   4623 wel] fulle J;   þou seist] quod scho J.   4624 Fairere] Fayre JO;   thing] -es O;   may I] *trs.* S. 4625 thinketh] thynke JM;   but] ȝif *add.* J.   4626 þerof] *with* goodname *mar.* G³;   haue] *(2nd a ins.* G³);   foryifte] forgiffynge JMO;   þerof] *scribble o. er. of* þer of O;   þerto] *with* restittusiou*n mar.* G³.   4627 shame] schaame *(2nd a ins.* G³) G;   I²] *with* detra{cci}ou*n mar.* G³;   haue] *(2nd a ins.* G³).

4628 Orguill] *with* pride *mar.* G³, Pride M, And orguell S; she²] *om.* JMO; acorde] (e *ins.* G³); hire] restitucioun *mar.* G³. 4629 to hire] *om.* J. 4630 good] *om.* S; name] (*2nd a ins.* G³); herde] herkenede C, *with* herknede *mar.* G³. 4631 þerof] *with* scilicet good naame *mar.* G³; Serteyn] Certaynly J; þe] þis same S; noueltee] þerof *add.* C. 4532 I tolde] þerof J, I take MO; þee er] (*1st e ins.* G³), I take J, þer of MO; now] and J; turne] tourned S; name] (*2nd a ins.* G³). 4633 norishe] norisshed S; thinketh] thynk JMO. 4634 ne] *om.* JMOS. 4635 Serteyn] Certis J; Werse þan helle] For I am JMO, wel wisse S; I am] than helle JMOS. 4636 or] other GS. 4637 withinne] in JMO. 4638 noon] neu*e*re JMO; harm] have J; haue] (*2nd a ins.* G³), harme þerof J, þer of *add.* MO; þe] For the J, *om.* MO; grete] *om.* JMO. 4639 make him shadwe] schadowe hym J. 4641 spere] (*2nd e ins.* G³); þe] *om.* G; and] *om.* JMO. 4642 þee] þat *add.* O; of] so J. 4643 it] *om.* JMO; nouht] of gude lyuyng *add.* M; eerþe] (*2nd e ins.* G³); of my spere] he schulde hafe J. 4644 he ... haue] (*2nd a .ins.* G³), of my spere J, I shoulde haue S; and] if M. 4645-6 him ... smiten] *om.* JMO. 4645 haue¹,²] (*2nd a ins.* G³). 4646 þerinne] *with* heuene *mar.* G³; And] also *add.* C; þat also] (also *subpuncted* C), *trs.* JS. 4647 now] *om.* M; holde] hoolde (*1st o ins.* G³) G; me] stille *add.* J; I ne] *trs.* J, þen I MO; make] (*2nd a ins.* G³), gerre J. 4648 doun] (*final e ins.* G³), adoune S. 4649 Smite] þou *add.* J. 4651 shal he] *trs.* J; mown] *om.* J; escape] askaape (*3rd a ins.* G³); if] bot ȝif J; ne] *om.* J; haue] (*2nd a ins.* G³); riht] an *add.* CS, a right J. 4652 þat ooþer] *with* detraccioun *mar.* G³. 4653 þee] first *add.* S; þat¹] *om.* S; of] out of CJ; þe] his S; we] *om.* J, make S; make] we S; first] *om.* JMOS; ouerthrowe] tumbille J, ouerthrawn M. 4654 ride] Takeþe heede nowe howe þe pilgryme soekeþe to Traysoune and / busily askeþe of hir what is hir name *add.* S. 4655 Whan] *prec. Capitulum* Cxlj (Cxlii, *1st i erased* C) *mar.* CG, {*Capitulum*} *xviij mar.* S; þese woordes] (*2nd o ins.* G³), I herde J, I þier wordes MO; I herde] þir wordes J, herd MO; thouhty] alle thoghtfulle J, þoghtly O; and] *om.* S. 4656 ne thouhte] (*2nd e ins.* G³), that J, nouȝt *add.* MO; to haue] (*2nd a ins.* G³), I J; hors] a horse J; Þou] *om.* JO; what] hattest *add.* C, hattest þou *add.* GS, hate *add.* JMO. 4657 Haue] (*2nd a ins.* G³); hors] a hors J. 4658 she] *with* detraccioun *mar.* G³, þan J, þou MO, he S; þis] þus OS; If þou] *om.* J, waite M, wylt O; it me] me sone J; Resoun] Quod scho J. 4658-9 quod she] *with* detraccioun *mar.* G³, resoun J; with] of J, to MO; þat] thought JM, thogh O. 4660 of ... name] (*2nd a ins.* G³), es alosed J; is renomed] renowned C, of goode name J, renamyd M. 4661 haue] (*2nd a ins.* G³); foure] *with* iiij *mar.* G³, iiij O; eche] ilke JM, euerych O. 4662 hadde] but *add.* S; thre] iij *over with* iij *mar.* G³; or¹,²] other G; tweyne] ij *over with* ij *mar.* G³, twa JMO; mo] me O. 4663 wel] *om.* CJ; on ... hors] (an hors *marked for gloss* G³), rade J, on swilk an hors M. 4663-4 were² ... uppe] on swilke an hors J. 4664 That] *prec. Capitulum* Cxlij *mar.* CG, *om.* J; oon] 1 *over* G³; þilke] that JM, þe O; þat] þat *add. ins. mar.* O³; haue] (*2nd a ins.* G³). 4665 evell] ille J; haue] (*2nd a ins.* G³); fame] (*2nd a ins.* G³)i; Þat ooþer] ij *over* G³, Anoþere fote J. 4666 not] *ins. mar.* G³, *om.* S; condicioun] thralle J; of thraldam] condicioun J; Þe] that J; thridde] iiij *over* G³. 4667 engendred] in lawfulle matrimonye J, born M, *om.* O; in ... mariage] geten*e* J, in þe in legityme matrymoygne S; feerþe] iiij *over* G³; þat] is þat CJO; haue] (*2nd a ins.* G³), be J. 4668 no] nouȝt J; ne¹] hafe *add.* J, no *add.* S; woodshipe] wodnesse J, worship*pe* O; haue] (*2nd* a *ins.* G³), has JMO. 4669 foure] iiij *over* G³, þe foure S. 4670 witnesses] witnes JMO; þat] *om.* JMO. 4671 sister] *with scilicet* tresou*n mar.* G³; spoken] (*2nd* o *ins.* G³); to] til S; ouerthrowe] caste J; þee] (*1st* e *ins.* G³); I] *with* detraccioun *mar.* G³. 4672 And] *prec. Capitulum* Cxliij (*1st* i o. *er.* C) *mar.* CG. 4674 song] Sayinge J. 4675 Israel] Jacob J, I · seke O; of Daan] of dante (e *subpuncted* G³) GS, Sange J; song] of his sone J; Fiat ... via] fiat dan*te* coluber in via *ins. mar.* (*caret and space in text*) G³, Say · Fiat dan Columber in via Se rastes in Semita &c J, et caetera *add.* M, *om.* S. 4676 Daan] dan (*with* dant *mar.* G³) G, *om.* S; go] gase JMO; nouht] *om.* O. 4677 bi] þe C; euene] þeeven S; þat] *om.* S; bite] bytes JMO; stelth] sculkery J, stolth M. 4678 bihynde] beo byhinde behinde S; nailes] and the hufe *add.* J; þat he hath] *om.* JMO. 4679 trowe] that *add.* J. 4679-80 þat¹ ... shal] *ins. mar.* O³. 4679 þeraboute] thareaboutes J. 4680 as] there J, wher MO; apperceyue] per*s*ayfe JMO. 4680-4 of ... apperceyue] *ins. foot of page after rub.* ✚ *also in mar., black caret in text* O³. 4681 me] (*2nd* e *ins.* G³); felt] to be felyd J, felid M, fell O. 4682 and þat] or 3if J; in apert] I bate hym J; I bite him] in a perte J, I boote him S; yrened] yren S. 4683 yiue] *om.* S; þe] *om.* O; hauen] (*2nd* a *ins.* G³); no] (n *subpuncted* C); doon] nou3t *add.* J. 4684 He] *with scilicet* pilgrim *mar.* G³; nothing] no thyng*es* M; apperceyue] per*s*ayfe JMO; tooth] teeth JM; biteth] hy*m. add.* JM. 4685 forto] til C; he¹] make hy*m.* JMO; falle] to falle J; al] *om.* JMO. 4686 Now] come *add.* C, Comme nowe J. 4686-7 hider þanne] *ins. mar. after rub. caret also in text* O³, quod scho *add.* J, hider S. 4687 It] *om.* S; þat þou] *ins. mar. after rub. caret also in text* O³; hast þus] *om.* M. 4688 exposed] expowned CJ, expownes M, expose F; seyinge] saync*es* M. 4689 And] *prec. Capitulum* Cxliv *mar.* CG, *om.* M, *ins. mar.* O³; upon] on JMO; spere] (*2nd* e *ins.* G³). 4690 sithe] Seyne JM, syne *over* O³; with open] *ins. mar. after rub. caret also in text* O³; throte] mowth J, *om.* O; toward me] to mewarde J, towardes me S; wood] woodeman or S. 4691 womman] & *add. ins.* C, and *add.* J; with ... took] *ins. mar.* O³; þe¹] hir J; þe²] my JMO; nailes] hufe J; made] gerte J. 4692 sore] *ins.* O³; spared] she OS; she] *om.* J, spared OS. 4692-4 with ... Doun] *ins. foot of page after rub.* ✚ *also in mar. and rub. caret in text* O³. 4693 Wel] scho schewed J; she shewede] (scheewed *1st* e *ins.* G³ *in* G), wele J; hire] *om.* JMO; þat] *om.* J. 4693-4 of ... kynde] scho was J, of dragon kynde MO, of þe dragouns kynde S. 4694 she was] of dragou*n* kynde J; sorweful] Inowe *add.* J. 4694-5 but ... nouht] *om.* J. 4695 Euene] *ins.* O³; meward] (*2nd* e *ins.* G³), -es S; Envye] and *add.* C, *add. ins. mar.* G³. 4696 tweyne] twe3 JMO; speres] with thay*me add.* J; putte] she shof C,⸱ i putt (*with* sche schoff *mar.* G³) G. 4697 longe] *marked mar.* C; hire] his J. 4698 rounginge] (o o. *e.r. with* er. *mar.* C), ruggande JMO; she] tuke J; heeld] scho J; oynement] -es O. 4699 oon] 1 *over* G³; enoyntede] enoygnted (g *ins.* G³) G, did ennoygnte S. 4700 in þe wombe] schowfed me J, *om.* O; she shof me] in the wambe J, she shaff S; with] *ins. mar.* G³. 4701 Þe] thane the J; olde] (*2nd* o *ins.* G³), delle *add.* J; grete] (*2nd* e *ins.* G³); neighede] come nere J. 4702 þee] quod scho *add.* J, now *add.* M; miht] may J. 4703 þanne] (e *ins.* G³). 4704 to¹] and J; me²] (*2nd* e *ins.* G³); to³] *om.* C. 4705 if ... discounforted] it is na wounder*e* þow3 J, if I wer gretely discomfyte M. 4705-6 it ... aske] I ware gretly disco*m*forted J, it neodeþe nought for to aske S. 4706 wel] I myght J; I mihte] (e *ins.* G³), wele J; Peresce]

with sleuthe *mar.* G³, and gret cause J, þei MO;   hadde] I had J.   4707 respyt]
laysere J;   to ... hire] *ins. mar.* G³, *om.* JMO, de soi pener F;   at] to M.
4708 ne] and J, *om.* O;   mihte] ne myghte O;   Algates Neuertheles J.
4709 euene] heuene (*with* eeuene *mar.* G³) G;   not] *om.* S.   4710 trist] trust
GOS;   þat] *ins. mar.* G³, *om.* S;   þerbi] þat *add.* S;   afterward] -es S;
escape] askaape (*3rd* a *ins.* G³) G, if god wold *add.* M, *and* Þe descripcion of Ire
· and hir lynage · what þei er · *add. rub.* M.   4711 As] *prec.* Capitulum Cxlv
mar. CG, capitulum xv *rub. mar.* M;   was ... I²] *om.* JMO.   4712 toward]
-es S;   renne] com J;   and come] Rynnande to mewarde J, *om.* M;   old oon]
oold onn (*2nd* o *ins.* G³) G, *om.* J.   4713 to þe ooþere] o. er. C, (*3rd* e *ins.*
G³), to the totothere J;   Hold him faste] *ins. mar.* G³, *om.* JMOS;   for] forte
(te *subpuncted* G) GS, telle J, vnto MO.   4714 bi] þorowe J;   whiche] that
J.   4715 Þilke] That JMO;   olde] (*2nd* o *ins.* G³), delle *add.* J;   disgysee]
disgysed JMOS;   poyntes] prikkes J.   4716 armed] (*2nd* a *ins.* G³);
aboute] -s S.   4717 siþe] hyngande J;   handes] hed J, hand M;   she hadde]
om. J;   caliownes] *id est* flintes *over* C, *with* scilicet flynttes *mar.* G³, gray
JMOS;   greye] And *add.* CJ, and *add. ins. mar.* G³.   4719 wel] I telle ȝowe
J;   I telle yow] wele J;   al were] it *add.* C, ȝif alle ware J;   þat] *om.* J;
she] *om.* J.   4720 was] *om.* J;   mouth] also *add.* J;   sawe] (*2nd* a *ins.*
G³).   4721 doone] *ins.* J;   with] þer with COS;   I ne wiste] wiste I neuere
J;   if first] ay tille efterwarde that J, forst of M, Fyrst O;   ne] *om.* JO;   askede]
spirrid J.   4722 Thow] *prec.* Capitulum Cxlvj *mar.* CG, Harstowe J;   olde]
tratte *add.* J;   nygh] nere J.   4723 and¹] swilke *add.* JO;   hattest] hate
JMO.   4724 me] nouȝt *add.* JS;   nothing] for *add.* J;   fayn] I walde J;
I wolde] fayne J;   it] *om.* M;   albe] it that *add.* J, it *add.* MO;   haue] (*2nd*
a *ins.* G³), diseese *add.* J.   4725 hire ... caliowns] (*with* stones *mar.* G³), scho
smate to gedyr J, hir two stonys MOS;   she smot togideres] hir twa flynt stanes
J, scho smote to gydir MO.   4726 made] garte J;   flawme] low M;   lepe]
leepe (*2nd* e *ins.* G³) G;   Serteyn] Certaynly J.   4727 of my craftes] I wille
anane make the to fle and to fele J;   I ... feele] (*2nd* e *ins.* G³), of my craftes J.
4728 name] (*2nd* a *ins.* G³);   divise] telle J;   I am] *prec.* Capitulum Cxlvij *mar.*
CG, þane S;   olde] (*2nd* o *ins.* G³);   kembed] kennyd O, kept S.
4729 evele] ille J;   tressed] trestid M;   rownded] rounde JMO;   togideres]
to gydere JMO.   4730 wiche] wheche (*2nd* e *ins.* G³);   him] *om.* M;   for]
of S.   4731 to] *om.* J;   ende] also *add.* J;   any wiht] anymann J.
4732 neighe] neghed S;   þat] *om.* J;   haue] (*2nd* a *ins.* G³), prikkynge *add.*
J, of som broch M;   of sum broche] hange M.   4733 seeche] (*2nd* e *ins.*
G³);   haue¹,²] (*2nd* a *ins.* G³);   þilke] tha JMO, I wol haue of alle þilke þat
add. dittography S;   misdoo] mysdone *add. can.* O.   4734 kindelinge] Fir
add. ins. mar. C³, *with* fure *mar.* G³;   ayens] agayne JMO.   4735 wel] þat
he has *add.* J, þat *add.* MO;   is] *ins.* G³, *om.* J, he MO;   taken] taake (e *ins.*
G³) G, *om.* J, has MO.   4736 hond] *with* god *mar.* G³;   haue] (*2nd* a *ins.*
G³).   4737 hateful] hastyf S;   impacient] vnpacient O.   4738 brambere]
brymble brere J, bremble S;   or¹] other GS, *om.* O;   or²] other GS;   greisiler]
scharpe whynnes J.   4739 his] hire J;   a] *om.* O;   hegge] heggys O;
me] (*2nd* e *ins.* G³).   4741 Noli Me Tangere] *ins. mar. there being space in text*
G³, *om.* S;   haue] noli me tangere *rub. mar.* MO;   anoon] als Sone J;   carmen
in ve] sorwe in weylinge CG³ (*mar. there being space in text* G³), carmen and ve and
J, curamen in ve O, *om.* S, carmen en ve F;   þat²] *om.* S;   with] for J.
4742 a¹] *om.* JMO;   make] -s JMO;   a³] *om.* MO;   upon] *om.* JMO;   þe
poynt] *om.* J;   in] *with* er. *mar.* C.   4743 þilke] thayme J, þo MO;   was]

ware J;   freend frendes J.   4744 howlinge cattes] owles J, howling hattes
S.   4745 hem³] in add. ins. C, and add. JMO.   4746 of¹] om. J;
greynes] erbes J.   4747 greene] (2nd e ins. G³);   yive] ȝeue (with ȝyue mar.
G³) G;   hem²) þo O.   4748 flewmatyk] followed by space in text G (see
note).   4750 thing] with wordle mar. G³;   round] (final e subpuncted G);
cleped] called JMO;   reise] I reise CJMO;   þe] om. JMO;   and] þe add.
MO.   4751 and²] om. JMO;   withdrawe] to with drawe J;   and³] her add.
MO, also vnto add. S.   4752 vnderstondinge] vnderstondyngynge G, schadows
J, Ira rub. mar. O², lyke an envenomed / Tode · cosine to frenzye mar. O³;
shadewed] hir vndirstandynge J, shadowes MO.   4753 rivelede] runkilde
J.   4754 mooder] the modere JM, om. O;   of houndes] om. O;   of swet-
nesse] has nathynge in hir J;   hath ... nothing] swetnes J.   4755 hastyf] hasty
JMO;   þan¹] hoote add. S;   soure] bitter JMO;   þe] om. C, subpuncted
G.   4756 kyndlinge] em. ed., hydinge CGJMOS;   þe] om. JMO;   fyre]
fure (e subpuncted) G;   whan] of S;   assaileth] whane þey assayle S.
4757-8 toward me] to me ward O, towardes me S;   þat ... ne] þat anoon CS, (ne
ins. mar. G³), that ne onane J, þen onoon MO;   caliouns] stanes to gedyr J, stones
MO.   4759 and smyte] om. J;   lepe] stones mar. G³;   out] vp JMO;
drye tunder] I had J;   I hadde] drye tundyr J.   4760 putte anoon] trs. J;
þe] om. J;   Despyte] despectus · chydyng rub. mar. M, Dispite / Chidyng rub.
mar. O.   4761 oon] 1 over G³;   þe] my JMO;   caliouns] stanes JMO;
þat ooþer] the toothre (with toother mar. G³) G;   cleped] called JMO.
4762 þilke] þa JMO;   togideres] to gedyr whene JMO;   twey] commoun add.
J;   þat²] om. JMO.   4763 iugement] þe Jugement S;   whiche] whedir J;
hadde] schulde haue J;   chyld] Howe þat Yre declareþe to þe pilgryme more of
hire power add. S.   4764 With] prec. Capitulum Cxlviij mar. CG, Capitulum
{xix} mar. S;   þese] thir twa J, two add. MO;   caliouns] stanes JMO;   sawe]
saawe (e ins. G³) G;   which] that J;   haue] (2nd a ins. G³).   4765 þilke]
with cayloun mar. G³, that stane J, þat MO;   cleped] called JMO.
4766 anevelte] stithy JMO;   þe²] Impacience rub. mar. M.   4767 taken] (2nd
a ins. G³);   maad] (final e subpuncted G³);   more] more add. subpuncted.
G.   4768 þe¹ ... men] om. JMO;   heten] heeten (2nd e ins. G³) G, om.
JMO;   it²] om. JMO.   4769 made] it add. JMO;   sumtime] and add. JO,
and end (end can.) M;   endente] -d JM, enuent (u. o. er.) O;   it] om. S;
now herkene] trs. J.   4772 name] (2nd a ins. G³);   cleped] called JMO;
þat²] it J, þis M.   4773 þe¹] a JMO;   sinne] correccioun rub. mar. M;
ne] om. J;   suffre] nowthere J.   4774 neiþer] Suffyr J;   þat] þen MO;
it ne] trs. J, it MO;   awey] thayme add. J;   and¹] ne S.   4775 haue] (2nd
a ins. G³);   me] with ire mar. G³;   out] off J.   4776 yren] with id est
pacience mar. C³, with scilicet Impacience mar. G³.   4776-7 of ... yren] om.
J.   4776 which] of whych add. can. O;   haue] (2nd a ins. G³);   þee] om.
MOS.   4777 She] with scilicet Justice mar. G³;   wende] wond alt. wou\l/d
O;   haue] (2nd a ins. G³) G;   fyled²] scho fulid MO; | and] thus es add. J;
endented] -ed G, it J.   4778 it¹] endented J;   haue] (2nd a ins. G³);   þerof]
as add. J;   it²] om. J;   Hise] the JMO, Odium rub. mar. O.   4779 as] fanges
add. J;   of] om. O;   Þe ... cleped] Odium JMO;   Hayne] haingne (with haate
mar. G³) G, es the Sawe called J, þe saw is called MO, odium rub. mar. MO;
whom] which C, with whech mar. G³.   4780 disioynct] es disioynd JM;   þe
onhede] is ysawed þe onhede C, {is} saawe and the onhede ({i}s saawe ins. mar.,
and subpuncted G³) G.   4780-1 of ... sawen] of oonhede C, of vnyte is saawen
(vnyte with oonheede mar., is saawen subpuncted G³) G.   4781 and] in add.

JM;   seyn] eseyne S;   figure] no*ta* de Iacob *et* Esa{u} *rub. mar.* M;   I] *with*
ire *mar.* G³.   4782 vnioyned] disioyned JMO;   boþe ... ooþer] (ton *has* 1
over G³), sente and disseuered J.   4782-3 I ... fer] the tane ferre fra the toþere
J.   4783 haue] (*2nd* a *ins.* G³);   many annoþer] done J, many odir M;
doo] many anothere J.   4784 telle] dwelle and telle S;   I] *prec. Capitulum*
Cxlix *mar.* CG;   with] Inne *add.* S.   4785 I¹] Pater no*ster rub. mar.* O;
sey] seo S;   Pater Noster] *ins. mar.* G³ *there being a space in text*;   be] *om.*
S.   4786 preye] preeye (*3rd* e *ins.* G³) G;   he] *with* god *mar.* G³;   on]
of S.   4787 þilke] *marked for gloss* G³, thay*me* JMO;   of] to C, *with* to *mar.*
G³, for J, þem MO.   4788 I¹ ... nothing] (for3eue *with* 3yue *mar.* G³ *in* G),
I giffe tha · nathynge, forgiue, or thy prayer is against thee *mar.* O³;   ayens] agayne
JMO.   4789 to meward] towarde me J, -s S;   Ther] *prec. Capitulum* Cl *mar.*
CG;   riht] *om.* J;   of] *om.* J.   4790 wurshipe] *om.* J;   prys] *om.* S;
or] of *add.* S;   þat²] so J;   be] es J.   4791 him] *om.* S.   4792 dwelleth]
Sathanas J;   þe Sathanas] Sathanas CMO, dwelles J;   thinke] thenke (*2nd* e *ins.*
G³) G.   4793 it] *om.* J;   and²] *om.* JMO;   sithe] Syne JM, *om.* O.
4794 afterward] eftere JMO;   gerde] gurrde (e *ins.* G³) G;   syþe] þat *add.* CJM,
spitte S;   haue] (*2nd* a *ins.* G³).   4795 þilke þat] that J, þat that MO;
I... murdreres] I gurdde mu*u*rdredres G, whare wi*th* J;   with] I girde Man
morthyrrers J.   4796 knyghtes] knight S;   gert] abowte hym J;   sumtime]
Sum tyme girded J.   4797 Homicidye] *with* manslawghter *mar.* G³, Homicidiu*m*
JMO;   cleped] called JMO;   his] the J.   4798 name] (*2nd* a *ins.* G³), or
mannes slawht*er add.* J;   and Occisioun] *with* sleynge *mar.* G³, *om.* J;   is]
homicidiu*m rub. mar.* MO;   þilke þat] *with* syythe *mar.* G³, þat that JM, þat O;
moweth] moweveþe S.   4799 þilke] *om.* J, þat MO;   þe²] *om.* J;   targeden]
targe3 MO.   4800 hem] with *add.* G, which *add.* S;   þe] there J;   not]
na J.   4801 siþe] spithe S;   and] to J, to *add.* MO.   4802 wodes] worldes
S;   perilous] piloures C, *with* pyloures *mar.* G³, perilleuses F.   4803 cuntre]
þe cuntre CJM, cuntreys S;   to] Atte J.   4804 to] *om.* J;   hert] owthere
J, þe hert OS;   or¹] other GS, *om.* J;   or²] other GS;   bor] hare J;
pilgrime] A pilgryme JS;   am] haue CJMOS, sui F.   4805 þi] þe C.
4806 now] *om.* CG;   lyfe] How Memory brynge3 armo*u*r agayn to þe pilgrime
add. rub. M.   4807 As] *prec. Capitulum* Clj *mar.* CG;   þat] *om.* JMO;
I²] *om.* JMO.   4808 Memorie] I Sawe J;   I syh] Memorye J;   þat] whilk
J, *om.* S;   seide] (*2nd* e *ins.* G³), *om.* S;   me²] to me C, *om.* S, vnto me J;
Sey] Memory *and in another hand* in tyme of necessitie *mar.* O³;   me³] now *add.*
CS, now *add. ins. mar.* G³;   whi] *em. ed.*, sey me CGM, S*a*y me quod scho J,
quod she S.   4809 swich armures] hadde 3e nouht be bett*er* hafe taken J;
þow ... of] this armo*u*r J;   þee] (*1st* e *ins.* G³);   miht] may J, þou S;   þou]
might S.   4810 faste] *om.* S.   4810-1 and ... woldest] *om.* J.
4810 haue] (*2nd* a *ins.* G³);   armure] -s S.   4811 woldest] wold MO;
Lo] looue S.   4812 þi] *with* thyn*e* erased *mar.* G³;   haue] (*2nd* a *ins.* G³);
shame] schaame (*2nd* a *ins.* G³) G;   þerbi] *om.* S.   4813 and] if M;   abide]
here *add.* J, abode MO;   lengere] lange J;   shame] þat *add.* M;   so longe]
beden*e* J;   abide²] so lange J.   4814 noon had] nane J, *trs.* O;   er] *om.*
M.   4815 þilke] the foule JMO;   olde] holde (*with* oolde *mar.* G³) G, tratte
add. J.   4816 hauen] hauue (*2nd* a *ins.* G³) G, hase JMOS.   4817 þus]
om. J;   argued] reprufed J, reproeued S;   and vndertook] *om.* O.   4818 me]
on this wise *add.* J, *om.* O;   a] *om.* JMO;   lengere] I schulde ligge J.
4818-9 I³ ... ligge] langer*e* J.   4819 my] myne (ne *subpuncted*) G;   and as]
atte J;   seith] say JMO;   aroos] I rase JMO.   4820 Slowliche] fowlich

S; for²] be cause J. 4821 haue] (2nd a ins. G³). 4822 Peresce] with slewthe mar. G³, Slewth J; bifore] me add. JMO; manasinge] om. JMO; me seide] sayde J, trs. MO. 4823 of hire ax] I schulde have J; I ... haue] (2nd a ins. G³), of hir Axe J. 4824 Hire] I dredde J; I dredde] hire J; dide] to the armour add. J, dede M, deth O; Hire pley] I had lerned J. 4824-5 I² ... lerned] hir play J. 4826 powere ... more] om. S; haue¹] (2nd a ins. G³), I MO; I¹] haue MO; in me] na more J; no more] in me J; haue²] (2nd a ins. G³); me²] (2nd e ins. G³). 4827 triste] truste (e ins. G³) GOS; þe] fayth add. ins. mar. O³. 4828 riht] om. J; to] om. JMO; I dar] trs. JM. 4829 þe] my S. 4831 Euele] In ille tyme J; leevede] trowed M, lyvyng O; I] om. O; Oyseuce] ydylnes over C³, with idelschippe mar. G³, ydilschippe JMO. 4832 desceyuede] me ins. M; me] dissayued M; leeuede] trowed M. 4833 þese] thire JM; olde] (2nd o ins. G³). 4834 espyowresses] Spiers J, espiers MO; shulde] moun J, shal MO. 4835 if] bot ȝif J; of Grace Dieu] I have Succoure J, of dame Gracedieux S; I ... socowr] I ne hadde socowr C, of Grace dieu J, How þe pilgrime goes furth by a depe valey add. rub. M, I haue no socour S and Takeþe hede howe þe pilgryme is soore abayssed and ferde of his parayllous wey add. S. 4836 As] prec. Capitulum clij mar. CG, Capitulum xvij rub. mar. M, Capitulum {xx} mar. S; waymentinge] Wepande and J; rounginge] (o o. er. with er. mar. C); on] with JMO. 4836-7 a valye deep] a valeye deep (2nd, 4th e ins. G³) G, I Sawe byfore me J. 4837 ful ... wylde] adepe valaye J, ful of hydous busshes horryble and wylde S. 4837-8 I ... me] fulle of Buskes hidous horible and wilde J. 4838 which] þe which S; passe] I muste nedes J; I muste] passe J; go] om. O. 4839 was] gretly add. J; for] ofte tymes add. J; wodes] offtymes add. S; hauen] (2nd a ins. G³), men O; men] has O; wey] -es S. 4840 many] money (with manye mar. G³) G; ben] þer er (er ins. M) JMO; alloone] by thaim ane · as of J. 4841 theeves] of add. J; murderes] moourdredres G, and of add. J; bestes] that add. J; duellen] beoþe S. 4842 ofte-times] ofte tyme O. 4843 thing] (final e subpuncted G), thyngys JMOS; as¹] om. JMO; whan] as M; as²] om. C, subpuncted G; yow] efterwarde add. J. 4844 bifore þat] ar J; heerof] þerof J; it] I S. 4845 nouht] ne disease ȝowe add. J; heere] om. O; niht] myght O. 4846 restinge] tille add. J; if] that J; wole] om. J; come] -n (marked for gloss) G; and] om. CMO, subpuncted G, Et F; þanne] om. O. 4847 heere] (2nd e ins. G³); ynowe] I schalle telle ȝowe J; I ... yow] myschefes J; of mischeeves] I newe J; and] of add. MO. 4848 encumbraunces] encumbraunce JMO; fond] so that add. J; pitee] ȝe schalle hafe J; ye ...haue] (2nd a ins. G³), pitee J. 4849 taketh] taake (with taaketh mar. G³) G, om. J; keep] om. J, ? felix certe mar. O³; eche] ilke man JM, euerych O; as] om. JM; ayens himself] that es wise J, agaynes his self M; for of] om. J; þe] om. J, þis M. 4850 mischef] om. J, mysciefs MO; of anooþer om. J; eche] om. J, ilk man M, euerych O; maketh] may make C, may maaketh (may ins., th subpuncted G³) G; a mirrowr] armur O; for] to JMO. 4851 Heere ... book] om. GJMOS, Explicit pars Secunda J, Explicit secundus liber F. 4852 Heere ... book] om. GOS; Incipit pars tercia (and Pars iij top of page) J, Incipit tercia pars rub. mar. M. 4853 Now] prec. Capitulum j mar. GC; prec. Here is þe descripcion of Couatyse · and hir lynage rub. M, prec. This Monster is called Coveteousnes · and is deuided into seuerall branches · as Rapyn, Theft · Vsury · Faytory · Symony · Deceipt · Periury etc. at foot of page O³, HErkenes J; herkeneth] nowe J; auentures] aventur O. 4854 was] Behol{de} reedeþ *mar.* S; and] *om.* J; euele²] eeuelle (*4th* e *ins.* G³) G, *om.* J; led] leadd (e *ins.* G³) G, *om.* J; in] to *add.* JMO; þe] here begynneth good Readyng *mar.* O³; haue] (*2nd* a *ins.* G³), *om.* J. 4855 spoke] Spake be fore J; Als] þat *add.* S; and aualede] *om.* O. 4856 olde] (*2nd* o *ins.* G³), theffe *add.* J; manere] -s J, Sorcerye and hir vsery *mar.* O³; of³] and of JO. 4857 þan] that J; hadde sette hire] sche had Sette hire J, In my wey O. 4858 in my wey] she had sette here O; shrewedliche] in my waye *add.* J; she was] *ins. mar. after rub. caret also in text* O³; it] Inchantm*ents mar.* O³; þat] as *add.* O, *om.* S. 4859 hire] þat S; þat] *om.* J; upon me] (*2nd* e *ins.* G³), scho walde renne J. 4859-60 renne she wolde] vp on me J. 4860 thing] a beste J, beste F; so] fowle *add.* JMO. 4861 þe] *om.* JMO; I¹] *om.* O; bithinke] þink O. 4862 wrong-] yuell M; shapen] schaapen (*2nd* a *ins.* G³) G; and²] *om.* J; enbosed] bouge bakked J. 4863 cloþed] cledde JMO; an] -y J; old] *om.* M; with² ... old²] *om.* O. 4864 cloth ... she] *om.* O; hadde] *ins. mar. after rub. caret also in text* O³; at] on JMO. 4865 wel] It Seme J, and wele M; it seemed] (*final* e *ins.* G³), wele J; þat] *om.* J; make flight] scho keste noȝt J; wolde she nouht] to flye J. 4866 it] vp *add.* J. 4867 drawen] *erased u.v.* C, drawyng O; þerto] faste J, *om.* M; faste] þerto J; was] she had vj handes not one to doe good *mar.* O³; mesel] *with* leepre *mar.* G³. 4868 foule] foulle (e *ins.* G³) G, fowly J; Sixe] vi *over and* vi *mar.* G³; hadde] has J; tweyne] twey (ij *over* G³) GJMOS. 4869 Þe] *om.* JO; tweyne] twa of hir J, two MOS; nailes] apon *add.* J; whiche] (e *ins. and with* hondes *mar.* G³); oon] 1 *over* G³. 4870 was] *om.* O; bihynde] hir*e add.* J, 1 *over* O³; straunge] stronge MO; In] and in J; oon] 1 *over* G³, 2 *over* O³. 4871 heeld *o. er. with er. mar.* C, had O; þouh] ȝif J. 4872 balaunce] 3 *over* O³; peisede] weyed J; sunne] son*er* J. 4872-3 in ... entente] als bisily right as scho scholde J. 4873 to¹] *om.* J, and M; in ... hand] scho hadde J, 4 *over* O³. 4873-4 she heeld] in a nothe*re* hande J. 4874 þe fifte] v *over* G³O, Ano*þere* hande J; hadde] (e *ins.* G³). 4875 made] gerte J, make M. 4876 biholde] luke J; downward] -es S; sixte] vi *over* G³O. 4877 hye] vp J, *om.* MO. 4878 Whan] (han *erased* C), *prec.* Capitulum ij *mar.* CG; swich] which C; old] (*2nd* o *ins.* G³); oon] delle that was J; so foul] and so vggly *add.* J, *om.* M. 4879 I sigh] *om.* J; bi hire] I must nedes passe J; passe I moste] bi hir J, paas mooste S; ynowh] *om.* O. 4880 al] ful C, *with* full *mar.* G³, tout F; wery] of *add.* C, (*2nd* e *ins, and* of *add. ins. mar.* G³); bifore] for nuy and disease J; for ... anoye] that I hadd before J; for to] for S; haue¹] (*2nd* a *ins.* G³), more *add.* C, *om.* S; anoye] al þe annoye S; haue²] (*2nd* a *ins.* G³); seid] talde ȝowe J. 4881 Harrow] *om.* J; quod I] lorde J; God] Quod I J; am] but *add.* S. 4882 þis] ȝone J; beste] beest (*1st* e *ins.* G³) G; þese] thir J. 4883 she] he (*with* sche *mar.* G³) G; drede] dreede (*1st* e *ins.* G³) G; me²] þat *add.* S. 4884 am] but *add.* S. 4885 In] *prec.* Capitulum iij *mar.* CG; þilke] the J, þat MO; poynt] Same tyme J; þe] þat O; olde] delle *add.* J; toward me] to me ward O, towardes me S. 4886 seide] scho saide vnto J, þus *add.* M, to *add.* M; my] mamon *mar.* O³. 4887 leeue] trow M; abod] habide J, of *add.* S; haue] (*2nd* a *ins.* G³); it] *with* deth *mar.* G³, thy deed JMO. 4888 Euele] For yuell M; heere] hedir J; Þou ... dye] for here J; heere²] schalle þou dye J. 4887 do] make J. 4890 alosed] louyd MO, cleped S; cleped] called JMO, aloosed S. 4891 þilke] *with* mahoun *mar.* G³, ouer alle J, *om.* MO; whom] hym JMO; is preysed] in erth JM, Riches, the god of wretched men. *mar.* O³;

in eerþe] es praysed JM.   4892 þilke] I Am scho J, Scho I am MO;   whiche]
whom O;   grete] (2nd e ins. G³);   and] er add. J;   cleped] called JMO.
4893 needeth] it needeth C, þou muste nedes J, nedis þe MO, þat add. S;   þou
submitte] submitte J, to submyte MO;   him²] Serue J;   to serue] hym J.
4894 sette þee] mahoun mar. G³, om. J;   sithe] seyne JMO;   shamefulliche]
I shal make þee CJMO;   I ... þee] shamefullich C, fully JMO.   4895 vileyne-
sliche] & vileynesliche C, om. JMO;   dye] to dye JMO;   Whan] prec. Capitulum
iv mar. CG;   þe] this J;   olde] (e ins. G³), tratte add. J;   took] by gan to
speke J.   4896 sey] me J;   þer ... lust] me list nathynge J, þen tuke me no
list MO;   but wel] Neuertheles ʒit J;   wold of sooth] desired J.   4896 wite]
to wit J;   name] (2nd a ins. G³);   and ... were] om. J;   olde] (2nd o ins.
G³), tratte add. J.   4898 name] (2nd a ins. G³);   art] and add. MS;   wherof
... seruest] om. S;   of] and of O, om. S;   what] om. S.   4899 linage] om.
S;   of¹] and of JMO, om. S;   what¹ ... art] om. S;   regioun] Also add. J;
who] she S.   4900 woldest] walde JMO;   I] om. S.   4901 not] na J;
þat¹] I add. J;   a] that J;   and] om. MO.   4902 I ... omage] ne that I that
es of nobele lynage J.   4902-3 þat ... lynage] long passage marked mar. C, make
hym homage J.   4903 if] it add. JMO;   shulde] schalle JMO;   to] do
JMO;   serue] Servise JMO.   4904 and] yit add. O.   4905 wite] I wille
J;   soothli] wete J, I wol S;   I wole] Sothely JS, om. M;   whens] wheyne
JM, of wheyne O, þou come add. S.   4906 anoon] euen M;   And] prec.
Capitulum v mar. CG;   olde] (2nd o ins. G³) G, delle add. J;   answerde] me
add. C;   Sithe] Seyn JMO.   4907 anoon] om. J;   soone ynowh] quod scho
· I wille telle it the J;   I² ... þee] Onane J.   4908 shewe] itt add. G;   þee]
Sumwhate add. J.   4909 leeue] trow M;   bettere] of the remenaunt J;
þer] whare JMO.   4910 and] than scho wente downe into the valey and beganne
to add. J;   now] om. M;   see] (2nd e ins. G³);   sorwe] -fulle JM;   of] om.
J, be M, be of O.   4911 of¹] the Jo, be M;   weylinge] with heu under
rubrication mar. G³;   ful of sorwe] and J;   sighinges] sighynge JM.
4912 lamentacioun] almentacioun O;   seeth it] sittes JMO;   noon] here quod
scho add. J;   þat ne] that ne he J, þen he MO;   Harrow] allas and that J;
which] with JMOS.   4913 woodshipe] is þis add. C, is thys add. ins. mar.
G³.   4914 And] prec. Capitulum vj mar. CG;   þe olde] (2nd o ins. G³), scho
J;   gon] to gange J.   4915 beholde] þere I biheeld C, (2nd o ins. G³), I be
helde J;   chirche] khrk kirk (khrk can.) M;   founded] efouned and S;   bisides]
be syde JMO.   4916 wher] there (2nd e ins. G³), om. JMOS;   ches] manyyʒ
add. J;   grete] (2nd e ins. G³);   smale] (2nd a ins. G³);   which] wheche (2nd
e ins. G³) G.   4917 rookes] booþe gret and smale add. S;   þe king] kynges
JS, -es MO;   þat] whiche C, with wheche mar. G³;   ledden] bare J.
4918 Eche] Ilkane JM, everych OS;   me] a add. J.   4919 for] om. J;   ooþer
times] of Sum tyme before J, othir ryme MO;   and] bot J.   4920 hadde] I
had J;   þat was] om. JMO;   swich] that J;   manere] araye J, A prophetique
dreame of the church of O³;   Here] with chess under rubrication mar. G³.
4921 chercheward] kyrke wardes JS;   bete] beete (2nd e ins. G³) G.
4922 first] wente freste J;   bifore wente] byfore J.   4923 foundement] þerof
and the grounde and add. J;   he made] they made J, þeyr hows and pycoys O.
4923-4 his¹ ... pikoyse] pikke and schouelle J, þey made O.   4924 Pikoise] the
scharpe ende was J, þe pycoys O;   was ... ende] the pik J;   howwe] the croked
end J, þe howe O.   4924-5 was² ... ende] the schouill J.   4925 þat I] om.
J.   4926 see þere] om. J;   Am I] trs. JMOS;   abasht] gretly abaiste J, sore
abaysht quod I S;   meetinge] (2nd e ins. G³), a metaile J;   or¹] other GS, or

a J;   faireye] fair MO;   or²] other GS, *om.* O.   4927 or] other GS;
ve] sorwe CS, *space in* G *with* sorewe *mar.* G³, ve F;   heu] weylinge CS, *space
in* G, heu G³, *with* weillynge *mar.* G³;   of] *om.* J.   4928 which] *om.* J, while
ere *add.* S;   þow] *om.* J;   speke] *tiny illegible word mar.* G³, *om.* J;   me of]
to me C, *om.* J, me of such (of such *can.*) O, to me of S;   It is þis] *om.* J, þis is
MO;   certeyn] quod sche *add. can.* C, *om.* J, *quod* sche certayn MO.
4929 soothliche] *om.* JMO, Certis quod I S;   þis] *om.* JMO;   is¹] *om.* JMO;
heu] weylinge CS, *space in* G *with* weylynge *mar.* G³, *om.* J;   ve] sorwe CS, *space
in* G *with* sorowe *mar.* G³, the ve J;   is²] the *add.* J.   4930 þat] interieccioun
mar. O³;   lusteth] likes J, liftes M, lystys O, Nowe þe olde tolde þe pilgryme þat
þis was þe sorouful thinges þat sheo hade spoken to him of to fore *add.* S;   And]
prec. Capitulum viij *mar.* CG, *om.* J;   Capitulum {xxj} *mar.* S.   4931 þanne
þe] *om.* J;   olde] (*2nd* o *ins.* G³) *om.* J;   seide] *om.* J;   me] *om.* JMO;
It is treweliche] This J, It is treuth M;   þis] is it trewly J;   haue] (*2nd* a *ins.*
G³).   4932 þee] of *add.* O;   king] -es O;   cheker] *with* earth *mar.* O³;
and¹] *om.* MO.   4933 hauen] (*2nd* a *ins.* G³);   þe] here awne J, þer MO;
hem] *om.* JS.   4934 ordeyned] assigned S;   hem] *om.* O;   in] of O;
þe] þat M;   Ynowh] thay had land J;   þei hadden] I nowe J.   4934-5 of
... lond] of thayre awene J.   4935 getinge] gretynge (*with* getynge *mar.* G³)
G;   ooþeres] oþere JMO;   ne] warne J, ner S;   were I] *trs.* JS.
4936 haue] (*2nd* a *ins.* G³);   sufficience] souffieceaunt S;   binemynge] takynge
J;   ooþere] mennys *add.* J, mennes gude *add.* M.   4937 sende] sent O;
þilke] that JMO;   nygh] nere JM.   4938 delue] delude S;   bineme] take
J, withdraw M;   kyng] kyngis vse J, -ys O.   4939 haue (*2nd* a *ins.* G³) G;
take] taake (e *ins.* G³) G, þaim *add.* J;   a tool] toles J.   4940 do] with *add.*
J;   cherles] carles J, þe cheorlles S;   werk] -es JMO;   is] atte Say *add.* J;
bishoppes] bischoppe JMO.   4941 howwe] pikke J;   and] or M;   pikois]
schouelle J;   bisshopes] bisshopp MO.   4942 wurshipful] tille a bischoppe
add. J;   a] *om.* M;   thing] a thynge J, *om.* MO;   diche] dike JMO.
4943 to¹] *om.* O;   foundaciouns] fundacione M.   4944 hauen] (*2nd* a *ins.*
G³).   4945 dicheth] dikes JMO;   he²] *om.* JOS;   howwe] schouel and
makes a schouell J, a Crosier staff *mar.* O³.   4946 bicom] he came S;   shulde]
scholde (e *ins.* G³) G.   4947 Cherl] A churle J, þe Cheorlle S;   is] also J;
also] he es J;   þe¹] *om.* S;   hornede] bischop J, honoured S;   whan] he takeþe
add. S;   þe²] his J;   which] wheche (*2nd* e *subpuncted*) G;   his cherche]
he schulde susteyne and gouerne J, þe kirke M, is þe chirche O.   4948 is¹ ...
gouerned] is susteened with & gouerned G, haly kyrke J;   whiche] wheche (*2nd*
e *subpuncted*) G;   taketh] he taketh CMS;   *om.* J, take O.   4949 it] *om.*
CJM;   þilke] thayme JMO;   þerof] þayre JM;   pikoys] pikke J, þeir pycoys
O;   howwe] schouelle þerof J, þeyr howe O, howes S.   4950 nygh] nere
JMO.   4951 cheker] eschekar M;   cherl] a cheorlle S;   ooþer] es wele *add.*
J, is *add.* S.   4952 which] whedere J;   pike] pykoys MO, pykoys *add.* S;
howwe] schouell J;   and delueth] *om.* S.   4953 sorweth] þat he so delueþe
add. S;   hornede] bischoppe J;   deliuereth] *twice* S.   4954 to] and J;
burdoun] staffe J.   4955 him¹] *om.* JMO;   whan] *om.* MO;   þe cherche]
he enbaundounes J;   he abaundoneth] the kyrke, Jeremye *mar.* O³;   him²] tille
hym J.   4956 sumtime] the prophete *add.* J;   he] his S.   4957 how-
weden] grubbed J;   þat] For J;   she] *with* chirch *mar.* G³, it O.
4958 subsidies] dymes J, subsyde O;   dimes] and Subsidies J;   extorciouns]
extorcioun O;   He] *with* Jeremie *mar* G³.   4959 compleyninge] complayned
J;   was] lady and *add.* J.   4960 folk] -es S;   and¹] *om.* S;   þe] *om.*

CJS;   maistresse] *om.* S;   was] note *mar.* O³;   bicomen] thralle and *add.*
J.   4961 as] Also M, þat as S;   þouh] wha JO, so M;   he¹] *om.* JMO;
wolde] wull (*with* wolde *mar.* G³) G, *om.* JMO;   seye] seyeth O;   he ouhte]
hym awht J.   4962 Now] *prec. capitulum* ix *mar.* CG, *passage marked mar.*
C;   haue] (*2nd a ins.* G³).   4963 bifore] For J;   aboute] alle aboute J;
lakketh] þat *add.* S.   4963-4 it ne is] ne it es J, it is nouȝt MO.   4964 eche]
ilke a J, ilk M, euerych O;   þe] booþe S.   4965 boþe] knyght *add.* J, *om.*
S.   4966 þat¹] euere *add.* J, that *add.* O;   þei don¹] *om.* J;   don²] it *add.*
J;   do¹] doon (n *subpuncted*) G, to do J.   4967 of] *om.* JM;   ben] haue
be O;   Strengthe ... neiþer] thare es nowthere kynge nor knyght ne roke J.
4968 kyng ne rook] that has strenghe to *with*stande me J, kyng ne knyght ne rooke
MO;   þat þei ne] that ne thay J, þen þei MO;   to] vnto M, *om.* S.
4969 raþe] arely JM;   Jeremye] ȝif þou lefe noȝt me J, and þou leeve not me
S.   4969-70 and ... me] Jeremye JS.   4970 witnesseth] witnys JMS;
þat] *ins. mar.* G³, *om.* JMO.   4971 Michel abasht] *prec.* Capitulum x *mar.* CG,
And than I answerde hir and sayde · Forsoth quod I þou make me J;   quod ...
me] gretly abayst J;   if] bot ȝif J.   4972 nouht] *om.* J;   may] can CJ, *with*
kann *mar.* G³;   miht] schulde J;   haue] (*2nd a ins.* G³).   4973 swich] soo
grete J, *om.* MO;   power] For *add.* J;   þee] *ins.* M;   cloþed] eclooþed S;
misshapen] myschapen (*with* mys schaapen *mar.* G³) G.   4974 and¹] *om.* J;
embosed] bouche makked J;   mawgre] a gaynes J;   nature] kynde J, mishapen
and *add.* S;   forthouht] furth brought J.   4975 how] thayn *add.* J;   haue]
(*2nd a ins.* G³);   kynges] dukes *add.* J.   4976 erles] Errlys (*1st* r *ins.* O³)
O;   to] ouer J, of MO;   ben] ert nouȝt (ert *o. er.*, nouȝt *ins.*) M, engendred
O;   engendred] kyndely J, ar O;   bi nature] engendrid J.   4977 born]
yborn C;   And] *prec.* Capitulum xj *mar.* CG, than *add.* J;   it] *om.* JMO.
4978 shuldest] schalle J;   þilke] scho JMO;   haue] (*2nd a ins.* G³).
4979 biwicche] be gyle JMO;   þe] *om.* J;   plesaunt] and *add.* S.
4980 plese] -d JO;   þat¹] thus J;   þat²] whilk M.   4981 biwicche] be swike
JM, beswynk O;   erles] Kynges M, Dukes S;   dukes] Eerles MS.   4982 prin-
ces] kynges and J, Dukes M, kyngys O;   kynges] princes JMO;   þat] ne *add.*
J, þen M, but þat O;   bi] *ins. mar.* G³;   sorceryes] sorcery JMO;   doon] thay
do J.   4983 comaundement] -es CS;   Apemendeles] *om.* J, ape nedeles
S.   4984 haue] (*2nd a ins.* G³), has JMO;   þat] Besachis apenmendales *mar.*
O³;   lawhe] doo S.   4985 it] *with* sory *mar.* G³, Sary JMO, yit S;   þat¹]
he S;   þat²] *om.* J;   I²] me J;   do] to do I.   4986 make] (*2nd a ins.*
G³), -s JO;   yive] to gefe J;   þus] this JO;   ywriten] schalle þou fynde J,
writyn MO, {Behol}de þe taale *mar.* S;   þou ... it] wretene J, þou shall fynde
MO.   4987 secunde] buke of *add.* JMO.   4988 longe] (e *ins.* G³);   his¹]
om. J.   4988-9 al his tresore] he toke hire J.   4989 he took hire] alle his
tresoure J;   needy] and *add.* J;   þe²] *om.* M.   4990 religious] religiouns
G;   Liberalitee] Scho hight J;   she hyghte] liberalite J;   and was] *om.* O;
sumtime] and *add.* O.   4991 and] as M;   þilke] scho JMO;   louede] the
kynge JMO;   þe kyng] luffed JMO.   4993 him] þarof J;   þerof] tille hym
J;   riht] *om.* J.   4993-4 He ... þerbi] *om.* CO, and mikille worschepe and
prise J.   4994 michel ... prys] and pris CO, he gate þereby J.   4995 ynowh]
aye mare and mare J.   4996 good] *om.* S;   and] *om.* JMOS;   profyte] *om.*
JMO;   þilke þat] that J, þat whilk M, þat · that O;   lyth] is M.   4997 riht]
om. O;   þat ben] *om.* S;   yiven] or weele elent *add.* S;   more worth] better
S.   4998 hepede] keped J, or hidd *add.* M, tresore *add.* S;   Now] *prec.*
Capitulum xij *mar.* CG, *om.* J;   I telle þee (*4th* e *ins.* G³), And J;   hire ... kyng]

þat þe kyng M.   4999 wurshiped] hir *add.* M, was whorshiped S;   of] on
J;   poyntes] wyse J.
5000 So I dide] and as I thought J;   as I thouhte] So y did J.   5001 kinges]
kynge J;   entrede] and *add. ins. mar.* G³, and *add* J;   bi] thorowe J.
5002 entre] *om.* O;   bed] bedde (*2nd* e *subpuncted*) G;   I wente] *om.* S.
5003 þere] there (*2nd* e *ins.* G³) G;   withdrough him hire] withdrough hir*e o. er.*
(*with* drough *mar.* C³) C, I with drewe hir*e* fra hym J;   stal] (*final* e *subpuncted*
G).   5004 him hire] hire fro him C, hir*e* JMO;   out ... chaumbre] drewe
hir J;   I ... hire] out of the chaunbre J.   5005 vnder keye] I putte hire J;
I putte hire] vnder*e* look J;   is] ȝit *add* J.   5006 into ... bed] I wente J;
I entrede] in to the kyngis bedde J;   and] *om.* M;   in ... place] (*2nd* a *ins.* G³),
layde me J.   5006-7 I² ... me] thare · scho lay J.   5007 He] *with* s*cilicet*
kynge *mar.* G³, and he J;   I¹] þat I M.   5008 biwicchede him and] *om.*
JMO;   him²] and *add.* JMO;   þat] *om.* JMOS.   5008-9 his tresorere] I was
J.   5009 I was] his tresoure J;   I³] and J;   keepe] keped JMO;   and¹] *om.*
MO;   al²] *om.* JO;   and²] all *add.* MO.   5010 He] *with* {k}ing *mar.* G³;
but I do] *om.* J;   him²] *om.* JM;   gret] *om.* JS.   5011 vnwurshipe] *om.* J;
al his lyfe] schalle do J, al his lyfes tym M;   shal ... him] alle his lyfe J;   while]
-s JMO;   of me] he makes J.   5011-2 he maketh] of me J.   5012 haue]
(*2nd* a *ins.* G³).   5013 auoir] Beholde howe þis foule olde horned spekeþe here
to þe pilgryme of hir name *add.* S.   5014 If] *prec.* Capit*ulum* xiij *mar.* CG,
Capit*ulum* x{xij} *mar.* S;   whens] wheyne JMO;   is] Sorcery, the place
of hir byrth and whoe was hir father *mar.* O³.   5015 name] (*2nd* a *ins.* G³);
shuldest] schalt JMOS;   vale] -ye S;   þe] *om.* M;   derke] depe J.
5016 Þe] -re CS, *om.* JMO;   engendred] engendre C;   þens] fro þens C, brought
me J;   he ... me²] theyn*e* J.   5017 norishede] mysteryd M;   vserere]
vsurere · Or couetise · Or auerice · *rub. mar.* O.   5018 cleped] called JMO;
clepen¹,²] calles JMO.   5019 Auarice ... and] *om.* CGS;   coueyt] Auaricia
rub. mar. M;   ooþeres] oþere mennes J;   and] *om.* O.   5020 I am cleped]
om. C, *subpuncted* G, I am called JMO;   Clepe] Call JMO.   5021 abasht]
aferde M;   þus] al *add.* M;   toragged] ragged J;   and²] *om.* O.
5022 toclouted] clouted JMO;   euele] ille J;   cloþed] for *add.* C, for *add. ins.*
mar. G³, soo *add.* S;   shuldest] schalle JS.   5023 yive] ȝeeue (*with* ȝyue
mar. G³) G;   of] þat *add:* S;   myn] is *add.* S;   with] wytte wele O;   haue]
(*2nd* a *ins.* G³);   ynowe] y nowgh (*with* nowe *mar.* G³) G.   5024 raþere]
om. J;   alle¹,²] (e *ins.* G³);   to] *om.* JMO.   5025 I or] *om.* J.
5026 good] *om.* C, (*final* e *ins.* G³);   if] ȝyue (*with* ȝyff *mar.* G³) G;   cowþe]
kooude (*2nd* o *ins.* G³) G;   ariht] departe J, right MO;   departe] right J;
myn] of gudes J, of myne MO.   5027 serueth] semeth S;   am] Narraci*on rub.*
mar. O;   lich] *om.* M;   þe²] *om.* J.   5028 any] ma*n*n *add.* J;   hand] to
take þereof *add.* J;   abayeth] bayes J.   5029 he] *with* hound *mar.* G³;
noon] not S;   I] *prec.* Capit*ulum* xiv *mar.* CG;   haue] (*2nd* a *ins.* G³);
ynowe] and *add.* J.   5030 gripe] take J;   with¹] alle *add.* J;   haue] (*2nd*
a *ins.* G³);   none] (e *ins.* G³);   þe] My JMO;   hondes] hande J.
5030-1 of my yivinge] of my ȝeuynge (*with* ȝyuynge *mar.* G³) G, whilke I schulde
gyffe with J, forto giff with MO.   5031 kitte] off *add.* J;   and doon] *om.*
O;   þou seest wel] *om.* CS.   5032 I haue] *om.* CS, (*2nd* a *ins.* G³);   but
þe stumpes] *om.* CS;   me] any *add.* J.   5033 hepes] heepes (*1st* e *ins.* G³)
G;   of] nobles and *add.* J, and S.   5034 Sixe] vi *over* G³;   haue] (*2nd* a
ins. G³);   gripe] take J;   hem] *om.* CS, *subpuncted* G, penyes J, wyþ O;
with] þai*m* O.   5035 in¹] on J, *om.* O;   sixe] vi *over* G³;   hem¹,²] *om.* CS,

subpuncted G; glene] gloue O. 5036 peise] *om.* J, þem *add. can.* M, preyse S; me and] *om.* J.; charge] to charge O; me²] with *add.* C, with *add. ins. mar.* G³; þat²] *ins. mar.* G³; if] *om.* S; falle] shall S. 5037 adoun] downe JMOS; haue] (*2nd* a *ins.* G³). 5038 haue] (*2nd* a *ins.* G³); Vnstaunchable] (unchable *o. er.* C), vnchangeable and vnstanchable M; is my] *o. er.* C; wille] *o. er.* C, *with* to haue *mar.* G³. 5039 fulfillinge] fullyng O; grete] Coueteousnes neuer satisfied *mar.* O³. 5040 anything] castynge oute agayne J. 5040-1 castinge out ayen] if any thynge J, agayn castyng oute M. 5041 and²] ne S. 5042 cometh] castes J; and¹] to S. 5043 peise] charges J, to peyse S; swich] which S; as I see] *om.* JMO; peiseth] charge me J, payse me MO. 5044 which] þe which S; blok] clogge J, *om.* O; and a] *om.* O; stake] staff MO; tye] byndes JMO; me²] *om.* M. 5045 rihtfulliche] by goode right J; cleped] called JMO. 5046 kepe] se O; it¹] *with* clog *mar.* G³, the clogge JMO; it²] *with* blokke *mar.* G³. 5047 me¹] *ins. mar. after rub. caret also in text* O³; I] it S; doun] haldes me J; it ... me²] downe J; doun²] weyes J. 5047-8 it ... me] it peiseth him C, me downe J, payses me MO; nota de Iuda *rub. mar.* M. 5048 þi] þe MS; blok] clogge J; sumtime] I hynged J. 5049 I heeng] Sum tyme J; purses] purs JMS; putte] sente JMO; in²] tille *add.* J, to *add.* M. 5050 sakkes] sekke JM, stackys O; hye] (e *subpuncted* G); lowe] (e *subpuncted with* lowgh *mar.* G³); made] (*2nd* a *ins.* G³) y made *add. subpuncted* G; falle] to falle J. 5051 into] in telle J, depe *add.* M. 5052 Now] *prec.* Capitulum *xv mar.* CG; I wole] *trs.* J; gripe] with *add.* G, and take *add.* J. 5053 metalles] metall MO; haue] (*2nd* a *ins.* G³). 5053-4 as I trowe] in þy lyfe J, in al þi life M, I trowe O, *om.* S. 5054 in þi lyfe] I trowe JM; founde þou] *trs.* J. 5055 it] þayme J; firste] furste (e *ins.* G³) G, hande *add.* JM; nailes] þe nayles S; griffoun] a griffoun J, þe Griffoun S. 5056 is] þat is O; cleped] called JMO; Rapyne] Rauen J, rapina O; whiche] Rapina *rub. mar.* MO. 5057 to] *om.* J, the first hande of his Monster force · Rapine Cum priuilegio *mar.* O³; take] (*2nd* a *ins.* G³), *om.* J; him²] *om.* J. 5048 goth] And *add.* J; and¹] he J. 5059 haue] (*2nd* a *ins.* G³). 5060 me] the JMO; it] *with* hond *mar. under rubrication* G³, that this hande JM, þis hand O. 5061 and¹] *om.* J; graspe] grape M; al¹] *om.* M; take] (*2nd* a *ins.* G³). 5062 grucche] gruches JOS; is] that es J; him] *om.* JMO. 5064 puttok] pittok C; kaccheth] takes JMO; chikenes] chikes J; taketh] makes J. 5065 hors] -es J; kartes] carte M; puruiaunces] puruyaunce JMO; goode] (e *ins.* G³). 5066 vsage] vse J; haue] *om.* O; oxe] ane ox J, *om.* O; or] other G, *om.* O. 5067 swyn] a Swyne JM, *om.* O; to ... his] *om.* O; store] warnestore J, *om.* O; she] *with* hond *mar.* G³, *om.* O; taketh] makis J, *om.* O; it] thaim J, *om.* MO; and ... reccheth] *om.* O. 5068 hire] *with* honde *mar.* G³, *om.* JMO, ne hir S; þouh þe poore] *om.* O; man] *om.* O, men S; cote] clathes J. 5069 his] hire CS, son F; lust] liste J; fulfilled] and his wille *add.* J; With] *prec.* Capitulum *xvj mar.* CG; kerue and] *om.* JMO. 5070 it] I JMO; araseth] arace JMO; breketh] brekes JMO; þe²] *om.* J. 5071 at] *om.* J; skorche] shorte M, shere O; anything] any JMO. 5072 yrayne] *o. er.* (or a loppe *over* C³) G, ravyne J; or] other G, *om.* O; marigh (righ *o. er.* C); be] is CJMOS (*o. er.* C). 5073 flye] flesshe S; it¹] owte O; pulleth] pluckys O; it²] *ins. mar. after rub. caret also in text* O³. 5074 skorcheresse] scorgeresse JM, sercheresse O; baconresse] bacouresse CG, faconeresse J, faucoresse MO (*see note*); seecheth] (*2nd* e *ins.* G³). 5075 bineme] take JM,

bynde S.   5076 skorched þus] *trs.* JMOS;   topulled] pulled J.
5077 and²] þus *add.* M;   whoso] who O.   5078 fynde] to fynde JMO.
5079 of þee] *trs.* MO;   dispense] and *add.* J, -s to S;   marigh] blude J.
5080 blood] merght J;   with] by S.   5081 fyve] v *over and with* v *mar.* G³;
sey] *marked mar.* O³.   5083 That] *prec. Capitulum* xvij *mar.* CG.
5084 straunge] strong MO;   meward] -es J.   5085 and] *om.* J;   ooþeres]
ooþere CS, oþere men J;   is] þe aunswere and *add.* S.   5086 eren] ere
JMO.   5086-7 Coupe Bourse] F, Coute burse C, Cutte purs JMOS.
5087 cleped] called JMO;   Larescyne] Latrosynie (*o. er. with* {Latro}synie *mar.*
C³) CS, *with* theffte *mar.* G³, thifte JM, theef O.   5088 dar] thar MO, Cutpurs
id est furtum *rub. mar.* M, Furtum *rub. mar.* O;   to] forto M.   5089 it] *with*
hond *mar.* G³, he J;   nihte] þe nyght O;   moone] (*1st* o *ins.* G³);   the second
hand, theft *mar.* O³;   shineth] schewes J.   5090 ooþer] toother dooth (dooth
subpuncted) G;   hath for] *ins. mar.* G³, note *mar.* O³.   5091 she] it CS, it
ins. mar. G³;   accroches] draweth to hir CS, draweth to hir *ins. mar.* G³;
encroches J, acroches F;   whan ... ooþer] *ins. mar.* (as¹ cropped) G³.
5092 dooth] or more CS, or more *ins. mar.* G³;   cometh] with out priuiledg *mar.*
O³;   so²] *om.* J.   5093 knowleche] knawelachynge J;   is] So that hir draght
commes to *add.* J;   mischaunce] myschefe J;   Manye] Monye (e *ins.* G³)
G.   5094 accrocheres] encrochers J, crocheris MO;   and] of *add.* JO, *om.*
M;   kaccheres] *om.* M;   if] and J.   5095 apperceyued] persayfed JMO;
þei²] þam J;   haue] to haue MS;   to¹] atte J.   5096 to¹] *om.* J;   him]
hem (*with* hym *and* kynge *mar.* G³) G;   bineme] byen CS, take JM;   ooþeres]
thing *add. into mar.* C, othere men ys gudes JM, oþer thing S.   5097 owene]
ins. mar. G³;   hole makere] vnmakere CS, brekere J, ill maker MO, pertuiseresse
F.   5098 and] of *add. subpuncted* G;   vnhelere] and *add.* CS;   a¹] *om.*
CS;   and²] *om.* M;   roungere] (o *o. er.* C).   5099 and¹] a *add.* JMOS;
of seles] *ins. mar. after rub. caret also in text* O;   graueresse] grauer J.
5100 lokyere] (*2nd* e *ins.* G³), *om.* J;   and a fals] *om.* J;   fals³] falsse (e
subpuncted) G.   5101 tellere] clippere J, toller M;   pens] (*2nd* s *erased* C);
dispoileth] dispooseþe S;   dede] folk *add.* M;   clos] -d M.   5102 into] vnto
JM;   haue] (*2nd* a *ins.* G³), grapid *add.* M;   glened] glouued S.   5103 þat¹]
al CS;   Þilke] *with* hond *mar.* G³, Scho J;   executrice] þexecutryce S;
dispendere] þe despender J.   5104 wherof] warefore JMOS.
5105 accroche] encroche J.   5106 bi] *om.* J;   nihte] mihte C, venyson on
nyghtertale J.   5108 millewardes] Milneres JMO.   5109 withoute] (oute
ins. G³), with JMO;   clepinge] callynge JMO;   Resoun] Fals scheperdes also
that falsly Serues þaire maistres false baxteres and brewsters also that falsly bakes
agayne the assise and delyueres þaire brede and thayre ale with fals mesures *add.*
J.   5110 false tailowres] Also J;   also] false taylours J;   folk] of crafte J;
ooþeres] ooþere CMS, oþere men J.   5111 wist] knowen M;   hand selfe]
(selffe *2nd* e *subpuncted* G), *trs.* CJMOS.   5112 hem] him S;   þanne] thy
J;   hanged ... be] atte the laste JMO;   at þe laste] they schalle be hynged J,
hangyd þei shall be MO.   5113 haue] (*2nd* a *ins.* G³);   laste] (e *ins.* G³).
5114 haue] (*2nd* a *ins.* G³);   How] Now CS, whate J, *prec. Capitulum* xviij *mar.*
CG.   5115 hangestere] hange man J;   Ye] ȝis M;   certeyn] forsoth J;
she] *with* coueityse *mar.* G³.   5116 Peresce] *id est* slowthe *over* C³, *with* slowthe
mar. G³, and Slewitȝ J, Sleuth MO;   me] that *add.* J;   And þanne] *om.* J.
5116-7 she seid me] *with* coueityse *mar.* G³, For Soth J.   5117 Certeyn] quod
scho J, quod scho *add.* MO;   she] so J;   it is] & true O;   treweliche] *om.*
J, trew M, it is O;   of] to M.   5118 but] *om.* J;   I] *with* coueityse *mar.*

G³, *om.* J; am ... of²] *om.* J; þe²] *om.* JMO; soule] *om.* J. 5119 keepe] the J; þee] helpe J; sey me now] *om.* J; heeng] (*2nd* e *ins.*, *final* e *subpuncted* G³). 5120 she] *with* coueityse & slewthe *mar.* G³; God keepe me] name J. 5121 but] if *add.* O; I] neuertheles I schalle *add.* J; þee] the sothe *add.* JMO; putte ... knotte] to gedyr J. 5122 togideres] putte the rape aboute his nekke J; ne hadden] had nou3t J; myne] (e *subpuncted with* coueityse *mar.* G³). 5123 Peresce] *with* slowthe *mar.* G³, Slewth JMO; him] so *add.* JMO. 5124 peysede] so heuy *add.* J; þat] þerfore it J; longeth] langed JMO; þerfore] for this cause J. 5125 principalliche] *om.* J; hand] -es JMO; leue me] wille do goode counseile J, trow me M. 5126 swich] suche (e *subpuncted*) G; an] *om.* JMO; hand] hende J, ende O; þe] þi M, *om.* OS; rerewarde] (rerewar o. *er.* C), Reerewarde (*3rd* e *ins.* G³) G. 5127 she¹] *with* coueityse *mar.* G³; sithe] Seyne JMO; she²] iij *mar.* O³. 5128 hem] Onane *add.* J, howe þat vserer telleþe þe pilgryme what hir oþer hande meneþe takeþe heede *add.* S. 5129 Of] *prec.* Cap*itulum* xix *mar.* CG, If *prec.* {Cap}*itulum* xxiij *mar.* S; I wole] wille I nowe J. 5130 lust] liste JMO; hand] vsura *rub. mar.* O; whiche] wheche (*2nd* e *ins.* G³) G; and] I M; togidere] and hepes J. 5131 and hepe] to gedire J; hauen] has JMO; conquered] geten JMO; here] *om.* J, the third hande vsery. lyke a fyle cutts by degrees till al be consumed *mar.* O³. 5132 swetinge] swynke and swete J; is] was S; ayens] agayn M. 5133 bras] brusche J; yren] yrnes JO; to²] for to O; brode] breede GJMO, couver F. 5134 pondre] powdir MO; maken] (*2nd* a *ins.* G³); ammenuse] to emmenu3 J. 5135 þis] it S; encrese] to encreesse JMO. 5135-6 An enchauntouresse] Scho es J. 5136 she is gret] ane enchauntresse and that agrete J; she²] for J. 5137 conuerte] to conuerte JO, couert S; into] marked *mar.* C, and turne in to J; paresis] *with* moneye *mar.* G³, many JO, monye M; of fyve] v *over* G³, in to sixe S; maketh] gers J, scho makes MS; bicome] *om.* S. 5138 sixe] vi *over* G³ fyve S; kyne] koyn CS, kygne GJ, kynges M, *om.* O, Vaches F. 5139 Kyne] koyn CS, kygne GJ, kyng MO, Vaches F. 5140 maketh] gers J; clepe] calle JMO; and] *om.* J; hath] also *add.* J. 5141 til] forte G, to JMO; greyn] corne JM; hire corn] scho selles J. 5141-2 she selleth] hir corne J. 5142 dubble¹] valewe *add.* J. 5143 fyle¹] *followed by misplaced caret* G, with *add.* J; for to fyle] *om.* S; with] *ins. mar.* G³; ooþeres] oþere mennes J, oþer S. 5144 waste] to waste J, wasteth S; it²] *with* hond *mar.* G³; rounginge] (o o. *er.* C); ooþere] or MO; comynge] commonynge J, to mony M. 5145 and] or in J, *om.* M; biside it] myght endure J, *with* hond *mar.* G³; mihte endure] beside it J; þat] þen MO. 5146 ne] *om.* JMO; bi¹] my J; name] (*2nd* a *ins.* G³); cleped] called JM. 5147 hire] him CS, (*with* hym *mar.* G³); lyf] lesse O; þilke] hym JMO; here] (*2nd* e *ins.* G³), *om.* J, hir (r *alt.* s) S; his] vsura *rub. mar.* M, hir (r *alt.* s) S. 5148 so in vsage] it ware no3t J; it ne were] *with* vsure *mar.* G³, soo in vsage J; eche] Ilke a J, ilk M, euerych O. 5149 agast] ferde JMO; of it] *with* vsure *mar.* G³, thereof J; soo in vse] it es so J; bicomen it is] becommen in vse J. 5149-50 in feyres] it es knawen J, vn to feyrys O, and chepinges *add.* S. 5150 knowen it is] into faires J; þe¹] *om.* JM; þe²] *om.* J; vsinge it] *with er. mar.* C, *with* {v}sure *mar.* G³. 5151 alle] (e *ins.* G³); fylinge] it *add.* S; þer] -e C. 5152 ayens-seith] (a *and* seith o. *er. with er. mar.* C); to] *om.* JMO; here] *with* ? usurores *mar.* G³. 5153 Sey] *prec.* Cap*itulum* xx *mar.* CG; balaunce] Balance *mar.* O³; in] with JMO. 5153-4 with ... entente] So besyly J, in so grete entent MO. 5154 peisest] weyes J; thing] a thynge J. 5155 I] hafe grete *add.*

J;   Lerne] nowe *add*. J.   5156 of] the J, þe of MO;   aboute þe zodiac]
Sum tyme JMOS.   5157 sumtime] made the Sunne to schyne J, aboute þe ʒodiak
MO;   sette ... shyne] aboute the ʒodeac J, made þe son to schyne MO;   eche]
ilke a J, ilk M, euerych O;   be] *om*. JMO.   5158 commune] comen JMO;
it] þat it M.   5159 Now] Bot J;   þat þat] that JO.   5160 which] *om*.
J;   not] nathynge J.   5161 þat] *om*. CS;   if] þaughe S;   not[1]] *om*. JM;
it] *with* tyme *mar*. G³.   5161-3 right ... me] *ins. mar. after rub. caret also in*
text O³.   5162 I] *om*. O³;   and ... fylen] *om*. M.   5163 approprede] it
add. O³.   5164 made] maade (e *ins*. G³) G, þem *add*. MO;   myn[1]] (*final*
e *subpuncted* G);   outrage] swete grace ʒif J.   5165 haue] (*2nd a ins*.
G³).   5166 bi²] *om*. S;   vtaues] vtases CJ, vtawes G, vtas MO, *om*. S;
monethes] moneyes S.   5167 þe pound] (*final* e *subpuncted* G), for ·xx· penys
J, all hole *add*. M;   for ... pens] the pounde J.   5168 or] other G;   ten]
marked for gloss G³;   þat] *om*. J.   5169 eche] ilke JM, euerych O;   taketh]
(*2nd a ins*. G³), take M;   it¹] *om*. O;   it²] *ins*. G³, *om*. M.   5170 Now]
prec. Capi*tulum* xxj *mar*. CG, Say me J;   sey me] nowe J;   quod I] *om*. S.
5171 ago] Seyne gane J, go MO.   5172 is] quod schalle be J;   þin] thyne (e
subpuncted) G;   thretti] xxx *over* G³;   anoon] pay me J.   5172-3 make
...payment] maake mee þe payement (*1st a 2nd* e *ins*. G³) G, nowe in hande J.
5173 to ... ende] (ende *ins. mar*. G³), þowe wille abide J, to þe ʒeer MO, to þee
þat eende S;   þou wolt abide] to the ʒere ende J.   5173-4 for ... shillinges]
xl *over* G³, þowe schalle giffe þerfore J, I moste selle it þee S. | 5174 I¹ ... it]
·xl· schelynges J, I sell it MO, for fourty shillinges I most selle it S;   if] whethir
J;   þilke] he JMO.   5175 peysede] weyed J;   and] that JMO;   it] or
noʒt *add*. J;   I wole] *trs*. J.   5176 as I haue] *om*. J;   herd] *om*. JS.
5177 here] the JMO;   þe] *scribble and* Nowesey *mar*. S³;   stok] stikke (e
subpuncted) G, stouene J;   haue] (*2nd a ins*. G³).   5178 anoon] hastely J;
yive] ʒeue (*with* ʒyue *mar*. G³) G;   swich] suche (e *subpuncted*) G, So J;   prys]
mekille J.   5179 yeer] ende *add*. CJ, ende *add. ins. mar*. G³, yeres eonde S;
for ... pris] I muste selle it J;   I ... it] for grete price J, me must sell it MO, *om*.
S.   5180 yeer] ende *add*. J, yeres eond S;   shulde¹'²] schalle J;   þerafter]
there after (*2nd* e *subpuncted*) G, þerfore J;   be] the mare J.   5181 þe more
worth] beworth J;   þus he] *trs*. J;   þee be] the JMO;   þilke] *om*. JMO.
5182 as bi] *om*. JMO;   þat] *om*. JMO;   if] and J.   5183 doun] felled downe
J;   and hewen] *om*. J;   were weyen] *ins. mar*. G³, *om*. JMO.   5184 not]
om. J;   for ... time] the thynge es Salde J.   5185 þe¹ ... sold] For lange tyme
J;   sold] þane *add*. S;   peysed] and weied *add*. J.   5186 and leeue] *om*.
JMO.   5187 oonliche] euylle J;   peysed] weyed J, weyed · peysed M.
5188 seelde] (*2nd* e *ins*. G³), Seldom JMO;   þe¹] here CS;   but] *om*. M;
stokkes] stouene J, stokk MO;   þei] the trees maye J;   liggen longe] lange ligge
on the grounde J.   5189 maketh] (*2nd a ins*. G³), *om*. O.   5190 payed] fore
add. J.   5191 sei þee þat] *o. er. with er. mar*. C, say the quod scho J, say þe
MO;   availe] vayle S;   what] that G, it *add*. S.   5192 diden ... of] felled
nouʒt J.   5193 þat] *om*. J;   wel] full JMO;   time] perauenture *add*. J.
5195 hewen] felled J.   5196 seye] thus gatys *add*. J.   5197 and] *om*. S;
hens] henne GJ.   5198 þerfore] (e *ins*. G³);   it] in O;   for] the *add*. J.
5199 selleres] selles S;   felle] selle OS.   5200 wodes] wodd MO;   make]
gerte J, do MO;   hem¹] it O;   and araye] *om*. J;   hem²] *om*. J, it O.
5201 of timber] hadde nede J.   5202 hadden neede] of tymbyr J;   þat] *om*.
J, th that *mar*. S³;   wolden] of J, þey wolden S;   brenne] brennynge J;
þerfore] (*2nd* e *ins*. G³);   ouhten] owghte (e *ins*. G³) G, thaye JO, þem M.

5203 þei¹] aught JMO;   leese] to lese JMO, at lees S;   for ooþere] thay J;
þei haue] for othere J.   5024 hewe] ehewe S;   haue] (2nd a ins. G³);
amended] mended JOS.   5205 þe derrere] that they may selle it J;   þei ...
it] the derrere J.   5206 no] om. JMO;   ne] for add. MO.   5207 in swich
wise] with in gyse mar. G³, ȝif thay do J;   sellen] payse J;   peisen] Selles J.
5208 it²] om. J;   haue] (2nd a ins. G³).   5209 acustomed] custommed
JMO;   þat³] om. O.   5210 wel] as þou wille JMO;   expose] expownde CJS,
wey J, compowne O, expose F.   5212 Of] for of J;   I wole] trs. J;   þee]
(1st e ins. G³);   tidinges] þinges O, and Trawandise · Or faytury · Or maunge
· Payne rub. mar. O³.   5213 This] prec. Capitulum xxij mar. CG;   heere] om.
JMO;   cleped] called JMO;   Coquinerie] om. JMO;   Trewaundrie] trow-
andyse or Fayturry JMO;   bi name I] om. JMO.   5214 cleyme it] om.
JMO;   and] or M, as S;   I] om. S;   clepe] calle JMO;   it²] Faitoury rub.
mar. M;   þilke] with hond mar. G³, þat JMO.   5215 brybes] brybory O;
his] om. JMO;   sak] Sacchelle JMO;   manye] with brybes mar. G³;   þer]
they JMO;   mowled] thay waxe J;   þei waxen] mowled J.   5216 wiht] body
J;   þilke] with hond mar. G³, þat JMO;   biseecheth] askes JMO;   bred] om.
S.   5217 and] in add. erased M;   place] (2nd a ins. G³);   scotte] no scott
(nor alt. no) M, þescotte S.   5218 she] with hond mar. G³, thay JMO;
dispendeth] Spende J, dispende MO.   5219 amende] be amendid JMOS;
hire] with hond mar. G³, the iiij hande mar. O³.   5221 if she wolde] For she
mihte CS, with for sche myghte mar. G³.   5222 wenne] werke J;   Þat] it J;
þilke] scho JMO;   þus] -gates J;   toragged] ragged JMOS.
5223 toclowted] clowted JMO;   It] with hond mar. G³.   5224 and paute-
neers] om. JMO;   and²] om. O;   bere bribes] trs. MO.   5225 me¹] -n S;
She] with hond mar. G³;   þe²] om. O;   þere] whare JMO;   þe³] om. J.
5226 weifareres] wayfernade menn JMO, wafurers S;   þe] om. J;   or] ooþere
add. CS, other G, and JMO;   shulden] om. JMO;   passen] passes JMO.
5227 þere] (2nd e ins. G³), om. O.   5228 þat] om. J;   mowe] haue þe gretter
pite of me add. can. rub. and black M;   þe] om. CM.   5229 þe] om. M;
maketh] (2nd a ins. G³);   me²] ins. mar. G³.   5230 þe thridde] iij· MO;
part] -es MO;   and more poore] om. J;   þerwith] ȝit add. JMO.   5231 þee]
om. JMO;   art] artt (with aarte mar. G³) G, crafte J;   me] ins. mar. after rub.
caret also in text O;   withdrawe] -s JO;   with] om. JMO.   5232 and²]
makes me add. J;   go] to go O;   and³] cause mar. O³.   5233 resoun]
chesoun JO, enchesoun M;   haue¹] ne resoun add. S;   and²] haue add. CS,
haaue add. ins. mar. G³.   5234 hye] stille J;   or] other G;   lowe] lowde
J;   curse] and banne add. J;   hem] hym JMO;   failen] fayles JMO;   me]
and giffes me nouȝt add. J.   5235 This] prec. Capitulum xxiij mar. CG, I add.
JMO;   borwen] I borowe JM, I borwed O;   ofte] tymes add. J.   5236 hauk-
inge] houging S;   it] om. M, onn O.   5237 it² with mangepaigne mar. G³,
maungepayn CS, la F.   5238 þese] the J;   religous] religions GS, religieus
F;   it] and putteȝ it furth add. J.   5239 hauynge] shame O;   shame] (2nd
a ins. G³), havyng O;   Now hider] Sum askes J, Nowe hyde hire S;   skinnes]
calfe skynnes J;   for] to make of J.   5240 hoodes] þei seyn add. CS, they seyne
add. ins. mar. G³;   and¹] Sum biddes J;   me] þayme J;   if ... and] Sum J;
peyre] of add. JMO.   5241 gessis] iesse MO.   5241 and¹ ... of¹] Sum askes
J, and I haue grete nede both of M;   a¹] ins. G³, om. M;   brod] om. M;
and of] For hounde J.   5241-2 a coler] hounde J, coler M;   to my grehound]
colers. Sum says J;   Make] om. J, ins. mar. after rub. caret also in text O;   yive
... cheeses] (ȝeeue with ȝyue mar. G³ in G), I pray ȝowe J, Makeþe and give me

of youre gessis S.   5242-3 I ... yow] giffe me of 3our goode chese J.
5243 and] Sum says I praye 30we J;   ne] *om.* CS;   gowne] garmente J;
russet] lyuerey (*o. er. with er. mar.* C) CS, clethynge J.   5244 abbeye] Sum askes
gloues · Sum knyfes · Sum says I am a beggere and hafe stotte or twa to my plught
Sayse me buse make a Journey · I pray 30we *add.* J;   me] for *add.* J;   eighte]
with viij *mar.*, *though unmarked* G³;   dayes] or nyne *add.* J;   and] or J;   for]
om. J.   5245 on] vpone JMO;   I prey yow] Sum pray lene thayme J;   lede]
leede (*2nd* e *ins.* G³) G;   my] thare J;   wode] or othere cariage *add.* J;   and]
Sum J, *om.* M.   5246 plowes] or thre O;   or thre] iij *over and mar.* G³, or
two J, plowes O;   for] *om.* J;   ere] with *add.* S;   my] þayre J;   lond] and
sayse *add.* J, and *add.* O;   ye] thay J;   shule] should S;   haue] (*2nd* a *ins.*
G³).   5247 ayen] Onane J;   withinne þe moneth] Sum forto spare with thayre
owne purse when thay passe thorowe the cuntre · leves ostries and ynnes and goode
townes and lyes atte abbayes · Sum with X hors · Sum with XX· and thare thay muste
be serued with alle the deyntees that may be getene · And but 3if thay be · thay schalle
wayte the abbaye with ane euylle turne *add.* J.   5249 þere] whare JMO;   haue
(*2nd* a *ins.* G³);   of ... owene] ouer þer awne *ins. mar. after rub. caret also in text*
O.   5250 not] *om.* J;   þat] *om.* O;   abbeyes] þe abbais M;   hauen] (*2nd*
a *ins.* G³).   5251 wherof] For thy J, wherfor O;   woldest] walde JMO.
5252 þat þat] þat MOS;   hauen] as the J.   5253 of] *om.* J;   þe] *om.* J,
þeir MO;   hous] *om.* J;   Now looke] *trs.* J.   5253-4 þei ouhten] þam aght
JMO.   5254 to¹] for to O;   þus] *om.* M;   to²] *om.* MO;   of] *om.* O.
5255 trewaundes] trewaundise CS, *om.* O, truans F;   and] *om.* O;   putte] -s
JM, *om.* O;   hem] here CMS, *om.* O;   hand ... with] *om.* O.   5256 my
sak and] *om.* O;   with] *om.* JMO;   my dish] *om.* O;   at] and S;   It] þis
S;   a] -n C.   5257 noblesse] gentilmen J, nobles MO;   seecheth] (*2nd* e
ins. G³), thus JMO;   þus¹] Sekes JMO;   his] thaire JMO;   þat þus] thay thus
J.   5258 it is] er J;   thral] all (*with* thrall *mar.* G³) G, charll O;   am] þus
add. S;   and] an S;   hoor] whate hared J, hored M, horyd O, Takeþe heede
now · how þat falsnesse declareþe to þe pilgryme of þe hande with Crochette and
what hit signefieþe *add.* S.   5259 Of] *prec.* Cap*itulum* xxiv *mar.* CG, Cap*itulum*
xx{iv} *mar.* S;   quod I] *om.* M, I pray the *add.* J;   sey] telle J;   litel] Symony
rub. mar. and the v· hande· of Symonmagus *mar.* O³;   if] *om.* J.   5260 þou
wolt] *om.* J;   of] *om.* J.   5262 hand] quod scho *add.* J.   5262 fisshed]
ficched JS, fecchid M;   þe derk] *om.* J;   Giesy] nota de Symone mago *et* Gye3i
rub. mar. M.   5263 þe crook] Symoun J.   5264 hire] *om.* JMO;   Simon]
the cruke J;   of¹] *om.* J;   figure] lett*er* M;   his] þis CS;   cheuenteyn] the
firste letter J.   5265 As ... figured] and that is ·s· J, ·s· *add.* MO;   þou ...
wel] *om.* J;   S] *om.* CGS, *ins.* O;   it is nempned] es this cruke J.   5266 þis
crook] called J;   Þis crook] *om.* O;   S] *ins.* G³, Symoun S.   5267 of] *om.*
J;   a] the JMO;   liven] haues lyuyd M.   5268 þis¹] *o. er.* C;   et ce] *em.*
ed., S· & C, esce G, ·s· JMO, et ce F;   Simon] the ferste lett*er*e of Symon J;
þis hand] es this hande J;   called J, Symonia *rub. mar.* M, is S.   5269 breches]
creuyce3 J, *om.* M, brekynges O.   5270 and¹] by *add.* JM, by fals *add.* O;
theeves] cheuys O;   whan] *om.* S;   withinne] it has ledde thaim J, *om.* S;
it ... hem] with in J, *om.* S;   and³] *om.* MS.   5271 with hire] *om.* S;   crook]
crukes JMO, *om.* S;   hooked] *om.* S;   of ... crooses] scho makes þaim J.
5272 she ... hem¹] of hir cruked crochettes J, *om.* S;   and] *om.* S;   pastores]
with heerdes *mar.* G³, herdes and pastures J, *om.* S;   of sheep] *om.* S.
5273 Pastores] *om.* O;   þilke] thay J, þo MO;   it ben] are the pastowrys J, þei
er MO;   so] *om.* J;   hem] selfe *add.* J;   doon] so doon with hem CS, so doon

with hem *ins. mar.* G³. 5274 so michel] þat CS, doon so muchul that (so muchul *subpuncted* G³) G, on that wyse that J; bettere] men J; men mihten] better J; clepe] calle JMO. 5275 keeperes] hirdes J; here] note þe abuse of tymes paste, in þe Church *mar.* O³; croses] croyse O; bi] with JMO. 5276 and disencresen] *om.* JMO; þe] hir JM, his O; throne] tresore CS, throsne G, and *add.* JMO; hire] his O. 5277 Oon hour] Atyme J; biggeres] beggers MO. 5278 wagen] (*2nd* a *ins.* G³); hemself] þair self O. 5279 þe] to JMO. 5280 thinketh] thynk M; wel] þat *add* S; waged] (*2nd* a *ins.* G³), salde J, 5281 leyd] in wedde *add.* J; so] *om.* S; thing] Monye taken \by/ the preists for prayers, and Masses, and such lyke Symony *mar.* O³; apayed] payde JO; ne it] *om.* JMO. 5282 lusteth ... wel] *om.* JMO; þilke] he JMO; she hath] es JMO. 5283 þilke] Swilke JMO; This] *prec.* Cap*itulum* xxv *mar.* CG. 5284 crochet] -s JMOS; and²] of *add.* JM; oon houre] atyme J. 5285 biggeth] and *add.* MO; anooþer] the toother G, tyme *add.* J, hour *add.* MO. 5285-6 þerfore ... Giezitrye] *ins. foot of* þ. G³. 5285 þerfore] *om.* JMO. 5286 speke] þere of *add.* JMO; whan it selleth] it is called *add.* J, Gieziterye it is called MO, *om.* S; Giezitrye] when it sellis MO; it²] *om.* S; Symonye] it es called J. 5287 it is seyd] *marked for gloss* G³, Symony J; þe] bathe the JO, both þies M. 5288 swich] this J, whiche S; hand] *om.* MO; þilke] thay J, þo MO; maken] gers J; masses] messe MO. 5290 þe¹] *om.* MO; ben] þay er JMO; þe²] *om.* JMO. 5291 Ihesu] iesu (*with* ihe*su mar.* G³) G; yit] *om.* JMO; þat²] thaye er *add.* J, nota de Iuda proditore *rub. mar.* M, *om.* S. 5292 Judas þei ben] he J; he¹] *with* Judas *mar.* G³. 5293 euele] amysse J; þei] id est prestes *over.* C³, *with* prestes *mar.* G³. 5294 neuere] *om.* JMO. 5295 yilde] to ȝelde JS; if] the cause why J, þe cause MO; þe cause] ȝif JMO. 5296 þee] and *add.* S; wite it] *om.* JMO. 5297 which] þat J; at my nekke] at myn nekke C, I bere J; I bere] atte my nekke J; yate] (*2nd* a *ins.* G³); what] thynge *add.* J. 5298 may] ne may CS; maad] emade S; a] it JMO. 5299 were] ware JMO; for¹] to JMO; fysh] with *add.* J; entree] Entres JS; þer is] *trs.* J. nouht] is þere nane J, noone S; for þat] þerfore CS, *with* ther fore *mar.* G³, for J. 5300 þilke] *om.* JMO; hauen] hauem C, (*2nd* a *ins.* G³); or] other G, *om.* MO; borwen] er drawen with JMO; mosten] moten S. 5301 conquere] gete JMO; for þat] But CS, *subpuncted with* butte *mar.* G³. 5302 nothing] -ys O; of þe sak] *om.* M; moste] nedes *add.* J. 5303 Whan] *prec.* Cap*itulum* xxvj *mar.* CG; seid] me *add.* CJS. 5304 despyte] the sixt hand *mar.* O³; thinketh] thynke JM; after] I prayed hire J. 5304-5 I ... hire¹] efterwarde J. 5305 and ... hire] *om.* J, and sayde S. þat²] the JMO. 5306 ooþer¹] Sexte J; ooþer²] *om.* J. 5307 cleped] called JMO; Baret] *om.* JMO; Treccherie] Trichery · or · dissayuyng *rub. mar.* MO; Tricot] tryced O. 5308 Disceyuaunce] *with* deseyte *mar.* G³; alwey] avauntage her O, -s S; avaunceth] besies J, alway O; hire] him S. 5309 þilke] þa JMO; nyce] prentise J. 5310 marchaunde] -s J, marchaundyse MO; and] *om.* M; balaunces] scho vses *add.* J, balaunce MO. 5311 mesures] scho vses J; she vseth] *om.* CGS, and fals mesures J; and ... biggeth] *om.* CGS; or] *om.* CGS, and M; selleth] *om.* CGS. 5312 of] *om.* CGS; eche] *om.* CGS, ilk ane J, ilk M, euerych O; metyerde] metewande J. 5313 and] *om.* MO; þat³ ... selle] þat þat she selleth CS, with the smalle J, with small mesur MO. 5313-4 with ... mesure] that atte scho selles J, that scho sellis M, *om.* O. 5314 she wole mete] *om.* JMO; with balaunces] sche duse J, with balaunce MO, with þe balaunce S. 5314-5 she

dooth] with balaunces J.   5315 weyhtes] wightes G;   she] can J.
5316 can] scho J;   of] in S;   5317 Neuere] Scho J;   she] neu*ere* J;   ariht]
right JMO, n*ot* any *mar*. O³.   5318 weyghte] wighte G, to na wight J;   thing]
thynges MO;   God] grete *add*. J.   5319 writen] *ins. mar.* G, *om.* MO;
Prouerbe] the pr*ouer*bes J;   This] *prec.* Cap*itulum* xxvij *mar.* CG;   stenderesse]
steynoresse CS, extendres*se* J, stenour M;   of corteynes] and a maker S.
5320 and a makere] merker O, of courtyns S.   5321 coloures] colour M;
þe²] *om.* JMO.   5322 þee ... þat] *o. er. with er. mar.* C;   riht] *om.* J;   ofte]
tymes *add*. J;   sheweth] scheeoweth (*2nd, 3rd* e *ins.*, o *subpuncted* G³) G, ry3t
add. JO;   goode] (e *ins.* G³).   5323 afterward] efterwardes J;   oo þere] *om.*
O.   5324 diliuereth] to *add*. JMO;   biggere] byers JMO;   Manye] *prec.*
Cap*itulum* xxviij *mar.* CG, Monye (e *ins.* G³) G.   5324-5 dooth ... harmes]
harmes dooth þis hand (*o. er. with er. mar.* C) CJMOS.   5325 O] 1 *over*. G³;
þe] -m MO.   5326 badde] to the *add*. J, and to sight *add*. M, to *add*. O;
wolen] schalle J;   time] *om*. J;   bi] in J.   5327 selleth] scho selles J, to selle
O.   5328 sheweth] scheeweth (*1st* e *ins.* G³) G;   þe] *om*. JMO;   folk] -es
S;   haue] (*2nd* a *ins.* G³), gete thayre J.   5329 falsliche] And *add*. M;
time] *om*. J;   taketh] scho takes JM, makys O;   þese] þe CJMOS, this G, ces
F;   cherches] kyrke JMOS, moustiers F.   5330 hem] *om*. JMO;   hed]
handes or in oþere parties of tha*i*m J, hand M, handys O.   5331 winne] to wynne
J;   or¹] other G, *om*. S;   whiche she hath] *om*. M.   5332 rediest] redreste
J, *om*. M, redy O;   in] with in M;   þat¹] *om*. J;   þat²] A good note for all
Miracle-mongers *mar*. O³.   5333 descendeth] (esce *o. er.* C);   it²] *with* ymage
mar. G³, is *add*. JMOS.   5334 þe olde ymage] (*2nd* e *ins.* G³), it may beo sayde
and nempned S;   mowe be named] þat þe olde ymage S;   to do] dooþe S;
Þanne] (ne *ins.* G³);   speke] and spekes J.   5335 þe trewaundes] Faito*uri*s
J, trowandes MO;   to seeme] this monke was no frend to the Church of Rome
mar. O³, seyne þat S;   embosed] *mark over and passage marked mar.* C³, enboosed
(*1st* o *ins.* G³) G, embodied J, or] other G, *om*. S;   contract] *om*. S.   5336 or¹]
other G, *om*. S;   deff] defayte S;   or²] other G;   dowm] hit heleþe *add*. S;
swich] suche (e *subpuncted*) G.   5337 Las] Allas CMOS, A · a · ha· J, las F;
hele] heele (*1st* e *ins.* G³) G;   After] For eftere J;   in yow] I haue JMO.
5338 I haue] (*2nd* a *ins.* G³), in 3ow JMO;   grettest] maste JMOS;   feith] tryste
J;   al hool] I make hym J;   I reise hem] alle hale J, raise hym M, I rayse hym
O.   5339 I shewe hem] I schewe hy*m* JO, hole M;   hol] *ins. mar.* G³, *om*.
JO, I shew hym M;   But] Note *mar*. O³, no *add. ins.* O³;   wunder] it es na
J.   5339-40 is it nouht] wondere þow3 he be hale J, it is nou3t M, is it O.
5340 harm] he hadde J;   hadden þei noon] na harme before J, hadd he noon
MO;   ne] na *add*. J;   al] bot alle J.   5341 euel] eeuell (*2nd* e *ins.* G³)
G, sekenes J;   þei hadden] *om*. J;   arretten] rett MO.   5342 preest] or the
perso*u*n *add*. J;   winneth] conneþe S;   and þe folk] *om*. S.   5343 feste]
Noat *mar*. O³, fayte S;   Many] *prec.* Cap*itulum* xxix *mar.* CG;   anooþer] oþere
JO, swilk odir M;   harm] -es JO, *om*. M;   þe] this JMS;   alle] *om*. J;
þe²] *om*. CJMOS.   5344 dayes] 3it does J, day MO;   yit dooth] day by day
and nyght by ny3t J;   but ... now] *om*. J;   for] *om*. J, all þogh (þogh *cramped
over*) O;   I haue] (*2nd* a *ins.* G³), *om*. J.   5345 ynowh ... yit] *om*. J.
5346 At þe leste] *om*. J;   quod I] Telle me nowe J;   þou ... me] q*uo*d I J;
if þou wolt] *om*. J.   5347 cause] (*2nd* a *ins.* G³);   þe¹] this J;   þe²] thy
J;   þat] and why J, and MO;   halteth] þou haltes thus J, hal*tes* MO.
5348 it] the hande J;   approcheth] a proocheth (*2nd* o ins. G³) G;   to] *om*. J;
þe] thy J;   mesel] *with* leepre *mar*. G³, lepre meselle JO, lepre M.

5349 Serteyn] Certaynly J.   5350 cleped] called JMO;   Periurement] forswer-
inge *over* C[3], *with* forswerynge *mar.* G[3], periury or Forswerynge J, *with* periurium
et mendacium *rub. mar.* M, Periurium Mendacium *rub. mar.* O;   I] es JMO;
clepe] called JMO;   Mensonge] mensoige (gabbinge *over*) C, *with* gabbynge *mar.*
G[3], mendacium or lesynge J, Mendacium · lesynge MO, mensongerie S.
5351 of] -t M;   tweyne] twa JM, ij *ins.* O, twey S.   5352 freend] frendly J;
hem] thaymwarde JMO.   5354 Menterye[1]] lesinge *over with er. mar.* C, lesynge
mar. G[3], lesynge JMO;   am] was O;   spaveyned] spayned M;   Menterye[2]]
lesynge *mar.* G[3], lesynge JMO;   is also] *trs.* JMOS.   5355 Periurement[1,2]]
with forswerynge *mar.* G[3], for swerynge J;   and engendred] *om.* O.   5356 if]
om. M;   Mensonge[1]] (n *alt.* i *with er. mar.*) C, lesynge JMO;   make him come]
bere hym J, make hym MO;   and[1]] *om.* JO;   in] *om.* J;   Mensonge[2]] (n *alt.*
i *with er. mar.*) C, *with* lesynge *mar.* G[3], *om.* J, beryng MO;   in[2]] *om.* S.
5357 Periurement] *with* forswerynge *mar.* G[3], forswerynge J, it *add.* S;   máy not
be] *ins. mar. after rub. caret also in text* O[3], bot *add.* J;   þat ... is] that ne þere
es J, þen þer is MO;   thre] iij *over* G[3].   5358 of] ane *add.* JM;   is þe] *twice*
J;   cause] (*2nd a ins.* G[3]) G.   5359 whiche] whi MO;   lened] lenande J;
for which] why J.   5360 visite] perjury & lijng in the *mar.* O[3];   tunge] Howe
þe pilgryme · askeþe of þe oolde · why þe tung is cleped pariurement *add.* S.
5361 Now] *prec.* Capitulum xxx *mar.* CG, Telle me J, Capitulum x{xv} *mar.* S;
sey me] nowe J;   how] why J;   seist] calles J, of *add.* MO, þat *add.* S;   þi]
þe MO;   tunge] hatte *add.* S.   5362 Periurement] forsweryng *mar.* G[3], for
swerynge J;   and whi þou] *om.* J;   clepest] *om.* J, calles MO;   spaueyned]
saveyned S.   5363 Menterye] lesyng *mar.* G[3], lesynge JMO;   sumtime] quod
scho J;   quod she] Sum tyme J;   Verite] *with* soothnesse *mar.* G[3].
5364 Equite] *with* eeuenesse *mar.* G[3], that es atte saye with sothfastnes and euenhede
add. J;   souhten] wente to begge J;   and] For thay J;   Þei] J;
5365 freendes] frende J;   ne[2]] *om.* JMOS;   hauen] (*2nd a ins.* G[3]);   me] (*2nd*
e *ins.* G[3]);   thinketh] thynke JM;   Whan I] *om.* S.   5366 sih ... turned]
al *add.* M, *om.* S;   aweyward for] *om.* S;   for] *om.* S;   wel I] I wille wele
&J, *om.* S;   wiste] *om* S.   5366-5367 winne of hem] wele that I myght
nathynge J, þat wynne of þaim O, *om.* S.   5367 mihte I nothing] wynne of thaym
J, *om.* S.   5368 bi] thurth J, fro O, feildes *mar.* O[3];   holdinge] of any *add.*
J;   wey] and *add.* J;   molle moldewerpe J.   5370 hool] hoole (*2nd* o *ins.*
G[3]) G;   ne[2]] *om.* CJMOS, *subpuncted* G;   day] the dayes J;   wronge] haltinge
(*o. er. with er. mar.* C) CS.   5371 haltinge] wronge (*o. er. with er. mar.* C)
CS;   virly] weyrey M, wery O;   I] *om.* S;   hippinge] hoppande my name
J, hoppyng MO;   my] *om.* MO.   5372 I clepe] calle I J, I call MO;
Mentirye] *with* lesyng *mar.* G[3], lesynge JMO.   5373 algates] neuerþeles J.
5374 to doone] atte do J, for to do O;   Soneste] My Sekke is J;   my ... filled]
Soneste filled J;   and] *om.* JMO.   5375 soonest ... þerwith] *om.* JMO;
riht[2]] wente J.   5376 wente] ryght J, I went MO;   ne ynowh] as I do J.
5377 comen] þere comes nowe J;   wolden gon] than wille ga J;   here wey] forby
J;   hem] me M.   5378 Now] *prec.* Capitulum xxxj *mar.* CG;   þus lyinge]
om. J.   5379 þer] þat O;   hete] heete (*2nd* e *ins.* G[3]) G.   5380 gret[1]]
om. O;   of] and J, to M;   wilnynge] willynge JO, will M;   yit] *om.* JM.
5381 of] *om.* JMO;   auoyr] *om.* J, an nodir MS, an eyr O;   out] I muste nedes
drawe J, wyþoute O;   I[2] ... drawe] oute J;   tunge] toonge (*2nd* o *ins.* G[3])
G.   5382 court] kings courte *mar.* O[3].   5383 herd] and *add.* M;   and[1]]
om. MO;   þat] and J;   wole be] be com J.   5384 ples] pleys O, pleederys
S;   wole] *om.* J;   þe] my S;   ooth] tong S;   þat my tonge] that I wille stere

J, þat myn O, Westminster Hall mar. O³, by ooþe þat S.   5385 I ... drawe]
my tunge J, I wil drawe MS.   5386 þe style] I hafe J, þe stilt M;   I haue]
the tile J;   lesinges] lesynge JMO;   and²] om. J.   5387 lyinge] om. J, -s
S;   euere] om. M;   my tunge] my toonge (2nd o ins. G³) G, I for bere nouȝt
J.   5387-8 I ... forbere] my tunge J, I nouȝt forbere MO.   5388 þat I ne]
that ne I J, þan I MO.   5389 þee] (1st e ins. G³);   þat] om. J;   riht so]
I do J;   I doo] riht J;   þe] a JMO.   5390 to] ins. M;   þilke] that JMO;
of] om. J;   þe¹] om. JMO;   peys] weyes J.   5390-1 hath ... part] heyere
J, -y MO;   5391 þere] whare JMO;   see] the add. JMO.   5392 tunge]
toonge (2nd o subpuncted, u over) G.   5392-3 as I see] whare JMO, in places
of gayne mar. O³.   5393 þer] I Se JM, om, S;   ben] maste penyes (e ins.)
J, lenys (? leuys) MO, om. S;   most pens] lese J;   summe] somtym M.
5394 me¹] diuerse folk add. M;   helpe] -d CS, aidesse F;   of] in J.
5395 witnesse] -d CGS, tesmoignasse F;   swere] swoore CGS, feisse F.
5396 wost] wate JMO;   þanne] thaim J;   Be] þou add. J.   5397 whan] ins.
mar. G³;   moneye] they tuke me J, þei money MO;   þei tooken me] marked
over and mar. C³, monee J, tuke me MO;   for] om. J;   in] to add. S.
5398 þe] thaire JMO;   hadden] haue M.   5399 þat] om. O;   with good
riht] they pledid J;   þei plededen] with gude right J;   veriliche] om. J.
5400 al] om. O;   ooþerweys] oþere wise JMO.   5401 Swich] prec. Capitulum
xxxij mar. CG, lange add. J;   langwetynge] (ety o. er. with er. mar. C), motynge
J, langueryng M, langwaging S;   of²] om. MO;   stiringe] stutinge CS, stryfynge
J.   5402 riht] and add. JMO;   to ... with] om. JMO.   5403 to my sak]
Sum siluere J;   sum siluer] to my sekke J;   sheweth] schoweth (alt. scheeweth
G³) G;   þe] my J;   seid] om. J.   5404 and¹] om. JMO;   cleped] called
J, om. MO;   Periurement] with forswerynge mar. G³, For swerynge J;   mesel]
with lepre mar. G³, scho es J;   she is] mesell J.   5405 bi¹] thurgh J;   and
bi] of J;   and²] om. O;   brennynge] desire add. J.   5406 ooþeres] oþere
mennes J, oþer OS;   goodes] and add. M;   languetinges] with spekynges mar.
G³, spekynge JMO, langageynges S.   5407 sweringes] Swerynge JMO.
5408 languetted] with spoken mar. G³;   neuere] (3rd e ins. G³);   bileeued] ne
trowed add. J, nor tristed add. M.   5409 Bi] Bot M;   it] with tonge mar.
G³;   tunge] a tunge J.   5410 is] nys S;   yifte] the gyfte J;   or] other
G.   5411 with þe tunge] yrne or brasse J, with tonge M, wyþ tong of O;
yren or bras] yren other bras G, with thayre tunge J;   and do] addid J;   þerwith]
with tonge mar. G³.   5412 hand] hound MO;   and] Lijng no kind to Nature
mar. O³;   miht] may JMO.   5413 not] no thyng M, om. OS.   5414 werch-
inge] makynge JMO;   bettere] þou schulde wete it J;   þou ... it] bettere J.
5415 bowche] bouche (e subpuncted) G, bouge J.   5416 wel] my wille Fully
J;   entencioun] entente J;   make] telle J.   5417 collacioun] a collacioun
MO. and ... mawmete] om. JMO.   5417-8 of which] om. JMO, þat S.
5418 þou ... me] om. JMO, haste spoken to me of to fore þis · Howe þe pilgryme
demandeþe of þe oolde what þe bouche signefyeþe S;   My] prec. Capitulum xxxiij
mar. CG, Capitulum x{xvj} mar. S;   bowche] boouch (e subpuncted) G, bouge
J;   þilke] that JMO.   5419 bowched] with bouched mar. G³, bouged J.
5420 superflue] Superfluyte J.   5421 alle] (e ins. G³);   bowchede] boouchede
(2nd o subpuncted) G, bouged J.   5422 shuldest] schalte J;   wite] also add.
J, wyþ O;   þilke] with Bouch (and bouche under rub). G, it is J, that MO;
it is] that J;   be] to be J.   5423 at] thurgh J.   5424 bouche] bouge J;
Whan] Sen J;   man] men JMO;   þe] þis M.   5426 bitwixe] betweene
GJO;   þe] þaim JMO;   tweyne] twa JMO;   bouche] a bouge J, a bouch

MO;   he] hym J.   5427 wel] to wete J;   to wite] wele J;   if] bot ȝif J;
ne be] be J.   5428 oþer] O lesse þan J, or MO, ellys *add.* S;   he muste] he
moste (*2nd* e *ins.* G³), he do J;   his] the J;   Man] A man J, Men M;   þat]
with er. mar. C.   5429 by a vow] *om.* JMO;   or] other G, *om.* JMO;   þat]
þat] that J.   5430 and] *om.* J;   þat] *om.* J, þe O;   whiche he] *om.* J;
hath] *om.* JO;   renounced] forsaken M.   5431 seye] before *add.* J.
5432 þe] his J;   as²] *om.* G;   bouche] boouche (e *subpuncted*) G, bouge J;
This] *prec.* Cap*itulum* xxxiv *mar.* CG.   5433 is] called *add.* J;   Propertee]
prop*er*ly O;   hire phisician] *om.* M.   5434 for] that *add.* JMO;   tobreste]
briste JMO.   5435 nouht] a thynge J, no M;   thing] vnhable J.
5436 maketh] (*2nd* a *ins.* G³);   good] *om.* JMO.   5437 take] -þ O;   him]
it JM, *om.* O;   She] *with* proprete *mar.* G³.   5438 it] *with* pou*er*te *mar.*
G³;   also] als J, note his opinion of the Clergie *and marked for 12 lines mar.* O³;
bowched] boouched (*2nd* o *subpuncted*) G, bowged J.   5439 bouchede] (*2nd*
o *subpuncted* G), bouged J;   enbosede] enboosed (*2nd* o *ins.* G³) G, bosyd O;
þese] this JMO;   cloistres] cloystir JMO.   5440 and¹] my *add.* J;   cosyns]
confynes M;   ben] es J.   5441 bouched (*2nd* o *subpuncted* G).   5442 redres-
sere] redresse M, vndertaker O;   vndertakere] redresse O.   5443 no] (*final*
n *subpuncted* G);   Whan þou art] Here eft*er* J;   heerafter] when þou erte of
ane J;   my] me C;   bouchede] bouched C, bouche O.   5444 þat] *om.* J;
if] and J.   5445 a woord] *om.* J, ydolle *mar.* O³;   mawmet] *om.* JMO, and
mawment S.   5446 which] that J.   5447 Now] kepe the J;   keepe þee]
(*4th* e *ins.* G³), nowe J;   al] ȝif alle J, þof al M, all if O;   haue þou] *trs.* JMO;
he shal] *trs.* J.   5448 boongree mawgree] niltowe wiltowe J, mawgre þe MO;
Myn] *prec.* Cap*itulum* xxxv *mar.* CG.   5449 gold] þe gold O, Behold { ... }
mar. S;   siluer] þe siluer O;   enpreented] *printed* JMO;   þe] þy J;   figure
of] *om.* JMO.   5450 þe¹] þy J;   hye] god and *add.* MO;   lord] *om.* J, þe
lord O;   of ... a] *om.* J;   ofte be] *trs.* S.   5451 swaþed] Swetheled
JMOS;   þat] & þat O.   5452 vncowche] (ow *o. er.* C);   in²] and in JMO,
in in S;   in³] *om.* O.   5453 eerþe] the erthe JM;   wel] fulle JMO;   Þat]
It J.   5454 god] goode S;   hem] hy*m* JMO;   turnen] turnes JMO;   here]
his JM, *om.* O.   5455 stowpe] enclyne J;   into] vnto J;   þe] *om.* O.
5456 moldewerp] moldwarpes O;   þilke] he JMO;   þe] *om.* J;   bouched]
bouged and enboced J;   or] other G.   5457 difigured] disfigured GJMS;
me¹] *om.* J;   defamed] defaced J;   He] *with mark mar.* C.   5458 algates]
neu*er*theles J.   5459 so²] mekille he *add.* J;   in] the *add.* J.   5460 do]
om. O.   5461 þat I ne] that ne I J, þen I MO;   do it] *om.* G.   5462 made]
(*2nd* a *ins.* G³), gerte J;   Laurence] Saynte laurence JO;   þe coles] aroste yren
J.   5463 binome] reft M;   it¹] *om.* O;   it²] *om.* OS;   fro me] *trs.* O.
5464   cote] witte JMO.   5465 many] woundes *add.* S;   merelles] merell
O.   5466 go] to ga J.   5467 and] *om.* MO;   þat] also MOS;   also]
þou J, þat MOS;   þou] also J;   him²] *om.* O.   5468 and þat] *o. er. with*
er. mar. C.   5469 Now looke] *trs.* J;   þou shalt] *trs.* M;   no] haue O.
5470 more] no O;   haue] lenger O;   anoon] blyue J;   degrees] with all þi
diligence *add.* M;   þee] (*1st* e *ins.* G³).   5471 him] for perill þat wil come
after *add.* M, Here he tellis þe descripcion of Glotony and also of lychery · and of
þer lynage as it followes *add. rub.* M, Auaryce *mar.* O³.   5472 As] *prec.*
Cap*itulum* xxxvj *mar.* CG;   Auarice] this *add.* J, þat Auaryce S;   me¹] þus
add. S.   5473 ydole] -s CGS, mawmet J, idole F;   lowe] *om.* JMO, lowde
S;   with] an *add.* JM.   5474 with] an *add.* J, *om.* MO;   teene] tone JM;
felawe] felaus JMO;   þe] þi CGMS, yon O;   þat I see] *om.* J.   5475 þere]

om. JMO;   nothing dooth] *trs.* J.   5476 shame] schaame (*1st* a *ins.* G³)
G.   5477 She] hire J;   wel] þerfore *add.* J.   5478 nice] vyce S;
Serteyn Certaynly J;   answered] quod J.   5479 Now] *om.* J;   do we peyne]
Enforce we vs alle þat we maye J, Do we hym payn MO;   of] *om.* J, fro MO;
oure handes] *om.* J;   nouht us] *trs.* CS, nouȝt fra vs J, nouȝt MO.   5480 ded]
here *add.* J;   Whan] *prec.* Capitulum xxxvij *mar.* CG;   swich wordes] I herde
J;   I herde] Swilke wordes J.   5481 more] I was JS;   I was] mare JS;
bifore] I was are J, I was before O.   5481-2 take þe flyght] fledde a waye J, taken
flight MO.   5482 if ... hadde] hadde I nouȝt J;   þe²] *om.* JMO.
5483 me] A ha\r/d thing for our frayle flesh to recou*e*re þe right waye, being Misled
mar. O³;   biheeld] luked J;   sigh] I see MO;   gret] *om.* J;   oon] delle
J.   5484 þat] with M.   5484-5 a ... perced] helde with hir teeth J, a foule
sacke depe and parted O.   5485 heeld ... teeth] a fowle Sekke depe and perched
J, and held it with hir teth M.   5486   tonell] fonelt CS, *with* fonell *mar.* G³,
entonnour F;   strangle] swalow M;   shoop] keste J;   manere] *om.* J;
ayens] a gayne JMO.   5487 strauhte] scho strekked JMO;   handes] hand
O;   me] trowthe scho *mar.* G³;   trowthe] the troweth that J.   5488 þe]
my O.   5489 Anooþer] *prec.* Capitulum xxxviij *mar.* CG, also *add.* J, old oon
add. M, and anoþer O;   after] hire *add.* J;   michel more] made me J;   made
me] mekille *mar.* J;   affraye] -d CJMOS, fremir F.   5490 fauce] faux (*with*
fals *mar.* G³ *but* faux *unmarked*) G;   ifigured] figured JM, fyngeryd O;   in
...hand] scho bare J;   she bar] in hir lyfte hande J.   5491 as ... targe] scho
did þerwith J;   dide þerwith] as with atargat J, scho did þerwith MO;   on] opon
M.   5492 arayed she was] ryght fayre and gayly J;   wel faire] scho was arayed
J, ful fair MO.   5493 shadwede] shewed O.   5494 facioun] face J;
hadde] in hire hande *add.* J, bare O.   5495 all bifore] lange are J;   þat] *om.*
J;   to hire] *om.* M;   it] *with* darte *mar.* G³;   To] and in to J, into M, vn to
O.   5496 herte] (*2nd* e *ins.* G³);   com] coome (e *subpuncted*) G.
5497 on] apon*e* J;   armed] armes S;   upon] on JMO;   myne] (e *subpuncted*
G);   Afterward] Affterwardes S.   5498 on] up on CS;   þe] myn*e* O;
me²] I JMO;   hadde] had *add.* J;   needed] nede of JMO.   5499 and ...
on] *om.* JO.
5500 But] The wyse man flyes þe wayes of wickednes, but þe foole abydes tyll he
be hanged *mar.* O³;   þe¹] *om.* JO;   fool] fules J;   abideth] leues J;   nouht]
nou*e*re J, will O;   til] forte G, her J, bifore M, þat O.   5501 he honge] he
be hanged JO, he be be hongid M;   Whan] *prec.* Capitulum xxxix *mar.* CG;
yhurt] hurte JMOS.   5502 cheere] (*2nd* e *ins.* G³);   þat] *om.* M;   for] (*final*
e *subpuncted* G).   5503 bi þe throte] I Schulde be halden*e* J;   I ... holde]
by the throte J;   ne] wiste J.   5504 wiste] nouȝt J;   to thinke] I myght
do J;   to doo] I myght thynke · And J;   wel] *om.* J.   5505 to¹] forto
JMO;   and] or forto JM, for to *add.* O, ne to S;   shulde] it shuld O;   nouht]
helpe me ne *add.* S;   be woorth] be avayle O;   note] A · A· *add.* J.   5506 I]
to my self *add.* J;   euel] Sorowe J, *om.* S;   it] *om.* JMO.   5507 þe] thee
(*1st* e *ins.* G³) G, to þe M, þe to O;   certeyn] -ly J;   alowh] *om.* J, Allas M.
5508 at þe firste] þou atte the fyrste J;   þou haddest] hadde J, þou had MO;
leeued] lefte J.   5509 þe] this J;   Now] *om.* O.   5511 miht] maye J;
not] *om.* O.   5512 shuldest] shall M;   þat²] this JMO, harome *add.* S.
5513 Þou] *with* pilgrim *mar.* G³;   olde] theefe *add.* J;   þe] that JMO.
5514 foule] -d CS;   sak perced] *trs.* J;   in] þou this in J.   5515 smytinge]
of *add.* J;   þou wolt] wille J, *trs.* S;   þus] *om.* JO, make S;   make] þus S;
dye] to dye JS, Takeþe hede · howe · þe pilgryme askeþe of þis olde verrayly hir name

add. S.   5516 And] prec. Capitulum xl mar. CG, Capitulum xx{vij} mar. S;
þe] that J;   olde] tratte add. J;   If] And if S;   wost] passage marked mar.
C, wiste quod scho wist MO;   ben] ware JMO;   Epicurie] Ipocrecy O.
5517 shuldest] shalt S;   haue be] be JS.   5518 Who ben] Quod I J, Who is
MO;   quod I] wha er J, þat beon add. S;   Epicurie] Ipocrecy O;   ben] is
JMO;   quod she] a folke JMO.   5519 a folk] quod scho JMO;   maken]
(2nd a ins. G³);   in] om. JMO.   5520 thouht] -es M;   it¹] with sak mar.
G³;   for] and JMO.   5521 an] om. J, on S;   hol day] þe halyday S;
and more] om. CS, subpuncted G;   roste] (e ins. G³).   5522 or¹,²] other
G;   disgisee] om. J.   5523 if] om. JMO;   mete] etynge J;   and] or
MO;   drink] drynkynge J, if add. O, whan add. S;   þei hauen] om. JM.
5524 it] om. JM;   þat] þey holden S;   þei holden] trs. J, þat S;   a delite]
oonlich S;   oonliche] a delyte S.   5525 hattest] hate JMO;   hire] þen add.
M.   5526 my] þe S;   percede] (3rd e subpuncted G);   putte] Glottonye
mar. O³;   foul] gula rub. mar. M.   5527 tweyne] ij over and mar. G³;
or] other GJMO;   thre] iij over and mar. G³.   5528 wel] oþer whyle S;
sakkes] sacke S;   wistest] (wi o. er. with er. mar. C), knewe J, wist MO, knowest
S.   5529 wel] om. J;   wast] and add. J;   outrages] Outrage JMOS;
of metes] in a 3ere J.   5529-30 in þe yeer] of metes J.   5530 þou woldest]
properly J, þou myght M, þou wold O;   properliche] þou wolde J, say OS;   sey]
call me M, properly OS;   I were] that I ware JS, om. M;   and] om. M.
5531 clepe] So þou wolde calle J, om. M, calle O;   me] om. M, soo add. S;
And] om. J;   what is] Castrimargi J;   Castrimargye] whate es that J.
5532 and] om. I;   drenchinge] drownyng or deuowrryng M. om. O;   morcelles]
morsell M.   5533 lopyns] morselles J, in another hand M³.   5534 drenche]
drownes M;   neuere] om. J.   5535 haue] om. J;   oon] morsell add. ins.
M³;   þat²] whilke J;   needes] castene out agayne J.   5535-6 cast out ayen]
as y nedes muste J.   5536 put] thaym add. J;   trases] (2nd a ins. G³);
dunge] tham J.   5537 stinkinge] wrecche add. J.   5537-8 Go ... spekinge]
speke na mare J.   5538 thing] a thynge J;   abhominable] that as foule J;
and¹] om. MOS;   and²] om. J.   5539 reprouable] to here J;   Serteyn]
Certaynly J;   þou seist sooth] om. J.   5540 whan] Sene J;   sey] telle J;
it²] om. M.   5541 clepe] calle JMO;   and¹] 3if add. J, for M;   þat] om. M.
5542 swelwe] swelle CS, to add. JMO, gloutoie F;   hele] layne J, hide M.
5543 wode] (2nd o subpuncted G).   5544 make] gerre J.   5545 deuow-
reth] o. er. with er. mar. C;   þat] om. M;   kichenes] þe kychins S;   þe] om.
JMO.   5546 seeche] serch M;   and²] om. JO;   trace] om. J, seke M, om.
O;   huntes] hunters J, hunter M, hounde O.   5547 hound] of an hunter O;
þe] om. O.   5549 showve] schoowe (with schowue mar. G³) G;   in] in to
JMO.   5550 Sey] prec. Capitulum xlj mar. CG, Telle J;   if] om. S;   it]
with sake mar. G³, ow3t J; | ouht] thy Sekke J.   5551 if] om. JMO, þaughe
S;   or] other G;   bred] om. S;   þou madest] trs. J.   5552 gret] to swelle
S;   Wite] þou add. J;   þe] þis for O, om. JS;   trouthe] is add. C, om. JS.
5553 as well] om. O;   I haue] (2nd a ins. G³), trs. J;   customed] in custome
J;   as²] and JMO;   to ete] to seke JM, to seke ins. mar. after rub. caret also in
text O³.   5554 metes] as white brede or metes of grete price add. J;   As]
And als J;   wel] wille J;   rudesse] rudenesse CS, ruydeste JMO;   þe²] om.
M;   curiowstee] curyoseste J, curiouse metes whilk M, curyous & O.   5555 of
... þat] om. S.   5556 ende ... me] om. S;   guste] savouringe GJMO (with
gouste mar. G³), taaste alt. guste S.   5558 guste] with scilicet {goute} and
sauorynge mar. G³, that is at Say Sauour or rastynge add. J, sauour M, I · sauer

add. O; þat] *om.* O. 5559 bi] the J; þat²] *om.* O; wherinne] in þat O; is] al *add.* S. 5560 It] *with* goust *mar.* G³; þe] by S; bouchinge] boowchinge (*with* bouchynge *mar.* G³) G, bougeing J; which] the whilke J. 5561 it¹] I O; bi] my *add.* JMO; towchinges] touchynge JMO; twey] twa JMO; fyngres] fygurys O; of] on J. 5562 were] mesured S; mesured] mette J, were S; I wolde] *trs.* J, þat *add.* O; lengere] longere (*with* lengere *mar.* G³) G. 5563 nekke] *om.* J; heroun] or of a Swanne *add.* J; wel] þat *add.* CJS. 5564 þere] *om.* JMOS. 5565 horse] horsse (e *subpuncted*) G; or] other G, ware I J. 5566 þe] that the J, þat MO. 5567 grete] gretly J; brennynge my guste] My guste brennynge CS, (c, a, b *over respectively and with* sauour *mar.* G³); oon] wille delyuere hym *add.* JMO; and] *om.* JMO; þat²] *om.* JMO. 5568 ooþer] *om.* MO; wolen] wille J. *om.* MO; al] nouȝt J, *om.* MO; as michel] *om.* JMO; or] other G, *om.* JMO; more as þe] *om.* JMO; guste] goust *marked for reversal* G³, *om.* JMO; may] *om.* JMO; gusten] gouste *marked for reversal* G³, *om.* JMO; þe²] *om.* JMO. 5569 eye ... him] *om.* JMO; vnmesurable] vnresonable O; þe] *om.* S. 5570 eiþer] the eye of a glotton biger þan his belly *mar.* O³; long] broode M; or] other G; brod] longe M; as] es J; anything ... þe] *om.* J. 5571 paunche ... thing] *om.* J. 5573 superflue] perilous JMO; morselle] no*t*a *mar.* G³; And] *prec.* Capi*tulum* xlij *mar.* CG. 5574 þou] þanne *add.* S; in] the *add.* JMO, þer Inne S; morselle] -s CS; þat is] *om.* CS; soo] *ins. mar.* G³. 5575 so pestilencial] So pestilencious J, in my mouþe S; a touche] a toth O, so pestylencyal S; in my mouth] a touche S. 5576 hath] had J, is M; it¹] I J; taketh] hafe J; reuelle] a delite, reule MO; in it] þere in J. 5577 to þat ooþer] it touched nouȝt J, þe toþer O; it ne touchede] anoth*er* J, ne touche it O; of] my *add.* JMO; it²] I JMO. 5578 shulde be] were O; Pat oon] þan O, and so þat S. 5579 It] *o. er.* M, I *add.* O; reccheth] reche *o. er.* M, recce O; him] *o. er.* M; neuere] *mark over and passage marked mar.* C³. 5580 haue] has J. 5580-1 it ... cleped] that touche J, it is named M, is ne*m*pned O. 5581 þilke touche] es called J, þat touch MO. 5582 wichche] witte JO, wight M; fleinge] felyng O; messanger] (anger *o. er. with er. mar.* C), messynger (*with* messenger *mar.* G³) G, messager S; seith] sees O; to] *ins.* O. 5582-3 þat þat] that JMO. 5583 þe¹] *om.* S; Malevoysigne] Male voysoyne (*with* voisygne *mar.* G³) G, malebosyn *id est* dronkynhede M, male bosyn O; þe²] *om.* M. 5584 folk] men M; clepen] calles JMO; gladliche] Ebrietas *rub. mar.* M. 5587 quod I] I vyntere J, a vynter S; a vintere] quod I JS; to assaye] assayes JMO; entermeteth hire] *om.* JMO, doþe entremeetre hir S. 5588 What] that JMO; is she] *trs.* JMO; Panne] and J, *om.* O; she seide] *om.* J; Pere] *with* wynes *mar.* G³. 5589 vnmesurable] vnresonable O; cleped] called JMOS. 5590 She putteth] *om.* J; me¹] *om.* J, him S; to] *om.* J, vn to O, in S; vnwurshipe] wurshipe CS, *om.* J; and] *om.* J; binemeth] *om.* J, birefes M; me boþe] *om.* J. 5591 prys and wurshipe] *om.* J; tonell] fonelle CS, *with* fonell *mar.* G³, entonneur F; in my sak] þou Sees bouged J. 5592 þou ...bouched] in my Sekke J; It] *with* fonell *mar.* G³; tunneth] turnes JMO; thoruh] of So grete J, by M. 5593 it] *om.* J; neiþer] neu*er*e J. 5594 me] right *add.* J; bed] bedde (*2nd* e *subpuncted*). G. 5595 to hire] *om.* JO; thing] a thynge JM, she O. 5596 gouernement] gou*er*naunce of J. 5597 if] and J; wistest] knewe J, wist MOS; riht] *om.* JM; al myn] the (*with* all my *mar.* G³) G, the JMO, my S; gouernaunce] of me *add.* J; haue] The effect of drunkenness, & gluttonye *mar.* O³. 5598 chewed] shewed

OS;   metes] mette O.   5599 to¹] of S;   Resoun] Note *mar*. O³.
5600 anoon] *om*. JMO;   sey] bidde hir*e* J;   Justice] ryghtwysnes J.
5601 þouh¹] *om*. O;   Equite] *with* eeuenesse *mar*. G³;   þouh²] *om*. O;
þouh³] and O;   alle] (e *ins*. G³).   5602 putte] *om*. O;   ayen] -s O.
5603 Attemperaunce] temp*er*aunce JMOS;   shulden] ȝif thay come to me schulde
J, þei shuld MO;   but] hoote S.   5604 of] at J;   make] gers J;   drive]
tham J;   hem²] Be dreuen*e* J.   5604-5 is entred] entres JO.   5605 as¹]
also J;   vnicorn] ane vnicorne JMO.   5606 wole] wold S;   eche] ilke a J,
ilk M, everych O;   oon] and *add*. J, and M;   roile] rolle JMS, rewle O.
5607 not] nowght (*with* not *mar*. G³) G;   nouht] nyte O;   for] *om*. CS, a *add*.
JM;   butour²] *om*. CS;   þis] that JO;   bifalleth] me *add*. M, fallys O.
5609 How] why J;   twey] twa JMO;   Ye] forsoth *add*. J.   5610 þat¹] and
they J, þer M, þey O;   genderes] engendred JM, gendryd O, genderiers S;
of¹] *om*. S;   Dame Venus] þe synis O, *om*. S;   me] *om*. J;   heere] hir*e* J,
Venus *rub*. *mar*. M;   which] swilk MO, þe which S.   5611 Yueresce] drunke-
shipe *over* C, *with* dronkschippe *mar*. G³, drunkun schepe JMO;   oon] *with* wombe
mar. G³, to O;   seid] *om*. JS, syde MO;   Gulf] gluf J.   5612 euere] ay
M, evermore O;   firste] furste (e *ins*. G³), the tane JMO, day *add*. S;   hath]
is has (is *can*.) M, I S;   stinte] lefte J;   and] *om*. O.   5613 apperseiued]
p*er*sayfed JMO;   5615 seyth] sey O;   I] *om*. S;   reuye] reue J, yerne O, rouþe
S;   it] is þat *add*. S;   oones] ne *add*. M;   hem] hym JMOS;   no] *om*.
MO.   5616 certeyn] *om*. JMO;   wolen] he wille J, will MO.   5617 þat¹]
it JMO;   haue] *om*. O;   Eche] Aythere of tham J, Ilk M, everych O;   last]
þe laste S.   5618 to] for to S.   5619   til] forte G;   þe¹] *om*. MO;
put to] atte J, brought to O;   þe²] an J;   twey] twa JMO;   Dame] þai*m*
O.   5620 reuelle] to reuell J;   hem] Gluttony breeds lust *mar*. O³;   and
to] *om*. JMO;   doon] *om*. JMOS;   euele] *om*. JMO.   5621 lest ... most]
om. JMO;   she] *with* venus *mar*. G³;   nygh] nere J, neste O.   5622 Bi]
om. JMO.   5623 thinketh] hopes J;   þat] *om*. M;   þilke] þam JMO.
5624 whiche] þat JMO.   5625 sithe] Sen*n*e JMO;   hider] nowe beholde heere
howe · Gloutony tooke þe pilgryme by þe throte and seesed him *add*. S.
5626 And] *prec*. Cap*itulum* xliv *mar*. CG, {Cap*itulum*} xxviij *mar*. S;   boþe] hire
add. JM.   5627 Sithe] Sen*n*e JMO;   wite] þou *add*. J.   5628 þe] *om*.
JM;   and ... cruelle] more cruell G, þou schalte fynde me J, mykill mare cruell
M, and þe more cruell O.   5628-9 þou ... me] and mekill mar*e* cruell J, now
add. M.   5629 Allas allas] allas *add*. CS, ha las, ha las F.   5630 me] go
add. O;   speke] speeke (*2nd* e *subpuncted*) G;   þilke] hire JMO;   I see] *om*.
JMO;   go] gase JMO;   hath] smitted me and *add*. O.   5631 I shal] *trs*.
J;   bitake] takyn*e* JMO.   5631-2 if of sooth] bot ȝif J.   5632 ne] *om*.
J;   wite] wyste O;   And] than J;   In þee it] *om*. J.   5633 is] *om*. J;
þat] quod J;   sei] telle J;   but] tryste it wele *add*. J;   askape] fra *add*.
J.   5632 sithe] senn JMO;   I²] *with* gloutonye *mar*. G³;   nigh] nere J.
5635 And] *prec*. Cap*itulum* xlv *mar*. CG;   to] of JMO.   5636 þou] quod I
add. J;   þilke] that JMO.   5637 thinketh] thynke JM;   bronnched] mouf-
fled S.   5638 Serteyn] Certaynly J;   þilke] scho J, þat MO;   þat] *om*.
O;   make] -s JMO;   dwelle] to dwelle J.   5639 and enhabite] *om*. JMO;
as] and S;   þere] -in JMO;   of] in S.   5640 and¹] *om*. O;   of¹] in S;
of² ... countenaunce] of countenau*n*ce JMO, also S;   also] of hir cou*n*tenaunce
S.   5641 of] luxuria *rub*. *mar*. M, venus or lust note *mar*. O³;   Dame] *om*.
JMO;   Glotonye] *mark over and passage marked mar*. C³.   5642 maistryeth]
maistreth (*with* maystreith *mar*. G³) G;   Longe agon] It es lange Sen*n* J, Longe

sithen M, *om.* O;   putte] drawe O;   drof] putte O.   5644 sithe] Seyne
JMO, weel S;   wel] with S.   5645 noses] nose JMO;   which] with S;
thing] tunge S;   wolden] waylde J.   5646 grettere] grete M;   þerinne] *o.*
er. G.   5647 withoute] any *add.* M;   stintinge] stynkyng O.   5648 Ne
... she] Hadde Scho nou3t J;   and ... in] into CJS, muciee ... et F.   5649 now]
þis CS, this tyme J;   deth] the dede JS;   castel] *with* Religioun *mar.* G³.
5650 muse] oute J;   was] it byfelle J.   5651 oon] þat *add.* C, i *over and* that
add. ins. G³, þat hade *add.* S;   hadde] he M, *om.* S;   he¹] thay J, hadd M;
be] gone owte O;   if] *om.* O;   out] þaye had nou3t gane J, noght O;   he²
...goon] oute J, ben he had O.   5652 anoye] ne disese *add.* J;   but] note
mar. O³;   he] scho JMOS;   at] of S.   5653 What] *prec.* Cap*itulum* xlvi
mar. CG;   þei] the J, þo MO;   tweyne] twa JMO;   misdoon] trespaste to
J, done mys O;   þee] *om.* O.   5655 I] *with* veus (*for* venus) *mar.* G³;   inne]
me S.   5656 þat I ne] Pat ne I J, þen I M, þanne but I O.   5657 which]
that J;   binome] refte JMO.   5658 and] for M, *om.* O;   seith] scho seyes
JMO;   lace] JM, lose my lyf & O.   5659 ly] be JMO;   bi] with JMO;
haue] hadd M.   5660 an] *ins. mar.* G³;   How] Quod I J.   5660-1 quod
I] howe J.   5661 white] grey S, or *add.* O;   greye] whyte S;   or] other
G, & O.   5662 yolden] 3eelden (*with* 3eeldene *mar.* G³) G.   5664 maketh]
2nd a *ins.* G³);   here] (*2nd* e *ins.* G³).   5665 þanne] (e *ins.* G³);   she]
þou sais *add.* M.   5665-6 for þat] þerfore JMO.   5666 þe¹ ... hire] *om.*
J;   and] I C, *om.* J;   am] *om.*: J, ay O;   þe more²] *om.* J;   sharp] *om.* J,
-ly O.   5667 ayens] *om.* J, asaylys O;   hire] *om.* J;   Whi¹] *prec.* Cap*itulum*
xlvij *mar.* CG;   Whi²] videce *mar.* S.   5668 þou¹] þat *add.* O;   sithe] Senn
JMO;   I am] þowe erte J;   nyh] nere J;   þee] me J.   5670   al] weele
add. S;   Whan] whanne (e *ins.* G³) G, why J;   whoeuere] whene so euere J,
when euer MO.   5672 from] fra JO.   5672 kembt] A maske fitt for a fowle
face *mar.* O³.   5673 seist] semes J;   If ... it] if þou ware J, *ins. mar. after*
rub. caret also in text O³;   þou ... not] I trowe noght J, þou wold nou3t MO;
as] *om.* J, aske *ins. mar.* O³;   I trowe] thowe walde J;   þee] so *add.* M.
5674 Now vnderstonde] *trs* J;   quod she] a litille J;   a litel] quod scho ·
Certaynly J;   wel] *om.* J.   5675 þat] *om.* S;   þus] this J;   me] me me
(*1st* me *can. and partly erased*) M.   5676 þat þouh] *trs.* JS;   þus] fir *add.*
M;   a] *om.* S.   5677 queyntrelle] quaynte M;   am] *om.* S.   5678 and
slauery] stynkyng O;   foule] *om.* JMO;   stinkinge] and slauery O;   vile]
lothely O.   5679 bi] *om.* O;   ynowh] thought J, *om.* O;   dar] can
JMO.   5680 me¹] *om.* S;   me²] mee (*2nd* e *ins.* G³).   5681 recche] ryche
S;   ooþer] -es CM;   place] (*2nd* a *ins.* G³);   þer] wher M.   5682 bi¹]
my *add.* S;   turnynges] turnynge J;   seche] *om.* J, I sekke M.
5683 hydinges] *om.* J;   and corneres] *om.* JS;   and²] *om.* J;   se] I see JM;
at ful] aboute JMO;   and³] *om.* M.   5684 haue] I hafe JMO;   thouht] youþe
S;   putte] (e *ins.* G³).   5685 doo] fulfille J;   which] what O.
5686 place] -s J;   ofte] *ins. mar. after rub. caret also in text* O³;   woldest] walde
JMO.   5687 þat riht] *om.* JMO;   woldest] walde JMO.   5688 I] *prec.*
Cap*itulum* xlviij *mar.* CG;   ride] on *add.* JO, opon *add.* M;   for] So JM;
pas] place J, passage O.   5689 is as] *trs.* C, thare maste felthe J, *om.* S;
most filthe] es J, -ye S;   his] es awene J;   him] downe *add.* J;   Þe] *om.*
G.   5690 is ... Wil] es ille J, is euyll MO, þat bereþe me S;   þat ... me] is
cleped yuel wille S;   and] aye *add.* J;   to ley hire] to lay hym J, where dong
is O.   5692 þere ... is¹] thare dounge es J, for to lay here O, Lust & þe filthynes
þer of *mar.* O³;   and] euere mare to J;   bidunge] be dungande J, bedongyng

O;   hire] *om.* J, him S.   5692 eerþe] alway *add.* J;   musell] morselle
CJS;   Þeras] thare whar*e* JMO;   himself] þer *add.* S.   5693 it] that J;
place] (*2nd* a *ins.* G³).   5694 and¹] *om.* O;   and³ ... in] *om.* JMO.
5695 abstracto] *em. ed.* storpaile CS, *space in text (with* stoppaile *mar.* G³) G, *om.*
JMO;   concreto] hideles CS, *space in text (with* hudles *and in another hand* couerte
mar. G³), coverte JMO;   I am²] *om.* S.   5696 peynted] fals JMO, face a *add.*
S;   fauce] paynted JMO.   5696-7 for ... visage¹] *ins. mar. after rub. caret*
also in text O³.   5697 a] *om.* CS.   5698 cleped] called JMO;   with] by
JMO, Faydrey *rub. mar.* M;   eelded] (*2nd* e *ins.* G³);   riueled] rou*n*cled J.
5699 me] my M.   5700 make] (*2nd* a *ins.* G³).   5701 for] to M;   alle]
(e *ins.* G³);   þilke] tha JM, þe O;   þe] by tis J;   dung-hep] dungeschip
JS.   5702 weylate] wey or a dungheep*e* S;   þer] þat S;   eche] *mark over*
and marked mar. C³, ilke man J, ilkon M, euerych O, yche body S;   at] in JM,
om. O;   his time] *om.* O;   to] and JOS.   5703 I² ... neuere] nowe JMO;
now] rekke I neue*re* J, I rekk neu*er* MO;   þi knoweleche] the J, Note *mar.* O³.
5704 þee¹] thy knowlage J;   now] *om.* J;   and] also *add.* M;   to] forto
JMO;   haue] (*2nd* a *ins.* G³), halde JO.   5705 is] it is MO, nis S;   nouht
but] but OS;   gret] a velany and J, Takeþe heede I prey yowe howe þe olde spekiþe
with þe pilgryme *add.* S.   5706 Serteyn] *prec.* Ca*pitulum* xlix *mar.* CG,
{C}a*pitulum* xxix *mar.* S, Certaynly J;   if] and J.   5705 þat] whilke J;
hid] *om.* J, had O;   cote] (*2nd* o *ins.* G³);   if þow ne] bot ȝif þ*ou* J.
5708 michel] *om.* J;   þe] þei C, thy JMO;   sholdest] *o. er. (with* schuldest *u.v.*
mar. C³) C;   michel] the *add.* JMO.   5709 me²] (*2nd* a *ins.* G³).
5710 to] þer *ins. mar.* O³;   hire] The Instruments of lust *mar.* O³;   nempned]
called J.   5710-3 Þat ... nouht] As þer of q*uo*d sche · þei ben nouht honeste to
shewe · ne CG³s (*at foot p.* G³), can. G.   5710 Þat] *om.* J.   5711 oon]
1 *over* G³;   hatte] es called J; | raptus] *space (with* raptus *mar.* G³) G;   þat
ooþer] anoþ*e*re J, Rapt*us* · stupru*m* ince{stum} adult*er*ium · Fornicacio *rub. mar.*
M, is sayde *add.* O;   stuprum] *space (with* stuprum *mar.* G³) G.   5711-2 þat
ooþer] the thridde J.   5712 incestus] *space (with* incestus *mar.* G³) G;   þat
ooþer¹] the ferth J;   is seid] *om.* JO, is called M; adulterium] *space (with* adulterium
mar. G³) G;   and] *om.* JO;   þat ooþer²] the fifte J, an othir M.   5713 forni-
cacioun] *space (with* fornicacioun *mar.* G³) G; | of¹] and J;   þat ooþer] the Sexte
J;   it] it is O;   for] *om.* O;   of] for O.   5714 may wel] Suffise the J;
suffice þee] wele I nowe J;   hem] *om.* M.   5714-5 now ... hem] *om.*
JMO.   5716 apertliche] *om.* S;   for²] be cause of J.   5717 vnthrifty]
vnthrift M;   here] *om.* JMO;   yit] neu*er*theles J;   algates] algate G, ȝit J,
wele MO;   wel] I can J, algates MO.   5718 I kan] I welle J;   leiser] and
add. J.   5719 but] ȝif *add.* JM;   flee] þe faster O;   fastere] flee O;
or] and J;   go] fastere *add.* J;   tigre] a tigre CS, the tygi*er* JMO;   sithe] Sen
JMO.   5720 of] fra JMO;   þi] *om.* JMO;   flight] felthe J;   drede me]
doute J;   nouht] that ne *add.* J;   Of me] þou schalle J;   þou shalt] hafe it
J.   5721 haue it] of me J;   þou shalt] *trs.* J; ·   ferþere] farrer M.
5722 And] *prec.* Ca*pitulum* l *mar.* CG;   olde] theeffe *add.* J;   with a darte] to
the herte J;   to þe herte] with a darte J.   5723 michel] for *add.* JS;   doun]
scho schoke me J.   5723-4 she ... me] downe J, she stroke me O.
5724 Auarice] also *add.* J;   þei] *om.* CS;   nouht] that they hadde J.
5724-5 þat þei hadden] nouȝt J.   5725 gowtes] þe gowte CJMOS, goutes (s
subpuncted) G, goutes F;   eche] For ilke ane J, Ilkon*e* M, euerych O;   at] in
J.   5726 armure] wapen J, weepens S;   she] thay JMOS;   Binome me] than
J, Reft me and takyn from me M, berefte me M;   þanne was] was my burdou*n*

J, *trs*. M;   my bordoun] refte me J.   5727 wel] þay scholde *add*. J, to *add*.
O.   5728 at ... poyntes] they hadde J;   þei hadden] at alle poyntes J;   slayn
me] *trs*. MO;   Whan] *prec*. Cap*itulum* li *mar*. CG.   5729 bitrapped] and *add*.
J;   smyten] and *add*. JMS;   hurt] greuously *add*. J;   whan] and þat J, bot
M, and O;   my burdoun] thus loste J, þus my burdon MO.   5730 lost] my
burdou*n* J, left M;   reise] rise (*with* Reyse *mar*. G³) G;   neuere man] I trowe
J.   5730-1 as I trowe] þere was neuere man J, I trowe O.   5731 was more
desolat] more desolat J;   þan I] was *add*. J;   shalt] schalle JMO.
5732 þou¹] I JMO;   shalt] schalle JM;   þou²] I J.   5733 comen] hic dolet
peregrinus rub. mar. M;   were] was J;   þou] *with* body *mar*. G³;   euere] so
hardy to by come a J;   pilgrime] quasi ? mort*uus mar*. O³.   5735 me] soule
over C³;   þou haddest] soule *mar*. G³, I had JMO.   5736 þee¹,²,³] me J.
5737 Þow] I J, þat O;   hast] hafe JO;   þi] my J;   Aa] Ellas S.
5738 made] had J;   passe] thurth *add*. JMO;   þe] ʒoure J, þi M;   thorny]
horny G, *om*. JMO;   hegge] egre O.   5739 now] *om*. J, be O;   be] now
O;   me] to me JMO;   ful] weell J, *om*. MO;   sweete] (*2st e ins*. G³);   and]
fulle *add*. J;   ne] werne J;   were I] *trs*. J;   so] ferre *add*. J.
5740 aloyned] withdrawen M;   straunged] strayed J.   5741 youre¹] *om*.
J;   prikkinges] *om*. J, prikkes M, pylgrimis O.   5742 oynement] nowe J, -es
MOS;   now] oyenementes J;   to] For J;   riht] *om*. JMO;   He] Oo ye CS,
A · A · JMO, He F.   5743 I ouhte] wele aught me J, wele *add*. MO;   biweyle]
to wayle For J, to make sorow for M, to be wayle O;   lyfe] tyme *add*. J;   livede]
schulde lefe J.   5744 enoorned] armed JMO, anoured S.   5745 it] I J;
nouht] so *add*. J.   5746 I] he S;   haue] (*2nd a ins*. G³);   me] (*2nd e ins*.
G³), *om*. J;   sithe] þerfore J, þerby MO.   5747 þerbi] Seyne JMO;   riht]
om. JM.   5748 He] Oo þou CS, A · A· JMO, He F.   5749 preyse] -d O;
þee¹] (*1st e ins*. G³);   haue] (*2nd a ins*. G³).   5750 sithe] Senn JMO;
haue] (*2nd a ins*. G³);   lost] left M;   whiche] the whilke JO.   5751 was¹]
haue M;   He] Oo þou CS, *om*. GJM, the O, Hee F;   was²] stirred and *add*.
J.   5752 excited] stirryd M.   5753 bihight] hight JMO;   þee²] *om*.
JMO;   wolde] schulde J.   5754 do þe viage] ga to the J, do my viage MO;
to þee] (*1st e ins*. G³), in pilgr*i*mage J;   þat] *om*. J.   5755 clere] cleen M;
Now] bot nowe J;   on] opon M.   5756 is] weel *add*. S;   forueyed I] ʒode
I oute of my hye way J, went I M, forfeted I O, *trs*. S.   5757 shal] mou*n* J;
þee] How grace dieu app*er*es to þe pilgr*i*me in a clowde · and comforteʒ hym *add*.
rub. M.   5758 As] *prec*. Cap*itulum* lij m*ar*. CG, cap*itulum* iij *rub. mar*. M;
I¹] *om*. O;   me] þus *add*. J;   biweyled] Sorowed J, wexid sorow for M.
5759 cloude] clowdid M;   reysed] out *add. ins.* (*with er. mar.* C³) CS, on hight
out *add*. J.   5760 þe wynd] *scilicet* cloude *mar*. G³, come J;   com¹] a wynde
J;   also] and J, as M, as *alt*. also O;   She com] it J, it come M, *ins. mar. after
rub. caret also in text*; midday] and *add*. J;   she] it J.   5761 tariede]
houed J;   þere] *om*. J;   a] litille *add*. J;   made] (*2nd a ins*. G³).
5762 for] ? Will top *of p*. C³;   as] I hadde bene *add*. J;   ded] *final e subpuncted*
G;   5763 lyfe] *om*. O;   hadde] was JMO;   þe] my JMO;   Now vnderstond-
eth] *trs*. J.   5763-4 so ... yow] and behaldes J.   5764 loth] þat *add*. O;
departeth hire] es to p*ar*te J, is to departe O.   5765 socoured] socours S;
whan ... hath] *om*. J;   bifalle] *mark over and marked mar.* C³, *om*. J.
5765-6 hem ... hem] *om*. J.   5766 whan] þat *add*. O;   Of] Fra J, Oute of
M;   þilke] that JMO.   5767 cloude] þere *add*. J;   me] *om*. JMO, þus S;
þus] on this wise J, to me S;   Now] Ryse vp J;   up] nowe þowe J;   wrechche]
wreched J.   5768 now] ryse J;   To michel] alle to lange J;   þou hast] *trs*.

J.   5770 to] for to S;   releue] deliuere CS.   5771 Entende] Take hede
J;   þee¹] Agayne add. J;   þee²] agayne add. J, to þe M.   5772 stablisshe
it] establysched G, stablys J, establissh MO;   þi deth] þider S;   albeit] that add.
J, þof if be so M, all þogh it be O.   5773 hast] hafe JMO;   me] -n S;
wole] þat add. O.   5774 þat þou] om. J;   Whan] prec. Capitulum liij mar.
CG;   swiche woordes] I vndirstode J, I slike wordes MO.   5774-5 I vnder-
stood] thire wordes J, vndirstode MO.   5776 arauhte] reched J, raught M;
me] to me O.   5777 she] So J.   5778 Haa] Aa CJMOS, He F;   God]
lorde J;   I] my goode and my makere add. J;   Neuere] I disserued J.
5778-9 deseruede I] neuere J.   5779 Now riht] trs. JMO.   5780 ne
hadden] hadde nouȝt J;   Sithe] Senn JMO;   my burdoun] ȝe ȝelde me J.
5780-1 ye² ... me³] my burdoun J.   5781 and] om. J;   ye¹] om. J;
areechin] reches JMO;   me³] (2nd e ins. G³), my J.   5782 þe] my MS;
Graces] Grace JMO;   and²] of S;   thankinges] thankynge JM.   5783 He]
Aa CJMO, A ha S, He F.   5784 now] See wele J;   I see wel] nowe J;
yit] om. CS, giff G;   not at] atte add. J, nat O, at S.   5785 forsaken] forsaake
(2nd a ins. G³) G;   me¹] om. C, nought me S;   at þe neede] schewed ȝowe redy
J, at nede MO;   shewed yow redy] to helpe me J, shewed yow tendrely S;   to
... me] atte my nede J.   5786 if it ne] bot ȝif it J;   long] along CS;   on]
of JMOS;   I wot neuere] om. O;   whens] wheyn J, om. O   5786-7 þis
...yow] þis coome þow M, om. O.   5787 but] all onely add. O;   youre] awne
add. JM;   haue] (2nd a ins. G³).   5788 I leeuede] trowed I J, I trowid
MO;   neuere] and þerfore add. J.   5789 me] to me JO.   5790 sey]
grauntes J, I say M;   gilt] and add. J;   bihote] be hoote (1st o ins. G³) G, hete
JMO.   5791 foryiueth] it add. (can. and subpuncted C) CJMO;   me] atte
add. J.   5792 time¹] and add. S;   anooþer time] om. S;   leeue] trist in
M;   yow] your rede O;   Redresseth] relesse O.   5793 riht] om. J;
michel] ille J.   5793-4 To þe hegge] Euene J.   5794 euene] to the hegge
J;   I wole] trs. J;   bi yow] I be delyuered J;   I haue deliueraunce] (haaue
1st a ins. G³) be ȝou J.   5795 wole] wulle (e ins. G³) G;   hens] heyne J,
Takeþe heede nowe a whyle I preye yowe howe Gracedieux aunswereþe þe pilgryme
· of þat he desyreþe of hir add. S.   5796 And] prec. Capitulum liv mar. CG,
{Capitulum x}xx mar. S, om. M;   þanne] (e ins. G³), dame add. S;   answerde]
and saide to me add. M;   sey] telle J;   riht] om. J.   5797 fair] gude J;
þilke] scho JMO;   toward] -es S.   5798 sone] nota de Elemosinar id est Sancta
Maria rub. mar. M;   she] and scho JS, om. M;   is] om. JM;   his mooder]
om. M.   5799 to¹] om. JMO;   yit²] but O, but S.   5799-800 þou
shuldest] weel S.   5800 wel] þou shouldest S;   lede] leede (1st e ins. G³)
G.   5701 woldest] walde JMO;   from þee] a waye J;   þe] þy CS, tha J,
torment] -ours that so has defouled the J, -ours MO;   And] om. J.   5802 þilke]
that JMO;   to ordeyne] (to can. and subpuncted) C, es ordaynere J, ordeyned
S;   of yow] and awmoinere J;   is lady] of ȝowe J, is a lady MO, his lady S.
5803 lady] quod add. J;   whan] om. J;   she²] that J.   5804 Serteyn]
Certaynly J.   5805 herte] (2nd e ins. G³);   mercy] For add. M.   5806 I
wole] þat I O;   þee¹] om. MO;   at] as O;   þis] is O.   5807 haue¹] gude
add. M;   wil] welle J;   er now] schewed the J;   shewed þee] ar this And
J.   5808 þe] this J, þy S;   defawte] þer es in the add. J;   shame] schaame
(2nd a ins. G³) G.   5809 þee¹] For add. J;   ooþer] many J;   times] atyme
J;   kast þee and] om. JMO.   5810 many] monye (e ins. G³) G;   yuel] om.
J.   5811 I haue] om. M;   þee] to the JMOS.   5813 ne ne] ne CJOS,
ne I M;   took] (1st o ins. final e subpuncted G³);   no] om. O;   keep] hede

O;   of hire] ʒe spake J;   ye speken] of hire J.   5814 of sum ooþer] ʒe had
Spoken J;   ye ... spoken] of Sum othyr J;   to] vn to J;   þat] and J, and þat
MO.   5815 sithe] Senn JMO;   to] *om*. JO. so M;   my charbuncle] *om*.
M.   5815-6 I wole] *twice and* Pars iij *top of p*. J.   5816 herte] (*2nd* e *ins*.
G³);   preye] pray (*with* peye *mar*. G³) G.   5816-7 as I can] here JMO.
5817 to hire] as I can JMO;   if] and JS;   yive] ʒeue (*with* ʒyue *mar*. *under rub*.
G³) G;   me¹] (*2nd* e *ins*. G³);   shewe] þe *add*. *can*. M.   5818 biseeche]
praye J;   hire] *om*. J;   right gladliche] I Walde J;   I wolde] right gladly
J.   5820 And] *prec*. Ca*pitulum* lv *mar*. CG;   of þe clowde] scho keste me
J, oute of þe clowed MO;   a scripture] A Scripture J;   she ... me] oute of the
clowde J.   5821 seide] vnto *add*. J;   me] *om*. S;   heere] (*2nd* e *ins*. G³),
Quod scho the fourme *add*. J, *om*. M;   boþe] *om*. JMO.   5822 alwey] altymes
M;   semblable] Swilke JMO.   5823 in ... hondes] þou schalle be J;   þou
... be] in the handes of Swilke alde theues J.   5824 verrey] trewe J.
5825 bihoote] be seeche (*with* heete *mar*. G³) G, hete J;   þou¹] *om*. S;   good]
trewe J;   and] *ins*. *mar*. G³.   5826 þere] whare JMO;   þou] fyndes or *add*.
O, for *add*. S.   5827 paas] pathes M;   Now] *prec*. Ca*pitulum* lvj *mar*. CG;
I¹] wil *add*. MS;   yow] of *add*. S;   þe] *om*. S;   I²] *om*. MO;   vndide]
opened J, *om*. MO, it *add*. S;   and] *om*. J;   vnplytede] *om*. J.   5828 it¹]
om. J;   and²] þus *add*. M;   alle] (e *ins*. G³).   5829 and¹] *mark over and
passage marked* C³;   in þe] *om*. S.   5830 Grace] dieu *add*. CJMOS, Grace
F;   hadde] bade me S;   seyd] wretyne J, I sayde S;   Þe] manere and *add*.
S;   þe] this J;   ye shule] crye J.   5831 A.B.C.] *space* (*with* a b c *mar*. G³)
G, ʒe can welle J, A.B.C.D. M, þabece S;   wel ye kunne] the .A.B.C.E. J, yee
conne weel S;   wite it] ʒe may J, yee may weel S;   ye mown] lightliche J,
vnderstonde and S;   lightliche] cunn it J, vnderstonde it *add*. S.   5832 for
to sey] it *add*. O, *om*. S;   if it be] when ʒe hafe J.   5833 Incipit ... alphabeti]
? Wyl *foot of p*. C³, *om*. GJMOF, *prec*. nota *mar*. S.   5834 Almihty] *prec*.
Ca*pitulum* lvij *mar*. C, ca*pitulum* iv *mar*. M, *2 grotesques with good stuff between
them, a 3rd below in another hand* O³, *nota* Chauc{er} *mar*. *but not Shirley's hand
or ink* S³ *and in Shirley's hand* Devotissima ora*tio* {ad} Mariam · pro *om*ni ten{tatione
et} tribula*cio*ne necess{aria} angustie *mar*. S.   5825 þat] *om*. JO.
5836 of²] *om*. JO, and MS;   and] of G;   teene] (*2nd* e *ins*. G³).
5837 floures] swete *add*. M.   5838 flee] crye S.   5839 releeue] relesse
JMO;   mihti] and *add*. O.   5840 of] on CS.   5841 Venquissed] when
cused O;   me hath] *trs*. JMO;   aduersaire] aduersarie GMOS.   5842 þin]
thyne (e *subpuncted*) G;   his] *om*. JMO.   5843 wolt] wille JM;   my] his
S.   5844 good] (*final* e *subpuncted* G).   5845 herte] (*2nd* e *ins*. G³).
5846 largeese] larged O;   pleyn] alle JMO.   5847 of²] *om*. MO.
5848 þat] that *add*. *subpuncted* G, *om*. J;   theeves] þeuys (theues and latones *over
in different hands* O³;   sevene] vij *over* G³;   mee] *id est* seven dedly synnes
mar. S.   5849 tobreste] breset J.   5850 yow] the JM.   5852 Which]
wiche (*with* wheche *mar*. G³) G;   ouhten] owghte (e *ins*. G³) G;   þi] þe M;
appeere] to appere MO.   5853 Han] Has JMO;   on] of MO.
5855 mihten] myghte (e *ins*. G³), may J, may right MO.   5857 Nere] Ware
ne JM, Ne were O;   merci] ware *add*. J;   you] the J, þe wer M;   blsiful]
heuene *add*. CS, blessydful O.   5859 Þat þou nart] that ne þou erte J, Þan þou
ert M, But þou art O, þat þou art S.   5860 vouched] vouche J, vouchis MO;
þee] thee (*1st* e *ins*. G³) G.   5861 Crystes] lady and S;   blisful] blyssedfull
O.   5862 þe] *om*. J, þi O;   bent] i · bent G;   swich] suche (e *subpuncted*)
G, a *add*. M.   5863 justice] riʒtwisnes J.   5864 God] *om*. S;   nolde]

walde JMO; no] þas J; heere] here (*with* audire *mar*. G³) G. 5867 For] *om*. O; a] *om*. M. 5868 Hast] As O. 5869 þe] þy J. 5870 Hye] by M. 5871 litel] fruit *add*. CS, goodnesse *add*. J; shal þanne] in me J; in me] þan schalle J. 5872 Þat] *om*. J; er] *om*. M; day] *ins*. G; correcte] me *o. er*. C, help M, me weel S; vice] *em. ed*., chastyse (chasty *o. er*. C) CS, mee GO, me folise J, me þat in syn*ne* lyse M. 5873 Of] thurth J, *om*. O; verrey riht] *om*. O; werk] -es JO; me] (*2nd e ins*. G³), wille JMOS; wole] *with* wull *mar*. G³, me JMS, me þan O; confounde] Eeuere to haaue ther by helle grownde (*2nd a ins*. G³) *add*. G. 5874 þi] þe O. 5875 from] for O; tempeste] -s J; dreede] (*2nd e ins*. G³). 5876 Biseeching] Be seekynge (*with* besechynge *mar*. G³) G; yow] þe JM; ye] þou JM; you] the JM. 5877 wikke] -d JM; O] AA J, *om*. M; help yit] *trs*. JO. 5878 Al] waye *add*. J; haue] þof M; and] in *add*. G. 5879 þi] *om*. J; grace] (*2nd a ins*. G³). 5880 myn] yit *add*. S. 5881 my] the J; in poynt] es J; is] in poynte J; chace] chaase (*1st a ins*. G³) G. 5882 mayde] maiden*e* J, modir M; mooder] mayden M; þat] þer O; neuere] euer S. 5883 Were] was JMO, Was neuer youre S; bitter] bett*er* JOS; neiþer] *om*. OS; nor] ne JMO, neyþer S; in] the *add*. J; see] *with* mare *mar*. G³. 5884 But] Both O. 5886 þou] *om*. J; for] euer *add*. S; ne] *om*. JMOS; ysee] See JMOS; 5887 þer] þat J, þe MOS. 5888 certes] certaynly J; but] if *add*. CS, (t *ins*. O³). 5889 stink eterne] lastande Paine J. 5890 tel him] *om*. JMO; as] it *add*. JMO; his] fre *add*. M. 5891 Bicomen] To become O; a] *om*. JMO. 5892 And] *om*. JMO. 5893 as] *erased* G. 5894 eueryl] eu*e*rylke J. 5895 þou] for vs J, our socour M; for us] þ*o*u JM; praye] be ay M. 5896 þou] *om*. O; boþe] *om*. J; his] *om*. G, oure S. 5897 make] (*2nd a ins*. G³); foo] faes J; his] þair*e* J; praye] preye (*with* praye *mar*. G³) G. 5898 wolt] *om*. O. 5900 a soule] we JMO; falleth] falle JMO; in] any *add*. J. 5901 him] vs JMO. 5902 Þanne] So JMO; his¹⁺²] oure JMO. 5903 him] vs J. 5904 þee] thee (*1st e ins*. G³) G, loues J, he O; loueth] the J. 5905 as] when JMO; he] *om*. S. 5906 enlumyned] illunynde J. 5907 lighted] lithned J. 5908 yow] the J, þe by M. 5909 thar] dar G; lame] (*2nd a ins*. G³). 5910 sithe] Sen JMO; þat] þe JM. 5911 seeche] as *add*. JMO. 5912 no more] my wounde JMOS; my wounde] na mare JMOS; entame] vntame CS. 5913 þin] the J. 5914 kan] ne care S. 5915 þe] thy Sone J. 5916 boþes] bather J, both MO; peynes] penaunce S. 5917 alder] alþ*e*re J, old MO, aldres S; his] vs O; bobaunce] bokau*n*ce JM. 5919 Conuict] Committe JM. 5920 erst] ar J, þou M; þou] ert M; ground] crowned O. 5921 Continue] Open*e* J, Conteyn MO; pitous] pitifo*us* JM. 5923 þer] *om*. J, þat MS; a] oon S; stikke] qwist J. 5925 which] wheche (*2nd e ins*. G³) G. 5926 þe] *om*. M. 5927 afyir] on fuyre S; in] a JMO. 5928 þou] *om*. J; defende] denfende C. 5929 Which] *om*. J; eternalli] endelesly J; shal] *om*. J; dure] endure J. 5930 neuere] ȝit *add*. JMO; haddest] hadde JMO. 5931 Certes] *om*. O; in us] be J; bee] in vs it comes þorow þe J, be it c*o*omys of þe MO. 5932 Þat ... þee] þ*o*u *add*. CS, Thow erte JO, Pat ert M; Cristes] awyne *add*. J, our lord*es* awn *add*. M. 5933 or] no oþ*e*re J, ne odir M, ne none oþer O. 5935 aduocat noon] *trs*. J; wole and] *om*. S; so] þanne S. 5936 for] so *add*. MO; hire] here M. 5937 tweye] twayne JMO. 5939 rest] lust CGS; of] and J; and] of *add*. JM. 5941 Þee] þou J, *om*. M; to] *om*. JO, his *add*. M; humblesse] mekeness*e* J, humblenesse MO.

VARIANTS
325

5942 he] *om.* J; þe] thee (*1st* e *ins.* G³) G, yowe S. 5943 for] *om.* S; beede] lede MO. 5944 awaiteth] hase waite J; on] in MO. 5945 ne] *om.* JMO; neuere] na *add.* 5946 for] *om.* MO. 5947 and whi] *om.* O. 5948 Gabrielles] *o. er.* C, Gabriele J; to] vn to CS. 5949 werre] wern (n *o. er.*) M, wery O. 5950 sithen] seyn JMO. 5951 us] *om.* MOS; for] *om.* J; saue] (*2nd* a *ins.* G³), haue S. 5952 not ... ouhte] noȝte JMO. 5953 Doo] To J, Vs aught to MO; penitence] ga *add.* JMO; axe and] *om.* JMO; haue] (*2nd* a *ins.* G³). 5954 me] (*2nd* e *ins.* G³). 5955 agilt] hafe JMO; haue] offended J, agilte MO; boþe] offt *add.* S; and] also *add.* M. 5958 shal] to thy Sonne J; vnto þi sone] schalle J, to þi sonne MO; mene] meene (*1st* e *ins.* G³) G. 5959 þat] þou O; art] of pitee J; of pitee] ert J. 5960 on] of JMOS. 5962 and] þowe *add.* S. 5963 faderes] fadere J. 5964 Pat] *om.* J. 5965 is] hys *add. ins. mar.* C³, þat *add.* JMO, þe *add.* S; rihtful] rihful C, rewfulle JMO. 5966 to] *om.* JM. 5967 ye] þou JM; eek] eeke (*2nd* e *ins.* G³) G, also JMO; soules] Sawle JMO. 5968 you] the JM; is] I JMO; pitee] putte myne JMO; haboundinge] habidynge JMO. 5969 To] *om.* J; eche] *om.* J, ilk M, everych O; þat wole] Off Petee J; of pitee] of whilke I J; you] the JM. 5970 is] it is JMO; ne] *om.* JMO. 5971 þee] you O. 5972 but] ȝif *add.* JMO; vnto] to JMO. 5973 þee maked] *trs.* J. 5974 þis] þe CS; eek] also JMO. 5975 he] erth J; represseth] empresse J. 5976 in] I M. 5977 þee corowned] *trs.* J; rial] a *add.* JS. 5978 þer] where in J, wher MO; his] *om.* J. 5979 which] wiche (e *subpuncted*) G; misbileeued] mysbeleuande J; depriued] pryued JMO. 5980 you] the JM; bringe] to ȝowe me *mar.* G³. 5981 I] ne *add.* S. 5983 acursed] cursed JMO; was] *om.* O; ful] fell O. 5984 I] As *alt.* I S; am] So J; so] *om.* C, Am J, soore S; ye] þou J. 5985 almost] *om.* S; it] JMO; smert] me *add.* S. 5986 art] So noble J, is MO; so noble] es J. 5987 Ledest] And ledest CS, Led JMO; into] vnto JMO; þe] þin OS; hye] *paradis add.* J; tour] of paradise *add.* MO. 5988 Of Paradys þou] þou JMO; me wisse] wisse me lady J; and] me *add.* J. 5989 How] On whate wise J, Þi grace and þi socour M, Of what wyse O; þi¹ ... socour] on what wyse M, þi grace and socour O. 5990 filthe] fyghte O; in²] *om.* JMO. 5992 cleped] called JM; þi] *om.* O; bench] benke JM, bouche O; O] of a JM. 5993 Þeras] there as (*2nd* e *ins.* G³) G, thare whare J; þat] *om.* JO; euere] Schalle JMO; shal] eueremore J, euer MO. 5994 Xpc] ? Xpistus J, Xrist MOS; alighte] (e *ins.* G³), lith J, light M. 5996 eek] *om.* J, also MO; þat] *om.* M. 5997 made] (*2nd* a *ins.* G³); to] forto J; adoun] downe JMO. 5998 And] *om.* S; al] So was it S; þis] þus O, al S. 5999 And] *om.* JMO; I] To hym J; to him] I J; eek also JMO. 6001 yow] the JM. 6003 forforth] JO. 6004 him] he J; ne rouhte] rought JMO. 6005 soo] *om.* O; lust] as a lambe J, as lambe MO; as a lamb] liste JMO; to] *om.* J, forto MO. 6006 ladi] I pray the J; ful of merci] lady J; I yow preye] Fulle of mercy J. 6007 Sithe] *o. er.* C, sith (*with* syththe *mar.* G³) G, Senn JMO; he] *o. er.* C; his] *o. er.* C, es JOS; merci] *o. er.* C. 6008 ye] þou JM; and] *om.* J; seye] softly J. 6009 ye ben] þou erte J. 6010 yow] the JM; clepeth] calleȝ JMO; þe] an M. 6011 To] the O; wasshe] wasche (e *ins.* G³) G, whylk of O; soule] *followed by er.* J, sowlys O; out of] excusys O; his] þe O. 6013 nere] ware noȝt J, wern M, ne were O; herte] wer *add.* M. 6014 sithe] Senn JMO; and] eek *add.* S. 6015 Adam] so *add.* M. 6016 Bring] And

bring J, So bring S; þat] thy JO; palais] place JMO; bilt] bryght O.
6017 penitentes] Penitence J, penitent MO; ben] to thy mercy J; to ... able]
are able J, mercy able M; Amen] quod Bennett add. M, om. OS. 6018 Explicit carmen] om. GJMOS, Here grace dieu giffes þe pilgryme his burdon · and raises
hym agayn add. rub. M. 6019 Whan] prec. Capitulum lviij mar. CG, capitulum
v rub. mar. M, (Capitulum) xx mar. S; þus] I had J, I þus M; I hadde] þus
J, hadd M. 6020 dispensere] Spencere J; Grace] dieu add. JMOS; hye]
om. JMO; heef] lifte vp J, vp add. MO. 6021 Grace] dieu add. JMOS;
haue] (2nd a ins. G³); goodshipe] goodnesse JMO; raught] rechid J.
6022 to Grace] I Sayde J, dieu add. MOS; I seide] vnto Grace dieu J;
thinketh] thynge J, thynk M; riht] om. J. 6023 now] quod I add. J.
6024 þat] ins. mar. G³, om. JMO; haue] (2nd a ins. G³); if] ȝif ȝe JMO.
6024-5 ye enoyntede] enoynted JMO, ye wolde enoynte S. 6025 my] þe
JMO. 6026 þe bocle] om. J; ye] om. O; þat] þe O; he] she o. er.
with er. mar. C³. 6027 yow] om. J; helpe] to add. G; þilke] þa JMO;
or] other G, of S. 6028 Excuse yow] ȝe maye noȝt J; of dispenseer] excuse
ȝowe J, of þe despenser S; ne of awmeneer] of Spensere J; mown ye not] ne
of awmoynere J. 6029 wole] þat add. CS; ye] om. MO; haue] (2nd a
ins. G³), no add. M. 6030 of yow] I hafe J. 6030-1 I haue] mark over
with mark mar. C³, (2nd a ins. G³), na Socoure J. 6031 no socour] of ȝowe
J; holt] comes J; Helpeth] ȝif ȝe helpe J, help ȝhe MO, and add. S.
6032 She ... me²] om. J; And] prec. Capitulum lix mar. CG. 6033 rauhte]
tuke J; oon] on (1 over G³) G, my J; Sithe] Sene JMO. 6034 hast] quod
scho So add. J, so add. MO; to] in JMO; þi] the G; fynger] hande J.
6035 to] om. J; þe] om. J, þi MO. 6036 Þou ... finger] and bot ȝif þou helpe
thy selfe to ryse J, reche me þy finger S. 6036-7 but ... þiself] it Serues of
nouȝt reche my thy hande J 6036 but if þou] and S. 6037 helpe] help (with
heelpe mar. G³) G; reise] rise (with Reise mar. G³) G; þanne] so S; my
fynger] I tuke hire J; I ... hire] my hande J. 6038 burdoun] finger S;
So ... I] om. J; strengthede] om. J, trenkeþed S; me and so] om. J.
6039 michel she halp] om. J; me] om. J, also S; to] om. J, all add. M;
olde] theues add. J, þat I saw bifore add. M; it] om. J; forthouhte] that I come
thare and add. J, þem gretely add. M; Eche] ilkane of thaym J, Ilkon M, everych
O. 6040 here¹] þe O. 6041 sithe¹] Seyne afterwarde J, sithen MO;
sithe²] efterwarde J, sithen MO; annoy] and grete anger add. J. 6042 I
trowe] I gabbed noȝt J; I² ... gabbe] I trowe J, For trewly it was to me grete disesse
and sorow so to be torment with swilk old mysshapyn · as I haue spoken of bifore
·And ȝit I am abasshid of þe remanentes · bot I will triste sadly in grace dieu and
also in þe awmner þat scho has tolde me of · þat is so bowntyuouse · and I wil also
haue mynde of my prayer · þat scho has taught me add. M. 6043 And] prec.
Capitulum lx mar. CG, capitulum vj rub. mar. M, om. M; me] with er. u.v. me
mar. C³; hy] om. M. 6044 place] (2nd a ins. G³); An eye] with oculum
mar. G³, apon that roche ther was J, onn hygh OS; upon ... was] ane eghe J,
opon þat roch was MO; þat] om. S; droppede] alway was droppande J, drepyd
O. 6045 of water] ins. mar. G³, om. MO; a kowuele] a koowele (with coouele
mar. G³) G, be nethe it J; þer was] byneþe S; binethe] a fatte J, it add. MO,
þer was S. 6046 þe²] ȝone J; kowuele] fatte J. 6047 þou] muste J,
þe O; mustest] þe J, myst MO; hele] heele (1st e ins. G³) G, helpe J.
6048 for] om. S; Seith] prec. Capitulum lxj mar. CG. 6049 whens ...
cometh] I pray the J; I preye yow] wheyne the water comys J; þilke] the
JMO. 6050 me] gretly add. J. 6051 vnderstonde] vuerst and J; to

me] þine eer O.   6051-2 þin ere] to me O, For *add*. S.   6052 Þilke] ʒone
JM, þe O;   seest] ʒonder J;   þeere] Sees J, *om*. O;   herte] (*2nd* e *ins*. G³);
þilke] thayme J, þo MO.   6053 hath] hafe JMO.   6054 his] thayre JM,
þe O;   errour] -s JMO;   roche] a roche JMO;   þee] (*1st* e *ins*. G³).
6055 it] him CS, *with* hym *mar*. G³;   I am] sumtyme O, þe harte of man compard
to a rock *mar*. O³.   6056 sumtime] taken J, I am O;   take] Sum tyme J.
6057 and] *om*. MO;   turne] *om*. MO;   to] *om*. JMO;   himself] *om*. MO;
shulde] beholde S;   biholde] shoulde S.   6058 hath] hade S;   hardshipe]
hardnesse J.   6059 harde] *om*. J;   weepe] faste *add*. J.   6060 A] and
JMO;   welle] well (*with* welle *mar*. G³) G, fulle JMO;   be for to] *om*. JMO;
it] *with* herte *mar*. G³, for *add*. S;   softe] sauf O.   6062 þis kowuele] I hafe
Sette J;   I ... set] this fatte J;   take] kepe J.   6063 I¹] For I J, þat MO.
6064 lost] for *add*. S;   make] of *add*. J;   þilke] þa JMO;   hath] er J, hurt
and *add*. M;   mayme] -d J.   6065 þe] -r M;   a] þe S;   cristeninge]
baptym;   with] Repentance & teares A second crystning *mar*. O³;   which] with
C, Dame *add*. J, *om*. S.   6066 lye] lowt M;   bowkynge] nota de Maria
magdalena *et* de *sanc*to Pe{tro} *rub*. *mar*. M;   baþed] (*2nd* a *ins*. G³).
6067 þe Magdeleyne] Sum tyme J, Magdaleyen MO;   sumtime] the mary mawde-
leyne and J.   6068 Marie] *om*. JMO;   also] *with* er. *mar*. C³;   manye]
monye (e *ins*. G³) G;   þat I] *om*. J.   6069 sey] (*final* e *subpuncted* G), *om*.
J;   nouht] *om*. J;   seid] *marked for gloss* G³, before *add*. J;   woldest] walde
JMO.   6070 þerinne] þou moste be waschyne J.   6071 þou ... wasshen]
(est *o*. *er*. *with* er. *mar*. C), þerin J, þe must be wasshyn M, þou muste OS;   It]
for it JM.   6072 place] (*2nd* a *ins*. G³) G.   6073 þere] that J.
6074 wel] quod Scho to J.   6076 Now] *prec*. Capitulum lxij *mar*. CG, Than
J;   I¹ ... yow] *om*. J;   þider] I wente J;   I wente] þedere J;   for] by J.
6077 hire] Grace dieu J;   vnder þe clowde] scho was hid J;   she was hid] vndere
a clowde J.   6078 come] (e *subpuncted* G);   þe kowuele] I Sawe J;   I sigh]
the fatte J.   6079 I] than *add*. J;   heer] heere (*1st* e *ins*. G³) G;   is] note
and passage marked O³.   6080 wherinne] Forto J, warme S;   I ... wasshe]
wasche me *with* J, Inne *add*. S;   wel] fulle JMO;   litel] þerwyþ for *add*. O;
of] a bath J, with M, *om*. O.   6080-1 a bath] off J.   6081 lowe] lowgh
MOS;   abeescede] stoupede *over* C³, a beescede (c *ins*., *and with* stoowpede *mar*.
G³) G, *om*. M, a baysched *ins*. *mar*. *after rub*. caret *also in text* O³, abasshed S;
a yerde] a ʒeerde (*final* e *ins*. G³) G, and tuke in to hir hand M.   6082 þat
...hand] (that *subpuncted* G, *om*. CS), a ʒeerde M;   take] (*2nd* a *ins*. G³), *om*.
M;   it] *ins*. M.   6082-3 I wot neuere] wate I nouʒt J, I wote nouʒt M, I note
O.   6083 I hadde not] *om*. J;   bifore] afore M;   whereof] wherfor MO;
abashed me] was gretly J, de virga Moyses *rub*. *mar*. M;   michel] a baiste J.
6084 thouhte] Supposed J;   þat] *ins*. *mar*. G³, *om*. JMO;   Moiseses] it was J,
Moyses MOS;   it were] moyses ʒerde J, his ʒeerd *add*. M.   6085 deserte]
and *add*. J;   hele] heele (*1st* e *ins*. G³) G, Slokene J.   6086 thrist] of the
childere *add*. J, thrifft S;   it was þat] *with* ʒerde *mar*. G³, trewly J;   treweliche]
the same it was J;   sigh] þat *add*. S.   6087 dede] grayth J, my *add*. O;
euident] euydence J;   þilke] that JMO;   yerde] ʒeerde (*final* e *ins*. G³) G;
she] he (*with* sche *mar*. G³) G.   6088 cowuele] fatte J.   6089 and ... cam]
om. J;   his] the J, hir MO.   6090 þou hast] *trs*. J;   6090-1 be wasshe]
twache the with J.   6091 þerinne¹] in J;   and] *om*. J, note *mar*. O³;   wasshe]
om. J;   þee] *om*. JS;   þerinne²] *om*. JM.   6092 a poynt] *om*. J;   it] *om*.
M;   þee¹] (*2nd* e *ins*. G³), warme J, *om*. S;   warm] to the J;   To þe cheekes]
Putte þe there in J, Vnto þe chekis M, to þi chekys O.   6092 put þee in] put

þee þerinne CS, putt the ther Inne (ther *ins. mar.* G³) G, to the chekes J. 6093 for] to J.   6094 withoute] *om.* M, (out *ins.* O³);   taryinge] *om.* M; in] to the Fatte *add.* J, me S;   bathed] (*2nd* a *ins.* G³).   6095 It ... me] (heeled *1st* e *ins.* G³ *in* G), I trow J;   I trowe] it hadde alle heled me J;   if] *om.* J; I hadde] *trs.* J.   6096 it] lange J;   but] *om.* MO.   6097 lerned] before *add.* J;   lych] liche (e *subpuncted*) G;   to] him *add.* S.   6098 made] (*2nd* e *ins.* G³);   bath] -es JMO;   nihtes] night S;   and] did *add.* S;   shedde] wette J.   6099 hem] his bedde J;   upon his bed] with thay*me* J;   Whan] *prec. Capitulum* lxiij *mar.* CG;   þus] comen oute J;   comen out] thus J. 6100 seide] *ins.* M;   me] vnto me J, to me M;   þou¹] quod scho *add.* J, þat *add.* MS;   so soone] hale J;   hool] so Sone J, helid M.   6100-1 into thornes] I putte the J.   6101 I ... þee] in the thornes J.   6102 haddest] has JMO; woldest] walde JMO.   6103 a ... water] myght nouȝt Suffy*re* a litille while J.   6103-4 of ... hele] a litelle wate*re* J.   6103 þou] note *mar.* O³;   þee] *ins. mar.* G³, *om.* O;   for] *om.* O;   þin] þe M.   6104 hele] heele (*1st* e *ins.* G³) G, helpe O;   þou ... while] of Swilke þou scholde be fayne for the hele J; mihtest] myght JMO.   6105 hegge] *-es* M, A hard matter to forake þe plesures of þis life & to pass þe hedge of repentance *mar.* O³.   6106 and¹] *om.* J;   and²] mare *add.* JMO.   6107 firste] furste (e *ins.* G³) G;   bathe] (*2nd* a *ins.* G³).   6108 Go] *om.* S;   wolt] and *add.* J.   6109 to¹] in J. 6110 not] *om.* M;   it] *with* worthy *mar.* G³, worthy JMO;   whan he] þat O; þe] a MO;   stour] skarmusshe S.   6111 eschawfed] chawfed CJMOS, eschaufe F;   þe¹] *om.* MO;   after] -wardes J;   þe²] *om.* JO.   6112 knight-lich] will do *add.* M, And *add.* O;   so] be J, do M;   doost] so JM;   be] more *add.* S.   6112-3 with ... wil] (thee *final* e *subpuncted* G³ *in* G), helpe þe J. 6113 I ... þee] with the bette*re* wille J, wole helpe þe O;   algates] neue*r*þeles J; at þis time] þou schalle J.   6113-4 þou shalt] see me namare J.   6114 no ... me] atte this tyme J;   I¹] will *add.* J;   go] and *add.* JM;   wole] shall O.   6115 wey] þat *add.* S.   6116 Whan] *prec. Capitulum* lxiv *mar.* CG; þat¹] *om.* J;   þus] hir*e* Say J, scho saide me MO;   she ... me] thus JMO; in ... wise] scho did J, in þis wyse S.   6117 she dide] on swilke wise J;   and] gretly *add.* J.   6118 þou] I JMO;   allas] to *add.* J;   side] way S. 6119 where] whider M;   shal] Schulde JM.   6119-22 I³ ... wey] *om.* S. 6120 I] am *add.* J;   God] goode J.   6121 me] fayth & hope, a happy help in tyme of need *mar.* O³;   and] I O.   6122 see] y see G;   is] my way J; my wey] es J.   6123 shinynge] Schyne and J.   6124 lighte] lithen J, lede O;   bi] *om.* JMO;   where] þat *add.* S;   oon] oo (l *over* G³) G, þe JMO. 6125 which] wheche (*2nd* e *subpuncted*) G, þat *add.* S;   haue²] has J;   had] in *add.* M.   6126 To] Vnto M;   holde] (*2nd* o *ins.* G³).   6127 me] not *add. ins.* O³;   lost] I am J;   I am] loste J;   So] *om.* J.   6128 preyede] made my pr*a*yere to þam*e* J;   I ... left] the hegge J, I left MO.   6128-9 þe hegge] I lefte J, þe hepe (*with* hedge *mar.* O³) O.   6129 gesse] gessynge J; go] to the right waye *add.* J.   6129-30 litel or nothing] I schulde fayle þer-of J.   6130 I¹ ... þerof] litille or nouȝt J;   To] Vnto M.   6131 ynowh] I thought J;   empechement] grete ympedymente J.   6132 how] he *add.* J, *om.* O; day] tyme S.   6133 a] *om.* J;   restinge] as nowe *add.* S.   6134 Heere ...book] *om.* GMO, Explicit Pars iij *rub.* J.   6135 Heere ... book] *om.* GO, Incipit Pars quarta *rub.* J, Incipit iiijᵃ *pars rub.* M, & begyn*n*e þe feorþe S. 6136 Now] *prec. Capitulum* j *mar.* CGMO (*rub.* M);   I wole] *trs.* J, I O;   yow] my *add.* S;   fond] (*final* e *subpuncted* G);   empechement] inpedimente JMO.   6137 I ... yow] Firste J, I will tell M;   withoute more] I wille telle

ʒowe J;   þat þat is] the J.   6138 to me] *om.* J;   and[1]] that *add.* J;
valeyes] valeis (*with* valeyes *mar.* G[3]) G;   in[2]] on J, *om.* M.   6139 disgisy]
om. J;   whiche] wheche (*2nd* e *subpuncted*) G.   6140 and] *change of scribe*
O;   anoye] disese J.   6141 to[1,2]] *om.* JM;   þilke] thaym J, þo MO;
Now] (N *decorated as for new paragraph, can.* G[3]).   6142 a[2]] grete *add.*
M.   6143 wherinne] whech S;   was[1]] our life in \this/ world a sea of many
miseryes *mar.* O[3] (this *in another hand*);   michel] drede *add.* CS, thynke *add.*
J, thynge M;   Tempested] trubled J.   6144 of[1]] with J;   grete] (*2nd* e *ins.*
G[3]), hude J, tempestys O;   tempestes] gret O;   of[2]] *om.* J;   wyind] wyndes
JM;   þer] (*final* e *subpuncted* G).   6145 þat] *om.* S;   al cloþed] Swamm
ther in J;   swommen þerinne] alle cledde J, *om.* S;   here] heere (*2nd* e
subpuncted) C.   6146 aboue] þe water *add.* J;   I sigh] no more MO;   no
more] na thynge else J, I see MO;   Ooþere] thare *add.* J;   upriht] vprightes
JO.   6146-7 of [2] ... wynges] & semed þay wolde haue flowne O.   6147 and
... flowe] (*2nd* a *ins.* G[3]), for some of þam had wengys O.   6148 ne hadde] nad
(*with* ne hadde *mar.* G[3]) G;   empeched] letted JMO.   6149 faste] (e *ins.*
G[3]);   bounden] bone O;   erbes] wedes J.   6150 þat] wheche S;   michel]
gretly J;   anoyed] nuyd J;   I sigh] ware J;   bended] blynded JO.
6151 ooþere] *om.* O;   ynowe] i nowe (e *ins.* G[3]) G;   which] wheche (*2nd* e *ins.*
G[3]) G.   6152 holde] held O;   as] *om.* JMO;   time] Her saw þe pilgryme
an horrible beste in þe see *add. rub.* M;   Whan] *prec.* Ca*pitulum* ij *mar.* CGM;
thinges] thing (*with* thynges *mar.* G[3]) G.   6153 afrayed] I was gretly J;   I
was] Affrayed J;   gretliche] *om.* J.   6154 thing] *om.* J;   is þis] may this
be J;   a] *om.* G;   see] (*2nd* e *subpuncted with* mare *mar.* G[3]) G, seght O.
6155 swich] *with* er. *mar.* C[3], suche (e *subpuncted*) G;   see] (*2nd* e *subpuncted*
G), a See J, syghtis O;   fish] *mark over and passage marked mar.* C;   thinketh]
thynke JMO.   6156 wel] *om.* J;   I muste] me buse owthere J, me must
MO.   6157-8 I muste] i moste (e *ins.* G[3]) G, else J, *om.* MO;   heere] (*2nd*
e *ins.* G[3]), abyde J;   abide] here J;   in] *om.* J;   putte me] be put O;
þerinne] in to the see J.   6158 am] be J;   dreynt] drou*n*ded onane J, drounyd
M, drownkyned O;   coste] coostes S;   go[2]] *om.* O.   6159 anoon] belyfe
J;   if] bot ʒif J;   ne] may J;   founde] fynde GJMOS (*with* fonde *mar.* G[3]);
who] Sum J;   þat] *om.* MOS;   yeue] ʒyue (*with* ʒeeue *mar.* G[3]), may giffe J,
shall gife MO, wolde gif S;   avyis] counsayle J.   6160 God] quod I *add.* J;
if] bot ʒif J;   I ne haue] I hafe J.   6161 þe] *ins. mar.* G[3];   to] by JMO.
6162 þere] theere (*1st* e *ins.* G[3]) G, I abade J, I þer M S, þat O;   I abide] thare
J, abode MS;   winne] I myght J;   mihte I] wynne J, *trs.* MO;   nouht]
nathynge J.   6163 lasse] I schulde wynne J;   I[2] ... winne] lesse J;   thouhte]
thowghte (e *ins.* G[3]) G, though J;   þat[2]] *om.* JMO.   6164 upon þe stronde]
I walde walke J, apon strond M;   I wode go] on the Sande J;   miht] myghte
(e *ins.* G[3]) G;   fynde] ouþer owþere *add.* J, *om.* O;   boot] bote (e *subpuncted*)
G.   6165 mihte] myghte (e *ins.* G[3]) G;   and go] *om.* J;   ouer] the See
add. J.   6166 withoute] (e *ins.* G[3]).   6167 al] *om.* JMO;   stronde] sande
J;   nouht] na J;   riht] fulle J, *om.* O.   6168 viage] iourne J;   O] The
deuill mente by this Beast, whoe goeth aboute seeking whom he may deuouer, fishing
in troubled waters *mar.* O[3];   sweete ... yow] a foule beste J, sweete folk þat blesseþe
yowe S.   6168-9 a ... beste] Swete folke blesses ʒowe it was so foule and So
horrible J.   6169 alle ... þat] wha So J, alle þat MO;   wel hadden] *trs.*
JMO.   6170 for] by O;   alle þe times] ay J, all þe tyme MO.   6171 þat]
when J;   þeron] þerof J;   Þilke] that JMO.   6173 speke] Spake to
JMO.   6174 peynted] it be J;   it be] paynted J, it by S;   heere] *om.* J,

hir S; who] *ins. mar. after rub. caret also in text* O³; þat³] so JM, *om.* S.
6175 it] *om.* MO; ooþerweyse] Othere wyse JMO; chevice] schewis O,
cherisshe S; me] *om.* J, yow O. 6176 Alweys] *prec.* Capi*tulum* iij *mar.* CG,
Alle waye JM, so myche O; so michel] all ways O; see] (*2nd e subpuncted*
G). 6177 lyne] -s J. 6178 hanged] hyngand JM; at] a boute J.
6179 a¹] of (*with* a *mar.* G³) G; a²] of O; nette] (*2nd e subpuncted* G), -s
O; had] *with er. mar.* C³; hanged] at his nekk *add. can.* M. 6180 see]
with mare *mar.* G³; anoon] he begane to blaw O. 6180-1 he² ... blowe] onone
O. 6181 to²] *om.* J; houpe] powpe J; to³] *om.* O; strecche] steke
J. 6182 redyinge] ryding S. 6183 abasht] I was gretly J; I was
gretliche] (itt *with* y *mar.* G³ *in* G), a baiste J. 6183-4 for ... be] *om.* O.
6183 wel] I Sawe J. 6184 taken] I Schulde be J; schulde I be] takene
J. 6185 do] a *add* O³; Schrewede ... fynde] I wende neu*er*e oute of this
place J; whider ... go] bot ʒif I hafe of thy grace J. 6186 I¹ ... place] (plaace
2nd a *ins.* G³ *in* G), schrewed way I fynd J. 6186-7 if ... Grace] withere So
Iga J. 6188 In] *prec.* Capi*tulum* iv *mar.* CG, I beying in S; poynt] Same
tyme J; come] *om.* JMO, an olde on S; an olde oon] on old O, come S;
rennynge] faste to mewarde *add.* J. 6189 bakward] bacwardes S; thwart-
ouer] ou*er*twerte J; and] *om.* MO. 6190 asqwynt] sqwynt G, as sche went
O; was²] *om.* J, þe diuell is þe faþer of blynd herisy · a stumbleing block to all
good intendments *mar.* O³. 6191 nygh] com*m* nere me J, me *add.* M, now
hidyr neghe O; Now] Come J; hider] -warde come S; she] and *add.* JS;
þee] (*1st* e *ins.* G³); And] *om.* J; who] whate JO. 6192 I shulde] *trs.*
OS. 6194 I hatte] my name is S; anoon] also so sone J, Heresy *rub. mar.*
M; I] *om.* J. 6195 come] and *add.* CS, to *add.* JMO; areste] þe *add.*
MO; pilgrimes] The world is father vnto pryd *mar.* O³. 6196 vnscrippe]
reue J; of] *om.* J; hate] and luffes nouʒt M; scrippe] the scrippe JMOS;
alle] (e *ins.* G³) 6197 thing] thynges MS; I¹] and that I J; it þee] the
J, *trs.* M; wel] right sone J; bineme] refe JMO. 6198 þyn] *o. er.* (*with*
þyne *er. mar. u.v.* C³) C, (*final* e *subpuncted* G); tobreke] rife it in Sundir J,
breke it MO. 6199 my] *om.* O; biholdinge] sight JMO; poynt] trewe
add. J; writen] wreten (*with* wryten *mar.* G³) G, wryttyng O. 6200 þou
...cursede] quod I Ĵ, In holde þe (*n can.*) O; quod I] þow alde cursed caytiff for
J. 6201 aright] right JMO; lokest] bukis O, The flesh father to our wilfull
affections, as *mar.* O³; ariht] right JMO. 6202 thwartinge] a twartynge
G, ou*er*thwertande J; be hool] (*final* e *subpuncted* G), be euyn J, bihold M, be
loking S; lookinge] aright S; Me reccheth] I rekke J, me reche O.
6203 wel] for J; wole] wote MS; þat²] *om.* J. 6204 and] alle *add.* J.
6205 bacward] with *add.* J, -s S; heeles] before *add.* J; and²] *om.* M; sewe]
folwys JM, se O. 6206 not²] *om.* JMO. 6207 hauen] hafe bene JO;
Brent] Be brent M; I shal be] So schalle I be J, I shall M. 6208 into] to
J, in MO; fyir] fuyre (e *subpuncted*) G; þis] thus J. 6209 heere] *om.*
J; al] forto be J; for] *om.* J; fyir] fuyre (e *subpuncted*) G; sooth] now
J; now] the Soth J, *om.* MS. 6210 olde] ane *add.* J; madest] gerte J;
Templeres] no*ta* de Templarii{s} *et* de Augustine d{ ... } *rub. mar.* M.
6211 soothliche] for soth J; shuldest] schalte JMO; also wite] *trs.* J.
6212 þilke] scho JMO; ayens] a gayne JMO; Augustyn] Seynt austyne J.
6213 pilgryme] S*t* Augustyn did maintaine his fayþ *mar.* O³; mihte] myghte (e
ins. G³) G; bineme] refe JM. 6214 him¹] and so *add.* J; my] mekill
J; shame] schaame (*1st* a *ins.* G³) G, shaame (p *alt. 2nd* a) S; departede] partyd
M. 6215 A] Amikylle J. 6216 assailest þou] assaylest G; þou²] *om.*

O.   6217 be] *ins.* O³;   he] she S;   certeyn] Forsothe J;   but] *om.* S.
6218 þat¹] *om.* J;   sithe] Sen*e* JMO;   þat²] *om.* MO;   þee²] me thynk *add.*
J.   6219 to] towarde J, no *add.* S;   manward] man J, -s S.   6220 Alle]
that J, þou MO, ne *add.* S;   hauen] haaue (*1st a ins.* G³) G, has JMO;   I] For
I J;   sithe] sith (*with* syththe *mar.* G³) G, Seyn JMO;   founde] mette with fulle
J, fundyd O.   6221 þat] whilke J;   hem] thayres J;   of] *om.* J.
6222 Hider] Co*m*m J;   now] nowe heder*e* and J;   quod she] *om.* J;   withoute]
mare *add.* J.   6223 certeyn] quod I J;   quod I] certaynly J.   6224 swich]
Sum J;   þer was] *om.* J;   þat¹] *om.* JMO;   agast] ryght ferde J, ferde MO;
þat²] *om.* MO.   6225 binome] refte JM, restyd O;   þe] my MO;   or] other
G, and J;   broken] refen*e* J.   6226 þerof] of it O;   Neuerþeles] natheles
G;   bleynte] blenked JMO;   smoot] I Samte JMO.   6227 made] (*2nd a*
ins. G³);   place] (*2nd a ins.* G³);   þanne] dame *add.* S.   6228 þat¹] *om.*
JMO;   doon] i doon G;   hadde²] so *add.* S.   6229 me¹] So *add.* J.
6230 me] Her gr*a*ce dieu techis þe pilgr*i*me of diu*e*rse folk þat wer in þe see ꞉ *and*
of þe foule beeste *add. rub.* M, Howe þat þe pilgryme thankeþe Gracedieux of þe
coumfort þat she did and shewed him *add.* S;   Ladi] *prec.* Ca*p*itulum v *mar.* CG,
prec. ca*p*itulum iij *rub. mar.* M, Ca*p*itulum se{cundum} *mar.* S.   6231 of] *om.*
JMO;   be] *om.* JMO;   þat² ... me] ȝoure beheste J, þat · þat ȝhe hight MO;
and²] þat ȝe have *add.* J.   6232 counforten] comforthed JM;   in þis hour]
onane J.   6232-3 if ye hadden] had ȝe J.   6233 þilke] that JMO.
6234 me¹] o. er. O;   see] (*2nd e subpuncted with* mare *mar.* G³) G;   hadde]
om. J, also S;   also] hade S;   maad] (*1st a ins.* G³);   al] *om.* O.   6235 if]
bot ȝif J;   of ... tauht] ȝe teche me J, of you it ne be thaght O.   6237 þese]
þier MO, suche S;   mown] quod scho J, wele *add.* M;   quod she] may J;
wel] I nowe *add.* J, *om.* S.   6238 þee¹] ȝowe J;   seyn] telle J;   þee²] alle
add. J.   6239 þese] þier MO.   6240 Now] *prec.* Ca*p*itulum vi *mar.* CG,
om. J;   I] *with* pilgr*i*m *mar. under rub.* G³, quod I · I O;   telle yow] *om.* J;
þat¹] þan J.   6241 hadde] has O;   stended] stented C, extended J, lent S;
him] his J.   6242 passeden] we passed JM;   it euere] *trs.* JMO;   durste]
(e *ins.* G³).   6242-3 were ... litel] for grace dieu J.   6243 for ... Dieu] ware
it neu*e*r so litille J;   whiche] for J;   he] the J;   dredde] that he had of hir*e*
add. J;   After] By J.   6243-4 þe see] (*3rd e subpuncted with* mare *mar.* G³),
the coste of J.   6244 costynge] the See J;   Grace Dieu] come O;   com]
grace dyeu O;   to] with JMO.   6246 þat] *om.* J, þen MO, but þat S;   þer]
om. J;   ne is] with owten J, is MO;   torment] tu*r*mentes JO, tou*r*mentynge
M;   for] *om.* S;   Veynglorie] when glori O, *om.* S;   whiche bloweth] *om.*
S.   6247 þerinne] *om.* S;   beligh] belwes J;   Orguill] *with* pride *mar.* G³,
pride JM.   6248 agoo] gane J;   eye] þe eye CS;   see] se (*with* mare *mar.*
G³) G.   6249 aboue] vpwarde J.   6250 þilke] þa JMO;   þat²] þat þat
(*1st* þat *can.*) C;   þe¹] *om.* JMO.   6251 couenable] to bere *add.* J;   see]
se (*with* mare *mar.* G³) G, the See JMS;   þe] *om.* J.   6252 it¹] It *add.* JO;
þilke] þa*i*m J, þo MO;   maketh] gers J;   him] þam JMO.   6253 he] thay
J.   6254 forto] vn to CS, tille J, for MO;   ley] ly MO;   al¹] the Sekke J;
al²] *om.* JM.   6255 upriht] -is JM;   wite wel] thowe schalte vyndyrstande J,
wyt ȝe wele O.   6256 oonliche] þer sustenaunce O.   6256-7 here sustena-
unce] onely O.   6257 hauen] (*2nd a ins.* G³);   here trist] alle anely J, treste
O;   in God] tryste J;   al oonliche] in godde J.   6258 see] se (*with* mare
mar. G³) G.   6259 see] for *add.* J.   6259-60 in ... place] þey schulde hafe
it J, -s S.   6260 þei ... it] (*2nd a ins.* G³), in other*e* place J, þei shuld haue it
MO;   gon] has J.   6261 upriht] vpritȝ JM;   Þe] thar J.   6262 lich]

tille *add.* J, *ins. mar. after rub. caret also in text (misplaced after* a) O;   þat
Ortigometra] *om.* J.   6263 I clepe] *om.* J, is called MO;   for] *om.* J;   he]
she O;   shulde] schalle J;   see] (*2nd* e *subpuncted with* mare *mar.* G³).
6263-4 ane ... him] (see *2nd* e *subpuncted with* mare *mar.* G³), *om.* J.
6264 swimmynge] slying O.   6265 strecccheth] strikes (g *alt.* k) J, strengthes
M, strenght O;   wynge] -es on brede J, -es MO;   maketh] (*2nd* a *ins.* G³);
þerof] of tham J.   6266 soo] *om.* J;   mowe] be redy forto *add.* J.
6267 þe] *om.* O;   see] se (*with* mare *mar.* G³) G, *om.* O, in þe heyre *add.* S;
Right] ryche O;   of] þay J, þo MO;   þilke] of JMO;   whiche] *mark mar.*
O³, þat *add.* S.   6268 speke to] telle J, speke MO;   see] se (*with* mare *mar.*
G³) G;   for] by JS.   6269 here] hertes & payre *add.* J;   elleswhere] thay
haue J, werher O;   þei haue] (*2nd* a *ins.* G³), else whare J.   6270 Of] *prec.*
Cap*itulum* vij *mar.* CG;   þat] *ins.* O³;   bi þi feet] er bounde J, by þe foote
M;   ben bounden] by the fete J;   þe²] *om.* O.   6271 erbes] wedes of þe
see J;   wite wel] þou schalte wit J, wyt ȝe wele O;   it] *om.* M.   6272 affec-
ciouns] affeccioun S;   ydel] in oþer S.   6273 better] the *add.* J, þe seculer
neddis & *add.* O.   6274 children] vse *add.* J;   mariages] mariage JMO.
6275 wounden] bunde JMO;   bi¹] þe *add.* J;   bi²] the *add.* J, *om.* M;   How
... flee] I wate neu*e*re J.   6275-6 I wot neuere] howe ȝe schulde flye J, I not
S.   6276 þei] that J;   haue] has J;   to¹] at J;   to²] hy*m* J, for to S.
6277 Of] *prec.* Cap*itulum* viij *mar.* CG;   han ... eyen] er J;   as] *o. er.* G, *ins.*
O³.   6278 wite wel] þow schalle wit that J, witt ȝe wele O;   kyn] -de CS,
þer kynne J;   and] *o. er.* (*with er. mar.* C³) C;   in²] *om.* O.   6279 thing]
thynges þat JMO;   withoute] And *add.* CS, and *add. ins. mar.* G³;   Albeit]
þat *add.* S;   world] warld (r *ins.* O³) O.   6280 blyndfelled] the foles J;
þei ... hem] makes þay*m*e J.   6280 þe fooles] blyndfelde J.   6281 a] *om.*
CS;   fairnesse] þat *add.* J;   it] *with* wordle *mar.* G³;   Salomon] (lo *ins.*
O);   sumtime] *mark over with passage marked* C³;   6282 þat] *om.* M;
veyn] veingne (*2nd* e *subpuncted*) G, vanite J;   þe²] *om.* MS.   6283 þei haue]
om. J;   bended] *om.* J, bounde MO;   hem] *om.* J;   þat] *o. er.* (*with er. mar.*
under rubrication C³) C, *om.* J;   þat ... and] *om.* J;   blynded] *om.* J, blyndfeld
M.   6284 hem] *om.* J;   Eyen] þay hafe J;   þei haue] eghn*e* J;   which]
wheche (*2nd* e *ins.* G³). G.   6285 þat²] *om.* M, & O.   6286 þou] in O.
6287 nothing] Sey the J, no more M;   sey þee more] sey thee namore G, na more
J, say þe O.   6288 anything] hire J;   heere] any thynge J, *om.* O.
6289 on] in J.   6290 withoute] more *add.* CGS, *om.* M;   lesinge] leesynge
(*1st* e *ins.* G³) G, *om.* M;   Þilke] That JMO;   Sathan] -as JMO.
6290-1 dooth ... entente] besies hy*m* in alle that he may J.   6291 haue] no*ta*
de Sathan{*as*} *rub. mar.* M;   alle] (e *ins.* G³);   þilke] þa JMO;   see] se (*with*
mare *mar.* G³) G;   bi] thurgh J.   6292 bi] *om.* J;   hookinge] hookynge
(*1st* o *ins.* G³) G;   lyne] -s J;   with²] *om.* O.   6293 temptacioun] -s CJOS,
temptation F;   to] the *add.* J.   6294 oon] j *over* G³;   him] no waye
vnatemtpted to catch þe wandering sowle (*2nd* t *can.*) *mar.* O³.   6295 and¹]
om. JMO;   draweth] (*2nd* a *ins.* G³) G.   6296 for he] he J, forhe for he (forhe
can.) M.   6297 for þat] *trs.* S;   þe¹] *om.* J;   ees] eyeghes S;   of] þe *add.*
S.   6298 temptacioun] -s OS;   taketh] (*2nd* a *ins.* G³).   6299 breide]
om. J;   to²] *om.* MO.   6300 feþeren] *vertues over* C³, *with* vertues *and* vertues
mar. G³;   fleeinge] fleeting S.   6301 haven] (*2nd* a *ins.* G³) G;   wynges]
(wy *o. er. with er. mar.* C³), *with* vertues *mar.* G³;   and] stinted hie nette *add.*
S.   6302 stended] stented C, *om.* J, steddyd O, tight S.   6303 þei] þow
J;   ne] and JMO;   for ... him] *om.* JMO.   6304 thinketh ... þe] *om.*

JMO;   see] se (*with* mare *mar*. G³) G, *om*. JMO;   hunte] -r also J, -r MO.
6305 stended] stented C, extended J, stedyd O, tented S;   bifore] in J.
6307 þat he ne] that ne he J, þen he MO;   arresteth] arested thaim J, þem *add*.
MO;   or] other GJMO.   6308 or] other G;   neuere] hym O;   yrayne]
(yne *o. er. with er. mar*. C³), neuer O;   made] (*2nd* a *ins*. G³).   6309 snares]
snare O;   for] *om*. O;   þe] *om*. JMO;   flyes] *om*. O;   ne þat] *om*. S;
sette] did J.   6310 þis] þat O;   bisyeth him] duse J;   bynde] the *add*.
J.   6311 werpeth] wrappis M;   breideth hem and] *om*. JMO.   6312 ster-
cheth] strekes J, strecchis MS, strenghtes O.   6314 certeyn] Sekerly J;   þat
he] *om*. J.   6315 hadde] *om*. J;   strenges] strengthes C.   6316 cop-
webbes] erayne thredes J, arayn webbis MO.   6317 flyght] wight S;   gret]
God strength \us/ to resist the temptation of the deuill *mar*. O³;   þat þer] *trs*.
marked for reversal O.   6318 him] *with* sathan *mar*. G³;   ne] but S;
withholden] haldene JMO;   bondes] bandes JO, handes M.   6319 feeble]
bebille J.   6320 I sey] *trs*. J;   þee] *om*. J;   nouht] this *add*. J;   þat þou]
þat ne þou J, þen MO;   riht ... wysliche] kepe þe J.   6320-1 ne ... þee] ryght
bysily and wisely J.   6321 hath] had J;   a thowsand] *with* M¹ *mar*. G³;
artes] and gynnes *add*. J, craftes M.   6322 and¹] 3a J;   thowsand¹] *with* M¹
mar. G³.   6323 fauce] faux (*with* fals *mar*. G³) G.   6324 dissimuleth]
faynes JMO;   he] *ins*. O;   briht] gude J;   not] for *add*. S.   6325 þee]
(*1st* e *ins*. G³);   heremite] armet O.   6326 appeerede] apeered (*1st* e *ins*.
G³) G;   with] Beholde þe { ... } *mar*. S;   fauce] faux (*with* fals *mar*. G³) G;
a good] *om*. J.   6327 messanger ... a] *om*. J;   Þe deeuel] he J;   seide] speeke
S;   to] vnto MO.   6328 heremite] *om*. O;   þus] on þis wyse J, *om*. S;
quod he] *om*. S;   war] þat *add*. J.   6329 supprised] Suppressed J;   þee]
(*1st* e *ins*. G³);   tomorwe] (to- *ins*. O), to morne JMO;   and] he *add*. J.
6330 þee] that J;   hindre] himdre C.   6331 first] faste JS;   On] Vpon
JM;   morwe] morne JMO;   his] *with* ermyte *mar*. G³;   com] coome (*2nd*
o *ins*. G³) G;   to him] *o. er*. (*with er. mar*. C³) C.   6332 him¹] for *add*. J;
sone] when *add*. J;   him⁴] *om*. M.   6333 ded] Loo how *add*. J;   Subtil-
liche] Sodeynlich S;   Sathan] -as JMO;   but] alle *add*. J.   6334 late] (*2nd*
a *ins*. G³);   apperceyued] persayfed JMO;   þee] (*1st* e *ins*. G³);   leeue] (*2nd*
e *ins*. G³), loue S.   6335 settinges] settyng M, sekynges O, lettinges S;   from²]
om. S;   þilke] he JMO.   6336 what] wham JMO.   6337 take] *om*. JMO,
kacche S;   and] *om*. JMO;   many] monye (e *ins*. G³) G;   wises] wise
JMO.   6338 and¹] *om*. O;   maneres] maneeres (*1st* e *ins*. G³) G, *om*. O;
many sheep] mankynde J, manhede MO.   6339 fro þe brest] the hede fra the
body J;   strangled] worowed M.   6340 not] plese the J;   plese þee]
nothynge J;   anoyeth] nuys J.   6341 I ... shortliche] I passe schortly JM,
þat I were þe noght O;   þat ... nouht] for I passe shortly O.   6341-2 to ...
þerof] *om*. O, Howe þat þe pilgryme seghe a wounderful wounndir *add*. S.
6343 As] *prec*. Capitulum ix *mar*. CG, *prec*. capitulum iv *rub*. *mar*. M, Capitulum
te{rtium} *mar*. S, þat dame *add*. S;   spak] þus *add*. S.   6343-4 þat ... bal]
(bare a *subpuncted* G), nyse she semyd O.   6344 Nice she seemede] þe whech
bar a ball O, Nicelich she shewed hir boþe S.   6345 as] *om*. O;   dowve] *with*
columba *and* doowue *mar*. G³;   To] Vnto M;   wolde speke] Spake J;   hire]
om. J, vnto hir M.   6346 Damisele] *mark over with passage marked mar*. C³,
quod I *add*. J;   thinketh] thynke JMO;   þat] rit3 *add*. J.   6347 If] *em*.
ed., yis CGJMOS;   wost] wate JMO;   whereof²] þou seruest yis quod she þowe
woost wher of *add. dittography* S.   6348 serue] and *add*. J;   manere] -s J;
not] Speke J, nowdir MO;   speke] nowþere J.   6349 agast] þowe schulde be

J, ferde MO; of me] fered J; þou ... be[1]] of me J; be ye] beoþe S; gentel] creature *add*. J, damysell *add*. M. 6350 which] of whilke J; made of you] made J; mihte] na man liffande J; no man livinge] myght J. 6351 yow[1]] *om*. J; of] *om*. J. 6352 but þat] ʒif J; it] *om*. M. 6353 wikkede] euylle J; doinge] doyinges J; hatte] am namede M, had quod she *marked mar*. O[3]. 6354 Jeonenesse] Jolyfnesse CS, *with* ʒowthe *can*. *and* ʒougthe *mar*. G[3], or ʒonghede *add*. J, youth to say in englissh *add*. M; þe lyghte] I am right light and nouʒt heuy M, Iunenesse i*d est* youth *rub*. *mar*. M; tumbistere] tembelere JMO; þe fonne] *om*. JMO. 6355 þe lepere] *ins*. *mar*. *after rub*. *caret also in text* O[3]; sette] -s JMO. 6355-6 I come] *ins*. *mar*. *after rub*. *caret also in text* O[3]; I flee] *om*. S. 6357 þe] *om*. CS; diches] dykes JM. 6358 joynpee] ioynepe J, Ioggipe O, Joynedpee S; caste] at *add*. J; þe[2]] *om*. J; ferþeste] ferreste JMO; abasshe] a baischt (*with* abaysche *mar*. G[3]) G. 6359 dych] dykes JM, dychys O; hegge] -s JM; wal] -les J. 6360 apples] fruytes S; in[1]] & O; gardynes] *with* yardes *mar*. O[3]; haue] parte *add*. J; am lopen] alopene J; in] to *add*. M; an] all (11 *subpuncted*) G, þe M. 6361 lightliche] *om*. JMO, anoon S; anoon] lightlich S; I] it S; am] is S; for nouht] *om*. O, þat I am þus *add*. S; on] in MO; þe] *om*. JO; feet] fote J. 6362 where I wole] *om*. O; hauen] haaue (*2nd a ins*. G[3]) G. 6363 wynges] as *add*. J; it] wele J; at] þe *add*. C, þyne *add*. S; eye] E O; bar] (*final e subpuncted* G). 6364 abouhte] bought JMO; To] Ou*er* M, oure O; gret] mekille J; lightnesse] (t *ins*. G), nota de Asael *rub*. *mar*. M. 6365 Oon] i *over* G[3], and J; þan] þat C; foure] *with* iiij *mar*. G[3]. 6366 er þis] *om*. JMO; Holicherche] hase JMO; hath] *om*. G, haly kyrke JMO. 6367 þat] wher O; were] be J. 6368 ne] he J; hadde] hafe J; go with] stable hy*m* J. 6369 footed] (*2nd o ins*. G[3]). 6370 staf] *om*. O; me lakketh] to me langes J; cholle] iape J; and] *ins*. O[3]; to[2]] forto MOS. 6371 croce] crooke S; I hadde] *with* s*cilicet* croce *mar*. G[3], had hadde (had *can*.) M. 6372 for my feet] *om*. J; not] be leyde in ne *add*. S; stiringe] striringe C, strythyng O. 6373 ne ne] ne CJM, *om*. O, þey S, ne ne F; wolden not] *om*. O; haue] hadde J; not] neu*er* J. 6374 boules] and *add*. JM, ballys & O; to bigile] *om*. JM, wyle O; to[3]] go *add*. M; pleye] at þe kayles at þe dalyes at þe dees *add*. S; merelles] merelle J, morelles \&/ at þe sticke S. 6375 to] and J; heere] (*2nd e ins*. G[3]); seeche] her O. 6376 disport] -is OS; bal] halle J. 6377 or] other G; in] *om*. S; euere[2]] oþer S. 6378 I[3]] & O; pleye] me *add*. O. 6379 I] and S; thouht] thing O; but] for *add*. O; and] to *add*. J; my[2]] me O. 6380 quod I] of any thing CSG; of anything] more CS, q*u*od y G, of nathynge J; more] quod I CS, elles J; þou] Schalle J. 6381 shalt] þou J. 6381-2 quod ... þee] *om*. S; bi ... see] *with* mare *mar*. G[3], bere the J. 6382 bere þee] by the See J. 6382-4 Shal ... þee] *om*. CGS. 6382 Shal ye] *trs*. O; me] me quod I Damyselle J. 6382-3 seyd ... I] sayde J. 6383 speke] spak O. 6384 Yit] ne O; oþer] or JMO. 6385 soone] Mors *mar*. O[3]; þilke] that JM, it O; þat] I J; shal] shuld M; do] parte J; þe[1,2]] thy JMO. 6386 men clepe] *o*. *er*. *with er*. *mar*. C[3], men calle JMO; Mors] *with* deth *mar*. G[3]; quod I] es mors J; is Mors] *marked for gloss* G[3], quod I J. 6387 quod she] wit J; wite] elde *mar*. G[3], quod scho J; Vilesse] else JMO, vylenesse S; þat] than JMO. 6388 bicomen] come J; in] to J; þee] Sone *add*. J; Vilesse] elde JMO (*with* age *mar*. O[3]), vylenesse S. 6389 dwelleth] dwelle J; In] when J; time] comes *add*. J, coming *add*. S. 6390 not] *o*. *er*. C. 6391 hand] For *add*. J; bi þe see]

with mare *mar.* G³, bere the J;   I² ... þee] by See J;   þere] where JMO.
6392 ne slepe] slepe no3t J;   or] other G, ne JMOS.   6393 And] *prec.*
Capitulum x *mar.* CG, *prec. capitulum* v *rub. mar.* M.   6394 sette me] me in
hir neke O;   in ... nekke] she sete O;   sithe] Syne JMO;   to] *om.* JMO.
6395 flee] (*2nd e ins.* G³), flyght JMO;   þe see] *with* mare *mar.* G³;   nouht]
ne sekyre *add.* J.   6396 þat] *om.* M.   6398 foolisshe] folye (e *ins. with*
foolesche *mar.* G³) G, *om.* JMO;   manere] maners J;   and¹] *om.* MS;   and²]
om. S.   6399 periles] perill O;   made] garte J;   feele] (*2nd e ins.* G³), fly
O.   6400 witen] wate JM.   6401 thre] iij *over* G³;   shewe] scheewe (*2nd*
e *ins.* G³) G;   it] 3owe J;   þou] all J.   6402 more] to passe J;   ooþer]
an ooþer CGS (an *ins. mar.* G³);   eende] thynges J.   6403 Cirtes] *prec.*
Capitulum xj *mar.* CG;   propre wil] *om.* J;   þat] *om.* J, þer O;   as] *om.* JMO,
. haþe S;   sond] a sond CJMOS;   assembled] that es gadered to gedire and J,
and *add.* S;   maketh] (*2nd a ins.* G³), in þe see O;   an hil] makis O.   6404 in
þe see] *with* mare *mar.* G³, a hill O;   whiche] the whilke J;   muste] nedes *add.*
J.   6405 stintinge] and breke thare and it betakens propyre wille *add.* J;   If]
For 3if J;   I] 3e J;   sigh] sey (*with* sygh *mar.* G³) G, owthere *add.* JM, outhir
add. O (u *ins.* O³);   man] men J, a man O;   or] other G;   womman] wommen
J;   gaderede] gaders JM;   hepede] hepes JM, kepe O.   6406 willes] to
gydere *add.* J, wyll OS;   to¹] ouer J;   þat] *om.* J;   kepte] kepes JM;   to²]
om. G;   ooþere] wille *add.* J;   I] 3e J, *om.* MO.   6407 wolde] may J;
þus] *om.* J;   grauel] (*2nd a subpuncted* G).   6408 þe¹] þat O;   see] *with*
mare *mar.* G³;   bouched] bouged JO, benched S;   binemeth] lettes J, takes
M.   6409 þe weye] away M;   þe see] *with* mare *mar.* G³.   6410 þee]
3owe JS;   from] þere J;   him] fra J, it MO;   He] For it J, it MO;   dredful]
paryllouse S.   6411 Caribdis] *prec. Capitulum* xij *mar.* CG;   þe¹] *om.* O;
wysdom] knawynge JM, *om.* O;   and] *om.* MO;   þe²] *om.* JM;   kunnynge]
om. M.   6412 seculere] seculere O;   alle] mark *over with passage marked*
mar. C³;   swiche] *om.* JMO.   6413 alday¹] alway J;   turnen] toournen (*2nd*
o *subpuncted*) G;   alday²] all M, alweyes S;   alwey²] and S.   6414 comen]
subpuncting with illegible gloss mar. all erased G³;   ayen] agaynes J;   holden]
all thinges in þe world haue þer change · and all is vanitie *mar.* O³;   hem] *om.*
O.   6415 sercelich] serclelich C;   firste] begynnynge J.   6416 no] ne
(*with* na *mar.* G³) G, *om.* J;   þe] a J, a round M.   6417 dureth] lastes J;
water] or wynde *add.* S;   of Salamon] 3e be thynke 3owe J.   6417-8 ye ...
yow] how Salamoun Sayde J, 3e be thynk O.   6418 how¹] *om.* J;   he¹] *om.*
J, it S;   souhte ... alle] *om.* J.   6419 and how] *om.* J;   it] ilke J, ild a M,
Iche O;   veyn] veyngn (*with* idell *mar.* G³) G;   and²] *om.* S;   torment]
toourment (*2nd* o *subpuncted with* tourmente *mar.* G³) G.   6420 and¹] *om.*
J;   ensaumple] ensawmpleis O.   6421 þe²] *om.* O;   a¹] *om.* J;   wrong]
strange J.   6423 In] *prec. Capitulum* xxij *mar.* CG, Of J, *om.* MO;   Bitalasso]
Bythalassum J, batalasso OS;   but] *om.* JMO, beoþe S.   6424 noon] now
O, howe S;   is seid] betokyns J;   aduersitee] and *add.* J;   Bitalassus]
batalassus O, Batalasso S;   It] they JMO;   sleyhtes] the Sleightes JM, þe flyghtes
O;   whiche] wheche (*2nd e ins.* G³) G;   wheel] whele (*2nd e subpuncted*) G;
turne] to turne JMO.   6426 it¹] to *add.* JM, at *add.* O;   it²] to *add.* J;
doun] adowne S.   6427 peynted] depeynted S;   ye] prosperitie & aduersiti
spokes in þe wheele of fortune · one tuurning vp · and þe other downe *mar.* O³;
it²] itt itt G;   wel] I nowe þerfore *add.* J.   6429 goth] *om.* S;   him] *with*
aduersitee *mar.* G³;   he] *om.* S.   6430 see] *with* mare *mar.* G³, tempested
and *add.* S;   possed] passyd O;   abayinge] by and J;   upon] on JMO.

6431 murmuringe] gnaystande J; of] on M; doinges] doynge JMO; It] *with* aduersite *mar.* G³. 6432 many] *om.* J; dreden] dreeden (*2nd* e *ins.* G³) G; þerinne] in O. 6433 ooþer] prosperite *over* C³, *with* properite *mar.* G³; drede] dreede (*2nd* e *ins.* G³) G; whoso] he so (*with* {h}o *mar.* G³) G. 6434 cleyey] ful of cley *o. er.* C, *om.* JMO, ful cleyee S, argilleus F; and²] *om.* JMO; and³] of J; glewy] (e *ins.* G³), glue JMO; is] *om.* JO, it is M. 6435 þilke] *with* prosperite *mar. under rub.* G³, *om.* JMO; richesse] riches JMO; of²] or M; of³] *om.* J; of⁴] *om.* J. 6436 fairnesse] so *add.* CS, so *add. ins.* G³; þat¹] *ins. mar.* G³; þilke] he JMO; ne is] es nouȝt JMO. 6437 bi it] þare by J; Sirena] *prec.* Cap*itulum* xiv *mar.* CG; þe which] whilk M, *with ins. mar. after rub. caret also in text* O³; with] þe weche O; hire] *om.* JMO. 6439 to] þe S; joenenesse] jolyfnesse CS, *with* ȝowt *can. and* ȝougthe *mar.* G³, ȝougthe JMO; me²] Cyrena worldly solace *mar.* O³; ofteste] ofte JMO. 6440 þat] *om.* JMO. 6442 Now] *prec.* Cap*itulum* xv *mar.* CG, cap*itulum* vj *rub. mar.* M, *om.* J; I ... yow] *om.* J, I will tell yow M; a ... while] borne thus J, right a grete while M, a grette while O; born þus] a grete while J. 6443 oon] 1 *over* G³; rood] on *add.* J; wawes] wayse O; see] *with* mare *mar.* G³. 6444 skin] barme Skynne J; hire] the ta J. 6445 and] in the tothere *add.* J; peire] of *add.* JMO; wich] wheche (*2nd* e *ins.* G³) G. 6446 me] and threete me *add.* J; harde] (e *ins.* G³), faste J, as I herd M, *om.* S; fro fer] o ferrum J, for fere O, from a fer S. 6447 doun] adoune S; þou mustest] the buse J, þe must MO; to] atte J, forto M. 6448 see] (*2nd* e *subpuncted with* mare *mar.* G³); ooþere] folk *add.* O. 6449 name] (*2nd* a *ins.* G³). 6450 I] þow alde tratte *add.* J; hattest] hate JMO. 6451 þat] and CGS, qui F; to] *om.* JMO. 6452 skin] barme skynne quod Scho J; tonges] hamer M. 6453 hamer] tongis M; been] es J. 6454 faileth] lakkes J; an anevelte] a stythy JM. 6455 wel] wo O; is it] *trs.* C, es JMO; bifalle] þe O; þee] bestillyn O; haue¹·²] (*2nd* a *ins.* G³); if²] *om.* J; oon¹·²] *with* aneveld *mar.* G³. 6456 þeron] þer wythe O; hast] haue JMO; it²] *with* aneveld *mar.* G³, *om.* JMO. 6457 not] nane JM; euele welcomed] þou schalle be J; shalt þou be] (schalte e *subpuncted*, thow *ins. mar.* G³), euylle welcomed J; anoon] and that right Sone J; Mi] þat my O; strook] strakes J. 6458 idel] vayne · For owþere J; upon þee] *om.* CS; or] *om.* CS, other G; þe] a JMO; anevelte] stythy JM; it] they J. 6459 And] *prec.* Cap*itulum* xvj *mar.* CG; þat] þe lady *add.* S; 6459-60 in hire hous] had giffene me J. 6460 hadde ... me] in hire hous J; anevelte] stethy JM. 6461 bithouhte] vmbethouȝt J; to laate] it was J; it was] to late J; I hadde it] it was J; on] vpo me J. 6462 he] it S; cometh] comme J; arme] harme S; him] me S; first] *ins. mar.* G³, *om.* JMO, frost S; is] *o. er.* (*with* is *u.v. mar.* C³) C³; into] þe *add.* MO. 6463 tournement] torment CS, tournoi F. 6464 tauht it] tasted S; seide] talde J. 6465 goldsmithesse] golde smyth JMO; forgeresse] forgier M, forgereres O. 6466 make] (*2nd* a *ins.* G³), -s JMO; forge] -s JMO. 6468 a] hate *add.* J, *om.* M; of] *om.* O. · 6469 Oon] on (*with* j *mar.* G³) G; with þe tonges] I take it J; I take it] with the tanges J, I taake S. 6470 platte it] penes it oute J; and¹] I O; it²] in plate *add.* J; and²] *om.* JMOS; anooþer] tyme *add.* J; hepe it] beet it to gedire agayne J, hepe M; þe] a J. 6471 with ... it] *om.* J; I²] *om.* O. 6471-3 make ... scriptures] *ins. mar. after rub. caret also in text* O³. 6472 wikkede] euylle JO; make] (*2nd* a *ins.* G³), mad O; cleped] called JMO. 6473 scriptures] scriptour O; approoved] comprovyde O; My] Tribulacio · et persecucio *rub.*

mar. M; Persecucioun] es called J; is seid] per*se*cuciou*n* J. 6474 oon]
on (*with* j *mar.* G³) G; smite] *mark over and passage marked mar.* C³; hem]
hym (*with* hem *mar.* G³) G; time] with *add.* M. 6475 a strok] strakes I
gyffe tha*i*m J; þe ... hath] þay hafe nou3t on J, þe pourpoynt & þe anueld wych
memori has O. 6475-6 he ... on] (haue *o. er. in* C *with er. mar.* C³), (*2nd a
ins.* G³), the pu*r*poynte whilke memory beres J, he haue notte a poynte O.
6476 he is] thay er*e* J, but *add.* S; it] I S. 6477 þilke] *om.* J, þo MO;
of] that er contended in J. 6477-8 þat ... litel] (itt *with* kalender *mar.* G³), *om.*
O. 6478 þei] þou O; ne hadden] had nou3t J, ne had O.
6479 anevelte] stethy JM; riht] dewe (*o. er. with er. mar.* C³) CS; grete] (*2nd
e ins.* G³). 6480 smot] gafe J; delay] Howe trybulacioun tolde here to þe
pilgryme what hir tanges signefyen *add.* S. 6481 My] *prec.* {Cap*itulum* xvij}
mar. CG, *prec.* {Cap*itulum*} quartum *mar.* S; þe²] *om.* J; anguishe]
anguyesse3 J. 6482 presseth] the *add.* J; troubel] -ed JMO; it¹] *om.*
O; thinketh] thynke that J, þat *add.* S. 6483 with] in JMO; loken] *om.*
J; as drestes] *om.* JMO, as destes S; defouled] fulled oft J. 6483-4 of
which] wher of CS, *with* wher of *mar.* G³. 6484 haue] (*2nd a ins.*
G³); wel] fulle JMO; þat] *om.* CS, *subpuncted* G; bi] es JM, *om.* O;
þe] a J, *om.* MO. 6484-5 teres ... messangere] *crosses over in* G (*with* G³'s
version of the passage at foot of p.). 6484 teres] it CG³S, the teres G.
6485 descend] -eth CG³S; a] thurgh J; pressinge] presserage of teres CG³,
presserage of þe teeris S; which] þat CG³S; of þe sorwe] ere messangers J;
is messangere] of the grete sorowe J, is messagier S. 6486 The] *prec.* Cap*itulum*
xviij *mar.* CG, She (*with* the *and* T mars G³) G; barm-fell] barmclathe JMO;
I clepe] es JMO; Hountee] *with* schaame *mar.* G³, schame JMO.
6487 acloyed] anuyd J, clooþed S; beten] him *add.* CG. 6488 and] with
J; hamered] him *add.* CGS, ha*m*mere J; rihtfulliche] rightwisly J; or]
other G; wrongfulliche] wrangwysely J. 6489 or] other G; on] in
JMO; þe²] *ins.* O³. 6490 his] þe O; bi] thurgh J; shame] schaame
(*1st* a *ins.* G³) G. 6491 .....] uacat CS, *space* (vacat *over* G³) G,
Skynne JMO; and] I O; skin] schame JMO. 6492 þilke] *with* that ibete
mar. G³, he JMO; knoweth] *o. er.* G; I am] with t*ri*bulacioun *mar.* G³;
þat] *om.* J; doo annoye] nuy J, anoye MO. 6493-5 men ... doinges] *om.*
O. 6493 him] his J; is] cometh CS (*o. er.* C), at JM; my] *o. er.* C.
6494 confusioun] he has J; he hath] confusioun J; shame] schaame (*2nd a ins.*
G³) G; sette] leet S. 6495 doinges] doynge M; make] (*2nd a ins.* G³);
barm-fell] barmskynne J; þerof] *with* skyne *mar.* G³. 6496 shame] schaame
(*2nd a ins.* G³) G; þe] A JMOS. 6497 of] on J. 6498 make] (*2nd a
ins.* G³); barm-fell] barmskynne J. 6499 þe¹,²] *om.* J; upon] *om.* O.
6500 þee] *om.* J; oþer] or elles J, or JM; sowne] soone MO; hye] by O.
6501 is] nis S; men] murmur *mar.* O³; it ... thing] *om.* J. 6502 I wot]
om. J; it] *om.* JS; wel I] *om.* J; haue] (*2nd a ins.* G³), *om.* J; assayed
it] *om.* J; to] *om.* G. 6503 to] *om.* G; he] sche G; me²] (*2nd e ins.*
G³). 6505 I] þat *add.* S; if ... sooth] and thy Powere J. 6506 also
þi power] that I may See whedere þou Say Soth or nou3t J, and þi power MO;
no] *ins. mar.* G³, *om.* JMO 6507 if I ne] bot 3if I J; it¹] *om.* S; and]
ne S. 6509 seide] vnto *add.* J, to *add.* M; þee] (*1st* e *ins.* G³); nouht]
quod scho *add.* J. 6510 anooþer¹] co*m*mission *add.* J, *om.* MO; of anooþer]
om. MO; yit] *om.* JMO. 6511 afterward] here afte*r* M, efter O; Þilke]
Quod I J, þat MO; quod I] that J; I wole haue] wille I See J; also] than,
add. J. 6512 sigh] loked J; boþe] Reade þis Commission *mar.* O³ *and in*

another hand Commyssioun of (*illegible*) O³; of whiche] þe tenour of J; firste] furste (e *ins.* G³) G; was writen] wrot G, was J. 6512-3 in þis manere] this J, on þis maner O. 6514 Adonay] *prec.* Cap*itulum* ix *mar.* CG; iustice] rightwysnes J; which] p*ri*ma commissio *rub. mar.* M; þe¹] *om.* J; þe²] hye *add.* O; eclips] clipse JO. 6515 emperour] þe f{irst comy}ssyone { ... } *mar.* S³; rewme] kyngedom M; dureth] lastes J. 6516 Greetinges] gretyng MO; Tribulacioun] -s S; ouhten] awe J; sende] to *add.* J. 6517 Of] Nowe of J; stepdame] stepmodere J. 6518 in] on S; kingdom] kyndom (*with* kyngdom *mar.* G³) G. 6519 hoodes] (*2nd* o *ins.* G³); þe] thye J; visages] visage MO. 6520 armures] armour J; binome] reste JO, reft M; and²] thayre *add.* J. 6521 withoute] with M; abidinge] *o. er.* (*with er. mar.* C³) C; with] the *add.* J. 6522 she] he (*with* schee *mar.* G³) G, it JMO; uoided] avoided M, a voyde it O; þe] *om.* JMO. 6523 I] we C, (*with* wee *mar.* G³). 6523-4 my ... Paradys] G³'*s version of this passage at foot of p.* 6523 my] oure CS; sette sum time] hadden bifore þis time put CG³S. 6524 where] wher thoruh CG³S, *om.* G; we ... castelles] *om.* G; in which] þer as CG³S, *om.* G; we²] *om.* G; hadden] many *add.* CS, noon *add.* G³, *om.* G. 6525 goode vesselles] *om.* G; wherinne] in whiche CG³MO (*scilicet* kastelles *over* G³), where G, in þe which S; fulfillinge] fillinge CG³S. 6526 of þe] in S; grete] grace O; tresores] tresour G, *om.* JMO, tresorieres S; 6527 þe] oure S; oynture] enoyentur M; is] a *add.* C; tresour] *om.* O. 6528 siluer] or *add.* J; or] other G, precious *add.* J; oure macier] oure mootiere CS, oure matiere G, þou erte J; þou art] oure mascere J. 6529 and¹] in O; sergeauntesse] Sergeaunt JMO; þee¹] (*1st* e *ins.* G³); comitte] to *add.* J. 6530 seeche] after *add.* M; Prosperitee] *ins. mar.* O; þat²] *om.* O. 6531 hire¹,²] hym GJMO, la F; þat²] and S; she] he GJMO. 6532 ne rebelle] *om.* O, and rebelle S. 6533 committe] to *add.* J; afterward] þou ga J, affterwardes S; þou hurtle] efterwarde hurtille J; þilke] þay J, þo M, þe O; so cruelliche] *om.* J. 6534 þat¹] þey *add.* S; hauen] haue S. 6535 blyndfelled] and bete tham So cruelly *add.* J; þat²] *ins.* G³. 6535 so] *om.* O; to þe] *mark over and passage marked mar.* C³, tille J. 6537 ne] and S; ne] *om.* J; bended] benden (*with* bended *mar.* G³) G, *om.* J, blyndid MO. 6538 armure] armores M; mailes] þat *add.* M. 6539 tobroken] brokene JMO; soone] Syne JM. 6540 hem¹] to *add.* J; haue made] make J. 6541 goldsmithesse] goldsmyth JMO; Afterward] efterwardes J; sende þee] wille J; in] to *add.* J. 6542 and¹] *om.* J; holde] *om.* J, hande O; alle¹](e *ins.* G³); disportes] disporters J; solaces] solace O; alle²] *om.* M. 6544 þat¹] *om.* JM; þat²] *om.* O. 6545 yiven] ȝeeue (*with* ȝyue *mar.* G³) G; þee] (*1st* e *ins.* G³). 6546 vesselles] vessell J. 6549 þis] thus JMO; yiven] ȝeeue (*with* ȝyue *mar.* G³) G; þee] (*1st* e *ins.* G³). 6550 alle] bathe *add.* J; grete] (*2nd* e *ins.* G³); smale] (*2nd* a *ins.* G³); þee] (*1st* e *ins.* G³). 6551 obeisaunt] obedient MO; ayenseyinge] agayne Standynge J, any gayne sayynges O; maad] (*2nd* a *ins., final* e *subpuncted* G³), in *add.* J. 6552 Adam] (*final* e *ins.* G³). 6553 ye ... heere] (heere *2nd* e *ins.* G³ *in* G), Schalle ȝe hiere J, wyche was note syche O, { ... } of þat oþer {comysy}oun *mar.* S; if ye wole] *o. er.* C, ȝiff ȝee wulle (*3rd* e *ins.* G³) G, *om.* JMO. 6553-4 which ... swich] (which is not *o. er.* C), off whilk the tenour es nouȝt Swilke J, ȝe schall here O. 6555 Sathan] *prec.* Cap*itulum* xx *mar.* CG, -as J; see] *with* mare *mar.* G³. 6556 kyng] secunda commissio *rub. mar.* M, Commyssion de *mar.* O³ *and in another hand* The commission of Sathan. reade. *mar.* O³; iniquitee] *with* w{i}ckydnesse *mar.* G³;

persecutour] *with* ? folewere *mar*. G³, Pursuere J, persecusion O;   equitee] *with*
? honeste *mar*. G³.   6557 suich] suche (e *subpuncted*) G;   mown] nowe
J.   6558 of] *om*. O;   neewe] now O;   thinketh] thynke JMO.
6559 pryded] proude JMO, pricked S.   6560 resceyued] agayne *add*. JMO;
to] and restored to J;   place] (*2nd* a *ins*. G³);   from which] whilke J, frome
þe which S;   we ben fallen] we er fallene fra J;   and] þat *add*. JMO.
6561 eche] ilkane JM;   hauen] (*2nd* a *ins*. G³);   taken] taake (*1st* a *ins*. G³)
G, hym *add*. J.   6562 seyinge] *om*. JS;   viage] make *add*. J.   6563 comaun-
dinge] commaundes the J, comaundes O;   þider] þou ga J.   6563-4 þou go]
thedere J.   6565 þilke] tha JMO;   þat] *om*. O;   clymbe] clene O;   of
heres] as þou may fynde J.   6565-6 as ... fynde] of thayres J.   6567 Bineme]
Refe J, Take fro M.   6568 to¹] in to JMO;   þe¹] thayre J.   6569 to] *om*.
J;   here²] *om*. MO.   6570 as] did *add*. J;   of] the *add*. J;   hemself] (*final*
e *subpuncted* G);   hise] thyse JO.   6571 þilke] þe JM, þat O.   6572 of]
the *add*. J;   maade] (*1st* a *ins*. G³);   stye] to steigh JO;   heuene] Her smytes
Tribulacion þe pilgrime · and youth gose hir way *add*. *rub*. M.   6573 Whan]
prec. Capitulum xxj *mar*. CG, *prec*. capitulum vij *rub*. *mar*. M;   þese com-
missiouns] I had Sene and redde diligently J, I þier commissions M, þer commiscioun
O, þees two Comissyouns S;   I ... red] þire commyssions J, hadd diligently redd
and M, & *add*. O.   6573-4 seyne and herd] *om*. J.   6574 foolded] folode
O;   and¹] & and (& *subpuncted*) G;   hem²] to hire *add*. CS, hir þam J;
þanne] *om*. J.   6575 I¹] *om*. J;   seide] vnto *add*. J;   þee] ȝowe J;   now]
om. M;   if þou] *o. er*. O.   6576 of¹] thaim J;   of²] whedere J;   wheþer]
of þaim J.   6577 nouht] bathe *add*. J;   triacle] venym J;   venym] treacle
J.   6578 Whan] quod Scho J;   I shal] whenn J;   quod she] y schalle J;
and] I O.   6579 of whiche] whedere J, whilk M;   þe tweyne] thaim J, þier
two M, two O.   6580 sey] (*final* e *subpuncted* G), ȝelde J;   ne] and (*with*
ne *mar*. G³) G, nat JO;   sowne] soune *alt*. sounde M;   no] ne na J;   in
yildinge] ȝeldes the J;   thankinge] -s S.   6581 miht] may J;   wite] say
JMO;   of] on J;   sooth] Sothfastnes J;   I] am *add*. M;   þe] (*2nd* e
subpuncted G).   6582 with] *om*. JOS;   of] and J.   6583 vnscrippinge]
vnscrippe CGJS.   6584 þee] (*1st* e *ins*. G³);   castinge] caste J;   dide]
theophille J.   6585 Theophile] did J;   þou miht] may þou J, -est S;   þe]
thyne JM, *om*. O.   6586 holt] es lange JM, long O;   of which] whedere
J.   6587 al] *ins*. *mar*. O;   in] the *add*. J;   men] man O.   6588 þe¹]
ins. O;   dunge] doynge (*with* donge *mar*. G³) G;   softeth] the *add*. JMO;
wex] way O.   6589 of me] I maye Say J;   I may sey] of me J;   þat²] þat
add. C, *om*. JM.   6591 Now] kepe the J;   keep þee] (*3rd* e *ins*. G³), nowe
J, keepe yowe S;   me] For *add*. J.   6592 me] my hende J, *om*. O;   I ne]
ne I muste J;   Anoon] *prec*. Capitulum xxij *mar*. CG, *prec*. {Cap}*itulum* quintum
mar. S;   so] Sayde J;   seyd] this wordes J.   6593 and¹ ... hire] *om*. J;
couenaunt] *om*. J, conand O;   and smot me] *om*. J;   þat] So that J.
6594 see] *with* mare *mar*. G³;   she] ȝougthe *mar*. G³;   Joenenesse] jolyfnesse
CS, ȝouthhede J, þat is to say youth *add*. M.   6595 flygh] fledde J;   Ne
hadde] had nouȝt J.   6596 dreynt] drowned J, dronkenyd MO;   To it] *with*
bourdoun *mar*. G³, I helde me J;   I ... me] þereto J;   for] *om*. J;   swimme]
ne *add*. S.   6597 I miht] y myghte (e *ins*. G³] G, wele O;   wel] I myghte
O;   haue] a O;   it] *om*. JS;   ne hadde] had nouȝt be J.   6598 to] *mark*
over with passage marked *mar*. C³;   aslewthed it] slawe J, a flewd it O.
6599 certeyn] certaynly J;   strauhten] strecch MO.   6600 poore] putte
S.   6601 ooþere] happye are þei þat haue learned to Swime in þer yeouth, that

þei sincke not in þer age · \not/ lyke þem þat neuer did good all þir lyfe long, yet presumes on þir saluation at þe last gaspe þrough fayth. etc. but blessed are þei þat haue both, þat liue in good workes, & dye in good fayth mar. (and foot p.) O³. 6602 viages] viage MO;   pilgrimages] pilgrymage MO.   6603 is] was J; þilke] þe JMO;   see] with mare mar. G³.   6604 soo] om. J.   6605 wente] (2nd e ins. G³).   6607 in] and J;   presse] -d me J.   6608 thouhte] that add. J;   in] suche add. subpuncted G.   6609 for litel] alle maste J; burdoun] falle and add. J;   dounward] with add. J, to add. M, in add. O; see] ga add. JMO.   6611 in ... perile] I Sawe me J;   I sigh me] in swilk perille J;   preyede] cried;   to] om. J.   6613 my¹] ins. O;   and] om. O;   in²] om. JS;   haue] (2nd a ins. G³).   6614 bi] om. JMO;   Joenenesse] iolyfnesse CS, with 30ugthe mar. G³, schewed J, giffen to youth M;   my lyf] 30weuth J; vsed] ins. mar. G³, om. JM, lede O.   6615 and] om. CGS;   certeyn] om. CGS, Sothely J, certaynly O;   wel] om. CGS;   I auhte] om. CGS, me awhte J;   repent] om. CGS, to repente J, so for to do O.   6616 me¹] om. CGOS; þerof] om. O;   Joenenesse] iolyfnesse CS, 30ugth JM, marked mar. O³;   bifore] be fore (2nd e subpuncted) G.   6617 sotte] fule JMO;   condyed] conuayde J.   6618 hire] with 30ugthe mar. G³, 30ughehede J, to add. S;   she] om. O.   6619 I am] trs. JM;   is it] om. J, trs. MO.   6620 southliche] om. J, sutelly O;   misbifalle me] per\s/ched J;   If] bot 3if J;   þou] with god mar. G³;   redy] redily J;   ne make] make J;   me²] refuyte J;   a refute] to me and Succoure me J.   6621 þi] þe J, þe alt. þy S;   to] vn to S;   of þe] om. M;   þou] om. J.   6622 seest ... peresshed] om. J;   me] ins. mar. G³, om. M.   6623 and¹] an add. subpuncted G;   restinge] place add. M; in] to M;   which] wheche (2nd e subpuncted) G;   showue] shew MO. 6624 of þee] I may nou3t make it J;   I ... it] of the J;   þe] om. O. 6625 leste] (2nd e ins. G³);   God] I be seke the add. J;   it] att add. ins. G³; þat] aboute add. CG³S (ins. mar. G³).   6626 it] 3it J;   was wont] trs. marked for reversal C;   me] om. CS, amen J, to me M, Her Tribulacion ledis þe pilgrym agayn to grace dieu add. rub. M.   6627 As] prec. Capitulum xxiij mar. CG, capitulum viij rub. mar. M;   made] (2nd a ins. G³), thus J;   þus] made J; herde] (2nd e ins. G³).   6628 me] to me JM, þat add. O;   sithe] Sene JMO;   leyd] (d ins. G³).   6629 to¹] om. M;   leede] (2nd e ins. G³); and ... me] om. JMO.   6630 riht] als lyght JMO;   þe] in þe tyme of tribulation, holde fast thy fayth, & call vppon the name of þe Lord. mar. and foot p. O³;   wynd] (e subpuncted G);   ledeth] beres J.   6631 and] om. M. 6632 into] to JMO;   skyes] clowdes J, sky O;   afterward] affterwardes S; hapneth him] trs. J;   to falle] om. J;   oþer] om. J, or MO.   6633 mishap- neth] om. J, hym add. MO;   he¹] hym J;   hath neede] nedes J.   6634 and¹] a add. JMO;   into] a add. M.   6635 place] (2nd a ins. G³);   þilke] scho JMO.   6636 þilke¹] swilke JMO;   craft] -es JMO;   þilke²] þa JMO. 6637 þilke¹,²] þa JMO;   to] om. M.   6638 forueyed] goon wrong M;   wey] the waye JMS.   6639 hadde founden] fande in JMO.   6640 drawe] (2nd a ins. G³);   pitee of] om. O.   6640-2 of² ... Tresmountayne] om. S. 6641 ooþere] or JMO;   leede] (2nd e ins. G³) þam add. J;   þe¹] his J. 6642 Summe] otheɾe add. JMO.   6644 lede] leede (2nd e ins. G³);   þilke] that JMO.   6645 alwey] þou hase JMO, alwayes S;   þou hast] alle waye JMO;   alle] (e ins. G³);   leede] (2nd e ins. G³), wille lede J.   6646 þee¹,²] (1st e ins. G³);   peyne] peygne (g ins. G³) G.   6647 As] prec. Capitulum xxiv mar. CG;   made] (2nd a ins. G³).   6648 nyh] nere J;   þe ryuaile] id est hauene over C, þaryvaylle S;   I²] om. O.   6649 sih] thare add. J;   þat] she *add. ins.* S; hire[2]] *om.* JMO. 6650 was] come J; nyh] nere J; Hider] hyre nowe J, Now MO; be] and *add.* J; Whens] When GJMO. 6651 I wende] þat *add.* M. 6652 longe] *om.* JMO; wel] Fulle JMO. 6653 take] (*2nd* a *ins.* G[3]); hardement] hardnesse J; saue] (*2nd* a *ins.* G[3]). 6654 þee] (*1st* e *ins.* G[3]). 6655 Whan] *prec.* Capitulum xxv *mar.* CG; sigh] þat *add.* M; argued] reproued J. 6656 hire] to hir M; soothliche] and *add.* J, sutely O; I ... yow] and folily J. 6657 and foliliche] I departed fra 3ow and J; I haue] (*2nd* a *ins.* G[3]), hafe A J, sythen M, *trs.* S; sithe] Seyne J, haue I M; abouht] bought JMO; algates] neuertheles J. 6658 confesse] graunte J; and] *om.* MO; biknowe] confesses J, *om.* MO; þat] *om.* MO; grete] (*2nd* e *ins.* G[3]); goldsmithesse] *with* tribulacioun *mar.* G[3], Smethiere the golde Smyth of heuene J, goldsmyth MO; led] brought M. 6660 me[1]] myne J; Driveth ... me[2]] I pray 3owe J; I prey yow] dryfe hire fra me J. 6661 cornere] rescues CS, *with* Rescous *mar.* G[3]; for] fra JMO; sufficeth] suffice MO; wel] and likes me *add.* J, *om.* S. 6662 sithe] Sene JMO; hath] *om.* J; turne] toourne (*2nd* o *subpuncted*) G; to yow] *om.* JMO; I] A *add.* J. 6663 hope] that *add.* JS; me] Her grace dieu tellis þe pilgrime þe way to þe cite · þat he desires to *add. rub.* M; In] *prec.* Capitulum xxvj *mar.* CG, *prec.* capitulum ix *rub. mar.* M, *marked mar.* C, And as I J; makinge] thus J; þus] made J; my] me J. 6664 goldsmithesse] goldesmyth JMO; hire[1]] *om.* J; bar] haþe S. 6665 not] nathynge J; sori] *om.* J; weryere] weeryore (*1st* e *ins.* G[3]) G, were þer O. 6667 me] to me JM. 6667-8 Now ... michel] *om.* JMO. 6667 riht] *om.* S. 6668 so] a mane S; man] so S; lyth euele] *om.* S; as] liche S; a] *ins.* G[3]. 6669 Þou hast] Alwey MO; alwey] quod scho *add.* J, þou has MO; wold] *om.* JMO; so michel] melled the JMO; medle þee] (*3rd* e *ins.* G[3]), in So mekille J; haddest] has J. 6670 reste] (*2nd* e *ins.* G[3]); feeld] flude J. 6671 left] (*final* e *ins.* G[3]); am] *om.* J; refute] (t *alt.* g O); Sorweful] Sary J. 6672 woldest[1,2]] walde JMO; flee] whethir & *add.* O. 6673 annoy] angere and disese J; I] *with* grace dieu *mar.* G[3]; þi shadewe] *om.* JM, ner þe & O. 6674 Wrecche ... now] *om.* JMO. 6675 þee] (*1st* e *ins.* G[3]); if þou ne] warne ne þou J. 6676 Certeyn] *om.* J; and] *ins.* O[3]; aryued þee] (*3rd* e *ins.* G[3]), brought the J, tyle a sherwed hauyn O. 6676-7 a ... hauene] tille a schrewed heuene J, areuyd þe O. 6677 shulde] happye man, whom grace doe comfort in tyme of tribulation *mar.* O[3]; haue] (*2nd* a *ins.* G[3]), a O; þilke] that JMO; þere] *om.* J. 6678 she] þou J; hath] has Sene J; longe] goon *add.* M; þat] Sene J. 6679 hise] nettes and his *add.* J; take] (*2nd* a *ins.* G[3]); with] folke J; þe folk] with J. 6680 and[1]] if M. 6681 yit be] *trs.* J; þee[2]] to the JM, þi O; a] *om.* O. 6682 lede] leede (*2nd* e *ins.* G[3]) G; riht] *om.* JMO; þer] whilke J, wher MO; menest] desyres J. 6683 woldest] walde JMO; it] to that *add.* J; to go] *om.* J. 6684 þe] þat M; wolde] wille J; wel] *om.* JO. 6685 withoute] (e *ins.* G[3]). 6686 þanne] thy J; equipollence] thare schulde J; þer ... be] equipollent J, (þer *ins.* O); Penitence] penaunce for J. 6687 maylettes] maliet J; places] (*2nd* a *ins.* G[3]), place O. 6688 effectuelliche] effectuously JMO; holde þee speche] Spake to the off J, hold þe spekyng MO. 6689 lasse and] *ins. mar.* G[3], *om.* JMO. 6690 to[2]] vn to S; þer] þat J, wher MO; woldest] walde JMO; so] and J; þerof] therfore J. 6691 þou[1] ... answere] telle me J; me] ane aunswere For J; herd] her to S, Howe þe pilgryme reioyseþe him miche of þe coumfortable wordes þat dame Gracedieux speek to him *add.* S; Whan] *prec.* Capitulum xxvij *mar.* CG; capitulum x *rub. mar.* M, Capitulum {vj}

mar. S, Þane S.   6692 þese woordes] I herde J;   I herde] thyse wordes J;
al] *om.* O;   fulfilled] and *add.* J.   6693 þe¹] þere J;   abbregginge] breg-
gynge MO.   6694 it] *om.* JMO, is *add.* S;   me¹] *om.* O;   of þat] because
J, for O, þat *add.* S;   she¹] *with u.v.* she *mar.* C³;   yit] *om.* M.
6695 wolde] sette to hand and *add.* S.   S;   a] *om.* MO.   6696 and¹] for
S;   recreaunt] reaunt O;   and²] sore *add.* S.   6697 shorte] *with* wey *mar.*
G³, waye *add.* JMOS;   I¹] wille J;   wole] wolde CS, I J;   gladliche go] *trs.*
S.   6698 sheweth] scheeweth (*1st* e *ins.* G³) G;   þouh] there of þowȝ J, þof
M, þer of O;   þer be] þer by O;   equipollence] equipollent J.   6700 In]
prec. Cap*itulum* xxviij *mar.* CG;   þilke] that JMO;   a ship] I Saw J, I stonding
seeghe S;   riht gret] (*final* e *subpuncted* G), A Schippe JS;   and wunderful]
right grete JS;   I sigh] and wondyrfulle JS.   6701 see] *marked for gloss* G³;
wel] (*2nd* e *subpuncted* G);   nygh] nere J;   arryuaile] riuale J;   al redy] and
redy JMO, *om.* S;   to] for to S;   make] (*2nd* a *ins.* G³).   6702 hoopes]
(*1st* o *ins.* G³);   al ... faste] *om.* J.   6703 fretted but] *om.* J;   summe ...
hoopes] *om.* JS;   weren] *om.* S;   slaked] waxoruer Slakk J, *om.* S;   for ...
of] *om.* S.   6704 oseres] ou\e⁄rseeres (*1st* e *ins.* O³) O, *om.* S;   to¹] *om.* J;
weren²] *om.* M, al *add.* S;   to²] *om.* JMO.   6705 þe¹] *om.* J;   þe hoopes]
faute was nouȝt in J;   hadden ... wrong] the hopes J.   6706 þilke] that
JMO.   6707 dwellinges] dwellynge places J;   and²] whilke J.   6708 wel]
to be *add.* J;   Þer weren] þat weren CGS, Il y avoit F;   and²] *om.* JOM.
6709 kernelles] kyrnell O;   aboue] aboute O.   6710 heeng] the Sayle J;
þe seyl] hange J;   ystreight whiche] *om.* JMO.   6711 ooþerweys] *om.* JMO,
in oþer langage S;   is cleped] *om.* JMO;   veyle] *om.* JMO, þe veyle S;   to]
for to S;   but] if CS (*o. er.* C), So J.   6712 Seest] *prec.* Cap*itulum* xxix *mar.*
CG;   þou] nowe *add.* JM, nowe þu O.   6713 þilke] that JMO;   þere] *om.*
JMO;   parde] pardey (e *ins.* G³) G, forsothe J.   6714 but] gretly *add.* J;
I am] abasshid MO;   abasht] I am MO;   neuere] are O;   erst] nane Swilke
J, afore M, neuer O;   noon swich] ar now J.   6715 quod she] Schalle þou
J;   þou shalt] quod scho J.   6716 þere] whare JMO;   þe] *om.* J.
6717 þerin] *o. er. with u.v.* yn *mar.* C;   Seith me] Lady q*uo*d I J;   now] *om.*
JS;   quod I] I pray ȝowe telle me J.   6718 hatteth] at O;   and¹] *om.*
MO;   it] *ins. mar.* G³, is *add. ins.* O³;   þerinne] er with Inne S.   6719 see]
mare *mar.* G³;   Þe ... bi] *o. er.* C;   his] *o. er.* C, hire JMO;   name] (*2nd*
a *ins.* G³).   6720 cleped] called JMO;   bounden ayen] *om.* JMO;   fretted]
fast *add.* S.   6721 obseruances] obseruaunce MO, nota q*uo*d nauis est dom*us*
religiones *rub. mar.* M, Religion, þe shipp betokens *mar.* O³;   is] *om.* G, *ins.*
O³.   6722 Bynde] b\r⁄yng (r *ins.* O³) O;   cleped] called religiou*n* J, called
MO.   6723 in] *om.* JMO;   ben bounden] bynde JM, b\r⁄yng (r *ins.* O³)
O;   ayen] *om.* S;   and] þe *add.* MOS;   soule] saules S.   6724 þilke]
þat J, hym MO;   þat] *om.* J;   grete] greete (*2nd* e *ins.* G³) G;   þe²] ȝe O.
6725 olde] hold O;   whiche] wheche (*2nd* e *ins.* G³) G;   religiows] Religioun*s*
(n *subpuncted*) G, religiou*n* JMO, religyons S;   þeron] on O.   6726 kept]
keptte (*2nd* t *ins.* e *subpuncted* G³) G;   wel²] *om.* M;   at here rihtes] *om.*
JMO.   6726-7 shulde ... faile] in natyme JMO.   6727 in no time] schulde
fayle JMO;   for] and *add.* JMO;   mihte] *mark over with passage marked*
C³.   6728 summe] some (e *ins.* G³) G;   smale] (*2nd* a *ins.* G³);   oseres]
estates or osieres S.   6728-9 þat bynden hem] *with* hopes *mar.* G³, *om.*
JMOS.   6729 þat] *om.* S;   þe] *om.* OS;   ship ... thing] *om.* S.
6730 þat ... nouht] *om.* S;   but] *om.* S;   if þe oseres] *om.* OS;   fastne] bynde
J, *om.* O;   hem] to gidders *add.* J, *om.* O.   6731 clepe] calle JMO;   smale]

sale S; whiche] wheche (*2nd* e *ins.* G³) G; restreynynge] restreyners S.
6732 grettere] grete JMO; seye] the *add.* JMO; who] So *add.* JMO; þat]
So J, *om.* MO. 6733 hem¹] *om.* J; or] oother G, and M; looseth] (*2nd*
o *ins.* G³), soweþe S; hem²] *om.* J. 6734 shulen] Solde JM, shuld O;
grete olde] greete olde (*2nd* e *ins. with* comaundemens *mar.* G³) G, obseruaunces
add. J, grett hold O; if] *with* er. *mar.* C³. 6735 summe] *om.* JMO; lighte]
litille JMO; comaundementes] Neglect of holly commandem*ents* · vynbyndes þe
frame of ou*r* religion *mar.* O³; wise] manere J, vyse O. 6736 smale] (*2nd*
a *ins.* G³); þe kyng] *om.* J; þat] þe *add.* MO. 6737 swich] suche (e
subpuncted) G; it] *ins.* G³, scho M, *om.* O; whan] atte the begynnynge JM,
þe begynnyng O; at þe biginnynge] when JMO; took] *om.* J.
6738 byndinge] byndynges JMO; noone] (*2nd* o *ins.* G³). 6739 smale] (*2nd*
a *ins.* G³); þe²] and J, *om.* M. 6740 þe ship] *om.* M. 6741 þe¹] *om.*
JMO; perilowse] in p*er*ile O; þe²] *om.* O; Nouht] note *mar.* O³.
6742 blame] (*2nd* a *ins.* G³); it ne¹] *with* religiou*n* *mar.* G³, and J, it and M;
dispreise] depraue J; ne ... it³] *om.* JMO; yit] þer ere JMO; þer ben] ʒit
JMO. 6743 of] *om.* J. 6744 hem] any *add.* S; oseres] osyere S;
it] *with* schypp *mar.* G³, this Schippe J; am I] *trs.* JMO. 6745 conduyeresse]
ledare JMO; mast] most O; which] that J, wit þat O; is] is is S.
6746 þe] *om.* JM; crossed] cressed J; amidde] y myddes JMO; me] (*2nd*
e *ins.* G³). 6747 it] *with* schyppe *mar.* G³; wynd] (*final* e *subpuncted* G);
Þe] this J; þe cros] the crosse (*2nd* e *subpuncted*) G, þer O. 6748 Gost]
with *add.* S; as] the *add.* J. 6749 Gildenemouth] Iohn with gilden mouth
M, John with þe gilden mouthe S; seith] we *add.* J, we *add.* J; mown] *om.*
J; to] gud *add.* J, þe *add.* O. 6749-50 into Jerusalem] þou wille ga J.
6750 hastliche] to Ier*us*alem J, þu wyll go O; þou ... go] hastily JO; þou²]
þe M; mustest] muste JMO; hider] thiddyre JMO. 6751 logge] the *add.*
J; oon] i *over* G³; Cliugni] elmgru S; or] *om.* CGS; of³] *om.* O;
Cistiaus] cristians S. 6751 or] other C; annoþer] any othir O; þidir]
with Jerusalem *mar.* G³. 6753 ben] þai *add.* O. 6754 þerinne] *om.*
JMO; boþe] *om.* O; enemy] entre CS; þere] to *add.* CS, *om.* JMO.
6755 or] other G; sheete] scheete (*1st* e *ins.* G³); if it ne] bot ʒif it J.
6757 bi] þi O, for to beo S; swymmynge] For *add.* JMO. 6757-8 þei ...
perile] þa that passes by Swym*m*ynge J, þei þat passe by swym*m*yng MO, *om.* S.
6758 þilke ... swymmynge] er i*n* p*er*il JMO, *om.* S; and] *om.* J; vnneþes]
vnneth M, vnes O. 6760 And] *prec.* Capitulum xxx *mar.* CG.
6761 castelles] castell MO. 6762 seide ... I¹] bade me J; wente] wende J,
me *add.* MO; where] to whilke of tha*i*m So J; al] *om.* J; my] awne *add.*
J. 6763 entre] to entre J. 6763-4 As ... anoon] And Onane atte the entre
I Fynde the · Portere J. 6763 As] and MO; I¹] *om.* MO. 6764 Þe
...entree] whilke bare in his hande a hevy mace J; fond] (*final* e *subpuncted*
G). 6764-5 which ... maace] And as Scho bade me I chose ane and to entre
I stirred me J. 6764 an] and S. 6766 þis] the J; led] ladde (a *sub-*
puncted e *over* G). 6767 if] and J; þat] *om.* JMO; it] were *add.* J.
6768 þee] (*1st* e *ins.* G³). 6769 þerinne] þere J. 6770 heere] (*1st* e *ins.*
G³). 6771 me] (*2nd* e *ins.* G³); if I ne] bot ʒif I J; king] ware *add.*
JO. 6772 me] (*2nd* e *ins.* G³); is¹] a *add.* M, þe *add.* S. 6773 Paradys]
dred of god þe porter *mar.* O³; cleped] called JMO; I] *ins. after rub. caret*
O. 6773-4 Paour de Dieu] id est drede of god *over* C, *with* drede of god *mar.*
G³, Drede of godd JMO. 6774 and] I *add.* J; biginnynge] Timor do*mini*
rub. mar. M. 6775 and¹] þe *add.* S; foundement] grounde J; of] alle

add. J;   I ... sinne] I heve out sinne C, (haaue *1st* a *ins*. G³ *in* G), also J, I hold owte synne MO, I hyre oute synne S;   also] I halde oute Synne J.   6776 þilke] this JMO;   ne] *om*. JMO;   him] *with* synne *mar*. G³.   6777 þis] his CS; to] Forto JMS;   herinne] there in JMO.   6778 myn] me CS;   maace] (*2nd* a *ins*. G³);   cleped] called JM.   6779 Þe¹,²] *om*. JMO;   Gryselichhede] gryselynesse J.   6780 auhten] me aght J;   haue] (*2nd* a *ins*. G³), to hafe JM;   drede] dreede (*2nd* e *ins*. G³) G, þarwith *add*. J;   and¹] I O;   and chastice] the folke J, *om*. M;   þe folk] and chastise þaim J.   6781 þat] *om*. G;   eche] men J, ilkon M, I S.   6782 preyse ... litel] sette litille by me J. 6783 Shalt] if þis mace ware not, ech wight would sett little by me *mar*. O³;   Ye] I wysse *add*. J;   he] and *add*. J.   6784 þou shalt] Schulde þou J, þou shuld MO;   þanne] (e *ins*. G³).   6785 biholde] be hoolde (*1st* o *ins*. G³) G, þe lady *add*. S;   seide hire] tille hire I Sayde J, saide to hir M;   þus] on this wyse J. 6786 lady] quod I *add*. J;   thinketh] thynke JMO;   þe entre] *om*. S;   so] *om*. J;   abaundoned] esefulle J.   6787 And ... she] *om*. O;   answerde] me *add*. CS, ansswerede (*3rd* e *ins*. G³) G, *om*. O;   and seide] *om*. O, me S;   me] on this wise J, *om*. O, and sayde S;   þou] *ins*. *mar*. G³.   6788 foryete] quod Scho *add*. J;   fynde] it *add*. MO.   6789 equipollence] equipollente J;   Stroke] *ins*. *mar*. ? C³, þe strooke S;   of²] þe *add*. *ins*. (*with er. mar*. C³) ? C³, the *add*. JMOS.   6790 is] nys S;   not] *ins*. O³;   smite] *mark over with passage marked mar*. C³;   þee] (*1st* e *ins*. G³);   þat þou ne] but þat þou CS, þen þou MO.   6791 mown] *om*. JMO;   not] yit *add*. S.   6792 þe maace] *om*. J, of *add*. O;   oweth] awht JM, aght he O;   wel] for *add*. S;   colee] the mace J, *om*. MO.   6793 into] the *add*. J, a *add*. MO;   stour] scarmusshe S;   or] other G;   haue] (*2nd* a *ins*. G³);   of] or J;   Is it] *trs*. (*with* is it *mar*. G³) GJMO.   6794 Ye ... And] *om*. JMO;   þerinne] *om*. JMO.   6795 quod I] *om*. JMO;   þat] *om*. J, at O;   I² ... first] *om*. J; Goth bifore] entre ȝe furste and J.   6796 sewe] folow M, se O;   anoon] in aftere ȝow J;   after yow] onane J, Howe þat Gracedieux in coumfortyng þe pilgryme entred first in to þe Castel · & þe pilgrime affter *add*. S;   Thanne] *prec*. Cap*itulum* xxxj *mar*. CG, Cap*itulum* {vij} *mar*. S.   6797 was] so *add*. S;   nygh] nere J.   6798 Swich] suche (e *subpuncted*) G;   made] maade (e *subpuncted*) G, gerte J;   doun] he *add*. CJOS.   6799 gronded] felled J;   ne hadde] had nouȝt J;   be] y bee G;   Alle] the *add*. J.   6800 hauen] haaue (*2nd* a *ins*. G³) G, resyfes J;   swerdes] the ordere J;   resceyuen] has J, receyued MO; colees] buffettes J.   6801 it were] and profit JMO;   and profyte] it ware JMO.   6802 Now] *prec*. Cap*itulum* xxxij *mar*. CG;   was] *om*. M;   forth] (*2nd* o *ins*. G³).   6803 haue] (*2nd* a *ins*. G³), are J, *om*. O;   nempned] spoken of M.   6804 whiche] wheche (*2nd* e *ins*. G³) G, the whilke J;   thouhte] thowghte (e *ins*. G³) G;   faire] (e *ins*. G³);   Þer] Clere JMO;   cloystre] dortour JMO.   6805 dortour] clostere JMO;   chirche] and *add*. MO;   I sigh] also JMO;   also] ane ostry J, ostry MO.   6806 ostelrye] ostrye G, I Sawe JMO;   oon] i *over* G³;   fermerye] afermery JO, þe firmary M, by þat oþer *add*. S;   To] Vnto M, I went S.   6806-7 þe ostelrye] the ostry JMO, to S.   6807 I wente] Charitee *mar*. O³, þe hostellerye S;   at] *om*. J, by S; þe] *om*. JO;   firste] furste (e *ins*. G³) G;   þere] And *add*. M.   6808 þat] and C;   serued] *om*. JMO, herberowed S;   and] *om*. JMO;   herberwede] serued S;   þe] *om*. J.   6809 yate] ȝaate (*1st* a *ins*. G³) G;   to²] for to M;   feede] (*1st* e *ins*. G³) G;   folk] þat *add*. CS, that *add*. *ins*. *mar*. G³;   haue] (*2nd* a *ins*. G³).   6810 spoke] talde J to *add*. MS;   of] bifore of M;   heerbifore] heere be fore (*1st* e *ins*. G³) G, hire M, here a fore S;   scripture] testament J;

of²] the *add.* J. 6811 yaf] spak (*with* ʒaff *mar.* G³) G; departede] delte J; releef] relesse J; Foorth] (*2nd* o *ins.* G³), Seyn I passed J, for S. 6811-2 I passede Forth J. 6812 and¹] *om.* J; to] in to JM. 6813 fond] (*final* e *subpuncted* G); whiche] wheche (*2nd* e *ins.* G³) G; wot] knawe J; þe names] (*2nd* a *ins.* G³), alle J. 6814 of alle] the names J; for] *om.* J; mo] me O; of ... herte] I asked Grace dieu the names J; þat] it O; at] to MO. 6815 and ... most] of tha that Sate me maste tille herte J; I² ... Grace] and of whilke I woundred maste J; names] (*2nd* a *ins.* G³), of alle for with outen mo of hem þat siten deere to me I asked þe names *add. dittography* S; of²] dame *add.* S; Grace] dieu *add.* MOS. 6816 Tweyne] Twa JMO; degrees] grece JMO; dortour] dortoour (*3rd* o *subpuncted*) G. 6817 togideres] to gidere JO; oon] j *over* G³; hadde] on *add.* J; gambisoun] *with* garnement *mar.* G³, was at þe grees *add.* S. 6818 Pilke] Scho JMO; þere] *om.* JO; she] *om.* JMO. 6819 cloþes] S· chathes J; saue] of *add.* CS, of *add. ins. mar.* G³. 6820 ooþer] (*2nd* o *ins.* G³). 6821 glooued] (*2nd* o *ins.* G³); with glooues] (*2nd* o *ins.* G³), *om.* JMO; and²] *om.* J; rochet] white J; riht] *om.* MO; whyt] rochet JMO. 6822 arayed] nobilly J; wel nobleliche] arrayed J, full nobly M, full noble O; Tweyne] Twa JMO; togideres] to gedir O. 6823 go] towarde the chapetre JO; toward þe chapitre] thay wente JO; of] the *add.* J; þat] þat *add.* S; oon] i *over* G³. 6824 fyle] wele *add.* J; steled] stiked C, stiking S; bitwixe] be tweene GJMOS. 6825 targe] -t J; Anooþer] *prec.* Cap*itulum* xxxiij *mar.* CG. 6826 croumed] muled J. 6827 and þer] *om.* O; sewede] folowed JM, *om.* O; hire a whyt] *om.* O; culuer] doufe JM, *om.* O; in þe eyr] fleande J, *om.* O. 6828 fleeinge] in the ayre J, *om.* O; after] *om.* O; hire] *om.* MO; Anooþer] *prec.* Cap*itulum* xxxiv *mar.* CG; yit] *om.* JMO; go] -ing S. 6829 toward] -es S; it ... me] me thought J, me semyd M. 6830 hire] þe CS; Anooþer] *prec.* Cap*itulum* xxxv *mar.* CG. 6831 hadde] *om.* S; streiht] strenght O; for] *om.* JMO. 6832 skyes] cloudes J; an awgere] a wymble J, it O. 6833 I ... michel] me thoght grete ferly J; serued] *o. er. with er. mar.* C. 6834 dede] *o. er. with er. mar.* C, deede (*1st* e *ins.* G³); þat¹] whilke J; þat²] *om.* JMO. 6835 seruice] that *add.* J; made] (*2nd* a *ins.* G³); hem] to *add.* J; bicome] whilke as it semed *add.* J; onlyue] a lyue G, qwikke JMO; Anooþer] *prec.* Cap*itulum* xxxvj *mar.* CG. 6836 þerinne] *om.* J; and] *om.* J; made] whare in J; þerinne] Scho made J. 6837 organes] hornys O. 6838 jowgleresse] mynstrall JMO; to] þe *add.* JMO. 6839 Whan] *prec.* Cap*itulum* xxvij *mar.* CG; seyn] alle *add.* CS; by haldyne J; þese] thire JMO. 6840 þese] thyr JMO. 6841 to hire] *om.* J. 6842 ben] thire ladyes JMO; þese ladyes] ere JMO; abasht] ferde J. 6843 þat þou see] fyrste quod scho J; first] þat þou See J. 6844 at] þe *add.* CS, *om.* O; eye] *om.* O; men] thay J; þat] *om.* J. 6845 þou see] in J; dortour] and in othere places *add.* J; hire] Than *add.* J. 6846 wenten] -t S; I] *om.* S. 6847 on] opon M; hem] *om.* S; and²] *prec.* Cap*itulum* xxxviij *mar.* CG. 6848 felawe] (e *ins.* G³); þe] -r S; swich] suche (e *ins.* G³) G. 6848-9 I wole singe] *twice* O. 6849 doon] to do J; bere] wille bere J; At] *mark over with passage marked mar.* C³. 6850 withholde] haldene abak J; In] *prec.* Cap*itulum* xxxix *mar.* CG. 6851 afterward] afftwardis S; of whiche] I was mekille mare abayste J. 6851-2 I² ... abasht] (*2nd* o *ins.* G³), off J. 6852 dede] deede (*1st* e *ins.* G³) G; mete] brede (br *o. er.*) M. 6853 on knees] *om.* O. 6854 gorgier] þat *add.* CS, that *add. ins. mar.* G³; was] (t *alt.* s C³); fretoreere] þe frayturrere þere of J, þer of *add.* MO;

she] *om.* CS.   6855 filled] Fulfilled J;   hem] *om.* JMO.   6856 Now]
prec. Cap*itulum* xl *mar.* CG, *capitulum* xj *rub. mar.* M;   I wole] *trs.* J.
6857 place] (*2nd a ins.* G³);   þat] at *add.* JMOS;   heerinne] here Inne (*2nd*
e *subpuncted*) G.   6858 þe strenges] *om.* J, and þe strynges *add. can.* (and
erased) M;   and¹] *om.* J.   6859 þe] *om.* J;   me] (*2nd e ins.* G³), *om.*
M.   6860 þe] *om.* J;   cloystreres] clostirs O;   hondes] hende J, þe handis
O.   6861 prisoneeres] in *prisounes add.* S;   dores] (*2nd* r *subpuncted*
G).   6862 nempned] *om.* JMO, cleped S;   and¹] *om.* JMO;   cleped] called
JMO, named S;   cordes] Obedience a bond to free will *mar.* O³.   6863 hire²]
om. JMO;   diuerse] obediencia *rub. mar.* M;   whiche] wheche (*2nd e ins.* G³)
G.   6864 it] he J;   doo] *ins.* O³;   of] at J;   his] *om.* O;   owen lust]
with at wille *mar.* G³.   6865 hire] his M.   6866 laaces] lace O.
6867 The] *prec.* Cap*itulum* xli *mar.* CG;   she] *om.* JS, discipline Ladye of order
mar. O³;   cleped] called JMO;   name] discipline *rub. mar.* M.
6869 hardy] for *add.* S;   in hire] *om.* S;   mouht] teeth J, *om.* S.   6870 it]
om. JO;   Vndernemynge] vndyrtakynge and Snybbynge J, vndirstondyng MO;
leueth] bereþe S;   nothing] (*2nd* o *ins.* G³);   þat she ne] *with* {di}sciplyne *mar.*
G³, þat ne scho J, þen scho M, þam she O.   6871 correcteth] it *add.* JMO;
skowreth] it *add.* JM;   forbisheth] it *add.* J, forbysh MO.   6872 thinge]
thynges JMO;   a poynt] atte alle poyntes J;   þat] at O.   6873 þe] that
JO;   targe] -te J;   hast] *om.* J.   6874 name] (*2nd a ins.* G³), þer of *add.*
J;   haue] *om.* J;   seid] talde J;   þee] byfore *add.* J.   6835-75 to ... it]
it *add.* C, it nedes nou3t J, to reherce nowe S.   6875 were ... woorth] to reherce
it J, it is lytell worthe S.   6876 She] *prec.* Cap*itulum* xlij *mar.* CG;   hath
seid] as J, Wilfull pouertye *mar.* O³, pouerte *rub. mar.* M.   6877 hire] awne
add. J;   goode] (e *ins.* G³);   left] (*final* e *subpuncted* G);   goodes] gud
O.   6879 alle] (e *ins.* G³);   vncloþed] vncledde J.   6879-80 riht ... hire²]
om. J.   6880 naked] (*2nd a ins.* G³);   on] *om.* O.   6881 bi lachesse] thow
J, by lachis (lachis *o. er.*) M;   þou took] of thy Selfe take J;   to²] forto J.
6882 clepen] calles JMO.   6883 hire] or lette hire *add.* J.   6884 þe] this
J;   þere] whidere J, wher MO;   wolde] wol S;   to²] *om.* J;   It needeth]
þer while CS, (*1st* e *ins.* G³);   þee wel] needeth þou C, weel thee *marked for reversal*
G, the gretely J, ne wele O, neodeþe þe S.   6885 þou¹] to JMOS;   þee] wele
add. J;   þat þou] to J.   6886 boþe þine] *trs.* G;   she] *om.* O.
6887 mowe] myght JMO;   soo] with hir *add.* S.   6888 Of] *prec.* Cap*itulum*
xliij *mar.* CG;   I sey þee] (*2nd e ins.* G³), also J;   also] I Say the J, *om.* MO.
6889 maketh] (*2nd a ins.* G³), Chastitye or dame Blaunch *mar.* O³;   make] hire
add. CJS, (*2nd a ins.* G³);   lyue] tyme *add.* M.   6890 þi] *om.* S;   bed]
-des S;   alle] (e *ins.* G³), ilke J, þe *add.* O;   nihtes] nyght JO;   and þat þou]
om. J;   make ... place] maake here a plaace (*5th a ins.* G³), to ligge J, make hir
plese (es *o. er.*) M, mak hir place O.   6891 þee¹] For *add.* J;   with þee²] *om.*
MO;   times] the tymes J.   6893 dortorere] adorturore JMOS;   wenche]
adamyselle J, a wench MS;   and] to J, a *add.* MS.   6894 come] (e *ins.* G³);
into] *with* er. *mar.* C³.   6895 hire] here (*2nd e ins.* G³) G;   wolde] wole C,
not *add.* S;   ligge] to ligge C.   6896 peny] gude J;   wite] wille wit J, wote
M;   not] *om.* J.   6897 it is] *om.* JMO;   and þe resoun] *om.* JMO;   swich]
this JMO;   for] þat *add.* S.   6898 seith] talde the before J;   and putte
hire] (*1st* e *ins.* G³), oute of the worlde J;   out ... world] and putte hir owte þer
off J.   6899 wherfore] þer fore S;   ayenward] -es S.   6900 cleped] called
JMO;   þilke] Scho JMO.   6901 of no wiht] sette be J;   hath cure] na wight
J;   if he ne] bot 3if he J, if she ne S.   6902 ooþerweys] *om.* J, odir wyse

MO; nempne] calle JMO. 6903 þou] *om.* J; miht] *om.* J, may M; clepe] *om.* J, call MO; hire] *om.* J, Chastite *rub. mar.* M. 6904 querelle] awblaster*e* J, balestrier S; she ne] *trs.* J; and] *om.* JS. 6905 neiþer arwe] qwarelle *add.* J, *om.* O; darte] (*2nd a ins.* G³). 6905-6 with þe gloouen] and glofed J, with glouys MO. 6906 and gloloued] with gloues J; is] *ins.* O. 6907 assaute] ascent JO; with hand] armed J; armed] on the hend J; ofte] *om.* JMO; michel] þe michel CS. 6908 wost] knawes J, wote MO; name] (*2nd a ins.* G³). 6909 it] *om.* M; þee] (*1st e ins.* G³); myn] (*final e subpuncted* G); were] was JMO. 6910 þou] were when þowe *add.* S; vnglooudest] glouedest S; hard] to the *add.* J; haue] (*2nd a ins.* G³), gette J. 6912 The] *prec.* Cap*itulum* xliv *mar.* CG; cloistre] Study · Lady of holy writt *mar.* O³. 6913 upon] the *add.* J; of] þis place *add.* O; and] eeke þe *add.* S. 6914 suthselerere] Southecelleress*e* JO; yiveth] ȝeueth (*with* ȝyueth *mar.* G³) G; mete] *passage marked mar.* O³; and ... it] þat it hongyr note O. 6914-5 þat ... nouht] þat it hu*n*gr*e mar.* G³, & fedes it O. 6915 filleth þe herte] fulfilleth þe herte CS, *with* fullfulleth the herte nowght the wombe *at foot of p.* G³. 6915-6 with ... mete] nouht þe wombe CS, (heere *2nd* e *subpuncted* G), with hir gude swete mete M, withe gud swet mete O. 6916 nouht þe wombe] with hire goode and sweete mete CS, *subpuncted* G, For *add.* J; cleped] (*final e subpuncted* G), called JMO; and] or MO, *om.* S. 6917 Studie] *om.* S; rihte] *om.* J, lesson · and study *rub. mar.* M; name] (*2nd a ins.* G³); nempned] called JM, clepyde O. 6918 and] *om.* J; vessel] -ls O. 6719 not¹] *om.* O; shede] scheede (*2nd e ins.* G³) G, Skatter J; mihte] myghte (e *ins.* G³) G; not²] *ins. mar. after rub. caret also in text* O³; ne] & OS; faire] (e *ins.* G³). 6920 in] none *add.* O, with S; ooþer] man*e*re of *add.* J; hire] also *add.* J; þou] the (*with* thow *mar.* G³) G, the þow J, þe MO, do *add.* S. 6921 þe] *om.* O. 6922 and²] *om.* S. 6923 as] in likness*e* of J; a ... culuer] aqwaynte doufe J, a white dowfe M. 6924 biyonde] vesand O. 6925 cometh] to *add.* CJMS, to *add. ins.* O³; þilke] þa JM, þe O; seeth] says O. 6926 feedinge] fedyng*e*s O. 6927 Now] *prec.* Cap*itulum* xlv *mar.* CG; telle] say MO; yit after] *om.* J; þat] that *add.* JMOS; gorgiere] note *mar.* O³. 6928 ladi] *om.* J; and] a J, *om.* OS. 6929 freytoureere] and *add.* J; Abstinence] Abstenau*n*ce Sobirness*e rub. mar.* M, Abstenau*n*ce Ladye *mar.* O³; clepe] calle JMO; to hire] þou wille speke J, þou to hir M, þu till hir O, þat *add.* S. 6930 þou ... speke] (speeke *2nd* e *subpuncted* G), to hire J, will speke MO; Hire] *om.* M, þe O; Sobrietee] Sobrenesse JMO; þou ouhtest] the aught J, þou aught MO. 6931 wite] to wit JMOS; it¹] welle I now *add.* J; if] bot ȝif J; ne haue] (*2nd a ins.* G³), hafe J; seide] talde JS. 6932 dede] deede (*1st* e *ins. with* Mortuos *mar.* G³) G, Folke *add.* J; and feeden] þe whike O; þe quike] & fedis O; withouten] *om.* J. 6933 lessinge] *om.* J; þe] *om.* JMO; gon] passed J. 6934 han] haauen (*2nd a ins.* G³) G; yiven] *om.* S; here] heere (*2nd e subpuncted*) G. 6935 Serteyn] Sothely J. 6935-6 þilke were] ryght nyce J, he wer MO. 6936 riht nice] he ware J, nyce and right fonde M; wiste nouht] walde noȝt knawe that J; he] þey S; dede] deede (*1st* e *ins. with* Mortuous *mar.* G³) G, folke *add.* J. 6937 and] þat *add.* CS, that *add. ins. mar.* G³; withoute heres] bot ȝif thares ware on happes J; shulde] he shulde CS, schall (*with* he scholde *mar.* G³) G, þay schulde J; of²] for JMO. 6938 seruice] men takes J; men taken] takes Seruyce J; of hem] *with* {ded}e *erased mar.* G³; þouh] *om.* JMO. 6939 hem²] *with* dede *mar.* G³. 6940 knees as] knesis O. 6941 owres ye liven] booþe youre hondes S; with

... handes] for with oures yee lyven S;   preyeth] *om*. S.   6942 for us] *om*.
S, Yit Gr*ac*edieux enfo*ur*meþe þe pilgryme þe signefyaunces · of moo oþer thinges
þat he sawe in þe Castell *add*. S;   Now] *prec*. Cap*i*tulum xlvj *mar*. CG, *prec*.
{Cap*itulu*}m viij *mar*. S;   she] *om*. O;   þat] þis J.   6942-3 heerinne ...
dede] *om*. O.   6944 is] Prayer *rub*. *mar*. M, Ladye Orison, our sow*le*s Messenger
mar. O³;   which] þat CS;   a] þe CS.   6945 messangeres] messanger O;
it] *om*. J;   hem] *with* dede *mar*. G³.   6946 eche] ilkane J, ilk M, of hem *add*.
S;   deserueth] (de *ins*. O);   augere] wymble that J, þat *add*. MO;   hast seyn]
Sawe hir*e* hafe in hir*e* hande J.   6947 perceth] perischeth (*with* perceth *mar*.
G³) G, p*ar*tys O;   she maketh] *om*. O;   goodshipes] goodenesses S;   þat²]
and S.   6948 hem] *with* Mortuos *mar*. G³;   here] *with* Religious *mar*. G³;
lyfes] lyflode CS, *with* lyfflo{de} *mar*. G³;   awgere] wymble J;   seid] called
J;   name] (*2nd* a *ins*. G³);   Feruaunt] Fuerant (e *erased*) C, fuerunt G.
6949 Continuacioun] continuau*n*ce JO;   bi] Feruens continuacio *rub*. *mar*. M;
maketh] (*2nd* a *ins*. G³).   6950 perce] to perce CS, to be p*er*ched J, p*er*chid
M, p*ar*te O;   hem] *with* Mortuos *mar*. G³;   mete] *with* preeyeres *mar*. G³;
and sweeteliche] *om*. JMO.   6951 abaundoneth it hem] *om*. JMO;   Halfpeny]
Peny JO;   peny] halpeny JO;   haue] (*2nd* a *ins*. G³), *om*. O.   6952 it ne
is] ne it es J, þen it is Mo;   guerdoned] rewarded JM, be wardid O;   hundreth-
fold] *with* C *mar*. G³.   6953 shal neuere] *trs*. J;   þouh] as O.   6954 hem]
with de{de} (qwyke *erased u.v.*) G³, For *add*. J.   6955 ayen] *om*. JMO;
apertliche] ap*er*ly J, dep*ar*tely O;   maketh] (*2nd* a *ins*. G³);   hem²] hem *add*.
erased C;   rise] ageyne *add*. S;   deth] to lyfe *add*. J;   bi] for JMO.
6956 dooth] haþe doone S;   and] of *add*. O.   6957 and] of *add*. M;
peynes] pey peynes S.   6957-8 of þe lady] þou wille wit the name J, of þis lady
M.   6958 þou ... name] (*2nd* a *ins*. G³), of the lady J;   sumtime] oracio *rub*.
mar. M.   6959 cleped] called JMO;   Preyere] priere (*with* preyere *mar*. G³)
G;   in ... manere] *om*. JMO.   6960 soone stye] up *add*. CS, *trs*. J;   into]
to J;   soone²] do JO.   6961 doo] sone JO;   is] his J, scho is M.
6962 is] for *add*. S;   to see] *om*. JMO;   him] *with* god *mar*. G³, *om*. JMO;
rediliche] *om*. J.   6963 him] hire JMO.   6963-4 þat þat] *with* orisoun *mar*.
G³, that J.   6964 him] *with* king *mar*. G³, *om*. JMO;   but] So J.
6965 procuracioun] procurassye J.   6966 hire] *with* orysoun *mar*. G³;   from]
for O.   6967 wolt] thynkes to J;   kunne] *om*. MO;   a] *om*. JMO.
6968 þereas] þare whare JMO;   make] (*2nd* a *ins*. G³).   6969 not] na J;
þi] þe S;   þider] ne be wiste *marked for reversal* O;   ne be wist] þidir *marked*
for reversal O.   6969-70 þer ... bifore] *om*. MO.   6970 þe] *om*. J;   ne
hadde] ne he J, he nade S.   6971 þat] no*ta* de latr*one* cum Ih*esu* crucifixo, *rub*.
mar. M.   6973 and] if M;   þou²] *om*. S;   neede] (*1st* e *ins*. G³).
6975 The] *prec*. Cap*i*tulum xlvij *mar*. CG;   hast] *om*. JO;   and] that *add*.
J.   6976 þat¹] she S;   awaketh] wak*en*s JMO;   king] at *add*. S;   times]
La: Latrina *mar*. O³.   6977 þat he slepeth] by hir*e* blawynge JM, w*ith* hir
blawyng O;   bi ... blowinge] whe*n*e he Sclepes JMO, and *add*. S;   cryinge] for
add. S.   6977-8 if ... michel] Scho makis hym ryse J.   6968 she ... rise]
(maaketh *1st* a *ins*. G³ *in* G), ȝif he ligge to lange J;   Latin] *om*. J;   Latria]
Scho es J, latrina O;   she is] latria J.   6979 cleped] *om*. J, called MO;
bi name] (*2nd* a *ins*. G³), *om*. J;   and nempned] *om*. JMO;   Þe] *om*. JMO;
Inuocacioun] vocacio*un* O.   6980 Dieu] godde that es at say J, god i*d est* MO,
om. S;   In adiutorioun] Deus inadiutoriu*m* meu*m* intende J, Deus in adiutorium
MOS;   euery] eu*er*ylke J;   withoute] *mark over with passage marked mar*. C³,
om. O;   weeryinge] *om*. O.   6981 sithe] Seyne JMO;   she] *om*. M, gose

add. M, for to S.   6982 aplyeth] applye S;   to¹] in JMO.   6983 taketh]
(*2nd a ins.* G³);   hire] and mellys J;   entermedlinge] hire J.   6984 and]
of melody & all so *add.* O.   6985 Þus] thus er J;   ben cleped] neuende J,
er namyd MO;   and ... names] *om.* JMO, and nempned by hir name S.
6986 þese] thire JMO;   ben þe] *om.* JMO;   þat] *om.* JMO;   þe king] god
S.   6987 swich²] suche (e *subpuncted*) G;   and²] *om.* JMO.   6988 swich
jogelorye] *om.* JMO;   þat] *om.* JMO, þat *add.* S.   6988-90 he ... wel] *om.*
S.   6989 þilke] þay*me* JMO;   and doon it] *om.* JMO.   6990 and ...
jogeloresses] *om.* JMO;   thing] thynges JMO.   6991 as ... blowen] *om.* JMO.
Here byndes þe Prioresse þat is callied obedience ⁚ þe pilgrym vnto religion *add. rub.*
M.   6992 As] *prec.* Cap*itulum* xlviij *mar.* CG, ca*p*itulum xij *rub. mar.* M, Right
as þat S;   þus] to me J;   to me] on this wise J.   6993 byndinges] and þe
cordes *add.* J, byndyng MO;   þat] *om.* JMO;   she] schee (*1st* e *ins.* G³) G;
to me] euyn MO;   euene] warde J, to me M, streght S.   6994 who] what JO,
whare M;   in] oure *add.* JMO, þe *add.* S.   6995 Whider ... þou¹] *with*
{...} þ*ou erased u.v. mar.* C³;   I wole] *om.* J, þat *add.* S;   sey it] telle J.
6996 wot ... wheþer] trowe J, I wot euell wheþer S;   espye] Spyes J;   I] I doo
add. S;   espye] Spye J, *ins. after rub. caret also in text* O³.   6997 wole] *om.*
J, weel S;   I nouht] enoughe S;   shulde] walde J, shall MO;   Jerusalem] the
citte of J;   þe citee] ie*ru*sal*e*m J.   6998 for] *om.* S;   abbregge] abrayge (*2nd*
a *subpuncted*) O.   6999 and ... it] *om.* JMO;   not] *om.* J;   seid] talde J;
þee] (*1st* e *ins.* G³).
7000 heerinne] þou schall Fynde J;   þou ... fynde] here in J;   bed] -des J.
7001 seemeth] Seme JMO;   swich] suche (e *subpuncted*) G, so J.   7002 if]
and J.   7003 þou ne] that ne þou J, þen þou MO;   do] it *add.* JMO;   wel]
I now *add.* J;   ne be] be nou3t JM.   7004 holt] standes J;   and ... good]
or nou3t J;   it] *with* will *erased u.v. mar.* G³;   to proof] I wille J.   7005 I
wole] proue J;   þee] *om.* JMO;   Hider] Cum nowe J;   cum forth] hedire J;
she] and *add.* J.   7006 hider] me J;   handes] hende J;   feet] For *add.*
JM;   sette] fette S;   as] *with* as *erased u.v. mar.* C³.   7007 faucoun] a
faucoun CJS;   gesse] -3 J;   Whan] *prec.* Cap*itulum* xlix *mar.* CG;   swiche
woordes] (*1st* o *ins.* G³), I herde J;   I herde] swilke wordes J;   riht] *om.* J.
7008 gretliche] I was gretly J;   I was abasht] a baist J.   7009 Flee] ne *add.*
S;   þat] whilke J, *om.* S.   7010 hadde] has J;   led] *ins. mar. after rub. caret
also in text* O;   þe] that JMO;   place] (*2nd* a *ins.* G³) G;   Hider] Comm
now J;   now] heydre J;   I] *ins. mar. after rub. caret also in text* (*and overwritten
rub.*) O³;   dooth] and do J.   7011 abaundoned] Obediente JMO;   durste]
dare JMO;   not] *om.* S;   contrariows] contrare O.   7012 to thing] þat *add.*
CJM, to thing that *add.* S;   wel] encensed me J;   avised me] wele and talde
me J.   7013 shal] Scholde JMO;   þis] þe O;   place] (*2nd* a *ins.* G³);
of] to M.   7014 hegge] -*es* O;   And] *prec.* Cap*itulum* 1 *mar.* CG;
byndinges] handes and hire cordes J.   7015 bi þe feet] bande me J;   bond
me] by the fete J;   so] *om.* JMO;   in] þe *add.* MO.   7016 with¹] in J;
grinnes] gyn*n*es JMO, las courant(s) F;   byndinges] bandes J, byndyng M;
hadde] *om.* JM.   7017 me] wythe me *marked for reversal* O.   7018 þat]
om. J, þan MO;   whan] *om.* J;   oo wey] *with* j *mar.* G³, away JMO.
7019 afterward] -es J;   wel] I nowe *add.* J;   of] at J;   þat] tyme *add.* J;
strof I] *trs.* J;   nothing] (thyng o. er. M);   haue] hade S.   7020 þan] for
to *add.* S;   heere] (*2nd* e *ins.* G³);   in my book] *om.* J.   7021 Afterward]
Seyne aftere J, -es S;   me] *om.* M;   þat] *om.* MO.   7022 werkes] þat *add.*
CJMS;   if] *om.* GS.   7023 yit] also J, she made S;   she made] sche dyde

make O, yit S;   me] to *add*. J, *om*. S;   a byndinge] scho putte J.   7023-4 she putte] a bande J.   7024 me¹] *om*. CJMS;   seyde] bade J;   me²] *om*. JO.   7024-5 if ... speke] with oute*ne* leue of hire J.   7024 bi hire] I ne by hir M, ne by hir O, I by hir S.   7024-5 I ne speke] ne spake M, I spak O, ne speeke S.   7025 byndinge] bande J;   cleped] called JMO;   Silence] Silenci*um* *rub. mar*. M, silence · but only to speke, or doe good þinges *mar*. O³. 7026 þis] *ins. mar*. G³, *om*. JMO;   is ... þat] *om*. JMO.   7026-7 Of ... Dieu] Neu*er*theles J.   7027 I sey nouht] to gr*a*ce dieu J, I say it note O;   ne of¹] and J, hem] þat *add*. CMS, thay that J;   ne of²] and J;   ooþere] þat *add*. CJMS.   7028 se] þat to hem þowe might see *add*. S;   þat ... ne] þat to hem þou CS, thow J, þen to þem þou MO;   miht] may JO, shall M;   anything] þou wille aske tham*e* J.   7028-9 þou² ... hem] any thynge J, whilke þat may torn þe to any edificacion of soule · þis silence is a speciall frende vnto religiouse men and women kept in dew tyme *add*. M, þowe wolde aske hem S.   7030 Whan] *prec*. Cap*itulum* li *mar*. CG;   þus] the Prioress*e* J;   þe Prioresse] has thus J;   hadde sette] bu*n*de J;   bounden] Sette J.   7030-1 as hound] leessed J, as a hond M, and honde S.   7031 leced] as a hund J;   gret] *marked mar*. O³; afterward] eft*ere* JMO, -es S;   tweyne] twa JMO;   olde] anes co*m*m to me warde J.   7032 michel] I was gretly J;   I ... me] abaiste J;   oon] *with* j *mar*. G³.   7033 she hadde¹] (sche *alt*. he G³ *in* G), fete of leed J;   'feet of led] Scho hadde J;   and²] *om*. MO;   she hadde²] *om*. J;   bihynde] Messengers of death. þe one Infirmity, our Remembrancer. þe other olde age, ou*r* destroy*er mar*. O³.   7034 as] scho ware *add*. J;   was] also J;   also] semed J.   7035 upon] on J;   heed] *can*. G³, scho *add*. J;   in] vndire J.   7036 wrastle (e *alt*. a C);   To] Vnto M.   7037 comen] bath *add*. J;   seyden] vnto *add*. J;   Þe] *om*. JMO;   Deth] q*uo*d thay *add*. J;   sendeth] Sende J.   7038 for to tourneye] with þe *add*. J, *om*. O.   7039 seid] co*m*mau*n*ded J, sende S; us¹] *om*. M;   and] *om*. O;   enioyned] bidden*e* J, ioynide M, *om*. O;   us²] *om*. JO;   from þee] we departe no3t JO;   we ... nouht] fra the JO.   7040 to þe eerþe] felled the J;   felled þee] to the erthe J.   7041 She] he (*with* sche *mar*. G³) G.   7042 þee] to þee CMS;   and] *om*. JMO, Howe þe pilgryme askeþe of infirmitee · and of deeþe hir names proprely *add*. S;   Who] *prec*. Cap*itulum* lij *mar*. CG, *prec*. {Cap}*itulum* ix *mar*. S;   anoon] than J.   7043 neiþer] of *add*. JMO;   þe] 3it J, *om*. MOS;   she] *with* deth *mar*. G³; if] whedire J;   Deth²] *om*. J.   7044 maistresse] maistere J;   I wole] also J;   also] I wille J.   7044-5 if ... hire] yo*u*r names and whereof 3e serue J.   7044 tweyne] *with* ij *mar*. G³, two M.   7045 hire] *with* deth *mar*. G³; wherfore ... wole] and whedire 3e bathe be with hire or nou3t J.   7045-6 and ... seruen] and þerfore telles this onane J.   7046 seiden] answerde J;   me] to me S;   Þe] thyne JMOS.   7047 þe] thy JMOS;   thuartinge] (thu *o. er. with er. mar*. C³), thwartynge (h *ins*. G³) G, wrenchynge J, writhyng M, wepyng O;   ayens] agayn MO.   7048 noon] nowdir man nor beste M;   þat may be] *om*. J;   we ne] *trs*. J;   abaaten] bayte O;   him] his strenghe J;   of] atte JMO.   7049 come] coomen (*2nd* o *subpuncted*) G;   Þe] *om*. J; lordshipe] wirship O.   7050 in ... bodi] *om*. O.   7051 hire] *with* deth *mar*. G³;   doon] pur men dus or S;   smale] (*2nd* a *ins*. G³), *om*. S.   7052 she] *with* deth *mar*. G³;   no] *om*. JMO.   7053 places] place MO;   þere] whare JMO;   soo] Note *mar*. O³.   7054 don] schewed J;   curteysye] the J; to þee] curtasy J;   come] to come J, to þe *add*. M;   bifore] for O.   7055 hastliche] in haste J.   7056 hire] *with* deth *mar*. G³;   special] -ly COS;   Eche] aythere J, Ilkon M.   7057 sey] telle J;   hire] his J;   owen

name] (*2nd* a *ins*. G³), name awne *marked for reversal* O.   7058 þanne] *om.*
S;   þilke] scho JMO;   spak] bare the bedde on hir*e* heued J;   þat ... heed]
& Semed a wristelere J, þat bare þe bedd on hir hede MO.   7058-9 and ...
wrastlere] Spake vnto me and saide J.   7059 Infirmitee] *with* syknesse *mar.*
G³, or syeknes *add.* JM, Infirmitas *rub. mar.* M.   7060 þer] whare JMO;
hele] heele (*1st* e *ins.* G³) G;   sette] -s JMO;   him] *with* hele *erased u.v. mar*
G³.   7061 ouertrede] ouerthrawe J;   Oon] *with* j *mar.* G³;   she] (s *sub-*
puncted C), *with* he *mar.* G³, he M;   him²] me CMS, *with* mee *mar.* G³.
7062 and] *om.* CS;   time] *om.* JO, houre S;   him] *with* {h}ere *mar.* G³, hir
alt. hyme S.   7063 me] *with* syknesse *mar.* G³;   ne] *om.* J;   were] oon
þat cleped is *add.* S;   Medicine] ware *add.* JM.   7064 bore] ordayned J, for
add. S;   Ofte] of O.   7065 fynde] *om.* S;   hire] *with* medicine *mar.* G³;
I] *with* syknesse (deth *erased*) *mar.* G³.   7066 do] to do M;   or] elles *add.*
J.   7067 þe] hir*e* J.   7067-8 and hise¹] *with* medisine *mar.* G³, and hire
J.   7068 emplastres] plastres J;   and¹] *om.* J;   hise²] hir*e* J;   and²] *om.*
S;   hise³] hir*e* J, *om.* S;   empassionementes] pocions JMO, *om.* S.
7069 couple me] compleyne CS;   to] on J;   þilke] hym JMO;   which] wheche
(*2nd* e *subpuncted*) G, to whilke JMO;   Deth] *om.* O.   7070 to] *om.* JMO;
ouerthrowe] caste JMO.   7071 mary] ne bloode *add.* S;   þat] *om.* J, þan
O;   I ne] *trs.* J;   souke] it oute *add.* J, it *add.* MOS;   His blood] and S;
I²] *om.* S;   drinke] and *add.* J;   his flesh] ete J.   7072 I ete] his flesche
J, I haue etyne M;   he] I J, *om.* O;   hath] lefe hym J;   þanne] (e *ins.* G³).
7073 þat I haue] *om.* JMO;   Deth] I may *add.* J.   7073-4 his lyfe] to drawe
oute J.   7074 to drawe] his lyfe J;   withoute] wyth O;   to³] at J, for to
S.   7074-5 Thou art not] *prec.* Cap*itulum mar.* CG, Nowe in faith quod I
J.   7075 quod I] þou arte na J;   ouhten] awght to J, owe to MO;   make]
(*2nd* a *ins.* G³).   7076 Yis] þis S;   þat] forsothe J;   I am] *trs.* J;   she]
is *add.* S.   7077 þilke] scho JMO;   make] -s men to J, -s MO, þee *add.* S;
remembre] remembrance MO;   on] of JMO.   7078 þilke] Scho JMO.
7079 setteth] (? th *subpuncted* G);   in] to M.   7080 þilke] he JM, hym O;
made] acto*ur* and makere of J;   sigh] *om.* J;   ne] *om.* J.   7081 nouht] *om.*
MO.   7082 clepede] called JM;   me¹] tille hy*m add.* J;   seide] bad J, to
add. M;   Go] quod he *add.* J;   þilke] ȝone JMO;   wordliche] weldly J.
7083 bete] beete (*2nd* e *ins.* G³) G;   fyndest] mee *add.* subpuncted G.
7084 for] because *add.* CJS, by cause *add. ins. mar.* G³;   haue] (*2nd* a *ins.* G³);
hele] heele (*1st* e *ins.* G³) G;   preysen me] Sette litille J, but a *add.* S;   litel]
by me J.   7085 foryetinge] forȝetynge (*2nd* e *ins.* G³) G.   7086 beddes]
bedde O.   7087 arise] ryse JMO;   hem] at hem *add. subpuncted* G;   leese]
(*1st* e *ins.* G³).   7088 etinge] mete J;   þilke] that JMO.   7090-1 and
... hem¹] *om.* S.   7090 entenden] bysy tha*i*m, take hede O;   saue] (*2nd* a *ins.*
G³);   Þe] *om.* J.   7091 eche] ilkane JM;   hire] him CGOS.   7092 þee]
(*2nd* e *ins.* G³);   nouht] I Sette nouȝt by the *add.* J.   7094 arayed] redy J;
his] this JO.   7095 lauendere] penitence *mar.* O³;   maad] (*1st* a *ins.* G³),
had J;   be] bi C, *om.* J, bende M, bene O.   7096 Now] *prec.* Cap*itulum* liv
mar. CG;   þat] *om.* JO;   he] *with* makere of nature *mar.* G³.   7097 me]
with syknesse *mar.* G³;   soone] *om.* M;   in] vndyr*e* J.   7098 haue] (*2nd*
a *ins.* G³).   7099 haue] (*2nd* a *ins* G³);   wrastlinge] strangeling S.
7100 haue] (*2nd* a *ins.* G³);   maad] (*1st* a *ins.* G³), gerte J;   wole I] *trs.* JS.
7101 lasse] therfore *add.* J.   7103 That] *prec.* Cap*itulum* lv *mar.* CG;   to
hire] *om.* JMOS;   shal first] as couenau*n*t is S.   7103-4 as ... is¹] as þe
cowuande is J, shall S.   7104 sey me] telle me J, seye me first S;   who] what

S;   wole] *graunte* J;   þanne] *ins.* G³, *om.* MO.   7105 þilke] scho JMO;
þou ... bore] ʒouthhede J.   7105-6 with Jeonenesse] with iolyfesse C, with
Jeoneusse (*with* {ʒ}owthe *mar.* G³) G, bare the J, with Jolyvetee S.
7106 wendest] wend *o. er.* O;   haue] (*2nd* a *ins.* G³), hadd M. *o. er.* O;   seyn]
o. er. O.   7108 softe] softly J;   haue] (*2nd* a *ins.* G³).   7109 þee] (*1st*
e *ins.* G³).   7110 haue] (*2nd* a *ins.* G³);   go] softe O;   softe] Softly J, I
go O.   7110-1 but ... softe] *om.* S.   7110 gon] by *add.* J.   7111 be
comen] ga JMO;   softe] Softly JMO;   algates] neu*ere* þe J.   7112 ouertake]
(*2nd* a *ins.* G³), ou*er*geten JMO;   þee¹] (*1st* e *ins.* G³);   bringe] (e *ins.* G³);
Þe] *om.* O.   7113 nouht] na man J, no thing S;   Hire messangere] I am
J.   7114 I am] hire messangere J.   7115 verryliche] Infirmity somtyme
doe mistake hir message · but olde age is certaine *mar.* O³;   felawe] *with* sikenesse
mar. G³, Sikness*e* *add.* J;   sumthing] some thyngis O.   7116 to do] say O;
me] Elde *rub. mar.* M, -n S.   7117 empeche] lette JMO;   Vilesse] Viletee
CS, *with* eelde *mar.* G³, Elde JMO.   7118 rivelede] runcled J;   þilke] scho
JMO;   hath] the heued J;   þe hed] has J;   hoor] white hared J;   wel] bien
F, fulle JMO.   7119 ofte] souvent F, softe CGS;   þilke] Scho JO, I am scho
M;   folk] (*final* e *subpuncted* G), men M.   7120 bere] do JMO;   gret] *om.*
JMO;   haue] (*2nd* a *ins.* G³).   7121 and yuel] proued J;   preeued] proued
(*with* preeued *mar.* G³) G, and euyl also J;   Þis] (*final* e *subpuncted* G);   is]
beeth *subpuncted* G, *ins.* G³, teches J, bithechis M, betyche O;   glose] -s G.
7122 þilke] I am scho J, scho MO;   bi] þe *add.* S;   þe] thir J, *om.* S.
7123 no] the JMO;   if he ne] bot ʒif he J;   haue] (*2nd* a *ins.* G³).
7124 Neuerþelees] natheles G;   ofte] it falles J, of it M;   bifalleth] ofte J;
and] þat J;   hele] layne J, hide M;   it²] *om.* J.   7125 albeit] þowh alle J;
þat²] *om.* J;   haue] (*2nd* a *ins.* G³);   ynowh¹] mekille J;   ynowh²] note *mar.*
O³.   7126 albeit] þof alle J, þat *add.* M, by it þat O;   haue] am M;   wel]
om. M;   winter] of age *add.* J, in age *add.* M;   I²] ʒit I JM.   7127 rewe]
rule S;   þe²] *om.* O;   laste] (e *ins.* G³).   7128 counseil] *with* *add.* J;
is] was J;   for] of (*with* for *mar.* G³) G, *om.* J;   which] and the skille why J,
why MO;   Ysaie] y sey (*with* ysaye *mar.* G³) G, I say · ysai O;   cursede]
counsayled JMO.   7129 whan] *om.* O;   me] Howe þe pilgryme demaundeþe
infirmitee of þe potentes *add.* S.   7130 Sey] *prec.* Cap*itulum* lvj *mar.* CG, *prec.*
{Ca}*pitulum* x *mar.* S;   þe] þa JMO;   potentes] poyntes that þow beres J;
anoon] *om.* J.   7131 hens] thy way J;   sithe] for Sen*e* J, And sithen MO;
þin] (*final* e *subpuncted* G);   me] I J;   liketh] kepe J;   nouht] na langer*e*
J.   7132 Like ... like] like other nowght lyke G, Quod scho J;   quod she] lik
or nouʒt lyke J.   7134 fro þee] *om.* S.   7134 haue] efter *add.* J.
7135 Courbe] and croked *add.* J;   make] note *and passage marked mar.* O³;
strokes] þat *add.* JM.   7136 shal] wol S;   Neuerþelees] natheles G;
auauntage] vauntage MO;   þou shalt] *trs.* J;   haue] (*2nd* a *ins.* G³).
7137 þou] S *ends, one leaf wanting*;   twey] twa JMO;   potentes] *om.* O;
lene] leene (*2nd* e *subpuncted*) G.   7138 take] þe O;   þee] to þe M, take
O.   7139 bineme] refe JMO;   with] *om.* J.   7140 ben] þei ben C, with
J, *om.* MO.   7174 dide make] made JMO.   7142 trussed] dressed JMO;
Curteys] Curtesy JO.   7143 nouht] also *add.* J;   þat¹] *om.* JMO;   oon]
j *over* G³;   ne] *with* er. *mar.* C³, *om.* JMO.   7144 if] and J.   7145 fallen]
falle (e *ins.* G³) G;   so¹] *om.* O;   so þat] tharfore J, n *add. can.* M.
7145 now] take tham J;   take hem] nowe J;   wolt] For *add.* J;   þei] the J;
neede] þe O;   þee] þaim J, nede O;   wel] *om.* JMO.   7147 tweyne] *om.*
JO, two M;   mi ... ben] forto bere J, my strokes M, my strok*es* two O;   sore

to bere] my strakes J, forto forbere M, for to ber O. 7148 if I ne] olesse than
I J; Hider] Cum nowe J; now] hedire J; she] *with* eelde *mar.* G³; felawe]
with sikenesse *mar.* G³. 7149 annoye] dissese J. 7150 ligge] to ligge J;
þi] his JMO; and²] *om.* O. 7151 annoye] (ann *o. er.* C); to] att J;
And] *prec.* Ca*pitulum* lvij *mar.* CG. 7152 maaden] gerte J; anoon] falle
downe J; falle doun] onane J. 7153 harde] hery O; pinche] pyne
JMO; me²] *om.* MO; braye] and grane *add.* J. 7154 wel] but *add.* J;
In ... þe²] *om.* J. 7155 laste ... me¹] *om.* J; and¹ ... me²] *om.* CJ; and
seiden] *om.* J; me³] to me CM, *om.* J; Araye] *om.* J. 7156 þee¹] (*1st*
e *ins.* G³), *om.* J; Þe] *om.* JMO; Deth] *om.* J; cometh] *om.* J; she] he
MO. 7157 on] of M; haue] (*2nd* a *ins.* G³). 7158 As] *prec.* Ca*pitulum*
lviij *mar.* CG, ca*pitulum* xiv *rub. mar.* M; on] in JO. 7159 a] *om.* M.
7160 a visage] benigne J; benigne] and a plesaunt J; and plesaunt] visage
J. 7160-1 hadde ... out] ane of hire pappes J. 7161 hire oon brest] (j *over*
and mar. G³), scho had drawen oute J, hir brest O; bi ... cote] (*2nd* o *ins.* G³),
of hir bosum J. 7162 corde] (e *ins.* G³); þouh] ʒif J; hey] the hay
JMO; To] Vnto M. 7163 hire] *om.* JMO; þanne] *om.* J; seyde] vnto
add. JM. 7164 Hider now] Cum J; come] hedire quod scho J.
7165 seide] aunswerred J; lady] quod I *add.* J; bihoote] be heete (*3rd* e *ins.*
G³) G. 7166 and ... yow¹] *om.* J. 7167 teche] teeche (*2nd* e *ins.* G³)
G, telle J. 7168 And] *om.* J; quod she] telle the gladly J; sey it þee]
quod scho J; of] þou J; sooth] Sothly J, suche O. 7169 þilke] scho
JMO; I²] *om.* JM. 7171 doon] giffene J; jugement] -es O; and] whilk
was M; put] þame *add.* J. 7172 bi] for J; maade] (*1st* a *ins.* G³);
leue] to rewe J, lene O; of] on O; hand] werke *add.* J. 7173 for ...
bileevinge] (*2nd* a *ins. and* beleuynge *with* vengeaunce *mar.* G³), in takenynge þerof
J; maade] (*2nd* a *ins.* G³). 7174 withoute corde] in heuene J; in þe
heuene] with outen corde J, in heuyn O. 7174-5 With ... I²] (haaue *2nd* a *ins.*
G³) *om.* JMO. 7176 drawe] (*2nd* a *ins.* G³). 7177 accordeth] acorde
O; Resoun] Mercy *rub. mar.* M. 7179 foul wrecchedness] *trs. marked for*
reversal O. 7180 thredere] Spynnere J. 7182 Why] *prec.* Ca*pitulum* lix
mar. CG, when J; haue] (*2nd* a *ins.* G³), *om.* MO; ye drawe] ʒe ʒour pappe
J, *trs.* MO; youre brest] *with* teeter *mar.* G³, drawene J. 7183 yive] ʒeue
(*with* ʒyue *mar.* G³) G; me] at *add.* J; Ye] forsothe *add.* J; yit] mare *add.*
J; þan] owþere *add.* J; or] other G. 7185 of] *om.* JMO; Pite] *with*
brest *mar.* G³, It hatte J; it hatteth] pete J; needeth wel] es fulle nedfulle J;
to] *om.* O; yive] at *add.* JO. 7186 with] *om.* O; to²] *ins.* G; þe¹]
om. J; poore] pite *rub. mar.* M; yive] ʒeue (*with* ʒyue *mar.* G³) G; þerwith]
at Sowke J, souke MO; sowke] þerewith JMO. 7187 þilke þat] that J, þo
þat MO. 7189 remeved] chaunged JMO; maad] (*1st* a *ins., final* e *sub-*
puncted G³); al] *om.* JMO; whyt] white (e *ins.* G³) G; heete] (*2nd* e *ins.*
G³). 7190 his] the J, hir MO; rednesse] þerof *add.* J. 7191 shuldest]
Schalte J; þat] *om.* O; nouht] no thyng O. 7192 þe] *om.* M; whiche]
wheche (*2nd* e *subpuncted*) G; whyt] (*final* e *subpuncted* G); boiled it] *with*
it seeth *mar.* G³. 7193 whyt] white (e *subpuncted*) G; bicometh] es by
commen JMO. 7194 þilke] he JM, *om.* O. 7195 swich] suche (e *sub-*
puncted) G; foryiveth] forʒeueth (*with* ʒyue *mar.* G³) G; þat men] *trs.*
JMO; han] haaue (*2nd* a *ins.* G³) G; To] Vnto M. 7196 wel sittinge]
Swilke apappe J, wele symyng and fytyng O; swich a brest] wele Sittande J;
and wel auenaunt] *om.* JMO. 7197 vnwarnished] vnwarshed C, with oute
Swilke mylke ne w*i*thoute J. 7198 of] *om.* J; brest] pappe J; al were it]

alle ȝif it ware J;   maade] (*1st* a *ins.* G³), lette J.   7199 riht] *om.* J;   þe
side] *om.* S.   7200 neuere] so *add. into mar.* ? M³;   mooder] (*2nd* o *ins.*
G³);   ne²] *om.* CO;   so michel] *om.* O;   hire] his M;   chyild] childe (e
subpuncted) G.   7201 brest] *with* pitee mar. G³;   to] and to J, vnto M;
eche] ilkane J, ilk man M;   seide] as in þis maner it shuld say M, it a sayd O;
Come forth] Comforth JMO.   7202 wole] comfortȝ *add.* J;   come forth] *om.*
JO, and take ynowh *add.* M;   more] maner of J.   7203 remeeved] chaunged
JMO;   it²] *om.* C.   7204 for] the *add.* JO;   non] *om.* O;   ne] -r M.
7205 brest] *with* teete mar. G³, pappe J, a breste M;   Now] *prec.* Capitulum lx
mar. CG;   þat] *om.* C;   yive] ȝeue (*with* ȝyue mar. G³) G, at *add.* JO.
7206 þilke] þa JMO.   7207 shuldest] schalte J;   þat] I *add.* J.
7208 alle] (e *ins.* G³);   places] (*2nd* a *ins.* G³), place MO;   þat¹] whare J;
anoon] *om.* J.   7209 him] þam JMO;   bred] bathe J;   I¹] *om.* J;   yive]
ȝeue (*with* ȝyue mar. G³) G, gesse J;   haue] (*2nd* a *ins.* G³);   foysoun] (u *alt.*
y *with* y mar. C³).   7210 any³] or J;   vncloþed] vncled J.   7211 cloþe]
(*2nd* o *ins.* G³);   and¹] also *add.* M;   hem²] *om.* JO;   hem³] þan O.
7212 I] *marked for gloss* G³;   in] to *add.* JMO.   7213 is] lies J, in prisoun
MO;   in prisoun] is MO;   go] and *add.* J;   visite] -s J.   7214 leste] leeste
(*2nd* e *ins.* G³) G;   Þilke] þa JMO;   dede] deede (*1st* e *ins.* G³) G;   þilke]
þa JMO;   lyen] been C.   7215 in] þer *add.* M;   bedde] beddis M;   in
humblesse] mekely J, in mekenesse M, wythe meknese O.   7216 hath] grace
dieu O;   Grace Dieu] has O;   maad] (*1st* a *ins.*, *final* e *subpuncted* G³);
enfermerere] Fermerere J.   7217 þe²] also M;   ofte] tymes *add.* J.
7218 ayen] þaire beddes J;   here beddes] agayne J;   endure] hafe J, to endure
M;   defaute] -s M.   7219 with me] þou wille come J, (with *ins.* O);   pou
... come] with me J;   redy] and gladd *add.* M.   7220 quod I] hafe I J;
haue I] (*2nd* a *ins.* G³), quod I J;   ne] wate J.   7221 wot] nouȝt J;   þese]
thir J;   nih] *om.* JMO;   may not] ne may C.   7222 If] and J;   diden]
walde do J;   gret bountee] ȝe did mekille J;   ye ... me] fram me & for me J,
ȝhe did to me M.   7223 awey] fra the *add.* J;   corde] -ȝ M.   7224 lede]
leede (*2nd* e *ins.* G³) G;   þee] me *alt.* the M;   reste] the *add.* J.   7225 wel]
thay wille J, þei will *add. into mar.* M³;   nouht] to *add.* O.   7226 bifore
...come] ne forbere the J, bifore dede come MO;   ne ... þee²] before dedd come
J;   And] *prec.* Capitulum lxj mar. CG.   7227 corde] (*2nd* o *final* e *ins.*
G³);   bond] feste J;   me] (*2nd* e *ins.* G³);   forth] (*2nd* o *ins.* G³);   olde]
(*2nd* o *ins.* G³), twa alde anes J, & þe old O.   7228 comen] (*2nd* o *ins.* G³);
nouht] nathynge J;   glad] -er MO;   Þe] *om.* C.   7299 myn] (*final* e
subpuncted G);   and] *om.* JMO;   amende] mende JO.   7230 Whan] *prec.*
Capitulum lxij mar. CG, capitulum xv rub. mar. M;   to þe fermerye] I was J;
I was] in the Fermery J;   and] I O;   hadde] *om.* J;   leyn] lefe O.
7231 and a soursaut] *om.* JMO;   was clumben] clamm JMO.   7232 an hy]
om. J;   I] *om.* O;   afryght] Fered JM, fered wyt\h/ O.   7234 and] in hire
nekke *add.* J;   cheste] (*2nd* e *ins.* G³) G.   7235 anoon] als sone J;   she
hadde] *trs.* J;   oon] j *over* G³;   hire] heere (*2nd* e *subpuncted*) G;   upon]
on JO.   7236 Ho ho] A a M.   7237 þat] *ins.* O;   place] (*2nd* a *ins.* G³)
G;   twey] ij *over with* ij mar. G³, twa JMO.   7238 haue] (*2nd* a *ins.* G³);
Sey] *prec.* Capitulum lxiij mar. C;   now] on J;   þanne] *om.* J, one O.
7238-9 quod ... anoon] *om.* CG.   7238 she] þan *add.* J.   7239 anoyeth]
diseses J.   7240 to go] els whare J;   elles where] to ga J;   And] *prec.*
Capitulum lxiij mar. CG;   com] Grace dieu J;   Grace Dieu] grace C, come
J.   7241 sweeteliche seide] *trs.* J;   me] *om.* J, to me M;   wel] quod scho

J; þe] tho (*with* the *mar.* G³) G.   7242 þi] þe C;   Þe] *om.* JMO;
comen] to the *add.* J.   7243 þe¹] *om.* J.   7244 in] to *add.* S.
7245 sithe] Syne JMO;   in] to *add.* JM;   coffyne] cooferre JMO;   þi bodi]
scho wille putte J;   she ... putte] (*3rd* e *ins.* G³), thy body J.   7246 take]
make J;   stinkinge to] *trs.* JMO (to *ins.* O);   is al] shall M;   commune] com
M.   7247 eche ilke JM.   7248 today] þis day M.   7249 and] com
JMO;   drye is] it es drie JMO.   7250 reynes] rayny O;   þou mostest] the
buse J, ye must M, þe moste O.   7251 tobroke] breke JMO;   twey] *with* ij
over and mar. G³, twa JMO;   oon] j *over* G³.   7252 ooþer] es *add.* JMO;
Þei] þat M;   mihten] may JMO;   togideres] to gedyre JMO.   7253 sithe]
seyne JMO;   afterward] efterwardes J.   7255 general] resurreccioun and *add.*
M;   assemblee] asemblynge JMO;   Now] loke J;   looke] (*2nd* o *ins.* G³),
now J.   7256 wel] in goode J;   apoynted] poynte J;   and] wele *add.* J;
If it ne] (ne *ins. mar.* G³), Bot 3if it J;   be] *with er. mar.* C³;   on] of M.
7257 whiche] wheche (*2nd* e *ins.* G³) G.   7259 and] or O.   7260 withinne]
in to it J;   wel] fulle JMO;   þilke] that JMO.   7260-1 at þe first] (furste
has e *subpuncted in* G), when þou sawe it JMO.   7261 whan ... it] furste
JMO;   algates] neuertheles J.   7262 in] and J;   biheetinge] be thenke J;
þouh] 3if J.   7263 doon] (*2nd* o *ins. and final* e *subpuncted* G³) G;   hire]
o. er. C, suffy3aunce O;   sufficience] to hir O.   7264 hire] *om.* C;   þere]
(*2nd* e *ins.* G³), whare JMO;   too] *The long prose and verse addition known as 'The
Pilgrim's Lament' add.* M (*see Appendix* A).   7264-8 Now ... suprysed] *om.*
M.   7264 Now] *prec.* Capitulum lxiv *mar.* CG;   if] and J, þat if O.
7265 haue] (*2nd* a *ins.* G³);   maade] (*2nd* a *ins.,* e *subpuncted* G³);   many]
money (e *ins.* G³);   demaundes] demawnde O.   7266 for] *om.* J.
7267 Whan men weenen] *om.* J;   þat] *om.* J, þe O.   7268 Þe] *om.* JM.
7269 maade (*1st* a *ins.* G³), make J.   7271 Þus] as M;   me] *om.* O;   as
I mette] in my dreme J, *om.* M, as me mett O;   but] And J, Þen M, *om.* O;
as] *om.* M.   7272 torment] þat onoon *add.* M;   herde] (*2nd* e *ins.* G³).
7273 for] vnto J, afore M;   þe] *om.* J;   awook] wakynned J.   7274 I¹] *twice*
O;   my meetinge] (*1st* e *ins.* G³), my metynges J, þat whilk J hadd seyn M;
gretliche] right J.   7275 thouhti] þouthfulle JMO;   Algates] And 3it M;
me] *om.* JMO.   7276 wente] me *add.* M, Infirmity, & owld age, þe end, of our
pilgrimage *mar.* O³;   weery] (*2nd* e *ins.* G³).   7277 fichched] sett M, *with
fixed mar.* O³;   to] on J;   þat¹] atte *add.* JMO;   met] in dreeme *add.* J, seyn
M.   7278 me] (*2nd* e *ins.* G³);   do] thynkes J.   7279 cuntre] lyfe J;
he] *with* dedleche *mar.* G³;   swich] suche (e *subpuncted*) G.   7280 haue] (*2nd*
a *ins.* G³);   it] *om.* O;   wise] manere J;   mette] saw M.   7281 haue]
(*2nd* a *ins.* G³);   sett] sayde JMO;   for] than *add.* J;   shulde] þen *add.*
M.   7282 If] *prec.* Capitulum lxv *mar.* CG;   þis metinge] I hafe nou3t welle
mette, þis dremyng M;   I¹ ... ymet] this metynge J, I haue nou3t wele mett MO;
preye] 3owe *add.* J, all *add.* M;   to riht] it mot be J;   it be] ryghthede and J,
it may be M, it mot be O.   7283 of] by J;   þilke] hym JMO;   meete] þen
I M;   or] other G, *om.* M;   þat bettere] *om.* M.   7284 mown make it] *om.*
M;   lesinge] leesynge (*2nd* e *ins.* G³) G, or errour *add.* J;   þer] *om.* JMO.
7285 þat] *om.* J;   meetinge] dremynge JM;   it] mot *add.* J, may *add.* M;
be] notte *add.* O;   arretted] rectyd (*with* imputed *mar.* O³) O;   meetinge]
dremyng M.   7286 alle] the *add.* J;   be shewed] *trs.* MO;   noon] none
(e *subpuncted*) G.   7287 haue] (*2nd* a *ins.* G³).   7288 meetinge] dremyng
M, thyng O;   þat] *om.* GO;   haue] (*2nd* a *ins.* G³);   ryghteden] shuld right
M.   7289 kepten] kepe M;   to forueye] from forueyinge CJ, to forneye G, fro

gangyng wrong M *followed by* For it is foly to abyde to þe nede · When men wenys þe deth be right farr ⁝ he abydes at þe post*erne* *add. can.* M, fro for fettyng O; he] *om.* G, be J. 7290 errour] -s O; forueyinge] gangyng wrong M, forfettyng O. 7291 eche] ilke man JM, man *add.* O. 7292 þilke] that JMO; ende] *om.* M; þe ... and] (guer *o. er.* C), *om.* JMO. 7293 þe^{1}] *om.* J; of] high *add.* M; God] of his grace *add.* J; grawnte] graunte (e *ins.* G^{3}) G; to] that J, vs O. 7294 alle] crysten*e* *add.* J; Amen] q*uod* Benett *add.* M. 7295 *The 'explicit' is rub.* C, *bookhand* M, *rub. bookhand* J, *underlined rub.* M, *in smaller script* O; of þe monk] þ*at* amou*n*ke made J, -ȝ M; of Þe] *om.* M. 7296 þ^{1,2}] his M; Lyfe] and *add.* M; which] wheche (*2nd* a *subpuncted*) G, *om.* M; is ... good] *om.* M; pilgryme] Pilg*r*imes J, *om.* M; þat in] *om.* M. 7297 þis] *om.* M, *ins.* O^{3}; world] *om.* M; swich] whilke J, *om.* M; wey ... hauene] *om.* M; and] *om.* JM. 7298 þat] *om.* JM; he] *om.* JMO; haue] (*2nd* a *ins.* G^{3}), *om.* JM; of ... ioye] *om.* JM; Taken] *om.* M; upon] off J, *om.* M; Þe ... þe^{3}] *om.* M. 7299 Rose ... of] *om.* M; loue] lyfe J, *om.* M; is] *om.* M; al] *om.* JMO; enclosed] *om.* M; Preyeth] *om.* M, *Pray* ȝe O; for] *om.* M. 7300 þilke] hym JO, *om.* M; þat^{1} maade it] For hym *add.* J, *om.* M; hath ... it^{2}] (it *ins.* G), garte it be made J, *om.* M, had made it by mad · & And gartte writt it (it *alt.* &) O; and] also For hym that *add.* J, *om.* M; wrot it] *om.* M; Amen] *om.* G, in the yeare ·1331· O^{3}.

END OF PAGES